Lola on Fire

ALSO BY RIO YOUERS

Halcyon

The Forgotten Girl

Lola on Fire

A Novel

Rio Youers

HARPER LARGE PRINT
An Imprint of HarperCollinsPublishers

LOLA ON FIRE. Copyright © 2021 by Rio Youers. All rights reserved. Printed in the United States of America. No part of this book may be used or reproduced in any manner whatsoever without written permission except in the case of brief quotations embodied in critical articles and reviews. For information, address HarperCollins Publishers, 195 Broadway, New York, NY 10007.

HarperCollins books may be purchased for educational, business, or sales promotional use. For information, please e-mail the Special Markets Department at SPsales@harpercollins.com.

FIRST HARPER LARGE PRINT EDITION

ISBN: 978-0-06-306237-5

Library of Congress Cataloging-in-Publication Data is available upon request.

21 22 23 24 25 LSC 10 9 8 7 6 5 4 3 2 1

This novel is dedicated to
Lily Maye Youers and Charlie Samuel Youers
All you have to do is dream . . .

Lola on Fire

PROLOGUE

The
Unstoppable
Lola Bear

(1993)

The car boomed toward Lola, its headlights cut so that she wouldn't see it in the darkness. The driver didn't factor in the engine noise, though. Or maybe he did but gambled on her not hearing it above the gunfire. He for damn sure didn't factor in the streetlight reflecting off the windshield, clear as sun-flash off a sniper's lens.

No time to think. An overworked expression, and one that riled Lola. It applied to reflex, not survival. To *not think*, Lola knew, was to lie down and die.

She calculated: Four seconds until the car was on top of her. It might not kill her outright but would do enough damage to render her ineffective.

Four seconds. She had time.

Tony Broome was taking cover ninety feet away, tucked behind the front wheel of a stationary Buick, which was smart, but every time he inhaled, the top of his head lifted above the hood. Not by much, only an inch or so, but an inch was enough. Lola liked Tony. They'd worked numerous jobs together. He was good people.

It would take a second to steady her hand, aim, pull the trigger. 0.08 seconds for the bullet to meet its target. Then two seconds to move.

Lola leveled her pistol, pumped off a shot. The peak of Tony's skull disappeared in a splash of blood. With that threat erased, Lola turned back to the car. Its engine snarled like a wild thing caged. She would clear more distance by rolling, but it would take longer to reset. So she pirouetted, staying on her feet, her gun hand still poised. ¶ a whirling of the body

The car missed her by a gasp, the distance between her and it tight enough to trap a sheet of paper. She lifted details—some crucial—as it whistled past: a 1992 Mercury Sable in reef-blue metallic. A cracked windshield. A dented fender. Paul Mostly rode shotgun (his surname the fuel for many inane gags: Paul *mostly* doesn't know shit from Shinola; Paul *mostly* has his thumb jammed up his ass). He had a custom bullpup M14 across his thighs. Some jerkoff she didn't know was behind the wheel. He had a cornerstone jaw sprinkled with beard and wore a patch over his left eye. Jimmy wouldn't usually hire someone with an eye patch. It exposed how desperate he was.

A good sign.

Lola aimed and fired twice at the back of the driver's headrest. The second shot was for insurance, in case the first was deflected on its passage through the rear windshield. The Sable ran out of blacktop with the driver too dead to react. It mounted the sidewalk and struck a steel security fence with a concertina boom. ~~Fold~~ The passenger-side door dropped off its hinges a moment later and Paul reeled out, spitting teeth from his blood-filled mouth. He flailed with the bullpup. Spent rounds glittered like broken glass.

Paul *mostly* misses with every shot.

Lola sighted down the barrel of her Baby Eagle: 9mm, Israeli-made, and decidedly lethal for something so daintily named.

Paul *mostly* dies from a gunshot wound to the throat.

The quickest way onto Jimmy's property was to vault onto the Sable and over the fence. It was also a guaranteed way to get herself perforated. *Pierced with holes* The crash— not to mention the gunfire—had announced her arrival like a railroad flare. Too many sights focused on that point. Lola could use it as a diversion, though. She knew Jimmy's property. There were other ways in.

She skirted the eastern wall where shadow kept her hidden. There'd be men posted here. Two, maybe three. Lola would hear them first—their quick, unsteady breathing in the darkness, in sync with the jitter of their hearts. She paused, listening, then moved on. Tony (another Tony) Marconi stood sentry midway down, trying to look everywhere at once, not trusting his peripheral vision, his hearing, his instinct. Tony M. was a twenty-eight-year-old brute with a skull as tough as quartz. He had black belts in judo and tae kwon do. Lola could drop him with a bullet, but a bullet would betray her location.

She had to strike silently.

Timing her movement, Lola hit him like rain, first across the right wrist, disarming him, then with a punch to the throat that disabled his vocal cords. She brought him down with a low kick that exploded his kneecap. A fourth strike, delivered with bewildering force and precision, snapped his neck like wet bark.

. . .

Lola took a breath and felt the blood rushing through her body. She waited a minute for it to slow. There were shouts from beyond the wall—Jimmy's men on alert, panicked crows with semiautomatics clutched in their trembling claws—and the throaty, wheezy snarl of Doberman pinschers. There were seven of them, named after the seven samurai from the movie of the same name, still on their leashes, judging from their frequent yelps and yowls.

She imagined Jimmy with his hands nervously flexing, stealing glances out the window, a bluish vein ticking in the hollow of one temple.

You can do this.

Lola gritted her teeth. She had no patience for positive reinforcement—a cousin to weakness.

It's already done.

She crept through the shadows toward the rear of the house. Benjamin Chen, her Xing Yi Quan instructor, floated to mind. Shifu Chen was beautiful and ocean-like and always welcome. Lola once asked him—appealing to his passion for metaphor—how to stay dry when caught in a storm. Shifu Chen had responded with a question, and a metaphor, of his own:

"How do you fly a kite?"

Lola had waited with everything open, eager for education, for betterment. Shifu Chen looked at her for a second, then made a kite out of his left hand.

"You ride the wind," he'd said, making his hand sway and swirl. "You gauge its strength, make adjustments. In a sense, you become the wind."

"Right."

"So, to keep from getting wet . . ."

Lola finished for him, "You become the storm."

Another thug she didn't know guarded the south gate. He didn't wear an eye patch but may as well have; Lola came up on his blind side and drove the heel of her palm into his face. It was a direct, efficient strike, ninety-eight percent of her internal power funneled into the end of the move. The thug's face bones caved. Eggshell splintered his brain. He collapsed and foamed at the mouth and his long limbs jangled.

Lola slipped through the gate. The house glimmered beyond the elms, a contemporary multimillion-dollar structure purchased with blood and wile. Every window was illuminated. Muscle barricaded the doors. She heard a sound to her right and found cover in the shadows. It was Mickey Grieco, searching the grounds with the help of Katsushiro—one of the Dobermans. The dog caught her scent and pulled Mickey close. Lola took off her jacket, placed it on the ground, and moved. Katsushiro found her jacket and showed all his teeth, and when Mickey picked it up with a puzzled expression, Lola struck from behind. Mickey died quickly but Katsushiro took longer. She strangled him with his own leash.

Lola pulled her jacket back on and moved toward the house.

She had sent a message through Carver City's grimy underbelly, using call girls and bootblacks and crooked cops, but also painting it across the exterior walls of the Steel Tiger, where every mobster and degenerate was certain to see it.

I'M COMING FOR JIMMY AND YOU KNOW WHY
GET IN MY WAY AND I'LL KILL YOU TOO

. . .

She left a trail of bodies—human and canine—on her way to the house, most of them on the lawn, Heihachi in the pool, which had turned from aqua to cherry-red. She maintained stealth for as long as she was able but had to switch to the Baby Eagle. That was okay. Let Jimmy hear the gunshots. Let him hear the panic, the screams.

Lola entered the house through the three-car garage and took a bullet to the shoulder.

It was Marco Cabrini—the first soldier she'd worked with, a know-it-all motherfucker born into the life—and he'd positioned himself at the far corner of the foyer, in the perfect amount of shadow. Lola saw the zeros of his eyes but too late. Marco fired four times and the third shot found her. She slammed back against the door with a white-hot coal burning into her left shoulder and a new weakness in her legs. Her return fire was lucky in that she only half aimed. She caught Marco in the shin and he dropped shrieking. Lola reloaded and popped one into his skull.

She holstered her pistol and examined her shoulder for an exit wound. It was there, a raw pocket of exposed tissue beneath a hole in her jacket. Lola nodded grimly, recalling an axiom of her grandfather's: *Entry wound bad. Exit wound good.* She smeared blood and sweat from her brow, readied her gun, and pushed deeper into the house.

Then Jimmy came at her with a flamethrower.

...

Jimmy Latzo had always been a crazy son of a bitch. Lola used to think it was all for show—to color his reputation—but the more she got to know him, the more she realized that he was hardwired that way. Or perhaps it was a short circuit, some synapse in his brain that struggled to connect to a considered response. Either way, Jimmy was a loose cannon. He once took a chainsaw to a man who'd cheated him out of $3,600 in a poker game. It wasn't the money—$3,600 was a piss in the ocean for Jimmy. It was the fact that he'd been *cheated*, that somebody thought he'd be stupid enough not to notice. On another occasion—shortly after Lola started working for him—he roped a snitch to the back of his Cadillac and drove him through the city streets, like some outlaw from the Wild West being drawn by a horse.

Jimmy had butchered, bribed, and hair-triggered his way up through the ranks of Carver City's criminal empire. He had crooked cops and politicians dangling from strings and would make them dance to whatever tune he was playing. He always got what he wanted.

With one exception . . .

Lola smelled the diesel first, so out of place in Jimmy's pristine house. A warning light flashed in her mind and she made the connection at the same moment she heard the click of the ignition charge. Jimmy had bought the flamethrower eighteen months ago—a reconditioned M2, World War II era. He sometimes wore it to business meetings and when addressing subordinates. "Burn, bitch," he squealed now, and a thirty-foot jet of flame squirted across the living room. It set fire to the silk drapes and the sectional sofa. It lapped across the walls and ceiling in red and orange tongues. Lola hit the deck and rolled.

The hole in her shoulder limited her speed and movement. She felt her skin prickle in the heat.

Pain bolted through her. She watched fire purl across the ceiling. *Crazy bastard,* she thought. But that was Jimmy. He wouldn't blink an eye at burning his house to the ground if it meant she would burn, too.

"Fucking *bitch!*"

Lola dived and rolled again as Jimmy lashed another rope of fire across the room. She positioned herself behind a pony wall with antique vases displayed on it, each of which exploded in the heat. Flames curled around and over the wall. Her clothes caught in several places and she doused them with her gun hand. Jimmy triggered another ignition cartridge. She heard him cackle before a third cord of flame scorched the air.

Her lungs contracted. She felt a tight collar of panic, as alien to her as an exoplanet. *How do you fly a kite?* she thought, the heat pushing down on her like a predator pinning its prey. She ran multiple scenarios through her brain, along with probable outcomes. *Six seconds.* Lola latched onto this with all the fury in her soul. *Six seconds of burn time in that old M2. That's all.* Blisters bubbled across the backs of both hands and she felt her jacket melting into her skin. She covered her mouth and nose against the burning fumes and calculated. Jimmy had fired three bursts, totaling four seconds.

Two seconds remaining. Then he'd be spent.

Flames snapped at the walls and rippled across the ceiling. The living room was a furnace. Above all else, Lola knew she had to break cover and move. Her body could ignite at any moment.

She sprang from behind the pony wall, pushed through a window of flame. Fire crawled up her back and caught the tips of her hair. In that lunatic moment she heard two sounds clearly: the strings of Jimmy's grand piano snapping with odd melody, and Jimmy's whooping, victorious laughter. He squeezed another thread of fire toward her, thinking she had nowhere to go, but she hit the double doors leading into the dining room.

The heat blast pushed her to the back of the room. It pushed her free.

· · ·

Lola yanked off her smoldering jacket. She slapped at her hair and legs. Her pants had burned away in places, revealing patches of reddened skin. There was small comfort in knowing that it could've been worse.

It was a long way from over.

"*Bitch!*"

The double doors Lola had crashed through burned like phoenix wings, keeping Jimmy at a safe distance. For now. There was another entrance into the dining room—an arched opening that led to the front hallway. Lola pushed herself to her feet and staggered through it just as Jimmy reached the hallway from the living room side. She raised her gun and fired awkwardly, managing two shots before Jimmy let loose with the flamethrower again. Lola retreated into the foyer. She tumbled over Marco Cabrini's corpse, half pulling him on top of her as the air crackled.

"It's all over, Lola," Jimmy cried. She saw him at the far end of the hallway, bordered by flame. He shimmered, appearing taller, *smokier*, closer to the devil he was. "No vengeance for you. Dumb fucking skeeze."

She'd get off a shot, but her right arm was underneath Marco, and even if she could aim with her left—if she didn't have a goddamn tunnel running through her shoulder—how accurate would her shot be? Jimmy flickered and swayed. He didn't look real.

Six seconds, she thought.

"I mean, I'm Jimmy fucking Latzo. I don't lose. You fucking *know* that. And guess what, baby doll . . . you tried to bring me down—fucking *end* me—and I brought *you* down. The unstoppable Lola Bear. I'm going to go from legendary to godlike."

And if he killed her, he probably would. It didn't matter that his army was torn apart and his house in ashes; killing Lola Bear would add considerably to his résumé.

Six seconds.

He started down the hallway with fire boiling around him, looking for all the world like some madman spat from hell. Lola watched him advance, her mind whirring. She needed time to clamber from beneath Marco Cabrini, steady her aiming hand, and put a bullet through Jimmy's heart. Her having that time depended solely on whether those fuel tanks were spent.

Jimmy stopped at the threshold between the hallway and foyer, twenty feet from where Lola lay. She saw his face clearly, his pig-mouth drawn downward, his eyes alight. He winked and aimed the flamethrower at her.

The house burned behind him. Windows shattered and chunks of the ceiling fell. Smoke mushroomed.

"You could've had everything," he said.

...

Jimmy ignited another cartridge and a bright pilot flame sizzled at the tip of the flamethrower's muzzle. Lola got ready. She pushed with her strong shoulder, easing herself from beneath Marco's corpse. With equal effort, she raised the Baby Eagle. The sights wavered. Jimmy still shimmered.

He roared maniacally and hit the firing trigger, but instead of a long strip of burning fuel, there was only an anticlimactic dribble of fire. His expression collapsed. "Motherfucker," he gasped. He shook the flamethrower's wand and jiggled it up and down, like rattling a spray paint can to eke out the last few squirts.

Nothing.

Lola looked at Jimmy down the sights of her gun. She got to her feet and stumbled closer. She didn't want to miss.

"You're out, Jimmy."

"Out," he repeated numbly.

"Out of fuel. And shit out of luck."

Lola pulled the trigger.

...

She shot him where it wouldn't kill him—not right away—but where it would cause excruciating pain: in the gut. She imagined the bullet ripping through the soft mass of his stomach, spilling acids and bacteria, then barreling on to his colon, perhaps his spleen, before lodging in his kidney.

Jimmy screamed brilliantly, falling to his knees, then onto his back, where he rocked this way and that on the flamethrower's tanks. Lola stood over him, the gun targeting his face now.

"You couldn't let me have that one thing," she said. "You had to take it away."

"You don't know it was me." Blood bubbled from Jimmy's mouth. The tendons in his throat were as tight and thick as bass strings. "You don't know shit, honey."

"But I do."

The fire had spread down the hallway, jumping between the walls and ceiling, snapping across the floor. Something in the living room came down with a spectacular crash. Sparks flashed like lightning in roiling clouds of smoke. Lola blinked and spluttered. She'd have to do this soon.

"Love letters," she said, reaching into her pocket with her left hand. Pain corkscrewed from the hole in her shoulder, all the way to the tips of her fingers. "Beneath his tough exterior, Vince was a hopeless romantic. He used to write these little notes and leave them in places I'd least expect: under the sun visor in my car, so it would drop into my lap while I was driving, or inside a box of ammunition. Sweet nothings, you know: *Crazy about you, girl . . . Love you madly.* That kind of thing."

"Gah, I'm gonna fucking puke."

"His favorite hiding place, though"—Lola coughed and tilted away from the gathering smoke—"was inside my left shoe, beneath the insole. Always the left, because it was closer to my heart."

"*Gah.*"

"When I picked up Vince's . . . personal belongings from"—she coughed again—"the coroner, I noticed the insole of his left shoe was sticking up just a bit. So I lifted it, and sure enough, I found a little note beneath."

Lola took her hand from her pocket, a folded piece of paper clasped between her trembling fingers. "Not a love letter, though. Not this time." She unfolded the paper and showed Jimmy what was written there. A single word in smeared, brownish uppercase:

JIMMY

Another crash from the living room, the sound of breaking glass, the tuneless thud of the grand piano collapsing. More smoke dirtied the air above Lola. In a modest house with narrower spaces, she probably would have died from smoke inhalation by now.

"And yeah, Jimmy, it's written in blood. Vincent's blood. I had it checked." Lola crouched, in part to breathe the fractionally cleaner air, mostly to jam the pistol's muzzle beneath the ridge of Jimmy's jaw. "He must've found time to write this after you cut his ears off, but before you plugged a bullet in the back of his skull."

Jimmy gagged and gurgled and spat blood. His eyes were spinning records, playing some shocked, disbelieving tune.

"You couldn't stand that I chose him over you," Lola said.

"Fuck you."

The fire had reached the foyer, climbing the high walls, blackening the windows. Something popped and sizzled. The door to the downstairs bathroom burned off its hinges and fell with an oven-hot clap.

"You couldn't stand losing. But here's a news flash for you, Jimmy." Lola straightened, retreating a step in the heat. She kept the sights locked on Jimmy. "You were never in the running."

"Bitch, kill me if you're going to."

"I don't have to kill you, Jimmy. You were brought down by a woman—one woman. Even if you survive that bullet in your stomach, your reputation is in pieces. You won't recover from this."

"*Gah.*" Jimmy kicked his legs in agony. His right hand was clapped to his gut, knuckle-deep in blood. His left hand was splayed, trembling, on fire. He didn't appear to notice.

"But I didn't suffer these burns, and kill all your men"—Lola looped her finger around the trigger—"just to let you live."

Smoke ballooned, obscuring Lola's vision. She waited for it to clear, although her eyes were red-raw and watering.

"You lose, Jimmy."

She fired twice and saw both bullets hit. Jimmy's body hopped like he'd taken a couple of quick zaps from a defibrillator. He tensed for a moment, as if all the feeling in his body were rushing toward one point, then slumped.

Lola tossed the last note Vince Petrescu ever wrote onto Jimmy's chest, where it curled and browned. She staggered backward, then butted through the front doors and out into the night. The first gulp of clean air pushed a wave of dizziness through her. She folded to her knees and vomited.

Sirens blared, extremely close.

Lola hurried from the scene, burned and limping. Blood trickled down her arm and dripped from her sleeve.

Become the storm, she thought, looking at the sky.

PART I

One-Inch Punch

Chapter One

The "gun" was a Zoraki M2906, a replica, a prop for movies and training. It had the heft and feel of a real pistol, all working parts, except it fired blanks, not live rounds. The orange cap lodged into its muzzle, distinguishing it from handguns of a more lethal variety, had been removed a long time ago.

Brody Ellis sat behind the wheel of his shitbox Pontiac, parked in the shadows. His gaze switched between the stale yellow glow of the convenience store and the replica handgun lying on the passenger seat. The clock in the dash—part of the stereo, which had a CD and cassette player; that's how old and shitty his shitbox was—displayed 4:28. Brody had read somewhere, or maybe one of his loser buddies had told him, that four-thirty to five A.M. was the best time to rob a convenience store. The cash register would be fatter, for one thing. More important, the cashier, not to mention any cops in the vicinity, would be nearing the ends of their shifts, and were likely to be tired, not as responsive. Brody wasn't sure if this was reliable information. Maybe some cops started their shifts at four A.M., and some no doubt became more focused as the hours wore on. But it sounded plausible, and Brody needed every advantage he could get. He'd never robbed a convenience store before.

And you don't have to now, he thought. *You can still back down from this shit.*

Yeah, he could, but what then? Tyrese was hounding him for half the rent. Same as every damn month, only this month Brody was out of cash. His overdraft was maxed and his credit rating was for shit. There was nowhere to go for the money, and Tyrese was not a man of limitless patience.

"I'm just a big ol' teddy bear," he'd said when he showed Brody around the place, but yesterday that big ol' teddy bear had pinned Brody to the wall. "Get your half to me, or you and your damn sister will be out on your asses. I'm not fucking around." The muscles packed into Tyrese's arms had thrummed with dangerous energy.

Brody had pondered how different life would be if he were on his own. Jesus Christ, it was 2019, and at twenty-four years old, he could be the goddamn poster boy for free-spirited millennials. He could live out of his car, if needed, or crash on a friend's sofa. Just for a couple of weeks, until he found a job and pulled enough scratch together to get another place. But he wasn't on his own. Molly complicated things. She needed comfort and care, much of which came by way of her medication. How many more nights would he lie awake with her, holding her while she cried with the miserable pain of it all, the muscles in her delicate legs trembling and jerking?

...

4:34. The convenience store's light spilled across Independence Avenue like it had been tipped from a barrel. Buddy's, it was called. 24-HR VALUE WITH A SMILE! The owner's name wasn't Buddy. It was Elias Abrahamian, a middle-aged Armenian with a gold tooth and a neck tattoo. Drove a Beamer. Never smiled. Elias would be at home sleeping next to his young wife while reliable, bespectacled employee ANT—HERE TO HELP worked the register. Ant—130 pounds of piss in skinny jeans—would be fading, playing *Candy Crush Saga* on his phone to stay awake. Nobody had been in or out of the store for twenty-three minutes.

...

4:41. Brody picked up the replica, leveled his arm, aimed at the windshield. His hand trembled. He cupped his right wrist with his left palm, which helped but only a little.

"Empty the fucking register, motherfucker! Right fucking now!"

Should he scream, like a hair-trigger sociopath, or make his demand in an even but menacing tone, as if blowing Ant out of his Vans were all in a day's work?

"You know what to do, kid. Don't give me a reason."

He preferred the latter option. Keep it cool, controlled, and quick. But he'd never sell cool if he couldn't keep his goddamn hand from shaking.

Brody tried again.

"Let's fucking do this—"

Again.

"Gonna ask you once—"

Brody had done his homework. He'd reconnoitered Buddy's and several other stores this side of the Freewood Valley delta. They all had pros and cons, but Buddy's came out on top. No bulletproof glass. Only one employee running the night shift (Ant on Mondays, Tuesdays, and Thursdays). Clear routes in and out. Busy enough to put some stacks in the register, but quiet enough—particularly between three and five A.M.—for the store to be empty for longish periods.

"One wrong move and I'll—"

Three miles from the nearest police department, which didn't account for patrols, but Brody was hoping for some luck. Christ knows, he was due. Only two surveillance cameras, one above the checkout counter, the other at the back of the store. It was possible that Ant had an alarm button or .45 beneath the counter, but Brody depended on him being too shit-scared to use them.

"Don't be a hero, kid—"

. . .

Brody had bought the replica from a wheelchair-bound meth-head who was done with rolling the dice.

"Every time I stick someone up," he said, "you can see 'em weighing up their chances. As if having no legs makes a bullet slower."

"But there are no bullets," Brody said. "Right?"

"Shit, *they* don't know that. I mean, the Zoraki is a grade-A replica. They use that shit in movies."

"But it's harmless? I don't want to . . . you know, *hurt* anybody."

"Harmless to everybody except you. Cop sees you waving that around, you're going to catch a bullet."

"Don't I know it. So what's your asking price?"

"That model sells for about one-fifty on eBay."

"One-*fifty*? Fuck that. I was thinking, like . . . twenty bucks."

"Get the fuck out of here with twenty bucks. Jesus."

"Hey, man, I can probably get the job done with my hand in a paper bag."

"Good luck with that. See how confident you feel with your hand in a goddamn paper bag. That's what I'm selling here, man. *Confidence*."

"Shit, I'll give you fifty."

"I'm looking at a yard, man. At least."

"A yard? You want to buy a yard?"

"No, a *yard*. You know, a hundred bucks."

"Right. Yeah. I can give you sixty, man. That's all the money in my world."

"Sixty and that Panthers lid."

"Deal."

. . .

4:48. Brody put his gloves on.

Go time.

. . .

He popped the car door and kept to the shadows until there were no shadows, only that lemony splash of light from the store. Approaching the automatic doors, he hooked a ski mask from his jacket pocket and rolled it over his face. The replica gun was in his other pocket, snug beside his wallet. Before reaching for it, a voice at the back of his mind once again insisted that he didn't have to do this, that he could back out and find another way. It wasn't the memory of Tyrese pinning him to the wall that kept him going, but of Molly trembling in his arms, trying hard—trying *so* damn hard—to be brave.

"Do it," he whispered to himself. "In and out. Thirty seconds."

A quick glance to his left and right before entering, to make sure no cars were pulling into the lot. Brody snatched the replica from his pocket and the weight of it in his hand—here, in the store lights, in the *open*—sent his heart cannonballing into his throat. He fumbled the gun, nearly dropped it, reeled into Buddy's with his lips peeled back behind the ski mask, his right hand jitterbugging, the tip of the barrel swaying like a metronome. The colors—all the boxes and packets and labels—were too bright and the fluorescent lights had sunlamp intensity. Brody wondered, had the gun been real, if he might have pulled the trigger in the sheer rush of it all.

Ant saw him and shrank, his thin arms crossed over his face.

"Jesus Christ, man. No, please—"

"You know what to do. Make it quick."

"Aw, Jesus. Aw, fuck."

"*Now.*"

It didn't matter that Brody's hand trembled, because Ant couldn't see it. Ant cowered behind his crossed arms, knees knocking. He'd started to make a squeaky-door sound—*reeee, reeeeeee*—and his shoulders jerked with every shrill breath. Brody was the apotheosis of cool in comparison.

"The money, dickwad." Brody rapped the butt of the replica on the counter. "I'll put a bullet in your knee, I swear to God."

Ant yelped and curled into a loose ball. He made no move for the cash register. Brody clenched his jaw and looked behind him, checking that no one had slunk into the store. He scoped the lot, too. No headlights. No early birds heading to Buddy's for a pack of smokes and a shitty cup of coffee. It was just a matter of time, though.

"*Reeee, reeeeeeee—*"

Abort mission, the voice at the back of Brody's mind snapped. *This isn't working. Get the hell out.*

But he didn't want to abort mission. He'd come this far, and he wasn't sure he could muster the moxie to do it all again.

So what are you going to do? Give Ant a cuddle? Ask nicely?

Ant's keycard hung from a lanyard around his neck, twirling slowly as he trembled. Brody had watched the store's cashiers use their keycards on previous occasions, touching the QR code to the scanner to open the register. It was that simple.

"*Reeeeeeeee—*"

Brody vaulted the counter in a wild, liquid move. Heart revving, he snatched at the plastic card around Ant's neck. Ant squealed and flailed with one arm.

"*No, please . . . nooooooo—*"

Ant's right elbow glanced off Brody's jaw. It didn't hurt but Brody staggered backward. He reached for the keycard again, grabbed it in one fist, and yanked. The lanyard didn't break.

"Mother*fuck—*"

Brody gave it another firm tug but the card remained around Ant's neck, and now Ant—probably unaware of what he was doing—grabbed a fistful of Brody's ski mask, trying to push him away, but succeeding only in shoving the mask up and revealing half of Brody's face to the surveillance camera. Brody growled, one eye rolling toward the front doors. How long before they opened and someone entered the store? How long before Ant realized that his assailant was a bumbling amateur who had no intention of using the gun?

Brody looked from the doors to the camera above the counter. There was a small black-and-white TV beside it, and Brody—the left half of his face uncovered—was the star of the show.

"*Reeee, reeeeee—*"

This (attempted) robbery had been somewhat planned, but what happened next was raw impulse. Brody raised the replica and brought the butt down on Ant's skull. It wasn't a shocking, forceful blow, but the skin cracked and blood flowed. Ant let go of Brody's mask and flopped backward. His eyes rolled in a giddy way that made Brody feel sick inside.

"Stupid asshole." Brody pulled his ski mask down. "You *made* me do that."

He looped the lanyard from around Ant's neck, leaped to the cash register, scanned the card. The drawer opened, revealing coins and banknotes— mostly tens, nothing larger than a twenty. None of the stacks were deep. Brody guesstimated a take of about two hundred bucks.

You're shitting me? he thought deliriously. *All of this for two hundred dollars.*

He grabbed the money, stuffing it into a paper bag he'd pulled from beneath the counter. It took seconds. Ant groaned and squirmed on the floor behind him. Brody was about to haul ass when he noticed the cash tray shift loosely. A tiny bell in his mind chimed, cutting through the chaos. He lifted the tray and tossed it, scattering coins. Beneath were more coins in neat rolls, and receipts and vouchers—also a bundle of bills with Benjamin Franklin's kindly face on the front. He was neighbored by more presidents in fatter stacks. Brody stared at the money for several out-of-body seconds, wondering if there was usually this much in the register, or if Elias had neglected to drop the day's take at the bank. Although it could have been two days' take—shit, a whole *week's*. There had to be two thousand dollars in there. Maybe three.

Brody removed the cash with an odd mix of euphoria and guilt. He considered, very briefly, leaving some behind, but took it all, even the four rolls of quarters—another forty bucks there.

"I'm sorry, brother," he said to Ant. "I hope your head's okay. I just . . . just . . ."

"Fuck you, man. My boss is going to kill me."

"Yeah." The bag in Brody's hand was quite full. "Dude's going to be pissed."

"*Reeeeee—*"

Brody twisted the top of the paper bag to close it, rolled over the counter, and headed for the doors. He moved quickly, sneakers skimming over the floor, his pulse echoing through his quavering limbs. Above the euphoria and guilt was the knowledge that he would never be able to undo what he had just done. Maybe later he would analyze how that made him feel—try to find some peace in it.

The doors opened. He stepped outside.

The girl came out of nowhere.

. . .

Brody collided with her. She staggered backward and he instinctively reached to steady her. "Sorry, I . . . I . . ." They danced awkwardly for a second or two, then she looked up—noticed the ski mask, the gun in his hand. Her eyes widened and she jumped back, and in that moment Brody registered how striking she was. Not pretty, but unusual, with penciled eyebrows, wagon-red lipstick, a scar beneath her left eye. She wore an Oakley beanie, purple hair looping from beneath it, framing her jaw and slender neck.

"Jesus!"

"Sorry," Brody muttered again. He bolted past her and ran without looking back, into the shadows where his car was parked.

. . .

He drove a mile with his head pounding, vision swimming, and finally pulled over on a side street lined with dark, dozing houses and mature trees. He killed the engine and inched the window open, listening for sirens. The city of Freewood Valley was silent, but for the sporadic hiss of traffic on Kimber Bridge.

Brody waited there until the sweat coating his body had dried, then he wiped his eyes—he'd been crying a little—and drove the nineteen miles to Rebel Point, the town he called home.

. . .

There was a twenty-four-hour CVS on Century Road. Brody swung into the lot and parked out of the spotlight. He fished the paper bag loaded with cash from the passenger-side footwell, dug his hand inside, and took out a sheaf of mixed bills—enough to cover Molly's prescriptions. He reached for his wallet with his other hand, but it wasn't in the pocket he thought it was in. Brody frowned. He remembered it being there, snug beside the replica. Hell, he'd *felt* it as he strode toward Buddy's.

"What the—"

Brody's heart dipped. A cold, unpleasant feeling leaked to the balls of his feet. He checked his other pocket. Maybe he'd switched it at some point—a little detail he'd forgotten in all the excitement.

No wallet.

"Shit." Brody tossed the bills into the passenger seat and rooted in both pockets again, going as deep as the stitching would allow. He found a candy wrapper and a bottle cap and an old receipt for breakfast at Applebee's. He bounded from the car, rifled his jeans. There was a firm rectangle lodged into his back pocket. A second's relief washed through him, but no, that was his phone.

"Jesus Christ, *no*."

Brody checked the car next: beside and beneath the seats, the center console, the glove compartment. He even checked the backseat. There was no sign of his wallet, which meant he'd dropped it, probably while pulling the replica from his pocket, but maybe while tussling with Ant. It was somewhere on the scene, and he couldn't exactly go back to look for it. His only hope was that it hadn't been found, but he thought it more likely the cops had it in their possession and were comparing the face on the driver's license with

the clumsy, half-masked assailant on the store's surveillance video.

· · ·

He bought Molly's pain management, antidepressant,
and antispasticity medications, pulling the crumpled
bills from the front pocket of his jeans and handing them over with trembling hands. The pharmacist
asked if he was okay. Brody vaguely replied that he'd
just come off a night shift and was dog-tired.

Two long miles to Palm Street, to the shotgun house
he shared with his sister and teddy bear Tyrese. He
expected to see police parked outside, two cruisers
blocking the tight driveway, lights beating. The street
was quiet, though, accented by a colorful wisp of
morning light in the east.

Brody sat for a while, then gathered his things and
went inside.

Chapter Two

The house was laid out like a trailer, and not much bigger. The living room backed onto the kitchen, then a tiny bathroom, then two bedrooms fronted by a narrow hallway. Brody and Molly shared a room. A curtain divided the space, affording each of them a degree of privacy, although it was, altogether, too confined a house for secrecy.

Brody snuck in just after six A.M., faced with the challenge of hiding the bag of cash somewhere Molly or Tyrese would never find it. He didn't want their questions or accusations. Dealing with the police would be enough. His lame strategy, when they came, was to deny everything, let his public defender fight the battle. It was likely a losing battle, but denial was all Brody had. He'd already dumped the ski mask—

threw it into a storm drain at the edge of town. Now he had to hide the cash.

He tipped the armchair and used the replica's barrel to punch a hole through the gauzy fabric beneath, then stuffed the cash and replica inside. It wasn't perfect, but it would do for now. He then walked as silently as possible into the bedroom he shared with Molly and placed her meds on the shelf above her headrest. He watched her sleep for a minute. She had two melted ice packs and a damp towel wrapped around her left leg.

Brody wanted to sleep, too—God, he was *exhausted*—but knew he couldn't. His mind was too active. He went back into the kitchen instead, made himself coffee, peered through the living room blinds as the day warmed, checking for cops. Tyrese woke at seven-fifteen, poured himself a monstrous bowl of Cheerios, dropped his considerable ass into the armchair in which Brody had stashed the cash and replica pistol.

"I want to see some money today," he grumbled.

"I'm on it."

"Better goddamn be." And a moment later Tyrese narrowed his eyes and asked, "What are you looking at?"

Brody lowered the blinds and stepped away from the window.

Molly hobbled in after Tyrese had left for work. At twenty-one, she was three years younger than Brody. Sometimes she seemed like a kid to him still, with a glimmer in her eye and a hopefulness in her demeanor. Other times she looked older, wearier. This was one of those times, and not only because she'd just woken up. She stood in the kitchen, propped on her crutches, looking at the stacks of dirty dishes, a bundle of laundry on a folding chair, the overflowing garbage, a calendar that hadn't been flipped since June.

"This shithole," she said.

"I'll clean today."

She nodded, went back to their bedroom, and returned a few minutes later with her medications. She set the boxes down hard on the kitchen table and for some time Brody couldn't look at her.

. . .

Molly had been born with the umbilical cord knotted around her throat and was deprived of oxygen for two and half minutes. MRI scans indicated mild brain damage. At age two, she was diagnosed with spastic cerebral palsy. Brody had an early memory of visiting his little sister in the hospital, her legs wrapped in casts from the knees down, still drowsy after what would be the first of her five surgeries. As Brody sat at Molly's bedside and cupped her small hand in his own, he knew that she would one day be strong enough to walk on her own, but that if she ever needed someone to lean on, he would be there.

She fell often. She picked herself up. The walker she used until she was six years old became a hated thing. She graduated to forearm crutches, which she still used. Molly was capable of walking unassisted, but not very far, and falling, she said, became tiresome. The left side of her body lacked response, but her ambition had no boundary. She could skateboard, drive a car, ride a horse. "Disabled?" she'd say. "It's just a matter of perspective, right?"

She was Brody's world. His whole damn world.

"You want to explain this to me?"

Molly took a seat at the kitchen table, opposite Brody, who regarded her with raccoon-black eyes and a not-now expression. His gaze jumped to the three boxes of medication—Motrin, Lexapro, Lioresal—on the table in front of her.

"I picked up your meds," he replied dryly. "Three cheers for Brody."

"You know what I mean."

"The money?"

"Yeah, the money." She sat back in her seat, arms crossed. A vein in her forehead pulsed. "Tell me you didn't steal it."

"I didn't steal it." He looked at her briefly. "I won it in a card game."

"Bullshit."

"What can I say? I got lucky."

Her speech was slurred, the left side of her mouth pulled downward. Her words were often incomplete—the result of muscle weakness, not lack of intelligence, as many people thought. Brody understood her perfectly, always had. As he often said, he was fluent in Mollyese.

"You need money to win money." She had no problem conveying attitude. Skepticism, for instance, or outright disbelief. "Even scratch cards cost a dollar."

"Threw my car keys into the pot." Brody had thought this lie out. "That old shitbox is worth a hundred bucks. Probably."

The kitchen window was broken, wouldn't latch, so they heard more neighborhood sounds than they wanted to. TVs and cell phones, conversations, fights, sometimes gunshots. Now they heard a car turn onto Palm Street and drive toward their house, slowing as it approached. Brody tightened inside, his hands clenched beneath the table. He imagined a Rebel Point cruiser easing to a stop outside, doors opening, two broad-shouldered cops stepping out and heading toward his front porch. He held his breath, but the car passed by and was soon out of earshot.

They would come, though. Surely.

"You're not in trouble, are you?" Molly asked. "Jesus, Brody, I couldn't stand to lose you, too."

. . .

He reached across the table and took her hand, and would wonder later if this was more for his comfort than hers.

"Everything's going to be fine, Moll."

She pressed her lips together, her fingers tightening beneath his palm. Brody thought she would pull away from him but she didn't. Her eyes dropped to the medications. She'd already taken the Motrin and Lioresal, and that was good.

"I came into some money." He cleared his throat, looked reflexively toward the armchair, then the window. "Enough to get Tyrese off our backs. Enough to make ends meet until I get another job."

Now she pulled her hand away.

"It'll be an entry-level job. Shitty hours. Minimum wage." Brody spread his hands, looked at her earnestly. *Whatever it takes, sis.* His jaw trembled. "But I'll keep my head down, stick at it. We'll get out of here—get our own place."

"It's hard to believe you."

Their mom had bailed on them in 2007. Brody—a deer-eyed twelve-year-old—had kissed her good night, as usual, and when he woke up in the morning she was gone. His starkest childhood memory was of trying to pacify Molly while she bawled, banging her crutches against the wall, blaming herself. Their father had shouldered the extra load, and he never complained, never faltered. Brody believed him superhuman.

Seven months ago, Ethan Ellis leaped from the roof of the Folgt Building—fourteen stories, 160 feet—and hit the road below like a moth hitting the headlight of a speeding Mack truck. His suicide was too much to come to terms with, not least because it made no sense. "If the world made sense," the police officer who'd delivered the death notification said to Brody and Molly, "I'd be out of a job."

Brody had been working at Wolfe Aluminum in nearby Racer, a non-unionized catch basin that had him pulling twelve-hour shifts for chump change. He buckled, understandably, after his old man's death, and found solace at Rocky T's—a dive bar on Carbon Street. His boss at Wolfe held his job for all of a week, then cut him loose. Brody bounced then from washing dishes at the

Watermark to serving coffee and donuts to delivering Domino's. His last job was working the drive-through at Chili Kicks, but he got fired after launching a Hot Tamale Burger at a customer who'd flipped him the bird.

He was a young man—he'd turned twenty-four in August—who struggled to balance his grief with the responsibility of looking after his younger sister. Evidently, he'd made some bad decisions. Robbing a convenience store—dropping his goddamn wallet at the scene—was just another.

A mud dauber buzzed at the kitchen window, trapped between the torn screen and the glass. The sky beyond was metallic blue scuffed with cloud. Brody looked at it wistfully, then wiped his eyes.

"Not just out of *here*," Molly said. She gestured at the cramped, dirty kitchen and everything else. "I want out of this town. Somewhere brighter. Cauley, maybe. They have the river."

"Buster's Ice Cream."

"Parade Park."

"Dad used to take us there." They said it at the same time, then found their smiles, which, despite Molly's palsy, were identical.

"Can we?" she asked.

"Sure." *If the cops don't bust my ass.* "We set our legs. Balance."

"One-inch punch this."

Molly had suffered a succession of bullies, from the moment she took her first awkward steps, spoken her first awkward words. The worst was Trevor Hyne, with his barbed-wire attitude and broad neck. It was hard to call a kid heartless, given they're always shaped by their nearest and dearest, but if ever a child was born with a hole in his chest, with nothing to influence, to warm or nurture, then that child was Trevor Hyne. It wasn't just that he mimicked Molly's way of walking, ridiculed her way of talking. He would elbow her, pull her hair, kick the crutches out from under her. Brody stood up to him several times, but Trevor—heavier and so much stronger—mowed him down like dead grass. "I want to learn karate," Brody had said to his dad. He was ten years old at the time. Too young to get into fights, but old enough to look after his little sister. "I need to get tough." But his dad insisted that fighting was never a solution. His mom apparently disagreed, and directed him quietly toward a YouTube video that offered step-by-step instructions on how to master Bruce Lee's one-inch punch. Brody watched the video over and over, learning how and where to position his body, how to twist his hips and flick his wrist upward a millisecond before impact. He practiced on a pillow duct-taped to a post in their backyard, gradually generating more and more power at extremely close quarters. "Strike just once with this punch," the grandly mustachioed instructor said, "and *if* you get it right . . . your opponent will think twice before confronting you again." Brody never got to use the punch on Trevor, though, because Trevor was crushed to death by a fifth-wheel trailer when Hurricane Ernesto cut across Salamander County (hard to argue with the gods on *that* call). Brody never forgot the instruction video, though, and the phrase—"one-inch punch"— had become his and Molly's euphemism for rallying against the odds, for making something out of nothing.

...

Midday rolled around and still no sign of the cops. Brody started to believe he'd dropped his wallet a safe distance from the store, and experienced the first sliver of hope, although he couldn't keep from peeking between the blinds every time he heard a car on Palm Street.

Molly had a part-time job at Arrow Dairy, punching sales data into a Mac. It earned enough for her to contribute to the bills, pay for her cell phone, and make occasional—but always practical—clothing purchases. She left for work shortly before one P.M. With the house to himself, Brody grabbed the bag of cash from inside the armchair, made some space on the kitchen table, and spread the notes out. He counted $2,360. There'd be no wolves at the door for a couple of months, at least. Molly would get her prescriptions, perhaps a few physical therapy sessions, which she hadn't had since Dad had died. Tyrese would get his rent. If Brody found a job quickly, he might even have enough for the deposit on a place in Cauley.

He counted the take again. Still $2,360.

Brody pushed $400 in tens and twenties into the front pocket of his jeans. He put the rest in the paper bag and found a new hiding place, beneath a loose floorboard at the back of his closet. He stashed the replica there, as well. Brody had no plans to use it again, but couldn't bring himself to toss it in the trash. It had cost sixty bucks, after all.

With that sliver of hope broadening, Brody sat on the front porch with one of Tyrese's beers and watched Palm Street breathe. Tiredness caught up with him, though. He dozed while the sun inched westward and the shadows grew—woke up to the sound of the bottle slipping from his hand and hitting the porch boards.

It was after four and still no cops.

. . .

"I ain't even asking, man." Tyrese counted the money, his deep eyes throwing quick, mistrustful glances at Brody. "Shit."

"It's all there, T. I even threw in a little extra for your troubles—oh, and because I helped myself to one of your beers." Brody jammed his hands into his back pockets and exhaled. "Think you might get off my ass now?"

"Well, you know, I been thinking, man." Tyrese peeled off the last twenty, considered for a moment, then started counting again. "This is the third month in a row you been late. Shit, man, you only paid on time once since you been here."

"Yeah, well . . . I had some bad luck."

"I hear you, brother, I do. But your bad luck is becoming *my* bad luck, and that shit don't seem fair to me."

"Right, but"—Brody pointed at the notes in Tyrese's hand—"things have really turned around for me. It'll be better from here on out."

"Heard that song before."

"I know, T, but—"

"All things considered," Tyrese interrupted, "I think it's time you find yourself another place to live."

Brody nodded slowly, feeling something cold swim through his gut. He told himself this was no big deal.

He and Molly were going to ditch this shithole, anyway. It was just a question of when. He had a little money now, and that was good, but he'd never secure an apartment in Cauley, or anywhere, without first getting a job. He'd need to prove earnings, to build his credit rating. It would take time.

"You'll, um . . ." Brody puffed out his cheeks and looked up at Tyrese. "You'll wait until I've got a new place first, right? I mean, you're not going to throw me out on the street . . ."

"You got until October tenth."

"Shit, T, that's two fucking weeks."

"And that's what happens when you're two weeks late with your rent." Tyrese finished counting the notes for the second time. He nodded and tucked the bills into his pocket. "I warned your dumb ass time and again. You only got yourself to blame."

"I'll give you another month's rent today," Brody countered. "Like, right fucking now. That'll give me until November."

"Not happening." Tyrese shuffled into the kitchen, pulled a jumbo bag of Cheetos from the cupboard, and poured them into his mouth. Bright orange crumbs popped from between his lips when he spoke. "I'm tired of your shit, Brody. It's over."

"Jesus, Tyrese—"

"I'm sorry as hell to be doing this, with your sister and all. Maybe that's why I gave you so many chances." More crumbs exploded from his mouth and peppered his sweatshirt. "I just can't afford to carry your ass no more. Shit, man, I work at Starbucks."

...

Brody helped himself to another of Tyrese's beers. He'd paid for it, after all—given the son of a bitch an extra ten bucks, for all the good it did. He drank it in a gloomy corner of the living room, mind pinwheeling, his anxiety amped.

Two weeks, he thought. His fingers tapped a mad rhythm on the bottle neck. *Out on our asses, if I'm not already behind bars.*

Brody knew only a tiny portion—five percent, maybe—of his anxiety could be attributed to Tyrese. The rest was down to the missing wallet. Sure, the police hadn't come knocking, but that didn't mean they wouldn't. They were probably trying to make him sweat. He'd be easier to break that way.

Another, more terrifying possibility occurred to Brody, and one he couldn't shake: Buddy's owner, Elias Abrahamian, hadn't called the cops because he'd decided to take matters into his own hands. He knew where Brody lived, of course, and tonight, or tomorrow night, or a week from now, he and his friends from the Armenian mob would pay him a visit. They'd kick down his door, put a bullet in Molly, then knock the shit out of Brody and cram him into the trunk of Elias's BMW. Brody would wake up in a damp cement room, peering through bruised eyes. *Steal from me, you fuckin' piece-of-shit, skinny-ass bitch?* Elias would say, selecting one from a multitude of torture implements arranged on a wooden bench. *Let me show you what I do to motherfucks who steal from me.*

Brody tossed the beer without finishing it, then dashed to his room and checked the jacket he'd been wearing yet again. He checked his jeans, too, front pockets and back. No wallet. He ran out to his car and went through it, using the flashlight on his cell phone to peer into all the small corners.

Nothing.

He drove to Freewood Valley and parked down the street from Buddy's, exactly where he'd parked some fourteen hours before. Knowing it was desperate, and pointless, he kicked at the trash and dead leaves at the edges of the sidewalk, and in the shallow gutter running beside the road. He ventured all the way down to Buddy's lot, and might have gone farther, but stopped when he saw the black-and-white cruiser angled in

one of the parking spaces. A coincidence? Maybe.
But Brody thought it more likely that the FVPD had
finally gotten around to investigating the robbery,
and were in the process of viewing security footage
of Brody hitting Ant the salesclerk with the grip of
his pistol, then lifting two-thousand-plus dollars from
the cash register.

...

Molly said, "You didn't clean," which was a kinder
way of saying what she *really* wanted to: *Jesus, Brody,
can't you do anything?* She sat on the sofa and started
to cry. Brody went to her. He held her, but his arms
felt thin and feeble.

"It'll be okay." His words were feeble, too.

"October tenth. That's fifteen days away."

"I know. I'll think of something."

He couldn't see beyond the more immediate problem, though: jail time or the Armenian mob. If, by
some miracle, he came out of this unscathed, then he
could think about a long-term living solution.

"What are we going to do?"

Running was an option, he supposed—shacking up
at a Motel 15, a long way from town, until this whole
crazy shitstorm blew over.

"Brody?"

"I need time to think." He kissed Molly's wet cheek and touched his forehead briefly to hers. When he stood up to go into the bedroom, his phone started ringing.

. . .

Unknown number. Brody stared at his phone's screen for a long time. He imagined Elias Abrahamian at the other end, snarling, his gold tooth winking. *I'm coming for you, bitch*, he'd say as soon as Brody answered. *Like a jackal.*

He let it go to voice mail, then checked his messages. There were none. His phone rang again ninety seconds later. The same number. This time Brody answered.

"Hi, Brody."

"Who is this?"

It wasn't Elias Abrahamian, that was for sure. The voice was female, high-spirited. He imagined it belonging to a punk-haired Manga character or sk8er girl, somebody tattooed and pierced and unafraid.

"Your new best friend," she said, and giggled.

"I know who you are." Because he did. He drew a quick and accurate line from the robbery to this moment, and saw a girl with purple hair looping from beneath an Oakley beanie, wagon-red lipstick, a scar beneath her left eye. He'd collided with her on his way out of the store.

Brody smiled, despite everything. He sensed a beat of excitement across the line—of *daring*.

"So," the girl said, and giggled again. "Do you want your wallet back?"

Chapter Three

Nothing ever changed at Rocky T's. It was the same colorless décor, the same dour faces lining the bar, the same heartland rock on the jukebox. Even the bartender, Macy, was the same. She'd served every drink Brody had downed there, no matter the time of day, and never with a smile. Brody wondered if she kept a sleeping bag behind the bar that she rolled into when Rocky T's closed its doors at three A.M., and rolled out of again to begin work a few hours later.

He ordered a Bud Light and took a seat at one of the booths. TVs ran sports highlights and Bob Seger sang about—what else?—that old-time rock and roll. Brody looked around without making eye contact with anyone. There was no sign of the girl with the purple hair.

Brody was early, though. Twenty minutes early. His relief that the cops didn't have his wallet was enveloped only by his need to get out of the house. He couldn't stand to look one minute more into Molly's sad eyes.

. . .

"Waitin' for yer date to show?" Macy asked when he ordered his second beer ten minutes later. Her bleak eyes found his for a moment, then dropped like weights. She had a fat lip on its way to healing— somebody had clearly popped her in the kisser. "You finally hit up Craigslist, find yerself a cum dumpster?"

"Jesus, Macy, you found your calling in customer service. No doubt about it." Brody threw a five on the bar. "Keep the change."

He returned to his booth, sank half of his beer in a single draw. Tom Petty belted from the juke—"Don't Do Me Like That."

The girl with the purple hair arrived in a dropkick of color.

. . .

Not a beanie but a yellow headband that lifted her hair into a vibrant sheaf. Her earrings and jacket were the blue of a new pool table. Shockingly red lipstick. The scar beneath her eye caught the light like broken glass.

She slid in across from Brody and everybody turned to see.

"Heya."

Brody nodded and made a tight sound in his throat. He had hoped to appear strong. Badass. He had failed already.

"You look," she said, "*so* different without your ski mask."

"Jesus Christ." A glance toward the bar. All eyes on their booth. Even Macy was looking, her fat lip curled. "You want to lower your goddamn voice?"

"Whoops. Sorry." Her eyes shimmered. She whispered, "*You look so different when you're not robbing a convenience store.*"

"Jesus Christ."

Brody didn't have a game plan, but he thought he might play ignorant, deny all knowledge of the robbery, grab his wallet—give Miss Purple Hair a $20 reward—and go home. He saw now that this wasn't going to work. The girl was sharp, and all sharp things had to be handled with care.

He said, "You have something of mine."

The girl nodded, reached into her jacket pocket, and took out a Chase Bank Mastercard. She pushed it across the table. It was *his* Mastercard, of course, with its 23.9 percent APR and $7,500 limit (maxed).

"Where's the rest?" Brody asked.

"I have it. Not with me. But it's safe. I brought this"—she tapped the card with one bright pink fingernail—"so you'd know I'm not lying."

Brody sat back in his seat and looked at her through narrowed eyes. His chest tightened with impatience. He knew what she wanted: a take of the money. And how could he blame her? In her situation, he'd do the same thing.

"How much?"

"What?" She attempted an innocent expression, but there was too much mischief to cover. Her red lips twitched.

"Your cut," Brody said. "To keep quiet. That's what this is all about, right?"

She barked a short, hollow laugh. "Shit, Bro, do I look like I need money? These boots . . ." She lifted her right leg and clomped her boot on the table. It had a block heel, glimmering studs and buckles. "Valentino Garavani. Fifteen hundred dollars. This jacket. Seventeen hundred dollars. A birthday present. And you know what? I was pissed when I opened it because I wanted the one with the silver buttons."

Brody angled his head, his eyes still narrowed. He wondered what a girl who wore $1,500 boots was doing, alone, at Buddy's Convenience Store at 4:55 in the morning. The question touched his lips, but instead he asked:

"So what *do* you want?"

"You can start by buying me a drink." There was a dog-eared drinks menu on the table. She grabbed it, danced her finger over the cocktails. "Eeny, meeny, miny, moe." Her finger came down. "Sex on the Beach. Lucky me."

"That's an eight-dollar fucking cocktail," Brody gasped. "How about a shot of Tiger Breath? Tastes like shit, but it's only a buck fifty."

"Tempting, Brody. Very." She dropped a wink that pulled at something inside him. "Sex on the Beach. Make it snappy."

Brody rolled his eyes, went to the bar, ordered the drink.

"Shit, boy," Macy remarked. Still no smile, but her broken lip lifted. "She's got you wrapped around her finger."

"You don't know the half of it."

Macy mixed. Brody waited, looking at his sneaker tops, not at the old drunk next to him who'd started to sing along to Mellencamp, getting the lyrics wrong—

". . . *hold onto six piece, long as you can, Chinese come around real soon mixing women and men . . .*"

—and then Macy pushed the cocktail toward him,

tall and orangey-red and served in a murky glass. Brody thanked her with a nod, reeled away from the bar, handed the drink to the girl with the purple hair as he took his seat in the booth. She closed her lips around the straw, cheeks dented as she sucked. "Dee-fucking-lish." She giggled, sucked again, and Brody, male, red-blooded, flushed from the groin out. He cleared his throat and mopped a film of sweat from his nose.

"I know a little about you, Brody," the girl said a moment later, swirling her drink with the straw. "I looked you up on Facebook. Everybody's favorite glory hole."

"Cute."

"Twenty-four years old. Star sign, Virgo. Dropped out of high school at seventeen—"

"To help my old man pay the bills."

"You like Foo Fighters, Arcade Fire, and *Stranger Things*. Is *The Matrix* really your favorite movie?"

"It's a classic."

"Seventy-nine friends. (By the way, some of them aren't *really* friends.) Relationship status: *nada*. Worked at Wolfe Aluminum—past tense. Your sister, Molly, has cerebral palsy."

"And yet I know nothing about you." Brody swigged from his beer, warm now, and flat. "I don't even know your name."

"Blair."

"As in, Witch Project?"

"Oh shit. That's an *old* one, Bro." That short, hollow laugh again. "I expected better from you."

"I guess I left my A-game at home." Brody sneered. That was the second time she'd shortened his name, or perhaps she was calling him *bro*, as in *brother*. Either way, it felt too familiar, too goddamn chummy, and he didn't like it. "So what *do* you want, Blair?"

"I'm getting to that." She sucked on her straw again, managing to smile at the same time. Her eyes had a cunning he couldn't help but find alluring. "You know all about loss, don't you, Brody? That deep, soul-sucking hurt. I'm guessing you still feel it."

Brody cleared his throat again.

Blair said, "Your father died seven months ago. Suicide. I read about it online. He jumped off the Folgt Building."

"What does any of this have to do with my goddamn wallet?" Brody leaned across the table. He gripped the edges with hands that had started to tremble.

"Your mom's not around, huh? Did she run away with her boss? Her brother-in-law?" Blair leaned across the table, too, her eyes digging into his. The glow around her dimmed. "Is she dead?"

"Dead to me." There were sparks in Brody's voice. He let go of the table and flexed his hands. "You know what, keep the wallet. I don't need this shit."

"I'm not going to keep it, Brody. What the fuck do I want with an empty wallet?" Blair sat back, sucked playfully on her straw, all candy and rainbows again. "I'll just hand it over to the police, tell them where and when I found it. Armed robbery is a felony, Brody. I think you know that. But did you know that here, in South Carolina, it carries a mandatory minimum sentence of ten years in prison?"

Brody covered his tired eyes.

"Up to thirty years. Thirty fucking years, man, with no shot at parole for the first seven." Blair whistled through her teeth. "Who's going to look after your sister while you're stamping license plates at the state pen?"

"The cops'll want to know why you didn't hand the wallet over at the time," Brody ventured. It was a desperate, straw-grasping plea, but it was all he had. "Withholding evidence—obstruction of justice—is an offense, too, Blair. Is that a chance you're willing to take?"

"I'll tell them I feared for my life," Blair said, and grinned. "You'd seen my face and . . . yeah, you had this *crazy* look in your eyes, and . . . well, I was just so *scared* you'd find a way to track me down." Her grin disappeared. She turned her lips down and her eyes swelled—huge brown O's brimming with guileless-ness. "In the end, and despite the danger, I decided it was the right thing to do."

Brody groaned. He felt drained.

"You know, I think they'll be so jazzed with the evidence, and so busy dealing with you, that they won't bother with me." She grinned again. "Or maybe not. But hey, is that a chance *you're* willing to take?"

The jukebox switched tracks. The pinball machine flashed. Someone at the bar cracked a joke and there was a clamor of laughter. Macy didn't smile. Brody took all this in with his tired eyes.

"I've got you where I want you," Blair said.

"Okay." Brody opened his arms, expanding the target. "So what's this about?"

Blair leaned across the table again. Everything about her was reckless, dangerous, exhilarating. She touched his hand—stroked it, suggestively, and Brody's heart clanged like a rock against an empty barrel.

She said, "I want you to steal something for me."

• • •

"I'm not a thief."

"There's surveillance video at Buddy's Convenience Store that says differently."

"That was a one-off. I was desperate."

"You're *still* desperate."

Brody had no answer to that. He tried to hold her gaze—to show some damn backbone—but she outshone him, as intense as a light in an interrogation room. He stared at the dregs of his warm beer instead, his fingers drumming idly on the tabletop. When he looked up again, Blair had slumped back in her seat. Her head was down.

"I know about loss, too." Her voice was almost too soft to hear. She had switched from manic to forlorn in a matter of seconds. "I can't remember the last time I had a good night's sleep. And all this . . ." She gestured at her purple hair and savagely colored lips. "It's a mask, Bro, hiding that deep, soul-sucking hurt I was talking about. Sometimes it feels like an anchor strapped to my ankle. I can float. I can ride the waves. But I'm always stuck in the same place."

"You've known me twenty minutes," Brody said. The iciness in his voice was a barefaced attempt to jump on her when she was down—to take back an iota of control. "You can call me Brody."

"Well, ex*cuse* me, BRO-*deeeeee*." She rolled her eyes, then lowered them again. "My mom died nineteen months ago. February twenty-sixth, 2018. One year—to the day—before your dad died, in fact. So I guess, despite the sugary frosting and Valentino Garavani boots, we've got something in common."

Brody's jaw throbbed. His throat was so dry that he drank the dregs of his beer anyway, and shuddered all the way to his pelvis.

"She had bone cancer," Blair continued. "It took her out quickly. From diagnosis to dead in four months. She was forty-six years old."

"I'm sorry. That's . . ." Anything Brody said would be redundant, so he closed his mouth.

"There are a few things you need to know." Blair looked up again. Some of the flare had returned to her expression. "First, my mom was my best friend. We did everything together, and her death stopped me in my tracks. I attempted suicide three times, and came close once—had to have my stomach pumped at a hospital in Munich. The second thing you need to know is that my asshole father was cheating on her—even during her illness—with a woman named Meredith. Now, you've never met Meredith, but you *know* her. Just picture every hoity-toity, money-grubbing bitch you've ever seen in any movie or soap opera, like, ever."

Brody gestured to indicate he had such a picture in his head.

"That's Meredith," Blair snapped. "She's a fucking vile human being. An upper-level *biznatch*. And get this . . . she's my stepmom now."

"Well, shit, I'm sorry about your luck." Brody rubbed his eyes. "With that, and not getting the exact seventeen-hundred-dollar jacket you wanted, my heart just fucking bleeds for you."

"Asshole."

"You want to cut to the chase?"

"Oh, I'm sorry, do you have somewhere else to be?" Blair raised her voice. "JAIL, maybe?"

Brody stiffened in his seat, then looked the length of the bar to see if Blair had drawn any extra attention. She had; several whiskery faces had swiveled their way. "Punch her in the eye," one of those faces growled— Brody wasn't sure which one. "Mind your goddamn business," he barked back emptily. "I'll punch *you* in the eye."

"The third thing you need to know," Blair continued, unruffled by the attention, "is that my mom promised me her diamonds. It wasn't in her will or anything. It was something we talked about—an understanding between the two of us." She gestured at her ears and throat. "A pendant. Matching earrings. From Harry Winston. Not their top-of-the-line set, but probably worth fifty thousand dollars."

"Jesus," Brody said.

"They were a graduation gift from Nancy Reagan."

"Holy shit. Really?"

"My mom was from good stock, Brody." Blair finished her drink, looking away from him, and for just a second he saw the hurt in her eyes. "The idea was that I'd wear them on my wedding day, so that some small part of Mom would be with me." Blair blinked, scuffed the back of one hand across her cheek. "And then my daughter, or daughter-in-law, would wear them on *her* wedding day, and so on . . ."

Brody nodded. His old man didn't have any money, and didn't leave them much beyond a closet full of faded clothes, a vinyl collection from the 1980s, and a five-year-old Chevy Malibu with monthly payments they couldn't meet. Brody sold what he could and took the rest to Goodwill. He kept one thing, though: a leather biker jacket that his dad had bought as a teenager, fully intending to one day buy the motorcycle to go with it—a Harley, of course—and ride from New York City to Los Angeles. Sadly, this life goal was never accomplished, but that didn't mean it couldn't be reinvented. Sorting through his old man's things, Brody found the jacket, hung it in his own closet, and had fostered ever since the fantasy that he might one day zip himself into it, and make the cross-country journey for them both.

He understood, as well as anybody, that people can survive in the things they leave behind.

"I took off after Mom died," Blair said. "I couldn't handle that shit. I went to Europe, India, Thailand. I was gone for eleven months, and when I returned to America, Dad and Meredith were married. And do you know what Daddy's gift to Meredith was?"

"Mommy's diamonds," Brody said.

"Ding-ding-ding. We have a winner."

"I've got to admit." Brody looked at her with some sympathy. "That's an asshole move."

"You're damn right it's an asshole move."

"And, what . . . you want me to break into your parents' house, steal the diamonds for you?"

"Ding-ding-ding." Blair beamed. Her smile was off slightly—a few crooked teeth—but brilliant, nonetheless. "Shit, Brody, maybe you *did* bring your A-game."

"Maybe. And it's telling me to stay the hell away from this."

"Why?"

"Listen, I dig your bouncy rebel vibe, I really do, and I even feel a shred of sympathy for you." Brody held his thumb and forefinger half an inch apart. "But don't you think, when the diamonds go missing, that you're going to be prime suspect *numero uno*?"

"No, because I'm going to be with my dad when you steal them." Blair was still beaming. "The perfect alibi."

"But you won't be able to wear the diamonds. Or flaunt them. Or whatever the fuck else you do with diamonds. So what's the point?"

"The point, Brody, is that they'll be in the possession of their rightful owner. It's a matter of principle." Blair pushed her empty glass to one side, propped her elbows on the table, and leaned closer. "And no, I won't be able to wear them, but I've rented a safe-deposit box at a bank in Freewood Valley. That's where they'll stay, at least for the foreseeable future. And then, when God finally answers my prayers and strikes Meredith dead, I'll wear them to her fucking funeral."

Brody fetched an exhausted sigh. In lieu of sleep, he bought another beer. He bought Blair a drink, too, the same eight-dollar cocktail. Macy served him without comment. The old drunk mumbled along to Springsteen.

"Thanks." Blair nodded at the drink.

"Sure."

A strange silence seeped between them as they tended to their drinks—strange in that it was comfortable. Despite Blair's brash, brattish exterior, Brody had warmed to her. Just a little.

"This is not an impulsive thing, Brody. You should know I've been thinking about this for a long time." She licked her lips and shrugged. Her eyes, Brody noticed, were subtly different colors: brown and a lighter brown. "I thought about hiring someone. An ex-con, you know? But shit, I don't know anybody like that. I'm just a spoiled girl from the Valley. And then, when I bumped into you and your wallet dropped at my feet . . . well, I guess I saw that as a sign."

"Right." Brody glugged his beer, wiped his mouth, nodded. "I can see that, I guess. But, Blair, I'm *not* a thief. I know what I did, and I know what I'm capable of. And trust me, you need a professional, someone with lockpicks and wire cutters and . . . Jesus, whatever else thieves use. I'm just a jerkoff with a fake gun. I *will* fuck this up."

"Next Thursday. October third. One of my dad's business interests is throwing him a big, swanky party at the country club." Blair raised her penciled eyebrows. "I'll be there with my dad and Meredith. Our house will be empty."

"And I'm guessing that empty house will be rigged with a high-end alarm system and light sensors. Maybe a guard dog."

"No dog," Blair said. "Light sensors in front only. And yeah, there's an alarm system, which *will* be activated if you go through any doors or break any glass. Sunrise Security will be on the scene within five minutes." Her cheeks pulsed as she sucked on her straw. "But I've planned this out, Brody. Every detail. You're going to ghost in, then ghost out again. Invisible. You won't even need your ski mask."

"Good," Brody said. "Because I've already dumped it."

"My bedroom window will be unlatched," Blair said. "It's on the south side of the property. Second window from the right. You can access it by climbing onto the pool house. It's an easy climb. I've done it myself, like, a *thousand* times."

"Sneaking in from all-night parties?"

"You know it." She grinned and touched his hand again. "Bad girl, right?"

"I guess." He lowered his eyes.

"Okay, so once you're in my room—and oh, excuse the mess, by the way, it's just, *ugh*, like, you know . . ." She threw her hands up, exasperated, as if troublesome pixies snuck into her room while she wasn't there and threw her shit all over. "Anyway, go straight through and on to the landing. My dad and Meredith's room is to the right, the double doors at the top of the stairs. Oh, and I'm *sure* I don't need to remind you to wear gloves, so you don't leave any paw prints on the door handles."

"I may not be a thief," Brody said, "but I'm not an idiot, either."

"You dropped your wallet at the scene of a crime, so . . ."

Brody rolled his eyes and gestured for her to continue.

"Their room is *hyooooge*. Two walk-in closets, his-and-her bathrooms, a bed the size of Alaska. I'm not kidding, Bro, they'd need GPS to find each other and fuck."

"Wow, so . . . elegant. So refined."

"Always." Blair smiled and lifted her chin. Her sheaf of purple hair swished. "Okay, the important part: Meredith keeps her jewelry in her dresser. It's the one against the far wall, between the two picture windows. It has three mirrors and a stool in front with a gold cushion. There are hair-spray cans and makeup boxes and a few other things on top. I suggest throwing all that crap on the floor, emptying the drawers—"

"You want it to look like a robbery," Brody said. "Like the thief was after anything of value, not just your mom's diamonds."

"Exactly." Blair snapped her fingers. "I knew you were the right man for the job."

Brody slurped his beer and shrugged.

"The diamonds are in the top middle drawer on the right-hand side." Blair said, just above a whisper. "That drawer will be locked, but you can jimmy it easily with a flathead screwdriver. Now, I've served this on a platter for you, Brody—given you a blueprint for success. But you're going to have to bring your own screwdriver."

An imperceptible nod, but he hadn't agreed to anything. Not yet.

"The diamonds are in a black case with the Harry Winston logo on it. That's an uppercase *H* above an uppercase *W.* Leave the case, but grab the pendant and earrings. It'll look like you weren't after that case, specifically. You feel me?"

"I feel you."

"I'm stating the obvious here, but don't just take the diamonds. That *would* look suspicious—like, you know, I'd hired someone to steal them."

"Or blackmailed someone."

Blair's face, already cartoon-bright, lit from within. She smiled and everything shone. "Damn, I *like* you, Brody. You're so cute. Maybe, after all this, we can get together and paint the town a wicked shade of red."

Don't count on it, Brody wanted to say, but the words wouldn't come. Blair was heedless and loud and utterly refreshing. He thought going on a date with her would be like swimming with a stingray or BASE jumping from El Capitan, but it might be just the kick in the ass his dismal life needed. So he shrugged and lifted one eyebrow.

"Maybe," he said.

"Take whatever else you want," Blair continued. She took a long pull on her straw and a third of the drink disappeared. "Meredith has a lot of jewelry. *Too* much, that goddamn pig. Do whatever you want with it. Pawn it, give it to your sister, I don't give a fuck. All I care about are my mom's diamonds."

Brody tried to resist, but couldn't keep from indulging in a brief fantasy: hitting up several pawnshops across the state, racking up the stacks, then checking in to a safe, clean hotel (not the Motel 15, with its invariable assemblage of crackheads and whores) and staying there until he'd turned things around. If everything worked out, he and Molly could be in their new apartment—in Cauley, of course, maybe overlooking the river—by Christmas.

Brody pursed his lips. He knew it was foolhardy to give this fantasy even brief life. But if—just *if*—Blair's plan went as smoothly as she said it would . . . well, things could really work out.

"Bring me the diamonds," Blair said now, rattling her pink fingernails against her glass, "and you'll get your wallet back. If you *don't* bring me the diamonds—shit, if you can't do this for me, Brody, then I'm going to the police. And don't think for one second that I won't do it, because I will."

Of this, Brody had no doubt. He finished his beer and said, "I guess you really do have me where you want me."

Blair made a pistol out of her right hand. She aimed at Brody, pulled the trigger.

"This is crazy shit," Brody said. He ran his hands through his hair. His scalp was slick with sweat. "My dad always told me that two wrongs don't make a right."

"But maybe two wrongs *can* keep your ass out of jail." Blair drained her glass of everything but the ice cubes. "I've made this very simple for you. Do exactly what I say, and it can't fail."

"I guess you've never heard of Murphy's Law."

"'Whatever can go wrong, will go wrong.' Yeah, I've heard of it. And it's pessimistic bullshit."

"You're talking to a guy who dropped his wallet the *one fucking time* he robbed a convenience store, whose mom ran out on him when he was twelve years old, whose dad decided to swan-dive off a fourteen-story office building. Trust me, Blair, I'm very used to things going wrong." He took a deep breath and looked at her squarely. "Jesus Christ, I should change my last name to Murphy."

"Yeah. So sad. Did I mention the ten-year minimum sentence?"

"Would you cut me some slack?"

"I'm cutting you a *deal*, Brody. That's how things get done." Blair counted off the pros on her fingers. "You get your freedom, my dad gets a sizable insurance payout, and I get my mom's diamonds. Everybody comes out on top."

"Yeah, right."

"So what do you say?"

Brody slumped in his seat. So many thoughts ricocheted around his mind. He pressed the heel of his hand against his forehead and sighed.

"This is a no-brainer, Brody, but I can see you're tired—probably not thinking straight—so here's what I'm going to do." She tipped a wink and flashed her smile again. "I'm going to let you sleep on it. *That's* the kind of girl I am. But I *will* call you tomorrow morning, bright and breezy. And if you don't pick up the phone, or if you *do* but don't tell me what I want to hear . . ."

She made a siren sound—"Weeooooow-weeooooow"— and used her forearm to mimic a cell door slamming. "*Bam!* Don't drop the soap, brother."

"There must be another way," Brody muttered. "I'll wash your car for a year . . . I'll clean your goddamn room—"

"I've told you what I want." Blair got to her feet, standing all of five-five in her designer boots, but appearing so much taller. She leaned over and dropped a moist kiss on his cheek, very close to his lips. "I wasn't kidding when I said you were cute."

Brody squeaked something in reply, then she was gone, bounding exuberantly from the bar, leaving nothing behind but the print of her lipstick on his face.

. . .

He'd made his mind up before the door had even closed behind her, and became certain of his decision on the long walk home—to the point where he nearly pulled up her number on his phone and called her back. He didn't, though, because he was tired, and she was something else, and he wanted a clear head the next time he spoke to her.

Molly had fallen asleep in the armchair, her crutches resting against the cluttered coffee table, within reach. Brody sat on the arm beside her, brushing strands of light brown hair—the same color as his—from her brow. He recalled that memory from so long ago, its power refusing to fade over time: of standing resolutely beside her hospital bed, his hand joined to hers, promising to be there if she ever needed someone to lean on.

Brody lost himself to sleep soon after and dreamed brightly.

. . .

His phone rang a little before nine A.M. He was already awake, propped against his pillows, waiting.

"Did you dream about me?"

"I don't dream."

"Everybody dreams, Brody."

He smiled—yes, this was true—and listened to her breathing over the line, the near-silence of anticipation.

"So?"

He imagined her in her messy room, cross-legged on the bed, colorless without makeup but vibrant within, maybe dressed in Winnie-the-Pooh pajamas and chewing her lower lip.

"So," he said.

"You going to do this?"

"Yeah."

"The right decision."

"We'll see."

He heard Tyrese singing in the shower, the neighbors quarreling, Molly's crutches thonking across the kitchen linoleum. These were delightfully normal, unexciting sounds, and Brody thought in that moment that he could listen to them forever.

Blair said, breaking the ordinariness, "I live at 1186 Windsor Grove. That's in Freewood Valley. The Laurels. You know it?"

"I know it."

"Okay." Blair took a deep breath. "I'm going to run through the plan one more time. Are you listening?"

"I'm listening."

"Good."

Chapter Four

B rody had been to the Laurels only once in his life. His father had driven him and Molly through it shortly after their mom took to her heels. "A possible future," he'd said, rolling their old car past multimillion-dollar homes set back from the roads (private roads, not a crack or pothole to be found), pointing out the multiple-car garages and lustrous lawns, the security gates at the ends of long driveways, the fountains and sculptures. "You can live in a place like this if you work hard, if you go to college and give it everything you've got." From the get-go, he took his single-parent responsibilities seriously. Indeed, the only big fight he and Brody had—it nearly came to blows—was when Brody dropped out of high school to get a job, help out with the bills. "You can kiss your house in the Laurels goodbye," his dad had stated resignedly, and there were tears in his eyes.

Brody didn't think he'd ever return to the Laurels, but his life's script had been flipped again.

He was back, not to buy a house, but to steal from one.

...

He parked half a mile from Blair's house and walked across Poplar Common—just a regular dude out for an evening stroll. The car being so far away didn't bother him; if this went the way Blair insisted it would, he wouldn't need to make a quick getaway.

Windsor Grove bordered the common on its northwest side. Blair told him that the simplest way onto her property—to avoid being seen or triggering the light sensors—was to cut through the dense woodland that ran between the common and her backyard (although "yard" was an extremely modest term for an area of real estate that could host the next Panthers game). "Those woods are thick," Blair had warned him. "I suggest you navigate them early evening, while there's still some light in the sky, then hang loose until it gets dark. We'll be out of the house at seven, and home by nine-thirty. That gives you plenty of time."

Brody crept into the woods a full hour before sunset. He twisted through an acre of crowded trees and blackened brush, and soon arrived at the perimeter of Blair's backyard. An eight-foot chain-link fence stood in front of him, but didn't present a problem. Chain-link fences were designed to be climbed, with their numerous little rungs and handholds, and the house was so distantly removed from its neighbors that no one would see him do so.

Hopefully.

He remained between the trees and scanned the back of the property. The light was dropping fast, but he saw the soft, greenish shimmer of the swimming pool and pool house beyond. Just like Blair said, its position offered easy access to her room—the second window from the right. He nodded. Her intel had, so far at least, been accurate.

Yeah, that's great, a voice in his mind spoke up— the same voice that had advised him to back down at Buddy's Convenience Store. *But you're not even on the property yet. Anything can go wrong.*

"Thanks for the vote of confidence," Brody whispered.

She's a loose cannon. You can't trust her.

"I have no choice."

He checked his phone, shielding the light with his hand just in case someone caught a flicker of it from the house. 6:29. He retreated a few feet, found a dark space between the trees, and waited.

He scaled the fence at 8:10.

. . .

His heart hammered as he crossed the sloping lawn toward the pool house, moving on loose legs, the breaths punched quickly from his lungs. *I can't believe you're doing this again,* the voice in his mind persisted. *Are you fucking crazy?* He provided an answer by imagining—for the thousandth time—his and Molly's cool new apartment in Cauley, their beds separated by a wall, not a flimsy curtain, Molly wearing nice clothes, eating healthy foods. A rainbow of possibilities arced through his mind as he wobbled across the grass, around the pool, and pressed himself tight to the pool house wall. He wasn't doing the right thing here, he knew that. But there was sometimes a difference between what was right and what was necessary.

The voice in his mind fell silent.

Brody took a moment to work the jitters out of his legs and steady his breathing. His ungainly bustle across the lawn had triggered no lights or alarms, summoned no dogs. So far, so good. He plucked his gloves from his jacket pocket and pulled them on, then peered around the side of the pool house. A single spotlight shone on the water, coaxing a kaleidoscope of inviting reflections. More lights burned inside the large house, probably to offer the illusion that someone was home. Brody was caught, briefly, by the grandness of it. Old stone and rich timber, its faux-rustic structure offset by an extravagance of glass. He peered through this glass and saw Oriental rugs hanging on the walls and modern sculpture and a vast aquarium bristling with exotic fish. Blair's old man may as well have decorated the joint with hundred-dollar bills.

Brody watched for movement and listened for any sound—a TV playing, a creaking floorboard, a running faucet—that would indicate somebody was home.

Nothing. The exotic fish were the only sign of life.

"Okay." He took another deep, draining breath. Silvery spots flashed across his field of vision. "Let's do this."

He ducked around the other side of the pool house and used two solid pipes to clamber onto a heater the size of a refrigerator. From here he pulled himself onto the roof, then crawled carefully toward Blair's bedroom window. This provided the biggest challenge yet; the roof was slick and pitched at an angle. He came close to slipping twice. It would be just his luck—Murphy's Law in full effect—to slide off the goddamn roof and impale himself on the flathead screwdriver he'd tucked into his jacket pocket. He imagined Blair's bitchy step-mom stepping out for her midnight skinny-dip, and discovering him moaning, near death, bleeding into the pool.

He grasped the window ledge with both hands. When he was sure he had his feet beneath him and that he wasn't going to slip, he transitioned his grip to the bottom of the frame. Blair had told him she'd leave the window unlatched. He closed his eyes and lifted.

A part of him wanted the window to be locked in place. That way he could abandon this nonsense. *Hey, I tried,* he'd say to Blair. *You forgot to leave the window unlatched. This shit is on you, honey. Now give me my goddamn wallet back.* Another part expected an alarm to sound—for a helicopter to appear suddenly and hover overhead, its searchlight covering him.

Neither of these things happened. Blair's bedroom window slid up smoothly. Her lacy curtains billowed against his face.

"Shit," Brody said.

He went inside.

. . .

Another reliable piece of intel: Blair's room really was a mess. It may once have been the over-pink refuge of a spoiled Valley teenager, but had deteriorated since into mayhem—*fashionable* mayhem, as if an F3 tornado had spiraled through a branch of Nordstrom. There was a suggestion of the rebel inside: posters of Jim Morrison and Che Guevara, an Ayn Rand quote stenciled on her closet door: THE QUESTION ISN'T WHO IS GOING TO LET ME; IT'S WHO IS GOING TO STOP ME.

Brody picked his way across the room, wondering why she hadn't cleaned up at least some of this shit, given she was expecting a "guest." But then, maybe such uncharacteristic behavior would arouse suspicion. If this was the case—as opposed to pure laziness—then Blair really had thought of everything.

"I'm beginning to trust you more and more," he said under his breath, opening her bedroom door and skulking onto the landing.

This trust would last another ninety-eight seconds.

...

A light at the far end of the landing illuminated the double doors to the master bedroom. There was a potted yucca to either side and to the right a framed Warhol-style painting, not of Marilyn Monroe, but of a middle-aged woman with the same teased hair and sultry expression. This, Brody assumed, was Blair's stepmom, and in that moment he believed everything Blair had said about her to be true.

He paused on the landing for a second or two, listening to the house, for any whisper of life. He heard a dim, motorized buzzing. The refrigerator, perhaps, or the aquarium. Other than that . . . a perfect stillness. Brody scurried toward the master bedroom. The right door was ajar. He pushed it, tiptoed into darkness, stroked the wall for a light switch.

Click.

Brody's jaw fell two inches and he turned a full circle, awed. The house he shared with Molly and Tyrese would fit twice in here, with enough room left over for dancing. The bed was indeed Alaska, with its mountain range of greige pillows and glacier-white comforter. There were three chandeliers, several animal-skin rugs, a balcony with a hot tub and a Glassy Mountain view.

"Jesus Christ."

This was all so far removed from Brody's world that it took him a moment to notice the blood splashed across the hardwood floor. He almost stepped in it, in fact, drawing his foot back with a surprised gasp.

"What the—"

All thoughts of Blair's diamonds vacated his mind. His jaw still swaying, Brody followed the blood across the room—its pattern beguilingly signpost-like—and everything inside him turned cold when he rounded the side of the bed and saw the corpse.

. . .

It was the woman in the Warhol-style painting, easily recognizable with her teased blond hair and Botox lips. She was slumped in the corner, one arm tucked behind her head, her body twisted at an unnatural angle. Her bathrobe had rucked up to her thighs, which were smeared with blood. There was more blood on the walls and a circular puddle on the hardwood floor. It ran down her arms and drenched her body. She'd been stabbed multiple times. The knife—a *big* knife—was still lodged in her chest.

Brody's legs crumpled. He fell to his knees with a deep moan and stared at the dead woman until an increment of awareness returned. "Oh Jesus. Oh fuck." It took several weak attempts to get back to his feet but he managed, using the bed for support. "Jesus . . . this isn't . . . oh shit."

What was happening here?

A memory surfaced, clear and bright. He saw Blair sitting across from him at Rocky T's—punky, rebellious Blair, with her burning lipstick and dangerous eyes. *And then*, she said, talking about her precious diamonds, *when God finally answers my prayers and strikes Meredith dead, I'll wear them to her fucking funeral.*

"Blair," Brody said in a small, cracked voice.

The voice at the back of his mind was firmer. *Time to haul ass, Brody.* It jerked him to his senses, as potent as ammonia. *I told you she was a loose cannon. Now get the fuck out of here—this isn't your shit to deal with.*

"Blair," he said again. He shook his head. Could she really . . . ?

GET OUT!

Out. Yes. Right now. To hell with Blair and the diamonds. To hell with his wallet. He floundered backward. His sneaker slipped in Meredith's blood. "Gah . . . Christ." He wiped it thoroughly on one of the rugs. He'd seen *CSI;* leaving a footprint—even a partial footprint, the barest edge of one sneaker—could unfold badly for him.

Brody loped across the large room, through the double doors, and onto the landing. The staircase curved before him, leading to a lavish entranceway—to a door out of this place. He lunged down five steps before remembering something else that Blair had told him: that the alarm system would be triggered if he went through any doors or broke any glass. It didn't matter that he'd left no prints behind; this would still unfold badly if Sunrise Security caught him trying to climb over the front gate.

He had to go out the same way he came in.

Brody bounded up the stairs and back onto the landing. He took a single step toward Blair's room, then froze when he heard that buzzing sound again. He'd thought before that it had come from downstairs—the refrigerator, perhaps, or the aquarium—but no, it was closer than that, and smaller.

It sounded like a cell phone vibrating on a flat surface, or like the motorized zoom on a digital . . .

"Camera," Brody groaned.

It was positioned in the right-hand corner, focused on the staircase and doors to the master bedroom. Brody hadn't noticed it before because of the angle of the wall.

"What the fuck?" Here was something else—along with the corpse in the bedroom—that Blair had failed to mention.

That sly bitch, he thought, and on the back of this a single word that jumped on his brain like a fat kid on a trampoline. *FRAMED . . . FRAMED . . . FRAMED . . .*

The camera buzzed again. A small but serious red light blinked on one side. Its blank eye stared at Brody, full of accusation.

He had no strength in his legs but ran anyway.

. . .

Blair's window was still open and he all but dived through it. He hit the pool house roof on his shoulder, rolled twice, and fell to the stamped concrete below. With his only stroke of good fortune that evening, he landed like a cat, feetfirst.

Around the pool, across the broad lawn, thunder in his mind and booming through his limbs. He didn't stop running until he hit the chain-link fence. It catapulted him backward and he landed on his ass with a grunt. Slowly, crying now, he regained his feet and jumped at the fence, made it over in a mad, trembling scramble.

"What the fuck?" He'd whimpered this—and variations thereof—since he noticed the surveillance camera. "What the *fuuuuck*? What the actual fuck?"

Thin branches whipped and snagged at him as he crashed through the woodland, swinging his arms like machetes. He collided with trees, stumbled over roots, fell numerous times. Blood leaked from a shallow cut on his neck and his left glove was torn, hanging from his wrist by a strip of fabric. He got lost twice and had the presence of mind to use the Google Maps app on his phone. Eventually he wavered from the tree line and onto Poplar Common, bedraggled and breathless.

Ornate lights swept across the common, illuminating paved walkways dotted with people. Brody stuck to the shadows, brushing burs and leaves from his clothes as he moved. He climbed the wall and dropped onto Cardinal Street, then briskly walked the two blocks to where he'd parked his car.

His heart pounded. Tears dripped from his eyes.

What the fuck?

He got behind the wheel, worked the key into the ignition, but didn't crank it. He was in no condition to drive. Not yet. A short, tight scream ripped from his chest. He knotted his hands into fists and cried until his head was empty.

It was 9:27, according to the clock in the dashboard. For the next ten minutes, Brody tried to think through the situation. Should he go to the police? Would they believe him, a street kid from Rebel Point, who'd robbed a convenience store less than a week ago? Or would they believe Blair, whose mom had known Nancy Reagan, and who was clearly from good stock?

Would *not* going to the police make him look more guilty?

There were answers, he was sure of it. But they defied him, at least for now. His mind whirred hopelessly. It was like a computer that kept shutting down every time he issued a command.

"Help me," he cried.

9:33. His cell phone rang. He snatched it out of his pocket and saw Blair's number on the screen. A searing rage flared inside him. He clenched the device so tightly the casing cracked.

You bitch. You goddamn—

Brody pushed the green answer button and lifted the phone to his ear.

"Blair," he growled. He wanted to scream but his throat seized.

Nothing for a moment. He heard her breathing— imagined her sitting somewhere, her stupid fucking boots propped on the arm of a chair or on a table, a dirty smile tilting one side of her mouth. And then she spoke. Her voice was like battery acid.

"Heya, Bro," she said.

Chapter Five

Brody drove home with his mind slowly returning, like daybreak in a forest, gradually uncovering the dewy understory and the shapes of leaves, but predominantly illuminating the trees—so many tall and twisted trees—that he would have to navigate. They'd always been there, of course, but now they were deeper, denser, more uncertain.

And now there were wolves. Hungry . . . predatory. They had his scent. They were coming.

He ran a red light on Musgrove Road—pure absentmindedness—and his heart skipped at least five beats, but there were no cops in sight. All the Rebel Point cruisers would be nosing around Tank Hill, *his* neighborhood, where he was headed. But they weren't looking for him.

I've got some good news, some bad news, and some real bad news.

Tyrese's car was parked in their driveway, but positioned so that Brody couldn't pull in behind it. There was space for two if they went bumper-to-bumper. Tyrese was already reclaiming his turf, and that was fine. Brody didn't need until October tenth. He and Molly would be out before Jimmy Kimmel had finished his opening monologue.

Brody parked on the road and went inside. His front door key still worked, so there was that.

"Sup?" Tyrese asked without looking at him. He was watching *Thursday Night Football*, one hand wrapped around the remote control, the other dipped inside a bucket of KFC.

Brody ignored him. He shuffled through to the bedroom he shared with Molly. She was on her side of the curtain. He heard the unsteady clomp of her crutches across the floor, then the creak of the bedsprings. He stood for a moment, mopping tears from his eyes with his sweatshirt.

"Brody? That you?"

He took a jittery breath, fanned at his damp eyelashes with one hand. "Yeah, it's . . . it's me."

She heard it in his voice, of course, in those few brief, broken words. His anguish. His pain. The bedsprings creaked again. The curtain skated open and Molly was there. Without another word, she pulled him into her arms. Brody was straighter than her, his muscles were more firmly developed, but in that instant—as in so many other ways—she was the stronger of the two. She closed herself around him, her arms crossed behind his back, and held him like she'd never let go.

He cried onto her shoulder.

"Brody," she said. "What's wrong?"

Beat feet, Bro. Out of town. Out of state. Nowhere is too far.

"Moll," he managed between sobs. "I'm in so much trouble. And I think you might be, too."

. . .

The call had lasted almost seven minutes, according to the readout on his phone. In that brief time, Brody went from being utterly directionless to having his immediate future determined.

"Heya, Bro."

She said it just once but he heard it dozens of times. It dripped onto his brain—*drip-drip-drip*—and trickled into all the important grooves and crevices. The air inside his car turned acrid. He struggled to breathe.

"What did you do?" he managed at last.

"What I needed to," Blair replied. Her voice was remarkably controlled for someone who'd just knifed her stepmom to death. "Meredith was a gold-digging bitch, and my dad was blind to it."

"Jesus Christ, I know what you *did*." Brody's vision tripled. He blinked rapidly but it didn't help. "I mean, what did you do to *me*?"

"It's nothing personal, Brody. You dropped your wallet at my feet. I saw an opportunity and took it."

"You *took* it? You just fucking—"

"You're a high school dropout with no future. They used to send guys like you to Vietnam. To fucking *die*." She shrugged. Brody couldn't see this, of course, but he sensed it. She shrugged those wealthy, trouble-free shoulders. "You've taken the fall for the greater good. You're a sacrificial lamb."

"A sacrificial . . ." Brody gasped and spluttered. He had to thump his chest to get talking again. "You won't get away with this. I'll fight you every step of the way. I'll fucking *bury* you."

"Your public defender against the best lawyers in South Carolina. Good luck with that."

"You dumb bitch," Brody snarled. "I've got your calls logged on my phone. Your number. Times and dates. That proves—"

"It doesn't prove shit, Brody. I've been using a burner, which I'll destroy after this call." Blair spoke with such unnerving confidence that Brody didn't doubt her for a second. "I've spent so much time planning this, putting the pieces into place . . . do you honestly think I'd be stupid enough to call you on my cell phone?"

No, he didn't. He recalled her sharpness when they'd met at Rocky T's, and thinking that he'd have to handle her carefully. But he hadn't, and he'd been cut. Deeply.

There was something else, though . . .

"We were *seen* together," he said, unable to keep the desperation from his voice. "At Rocky T's. Jesus, you turned heads. *Everyone* saw you."

"Half-drunk assholes."

"The bartender wasn't drunk."

"Okay, but what did she see? You talking to some punk chick with purple hair." Blair made a sound, almost a giggle, mostly an exasperated sigh, as if she couldn't believe Brody's gullibility. "I don't *usually* look like that, you silly boy. I was incognito."

"I'll find something," Brody vowed, and then it came to him. He snapped his fingers. "Shit, yeah. Time of death. It won't match the timestamp on the surveillance footage."

"It'll be close enough," Blair responded coolly.

"I'll also take a lie detector test," Brody said. "I'll *insist.*"

"Go for it. I've heard polygraph testing is only sixty-five percent accurate. At best."

"I'll make sure you take one, too."

Now she did giggle. A maddening sound. "Oh, Brody, I admire your spirit, but you've got nothing on me. If you squawk, it'll be your word against mine. And who's going to believe you? You're just a dirtbag from Rebel Point."

Brody closed his eyes. It felt like he was sliding down a steep embankment, grabbing at roots and rocks that appeared solid, only to have them come away in his hands.

"My bases are covered," Blair said. "But we're getting *way* ahead of ourselves. Listen a sec."

"I don't want to listen to you."

"I've got some good news, some bad news, and some *real* bad news."

Brody wanted to cut the call, but two of those words—"good" and "news"—sank their shiny hooks into him, dragged him along.

"The good news," Blair revealed, "is that the police are not looking for you. Well, not you *specifically.* My dad didn't submit the surveillance footage as evidence. He removed the tape before the police arrived."

"Why?" Brody asked. This didn't sound at all believable, but he stiffened attentively, like a starving fox that has caught the scent of food.

"That leads me to the bad news," Blair said, and sighed. "My dad has never been a huge admirer of our nation's judicial system. I mean, sure, you can get the death penalty in South Carolina for murder, and our lawyers would push for that to happen. But you could live a long time before they stuck that needle into your arm. Shit, my dad would probably die before you, and what kind of justice is that?"

Brody gritted his teeth. He knew where this was going.

"He's coming for you himself, Brody." Her voice conveyed an uncharacteristic gravitas, as if she'd gone from strewing flowers to pounding nails. "He wants to take matters into his own very capable hands."

"Capable," Brody repeated. Not really a word, more a vague grunt.

"And so we come to the *real* bad news."

"Don't tell me," Brody said. "Your old man is a former Navy SEAL badass. He cracked skulls in the Middle East—put the bullet in Bin Laden."

"Hmm, he's a badass, but he's no hero." A pause. Brody imagined her somewhere quiet, out of the way, while police and forensic units worked inside her house, snapping photographs, dusting for prints. "You never asked what my surname was—and to be fair, I'd have lied if you had. But I can tell you now: it's Latzo. My father is Jimmy Latzo. Have you heard of him?"

"No." Brody pressed a hand to his forehead. "I don't know. Maybe. I'm not exactly thinking straight right now."

"He's . . . a man of influence."

"A mobster, you mean."

"He doesn't like that word." Blair made a *tut-tut* sound, as if Brody were four instead of twenty-four. "Google him. There's a whole bunch of stuff online. Not all of it is true, of course. That whole thing about him tying some guy to the back of his Cadillac and driving him through town—heck, I don't believe *that*."

"Jesus," Brody said. His vision tripled again. He cranked the window and took a chestful of night air.

"Feel kind of sick, huh?"

"Oh Christ. What have you done to me?"

"Aw, come *on*. I never asked you to rob that convenience store. You brought at least some of this on yourself." She tutted again. "*Bad* Brody."

"You're evil," he whispered. "You're the devil."

"I have my moments," she said. "But anyhoo, back to the matter at hand: Believe all of what you read about my father, or none of it. I don't care. But take it from someone who shares a house with him . . . he is one mean son of a buck. And he's looking for you."

Brody's vision had cleared, but it dipped and swayed. He tried to focus on a single point: the black and yellow Waffle House sign on Carnation Boulevard. It bent like a tree in a storm, leaving pretty streaks against the sky.

Blair continued, "He knows what you look like, but he doesn't know *who* you are—"

"Yet."

"Right. But he's already got people working on it. His top guys. It'll likely take them a couple of days to track you down. No longer than a week. You should use this time to get the hell out of Dodge."

"Why are you telling me this?"

"I don't know. Maybe I'm not the devil you think I am."

He blinked hard. The Waffle House sign bent the other way.

"Or maybe," she said, "some part of me really *did* want to paint the town red with you. Either way, consider this a courtesy call. I don't know, Bro, it kinda feels like the least I can do."

"You're going to hell," he said, and cracked a mad smile.

"And talking of courtesies . . . this may seem trivial now, but I took the liberty of destroying your wallet. Soaked it in gasoline and set that sucker on fire. No chance it can be used as evidence, so you don't have to worry about that little convenience store thing anymore."

"Oh," Brody said. Should he be grateful for this? Maybe, but it felt a little like Blair had handed him a Kleenex to wipe his boogery nose, moments before blowing his brains out with a shotgun.

"Run," she said now, the pounding-nails tone back in her voice. "I'm serious, Brody, if my dad finds you, he's going to hurt you in a hundred different ways. And then he'll hurt you again."

"My sister," Brody said weakly. More tears crept from his eyes.

"If you're lucky, he'll kill you first."

"I hate you."

Silence between them. Ten seconds. No longer. The Waffle House sign bent all the way to the Waffle House parking lot, then snapped back, straight as a flagpole. The flash it left behind was breathtaking.

"Beat feet, Bro. Out of town. Out of *state*." Her voice was still remarkably controlled. "Nowhere is too far."

"Yeah."

"I have to go. The police need to question me."

"Yeah," he said again, but she'd already gone. He lowered the phone, looked at the screen. Call duration: 6:46. His eyes flicked to the cracked, faded dashboard and the cassette/CD player and the fat odometer, and he wondered how far this old shitbox could take him.

...

Molly tried to hold on but he broke away from her, not wanting to—*needing* to. He dropped to one knee, grabbed an old gym bag from beneath the bed, and placed it in Molly's arms.

"Pack anything you absolutely can't do without," he said. His voice was a little firmer now. "Leave the rest."

"Brody, what—"

"We have to go. Tonight."

She stared at him. Her mouth formed a trembling, downturned line that had very little to do with her palsy. "What are we running from?"

Not what—who. He had Googled "Jimmy Latzo" shortly after his call with Blair, when a fraction of his mind had returned and his hands had stopped shaking enough for him to punch the letters into his phone. He didn't go deep, though. He *couldn't*. Partly because time wasn't on his side. Mostly because the first thing he read put him off digging any deeper.

Blair had told him that not everything he read would be true, but the source—*The Mighty Penn Online*—appeared credible. There was a photo of Latzo, circa 2010. He was dressed like Gotti, had the same pompadour hairstyle, but terrible facial scarring. They looked like burn scars, Brody thought. The accompanying article reported that Latzo was being questioned by authorities in connection with the brutal murder of Art Binkle, a music industry executive from New York City. Binkle's label, Purple Mule Records, had allegedly declined to sign Latzo's nephew (not named), despite a generous monetary "contribution" from Uncle Jimmy. Soon thereafter, Binkle wrote an email to his close friends and business partners, saying that he feared for his life. He was found decapitated in his studio a week later, his severed head mounted on a turntable and spinning at 45 rpm.

"I'll tell you everything soon. I promise." Brody kissed Molly on the cheek. "Please, sis. Pack as quickly as you can. We need to get out of here."

"Are we coming back?"

"No."

"Never?"

"Never."

"But . . ." Tears shone in her eyes. "I have work tomorrow."

"Not anymore."

He left her standing with the gym bag in her arms, and walked through to the living room. The football game was on commercial break. Tyrese was using that time to rifle through the bones in his bucket, looking for any pieces of deep-fried bird he might have missed. He didn't know he had company until Brody said:

"We're out of here."

"Whu?" He had a bone in his mouth, too.

"It's what you wanted, right?" Brody's hands were still shaking. He rammed them into his back pockets. "Well, you got it. We're taillights."

Tyrese spat the bone from his mouth. "When?" He licked his lips and his fingers.

"Tonight."

"Whoa, damn. Really?"

"Really. We're just throwing some shit together, then we're out of your hair for good."

Tyrese considered this, then shrugged and shook his bucket. Bones rattled. He dug a greasy hand in and came up with half a thigh. "Where you going?"

"What's it to you?"

"Shit, man. Just asking."

Brody took his hands from his pockets, folded his arms, shuffled his feet. "Sorry, T, it's just . . ." He lowered his gaze. "We're going to Maine. I have an aunt there who—"

"You told me you don't have no family."

"Right. And we don't. She was a friend of my dad's. A close friend. We just called her aunt, you know? Aunt . . ." His mind blanked. A name. A female name. *Any* female name. ". . . Cherry. Aunt Cherry."

"Cherry, huh?"

"Cheryl, actually." Brody wiped his eyes. They were still damp. "Anyway, she said we can crash with her for a while, and she knows a guy who can set me up with work. Basement conversions, I think."

Tyrese nodded, sucking meat through his teeth, wiping his fingers down the front of his sweatshirt. "Right on."

"So, yeah . . . our bus leaves at midnight."

"You ain't driving?"

"Shit, my car wouldn't make it to Rock Hill, let alone Maine." Brody pushed out a laugh. His chest hurt. "I sold the car. Got two hundred bucks for it. The buyer's picking it up outside Rebel Point Central."

The commercial break ended. Joe Buck's voice welcomed viewers back to the game. Tyrese turned up the volume. "Okay, brother. Sure." He flapped a hand in Brody's direction. "Take her easy, man."

Fuck you, Brody thought. He returned to the bedroom. Molly packed silently and wouldn't look at him. He dragged a second gym bag from beneath his own bed and started throwing stuff in. Underwear, a pair of jeans, a few tees and sweatshirts. His dad's leather jacket wouldn't fit in the bag, but he refused to leave it behind and so put it on. It was too large for him; his dad had been bigger, even as a younger man.

Brody pulled the curtain for privacy, lifted the loose floorboard at the back of his closet. The last things he packed were the replica handgun and the fat bag of cash that had gotten him into this mess.

"You ready, Moll?"

"Nearly," she said coldly.

They were on the road fifteen minutes later.

• • •

They drove southwest, away from Blair and her mobster daddy (and in the opposite direction from Maine and their fictitious Aunt Cherry). Molly didn't ask any questions, and for that Brody was grateful. She took her medication and eventually drifted off to sleep. By midnight they had passed over the Tugaloo River into

Georgia, the first of many state lines Brody hoped to cross within the next few days.

He fueled up west of Gainesville, wondering wryly which would last longer, the car or the tank of gas. They rumbled through the suburbs of Atlanta an hour or so later. The engine groaned and clattered but the car kept running. Brody angled the rearview so he didn't have to look at the shocked, unhappy man staring back at him. He focused on the road ahead, locked to the speed limit. He wanted to make the Alabama state line before stopping for the night.

Molly slept, occasionally half waking to stretch and knead the stiffness out of her legs.

. . .

Stardust Motel. Mallory, Alabama. Sixty rooms off a litter-strewn parking lot, this populated by aging pickup trucks and cars with expired inspection stickers. The rooms were off-white boxes with insincere splashes of color: fire-orange blankets on the beds; a russet carpet; paintings of birds. It was no different from the Motel 15 chain dotted across South Carolina, or the thousands of other motels across the Lower 48. The disadvantages with places like this—quite aside from the lack of comfort—were the vomit and/or piss in the stairwells, the junkies that oftentimes loitered in their doorways, the stained towels and sheets. The (only) advantages were the price and the fact that all they required was cash up front. No ID. No credit card.

"What are we doing here, Brody?"

"I messed up, sis." Brody ran his thumb over a cigarette burn on the nightstand. "I don't know if there's a way out of this, but if there is, I'll find it."

Brody's phone had switched over to central time. Two-ten A.M. They ate corned beef subs and Twinkies that Brody had bought at the gas station. He slept afterward, but woke early from a shocking nightmare. No chance of getting back to sleep, so he showered, then sat at the window and watched daylight spill across the parking lot and Interstate 20 beyond.

They were 220 miles from Rebel Point but he didn't feel safe.

· · ·

The TV was small, Clinton-era, bolted to the wall. Brody flicked through the news channels, but there was no mention of Jimmy Latzo's murdered wife. The stations were out of Alabama and Georgia, though. Perhaps they weren't interested in out-of-state news. Or perhaps—and Brody prayed this was the case— Latzo's infamy wasn't as far-reaching as Blair had led him to believe.

He checked South Carolina's WIS and Live 5 websites on his phone, scrolled through several pages, but found nothing. Now Brody wondered if Latzo had used his influence to keep his wife's murder out of the press—at least until the guilty party had been tracked down. Bad for business, maybe.

Molly woke up at 7:37 with a numbness in her left hip and her leg shrieking in pain. Brody gave her two Motrin and helped her with some basic range-of-motion exercises. She swore at Brody throughout—told him she couldn't do this, she was going home.

"We don't have a home," Brody said.

Once the pain had faded and most of the feeling had returned, Brody helped Molly into the shower. He held one hand behind the curtain while she washed herself with the other. After she'd toweled off, Brody gestured at her cell phone, placed on the nightstand between the two beds.

"You can't tell your friends," he said, "where we are, or where we've been. No texts. No photographs. Okay?"

Molly nodded.

"If they ask—if *anybody* asks—tell them you've gone to live with your Aunt Cherry in Maine. Your brother got a job opportunity. Too good to pass up."

Tears filled her eyes. She dropped onto the bed and wept silently. Brody gave her a minute. When he tried to hug her, she pushed him away.

"I don't understand," she said irritably, "why we can't go to the police. They can help us. *Protect* us."

"Not an option."

"Why? Is that who you're running from?"

"No. Not exactly." Bitterness swished through his stomach, as brown as the nicotine stains on the ceiling. "I'm going to tell you everything, Moll. But first we need distance, then I have to figure out what we're up against."

She gave him a look, as if the room she had in her heart for him were diminishing. "I miss Dad." She wiped her eyes on the bedsheet. "He'd know what to do."

Yeah, good old Dad. But let's not forget that he started this shitball rolling when he killed himself. Brody pushed his hands through his hair, clenched them behind his head.

"Let's go," he said. "I want to be at least two states west of here before the sun goes down."

. . .

They were midway across Mississippi when Jimmy's men caught up to them.

Chapter Six

The car gave up on the outskirts of Bayonet. It spluttered and lurched, gradually losing speed, until it surrendered with a disagreeable cough on the shoulder of Route 82.

"What now?" Molly asked.

Brody struck the wheel. His only plan had been to put at least a thousand miles between them and Jimmy Latzo. He'd been considering Oklahoma. A small town in the Panhandle, perhaps, where they could catch their breaths and contemplate their next move. Maybe they'd assume aliases and stay awhile. Brody could find work under the table—hang at the corner of a Home Depot until some contractor picked him up for eight bucks an hour.

But could they do that here, in Bayonet? THE SHINING LIGHT OF MISSISSIPPI, according to the sign at the edge of town, but also famous for the Byrnes Theater Massacre. It seemed an ominous place to hang their hats. Moreover, they were only five hundred miles from Rebel Point.

Not far enough.

"Talk to me, Brody."

"I'm thinking."

Two choices: ride the Greyhound, or repair the car. The former was appealing; they could sit back, talk things through, maybe sleep awhile. Brody was reluctant to give up the car, though. It was chewed by rust and breathing its last, but they might have to live in it, at some point.

He flipped a coin in his mind. It came down tails.

"Brody?"

"We get a tow to the nearest garage." He fished his phone from the console in the dash. "See how much it'll cost to get this shitbox back on the road."

. . .

The tow set him back $110—a sixty-dollar hookup fee, then another fifty bucks to pull his car three miles to Kane Bros. Auto. Brody was certain he'd been stiffed, but the tow-truck driver had an air of misery about him, so he elected not to contest.

The brothers Kane weren't much cheerier. Silas and Mort, whippet-thin twins with black greasy hands extending from the sleeves of their coveralls, their Adam's apples as stark as elbows.

"Prob'ly the fuel pump," Mort said.

"Yup," Silas agreed soberly. "The fuel pump."

They had arrived at this diagnosis without popping the hood. They simply circled the car, rubbing their whiskery throats, frowning.

"How much?" Brody asked.

"Shoot," Mort said. He leaned his narrow frame across the hood, looked at the VIN stenciled at the bottom of the dash. "She's a '99. Old."

"Old," Silas echoed.

"We can check Timmy's Salvage—might get lucky and pull a halfway decent replacement from a junker. That'll save you heartily. Otherwise, we'll have to call our supplier, see if we can get something reconditioned."

"Cheaper than new," Silas said. "A mite, at any rate."

"A mite. Yup. And besides, new won't matter much." Mort's Adam's apple yo-yoed as he spoke. "That'd be sorta like giving a new hip to a man with terminal cancer. If you follow me."

"I follow you. But how much?" Brody spread his hands. "Can you ballpark it?"

"Nope. Too many variables." Mort touched the wheel arch with the tip of his steel toe cap and rust sifted down. "Leave a number and we'll call you tomorrow."

"I'm paying cash," Brody said.

"All to the good, but that don't make us work no faster." Mort stepped around the hood and clapped an oil-dark hand on Brody's shoulder. "We'll get you moving as soon as. In the meanwhile"—he pointed south—"if you're looking for a place to rest your head, Katie's Motel has beds. Go five blocks on Main, then hang a right on Biloxi. She's across from the flea market."

Molly had absented herself from this conversation, and Brody wished he could have done the same. She stood to one side, shielding her eyes from the late afternoon sunlight. With business concluded, at least for now, the brothers turned their attention her way. They nodded curiously, scratched their bristly faces, and didn't quite whisper.

"Crutches, huh?"

"Yup. Crutches."

. . .

Katie's was of marginally higher quality than the Stardust Motel. There were no used condoms under the bed, no rat turds in the back corner of the closet. It was also more expensive: $69 a night. Katie—in her late fifties, but with the cut biceps of a professional arm wrestler—asked for a credit card to cover incidentals.

"What incidentals?" Brody asked. "Minibar? Valet parking?"

"We got cable." She cocked an eyebrow and smirked. "Adult entertainment."

She settled for an extra $20 cash, which put the room a buck shy of $90. Added to Mr. Happy's tow charge, Brody's bag of cash was $200 lighter than when he'd set out that morning. It was worrisome, not least because he still had to pay for repairs on the car, and they were still a long way from the Oklahoma Panhandle.

"How much cash do you have left?" Molly had always been able to tune in to his concerns. "You know . . . your winnings."

"Enough," Brody replied. "Don't sweat it."

He ordered pizza that night and they wolfed it down watching *Happy Days* reruns on TBS. They didn't laugh often, but when they did it was from deep down and wonderful. Several times, Molly started to say something to him, then stopped herself, at least until she'd taken her medication and pulled herself into bed.

"I know what it is." She looked at the ceiling, painted the same drab tan as the walls. "You know . . . the reason you're in trouble."

"You think you do," Brody said. "But believe me—"

"You didn't win at poker. You cheated. I don't know how, but you did. And the people you cheated . . . they're heavy guys. Mobsters, maybe."

Brody stripped to his boxers, climbed into his own bed. The sheets were cold, clean. They felt good.

"You fucked with the wrong people, Brody."

"Maybe. Or maybe I was just in the wrong place at the wrong time."

"The police can help. Think about it." Molly puffed up her pillow and lay down with her back to him. Brody sat against the headboard, knees drawn. He had to tell Molly everything, and soon. It wasn't fair to have dragged her into this without telling her why. But doing so meant confessing to robbing Buddy's Convenience Store, an act he was desperately ashamed of. Molly would be disappointed in him. Heartbroken, even. On top of everything else, he wasn't ready for that.

He flicked the TV off. Motel ambience filled the air: a shower running in a nearby room, a car pulling into the lot and idling, muffled voices from behind thin walls. Soon Molly's light snoring joined the chorus. Her body barely moved beneath the sheets.

Brody closed his eyes. He slept, but only for a moment. He awoke with his knees still drawn, his gaze fixed on the window. The aqua neon of Katie's sign showed through the curtains. He rolled his head, looked at Molly. She hadn't moved.

Five hundred miles from Rebel Point. Not enough distance. But perhaps enough to dig a little deeper into Jimmy Latzo's infamy. If Brody had any hope of getting out of this, he needed to do his homework.

He picked up his phone.

. . .

While the Gambino family—with John Gotti at the helm—called the shots in New York City, Don Esposito held sway over western Pennsylvania. This was in the mid- to late 1980s. Jimmy Latzo was, at that time, a young soldier with Rudy Tucoletti's crew, who controlled the action in Carver City, a remodeled commuter town south of Pittsburgh. Even then, Latzo was known for his short fuse. He once ran three teenagers through an industrial meat grinder for vandalizing a hardware store on Tucoletti's turf.

Allegedly.

In those early days, Latzo's reputation gave pause to anybody who thought to challenge him. A soldier from Nicky Scarfo's South Philly Mob had suggested that

Latzo's methods lacked finesse, and that he brought shame to La Cosa Nostra. Soon afterward, this soldier was found strangled by his own large intestine, his mouth crammed with bull feces.

Jimmy Latzo feared no recriminations. Thirty years old, stylish, ostensibly untouchable. He was one of Tucoletti's big earners.

"This fucking kid didn't like to lose," Michael De-Cicco wrote in his controversial memoir *Point Blank: A Keystone State Mob Story.* "And I mean at anything—business, gambling, women. I once saw him shoot some chick in the kneecap after she refused to dance with him. Boom. Down she went. And everybody turned a blind eye because of who Jimmy was, and what he might do. I swear to God, the kid was a fucking powder keg."

The consensus was that Latzo would blow himself up. It was simply a matter of *when.* In 1989, Rudy Tucoletti got himself whacked with the cancer stick and was dead within months. His cousin Frankie—"A fucking gutless pussy bitch," according to Michael De-Cicco in the same tell-all—took the reins in Carver City. He didn't last long. Frankie was gunned down on the eleventh hole at Pin High Country Club, by order of Don Esposito's consigliere, Alfonso Monte, who'd heard that Frankie was in bed with the Feds. Jimmy

Latzo—reckless, yes, but his ambition couldn't be questioned—was promoted to caporegime and given control of Carver City.

He was thirty-three years old. A 1990 article in the *Carver City Herald* referred to Latzo as "the Prince of Pennsylvania." Other monikers included "Chainsaw Jimmy" and "the Italian Cat," this latter on account of him always getting the cream. Certainly he lived the high life for the next few years. Fast cars, beautiful women, associating with celebrities and politicians. Carver City officials—those with enough clout to matter—ate from the palm of his hand. Not out of hunger, but fear.

Most of the legends regarding Latzo stemmed from the three years he presided over Carver City. They were many and colorful. Among them: setting fire to a restaurant in Greensburg that had refused him entry to a private function; the beheading of an associate who'd ill-advisedly described Latzo as having "little legs, even for a wop"; tying an alleged informant to the back of his Caddy and driving him through Carver City until only "rat scraps" remained (Blair had said she didn't believe this particular story, but Brody wasn't so sure). It was the suggestion of violence, too—the countless threats and intimidation. Several sources claimed Latzo occasionally wore a World War II–era flamethrower to business meetings to ensure proceedings went the way he wanted them to.

Such violence and arrogance garnered a multitude of enemies, some of whom tried to take him down. There were several failed hits, apparently, and a year-long racketeering trial that went quickly south following the apparent suicide of an FBI informant.

But no one is truly untouchable.

Accounts of what happened in 1993 were varied and unreliable. The authorities suspected gang warfare—Latzo had, on numerous occasions, overstepped the mark with the Russian mob and the tongs, and his actions may have caught up to him. Other sources claimed it was dissent in the ranks; with both Little Nicky and John Gotti behind bars, the East Coast families were in disarray. Folks were squealing left and right, trying to cut deals. There was inevitably bloodshed. Another theory—favored among those on the inside—suggested it was the work of one person. An unnamed soldier with an ax to grind.

Whatever the cause, it resulted in Jimmy Latzo's downfall. Most of his crew was wiped out, and his luxury house in Carver City was burned to the ground. Firefighters pulled Latzo from the flames. He suffered second-and third-degree burns to thirty percent of his body. He'd also been shot three times.

There followed a long process of surgeries, reconstructions, and convalescence. Latzo was rarely seen. Brody found one picture of him at a hospital in New York City, hooked up to numerous machines, wrapped almost entirely in bandages. It was haunting. Several cases were brought against him during this time, but all collapsed due to lack of evidence. No one turned on him, probably because he still had protection from Don Esposito, and there were bigger fish—and better deals to be cut—in Jersey and New York City.

Latzo wasn't finished, though. He was back on his feet by the late nineties, a "legitimate businessman" with interests in commercial real estate and property development. Over the next two decades his name was linked to multiple misdeeds, including insurance fraud scams, a counterfeit money operation, illegal gambling, and the murders of several high-profile businesspeople, with Art Binkle (his severed head spinning at 45 rpm) being the most gruesome and well-known case.

Latzo maintained his innocence, and always managed to slip the noose. He claimed he was being victimized because of previous and deeply naïve business dealings, and had worked to counter this with his "openhearted community efforts" and donations to local charities. According to the last article Brody read, Latzo continued to operate out of Carver City, but had homes across the United States.

"A lot of guys got away with shit back then," Michael DeCicco wrote at the end of his chapter on the Carver City mob. "But Jimmy wasn't one of them. The kid answered for his crimes, and he's got the scars to prove it. Okay, maybe he isn't at the bottom of the Ohio River or pulling laundry shifts in Marion with the Teflon Don, but he still has to look at his burned-up face every day, and I know that fucking kills him."

. . .

They ate breakfast at a family restaurant called Missy Lean's. It was southern home style—biscuits and gravy, country-fried steak and eggs, everything served with a generous helping of "God Bless America." Molly ate like she hadn't seen food in a week. Brody, quite the opposite. His appetite was history. He nudged his food around the plate and glanced out the window every time a car pulled into the lot.

"You going to eat that?" Molly pointed at his cheese grits.

"Knock yourself out."

Most of the vehicles were Buicks or Chryslers driven by octogenarians wearing plaid shirts and baseball caps. Some were pickup trucks with either a rebel flag on the tailgate or a shotgun racked on the back glass. Occasionally a late-model Toyota or a loaded SUV pulled into one of Missy Lean's parking spaces, and that was when Brody clenched inside. He expected all four doors to open and the cast of *The Sopranos* to roll out. His late-night reading had influenced his imagination, hence the loss of appetite.

He hadn't slept much.

Reading about Jimmy Latzo was one thing, but knowing what to do with that information was another. The dude wasn't simply a corrupt businessman, he was a *mobster*, a fully fledged omertà-swearing-hanging-out-with-John-fucking-Gotti wise guy. How could he, Brody, neutralize that? Hide in Oklahoma and hope for the best? Informants went into witness protection to escape the mob. New towns, new identities, new lives. They had a practiced team behind them, and a shitload of money to set them up. All Brody had was a movie-prop handgun and a crapped-out Pontiac.

"Hey, remember that guy who used to visit when we were younger? A friend of Dad's, I think." Brody raised a hand above his head, indicating a greater height. "Tall. Six-three, maybe. Boston accent."

"*Bawston*," Molly said, and smiled. "Yeah. Karl somebody. Janko, maybe? Or Jankowski?"

"Karl Janko." Brody snapped his fingers. "That's him."

"Always wore tight T-shirts." Molly wiped cheese grits from her chin. "He was Mom's friend, not Dad's."

"Oh. Right."

"Why are you asking?"

"Options, I guess. Keeping them open." Brody picked up a piece of toast, considered it, then dropped it back on the plate. "I'm putting together a mental list of people we know."

"In case we need a favor?"

"Right."

"Okay, but there are people we know, and people who, maybe, would help us. Not too many names on that second list."

"Tell me about it."

"And Janko is a bad dude. I remember Dad telling me he'd been to jail a couple of times."

Brody shrugged vaguely, as if he'd forgotten this detail, when in fact it was at the forefront of his mind. A man like Karl Janko might know a place they could lie low for a while. He might even know someone who could hook them up with false papers. It was a long shot, no doubt, but maybe their best, if not only, shot.

Molly finished her breakfast, then swiped the toast from Brody's plate and finished that, too. Brody looked out the window. A truck pulled in, USA flag rippling from the antenna, country music making its panels quake. Right behind it, a tar-black Yukon with tinted glass. A stone dropped into the pool of Brody's gut and sent unpleasant ripples through his body. He watched the Yukon muscle into a tight space, then the driver and passenger doors opened. The passenger was thirty-something, tan, dressed in an open-throat shirt and mirrored aviators.

Oh fuck.

The driver was older, in his fifties, silver-haired.

Oh fuck. Oh fuck.

"Brody? You okay?"

The rear doors opened. Brody waited for more wise guys to spill out, smoking Padróns, shooters wedged into the waistbands of their slacks. It was two women, though, the same age as the men, dressed more casually. The older woman wore an Ole Miss Rebels sweatshirt. They joined their men and the two couples walked hand in hand toward the restaurant.

"Brody?"

A sweet, relieved sigh escaped him, and he cursed himself for being so damned paranoid.

"I'm fine," he said.

He got the check.

...

Mort Kane called a touch before ten with good news, he said, and not so good.

"We'll get you on the road by midafternoon. Say, three. That's the good news. Unfortunately, we couldn't yank the parts at Timmy's, and our supplier can only get his hands on aftermarket."

"Aftermarket," Silas said in the background.

"You're looking at six hundred bones, parts and labor. If you're still paying cash, we can bring that down a mite."

Brody closed his eyes, imagining his dwindling bag of cash. He'd been thrifty since emptying the register at Buddy's, but there'd been expenses: food, gas, motels, Molly's medication, paying Tyrese. He'd have to count, but he guessed this repair bill would drop him to below a grand. And that was it. All they had left.

"How much would you give me for the car?" he asked Mort. "You know . . . take it off my hands."

Mort laughed. "Shit, son, you dropped a ton and a half of garbage onto our lot. You'd have to pay *us* to make it go away."

"Pay you?"

"Hundred should do it."

Silas: "Hundred."

"But you could fix it up," Brody said. "Sell it for a profit. Easy money."

"Nothing easy, son. We'd spend a grand fixing her up and sell her for five hundred. That's all she's worth, running smooth-like."

"Shit," Brody said, thinking that the six hundred bucks he was faced with spending was too much for a five-hundred-dollar boneshaker, but that the Pontiac Motel might be their go-to domicile in the weeks to come.

"What you wanna do?" Mort asked.

"Fix her up," Brody said.

Checkout was midday, but Molly, leaning heavily on her crutches, persuaded Katie to extend it to three—no additional charge. At 2:40, Brody covertly took six hundred bucks from his haul, pulled on his jacket, and started for the door.

"I'm going to get the car."

"Okay," Molly said.

"I'll be twenty minutes, give or take, then we're getting out of this shithole." He ran his hand along an imaginary highway. "Next stop: Oklahoma."

"I'm not going," Molly said.

"What?"

"You heard me."

"Yeah, but . . ."

Molly sat on her bed, hair strung across her face, one hand scrunching the sheets. Her crutches leaned against the nightstand. She grabbed one of them and threw it on the floor at his feet.

"I'm not leaving this room until you tell me what's going on." Spots of color found her cheeks. "Fuck you, Brody. I've got a right to know."

He picked up Molly's crutch, placed it on the bed next to his bag, neatly packed, ready to go. Molly's stuff was still dotted around the room.

"Yeah," he said. "You do."

"So?"

He ran a hand down his face, shook his head, and sighed. "Okay, listen, sis." He didn't know where to begin. What he *did* know was that he wasn't having this conversation now, in the motel room. "We've got six hours until we hit the Oklahoma state line. That's a long time, and a lot of highway. I'll tell you everything while we're driving. *Everything.* You have my word. But please, let's just get the hell out of here."

"No. Tell me now."

"There's not enough time. We've got to hand the key in at three." It was moments like this that he wanted to appear strong, show her that he had everything under control. Instead, his chin quivered, his shoulders slumped. "Please, Moll. Let's hit the road. I'll tell you everything, I swear."

She brushed the hair from her eyes and looked at him. He hated doing this to her. She was his best friend, his single source of light. He didn't know then that it was about to get much worse.

"I'm finding it harder and harder to believe you."

"I'm doing the best I can."

His phone chimed. Mort Kane. "Your car's ready," he said, and Brody told him that he'd be right there. He looked at Molly, his chin still quivering. She nodded.

"Don't fuck with me, Brody. You'd better tell me every goddamn detail, or I swear to God I'm jumping out on the move."

She'd do it, too, to prove a point, that she didn't take shit from him—not from *anybody*. He imagined her popping the door lock and bailing on Interstate 40. There one second. Gone the next. And he'd see her in the rearview, tumbling across the inside lane, crutches kicking sparks off the blacktop.

...

Repairs were $540 cash, but Brody haggled them down to five even. A minor victory. The car started like a champ, purred for a time, then everything started to rattle and smell, reminding him that it was still the same old shitbox, after all.

He drove to the motel and rolled into the space outside their door. As he stepped out of the car, Katie hollered to him from the main office.

"Good timing, kid. You got a phone call."

Brody frowned. Exactly nobody knew he was here, and his very few acquaintances—should they call— would hit him up on his cell.

"Got the wrong kid," he hollered back.

"Don't think so. She described you pretty good, right down to the shitty car and crippled sister."

This hooked him. Any anger he felt at Katie describing Molly as crippled was dissolved by her use of the word "she." He didn't have a girlfriend. His mom had deserted him. His buddies—such as they were—were all male. He knew women, of course, lots of women, but only one who would call him.

"Blair," he growled down the phone. It seemed he couldn't speak her name without growling.

"Listen to me, Bro—"

"How do you know where I am?"

"That's the reason I'm calling, you dick. I know where you are because *they* know where you are."

"What?"

"It didn't take my dad long to figure out who you are. Your face is *way* clear on the security footage."

"They know where I am?"

"As soon as he had your name, he had your cell number. You ever hear of geolocation, Brody?"

"Geo *what*?"

"Location. It's a way of tracking the exact whereabouts of a web-based computer or cell phone. There are *programs*. I can't believe you didn't dump your phone. How fucking stupid are you?"

Very fucking stupid, Brody thought. He felt the awkward shape of his cell in the ass pocket of his jeans—imagined it sending out signals, bleeping, like a dolphin with a tracking device strapped to its skull.

"What . . . ? How . . . ?" He shook his head. Too many thoughts, so many questions, hijacked his mind. He looked vacantly around Katie's office, her smelly plastic phone pressed to his face. There was an Alberto Vargas calendar on the wall, a dog in the corner, curled up like a dropped scarf, that startled him when it yapped. A half-eaten TV dinner was pushed to one side of Katie's desk, next to a thick novel with a bookmark parked midway through—Faulkner, Brody noted, which surprised him as much as the dog.

He gathered his thoughts.

"Why are you tipping me off?" It didn't add up—something was wrong with this picture. "You framed me. Why not just let me hang?"

"Maybe I like you more than I thought," Blair responded. There was no warmth in her voice. "You probably don't believe me, but I want us both to get away with this."

He *didn't* believe her. Something else was going on.

"How long have I got?" he asked.

"I don't know. Just get out of there. Right now. And if you know anybody who might protect you, now's the time to look them up."

"No shit."

"And dump your fucking phone. My dad will hack it for contacts, which is why I'm calling you on the motel's landline."

Brody slammed down the receiver and reeled from the main office, bumping his hip on the edge of Katie's desk and knocking her TV dinner to the floor.

"You *shithead*," Katie shouted as he ran across the lot. "That's an incidental!"

He made it to their room in a series of bounding, Impala-like strides, shouldering the door open—

"Molly," he gasped. "We've got—"

Brody froze. Everything appeared in stale snapshots. The tan room and crappy, mismatched furniture. His and Molly's bags on the bed—she'd packed up at last— ready to go. The slick mobster grabbing Molly from behind, with one forearm around her throat and the muzzle of a semiautomatic pistol locked to the conch of her ear.

"Man of the hour," he said, and ran his fat, pale tongue across Molly's brow. "Welcome to the party, motherfucker."

Chapter Seven

"Let her go," Brody said, both hands raised. "Please, man. She's got nothing to do with this. I'm the one you want."

"Shut your mouth, kid. You're in no position to deal."

There was a second mobster behind the door. Brody didn't see him until the door banged closed and he grabbed Brody by the upper arm. He was wide and sweaty, his puffy face crowned by a mop of black, boyish curls.

"Ain't nothing to this kid, Leo. Look at him—scrawny little bitch." The thug shook Brody by the arm. "I could break him in half, throw him in the trunk."

Molly squirmed against Leo. Shaky, terrified breaths rumbled from her chest.

"Please," Brody said. "I'm begging you, man. Leave her out of this."

Leo responded by tightening his hold on Molly, squeezing so hard that her feet left the ground. Her eyes swam with helplessness, fear, confusion. It was how she'd looked when the cop told them that their father was dead.

"Come on, man," Brody implored. "Just let her—"

"This is how it's going down," the mobster gripping his left arm interjected. His face was close enough for Brody to smell the nicotine and cooked meats on his breath. "You two assholes are coming with us. You, shit-for-brains"—he shook Brody again—"are riding trunk-class. Play nice and we only have to tie you up and gag you. Try anything stupid and we start breaking bones. That'll make the long trip to Pennsylvania even longer."

Pennsylvania, where Blair's daddy was waiting.

"Please, guys, *please*—"

"The cripple can ride in back with me. But one wrong move"—the mobster jabbed a finger toward Molly—"and into the fucking trunk she goes."

Brody shook his head. There was no reasoning with these thug assholes, and he wasn't going down without a fight. That might result in broken limbs, but it was better than being led like a sheep to Jimmy Latzo—to a long and miserable death.

He had to do something.

His eyes scanned the room. Could he grab Molly, hit the bathroom, lock the door, and jump out the window? Could he bounce the TV off Leo's skull, snatch the pistol, shoot them both in the legs so they couldn't give chase? *The pistol*, he thought, and his gaze flicked to his gym bag. The replica was inside, tucked toward the bottom. Having it in his hand would turn this into a different conversation.

"Let's go," Leo said. "Right fucking now."

"Yeah," Brody said, and yanked his left arm free of the mobster's grip. At the same time, he curled his right hand into a firm knot and launched it. His knuckles connected with the big guy's mouth—smashed his lips against his teeth. It wasn't a lights-out punch by any means, but it knocked him back a step. Brody lunged for his gym bag, and managed to get it unzipped before a sweaty hand grabbed him by the back of his neck, squeezed hard, turned him around. Another hand smothered his face, pushed him backward. Brody's head thudded against the door and stars shimmered.

"Son of a *bitch*," the thug bellowed. "I should pop this motherfucker, Leo, I swear to fucking God."

"You can't pop him, Joey."

"I'll break his fucking teeth."

The stars dispersed. Brody saw the big mobster, Joey, directly in front of him, eclipsing the room, but what he *really* saw was a bully, mean and mindless—a grown-up version of Trevor Hyne, who'd relentlessly mimicked Molly's way of talking, who'd pulled her hair and kicked the crutches out from under her. A gallon of anger raced through Brody. He recalled a certain video on YouTube, in which a lavishly mustachioed instructor tutored the technique behind a punch made famous by Bruce Lee. Brody also recalled a pillow duct-taped to a fence post in their backyard, hit so many times it had to be doubled over and taped again.

Blood filled the gaps between Joey's teeth. His eyes were flames. "I'm gonna take your fucking—"

Brody moved so suddenly it surprised even him. He formed a fist with his right hand and thrust forward, covering four inches—not one—with improbable force and speed. Maybe it was muscle memory, or pure luck, but his form was exquisite. The power didn't come from his wrist, or from his right arm, but rather from his entire body, transferred from the ground up, channeled into a fist-sized pocket of explosive energy.

It worked.

Joey—easily a hundred pounds heavier than Brody—spilled backward like he'd taken a sledgehammer to the gut. On another day, he might have dropped to one knee and recovered after several deep breaths, but this was not that day. His feet tangled and he fell with the density of a dropped cylinder block. The back of his skull met the edge of the nightstand with a tremendous crack. His eyes fluttered before he lost consciousness.

Good night, Joey.

Leo's face was a stupid question mark. The pistol slumped in his hand. Brody, meanwhile, didn't miss a beat. He pounced at his gym bag, dug his hand inside, came up with the replica. It felt immediately powerful, dependable, *good*—the opposite of how it had felt when he'd robbed the convenience store.

Brody pointed it at the mobster. His hand was remarkably steady.

"Okay, you son of a bitch," he said. "Let's deal."

• • •

Could Leo tell, from across the room, that Brody's gun was fake? Was there an obvious giveaway that someone who knew his way around a firearm—a mobster, say—would pick up on immediately? He studied Leo's face, waiting for him to crack a smile or roll his big brown eyes.

He did neither. Nor did he back down.

"Bad fucking move, kid," he said.

"Let her go."

"You don't get to call the shots." Leo curled his lip, adjusting his hold on Molly so that she covered more of his body. "Drop the piece, or I'll put a bullet in this bitch's eye."

Brody took a step closer and leveled his arm to more determinedly aim at Leo. He cracked a smile of his own; Leo couldn't tell that the gun was a fake. That was good. He also believed that Brody had killed Jimmy Latzo's wife, and a man crazy enough to do *that* should be approached with extreme caution.

This was the advantage he had to press.

"You really want to negotiate with *me*?" Brody's eyes and nostrils flared. He gestured at Joey. "Why don't you ask this fat fuck how negotiating with me works out?"

Leo's gaze flicked toward Joey, who was slumped against the nightstand, his neck bent at an awkward angle.

"Now let her go, or I'll shoot you right between the eyes." Brody showed his teeth, his lips still tilted into a kind of smile. "You know I'll do it."

"Maybe you will," Leo said, lifting Molly a little higher. "Or maybe you hit her instead."

"I doubt it," Brody said. "But that's a chance I'm willing to take."

Molly cried out and shook her head. She looked at Brody, still with the fear and helplessness in her eyes, but there was something else . . . a bewilderment, a distance, as if she were seeing something she thought was red, but had just learned was actually blue. This hurt Brody more than these goons ever could. He wondered if she'd ever look at him the same way again, or if he'd lost some vital piece of her forever.

"You need to think about the situation you're in," Leo said, and maybe he sensed a frailty in Brody; he appeared to expand beyond Molly. The gun at her ear was darker, deadlier. "There are more of us on the way. Another carload. Bad hombres. They'll be here any moment. You can't take us all on, kid."

"I'll worry about that," Brody said, "when they get here. *If* they get here."

"Oh, they'll get here. Jimmy wants you. And Jimmy always gets what he wants."

Brody flinched at the mention of Jimmy's name, betraying just how scared he was.

"And what are you going to get?" he asked Leo. "A bullet in your skull?"

"I don't think so."

If there was a balance, it had shifted in Leo's favor.

It wasn't just that he had backup en route, but that he was becoming more confident that Brody wouldn't—or couldn't—pull the trigger.

This standoff had to end.

"Let's talk about *your* situation," Brody said. "You have a gun to my sister's head, but you're not going to pull the trigger. You're not going to shoot me, either. Why? Because Jimmy wants us alive. Those are his orders. And Jimmy always gets what he wants."

Leo snorted and said, "You better goddamn believe it."

"I killed his wife, right? That's what you think. Stabbed her, what . . . fifteen times? Twenty?" Brody couldn't look at Molly when he said this. He kept his gaze riveted to the mobster. "I'm a crazy son of a bitch. Approach with caution, am I right? So tell me, Leo, how confident are you that I won't pull the trigger?"

"I don't know about crazy, but you *are* a stupid son of a bitch." Leo tensed his forearm, drawing Molly yet closer. "You really think I'm scared of you?"

"You should be," Brody said. "Because I'm exactly three seconds away from splashing your brains all over these fucking walls."

"Fuck you, kid. You won't do it."

"You sure about that?"

Leo sneered and dragged the pistol from Molly's ear to her cheekbone, pressing so hard that her eye closed.

"Let her go," Brody said.

"You got some fucking balls."

"One."

"Jimmy only wants *you* alive, you stupid fuck. He don't care about the cripple."

"That's my sister, you asshole." Brody took another step forward. The tip of the replica was threateningly close to Leo. "Two."

It wasn't only that Brody's hand was steady; in the last few seconds, he became aware of a change *inside*, something running through his veins. It paralleled his fear, then overtook it—as cold as steel, and as solid. He was quietly confident that he *could* shoot Leo, if the gun were real, then turn and bang a round into Joey. The abruptness of this realization unnerved him, but didn't stop the imagery from flowing through his mind: pulling the trigger twice, two deafening reports, two Italian corpses.

"You're dead," he said, as if the things he'd seen in his mind had come to pass.

Leo must have sensed this hard shift in Brody, because he lifted the gun from the side of Molly's head and raised both hands. "Bad fucking move, kid," he said for the second time, taking a step backward.

Brody exhaled. Every muscle in his body clicked down a couple of notches. He kept the gun locked on Leo, though.

"Come on, Moll."

He thought Molly might collapse on the bed in tears, and he'd have to pull her from the room. But, always full of surprises, she grabbed her crutch from where it rested against the nightstand, held it like an oar, and drove the tip into Leo's gut.

"Who's a fucking cripple?" she said.

Leo doubled over, his cheeks blown out. Molly switched hand position on the crutch, holding it more like a baseball bat now. She placed her weight on her stronger right side and swiveled. The crutch whistled through the air and the tip clocked the ridge of Leo's jaw. His head rolled sharply to the right. He dropped to his knees.

Molly staggered toward Brody. She fell into his arms.

"Get us out of here," she said.

Brody grabbed their bags from the bed and together they spilled from the room. Before the door closed, he saw Leo getting to his feet and taking one groggy step forward. Blood smeared his mouth and chin.

The car—thank God for fleabag motels—was right outside, seven feet away. Brody opened the passenger door and Molly flopped across the seat. He loaded both bags on top of her, then slammed the door and rolled across the hood to the driver's side. As he jumped behind the wheel, the motel room door opened. Leo staggered out, one hand looped around his pistol.

Brody yanked the keys from his pocket and gunned the ignition. The car started like a champ again. He threw it into reverse, backed out of the space. Leo took a shot at the front tire and missed.

Molly screamed, scrabbling at her seat belt. Brody didn't wait for her to buckle up. He cranked the wheel and whipped the front of the car around. In the rear-view, he saw Leo raise the gun to take another shot, then think better of it and rush toward his own car.

"Go, Brody!" Molly yelled.

"I'm *going!*"

He jammed the transmission into drive, plugged his foot to the floor, and lurched out of the lot. An on-coming Jeep Cherokee swerved and missed them by a beat. Brakes hissed. Horns howled. Brody raced east on Biloxi, turned left on Main, and ripped toward the edge of town.

A glance in the rearview showed not one car in pursuit, but two.

There are more of us on the way, Leo spoke up in his mind. *Another carload. Bad hombres.*

"Shit," Brody said.

They'd catch up to him on Main—four lanes of straight blacktop. They'd shoot out his tires or go one in front, one behind, and force him to a halt.

"Shit, *shit.*"

The light at the next intersection was red. Brody slowed but didn't stop. He steered between traffic—horns everywhere—and hit the gas on the other side. "Got to get off this road," he said, then made a sliding right onto a side street lined with parked cars. He traded paint with a few of them, then found his lane and floored it.

The mobsters weren't far behind. They appeared in the rearview and gained fast. Molly looked over her shoulder.

"Oh shit, Brody."

"Yeah." He gripped the wheel. "I know."

"If we get out of this, I'm going to kill you myself."

Brody made another sharp turn, then another. Both cars followed, smoke pouring from their tires. The rush of air past Brody's window, the engine clatter, the overworked grumble of the exhaust, were nothing compared to his sister, who looked over her shoulder again and screamed through the rags of her hair.

"Faster, Brody. Go . . . *go!*"

Chapter Eight

Blair's phone rattled against her right hip. She plucked it from her pocket, glancing at the screen as she slipped from the room to answer.

"Where is he?"

"Tear-assing out of Bayonet," Leo replied. Blair heard his car's engine roaring in the background. "Keeping to the backstreets. A better chance of losing us that way."

"Is he scared?"

"Kid's got some fucking balls."

"Is he *scared*, Leo? Tell me you put the fear of Christ into him."

"Are you kidding me?" A horn blared. Tires shrieked. "I took a shot at his front tire. Missed on purpose. But yeah, he's pissing in his pants right now."

"Okay." Blair closed her eyes and smiled. This whole thing was playing out exactly as she'd planned. "Back off. Let him lose you at a red or something. We'll see where he goes, what he does next."

Leo started to say something, but she ended the call and stepped back into Jimmy's office.

"What's going on?" Jimmy called out.

The massage table was erected in the center of the room and Jimmy lay facedown on it, his hairy ass covered by a white towel. Puccini floated from the Echo on his desk. The air smelled of jojoba and sandalwood.

"He's on the move again," Blair said.

"On the move," Jimmy muttered. "Jesus, Blair, you better pray you don't lose him."

"We've been glued to this kid's ass for five months," Blair said. "Monitoring his cell phone, his email. We've got a tag on his car and Eddie the Smoke has been tailing him since he left Rebel Point. We won't lose him."

Today's masseuse was Celeste. Long eyelashes. Strong wrists. Oiled to the elbows.

"But you keep rolling the dice. You keep taking chances." Jimmy grunted as Celeste pressed knuckles into his sacrum. "I mean, why . . . *ungh* . . . why ambush the motel room?"

"To terrify the little fucker." A proverb occurred to Blair—the one about old dogs and new tricks. She couldn't help but smile. "We can't afford to let Brody relax. We're *herding* him, Jimmy. Not following him."

"Herding. Right . . ."

The Puccini encouraged a thoughtful, relaxing vibe, but the atmosphere in Jimmy's office was anything but. Physically, he was prone, glistening with essential oils. Energetically, he was like a shark in a tank, circling for the scent of blood.

"You need to be cool, Jimmy." Another proverb surfaced in Blair's mind, one she felt impelled to share: "Slow and steady wins the race."

"Not in my goddamn world," Jimmy snapped. "In my world, if you want something done, you've got to . . . *ungh* . . . grab it by the balls."

"But this isn't your world. It's mine." The smile left Blair's eyes, yet her lips crept higher, showing teeth. "This is my show, remember? I told you that I'd deliver Lola Bear, and that's exactly what I'm going to do."

. . .

Jimmy had trusted her with this, but it wasn't his style to play the long game. Direct force had always been his modus operandi. Blair was not opposed to violence— she'd employed it herself on many occasions—but was it effective when it came to procuring information? Jimmy certainly believed so, but the numbers suggested otherwise. In the twenty-plus years that he'd been searching for Lola Bear, his methods had netted only one crucial lead. A two-bit gun dealer out of Memphis had attempted to sell information—"Fifty Gs and I'll tell you what I know"—but had shown an eagerness to negotiate after Jimmy had taken a chainsaw to his left foot: "*Little Rock, Arkansas. Calls herself Jennifer— ARRGH CHRIST JESUS FUCK SHIT—Jennifer Ames.*" Jimmy's top guy, Bruno Rossi, had gone to Little Rock and tracked "Jennifer Ames" down—sent Jimmy a photo of her buying groceries at a Harps Food Store. The next photo Jimmy received was of Bruno slumped in the corner of some brick room, a small, ragged bullet hole over his left eyebrow. It was accompanied by the message: *Back off Jimmy!* But Jimmy hadn't backed off. He sent more men to Little Rock, but Lola had blown town by the time they got there.

Other leads had gone nowhere, and then, nine months ago, one of Jimmy's lawyers, Aldo Perera, had tracked Lola's family to South Carolina. "By going back and cross-referencing old files, and with some black-hat-level hacking and old-fashioned cunning, I was able to link Vincent Petrescu's last will and testament to a general practice lawyer in Minnesota. Turns out

Vince's sister, through her company, wired three payments of ten thousand dollars each to the Juniper Law Firm in Minneapolis—no doubt money that Vince had indirectly willed to Lola. From there, I joined the dots to a divorce lawyer in South Carolina. The details will numb the shit out of you, but the upshot—the divorcé: Ethan Ellis, a foreman at Blackridge Auto. Two kids. Brody and Molly. You'll find them in Rebel Point, a little shitburgh in the upstate region." So Jimmy had sent a team to Rebel Point and they watched the family for six weeks—too fucking long, by Jimmy's reckoning. There was no contact with Lola. Not even an email. Boiling with impatience, Jimmy had sojourned to Rebel Point with his direct-force strategy. A fruitless excursion, as it turned out; Ethan Ellis had no idea where Lola was, and in Jimmy's experience, people tend to speak truthfully when being dangled from the rooftop of a fourteen-story building.

Dropping the divorcé from the rooftop of a fourteen-story building hadn't worked, either. Jimmy had thought it would draw Lola—a vengeful cunt if ever there was one—out of hiding. But no beans.

"So we grab one of the kids." Jimmy's eyes had been wild and black in the scarred rag of his face. "Shit, *both* of them. Make the little fuckers talk."

At which point Blair had intervened.

"You think that'll work, Jimmy?"

"Sure. If they know something—"

"But they don't. You *know* they don't. Torturing them gets you nothing but a mess to clean up." Blair knew how to handle Jimmy—an intuitive understanding of his ugly, yet delicate, clockwork, and what it took to make him tick. "Maybe it's time for something other than brute force."

Jimmy's eyebrows had been burnt off in 1993 and the muscles across his brow were partially paralyzed. He conveyed many expressions, including doubt and consternation, by tilting his head and pressing his tongue to the inside of his cheek.

Blair said, "We need to use our brains, Jimmy."

His tongue had remained lodged in place for a full twenty seconds, then he retracted it and exhaled through his nose. "Brains, huh?" He struck a light to a cigar, reclined, and propped his expensive Italian shoes on his desk. "So tell me, Blair . . . you got any ideas?"

· · ·

To begin with, she wasn't Jimmy's daughter.

The Strawberry Avenue Massacre, in which thirty-three rival gang members killed one another in a storm of semiautomatic gunfire, had been entirely Blair's doing. Unlike Jimmy, she saw value in the long game.

"You singlehandedly eliminated Swan Grove's gang problem," Jimmy had said to her. This had been several years later, after he'd taken Blair under his wing and spent tens of thousands of dollars training her to be a fighter as well as a thinker. "You did what the Feds couldn't. How?"

"Time and patience," Blair had replied.

She'd been born on a bed of damp cardboard, gasoline stench in the air, a bleak December wind howling through the broken windows of her momma's trailer. Momma was a tweaker and penniless. Daddy was gone, taken by a gator while harvesting hallucinogenic mushrooms in the Wasino Bayou. Daddy was a small man—not an inch over five-three—and the rumor went that the gator had swallowed him whole. He'd left Momma only a sack of burdens.

The trailer was run-down and let in the rain but had no lien against it. The same couldn't be said for Blair's momma, who owed more than she'd ever have. She chipped away at her debts, usually with her body, but it was all too little. By the age of eleven, Blair was earning, too. Typical of Blair, she used her wile, not her body. She rode the bus to New Orleans and petitioned tourists on Bourbon Street: *My granddaddy died and I'd so dearly like a rose for his grave. A yellow rose. Uncle Bloom's on Toulouse sell 'em for a dollar apiece.* She graduated from grade-six mooching to picking pockets, then to ferrying Class A narcotics for the Black Lizard Boys.

Swan Grove had none of NOLA's allure and all of its dirt. Located in the mire southeast of the city, it was sometimes referred to as the Big Easy's dim-witted stepchild. It had three sleazy blues bars, a strip joint, a riverboat burlesque. It also had two gangs: the Cajun Warlords and the Black Lizard Boys.

Dakota Mayo—Blair's momma—was in deep with the Lizards. She owed mainly for her meth addiction but had borrowed five thousand dollars over the years and, for all her whoring, had repaid only a touch of it. The Lizards' *veterano* was a hotheaded Mexican called Lupe "El Martillo" Paez. Lupe was unblessed in the smarts department, but commanded deference by way of his fists. Dakota was his plaything. His *perra.* "For as long as you owe me," he told her, "I keep the leash tight."

Employing Blair was part of the arrangement, but for how long would she remain a mule?

"How old are you, *chiquita*?"

"Twelve."

Blair was stringing washing in what passed for their yard. Lupe watched her from the hood of his Caddy, his legs spread, the tips of his Old Gringo boots flashing in the Louisiana sunlight. He rubbed his chin and nodded.

"*Sí . . . te veo pronto.*"

Blair was not yet a teenager but intelligent enough to know a couple of things: that the only way to slip El Martillo's leash was to cut off the hand holding it—an act that required considerable force. Also, the Lizards were not a one-man operation; Lupe had an army around him, and lieutenants who were more than ready to step into his Old Gringos.

Blair needed an army, too.

The Cajun Warlords ran the west side of the Grove. A rabble of rednecks, they'd had it all until the Lizards slithered in, and there was no love lost between the two gangs. There'd been bloodshed, and then compromise: the Lizards controlled hard drugs, firearms, and prostitution, and the Warlords controlled everything else. This included marijuana, moonshine, and gambling— primarily by way of underground fighting. Something else Blair knew, because she'd heard one of those clever women on *The View*—maybe it was Whoopi—say it once: A compromise is an agreement whereby both parties are equally dissatisfied.

Big Trapper Neal was boss of the Warlords. A former Creole State boxing champion, he conducted most of his business at his gym on Strawberry Avenue.

The basement was one of several venues used for his lucrative Fight Nights. Upstairs, his spacious office (a rebel flag in one corner, a photo of Trapper meeting Sylvester Stallone on the wall) doubled as the Warlords' boardroom. This was where Blair first met Trapper. She just dropped by one day.

"Well, shit, girlie. Lookit you."

"I want to box," Blair said.

"I respect that, but I don't train girls."

"That's some bullshit, mister. Girls can box, too. You ever hear of Laila Ali?"

"I sure have. Heard of her daddy, too. But that don't change shit. You could tie the leather on, but the fact remains that I don't train girls. That means you ain't got no one to spar with."

"So?"

"No winner was ever made from just punching a bag."

"Do I look like I just want to punch a bag? Shit, mister, put me in with the boys."

Trapper was as wide as a truck's grille and when he laughed the floorboards trembled just a bit. He wiped eyes made bleary by years of taking leather, and even more years of guzzling his own hooch. "I tell you what." He slapped a hand on the table. A breeze from somewhere made the rebel flag shiver. "I could use some help around the place. Someone to drag a mop across the floors, to clean out the spit buckets. You do that, and maybe I'll show you a thing or two."

Going in, Blair had hoped things would move swiftly, but it soon became apparent this wouldn't be the case. She was still twelve when she first picked up a mop at Trapper's gym, and thirteen when she felt ready to plant the first seed. She'd been sparring with a knucklehead named Lorne Franco, four years older but built like a length of rope. She'd let Lorne knock her around, and between rounds the trainer, Ducky Rose, asked what was wrong.

"Nothing," Blair had responded. "Don't want to talk about it."

"You're getting schooled in there." Ducky was high up the Warlords' chain of command and Blair knew it. "Flash some goddamn leather. I got better things to do than watch this beanpole make a monkey out of you."

"I'm fine."

But she took a knee twice in the next round and the second time Ducky stopped it. "Left your pluck at the trailer park, kid," he said, snipping the tape off her fists. "That's not like you. Want to tell me what's wrong?"

"No."

"Drop the tough-girl act." Ducky stopped snipping and held her reddened hands firmly. "I'm talking to you as a friend now, not as a trainer."

At which point Blair dropped the tough-girl act and turned on the waterworks. It was easy to fake-cry with the sweat on her face and her eyes still puffy from Lorne's gloves.

"Come on, kid." Ducky handed her the same towel he'd tossed into the ring not five minutes before. "Don't let the boss see you crying. He'll get you back to dragging that mop around."

"Yeah. I know. Sorry." Blair ran the towel across her face. "It's just . . ." And she told Ducky the story she'd devised—how the Mexicans were tightening their stranglehold on Momma. "I guess she owes them big." And how, last night, eight of them had come over, stinking of tequila, and made her pay her dues. "I got the heck out of there. I couldn't—"

"Dirty goddamn spic assholes."

"Momma was still tweaking this morning. It's how she deals, you know?"

Ducky nodded.

"Bitch threw a glass at me. Just missed."

"Christ."

"And things'll only get worse." Blair wiped her eyes again and said, very clearly, so there was no way Ducky would misunderstand, "I overheard a couple of those beaners saying how more of them were coming to the Grove."

"More?"

"Lupe's cousins, I think. *Primos.* That's the Spanish word for cousins, right?"

"Fuck if I know."

"Some from New Mexico. Some from Veracruz."

"That so?" Ducky cleared his throat.

"Yeah. Something about Lupe wanting to expand his territory."

Seed planted. Blair stopped fake-crying and started counting. One-Mississippi. Two-Mississippi. She got only to forty-five-Mississippi before Ducky tromped his way upstairs to Trapper's office.

Blair let the seed gestate. She went about her business—just another luckless kid from Swan Grove—and on a warm September night, five weeks after her heart-to-heart with Ducky, she spray-painted WETBACK MO-FUCKS EAT SHIT!!! on the sidewalk outside the Lizards' clubhouse, and she was careful to leave the fat ass-end of a joint packed with Purple Widow—one of the Warlords' famed strains—in the gutter nearby.

Tensions between the gangs escalated. There was much crowing and flexing of muscle. Nothing more than that, but Blair knew it was just a matter of time. She watched and waited, occasionally fanning the flames. A whisper here. A comment there.

"Those damn Lizards really *are* cold-blooded," she said to Otto Dickinson during one of their morning training sessions. Otto wasn't as many rungs up the Warlords' ladder as Ducky, but he had a big mouth and he liked to run it. "Bunch of them at Shooter's last night saying how they'll soon be using rednecks for gator bait."

And to Héctor, her momma's meth dealer, she said, "Nope. No sparring today. Gym was closed." Héctor was a former student of the sweet science, before his life hit the shitter, and he regularly asked Blair how her training was coming along. "Trapper was at the range. Word is, some damn fool redneck shot his left foot clean off while trying out one of the Warlords' new guns."

Héctor and Lupe were very close. Héctor was a good earner. "Guns?" He pronounced it *gonz*. "What kinda *gonz*?"

"All kinds." Blair shrugged. "Whole crate of them came in last week."

Blair was careful how and when she leaked these deceptions. She understood that they needed to work their way beneath the skin. She also had to ensure nothing came back on her. Even the "innocent" observations of a teenage girl would arouse suspicion if divulged too frequently. What Blair never expected was for both gangs to own these fabrications with an odd kind of pride. Neither side denied anything, as if to do so would show weakness.

Her final move, and crowning achievement, was to deface Josephine Neal's grave. And Lord, how Trapper loved his momma! The Warlords' top dog visited Cedar Hill Cemetery three times a week and set a bouquet of lavenders—Momma's favorite—at the base of her stone, and he'd tell her that, by Christ, he missed her so, and that he was half the man without her (hard to imagine, considering he was pushing four hundred pounds). Sometimes he'd sing Jimmy C. Newman songs to her as the stone angels looked down. One night, Blair, now fourteen years old, left her trailer and walked the two and a half miles to Cedar Hill. She clambered over the wall, found Josephine Neal's grave, and went to work.

The cemetery caretaker cleaned up most of the mess, but he couldn't attach the heads back on the angels, and he was still scrubbing the word PUTA off the stone when Trapper showed up.

And so began the bloodshed.

Casper Morales—Lupe's primary link to La Eme at Orleans Parish—was gunned down while gassing up his Grand Marquis at the Fuel King on Delray Avenue.

Little Rocky Carson—Trapper's second cousin on his daddy's side—was knifed to death in the entranceway of his apartment building. A six-year-old kid found the body.

Héctor Alonso—meth dealer and failed human being—had his throat cut on the 270 bus between Alligator Creek and the Grove. No witnesses.

Not that witnesses were necessary. The whole town knew what was going down. Drunk off his ass at Rooster Wilson's, even Swan Grove's chief of police was heard to remark, "Those goddamn assholes are going to wipe each other out, and I for one say let them get on with it."

The chief of police was a lazy slob who rarely did anything of note, but he was right on the money on this occasion. On October 5, 2008, fourteen months after Blair planted her first seed, five large sedans with blacked-out windows rumbled onto Strawberry Avenue. What followed could have been ripped from a Wild West movie, with store owners slamming their doors and rolling down their shutters, and parents dragging their kids in off the street. The Warlords opened fire first. Otto Dickinson had snuck onto the roof of Trapper's Gym with a Hi-Point carbine, and he ripped a .45 through Cristóbal Ayala's chest. A single, startling shot—*crack!*—and Cristóbal was dead before the echo faded.

The air filled, then, with the cacophony of gunfire, of dying men's screams, of the shattering of things. Blair heard the shots from her trailer two miles west. Her momma, roused from some meth-induced stupor, stepped from her bedroom and cocked her ear at the noise.

"What *is* that?"

"The sound of your debts being paid," Blair replied.

Once the bodies had been zipped into bags and the dust had settled, Blair tried to persuade her momma to sell the trailer and get the hell out of the Grove. "Let's go where nobody knows us. We can start again." But Momma's rut went deeper than her debt to the Black Lizard Boys. She found a new meth dealer in New Orleans and went right back to where she was before.

She was dead inside of two years, but Blair had already made plans of her own. She'd gone back to pickpocketing tourists on Bourbon Street and had saved enough coin for a bus to Philadelphia and a dirty room in the basement of an ex-boxer's house. Before long, she was back in the ring, fighting guys thirty pounds heavier than her in illegal bouts. She had nine fights and won four of them, using her smarts to wear her opponents down before blazing leather into their faces. Her longest fight went twenty-two rounds.

Jimmy discovered her after one of her losses. She'd taken a right hook from a lightning-fast welterweight that dropped her cold. She came to in the locker room with Jimmy's scarred face leering down at her.

"You were doing good," he said, "until he knocked you out."

"Shit happens." She touched the deep cut beneath her left eye. "Who the fuck are you?"

"A man who recognizes your talent. I'd like to train you to be a real fighter."

"I am a real fighter."

"I'm not talking about boxing . . . or whatever this is."

Blair didn't exactly jump at Jimmy's offer. She wanted to find out more about him first, which wasn't difficult, given his reputation. Two months later, he showed up at another fight (another loss). He offered her a job—his personal assistant, he said—and a room at his house in Carver City.

"Why me?" she asked. "I'm nothing special."

"I think you are," Jimmy said. "And I'm usually right about these things."

Two days later, she was in the back of a limo on her way to Carver City, her single bag of possessions on the seat beside her. Jimmy met her at the front door of his showy, modern residence, then led her to his office. It was large and clean, with an open fireplace and a cello in the corner that looked as if it had never been played. A forty-something male with muscles packed into a black T-shirt stood by the window. Jimmy nodded at him, then took a gun from the top drawer of his desk and placed it in Blair's hand.

"You know what that is?" he asked.

"A gun," Blair said. "A pistol."

"It's a Beretta M9. Italian, semiautomatic. This means the gun will reload itself, but pulling the trigger will only fire one bullet at a time. It's a fifteen-round mag, though, so you can do a lot of damage before you have to *stop* pulling the trigger. How does it feel?"

"Heavy."

"Won't feel that way for long. Howie is going to show you how to use it." Jimmy gestured toward the man with the muscles. "By the time he's finished with you, you'll be hitting targets from twenty yards with a blindfold on."

Blair looked from Jimmy to the pistol, turning it over in her hand, getting a feel for its weight. "You said I was going to be your personal assistant."

"And you are. I just didn't tell you what you'll be assisting me with." Jimmy smiled and clapped her on the shoulder. "Welcome to your first day on the job."

Howie was ex–Special Forces. He'd spent eleven years in the Middle East working counterinsurgency and counterterrorism operations, and another eight years training snipers at Fort Benning. As well as fire-arms, he was proficient in knife and weapons combat. It took time, but he taught Blair everything he knew. By the age of eighteen, she could field-strip an AR-15 in under thirty seconds and hit a moving target from sound alone. Jimmy was pleased with her progress, but it was not enough. He financed her intensive schooling in kendo, kung fu, and Krav Maga. *I'd like to train you to be a real fighter*, he'd said when they first met, but what he actually wanted was a killing machine.

And Blair knew why; Jimmy had told her all about Lola Bear, in painful and intimate detail.

"You were in awe of her," Blair said. She looked at Jimmy, seeing Lola in every scar, in the black torment of his expression. "Maybe you even loved her."

"No maybe about it."

"Is that what this is about? My training?" They were in Jimmy's orchard, Blair throwing knives at a series of targets she'd set up between the trees. "Are you trying to create a new Lola Bear?"

"No." Jimmy shook his head vehemently. "You're going to be better than her. Stronger than her. And you're going to help me bring her down."

"So this is a fight-fire-with-fire situation?"

"Exactly." Jimmy's chest swelled and his eyes glimmered in the hazy afternoon light. "Think you can handle that?"

Blair plucked a knife from her belt, threw it without looking, and struck a man-shaped target in the throat.

"I can handle anything," she said.

. . .

Blair had pointed out the obvious (although she couldn't be sure Jimmy had considered it): Brody and Molly Ellis were too valuable a bridge to burn. "We need to compromise them in some way," she'd said. "Make *them* do the work for us."

"Go on." Jimmy puffed his fat cigar.

"They need to feel threatened, scared, but with room to move—to *think*. If we play it right, they'll draw on contacts they wouldn't ordinarily consider. And maybe, just *maybe*, one of those contacts will lead them to Lola Bear."

Jimmy pushed his tongue to the inside of his cheek again, smoke leaking from the edges of his mouth. Then he shook his head. "No. Too much can go wrong."

"I think it'll work."

"Maybe." Jimmy shrugged. "But if they have information—contacts, addresses, phone numbers—

it'll be quicker to beat it out of them. Shit, I'll take a tire iron to the cripple's leg, and you'll see how quickly the brother squawks."

"Brains, Jimmy, not brawn." Blair placed her fists on the desk and leaned toward him. "No one can think clearly while getting the shit kicked out of them, or while watching someone they love get hurt. It's not as effective as you like to believe. And twenty years of chasing Lola Bear, torturing her contacts, *still* not finding her, proves that."

Jimmy made a rumbling sound in his chest. Ash fell from the tip of his cigar and powdered his white shirt.

"Also," Blair continued, "they may not *have* those contacts yet. They may need to think laterally, ask around. It might require some footwork."

Jimmy considered this for a moment, then his eyes widened and he snapped his fingers. "Well, shit, I can think laterally, too. Let's kidnap the sister. We'll put her on camera and send the video file to the kid."

"By email?"

"Shit, no. We'll put it on a flash drive and mail it anonymously. And we won't incriminate ourselves in the video. It'll just be the girl talking to the camera. She'll need to be beaten up a little—or a *lot*—but still able to deliver the message: *Find Lola Bear, dear brother of mine, or these very bad men will do very bad things.*"

"Okay." Blair nodded. "That's better, Jimmy. Smarter."

"You like that?"

"I do, and I'd say go for it, except . . ."

"Except?"

"The sister is the brains of the operation." Blair stood up straight and folded her muscular arms. It was often necessary to adopt such unwavering body language when dealing with Jimmy. "I don't think Brody can find Lola without her. Also, he might go to the police."

"Let him," Jimmy snorted. "They won't be able to link the video to us."

"You're missing the point." Blair said patiently. "For as long as Brody is relying on the police to find his sister, we can't rely on him to find Lola."

Jimmy took a long pull on his cigar. The tip bloomed and sizzled. "Okay, so we threaten to kill his sister if he goes to the cops. Problem solved."

"I don't think so. Brody will be too rattled. He'll still think he's got a better chance with the police." Blair relaxed her posture, but wrinkled her brow contemplatively. "I'd prefer to remove law enforcement from the equation. Then it's just him and us."

Jimmy made that rumbling sound again.

"I'll find a way to set Brody up," Blair insisted, and a word popped into her mind. She wasn't sure it was the correct word, but it had a wonderful, sinister ring. "*Artifice*. It's what I do best. Then we just sit back and wait."

"I'm not convinced."

"Give me this, Jimmy. Six months, that's all I ask. And if I can't deliver Lola Bear, *then* we kidnap the cripple. You can beat the shit out of her, put a bullet in her eye. Whatever you want."

Jimmy exhaled smoke and grinned.

"Six months," Blair said. "Then we do it your way."

. . .

Blair found out everything she could about Brody: where he'd lived, gone to school, his interests, favorite movies and music, his employment history, his friends and exes. Then she started watching him, day and night, assuming various disguises to avoid suspicion. She soon devised a scheme to enter his life, seduce him, then persuade him to steal her "stepmother's" diamonds and frame him for her murder. Jesus, didn't one of Jimmy's loaded poker buddies own a house in Freewood Valley? What a serendipitous fucking opportunity! They could use it to stage the crime, and Jimmy's accountant, Cynthia Gray, could play the part of the wicked stepmom. All she had to do was play dead for a few minutes. She even had one of those fucking hideous Warhol-style paintings of herself that they could hang on the wall for added effect.

Was it a shitfuck crazy plan? Well goddamn, yes it was. It *was*. But the craziest plans netted the biggest rewards, and framing Brody would keep him from going to the police.

"His old man is dead," Blair had said to Jimmy, having outlined her extravagant scheme. "We eliminated *that* source of support. The few friends he has are airheads and stoners—fucking useless, all of them. He has no immediate family, other than his sister. His landlord doesn't give a shit—"

"The kid has no one," Jimmy cut in.

"Right. At least not on the surface," Blair said. "But with his back against the wall, he's going to start digging."

Blair was about to make her move when a new development inspired a change of plan: Brody had started reconnoitering convenience stores in the early hours of the morning. With no job and barely a penny to his name (hacking his credit information and bank activity had confirmed this), it was obvious that he was going to rob one of them—probably Buddy's on Independence Avenue, which he'd cased three times.

Blair waited in the wings, recognizing how to use this development to her advantage, and relishing the opportunity to apply her pickpocketing skills once again.

"You're making this too easy, Brody."

After all, why fuck him when she could blackmail him?

...

Celeste had packed up and gone, leaving only a musk of sandalwood and jojoba. Jimmy sloped awkwardly across his chaise longue. The massage hadn't relaxed him at all.

"Alexa," he groaned. "Play Vivaldi."

Vivaldi's *The Four Seasons* floated from the Echo. Jimmy shifted stiffly, eyes closed. Blair stepped toward him and loomed until he cracked his eyelids and acknowledged her.

"I like how this is working out," she said, and displayed the same smile she'd used on Brody: coquettish, with a hint of devilry. Men, she'd learned, were a sucker for that smile.

"Good for you, but your six months is up at the end of October. That's . . ." Jimmy counted on his fingers.

"Twenty-six days, then I'm pulling the plug on this goddamn cat-and-mouse and doing it my way."

"Chainsaw Jimmy. Always looking for blood."

"I prefer to be called the Italian Cat." Jimmy showed his teeth. "Nobody fucks with me. Even dogs run away."

Vivaldi stirred the room like a breeze. Dead leaves spiraled beyond the windows. Blair stooped, still smiling, and hooked a lock of silver hair behind Jimmy's ear.

"Bitch ruined me," he snarled. "All these years of searching, waiting for my moment—my revenge."

"You'll have it. Soon."

"I wish I had your confidence." Jimmy's fists trembled at his sides. "Goddamn it, Blair, this kid had better come through."

Blair dropped to one knee and leaned close to Jimmy. Her lips whispered against his cheek.

"Trust me," she said, and there was devilry in her voice, too. "A scared little boy will always find his mommy."

Chapter Nine

"Faster, Brody. Go . . . *go!*"

Brody ripped through a four-way stop without slowing. A dusty old Buick puttered in front of him and he swerved right—drove fifteen yards with two wheels on the sidewalk, then swerved again to avoid a telephone booth. Molly took a sharp breath, her body pressed into the passenger seat.

"This is all a dream," she hissed. "A bad fucking dream."

Brody's eyes flicked to the mirror. The mobsters had fallen back. They negotiated the four-way stop more cautiously, then gunned it once they were through.

"I'll get us out of this," he said.

Another intersection loomed ahead. There was roadwork on the other side, traffic packed into a single lane. Brody touched the brake and turned left, timing his move to cut in front of a tractor-trailer. It howled at him, leaving rubber on the blacktop. Brody eased off the gas so that the truck flooded his rearview, then made an abrupt right turn, hoping the long trailer masked the maneuver. He jammed his foot to the floor again, blew a red light, then turned into the parking lot of a furniture store. Another glance in the mirror. No sign of Jimmy's guys. He zipped between rows of parked vehicles, then around the back of the store where the loading docks were. Brody considered tucking his car into one of the docks beside an empty trailer—hoping Leo and company wouldn't think to look back here— but noticed an access road leading across a patch of scrub, framed with chain-link. He took it at speed, came out on a quiet road that veered north out of town. Several tense glances into the mirrors showed nobody in pursuit. Brody took a series of arbitrary right and left turns before pulling into the gap behind an empty cattle shed.

"We lost them," he gasped. "Holy *shit*."

Molly said nothing. She had her face buried in her hands, crying and trembling copiously. Brody cranked the window, took a deep breath. The air smelled of cow shit but it was still fresher than the stifling stench of fear inside the car.

His nostrils flared. He gripped the wheel to steady the earthquakes in his hands. *Lost them,* he thought, but something about that didn't seem right. He, Brody Ellis, had outmaneuvered Jimmy's goons in his crapped-out Pontiac. Even back at the motel, he'd outwitted them. It shouldn't have been that easy.

Molly lifted her face from her hands and looked at him. He didn't want to meet her gaze but, eventually, he did. He *had* to.

"What the fuck, Brody?"

"Give me your phone," he said.

...

He stepped out of the car with his own and Molly's cell phones in one hand, and the replica pistol in the other.

"What are you doing, Brody?" Molly struggled to get out on her side, clumsily gathering her crutches while pushing the door open. Brody had yanked the phone from her pocket when she refused to give it to him. Now he tossed it on the stony ground, dropped to one knee, and smashed the screen with the butt of the pistol.

"What the *fuck*?" Molly fell out of the car, picked herself up, and hobbled around to Brody. She hit him twice with one of her crutches, then lost balance and stumbled backward. By this time her cell phone was a mess of plastic and broken glass. Brody picked up the pieces and threw them into the trees behind the cattle shed.

"Brody?"

"This is how they found us. How they're tracking us." He waved his own phone at the satellites before dropping it at his feet. "Jesus, Moll, haven't you heard of geolocation?"

"Of course," she said. "It's a way of determining the location of any web-based device."

"It's . . . well, yeah." Five furious strikes with the pistol grip ended his cell phone's life. He flung the ruptured casing as far away as he could.

Molly sat on the hood of the car. Her eyes were heavy but she was out of tears. "Who are 'they,' Brody?" She was sad, angry, and scared, but Brody knew she was more disappointed than anything. "And why do you have a gun?"

Brody sighed. He aimed the pistol at the sky, pulled the trigger. Nothing happened.

"It's not real. It's a replica. I used it to rob a convenience store." He lowered the gun, then lowered his head, deeply ashamed. "That's where I got the money from."

He told her everything.

...

Brody's response to Molly getting bullied was to ask his dad if he could learn karate, and then to master the one-inch punch. Violence. His go-to solution, and one that mankind—with an emphasis on *man*—had favored since it dragged its knuckles along the ground. But Brody had bullies, too. Mainly on the inside. He'd had insecurity issues throughout his teens, which started when his mom hit the road, and manifested by way of nightmares, mood swings, and feelings of inadequacy. Molly had helped him through the worst of it, and while she occasionally expressed her frustrations by lashing out with her crutches, her default approach to problem solving was through conversation.

As it was now.

"There must be *something*," she said. She had calmed down, but there was still a flush of color on her cheeks. "A detail, a flaw in the plan—something that Blair forgot, and that we can use to prove your innocence."

"The police are not an option, Moll." They sat on the ground, their backs against the Pontiac's freshly dented fender. "Blair is smart on a different level. A *dangerous* level. Like a shark. She's thought of everything, and even if she hasn't—if there *is* a flaw in the plan—I don't fancy my public defender's chances against Jimmy Latzo's big city lawyers."

Molly sighed and rested her head on Brody's shoulder.

"And if, by some miracle, I *can* prove that I was framed," Brody continued, "I don't think Chainsaw Jimmy would let it lie. I broke into his house, after all. That's an irrefutable fact. Caught on tape. He'll kill me for that, if nothing else."

It was growing dark. The early October sun touched the horizon, pushing a rusty light through the trees and buildings. Power lines underscored the view. A breeze set everything flickering. It made the cattle shed creak and whistle.

"We need to run," Molly said. Even with her ability to strip a problem to its component parts and reassemble it into something hopeful, she still arrived at the same conclusion as Brody.

"To hide," he said.

"Not just hide. Disappear."

"Right."

"But we can't do that on our own. We need help."

Brody closed his eyes for a moment. She was still with him, at his side, despite everything. He wanted to throw his arms around her, drag her into the kind of hug that made small bones pop. He didn't, though; it seemed an incommensurate way of showing gratitude for such strength. So he exhaled from deep within his chest and blinked at tears and absorbed the delicate weight of her head on his shoulder.

"You mentioned Karl Janko earlier. Mom's friend." Molly lifted her head from Brody's shoulder and looked at him in the reddish light. "You think he can help?"

"It's worth a shot," Brody said. "I remember him more than I was letting on. And he was totally sketch. Someone like that might be able to help us . . . you know, disappear."

"He's probably in prison." Molly shook her head. "Or dead."

"Maybe. But it's somewhere to start."

"We know anybody else?"

"Johnny Frye—"

"The pest control guy?"

"He used to sell Ecstasy to high school kids."

"No. Absolutely not. Anybody else?"

"Christy Beale. She's cleaned up her act, but . . ." Brody shrugged, then started plucking clumps of yellow grass out of the dirt. "Kieran Houser. Franklin Ogg. Macy Zerilli—"

"The bartender at Rocky T's?" Molly rolled her eyes. "She wouldn't piss on you if you were on fire."

"This is true."

"These are shitty options, Brody. In fact, they're not options at all." Molly leaned to her stronger side, grabbed one of her crutches, and hoisted herself to her feet. The pain clearly bolted through her, because she grimaced, but nothing more than that. "So I guess we need to track down Karl Janko."

Brody nodded. "Like I said: a good place to start."

"The only place to start." Molly tapped the tip of one crutch against the Pontiac's buckled hood. "We also need to dump the car."

"Dump it? You're kidding, right?" Brody jumped to his feet, slapping dirt from the seat of his jeans. "I just spent five hundred bucks on a new fuel pump. And we might need to sleep—"

"Christ, Brody, do you really need me to spell this out for you? Jimmy Latzo's men are *looking* for this heap of shit." The way she squared her shoulders assured Brody this was not open to negotiation. "There aren't too many '99 Sunfires on the road today. It's distinctive, not to mention unreliable. We're dumping it."

A large bird signaled from somewhere. Smaller birds peppered the western sky, dark as drops of water on red cloth.

"Let's get out of here." Molly thrust her crutches into the dirt and started walking.

"Wait. Christ, Molly. *Wait.*" Brody loped toward her, gesturing inanely at his car. "We're *walking*?"

"Sure."

"But—"

"Grab our bags, and whatever else we need. I think"—she pointed one crutch at a sprinkle of lights to the north—"that's Elder. I saw it on Google maps coming in. About three miles away, I'd say. We'll leave the car here, cut across the fields. Should be there in a couple of hours."

"Molly, I really—"

"I'll be fine." She pulled Motrin and Lioresal from her jacket pocket, popped one of each into her palm, and swallowed them with a single, practiced click of her throat. "Let's go."

It was arduous going. The fields dipped and rose, in places marred with flints and potholes, and elsewhere with long, dry cogongrass that pulled at their heels. At one point they had to cut through a bedlam of leaning trees that conspired with the darkness, messed with their sense of direction. Molly fell twice. The first time she wouldn't accept Brody's help but the second time she did. They rested until they'd caught their breaths, pushed on, and eventually emerged on the edge of a stream with Elder's lights not quite where they thought they'd be.

They crossed the stream carefully, not bothering to take off their sneakers and socks. The landscape was easier on the other side and they pushed on eagerly. A skim of moon shone. Molly remained three or four paces ahead, digging her crutches into the dark ground.

Brody breathed hard and watched the accent of her back, the rhythmic tick of her legs. He shifted the weight of their bags from one shoulder to another.

"I'll say this just once." She stopped, turned to look at him. Elder's lights framed her. He could see a strip mall and an overpass and an illuminated billboard that promised the most competitive insurance rates in the Magnolia State. "This is on *you*, Brody. You own this shit. I don't ever want to hear—not fucking *once*—that you did this for me. You feed me that line of horseshit and I swear to God you'll never see me again."

BEFORE

Lola had wanted to make the room as comfortable as possible: fresh, colorful carnations, pictures of his wife and son—both long dead—on the bedside table, Tin Pan Alley music playing softly in the background. But Grandpa Bear was a stubborn old mule, even now, and all he insisted on was a glass of cold water and the TV tuned to CNN.

She watched him sleeping for a moment, supported by large pillows, his eyelids fluttering. All the muscle had been stripped from him. His body had been reshaped—the austere angles replaced by shadowy hollows and weak lines. To see him like this was unthinkable. This was the man who had taken care of her since she was fourteen, who'd taught her how to spot a concealed handgun, how to field dress a deer, how to tighten her shot groups at the range. And more, so much more. He was the beginning of everything she'd become.

Lola stepped farther into the room, suppressing her emotion, as she was inclined to do, but feeling that, at twenty-four years old, she was too young to lose the most important person in her life, and one of only two people that she actually cared about.

He opened his eyes suddenly, then turned toward her, noticing her there. His peripheral vision was still precise.

"Lola," he said warmly.

"Hey, Gramps." She found a smile, albeit a delicate one. "Just checking in. You need anything?"

He returned her smile—his a little stronger—and pondered the question for several seconds. "No," he croaked, and coughed, clearing his throat. "But *you* do." He drew one hand from beneath the sheets and pointed at the dresser against the far wall. "Bottom drawer."

Lola walked to the dresser and opened the bottom drawer. There were a few folded sweaters inside— clothes that Grandpa Bear would never wear again— and a brown faux-leather folder. She took it out.

"What is this?"

"Don't ask questions," Grandpa Bear said. "Just take it. Put it somewhere safe."

Lola opened the folder. Inside were driver's licenses, Social Security cards, and birth certificates. Three of each. Lola's photograph graced each driver's license. She looked at the one from North Dakota. The name stamped across the front read WARD, MARGARET NAOMI. The other names were Natalie Myles and Jennifer Ames.

"How can I not ask questions?" There was surprise in Lola's tone.

Grandpa Bear coughed again and adjusted his pillows—or *tried* to; he couldn't get the angle. Lola did it for him. He had been diagnosed with aggressive non-Hodgkin's lymphoma two and a half years earlier. Doctors gave him three to six months. He'd battled like he had in Europe, Korea, and Vietnam. Three wars' worth of toughness and experience. The fight was almost over, though.

"I know you work for Jimmy Latzo," he said, and coughed yet again. Lola handed him water and he sipped gratefully. "If I thought I could talk some sense into you, I would. But you are a stubborn young lady."

"That I am." She took the glass away. "Wonder where I get that from."

"Must be a Bear thing." The old man gave his head a little shake. "You could've been a cop, Lola. A damn good one."

"Sure, and get a psychiatric evaluation every time I fire my service pistol." Lola took out another driver's license. Same photograph. Different name. "Besides, all the sitting around, and all the paperwork, would drive me crazy."

"Like I said, there's no talking sense into you, so all I can do is protect you, give you an exit." Grandpa Bear tapped the folder. "Three exits, actually."

"Fake IDs?"

"No. Think of them as resets. New beginnings." Grandpa Bear coughed once again, fumbling for the glass. Lola held it to his lips and he took a long drink. He raised one finger when he'd had enough, then continued. "Working for Jimmy, there'll come a time when you have to run, either from the law or from Jimmy himself. That's the nature of the life you've chosen."

"Maybe."

"No maybe about it. This isn't a long-term career, and you'll make enemies. So I've given you three new starts. When the time comes, get as far away as you can, choose an identity, and live a different life. If you're ever compromised, ditch that identity, and move on to the next one." Grandpa Bear breathed deeply. His throat crackled. "Three should get you through, if you're careful."

Lola looked at Natalie Myles's Social Security card. "This is good work. Everything looks legit."

"I pulled a favor with an old friend, ex–Marshals Service. I saved his life in Iwo Jima. Just doing my job, but he promised to repay me somehow." Grandpa Bear tapped the folder again. "All these names are in the system. If you need to renew a driver's license, or apply for a passport, you can go through the legitimate channels. You can also vote, get a job, get married—"

"Married?" Lola smiled. "Vince will be happy."

"No. Not Vince. You'll be escaping your old life and everyone in it." Grandpa Bear settled back into his pillows. His chest pumped out another rotten cough. "The moment you assume one of those identities, you start living a lie. And it's a lie you can never *unlive*."

"Let's hope," Lola said, "it doesn't come to that."

"It almost certainly will." Grandpa Bear said nothing for a while. His chest climbed, then sagged. He looked unspeakably lovely, Lola thought. Large enough to have survived three wars, yet small enough to cradle.

"You should get some rest," she said.

"Soon. Listen . . ." He urged her closer. She smelled the medicines on his breath. "I want you to open bank accounts in all three names. Do it in the states the driver's licenses are issued in, so you don't raise any flags. And don't wait too long."

"I can do that," Lola said.

"Good. You'll come into your inheritance . . . any day now." Grandpa Bear allowed a tight, sad smile. "Divide it between your accounts. But launder it first, so there's no paper trail. And launder it again if and when you relocate. I have a contact who can help with that."

"Okay," Lola said.

His bleary eyes fluttered, rolled to the ceiling, then slowly closed. Sunlight fell through the window in an even yellow bar, while a TV in the corner silently re-layed the news: riots in Los Angeles after four police officers were acquitted in the brutal beating of Rodney King.

"I said . . . get married, that you . . ." He mumbled, drifting into sleep. His lips made slight shapes. "But don't . . . don't . . ."

"It's okay, Gramps." Lola took his hand and squeezed gently. "Sleep now."

"Don't get married." He looked at her. There was something in his eyes. Pain or disappointment. It didn't matter which; both broke her heart. "Don't put down roots, or make anything that you can't leave behind."

Lola wondered what kind of life that would be, one without stability, without expectation or legacy. Was that really the track she was on? Or was there a brighter path ahead?

Grandpa Bear muttered something else—she didn't catch it—then drifted back off to sleep. Lola leaned over and kissed his forehead.

"I'll be okay," she whispered, more to herself than to Grandpa Bear, who'd given her so much, and had never let her down.

She tucked the folder beneath her arm and left the room.

Chapter Ten

Brody and Molly cut across farmland and entered Elder on its southwest side. The dark streets made surveying for suspicious vehicles and people difficult. When, after several minutes of walking, nobody had jumped them, Brody relaxed just a little.

"What's the plan, Moll?" He was content—relieved, even—to let his sister take the reins for a while.

"We're too close to where we lost them," Molly said. "They might have eyes on this place. So we need a ride somewhere else—forty, fifty miles away, at least. From there, we can catch a bus or train and go . . . shit, anywhere. As long as it has a motel and a library."

"A library," Brody repeated. "You plan on doing some reading?"

"Online reading, yes. Libraries have computers. I need to find Janko, remember, and I don't know how long that will take."

Molly approached a young woman outside a small theater, speaking slowly to make herself understood, this—quite deliberately—emphasizing her palsy. She explained that her phone was out of charge, and asked the woman if she would call a taxi for her.

"What's wrong with his phone?" The woman gestured at Brody, hovering just beyond the marquee's lights.

"Doesn't have one," Molly said, and shrugged. "Says he's a technophobe, but that doesn't stop him playing video games with his loser buddies."

"Uber's better. Cheaper," the woman said after a moment, accessing her app with impressive speed. "There are four in the area."

"Okay. Whatever. I can—"

"You can give me the cash."

"Yeah. Absolutely."

"Where are you going?"

Molly blanked, shook her head. "I don't . . ." She shifted her weight from one crutch to the other. "How far is Tupelo?"

The woman lowered her phone, her eyes floating between Molly and Brody. "Maybe a hundred miles."

"That's a little far," Molly said, thinking of the dwindling cash in Brody's brown paper bag. "Somewhere closer. But not *too* close. And big enough to have a bus or train terminal."

"Sparrow Hill is forty-five minutes north."

"Okay." Molly nodded. "Perfect."

The woman tapped her phone, stepped furtively toward Molly, showed her the screen. On it she'd written: *Want me to call the police??* Her eyebrows twitched in Brody's direction.

"No. He's my brother," Molly whispered. She touched the woman's elbow briefly, gently. "Thank you, though. We just need to get out of town."

"You sure?"

"Yeah."

The woman nodded stiffly and returned to her app. "Eighty bucks to Sparrow Hill. Driver will be here in three minutes."

"Thank you." Molly offered her a warm, grateful smile, then she added, not sure if she had to but wanting to be doubly careful, "And please, if anyone asks, you didn't see us."

. . .

Fifty miles to Sparrow Hill, I-55 most of the way, the highway like the blank, non-REM stages between dreams. Brody and Molly sat in the back so they wouldn't have to talk to the driver. He was as chirpy as a bird to begin with, but took the hint after a string of uninterested, monosyllabic replies. He dropped them, as requested, at the bus depot on Burlington Avenue. The last thing he said was, "Going anywhere exciting?" To which Brody replied, "I hope not."

. . .

Brody counted his money in the bus depot's restroom, holding the bills the way he'd hold an injured mouse. $940. Bleak. Very bleak. At this rate, they'd be down to their last few dollars by the end of the week.

Six buses were leaving in the next hour. Molly wanted to go to New Mexico. Brody opted for Jefferson City, Missouri. A quicker, less expensive ride, and more central—potentially more convenient to wherever they had to travel next.

"It's still four hundred miles away," he said. "That's a good distance."

They paid cash for their tickets and were in Jefferson City by four P.M. the next day.

. . .

Brody had slept on the bus. Not well, but better than he expected to, and more than he *wanted* to. He'd planned to gaze meerkat-like out the rear window to remain certain they weren't being followed. There was no way, of course—they would have been jumped by now—but better to stay vigilant. It was too dark to see anything but headlights, though. Eventually he gave up. Sleep took him.

They found a motel called, laughably, Cozies, a step above Motel 15, with its crack whores and gunshots, but not a broad step. Still, it was $48 a night, no credit card required. The beds were as hard as tortoiseshell.

...

They spent what remained of that day resting. Molly gulped meds. The bus journey, not to mention the miles they'd traveled on foot, had been hard on her. Brody massaged her legs and feet, circled a damp towel around her left thigh. She cried a little bit but tried to hide it.

They watched shit TV. Ordered Chinese food. Their new life.

...

And eventually they slept. Brody startled awake in the small hours when headlights swept across the thin curtains.

They're here. Oh my God. Jesus Christ—

He sprang out of bed, rushed to the window, peered between the wall and the curtain. But no, it was just a car turning around. Brody watched as it pulled out of the parking lot and drove away.

"Jesus."

He went to Molly, gazing at her while she slept. "I'm sorry." He cried, covering his eyes, even though she couldn't see, then dropped to his knees, placed his head in the nest between her arm and rib cage, and fell asleep.

He woke several hours later, his head now resting on a fold in the bedsheets. Molly had gone.

A note on the nightstand read: *At library.*

• • •

The paranoia was hard to shake. He sat in the gloom, curtains drawn, attuned to every sound. Cars hissed. Doors slammed. A couple in an upstairs room fought colorfully, then kissed and made up. Their bed thumped for thirty-seven tireless minutes.

Brody paced, counted stains on the walls, watched infomercials with the volume down. There were some left-over noodles and he ate them cold, grimacing at every soggy mouthful. He finally left the room and walked with his face turned to the sun, breathing the fumy air and sometimes flinching at the city's angry clatter.

• • •

How?

That was the question. He and Molly had destroyed their cell phones, ditched the car, paid for transport and accommodation with cash. No footprints. So how could Jimmy's men track them down?

"There's no way." Brody sat on the bleachers in an empty baseball park, the sun behind him now, throwing his shadow across the diamond. "We lost them in Mississippi. End of story."

Right. He'd outmaneuvered them, as improbable as that seemed, and had avoided them for forty-eight hours, 460 miles. With no way to follow, the mobsters had likely resorted to interrogating his and Molly's few acquaintances: Tyrese, Molly's colleagues at Arrow Dairy, their handful of friends—who'd hopefully diverted them to "Aunt Cherry" in Maine.

So . . .

"There's no way," Brody said again. He closed his eyes, though, considering every possibility, however unlikely.

How?

. . .

Brody walked back to Cozies in the near-dark, less wary of every sudden noise and shadow. The time to himself had been needed. He'd had space to think, and had subsequently started to believe they were in the clear.

At least for now. The moment they showed their faces, used their names, left a footprint, Jimmy's men would swoop. Maybe they weren't following, but they *were* looking.

Yet another "how" question surfaced when he returned to the motel room, recalling the paranoia like a foul taste: How long did it take Molly to search for someone online?

"You here, Moll?"

It was a boxy room with a cramped bathroom attached. He could *see* she wasn't there, but anxiety drew the question from him. A dusty alarm clock on the nightstand displayed 17:48 in faded numbers. She'd been gone all day. Brody ran a hand across his face, trying to convince himself that Jimmy's men were looking for *him*, not her, but paranoia was a slippery, wicked snake. He turned the TV on, hoping it would distract him, but it didn't. He imagined how Molly would scream when Jimmy pulled the starter rope on his favorite chainsaw.

"I can't stay here," he said, staggering from the room, slamming the door just as a taxi curved across the lot. It pulled into a space close to their door. Ranchera boomed from the driver's open window.

Then a rear window opened and Molly's face appeared. She looked tired, but never more beautiful. Relief crashed through Brody.

"Moll. Jesus. You were gone a long time."

"Yeah. Digging deep." She gestured at the empty seat beside her. "Get in. Let's grab a bite to eat. Talk."

"Did you—"

The window closed again, but before it did he heard her say, "I found Janko."

...

King Elvis was a themed burger joint on East High Street—more money than Brody wanted to spend, but Molly insisted. "I'm hungry, dammit, and I'm not going to Mickey-fucking-D's." Brody knew better than to argue. The closest he came to an objection was whistling through his teeth when Molly ordered an $18.99 Teddy Bear Burger.

"Karl Janko is dead," she said as soon as the waiter had left their table. She pulled several dog-eared sheets of paper, covered with her handwriting, from her purse, and shuffled through them. "Died twelve years ago. Murdered. Beaten up and drowned in a barrel."

"Christ," Brody said. He brought Janko to mind— had a clear memory of playing catch with him in their backyard in Minneapolis. "In a *barrel?* That's some medieval shit."

"No doubt. But he knew a lot of bad dudes. Shit, he *was* a bad dude. Some sources claim he was connected to the mob." Molly riffled through her notes and came up with the page she was looking for. "I started my search the same place everybody searches for people these days: social media. No luck there, so I Googled 'Karl Janko,' got half a million hits, then narrowed the field with key words and filters. That's when I found his obituary."

"That's good work, Moll," Brody said, and sighed. "Doesn't help us, though."

"The obit led me to other stories: sixteen months served in 1985 for grand theft auto; another stint in 1988 for aggravated assault. There were several charges he was acquitted of, or that were suddenly dropped, including criminal harassment, arson, and manslaughter in the first degree."

"What a swell guy," Brody said.

"I know, right? And he must have got in with some bad people. His murder was . . . *savage.* His thumbs had been cut off, his teeth were smashed in. There were abrasions around his wrists and ankles from where he'd been tied up—"

Molly stopped suddenly, lowering her notes into her lap. Their server had arrived with their drinks. He set them down mutely, then retreated to the bar. Molly sipped her vanilla milkshake with fluttering eyelids. "Oh wow. Yummy." She licked her lips, returned her notes to the tabletop, and continued:

"I read a few articles regarding the investigation. The police had very little evidence, followed a lot of dead ends. They believed—from the deliberate nature of Janko's injuries—that he'd been tortured for information."

Brody sighed again and shook his head. The only reply he could muster.

"I didn't dig too deeply," Molly went on, looking up from her notes. "I figured it was a waste of time. The dude's dead, right? But from what I could tell, his killer, or *killers*, were never found."

"Too many enemies," Brody muttered, thinking that he, unjustly, had an enemy, too, and one that was capable of something similar. Or worse.

"Janko was buried in his hometown of Cambridge, Massachusetts. No wife. No children." Molly sipped her milkshake, flipped through a few pages. "He was survived only by his stepbrother, Wendell."

"Tragic," Brody said, running his hands through his hair. He wondered how many diners would vacate their tables if he pummeled the back of his skull and screamed his frustrations at the Elvis portraits on the walls. Instead he sipped his Pepsi and whispered, "So what do we do now?"

"Our options are . . . limited," Molly said. "And none of them are good."

"Tell me about it." Brody linked his fingers. "We need a miracle."

"Exactly. Which brings me to Wendell, the step-brother. Something he said in one of the articles I read stayed with me—how he and Janko were thick as thieves when they were younger, but drifted apart in later life."

Molly sipped her milkshake again, making small delighted sounds. Those sounds alone were worth the price tag, Brody thought.

"I wondered if *he* might help us." Molly shrugged. "We knew his brother, right?"

"His *step*brother," Brody said. "And we *barely* knew him."

"Okay, but I figured Wendell doesn't need to know that. And if they were thick as thieves when they were younger, maybe they moved in similar circles."

"Had the same connections."

"Right. Someone who could help us disappear."

"Okay. A long shot, but worth exploring." Brody nodded. "Tell me about Wendell."

"He was tough to track down. He and Janko had different biological parents. Different surnames. Took a few hours, going through various genealogy and life-hacking sites. But I found him."

"And?"

"He's a Pentecostal minister."

"Aw, fuck."

"In Decatur, Illinois."

The tables around them had filled. King Elvis was in full swing. The air brimmed with dozens of voices, conversations, rich with aromas of barbecued animal and sarsaparilla. "Suspicious Minds" played through the speakers, just loud enough to hear. An Elvis imper-sonator sang "Happy Birthday" to a bucktoothed teen three tables away.

At some point their food arrived. Brody only no-ticed when Molly aimed ketchup at her fries, hit the table instead.

"Shit. Not even close."

"So what's Reverend Wendell going to do, Moll?" Brody smeared the ketchup away with a napkin. "Shelter us with angels?"

"First," Molly said, popping a fry into her mouth, "he was wrongly imprisoned in 1991, for murder, served eight years of a thirty-year sentence, so he may have some empathy for your—*our*—situation."

Brody looked at his meal—ribs, partly charred, glazed with sauce—with zero appetite.

"Second, we knew his stepbrother. There's a family connection. And he's close; Decatur is half a day's bus ride."

Brody said, "Feels like grasping at straws."

"We're lucky to have a straw to grasp." Molly went back to her milkshake but this time there were no delighted sounds. "Bottom line: the Reverend Wendell Mathias is duty-bound to provide guidance to those in need. And we are most certainly in need."

Brody yanked a rib, looked at it as he might a small, live fish, and dropped it back on the plate.

"And maybe he can't help us the way we *need* to be helped." Molly inhaled. Her thin chest trembled. "But he can at least pray for us."

...

Sleep didn't come quickly for Brody. It wasn't paranoia that kept him awake, but the Cadillac-sized concerns regarding their immediate future. The money was only part of it. More urgently, what would they do—where could they turn—after Janko's stepbrother offered prayer, then shooed them away?

What an ugly mess, he thought, wondering at which point his life had transitioned from generally shitty to totally fucked up. When he decided to rob Buddy's? When he—literally—bumped into Blair Latzo? Or maybe it was earlier . . . when his old man committed suicide, or when his mother . . .

"Mom . . ." he murmured.

Memories of her shimmered at the edges of his mind, and it occurred to him that maybe . . . he could find her . . .

"Mom."

. . . track her down. She was out there somewhere. She . . .

It took a long time, but when sleep came, it was as heavy as lead and just as gray.

...

They were on the road before ten, the first of two buses to Decatur. They faced a ninety-minute layover in Jacksonville, so wouldn't reach their destination until eight P.M.

"Prayer won't cut it," Brody said sharply.

They hadn't spoken much that morning—a few sentences mumbled over breakfast, a couple of grunts and sighs while waiting to board the bus—so this statement rang like a ball-peen hammer on steel.

"I know," Molly said.

Sunlight flashed across the windows, highlighting

handprints and grime. Two seats ahead, a little girl pulled bubble gum from beneath the armrest while her mother slept. Somewhere behind, an elderly fellow with an interdental lisp extolled Trump's qualities in a loud, know-it-all tone of voice.

"We need money," Brody whispered. "And soon."

"You're not robbing anyone," Molly whispered in return.

"I was actually thinking," Brody began, "that I—we—could get work on a farm. Picking apples or grapes or whatever. And some farms offer basic lodging—you know, for illegals who don't have anywhere else to live."

"And who work for next to nothing." Molly shook her head. "It's a step up from slavery, I guess."

"It's somewhere to start." Brody shielded his eyes from the sunlight. His forehead accommodated a low, dull ache. "We can slowly get some money behind us. Maybe make new contacts."

"Something *I* considered," Molly said, and what she offered next made Brody wonder if she'd read his mind as he drifted into sleep the night before. "Wendell and Janko were thick as thieves when they were younger."

"You mentioned that." Brody shrugged. "So?"

"So Wendell might know Mom."

Chapter Eleven

Eddie the Smoke was an independent. He had preferred clients, but allegiance to no one. *Like an assassin,* he often thought of himself. He went where the money was, and if this wasn't the first rule of business, it was certainly the most important one.

He began his tasteless professional life as a paparazzo (he took *the* notorious shot of a certain British rock star getting a blow job from a groupie in the parking lot behind the Viper Room), then moved from Hollywood to Philadelphia and became a private eye. It was dull, occasionally dangerous work. His clients were primarily insurance companies and lonely, suspicious wives (and in almost every case they had cause to be suspicious). "Cheats and pricks," he intoned of his job. "But Christ, they pay the bills." In

2006, he was approached by a well-known property magnate and hired to "tail" a competitor on a month-long tour of the Emirates. "I want to know where he stays, who he meets with, how often he takes a shit." Eddie the Smoke—then just Edwin Shaw—provided this information, and more besides, and at the end of the job was rewarded with a check for $30,000, plus expenses. At that point he determined that following people might be more lucrative than secretly taking photographs of them.

Over the years his clients included a former child star, a best-selling novelist, and more than one crooked politician. On official documents, under "occupation," Eddie usually wrote *tailer*, and nobody challenged him on the spelling.

. . .

He used technology, but didn't rely on it. Tracking devices were often lost or, worse, discovered. Geo-location was unreliable. Eddie favored the old-fashioned method of physically *following* his objective. He drove a dependable vehicle and carried a set of license plates from twenty-three states, magnetized for easy switching. He used multiple disguises, mainly hats and glasses. A baseball cap or pair of aviators altered not only his appearance but his character, too.

Eddie maintained a prudent distance when tailing, of course, but there were times when he couldn't help but get close. There were also occasions when it paid to get *very* close. He'd been an Uber driver since 2014, and in that time had given rides to twenty-nine of his targets. Uber was incredibly popular, and Eddie had the smarts to use it to his advantage.

"Going anywhere exciting?" he'd asked the kid, looking at his sad, purplish eyes in the rearview.

"I hope not," the kid had replied.

Eddie had worked for Jimmy Latzo several times. Knowing the way Jimmy operated, it was safe to assume that excitement was very much in this kid's future.

. . .

Followed State-Ways #1078 to Jacksonville, IL. Objective disembarked at 16:07. He and the cripple ate hoagies from Mac's on N. Main St. Boarded State-Ways #1211 to Decatur, IL. Disembarked at 20:04. Checked into Overnites on N. Water St. Room #17. Lights out at 23:02.

Text from Eddie the Smoke to Blair Mayo. 11:09 P.M. 10/08/19.

Chapter Twelve

It was 10:10 on a Wednesday morning. Church was not in session, but the New Zion Gospel Choir was in full, rapturous swing.

...

They heard the singing from half a block away and looked at each other like thirsty travelers within earshot of running water. The corners of Brody's mouth lifted. Molly nodded and thonked ahead. She'd been dragging her crutches since they'd left the motel but now the rubber tips came down with a clear and determined rhythm. Brody followed. He walked not faster, but straighter, his energy like a brightening coil in his chest. They ascended broad steps outside the church. A sign above the doors declared WHERE

GOD GUIDES HE PROVIDES. Molly threw her shoulder against the left door while Brody took the right. The doors swung inward. The singing cascaded.

It was rehearsal but the choir was nonetheless in its raiment of service: blue and white gowns, flashed with orange trim. Their voices boomed to the accompaniment of a slightly out-of-tune piano. A large and beautiful woman led them, one hand to the heavens, singing from the deep well of her solar plexus. "His divine *glory*, His *love*, His *mercy*," she bellowed. "Trust in the Lord and He *will* set you free." The New Zion Baptist Church was in a low-income neighborhood. Brody and Molly had passed boarded-over stores and crime scenes and thin, mistrustful children to get there, but there, throughout the choir, from baritone to soprano, every face was incandescent.

A cool tear tickled Brody's cheekbone. He scuffed it away, proceeded down the aisle on loose legs. He was not religious—God had not factored deeply in Brody's twenty-four years—but if nothing else came from this, then this moment, surrounded so profusely by song and faith, made the journey worthwhile.

The song ended in a crescendo of hallelujahs. A tall man with a smooth brown head stood up from the piano, took three strides toward his choir, then noticed the weeping white man and crippled woman standing wearily in the aisle.

"Brothers and sisters," he said, and even talking he had melody to his voice, "let your mercy fill this house like your song. Open your arms, your hearts, for the wretched are among us."

. . .

The hall was simple and elegant: white walls, plain doors. There was no stained glass or polychromed statues. The most elaborate aspect was the design: semicircular, with a sloping glass roof that shared views of the trees and sky from every angle. The pews faced a wide stage, a modest pulpit, and an altar overlooked by a thin, shimmering cross.

"We knew Karl," Molly said, then added, so there'd be no doubt which Karl she was referring to, "Your stepbrother."

"He was a friend of our mom's," Brody said.

The Reverend Wendell Mathias regarded them expressionlessly, as if waiting to hear more. Several seconds passed, then he pushed a hand across his shaved skull and flicked his eyes in a follow-me gesture.

"Florence," he called to the large woman on stage, "you'll have to do without my dazzling piano for a beat or two."

"A cappella for the Lord," Florence said, and chuckled. "Oh, we can do *that*."

Brody and Molly followed the reverend through a door behind the pulpit, into a windowless, utilitarian space annexed by a crowded office. There was a computer on the desk, files, papers, a stack of prayer books, a lamp that blinked and buzzed. A calendar pinned to the wall displayed Jesus, black and radiant, and a verse from Micah: *You will again have compassion on us; You will tread our sins underfoot and hurl all our iniquities into the depths of the sea.*

Reverend Mathias pushed aside paperwork and perched himself on the edge of the desk. Molly took the only chair. Brody leaned against the wall.

"You should know," the reverend said, "that I saw Karl only once in the years before his death. Our lives went in very different directions."

"We're aware of that," Molly said.

"So you'll excuse me for asking . . ." Reverend Mathias joined his hands, perhaps out of habit. "What exactly do you want from me?"

"To be a friend," Brody replied. "That may sound sad, or crazy, but you're about the closest thing we have."

"I don't even know you." A cry rose from the church proper: a holy high note. It was followed by baritone bass lines and percussive hand claps. Reverend Mathias listened for a moment, no doubt wishing he were out there, then looked at Brody and asked, "What kind of trouble are you in?"

Brody and Molly glanced at each other. Molly shifted uneasily. Brody ran a hand across the back of his neck.

"The long version," he said, "begins when our mother walked out on us. The short version begins when I decided to rob a convenience store."

It was the reverend's turn to shift uneasily. He separated his hands and raised one eyebrow.

"It wasn't even a real gun," Brody began in a dejected tone. "It was a replica. I bought it for sixty bucks."

. . .

The choir bounced joyously from "Break Every Chain" to "For Your Glory," then into something improvised and entirely sweet. Brody recounted the events that had spiraled them from Rebel Point to the New Zion Baptist Church. He spoke honestly and left nothing out. Reverend Mathias listened in silence, and Brody soon sensed a change in his demeanor, one of empathy. As such—and with the exception of his bald head—he looked hauntingly similar to October's depiction of Jesus Christ.

Molly swallowed a painkiller. The lamp hummed and flickered. Brody finished speaking, then joined his hands without thinking, as if in prayer.

"I know what you're thinking," he said after a moment. His tone was still miserable. "I'm the kind of bad news you could do without."

"I'm not thinking that at all," the reverend said. "And there's no such thing as *bad*, only misguided."

Brody nodded. "Even so, I'm sorry to drop this on your doorstep."

Molly said, "We had nowhere else to go."

. . .

The stack of prayer books had wobbled precariously as the reverend shifted his butt along the desk's edge. He took a few seconds to arrange them into stable piles, then turned again to Brody and Molly.

"My father married Karl's mother in 1977. Karl and I were the same age—eleven, only three weeks between our birthdays—but different in almost every other way." His eyes fogged as he regressed forty-two years. A smile touched his lips. "Heck, we shouldn't have gotten along as well as we did, but I think, in some ways, our differences made us closer."

"No sibling rivalry," Molly said. "Makes sense."

"Sure. Could be." The reverend nodded. "We grew up together. We went through a young man's rites of passage together. You know . . . bumbling into adolescence, discovering girls, dabbling in cigarettes and alcohol."

He blinked away the memories and smiled again. Molly looked at him with a fondness Brody recognized. Her posture, her body language, were at ease. She liked this guy. He was, in fairness, easy to like.

"I wanted to be a corporate accountant. Can you imagine?" The reverend looked to the low, dusty ceiling—what passed for heaven in this part of the church—as if to say, *What was I thinking?* "I got into Penn State and Karl followed me out a few months later. Not at the university; Karl wasn't of the academic persuasion. A job opportunity, he said. I welcomed having family so close, but it was clear our lives were bound for different points of the compass. Karl had started to get into trouble for petty crimes. Trespassing, disorderly conduct, possession of marijuana. I was concerned that his . . . misdemeanors might reflect negatively on my studies, so I put a little distance between us. He was my brother, though, and we still hung out from time to time. We watched the big college games together— Penn State all the way. We went to a few parties. We even went on a couple of double dates. But it wasn't like it used to be."

"Did you have mutual friends?" Molly asked.

"Sure," the reverend replied. "Not many, but yeah. Three or four."

Brody pushed off the wall, squaring his shoulders, like a man readying himself for a punch to the gut. "Did you know our mom?"

"What was her name?" the reverend asked.

"Natalie . . . Natalie Ellis."

"Her maiden name was Myles," Molly said.

"Natalie Myles?" Reverend Mathias cut a deep frown. "Doesn't ring any bells, and I'm pretty good with names. It's possible Karl met her while I was doing time."

The silence was awkward but blessedly brief, broken by the choir, all voices, full of glory.

"Karl was the problem child," the reverend said, feeling the need to clarify, "but the longest he served was twenty-six months for aggravated assault. I, on the other hand, served eight years for a murder I didn't commit."

Molly sat up in her seat, wincing as she shifted her weight. Brody looked from Reverend Mathias to October's Jesus, again struck by a likeness that went beyond the color of their skin.

The reverend continued, "The police picked me up three blocks from the scene of a fatal stabbing. A witness had seen a black man in a red jacket fleeing the area. Now, I wasn't wearing a jacket, but that was a minor consideration. Like the good officer said, it's easy to take a jacket off, even when running from the scene of a crime. Things went from bad to worse when the same witness IDed me in a lineup the following morning. And that, friends, was all it took. Thirty to life at SCI Graterford."

"Talk about wrong place at the wrong time," Brody said.

"That's some of it," the reverend agreed. "But *most* of it . . . well, let's just say that, for black Americans, it sometimes seems that the only place justice comes before prejudice is in the dictionary."

"I'm sorry you went through that," Molly said.

"Don't be sorry," the reverend said. "It's true what they say about God: He *is* everywhere, and I found him at Graterford Prison. He lifted me up—shone His light into some dark places. But God's tests are never easy. Faith, like everything, is worth more when you have to work for it."

Brody thought he'd give anything for a shot of faith. Faith that he and Molly would find a way through. Faith that the real killer—Blair—would be brought to justice. He didn't think it would come from God, though, but rather from an oversight on Blair's part. That, or a lightning strike of good fortune.

"I was pardoned by the governor of Pennsylvania in 1999, after the real murderer confessed, not only to the crime I was convicted of, but to several other serious misdeeds. He'd found God, too, apparently." The reverend's eyes rolled to the low ceiling again. Another smile touched his lips. *You sure work in mysterious ways.* "Anyway, I was out. I had nothing but a bachelor's degree I had no use for, and a few dollars in my pocket. By way of compensation, the state funded my re-education. I got my master of divinity degree, learned to play piano, and landed here in 2006."

"No looking back," Brody said.

"Oh, I look back often. And this may sound crazy, but I'd do it all again—"

"That *does* sound crazy," Molly blurted, then pressed her fingers to her lips. "Sorry. No offense meant."

The reverend waved it off. "I could have been an accountant working sixty-hour weeks, kissing corporate butt, never seeing my family. Now I live in God's light." He made a single gesture that encompassed his faith, his church, everything from the prayer books stacked behind him to the belief in his soul. "Furthermore, I know how it feels to be so low that you can taste the dirt when you breathe. And empathy is a valuable resource when it comes to forgiveness."

Silence from the hall as the choir closed out another timber-shaking number.

"What I don't know," Reverend Mathias said in that ominously still moment, "is how I can help you, other than through prayer."

Molly said, "That sounds like a good place to start."

"The man who's after me, Jimmy Latzo . . . he's well connected, merciless." Brody dragged a hand across his eyes. "I won't turn down the prayers, Reverend Mathias, but what I—*we*—really need is to get under the radar. To disappear. We were hoping you might still be in contact with some of your brother's acquaintances."

"His criminal friends?" The reverend pressed a thumb to his chin and frowned. "Someone who might provide you with forged paperwork?"

"Whatever it takes," Brody replied. "I'm not asking you to collude or break the law. Just point us in the right direction."

"The right direction is that way." The reverend pointed at the ceiling. "God is the answer."

Brody lowered his head despondently.

"He's the answer you need," the reverend said, and there was a different note in his voice, one of quiet resignation. "But I can see He's not the answer you want."

Brody lifted his eyes.

Reverend Mathias sighed. "I didn't know many of Karl's delinquent friends. Being in prison, ironically, distanced me from that side of his life. On the occasions he visited, I urged him to find distance, too. But he never did."

"Maybe he couldn't," Molly said.

"Maybe," the reverend said, nodding. "Some things have of a way of catching hold, and not letting go until they've dragged you all the way down."

"Tell me about it," Brody said wearily.

"Less chance of that happening"—the reverend dropped a wink—"when your focus is heavenward."

Brody realized there hadn't been any singing for a while, only muffled voices from the hall. The choir must have concluded their rehearsal, which made him wonder how much of the reverend's time they had used up. He was about to suggest to Molly that they hit the road, when the reverend stood up straighter. His expression cleared. He clapped his hands once, crisply.

"You look like you need a good meal. And Florence— my, she makes the most delicious soul-smothered chicken. Serves it with gravy and white rice. Mmm-mmm." All melancholy had left his voice. "I'll have her take you home, feed you up some—"

"Oh no," Molly said. "That's really not—"

"Hush, now. You're friends of the family. And you're not leaving here on empty bellies."

Brody and Molly displayed their identical smiles. Tired, but still lovely.

"That's very kind," Molly said. "Thank you."

"I can't help you beyond food and prayer," the reverend said. "But I do have some of Karl's possessions—cleaned them out of his apartment after he died. A small boxful of things. Photographs, old vinyl records and mixtapes, letters to his ex-girlfriend. I'll bring it over to Florence's house later. You're welcome to look through, see if you find anything that . . . points you in the right direction."

"Thank you," Brody said. "I guess you never know."

"You're in a dark place. I know how that feels." The reverend's voice was somber, but kindness sparked in his eyes. "A little light goes a long way."

"I hope so." Brody indicated the door behind him, the indistinct voices beyond. "We can come back later, if you need to finish up with—"

"I do, but you're not going anywhere yet." The reverend pushed himself off the desk, took Molly's left hand and Brody's right. "Now we do what you should have been doing all along. Now we pray."

. . .

Florence lived with her sister and mother in a small two-bedroom house, which seemed larger on the inside, despite the clutter. It boomed with personality, like Florence herself, so that the walls, with all their pictures, and the surfaces, crowded with figurines and curios, drew the eye and expanded, like a broadly detailed painting.

Tamla Motown flowed from the kitchen. Florence browned chicken and sang along, matching the greats—Diana Ross, Marvin Gaye, Smokey Robinson—note for note. Crockery rattled as she danced. Every now and then, Florence's sister—younger, smaller, louder—dueted from elsewhere in the house. Conversely, Florence's mother sat rocklike in the living room with Brody and Molly, watching them with a gaze that managed to be both discerning and comforting.

Brody ventured, "She may have smothered too much soul on the chicken." Molly cracked a smile, while Florence's mother retorted in a melodic voice, "Ain't no such thang as too much soul."

Family and friends joined them for dinner, a host of faces, all with cheerful voices. They filled their plates, found a spot at the table. They prayed, ate noisily, hummed along to the stereo still playing in the kitchen. Reverend Mathias arrived when a single piece of chicken and a spoonful of rice remained. He asked if everybody had eaten enough. Assured that they had, he gave thanks to his friends and to his God, then he ate.

When most of the company had left, and with Florence busying herself with the pots and pans, Reverend Mathias retired to the living room with Brody and Molly. He had the box of Karl's possessions in one arm—it was not a large box—and set it down on the coffee table, having to first clear a landslide of magazines and flyers from Kroger.

"I have memories," he said, pressing his finger to the side of his head. "But everything else is inside that box. Everything Karl left behind."

"Not much of a life," Molly observed.

Brody tightened inside, thinking that, if he were to die anytime soon, all he'd leave behind was a dusty leather jacket—one that had originally belonged to his old man. Twenty-four years of life, and all Brody had to show for it was a hand-me-down item of clothing. He sighed, dragged the box toward him, and fished out half a dozen vinyl albums and 45s—the kind of music college kids played while they smoked weed.

"I listened to Janet Jackson and Lionel Richie," the reverend said. "Karl listened to Pink Floyd and The 13th Floor Elevators. One of the many ways in which we were different."

Brody pushed aside dog-eared paperbacks, a signed baseball, a broken wristwatch. He found an old wallet with nothing inside.

"Already checked that," the reverend said.

There was an empty jewelry box, a martial arts magazine without a cover, a handful of mixtapes with faded cursive on their card inserts. Beneath these, a loose, creased photograph. Brody lifted it out carefully, turned it toward him. His heart plunged. Anger blew through him, unexpected and hot. He imagined it curling like woodsmoke from his skin.

"What is it?" Molly asked, seeing the change in his disposition.

"Mom."

She was young in the photograph. Early twenties. Sharp cheekbones. Light brown hair spilled across her shoulders. She stood next to Karl. They were in a bar or club, judging by the beer signs behind them. Both had their arms folded, their jaws firmed in a mock-intimidating expression, like a couple of linebackers posing for their TV shots. She was prettier than Brody remembered.

He passed the photo to Molly and forced several cooling breaths.

"That's really her." Molly shook her head. "Wow, Brody, she looks like you."

"Goddamn her," Brody said, then looked at the reverend. "Sorry."

Reverend Mathias cocked a disapproving eyebrow, then drew a pair of glasses from his breast pocket and slipped them on. They hid the creases around his eyes—made him look younger. "Let me see that." He held his hand out for the photograph. Molly handed it to him. "*This* is your mom?"

"Yeah." Brother and sister in unison.

"And what did you say her name was?"

"Natalie Ellis," Molly said. "Née Myles."

"Then I guess I *did* know her, but not well. Met her twice, maybe three times. I'm sure she said her name was Lola, though. You know, like that old song." The reverend sang a few bars of something neither Brody nor Molly had heard before. They regarded him with blank expressions. "I, uh . . . I guess you're too young. Anyway, yes, Lola Blythe. Or Byrd. Something like that."

Molly offered the slightest smile. "I thought you said you were good with names."

"Well, it was a long time ago," the reverend conceded, but looked at Brody and Molly through narrowed eyes, as if *they* might be wrong. "We were just kids. I was actually closer to your mom's cousin."

"Her cousin?" Molly said. She looked at Brody, who returned another blank stare.

"You didn't know she had a cousin?" the reverend asked.

"No." Brother and sister again.

The reverend gestured at the box. "Should be a photo in there."

Molly pulled the box toward her and swept through it. She lifted out the mixtapes and paperbacks, stacking them on top of the vinyls, clearing some space. "So much junk." She held up a Rhode Island fridge magnet, an empty video game case, a mini Rubik's Cube on a key chain. Two photographs followed. The first was a Polaroid of teenage Karl in a baseball uniform. The second was of a block-faced man with his stomach erupting from beneath a gray vest, probably Karl's father. Molly dug deeper into the box, uncovering more junk—a Michael Jordan bobblehead on a broken base, a VHS copy of *Top Gun*—before finding the photograph she sought. She studied it for several seconds, nodded, and handed it to Reverend Mathias.

"There she is," he said, and grinned. "Renée Giordano. Sweet as an apple."

Florence sang in the kitchen, occupying the pause as Reverend Mathias slipped away. His eyes were on the photo but his mind was in the past. Florence's mother slept in her armchair, a blanket across her knees. Her breathing was soft and sweet.

"We went on a few dates." The reverend broke out of his reverie. He sat upright, handed the photograph to Brody. "It looked, for a time, like it might develop into something good, something real. And then . . . well, then I took an eight-year vacation, courtesy of the state of Pennsylvania. Renée wrote me a few times, but the letters stopped after a year or so. I figured she'd found someone else. And so had I." He touched the crucifix around his neck. "We move on, you know."

The photograph was circa 1990, the colors mostly aged out of it. Karl sat at the head of a table loaded with barbecued meats. A young Wendell Mathias—with a high-top fade straight out of Kid 'n Play—sat to his right. The woman beside Wendell had a slender neck, coils of dark hair, eyes deep enough to demand gravity. She had one hand on Wendell's thigh.

"Renée Giovanni," Brody said.

"Gior*dano*," the reverend corrected.

The photograph was old, but the kindness hadn't seeped from Renée's face. It shone ahead of her beauty, in itself remarkable. But beauty fades, whereas kindness endures, and this—*this*—was what Brody homed in on, with the instinct of a butterfly to nectar.

He imagined her now. A successful crime novelist. A concert pianist. A senator. Did she live in a loft in Brooklyn Heights, or on a ranch in sunny Cali? Dreams hit his mind and rippled. He imagined Molly fanning shell grit from one hand, fowl squabbling around her ankles. He smelled morning coffee and freshly laundered towels. How would it feel to wake to a clean house, to the sound of livestock braying, or perhaps the Pacific roaring, before stepping down to breakfast with family? How would it feel to belong?

"Do you know where she is now?" Brody glanced at Reverend Mathias, but only for a second. Renée Giordano, even in an old photograph, was hard to look away from. "She's Mom's cousin, which makes her our, what . . . great-cousin?"

"Second cousin," Molly said.

"Right. She's family." Brody lifted his eyes again, rolled them toward Molly. "Blood?"

"Yeah," Molly replied, and then, "What's going through your mind, Brody? You think she can lead us to Mom?"

"I don't know." Brody shook his head. "I guess I'm thinking we can crash with her for a week or so, keep a low profile. We had no idea she existed, remember, so Jimmy Latzo won't, either."

"You can't be sure of that," Molly said.

"Where can we find her?" Brody asked the reverend.

He removed his glasses, slotted them back into his pocket. "I haven't heard from Renée in . . . more than twenty years. Heck, closer to thirty." Something flashed through his expression, maybe an alternate life, one where he hadn't been in the wrong place at the wrong time, and Renée's body had kept him warm at night, instead of God's light. "I looked her up a couple of times, out of curiosity, the way we do with the faces from our past. The internet makes that so much easier."

"That's how we found you," Molly said.

"I saw on Renée's Myspace page—that's how long ago this was—that she'd moved to Bloomington, Indiana, and landed a job with the Colts a short time later. Events coordinator, or some such. I wished her well, said a prayer for her, and moved on." The reverend angled his head to look at the photograph, still in Brody's hands. He inhaled sharply, then said, "Fast-forward a couple of years. Super Bowl Forty-One. Colts versus Bears."

"I remember it well," Brody said. "Manning was on fire."

"Don't I know it? We put up a big screen here in the hall, because you *can* follow God and the Bears. And then, after the game, with the Colts celebrating on the field, who should I see over Tony Dungy's shoulder but my old girlfriend, Renée Giordano."

Brody looked at Molly and nodded. He'd made up his mind.

"She looked happy," the reverend said. "Inside happy. Not just happy that the Colts had won. And I was happy for her."

He drifted again, eyes glazed. Brody drifted, too, imagining moonlight over the woodlands of Indiana, the silence of a safe neighborhood, drinking craft beers and playing Cards Against Humanity with family he never knew he had.

Florence clanged pots and pans. She sang along to The Temptations, "Ain't Too Proud to Beg," and her sister harmonized.

BEFORE

(2007)

AKA NATALIE ELLIS, NÉE MYLES

"Hey, Ethan—"

"Nat, Jesus, where—" His breath caught in his throat, an upsurge of emotion somewhere between relief and fear. "Where are you?"

She closed her eyes, the handset pressed to her ear. Traffic ripped by. A street she didn't know the name of. A city she was passing through. The phone booth smelled of cigarettes and plastic. There was a small bag at her feet.

"Natalie?"

"I'm not coming back, Ethan."

She had to be strong, and she had to sell her hardness. All those years of repressed emotions, of having sawdust in her heart, and these last thirteen, with Ethan and the kids, were an earthquake. She had laughed, cried, and dreamed with them. She had loved like a supernova, and been vital for every second.

"I'm leaving you," she said.

Her voice was a flatline. Not the merest blip, no hint of a heartbeat. It didn't matter; Ethan heard the words, not the deadness with which they were delivered. He started to contest, as she knew he would, to plead, like any person who faced the unknown, saying that things were great between them, that they had everything to look forward to, and couldn't . . . Jesus, Nat, couldn't they at least talk—

"Nothing to talk about," she cut in. Cold. Cold. Cold. And then she told him a miserable lie, and prayed she'd never have to tell a worse one. "I don't love you anymore."

She hadn't thought it would come to this, because Jimmy—that reptile, that walking fucking *cancer*—was supposed to die. He'd been in a coma and on life support, yet he'd clawed his way out and continued to breathe—to get stronger, in fact. "You need a backup plan in case anything happens to me," Karl had advised her, and for all her caution and intelligence, this was the best she could do: to leave her family, assume a new identity, and hole up in a different part of the country.

She told Karl to make sure *nothing* happened to him. "Stay close to Jimmy. I need your eyes and ears. But be smart." The years ticked along. Did they erode Karl's vigilance, his cunning? He usually called her on the first of every month, but when August and September passed without contact, she started to worry.

She gave him another week, then hit the internet. A report from the *Altoona Mirror*—found only minutes into her search—confirmed her fears. The headline alone had been enough.

ALTOONA RESIDENT FOUND BEATEN, DROWNED

He didn't squawk. Of that Lola was sure. Not Karl. Not ever. He'd suffered at Jimmy's hands, like so many before him, but he never gave Lola up. If he had, Jimmy would have found her by now.

But how long before Jimmy made the right connections, received accurate intelligence, and came knocking? He cast a broad net, and without Karl to keep her informed, Lola felt exposed. Worse, she felt that her family was exposed.

Her other option was to go on the offensive, like she had in 1993. But she was too unpracticed for a close-quarters assault. She could hit Jimmy from long range with a high-power rifle, but that wasn't exactly straightforward. To begin with, it would take weeks to learn his routine, which in turn would require getting dangerously close. Also, Lola would probably have to position herself in a built-up location. This wasn't like shooting from the window of a book depository in 1963; modern police, with all their tech, would have her surrounded within minutes of her pulling the trigger.

Every offensive measure required a talent she no longer possessed, or a risk she wasn't willing to take. Of course, the surest way to keep her family safe was to give herself up. Failing that, she had to run.

It broke her heart, though. It broke everything.

"This can't be happening," Ethan said. Poor Ethan, who had no idea who she was, and how dark and deadly her past. She'd filled herself with lies and allowed them to leak out over the thirteen years of their marriage. "Please, Natalie. Come home. Whatever's wrong, we'll make it right."

Hard, she thought. *Be hard.*

"Nat . . ."

It was one word, and not even a full word. One syllable of her false name. Yet she heard the brokenness in it, like something made of sand, cracking, sifting between his fingers. She closed her eyes again and covered her mouth, because her own emotion wanted to spill from between her lips—the feelings that had reshaped her, that had moved like a plane over her rough edges. She could count on one hand the number of times she had cried: when Grandpa Bear had died, when Vince had died, when her children were born. Tears threatened now. Her chest bubbled and ached. She shook her head.

Hard.

She would not allow Ethan one iota of her heartbreak. She had to distance herself completely. No forwarding address. No weekend visits. It was a stony foundation upon which to rebuild—for all of them—but infinitely safer.

"Your things are here," Ethan said. "Clothes. Bathroom stuff. Books." He drew a damp breath. She imagined him smearing tears away with the heel of his hand. "Everything."

"Nothing I need," Lola said.

There were a few essentials in the bag at her feet, some of it taken from a safe-deposit box that Ethan didn't know about: her Baby Eagle and two boxes of ammo, a change of clothes, basic toiletries, $420 in cash, the faux-leather folder that Grandpa Bear had given her fifteen years ago containing two new identities (there *had* been three, but she'd just expired one of them). Lola had considered taking a few photographs of the children, but her heart would shatter every time she looked at them.

Life had been easier without emotion. As it would be again.

As if channeling her train of thought, Ethan said, "Your children are here."

Her chest throbbed. A hardy tear squeezed itself from her closed eye and raced along her cheekbone. She imagined Molly sleeping with her crutches beside the bed, and Brody, with his toys boxed away and his favorite rock band posters on the walls, yet still young enough to want the bedroom door ajar. They had closed their eyes on a normal world, and would open them to it being fractured.

Hard.

"I don't need them, either," Lola said, and there it was, only minutes later: a worse lie, still.

Two cruisers barreled down the street she didn't know the name of, all lights and sound. A digital billboard flashed hypnotically, selling first Taco Bell and then, ironically, cholesterol meds. Lola looked at her watch. The train to St. Louis left at 1:35. She didn't think she'd settle in St. Louis, but she could shed Natalie Ellis's skin there—become one of the two women she kept in the folder Grandpa Bear had given her.

"You can't do this over the phone, Natalie. A *god-damn* phone." This was the first time Ethan had raised his voice. In fact, he'd seldom shouted in all their years together. He was gentle and bighearted. "I'm worth more than that."

"No," she said. "You're not."

Lola ended the call before he could say anything else, and stood for several long seconds staring at the grime and cigarette burns on the pay phone's handset.

Cold. Cold. Cold.

She then picked up her bag, walked three blocks of whatever street this was to the train station, and boarded the 1:35 to St. Louis.

On to the next life.

Chapter Thirteen

Jimmy had twice-weekly massages, regular mani-pedis, fine whiskey tastings, and poker nights (quality cigars required) with his associates. But the hour he spent every day in the gym would always be his favorite time.

Music thumped from in-ceiling speakers, something loud and angry, to get the blood pounding. Jimmy applied ten-pound weights to each side of the barbell, bringing the total to seventy pounds. He curled eight reps, strict form, not swinging his back at all. He counted to twenty, then curled another five. Not bad for sixty-two.

He looked at his reflection in one of the many mirrors, enjoying the way his muscles moved beneath the embroidery of scar tissue.

"The Italian fucking Cat."

Jimmy was not a spiritual man, but he believed the universe followed certain lines. As he looked at his scarred body, he remembered the old neighborhood—Chase Street, specifically, behind Sicily Pizza. Mario Antonutti would sometimes bring out burned calzones or leftover slices, and there'd usually be a rabble of kids hanging around to intercept those scraps before they hit the dumpster. Only this one time, Jimmy, maybe seven years old, was out back all by himself when the door opened and Mario came out with three-quarters of a Sicilian pie—a solid rectangular base, topped with spicy sauce and singed, salty pepperoni—and there must have been *something* wrong with it, but to Jimmy it looked like the greatest pizza in all of history. He sat cross-legged on the ground and wolfed down the first slice. Into his second slice, a cat leaped briskly onto a nearby trash can and watched him eat. Jimmy couldn't stop looking at the cat. Its left eye was sealed from fighting, it had half of one ear missing, and its calico fur was punctuated with scar tissue. "Nobody fucks with you," Jimmy said to the cat. "Even dogs run away." The cat responded with a hiss that sounded like paper tearing. Jimmy smiled and nudged the box—with more than half the pizza remaining—toward the cat and they ate it together.

...

Another eight reps at seventy pounds. Then five more. Jimmy dropped the barbell. It thudded at his feet with a forceful sound. The veins across his chest and in his throat bulged. He circled the gym and flexed.

"*Nobody* fucks with you."

He was not a big man, but he was strong. The son of an Italian steelworker, second-to-youngest in a household of twelve, he *had* to be strong. His old man would consistently drive him into the ground with the same force he'd use to shape steel, and Jimmy always popped back up. Sometimes he was hurt bad—a broken collarbone, six cracked ribs—but he rarely let it show and he never cried. Strength coursed through the Latzo DNA, as unequivocal as their olive coloring and brown eyes. "We were forged from the volcanic rock of Mount Etna," his Uncle Victor used to claim. Another family story recounted that, in 1878, while working on the Brooklyn Bridge, Luca Latzo—Jimmy's revered and respected *grande nonno*—threw four men to their deaths, reason unknown.

. . .

Lola Bear *had* fucked with him, however, and only the Latzo strength had kept his heart beating. Jimmy had no recollection of the three months he'd spent in a coma, or the sixteen months on life support. He didn't remember the trauma surgeon tweezering the 9mm round from his left kidney, or sawing a window into his skull to relieve the pressure on his swelling brain. His upper body had been slathered with silicone fluid, wrapped in gauze. Healthy skin had been removed from his legs and grafted to his face and shoulders. A machine had breathed for him. He had no memory of this.

The nightmares arrived soon after. Oil-like, narrow, confined. Lola Bear followed him. Sometimes she was a nimble panther that materialized out of the darkness and clawed. More often she spewed flames from her small ruby mouth and engulfed the world.

In one dream Jimmy caught the panther and slit its throat and pulled its surprised, beautiful head from its body.

It was three and a half years before he could speak, and the first words out of his cracked larynx were, "Where is she?"

He screamed the first time he looked in the mirror.

. . .

The doctors predicted a loss of motor coordination, impaired speech, and post-traumatic amnesia. Jimmy mixed gasoline with the nightmares and they fueled him. He hit the gym in 1997, four years after Lola tried to kill him. He curled three-pound wrist weights that first session—the kind of weights Beverly Hills housewives jogged with. After a month he was bench-pressing thirty pounds. After two months he was up to fifty. His arms and chest tightened with muscle.

Reinventing his body was one thing, but Lola had destroyed his reputation, too. Don Esposito had been good to Jimmy during his long convalescence. He supplied money, care, and protection in case that bitch returned to finish the job. He also provided a temporary residence when Jimmy got out of the hospital, seeing as Jimmy's house had been burned all the way to the fucking basement. But the Don giveth, and the Don taketh away, and he demoted Jimmy—fucking *excommunicated* him—when it became apparent that he was not going to die. From caporegime to civilian, just like that. Jimmy was pissed off, but he understood; Don Esposito was all about appearances, and Jimmy was weak back then, difficult to look at.

He was also a determined son of a bitch, and hell-bent on recuperating everything he'd lost. By the spring of 1998, he was able to form complete sentences and to speak without slurring too much. Duly emboldened, he donned three thousand dollars' worth of Italian finery and met with Hunch Calloway at the Tuscan Gourmet in Carver City—the clothes, the location, very much informing that it was business as usual.

Jimmy made no effort to hide his scars. A specialist in New York City had recommended a prosthetic mask that moved with his face, allowing some small expression. Jimmy declined. He despised his appearance, but the scars were a part of him, a reminder to everyone that it would take more than bullets and fire to put him in the ground. He thought regularly, fondly, of the cat he'd seen behind Sicily Pizza. *Nobody fucks with you. Even dogs run away.* This was precisely the message he wanted to present.

"What's the matter, Hunch? Can't look an old friend in the eye?"

"Jesus Christ, Jimmy. I *can*, it's just . . ."

"Look at me, Hunch."

"They said you were going to die."

"They were wrong."

Hunch Calloway had eyes and ears on every street corner from Pittsburgh to Providence. In the past, Jimmy had used him to procure the names of witnesses, jury members, and criminal informants. Hunch would turn CI himself ten months later, and would be executed for this foolish betrayal by Mykyta Dević, an enforcer for the Odessa Mafia.

"Where is she?" Jimmy asked.

"Lola?"

"Yes, Lola. Of course, fucking Lola."

"Nobody knows, Jimmy. She took off after . . . you know, after . . ."

"After she tried to kill me?"

"Right."

"And nobody knows nothing?"

"Right."

"What about Dane Greene, Johnny the Grease, Lucky Manzarek—those two-faced pricks she always kicked around with?"

"They've all gone, too. I heard Lucky went into witness protection, but I'm not sure." Hunch drank his water. He couldn't look at Jimmy for long. "Everything's changed, Jimmy. Guys are cutting deals and cutting loose. Don Esposito is keeping his head above water—he's got good people around him—but rumor is the sharks are circling. Not just the Feds. The fucking Ukrainians, the blacks, the spics. There's business to be done and they all want a piece."

Jimmy told Hunch to keep his ear close to the ground. "Catch a sniff of that cunt, and I want to be the first to know." He knew tracking Lola down wouldn't be quick or easy, but that was just as well; he needed time to prepare, physically and mentally.

Things were looking up, though. His lawyers had

already secured investments with commercial real estate and land development companies in western Pennsylvania, with designs on obtaining majority ownership—by whatever means—within eighteen months. Jimmy was on his way to reestablishing ties with commerce and community: the foundation from which to expand.

At the gym, he was bench-pressing one hundred pounds, curling twenty-five. Kid weights, but it was a start.

"Nobody fucks with you."

The Italian Cat was coming back.

...

The criminal landscape changed over the next ten years. By 2008, Don Esposito had lost ground in western Pennsylvania, but remained a key player. He'd opened his doors to new enterprises, and maintained a profitable relationship with Jimmy, although the prospect of bringing him back into the family and reinstating him as caporegime was never considered. Don Esposito had his reasons for this, and had shared them with Jimmy during a golfing weekend at Mar-a-Lago.

"You're doing great, Jimmy. You don't make that disgusting rattling sound when you breathe anymore, and your hands don't tremble as much. You've come a long way." Don Esposito was seventy-three but could get around Trump's course in eighty or better. There was nothing wrong with his eye, or his judgment. "You've still got a long way to go, though. And times have changed. The glory days . . . fuck, they died when Little Nicky went down."

"I know that, Don."

"You don't know shit. You've been out of it too long." Don Esposito hit a fifty-yard pitch shot and landed inches from the pin. "Ow, sweet. You like that, Jimmy?"

"A great fucking shot, Don."

"You need to appreciate that everything is different now. We're dealing with multiple business interests. It's volatile as fuck." Unlike the late Hunch Calloway, Don Esposito had no problem looking Jimmy in the eye. "This is a time for politics, patience, and diplomacy. Your short fucking fuse could undo a lot of good work."

Jimmy tightened his jaw. A vein at the back of his skull ticked arythmically.

"And let's not forget the other thing," Don Esposito continued. "The *big* thing: You were taken down— almost taken *out*—by a woman. One fucking woman."

"No ordinary woman," Jimmy said.

"That may be so, but you can see how a detail like this could reflect badly on me."

"I'm going to find that bitch, Don, and I'm going to kill her." Jimmy said this, trying to keep his voice from shaking with rage. "In the meantime, I respect your decision."

"Of course you do. Now hand me my putter and shut the fuck up."

. . .

He dreamed about Lola every night. She was sinuous and rotten. He hated and loved her. "I'm coming for you, Lola. I'll catch you outside of a dream. I swear to you." And there were not many daylight hours when she didn't cross his mind. He might see her in the black reflection of his TV or cell phone, or in the heat haze above Donegal Steelworks. She fueled every dollar he earned, every soldier he hired. "You've become my ambition. My purpose. And I will give you the glorious death you deserve. I'll catch every slow drop of blood in my mouth, and let the birds take your skin."

. . .

Jimmy finished his workout the same as always: with a line of Peruvian flake, snorted off the seat of his weight bench. He prowled the gym until his eyes grew as large as tulips.

The door opened. Blair stepped in.

"You can't fucking knock?" Jimmy snapped.

"I *did* knock." Blair pointed at the ceiling. "The goddamn music's too loud."

Jimmy turned down the volume and wiped his nose with the back of his hand, removing any excess coke. "What do you want?"

"I have news."

Blair had surpassed his expectations regarding adeptness and cold-bloodedness. He once saw her kill a man with a nail file after he'd roofied her margarita. It happened in a moment. He, the man, was surprised to find himself bleeding so magnificently. Blair also enjoyed chess, world cinema, and Filipino knife fighting.

"News?"

"Actually, it can wait until you've come down."

"Tell me now."

"No."

Men underestimated her. They disarmed themselves. Blair used this to her advantage. Lola had been the same. How many of their victims had fallen because they had surrendered the first—and only—shot? Jimmy maintained that Blair wasn't a replacement for Lola, but they were the same in so many ways.

Blair was more ruthless, however. More patient. This patience infuriated Jimmy sometimes. He needed it, though. It was the white to his black.

She caught up with him later, after he'd showered and his eyes were back to normal size.

"The latest from Eddie the Smoke," she said. "Brody and Molly have arrived in Bloomington, Indiana."

"Bloomington . . . ?"

"It's where Renée Giordano lives."

Jimmy pressed his tongue to the inside of his cheek and searched his memory, running through countless faces and acquaintances. People he'd worked with. People he'd hurt. The name was familiar, but he couldn't place it.

"Renée Gior—"

"I asked around," Blair cut in, seeing him struggle. "Drew blanks, until Joey Cabrini told me that she's Lola Bear's cousin."

"Her cousin?" Jimmy narrowed his eyes. "And did we get to her?" Then he shrugged, as if the question required no response. "I mean, of *course* we got to her."

"You had Karl Janko rough her up back in '97," Blair said dryly. "You were recovering at the time. Still too frail to do it yourself."

"Karl fucking *Janko*?" Jimmy's eyes went from

squinted pencil lines to wide, bright circles. "But he was working *with* Lola."

"You didn't know that then."

Jimmy blinked. He looked like he'd been slapped. "And have we got to the cousin since?"

Blair shook her head. "You crossed her off the list."

"Jesus Christ."

"It's an oversight, Jimmy, but put it out of your head. It's history." Blair paused, allowing Jimmy a moment to refocus. "Something we need to consider, though: Renée Giordano knows who you are, and almost certainly knows your history with Lola. The fact that you're now hunting Brody will seem like too great a coincidence."

"She'll know it's a setup." The glimmer in Jimmy's eyes shifted from ire to hunger. "So is it time to do it my way?"

"No. We hang tight." Blair stood rock-still and held Jimmy's gaze with impressive confidence. "If the cousin knows where Lola is, there's every chance she'll share that information with Brody."

"She won't share a damn thing," Jimmy snapped, "if she suspects it's a setup."

"I think she will," Blair said. "She has Brody and Molly to consider now. How else will she get them out of your crosshairs?"

Jimmy had been opposed to this bullshit cat-and-mouse since the moment Blair had proposed it. He'd acquiesced, though—soft touch that he was—and had spent six months on the sidelines with nothing to get excited about. He was ready to go back to doing it old school, but Blair's last two sentences had stirred something inside him. A maybe. A hopefulness. A morsel of enthusiasm no larger than a berry.

He didn't realize how tense he was until the muscles across his shoulders dropped a full two inches.

"Okay," he said. "How do you see this playing out?"

"The only way it *can* play out." Blair linked her fingers. Her nails were still streaked with the pink varnish she'd applied on the night she met Brody at Rocky T's. "Brody is about to realize he's been drawn into a war. He knows the cops can't help him—not that he'd risk turning himself in. Running is not a long-term solution. Leading you to his badass mom—who brought you down once before—is his only hope of survival."

Jimmy considered the likelihood of this. He paced his office, tongue lodged into his cheek. His heart fluttered, but that might have been the last of the cocaine.

"How—" he began, then that morsel of enthusiasm expanded greatly. It surged from his chest into his throat, tasting both vinegary and delightful. "How do you know the way things will play out? The way people will act?"

"It's human instinct, Jimmy." Blair spoke with the same detachment she'd adopted when opening Mr. Roofie's throat with a nail file. "In the face of an insurmountable threat, we seek security."

"Even so . . . you're exceptional."

Blair nodded. Her patience was only outgunned by her confidence.

Jimmy stopped pacing. He sat on the couch and dared a tiny smile.

"I think we're close," Blair said. "I really do."

"Maybe," Jimmy allowed.

"After so long . . . how does it feel?"

Jimmy closed his eyes to better isolate the feeling, but slipped instead into a post-cocaine, post-workout sleep, where many fires burned but their flames were lighter, comforting.

Chapter Fourteen

Brody had indulged in fantasy, knowing it would lead to disappointment, but unable to help himself. After scuttling from one flea-pit motel to the next, and living with Tyrese before that, he needed to believe that some degree of comfort was forthcoming. He'd imagined fragrant, bouncy towels, a bed with a memory-foam mattress, drinking freshly ground coffee, and watching Netflix originals with newly discovered family. Wonderful, nourishing things, when really, a comfortable sofa in a warm, safe home would have sufficed.

Renée Giordano's home was comfortable, in a way, and welcoming. Brody got the sofa, the freshly ground coffee, but he also got more.

He got truths, understanding, despair.

More than he could ever have imagined.

...

The bus rides from Decatur to Bloomington consumed thirteen long hours, including a four-hour layover in Indianapolis. Brody reflected that it would have taken three and a half in a car, and thought wistfully of his little Pontiac Shitbox, wondering if it was still parked behind the cattle shed on the outskirts of Bayonet. He liked to think it had been put to good use. Maybe a family of red wolves had appropriated it, a mother on the backseat nursing her litter. Or maybe some dusty vagrant had made it his own, the contents of his shopping cart distributed across the front seats and dash. One man's shitbox is another man's palace.

They arrived in Bloomington at 12:20 P.M. Molly immediately went to work. Brody went to Starbucks. He ordered a grande latte, dropped into one of the lounge-style chairs, and sipped it while flipping through the *Indy Star*'s sports pages. He then ordered a chai tea to go—for Molly—and by the time he'd walked to the public library downtown, she had located their second cousin.

"Not that it matters," she said, "but to give you a heads-up, Renée became a wheelchair user five years ago."

"Oh shit. What happened?"

"Motorcycle accident." Molly had her notes in one hand and her chai tea in the other. "Hit some wet leaves, lost control, got smoked by a Chevy Tahoe."

"Christ," Brody said, and swallowed a sour lump in his throat. "So how did you find her?"

"She's unlisted, of course, because nothing is easy."

"Right."

Molly sipped her tea. "I tried the usual social media suspects first. Nothing. Then I Googled 'Renée Giordano Indianapolis Colts.' It brought up, among other things, a newspaper article from 2014, about a charity fun run to raise money for Renée. It was organized by her friend, a woman named"—Molly consulted her notes—"Beth Livingstone. They'd worked together at the Colts. The run raised forty-six thousand dollars. Tony Dungy took part."

"Way to go, Tony."

"Now, Renée doesn't have a Facebook page, because, as you know, nothing is easy, but Beth Livingstone *does*. So I checked it out." Molly swept hair from her brow and took another sip of tea. "It's the usual shitshow of dog photos and Bible quotes, but I scrolled back to 2014 and found photos of the charity run. Renée is in quite a few of them. Then I jumped forward a few months and found a photograph of Renée behind the wheel of her new custom disability van, paid for, in part, with money from the run."

"Okay," Brody said.

"It's a red Honda Odyssey, a little Colts pennant in the rear window. But the most telling thing about the photo is the street sign in the background." Molly looked at her notes again. "Terracotta Avenue. So then I jumped onto Google Maps, took a virtual stroll down Terracotta Avenue, and there's the red Honda Odyssey with the Colts pennant in the back, parked in the driveway of number 1516."

"You should have been a private detective," Brody said, looking at his sister with something close to awe. "You're amazing."

Molly smiled sweetly. "Only on days that end with a y."

The library hummed around them, the sound of whispering, footsteps, pages turning. Children laughed in an adjacent room, full of color.

"Terracotta Avenue is a twenty-five-minute walk from here. So . . ." Molly finished her tea and grabbed her crutches. "Do you want to go meet our second cousin?"

Brody said, "Let's go."

. . .

The midafternoon sun broke through a webbing of cloud. It never got summer-day hot, but Brody's shoulders slumped and Molly pushed out every breath. Her crutches dragged.

It took forty minutes, not twenty-five, to reach Terracotta Avenue. There was a silver Toyota Sienna in the driveway of 1516—no Colts pennant in the window—and a Smart car parked behind this.

"You think she still lives here?" Brody asked.

Molly nodded, using her crutch to point at the ramp leading to the front door. "I guess she bought another minivan since the Google car zipped through the neighborhood."

A Hispanic man with deep eye makeup answered the door. He looked Brody up and down, and regarded Molly with a softer expression.

"Is Renée home?" Brody asked.

"Who are you?"

"Family."

He looked doubtful, but flitted away. Moments later, Renée rolled into the hallway. She didn't get far before stopping, tires squeaking on the hardwood. Her jaw dropped an inch.

"Brody," she said, and he detected the tightness in her voice. "I've only ever seen you in photographs, and the last one I saw was nearly thirteen years ago."

Brody had nothing. He opened his mouth, but . . . silence.

"And Molly," Renée said. "Your mother lost sleep for you, praying for you. And look at you now. So beautiful."

"Hello, Renée," Molly said.

Renée smiled, and Brody saw what Reverend Mathias must have all those years ago, and what had shone through in those old photographs. An unassailable beauty. A deep and penetrating kindness.

"Come in," she said. "Come in, come in."

. . .

Renée's caregiver, Manuel, he with the eye makeup, brought them sodas, then left them alone. Renée led them onto the rear deck. "You can never get too much fresh air." A wonderful old maple provided shelter from the afternoon sun.

Molly sat with a sigh. She dropped one of her crutches. It clattered to the deck and she left it there— flapped a weary hand at it—then plucked a near-empty strip of pills from her purse.

"Baclofen?" Renée asked.

"Yeah." Molly popped two into her palm and gulped them. "Lioresal."

"Me, too," Renée said. "I can't wilfully move anything south of my boobies, but sometimes my legs do the funky chicken. It's the darnedest thing."

"God bless pharmaceuticals."

"Amen."

"I'm on antidepressants, too. Lexapro. And Motrin for the pain."

"Celebrex here, and Prozac. Also, stool softeners and anticonvulsants."

"Where," Molly said dryly, "would we be without the miracles of modern science?"

"And how are you paying for these miracles?" Renée's gaze switched between Brody and Molly. "Excuse my bluntness, but you look like you just hopped out of a garbage can. I assume you don't have insurance."

Brody squirmed in his seat. "I, um . . . we . . ." He looked at the maple, leaves peeling from it in the breeze.

"I had a part-time job," Molly said. "In Rebel Point. It wasn't much money, but it helped."

"Right, and we had savings," Brody added. "Dad's savings, mostly. And we sold his car—"

"Which didn't cover the lien. Upside down, they call it in the car business. But we sold some of his other possessions—power tools, his vinyl collection, his stereo—and when the money ran out, Brody robbed a convenience store."

A crow called from the maple's high branches, accenting its pitch as if to question Molly's statement, if not her audacity. It was met with a silence that begged for someone to fill it. At length, Renée did.

"I guessed you were in trouble. Why else would you come here? But back up a moment." Renée made a rewind gesture with the forefinger of her right hand. "Your dad's savings? His possessions? Did something happen to him?"

"He died," Molly said.

"Oh my." Renée pressed the same forefinger to her lips. "He wouldn't have been very old."

"Fifty-four."

"I'm so sorry. That's just . . ." Renée shook her head. "Cancer?"

"Suicide," Molly said.

"Really?"

Something in the way Renée said this—a bleakly curious tone, rather than one of surprise—triggered an uneasy feeling within Brody. He might have dismissed it, but her further questioning didn't help.

She asked, "Do you mind if I ask how?"

"He jumped off a building," Molly replied.

"He jumped?" It was doubt, not curiosity, in Renée's voice now, and Brody didn't like it, not one little bit.

The crow called again and the maple's branches clattered as it flew away. That uneasy feeling settled close to Brody's heart. Renée gripped her armrests—clearly bracing herself—and asked the same question as Reverend Mathias.

"What kind of trouble are you in?"

. . .

Molly had told Brody on their short hike from Bayonet to Elder that this was on him. *You own this shit*, she'd stormed, and Brody intended to. It would have been easy to paint himself in a less damning light while relating events to Reverend Mathias, but he hadn't. He'd recounted his sorry tale with candor, shouldering the responsibility for his errant actions. He did the same with Renée. "I fucked up," he began, and started to tell her how he'd tipped his and Molly's precariously balanced world into the shitter. He added no filler, no shine, and paused only twice—once to take a long drink of soda, and again after mentioning Jimmy Latzo for the first time.

"I knew it," Renée said.

"What?" Brody asked.

The kindness in Renée's eyes faded, replaced with a knot of deep thought. Dark lines crossed her brow. Her irises flicked from side to side, as if she were viewing many things—incidents from her past, perhaps, replayed in clear and startling snapshots.

"Are you okay?" Molly asked.

"Yes, I . . ." Renée exhaled from the depths of her lungs. She blinked twice—coming back to herself—and looked at Brody. "Carry on."

Brody did, hesitantly to begin with, and with a set of questions tumbling through his mind. They tailed a notion that there was more to this, and that his part in it was relatively minor. Distracted, he stumbled through, still with candor, describing the fear and anxiety—looking over their shoulders every mile of the way, outrunning Jimmy's goons in Bayonet, dumping his old shitbanger and riding bus after stinking bus across the Midwest—before finishing on a sweeter note: their meeting the Reverend Wendell Mathias.

"He sends his fondest wishes," Molly said to Renée. "I think he still misses you."

"Wendell," Renée said. The kindness returned, not just to her eyes, but to her entire body. She sighed wistfully and appeared to expand in her chair. "Reverend?"

"He was pardoned in 1999," Brody said. "Found his calling with the church."

"He's the reason we're here," Molly said. "In fact, we didn't know you existed until he told us."

"Right," Brody said. He took another sip of his soda and leaned forward. "Why wouldn't our mom tell us about you?"

Renée hesitated, then shrugged and looked down at her hands. "I was a part of her old life. The life she ran away from."

"We *are* the life she ran away from," Molly said.

"No, sweetie." Renée shook her head. "This was before you came along."

"Before?" A shallow crease appeared in the center of Molly's forehead; she was lost in thought, but not for long. "Her name was Lola," she said suddenly. Her eyes brightened and she sat up straight. "Byrd or Blythe. Right?"

"Did Wendell tell you that?"

"Kind of. He thought he had Mom mixed up with someone else. It was a long time ago, but he said he was usually good with names."

Renée offered a small smile. "Bear, not Byrd. Her name was Lola Bear." She sat back in her chair and spoke her next sentence with an icy suddenness: "You may have been followed here."

The notion that there was more to this deepened, but it was too big for Brody to grasp. He pushed against it. "That's not possible. Jimmy's guys jumped us in Mississippi but we lost them. I told you that. Then we dumped my car, dumped our phones. We rode buses and used cash. We've been careful."

Molly must also have sensed something bigger at play, but didn't push against it. She asked, "What's going on, Renée?"

Renée's jaw tightened. She drew her shoulders in again and watched a leaf skate across the deck. "How much do you know about your mother?"

The sunlight shone through the rustling leaves of the old maple. Renée started talking, and by the time she stopped, it was close to dark.

Chapter Fifteen

At the height of his influence and infamy, Jimmy Latzo had twenty-six people on his payroll. They ranged from personal assistants, lawyers, and crooked cops to soldiers and enforcers. When a "situation" needed attention, Jimmy liked to go in strong, and he only hired the best: the most accurate shooters, the smartest negotiators, the deadliest fighters. Lola Bear ticked every box, and a few boxes that Jimmy hadn't considered. She joined his ranks in 1991.

"It was highly irregular—hell, totally *unheard*-of— for a woman to be on the front line," Renée said, adjusting her position in the wheelchair. "But your mom was special."

"She *worked* for Jimmy Latzo?" Brody's voice hit a rare pitch, reserved for his most disbelieving of statements. "She was a . . . a fucking *mobster*?"

"No," Renée replied. "Jimmy was the mobster. Lola worked *for* Jimmy. There's a difference."

"One degree of separation," Molly noted. "How did she get involved in that?"

"She fell in love," Renée said. A faint smile pinched the corners of her mouth. "His name was Vincent Petrescu, and he was everything to your mom. Her world entire, as the poets might say. She met him at the Western Penn 3-Gun, and it was Vincent who introduced her to Jimmy."

"I've got so many questions," Brody said. The uneasy feeling in his chest had turned into a cold hand. It squeezed and let go, squeezed and let go. "I don't know where to begin, but . . . who is Vincent Petrescu, and what the hell is the Western Penn 3-Gun?"

"It's a shooting tournament. Three different types of firearms. Rifle, pistol, and shotgun. Whoever hits the most targets in the shortest time is the winner." Renée spread her hands, as if the outcome of this competition were never in question. "Lola won by a considerable margin. Vincent finished second."

"Who was he?" Molly asked.

"One of Jimmy's most trusted soldiers," Renée said. "He was capable, strong, and he respected your mom. A lot of guys in the life treated their women like shit. But not Vincent. He was a gentleman."

Renée cleared her throat. She sipped from her glass and breathed the air for a moment. Her dark hair, shimmering white at the roots, moved lazily in the breeze. Brody and Molly looked at each other deeply, if only to see something familiar, something they knew to be true.

"Your mom started running errands for Jimmy," Renée continued. "She told me, on one of the few occasions she talked to me about that part of her life, that she only did it for the money. That may have been true, but there was more to it. Lola had a solemnness about her, a certain . . . *coldness*. I think working for Jimmy warmed her in some way."

"A coldness?" Molly frowned. "What do you mean?"

"She rarely showed emotion," Renée said. "She hardly ever laughed, and I never saw her cry. Everything was repressed, pushed down deep. Any psychologist in the world would point to her childhood, which was extremely tough."

"How so?" This was Brody.

"Lonely. Lacking. Abusive." Renée shrugged. A sad light touched her eyes. "Lola's father was killed in Vietnam, three months before she was born. Chloe—Lola's mom—struggled in every way imaginable. She took handouts, worked multiple jobs, sometimes leaving Lola at home—six, seven years old—so that she could earn enough money to put food in their bellies and clothes on their backs. They were hard times. Then Chloe met Mav Hamm, and they only got harder."

Molly glanced at Brody, all this information—these truths—passing across her face, evoking an expression he'd never seen before and couldn't quite name. A reddish leaf tumbled from the maple, landed in her hair, where it fluttered for a second, then blew away.

"Lola's stepdaddy, Mav Hamm." Renée lifted one eyebrow, as if the name alone were cause for mistrust. "Or Maverick Cooper Hamm, if you want to be formal about it. He was a nasty piece of work—a mean, *shitty* human being—and he shut down everything worth nurturing inside Lola. He may have even killed some vital part of her. But he brought something to life, too. Something dangerous."

More leaves swirled across the deck, brushing over the tops of Brody's sneakers and against Renée's legs. One caught beneath the hem of her jeans and tapped uselessly against her ankle.

"I mentioned that your mom rarely showed emotion," Renée continued. "That's true, but I don't want you thinking that she was emotion*less*. Believe me, she had everything inside her. It just took a long time to come out. But when it did, *when* she felt something, she felt it furiously. That worked for love—Vincent

Petrescu is proof of that—but it also worked for hate. For rage."

The cold hand inside Brody's chest squeezed tightly, and didn't let go for a long time.

"What did she do?" he asked.

"She beat Mav half to death," Renée replied. "Put him into a coma."

"A *coma*?" Molly repeated, her voice reaching a higher octave than usual. "Jesus Christ."

"He came out of it eventually, but . . ." Renée shook her head, as if to suggest that things were never quite the same for Maverick Cooper Hamm. "The crazy thing is, Lola was only eleven years old at the time."

Molly sat back with such force that her chair nearly tipped over. Brody had to reach to steady it.

Renée finished her drink and said, "It happened like this."

. . .

Chloe met Mav at the Lycoming County Fair. She'd taken Lola, then nine, because it had been months since they'd spent any real time together, and she had a few dollars in her pocket from the extra shifts she'd pulled at the car wash. Mav had been shoeing a pony, and afterward had handed Lola a brush and invited her to groom the pony's mane. She did, working carefully, with smooth, gentle strokes. "Nice and easy, girl, that's the way," Mav had said. "Say, Mom, I think you got a natural here." He'd looked at Chloe and winked and something inside her had fluttered in a way it hadn't for many years. He was not all the way handsome, Chloe thought. He had a chipped front tooth and a squint in one eye, but his voice was barrel-deep and his chest looked large enough to curl up on. Chloe made a point of passing by the pony pen later that day. She got talking to Mav. He was funny and charming. She saw depth in his eyes. He took her for dinner at Bello Italiano three nights later.

It was all peaches and cream for the first few months—holding hands, tender promises, long walks in the park. The warning signs only appeared after Chloe had confessed her love for him, although she didn't view them as warning signs at the time. They were more like . . . *mannerisms*, the curious traits of the Y chromosome. He had started to pinch the tender skin at the back of Chloe's arm to get her attention, and to switch the TV show she was watching over to whatever sport was playing. Yes, these boorish quirks were frustrating, and yes, Chloe believed she deserved more respect. But Mav was good to her in other ways.

He put new brakes on her car, always paid when they went to the movies or to dinner, and bought Chloe her very own Steelers jersey to wear on Sundays.

Besides, Chloe mused, no relationship was perfect. No *honest* relationship, at any rate.

Mav hit her once before they were married, but only because she'd stepped out of line. They'd been drinking at their local bar with Mav's friends, and Chloe had suggested Mav slow down just a bit—jeez, did he want to spend the night sleeping on the bathroom floor again? Just a joke, was all, and they all laughed, Mav hardest of all, but when they got back to Chloe's place, he socked her cleanly in the eye. Chloe sagged against the wall, holding her face in her hands. "Don't ever disrespect me in front of my friends," he'd snarled. "Take heed, Chlo, that gun was about one-quarter cocked. Next time, I'll take your fucking head off."

Chloe nodded and cried, partly at the pain, mostly at the miserable *surprise* of it all. That was the first time she'd been hit by a man that wasn't her daddy, and it was *scary*. She slept on the sofa that night—except she didn't sleep, of course; she lay awake with a bag of frozen peas pressed to her left eye, thinking it all through, and with a little perspective she concluded that she *had* disrespected Mav, and that was silly of her. Mav came down the following morning and she pushed a stack of strawberry banana pancakes in front of him—his favorite—and kissed his forehead and told him she was sorry.

Meanwhile, Lola drifted in the background, silently registering every degree of abuse. She was always a quiet girl—*contained*, Chloe often thought of her—but had become particularly subdued since Mav arrived on the scene. This didn't change, even when they moved into Mav's ranch house in Salladasburg. It was a nice place, if a little run-down, with a huge yard for Lola to run around in, and sometimes the cows would dawdle down from Clemons Farm, lift their big heads over the fence, and chew the tall grass on Mav's land.

"Isn't this a wonderful place to live?" Chloe asked her daughter, which was her way of skirting around the *real* question: *Do you like Mav?* Lola didn't reply, but the stillness that came over her, and the ice in her eyes, was all the answer Chloe needed.

She and Mav were married in July 1978. Things were better for a while—Mav showed flashes of his old charming self—but by Thanksgiving the bloom was truly off the rose. The little pinches that Mav administered to get Chloe's attention became harder and meaner, and left welts that didn't fade for days. On the plus side, the cold weather allowed Chloe to wear clothing that hid the bruising on her legs and throat, and when friends saw the broken arm that Mav had given her for Christmas, she explained in her best oh-silly-me voice that she'd slipped on the ice.

"He hurts you," Lola had said, which surprised Chloe, because her daughter rarely acknowledged Mav, let alone spoke about him. This had been on the afternoon of Lola's eleventh birthday. She and Chloe were eating chocolate cake in the kitchen. Mav was in the yard, changing the exhaust on his Ford truck.

Chloe had covered her mouth and felt a pang of hurt deep inside. Hurt and shame. She managed to say, "He does a lot of good things for us."

"Can he do those things without hurting you?"

"Everybody's different, Lola." This wasn't an answer. Not even close. "Eat your cake."

Lola did, and said no more. She went about her day-to-day in her usual solemn manner, but over the next couple of months Chloe logged a certain change. Her daughter would sporadically emerge from her containment, and always with unwavering focus. She read novels in a single sitting, smashed rocks, climbed tall trees. She spent all of one Sunday afternoon chopping wood, and didn't stop until both hands were blistered and bleeding. Lola even started a conversation with Mav—a rare phenomenon, indeed. "Do you know," she said across the dinner table, looking him in the eye, "that the human skull is made up of twenty-two pieces? It's like some crazy jigsaw puzzle." And Mav had wiped gravy off his chin and said, "That a fact?"

The snow melted. The trees wore pale green at the tips of their branches. Mav watched the Pirates play their preseason games and swore at the TV a lot. One night in late March, Lola walked out to Mav's tool-shed and selected a hammer from its place on the rack. It was the one he'd used to shoe the pony that day at the county fair. It wasn't too heavy—about the right weight for a purposeful eleven-year-old—with a blunt, square face and a squat claw. Mav called it his spanging hammer. Lola held it at her side and walked out of the toolshed, across the yard, and into the house. She went through the side door so she wouldn't have to pass through the kitchen, where Chloe was making corned beef sandwiches for Mav's lunch the next day—because how could she know that his days of eating solid food were behind him? Lola walked into the living room and crossed to Mav's armchair. He was too absorbed in the baseball game to notice her. Without breaking stride, she raised the spanging hammer and rang the blunt, square face off the side of Mav's skull. "Christ *that*?" he blurted. His muddy eyes rolled and a rivulet of blood raced from his hairline. He looked giddily at Lola and she spanged him with the hammer again, this time impacting his right cheekbone so deeply that his eye sagged in its socket. He sneered and tried getting to his feet but his legs noodled beneath him. "Oooh," he said, and dropped to one knee. Lola rapped the hammer off the top of his skull—right in the middle of the jigsaw puzzle—and she felt some of the pieces separate. Mav's entire right side started to jitter. The blood didn't trickle, it poured. The last coherent words he ever spoke were "Willie Stargell at the plate," then Lola whopped him again and this was lights-out.

· · ·

Birds called across the neighborhood, the first verses of evening song, and the sunlight had deepened to a coppery pink belt in the west. It was reflected in Brody's eyes.

"How do you know all this?" he asked.

"Chloe died at forty-eight. Breast cancer. She spent the last five weeks of her life with her sister—my mom—and I visited most days. I'd take her her meds, read to her, puff up her pillows, and in return she shared her story." Renée blinked and wiped her eyes. "I learned a lot about my Aunt Chloe during that time, and even more about Lola."

A stillness fell between them, with each lost to their own complicated emotions. It continued until Manuel brought out Renée's meds in a small plastic cup, along with a glass of water. "Five minutes," he said, and wagged his finger theatrically. "Then you come inside; it's getting cold."

"Yes, thank you, Manuel," Renée said, spilling the meds into her palm. "We're nearly finished here."

He nodded and clicked his Fitbit. "It's five twenty-seven. I leave soon."

"Okay." Renée smiled. "I'll see you tomorrow."

"Ten A.M." Manuel turned and headed toward the house, but before going inside he called over his shoulder, "Five minutes. *Cinco.*" He flashed five fingers and closed the slider behind him.

Renée downed her prescriptions and sipped her water. Molly, in camaraderie, dug Motrin from her purse and took it dry. Their eyes met. They shared a smile.

"I wish we could have met under happier circumstances," Renée said, looking from Molly to Brody. "But I'm so happy you're here."

Molly reached across, clasped Renée's hand, and held it with a meaningfulness Brody couldn't remember seeing before. He knew then that he would continue this wild journey—wherever it took him—on his own.

He needed more information, though. *We're nearly finished here*, Renée had said to Manuel, but Brody thought they were just getting started. There were so many questions left unanswered, so many blanks to fill in. He looked at the darkening sky and wondered where to begin, and it was Molly—always Molly—who led the way. How would he manage without her?

"What happened to Mom?" she asked, still holding Renée's hand. "You know . . . after Mav?"

"Cormorant Place happened," Renée replied, turning her face to the colorful old maple. "It's still there, right in the heart of Lycoming County, and if you visit their website it still professes to be a juvenile care facility. But it is now and has always been a psychiatric hospital for children."

Brody had an image of doped-up kids playing Connect 4, eating mashed potatoes with plastic spoons, watching non-stimulating TV—*Little House on the Prairie*, maybe—on a small set bolted high on the wall.

"How long was she there?" he asked.

"Just over three years," Renée said. She slipped her hand from Molly's and eased back into her seat. "She was discharged in August of 1982. That was when I first met her. We'd been living in Oregon, but moved back to Pennsylvania when my dad lost his job. I was thirteen at the time, crushing on Simon Le Bon and playing Atari. Lola was only a year older, but you'd think she came from a different planet. Her hair was short and scruffy, her skin was pale. She'd never heard of *Magnum, P.I.* or Duran Duran or *Pac-Man.* I'd talk to her but . . . there was nothing."

"Poor girl." Molly winced and stretched out her left leg, kneading the muscles in her thigh. "But things got better, right? *She* got better."

"Eventually," Renée said. "I like to think I had something to do with that. I saw her all the time—we lived twenty miles from each other—and it was good for her to be around a regular, happy kid. That was Grandpa Bear's idea. He was a smart old fella, and he was the real reason Lola . . . *developed* the way she did."

"Grandpa Bear." Brody dragged a palm across the stubble on his jaw. He might have laughed if he wasn't so tired. "Sounds like something from a fairy tale."

"It does. And he *was* kind of mythical." Renée took another sip of water. The glass flashed in the evening sunlight. "Frankie Bear. Lola's grandfather on her daddy's side. He used his influence to get Lola out of Cormorant Place."

"His influence?" Brody frowned. "Was he a mobster, too?"

"He was in the military," Renée said. "A decorated war veteran. *Wars,* actually—one of the very rare individuals to have served in World War Two, Korea, and Vietnam."

"He saw combat in 'Nam?" Brody asked.

"Not directly. He was a general, one of West-moreland's crew, then he stuck around to help train the ARVN. He came home in '72 and opened a shooting range in Altoona."

"You think he'd be sick of the sound of gunfire," Molly said.

Brody said, "Maybe it gets comforting after a while."

"Maybe," Renée said. She looked at the old maple again, then continued. "Chloe went off the rails after what happened with Mav. Alcohol. Antidepressants. She declared herself unfit to be a parent and Frankie took guardianship, then pulled the strings to get Lola out of that god-awful hospital. Good for Lola, but good for Frankie, too. He'd lost his wife in a traffic accident in the late fifties, and his only son was killed in Viet-nam. Lola was all the family he had, and he cared for that little girl with every piece of his heart."

"Why didn't he help before?" Brody asked. "When Mom was a little kid, and Chloe most needed help?"

"He *did*," Renée said. "He sent money on occasion, and dropped off a bag of groceries whenever he was in the neighborhood. It was never much, but Frankie was a hard-nosed old dog, and he believed that Chloe fending for herself would make her stronger. He was the same with Lola. To say he raised her tough is the understatement of the century."

Brody thought of the spanging hammer looping down on the jigsaw puzzle of Mav's skull and said, "I think she was already tough."

"She was tough inside," Renée said. "But she had no skills. Frankie changed that. Now, a cynical person might say that Frankie turned Lola into the ultimate trophy kid. I prefer to believe he was preparing her for all the harshness and mean-spiritedness in the world. He knew that he wouldn't be around forever, and that Lola would have to be tough to make it alone."

Renée yawned, then finished her water. A breeze knifed across the deck, much colder than it had been.

"So he gave Lola the benefit of his wisdom," she said. "And Lola—machinelike, unaffected by her emotions—learned extremely quickly. Frankie taught her how to survive in the wild. They'd go off for weeks and live in the mountains, with nothing but a sharp knife and the clothes on their backs. He taught her how to make smoke bombs and booby traps, how to camouflage herself, how to hunt with a bow. He shared his knowledge of firearms and close-quarters combat. He also introduced Lola to Benjamin Chen, one of the most renowned Xing Yi instructors in America."

"Xing Yi?" Molly asked.

"One of the martial arts," Renée responded. "Xing Yi Quan. It focuses on swift, direct movements with explosive power. Your mom held a third-degree black sash by the time she was seventeen—a rank that can take the serious student seven years to achieve. She did it in three."

Brody's upper lip twitched, the closest he'd come to smiling since arriving at Renée's house. A memory had floated into his mind: his mom steering him toward a particular YouTube video, and the subsequent hours he'd spent striking a pillow duct-taped to a fence post in their backyard.

"Additionally," Renée continued, "and off her own back, Lola learned kendo, judo, and kickboxing."

"Holy shit," Brody said. "It's like *The Matrix*."

"There was nothing Hollywood about it," Renée said. "It was bare-bones and ugly. She used to get up at four o'clock every morning and grind."

"That's unbelievable," Molly said, shaking her head.

"And then there was *me*, providing some degree of ordinariness by pinning John Stamos posters to Lola's bedroom wall and introducing her to the new Culture Club record." Renée drifted for a few seconds, her eyes shining in the early evening light. "We had some fun. It was nice to see her emerge. But she was more interested in becoming an elite warrior than she was in being a teenage girl."

A fire truck howled a few blocks west and faded somewhere toward downtown. Brody thought of Tank Hill, his neighborhood in Rebel Point, where the sirens were so commonplace he failed to hear them after a while, but the gunshots always woke him at night. *We'll get out of here*, he'd promised Molly—a promise, by pure bad luck, he'd managed to keep. But maybe this tranquil neighborhood, with its hushing trees and occasional sirens, might be the beginning of something, if only for Molly.

"Lola blew the roof off everything she did. The martial arts, the shooting, the weapons combat. I thought she was some kind of superhero." Renée brushed a fallen leaf from her lap and adjusted her position in the wheelchair again. "Then she met Vincent Petrescu, and if the first electrical storm of emotion she displayed was rage, at eleven, then the next was love, at twenty-two. My God, she was besotted."

Another breeze scraped across the deck. Brody cupped his elbows and shivered.

"Yes, it's cold, it's getting late, and I've talked for too long." Renée eased the brake off her wheelchair. "I'll say one more thing before we go inside. Vincent introduced Lola to Jimmy Latzo. I told you that. And it was Jimmy—twisted with jealousy—who took everything away from her."

"He killed Vincent," Molly said.

Renée nodded. "Not a smart move."

Brody's palms moved from his elbows to his forehead. Scraps of information flickered through his mind: Karl Janko beaten up and drowned in a barrel; his father plummeting to his death from the roof of the Folgt Building; Jimmy Latzo's fiery collapse in 1993. The authorities suspected gang warfare, according to the numerous articles Brody had read, but there was another theory: that an anonymous soldier had been responsible. The work of one vengeful man.

Or one woman, Brody thought.

"I saw Lola briefly before she left," Renée said, grasping the hand rims on her chair and wheeling smoothly toward the house. "That was the last time I saw her. I could still smell the smoke."

BEFORE

(2010–2019)
AKA JENNIFER AMES/MARGARET WARD

Jennifer Ames had lived for two years, seven months.

She was a librarian in Little Rock, Arkansas. She had shorter, darker hair than Lola Bear, and was about fifteen pounds heavier. She wore different clothes, too. Frumpy sweaters and leggings, and cheap jewelry from Banana Republic.

This invention of Lola's—this middle-American calendar girl—had been at the range, and had noticed some jackass checking her out. Because of her shooting, or because he wanted to jump her bones. Lola didn't know. But there was another possibility. Maybe he recognized her. Lola subtly pointed him out to Arlen

Stoat, whom she'd known since arriving in Little Rock. "Steer clear, Jen," Arlen warned her. "Jason Kazarian. Fancies himself a gangsta. You know, with an *a*. Sells shooters to street kids in Memphis." Lola remembered that Jimmy Latzo had associates in Memphis. He was part-owner of a restaurant on Beale Street. He'd likely circulated her photograph among the criminal element. Alarm bells chimed loudly. Lola spent the next week in a state of hypervigilance—making note of suspicious persons and vehicles with out-of-state plates, and checking the backseat of her car before getting in—and just when she began to believe that she was being paranoid, Bruno Rossi came to town.

Karl had warned her about Bruno in their final communication. "Jimmy's new guy," he'd said. "Fucking man-ape." A brief but fair description. Bruno was *big*—six-four, packed with gym muscle that would slow him down and expose weaknesses. Lola didn't want a fistfight, though. One bullet to center mass would do it.

She had led Bruno to a quiet industrial street in East Little Rock, with enough distance between them that she could park up and quickly hide behind a storage crate. He'd just exited his car when Lola jumped out, leveled her Baby Eagle, and took the shot. Bruno staggered back several feet and hit the blacktop. He shrieked, clutching his midsection, or so Lola thought. In fact, he was removing his .45 from where it was secured between his jacket and ballistic vest. As Lola approached to finish the job, he sat up and fired five times at her legs (he didn't want to kill her—oh no, that was Jimmy's privilege). Lola anticipated the move. She rolled to her right, feeling the rounds cut through the air only inches away. In a previous life, she would have completed the move by popping to one knee, aiming on instinct, and blowing a hole through Bruno's skull. In this life, she lacked that Jedi-like prowess. She *did* pop to one knee, but overbalanced, staggered, and had to plant one hand to steady herself. Another bullet rippled the air—Bruno firing behind him as he took up a better position. He got behind his car and kept low. He'd moved slowly, though. The ballistic vest had saved his life, but the impact of a 9mm round would have bruised or broken several ribs. Coupled with the fact that he couldn't kill Lola, this gave her a distinct advantage.

She zigzagged toward his car, giving him nothing to aim at, then slid across the hood in one slick movement. Bruno anticipated the maneuver, but she was too fast for him to guarantee a nonlethal shot. He used muscle instead, throwing himself at her, wrapping his thick arms around hers so that she couldn't raise her gun.

The trauma to his central mass had upset his power, though, and Lola made room to move. She simultaneously head-butted his chest and drove her knee into his groin, then freed her non-shooting hand and elbowed him in the throat. He spluttered and stepped away, sweeping his left arm downward, knocking the gun from her hand. They traded blows. Lola connected with his solar plexus and ribs, feeling the tight bind of the bulletproof vest. He answered with a punch that she blocked but that knocked her back anyway. It gave him the space he needed. Grimacing, clearly in pain, he raised his .45 and fired twice.

The first bullet fizzed between Lola's legs. If Bruno's aim had been steadier, he would have shattered her left kneecap and everything behind it. The second bullet ripped across her calf. She felt the burn of it, then the warmth of her blood. It dropped her to one knee.

"You're not so tough," Bruno gasped. He stepped closer, aimed at her other leg, pulled the trigger.

Click.

An eight-round mag. Bruno stared at his gun stupidly. Lola picked up hers. She thrust forward, close enough to plant a kiss on Bruno's surprised mouth, and shot him point-blank in the stomach—the ballistic equivalent of a one-inch punch (she thought, dazedly, of her son, from a lifetime ago, striking a post in their backyard).

Every one of Bruno's two hundred and thirty pounds was raised off the ground. He flew backward and landed hard. Lola stepped over him and shot him in the head. His blood made a satisfying pattern on the sidewalk.

. . .

She dragged Bruno's corpse into one of the warehouses, propped him in a corner, then used his phone to take a photo. The flash overexposed the shot and made the hole above Bruno's left eyebrow appear quite small. It also drew the last hint of color from his face and made his teeth shine. It was a grim arrangement, and told a certain truth: that Bruno Rossi had died in pain.

She sent it to Jimmy.

Lola pocketed the phone. It would be full of contacts, messages, web-browsing history, perhaps strategies. Information was power. She ripped the sleeve from Bruno's suit jacket and used it to bandage her bleeding calf. Her DNA was all over the scene—Lola's first public appearance since 1993, and hopefully her last.

She limped back to her car.

The first sirens howled as she pulled away.

. . .

She was on a bus to Austin three hours later, drowsy with painkillers. She'd left behind the frumpy sweaters, the cheap jewelry, the librarian's job. The small bag on the rack above her seat—the same bag she'd used when she left Ethan and the kids—contained a pair of jeans, a first-aid kit, her Baby Eagle with half a box of ammo, $216 in cash, and the faux-leather folder that Grandpa Bear had given her in 1992.

One identity remaining. One life. One more chance.

The bus moved southwest. Lola listened to the thrum of the wheels on the highway. A strange comfort. She slept beneath a shell-thin layer and dreamed angrily.

A ninety-minute layover in Dallas. This gave her the opportunity to change the dressing on her calf. She then limped to the nearest drugstore and bought hydrogen peroxide and a pair of scissors.

Later that morning, at a dusty motel in Austin, Lola burned Jennifer Ames's documents in the bathroom sink.

Dead. Done.

She cut and dyed her hair, and became Margaret Ward.

...

All but $118 of Jennifer Ames's money disappeared from her Chase Bank account. It was filtered through various businesses both at home and overseas, and gradually integrated (minus a five percent fee) into Margaret Ward's Bank of America account.

There was no link from Jennifer Ames to Margaret Ward, thanks to Grandpa Bear's money-laundering contact.

He'd thought of everything. Good old Grandpa Bear.

Lola didn't stay in Austin. It didn't feel like a good fit for Margaret. She moved to Oklahoma, then Colorado, and finally settled in Lone Arrow, Nebraska.

The years passed. She worked as a waitress, a farmhand, a builder's laborer, a store clerk. She watched her children grow via the marvel of social media. Neither Brody nor Molly were active Facebookers, but their occasional posts opened bittersweet windows into their lives. Lola missed them so much.

There were men. Two of them. She used the first for sex, an arrangement that suited them both. He was younger than her, as fit as a thoroughbred. It was easy breaking it off. The second relationship was deeper. Christian Mellor. A fifty-three-year-old English teacher. Smart, generous, and patient.

Lola recalled what Grandpa Bear had said to her—his final lesson: *Don't put down roots, or make anything that you can't leave behind.*

She cut Christian loose when she started to fall in love.

This hurt. Not as much as losing Vince, or breaking away from Ethan and the kids, but enough to question the point of it all. Was her life merely an exercise in survival? Was she allowed nothing to nurture and live for? Thoughts like these chipped at her soul. She felt haunted by her own ghost.

Owlfeather Farm—purchased eight years and two months into Margaret Ward's existence—was her rebellion against the emptiness, and against everything that had her in chains. Yes, it was another example of putting down roots, but they weren't *human* roots. Nothing could be scarred by her having to run. Besides, it was a prime location, with good visibility all around. It would be her stronghold.

If she needed it to be.

Fifty-seven acres, bordered on either side by farmland, to the north by a small but dense patch of forest, and to the south by Big Crow Road. Lola farmed beans and alfalfa. She had chickens, goats, cows, and horses. It was small, and lean in terms of profit, but it was hers, and she threw herself into it completely.

The days turned into weeks, the weeks into months. Margaret Ward's skin grew comfortable. She loved her work, played pinochle with the old folks every Thursday, and sometimes shot skeet with Butch Morgan. Her favorite thing, though, was to ride Poe, her horse, across her acreage, with the sun melting in the west—to inhale the endless sky and feel the wind ripple her hair. In those moments, she never felt freer, and it was possible to believe.

She never let her guard down, though.

Nine and a half years since she'd pulled a trigger in anger.

Chapter Sixteen

Despite everything they had learned, Brody slept deeply that first night at Renée's. Molly had the spare room. He took the sofa. It was long and soft and unfathomably comfortable. He sank into plush pillows, and though his mind reeled with information—everything from his mother's real name to her working for Jimmy Latzo—his exhaustion won out. A great gray cloud consumed him and he sank helplessly.

"How long do we stay here?" Molly asked the following morning. She had woken him with a mug of freshly ground coffee—the kind he'd been fantasizing about. It smelled rich and delicious and it lifted him, wide-eyed, into a sitting position. He took the mug, sipped from it, savored the taste.

"We need more information," he said. It wasn't an answer, but it concealed what he was thinking: that he planned to continue without her.

He showered for a long time and it was the greatest shower of his life. Pink steam ghosted around him, scented with lilac. He breathed it into his lungs and exhaled, like a man who has been trapped in a mine, stepping into fresh air for the first time in weeks. His skin prickled with cleanliness. Afterward, he used one of Renée's razors to shave. He had lost weight, there were shadowy crescents beneath his eyes, but he looked more like himself than he had in a long time.

His thoughts were still a knife-fight of words and images, though—glimpses of his mother's past and his own potential future. But out of the clash of everything in his head, he kept returning to two things. The first was how Jimmy Latzo had been taken down in 1993, his empire reduced to ashes. The second was Renée saying that she thought Lola was some kind of superhero.

Not *everything* in his mind clashed. Some of the pieces clicked. They had synergy.

For better or worse, Brody sensed the end was in sight.

...

Later that day, he went to Bryan Park with Molly and Renée. He pushed Renée's chair at an easy pace. Molly walked beside them, thumping along on her crutches. There were plenty of people around, walking through the rich fall scenery, running the loop, throwing footballs, and shooting hoops. The trees were alive with color, shimmering in the afternoon light. It was, by any measure, a picture-book October scene, but Brody was too distracted to enjoy it. He had taken to looking regularly over his shoulder.

"You can relax, Brody," Renée said. She'd noticed his agitation, even though he was behind her. "They're not going to jump us."

His arms were rigid, his hands clamped around the push handles. He wondered if Renée could feel the tension through the chair. "You still think we were followed here?"

"I think you should assume as much," Renée replied after a moment. "And proceed accordingly."

"But we were so careful."

"You're dealing with professionals."

They strolled for another minute or so, then Brody looked over his shoulder again. Molly did the same.

"Anybody look suspicious to you?" she asked.

Renée was right; Jimmy worked with professionals, people who could blend in, make themselves invisible.

The woman walking her dog, her phone welded to one ear, might be talking directly to Jimmy, or perhaps to another contact elsewhere in the park. *The target is approaching the basketball courts, heading your way.* Maybe one of the elderly men playing dominoes was Jimmy's uncle, still on the payroll. The guy taking pictures of trees might also be taking pictures of Brody. Or how about the hipster chick with the skateboard, the dude taking shots from the free-throw line, the crane-like woman doing tai chi?

"Everybody looks suspicious," he said.

There were fewer people farther along the path, and Renée took that opportunity to share what Brody already suspected: that Lola had singlehandedly dismantled Jimmy's empire back in 1993. She'd killed sixteen men and seven attack dogs, and had fled the scene with Jimmy's mansion engulfed in flames. Intent on revenge, Jimmy had spent the last twenty-plus years hunting Lola, tracking down and questioning—in many cases torturing—anybody who knew her.

"And I guess," Molly said, "that's how Karl Janko ended up in a barrel."

"You guess right," Renée said.

Now Jimmy was after Brody, and no, this wasn't a coincidence. It *had* to be a setup. Brody contemplated this, putting together an unlikely puzzle in his mind, but some of the pieces didn't fit.

"How would he know?" he asked. They had paused to watch two squirrels chase one another around the trunk of an elm tree. Both Molly and Renée giggled at their antics, then Molly turned to Brody and frowned.

"Say what?"

"I put myself in this position," Brody replied. "Jimmy didn't *make* me rob a convenience store. He didn't *make* me drop my wallet at the scene. So how can I have been set up when it was *my* actions that started this whole thing?"

"I wondered that, too," Renée said. "Everything with Blair's stepmom—the diamonds, the so-called murder, *that* was a trap, but the convenience store wasn't."

"Right," Brody said. "It doesn't make sense."

"It does, though," Molly said. "Because it *was* a trap, only one that you made and walked into yourself. You put yourself on a plate for them, Brody."

The squirrels had clambered into the higher branches, out of sight. Molly walked on. Brody was lost in thought for a few seconds—lost in space, Molly always said—then Renée snapped, "Giddyap!" and he blinked hard, pushed on.

"What do you mean?" he asked, drawing level with Molly.

"They were watching you," Molly said, and shrugged as if this were obvious. "How many times did you survey Buddy's Convenience Store before you finally robbed it?"

"Three, four times, maybe," Brody replied. "I wanted to make sure I had all my ducks in a row."

"I'm glad you put some thought into your stupidity," Molly said, and Renée snorted laughter, then clapped a hand over her mouth. "Meanwhile, this girl Blair—who clearly works for Jimmy—saw what you were planning. I mean, it's obvious, right? So she just sat in the wings, waiting for you to make your move."

Brody winced. Yeah, that logic held.

"Okay," he said, seizing something else. "But that doesn't explain . . ."

He was going to say, *that doesn't explain the wallet*, but the words faded as a memory swam to the front of his mind. Atlantic City, New Jersey, three years ago. He'd gone for a boys' weekend with his buddy Kieran. They'd been drinking in a bar on the boardwalk. It was a good time. No luck with the ladies, but they hadn't landed in any trouble, either. As they left for the night, stepping out onto the boardwalk, some snot-faced kid ran into Kieran, caromed off him, and kept running.

No excuse me. No apology. It was only when they got back to their hotel that Kieran noticed his phone was missing. He placed his hand on his empty front pocket, looked back in the direction of the boardwalk, and said, "That little motherfucker—"

"Pickpocketed me," Brody finished out loud. He stopped pushing Renée, and his eyes glazed with the same abashed, slightly hurt expression that Kieran's had on that night in Atlantic City.

"What?" Molly asked.

"Blair," Brody said distantly. He remembered reeling from Buddy's Convenience Store with the replica gun in one hand, the bag of cash in the other, and bumping into Blair. Or, more accurately, she—appearing from nowhere—had bumped into *him*. Brody had reached to steady her and they did a clumsy kind of two-step before she pulled away from him. "That bitch *pickpocketed* me."

He explained, again, how it went down to Molly and Renée. They agreed that Blair lifting his wallet from his jacket pocket was the most likely explanation. Really, the *only* explanation. Along with many other emotions, Brody felt a splash of vindication. He'd been carrying the weight of dropping his wallet at the scene of the robbery all this time. Apparently he hadn't been *that* stupid.

They started moving again and Molly said, "It was a setup, Brody. Jimmy is using you to find Mom."

Brody nodded. This knowledge offered small relief. Okay, so he was not the primary target, but he was still in Jimmy's crosshairs, and very much in danger. They both were.

"This explains why the stepmother's murder didn't make the news. Jimmy staged the whole thing." Brody recalled the blood—so much blood—and the body, sprawled with one arm behind her head and a huge knife implanted in her chest. "He did a *very* convincing job. Him and Blair."

"From what I know of Jimmy," Renée said, "I'd say Blair is masterminding this whole thing."

Brody flashed back to their meeting at Rocky T's. Punky, colorful Blair, with a cool cunning in her eyes and a sharpness he knew could slice to the bone. Blair, with her Valentino Garavani boots and $1,700 jacket, and hadn't he wondered then what a spoiled brat from the Laurels was doing alone at Buddy's at 4:55 in the morning?

Jesus, he'd been played like a hillbilly's banjo.

"It's all so elaborate, though," he said. He'd fallen behind Molly again in his deep thought, and put on a burst of speed to catch up. "If they think I have information, why *not* jump us? Why not beat it out of me?"

"Do you, though?" Renée asked.

"Do I what?"

"Have information," Renée replied. "Specifically, do you know where your mother is?"

"No," Brody answered curtly. "Of course I don't."

"And Jimmy knows that. So beating and torturing you is a waste of time. But if you're scared enough, and if you have nowhere else to run, maybe you'll look for her."

"Maybe," Brody said.

"You have a better chance of tracking her down than he does," Renée said. "At least, that's what he's counting on."

"Right," Molly agreed. "And all Jimmy has to do is follow."

Brody scratched the back of his head. It was a desperate strategy, yes, but more than twenty years of searching for Lola Bear, drawing blanks, had no doubt made Jimmy a desperate man.

"That whole thing in Bayonet," he said. "Getting jumped by Jimmy's boys, us getting away, them giving chase . . . that was just an act to . . . to *scare* us—get us to run in the right direction?"

"I don't know for sure, but . . ." The inflection in Renée's voice suggested she *did* know for sure, and now so did Brody.

A kid blazed across their path to catch an overthrown pass. He leaped theatrically, tipped the football, and it sprang away from him. His buddies jeered. Elsewhere, parents scanned their phones while their toddlers let loose in the playground, and a squat, bearded dude wrestled his French bulldog playfully.

Clouds had gathered in the north. They had bruised edges. Rain, for sure. Somewhere out there, Jimmy Latzo licked his wounds and hated, scouring the Lower 48 for a woman named Lola Bear.

"All of this," Brody said. "The pain, the fear, the running. It's all because of our mom."

"They're watching you," Renée said, gesturing not at the wide autumn sprawl of Bryan Park, but at the northern clouds, portending some doom. "The question is, how do you want to play it?"

...

"We need to talk about the elephant in the room," Brody said to Renée later that evening. "Or rather, the elephant in Spring Grove Cemetery."

Renée frowned and wheeled a little closer to Brody. It was just the two of them. Molly—complaining of hip pain after their walk in the park—had dosed up on Motrin and retired to bed. This presented the perfect opportunity to talk to Renée one-on-one, and to learn some harder, necessary truths.

"Did Jimmy Latzo kill my father?"

For all the hardship Brody had endured recently, none of it compared to the bleakest moment of his life—a sliver of time that he relived often, and never *more* often than on that day with Renée.

It happened on the evening of February 26, 2019, when a dour-faced police officer capsized his and Molly's life with two short, knife-like sentences. The first was, "I'd like you to steel yourselves." *Steel.* What a fabulous choice of word, Brody thought, and wondered if this cop wrote crime novels in his spare time. Brody nodded but didn't steel himself. He perched on the arm of the sofa and looked at the police officer as the second sentence was delivered: "I'm afraid your father is dead." There. Precise terminology. No vagueness. *Dead*—the most unambiguous word in the English language. Brody responded pathetically, by saying, "No, he isn't," as if "dead" could be disputed, after all, and he'd pointed at the latest edition of *Rolling Stone*, still open on the coffee table where his father had been reading it the night before.

In the weeks and months that followed, Molly asked questions like, *Why?* and *What now?* Brody's inner dialogue was one of denial, not that his father was dead—Brody had identified the body via photograph; Dad's face was covered on one side, but there was no mistaking his patchy beard, his Greek nose—but rather the manner of his death. Ethan Ellis had been a man of boundless love, encouragement, and optimism. Jesus, he'd held on to a biker jacket from his teens because he intended to one day buy the Harley to go with it.

He would never take his own life. *Never.*

That Jimmy had killed him had been on Brody's mind since learning about his mother's connection to the mobster, but the notion was so terrible that he kept pushing it away, focusing on other things. It was barbed, though, and would snag him. It would draw blood. He knew Molly had considered it, too. She hadn't spoken to him about it yet, because to face it would be to accept it, but it was only a matter of time.

Brody needed to face it, though. *The question is, how do you want to play it?* Renée had asked in regard to everything he'd learned, and getting closer to the truth about his father's death would factor heavily in his decision.

Now Renée lowered the armrest on her chair and transferred to the sofa. A smile touched her lips and eyes. That kindness again, never far away, and she patted the seat beside her, inviting Brody to sit. He did, and he held his breath.

"I can't say for sure," she said. "But taking everything into account, I'd say the probability is high."

Something inside Brody rattled with a cold, heavy sound. It felt like a chain strung through several of his ribs. He breathed around it with tremendous effort, then looked at Renée and nodded. She hadn't told him anything he didn't already suspect, but to hear her say it out loud was harder than he had anticipated. The first of his tears came. Renée rubbed his back and said nothing until he did.

"I'll be okay. It's . . ."

"Take your time."

Brody remembered his dad's smile, as welcoming as blue water, and the sturdiness of his arms. He'd had tough mechanic's hands, but a deft touch, so he could apply a Band-Aid, or wipe the goop from beneath Brody's nose, with a fabulous tenderness. A kind man, a hopeful man, and Brody's favorite place, as a child, had been in his arms, enjoying the warmth of him, listening to the blood rush through his kingly body.

"After the funeral, I went to the Rebel Point Police Department and asked them to launch a murder investigation. I had no evidence other than my absolute conviction that my father would never commit suicide." Brody took a Kleenex from the box Renée offered and dragged it across his cheeks. "The sergeant I spoke to told me that mental health issues present in many forms, and not all of them are obvious. He gave me the number for a bereavement counselor and sent me on my way."

Renée rubbed his back again. A small gesture, but it felt wonderful. He didn't think it possible to miss something he'd never had, but he missed extended family. How much fuller would his life have been with a host of aunts, uncles, and cousins?

"I went in for justice, but all I got was a business card." Brody wiped his damp eyelashes, then balled the Kleenex and tossed it on the side table. "I knew it, though. I fucking *knew* Dad was murdered. And now I know who did it."

Had Dad been accosted in the street, Brody wondered, dragged into an alleyway and sedated? Or maybe one of Jimmy's boys had hidden in the back of his Malibu, and as soon as Dad got behind the wheel: *Drive, motherfucker.* A northeastern accent. A .45 locked to his temple. *Do exactly what I tell you, and don't try anything stupid.* Brody pressed the heel of his hand to his forehead, trying to urge the images to the rear of his mind. What good would it do, to imagine Dad's fear, his consternation? How could it help, to envision Jimmy's goons balancing Dad at the edge of the Folgt Building's rooftop, with Jimmy snarling in his face?

Where is she, Ethan? And Dad desperately holding on with those tough, deft hands—the same hands that had applied Band-Aids to Brody's knees and wiped his nose. *You tell me what you know, or by God it's the express way down for you.*

"He must have been so scared," Brody said. "And confused. He died . . . confused. That's . . . I almost can't bear to think of that. Poor Dad. Poor, sweet Dad."

Renée handed him another Kleenex and he took it. He didn't want to use it, but to think of his dad in the closing moments of his life . . . Jesus, how many stunned, panicked thoughts had he processed in the three seconds it took to plummet fourteen stories?

He used that Kleenex and another two besides.

"Jimmy," he said, except he growled it, a sound like rocks tumbling down the chute of his throat. "Jimmy fucking Latzo. But this isn't just about him, is it? My mom has a lot to answer for."

"Brody—"

"She's caused so much pain. How could she do this to us?"

"She loved you, Brody." Renée adjusted her position on the sofa, tilting her upper body so that she could look Brody in the eye. "You and Molly. From the few notes and photographs she sent me, it's clear how much she loved you. It would have broken her heart to run away. But she did it to keep you safe—to move the target away from you."

"If she loved us," Brody said, "she would have given herself up. Or *fought* Jimmy. If she's such a badass, why didn't she fight him again?"

"Your mom did what she thought was best," Renée said. The kindness in her voice was laced with seriousness. "And she was careful. There was no way Jimmy should have tracked you down."

"I guess she wasn't careful enough."

"You were three random people with no connection to Lola Bear," Renée said. "I don't know how Jimmy found you."

"And you?" Brody broke her gaze for a second. He gestured at Renée's empty wheelchair. "Was it really a motorcycle accident, or did Jimmy get to you, too?"

"It *was* an accident," Renée said. "And it was entirely my fault; I was going too fast, and riding conditions were not good. But my lack of judgment, my fate . . . it does play a part in this. I appreciate now how breakable we all are, and how valuable life is. And knowing what had happened to Karl Janko, I made the decision that if Jimmy came for me, I'd tell him everything I know."

The chain strung through Brody's rib cage snapped tight. He managed a shallow breath and said, "You know where my mother is, don't you?"

And Renée said, "I have a pretty good idea."

...

Brody took Tylenol to manage the ache in his chest. Despite downing her own medication after dinner, Renée selected a bottle of Merlot—"For special occasions or maudlin moments"—and poured herself a glass.

"Jimmy spent two years in the hospital, and another two years convalescing. During this time, Lola Bear disappeared. *Poof!* Gone, baby." Renée snapped her fingers and sipped her wine. "With you and Molly filling in the blanks, I now know that she changed her name to Natalie Myles and moved to Minneapolis."

"Uh-huh." Brody nodded. "Nokomis East, close to the lake."

"I also know that she met and fell in love with a young mechanic named Ethan Ellis."

"And I was born in August of '95, twenty-three months after she tried to kill Jimmy." Brody lifted one side of his mouth, closer to a sneer than a smile. "She didn't waste any time, did she?"

"A family is the perfect cover," Renée said. "She threw herself into being a wife and mother just like she had everything else: quickly, and with passion."

"So we were . . . what? Camouflage?"

"Don't go down that road, Brody. Just because she fast-tracked the family life doesn't mean she loved you any less."

"I'll have to take your word for it."

Renée gave him a sideways glance, then continued, "Other than the occasional cryptic note and a few photographs of you and Molly, I never heard from your mom. She had severed all ties with her old life, except for one."

Brody recalled the visits from the tall guy with the tight T-shirts and Boston accent. "Karl Janko."

"Right. She and Karl were close, but Jimmy never knew that. They had kept their alliance under the radar—smart practice in an environment where so many people want to put a bullet in your back."

"It couldn't have been *that* under the radar," Brody remarked. "I saw a photo of them together, standing shoulder to shoulder, like a couple of old *hermanos*. Not exactly covert."

"It was normal to fraternize; they were colleagues, not enemies. But Jimmy had no idea how close they really were. I guess he was more focused on Lola's relationship with Vince, and how he might worm his way between them." Renée swirled the wine in her glass, then took a deep drink. "Lola stayed in touch with Karl after she blew the scene. He was her link to the western Pennsylvania crime scene, and, more importantly, to Jimmy. Karl informed her of Jimmy's every move. Where he went. Who he questioned. Lola was able to stay one move ahead."

"And Jimmy never questioned you?" Brody asked.

"He did, but not in person. This was twenty-two years ago, when he was still too weak. So get this: he sent Karl." Renée snickered, one hand over her glass to keep the wine from spilling. "I remember that day. Karl and I watched *Friends* and ate banana bread. I think he told Jimmy that he broke both my legs, and Jimmy was satisfied with that."

"You were lucky," Brody said. He thought of his dad again, dropping to his death, and Karl, upended into a barrelful of water with his arms tied behind his back. "He could easily have sent another of his guys."

"True, but even if he had, and even if that guy *had* broken my legs, or worse, I wouldn't have told him where your mother was, because I didn't *know* where she was." Renée shrugged, finished her wine. "Not *then*, anyway."

She set her empty glass down, then transferred back to her chair and wheeled over to a display case with a drawer in the bottom. With a little effort—and refusing Brody's offer to help—she opened the drawer and pulled out a folded manila envelope. She placed this in her lap, rolled back to the sofa, and eased into the seat beside Brody.

"I destroyed most of the notes your mom sent." Renée opened the envelope and withdrew a handful of photographs. She flipped through them while she talked. "They were veiled enough that I probably didn't have to—there was no name on them, certainly no return address—but I didn't want to take any chances. I liked receiving them, though. They offered a tiny window into your mom's new life, and let me know she was still alive."

Brody glimpsed some of the photographs as Renée flipped through them. Many were of her—a younger Renée, standing next to her date on prom night, sitting on the hood of an old Dodge with a beer in her hand, straddling a custom chopper with ridiculous ape hanger handlebars. There were tourist shots—Niagara Falls, Machu Picchu, the Eiffel Tower—along with snaps of pets and flowers and some well-known faces from her time with the Colts. A more recent photograph showed

Renée with her arm around a man with close-set eyes and babyish curls.

"Boyfriend?" Brody asked.

"Fiancé," Renée said, and rolled her eyes. "He called the engagement off after my accident. I guess he couldn't deal with the wheelchair."

"Some kind of guy, huh?" Brody said. "I think maybe you dodged a bullet."

"No maybe about it."

She flipped through a few more shots, pausing to look at one of her and Lola in their teens—Renée was holding a copy of *Bop* magazine, Lola had a hunting knife strapped to her thigh—before handing Brody a photograph of a baby swaddled in a *Sesame Street* blanket.

"Who's this?" he asked.

"It's you," Renée replied. "Four weeks old."

"Oh." A new pain rose in his chest. It hit his throat and dissolved, leaving a vapor of melancholy. The baby in the photograph was cradled in female arms. Her face was out of shot, but these were his mother's arms. Over the last couple of days, he'd learned that Lola Bear seldom showed emotion, but he saw only love in the way she held him, one hand tenderly supporting his tiny head.

To mask his own emotion, he said, "I was an ugly little bugger."

"You were beautiful. Here." Renée handed him another photograph, this one of Molly. She was maybe three years old—all curls and smiles—leaning on her walker.

"I remember that walker," Brody said. He blinked at tears. "Molly hated it."

"One more."

This final photograph was of Brody and Molly together, Christmas morning of 2006—their last Christmas with Mom. They wore matching sweaters and outstanding grins, surrounded by gifts and torn wrapping paper. Brody's melancholy deepened. He'd been happy once. He had a mom and a dad. Life was easy. It was good.

"Why are you showing me these?" he asked.

"You have a lot of anger toward your mom, and that's justified. But you need to know that she was proud of you. Of Molly, too. And she loved you very much. She wouldn't have sent me these photographs if she didn't."

"Maybe, but it changes nothing." Brody handed the photos back. "This is her war. She's been running for too long."

"I agree." Renée nodded and touched his knee gently. "You know I do. But without the truth, it's hard to make a decision that you can live with."

"What's hard is feeling like a pawn on somebody else's chessboard," Brody said. "I'm tired of being moved around. I need to take control."

Renée held up both hands, perhaps to illustrate that she was not controlling him at all, merely passing along information. She poured another glass of wine.

"This is going to my head. I should slow down." She took a big glug anyway. "Your mom sent a photo, or a note, every eighteen months or so. They stopped completely after Karl was killed: 2007. That's when she left you, right?"

Brody nodded.

"She must have felt that, without Karl, she couldn't keep her family safe. So she ran away, taking the target with her." Renée swigged wine and started flipping through the photographs again. "I heard nothing. For years. I thought she was dead. And then, last summer . . ."

She passed him a photo of a beautiful black horse with a splash of white on its nose. It stood in a field. There was a fence in the background, and what looked like the edge of a red barn, or maybe a silo. Brody flipped the photo over. A short message had been printed on the back.

I found Little Moon
Miss you, Pickle

"I don't understand," Brody said.

"You're not supposed to. It's *veiled*. Like all of your mom's messages." Renée took the photo back and looked at it fondly. "We'd spend hours watching TV, your mom and I. Eating popcorn, huddled beneath a comforter. *The A-Team, Three's Company, Scarecrow and Mrs. King.* My favorite was *The Facts of Life.* Your mom really liked *Little Moon Farm.*"

Brody stared at Renée vaguely.

"*Little Moon Farm,*" Renée continued after another hit of wine, "was about two teenage sisters—Sage and Pickle Moon—who moved away from the city to run a farm they'd inherited. It was nonsense. The kind of schlock that was everywhere on TV back then. But, you know, we kind of loved it."

"A guilty pleasure," Brody said.

"Yes, but without the guilt." Renée smiled, turning the photo over to read the message on the back. "We always said we'd buy a farm one day. It was our dream for a while."

"I found Little Moon," Brody mumbled, reading the first part of the message. "So she lives on a farm? Well, that's narrowed it down to, what, two million possibilities?"

"Silly boy," Renée said playfully. The wine was definitely going to her head. "This photo was sent in an envelope with a postmark from Lenora, Kansas. Now, your mom is too smart to mail anything from the town she's hiding in, but I figured she wouldn't travel *too* far to mail one photograph."

"Okay." Brody leaned a little closer.

"It was a long shot, but I had a realtor friend of mine search for all the farms in a seventy-five-mile radius of Lenora that had sold within the previous year." Renée sipped her wine and winked. "I told him I was thinking of writing a book about agricultural buying trends."

"Riveting," Brody said. "And?"

"I'd hoped to whittle it down to maybe a dozen properties," Renée said. "But he came back with a hundred and eighteen hits, everything from tiny chicken shacks to multimillion-dollar farms that had sold to huge corporations."

"That doesn't help much," Brody said.

"Right. I went through them, eliminating anything too rickety or expensive, but that still left me with forty or so, spread across northwest Kansas and into Nebraska. I didn't know how to narrow them down further, other than fly out there and wheel myself door-to-door. It all seemed too much, and I'd started to question why her location was so important to me." Renée sighed, and after a solemn pause added, "I knew why, of course. I just didn't want to admit it."

"You wanted that information," Brody said, "in case Jimmy came knocking."

"It's like I said . . ." Renée gestured at her ragdoll legs. "I appreciate how valuable life is, and how easily we break."

"I get it," Brody said.

"Anyway, I got lucky," Renée said. "I was idly going through the listings, looking at the photographs, when something caught my attention: a red barn. Well, not the *barn*, exactly, but the word 'Owlfeather' painted across the front in big yellow letters."

Renée showed Brody the photo again, pointing out the barn that had sneaked into the right side of the frame. He hadn't noticed before, but now saw the beginning of a letter that had been painted across the front. An *O*, yes, or maybe a *C*. Whichever, it was bright yellow.

"It's the same barn," Renée said. "I put the two photographs side by side. And it's not just the yellow lettering. The trees behind, the wooden fence . . . it's all the same."

"Okay," Brody said, and sat up in his seat. "That's good."

"Owlfeather Farm, two miles west of Lone Arrow, Nebraska. It was purchased in June of 2018 by a lone female buyer. I couldn't find any information about her, other than her name: Margaret Ward."

"At the risk of sounding like a misogynist dick," Brody said, "is it unusual for lone females to buy farms?"

"I asked my realtor friend the same question," Renée said. "And get this: only eight percent of farms in Nebraska have a principal female operator. So while it's not unheard of, it *is* unusual. This information, together with the photo . . . I'd say there's a good chance Margaret Ward used to be known as Natalie Ellis, and Lola Bear before that."

Questions elbowed and pushed in Brody's mind, all wanting to be heard first. How could his mom afford to buy a farm? How far away was Lone Arrow, Nebraska? How long would it take to get there on a bus? Brody placed a hand on either side of his head and squeezed, narrowing his focus.

"No guarantees," Renée said, going back to her wine. "She may have moved on since then, or maybe she sent a photo of somebody else's farm. But my gut tells me this is where you'll find your mom."

They sat in silence for several minutes. Brody mapped scenarios in his mind, trying to define the clearest, safest way through for him and Molly. Renée finished her wine, then pressed the cork into the bottle and took it, and her empty glass, into the kitchen.

While she was gone, Brody grabbed Renée's iPad from where it was charging next to the TV and started to gather information. Lone Arrow was 810 miles from Bloomington. The nearest major bus line served Kearney, Nebraska, thirty-five miles north. It was a nineteen-hour ride from Bloomington to Kearney, with changes in Indianapolis, Chicago, and Omaha. A long, ugly journey, and the thought of trading the comfort of Renée's house for a showdown with Jimmy Latzo was stomach-turning. On the flip side, to deliver this war to the woman who *should* be fighting it was his best—and perhaps his only—shot at getting free.

"Given what we know," he said when Renée returned to the room, "and what I'm potentially walking into, do you agree that Molly is safer here with you?"

"I do," Renée said. "I was actually going to suggest it. Not least because she's almost out of her prescriptions; I can share mine as required."

"You're an angel," Brody said.

"A tipsy angel."

"And there's no chance Jimmy will come here?"

Renée considered this for a few seconds, then shook her head. "Wherever *you* go, he'll follow. You're his focus. But if he comes here—which I doubt—I'll tell him what I told you."

"Then I'm leaving tonight," Brody said.

"Tonight?" Renée said, surprised. "Nebraska is a long way, Brody. Wouldn't it be better to get some rest, have a decent breakfast—"

"No, I want to do this quietly, while Molly's asleep."

"You're not going to say goodbye?"

"I'll look in, but I won't wake her. She'll want to come with me, and I won't be strong enough to say no. Nor would I have the right." Brody swiped the iPad's screen and accessed the timetable. "There's a bus to Indy at ten, and I can make the eleven-fifty connection to Chicago. With everything running on time, I'll be in Iowa by the time she wakes up."

. . .

Within minutes, Brody had his things packed and was ready to hit the road. A life on the run called for few possessions, he reflected, and there wasn't much more to say for it. At least Molly didn't have to run anymore.

He crept into the spare room. A night-light threw a purplish glow across the bed. Molly slept with her hair fanned across the pillow, the quilt pulled high and gathered beneath her chin. Her face was smooth and peaceful, in contrast to her waking face, which was tight and worked. She looked ten years younger.

Brody whispered goodbye and kissed the top of her head. That was when the magnitude, and the emotional gravity, of what he was about to do hit home. He went downstairs in a haze, put on his dad's leather jacket, and couldn't keep the tears from falling.

Renée saw him and wheeled to his side. She reached out of her chair to wipe his eyes with her fingers, and he let her, feeling childlike and cared-for.

"You don't have to do this," she said. "We can wait for Jimmy to come knocking—which he will if you're still here—and we'll tell him what we know. This doesn't have to be your fight."

"It does," Brody said, thinking of his dad. "It already is. But thank you, Renée. Thank you so much for everything."

"Be careful, Brody. Come back to us."

"Don't tell Molly," he said, indicating his tears and wildly trembling hands. "Tell her I was strong."

"I will."

"If she knows how scared I am, she'll follow." He glanced at his reflection in the hallway mirror. He looked so small in his dad's jacket. "It won't matter how many states she has to cross."

Chapter Seventeen

Rain fell in drab lines. It might have been revitalizing in the early morning, with the stained hue of the leaves and the silvery gleam off the blacktop, but by night it was spiritless. It slanted through the streetlights and droned, caring nothing for the long, warm days it had left behind. Moreover, it felt ominous, like a warning.

Renée had offered to call him a cab. Brody had refused, wanting the mile-long walk to invigorate him and clear his head of lingering doubts. He wished, now, that he'd taken her offer. The rain had really picked up since he'd left the house. He was shivering and miserable, and the night was unaccountably darker without Molly beside him.

She would wake in the morning to find him gone. Would she follow? Brody didn't think so. Molly would be hurt and angry, but Renée—who'd taken to Molly as if she were a long-lost kid sister—would convince her that this was the best way.

. . .

He heard a car behind him and turned, but the street was empty. The rain was haze-like in the distance. It swelled around the streetlights in heavy orange bags. A wet flag rippled outside an office building.

Renée's warning echoed in his mind: *You may have been followed here.* That had seemed implausible at the time, but now, having spoken more with Renée, and alone on these dismal streets, he knew it was true.

Brody wiped rain from his eyes and peered through the murk. A truck rumbled across the intersection two blocks west, spraying fans of water from its tires. Brody continued on. The bus depot was at the intersection of South Walnut and East Third Street, half a mile away. On the next block, a homeless kid mumbled for spare change from a barely lit doorway. Brody flipped him a quarter. A car appeared on the street behind them, moving slowly. "God's blessing," the kid said. Brody wondered if he worked for Jimmy, one of his many spies dotted around the city. Would he send a text after Brody had gone? TARGET HEADING EAST ON W. KIRKWOOD AVE. Brody kept walking. The car crept closer, its headlights working through the rain. Brody imagined it stopping beside him, one of the rear doors banging open, being grabbed and dragged inside. A pistol would be slotted beneath the shelf of his jaw. *We can take you any time we want, kid, put a bullet in your throat.* The car pulled alongside Brody and he flinched, but it kept going and soon its taillights faded.

. . .

Brody picked up the pace and eventually turned onto South Walnut Street. He saw the lights from the bus depot two blocks away. They offered no comfort, looking cold and clinical in the rain. Walnut was one way, three lanes flowing north. Vehicles crawled behind their headlights. Traffic signals blinked like robotic eyes. The sidewalks were empty, save for a single dim figure huddled beneath an umbrella, and a young couple tucked inside a doorway, waiting for the rain to let up.

Brody regarded them suspiciously, then noticed the SUV parked across the street. The side windows were tinted, but there was enough streetlight to determine movement in the driver and passenger seats. Two people. Brody imagined Blair to be one of them, smiling through her wagon-red lipstick, knowing that *he* knew it was a setup—that he'd put it all together.

No more games, he thought. *All cards on the table.*

Blair, with her designer boots propped on the dash, daring him with her eyes. Another ultimatum.

So what are you going to do, Bro?

He stared at the SUV for fully two minutes before the driver's window buzzed down and some blaze-eyed dude leaned his head out.

"The fuck you staring at, friend?"

A middle-aged woman in the passenger seat. Platinum hair and a missing front tooth. Not Blair. She blew a kiss, then flipped him off. Brody turned and took dizzy steps toward the bus depot. How close had he been to approaching the SUV and rapping on the window, telling the occupants everything he knew? *You don't have to do this,* Renée had said, and she was right. He could spill the beans and take a backseat.

But no. Things had changed. The game was different. There was more to this than just getting Jimmy off his back. *Much* more.

Brody had a new motivation: revenge.

He owed his mom nothing, but revealing her location would stack the odds in Jimmy's favor. His most ruthless enforcers would take Lola by surprise—probably at night, while she was asleep. They would overwhelm her, put a bullet in her knee, then tie her up and hand her to Jimmy. Brody couldn't let that happen. His mom's long and miserable death was not part of the game plan, and he for damn sure wasn't going to give Jimmy the win.

Brody needed to confront Lola Bear. But this was no mawkish family reunion. It was a battle strategy, to ready and deploy her.

He thought of his dad holding on to everything with those tough, deft hands, begging for his life, and the last face he saw was Jimmy Latzo's.

Brody crossed the road toward the bus depot. The hard rain pattered off his leather jacket.

"Now," he said.

Now was the time to steel himself.

PART II
Nebraska

Chapter Eighteen

The hands of time have no bias. They will deteriorate everything, and without mercy. From the sweetest fruit to the toughest mountain. Emotion, too. Some say that time heals, but it doesn't. It gradually degrades feeling and sense. The very opposite of healing.

Time is the great enemy of all, and cannot be defeated. Inactivity, Lola knew, was a lesser foe, but more quickly damaging. She had softened during her twenty-six years on the run, having traded hours in the dojo, and on the range, for numerous day jobs. A barista, a librarian, a waitress, a farmer. She had even been a mother, albeit a poor one.

I am an ordinary woman, Lola often thought, looking in the mirror at her softer stomach and looser arms—this fifty-one-year-old Pinocchio, who could be cut where once she was wooden.

Yes, she still trained, but not with the same discipline. She was still quick, but no longer breathtaking. She still had power, but her days as a force were behind her.

Benjamin Chen's voice ghosted to her from back in the day: "We are nothing without motion, Lola. Even the sharpest knife will rust."

. . .

Lola had just finished loading hay bales when her phone vibrated. Three quick thumps. *Brrrz-brrrz-brrrz.* She looked across the riding arena to the 175-yard driveway that stitched her property to Big Crow Road. The infrared sensor at the entranceway had been activated. Inside her comfortable little farmhouse, an alarm would have sounded. A single, high-pitched note. The sensor was also linked to her cell phone, for when she was outside the house. A different signal, but the same message: *You have a visitor.*

Unexpected visits were rare. Almost everything was by schedule or appointment, and that's exactly how Lola wanted it. Every now and then her veterinarian, Coot Birnie, would drop by to shoot the breeze, usually with a hot coffee and a boxful of pastries from Find's, because this was the country, and that's how country folk do. And canvassers approached on occasion, although most were deterred by the sign Lola had attached to her fencepost: I BELIEVE IN THE 2ND AMENDMENT TO PROTECT THE OTHER 26.

Lola might be a rusty knife, but she hadn't evaded Jimmy all these years by taking chances. She bolted from the trailer she'd just loaded, past the chicken coops and goat pen, to the back door of her house. She moved well, although she felt that rust, mainly in her knees and ankles. Adrenaline provided the oil. Her lungs ballooned, her eyes dilated. There was no fear. Only focus.

She burst through the back door and into the kitchen, whacked her hip on the table on her way to the hallway—she would have glided past not so many years ago—and took the stairs two at a time. The guest bedroom faced south, offering views of the horse barn, the riding arena, and the long, curved driveway. This room hadn't seen a guest since the previous owner had lived here. Lola had an exercise bike in one corner and a Weatherby Mark V bolt-action rifle in the window. She got behind the scope and sighted down the driveway.

...

She had been hiding from Jimmy, but he hadn't been hiding from her. He was not the high-profile player he used to be, but he still had influence and he liked to be heard. As such, it wasn't hard to track his business dealings and identify key employees. She had pinned the most recent photographs she could find to a bulletin board beside the window. Eight of them, including Joey Cabrini, son of Marco Cabrini, who'd shot Lola in the shoulder during her raid on Jimmy's house. Joey had his old man's curly black hair, as well as a small birthmark on his throat that would be visible through a rifle scope. There was Eddie "the Smoke" Shaw, a professional stalker, whose disguises included a variety of baseball caps and glasses, and false goatees in carrot and white. Lola was confident she could place and eliminate these men, along with other faces on her wall of fame. But Blair Mayo was a different story. Young, lethal in a way Lola used to be, Blair would require additional strategy, and would make nothing simple.

Lola glanced at the photographs now, noting distinguishing features: Joey's birthmark, the scar beneath Blair's left eye, Jared Conte's missing earlobe, Leo Rossi's crooked nose. She returned to the scope, looped her finger around the Mark V's trigger, and waited for her visitor to step into the reticle.

...

Would they advance down the driveway in broad daylight? Probably not, but they might think it was a crazy enough move to catch Lola off guard. The front of her property was a better option than the back, which was exposed between the woodland and her house, even more so after she'd hayed the long grass. Approaching under cover of darkness was smarter, of course (she had a Sightmark Night Raider scope for such an eventuality) but bringing the fight to her would always be a gamble, at any time. Jimmy didn't know what home security measures she'd taken. He was hotheaded enough to risk going in blind, but after all these years, would he take that chance?

Movement through the foliage. Lola held her breath, steadying the scope. The leaves winked yellow and gold, so magnified she could count their veins. She glimpsed blue jeans. Jimmy had always insisted his crew dress to impress. They represented him, and he was unconscionably vain. Perhaps having his face burned off had changed that.

The Mark V's muzzle inched right, mirroring her visitor's progress. Lola saw the collar of a black leather jacket, light brown hair, the flash of an ear, pink in the cold.

"Who are you?" she whispered on the exhale, then held her breath again. *And what do you want?*

She'd always believed that *if* they came, they would do so away from her property, negating any advantage she might have—alarms, vantage points, access to greater firepower, knowledge of the environment. They would ambush her on the way back from the Grocery King, perhaps, or on one of Lone Arrow's many quiet streets. It would be difficult for Lola to anticipate such an attack, but she was always prepared; she never left the house without a Glock 42 in her bra holster and a fixed-blade knife strapped to her strong side. Nebraska state law prohibited carrying a loaded shotgun in a vehicle, but she didn't drive anywhere without a sawed-off concealed beneath the dash, both barrels occupied. Would all this be enough? Lola had no idea. She knew only two things for certain: that Jimmy's crew would not kill her quickly (the boss would want to have his fun), and that they would come in numbers.

So who was this lone visitor? Not a canvasser; they only ever approached by vehicle, because her farm was so remote. Not someone looking for work, not when the ground was about to freeze. Whoever it was, he or she was nearing the apex of her driveway, and would soon come fully into view. And *if* his or her face matched one of those on the bulletin board, Lola would pull the trigger. Butch Morgan, who owned the property nearest hers, might hear the report, but gunshots weren't uncommon in the country. Butch would likely think Lola was firing a warning shot to scare off a—

All thought flew from her mind. It was as if her brain had been instantly detached and locked in a tight black box. She gasped and stepped away from the window.

"No," she said. "It can't be."

She reached for something—a scenario where this was possible, or at least made a modicum of sense—but her brain only produced small puffs of air. So she returned to the scope and watched numbly as her son, her beautiful son, advanced into the crosshairs, and back into her life.

. . .

There followed five slow seconds in which Lola felt Margaret Ward's comfortable existence slip from her shoulders like a borrowed cloak. Then she jumped into action.

She grabbed her Baby Eagle from the top drawer of her dresser, chambering a round as she broke downstairs, then through the kitchen (she didn't bang her hip on the table this time), and out the back door. Questions raised a racket in her skull. Lola ignored them—focused on the objective.

Brody.

Around the back of the farmhouse, using available cover: her pickup truck, a heap of firewood, the toolshed.

She sprinted from there to the barn, cutting through so that she could approach the driveway from the side and hopefully reach Brody without being seen. Lola had to assume Jimmy was hot on his heels. She wanted her son under cover before the bullets started to fly.

Sweat ran from her hairline. It latched her denim shirt to her back. The rust had slowed her down and set an ache in her joints, but the adrenaline was still there, producing responses that had been dormant for years. Lola felt freest when bringing her horse to gallop, but she felt fully alive in this moment. It was a familiar rush. Later, she would admit to having missed it.

She ran across the horse arena, exposed now but keeping low. The fence would mostly cover her at eye level. Brody continued toward the house, moving slowly, as if unsure. He hadn't seen her yet, but he would soon. One hell of a reunion.

Something caught her eye as she approached the driveway. A flash, quick as a blink, maybe a mile to the south. It might be sunlight winking off the windshield of a parked vehicle. Then again, it might be one of Jimmy's guys watching the farm through binoculars. She also considered the possibility of it being a tactical scope, although she didn't think so; they'd have to be quite the marksperson to guarantee nonlethal from a mile away.

They were looking for positive ID, then Jimmy's army would roll in. And she couldn't run—not with her son on the battlefield.

· · ·

Lola leaped the fence, took cover behind one of the ash trees, then broke and ran at Brody from the side. She hit him like a linebacker, carrying him across the driveway, to the cover of a tree on the other side. It happened too quickly for him to struggle. She held him down with her knee to his chest and placed the barrel of her handgun to her lips.

Mama says shhhh.

· · ·

No vehicle sounds. She waited. Brody started to squirm and she shot him a warning glance, the gun still pressed to her lips. Her other hand was on her phone, waiting for it to vibrate.

Nothing.

"Don't move, baby boy." She lifted her knee from Brody's chest and dashed to the other side of the driveway. From here, through the trees, she could see a section of Big Crow Road as it approached her property. She counted to sixty. Still nothing. Brody clambered to his feet. She held up one hand: *Wait*.

Another count. She heard the murmur of traffic on Highway 183, but that was all.

Might they advance from the north, having used Brody as a decoy? Unlikely. They would come from the front, probably in armored SUVs. They would come in force.

So where were they?

Lola moved back to Brody. He brushed dirt from his jacket (not *his* jacket—it was Ethan's; Lola recognized it immediately) and for a moment wouldn't, or couldn't, look at her. His teeth were clenched. Maybe he hadn't been followed.

"Talk to me," she said.

His eyes flashed across hers, then fixed on the branches above. His hands trembled. There were too many emotions for her to read. Just when she thought he wouldn't say anything—that she would have to do the talking, at least to begin with—he found his voice and blew her world apart.

"Jimmy Latzo found us. He killed Dad and I'm next."

He cracked, then. The strength went out of his legs and he sagged. He might have fallen if Lola hadn't caught him. She gathered him close, as she had a thousand times. He placed his head on her shoulder. A tired, scared boy.

"I need your help," he said.

Chapter Nineteen

Jimmy had offered her a room at his house rent-free—she was his *numero uno* and he wanted her close, he liked the extra security—but Blair insisted on her own space. Not just a room, but an apartment, a place she could kick off her boots and distance herself from work. She was a twenty-five-year-old woman, after all. Somewhere inside, behind the cunning and the knives, that twenty-five-year-old woman wanted to burn toast and sleep on the sofa and listen to her neighbors fuck, and it was important she had the opportunity to do just that.

More than anything, she needed time away from Jimmy. She was his power source, his battery. Just being close to him was draining.

Her phone buzzed at 11:48 A.M. A message from Jimmy: GET UR ASS HERE NOW!!! Uppercase. Three exclamation marks. There were rarely fewer than two, whatever the message. Such was his nature.

Blair waited a couple of minutes, then texted back: on my way

All lowercase. Not even a period.

She poured two half-empty glasses of wine down the sink, picked her clothes up off the floor. Memories of last night—or early this morning, to be more accurate—flickered through her mind. He said his name was Gary but she checked his wallet when he used the bathroom and it was actually Peter. He lived in Seven Springs, not Manhattan (liar), he was forty-one years old, not thirty-five (liar), and his business card revealed that he was an insurance broker, not a literary agent (liar). Peter was a competent lover, though, and he'd made her laugh more than once. A sense of humor was not as important as honesty, but it was a good quality, nonetheless.

"Should I call you?" he'd asked spiritlessly, rooting around for his socks at 6:03.

"No."

Blair often felt that these intimacies were as close as she'd ever get to feeling normal.

. . .

12:17 P.M.

WHERE THE FUCK R U!!!
the traffic sucks today
U DIDN'T TAKE THE EXPRESSWAY??
no. stopped at rite-aid. needed eyeliner
FUCKING EYELINE I TOLD U 2 GET UR ASS HETE!!!
be there in 15
FUUUUUCCCCKK!!!

Blair turned off her phone, cranked the radio, and made her way to Jimmy's. The traffic flowed smoothly and she hadn't stopped at Rite-Aid for eyeliner. These deceptions weren't in Gary the Literary Agent's league, but they were plausible, and necessary. When the boss was three-exclamation-marks excited, it was often prudent to vent him before getting too close.

...

His cigar was as fat as a table leg. Bluish brown smoke wreathed his head. Blair approached coolly. There was a smile inside the smoke—or what passed for a smile on Jimmy's damaged face.

"Here she is. At long last."

"What's going on, Jimmy?"

A smile, yes, but he wasn't fully vented. She could tell from the tension in his voice, and by the way the tip of his cigar jittered ever so slightly. Brad Lemke stood to his right. Lorne Dupont towered on the left. Six hundred pounds of muscle between them. *Maybe* enough IQ to fill an inkwell.

There was a stack of $2,000 straps on the desk in front of Jimmy. Fifteen of them. He gestured at the cash with an appraising nod.

"Yours," he said.

"Why?"

"It's a thank-you." Jimmy drew on his cigar and his smile lengthened. "We used to call it a 'bonus' back in the day. But whatever, you've earned it."

The penny dropped—the reason for Jimmy's excitement. Not anger, but elation. Blair looked at the money but didn't touch it. She hadn't earned it yet.

"Eddie should have contacted *me* first," she said, and curled her lip. Eddie the fucking Smoke, stealing her thunder. "I engineered this. It's my job."

"The fuck it is," Jimmy said. "You work for me, so it's *my* job."

Blair rolled her eyes. As if Jimmy—who had all the deftness of a land mine—could ever finagle something so intricate.

"Fine," she said.

Jimmy knocked ash from his cigar, grabbed his phone, swiped through a couple of screens. "Eddie sent me these an hour ago. They were taken this morning, between nine-fifty and ten o'clock central time."

Eleven photographs, crisp quality. The first five showed a middle-aged woman with bleached blond hair bucking hay onto a flatbed trailer. She wore black jeans, a blue denim shirt. Eddie's zoom was powerful enough to pick up the red Levi's tag stitched to the front pocket. The next three photographs were close-ups of her face, one of them in profile. The final three were of her running across a field, keeping low. White fencing provided some cover, but Eddie was elevated enough—probably positioned on the roof of his car—to see the pistol in her right hand.

"She dyed her hair, and her ass is a little rounder than it used to be." Jimmy puffed smoke and pointed at the phone in Blair's hand. "But that's her, all right. Lola Bear. We found the bitch."

"We?"

"Yeah, well . . . thanks to your crazy-ass plan." He pointed at her with the soggy end of his cigar. "But shit, Blair, it *worked*. The kid led us directly to his mommy."

"He did it knowingly," Blair said. "He's prepping her for a fight."

"And I'm going to oblige."

A distracted smile touched Blair's face. She wanted to revel in the satisfaction of having located Lola Bear, but the job was only ninety percent complete. Jimmy didn't appear to comprehend this. He pushed the money toward her—$30,000 in total—and said something about her spending it when they got back, then he laughed maniacally and banged the desk with his fist. Brad and Lorne laughed, too, with all the character of rocks in a sack. Blair looked from one face to the next. She didn't want to dampen the mood, but felt it important to point out that there was still work to do, and didn't they—

"Whoa, hold on just a second." Blair cut through her own train of thought. Jimmy's words had finally sunk in. "When we get *back*? Back from where?"

"Nebraska," Jimmy replied. His smile faltered. He flicked ash and nodded at the phone. "Lone Pine, or some shitkicking town like that—"

"Lone Arrow," Blair corrected him. She'd already scrolled to Eddie's message and clicked on the address. It brought up a satellite image of Owlfeather Farm. Blair zoomed in.

"*Arrow*. Yeah. Whatever." Jimmy's cigar sizzled as he pulled on it. "Leo and his boys are already in place. That's five. You three make eight. Jared Conte and the

Tucson Tank are meeting us at the airport. Ten will be enough. I've chartered a jet that will have us touching down at four-oh-five central."

"Jimmy, listen to me—"

"If all goes to plan, I'll be spilling Lola's blood—and plenty of it—before nightfall. I'm going to kill the kid, too. While she watches."

"*Jimmy.*" Blair didn't raise her voice, but she gave it a keen edge, and it sliced through the room like a guillotine. Jimmy sat back in his seat, the cigar parked between two fingers. The tip still jittered.

"What's the problem?" he asked.

"We're not going to Nebraska."

"Oh, but we are." He pressed his tongue against the inside of his cheek. This looked like so many of his expressions, but she'd been with him long enough to know it was frustration, bordering on anger. "We are going, we will make misery, and we will sing 'Beautiful *fucking* Nebraska' while we do."

"You're emotional. That's understandable." Blair took a deep breath, trying to control her own emotion. She hadn't orchestrated this whole maneuver for it to collapse now. "But you're not thinking clearly."

The tip of Jimmy's cigar crackled, or it might have been the fire in his eyes. "I have dreamed about Lola every night since dragging myself off life support.

Vivid, beautiful dreams. I have developed strength and endurance, and rebuilt my empire, for the sole purpose of making her pay for what she took from me. Now I know where she is."

"I know that, Jimmy, but—"

"Trust me, Blair, I have never thought clearer than I'm thinking right now."

"She'll kill us all," Blair said. She spoke softly, but her words chimed with a certainty that was hard to ignore. Even Lorne, who likely wouldn't feel a pool cue broken across his shoulders, looked uncomfortable.

Jimmy stubbed out his cigar with angry little jabs.

"Fuck you," he said.

"Look at this satellite image," Blair urged, holding his phone so he could see. She centered on Owlfeather Farm, then pinched and zoomed out. "A farmhouse, a barn, a couple of small buildings—all of it surrounded by open land. She'll see us coming and pick us off. One. By. One."

"Then we'll attack at night, while she's asleep." Jimmy looked at Brad and Lorne for support and they nodded hesitantly.

"We don't know her defenses. She's probably rigged the land with alarms and motion sensors. Jesus, she might have a bunch of redneck security guards armed with AKs." Blair kept the incredulity from her tone. It wouldn't do to make Jimmy feel as stupid as he actually was. "Of course, the biggest problem with infiltrating at night is that *we* won't be able to see her."

"We'll use night-vision equipment," Jimmy said. He banged his fist on the desk again, not elatedly this time. "We'll recon the property. Drive a fucking AFV through her front door. Whatever it takes."

"She'll kill us all."

Jimmy stood up quickly, sending his chair skating backward. It thumped against the wall hard enough to leave a mark. He balled his fists and discharged a broad variety of expletives. Lorne Dupont wisely shuffled several feet to the left, removing himself from Jimmy's radius.

Blair said nothing. She stood with her eyes to the front and waited for the flames to die. Eventually, they did. Jimmy dragged his hands through his hair, then stepped to the window and looked out.

"That oak has always been tenacious," he said plaintively. "Some of its leaves are still green."

It might have been the silvery light against his skin, or the set of his shoulders as he expanded his chest and breathed, but in that moment Blair thought she saw the man he used to be, before Lola Bear, before the scars. She tried to envision a different life for him, as a doctor or teacher, but such imaginings were beyond her. Jimmy embodied infamy and vice like a Maserati embodied speed. It was in the slope of his neck, in the bumps of his knuckles, in every motor neuron and sensory receptor. His destiny had been rifled like a gun barrel.

"What's the point of all this?" he said a moment later. He had relaxed his body but his voice was still tight and high. "What's the point of *you*, Blair? Or Leo, or Jared, or any one of the others? Why spend so much time and money on finding Lola Bear, if all we're going to do is stand back and see what happens next?"

"We're not going to stand back," Blair said, measuring not only her words, but the spaces between them. "This is when we make our next move."

"Oh right. *Another* move. You see, Blair, I think you're taking this 'patient approach' thing too far." He turned away from the window. The light, now, made him appear agitated and savage. "I say we go in full force and we get that bitch."

"It's your call, Jimmy," Blair said. Her voice fluttered—a touch of emotion sneaking through. "But if you do that, you can count me out."

"Fuck you, Blair. This is what I *trained* you for. The weapons combat. The Krav fucking Maga." He blustered toward her, wringing his fists again. "What are you, *scared?*"

"I am *not* scared of Lola Bear. I will dismantle that bitch. But taking the fight to her, on her turf, is suicide." Blair tapped two fingers off the side of her skull. "*Brains*, Jimmy."

"Fuck brains, and fuck you." Jimmy snatched his cell phone from her hand and looked at Lola's photograph. "We finally have her in our sights. This is the time for brawn."

He scrolled to another photograph and stared at it for a long time. The years passed across his face like silhouettes on a screen. The dreams he'd mentioned flickered in his eyes. "Lola," he breathed, then said it again, and again. His mouth glistened. Eventually, he turned off his phone, then pulled up his chair and dropped into it.

Blair steadied herself and tried once again to reason with him.

"You *will* need your army, Jimmy. Every man you've got. You'll need me, too. But we have to stack the advantages in our favor." She leaned across his desk, her fists knotted on the polished wood. "We have to bring the fight here."

Jimmy looked at her. He'd come a long way, but he was still wrecked inside. Too many open wounds. Only Lola could heal him completely.

"I appreciate the bonus, but the job isn't finished."

Blair pushed the money toward him. "I didn't say I'd find Lola Bear, I said I'd *deliver* her."

Jimmy smiled humorlessly and shook his head. "And how are you going to do that?"

There. She had him. Sweet relief. There'd been some tricky pieces, but they clicked into place, the same way they had when she got to Brody at Rocky T's. The feel-good chemicals—dopamine, serotonin—flooded her. This was why she lived. The mastery, the control, the breathtaking rush of it all. She tingled to the tips of her fingers and smiled. If only Gary the Literary Agent could see her now.

"You still want to go after the cripple?" she asked.

Chapter Twenty

All kinds of things were happening inside him. Fireworks. Meteor storms. Earthquakes. He was in his mother's arms. She held him like she used to, one hand just above his left hip, the other cupping the back of his neck. Beneath the hay and sweat, she even smelled the same. This should have induced a flood of memories, but there was nothing beyond the meteor storms and earthquakes. It lasted only seconds, perhaps, but it felt longer, and just when he started to get a sense of himself, she turned him around and planted her palm between his shoulder blades.

"Move your ass."

They dashed toward the house, Brody in front, Lola right behind. She glanced over her shoulder several times, pistol at the ready. In the aftermath of the fireworks, a curious concern surfaced in Brody's mind: What kind of life must his mother live, to be perpetually prepared for a situation like this? Her heart would be like a paperweight, he thought, keeping everything in order but essentially dead. Could she even dream when she slept with one eye open?

They went in through the back door. Lola locked and bolted it behind her, then took the lead. Pistol in hand, she checked the downstairs rooms and made certain the front door was locked (Brody had a feeling it was *always* locked) before going upstairs. She paused on the landing, attentive to every small sound, then opened the door to her bedroom. After checking the closet and en suite, she motioned to Brody.

"In here."

He nodded from a thousand miles away and entered the room. His mom glanced out the window, her gaze sweeping the land at the rear of her property.

"I need you to focus," she said, touching one shoulder and turning him toward her. "Can you do that for me?"

"Sure," he said with a cracked voice. He didn't think he could, though. His focus was still on the driveway, having been knocked from his body when she tackled him broadside.

"Okay. Good." She looked into his eyes. "You're here, Brody, with me, but do I need to worry about your sister?"

"No."

"You're sure? Where is she?"

"Safe," he replied. It seemed he could only manage one word at a time.

Lola stared at him a second longer—stared *hard*—then nodded and clapped him on the shoulder. "Stay here. I'll be right back."

She left the bedroom, still behind her pistol. Brody heard doors opening. He dropped his bag, sat on the edge of her bed, and looked numbly around. It was an unloved space, appropriate for an unloved person. There was no softness or delicacy. The walls were painted sunflower yellow (many years ago, judging by the water marks and discoloration), and were bare except for a small painting of a horse. The dresser housed no perfumes or makeup, only an iPad and a stack of magazines. Clothes were draped over the back of a chair. There was a paperback on the floor next to the bed. No nightstands. Brody felt an odd grief for her, then realized this wasn't his mother's room—his mother, Natalie Ellis née Myles, who'd laughed with him and loved him and sat him on the throne of her world. This was Lola Bear's room, and Lola was an obdurate killer with a paperweight for a heart.

"Killer," he mumbled through dry lips. And yes, that was why he was here, the *only* reason. This wasn't about reuniting with his mom like some desperate cub. It was about getting Jimmy Latzo off his back and avenging his father's death.

I need you to focus. Can you do that for me?

Brody stood up, blinked several times, breathed in through his nose and out through his mouth. Goose-flesh rippled his arms.

"I've got this," he said to himself, then Lola came back into the room and thrust a semiautomatic rifle into his hands.

...

She opened the window. A cold breeze lifted the curtains and puffed the hair from Brody's brow. It felt wonderful. Unlike the rifle he held—the very real, very lethal gun, which had never top-fired blanks, and couldn't be bought for sixty bucks and a baseball cap. A metallic taste flooded Brody's mouth. He pined for his replica.

Lola registered the dumbfounded expression on his face (he thought it must be hard to miss). "That's an MMR Carbine," she said. "Built on the AR-15 platform."

"It's a fucking *assault* rifle."

"Technically, it's not, because it's semi, not fully automatic. A bullshit distinction, if you ask me, because it'll still fire as fast as you can cycle the trigger." Lola swept the magazines onto the floor, spun the iPad onto the bed, and dragged the dresser over to the window. "It's designed to perform devastating damage, very quickly. So yeah, it's a fucking assault rifle."

Brody looked from the MMR, to his mom, then back again. "What do you expect *me* to do with it?"

"Do you know that one in five guns bought legally in this country is an AR-15, or variant? It's the nation's number-one choice for home defense." She gestured out the window. "So . . . defend."

Brody didn't move. The rifle wasn't heavy—it was surprisingly light, in fact—but lifting it was another matter.

"Listen to me," Lola said, stepping toward him. He edged backward, as if she were an animal with a tendency to bite. "Everything between the tree line and the house is my land. It's wide open. No cover. I don't think you'll have to pull the trigger. But if you *do*, don't worry about accuracy, just aim toward the assailant. Get anywhere close and they'll retreat or go prone. If there's more than one, alternate between them. I'll assist from the room next door, and

I'll also cover the front in case they come from both directions."

"I don't know if I can shoot *at* someone," Brody said, but recalled that he *could*, if sufficiently pushed. The incident in Bayonet dashed across his mind, and he remembered the hard shift he'd felt inside—the sudden and unnerving coldness in his veins. A little something he'd inherited from his mom, as it turned out. "I just . . . I . . ."

"It's time to snap into survival mode. Now watch." Lola knelt in front of the dresser, her arms poised, demonstrating position. "Four points of contact: shooting hand, supporting hand, shoulder, and cheek. Bring the sights to your eye, not the other way around. Use the dresser for stability, and don't grip the gun too tightly."

"This can't be happening," Brody whispered.

"Oh, it's happening," Lola assured him. "And if you need extra motivation: just know that anybody who approaches from that direction likely had a hand in killing your father, and that they're coming here to kill us both."

A blank expression from Brody. His mind was anything but; he imagined gray-faced mobsters accosting his old man, dragging him into the service elevator of the Folgt Building, then dangling him from the roof-top while Jimmy fired questions.

He imagined those same mobsters emerging from the woods at the back of his mom's land, weapons strapped to their bodies.

Lola grasped his shoulder—man, she was *strong*—positioned him in front of the dresser, kicked the back of his right leg so he dropped to one knee. "Supporting hand here, on the handguard." She moved his left hand into position, palm beneath and thumb over the barrel. "Shooting hand here, on the pistol grip." Same again, placing his right hand where it needed to be. "All fingers stay clear of the trigger guard until you have a target. Understand?"

"Yes," he said, and here came the adrenaline—bouncing and tumbling, like barrels going downhill.

"Now pull the buttstock into your shoulder. Here." She showed him, placing her hands over his and drawing back until the stock was tucked into the pocket of his right shoulder. "That's good. Keep it on the inside. Nice and secure. Remember: bring the sights toward you, don't hunker over the gun."

"Like this?"

"Yes, but you're twisting your body. Square your shoulders as much as you can, tuck your elbows in. That'll help with recoil and shot recovery—that's the adjustment your body and the rifle need to make between shots. The smaller the adjustment, the better."

"It's a lot to remember," Brody gasped. The window might be open, but there was less oxygen in the room, he was sure of it.

"The safety selector is here, just north of the pistol grip. You don't have to hunt for it; inch your right thumb up and you'll find it."

"This thing?"

"Yes. Thumb the switch down when you're ready to fire—*ready* being the operative word. Do *not* engage the safety until you have mounted the rifle and acquired a target."

"Which won't happen," Brody said. He glanced at his mom with big eyes. "They won't come this way, right?"

"I doubt it," Lola said. "But we need to be ready, just in case. Now, this is a semiautomatic rifle, which means—"

"I know what it means. One bullet for every trigger pull. There's been enough on TV about guns lately." He palmed sweat from his brow, then got back into position. "None of it good."

"When fatigue sets in—and it will, into your arms and legs—get up and shake it out. Stretch. Take five.

But keep your eye on that window. If you see movement at the tree line, it's probably a deer. Use the optic if you want to make sure." She tapped a knurled wheel on the riflescope. "This adjusts the magnification. Play around with it a little. Get comfortable."

Brody nodded, swallowed awkwardly. Lola stared at him for a second, then—unbelievably—kissed the top of his head and swept from the room.

"We need to talk," she called from the hallway. "We'll do it later. For now, I need your help to keep us alive."

. . .

His mom never asked if he'd been followed. Quite aside from it being an inane question, it was, in this instance, entirely redundant. His very presence had put her on high alert. Being holed up, scoping her acreage for threats, was not the retaliatory response he'd hoped for, but did he honestly expect her to smear greasepaint across her face, strap an RPG to her back, and take the fight to Jimmy? Okay, so he'd fantasized as much on the journey here, but the reality was different. They would need to withstand the impending assault, then pick up the pieces—hopefully Jimmy's—after the smoke had cleared.

The minutes stretched out. Twenty . . . forty-five . . . eighty. Lola called to him every so often. "Give me a status report," and, less militarily, "Anything, Brody?" This was obviously to keep him on his toes. On one occasion she asked, with a note of concern, "How are you holding up?"

"Been better," he called back.

More than once, he told himself that it had been a good decision to leave Molly with Renée. If he'd done anything right during this whole nightmare, it was that.

His adrenaline evaporated deep into the second hour. Brody set the rifle down, stood up, and stretched. His arms were on fire. Pain lanced from his knees to his hips. He paced the breadth of the room, working out the discomfort. Time trickled steadily by. Brody didn't know how long, but at some point he noticed the light had changed.

He mounted the rifle again, scoping from northeast to northwest and back again. How many times? Fifty? One hundred? All emotion drained from him, then exhaustion moved in. Brody stretched again, easing the stiffness from his arms and legs. Take five, his mom had said, so he did. The next thing he knew, he was climbing out of a light doze, his forehead resting on top of the dresser.

"Oh shit."

He snapped upright, looked out the window, certain he would see a troop of Jimmy's boys within twenty yards of the house. The sun had dipped westward, pushing its light into a pillow of cloud. It was murky out there, but he was able to see that his mom's acreage was as empty and featureless as it had been all day.

"Okay." Brody breathed, one hand on his chest. "No one there."

His mom came in several minutes later with packaged food. Potato chips, a Snickers, a can of Welch's Grape Soda. "It's not healthy, but the sugar should pep you up." Brody tore into the Snickers bar, nodding gratefully. He took a bite, swallowed, then pointed out the window.

"It's getting too dark to see."

Lola nodded, then left the room. She returned a moment later with a new scope, which she fitted to the MMR.

"That's a thermal scope," she said. Her hair was tied back, and the pistol she'd been carrying was now holstered to her right hip. "The clarity and magnification aren't as good, but you can pick up a heat signature at sixteen hundred yards. You'll see anything—or anybody—coming out of those woods."

"Right," Brody mumbled around a mouthful of his candy bar.

"A lot of wildlife here, especially at night. Deer and coyote, mostly." Lola cracked a tired smile. "Those coyotes are a pain in the ass. Feel free to get some target practice in."

The next few hours moved languidly. It was dark, cold, and uncomfortable. The sugar *did* lift him, but not for long. His exhaustion was as lumbering, yet oddly attractive, as a sea turtle, and it flopped across him by inches. He wondered how his mom was doing. Was she equally exhausted, or had she trained herself to operate without sleep, like an elite sniper? *Not this kid,* Brody thought, and closed his eyes for a second— maybe a couple of minutes, ten at the most—before returning to the scope.

He saw deer, or *thought* he did, a dozen of them, highlighted a hot white though the thermal optic— his tiredness underscored when they separated into a thousand brilliant particles and drifted across the darkness like dandelion seeds.

. . .

Brody slept, properly and deeply. He stirred in the early hours to find himself in his mom's bed, the covers pulled up to his chest. *She tucked me in,* he thought blearily. It was dark but he saw her outline at the window, scanning her property through the riflescope.

Chapter Twenty-One

"Tell me about Molly. Where is she?"

His mom stood in the space previously occupied by the dresser. She *was* tired, despite whatever training she'd had. Not even the vivid morning light could lift the pallor from her skin. Her eyes, though, sparkled with something Brody couldn't read, and didn't like.

"With Renée." He stepped out of the en suite, having just brushed his teeth and splashed his armpits with cold water. In terms of his morning ablutions, this would have to do.

"You didn't think," Lola said, "that she'd be safer here?"

"What? No. Jesus, no." Brody shook his head. He gestured at the gun in her holster, then at the bigger gun on the dresser. "Are you serious? This is a fucking war zone."

Lola narrowed her eyes, hands on her hips. Silence fell between them. Somewhere, a bird called.

"Listen," Brody began, as if this needed further justification. "I'm running short on cash. Molly was almost out of meds. All things considered, Renée is in a much better position to take care of her."

Lola pondered this for a moment, then nodded. "Okay," she said. It was the response Brody wanted, but he still didn't care for that look in her eye.

She left the room, heading back to her window. Brody started to follow—he wanted to dig into her odd curiosity; Jesus, shouldn't *he* be the one asking questions?—when an alarm sounded. A single high note.

• • •

Lola got into position: behind a rifle in the front window. A shooter's rifle, Brody thought, designed for power, distance, and accuracy. He stood numbly on the landing. Without breaking her sight picture, she said to him, "It's probably farm business, but if I give the go, grab the MMR and start laying down suppressive fire from the next room."

"Suppressive fire," Brody repeated. Four weeks ago, he'd been sprawled across Tyrese's sofa, watching *The People's Court* on Channel 62. He tried drawing a neat line from there to here, but couldn't. That line made no sense.

He moved, though, and with purpose. He grabbed the MMR from the dresser. It already felt familiar—comfortable, even. Engaging in any kind of conflict would knock that familiarity into a different time zone, but he didn't have to worry about that for now; his mom met him on the landing. She'd taken off her holster and tucked the pistol into the back of her jeans.

"Stand down, soldier," she said. "It's just Hudson."

"Hudson?"

"From the Country Market. He's here to pick up the eggs."

...

The window in the spare room was open and Brody caught snatches of his mom's conversation with Hudson. Her tone was convivial, and he detected a subtle change in her accent—a shift in her vowels—that deepened the Midwest connection. It was convincing, and Brody was impressed with how smoothly she'd switched from gun-savvy mom to happy-go-lucky cowgirl. Must be some kind of survival mechanism, he thought. Serial killers probably had the same chameleonic trait.

This show had drawn him into the spare room. He watched from the window for a moment, making sure he wasn't seen. Hudson had a ruddy face and Paul Newman eyes, and his posturing suggested he might have a soft spot for Lola—or Margaret, as he knew her. He licked his lips frequently, thumbs hooked into the belt loops of his jeans. It was an interesting display on both parts, but Brody didn't watch for long; his attention was claimed first by the bolt-action rifle set up in front of the window—it looked powerful enough to drop a charging rhino—and then by the bulletin board on the wall. Specifically, the photographs pinned to it.

"No fucking way."

Eight headshots, cropped and enlarged. Three of the faces were familiar: Jimmy Latzo's, with his Gotti hairdo and unmistakable scarring. This was the same photograph that accompanied the article in *The Mighty Penn Online*, reporting that Jimmy was being questioned in connection with the murder of Art Binkle, whose severed head was discovered spinning on a turntable at 45 rpm. There were photographs of Leo and Joey, too—Brody's nemeses from the motel in Bayonet.

Three familiar faces, and one other that was *very* familiar.

"Hello, Blair."

Hers was in the middle. A candid shot, no doubt lifted from some online source. Her hair was brown, sensibly pulled back from her face, not purple and punky. Without the wild makeup, she looked both older than the girl who'd sat across from him at Rocky T's, and younger. Brody might not have recognized her at all, but the cunning in her eyes was one hundred percent Blair. He recalled how she'd drawn him in—her clever fabrications, the sexually loaded body language—only to tear his world apart.

Hudson rolled out a big old country laugh. It was a pleasing sound, if not entirely genuine. Brody dragged his eyes from Blair's headshot and approached the window again. His mom appeared relaxed—just another Wednesday morning in Lone Arrow, Nebraska. He could see the shape of the pistol beneath her shirt, though. A suitable metaphor for the margin between lives.

"Say, Huddy," she said, stepping a little closer to him. "You get any out-of-towners through the store yesterday?"

"I'd say likely. We're right off the 183. See a strange face or two most days." Hudson tucked his hands into his back pockets. "Why'd you ask?"

"Had a fella come by here," Lola replied. "Pencil-pusher. From the Federal Highway Administration, he said."

"That so?"

"Asking questions about the land." Pronounced *lend* with the accent. "Boundaries and such. Says not to be surprised if I see surveyor types in the area. You see anybody like that on the way out here?"

Hudson removed one hand from his back pocket to rub his chin. "Hmm, can't say that I did."

"Likely parked up in SUVs, or some other corporate vehicle?"

Hudson snapped his fingers. "Shoot, Maggie, I *did* see a car parked out by Crandall's place. Not an SUV. A Nissan, or some other Jap model." He took a step back and peered from east to west, as if checking for traffic. "You think they're looking to buy you out, run a highway through here?"

"They'll do it over my bones," Lola said, and that earned another big old laugh from Hudson. Lola laughed, too—she was very convincing—and led Hudson around the side of the farmhouse, but not before casting a deep, searching stare at the driveway.

Brody stepped away from the window, thinking that Lola's performance as Nebraskan Farmer was second only to her performance as Loving Mother, which she'd kept up for twelve years. Anger flashed through him. A feeling of betrayal, too, and disjunction. He wanted to hold on to those negative emotions; to relinquish them would be to allow room for forgiveness, and he wasn't ready for that. Or so he believed. He looked at the bulletin board again—all those people who wanted her dead—then at the rifle. It was fixed to a hunting tripod, and it was this, the permanence of it, that struck him inside. This woman lived in fear, and had since Jimmy Latzo stepped onto the warpath. She'd spent most of her life looking over her shoulder.

She loved you, Brody, Renée had said. The kindness in her eyes had been deep. As had the honesty. *It would have broken her heart to run away. But she did it to keep you safe—to move the target away from you.*

Sympathy rose above all other emotions. It was unexpected, and disconcerting. Brody ran his hands through his hair and tried to recall the anger. A cold and dependable sentiment. But it had diminished. The size of a coin.

. . .

He checked the back window, scoped the tree line. His mom joined him minutes later.

"There's a car out near Crandall's place," she said. "About a mile from here. I think it's Eddie the Smoke."

"Is he dangerous?"

"Not directly. He used to be a paparazzo. Now he's a cross between a private eye and a stalker. He follows people, and watches them."

"And he's got eyes on us?" Brody asked.

"Right. And if we move, he'll follow."

"So we just stay here?"

"You got it." Lola managed a dry smile. "If you weren't here, I'd take Eddie out, then hit the road. I'm not sure where I'd go; I've run out of lives. But I'd find a way . . . somehow."

"Am I complicating your plans?" Brody cocked an eyebrow.

"If I run," Lola explained, "Jimmy will come after you, and I can't allow that to happen."

"Then take us with you," Brody said. "Me and Molly. We'll all start again—look out for one another."

"I care too much to subject you to this life." Lola shook her head. "That's the reason I ran away last time."

"You care?"

Lola didn't reply, but she lowered her eyes. A glimmer of emotion.

"So what do we do?" Brody asked, letting it go.

"The only thing we *can* do," Lola replied. "We wait."

She returned to her station. Brody crouched in front of the window and looked across her acreage. He saw movement, but didn't panic this time. It was more deer, at the edge of the tree line, a mother and her fawn. Brody studied them through the scope. They made him smile.

Satisfied the coast was clear, he left his window to join Lola in the spare room. She was curling twenty-five-pound dumbbells. Three sets of ten. Her biceps rolled behind her shirtsleeves, straining at the fabric. She was a year older than Renée, which put her at a spirited fifty-one. Brody watched her, feeling a jab of pride—this accompanied by the now-familiar sting of having been deceived.

"Hey," she said, setting the dumbbells down beside her exercise bike. Brody thought she might drop into a plank position, or start doing push-ups, but she stayed on her feet.

"Hey," Brody said. His gaze shifted around the room. Another unloved space. He lingered for a moment on Blair's photograph, then looked at the rifle in the window. "All clear out back. I think you're right; no one's coming that way."

"Probably not."

He took in the view: one hundred yards of open driveway, flanked by ash trees, curving east for another seventy yards or so toward the road. The horse arena was to the right of the driveway, and the barn—OWLFEATHER FARM painted above the doors in yellow letters—was to the right of this. He saw a strip of Big Crow Road, and then it was flat country all the way to the horizon.

"You think they'll come in cars?" Brody asked. "Or on foot, using the trees for cover?"

"Cars, I think," Lola said, joining him at the window. "At least until I hit their tires. Or take out the drivers, if they're not behind bullet-resistant glass. They'll get as close as they can, though, then they'll use cover."

"It'll happen quickly."

"Yeah, and it'll be over quickly." Lola sighed. "One way or another."

"At least you won't have to hide anymore." Brody ran his finger along the buttstock of the rifle. His other hand was clenched, drumming lightly against his thigh. "I had to come. You know that, right?"

"I know that."

"I knew I was bringing a war."

"You didn't bring anything that wasn't already here," Lola said. "Why do you think I have all this hardware?"

Brody nodded and looked down at the rifle between them. "What kind of gun is this?"

"It's a Mark V DGR," Lola replied. "DGR stands for dangerous game rifle."

"Dangerous? That's perfect for Jimmy."

"It's bolt-action, so it's slower than the MMR, and it only holds four rounds—one in the chamber, three in the drop box." Lola reached beneath the rifle and ejected a compact magazine. Cartridges glittered inside. "I can switch this out quickly, though, and the .300 Weatherby mag will stop anything that comes down the driveway."

"I remember when you used to bake muffins," Brody said.

"Yeah?" Lola clicked the drop box back into place. "I still bake muffins."

"Chocolate chip?"

"You know it."

They both smiled. It was strained, but mostly pleasant. Brody turned his attention back to the window. The ash trees shook their beautiful yellow leaves in the clear morning light. The goats bleated in their pen.

"You have an alarm?" he asked, remembering the shrill tone that had filled the house prior to Hudson's arrival.

"My early warning system," Lola said. "It's rigged to a sensor at the bottom of the driveway."

"So why bother watching the front?" Brody asked. "Why not just get into position when you hear the alarm?"

"If Jimmy attacks, he's going to come hard and fast. Every second is critical. I want to be behind that rifle, and ready." She drew an invisible line from her right eye to the point where the driveway curved. "And for your information, I've also been watching both sides—"

"If?" Brody cut in.

Lola stumbled on her words and looked at him. "Huh?"

"You said if Jimmy comes. *If.*" Brody frowned. "You think he's had a change of heart?"

"No, I don't. It's just . . ." More stumbling. Her eyes danced left and right, then settled on her boot tops. A wisp of hair had worked itself loose and fluttered across her brow.

"You're not telling me something," Brody said.

"Okay." She nodded, folded her arms. "But before I say anything, you have to understand that I'm hard-wired to analyze a situation and consider all possible outcomes. This means looking seriously at worst-case scenarios."

"And?"

"Jimmy's a goddamn pit bull. He has a small brain and a short fuse. Which makes me wonder why he hasn't attacked already."

"He's putting his pieces into place," Brody said.

"Even that's too smart for him," Lola said. "But yes, he's making moves, somehow, some way. He's waited a long time to get his hands on me, and he won't want to screw it up."

"What are you thinking?"

"Best-case scenario: he comes here hotheaded—hoping to take me by surprise—and I shoot him dead." She patted the top of the rifle as she might a dog. "*Real* dead this time. Then you and Molly can live here with me. You can feed the chickens, ride the horses. We all live happily ever after."

"Worst-case?"

Her eyes dipped again. "Jimmy gets smart, and he uses Molly to bait me out."

A cold feeling flooded from the pit of Brody's stomach. It went down his legs first, then it hit his heart, his throat, his brain. He gasped—every breath was a thin effort. Frost flowers bloomed across his mind. His mom reached for him but he knocked her hand away.

"That can't happen," he hissed. Their earlier conversation recurred—Lola asking where Molly was, and if he'd considered that she might be safer here, with them. Was this *his* fault? In his endeavor to do something absolutely right, had he in fact done something terribly wrong? He shook his head and pointed a trembling finger at his mom. "That *cannot* happen."

"Take a breath, Brody. Calm down."

He nodded. His gasps lengthened into short breaths. The cold feeling was replaced by a dull nausea.

"Listen to me," Lola continued. She reached for him again, this time taking his hand and squeezing reassuringly. "It probably *won't* happen. Jimmy has always been predictable, and holding Molly hostage doesn't fit his MO. He has the cruelty, but not the cunning."

On this last word, Brody's eyes snapped to the bulletin board. He shook off his mom's hand, stepped around the rifle, and tapped Blair's headshot.

"*She* has the cunning," he said. "And I think she might be running the show."

"You know her?"

"Yeah, that's Blair. She was the one who suckered me into this whole thing." He spoke through clenched teeth. "She's . . . slippery."

"And deadly," Lola said, looking at the photograph. "Blair Mayo. She's a two-time state boxing champion. She also has distinctions in kung fu and Krav Maga—"

"Krav what?"

"Maga. It's an Israeli self-defense system. Incredibly brutal. As if that wasn't enough, she's the first female to win the Western Penn 3-Gun since I won it in 1990."

"Jesus," Brody said. He recalled her coquettishness, the way she'd sucked on her straw—*Dee-fucking-lish*—and batted her eyelashes. A masquerade, obviously, but it was still a stretch to connect that Miley Cyrus version of Blair to the John Wick version his mom had unveiled. "I can't even . . ."

Lola pulled her cell phone from her pocket, opened her browser, then tapped on a series of links she'd bookmarked—stories from *The MMA Report, East Coast Boxing, The 48 Gun Club*. They featured various action shots of Blair: firing a semiautomatic pistol; throwing leather in the ring; hoisting a trophy after winning a kung fu tournament. The last link brought up a story about Blair putting an opponent—a fierce rival—into a coma with a roundhouse kick.

"Holy shit," Brody said. His nausea had abated, replaced by a fluttering that filled his rib cage like spooked birds. He wanted to run, to scream, to reach inside the photographs of Blair and Jimmy, and twist their necks until something broke.

Leo and Joey looked tame in comparison. He bounced the side of his fist off their faces.

"I know these motherfuckers, too."

"Leo Rossi and Joey Cabrini," his mom said.

"They jumped us in Mississippi, then let us go." He recalled the misery of seeing Molly with a gun locked to her head, and the hard shift this had encouraged inside him. "They were herding us toward you."

"We need to talk," Lola said, putting her phone away. "I want to know everything that happened. I *do*. But I have too many other things to think about right now."

Brody sagged against the wall. He hurt throughout. "Molly. Jesus, we . . . we need to warn her somehow. We can contact Renée—"

"Brody—"

"Or call the police—"

"Brody, *listen*." There was a snap to her voice that he recognized from when he was a kid—when he liberated brownies from the Tupperware on top of the fridge, or watched R-rated comedy skits on YouTube. "You've been here nearly twenty-four hours. If Jimmy wants to go after Molly, he'll have her already."

"And this worst-case scenario didn't occur to you yesterday?"

"I expected an immediate attack," Lola said. "When it didn't happen, I started to run through alternative strategies. Everything from his assembling a battalion to air-dropping teargas on the house. The Molly scenario occurred to me late last night."

"Jesus *Christ.*"

"The best thing we can do right now is stay focused. Stay strong." Lola's voice was taut, but not without compassion. "Jimmy will show his hand soon enough, and I *will* respond."

Brody nodded meekly, head low. She was a warrior—could hit without aiming, kill without qualm, dismantle armies. He wasn't going to cry in front of her, but he wanted to. And she must have sensed this, because she took him into her arms and held him until the spooked birds quieted.

"I'm not going to let anything happen to Molly," she assured him. "And I'm not going to let anything happen to you."

Brody nodded, feeling small and young.

"Do you hear me?"

"Yes," he croaked.

"Do you *hear* me?"

"Yes."

She continued to hold him—one hand just above his left hip, the other cupping the back of his neck—and he found comfort in her strength, her protection, while bleakly aware of the imagery: a deer and her fawn, viewed through a riflescope.

Chapter Twenty-Two

Brody cooked breakfast while his mom kept a lookout. This was her suggestion, and although he didn't have much of an appetite, he obliged; he was happy to escape that upstairs room for a while and apply his mind to something normal. He fried bacon and scrambled eggs, trying not to think about Molly. The view from the kitchen window helped: a scratch of dusty yard, the chicken coops, the edge of a field where cows cropped grass and jostled their big, beautiful bodies against the fence. Once or twice, Brody imagined living here—in a more peaceful time—waking early to feed the chickens and muck out the stables, then sitting down to a hearty breakfast while cows lowed in the background. It was a simple, pleasing fantasy, but broken every time his mom's footfalls thudded from one room to the next.

They ate in the spare room, the photos of Jimmy, Blair, et al., staring down at them, the rifle hoisted on its tripod, sentinel-like. Lola wolfed her food and left not a morsel. Brody nudged his with a fork.

"Good," she said, wiping Tabasco from her chin.

"You learn to cook in a hurry," Brody said, "when your mom runs away and your dad has to pull double shifts to keep the roof over your head."

Lola ignored this. She pointed her fork at his plate. "You need to eat."

"Not hungry."

"Don't care. Eat. Keep your strength up."

He ate, but listlessly, and didn't enjoy it. Afterward, he washed the dishes—laughably normal behavior, and he reveled in it—then returned to his post. He scoped the back of her property for three hours, stopping only to use the bathroom and stretch when fatigue set in.

"I thought it would be over by now," he said to his mom. He'd walked to the guest room to work the tiredness from his legs. "I should be either dead or free."

"Stay alert," Lola said. She sat cross-legged on the floor, weapons and paraphernalia arranged around her. There were three different pistols, a KA-BAR knife, a stun gun that looked like a cell phone, two cans of pepper spray. "Jimmy won't be able to hold out much longer. Here, load this." She tossed him an empty magazine and a box of 9mm rounds.

"I . . . what?" He looked at her. "I don't . . ."

"Let me show you." She stood and demonstrated. "This is the back of the mag. The flat end of the round goes against this. Now take your round, use it to push down on the follower—that's this spring-loaded plate—then slide it all the way back. These little lips will keep it from popping out. Use your second round to push down on the first, slide it back. Then repeat with the third round, the fourth, and so on."

Lola handed the magazine back to him. He sat on the floor, the box of ammo beside him, and started to slide the rounds in one after the other. It was tricky to begin with—a couple of the cartridges slipped between his fingers and pinged across the floor—but he soon got the hang of it. Once the mag was full, he handed it back to Lola.

"Thank you. Good job."

"You have any other guns?"

"A shotgun in the barn," she said. "I use that for shooting skeet with the neighbors. And I have a sawed-off in the truck, beneath the dash."

"No grenade launchers or RPGs?"

"Wouldn't that be nice?" Lola picked up her KA-BAR knife and started sliding it across a whetstone. "You can only buy that kind of firepower illegally, and I've been keeping off the criminal grid."

"So that you don't alert Jimmy?"

"Exactly." She looked, for a beat, quietly impressed, then went back to the whetstone. "The black market is big, but Jimmy has a lot of contacts. It's best not to take any chances."

Brody watched Lola sharpen her knife—noting her technique—and was about to ask if he could try when her early warning system sounded. They sprang to their feet. Brody started for the bedroom to grab the MMR, but Lola held him with a raised hand. She stood in front of her rifle, looking at her cell phone.

"Five of two," she said, coolly sliding the phone into her pocket. "It's probably Janey. She comes Wednesdays and Fridays to help with the horses."

Brody stood, locked in place. He felt his heartbeat in the balls of his feet. His mom scoped the driveway for what seemed an incredibly long time, then nodded and stepped away from the rifle.

"Yeah, it's Janey." She scooted around Brody, onto the landing. "I'll send her away. But listen, I'm going to need you to pull a few shifts around the place. These animals want looking after."

Brody smirked and shook his head. "You got me loading ammo and shoveling shit," he said.

"Welcome to my world," Lola said.

...

Janey was in her early twenties, dressed in old clothes, not a spot of makeup, and disarmingly attractive. Under different circumstances, Brody would have liked her to stick around—maybe she could show him how to groom and feed the horses—but this was certainly not the time and his mom was right to send her away. Brody watched Janey's truck rumble back down the driveway, around the curve, and out of sight. Not shy of fantasy, he imagined being in her passenger seat, the radio tuned to some country-and-western station, nothing but open road ahead.

"So," Lola said, joining him again. "About that horseshit."

He spent the next two hours mucking out the stables (the shit—and there was a lot of it—was wheelbarrowed to a dry stack behind the barn), then watering and feeding the horses and other animals. His mom gave him her cell phone with the instruction to return to the house, on the double, if it buzzed three times. "That's my early warning system for when I'm working outside." It *did* buzz, while he was feeding the chickens, and he tossed the sack of scratch down and bolted for the house. This time it was the vet, who'd come—a week early, apparently—to administer biannual cattle vaccinations. Again, Lola sent him on his way.

Brody finished his chores, then showered and took up his post. He scoped the rear of the property until sundown.

. . .

It had been a warm day, but by six-thirty P.M. the temperature had dropped to the midthirties, and with the window open (for optimum visibility), Brody was forced to put on his dad's motorcycle jacket. He studied the cold twilight through the thermal scope—which he had switched himself—but a heavy layer of disquietude had obscured his concentration. Brody tried to shake it off. He paced, stretched, and splashed his face with icy water, but his unease only deepened. So he wrapped the jacket tighter around his body and went to see his mom in the spare room. She was alert, as ever, not behind the rifle but sitting against the wall, rolling a quarter across her knuckles. It glinted in the subdued lamplight.

Brody stared at her, his arms folded.

"What is it?" Lola asked.

"I don't like doing nothing," he said. "Molly might be in danger, and we're sitting here with our thumbs up our asses."

She stopped rolling the coin, flipped it, snatched it out of the air. "Okay. So what do you propose?"

"Maybe we should take the fight to Jimmy."

No response. No expression, even. Brody sat against the adjacent wall, one knee drawn to his chest. They looked at each other, their breaths visible in the cold air.

"I know you're frustrated," Lola said at last. There was thoughtfulness in her tone, but her eyes were still blank. "And angry—"

"Yes, I'm angry," Brody snapped. "I'm fucking furious. And I'm still grieving my father—the kindest, best man I've ever known."

"I know."

"No, you *don't*. You ran away. You don't know shit." Brody sighed and said under his breath, "This is all your fault."

She heard him, at least he thought she did, but she showed no sign of objection. She slipped the coin into her pocket and watched her breath flower in the air.

"I'm sorry, I just . . ." He ran one hand along his stubbly jaw. "I'm scared for Molly."

"I understand," Lola said. "And believe me, I want us all to walk away from this, alive and together. But that won't happen if we take the fight to Jimmy."

"Why not? It worked last time."

"Last time was twenty-six years ago. I was reckless then. And talented." She lowered her head. "Things have changed."

"But we have to do something."

"We're outgunned, Brody, and outnumbered. This house, with its open land and good visibility, is the only advantage we have, and I don't want to give it up." Lola gestured at the rifle in the window—the defensive center of her operation. It appeared, at that moment, quite inadequate. "Jimmy is too impatient to hold out much longer. So we're going to sit tight and see what we're dealing with."

"If he was going to attack," Brody said, "he would have done it already."

"Maybe. Probably." She blew into her hands and rubbed them together. "But not definitely. We hold our ground, maintain our advantage. At least until we get more information."

The next few minutes passed without a word between them. Brody listened to the chickens bristling, the cows mooing, the evening breeze whispering through the ash trees. A truck bounced and rumbled along Big

Crow Road. He returned to his window, but only for a moment. The scene out back was dark and empty.

"Nothing," he reported.

His mom nodded, then looked at him—a double take, of sorts. A small, knowing smile touched her lips.

"What?" Brody asked.

"That jacket," she replied. "It was your dad's."

"Oh. Yeah."

"Jacket first, motorcycle later. Am I right?"

"That was the plan."

She stared for a long time, not at him, he realized, but at some memory induced by the jacket. This angered him a little, although he didn't know why. Perhaps because, until now, she'd barely mentioned his father, and had shown no remorse.

"You have my eyes," she said, coming out of her reverie with a long blink. "My mouth. But you have his profile. I look at you in that jacket and keep thinking it's him."

"Don't," Brody said.

"Don't what?"

"Talk about him." He shook his head. "You don't deserve that."

This drew a rare beat of emotion: *hurt*. Brody saw it in her eyes. Just a flash, then gone.

"Okay," she said. She took a breath that filled her chest and let it out slowly. "Then let's talk about you."

"You're suddenly interested?" Brody spread his hands. "You want me to summarize twelve years in . . . what, five minutes? Ten?"

"That's not what I meant," Lola said patiently. "I know what you've been up to. You took drumming lessons when you were fourteen and started a band called Righteous Mojo, but then broke your ankle wakeboarding on Lake Murray and never drummed again. You had a dog-sitting job for three days, but got fired after you lost the dog. You sold your PlayStation to buy Molly a ticket to see Lady Gaga. Your first car was a 1999 Pontiac Sunfire—"

"First and last."

"You dropped out of high school when you were seventeen—a year from graduation. And oh, Brody, I was heartbroken, but I *get* it, and I have no right to be mad."

"No right at all."

"You got a job bussing tables at Angel's Diner, then working the drive-through at the McDonald's on Aqua Street. You dated Emily Knowles for four months, and Bianca Ciaramella for—"

"Okay, okay, I get it." Brody held up his hands. "So you've been stalking my Facebook."

"Your Instagram, too," Lola said. "And your Myspace, when that was a thing."

"Doesn't make you Mom of the Year." Brody leaned against the wall, then dropped into a sitting position. He was still mad, but it was oddly comforting to know that his mom had been watching him from afar. *She loved you, Brody,* Renée spoke up in his mind again. *It would have broken her heart to run away.* He looked at her and shrugged. "Is this it? Are we talking now?"

"Yeah," Lola said. She checked the time on her cell: 19:46. "You can tell me the fun stuff later. Right now I want to know what happened to you, and how you found me."

. . .

The story itself didn't take long—he'd become adept at telling it—but he paused twice to scope the back of the farm (while Lola checked east and west), and again to fetch provisions from downstairs. By the time he'd finished, it was almost ten. The floor of the spare room was littered with empty juice boxes and assorted wrappers.

Lola sat pensively. Every now and then she blinked slowly, or creased her brow. Otherwise, she was still.

"Not one part of this has been easy, Mom," Brody said. "It's been a long, hard road. And scary. But here I am."

It occurred to him that this was the first time he'd called her "Mom" since arriving. There'd been no hesitation, no stuttering. The word had popped from his mouth with surprising ease, leaving a trail of odd feelings. Lola registered it, too; her eyes glistened with an ambivalent light, somewhere between happy and sad. She opened her mouth to say something, then closed it again.

"You," Brody added quickly, not wanting to dwell on these feelings, "are either my savior or my sacrifice. I had no choice but to find you."

The lamp hummed. A candy wrapper skittered across the floorboards, prompted by a breeze through the window. Lola stood, worked a kink out of her lower back, and walked slowly to the bulletin board. From the position of her head, Brody thought she was looking at Blair, not Jimmy.

"You did the right thing," she said.

Brody hadn't felt the cold for some time. The atmosphere in the room was not warm, but it had a blanket-like weight that covered every molecule of air. The same could be said of Lola's emotion. It couldn't be seen, but it was there—a heavy, volatile energy.

"I'm sorry for everything you've been through," she said. "And I'm sorry for what happened to your father. I did everything I could to avoid that."

"I believe you," Brody said.

She turned around and looked at him for a long time, or at his jacket, perhaps—his father, the memories dry but still bright, like drifts of dead leaves beneath the porch. He thought for one moment that she was going to hug him, cry on his shoulder, but she only nodded and turned back to the photographs of her enemies.

"Get a couple of hours' rest," she said. "If they come, it'll be between midnight and dawn. I want you alert and at that riflescope."

"Right," Brody said. He stood up, shuffled to his mom's room, and shaved the edge off his tiredness with a thin sleep. He then rolled out of bed and looked through the riflescope until a tangerine light edged into the east.

Nobody came.

...

They breakfasted, after which Brody collected the eggs, watered the animals, and shoveled more shit. Lola told him to expect the alarm to sound at nine A.M., and again at nine forty-five. It did. Farm business on both occasions. He kept working.

"It'll be today," Lola said when he came back in.

"Today what?"

"Whatever Jimmy is planning." Her face was gray. She looked so tired. "We'll find out today."

"How do you know?"

"Experience."

The UPS truck arrived that afternoon.

...

Brody assumed Lola had slept in increments—ten minutes here and there, just enough to recoup some drive. When he got out of the shower, he found her curled up on her bed. If this was a nap, it had gotten out of control; she was deep, and would likely sleep the entire day if he didn't wake her.

He couldn't bring himself to do it, though. Not yet. The early warning system would snap her out of her dreams—within seconds—if it went off. Her resting was to their advantage. He could hold the fort for now.

He managed eighty minutes; Lola had unnerved him when she'd predicted that Jimmy would play his hand that day, and Brody felt safer with her awake. So he brought soup and toast to her room, and gently woke her. She cracked one eyelid, looked at him, then jerked awake.

"How long was I asleep?"

"Not long enough." He placed the tray down on the edge of her bed. "I made you soup, inasmuch as I poured it from a can and heated it on the stove."

"Thank you." She smiled, but there was more to it—a softness in her gaze, a delicate hitch in her breath. She was *touched*, and in a way she hadn't been, perhaps, for some time. "Thank you, Brody."

"Okay."

He went to check the side and front windows, but before he left the room she said to him, "You were always a good kid, with a big and genuine heart. I'm so proud of you."

...

In the hour before the UPS truck rumbled onto the property, delivering the item that would incite a desperate and terrifying course of action, Lola and Brody sat together in the spare room. They talked. Not easy conversations, but a distance was narrowed as Brody began to determine the overlap between Lola Bear and her other personas.

He said, "There's so much about you I don't know, and may never know, but the one question I keep coming back to is, why? If your life is so dangerous, why did you get married and start a family?"

"The simple answer is because I chose to," Lola replied. "I didn't want to deny myself happiness, or the chance of a normal life. If I'd done that, Jimmy would have won. He would have killed me inside."

"That's a selfish answer," Brody said honestly.

"Your great-grandfather would agree," Lola said. "He warned me about putting down roots, but you have to remember that I thought I was in the clear. I met and fell in love with your father quickly. *Too* quickly. Jimmy was on life support at the time. Karl told me that his family—his brothers and sisters, there were eight or nine of them, I think, a big family . . . Karl told me that they considered pulling the plug, because even if Jimmy survived he would have no quality of life. He'd be brain-damaged—you know, eating baby food, buzzing around in a motorized chair."

"Jimmy wasn't ready to die, though," Brody said. "He had unfinished business."

"Don't I know it."

"Jesus, you should've put a pillow over his face while he was in the hospital. Gone back and finished the job." Brody looked at her, his expression puzzled. "Why didn't you?"

"There's more than one answer to that question," Lola said. There was a weariness to her voice, as if she'd had this conversation with herself on numerous occasions. "Firstly, sneaking into a hospital to kill someone isn't as easy as the movies would have you believe. There are people everywhere. Not just nurses and doctors, but orderlies, security personnel, other patients, visitors. *Witnesses*, in other words. There are also security cameras on every floor, in the stairwells and elevators. Additionally, Jimmy had people around him all the time—that big family I mentioned, and his other family, too. La Cosa Nostra. He was still a made man at the time, and the big boss—Don Esposito— made sure he was protected."

"Even so," Brody said, "a few security cameras and mobsters should've been no problem for Lola Bear."

"If he was at home, I would have risked it," Lola said, looking stormily at Jimmy's photograph on the bulletin board. "Soldiers or not. Shit, I'd done it before. But he was under constant surveillance in the hospital—first in Pittsburgh, then New York City. There was no way I could get in and out cleanly."

"Makes sense, I guess," Brody said, and shrugged. "Sometimes, being tough is not enough."

"It's never about being tough, Brody. It's *always* about being smart." Lola turned her gaze back to him, still stormy. "Which brings me to the final answer to your question: I didn't think I *had* to finish Jimmy off, because Jimmy was going to do that all by himself. Jesus, he had his last rites administered twice—*twice*! And when it became apparent that he wasn't going to die, I figured him being a vegetable for the rest of his life was a reasonable punishment. Perhaps even a *better* punishment."

"That didn't happen, either."

"Right. The Italian goddamn Cat." Lola breathed deeply through her nose. A muscle in her jaw twitched. "So he's back on his feet, making moves, building a crew. No longer with Don Esposito, but forging deals of his own. *That* would've been the perfect time to go back and finish the job, but I had you at my knee and Molly in my belly. I was in a different place—a different *world*—slowed down by two pregnancies, mentally and physically. I simply wasn't ready."

Lola rolled her eyes to the ceiling, remembering. It might have been the cold, but Brody noticed her hands were trembling.

"I used to go behind your dad's back," she continued after a brief but heavy pause. "Sneak off to the range every couple of weeks, try to stay sharp. But it wasn't enough, and I was terrified, Brody, for the first time in my life . . . terrified that Jimmy would not only come after me, but after my family, too."

"Yeah," Brody said. "That's a tough scene."

"I had Karl, though." A fragile smile touched Lola's lips. "We'd looked out for each other since day one. He was a good friend to have."

"Renée told me how close you were," Brody said. "She said you kept your alliance on the down-low."

"In that line of work, it helps to know if someone is whispering behind your back."

"Was he there the night you went after Jimmy?"

"No," Lola replied. "Him and a couple of other guys were in New Mexico, some counterfeit money thing that Jimmy was trying to get off the ground. Jimmy called them back—he wanted boots on the ground—but it was all over before their plane touched down in Pittsburgh."

"One of Jimmy's few surviving soldiers," Brody noted. "And close enough to keep you in the loop."

"I called him twice a day to begin with, fully expecting him to tell me that Jimmy was dead." Lola blinked brightly, dazedly, as if she still couldn't believe that Jimmy had pulled through. "That didn't happen, obviously, but Karl and I kept in touch—usually by phone, sometimes in person."

Brody nodded. "I remember him coming to the house."

"A few times, yeah. He'd play catch with you, have a beer with your dad, then he'd quietly tell me what was going on with Jimmy." Lola drew her knees up, looped her arms around them. "That's why we moved from Minneapolis to South Carolina. We said goodbye to a comfortable life—a nice house, a safe community, good jobs. But Karl told me that Jimmy had invested in a payday loan company in the Twin Cities, so that was it. We had to relocate."

"How did you swing that with Dad?" Brody asked.

"I didn't swing it. I told him I wanted to leave and he agreed." Lola smiled. "He was a good man. He loved me."

A horse whinnied, probably wanting to escape the stall; they'd all been stabled since Brody arrived. Crows called from the trees. Every now and then one would swoop past the window. The sky beyond was gray and carried rain. It all looked and sounded so ordinary out there that Brody couldn't imagine it changing.

"And there was Vince," Lola said. "It's probably not appropriate to talk about my first boyfriend with you, but he's important, because he awoke so many feelings inside me. I would not have fallen so hard and fast for your father if not for Vince."

"I get it," Brody said. "He taught you how to love."

"Yes, but that sounds so cliché." Lola paused, trying to find the words. Brody waited silently, watching the first raindrops streak the window, until she nodded and placed one hand against her chest. "*Balance*. That's what Vince gave me. You hear martial artists talk about balance all the time, but it applies to everything—to every pursuit. Talent, achievement, love . . . they represent the balance of heart and ability. When one aspect falters, you draw on the other."

"But you had talent," Brody said. "All those trophies you won. The shooting tournaments, the Xing Yi—"

"I had ability," Lola said. "*So* much ability. But without the heart, I was little more than a machine. I functioned, but didn't feel. Vince brought that part of me to life."

Brody said, "Something else that Jimmy crushed."

A dark look from Lola. "Yes. And his timing was . . . well, heartbreaking. Vince and I had hatched a plan to escape the life—to get away from Jimmy once and for all. We were going to move to Northern California. A brand-new start. No gunrunning, burying bodies, or trading bullets with drug dealers. We had it all worked out."

"And Jimmy found out you were leaving?"

"No, I don't think so," Lola said. "We didn't tell anybody. We were smart. But Jimmy had been pursuing me for years. I spurned his advances, of course, but jealousy got the better of him."

"Son of a bitch didn't like to lose," Brody said, paraphrasing a quote from one of the articles he'd read.

"We were *this* close to getting out." Lola sighed and held her thumb and forefinger an inch apart. "Vince and I had purchased one-way tickets on a flight to San Francisco. Adios, Carver City. Adios, Jimmy. Three days before our departure, Vince got called on a job to Philly. Not our territory, but you do what the boss says. This was at ten-forty A.M. By seven P.M. that evening, I was identifying photographs of Vince's body."

Other than lowering her eyes, she showed no sadness. It was there, though—a shadow on her aura. Brody never knew Vincent Petrescu. He didn't really know Lola Bear, either. This was, for all intents and purposes, a stranger's account, yet it was all he could do to keep from crossing the room and hugging her.

"Jimmy tried to make it look like a rival gang hit. The Badland Brothers used to cut the ears off their victims, and that's what Jimmy did to Vince." Lola nodded and looked at Brody, her eyes cold and certain. "I would always have *suspected* that Jimmy was behind it, because of who and what he is: a goddamn psychotic lunatic. But I had conclusive proof that removed all doubt."

"And then you went on the warpath."

"I did. I went through attack dogs, bullets, and flamethrowers to get to Jimmy. Nothing was going to stop me." Lola drew a deep breath into her lungs. "Although not a day goes by when I don't wish I'd stopped myself . . . just walked away."

The breeze whipped rain through the open window. It hit the wall in tiny droplets and shone in the pale light. Swallows and wrens had joined the crows' cawing. A peculiar discussion.

"I miss Vince. I miss your father, oh, so much. And I miss you and Molly." Lola wiped a speck of rain from the back of her hand. "I often think about the mess I've made, and how I didn't do anything right. But I look at you now and know that I did."

Brody scooted along the floor, took her hand. She squeezed firmly, as if to assure herself that he was actually here. Words drifted across his mind. He reached, found the right ones—*I don't fully understand, but I don't blame you, either*—but before he could open his mouth, the alarm system sounded throughout the house.

Lola removed her hand from his and got to her feet.

"I think this is it," she said.

. . .

Brody grabbed the MMR and took up position in the room next to Lola's. He didn't need the scope to see the large brown vehicle flashing between the trees.

"I see a truck," he called out.

"A UPS delivery truck," his mom called back.

"What should I do?"

"Hold position. Do *not* open fire unless I say."

He opened the window, mounted the rifle, watched the UPS truck round the curve in the driveway and rumble into view. Brody scoped. A male driver, in his forties. Nobody else up front. He wondered if Jimmy's boys were packed into the back. A kind of Trojan horse.

Thumb on the safety, ready. He felt his heartbeat through the rifle's stock, all the way to the handguard.

The driveway ended in a broad turning circle sixty feet from the front door. The driver steered through most of it, then stopped his truck with its rear doors facing the house. Brody imagined them banging open and Jimmy's army spilling out. Twelve, fifteen, twenty guys packing muscle and heat. And Brody would open fire—on impulse, if nothing else—and wouldn't stop pulling the trigger until the magazine was spent.

"Hold steady," his mom called. Maybe she'd read his mind.

He couldn't see the driver because of the angle he'd parked at, but the truck wobbled as he made his way from the front seat into the back. One of the two rear doors opened a few seconds later. The driver stepped out, on his own. He carried a small box beneath one arm. Brody watched him walk down the pathway that linked the turning circle to the front door. Three thuds as he mounted the porch steps—out of view now—and then the doorbell chimed.

His delivery made, the driver returned to his big brown truck and drove away.

...

"Is it a bomb?"

"No. It's not heavy enough to be a bomb. And Jimmy won't blow me up." Lola gave Brody a wry smile. "He wants to kill me slowly."

"Maybe a chemical device?" Brody ventured. "You know, like fentanyl, or some kind of knockout gas?"

The package sat on the kitchen table. A plain brown box, twelve inches long, seven inches wide. It was addressed, not to Margaret Ward, but to Lola Bear.

"Doubtful," Lola said, lifting one side of the box to look underneath it. "There's no crystallization at the edges, no oily marks or strange odor. The return address is bogus, though."

She pointed at the smaller label in the top corner. It read: IC INDUSTRIES, PHOENIX, 54558.

"Phoenix, Arizona?" Brody asked.

"It's a reference to the mythical bird that rose from the ashes. The zip is standard letter mapping, like you'd find on a phone keypad. It spells KILL U. The IC in IC Industries stands for Italian Cat."

"Jesus Christ." Brody took a step back. "It's from him. It's really from him."

"Yes, it is." Lola pulled a knife from the block on the counter behind her. "It's a message."

She carefully cut the packing tape and lifted the box's flaps. Inside, beneath a cushion of bubble wrap, was a dirty white sneaker with a crust of blood on the toe.

The ground opened beneath Brody. He swayed, clasped the edge of the table. Everything dimmed for the first—but not the last—time that day.

"Oh my God," he moaned. "That's Molly's shoe."

"No," Lola said. She took the sneaker out and turned it slowly in her hands. "It's a love letter."

Chapter Twenty-Three

Lola had seen both sides of Vincent Petrescu. There was the enforcer, who would snap the fingers of drugs and weapons dealers who were short in their earnings. Then there was the *man*, intelligent, loyal, a son and brother who made regular donations to the children's hospital in Reflection Park, and called his *bunica* in Romania every other Sunday. Lola would never deny her attraction to the bad boy with the .45 at his side, but it was the *man* that she fell in love with.

The man who uncovered a warmth inside her she hadn't known existed.

The man who put her first, in everything.

The man who wrote her love letters.

It would brighten her day when she found them, and encourage that new and wonderful feeling inside. *It's all better with you here*—written on a scrap of paper tucked between the pages of a magazine. *Addicted to what you give me*—on a Post-it note inside a CD case. *Thanks for being my Happy Place*—folded and tucked beneath the insole of her left shoe. This last was a favorite hiding place for his sweet nothings, and indeed the spot where he'd secreted his final note to her: one word—*JIMMY*—written in his own blood.

Jimmy knew this story. Lola had told him as he lay dying in the hallway of his burning mansion. And now he'd borrowed Vince's idea to send a note of his own.

Lola placed Molly's sneaker on the kitchen table. It was her left sneaker, of course—closer to her heart, as Vince would say—and when Lola lifted the tongue and looked inside, she noticed the insole sticking up at the back, eerily similar to how Vince's insole had been sticking up when she'd looked inside his shoe twenty-six years before.

Deep breathing sounds from behind her. Brody was doubled over, leaning against the wall. Lola glanced at him, then turned back to Molly's sneaker.

She lifted the insole, expecting to find a folded piece of paper, probably with an address written on it, almost certainly written in Molly's blood (Jimmy wouldn't miss *that* trick). Instead she saw that a rectangle of the cushioning had been cut out, and neatly filled with a USB flash drive.

Lola took the drive out and held it up, like an appraiser holding up a diamond.

"What . . . the fuck?" Brody gasped.

"You probably don't want to see what's on this," she said.

• • •

A single MP4 video file. Run time: 03:31. It opened on a shot of an oil-stained floor and scrolled slowly up to reveal a bare concrete wall. An abandoned factory or warehouse, Lola thought. The camera jigged left, lost focus, came back in. The same shot, except now she saw a man-shaped shadow against the wall.

Mumbling in the background: "Please . . . let us go . . . please." This was followed by a distinct, violent thud and then screaming. Both sounds cut through Lola. Next to her, Brody flinched. He'd chosen to watch. "I need to know," he'd said. Now he covered his ears and took a broad step back. "That's Molly," he said.

More screaming, followed by a muffled whimpering, closer to the camera. Two people, Lola thought, one of them gagged.

The shadow moved. Lola heard footsteps (she imagined expensive Italian heels clicking off the floor). A man stepped into the shot. It was Jimmy. Lola knew this, even though he wore a black hood over his head, eyeholes cut into it. She could tell from the way he walked, the cant of his back, his narrow, almost boyish hips. He wore leather gloves to hide the scarring on his hands.

"Hello, Lola." Even his voice was disguised, pushed through a filter, almost robotic.

"Is that Jimmy?" Brody asked.

"Yes, but there's no way of proving it."

"Why's he hiding?"

"To keep us from going to the police."

The camera followed Jimmy as he stepped left past two empty racks and a fire door and an old blue machine that probably hadn't worked for a long time.

"Hit that bitch again."

The same meaty thud and Molly screamed again—a hurt, hopeless wail, then tears and tears.

"Again."

Jimmy flicked his hand, suggesting the camera follow the action. It did. A quick snap left. A different scene: red-painted cinder block, heating ducts, a low yellow light. Molly was chained at the wrists to an overhead crossbar that sagged a little with her weight. Her weaker left leg was drawn inward, like a cowering animal.

"Don't watch," Lola said.

"I'm going to kill him."

Lola paused the video at 01:21. Still two minutes and ten seconds of this nightmare to go. She turned to Brody.

"Get the hell out of here."

"No. I need to see."

"You don't."

He said, "This is a goddamn *war*. I don't want to second-guess myself on the battlefield. I want every reason to put a bullet in Jimmy's brain."

"Brody—"

"Hit play."

She hit play. The camera jerked away from Molly, lost focus for a second, swam back, and here was the second person: Renée, strapped into her wheelchair, sobbing through the wad of flannel stuffed into her mouth. Blood flowed from her hairline and from a deep cut that looped from her left ear to her cheekbone.

Back to Molly. The camera zoomed in on her face. She had a broken lip and bruising around her eye. The camera jerked again, zoomed out. Another hooded person stepped into the shot, smaller in frame. No gloves. He or she carried a heavy-duty pipe wrench in one hand. *She*, definitely a she; Brody noticed the bright pink varnish on her fingernails and flashed back to Rocky T's.

"Blair," he said.

Blair raised the wrench and brought it down in a blur, smashing it against Molly's left leg, just above the knee. Molly screamed and thrashed, swinging from the chain. Blair hit her in the same place again.

Brody groaned, covered his eyes, staggered away.

Pause at 01:56.

"Get out of here, Brody," Lola insisted. "Please."

He cried out—a hurting, furious explosion of sound—and threw his fist against the wall, two solid thuds that made the window tremble in its frame. "I'm not going anywhere," he said. "This is on me. I won't back away."

"But you *can*."

"I'm the reason Molly and Renée are there."

"No, Brody. *I* am."

"I guess we're both to blame, which means we're in this together." He flexed his right hand, examined the grazed skin on his knuckles, then nodded at the screen. "If I'm soldier enough to fire an assault rifle from your bedroom window, then I'm soldier enough to watch this."

Lola lowered her eyes, recognizing the thick cord of resolve—stubbornness, Grandpa Bear would've called it—that ran through him. He truly was her son. Reinforcing this, their thoughts ran parallel; she had seen enough of the video, but for what she had to do, she needed to see more.

She turned back to her laptop and clicked play.

Molly drooped from the chain, turning a slow circle. A long thread of saliva hung from her mouth. The shot switched back to Jimmy. He stared at the camera for a long time.

"I need you, Lola," he said. "I need you very badly."

He took half a dozen slow steps to his right and stopped a yard or so from Renée's chair. He touched her hair and she shrank away from him. The camera operator adjusted his or her position to get all four of them in the shot: Jimmy and Renée in the foreground, Blair and Molly behind. Molly lifted her head and moaned. The chain rattled. "*Pleeeeeease*," she wailed. Jimmy reached behind him and pulled a semiautomatic pistol from the waistband of his pants. He pointed it at Renée's head.

"*No*," Molly screamed. "*Please, Pleeee*—"

Blair silenced her: one deft punch to the jaw. Molly went limp and spun on her chain.

"You know where to find me," Jimmy said to the camera. It looked for a moment like he was going to lower the gun but he pulled the trigger instead. The report was dull and shocking. Renée's head snapped backward and the right side of her skull opened in a hail of bone and matter. The force lifted her chair onto one wheel. It almost tipped, then it settled and rolled a few inches. The movement caused Renée's head to flop forward. Blood spouted from the entry wound and gushed from the exit.

Jimmy tucked the pistol into the back of his pants and stepped close to the camera. His eyes blazed through the jagged holes cut into the hood.

"Come get me, you bitch," he said.

End of video.

. . .

Ten seconds of painful, disbelieving silence, then Lola closed the laptop's lid with a loud snap. She turned toward Brody. His eyes were big and wet.

"We've got work to do," she said.

Chapter Twenty-Four

The message from Jimmy—the brutal, inhuman hand he had played—meant that Brody and Lola no longer had to scope the property. Nobody was coming, at any time of the day or night. Jimmy had been clear: he wanted Lola to go to him. This was hardly a source of relief, but they were at least free to suffer in their own way. Lola fell into an exhausted sleep. Brody was tired, too, but sleep wasn't in the cards. He wandered the farm, drifting in and out of himself, the most hopeless of ghosts. He'd find himself in the barn or the basement with no memory of how he got there. He fed the chickens at midnight.

The world returned, gradually. It felt like a wound both opening and closing. At 6:50 A.M., with a scratch of light in the east, Brody stripped off his shirt and ran.

He bolted across the yellowing land to the north—the very land he'd watched over since his arrival—and into the woods. He didn't feel the cold or the sting of the branches as they whipped against his skin. Deer sprang ahead of him in beautiful shapes.

The light climbed. A saffron mist clung to the understory. Brody broke from the woods and stumbled back to the house, bleeding and bruised. His mom was still asleep, curled up in an armchair in the living room. Brody draped a thick blanket over her and found one for himself. He sat in front of the empty fireplace and remembered Molly, age two, lying in a hospital bed, her legs in twin casts. He had cupped her hand and silently promised to be there if she needed him. *If.* She was such a determined girl.

Brody eventually succumbed to sleep, but his dreams were like the mist in the woods: thin and crowded by darkness.

• • •

On any normal day—or as normal as her life ever got under a constant threat—Lola would wake at five A.M., shower, eat breakfast, then go to work. Hers was a small farm but there was always plenty to do, and an early start occasionally meant that she could dedicate her afternoon to other pursuits, like riding her horse or getting off a few shots at the range.

Brody's arrival had derailed Margaret Ward's existence—ended it, in fact—but Lola woke late that Friday morning determined to play the role one last time. So she pulled on her dirty old denims and made her rounds. She groomed the horses and let them run in the arena. She cleaned and hosed the stables, mucked out the chicken coops, refreshed all the feeders and troughs. Hudson came at eleven and she gave him a vibrant, nothing-wrong-here smile, then handed him sixty fresh eggs stacked into two trays, just like she always did.

"Missed you at pinochle last night," he said as he climbed back into his truck, and she told him that she'd be there next week, even though she knew that her days of playing pinochle were well and truly behind her.

She spent some time with her cattle, looking for signs of disease: scours, coughing, nasal discharge. Maybe it was pointless, given what she was about to do, but doing something normal—even checking a calf for diarrhea—helped her cope with the many things that were *not* normal.

Brody was awake when she returned to the house, but not exactly alert. He sat on the floor in the living room, huddled in a blanket, rocking back and forth.

"I'll make us something to eat," Lola said.

"Not hungry."

"The worst thing we can do right now is deteriorate. We need to stay strong."

She went to the kitchen and started pulling eggs, meats, and vegetables out of the fridge. Brody joined her after a moment. He sat at the table, stared at the closed laptop for a second or two, then pushed it away from him.

"Is there any point," he said, "in going to the police?"

"No," Lola said.

"But if you show them that . . . that *video*"—he sneered when he said it, his hateful eyes directed at the laptop—"they'll have to do something. They'll at least investigate."

"You're right." Lola lifted a skillet out of the cupboard and dropped it on the stove with a bang. "But there's no way to prove it's Jimmy in the video. Investigators might question him, on suspicion, probably at his home while sipping cognac—he has friends on the force—but no arrest will be made without evidence."

"There has to be something in that video," Brody said. "Some small clue that—"

"Involving the authorities is a dangerous move, with little chance of success. It will only frustrate Jimmy, and then he'll do something worse to Molly."

"Kill her?"

"Not right away. She's his bargaining chip, but there's still lots he can do." Lola sprayed oil into the skillet and cranked the heat. "Eventually he'll tire of hurting her. *Then* he'll kill her. And then he'll come at me the old-fashioned way."

Brody stared at her, dark pouches beneath his eyes, his mouth slightly open. He had the hollow, dead look of a prisoner of war: a boy whose world has been upended, the few good things he had known tipped out.

Lola went to him, one hand on his face—which was cold, so cold—her forehead touching his.

"I'm going to take care of this," she promised him.

"Okay." A weak, cracked word.

"I told you," she said, "that when Jimmy played his hand, I would respond. And that's exactly what I'm going to do."

"I'm coming with you."

"I know."

"I'm going to kill that son of a bitch." Brody started to cry and she lifted him into her arms and held on tight. She felt a fluttering in her own chest but pushed it away.

"Listen to me, Brody—"

"*Kill* him."

"Listen: I have a plan, and it *has* to go off without a hitch." She held him at arm's length and drove her gaze deep into his. "I need you to do exactly what I say, when I say. Do you understand?"

A vague response.

"Do you *understand*?"

"Yes."

"Good." Lola lowered him onto his seat and returned to the skillet. "We leave in a few hours."

...

They drove into Lone Arrow proper. Population 5,100. Main Street was narrow, three stoplights, lined with the usual crop of small-town stores and eateries. There were no McDonald's or Starbucks. Savior came by way of the First United Methodist Church and the Bald Eagle Shooting Range.

Lola pulled her pickup into one of the spaces in the range's lot. It was a low-key establishment, with neat white lettering across the brickwork and two signs in the glass door. One read: NO MINORS UNLESS ACCOMPANIED BY AN ADULT, and the other: NO ALCOHOLIC BEVERAGES OR DRUGS PERMITTED ON THIS PROPERTY.

She said, "I'm going to do everything I can to keep you from pulling a trigger. You might have to, though. It's a good idea for you to know how."

Brody nodded, staring straight ahead.

"This place is better equipped than it looks. Fourteen lanes, good ventilation. Best of all, it has a tactical area, with cover and moving targets. The local police use it for training."

"Okay," he mumbled.

"I can't teach you much in the time we have." Lola shook her head. "You'll be as green when you come out as when you go in. Just a different shade of green. That's about the best I can do."

They got out of the truck. Lola lifted a carryall of firearms from the backseat: the MMR, her Baby Eagle, the Glock 42. She glanced across the street and saw a silver Nissan Maxima pull up outside Bricker's Hardware, a single male occupant, red goatee and a ball cap.

"Just put Jimmy in front of me," Brody mumbled. "I only need one shot."

"If only it were that simple," Lola said. "Come on."

...

They started on the lanes. A crash course in pistol shooting. Lola showed him arm and hand position. "Push out with your shooting hand, pull back with your support hand. Same mechanic as with the rifle; think of your right arm as the buttstock . . ." She helped with his trigger control. "Don't jerk the trigger. That will upset your aim. You want a nice, smooth motion. That gun should surprise you a little every time it goes off . . ." She explained the importance of sight alignment. "See the target, but focus on the front sight. I mean *really* focus. There's a magic point where everything on the periphery melts away, then you'll keyhole every shot . . ." Brody put round after round down the range, and Lola helped him make adjustments until his groups came back tight.

"Good," she said, showing him a target where every hit but one was within the inner ring. "I guess the apple doesn't fall far from the tree."

This earned a thin, wavering smile.

They proceeded to the tactical area, where Lola showed Brody cover techniques, how to shoot from prone and kneeling positions, and how to quickly transition from pistol to rifle and back again. Man-shaped targets swooped and popped up. "Same basics as stationary shooting," Lola instructed. "Focus on that front sight post. Smooth trigger pulls. But track the target through the shot, even after you pull the trigger." Brody missed and missed again. "You need to adjust your lead," Lola said. "Your shots are late. Think about angle, distance, and speed. That's a calculation you need to make instantly, and no two shots are the same."

Brody missed.

"Sight alignment. Smooth tracking."

He missed.

"You're jerking the trigger."

Brody clipped targets. He hit shoulders and thighs.

"Better. Try again, starting from cover. And think about your lead."

Six hits to center mass. Two to the head.

"Attaboy."

The hours ticked by. Two and then three. They took a short break, then headed back to the lanes.

"I don't know," Brody said, flexing his right hand, rolling his shoulder. "My fingers are killing me. And my *arm* . . ."

"What are you going to do if you take a bullet to the shoulder?" Lola asked. "Give up? Curl into a ball and hope the enemy doesn't see you?"

"No, I . . ."

Lola popped the top two buttons of her shirt and pulled it open enough to expose a knot of scar tissue on her left shoulder.

"Little present from Marco Cabrini," she said. "Joey's old man."

"You told me you got that scar falling out of a tree."

"Something else I lied about." She shrugged and buttoned up. "Let's keep going."

. . .

They shot side by side for fifteen minutes, then Lola handed Brody the MMR and two boxes of ammo.

"Switch it up," she said, removing her ear protectors. "Apply everything I've shown you. I want to see some tight groups when I get back."

"Where are you going?"

"I've got a little business to take care of."

She left the Bald Eagle via the back door and cut across the Dollar Tree lot to Station Road, which she followed north for two blocks, then took Main west, then Vincent Street south, approaching Bricker's Hardware from the other direction. The silver Nissan was still parked outside. Lola crept up on the passenger side, opened the door, and jumped in.

"Hello, Eddie."

Within one second she had the muzzle of her Baby Eagle tucked beneath his rib cage and she pressed hard.

"Oh fuck," he gasped, and then, thinking clearly, "I call Jimmy every hour. If he doesn't hear from me, he'll hurt the girl."

"Hurt her, yes. But he's not going to kill her. Not yet." She pressed even harder with the gun and he winced and shrank against the driver's door. "I think a little more pain is an acceptable trade for running a bullet through your internals."

"Fuck."

"I don't *want* to shoot you, though. Because you're a goddamn chickenshit asshole, and I derive no pleasure from shooting goddamn chickenshit assholes." She started to twist the pistol. He groaned and dribbled. "But, you know, if I *have* to . . ."

"Chrissakes," Eddie snorted. "What's this about?"

Lola smiled. "It's about you giving me what I want."

He breathed hard and a section of his false goatee came unglued. Sweat ran from beneath his ball cap.

"What *do* you want?" he hissed. "Just fucking tell me."

She told him.

. . .

Lola returned to the range to find Brody stripping the MMR and returning it to the carryall.

"Ran out of ammo," he said.

"Good." She nodded. "Any kills?"

"Just the same one," he said. "Over and over."

. . .

It was almost six P.M. by the time they got back to the farm. Brody took Advil for his shoulder and for everything else that ached.

"Grab whatever you need," Lola said.

They loaded up the truck and headed east.

Chapter Twenty-Five

They drove more than two hundred miles that evening, listening to the drone of the engine and nothing else. They were trapped with their imaginations. And maybe they deserved that, Brody mused. They had each played a part in putting Molly where she was. They should each conceptualize what she might be going through.

Brody distilled every harrowing thought into gasoline and dripped it into a bottle inside him. By the time they reached the Omaha city limits, that bottle was three-quarters full. He didn't know if he had the ability to do what needed to be done, but he for damn sure had the fuel.

...

An imperfect moon watched them over the Missouri River, into Iowa, then shut its eye behind a lid of soft cloud. Soon after, Lola exited the interstate and pulled up outside a hotel. It wasn't much, but it was multiple stars better than anything Brody had stayed in with Molly.

"I'm not tired," he said. "We should keep going. I'll drive."

"We've got nine hundred miles of interstate ahead of us," Lola said. "We need to rest."

She got out of the truck, stretched, grabbed her bags from the backseat—including the carryall filled with weapons. They were all in there: the pistols, the rifles, even the shotgun from the barn. Along with the sawed-off strapped beneath the dash, they were considerably armed.

Brody grabbed his own bag—he'd ditched the replica; the time for nonlethal had passed—and walked with his mom toward the hotel entrance.

"What do you need me to do?" he asked.

"Huh?" Lola rubbed her eyes.

"You said you had a plan, and that you need me to do exactly what you say, when you say." Brody winced as he heaved his bag onto his right shoulder. "What is it?"

"Right." She lowered her gaze and stepped ahead of him. "I'll tell you when we get there."

...

Despite the world and all its cruelty, and the bleak industry of his imagination, Brody fell asleep within seconds of his head touching the pillow. His dreams were as deep and quiet as the ocean floor.

They were on the road by six, after removing a skin of ice from the truck's windshield. One quick stop for gas, another for breakfast—McDonald's drive-through, convenience over nutrition. Brody's appetite was surprisingly lively. He wolfed all of his and finished what his mom couldn't.

"Still hungry?" she asked. "We can hit another drive-through."

"I'm good for now," Brody said. "Let's keep going."

They rolled east, into the new day, watching the red seam ahead of them first crack, then bleed, then spread into a dramatic apricot sunrise. Lola flicked the radio on, skipping through stations until she found something that rocked.

"That's some sunrise," she said.

With no delays, they would roll into Pennsylvania, and onto Jimmy's turf, sometime around eight P.M. If his mom's mysterious plan didn't work, he might be sleeping with the fishes by eight-thirty, making this the last sunrise he'd ever see.

"It's beautiful," he said.

"I watch the sun come up most mornings," Lola said. "I always take a moment, you know, just to breathe it in. And I still can't look at a sunrise without thinking about your dad. It was his favorite time of the day."

"I didn't know that."

"It's true." Lola nodded and cracked a faint smile. "Every two or three weeks we'd wake early, drive to the High Bridge in St. Paul, and watch the sun come up over the city. My memory is that it was always spectacular—the way it reflected off the high-rises downtown and shimmered on the Mississippi—but that might just be the way I choose to remember it. We sometimes skew our memories to suit us, right?"

"I guess so," Brody said.

"It was probably cloudy and cold, and I was probably cranky, pregnant, and desperate to pee. But in my mind"—Lola tapped her right temple—"it was always perfect."

Brody settled back in his seat, momentarily at peace. Maybe it was the sunrise coupled with the music, or the knowledge that they were on their way to ending this, whatever "the end" might mean. But he thought it had more to do with Lola—this new glimpse of her spirit and tenderheartedness. For the first time in years, he was beginning to feel like he had a mom.

"I have a lot of good memories," he said. "I don't think any of them are skewed."

"Like?"

"Like our camping vacation at Crow Wing Lake—"

"When your dad went fishing and capsized the kayak."

"Oh God, and that *storm*." Brody puffed out his cheeks. "That shit was biblical. Then there was the Christmas we all went carol-singing dressed as snowmen—"

"And snow*women*."

"Right, and nobody knew who we were. I don't think we got through one carol without laughing our asses off."

"Yeah, that was a good time."

"And remember when our TV broke, and we put on our own production of *The Simpsons*?"

"You stole the show," Lola said. "You were a great Bart."

"We were all great."

Lola smiled, tapping her thumbs on the wheel as the radio played. Brody looked out the window and lost himself to the past—to good memories and bad. He indulged them all, though; he wasn't running from anything today. The scenery flashed by. Flat farmland. A river. A water tower. More and more farmland. Brody finally snapped back to the present when a fleet of hot-air balloons drifted over the interstate, low enough to hear the roar of their burners.

Lola must have snapped out of her memories, too.

"That was the happiest I've ever been," she said.

Brody turned to her, expecting to see her usual noncommittal expression, but there was more now: a depth to her eyes, a trembling in her jaw, a crimping of her brow. It was as if her tough exterior layers were peeling away, revealing the hesitant, more tender person beneath.

"If I could go back to any time in my life," she continued, "it would be then, with you, Molly, and your dad."

"Really?"

"No doubt about it." She gripped the wheel firmly. Maybe her hands were trembling, too. "I had a difficult childhood. It was better with Grandpa Bear, but it wasn't normal. And Vince . . . I was happy with him, but we were working for Jimmy, and that was not a good scene. The last twelve years have been lonely, sometimes fulfilling, but rarely happy. And then there was Natalie Ellis, the opposite of Lola Bear, with her reusable grocery bags and rusty minivan, the years of changing diapers, baking muffins, the PTA meetings, the Little

League baseball games and swimming lessons. Of all the lives I've lived, that was by far the happiest."

Brody said, "If this ends well, maybe we can start again. The three of us."

Lola nodded, but flinched at the same time. Perhaps it was the sunlight in her eyes.

"I've endured some terrible things," she said. "I've encountered very bad people, lived through years of isolation, been pushed beyond my endurance. But leaving my family was the hardest thing I've ever had to do. That night, when I kissed you and Molly goodbye, thinking I would never see you again . . . I can't even put into words how much that broke me inside. And I've never been *un*broken since."

Another layer lifted away and now Brody thought she might cry (a phenomenon he'd never seen, not even when she was Natalie Ellis). She held the tears back, though. Her eyes were fixed dead ahead, unblinking.

"I thought about you all the time. Not just big stuff like school and relationships, but the little things, too: what time you got up in the morning, which superheroes were your favorites, if Molly still liked chocolate milk on her Cheerios." She pressed her lips together and drifted into the past again, but only for a moment. "I contemplated going home to you—three, four times a day I'd think about it. I even packed a bag on one occasion. I couldn't do it, though. I just couldn't put you into that kind of danger. If I'd known, of course, that Jimmy would find you anyhow . . ."

The interstate got tighter as they approached Des Moines. The landscape barely changed, though: a deep rolling green on both sides, punctuated by blue road signs and off-white buildings. The radio signal swam in and out. Lola hit scan a couple of times, found nothing to her taste, so shut it off.

"I was always a quiet kid. Not much of an ego, never really open with my emotions." Lola shook her head. "That changed, somewhere around ten or eleven years old."

Brody thought of Mav Hamm, the first to be introduced to Lola's ego.

"I developed strength, determination, and feelings," she said. "But I always felt divided—*torn*—between that sad, emotionally repressed little girl and the fierce, ambitious woman she became. This is how I've lived, and how I've made decisions. I didn't always make the right ones, but when it came to my family, I always tried."

A hawk circled above the interstate, then cut away to the north, where heavier clouds had gathered. It would rain before long. Lola looked in that direction, drumming one hand lightly on the wheel. Brody heard the quiver on her breath.

"I'm sorry, Brody, for bringing you into a life you don't deserve, and then running away from you. I'm sorry that all my shadows found Molly and your dad. And Renée. Poor, sweet Renée." A hitch in her breath. She blinked her cold, dry eyes. "I can't undo the suffering or make anything right. All I can do is stop the shadows, put an end to the pain."

"We'll get Jimmy," Brody said. "He'll pay for every horrible thing he's ever done, not just to you and me, but to everybody."

A shallow smile from Lola. "You've got some grit, son. I'll give you that."

"It's mostly rage," Brody said. "If this truck breaks down, I'll grab the guns and *run* to Carver City, and nothing will stop me."

The truck didn't break down. It rolled smoothly east, through Iowa and into Illinois, where they stopped to refuel and grab a bite to eat. Brody reflected on his recent trip to the Prairie State with Molly, how they'd staggered through the doors of the New Zion Baptist Church with gospel music ringing, and the Reverend Wendell Mathias had offered his hand.

It had been a hard journey, and it was about to get harder, but there'd been hope along the way, and kindness. Rare points of light in a cripplingly dark tunnel.

A hard rain followed them into Indiana. Lola worked the wipers. She didn't slow down. Understandably, their conversation got thinner as they chalked up the miles and the reality of what they were driving toward took hold. Brody closed his eyes and found a point in his rage—a bright, burning coal—that he could hold on to. He imagined that coal igniting a fire that started out small, but soon spread and set everything burning. With this in his mind—and with the lulling rhythm of the truck—he fell asleep.

It must have been a deep sleep, because it was dusk when he stirred and a nearby road sign revealed they were forty miles from Cleveland, Ohio, which put them about two hundred miles—and three hours— from Carver City.

Also, they'd parked, and Lola wasn't in the truck.

Brody sat up, wiping his eyes. He looked blearily through the fading light and saw they were in a rest area. His mom sat on a bench facing the interstate. He couldn't be sure, but it looked like she was crying.

· · ·

She pulled a shirtsleeve across her cheeks. Her rounded back bobbed and trembled. Brody approached slowly, knowing she wouldn't want him to see, but wanting her to know that he cared. He got to within fifteen feet and was about to speak when she beat him to it; she knew he was there, even without turning around.

"This was supposed to take two minutes," she said, watching the traffic rush by. "Just a brief spell, alone, with my thoughts. But it's been ten minutes and I'm *still* having that spell."

Brody pulled level with the bench. Even in the dull light he saw that her eyes were red and wet.

"I don't cry," she said, giving her head a little shake. "This is . . ."

"It's okay," Brody said. He sat beside her and looped an arm over her back. Such a simple thing, really— the act of reaching out and offering comfort. She had comforted him so often over the past few days. Now it was his turn, and it felt big and wonderful and not simple at all.

She leaned into him, her head on his shoulder. Cars and trucks zipped along the eastbound lane, a thousand lives moving at sixty miles an hour, each multifaceted, with challenges, burdens, and travails. Although none, Brody surmised, were quite like theirs.

Lola wiped her face, studied the tears on her fingers, as if evaluating their rarity. The trees around them rattled their naked branches.

"I'm not going to make it out of there," she said.

Brody considered her skill with firearms. He'd watched her at the range as she racked up headshots on moving targets—with zero effort, it seemed. He recalled how she'd tackled him on her driveway. One moment he was staring at the farmhouse, wondering if he had the right place, and the next he was flat on his back with her knee planted on his chest.

"You will," he said, and he believed it.

"I'm not what I used to be. Nothing like. I'm older. Slower." She wiped more tears away. "And I'm scared."

"I know. And that's okay."

Lola sat up, her eyelashes heavy and dark, her shoulders low. Brody rubbed her back and she looked at him gratefully.

"I can't say I'm glad you came, Brody," she said, and a sad smile played across her face. "Except I *am*. I wish the situation had been different, of course, but seeing you again has lifted my lonely old heart."

They embraced warmly and with meaning. Lola sighed, kissed the top of his head, and stood up.

"Okay," she said. "Let's go end this."

. . .

They crossed into Pennsylvania a few minutes shy of seven P.M., Lola's home state and the one place in

America she had vowed never to return to. She followed the turnpike to Interstate 79, then cut south toward Pittsburgh. The darkness felt different here, she thought. The open skies of Nebraska allowed for a nighttime that breathed. Here, it felt crowded and ugly, or maybe that had more to do with the individual she was going to see.

An hour outside Carver City, Lola veered off-route and pulled into a hotel parking lot.

"We're not stopping, are we?" Brody asked.

"No," Lola said. "I need to do something."

"Here?" Brody shook his head. "Can I help?"

"It's a female thing," Lola said.

She got out of the truck, walked across the parking lot, and into the hotel. It was not grand, but it had a waiting area with comfortable seats and reasonable privacy. She sat down, took out her cell phone, and brought up the information that Eddie the Smoke had provided while she had the muzzle of her pistol pressed into his ribs.

A telephone number with a western Pennsylvania code.

She started dialing but hit the wrong digit and had to restart, not once but three times. Deep breaths. Composure. She tried again and completed the number. A chill laddered her spine as she brought the phone to her ear.

He answered on the second ring. His voice was as stale and suffocating as the air from an old grave.

"I've been expecting you," he said.

"Hello, Jimmy," she said.

. . .

The final hour of their long drive passed in silence. The tension was too thick for conversation. Even breathing was difficult. Brody focused on that single burning coal, and the fact that, within hours, this would all be over. All the running. All the bloodshed. Lola reflected on her childhood, and how wonderful it had sometimes been to feel nothing.

The miles ticked by. The guns rattled on the backseat.

They soon saw the burnt fog of light pollution hanging over Carver City.

Chapter Twenty-Six

Thousands of dreams. Thousands of miles. Hundreds of thousands of dollars. And blood, of course. Gallons of blood. This was what had filled the valley between him and Lola Bear. A broad valley, but he had built his bridge one piece at a time. He had persevered when the wind howled and the storm raged. And he had crossed.

Jimmy sat in the front office of his Carver City warehouse. He'd owned this place for thirty-three years. Its location—behind the rail yard, and away from the other warehouses and units in the industrial zone—made it the perfect site to conduct business. Most of that business was legitimate, but it had stored and shipped out plenty of contraband over the years, and any number of corpses packed into barrels of sodium hydroxide—the last being Renée Giordano's. He sat with his right leg twitching, his jaw anxiously clenched. The only light came from the warehouse floor, and it shone through the office glass, just enough for Jimmy to see the scars on his hands. If he were to strip naked, he'd see the other scars—these disfigurements he'd carried. An indignity, but a mere gloss over the real wound, the one inside, the one that still bled.

"Even dogs run away," he whispered.

The clock on his cell phone read 20:11. Forty-seven minutes since Lola had called. Forty-seven minutes of nervous excitement and deep distrust. He'd vented and preened. He'd shadowboxed and prayed. A pinkie nail of coke—just a little bump—had aligned his self-control.

The bitch was coming.

All quiet on the warehouse floor. It ordinarily functioned around the clock but there were no employees tonight. Only soldiers, eleven of them (he'd drafted some extra muscle for this—he wasn't going to fuck it up), armed with machine pistols and AR-15s. There were more outside, some equipped with riot gear. He felt a strong sense of déjà vu, but the outcome would be different this time around.

The quiet lasted a moment longer, then Jimmy heard the hectic approach of a vehicle. Headlights splashed through the open bay door as Blair's SUV pulled to a hard stop outside. She cut the engine and got out. Remarkable Blair, who'd delivered on her promise. Implacable Blair, who wouldn't stop until the job was done. She entered the warehouse, passing in and out of the shadows. Her expression was harsh and focused. She had a .45 on each hip and a bandolier across her chest loaded with throwing knives.

Jimmy relaxed in his seat as she entered the office, to give the impression of cool. Everything inside him jumped, though.

"Got a call from Jared: a half-ton Sierra with Nebraska plates was just spotted on Corporation Boulevard. Eddie the Smoke confirmed it's her." There was no air of smugness about Blair. She was all business. "ETA is ten minutes, maybe fifteen if she catches all those red lights on Franklin."

Jimmy linked his fingers—cool, oh so cool—and asked, "Are you ready?"

"The guys are taking up position now: ten flanking the approach, four on the roof. There'll be two on you, and I'll fill in any gaps." She looked at him carefully. "Are *you* ready?"

"Nobody kills her," Jimmy said. It was an answer of sorts.

"Everything south of the knees," Blair agreed. "If that's what it comes to."

Jimmy licked his lips. Snapshots from a hundred dreams flooded his mind, all violent, all beautiful. "I'll take her hands tonight. Tomorrow I'll take her feet."

"You can take whatever you want."

He stood up, feeling a hundred feet tall, as if he might smash through the office ceiling, up through the warehouse roof, and stand like a giant over Carver City.

"Get the cripple," he said.

. . .

Carver City had been a benign commuter town until the western Pennsylvania mob gave it a face-lift. Rudy Tucoletti—who controlled the city until his death in 1989—encouraged multifamily housing and retail development, which escalated industry of a different nature. "Americans love waffles," Rudy used to say. "But we also love drugs and guns." Rudy had a lock on these, too (always kicking up to Don Esposito), and the inevitable rise in crime offered lucrative extortion opportunities.

Jimmy built on this during his brief tenure, and twenty-six years later—like Jimmy himself—the scars remained. Carver City held the dubious distinction of being the second most dangerous city in Pennsylvania, with a violent crime rate of 1,622 per 100,000 residents.

"You used to live here?" Brody asked, looking at the gray brick buildings and boarded-over windows, the overpasses sprayed with graffiti, the trash-lined streets. "Jesus, it makes Rebel Point look like Disney World."

"I *operated* here," Lola said. "I lived in Greensburg. A much nicer city."

They drove through the downtown core, where Brody saw the hunched shape of what might once have been a picturesque neighborhood. There was a colonial-style post office, an old movie house called the Fortuna, a broad park with two baseball diamonds and a water fountain. It was all run-down now. The cheerless streets were peppered with FOR LEASE signs, dive bars, and pawnbrokers. Call girls paraded beneath the Fortuna's cracked marquee.

"How far is Jimmy's house from here?" Brody asked.

"We're not going to his house," Lola said.

East off Main Street, and here were the fruits of Rudy Tucoletti's labors: strip malls, fast food joints, motels, and apartment buildings. Police cruisers prowled like sharks in shallow water. The industrial zone was beyond this, a nest of factories and warehouses, with a four-track railway running in and out, and smokestacks pumping refuse into the night sky.

"Where the hell are we going?" Brody asked.

Lola didn't respond. She bounced the truck across a scrub lot and veered onto a road with flex units on one side and loading docks on the other. This intersected a narrow lane that paralleled the length of a rumbling, smoky factory. Lola followed it around the back, then turned onto a gravel track marked EMPLOYEE AND DELIVERY ENTRANCE ONLY. There was a deserted rail yard to the left, enclosed by a sagging chain-link fence. Empty boxcars sat in the darkness. To the right, a posse of transmission towers stood protectively around a bleak, humming substation.

Lola drove slowly down the middle of the track. Vehicles had been parked along both sides. Halfway down, she brought the truck to a stop but kept the engine running. The headlights picked out the exterior of an isolated warehouse fifty yards away.

"Mom?" Brody asked, his voice cracking. "What's going on?"

She looked at him through a mask of fear and sadness—the face of a woman who has resolved to take a long, hot bath with a razor blade. "You said it yourself," she said. "I'm either your savior or your sacrifice. And I'm too old to be your savior." She grabbed her phone from where she'd slotted it in the cupholder, pulled up her recent calls, and tapped the number at the top of the list.

Brody heard the ringing tone through the phone's earpiece. It was picked up quickly, although the person at the other end was content to let Lola speak first.

"I'm here," she said.

"I know," came the reply.

Floodlights flared above the warehouse's bay door. A second later, a battalion of Jimmy's goons emerged from behind their parked vehicles and surrounded the truck with weapons raised.

· · ·

Brody counted ten mean-looking guys, with ten very serious guns. Joey—the meathead he'd one-inch punched in Bayonet—was on the left side, staring at him down the barrel of an AR-15. He was not acting this time.

"Jesus Christ." Brody's skin crawled, his muscles contracted. He was vaguely aware of the guns on the backseat, but knew if he lunged for one of them, Jimmy's guys would turn his mom's truck into a cheese grater.

What was the point of those guns if *this* was the plan? Or the time he'd spent at the range? *I'm going to do everything I can to keep you from pulling a trigger,* Lola had said. *You might have to, though. It's a good idea for you to know how.*

But a better idea, apparently, to just give up.

The bay door rolled open, spilling more light into the loading area. Molly limped onto the dock. She was being bolstered from behind by Blair, who held a pistol to her head. Seeing Blair again triggered a fresh rage inside Brody. It was like a shock wave, starting in his gut and radiating outward. Molly was the nullifier; if she hadn't been here, Brody would have erupted.

Two armed thugs followed. Leo—the other bozo from Bayonet—was one of them. Then came the star of the show, Jimmy Latzo, dressed in a sharp suit, his hair immaculately combed. He had a cell phone pressed to his ear.

"Welcome home, Lola," he hissed.

. . .

Lola tapped the mute button on her phone and turned to Brody.

"I told you," she said, "that I have a plan, and that I need you to do exactly what I say, when I say."

"I remember," Brody murmured.

"So here's what I need you to do." The humanness she'd displayed earlier was absent now. This was cold Lola. Machinelike Lola. "I need you to get Molly, and then get the hell out of here. Don't look back. Do *not* go to the police. There's not a cop in Carver City who'll come out here tonight, anyway. And you'll only put yourself back on Jimmy's shit list."

"You're giving up?" Brody said.

"You're free now," Lola said. "Both of you. Go back to Nebraska. The farm is willed to you, Brody. You and Molly. Look after it."

"I don't want the farm, I want . . ." He had no words. The air had been robbed from his lungs. He screwed his eyes closed and managed, "I want the three of us. *Together*. Riding the horses. Feeding the goddamn chickens."

"That's not going to happen."

Jimmy's voice came through the earpiece. "Get out of the truck, Lola. Hands in the air. Try anything stupid and I'll have Blair put a bullet in this little cunt's ear."

Lola unmuted the phone and spoke into it. "I'm not moving until my daughter is sitting in the backseat. You want to try shooting me out of here, go ahead."

Jimmy lowered the phone and said something to Blair. After a moment, she nodded, said something back. Her gun never left Molly's temple.

"This is how it's going to work," Jimmy returned, his voice clear in the stillness. "You're going to send your boy out to get her. While he's doing that, my men will remove any guns you're carrying from the equation. It's better for everyone that we don't have any nasty surprises."

"I agree," Lola said.

"Then your kids *slowly* get into the truck, while you *slowly* get out. My men will pat you down—again, no surprises—and the little tots drive away." Jimmy growled contentedly. Even this came through the earpiece. "Everybody's happy. Except you, Lola. You most certainly will *not* be happy. But you know that, don't you?"

"Let's do this," Lola said, her voice remarkably calm. She killed the call and tossed her phone into the cupholder.

Blair started to walk Molly toward the truck.

"Go get your sister," Lola said.

"Mom, I—"

"*Now*, Brody. You said you'd do exactly what I need you to do. This is what I need. So *do* it."

Brody felt something tear inside him. It was small, but vital. A connection between his heart and brain. Or his body and soul. It spilled emotion instead of blood: anger, grief, fear, sadness, confusion, relief, disappointment. A copious flow. He reflected on his mom's rare show of emotion—how she'd cried at the side of the road. And *this* was the reason why: because she was quitting, throwing in the towel, giving up.

"You can't do this," Brody whispered. "You can't let Jimmy win."

"Jimmy always wins."

"He killed Dad. You remember him, right? Ethan Anthony Ellis. You had two kids with him. Used to watch the sunrise together."

"Brody—"

"And Renée. Oh Jesus, she was so sweet and kind. And Jimmy killed her—just fucking *killed* her."

"Right, and I am not going to let him kill you." Lola's voice remained calm but there were sparks in her eyes. "This is the only way, Brody. Look out the window: sixteen armed guys *plus* Blair, who equals at least another five—"

"Sixteen?" Brody frowned.

"Ten surrounding the truck. Four on the roof. Two with Jimmy."

Brody looked at the warehouse roof and saw the outlines of four gunmen.

"We can't beat them all," Lola said.

"But if we'd planned something, hit them by surprise—"

"You're inexperienced," Lola said. "I'm old and slow. This was never a fight we could win."

"But I was willing to die trying."

"Right. You'd be dead, then Jimmy would kill

Molly, too. And I can't let that happen." She took a deep breath—as steady as her voice—and placed one cool hand on his face. "I left you twelve years ago to get you out of danger. I'm doing the same thing now."

Blair had walked Molly one-third of the way toward the truck and stopped. Her eyes—they were different shades of brown, Brody remembered—were narrowed, ready for anything.

"Go get your sister," Lola said again.

Brody nodded, and memories skated briefly through his mind: the old days with Mom, Dad, and Molly—magical Christmas mornings, camping at Crow Wing Lake, carol-singing dressed as snowmen. And more recent times, from their long conversations in the spare room to her teaching him how to load a fifteen-round mag.

He looked at her, his mouth open, and he was about to say that he didn't want to lose her again, then he bled out. No memories. No emotions. Only numbness.

He opened the passenger door and stepped outside.

· · ·

Two armed goons advanced on him. One wore a bulletproof vest and a riot helmet. "Hands in the air," he shouted. Brody did as he was ordered. The other gunman turned Brody around and pushed him against the truck. His hands were everywhere: in Brody's crotch, around his ankles, down both sides of his rib cage. He turned Brody again and frisked his front.

"Clear."

The goon in the riot helmet shoved Brody ahead of the truck. "Get moving." Brody reeled and fell to one knee. "Up. Get up." Brody got up. He started walking toward Blair and Molly. The goon followed, urging Brody along with the muzzle of his AR-15.

Blair gave a signal. Three more gunmen moved on the truck. They checked the cargo bed—empty—and opened the rear doors. One of them lifted the carryall of weapons from the backseat. Lola sat behind the wheel and didn't move. Jimmy's boys emptied their bags, spilling clothes everywhere. They checked beneath the seats, the center console, the glove compartment.

"Clear."

Brody had almost reached Molly by this point. Her clothes were dirty and bloodstained, and she wore only one sneaker. A heartbreaking detail, Brody thought. She looked at him through one eye—the other was bruised closed—and spoke his name softly.

Blair said his name, too. "Heya, Bro." She pushed Molly toward him, and Brody lunged to catch her.

"Molly," he said, lifting her, holding her. "Molly, I'm sorry. I'm so sorry."

"Oh, Brody," she said, placing her hand on his face where their mom had. "None of this is your fault."

They held each other a moment longer, then Blair sneered, "So sweet," and Brody looked at her. There was no anger in his expression, only that numbness—an empty, spiritless stare. This appeared to unnerve Blair just a touch. That wily glint in her eye faded and she pressed her lips together.

Brody had no words for her, either. No breath. He simply gathered Molly closer and turned back to the truck.

"Wait," Blair said.

He stopped, looked over his shoulder. Molly stumbled against him. He propped her up as gently as he could, fixing Blair with that same numb gaze.

"You did everything I wanted you to. You've earned this . . ." Blair reached into her back pocket, took out a worn black wallet, and offered it to him. "I told you I'd destroyed it. That was a lie. One of many, as it turns out."

This earned the slightest reaction; his left eyebrow twitched. He took the wallet, let it fall open. The face on the South Carolina driver's license was his. The name on the Social Security card, and on the numerous maxed-out store and credit cards, was his.

"This isn't your problem anymore," Blair said. "Get out of here. And don't even *think* about going to the

cops, or you'll be in a whole new kind of shitstorm—
one even I couldn't dream up."

Brody said nothing. He pushed his wallet into his
pocket, then he and Molly staggered back to the truck,
stepping into the glare of the headlights like two broken
characters walking into the sunset. The goon in the riot
helmet followed them the whole way, his rifle unneces-
sarily poised.

As Brody helped Molly onto the backseat, Blair
shouted, "*Okay, bitch. Out of the truck. And remember,
there are seventeen guns pointed at your kids.*" Brody
climbed in on the passenger side as his mom stepped
out on the driver's. "*Slowly. Hands where I can see
them.*" She didn't get the chance to raise her hands; four
bruisers—two in riot gear—jumped forward. They
threw her over the hood, her arms and legs spread.
One of them cracked her head against the hard steel.
The sound was loud inside the truck—a dull, metallic
thonk. They frisked her forcefully, their monstrous
hands probing, grabbing. As they lifted her, turned her
around, Brody saw a shallow cut over her eye. Blood
trickled from it, down her face, around her jawline. A
single drop fell and splashed on the hood. It stood out
on the silver paint with shocking clarity.

They searched her from the front, taking every opportunity to express their ugliness. One of them forced

her mouth open and ran his finger around her gums, checking for a cyanide pill, Brody thought.

"Clear."

Lola was turned around and marched toward the warehouse. She had a gunman on each arm, one in front—walking backward with his rifle in her face—and one behind. In the second before being led away, she had looked at Brody through the truck's windshield.

I love you, she had mouthed.

The other gunmen fell in behind. Two of them kept their sights locked on the truck. This didn't surprise Brody; the entire switch had been executed with military precision. Except for one small detail: they'd neglected to check under the dashboard.

"Brody . . ." Molly groaned from the backseat.

"I'm here, Moll," he said. But he wasn't. Not really.

He slid behind the wheel, started the ignition, and backed away.

. . .

He got as far as the lane that ran beside the rumbling factory, then stepped on the brake. It was the blood— that single drop of blood on the hood. Brody couldn't take his eye off it, the way it spread as the truck picked up speed. It looked like . . . like . . .

"Brody?" Molly said. "What are you doing?"

"Can you drive?" he asked.

"Can I . . ." Molly groaned. "Jesus, Brody. My left leg's messed up and I can only see out of one eye."

That drop of blood. It looked like the bright, burning coal that Brody had forged earlier—a symbol of his rage and resolve. With this association, the coal reignited. A spark, a flame. It melted his numbness.

"You work the gas and brake with your right foot," he said, looking at Molly in the rearview. "And you only need one eye to see."

"See? Brody, let's *go*." Molly lowered her head. "Can we . . . let's please . . . let's just go."

"I can't turn away from this, Moll," he said. "It's too big. I'll never be able to live with myself."

"I don't know what you're saying," she mumbled. "I just . . . I don't."

He pulled a thin wrap of notes from his pocket, turned in his seat, and handed it to her. "Two hundred and eighty-four dollars. That's all the money we have left. It'll cover some of your meds and a new pair of sneakers. Then get yourself a bus ticket."

"Brody—"

"Go to Nebraska," he said. "Owlfeather Farm. It's just outside a small town called Lone Arrow. Will you remember that?"

"Mom's farm," Molly said. Renée had obviously told her what she'd found, probably right before Jimmy came knocking.

"It's your farm now," Brody said. He clasped her hand and smiled weakly. "You'll love it. You have horses."

"I'm not going on my own."

His eye drifted back to the drop of blood on the hood. It had lost it shape, but not its color—its *redness*. And it was no longer just his mom's blood. It was his dad's, and Renée's, and Karl Janko's. It was every drop of blood that Jimmy had ever spilled. It was every vile thing he'd done.

"You have to," he said.

"I don't know what you're planning," Molly said, grasping as he pulled his hand from hers. "But I know it's something stupid."

"Yeah, it is." He reached beneath the dashboard. "This whole thing started when I did something stupid. I guess that's how it should end."

"Please, Brody . . . don't do this."

He grabbed the sawed-off shotgun and freed it from the clips holding it in place. The weight of it in his palm, its cold metalwork and the smooth wood of its stock, stirred the newly realized hardness in his veins.

"Jesus Christ, Brody," Molly grabbed the shoulder of his leather jacket. "This isn't just stupid. It's *suicide*."

Brody shook her off, opened the door, and hopped down from the truck. The night was icy and smelled sour. Smoke from the factory billowed overhead, a dirty shade of orange.

"*Brody.*"

"I love you, Molly. You're the best thing in my life by a thousand miles." Brody bypassed all the combative emotion—all the rage and grief—and gave her the biggest smile he could. "Now get out of here."

He started toward the warehouse, the shotgun clasped in one hand. Only two cartridges in the side-by-side barrels, but he only needed to kill two people.

. . .

Jimmy walked down to meet her, taking his sweet time, savoring every moment. His hair was now completely silver. The expensive oils he'd applied made it shine. No wrinkles across his brow or around his eyes, though. The scarring had kept his face from aging.

He stopped, looked her in the eye. They were the same height, five-foot-six. *Good for fucking,* he'd once snarled at her, laughing it off as flirtation when she knew he was being horribly serious. He didn't have fucking on his mind now, though. He curled the hard ridge of tissue that passed for his upper lip and spat in her face. His saliva was warm and it smelled and Lola didn't flinch.

"I was beginning to wonder if this day would ever come." His voice was raspier. He'd lost that Italian smoothness. Maybe his vocal cords had been damaged in the fire. "But here you are."

She said nothing.

"You have Blair to thank." He nodded toward Blair, who stood with her hands on her hips, close to her .45s—two of the many guns brought to the party. Lola thought that, if she moved suddenly, the jumpier soldiers would pull their triggers. There might even be some friendly fire. A small consolation, particularly if Jimmy got caught in the crossfire. At the very least, Lola would bleed out before he could have his fun.

"Go ahead," Blair said. "Thank me."

Lola looked at Jimmy and remained silent.

"She's like you, only better, stronger, faster." He pressed his tongue to the inside of his cheek. His eyes glowed, all but crackling. "And smarter. *Much* smarter. I'd put you in a cage with her, a fight to the death, for the sheer spectacle, but I fear it'd be over too soon."

"Oh, it would," Blair said.

Jimmy ran his palm across Lola's face, smearing the blood and spit away. "I want this to last a long, long time." He held his hand up for her to see, then licked the blood clean, not to shock her—he couldn't do that—but because he was thirsty.

"I've dreamed you," he said simply, sadly, then balled the hand he'd just licked and struck her across the jaw. He had terrific power for a man in his sixties—for a man who should have died twenty-six years ago, who'd breathed through a machine and navigated a coma. *I could never beat you*, she thought with bitterness and consternation. *I was foolish to ever think I could.*

She tried to stay upright but couldn't. The pain mapped a route from her jaw, to her spine, to her hips, then down her legs. She dropped heavily, blood leaking from her mouth onto the gravel.

This was just the beginning. There would be weeks of this. Maybe months. Lola spat more blood and sought out that desolate place inside her—that detached, solemn box she had lived in as a child—but instead found herself peering longingly down the gravel track. She frowned, then sighed. Her ground-level perspective showed her a pair of blue and white sneakers advancing behind the parked vehicles on the right-hand side of the track, moving stealthily from one to the next. Brody's sneakers, of course, because the goddamn kid didn't know when to quit.

"Fuck," she said.

No desolate place, no box. Not yet. Now she had to protect her child.

Now she had to fight.

Chapter Twenty-Seven

Brody expected to infiltrate the warehouse, sneak between crates and boxes, avoiding surveillance, until he found Blair and Jimmy. He'd envisioned a scenario where they were in a room together, unarmed, with no means of egress. Sitting ducks. Two shots. *Boom boom*, as John Lee Hooker famously sang.

Not the case. Blair, Jimmy, and his band of soldiers were still outside, forming a loose circle around Lola. Their weapons were lowered, but that didn't mean they weren't on high alert. One small sound—a sniff, a broken twig—and those barrels would be raised. The gunmen on the warehouse roof were a bigger problem. Their vantage point offered a greater probability of Brody being spotted as he closed in. For now, all eyes were on Jimmy.

Brody's were, too. He watched as Jimmy hit his mom—a bone-jarring right hook that dropped her to the ground. The coal inside Brody flared, its heat rising. He crept forward, using the parked vehicles for cover. He'd never fired a shotgun. The one thing he knew was that closer equaled deadlier. This was likely even truer with eighteen inches lopped off the barrels.

Gravel crunched beneath his sneakers. He stopped, held his breath, counted to ten. Nobody had heard; their attention was on the boss, holding court with his cruelty. Keeping low, Brody moved to the next vehicle—close enough now to hear Jimmy's voice.

". . . if you'll scream as loud as Vincent screamed. You know, Lola, for all his toughness . . ."

There were two more vehicles parked along this side, which would bring Brody to within range of his targets—lethal range, hopefully, depending on the shotgun's spread. He had a decision to make, though. Should he use the vehicles to get closer and risk being spotted? Or break cover and take the shot now, guaranteeing the element of surprise, but sacrificing the shotgun's effectiveness?

Closer, he thought. If this was his last act on this godforsaken earth, he'd for damn sure make it count. He wanted Blair—wanted to blast the cunningness out of her eyes. But what he *really* wanted was the man who had killed his father.

". . . and I will enjoy every moment, every drop of blood . . ."

The coal burned. Brody felt it in his fingertips, in the soles of his feet. It blazed through his heart. He shifted to the next vehicle. The nearest gunman stood with his back to Brody, maybe eight feet away. Brody could lift him out of his boots with one trigger pull.

Tempting, but no . . .

Jimmy kicked Lola in the ribs—a savage, eye-watering strike—and Brody used the distraction to move up to the final parked vehicle. This was it—as close as he could get. He took a moment to visualize what he had to do.

Two shots: Jimmy and Blair.

He brought his father's face to mind, then popped up from behind the hood, raising the shotgun. Lola moved at the same time. So did one of the gunmen on the roof.

The gunman fired first. The shot was desperate and missed Brody by a few inches, but it was close enough to stagger him. He jerked the front trigger and sent a comet of lead shot into the night sky. The report was formidable. The recoil more so. It knocked Brody backward and he sat down with a thud, behind the car and out of sight.

Another round zipped through the air where he'd been standing only a second before.

"Jesus," he gasped.

All hell broke loose.

. . .

In surrendering, Lola's only strategy was to exhibit no emotion, show no pain, and deny Jimmy as much satisfaction as possible. It was a disappointing end for a woman once revered for her mettle, but to fight would be to lose, and the only thing worse than dying would be to award Jimmy the glory of her defeat.

This was the plan, and she'd made her peace with it. Ever since viewing the three-and-a-half-minute video that Jimmy had sent, she knew that she had to bargain for her children's safety. And what else did she have to offer? Taking Brody to the range, packing all the guns and ammo, had been a precaution. Both Grandpa Bear and Shifu Chen had taught her to always be prepared, but she didn't think a single bullet would fly.

Her thinking changed when Brody reentered the fray.

She made her move only moments after Jimmy had kicked her in the ribs. It was not the optimum time in which to initiate an attack—by God, that kick had *hurt*—but Brody had provided a distraction, a tiny window in which to operate. He emerged from behind the nearest vehicle with her sawed-off twelve-gauge in his hands, raising it to shoulder-level. One of the gunmen on the roof registered the movement and re-acted quickly, getting off a shot before Brody could ad-equately position the shotgun. Every set of eyes turned away from Lola and toward Brody, who'd fired a shot of his own—a wild effort that threatened no one, but caused Jimmy, Blair, and a few of the soldiers to scatter. Brody teetered and dropped. Had he been hit? Lola didn't think so, and she couldn't contemplate the pos-sibility. She had to abandon any thought or action not directly connected to amassing a body count.

Step one in that thought process was to get a gun.

In the three-second window created by Brody's dis-traction, she had regained her feet and scanned the environment for opportunities. The gunman to her right had curled over when the shots were fired, making his rifle difficult to appropriate. The big bruiser to her left— Scott Hauer, aka the Tucson Tank; she recognized his face from the photo on her bulletin board—had dropped to one knee. He had an M4 carbine at the ready posi-tion and a Glock 19 in an open holster. He also wore a ballistic vest, making him the perfect shield.

Lola ducked behind him, lifted the Glock from his holster. Ideally, she would take out Jimmy and Blair first, but the gunman on the roof had fired at Brody again, and three more were closing in on his position. He only had one shell left in that twelve-gauge. If they flanked him—which they would—he'd be dead for sure.

She took out the gunman on the roof. One accurate shot. The way his forehead lifted indicated hollow points in the mag. A second later, one of the soldiers advancing on Brody's position was facedown with a bullet between his shoulder blades. Two dead before they realized what was happening—before the Tucson Tank realized that his gun was being used.

Lola took aim at the next gunman approaching Brody's position. The first shot hit his shoulder. It staggered but didn't drop him. He shrieked and turned sideways. Lola fired again and the left side of his face disappeared.

Three down.

Blair—so sharp—assessed the threat and rounded on Lola, both .45s engaged, looking for a nonlethal shot. She took it: a bullet to the kneecap. Bone and cartilage exploded. Blood flew. But not Lola's blood; Blair had shot the Tucson Tank—Lola's shield—in the knee. It had the desired effect. He howled and writhed and Lola had to fight to keep him in position. Blair fired again, missing her gun hand by an inch.

Only one option: Lola put the Glock to the Tucson Tank's cheekbone and pulled the trigger. She turned her face away just in time. Blood and bone fragments sprayed her hair and the side of her throat. The Tank flopped against her, one leg twitching.

Lola heaved the corpse to its feet as Blair fired between and through its legs. Another gunman had opened fire, thudding bullets into the ground. Lola squeezed off shots of her own—two of them at Blair, who deftly rolled and found cover beside the warehouse steps. The other gunman came up on Lola's side. In his panic, or inexperience, he chose the side with the gun. She halted him with a bullet to the chest.

Lola assessed the scene, peering from behind the shattered remains of the Tank's skull. Jimmy—the sly cat—had evidently ducked into cover. Five gunmen were dead. Others were scrambling or prone. If they all shot at once, they'd tear her apart. They'd been given a nonlethal directive, though, which made them hesitate.

Her shield was a heavy son of a bitch, and slick with blood. She would have to dump it and find cover. She looked first toward the row of parked cars where Brody had toppled from sight. As she watched, the last advancing gunman—it was Joey Cabrini, she saw now—slipped behind the back of an SUV. He'd reached his target.

Back-to-back shots rang out. One of them—the first, thankfully—was a shotgun.

Cover, Lola thought. She blind-fired the Glock until it clicked empty, seven erratic shots that bought her the time she needed. She retrieved the Tank's M4 from the ground, dragged his corpse several feet, dropped it, and broke for the vehicles parked on the near side of the gravel track. Bullets followed her, chipping at the ground around her boots. She lunged for the cover of the nearest car, and that was when she was hit. Not a bullet, a blade—one of the throwing knives from Blair's bandolier. It struck her left forearm with the power and suddenness of a scorpion's sting. That little bitch really was dangerous.

Lola scuttled behind the wheel and took a moment to center herself. Bullets splashed the car and blew out the glass. She looked at the knife in her arm but didn't remove it—let it stem the blood flow. Keeping low, she scurried farther along the rank of vehicles, and blended with the shadows.

. . .

Gunfire cracked against the night sky and blurred the few stars. Brody's first thought was to hide beneath the SUV he'd taken cover behind. A more compelling thought—in keeping with the coal that burned inside him, and the hard DNA passed down from Lola—was to use the one shell remaining in the shotgun. Remembering his crash course at the range, he maintained a short distance from cover to increase his movement and visibility. A peek over the hood confirmed Blair was too far away and Jimmy was out of sight. Several bodies were scattered across the warehouse's frontage. He couldn't see his mom at all, then realized—to his awe—that she was using one of Jimmy's guys as a shield. All the attention was on her.

Almost all. A familiar gunman marched toward the SUV: Joey from Bayonet. His directive then had been to intimidate—to terrify. Now his intent was to kill.

Brody recalled another lesson from the range. "Keep low," his mom had said. "Make yourself a smaller target. If you can go prone, do it." Brody dropped to his knees, then slowly to his stomach. The SUV's shadow fell over him like a blanket. He brought the shotgun to his shoulder and held it firmly, remembering its bright kick.

Joey advanced. Brody tracked his position from beneath the SUV. He shut out everything else—the gunshots, the screams—and focused on Joey's combat boots, getting steadily closer. He exhaled a jerky breath and curled his finger around the rear trigger.

It happened quickly. Joey slunk around the back of the SUV, paused for a second, then jumped out. He was crouched, looking down the barrel of his AR-15, its muzzle aimed several inches too high. Brody didn't hesitate. He pulled the trigger an instant before Joey pulled his.

Joey's shot missed. Brody's didn't.

The sawed-off hammered against his shoulder and voiced a devastating report. A cloud of shot erupted from the left barrel. It severed one of Joey's legs at the knee and left the other hanging from a thick cord of fat and muscle. Joey dropped as if someone had yanked a rug from behind him. He didn't scream—he grunted, shocked and pig-like, rocking on his belly with his eyes rolled to whites.

Brody repelled all emotion: horror, guilt, disgust. This moment was about survival. Later—if there *was* a later—he could anatomize the shooting and everything associated with it. He could be human again, but right now he needed his blood to run cold.

He got to his knees, turned the shotgun around, and cracked the butt against Joey's forehead. It took three swift, fierce strikes to knock him unconscious.

Brody yanked the AR-15 from Joey's limp grasp and soldiered on.

...

Lola flared inside. She tasted the fight, the thrill, the heat. A sound like ringing crystal flooded her mind. She hadn't planned on going to war, but here she was.

The unstoppable Lola Bear, locked and loaded once again.

The three remaining gunmen on the roof were open targets. All, to their credit, had gone prone, but their little pale faces still peeked up over the edge, and that was enough. Lola squeezed the M4's trigger twice and took two of them out. She moved to another vehicle—to get a better angle, but also to create confusion as to where the shots were coming from—and took out the third.

The rooftop threat had been eliminated. The ground threat remained: at least seven soldiers. And Blair. And Jimmy. They were scattered. Some were in cover. Shots rang from multiple directions. Bullets struck the parked vehicles with hammer-like sounds. Glass exploded. Tires hissed. Lola blind-fired toward the warehouse, then moved again. She peered through the tinted window of a Chevy Suburban and noticed muzzle flash from behind the vehicles parked on the other side of the gravel track. Staccato shots, directed at the warehouse.

Brody.

"*Keep moving,*" Lola shouted between shots. He was in the shadows, but if she had noticed his muzzle flash, Jimmy's guys had, too. Underscoring this logic, bullets rattled the hood and windshield of the car closest to Brody's position. Lola located the shooter. He was tucked into the deep shadow around the loading dock. She switched the M4 to three-round burst, rolled from cover, and squeezed the trigger twice. One of the six bullets found its mark. The shooter staggered from the shadows, clutching his bleeding gut. Lola switched back to semiauto, aimed, and removed a piece of his skull.

Back into cover. She moved.

Bullets continued to sting the air. The vehicles rocked on their flats, their paint jobs perforated. Another gunman broke from the shadows and charged Lola's side of the track, firing on the run. He'd clearly abandoned the nonlethal objective. Lola timed her move. She aimed through the broken windows of what had once been a Lexus and squeezed off a shot.

Nowhere near. Her support hand was weakening—that goddamn knife in her forearm, affecting her aim. She fired twice more, missed both times. Now the charging gunman—it was Jared Conte, another face from her wall of fame—had seen *her* muzzle flash and swung his rifle toward her.

She dropped just in time. Bullets sizzled over her head.

"*I've got you, bitch*," he screamed.

Lola rolled to the next vehicle along and took up a new position. Grimacing, she mounted the M4 and popped up over the hood.

Jared was no slouch. He was ready for her.

Lola's luck, her talent, whatever it was, had run out. The barrel of Jared's rifle looked enormous.

He was beaten to the trigger, though. Not by Lola, but by Brody, who'd broken cover on his side of the track. He fired once, hitting Jared in the back. A ballistic vest stopped the bullet, but the force of it knocked him to his knees. Lola finished the job. Her left hand trembled but she was close enough that it didn't matter.

She aimed for the middle of Jared's face but got his throat. Six or seven inches low, but the result was the same.

Another dead soldier.

Lola moved into deeper cover, clutching her wounded forearm. She didn't know how many of Jimmy's guys were still in the fight, or how many rounds were in the M4's mag—assuming there had been thirty to begin with. It was not like her to lose count. Another sign of getting old.

"Head in the game," she berated herself, wiping grime and blood from her face. She needed a pistol, that much was certain, so that she could aim and fire one-handed. Maybe then—

She felt that scorpion sting again, in her right thigh this time. It rocked her on her feet, and as she tried to back away another perfectly weighted blade plunged into her right hip, deep enough to chip bone.

"Shit," Lola whispered.

Blair crouched beside the foremost vehicle, an alligator grin on her face. She'd used Jared as a distraction—hell, as a *sacrifice*—and it had worked. As Lola watched, she plucked another knife from her bandolier and flashed it through the smoky air. Lola twisted sideways and avoided it by an inch. She raised the M4 one-handed and sprayed off a few hopeful rounds. Blair rolled to her right with a nimbleness that Lola hadn't had for twenty years. She came up with both .45s in her hands but wouldn't chance the lethal shot. Instead, she weaved toward Lola, closing the distance between them with daunting speed. Lola managed to squeeze off another round—it went well wide—then Blair knocked the M4 out of her grasp. It bounced off the hood of a nearby car and dropped out of sight. Lola threw an elbow and a knee, but Blair blocked both with no real effort, countering with a front kick to Lola's right thigh. It was a deliberate, exact strike that drove the knife there deeper into the muscle.

Lola folded at the knees and tumbled down a shallow embankment, stopping at the chain-link fence that separated the warehouse grounds from the rail yard. The night took a slow, frightening loop. Gunfire boomed and echoed.

Blair's outline floated on the bank above her, framed by dirty light.

"Jimmy wants you alive," she said. "But I want to give him your fucking head."

Chapter Twenty-Eight

The caustic odor of propellant choked the air, and gun smoke drifted in white rags. Jimmy Latzo had reappeared. He stepped around the bodies of his fallen soldiers, picked up a rifle, and fired into the sky until the mag was dry.

"*Motherfuckers!*" he screamed. His eyes were broad circles, and even from a distance Brody could see the damnation in them. "*You fucking fucks. I'll fucking kill you fuckers!*"

He threw the empty rifle away, picked up another, and pumped rounds into the line of vehicles behind which Brody had taken cover.

"*Motherfuckers!*"

Brody scrambled to a different position. The visibility wasn't as good but the cover was better. Until that point, he'd primarily been laying down suppressive fire, letting his mom do the heavy lifting, but seeing Jimmy set a rock tumbling through him. Everything shook. His blood chilled. It was all he could do to keep from leaping over the cars and running at him with his gun blazing.

Jimmy emptied this second rifle, picked up another. The remaining soldiers rallied to his side—five of them in a ragged line. Two had lower body wounds. One had blood pouring down his face. They still packed fire-power, though, and they could still use it. Leo Rossi—Brody's other friend from Bayonet, who'd held a gun to Molly's head—stood at the far end of the line.

Brody blind-fired to set them on their toes. They retaliated, all weapons smoking, spent shells helicopter-ing to the ground. Brody moved to yet a new position and braved a glance. The shooting stopped. The smoke lifted. Jimmy motioned his guys to flank the vehicles while he held the front. Brody halted them with a splash of gunfire. He hit one of them, a lucky shot, and the thug dropped, screaming, clutching his knee. It wasn't all luck, though. Leo Rossi had fired a couple of reflex shots. One went wide. The other punched through Brody's leather jacket and ripped through his side.

Shot I've been shot I've been—

The pain was like a forest fire in miniature. A raging, wicked thing. Brody hit the ground in a heap, then pushed himself against the wheel of the car. He clutched his side. Blood seeped through his fingers.

"*Come on, you motherfucker,*" Jimmy yelled.

Brody looked at the blood on his hand, then at the AR-15. He didn't know where his mom was, and couldn't depend on her now. This was down to him. One bullet. That was all he needed. One sweet, precise shot to blow the life out of Jimmy's body.

He nodded. This was it.

Fuck you, Jimmy, he thought, and broke from cover, bringing the gun to his shoulder. He rose through a haze of pain and anger. He even *heard* it. A wild engine sound. A kamikaze cry. Leo and the other thugs faded from view. The bodies, the blood, the warehouse . . . it all faded. Only Jimmy remained.

He expanded in Brody's eye. In that second, he was the entire world.

This was Jimmy Latzo. Mobster. Torturer. The Italian Cat.

This was the man who had killed his father.

Brody locked him in his sights and pulled the trigger. Nothing.

He pulled the trigger a second time. And a third.

Zilch. Zip. The gun was spent.

Brody sagged. His heart curled up and died. The rest of his body would follow, he thought, although he could still hear that wild engine sound, that ka-mikaze cry. Jimmy's guys mounted their rifles and prepared to shoot, but Jimmy raised one hand and held them.

"No," he growled. Craziness spilled from his eyes. His scars were flushed and glowing. "This mother-fucker is mine."

He lifted his rifle and took aim, then a bright white light covered everything.

. . .

Headlights—high beam—raced toward them. The police, Brody assumed, even though he couldn't see the splashy beat of their reds and blues. His mom had suggested they wouldn't venture out here, but this much gunfire, even in Carver City, surely couldn't be ignored.

Jimmy and his goons squinted, throwing up their hands to deflect the light. Brody did, too, but not before he saw that this wasn't the arrival of Carver City's finest. It was a pickup truck. A silver Sierra 1500. His mom's truck, no less.

Molly behind the wheel.

She took the gravel track at startled-cat speed, grit flying from the rear tires, the engine—that kamikaze cry—filling the night. She didn't stop. She didn't touch the brake. Brody caught a glimpse of her—or *imagined* he did: grinning deliriously, hair hanging across the bruised side of her face, hands gripping the wheel.

Leo was the first to be hit. The grille snapped him. His face met and collapsed the windshield and he spun away over the roof—launched so high that he was the last to touch down. The next three thugs were thrown to the sides, bouncing and breaking over the gravel. One of them hit the car Brody stood behind with fatal force. The unfortunate chump that Brody had shot in the kneecap—already on the ground—was pulled into the wheel arch and dragged along until Molly had concluded her brief terror drive.

The truck jounced and slowed, its momentum influenced by these external forces. It struck Jimmy at half the speed. He rolled over the hood and along the driver's side, coming to rest several feet away. The side mirror had ripped the jacket from his body.

Molly came to rest, too. The truck slewed, coughing up a curtain of dust, and crashed into the warehouse's metal siding. Smoke boiled from beneath the crimped hood.

Brody stood for too long with his jaw hanging, blinking his wide, wondering eyes. "Molly," he finally whispered, and started toward the truck, forgetting the bullet hole in his side—remembering when the pain speared through his body.

His legs betrayed him. He dropped.

"Molly," he said again.

He started to crawl.

. . .

It was all sound and haze. Lola breathed gunpowder and coughed. Stars winked through the smoke, or maybe that was the pain—fierce points of light mottling her vision.

Blair placed her boot on Lola's throat and pressed down.

"I thought you were special."

Lola twisted and struck with her stronger right hand, but could get no leverage, no power. Blair smiled and held her in place.

"I was in awe of you, even though I'd never met you. I revered your talent, and urged Jimmy—who *can* be a little hotheaded at times—to tread carefully. That all seems excessive, now that I've met you." Blair exerted more pressure, grinding at the heel. "You're really quite disappointing."

The knives in Lola's forearm and hip had come out when she'd toppled down the embankment. The one in her thigh was still there, driven deep by Blair's front kick. Lola gasped, eyes bulging, and dug her fingers into the wound. She plucked at the slick handle, working it loose by fractions. Pain bolted down her right side. It took everything she had to shut it out.

"I have this clear picture of walking back to Jimmy, carrying your head by the hair." Blair grinned and held up this imaginary trophy, rolling her wrist to mimic swinging it like some gruesome pendulum. "It's such a warrior-like image, isn't it? The kind of thing that inspires myths and legends."

Lola's vision grayed, but more stars appeared. The brightest, biggest stars yet. Her chest locked, needing oxygen that wasn't there. She teased the knife out another quarter of an inch.

"I mean," Blair continued, "Jimmy would be *pissed*, and I can understand that—he's waited a long time to kill you. But oh, that *image*."

Lola pinched at the knife handle, wiggling it inside the wound. Another fraction of an inch. She almost had it in her grasp.

"I'm torn, Ms. Bear." Blair pressed with her heel, harder still. A muscle in her jaw flexed. "Although I'm glory-bound either way."

There was a rush of insistent light somewhere behind Blair, an emphatic engine sound. It was all very dream-like . . . confusing. Lola wondered if it was death, its brightness and roar. *Not yet,* she thought. She hadn't expected to win this war, but she still had one move left. With every scrap of spirit left in her soul, she pulled the throwing knife from her thigh, and plunged it into Blair's left calf.

Blair never saw it coming. She didn't scream or hiss, but she *did* lift her boot from Lola's throat and stagger backward, and that was all Lola needed—to be able to move, to *breathe.* If she could get to her feet, or even to one knee, she had a chance. Blair was wounded now. The playing field was about twenty years from being level, but this fight wasn't over.

Become the storm, she thought, summoning the long-ago wisdom of Benjamin Chen. But a storm would not be enough here. She needed to engulf and destroy. *Become the fire.* She needed to burn.

Lola rolled over, got her hands beneath her, and pushed herself up—first to one knee, then to her feet. Blair immediately attacked, and she was still strong. A forceful punch, a looping elbow. Lola dodged the first, half blocked the second. She was able to counter, throwing a fist into Blair's rib cage, applying everything Shifu Chen had taught her: generating power through her body, letting it amass, then directing it into the final few inches of her strike. It was not the punch she hoped for—she lacked the strength for that—but it buckled Blair nonetheless, and broke ribs. Two, maybe three.

Blair twisted away from her, dragging in hurt breaths. She held her side and snarled. Lola put the fire into her feet and kicked. Once to Blair's upper arm, again to her injured leg. Neither kick landed cleanly. The women exchanged a clumsy fusillade of fists, knees, and elbows. Blair got the better of it. She blocked two high punches, set her feet, and threw a fist of her own. It cut through Lola's defense, smashed into her sternum, and sent her staggering backward.

Stars again, bright and piercing. Lola fell against the sagging chain-link fence—it bowed beneath her weight—and barked a jagged, burning breath. With room to move, Blair seized her opportunity. She drew her .45s and aimed.

Lola leaned backward, pushed with the balls of her feet, and flipped over the fence. Bullets whizzed beneath her; Blair was still going for leg shots. What little tension remained in the fence buoyed Lola's weight and she landed on her feet in the rail yard. She turned immediately and staggered away, melting into the shadows.

The yard was dark, full of cover. Boxcars hulked in silhouette. A cold locomotive stared blindly. Lola ducked behind a concrete buffer stop, covered her mouth, and stifled a scream.

Her head cleared. Not by much, but enough to focus on her objective: add to the body count, whatever it took. The rail yard had leveled the playing field a few more degrees. Lola could use the shadows. Use her experience.

Be the fire.

She watched as Blair hopped the chain-link fence and wiped something—blood, probably—from her mouth. She still held her guns.

"Okay, you tired old bitch." Her voice carried to Lola, laced with mania. "Now we've got a fight."

Chapter Twenty-Nine

Not again, Jimmy thought. *No fucking way.*

There was a bleak, watery pain in his hip. Something in there was cracked or dislocated. His left knee had been rearranged and his foot pointed at two o'clock rather than twelve. He was no stranger to pain, though. Oh no, he and pain were old compadres. Thick and thin. Ben and fucking Jerry. He dragged himself to one of the parked cars—which were supposed to provide cover for *his* fucking guys—and used it to get upright. Blood ran into his eyes. He gingerly touched his scalp and felt not hair but the top of his skull.

Not good. Not fucking good at *all*.

His left foot stabilized him, but couldn't bear his weight. He could limp, though, and did so, moving from the car to where Brad Lemke lay mumbling on the ground. Brad's legs were a mess of odd angles and sticking-out bones. One side of his face had met the gravel and been planed to a smooth red surface. His pistol was on the ground, out of reach.

"Glab-glab," Brad said. His eye locked on Jimmy, then flashed open and closed. "Glab-glab. Glab-glab."

"Yeah," Jimmy said. He bent his right knee— managed to reach down and hook Brad's pistol up off the ground. "It's all fucking bullshit."

He aimed unsteadily and shot Brad, twice, because the first bullet only clipped off one of his ears. The second was truer, though, upsetting the smooth red half of his face.

No more glab-glab for Brad.

Or for *any* of them. Jimmy looked around. Corpses everywhere. Corpses wearing riot shields and bullet-resistant vests, carrying semiautomatic rifles. How much goddamn protection did they *need*? And yet . . . corpses. He saw Scott Hauer—the Tucson Tank himself—with one side of his skull blown away. Jared Conte was facedown in a lake of blood. Leo Rossi's spine was L-shaped and his brains were waterfalling out of his open head.

No sign of Blair. She'd gone after Lola. There'd been gunshots from that direction but Jimmy had no idea which of them was still standing. Probably Lola, given the way this whole shitshow had gone down.

This was all horribly familiar.

"Not again," Jimmy insisted, and shook his head. This wasn't over. *He* was still standing, after all, and *he* was the only one that mattered.

He could still spill some blood, and dammit, he was going to.

Right on cue: the pickup truck's door clunked open and the cripple dropped out. She stood for a moment, then collapsed to her knees. Jimmy looked at her through the blood-mask of his face, thinking that a little eye-for-an-eye action was appropriate here. He checked the pistol. Eight rounds in the magazine and one in the chamber. He could kill the bitch nine times.

Jimmy shunted the mag home and wavered toward the truck. Pain rolled through him. He'd known, and survived, worse. It wouldn't stop him now. Still some distance away, he lifted the pistol and squeezed off a shot. The bullet punched a hole through the truck's fender. The girl screamed. She tried getting to her feet, but floundered and sprawled. Jimmy fired again and lifted a cloud of grit three inches from her left hand.

"*Bitch*," he screamed. His damaged hip, and the blood in his eyes, had affected his aim. He gritted his teeth and labored closer, stomping one foot, dragging the other. Five feet from the girl—close enough, goddammit—he took aim again, and was about to pull the trigger when two words flared at the back of his mind.

Bargaining chip.

He blinked. This was a Blair-like moment of ingenuity. If Lola was still alive, she'd likely be open to renegotiation. It was the reason this crippled little bitch was brought in to begin with. If Lola was dead, and Blair came back . . . well, shit, he would pull the trigger then. And happily.

"Get up," Jimmy sneered. He hopped the last few feet and pressed the gun to the back of her head. "Now. Right fucking now. Get up."

She didn't move. He rapped the barrel against her skull, hard enough to draw blood, and that did the trick. The girl whimpered, lifting one hand over her head, pushing herself up with the other. Jimmy helped, insomuch as he grabbed a fistful of her collar and pulled.

"Let's go. Fucking move it."

They started toward the warehouse, the girl in front, Jimmy behind. They stumbled and limped in peculiar unison.

"Look at us," he observed wryly. "Couple of hopalong assholes."

He eased her toward the loading dock steps and they struggled up slowly. Jimmy wiped blood from his eyes and fought a wave of wooziness. He could *do* this, by Christ. Just a little longer.

"Lola," he shouted, or *tried* to. His voice cracked—barely a sound came out. He moved the girl in front of the warehouse's open bay door and stepped behind her, the gun placed to her head. She gasped and squirmed.

"*Lola*." That was better. Much louder. He spat blood, took a breath, and shouted, "*Lola Bear. I have your daughter. Come and get her.*"

His voice carried across the lot.

He'd win this war yet.

...

Brody had the perfect shot—the center of Jimmy Latzo's spine—but didn't have a gun. By the time he'd acquired one (and checked to make sure it was loaded), Jimmy had scaled the loading dock steps and positioned himself behind Molly.

Jimmy called out to Lola—a desperate, frenzied cry. Or perhaps he always sounded that way.

Raising the gun—another AR-15 variant—Brody hobbled in front of the warehouse and faced Jimmy.

"Let her go," he groaned.

Jimmy looked at him. His face was a red horror mask. A flap of skin drooped across his brow. "Get the fuck out of here, kid," he snarled, "while you still can."

"Let her *go*." Brody staggered closer, tightening his grip on the rifle. He didn't have a shot, though. Jimmy was behind Molly, with only his bloody face exposed over her shoulder. And while it temptingly resembled the center of a target, Brody's hands trembled too much to risk pulling the trigger.

"Fuck you," Jimmy hissed. He extended the pistol and fired twice in Brody's direction. Neither bullet came close. He appeared to consider another shot— his gun hand shook as much as Brody's—then thought better of it, obviously deciding it was wiser to conserve ammo.

Brody stood his ground. He had hoped to appear stronger than he was, but his trembling hands betrayed him, as did his ashen face and the blood trickling from beneath his jacket. He wouldn't pull the trigger and Jimmy knew it.

Molly squirmed and Jimmy settled her again with another dull crack from the pistol barrel. Brody's finger hovered close to the trigger.

"You want this bitch," Jimmy said. "Go put a bullet in your mommy's back. Then I'll consider it."

"Only person I'm shooting is you," Brody said.

Jimmy snorted laughter. A wet, mad sound. Blood dripped from his jaw, onto Molly's shoulder.

"Go get your mom," he said. "Tell her I'm waiting."

He ushered Molly backward, through the open bay door, and slowly into the shadows. Brody watched them disappear. He waited for a moment, trying to smother his pain and fear, then he followed.

. . .

Lola's experience was offset by Blair's youth, and the fact that she wasn't as badly injured. She was wily, too; Lola listened for her footfalls through the rail yard, maybe a couple of hurt, rasping breaths. Blair made no sound at all, though. She was a ghost.

Lola waited, studying the darkness. She reached and grabbed the most basic, primitive weapon: a rock. It was the size of her fist, easy to grip and swing. Blair—with her .45s—had the advantage here, too, but up close it would all be the same.

. . .

The front of the warehouse was bathed in light. There was some deep shadow cast by the raised loading dock, but Brody couldn't enter the bay or side doors without being seen. Jimmy was always dangerous. He might have positioned himself behind a crate, using the top of it to stabilize his aim, ready to pull the trigger the moment Brody hobbled into view.

Needing another way in, Brody moved away from

the open bay door, then around the crumpled truck and along the side of the warehouse. It was darker here, but he found what he wanted soon enough: an office window. Brody tried opening it. Locked, of course. He shook off his dad's leather jacket—not without discomfort—and balled it like a mitten around his right fist. As he struck the window, he fired the rifle with his left hand, the stock tucked against his ribs—six loud shots that enveloped the sound of breaking glass.

Brody reached through the window, flipped the catch, lifted it open. He pulled his jacket on again—it was black; a good color for sneaking through the shadows—then leaned across the sill and let forward momentum carry him over, into the office. He landed on the tiles and broken glass with a crunch, clutching his side as the pain bloomed.

Getting to his feet was hard. He brought Molly to mind. And his dad. Renée, too. He held them there, poised above the burning coal like a ridge he could grasp on the updraft.

Sweat coated his body. The office rolled once—a gloomy, boxlike space with an uneven floor. Brody caught hold of the desk, steadied himself, then made his way into the warehouse proper. He heard Jimmy immediately, gasping and cursing.

Brody hugged the shadows and advanced from behind a row of crates stacked along one side, knowing he couldn't approach from the front or let Jimmy see him at all.

He needed to go past Jimmy, attack from behind.

. . .

Blair played the stealth game for a while, then switched her strategy, opting to draw Lola out.

"You can't beat me, Ms. Bear," she goaded, and brayed laughter—a sound full of color and confidence. "You're too slow. Too worn out. Too old."

There was a time for caution, and a time to throw down. Clearly, Lola had given her no reason to be afraid.

"Come on, bitch. Let's do this."

Lola moved, making no sound at all, relying on her experience; impetuousness was for the young. Every step was painstaking, lifting and softly placing her boots, taking an indirect route, but one that kept her hidden. She slipped between two buffer stops, crept into the shadow of a maintenance shed, crossed the tracks behind a rusty locomotive. As ever, she focused on one objective: increasing the body count. She'd lost blood. The pain was a blizzard. She still burned, though.

She saw Blair, mostly in shadow, standing on the tracks between two boxcars.

"I'm right here, Lola. Let's see what you've got."

Keep running your mouth, little girl, Lola thought. She edged closer, approaching on Blair's blind side. Fifteen yards away, she grabbed a handful of dirt and stones and threw it, not aiming for Blair, but for the boxcar beside her.

The debris struck with a rattling sound, diverting Blair's attention. Lola sprang from the shadows and attacked with the rock in her hand. She envisioned bringing it down on the top of Blair's skull and dividing it into three, drawing on an old memory featuring her stepdaddy and his spanging hammer.

Not this time. Blair heard—or maybe sensed—Lola's approach. She swiveled, avoided the downward swoop of the rock, countered with a humming fist that caught Lola square and dropped her.

"Like I said: Too slow. Too worn out. Too old."

Blair pulled her guns.

...

It wasn't all crates, shadow, and cover. There were walkways, doorways, broad lanes for forklift trucks to maneuver. Jimmy had retreated down the center gangway, shambling backward with the gun still rooted to Molly's skull. He wasn't hard to track.

"Nobody *fuuuuucks* with me," he bellowed. He'd

lost his mind as well as the top of his scalp. "Dogs run the fuck away."

Brody timed his moves, shuffling across the exposed areas, crawling from one crate to the next. He dragged his feet and breathed hard. Jimmy would have heard him if he hadn't been making so much noise himself.

"Nobody. *No-fucking-body.*"

Jimmy stopped walking. There was a row of forklift trucks behind him, open walkway to his left and right. Brody didn't think he could cross that space without being seen. Molly, however, provided a distraction. She pushed against Jimmy, rolling her head from side to side, flicking her hair into his face. While Jimmy dealt with her—a third sickening pistol whip—Brody crossed the walkway and snuck in behind the forklifts. He paused to let a wagon train of hurt pass through his upper body, then limped into position, rifle raised, eight feet from Jimmy's back.

A dark thought struck him, though, and he lifted his finger from the trigger. What if he shot Molly, too? With this caliber, at this range, it was entirely possible the bullet would tear through Jimmy and hit Molly's spine, or her lung, or her heart. Even a headshot, point-blank, could deflect badly. He had to get Molly away from him before pulling the trigger.

"*Nobody . . . fucking dogs.*"

Brody flipped the rifle around, buttstock forward. One good strike to the back of Jimmy's sick, bleeding skull would do it. He gasped and blinked through the pain, tightened his grip on the gun.

"*Dogs fucking run.*"

Brody edged closer.

. . .

Lola still had the rock in her hand. She threw it without thinking, without aiming, a hopeful pitch from the ground. It had little power, but devilish accuracy, hitting Blair beneath the jaw. Blair's head snapped backward. She reeled—almost tripped over one of the rails. Lola swept with her stronger left leg. Her boot met Blair's right ankle with a vicious thud.

She swept again . . . and again.

This third strike did it. Blair gave at the knee, then hit the ground. She fired both pistols and sent two bullets to the stars. Lola scrambled to her feet and pounced. She kicked one of the guns from Blair's grasp—it spun away into the darkness—then dropped a knee onto the damaged side of her rib cage. Blair screamed. It was the first time Lola had heard that sound, and it was wonderful.

Blood trickled from the knife wounds in Lola's left forearm, her right thigh and hip. There was nothing wrong with her right fist, though. She rained two full-blooded blows into Blair's face, smashing her cheekbone, breaking her nose. Blair's mouth gaped for air. She swung the other pistol toward Lola, but Lola batted it away. It toppled from Blair's hand and rang off the rail.

"Who's worn out now?" Lola sneered. "Who's slow?"

Blair twisted and struggled, trying to regain her feet. Lola scooped up a handful of gravel from between the crossties, rammed it into Blair's open mouth, and looped a punch to the underside of her jaw. Small stones and broken teeth flew.

"Who's fucking *old*?"

Lola reached for the gun. Blair—desperately, impossibly—saw an opening. She threw a punch of her own, connecting with Lola's left forearm. It jarred the wound there, causing Lola to sprawl. Her hand came down several inches from the gun. Blair spat a cloud of grit and got to one knee. She launched a volley of blows born out of pain and the unthinkable notion of defeat. Some connected. Others glanced off Lola's arms and face. The two women fought their way to their feet, lifted on an upsurge of adrenaline and defiance.

They rose together. They fell together.

Exhausted, hurting . . . Lola dropped to her knees and Blair fell against her. She rolled away, still coughing stones—snatched the last knife from her bandolier and threw it. Lola felt the blade bite through her jacket, into her upper arm, but it didn't have the velocity to stick. It fell to the ground, small and shiny against the black crosstie.

Lola picked it up.

There wasn't much on Blair's face besides blood and pain, but Lola thought, for just a second, she saw something that might be respect. It floated out of Blair's eyes, a haunted, somewhat childlike expression. Her mouth opened soundlessly. Blood and grayish saliva drizzled down her chin.

Lola threw the knife.

She threw it from her broken childhood, from a box of muted emotions, from twenty-six years of running. She threw it for all of Jimmy's victims, who were *her* victims, too. She threw it for her children, and for the uncompromising strip of fire that best defined her soul.

The knife hit Blair in the center of her forehead and plunged to the midpoint of the handle. It went through her skull and into her frontal lobe. Blair first squinted, then opened her eyes as wide as they would go. A rill of blood trickled down the middle of her nose.

"Mizzy Bear," she said, and almost smiled.

Lola wiped her face and breathed painfully. It took several efforts, but she eventually got to her feet. She looked toward the warehouse—it was eerily still over there—then back at Blair. Such an impressive woman, but too young, too dangerous.

"You gave me one hell of a fight," Lola said.

"Mizzy Bear."

A cold breeze howled between the boxcars. The nearby factory clashed and clanged. Blair's left eye spasmed to one side and she held out her hand. Lola didn't know what to do with this gesture, and it didn't matter anyway. Blair dropped her hand a second later and fell down dead.

Lola stepped around her and picked up the .45. She knew what dead was. She'd also known the dead to come back.

"You were the best I ever beat," she said.

Lola aimed the gun, pulled the trigger once, and blew Blair's skull wide open.

. . .

Jimmy gesticulated as he made his deranged announcements about dogs running away, waving the pistol between Molly's skull and anywhere else. A sudden knock to the back of the head could cause him to yank the trigger. Brody had to strike at the right time.

He wasn't quiet—he wheezed with pain and nervous energy, dragging his body like a heavy sack—but it didn't matter; Jimmy was lost in his own world, waiting for his nemesis to appear so that he could exact his long-awaited revenge. His white shirt was mapped with blood—continents separated by small bodies of water. He was canted to the right, his weight almost entirely on his good leg.

"Nobody *fucks*. Dogs *run*."

Brody got to within a foot of him. Close enough to smell the blood, the heat, the madness. Tendrils of steam danced from the gap in Jimmy's scalp.

"They fucking *run*."

Not this dog, Brody thought. He waited for Jimmy to lift the pistol from Molly's head, then he struck. It was a crisp, direct hit. The buttstock met the rear of Jimmy's skull with a force that sent a recoil-like vibration through Brody's arms. The sound was appalling—a damp, toe-curling crack. Jimmy wobbled. He fired two shots. Bullets pinged off the warehouse roof.

He was a tough old cat, though, and he didn't go down. He half turned and Brody hit him again, not as hard, but it was enough. Jimmy fell but took Molly with him.

They landed in a tangle. Molly tried to separate herself, but Jimmy held tight. His eyes were mad fog lights. They flicked every which way, then found Brody and swelled. He aimed the gun and pulled the trigger.

Too close; the bullet scuffed the shoulder of Brody's jacket. He flinched, then winced—the hole in his side protested at the sudden movement. There was no chance of returning fire, not until Molly was in the clear. She shimmied and fought. Jimmy struggled to hold on to her, still waving the gun in Brody's direction. Brody took a chance. He lurched forward and smashed the rifle's buttstock against Jimmy's injured knee.

Jimmy wailed. His arms flew out to the sides and his body jumped. Another bullet sizzled from his pistol. It skimmed harmlessly away, across the concrete floor. Molly scrambled out of his orbit.

Brody flipped the rifle back around, pulling the buttstock into his shoulder and peering down sights that doubled and swam. Jimmy—the solid old bastard—rose unsteadily to one knee. He leered through his red mask and took two more shots at Brody. The first flashed past Brody's right ear, hot and loud. The second did nothing. Just a gutless click. The gun was empty.

Brody made a sound deep in his chest—a relieved sob. He limped closer to compensate for his uncertain aim. He didn't want to miss.

"You killed my dad," he whispered.

"Dogs run away," Jimmy replied with the matter-of-factness of a four-year-old. His wide, mad eyes flashed.

Brody hooked his finger around the trigger, exerted the slightest pressure, then eased off. Did he really want to kill this man? Jimmy had nothing left, after all. No gun. No mind. Furthermore, did Brody want Molly to witness it—to *see* him take a life? Something like that would leave a constant shadow. It would scar and harm, and undoubtedly cause a rift in their relationship.

He looked at her. His beautiful, strong sister, always the voice of reason and wisdom. Always his hero.

"Do it," she said.

Brody did it.

...

Three shots, to remove all doubt. The same number of bullets his mom had fired into Jimmy. Brody's were more decisive, though. One to the center of Jimmy's chest. One to his throat. One to his head.

Jimmy went down, and down Jimmy stayed.

"No more lives for you," Brody said.

The Italian Cat was dead.

Brody dropped the rifle and went to Molly. She threw her arms around him and they cried together. He didn't know if the fight was over, if their mom was still alive, or how they'd deal with the aftermath. The only certainty was that he was in his sister's arms, and in that moment, that was all he wanted.

Chapter Thirty

Lola still burned, and would until she knew this was over.

She moved as stealthily as she was able, through the rail yard, then along the bullet-ridden line of vehicles on the left side of the gravel track. The only sounds came from elsewhere: the whirr of heavy-duty machinery, a loaded semi bouncing over a potholed road, the bangs and clonks from the factory. She had heard gunshots from the warehouse—and thought she'd heard Jimmy's voice at one point—but now the silence was complete.

The dead were scattered. Some lay in simple puddles of blood. Others were tangled and broken. Lola had readied herself to find Brody dead—an outcome she'd tried so hard to avoid, even to the point of sacrificing herself. When she saw her truck, though, crumpled against the warehouse's siding, her apprehension took an even darker turn: not one dead child, but two.

She looked at a row of broken bodies, including the one still under the truck. It wasn't difficult to piece together what had happened. Molly had returned, fast and furious, and taken out four, maybe five of Jimmy's guys. Lola recalled the rush of light she'd seen when Blair was standing on her throat, accompanied by a shrill engine sound. She'd wondered if it was death, and it *was*, but not for her.

Lola checked the truck. Empty. She shifted along the front of the warehouse, and here, tucked into the shadows, was her carryall of guns. She discarded Blair's .45 and grabbed her Baby Eagle. The fire spread inside her. She thought of the last few shots she'd heard from the warehouse and imagined Jimmy standing over the bodies of her dead children.

She ascended the loading dock steps and slipped through the side door. Silence at first, and then, proceeding toward the main throughway, she heard crying. It sounded like a child.

Not Jimmy.

Lola peeked around the side of a cramped storage rack. Overhead lighting illuminated the front third of the center aisle, and there, huddled where the light ran out, were Brody and Molly.

Jimmy lay several feet away, perfectly still and un-questionably dead.

Lola had never been quick to feel emotion, but she felt something then: a thrilling and immediate jolt to her heart. It staggered and invigorated her. It extinguished the flame. She dropped her gun and moaned, took a dazed step, then broke into a weary, shambling run.

Tears flowed from her eyes. They felt good.

She stopped a little short, thinking she should give them space, give them time. They had been through so much together. They had supported one another, warred, and ultimately triumphed. This was about them, and Lola wasn't sure that she belonged. She hovered close by, shuffling her feet and blinking the tears away.

Then Molly looked at her through broken eyes. She held out her hand, much like Blair had, but Lola understood this gesture.

A different fire kindled inside her.

Lola went to her children.

...

Carver City police were no strangers to violent crime. They put their lives at risk every day, but they knew where to draw the line.

The first reports of "multiple gunshots" at Dynasty Warehousing came in at 21:01. Average police response time in Carver City was sixteen minutes (a skewed average; it was only seven in the white neighborhoods). The first unit could have arrived on scene within this time frame, but was advised to wait for backup; Dynasty Warehousing was Latzo territory. This was gang-related, no doubt about it. Let the bullets fly, then go clean up.

At 21:29, six CCPD patrol cars and two special service vehicles rolled toward Jimmy's warehouse. A police chopper looped overhead. The news teams would undoubtedly follow.

Sergeant Maya Cornell drove the lead car. She stopped midway along the gravel track, tires throwing up dust. The cruiser's headlights illuminated the carnage.

"Jesus fucking Christ," her partner said.

Cornell nodded. "Tell the coroner he's going to need a bigger boat."

· · ·

Fifteen minutes, give or take, since the final gunshot. Quicker than Lola expected.

"*This is the Carver City Police Department. We have all exits covered and eyes in the sky. Lay down your weapons and come out with your hands nice and high.*"

"Can you walk?" Lola asked.

"Think so," Brody replied. "Slowly."

"I'll need help," Molly said. "And I can maybe put *one* hand nice and high."

"Good enough," Lola said. She pushed herself to her feet, took several steps toward the bay door, and called out as clearly as she could: "*We hear you and we're coming out. Two females, one male. We are unarmed and in need of medical attention.*"

She helped Brody and Molly to their feet, and the three of them made their way toward the exit, each depending on the other. The light outside was hot and fierce. Lola saw the outlines of multiple police vehicles and officers with assault rifles.

"Think we can take 'em," Brody whispered.

Lola managed a tired smile. She separated herself from Brody and Molly as they emerged through the exit, raising both hands.

Six officers approached. Two held position in the loading area. Four proceeded up the steps. One of them—Cornell on her name tag, three stripes on her arm—looked at Lola and said, "What the hell happened here?"

"I'll tell you everything," Lola said, "from the comfort of my hospital bed."

Molly stumbled. Brody tried to keep her up, but they both fell to their knees. Cornell nodded. Two of the officers lowered their weapons and stepped forward to help.

A news chopper had joined the CCPD air unit. They thundered overhead. More headlights—more news crews—bounced down the gravel track. One of the cops had broken position to head them off.

Sergeant Cornell looked from the choppers, to the bodies strewn in front of the warehouse, then back to Lola.

"Who are you?" she asked.

Lola shook her head. Too many answers to that question, and they reeled through her mind, each bringing its own flame, its own strength. A lover. A mother. A wife. A granddaughter. A student. A cousin. A friend. A killer. A warrior.

She was all of them. She was every woman.

"My name is Lola Bear," she said.

EPILOGUE

Maggie's Farm

(2020)

Poe was eight years old, a coal-black American saddlebred with a white brushstroke down his nose. He could rack at twenty-four miles an hour but preferred to canter, and that was fine with Molly. She guided him out of the arena, around the chicken coop and goat pen, then onto the field. A dry, used path ran toward the woods. Molly clicked her tongue, applied a brief squeeze with her legs, and Poe took his signal. He strode smoothly, his hooves tapping off a three-beat rhythm. Molly moved with him, always in control.

Alfalfa grew on both sides, knee-high and deep green. To the east, beyond Butch Morgan's fields of swaying corn, three new wind turbines reached into the Nebraska sky. They were a source of excitement and controversy among local famers; one of the first things

Molly was asked to do on her arrival at Owlfeather—
she was still bandaged and sore—was sign a petition
against them. Her signature made no difference. The
turbines were installed, and Molly didn't mind at all.
She liked them, in fact, admired their quiet power and
majesty. She sometimes rode Poe out there and sat listening to the lazy whoosh of their blades turning. It
had a certain calm.

Today, though, she rode west, around the three-acre
splash of woodland, to Assumption Creek, where Poe
drank noisily. Deer watched from the opposite bank
with their ears twitching. Molly kicked her heels and
got moving again. She followed the creek to the ruins
of the Church of the Resurrection, struck by a tornado
in 2007 and yet to be resurrected. Old timbers angled
toward the sky. Musk thistle grew among the pews.
Beyond this the land rose modestly, then dropped
away, and here the view was complete. No wind turbines or tumbledown churches. Nothing man-made
for miles. Only green, steady earth and a broad strip of
river, almost gold in the late sunlight.

. . .

She patted Poe's crest. "Good boy." He snorted appreciatively and switched his tail. Crickets hummed
in the long grass, and that, for a time, was the only

sound. Molly watched the river roll and lost herself to thought. She remembered Rebel Point, the police sirens, the neighbors constantly at odds, the thin curtain that separated her private space from Brody's.

She was so far from that now, literally and figuratively. Sometimes that distance took her breath away.

Poe's ears flicked, alerted to a sound from behind them that Molly, in her reverie, heard late. She turned and watched another horse canter around the church ruins. Autumn, a bay Arabian, and frequently feisty. Her rider was broad in the shoulders, wore a short beard and a white cowboy hat—a visual change indicative of the great distance that he, too, had traveled.

He pulled up beside Molly and worked the reins. Autumn flared her nostrils and champed, bumping against placid Poe.

"Whoa, girl."

Molly grinned as Brody walked a few figure eights and hushed his horse, finally getting her under control.

"What took you so long?" she said.

...

The river turned from gold to bronze, capped with silver where rocks broke the surface. The sun dropped slowly, like a hand bearing weight. A different light lined the horizon. It was beautiful. All of it.

"I was talking to Mom," Brody said.

"Yeah? How's she doing?"

"She's a little . . . *emotional*." Brody couldn't help but smile; this was not a word that had been used to describe their mom very often. "But she'll be okay."

"We'll *all* be okay." Molly gazed across the open land. "We've got this."

Brody nodded. "We'll one-inch punch it, right?"

"Always."

Their credo, still, and they embodied it, appearing basic and harmless, but packed with interior power. The press, following the shoot-out at Dynasty Warehousing (the "Second Carver City Massacre," some news outlets called it—the first being from 1993, also starring Jimmy Latzo) jumped on this: the David and Goliath angle. They knew only what Lola, Molly, and Brody had told the authorities, though, and Lola had insisted they keep everything low-key. Their line: they were victims and had acted in self-defense.

This was corroborated by the 03:31 video in which Molly was tortured, and Renée Giordano shot to death. The assailants were masked, but there was enough evidence to damn them. Molly's statement, for one. But also: the victims' hair and blood was discovered in a basement room of Dynasty Warehousing, owned and operated by Jimmy Latzo; the original MP4 video file was dug out of the hard drive of Jimmy's personal computer; forensic voice analysis matched Jimmy's voice, despite his efforts to disguise it. As if this wasn't enough, Renée's partially dissolved remains were discovered in a barrel of sodium hydroxide at a hazardous waste facility (also owned by Jimmy Latzo) two miles from the warehouse.

"Why you?" the FBI agent asked Molly after she had given her statement.

"Jimmy Latzo was after my mom," Molly replied truthfully. "I guess they've got history."

Lola downplayed this history, as well as any act of heroism.

She said: "Jimmy was convinced I had something to do with what happened in 1993. I *didn't*, of course, but I was forced into hiding—I changed my identity, my backstory. Jimmy is resourceful, though. He tracked my kids down, and after he sent that video . . . well, I went there to reason with him. Things turned bad."

"Eighteen dead?" the FBI agent said. "That's not *bad*. That's apocalyptic."

"They turned on each other," Lola said. "Some of them wanted to let us go. Some of them didn't. We did what we had to. No more. No less."

Certain evidence—a sawed-off shotgun with Brody's prints all over it; Blair Mayo's grisly corpse—invited further questioning, but the authorities were content not to dig too deeply. Some very bad people were dead. The victim's accounts held up. File under "closed" and move on.

There were no objections, no impassioned pursuit of the truth. A few of Jimmy's high-rolling "friends," business associates, and siblings came out of the woodwork, but they knew what Jimmy was about and were not at all surprised that his death came in a barrage of gunfire. They paid their respects and carried on as before.

The press kept him alive, though, for as long as they were able. They glorified the information they'd been given and disinterred old stories and legends. Jimmy's ignominy spread beyond the northeastern states. He had his fans, like any mobster or mass murderer (his subreddit had 32.6k subscribers) but the popular opinion was that the world was better off without him.

At the opposite end of the good-and-evil spectrum, a service was held for Renée Giordano in her hometown of Bloomington, Indiana. It was gloriously attended.

The Indianapolis Colts wore black armbands and observed a minute's silence at their next home game.

. . .

In January 2020, a donation of $2,800 was made to the pediatric ward of Freewood Valley Hospital, under the name of Buddy's Convenience Store. This was, give or take a few dollars, the amount Brody had stolen from Buddy's cash register. He had hoped this act of good-will would appease the universe and lessen the frequency of his nightmares. It didn't.

"How do you manage?" he'd asked his mom. This was shortly after getting out of the hospital, when he was still too sore for farmwork, and trapped with his thoughts for most of the day. "Do you shut yourself down and pretend it didn't happen?"

"It all comes down to balance," Lola had replied, and made weights out of her hands. "You can't let the darkness consume you. And you can't smile stupidly and pretend everything is A-okay. You shoulder the bad, you draw on the good. That's the only way to walk straight."

Janey had said something similar. "Make peace with what happened. You're a good man, and you protect what you love." Their relationship was one of the new lights in Brody's life, and had come out of nowhere. Brody had been grooming Autumn, who was unset-tled, stomping her hooves, when Janey—who still came Wednesdays and Fridays to help with the horses—stepped beside him, placed her hand over his, and gently guided the brush. "Long, easy strokes. That's how she likes it." Autumn settled, but Brody ran hot. It was the best he'd felt in quite some time.

He didn't tell Janey everything. There were details she didn't need to know, and that he was doing his best to forget. They were like bugs, though. They got into small places. They buzzed and scratched. And they were always busier at night.

There was blood in his dreams. Sometimes it was Jimmy's, or Joey Cabrini's (always accompanied by that pig-like grunting). Most of the time, though, it was Brody's blood. In the worst of his nightmares, he kept getting back up. He'd be shot through the leg or chest, and up he'd pop. He'd take a bullet to the head and keep on ticking, fueled by something inside that refused to die.

"I can't stay down," he'd said to Janey. She was curled into him, one hand on his chest. Three A.M. moonlight bled through a gap in the curtains. "I don't know if it will ever end."

"It will," Janey had replied, "if you get up stronger."

This brief and brilliant wisdom—get up stronger—complemented the "one-inch punch" philosophy. He carried both into his everyday and worked hard. The farm cradled him. It felt secure, a place from which to feed and grow. His days were spent spreading fertilizer, irrigating crops, spraying pesticides, tending the livestock. The work packed muscle onto his shoulders and arms.

He frequented the Bald Eagle Shooting Range. His mom's idea. "You won't control your fear," she'd said, "until you've bridled it." She was right. Brody had hammered rounds into waves of gunmen, goons, and mobsters, until gradually they morphed into twelve-by-twelve targets. Paper squares with a series of concentric circles and a bright dot at the center.

His arm got steadier, his aim truer.

The nightmares dulled but didn't stop.

Evenings were spent with family, or with Janey. Sometimes the four of them would ride across the fading countryside, the wind chasing through their hair, until even their horses were breathless. They cooked together, streamed movies, cheered for the local baseball team. They slept on bedrolls beneath the endless sky, with coyotes prowling nearby and bull snakes hissing in the grass.

Molly remained his light, without her having to shine it. She tackled her own nightmares with a fierce tenacity. Working on the farm helped (Molly loved those horses). She saw a therapist once a week. "Benign discussion," she called it. Also, Butch Morgan's son was tall and understanding, and in him she'd found a companion. They weren't as far along the romance trail as Brody and Janey, but the look in Molly's eye suggested she hoped they soon would be.

She and Brody had the same ghost. Not the bleeding, dripping characters that rattled their dreams, but a silent, forceful woman who haunted their waking hours.

Blair.

She lived in the corner of Molly's eye. Molly would be in the barn, or maybe the kitchen, and would turn quickly, certain she'd seen Blair standing in the doorway with a pipe wrench in her hand. Other times, she lingered in the darkness beside Molly's bed, only to disappear the moment Molly rolled over to look.

Blair haunted Brody in a different way. She lived in his wallet.

Her returning it had been an odd, unexpected gesture, and Brody thought about it often. Was it a genuine attempt at decency, or had she been mocking him—flaunting her absolute control? It was probably the latter, but Brody couldn't shake the notion that Blair had wanted to show him something beyond her cunning and cruelty: a redemptive quality that so rarely surfaced. He had searched though the wallet while lying in his hospital bed, expecting to find a note folded to fingernail size and tucked deep into one of the pockets. It would read, *Forgive me*, or maybe even, *Help me*.

There was no note.

Brody searched for her online, looking for a history of neglect or humanity—a skeleton for his ghost. He found nothing beyond the marksperson and martial arts accolades. No mention of a family. No social media presence. The press made no special mention of her in the aftermath of the shooting. She was just another redshirt in the Jimmy Latzo script.

Brody bought a new wallet. He filled it with a Nebraska driver's license, a concealed handgun permit, a credit card with a manageable APR, and with money that he'd earned through hard work. He kept his old wallet, though, and looked through it every now and then, remembering the girl with the purple hair and $1,500 boots, who had blazed through his life like a rocket.

. . .

Renée had said that she believed Lola was some kind of superhero, and she *was*, in many ways, but at her core she was fractured and wonderful and wholly normal. She was also, perhaps, the last person to realize this.

Lola held her children when they needed holding. She encouraged, comforted, and reassured them with a tenderness that was undeniably close to the surface. In these moments, it would be easy to believe she didn't have traumas of her own, but Brody recognized the ghosts behind her eyes.

She had told Brody that balance was the only way to walk straight, but sometimes she wavered, too.

"Is everything okay?"

Before riding out to meet Molly, Brody had walked into the kitchen to find Lola sitting at the table. Her cheeks were damp and she had a Kleenex balled in her fist.

"Oh hey, sweetie." She blinked her wet eyes. "I thought you were out."

"Leaving now." He and Molly were meeting at the place they called Resurrection Lookout. A serene, untouched stretch of acreage, where it was natural to reflect on what was, and what might be. "You didn't answer my question."

"I know you think I'm crying . . . and yes, I *am*, but . . ." She sighed, then managed a shaky smile. "Jesus, who am I kidding? I've actually cried a lot lately."

"I know."

"I think it's a sign I'm turning into a normal person."

"You've always been a normal person." Brody grabbed his hat from the kitchen countertop and placed it on his head. He hesitated for a moment—sometimes it was better to give his mom some space—but then took the seat opposite her at the table. "It's just that everything else around you was messed up."

"I suppose that's true." She wiped her cheeks and looked at him. He saw no ghosts in her eyes now, only honesty and trust.

"I know it's true," he said.

The clock in the hallway ticked dutifully into the early evening, emphasizing the Nebraska quiet. Even the animals had settled. Lola breathed over her upper lip and glanced at her hands. Her knuckles were callused from her training (or was it her therapy?): striking a solid wooden post in the barn until it bowed and had to be supported.

"I don't ever want you to think I'm not happy," she said, "or that I don't want you and Molly here. It's just . . . everything with Jimmy. I carried that weight for a long time, and now that it's gone, it feels like a part of me has been chipped away. That's a good thing, I know, but I still feel . . . *less*, somehow. Does that make any sense?"

"I guess so," Brody said. "You have a lot to unpack. We all do."

"It's complicated, huh?"

He reached across the table, took her callused hand, and squeezed. She looked at him gratefully and another tear flashed down her cheek.

"To complicate matters further, I also feel . . . well, *more*. More fulfilled. More complete. I'm a full-time mom again, which is the best feeling in the world. But it comes with its own perils, because now I'm worried about you. *Mom* things. Are you going to fall off that horse and break your neck? Are you going to get Janey pregnant—"

"Aw, Mom—"

"Is Cal Morgan going to look after Molly, because if he doesn't . . ." She trailed off, offering another weak smile. "I sometimes think it was easier being shot at. I know what to do about that, at least."

"Molly can look after herself." Brody grinned, his eyes glimmering beneath the brim of his cowboy hat. "And me? Well, I think I got all of the stupid out of my system."

"You better have."

"And these things you're feeling . . . yeah, they're scary. But they're healthy, Mom. They're *normal*."

"Normal," Lola repeated. "That word again. You know, this is the first time I've ever had a normal life.

I didn't have one as a kid. I didn't have one when I was working for Jimmy. And I didn't have one when you were younger, because the threat was still out there. But here I am, in my early fifties, and my life is finally my own."

"It's daunting," Brody said.

"It's breathtaking."

The kitchen brightened as the late sun touched the window and ran across the floor.

They said nothing else but held hands a moment longer.

...

Autumn bristled again but Brody gave the reins a tug and she settled quickly. He looked at Molly with one eyebrow raised: *Not bad for a city boy.*

Molly winked. Her smile was as curved and radiant as the river.

The minutes rolled by, and beautifully. They watched from their saddles as the sun splashed the horizon with warm paints and a thin moon appeared. Birds whistled. The crickets droned.

"Sure beats the smokestacks in Tank Hill," Molly said.

"Beats everything," Brody said.

Raw, deeper color, and then it all began to ebb. Molly opened her arms as if to embrace it, keep a piece of it for herself. Brody did the same.

"We're almost there, sis," he said.

Their shadows were long and blended with the land.

Acknowledgments

Writing *Lola on Fire* was a rush, a wild ride. I traveled solo for the first few drafts, which is just the way I like it, then brought in a host of friends and good people for subsequent drafts. They each played a part and helped make the journey more enriching and fulfilling. *Lola on Fire* is the result of the miles we clocked together.

To begin with, I had the best beta readers a novelist could hope for: Chris Ryall of IDW Publishing, and *New York Times* bestselling authors Christopher Golden and Tim Lebbon. They offered their enthusiasm, as well as suggestions and constructive criticism. I'm so lucky to have had their knowledge and expertise to draw on, and even luckier to have them as friends.

Joe Hill has supported my work in the past, and he was in my corner for *Lola on Fire*, too. Joe read a later (fourth or fifth) draft, then sent me a long email detailing the parts he liked, and the parts that still required a little TLC. It was exactly the email I needed. Applying Joe's suggestions made *Lola on Fire* a stronger, better novel, and I'm incredibly grateful to him for it.

Okay, I've name-checked three *New York Times* bestsellers so far. May as well make it four: Michael Koryta read *Lola on Fire* while delayed at an airport, then announced on Twitter how much he enjoyed the book. That may seem like a relatively small thing, but that Tweet grabbed my future editor's attention . . . and *that*, friends, is a big reason why this book is in your hands today. Thanks, Michael!

I have one of the best agents in the business in Howard Morhaim, who took me under his wing when I didn't have much to offer, and whose belief in me has never faltered. He cares about my work, he cares about my career, he cares about *me*. I consider him to be more than my agent. He's also my friend. Thank you, Howard, for everything. *Lola on Fire* is as much your book as it is mine. We did this together.

Also in the Morhaim Literary camp, my thanks to Megan Gelement, who makes everything so easy by being great at what she does, and a huge thank-you to Michael Prevett, who is representing *Lola*'s further fortunes in the sunny climes of Los Angeles.

And, of course, *Lola on Fire* would be nothing without my brilliant editor, Jennifer Brehl, who brought this book to life with unwavering excitement and endless faith. Working with her has been every bit the rewarding, educational, and wonderful experience I knew it would be. A mere thank-you is not enough. Suffice to say, Jennifer has been one of my favorite editors for many years, but now she's one of my favorite people, too. This giddy, dreamlike gratitude is extended to everyone at William Morrow. I'm so proud to be a part of the family.

Finally, love and thanks to my spectacular wife, Emily, whose support is nothing short of staggering, and whose belief lights my way. And to our children, Lily and Charlie, who inspire and elevate me in every possible way.

HARPER
LARGE PRINT

The good old days when a few mortals were giants.

R. Freeman Butts

No profit grows where is no pleasure ta'en;
In brief, sir, study what you most affect.

William Shakespeare,
The Taming of the Shrew,
Act I, Scene 1

It is in jeopardy until a great, long time from now when they will
begin to say, "Well, what a thing we had, why didn't we appreciate it? Why didn't we understand it? There is was and we
missed it!" Everything that is forward-looking and prophetic is
in danger at the time in which it occurred, and there has been no
exception to that rule.

Frank Lloyd Wright

William Heard Kilpatrick at Johns Hopkins University, c. 1900. (*Museum and Archives of Georgia Education, Milledgeville, Georgia*)

Kilpatrick Family in White Plains, Georgia, 1901 - 1. Margaret Louise Kilpatrick (daughter) 2. Clifford Elizabeth Hunter (cousin) 3. Helen Kilpatrick (sister) 4. Marie Guyton Kilpatrick (wife) 5. Mary Acton (cousin) 6. Sarah Kilpatrick (sister) 7. William Heard Kilpatrick 8. Susie Hunter (cousin) 9. Nellie Howell (cousin) 10. Edna Perrin Heard Kilpatrick (mother) 11. Howard Kilpatrick (brother) 12. Macon Kilpatrick (half-brother) 13. James Kilpatrick (father) (*H. K. Baumeister Collection*)

Teachers College faculty and student group, 1914. Front row, third from left, John Dewey; fourth from left, Dean James Russell; fifth from left, Edward Thorndike; and sixth from left, Kilpatrick.

Unveiling of Dewey bust by Jacob Epstein, 1928. John Dewey and Kilpatrick. (*Museum and Archives of Georgia Education*)

Margaret Pinkney Kilpatrick and Kilpatrick with Chinese student delegation presenting banner at Teachers College, c. 1930. (*Special Collections, Milbank Memorial Library, Teachers College, Columbia University*)

William Heard Kilpatrick - "Columbia's Million-Dollar Professor," c. 1932. (*Museum and Archives of Georgia Education*)

Kilpatrick, c. 1935. (*Museum and Archives of Georgia Education*)

Street scene from Teachers College, New York City, c. 1936. (*Special Collections, Milbank*)

Kilpatrick Award Ceremony, Horace Mann Auditorium at Teachers College, 1947. Left to right: George Counts, John Dewey, Boyd Bode, Kilpatrick, H. Gordon Hullfish.

Marion Ostrander Kilpatrick and Kilpatrick, c. 1950. (*Museum and Archives of Georgia Education*)

Kilpatrick with Eleanor Roosevelt, c. 1955. (*Museum and Archives of Georgia Education*)

Kilpatrick with grand-daughter Mary Baumeister, c. 1955. (*H. K. Baumeister Collection*)

1

A SOUTHERN YOUTH:
THE EDUCATION OF AN EDUCATOR

Heard was the best child in the world; in fact I believe he was
a perfect child — the only perfect child I have ever seen.
Mrs. T. D. Moore, Milledgeville, Georgia [1]

A Southern man with Eastern training became the prototype
of the ideal Southern professor. The Johns Hopkins
University of Baltimore, a school on the border between East
and South, became the gateway between ambitious Southern
youths and the cosmopolitan world of scholarship.
Edward L. Ayres in The Promise of the New
South: Life after Reconstruction [2]

Although the soldiers and horses of William Tecumseh Sherman passed by
the Georgia village of White Plains on their march from Atlanta to the sea, the
social and economic dislocation of the War between the States did not. White
Plains, located in Greene County in the northern portion of middle Georgia,
was originally called Fort Neil, but derived its later name from the grayish, bone
color of the sand and soil, which contrasted sharply with the deep-red clay
prevalent throughout the rest of Georgia.[3] In 1870 this agricultural village had
a population of 374, divided almost equally between blacks and whites.

White Plains would grow to 500 residents by 1890, but a decade later the
number fell below 300. The census of 1890 for Greene County showed a black
population of 11,719, out of a total of 17,051. The overwhelming African-
American majority in the county was caused by the fact that this region of
Georgia had a number of large antebellum plantations with significant numbers
of slaves. A prewar census showed a total county population of 11,781, of
which almost two-thirds were enslaved. (The figures did list 37 "free Negroes.")
A majority of the white residents of the area were descended from
Revolutionary soldiers who had migrated to Georgia from the Carolinas and

Virginia in order to receive land grants. The first settlement was established in February of 1786. Many of these colonists who settled in Greene County were descended from Scottish and Irish stock.[4]

William Heard Kilpatrick was born in the midst of Reconstruction, or what the South referred to as the "shadow of the War of Secession."[5] Georgia had been one of the eleven states that had seceded to form the Confederacy, and as a boy Kilpatrick often heard adults express their regret over the loss of the "good old days." Such a phrase usually meant the idyllic, aristocratic culture based on a way of life centered on the plantation. Unfortunately, such euphemisms, like "the peculiar institution" (slavery), were often justified through the Bible and based on the firm belief by whites that blacks were clearly inferior. Kilpatrick also remembered the use, usually in private, of the term "poor whites" or "poor white folks." This group, along with formerly enslaved people, comprised the majority of White Plains. At the other end of the spectrum were a mere five men and two women who were college-educated and were accorded a slightly higher level of recognition on the social scale.[6]

The years of Reconstruction were grave and difficult, in terms of both economic upheaval and social disorientation. High tariffs on cotton, the loss of enslaved labor, and the deep recession known as the Panic of 1873 all focused the attention of White Plains residents on the fact that they were living in dire times. The future was unpredictable, and they yearned for the "glorious past." With cotton the chief cash crop, the fortunes of small Georgia communities such as White Plains were closely tied to its success or failure. And yet there were other crops such as corn, wheat, oats, rye, potatoes, peaches, pears, apples, and grapes that helped to sustain the economy.

But one particular dark underside of the South did not touch White Plains. For both political and social reasons, racially motivated violence occurred frequently in the South over the last third of the nineteenth century. One historian has referred to "terrible scenes of inhumanity," which included brutal whippings, mass sickness, starvation, and death. The South became a "notoriously violent place." Lynchings, burnings, and other acts of violence against blacks continued unabated during Reconstruction. This violence was randomly visited upon former slaves who were either newcomers to a community or strangers. Since the African-American population in White Plains tended to be stable, this section of Georgia was spared much of the tragedy associated with these senseless acts. But there is little doubt that such violence created an inescapable, oppressive environment for the African-

American citizenry in the life of the community.[7]

There was little commercial or, for that matter, cultural diversity in White Plains. The Tappans, for example, a New Jersey family of Dutch ancestry, and owners of one of the town's three general stores, called Tappan Brothers, were the only "Yankee" family in White Plains. The Tappans were scrutinized, according to Kilpatrick, for differences in their speech, attitudes, and cultural practices.[8] But since the Tappans offered the best prices for cotton, few Greene County residents took their trade to Greensboro, the county seat, or to Augusta, located seventy-five miles away. Savannah was the state's chief city, but it was relatively inaccessible to the citizens of White Plains, while Atlanta had yet to establish itself as a major economic center. As no rail line ran through White Plains, the cotton made its way out of the village on an almost daily basis by wagon to Union Point and Crawfordville.

The social elite in Greene County was limited. Although there were several surreys in the area, only one resident owned a closed carriage. Architecturally, there were two "colonial" houses within five miles of White Plains. These were typical two-story antebellum houses with four to six Greek columns. The young Kilpatrick was quite taken with this architectural style and regretted, along with his brothers and sisters, that their father, James Kilpatrick, who opposed any hint of ostentation, had not built the family home in such a fashion. While James Kilpatrick may have eluded the trappings of the antebellum way of life, according to his son, he had believed deeply in the South's cause during the war. His son even heard him say that he had no wish to live in a defeated South: Had it been the "Lord's will," he and his family would have gladly followed the cause into death and oblivion. Paradoxically, although he was a slaveholder, James Kilpatrick did not regret that these men and women gained their freedom after the war. He found it a relief, even the "Lord's will," that enslavement had ended. Southerners never doubted the validity of their cause, but the elder Kilpatrick's regional feelings went far deeper and were more extreme than any others young Kilpatrick ever witnessed.[9]

A wing of Sherman's army, under the command of General John W. Geary, did move through Greene County in November of 1864, destroying a railroad bridge and burning cotton and corn. This division chased a few Confederate soldiers down the Oconee Road, the same road that, six months later, would find Jefferson Davis being pursued by Union soldiers as he fled southward. On the whole, General Geary was, according to historians, one of the more restrained military leaders of the federal troops that crossed Georgia.

A former governor of Kansas, he was later made military governor of Savannah during the occupation.[10] Still, while Greene County was spared the full brunt of Sherman's March, the Kilpatrick family was not entirely spared losses during the war. In a letter to James Kilpatrick, his brother, Washington, told of the destruction wrought by Sherman's army in Waynesboro in Burke County — where food, personal property, and animals were lost during the Union army's one week stop. "We have experienced all from the enemy that you feared, and a hundred times more," wrote Washington Kilpatrick.[11]

Only the most extreme Confederate would suggest that secession or war be revived — that was a closed affair. But there remained a peculiar loyalty to Southern culture, excluding both slavery and secession, that lingered with the younger Kilpatrick his entire life. For example, blacks celebrated the Fourth of July, while southern whites did not. For much of his life Kilpatrick would enter into his diary on Independence Day: "July 4, means nothing to me." Thanksgiving was not celebrated, as it was thought to be "too northern," and Easter was considered a rite of spring, rather than a religious holiday. And while the national flag was never shown disrespect, the Stars and Stripes were rarely displayed and the Confederate flag was used in all regional celebrations. The Confederate Memorial Day, April 26, was frequently mentioned in Kilpatrick's diary with a note of regret that, while it was imperative that slavery be abolished, something fundamental had been lost in Southern society. But the younger Kilpatrick's generation considered the national flag their flag. To illustrate the difference of viewpoints on the issue, Kilpatrick told of informing his father that his school in Blakely, Georgia, flew the national flag from its steeple. "I was greatly surprised when he demurred at what I had approved," wrote Kilpatrick many years later. "It was a clear difference between two generations."[12]

But among the citizens of White Plains, loyalty to the Southern cause was secondary to devotion to the Christian religion. Kilpatrick could not remember a single elderly adult in the village who was not associated with a church. An almost even numerical split existed between the membership lists of the Baptists and the Methodists, with the former just slightly in ascendancy. Only one woman in the village, a Presbyterian, reported being outside both folds. Kilpatrick remembers regretting, at about age ten, that he had failed to meet the only Jew who had once lived in White Plains. The religious regime was influential. The sale of intoxicating liquor was forbidden in the village and, by consensus, neither dancing nor card playing was permitted. If a student was caught with a pack of playing cards, their cards were burned, after which a

mandatory whipping took place. School adjourned early during local revivals, and class began each day with a prayer.[13]

Kilpatrick would spend the second half of his life devoted to the study of his family's genealogy. The name Kilpatrick is an ancient one, from the Scottish Kill (cell, small church) devoted to Patrick (Saint Patrick). Killpatrick became Kilpatrick by 1780. The Kilpatricks had emigrated from Scotland to Pennsylvania by way of Presbyterian northern Ireland. Kilpatrick's great-grandfather, Andrew Kilpatrick, was born (in 1746) in either Ireland or Pennsylvania. The family later moved to North Carolina and settled on the south fork of the Yadkin River.[14] Family records indicate that a relative, Joseph Kilpatrick, was killed by Indians in the battles of 1757.[15] Kilpatrick's grandfather, James Hall Kilpatrick, moved to South Carolina, where he served as a tutor in the school of Moses Waddell, and later journeyed to Nachez, Louisiana, where he opened the first English-speaking academy. He eventually joined the Baptist church, becoming a Baptist minister. Intertwining his Presbyterian background with a commitment to the thinking of the eighteenth century's Great Awakening, the newly ordained Baptist minister had a strong adherence to orthodox theology, foreign missions, an educated clergy, Sunday schools, temperance, and strict observance of the sabbath.[16]

After the death of his first wife in Louisiana, James Hall Kilpatrick returned to South Carolina, where he met Harriet Eliza Jones, twenty-nine years old, known equally for her great piety and her considerable wealth. Her father, Batte Jones (1754-1821), was descended from an English Cavalier family that had suffered at the hands of Oliver Cromwell and had emigrated to Virginia in the 1640s. Batte was one of five Jones brothers to fight with the American patriots during the Revolutionary War. Harriet Eliza Jones had attempted to return her inherited slaves to Liberia. But, so the story goes, they hid in the swamps near Savannah until the boat had departed. Before the next vessel arrived, she had married James Hall Kilpatrick in 1822, and under Georgia law he became the owner of her property.[17] He reversed her earlier decision by canceling plans for another boat to Liberia. (In all, he owned 14,555 acres of land and 24 slaves.[18]) The Joneses' religious heritage was a diverse mixture, according to one source, of Episcopalianism, deism, and indifference. For Harriet Eliza to join the Baptists was a distinct step of faith. The couple's fifth and youngest child, named James Hines Kilpatrick — who would become the father of William Heard Kilpatrick — was born in 1833.[19]

His father was reared, Kilpatrick later wrote, in "a puritanic evangelism of religion."[20] It was while he was a student at Mercer University in Macon,

Georgia, that James Hines Kilpatrick was "led to Christ." Like his father and older brother, James Kilpatrick felt a "call" to the ministry and soon entered his lifelong occupation. Although licensed as a Baptist minister after graduating from Mercer in 1853 and called to preach in Madison, Georgia, he began his career by teaching school in the village of White Plains. He did not enter the pulpit full time until after the local minister was felled by a stroke. Kilpatrick was twenty-one years old at the time, and would remain with the congregation for fifty-four years.

One of James Kilpatrick's first crusades as minister was a personal campaign to rid Greene County of liquor. He rode to Milledgeville, then Georgia's state capital, and lobbied the legislature to give White Plains the power of local control over liquor. The request for the charter was approved. James Kilpatrick was subsequently elected mayor of White Plains, and the town council voted to forbid the sale of intoxicants.[21] After the war, he moved from his 1,600-acre "plantation" (farm) into town. In addition to his ministerial functions, James Kilpatrick also assumed a variety of quasilegal roles, including writing wills, serving as executor of estates, and refereeing local disputes. He also reportedly pulled a few teeth.[22]

Kilpatrick saw in his father a propensity for extracting particular ideas from the Reformation — especially the exercise of reason and logic — and integrating these concepts within the practices of the Baptist church. When Kilpatrick wrote about this in his unfinished autobiography, forty years after the death of his father, he may have been looking for common ground with his own pragmatic, rational, experiential philosophy. He frequently quoted his father on the need for open-mindedness: "It is my understanding that the Baptist outlook allows for the acceptance of any new truth."[23] He admired his father's intelligence and often grouped him with John Dewey and Edward L. Thorndike as the three best minds he had ever known. Said Kilpatrick, "My father would constantly tell me, 'You must think, my son, notice what you are doing; think about it.' If anyone used bad thinking or bad logic, he caught the error and pointed it out."[24] Years later he concluded that while his father could not defend the Christian religion itself, he was "well nigh impregnable" in shielding the Baptist orthodoxy from attack by other Protestants. The son, when he was over seventy years old, wrote of the father:

> My father was the second great formative influence in my
> life. He helped me to believe in careful thinking as the great
> resource in all vicissitudes. He taught me, too, how to think

and his stalwart integrity showed me what a strong personality can be.[25]

The Rev. James Kilpatrick (later Dr. Kilpatrick, by virtue of an honorary degree from Mercer University, bestowed in 1882) became one of the most influential Baptists in Georgia. He was president of the Georgia Baptist convention, was a trustee at both Mercer University and Southern Baptist Theological Seminary, and was eventually included in *Who's Who in America*.[26] He wrote a number of tracts, including "Why I Am a Baptist," and a collection of his sermons, entitled *The Baptists, Their Doctrines and Life,* was published posthumously. And yet, Rev. James Kilpatrick had a human dimension. B. F. Hubert, president of Georgia State University, spoke of his own father's admiration for James Kilpatrick: "This man who drove a bay horse with slack lines . . . preferred to remain out in the open country as a shepherd of country folks although many flattering offers came from far off city parishes." Hubert added that his father's conversations with Kilpatrick "had the authority of an oracle, it mattered not whether he discussed religious or social questions that concerned the people of both races in the community."[27]

In May of 1856, the Rev. James Kilpatrick married nineteen-year-old Cornelia Hall. Over the next thirteen years, seven children were born to the couple, two dying in infancy. Cornelia herself died of pulmonary tuberculosis a week after giving birth to the seventh child, who was her namesake.[28] In a biographical sketch of his half-brother Macon, Kilpatrick wrote of his father's first wife: "Cornelia Hall was too young, too little experienced in worldly matters, too much overawed by the superior rearing, intellect, education, and piety of her husband to maintain herself against his overpowering individuality."[29]

Kilpatrick would find, through his mother, Edna Perrin Heard — born in Augusta, Georgia, in 1843 — an escape for whatever intellectual and personal impediments he himself encountered within his father's world. Her father, who died when she was a child, had been born in South Carolina, and her mother's family had been residents of New York City. Edna Heard's family had fought for the Confederacy and her oldest brother, a sharpshooter, had been killed during the conflict. In speaking of his mother's family in comparison with his father's side, Kilpatrick wrote in his autobiography, "My mother from her rearing was in respect of asperity a little farther along than my father, though his family would socially outrank hers."[30] Edna Perrin Heard studied at the Preparatory School of the Presbyterian College for Young Women. She

also studied in the Georgia towns of Greensboro and Covington, and finally in White Plains under Vincent T. Sanford. Edna's sister, Emma Heard, taught in White Plains and later married Dr. John Howell. Edna continued to teach in a variety of settings, sometimes as a private tutor, and at the Augusta Orphanage. She had met James Kilpatrick while a student in White Plains, but came to know him better while visiting her sister. Her son later wrote that his mother's eclectic religious background made her less doctrinaire than her future husband. In any case, she and the widowed Rev. James Kilpatrick were married on December 20, 1870, and moved into the White Plains house built that same year.[31]

William Heard was born eleven months later to the day, on November 20, 1871. Named for his mother's youngest brother, William Thomson Heard, he would be called Heard by the family. The use of his middle name was by his mother's design, as she wished to avoid having her son known by a nickname or derivation of William, such as Bill or Will. The namesake uncle gave Heard, at age two, a small chair which he used to slide across the floor, and upon which he took his first steps. Heard usually played with his sister Helen, two years younger than he. (There would be another sister, Sarah, five years younger than Heard; and a brother, Howard, seven years younger.[32]) The children usually played in the garden, where the walks were lined with hyacinths, daffodils, and jonquils, or under the house, built in the southern style so as to allow air to flow underneath it. There were occasional visits to nearby aunts and uncles. One particular visit before his schooling began left an indelible mark on Kilpatrick. He remembered seeing farmhands stripping the cornstalks into fodder and singing spirituals. "As I look back on that day," he later wrote, "with all it had and its possibilities, it made it seem then to me an ideal place in which to live." [33]

Samuel Tenenbaum, Kilpatrick's first biographer, described the relationship between mother and eldest son as idyllic.[34] A strong bond certainly existed; thirty-five years after her death, Kilpatrick never failed to note her birthday in his diary or to speak about the contribution she made to his life through her gentleness, kindness, and encouragement. "She helped me," he told Tenenbaum, "to learn not to be selfish, that I must give to others their just due." She told the children stories, and Kilpatrick particularly remembered a fictitious character she called "Little Bobby," who was very much like young Heard. He delighted in hearing of the adventures of this imaginary lad, and in how the stories allowed him to dream about his own future. Kilpatrick did consider his mother a "Victorian" in many of her attitudes, especially with regard to the treatment of females. He recalled receiving his last "whipping" from her when

he was nine: Heard, with the help of a friend, had carried his sister Helen "bodily" across the yard.[35] Years later he reminisced about his mother, saying that she "piloted me successfully through the fateful early years."[36] One of his earliest childhood experiences, though, almost took his life, leaving a handicap that remained with him into old age. At age nine months, little Heard placed his finger into an open box of lye concentrate used to wash clothes. As it burnt his finger, he was later told, he placed his finger in his mouth, and swallowed. The incident left strictures on his esophagus. Throughout his life, if he failed to chew his food well he would often be forced to leave the table in order to clear the troublesome passage in his throat.[37]

Kilpatrick attributed his later success as a teacher to his mother's sensitivity. An example of the gentleness he gained from her can be heard in a tape recording made in Columbus, Ohio, in 1949. Kilpatrick, after an address, asked for questions from the audience, with the gentle admonition, "Please, don't be embarrassed or uncomfortable, ask what you wish."[38] In 1912, his mother wrote to him, "If either you or I have in thirty years in any degree raised or quickened the voice in speaking to each other, save in gladness, I have no recollection of it."[39] From 1888, when he left for college, until her death in 1925, mother and son wrote to each other without fail once a week. Almost twenty years after her death, he wrote of her:

> My mother occasionally used a hairbrush or a peach switch. She was very kind otherwise and indeed never punished in anger. In my present language my mother was especially skilled and correct in maintaining a good balance between self-regarding and other-regarding tendencies. We learned from her well how to distinguish right from wrong on a better than authoritarian basis.[40]

In 1925, just after her death, he dedicated his book, *Foundations of Method*, "To the Memory of My Mother, Earliest and Best of My Teachers." He had planned the dedication all along, but her death occurred just before publication. The effect of Kilpatrick's mother on the future educator cannot be overemphasized. A decade after her death he wrote, "It was my mother, I think, who most of all made me what I am. The sympathetic regard for other people's feelings lies at the basis of my teaching, both intellectually in understanding how the other person thinks and sympathetically in knowing how he feels and wishes to be treated."[41]

Young Heard's relationship with his father was more distant — even, at times, strained. Kilpatrick remembered no dissension, harsh words, or raised voices in the home.[42] But also "with him," wrote Tenenbaum "there was no light talk, no banter, no frivolity." In later years the only two criticisms Kilpatrick would make of his father were the poor care his teeth received as a child and the lack of interaction on a deeper, personal level. "If I have any fault to find with my father, it would be his lack of association with his children. I cannot now recall any familiar personal conversation between the two of us at any time. When I left home for college . . . he never wrote me a familiar personal letter."[43] The elder Kilpatrick was indeed industrious to a fault. He read no novels, according to Kilpatrick, viewing the reading of novels as not necessarily wrong, but rather as a waste of time. Kilpatrick does remember his father reading *Adam Bede*, on the request of a clergyman friend, who had asked him to render an opinion. He valued it only slightly, reported Kilpatrick.

And yet Kilpatrick's father was no killjoy. Others were welcome to enjoy themselves, though he had no time for such diversions. He rarely sat on the piazza with the family, preferring to work in his garden or study. He kept meticulous records of his peaches and was known long after his death for the seedless Kilpatrick watermelon. Heard was spanked only once by his father: This occurred when he refused to take a dose of medicine, spitting it out twice. Rev. James Kilpatrick established a family devotion time at both breakfast and supper, when the Scripture would be read, followed by prayer. One of the children was then called upon to recite a Bible verse from memory. Shorter verses were frowned upon until a visiting minister, called upon for the recitation, employed the irreducibly minimal verse, "Jesus wept." The children around the table could hardly contain their amusement. In the arena of religious instruction, Heard learned songs both at home and in Sunday School. He recited "Now I lay me down to sleep" and then, when a bit older, The Lord's Prayer. Church attendance took place on the first and third Sundays of the month. Evening services were added when the children reached the age of twelve. Sunday was strictly observed, with no visiting, organized games, or swinging. Even cooking was halted for the sabbath. Cold meals were served, with only the coffee and gravy being heated — by the fireplace, not the stove.[44]

In August of 1886, tragedy struck when two of Kilpatrick's half sisters died of typhoid fever on the same day. This was followed the next month by the Charleston earthquake. The local Baptist congregation held a revival, and the teenage Kilpatrick, along with several of his friends, joined the church. The

effect of the conversion on Kilpatrick's life was evidenced by longer personal prayers and additional readings from the Bible. In addition, his father questioned him regularly as to whether his conversion might have included a call to the ministry. The reply from Heard was a respectful "no." His newfound religious regimen lasted until he entered college two years later.[45]

Kilpatrick noted in his autobiography that he was never close to any of his half brothers or half sisters other than Macon. He gave no specific reason, nor was there reason to believe he received any ill treatment from them beyond normal pranks of siblings. He does mention age as possibly being a factor and notes that a disparity of even four years made a great deal of difference in the children's relationships. One half brother, James, rejected the religious faith of his father and later named his own children after nonbelievers such as Darwin and Huxley.[46] Although Macon would stay in Georgia, the two other half brothers eventually left the state to begin new lives away from their father.

There had been no continuous public school system in antebellum Georgia. In the late eighteenth century the state had chartered an ambitious plan for a state university system consisting of a university in Athens with a complement of academies in each county. By 1837, though, the system, with few exceptions, had either disappeared or been incorporated with another group of schools. Young Heard Kilpatrick attended the local academy, later named the Dawson Institute, which had been established in 1838, and emerged from the White Plains School founded four years earlier. (Kilpatrick referred to it in his autobiography as the White Plains Academy.) In 1873, Georgia established a system of free elementary education for students aged six to eighteen. Since the state funded the school for only three months, the citizens of White Plains continued funding the academy on a tuition basis for the remainder of the academic year. Kilpatrick's father allowed his children to choose whether they wished to attend school prior to age eight. Then from ages eight to twelve they would be allowed to attend the free school (three months), but no more. From age twelve to college the Kilpatrick children were required to attend the whole year.[47]

Heard began school at age six. "My schooling opportunities I judge now to have been above the average of the time and region," he wrote many years later.[48] He learned to read by the "alphabet method," which consisted of memorizing letters as the teacher pointed them out — and also becoming familiar with the sounds. Next the students spelled from a book, pronouncing words syllable by syllable. Using a primer, the students began with short sentences of two-letter words, e.g., "It is an ox." Finally, each word was spelled

by students under their breath and then pronounced out loud. "It was a very poor way of teaching," wrote Kilpatrick, "and the non-verbally minded often had much trouble with it."[49] Those who were unable to read were often assigned to the teacher's home for further instruction. The White Plains school was a two-story structure which made use of only the first floor. Girls answered "present" and were seated away from the teacher, while boys responded "here" and sat closer to the front. There were no more than six students in Heard's class.

While the classroom was conventional, traditional, and no doubt boring at times, Heard never felt compelled to take exception to the regimen. "I followed, abided and agreed," he later said of his early schooling. One vignette of his school days stood out in his memory. In the schoolyard he accidentally stepped on a classmate's hand. The teacher asked him, "Ain't you ashamed of yourself to hurt a little girl in this way?" "I was sorry I had done it, but I wasn't ashamed," he later related. The episode impressed on him how not to treat children. "A teacher should find out the real truth before saying or doing anything," he commented.[50] Evidently his behavior was more than acceptable, in that he was placed in the corner only once for misbehaving. Heartbroken, he wept the whole time.[51] A similar episode occurred when Heard was twelve, during a spelling bee. The rules called for the student to say the word before spelling it. When Heard was instructed to sit down after failing to say the word first, although he had spelled it correctly, he became angry to the point of tears. He could not see the point of being removed from a spelling contest when he had not misspelled a word. The episode left a life-long impression on him, teaching him the danger of arbitrariness in the classroom.[52]

One particular episode proved far more embarrassing. As Kilpatrick tells the story in his autobiography, his "boy pants" had a small "convenience" opening in the front. Once, when he sat down, it came open and a fellow student shot a marble into the gap. The class broke out into laughter, and, upon arriving home that evening, he had his mother sew up the revealing "target." Another incident during his first year of school involved the use of improper language. On the playground several students were attempting to kill a large bug with stones. Young Heard had retrieved several stones from another part of the schoolyard and, returning to the group, shouted out, "Where's that damned bug?" While profanity was not unheard of in rural Georgia, it shocked the entire group of children. No one "told on him" as they were returning to the classroom, but one girl whispered to another, "Heard cussed." Overhearing this comment sobered the minister's son to such an extent that in his autobiography he claimed that he never uttered that particular word again, except in a quotation.

"That one instance," he wrote, "has sufficed me from that day to this."[53]

Mrs. T. D. Moore, who knew the Kilpatricks well, had nothing but praise for the young Heard. "He was sweet and obedient and thoughtful of everybody," she told a newspaper reporter years later, "He was loved by all with whom he came in contact." Her remembrances border on hagiography: "He had no bad habits as he grew older; he never drank and never used a curse word in his life. He was just about perfect." Mrs. Moore believed that Kilpatrick would have been successful if he had stayed in White Plains, but "he just had it in him to do something and he would have done it anywhere that he was."[54]

Outside of school Heard joined other children in the popular activity of pecan hunting. Once he volunteered to climb the tree to shake the nuts loose to those waiting below, with the understanding he would receive one-half of those which each retrieved. This meant his share was about ten times larger than the others', which became apparent after he climbed down. The group insisted on another division, to which he agreed.[55] Heard also enjoyed fishing and occasionally hunting with his half brother, Macon. As a boy he also utilized his primitive mathematical skills, surveying with his father (evidently another of James Kilpatrick's sidelines) and later teaching some of these skills at Mercer. At the time of his father's death, he carried out the survey of land left in the will. While he read widely in his father's extensive library, he also enjoyed the magazine *Harper's Young People*, especially the section on stamp collecting, a hobby he began at age ten.[56]

A child's education never takes place totally within the confines of the schoolhouse. Confederate sympathies produced pejorative racial comments, which frequently emerged in childhood rhymes. Kilpatrick noted the use of the term "nigger" in such a context and also remembered hearing the verse:

> Old Jeff Davis in a big armchair,
> Lincoln on a stool.
> Old Jeff Davis was a president,
> Lincoln was a fool.

Kilpatrick later wrote that he was highly offended, even at a young age, by these aspersions. It was thought in the South that, had Lincoln lived, he might have prevented the imposition of the "carpetbag era." By the same token, the Confederate president, Jefferson Davis, was "no hero" to some southerners, according to Kilpatrick. He could not believe that anyone would have called Lincoln a fool, saying that "these words seem incredible."[57]

While dancing and card playing were forbidden activities for the youth of White Plains, kissing games seem to have been acceptable. Kilpatrick remembered the opening lines of one song which commenced such activity:

Many many stars are in the skies as old, old as Adam,
Down upon your knees and kiss whom you please,
Your humble servant madam.[58]

In his autobiography Kilpatrick offered up a paragraph entitled "Teenage Love Affairs." These were chaste relationships which he described as follows: "A more empty and vacant courtship it would be impossible to imagine." There was certainly no kissing ("I never touched her person in any way whatever") and mutual feelings, if present, were never discussed. When he went off to college, all parties concerned apparently lost interest in these romances. In his diary during the early 1950s, he does allude to "making love" (a phrase having an entirely different connotation than today) to two girls, but once again these relationships were chaste and led to no long-lasting commitments.[59]

As preparation for college, a traditional course of study was followed by late-nineteenth-century schools. By age twelve the study of Latin and Greek was begun in earnest. Heard also studied algebra, geometry, some trigonometry, English, and a form of rhetoric. Kilpatrick found it remarkable that history was omitted from the curriculum.[60] Like his father and uncle before him, Heard entered Mercer University in Macon, Georgia. The year was 1888, and he was seventeen years old. At this time, the term "university" in the title was quite inflationary; the Baptist college had fallen on hard times — economically, intellectually, and spiritually, according to Tenenbaum. Kilpatrick tells of the disastrous post-Civil War economy and how it spilled over into the lives of young people, resulting in personal despair. For many of the young men at the time, their prospects often led them to drink. Kilpatrick was one of 100 students who were enrolled at Mercer, and an aged faculty that had long lost its intellectual vigor met the freshmen. One exception was a rather exacting professor of classical languages who would accept a translation of a phrase which, although different from the one found in the textbook, was preferable. Kilpatrick was taken with this man because he could "admit he made a mistake." But this rare show of openness accomplished little, and the classics professor was soon replaced by a "hard, exacting, dogmatic, and intellectually dishonest" professor. (The yearbook said of him, "He shall not receive mercy, for he showeth none.") As a result, Kilpatrick formed a negative attitude toward

both Latin and Greek from that point on.[61]

Kilpatrick's collegiate career had lasted a mere month when he was taken ill with a light case of typhoid and forced to return home until after the Christmas holidays. He also fell ill during the second semester, returning home once again, this time missing commencement. His mother blamed Macon's climate for his health problems and persuaded his father to let him transfer to the University of Georgia. "But I was too firmly united to my Kappa Alpha fraternity," Kilpatrick later wrote, and therefore the move to Athens never took place.[62]

Arthur Powell of Blakely, Georgia, a classmate at Mercer and future Atlanta judge, wrote about Kilpatrick in his autobiography, *I Can Go Home Again*:

> Even when we were with him at Mercer, he had begun to display that genius which later gave him nationally and internationally the reputation of being one of the world's educational leaders. I have never seen one of them [his students] who did not ever afterward show in his processes of thinking Kil's imprint upon him.

Needless to say, when Powell was offered the opportunity to room with "Kil" — a college nickname — the invitation could not be ignored. Powell accepted immediately.[63]

As important as college social life was to Kilpatrick, fraternity rituals often went to the extreme. Powell tells of a pseudojudicial process the fraternity had instituted, consisting of a "pillory" and a leather cat-o'-nine-tails. Various officers in the fraternity could be punished or even impeached. On one occasion Kilpatrick refused to divulge to his fraternity brothers the purpose of a black wooden block he had in his possession. They decided "to try and convict him," lashing him and asking after each strike, "Tell us what it is," to which Kil stubbornly responded "I refuse to tell." The affair went much too far, according to Powell, and Kilpatrick almost fainted. Feelings were hurt all around, although days later, forgiving them, Kilpatrick indicated that the object was a setting block for preserving butterflies. Powell also relates that he and "Kil" were involved in mock burials and painting phrases on campus buildings — some of which did not come off. Pranks aside, Powell concluded that of all the experiences during his college days, it was Kil who "taught me how to think more clearly than I had ever thought before."[64]

In the academic arena, an aptitude for mathematics and physics prompted Kilpatrick, during his junior year, to consider a career in engineering. But a crucial event in his intellectual journey overtook this potential vocational interest. He read Charles Darwin's *Descent of Man.* Kilpatrick wrote of the episode fifty years later:

> I took out of our Phi Delta Society library Charles Darwin's *Descent of Man.* As I read it, it gripped me, I found myself accepting it in full. This meant that I accepted fully the doctrine of evolution and . . . had to give up contrary doctrines which I had accepted from my youth. I made up my mind, right or wrong as the reader may differently judge, never to let my father know of my change of outlook. But the difference to me was very, very great.[65]

The change for Kilpatrick was indeed, as Tenenbaum has called it, "cataclysmic," the more so because his three older half brothers had all rejected religion. Therefore, to prevent further anguish for his father, he refrained from raising the issue at home. For Kilpatrick, the book meant "a complete rejection of my previous religious training and philosophy." As a result he repudiated the belief in the immortality of the soul and discarded religious ritual. With regard to this intellectual and spiritual upheaval, Kilpatrick told Tenenbaum:

> At the moment, I did not have anything to put in its place. It was rather a rejection of what I had previously thought. But, contrary to what many people have prophesied about such matters, it did not change in any way my moral outlook. I now had no theology, but my social and my moral life continued in exactly the same way.[66]

There was little doubt that Heard was influenced by his half brother, Macon, who was seven years older. Of him Kilpatrick later said, "He helped me form my mind."[67] Macon's two older brothers, according to Kilpatrick, "inherited from their mother (the first Mrs. Kilpatrick) a seeming antipathy to asceticism and were in constant collision with the severe spirit of the household."[68] The "severe spirit" was no doubt their father. Not as robust or healthy as his brothers, Macon did not share in the rougher life of rural Georgia. Shy and reserved, he played more with his sisters, becoming more introspective

and withdrawn as he grew older. The strict Calvinism of his father took a "serious hold on him," according to his half brother. Macon, wrote Kilpatrick, "sought a thing he now knew not, but a thing he would recognize when it came." As the search became more painful, Macon would pray seven times a day, study his Bible, and mourn over present and past sins. His bashfulness and awkwardness increased. Life became too serious for levity while he remained a lost sinner. Then, reading by chance some of his older brothers' atheistic tracts, Macon had what can only be termed a conversion experience of a reverse nature. At seventeen he rejected the whole scheme of God, sin, and salvation. "Macon found," recalled Kilpatrick, "a peace and joy the like of which he had never known." [69]

After this "conversion," members of the community no longer attempted to dissuade Macon from his tendency toward introversion. In fact, parents ordered their children to stay away from him. (An uncle had even warned his mother to keep Macon away from Heard.) He became, in Kilpatrick's words, a "marked man." When he left for college, an unfortunate episode occurred, apparently as a result of the best intentions. With what Kilpatrick describes as love and tender care, Rev. James Kilpatrick sent Macon off to Mercer in a suit too large for him and a shawl at least three decades out of date. All this was done at great financial sacrifice by the family. His poverty, the unfamiliarity with the new world he was entering, and his continued rejection of his father's religion all weighed heavily on Macon. His shyness and sensitivity returned at this crucial time, and, Kilpatrick cryptically wrote in a brief biography of his brother, "prevented him from being like other boys." [70] Macon, plagued with ill health, became a student at the Johns Hopkins Hospital in Baltimore. (At this time the medical school had yet to open.) His health broke several times, according to his brother. Of Macon, Kilpatrick wrote, "His mind was of the best, his range of interests broader than almost anybody's that I have known. He was one of the most progressively minded of men and the world has been a distinctly poorer place . . . since his death." [71] He also credited Macon with saving his life and that of their sister, Sarah, from typhoid fever in 1900. Macon's own health continued to deteriorate, and he died July 25, 1904.

Kilpatrick's own schooling at Mercer involved a mix of both acceptable and inferior teaching. He seems to have learned most from the poor examples of instruction, in that these experiences stayed with him the longest. He was most critical of those teachers who were unable to admit they were wrong or who failed to show a humane side in their teaching. During his junior year, Kilpatrick became deeply involved in his fraternity, and by the end of the year

he was elected its president. When he looked back, his only regret was the snobbishness that often attached itself to fraternity life.[72] The summer before his senior year, Kilpatrick taught in a school near Athens with Macon, who was earning money to return to medical school. During his senior year, Kilpatrick roomed again with Arthur Powell. Romantically, Kilpatrick had, as he described it, "close personal relations" with Deania McAndrew, though they never reached "a lasting agreement."

Although opposed to academic honors, Kilpatrick did rank second in his class and prepared the salutatorian commencement speech in Latin. Just after the Mercer graduation exercises in 1891, Dr. G. R. McCall, secretary to the board of trustees, approached Kilpatrick and suggested that he undertake graduate studies in mathematics and physics with the possibility of returning to Mercer to assist Professor Joseph Willet and eventually succeed him. Entering Virginia Military Institute and studying civil engineering was also a possibility. But Kilpatrick finally decided to borrow $500 from Macon and enter graduate study at Johns Hopkins University in Baltimore. Johns Hopkins University was indeed a "gateway" for many young, intellectually inclined scholars from the South. In 1901, 236 of the 465 advanced students at Hopkins had come from that region.[73] When Kilpatrick announced his decision to go to Baltimore to continue his education, two citizens of White Plains expressed their surprise and bewilderment. The town physician, I. D. Moore, advised strongly against the move: "I tell you Heard, if you don't look out you'll be just like Macon, study so long you can't get down to practice." But Dan Kilpatrick, a former slave of Kilpatrick's father, told him, "You mus' aimst to learn it all."[74]

Tenenbaum called Johns Hopkins the "most moving intellectual adventure of Kilpatrick's life." There free inquiry took precedence over custom and tradition. "Even by breathing the air," Kilpatrick told Tenenbaum, "I could feel that great things were going on. I have never been so deeply stirred, so emotionally moved before or since."[75] While highly intelligent, even brilliant, Kilpatrick did have difficulty holding his own academically when he first arrived. After he received a score close to a zero on a quiz in a mathematics course, his professor noted that Kilpatrick had studied differential calculus rather than integral calculus. Kilpatrick's entire undergraduate education, in fact, was questioned by this professor and considered mediocre at best. He was directed to "read" mathematics, something he had never done before. For the next two or three weeks he studied thirteen hours a day. After that, he never made a grade less than an A.[76]

At Johns Hopkins, Kilpatrick came into contact with higher biblical

criticism, a topic certainly not mentioned in any of his father's theological publications. The intellectual discourse and interaction with the university were invigorating. Kilpatrick heard lectures on politics, religion, and medieval history. One of the most memorable lectures he heard was by young Woodrow Wilson, who spoke of implementing the British parliamentary system in the United States. It seems that Kilpatrick became a Wilson devotee from then on. He also found time to spend a Thanksgiving day in Annapolis and attend the Army-Navy football game.

One classroom experience left an indelible mark on Kilpatrick. Rather than the traditional procedure of working through a set of mathematics problems on the board as a group and then going on to the next set of assignments, something quite different occurred. The professor said to the class, "Take any problem you found difficult, or any you have not yet worked, and attempt to solve it." The professor then moved about the room, assisting the students. Kilpatrick wrote in his autobiography: "For the first time in all my pupil-student experiences, the instructor was on my side. Such a reversal of school practices that many reading my account of the experience will fail to see what constitutes the reversal."[77] Kilpatrick then decided that he wanted to teach mathematics, or possibly science. With the initial encouragement of the Mercer trustee, he began, with great anticipation, to make preparations to return to Georgia.

At the close of the 1891-1892 academic year at Johns Hopkins, Kilpatrick and a friend, Charlie Barrett, left Baltimore by boat for Savannah. There they purchased rail tickets for Milledgeville, Barrett's hometown. After spending a day or two there in the old Georgia state capital, Kilpatrick traveled on to Macon. He found, to his great disappointment, that the hoped-for position on the Mercer faculty had not materialized. Still committed to teaching and yet unemployed, Kilpatrick faced the daunting task of finding a position before fall. In a stroke of good fortune, he then heard that there was a teaching position open in the southwest Georgia town of Blakely. And, as it happened, the father of his roommate at Mercer, Arthur Powell, was a member of the school board.[78]

2

THE EMERGENCE OF A PROGRESSIVE

In the summer of 1892, Kilpatrick arrived in Blakely as a
college mathematician, and three years later he departed as
a progressive educator.

> Donald D. Chipman
> "Young Kilpatrick and the Progressive Idea"[1]

In education there is much opportunity. I am mindful that it
means hard work . . . a subordinating of momentary
inclinations to the grand prupose.

> William Heard Kilpatrick to Marie Kilpatrick, 1902[2]

Kilpatrick would describe the residents of Blakely, a southwestern
Georgia town with a population of 1,200, as a mix of the intelligent and the
crude, though he was quick to add that the citizens were deeply interested in
their schools. But when "Kil," as his college classmates still called him,
arrived in Blakely, a minor problem arose. The school board believed
Kilpatrick's stature too small and his appearance too youthful for him to be
given the position of high school principal. A compromise was finally
reached when his Mercer classmate, John Wade, was made coprincipal with
Kilpatrick. Each man received a salary of $700 for the school year, with
Wade managing student discipline while Kilpatrick oversaw the curriculum.
To further assure the board of his abilities, Kilpatrick offered to attend
summer classes at the new normal school institution, Rock College in
Athens.[3]

The experience at Rock College was Kilpatrick's first exposure to the
academic study of education. As he wrote in his autobiography, "Hither I had
thought of education as the process of assigning lessons from a textbook and
then hearing the lessons."[4] Admittedly, much of what was taught at Rock
College was in keeping with this traditional point of view. But an episode
related to him that summer by Otis Ashmore of Chatham Academy in
Savannah, Georgia, dramatically changed Kilpatrick's view of the educative

process. Ashmore told of leaving his students unattended one day for a brief period of time. A visitor came by the classroom looking for Ashmore and found the students so engaged in their lesson that they were working without supervision. "I did not see that far into the future then," Kilpatrick wrote, "but this 1892 suggestion led to the 1918 'Project Method.' The idea that a class could and would work with no teacher watching came to be an ideal for me."[5] Such a practice contradicted the conventional wisdom of the time, which stipulated a highly structured approach based on student recitation.

Kilpatrick also began to immerse himself in the literature of educational theorists. Page's book *Theory and Practice of Teaching* (1847) strengthened his distrust of set rules of behavior. And Herbert Spencer's theory of "natural punishment" endorsed that concept and also suggested the guidance inherent in goal-directed efforts.[6] At this time, Kilpatrick began to read the writings of the German educator and originator of the kindergarten, Frederick Froebel. He was also influenced by the nineteenth-century Swiss educator Johann Pestalozzi, who had suggested that the teacher-student relationship was best conducted on a basis of friendship and humane treatment, rather than harsh discipline. "These ideals took a firm hold on me," Kilpatrick wrote almost sixty years later. The traditional approach under which he had been reared was now undergoing a radical reevaluation.[7]

When Kilpatrick began his coprincipal's duties in September of 1892, he had also agreed to teach mathematics, Greek, and Latin to the eighth, ninth, and tenth grades. (Blakely was one of the first schools in the state to use a graded program.) As Donald Chipman noted in his study of Kilpatrick's first teaching assignment, the staff appeared so young that the local newspaper suggested that the women teachers wear "long dresses and the two principals be required to wear false mustaches to distinguish them from the pupils."[8] On opening day, the new principals welcomed the 140 students in a new school building, the Blakely Institute, a two-story edifice containing ten classrooms. Kilpatrick quickly applied his newfound Pestalozzian ideals to his own classroom. Students were permitted to leave their desks and converse among themselves about the lesson. They were even allowed to leave the classroom without receiving permission. Kilpatrick never administered corporal punishment to his own students, although on occasion he was obliged to follow the abhorrent practice with other students in his role as principal when John Wade was absent.

As his practical experience was growing, Kilpatrick's theoretical knowledge of education also continued to expand. The following spring he

traveled to Albany, Georgia, to hear the principal of the Illinois State Normal School, Colonel Francis Parker. Parker, considered by many the father of progressive education, had become well-known through Lelia E. Partrige's book *The Quincy Method*, which related Parker's experiences in Quincy, Massachusetts. "Francis Parker was the greatest man that we've yet had to introduce the better practice into the school," wrote Kilpatrick. "Here indeed was a vision, but its light was as yet blinding. I could sense the direction, but saw only dimly."[9] Upon his return to Blakely, he read Partrige's book on Parker and began immediately to introduce even more progressive practices into the school, implementing new methods of teaching math and initiating field trips to study nature. The inspired young principal even managed to arrange an expedition to the Kolomoki Indian Mounds, ten miles north of Blakely.[10] He next abolished commencement, being opposed to the concept of honoring one student over another, and also organized a county educational conference allowing teachers to discuss problems and issues in education. (He notes in his autobiography that while black teachers were not allowed to become members of the organization owing to "dominant ideas then in vogue," they were permitted to attend the conferences.[11])

In his own classroom, he furthered the use of his progressive techniques. In his first geometry course, six of the twenty students failed. The next year he made the course as concrete as possible, using actual constructions, taking care that the students understood each succeeding step. One particular student had been judged by her fifth-grade teacher to be unable to learn arithmetic — the subject was thought to be simply "beyond her mind," Kilpatrick was told. She not only finished Kilpatrick's course but went on to college, where she performed especially well in mathematics.[12] The boldest experiment, though, may have been Kilpatrick's directive to eliminate the traditional report cards. In their place the staff sent out monthly written reports on progress and attendance. The next year, according to Chipman, the teachers were to act on the assumption that the parents would assume no news was good news. Thus, these reports were given to the students but not sent home. Kilpatrick told Tenenbaum that report cards set pupils against teachers; created animosity, feelings of inferiority, and frustration; and disturbed the "wholesome relationship between the child and the community." The "failing child," Kilpatrick insisted, "loses status not only with his classmates, but also with his parents . . . and oftentimes with himself." Undeniably, there was an element of Rousseau's philosophy in his thinking. "In dealing with human beings," he maintained, "one encounters difficulties, but certainly they are

not created by trusting children."[13]   Kilpatrick's interest in his students was genuine. Tenenbaum was amazed that Kilpatrick could, after sixty years, not only name his students at Blakely but tell of their interests at the time and what had happened to them in the intervening years. Tenenbaum wrote, "He was surprised that I was surprised. 'They were my girls and boys,' as if to say, what sort of parent would forget his own children."[14]

As Kilpatrick's second year at Blakely began (1893-1894), John Wade abandoned teaching to become a cashier at the local bank. Now on his own, Kilpatrick got to know the community better, boarding at the home of Mrs. Ella Alexander. There was even time for occasional recreation. The bicycle fad had come to Blakely, and one evening Kilpatrick, Arthur Powell, and several others decided to take a moonlight ride to the Chattahoochee River, nine miles away. Powell tells that midway through the trip Kil let out a howl of pain, jumped off his bicycle, and rapidly began to disrobe. Standing almost naked in the middle of the road, he yelped between jumps, "Bees, wasps, hornets, yellow jackets, spiders, something's stinging me! My trousers are full of them." What had occurred was that a tube of bicycle tire glue in his back pocket, carried because of the frequency of punctures, had broken and was blistering his buttocks.[15]

During his third and final year at Blakely (1894-1895) the school board allowed Kilpatrick to employ an assistant. As superintendent of the Baptist Sunday school, Kilpatrick felt compelled to hire a Methodist in order to maintain the all-important theological balance. He also learned embroidery while at Blakely. And there was a girlfriend who baked him cookies and cakes, although he was not planning to fall in love.[16]

Almost sixty years later, in the early 1950s, Kilpatrick returned to Blakely and was warmly greeted by men and women who still remembered his work in the community. Chipman noted that in the mid-1970s, when he was doing his research in Blakely, people were still talking about Kilpatrick. They spoke of his wit, penetrating mind, and skill in seeking the deeper meanings of life. Arthur Powell called it the "killectual skill." Chipman concluded that if the definition of a progressive educator included "the application of new pedagogical principles tailored to the individual's needs," then "to constantly refer to him [Kilpatrick] as simply Dewey's disciple is to misinterpret the life of young Kilpatrick."[17] Without doubt, the basic principles of progressive education were present during Kilpatrick's years at Blakely. The only contradictory evidence to Chipman's thesis on Kilpatrick's progressivism is the fact that at this juncture he continued to see himself as a

mathematician, rather than as an educator. He wanted to teach, but it was mathematics, not education.

By the end of his third year, Kilpatrick had saved enough money to both repay his brother Macon the $500 he had borrowed and to return to Johns Hopkins. In his autobiography he wrote, "I left Blakely after my three years of teaching there with the clear determination of returning to Hopkins for my Ph.D. in mathematics. My first year there had filled me with enthusiasm. There was no doubt in my mind as to my aims and my hopes."[18] When he returned to Baltimore, Kilpatrick roomed with a boyhood friend, C. Sterling Jernigan, who was studying medicine. They lived on McCulloch Street in a boardinghouse, and Kilpatrick became rather good friends with Naomi Auschitz, the daughter of one of the boarders. "She and I struck it off very well, almost too well," he wrote later. "We were soon holding hands, and when we went down in the hall we generally hugged — all of this in spite of the fact that she was currently engaged to a young ministerial student."[19]

Unfortunately, Kilpatrick's university studies did not prove nearly as interesting. His return to Johns Hopkins was disillusioning in that the intellectual novelty he had encountered four years earlier had vanished. The newer professors were not nearly as impressive. He had changed his minor from physics to astronomy, as that was closer to mathematics, and had thoughts of eventually traveling to France to study. Finally, Kilpatrick shifted his two minors to Greek and philosophy and his theological thinking continued to be in turmoil. A class in the history of philosophy caused his religious concepts to shift again. This was a personal debate with himself, not so much over the existence of God as over how to better understand what was meant by "God." "I had to reintegrate these ideas into my thinking," he told Tenenbaum. A liberal minister in Baltimore told him, "I have no advice, except that you keep on thinking; don't stop. Keep on and you'll come out all right."[20] "As I look back on this, my second year at Hopkins," he concluded years later, "it was a definite disappointment."[21]

After leaving Johns Hopkins, Kilpatrick thought his future might lie in Savannah. But just getting there proved a challenge. Yellow fever was rampant in the South, and proof was needed that he had not traveled via New Orleans, where the epidemic was especially severe. Upon gaining entry into Savannah, Kilpatrick was contacted by Otis Ashmore, his colleague from Rock College. Now superintendent of schools in Savannah, Ashmore asked Kilpatrick to become the principal of Anderson Elementary School. Kilpatrick accepted the offer at a salary of $1,500, an excellent figure for the

time. In addition to supervising nine teachers and over 400 students, he also taught seventh grade. Such large numbers forced classes to swell to over fifty pupils. As a result, Kilpatrick suggested that the teachers break the classes down into groups. "Impossible," came the response — rules forbade it. He approached the board of education, as he had in Blakely, and the rule was changed. And, once again, report cards and corporal punishment disappeared in quick succession.[22]

One of Kilpatrick's more amazing achievements in Savannah, which he related in great detail both to Tenenbaum and in his autobiography, dealt with bringing some semblance of order to a talkative class. He began by announcing to the class that he would leave the room for five minutes. When he left the room, "bedlam did break loose." Upon returning, he asked for a show of hands of those who had *not* "behaved as they should," as he put it. It was understood that there would be no punishment. When he asked who had not done the right thing, most hands went up. Kilpatrick acknowledged the situation and asked the class to do better the next day. Each day he left, and upon his return fewer hands went up. The students engaged themselves in the work at hand as the amount of time he left the room increased from five to ten to fifteen minutes. "In the end I could leave the room and they behaved as well as when I was there," he said.[23] The students' shifting from external to internal control was an essential element of Kilpatrick's philosophical outlook. In explaining this phenomenon, Kilpatrick referred to his belief in trusting children and to the child's psychological need for recognition:

> The strongest motivating factor in a human being is a desire for recognition. Other things being equal, they would rather have recognition that brings approval than recognition that doesn't bring approval. If a child can't get recognition for being the best boy in the class he's apt to try to get it for being the worst.[24]

But curricular traditions were not so easy to dispense with. The superintendent's test called for students to learn a mind-numbing bank discount chart. "I told my children frankly that I was doing the best to prepare them for this test. They at least knew why they were studying this outlandish material, but they also knew . . . that I was on their side."[25] In 1896, he had jotted down on an index card a seminal piece of his philosophy that he would find almost fifty years later and record

in his diary:

> The natural exercise of the functions of the mind are pleasant just as those of the body. To give the child plenty of such work as is suited to his condition is to win his respect and good will; and thus he will naturally behave as he should. This is especially true and important in the primary grades. We need not expect to require a pupil to put his mind on unsuited work without hurt to himself.[26]

At times there did seem to be a mysterious and unexplainable ambience surrounding Kilpatrick as he taught. Later, he would teach classes at Teachers College with 500 or 600 hundred students in an auditorium, and individuals would speak of feeling as though they were the only one in the room with him. Forty-five years later, a military officer who had been a student in Kilpatrick's class of seventh-graders testified: "Things got so interesting that even the boys wanted to come to school rather than play hooky. They were afraid they would miss something."[27] The citizens of Savannah at the time reported a remarkable change in their community, according to Kilpatrick:

> Parents came to me and said: "Our children are now different; they are kindlier, more considerate." The town and the neighborhood felt this difference. There was considerably less mischief around the neighborhood; gates stayed on better, fewer windows were broken; there was less vandalism. I appealed to the better in the children and I gave them an opportunity to act on that better self and then gave them recognition and approval for such behavior."[28]

As the school year at Savannah drew to a close, Dr. Pickney Daniel Pollack, president of Mercer University, visited Kilpatrick and offered him the position of professor and chair of mathematics and astronomy at his *alma mater*. Pollack had few concerns regarding Kilpatrick's abilities as a teacher or scholar, but the question of his religious views was raised. Kilpatrick responded that his second year at Hopkins had caused him to examine more closely man's spiritual nature and his place in the universe. As the minister in Baltimore had suggested, Kilpatrick was rethinking his religious position. Whether Pollack listened carefully to what Kilpatrick was saying is not

clear, but he seemed satisfied and matched the Savannah salary of $1,500.[29] For now, religion became an extraneous issue, an unanswered question for Kilpatrick, but one that would emerge again within a decade.

When Kilpatrick returned to Mercer, it was with a sense of both duty and family tradition. Then, as now, the idea of service was an important, if not overriding, motivation for faculty members associated with denominational institutions of higher education. In an undated, untitled article in his scrapbook, Kilpatrick addressed the role and freedom of the teacher in an institution such as Mercer. "The reason for its [Mercer's] being is found in the service that it renders," he wrote. While he admitted that there were limitations and restrictions upon the individual teacher, the faculty member must "deny self and selfish inclinations" so as not to damage the institution as it went about its objective of service. He concluded his essay on this topic with a rather circuitous argument: that the goal of Christian education was an environment where Christianity could embody its ideals through the lives of the students and faculty, who, in turn, would work for Christianity and the world. There is a noticeable lack of denominational dogma or orthodoxy in his essay; in fact, he speaks of the "delightful comradeship" he enjoyed with students from an interdenominational population, including Methodist, Episcopal, "and even Jewish" traditions.

The only man on the faculty Kilpatrick knew when he returned to Mercer was Professor Ragsdale, who taught religion. Despite this lack of acquaintance with fellow faculty members, he was elected secretary of the faculty. Kilpatrick almost immediately struck up a close friendship with the history professor J. R. Moseley. Kilpatrick described Moseley as the "completest saint that I have ever known." An example of this is the fact that Moseley had even given up golf for religious reasons: He was unable to watch an opponent play and wish him success. The two men became lifelong friends, with Moseley, years later, frequently staying with Kilpatrick in New York when his travels to religious retreats took him through the city. At Mercer, Moseley, who lived in his office and took his meals with the students, was an extremely popular figure on campus.[30] But Moseley's religious beliefs eventually caused him to resign from Mercer. Stricken with poor health, he began to delve into the teachings of Christian Science. Thinking this connection would embarrass the conventional dogma of the Baptist institution, he resigned, much to the consternation of faculty and students alike. As a result, Kilpatrick inherited the sponsorship of Moseley's Magazine Club. The club quickly moved into the area of philosophy and from there into

comparative religion. Kilpatrick told Tenenbaum that he saw no contradiction in "bypassing" an emphasis on moral and spiritual views while discussing theological points and church dogma and ritual. (He found himself most comfortable with the philosophy he termed neo-Hegelianism.[31]) And while regarding with skepticism any theological bent in the study of religion, Kilpatrick agreed to teach Sunday School and became active in the Y.M.C.A.

The affectionate moniker "little Kil" stayed with him when he returned to Mercer. His sensitive nature and warm personality made him extremely popular with the students. Tenenbaum's biography contains numerous testimonials from students about how he had "permanently enriched and ennobled their lives." It was a relational bridge that he was able to develop between himself and students. J. W. Norman was a student of Kilpatrick's at both Mercer and Teachers College who went on to become dean of the College of Education at the University of Florida. He spoke of visits to his former teacher in later years as "an exhilaration I get from no other experience that I have." Kilpatrick's assistance, companionship, and empathy with his students extended beyond academics. He would discuss moral, political, financial, and even personal problems with them. (In fact, his letters indicate that he may have been too generous in lending students money from his meager means.) At Mercer he became, as he would later become at Teachers College, a one-person personnel office, obtaining teaching positions for three-quarters of the Mercer graduates. One student summed it up quite simply: "Dr. Kilpatrick knew how to handle boys. He usually knew their problems and what they needed."[32]

Always an admirer of President Pollock, Kilpatrick came to be relied on more and more by Mercer's leader. At first an informal agreement between the two men led to Kilpatrick's becoming responsible for the internal affairs of the institution while Pollock devoted his attention to external matters. Eventually, at the age of twenty-nine, Kilpatrick was formally elected vice president by the Mercer trustees. The idea of a career in college administration did enter his mind. On a trip to the University of South Carolina, as he "stood and looked at the buildings, a very attractive sight, a premonition came to me that I would be president of that institution someday."[33] But for Kilpatrick this ambition was an aberration in the larger picture. He would have numerous opportunities in the future for presidencies or high academic office (especially during his years at Teachers College), but in the end, although he was a natural leader, administration never really appealed to him.

In addition to his professional activities, Kilpatrick's personal life took a

new direction.   He had been boarding with an attorney in Macon, Olin Wimberly, father of four children — all under the age of six — who was also on the faculty of Mercer's law school.   In January of 1898, Wimberly's first cousin, Marie Beman Guyton, met young professor Kilpatrick on a visit to Macon.   She was three years his junior.   They were engaged after a brief courtship, which included a summer visit by Kilpatrick to Marie's hometown of Marianna, Florida, a small town on the Florida panhandle, and were married there on December 27, at the Episcopal church.   "Our religious alignments were different," Kilpatrick later wrote; "She was an Episcopalian and I Baptist, but we had no difficulty on this point."[34]   After a trip to White Plains to visit his parents, the Kilpatricks returned to Macon to begin their new life together.

Marie was described as a "small, dainty, sweet person, who made friends easily."[35]   The rare photographs that survive do indeed show her to be a petite, attractive young woman with large eyes in a slender face framed by a high Victorian collar, her hair piled high on her head in the style of the time. Written in a personal manner rarely found outside his letters, this paragraph survives in Kilpatrick's unfinished autobiography:

> I think it would be difficult to find a married [couple] that
> lived together more happily. Any two people living together
> will find differences of opinions on particular points, but if
> there was ever any tendency to conflict in even the slightest
> degree I do not recall it. We loved each other, I might say,
> intensely and this in all ways.[36]

On January 10, 1901, a daughter was born to the Kilpatricks. She was given the name Margaret Louise, but her father called her Baby until she was three or four. A number of letters from Kilpatrick to his Marie survive, and they reveal deep feelings for both his wife and his daughter. The letters almost always began, "My Darling Wife," and concluded, "Your Devoted Husband." The following was written while he was away at summer school:

> I am so anxious to be again with my wife and child. I feel as
> if I am not living in any real sense so far away from you.
> After one has known what it means to enjoy the pleasure of
> living with such a wife as I have, he is not willing to be
> absent from her. I hope that we may keep our married life

free from real care. I believe that we are happier than most
others, and I believe that we shall continue so.[37]

In another letter, also from the Knoxville summer school, he wrote, "I
am getting homesick for my wife and Baby, especially my wife. I lie awake
at night and think of her and wish for her. I love you, my dear, and I miss you
so much."[38]

One idea about education that Kilpatrick brought from Blakely and
Savannah to Mercer was his opposition to formal grades. "I prevailed upon
the faculty to stop telling students their marks. As a compromise," Kilpatrick
later wrote, "it was agreed that if a student failed any course he would be
given his exact mark."[39] Mercer had already abolished graduation honors, a
practice that Kilpatrick had objected to even as a student. But a deeper and
more profound change in Kilpatrick's educational philosophy was in the
making. His work at Mercer in the area of mathematics led him to doubt the
theory of formal discipline, which held that the study of mathematics trained
the mind, much as exercising the body produces greater muscle tone. The
monotony of teaching mathematics year after year also made it difficult for
him to maintain his own interest, let alone that of students, in the subject. He
also had grave doubts as to whether traditional mathematics could be taught
"in conformity with a modern philosophy of education." Thus, Kilpatrick
told Tenenbaum that "find[ing] it difficult to maintain their [the students']
interest . . . I branched out into education, administration, and later into ethics
and educational psychology."[40] For the time being, though, the teaching of
mathematics left him empty.

Kilpatrick thus began to venture into the area of educational studies,
although the field itself was new. In fact, Mercer offered no formal courses
in the study of education as a discipline. In addition to the Magazine Club,
however, Kilpatrick inherited from Moseley a Saturday-morning discussion
group, which explored the educational problems of the day. In 1897, he used
a Herbert Spencer volume on education with the group, and in 1899, William
James's *Talks to Teachers*. He and John Dewey later wrote a new introduction
to James's book, a volume he always kept close at hand, according to
Tenenbaum.[41] In this volume, one heavily marked passage noted that "the
total mental efficiency of a man lies in the strength of his desire and passion,
the strength of the interest he takes." And another underlined passage said,
"To think, in short, is the secret of will, just as it is the secret of memory."[42]

Summer school programs, popular throughout the country at this time,

provided the busy young scholar with the opportunity to explore this new area of interest for himself. In 1898, he traveled north to the University of Chicago, where he took two courses — one in education and the other in mathematics. He seemed to enjoy the latter course for the rather odd reason that a mathematical problem given to him by the instructor proved so difficult that he began to doubt his intellect and his ability in the subject.[43]

The other course he enrolled in during that summer of 1898 in Chicago began, although inauspiciously, a relationship that would last for over half a century. The professor of Kilpatrick's education course was John Dewey who was then thirty-nine — twelve years his senior. Dewey had published *Interest As Related to the Will* and *My Educational Creed* and was beginning to impress people in the fields of both philosophy and education. But for some reason Kilpatrick, at least at this juncture, was unmoved by Dewey's course. Recalling this fact years later caused him both shame and puzzlement. "I can hardly recall anything about it," he wrote.[44] He told Tenenbaum:

> As I heard Dewey lecture, I thought of him as a very capable man. I honored and respected him, but I failed to get from him the kind of leadership in thinking that I wished. Professor Dewey is not a good lecturer, and he does not always prepare the ground, so that a newcomer can follow him.[45]

Two summers later, in 1900, Kilpatrick, along with Marie and his sister Helen, traveled to Cornell University in Ithaca, New York, for two more summer courses, once again, one each in mathematics and education. This time the outcome was just the reverse. The mathematics course was "a complete flop," while Charles DeGarmo's education course emerged as pivotal in Kilpatrick's thinking. DeGarmo used Dewey's *Interest As Related to the Will* (later to be retitled *Interest and Effort*). "This book opened up a whole new world to me, as no book ever before," he said. "The starting point in all education — the crux of the education process — is individual interest; further, that the best and the richest kind of education starts with this self-propelled interest."[46] "I could not thank Dewey enough for what he had done for me," wrote Kilpatrick.[47] Writing of DeGarmo and a now forgotten mathematics teacher, Kilpatrick recorded in an article fifty years later the revelation he experienced:

If there is such a thing as a spiritual rebirth in the realm of thought I then experienced it. Here all my gropings were brought together and enlightened. Every teaching ideal, every moral stirring in the field of teaching, every conception of method — all these and more were brought together in focus and given a burning zeal. That same summer — partly as a result of the most repellent teaching I had ever experienced — I turned my back on any idea of further study in mathematics. A new calling beckoned me.[48]

Thus emerges, possibly for the first time in Kilpatrick's thought, the debate over a strictly subject-matter track to the teaching and learning process as opposed to a more child-centered approach. Dewey had grappled with this issue in *The Child and the Curriculum* (though he viewed it not as a struggle between two mutually exclusive areas, but rather as a partnership) and would continue to discuss the apparently dichotomous issue throughout his lifetime. For Dewey it was yet another pernicious dualism, which could be ameliorated if "the prejudicial notion that there is some gap in kind (as distinct from degree) between the child's experience and the various forms of subject matter that make up the course of study" were abandoned.[49]

Kilpatrick may or may not have been influenced by *The Child and the Curriculum*. Owing to his attendance at various summer schools at this time of his life, he was certainly cognizant of the major works being published in education. If not directly influenced by this particular work of Dewey's, he was swayed by Dewey's ideas on interest and effort. In the following lengthy segment — in which Kilpatrick uses mathematics as his primary source of experience — one can detect the genesis of what has been interpreted by some as an anti-intellectual, anti-subject matter bias. It should be remembered, though, that these comments were made fifty years after the time his thinking was transformed:

In teaching math, I started out with what I wanted my students to master; in other words, I was trying to project my knowledge, my wishes, and my interests on them. I began to perceive that if we wanted rich, meaningful learnings we must start with the student's present knowledge, wishes, and interests, whatever they may be and wherever they may lead. This shifted my viewpoint radically. I was dimly

> beginning to perceive that the fundamental error of our
> school systems was that they first chose things that the
> teachers and the school thought important and then
> compelled students to master that material. They began in
> the wrong place; they began with fixed and set subject
> matter, when they should have begun with the student's
> present interests, purposes, abilities, and needs.[50]

The summer at Cornell with DeGarmo had indeed been crucial in Kilpatrick's thinking. "I found myself making what was to me an epoch-making decision, namely that I would give up the teaching of mathematics as my life work and would take up the study of education."[51] There would be a period of transition and, later, of preparation, but he had made the decision to move in a new direction.

On the way home to Georgia from New York state, the Kilpatricks visited Niagara Falls, Toronto, and then New York City. These southerners saw automobiles for the first time and visited the new Cathedral of Saint John the Divine, where two of the enormous arches had just been put in place. Kilpatrick later noted that although it was only blocks away, he failed to visit Teachers College and Columbia University.

His attendance at summer schools resumed in 1902, when, under the auspices of the Rockefeller Foundation and a $1 million grant to improve education in the South, Kilpatrick and 162 other Georgians traveled to Knoxville, Tennessee, to attend what became known as the Summer School of the South. Here he met men whom he considered to be first-class educators, including Wyckliffe Rose and G. Stanley Hall. Rose, a master teacher in the philosophy of education, later went on to assist in the founding of George Peabody College. Kilpatrick continued to be fascinated with the works of William James, desiring to begin scientific studies himself in connection with learning, possibly using his daughter, Margaret, as a subject. To Marie he wrote: "I have received a new impulse to study her. I want us to keep a diary of her and of the other baby that is to be, and put down various records of her development."[52]

He also began to compare himself with the conference leaders and found himself wanting. "I am a little disappointed in respect to one thing," he wrote to Marie; "I don't have quite the opportunity to mingle with the greater men — invited lecturers. I am too young, too inconsequential looking." He continued ruminating in this letter on the future and what it might hold for him:

What will it come to? I cannot say. I feel that in some way I am preparing for something yet greater, and I believe that my coming here has helped me in several important ways: I am stirred as I have not been in a long time, if indeed ever before; I have learned certain specific things; I have gained certain towering viewpoints; all of these will stand me in good stead.[53]

The transition from his career in mathematics to a possible future in the new field of education continued to be in his thoughts as he studied at Knoxville. One colleague that summer inquired as to why he had not studied education and, indeed, why no one in Georgia had pursued this sorely needed line of inquiry. He wrote again to Marie:

I am feeling much inclined now to take up some of this work [education], gradually breaking away from mathematics. I can teach mathematics, but there is no soul growth in it to me. In education, there is much opportunity (1) for soul growth, individual improvement, and (2) for influencing Georgia. I feel now that I have reached the time when I must map out my path and walk in it. I must systematically prepare for what I am to do. I am mindful that it means hard work; it means fixedness of purpose; it means a subordinating of momentary inclination to the grand purpose.[54]

He later wrote in his diaries that these letters to Marie during 1902 and 1903 provided the best insight into his thinking about the shift from mathematics to education. In the letters he sketched out a line of study as he prepared for his new vocation. His program included psychology, philosophy and history of education, and a knowledge of methodology. He also planned to study philosophy, ethics, French, German, biology, and poetry,[55] and he gave serious consideration to a year of study at Oxford. But his concrete plans returned to Teachers College of New York City. Although his goal had been to gain a Teachers College fellowship in the fall of 1903 and then return to Mercer to establish an education department, the serious illness of Dr. Pollock made it necessary for Kilpatrick to assume the institution's presidential duties on a temporary basis. "It is undoubtedly true that my temporary presidency is going to be of great help to me," he wrote to Marie

in the summer of 1903. "It will put me before the people . . . in a way that is pregnant with issue for the future. I do not think I am vain about this. I tell it to you, because I want to put my trophies at your feet."[56]

At the age of thirty-three, Kilpatrick still looked ten years younger — slender of build, blue-eyed, and with a full head of light-brown hair. The appointment, although temporary, was probably more popular with the students than with the faculty. Although shy and reserved in larger group settings, he had a magnetism which came alive when he dealt with people on a personal basis. At this time, the greatest burden for the young administrator, other than grappling with himself over the move to education, was recruiting a freshman class large enough to keep the institution afloat. This heavy responsibility came at a difficult time for the Kilpatricks. The young couple had lost an infant son in January of 1903. The child, named for his father, was born on New Year's Day; died a week later, possibly of tetanus, and was buried in Marianna. During that same year Marie developed the early stages of what proved to be tuberculosis. Kilpatrick moved Marie and their young daughter to White Plains that summer and then returned to Macon to begin the task of recruiting a class of young men to enter Mercer in the fall. He asked that Marie be patient with his father and brother Macon. "They are honest and hearty," he wrote to Marie, "if they do offend."[57]

Kilpatrick's letters to Marie from Mercer that summer of 1903 reflect his brimming schedule. A plea for assistance in the form of a P.S. in one of his letters said, "Cultivate all of the people with boys who might come to Mercer. You might get me three or four boys."[58] The pace was frenetic, and he continued to carry on much of the secretarial work connected with the presidency. He ran the mimeograph machine, answered correspondence, put together 600 copies of the catalog, and even placed 500 letters in envelopes. He also began to type when he lost his secretary. "Don't think that I am dictating my letter to my stenographer," he wrote his wife. "I am learning to use the machine myself . . . tho' likely I shall change to pen and ink before very long."[59] All of this was done on too little sleep and in the stifling heat of a Georgia summer. After a difficult summer of rising and falling expectations (he had generated 200 more names of potential students than Pollock had the year before) as to the eventual class numbers, the fall semester opened with the largest enrollment in the school's history. "I had made my success," he later said, proud but exhausted.[60]

Crucial academic issues, in addition to the recruitment of young men for the freshman class, emerged. The law school faculty resigned en masse over

a projected change in their status by the state legislature. Kilpatrick was also asked to review the state's examination questions for teachers and to serve on the Georgia Rhodes Scholarship Committee. The pace was hectic. He had lost 17 pounds from 1902 to 1903, going from 121 to 104, before going back up to 110 by the end of the summer. His only sustenance, it appears, would often be a few peaches before returning to the many tasks at hand.[61]

Tenenbaum concluded, in his biography, that if Kilpatrick had one weakness, it was overworking himself.[62] He did seem obsessed with his assignment at times. Even in letters to Marie in which he was proclaiming his love for her, the subject of the "boys" emerges:

> I love you too much darling, for the college or any of these
> things to come between us. My heart is fixed; you need
> never fear. If you love me, you will be in my life. You do live
> in my life more than formerly. For instance, your meeting
> with the boys on Saturday nights has brought you close to
> me, because you have some of the same interest in the boys
> that I have.[63]

During the school year 1903-1904, George Peabody College in Nashville and Kilpatrick explored the possibility of his taking a position there. For the next decade Peabody would come forth as a suitor and then retreat. Kilpatrick finally announced that he did not wish to have the Mercer presidency on a full-time basis. Withdrawing "leaves me free to talk, to observe, to laugh at any wire pulling, to feel independent," he wrote to Marie. While his relationship with the faculty had not been a disaster, he admitted to Tenenbaum that things could have been better. He had preferred that the faculty make their own decisions, based on their best thinking rather than on information he gave to them. But he had also removed himself from the presidency because he did not think that he could represent Mercer throughout the state. He wrote to his mother that he thought himself too young and lacking in experience at this time in his career to assume the office permanently.[64]

While he may have thought himself inexperienced for the position of president of Mercer, it was during this time that he began to give what were known as talks or lectures, mainly to local groups, even on occasion outside the county. One such talk suggested the force with which Kilpatrick could hold forth when he was at his full powers of influence and persuasion.

Speaking on the insipid topic of local taxation of schools for an hour and a quarter, Kilpatrick "began in fear and trembling. The sun was hot and the people would not sit in front, but stood in the shade all about. I soon caught the crowd and had unbounded attention."[65] His progressive ideas emerged in a talk he gave in 1904 before the Macon Athenaeum entitled "The Educational Progress of the Century," in which he spoke of the crucial need for education to be studied as a subject on its own, of the progress toward more democratic schools in terms of opportunity and compulsory attendance laws, and of the need to recognize that the child's nature must determine the method of teaching. He went on to quote G. Stanley Hall by saying that the education of the future would not focus on "the training of memory by information," but rather would "focus upon the feelings, sentiments, and emotions . . . which are the issues of life."

Although he had withdrawn himself from consideration for the permanent presidency at Mercer, the idea of a presidency had not left him. He had considered again going to Teachers College for a year and then in 1905 looked at Milledgeville, the normal college at Athens, and revisited Peabody. In the back of his mind was also the thought that the Mercer presidency would open up again in "seven years at most." And there was the inevitable political jockeying going on for the presidency at Mercer, especially among certain faculty members. But Kilpatrick's work went on. "The faculty are easy to manage, perhaps because I don't care to manage them," he wrote.[66] In the end the trustees selected, in 1905, Dr. Charles Lee Smith of William Jewell College as the new president of Mercer University. For Kilpatrick, the actions of the new president, along with the issue of his religious beliefs, would make the next few years one of the most trying periods in his life. Just as his philosophical, intellectual, and pedagogical theories were crystallizing, his professional and personal life was to undergo profound, even melodramatic transformations.

3

A HERESY TRIAL AND THE WILDERNESS

"The only place you can kick that Kilpatrick is up."
Comment by a Mercer University faculty member

As the year 1904 began, Kilpatrick, his wife Marie, and their three-year-old daughter, Margaret, resided at 657 College Street, Macon, Georgia. The acting president of Mercer University, at age thirty-three, initiated on January 1st what would become one of the more remarkable documents in the history of American education: he began keeping a diary. With only a few exceptions, it would be faithfully kept, with entries recorded each day for the next fifty-seven years. Kilpatrick wrote as a preface on the first page:

> In this book it is my intention to keep for my own satisfaction certain records of things that interest me, such as without committing them to writing would likely escape my memory; or at any rate be recalled in only an indefinite way. One main purpose is to record those things that I wish afterwards to recall with absolute certainty.[1]

Other factors which motivated the inception of the diary were his deep interest in family history and his wish to preserve a record of events for his children, if there were to be others in addition to Margaret. Almost forty years later, in his book *Selfhood and Civilization*, Kilpatrick quoted the Englishman William Jowett, who wrote "In every man's writings there is something like himself and unlike others, which gives individuality."[2] For the author, these diaries would provide that unique glimpse at both the man and his times.

Outside his administrative responsibilities, Kilpatrick taught the Sunday class for college men at the First Baptist Church, splitting the lessons between a study of the Old Testament and the words of Jesus. But his role was basically that of facilitator, keeping a very close rein on divulging what he himself believed. "I asked questions, but I answered no questions and at no point gave any opinion of my own."[3] Attendance was healthy, and the group, according to Kilpatrick, appeared to approve of the process. While developing in the young

men "a more rational and fruitful attitude toward the Bible," he also tacitly questioned the reliability of the Bible.[4] He would teach the class for six years, but by 1905 it had shrunk to a mere five students.

What were Kilpatrick's beliefs regarding religion during his years at Mercer as professor and administrator? It would be accurate to state that at this time his ideas were still in flux, although leaning toward a mild form of agnosticism. As the years passed, he would move further away from any system of belief in the supernatural. Tenenbaum may have best captured his thinking at this point in his life when he wrote that Kilpatrick "looked upon God as the spirit of goodness, and on religion as the unification of the spirit of man with this all-inclusive spirit of goodness." He had already come to "reject the traditional religious dogma, theology, and ritual."[5] Regarding his wavering from the theological Baptist party line, Kilpatrick later said that there may not have been a truly orthodox man on the faculty. He had shared his thoughts and beliefs with a colleague in the religion department, who found no reason for criticism. But his questions in the campus discussion groups (such as "What constitutes a religious experience?") lent credence to charges of apostasy by those to whom he referred in his diary as "heresy hunters."[6] With one exception, from this point on in his life, he cared little for preaching of any kind. "Staid to hear Dr. White, the local Baptist minister, preach one of his charac-teristic sermons," wrote Kilpatrick in his diary in 1904, "dry orthodox, narrow, bearing no message to me."[7]

One reason for Kilpatrick's impatience with what he viewed as Baptist orthodoxy was the diversity in his reading at this time. He read not only periodicals such as *The Nation, The London Spectator, The Outlook*, and *The Atlantic*, but also both new and traditional works of philosophy. "Read today . . . Royce's *Spirit of Modern Philosophy*, Paulsen (philosophy), Morrell (history), and Hume's *Enquiry Concerning the Human Understanding* . . . and some of Spinoza." He was also reading the works of Edward L. Thorndike, and John Dewey's *School and Society* for a second and third time, respectively.[8]

As Kilpatrick's own intellectual life was growing, there were also the internal politics of Mercer to be dealt with. In February of 1905 President Pollock had written to Kilpatrick that he intended to resign at commencement. Kilpatrick wrote that he thought (again) he would go to Peabody in Nashville or stay at Mercer as a regular faculty member. He had no wish for the presidency, nor would he seek it. Kilpatrick sensed that the atmosphere was becoming less hospitable. During the trustees' meeting that

May, resignations and decisions not to renew contracts were made regarding three professors in order, according to Kilpatrick, "to put in their places men of more active piety." [9]

Kilpatrick received a raise of $250 for the coming year and would be earning $1,800 when the new school year began. But the board's selection of Dr. Charles Lee Smith filled Kilpatrick with concern. He wished for a year's study leave, and his uneasiness was apparent. "I fear much that our relationship will not be harmonious. I cannot see much agreement on the spiritual side of things." When news of the formal election finally came in July, he tried to be optimistic but was apprehensive. "I know nothing but what is favorable," he wrote, "but in some way I fear." While not overly impressed when he first met Dr. Smith, Kilpatrick detected no major character flaws. Although Smith did not seem to have a sense of humor and seemed to enjoy talking about himself, Kilpatrick thought he could work "pleasantly with him," and, more important, that the new president did not appear to be a "heresy hunter." [10] These first impressions would soon change.

A week after this initial meeting, Kilpatrick noted in his diary that Smith had the "unusual wish to go into details of communication of his personal affairs" (e.g., the cost of his suits and hotel rooms) and called Smith an "egotist and lacking in deeper spirituality." And during that last week of July 1905, as if to bring closure to the situation, Dr. Pollock died. With his passing, Kilpatrick lost his most powerful advocate. A month and a half later, the situation began to deteriorate in earnest. Kilpatrick returned to campus in mid-September and found everything "upside down." "Dr. S. [Smith] seems inclined to put all the work that he can on others. I don't find myself drawn as much to him as formerly. I can hardly imagine what he can have been doing since I left Macon August 16th." [11] Three weeks later, the bottom seems to have dropped out: "He is a small caliber man. On the least provocation he shouts forth a verbal avalanche of shallow platitudes, the effect of which (on me) is to bring amazement and annoyance and even exasperation bordering on desperation. I can hardly stand to hear him. There is no such thing as discussion with him." By the end of October he found Smith "too much of the sissy . . . too much threatening in his manner." Smith's behavior was also found wanting compared with Dr. Pollock's, especially at chapel time. "I look for a deluge later on. I shall try to keep from being engulfed in it." [12]

Working with Dr. Smith was now becoming more and more difficult. On his thirty-fourth birthday, Kilpatrick expressed dissatisfaction with both Smith's management and his conduct. "I shall have to leave . . . for my own spiritual

welfare," he wrote. Two days later he resigned his position as vice president so that Smith would be able to choose his own person. He had discussed this with his father, and the elder Kilpatrick agreed that his son's contributions had not been fully appreciated.[13] During a chapel service held shortly after Kilpatrick's resignation from his administrative duties, a speaker made the innocuous statement that he had heard much advice, all of which he had forgotten. Kilpatrick applauded. Later that day, Smith confronted him and asked whether his applause was a reflection on him (Smith). Kilpatrick denied the charge, but wrote in his diary that it corroborated his previous judgment that Smith was a "sensitive fool, suspicious of everything, especially me." Chapel services continued to be a problem for the new president of Mercer. Two students scuffling before one service prompted Smith to deliver an extended diatribe on students' behavior, suggesting that they should always behave as if the president of the United States were present. This appeal, according to Kilpatrick, carried no weight with the audience: "He knows very, very little about managing students." The students later placed a cow in the chapel overnight and wrote several inane verses on the back wall of the building. The local paper carried the incident in both morning and afternoon editions. Smith summoned Kilpatrick the next day and, while not accusing him directly, implied that he had been behind the episode. Although angered, Kilpatrick held his tongue and was advised by a colleague to "swallow a measure of unpleasantness."[14]

The culminating incident occurred when Kilpatrick caught Dr. Smith's son Howell cheating. In early February of 1906, Kilpatrick went to Smith with suspicions that Howell had cheated on an examination. After meeting with his son, Smith told Kilpatrick that no dishonesty had taken place; Howell had merely memorized the portion of the examination in question. The next day, the issue came before a faculty meeting, where father and son, protesting innocence, implied that Kilpatrick's charge was an attempt to thwart Dr. Smith's own attempts to root out cheating in the college. The president marched up to the brink by intimating that Kilpatrick may have been lying. Kilpatrick then directly asked Smith if his veracity was being questioned. The Smiths both retreated and said no. After further evidence regarding the incident was heard from other faculty members, and failing to secure a confession from Howell, both Smith and Kilpatrick withdrew while the faculty deliberated this issue. While the faculty was cloistered, there emerged from the hallway hysterical screaming. Mrs. Smith appeared at the door, bellowing, "Gentlemen, you shall not make my son confirm to a lie, you shall not!" Dr. Smith quickly removed her from the room, where a straw ballot was taken,

finding Howell Smith guilty of cheating by a vote of seven to one. Upon hearing the decision, Dr. Smith burst forth in a tirade against Kilpatrick for not coming to him immediately over the situation and for having the ulterior motive of crippling his administration. Kilpatrick responded coolly that he had delayed speaking to Smith to save the feelings of Howell and that the faculty vote indicated that he had not erred. The younger Smith was expelled from the college.[15]

Unfortunately, this was not the end of the episode. Three days later, Smith lashed out with an even stronger attack against Kilpatrick and, in the heat of the moment, called another professor a liar. He apologized for the latter act but resumed his diatribe against Kilpatrick. Kilpatrick, having reached the limit of his patience, "burst forth uncontrollably: 'Dr. Smith, Howell Smith knows that I . . .'" whereupon a fellow faculty member took him by the shoulder and led him out of the building. The next day Kilpatrick went to see the mayor of Macon, who warned him to be careful. "They may try to unload on you," he was told. Within the week, Dr. Smith did essentially admit that his son was guilty, but he could not resist the opportunity to give Kilpatrick a patronizing speech in front of the faculty on how such cases should be handled in the future.[16]

That may or may not have been the end of the incident. A fellow faculty member told Kilpatrick in March that he thought the incident was over, and that the president would not take it any further. But the colleague did believe that heresy charges could emerge. He added, though, that Kilpatrick's standing with the faculty had never been stronger. Kilpatrick responded that he had thought of resigning and was "sick at heart" over the entire matter. But rumors had indeed begun to circulate regarding Kilpatrick's religious beliefs. Tenenbaum even hints that Dr. Smith had a role in the rumors, which began to build with a bout of paranoia on the part of the president — possibly instigated by talk of Kilpatrick's popularity with the students and suggestions that the young professor might even be the de facto president. What has been called a "witch-hunt," or the "heresy trial" of William Heard Kilpatrick began in earnest as the academic year 1905-1906 came to a close.[17] There is no evidence that Charles Lee Smith was behind this activity, but the disharmony between the two men, coupled with the loss of any support Kilpatrick might have had when Dr. Pollock died, made the environment a dangerous one for the young professor.

The heresy charges came from various sources, including a group of students who belonged to the Y.M.C.A. and who called Kilpatrick an "emissary from hell." There were also anonymous letters questioning his belief in the

deity of Christ and other theological precepts. One colleague he consulted urged him to respond in a way that would allow him to stay at Mercer. This man told Kilpatrick that "higher criticism" was a fad, a comment Kilpatrick found amusing.[18] But there had been threats from alumni that they would not raise further money for Mercer until the institution had "purged itself of infidelity." As the rumors grew more bizarre, Kilpatrick's first impulse was to resign. The board of trustees had made investigations, but nothing could be substantiated. In the spring, Kilpatrick met in Atlanta with three of the trustees and openly responded to questions, asking their advice as to what he should do. "They listened to me . . . but they had no advice to give me; they didn't seem to know what to do." Another colleague advised Kilpatrick to tender his resignation with the hope that the trustees would not accept it, thereby dealing a fatal blow to what this professor considered reactionary fundamentalism.[19]

But in the end, the board of trustees was forced to deal directly with the situation. Their meeting, which some have considered a trial, began at the end of the school year 1905-1906. According to witnesses, it was a remarkable event. Kilpatrick quoted Scripture, and his knowledge of the Bible was even called "expert."[20] Dr. P. A. Jessup, who witnessed the proceedings, later shared his remembrances with Guy Wells:

> I sat at Kilpatrick's trial for three days. Never in my life have I been in a class where I heard such good theology. He spoke honestly and frankly. I have never seen a man so completely confuse, confound, and astound the judges, particularly on the divinity of Jesus. For thirty minutes he quoted strong Scripture upholding one side and then took thirty minutes quoting Scripture on the other.[21]

In the end, the final blow may have been struck by a local Baptist minister, Dr. White, who had heard Kilpatrick say in a private conversation concerning the Virgin Birth, "I gave that up a long time ago." (During this conversation Dr. White had told Kilpatrick that Dr. Smith was supporting him, thought kindly of him, and recognized his worth as an educator. "I only smile at this," Kilpatrick wrote in his diary.) At the trial itself he told the trustees that, with regard to the divinity of Jesus, "Gentlemen, I must be honest and tell you that I don't know what the answer is."[22] In his diary, Kilpatrick wrote, " . . . many questions were asked, most of which I seemed to answer satisfactorily until the question of the Virgin Birth was sprung. I discussed it a little stating

my present rejection of it. I felt that the discussion carried the board with me and retired expecting an early vindication." He was mistaken. Echoing the words of Pilate, Jessup later said, "We really felt we could find no fault with him," but, "with tears in our eyes we made up our minds to let Kilpatrick go. But we knew he was a remarkable man."[23]

On June 6, 1906, the board of trustees accepted Kilpatrick's resignation, and word came to him while he was with his students. In what may or may not have been a related matter, the board also accepted the resignation of Dr. Charles Lee Smith. His problems with students, his arrogant behavior in faculty meetings, and the episode of Howell's cheating certainly did not make his brief tenure at Mercer a pleasant or productive one. Of his own resignation, Kilpatrick wrote, "I tell Marie and go to bed, nervous, sore at heart, not rebellious." Despite the usual stoic manner with which he held up during the ordeal, the process was hard on him. The next day, he broke down saying good-bye to his landlady.[24] A remarkable footnote to the entire episode was the fact that Kilpatrick's father, James Kilpatrick, sat on the Mercer board of trustees. Excusing himself from the proceedings, his father told the board, "I love my son, Heard, more than anything, excepting the Kingdom of Heaven. First, do what you think best for the Kingdom of Heaven, and second, for Heard." Ten years later Kilpatrick wrote that when he had stepped down as vice president and the act had gone unnoticed, his father had said that he was "mortified and ashamed at the way the brethren have treated you."[25]

The episode was reported in the *Atlanta Constitution* of June 8. The article pointed out that no students testified against Kilpatrick and that the charges concerned his belief in the Virgin Birth. The paper also noted that some students may have made allegations because they received poor grades in class, but this specific charge can be found in no other accounts of the event. For the most part there was substantial support for Kilpatrick among the faculty and, especially, among the students throughout the entire week. Rev. T. P. Bell, a staunch defender of conservative Baptist theology, wrote an editorial in the *Christian Index* which actually treated the incident with some sensitivity, although the tone is a bit high-handed and couched in rather overblown homiletic syntax. "This professor [Kilpatrick] came before the Board and told the story of a Christian experience that thrilled the hearts of many of the Trustees especially those who . . . had tremendous spiritual battles centering around the deeper doctrines of the Work." Bell concluded, "Acting like a true man and a high man, [he] solved the difficulty by presenting his resignation rather than to allow his brethren to be embarrassed on his account or permit the

possibility of the institution being injured in the eyes of the people."[26]

The event was one that literally would not go away. Seven years later, Kilpatrick, attending a conference in the South, was waylaid in the lobby of a hotel by Charles Lee Smith. He approached Kilpatrick, extending a hand, and said, "I am glad to see you. There was a time when you would not have expected to hear me say so, but I now feel so sincerely. You did me a greater service than I then knew; for my leaving Mercer was decidedly the best thing for me." Taken aback, and never one to pay an empty compliment — especially to someone who had treated him in a callous, if not unethical manner — Kilpatrick, finding it difficult to say anything, responded, "You give me too much credit."[27]

The lingering rancor of some Georgians over the heresy episode would erupt again during the "red scare" following World War I. In 1921 Kilpatrick, who was then widely known as one of the leading professors at Teachers College, received what can be described only as a piece of "hate mail" from Rev. R. L. Bolton of Madison. "They are getting your number down in Dixie," Bolton wrote. "The lightning is going to hit you some of these days. Look out. It got you at Mercer in '06." There was also a quotation from Bolton's weekly newsletter, a portion of which Kilpatrick entered into his diary. Bolton called him an infidel, an uncircumcised Philistine, and suggested that the colleges be cleansed of those who were "reeking with radical social doctrine."

For the most part, though, the wounds began to heal. Just a few weeks after the above outburst from his home state, Kilpatrick was called on by Mercer's President Weaver. He asked for James Kilpatrick's Bible and other books to be placed in the Mercer archives and invited Kilpatrick to lecture during the summer. According to Kilpatrick, Mercer's current president "certainly meant to cultivate cordial relations with me." Five years later, in 1926, Mercer bestowed the doctor of law (LL.D.) degree upon him.[28]

Still, Kilpatrick told Tenenbaum, over forty years after these events, he continued to feel "aggrieved at the unjust accusation and unjust condemnation." He also commented that at Union Theological Seminary the views he expressed would be considered middle-of-the-road, possibly even conservative.[29] And the issue really never left him. Once, thirty years after the episode, he was almost late to a class because he was retelling the story of his leaving Mercer to a student from West Virginia.[30] The official history of Mercer University, written in 1958, attempted to reduce the passion of the episode by providing the following reconstruction of history:

> In their alertness to advance in thought and in their spirit of
> open-mindedness and independent thinking, two or three
> professors were reported to have entertained views that were
> modernistic and at variance with the traditions and beliefs of
> the denomination, and that made them unacceptable to the
> college constituency. Because of these differences in points of
> view, some tensions developed that led to the withdrawal of
> Professor Moseley in 1900 and Professor Kilpatrick in 1906.

After relating Kilpatrick's rehabilitation, including the honorary degree, the history concludes, "His visits and his valuable contributions from year to year attest to the character and strength of this sustained and sustaining loyalty and leadership."[31]

As the summer of 1906 began, there was talk of a high position at the University of Georgia in Athens and also of an offer to go to Columbus, Georgia, as principal and mathematics teacher for a salary of $1,500. Kilpatrick had returned to White Plains and began to ponder his future. For reasons of health, Marie wanted to go to Highland, North Carolina, and so after leaving wife and daughter in Highland, Kilpatrick traveled to the University of Georgia, where he taught mathematics in the summer school program. A series of disappointments then commenced, as possible positions in Athens, Milledgeville, Savannah, Nashville, and other places either met with rejection or vanished. The religious controversy surrounding Kilpatrick's departure from Mercer clung to him in both subtle and not-so-subtle ways. Some thought that his difficulty in securing a position, especially in Georgia, was directly connected to the heresy charges and he received anonymous letters during the summer asking again about his belief in the Virgin Birth. In any event, he told Superintendent Gibson of Columbus that he wanted to go to Athens, but in late September, when the position in Athens (an adjunct professorship) was offered, Gibson agreed to release him only if a replacement could be found before school started. None was found, and so Kilpatrick held to his commitment to go to Columbus.[32]

Unfortunately, the North Carolina highlands did little for Marie's health, and in August of 1906 the family headed for Columbus, Georgia, by train. Because of public concern over tuberculosis, Marie was placed on a cot in the baggage car, next to a coffin. Kilpatrick sat in a chair by her side while five-year-old Margaret rode in one of the coaches. The symbolism of the journey was not lost on Margaret, who remembered the episode over seventy years later. Struggling to

find housing in Columbus, owing to Marie's condition, Kilpatrick finally came across the Howard sisters, who owned a large and rather imposing home in Columbus. Tenenbaum described the oldest sister as a "suffragette, a vegetarian, and an opposer of corsets" who took a liking to this supposed renegade of Baptist orthodoxy and welcomed the Kilpatricks into her home. Marie was provided with comfortable arrangements and fresh air on the enclosed second-story piazza, with Kilpatrick and Margaret placed in spacious rooms close by.[33]

Leaving the college setting for high school teaching and administration was a slightly different route from the one Kilpatrick had planned for himself. While Columbus was not a backwater, it was a rural town and it did take him out of the educational mainstream he had been striving for. Thoughts of Oxford or Teachers College ceased. He was not in exile, but it was, in a sense, the wilderness. On his thirty-fifth birthday he noted that life was taking on "an entirely different aspect than formerly. Now it is a struggle." At times he saw his new position as a step down. After one month he called high school teaching "refined cruelty under the circumstances" and told himself to "have courage and be brave." (These comments came after the superintendent had forgotten to ask the board to let Kilpatrick off for Christmas.) But he did throw himself into his work, improving Columbus High School according to his rudimentary progressive ideas, which included the abolition of his twin dislikes — honors and prizes. And, of course, there was the problem of punishment. He told one of his teachers that he thought placing a child in a corner of the room was "too aggressive." He was consistent on the issue, even with his own daughter. When Margaret, age six, was caught in an "untruth," as Kilpatrick put it, her punishment consisted of a moratorium on his reading to her and of sending her to bed thirty minutes early. Even these mild corrective measures disturbed him.[34]

It was in Columbus that Kilpatrick met Dr. Ashby Jones, a local Baptist minister of a definite liberal bent. He and Kilpatrick struck up an immediate friendship, which lasted for almost fifty years. The two men spent many hours discussing theology, religion, and life in general.[35] Kilpatrick wrote after an early meeting:

> I go to visit Dr. Ashby Jones at his new home. I am much pleased with him. He seems to think and think with freedom. I am hopeful if I stay in Columbus that he and I may become good friends. We discuss plans for improving the Sunday School and I promise to help him.[36]

Kilpatrick revisited his "neo-Hegelian spiritual concept of God," joined Ashby's congregation, and even taught Sunday school. For his diligent work with the Sunday School, the church gave him a watch fob at the end of the year.

It was also while Kilpatrick was in Columbus that he undertook his first organized interest in racial and cultural problems. Recent race riots in Atlanta had raised the consciousness of the population across the state regarding the issue, and the citizens of Columbus, led by Gunby Jordan, a local banker and industrialist, organized a group to examine the problem which Kilpatrick attended.[37]

Always a hard taskmaster on himself, Kilpatrick was a disciplined, structured man, almost to a fault in his later life. But his time in Columbus seemed to focus his activity as never before. While reading one evening "how Robert Burns ruined his life," Kilpatrick decided to list the characteristics by which he would henceforth attempt to abide. (He did add that he was already doing most of these things anyway.) The list included sweetness of temper, especially inwardly; absolute purity of loyalty in thought; work rather than selfish browsing; trusting in the power of love; and thoughtfulness for others.[38]

Marie's health continued to deteriorate as 1906 drew to a close. In late January the Kilpatricks had lost a baby boy, born two months prematurely. The infant's respiratory system failed, and he died almost immediately after birth. Kilpatrick had feared the birth and was relieved that Marie had withstood the trauma as well as she did. Her tuberculosis made it impossible for her to leave the house, and Kilpatrick devoted a great deal of his time to nursing her and reading aloud. He did accept dinner invitations, on occasion, from friends such as Dr. Jones, or attended public events with other teachers. On one occasion he was asked, innocently enough, if a colleague was his wife. "I must be careful not to embarrass any of my friends," he later confided in his diary.[39]

By spring, Marie's illness entered its final stages. The tuberculosis had left her thin, weak, and unable to stand for more than a few seconds unaided. In late May of 1907, when she inquired as to her condition, Kilpatrick told her she would not be with them much longer, at which she showed no regret. He told her that they would meet in "that other world," but she responded, "I am not thinking of that other world; I am thinking of this one. I want you and Margaret to be happy here." He left this tragic scene to return to school and later wrote in his diary, "Oh, the bitterness of leaving her! I weep aloud when I am by myself."[40] Marie's mother had arrived from Florida on May 28, and the next morning Kilpatrick was called to his wife's bedside at 2 a.m. Thinking that Marie was dying, he told her she was going. He begged for her to tell him of

her love, and she responded, "Oh dear, it has been the guiding star of my life." He massaged her feet, but she asked him not to sit up with her, as he had to work the next day. She grew weaker, and by 6 a.m. the end was at hand. He gave her sips of water with a spoon, rubbed her swollen face, and squeezed her hand. Her breathing grew distinctly shorter, and finally she was gone. Kilpatrick returned to his room, racked with pain, guilt, and despair:

> I . . . think with many heart pangs how often I failed to be as kind and loving and thoughtful as I should have been to her, who loved me so truly and thoughtfully. I thought how often her heart had been hungry for loving attention and I had been engrossed in other things. I thought of her bravery . . . her patience . . . her longing to have it over with. Her love of me . . . continued up to her very last spark of conscious life.[41]

That afternoon he had his infant son's body disinterred and made arrangements to take the bodies to Marianna. The service was held the next day, May 30, and after what Kilpatrick called "the too long ceremony of the Episcopal Church," Marie was buried between the two little graves of her infant sons in the churchyard where she and Heard had been married less than a decade before.[42]

4

JOHN DEWEY AND TEACHERS COLLEGE

"He's the best [student] I ever had."
John Dewey [1]

Nearing forty years of age and with his young wife dead of tuberculosis, Kilpatrick was forced to send his six-year-old daughter to live with his parents and sister in White Plains, Georgia. With the faith of his father shattered, and standing condemned for heresy, he had lost his university post and taken what some in educational circles might have considered a second-rate job. He still yearned for acceptance in Georgia, yet he was firmly convinced that his future lay elsewhere. Kilpatrick realized he would need to leave the South and pursue a doctoral degree in order to advance his career. And so he looked to the most prestigious graduate school in education in the nation, possibly the world — Teachers College of New York City. According to Tenenbaum, Kilpatrick was an unreconstructed southerner when he left for Teachers College in the fall of 1907.[2] While it would be accurate to label Kilpatrick "unreconstructed" in terms of cultural allegiance and pride of regional accomplishment, he did not support the Old Confederacy's war aims, nor its extreme racial attitudes. Most of all, he was a true son of the South in that he had neither plans nor a desire to remain in the North permanently.

After the death of Marie in May of 1907, Kilpatrick taught in the University of Tennessee's summer school. It was there that he met two Teachers College professors who were also on the summer staff — Edward L. Thorndike and Percival R. Cole. He enrolled in Cole's course on Herbart and Froebel, which was described as the study of the "two systems of education that have shown the greatest vitality."[3] In addition to teaching and attending classes, he began playing tennis and frequenting picnics, even the horse races, with a Miss Hansard, who was also taking classes that summer. The two also read together and conversed about their classes and events of the summer. During the summer Thorndike encouraged Kilpatrick to apply for a $250 Teachers College scholarship, which he did; and he was immediately accepted for graduate study. His plan was to study education and philosophy and to return to the South one day to teach on his native soil. At the end of the summer

he made plans for Margaret to enter school in White Plains for the first time. Kilpatrick wrote in his diary, with a mixture of hope and parental pride, that when mature she would be "rather pretty, well formed, attractive both to men and women, intellectual, graceful, good, naturally unselfish, not remarkable in any special way nor to any special degree, but still an unusual young woman."[4]

With personal matters settled in Georgia, he arrived in New York City on September 24, 1907, and the next day, his diary records, he met with John Dewey to plan his course of study. On September 26, he took his first "shower bath" and contemplated the future. Lonely and despondent, he was impatient to begin his work and get on with life. His talent and intelligence had made him the center of much attention during the past fifteen years of his educational career in small Georgia settings, but now he was in New York City. Attendance at a Sunday service in the incomplete cathedral of Saint John the Divine helped little. The canon's sermon on "not my will, but thine be done" touched a chord in terms of what he was going through at the time, but on the whole he concluded as he left the service, "Life just now looks a little blue to me." There was a glimmer of hope in his musings, though, as he concluded the first week at Teachers College that "it will come out well, I am sure, better than I could plan I daresay; but is hard to *feel* satisfied with what one thus is not persuaded of." The religious aspect of his previous life in Georgia emerged briefly as he joined a "pay Sunday School" at the Horace Mann School (at a cost of $15 per year), but he soon stopped attending.[5]

The move to graduate study at Teachers College was a significant demarcation for Kilpatrick, so much so that he would later entitle his unfinished autobiography *Two Halves of One Life*. Founded in 1887, Teachers College had become, even before its twenty-fifth anniversary, a Mecca for the study of education. Much of the credit for the institution's success belonged to Dean James E. Russell, who had come to Teachers College a decade after its founding and stayed just shy of thirty years. He had moved Teachers College toward the German model of graduate education and seminars. But education had not received formal acceptance as a traditional area of study in higher education — many university leaders and faculty members were unwilling to view this emerging field as legitimate. The year that Kilpatrick arrived, John Dewey wrote that to many, "pedagogy was the predetermined art of teaching teachers how to teach by the means of trivial devices and patent panaceas, all of which tend to make 'method' a substitute for knowledge of subject matter."[6]

Teachers College was located in a large red-brick Victorian building at 120th Street and Broadway, north of Columbia University. When Kilpatrick

arrived, the institution had a faculty of sixty-five, ranging from full professor to instructor, in addition to five professors from Columbia University, including Dewey from the Philosophy Department, who lent their services on a part-time basis. In 1907 Teachers College had more graduate students than any department at Columbia, with students representing thirty-two foreign countries. In comparison, by 1912 the University of Chicago had thirty doctoral students enrolled in education, while Teachers College had 300. The array of influential professors at Teachers College was impressive. First and foremost was Edward L. Thorndike, a student of William James and a pioneer in the classic stimulus-response formula of learning. Kilpatrick called Thorndike "young, brilliant, and vigorous" and was influenced by much of his earlier work in learning theory, though differences on the issue of measurement would eventually emerge. Intellectually, he always ranked Thorndike alongside Dewey.[7] Other professors included Paul Monroe, the educational historian; Frank McMurray, professor of elementary education, a former Hebartian who had converted to a more Deweyan approach by the time he came to Teachers College; Henry Suzzallo, an educational sociologist who would later go on to the presidency of the University of Washington; and John Angus MacVannel, a Scotsman via Canada, who taught philosophy of education.

And then, of course, there was John Dewey. Dewey had arrived at Columbia in 1904 after ten years at the University of Chicago. Although officially associated with Columbia University's Philosophy Department, Dewey did teach selected courses for Teachers College and served, on occasion, on doctoral committees. Kilpatrick's fall schedule included philosophy of education with MacVannel, Herbart and Froebel with Cole, history of education with Monroe, and history of modern ethical ideas with Dewey. In addition, the Georgian was also studying German on his own. A chart found in his diary sketches out a Monday-through-Thursday schedule in which he rose at 7:15, beginning a full day of classes and reading which lasted until eleven o'clock each evening. Fridays and Saturdays, he worked a half-day; Sunday mornings were left open and Sunday afternoons devoted to writing letters. His evenings on these days were spent reading until 10:30 or 11 p.m.

One of Kilpatrick's first tasks was to build a library. Purchasing used books at Dewitt and Wilson's, he assembled a respectable collection while spending anywhere from 50 cents to $2 per volume. His purchases included the works of philosophers such as Kant, John Stuart Mill, Descartes, Santayana, Hume, Erasmus, Martineau, and, of course, Aristotle and Plato. Literary selections included Goethe, Hawthorne, Emerson, Samuel Johnson,

Shelley, Ruskin, George Eliot, and Browning. A perusal of Kilpatrick's own later works, including his *Source Book in the Philosophy of Education* and *Philosophy of Education*, demonstrates that he not only purchased these books, but read and integrated them into his thinking and his life. Upon returning from one trip to the bookseller, he found a letter from Margaret awaiting him, written in her own hand: "Papa, I want to see you — Baby." "It brings tears to my eyes," he wrote.[8]

Striking up a friendship in the Teachers College community with a Japanese student named Kumamoto, Kilpatrick marveled at the international diversity he found. At a meal one evening he sat with a Canadian, a Japanese, a Chinese, a Colombian, two Turks, and an Arctic explorer. He also took up tennis again. The exercise was good for him, as he had gained weight since coming to New York. As vigorous as his exercise regime was the frenetic series of visits he made to the cultural high points of the city. Within a period of four months he visited the Metropolitan Museum of Art and went to see *Faust* at the Manhattan Opera House, Ibsen's *The Master Builder* at the Bijou, *Madame Butterfly* at the Garden Theater, and Maude Adams in *Peter Pan* at the Empire Theater. Of the latter he wrote, "I did enter frequently into the humor of the situation so thoroughly as to feel young a little bit." As for the Ibsen play, he wrote, "The ideal of marriage as true communion on a common plane was well presented."[9]

Kilpatrick "coached" (tutored) mathematics in the evenings, when time permitted. And he began the habit of taking what were to become his famous walks along Riverside Drive and through the environs of Columbia. At times, he would observe the crowded street scenes of New York City. "Stand for quite a while on 14th and Broadway and watch the moving throng," he wrote in his diary.[10] On occasion there was a novel experience associated with life in the first decade of the twentieth century: one morning he observed an "aeroplane" flying over the Hudson River. Ever-cognizant of world affairs and scientific advances, Kilpatrick pondered the future of this new machine: "Who can say that we are not on the verge of a great advance in navigation? For my part I confidently expect, if I live my expectancy, to see aerial navigation in a more or less successful common use."[11] He was correct, but it was almost a half century before he himself traveled aboard one of the successors of the Wright brothers' machines.

As for academics, he found Dewey's course "so far easy," he wrote; "I hope it will have more content than so far appears."[12] His semester examination questions, which he entered into his diary, suggest the severely traditional

substance of his program. One, for example, was "Show the educational significance of Goethe's *Faust*." And in another course a convoluted question was
aimed, rather tortuously, at bringing medieval history and education into
congruence: "What were the standards involved in the medieval conception of
chivalry, and what were the educational methods directed towards the
attainment of those standards?"[13]

Ever discerning of attractive women and sometimes cruelly blunt,
Kilpatrick noted being surprised at "the youth of certain ugly girls" in John
Dewey's class, some of whom were not yet twenty-one, he guessed. Although
Kilpatrick's diary is rather discreet concerning his personal life, he was, he
noted at one point, struggling with living "the virtuous life according to the
monastic theory."[14] Overall, though, he viewed himself as making progress in
this area, and he concluded his 1907 diary with these words:

> I am reaching in some measure the philosophic attitude of
> valuing the ethical above the transitory; hence in part at least
> the feeling of rest. I feel that during this year, I have made
> some real progress in virtue both as to subordinating the
> particular demands of the body to the general requirements of
> the spirit and as to care more for the happiness of others.[15]

In February of 1908 Kilpatrick journeyed to Washington, D.C., to attend
an education conference and heard President Theodore Roosevelt speak.
Kilpatrick's study was then suddenly interrupted by the grave illness of his
father. He returned to White Plains in late March and was there when the elder
Kilpatrick died on March 27. In a therapeutic act of memorialization, he
entered into his diary five and a half pages of painful detail regarding his
father's strengths, weaknesses, and character. He concluded that his father's
potential intellectual brilliance had been stifled by his religious beliefs, yet he
had been able to lead a stable and productive life, though his influence was
limited to Georgia Baptists.[16] That summer Kilpatrick again returned to the
family home in Georgia to visit Margaret, hunt blackberries, and eat peaches.
He traveled to Mercer to visit with former colleagues and to revisit the events
of two years before, wondering if he had acted too strongly by not compro-
mising. He then went to Columbus for a visit with Rev. Ashby Jones before
going on to Marianna, Florida. He concluded his summer in Athens, teaching
educational psychology, history of education, and mathematics at the
University of Georgia.

When Kilpatrick returned to Teachers College that fall — 1908 — he continued his work with Dewey, taking every course the philosopher offered and struggling over the selection of a dissertation topic. The plan had been to write on Spinoza, and he had spent a great deal of time indexing the philosopher's works on note cards. But then a topic in colonial educational history related to the Dutch schools emerged, which eventually became his thesis. In a research paper for Professor Monroe he had established that the date for the first Dutch school in Manhattan was not 1633 but actually 1637, or even 1638. The traditional date, 1633, was found in much of the literature on the subject and had even been emblazoned on a bronze tablet in the city. Professor Monroe was quite taken with this piece of detective work, esoteric as it was, and encouraged Kilpatrick to publish his findings, which he did, in the *Educational Review*, the most prestigious education journal of the time. The article in turn led to a number of invitations to speak on the local lecture circuit.[17]

The diary that Kilpatrick continued to keep is a historical document unique unto itself. Below is a full day-and-a-half entry from early November 1908:

> November 2 — Hear Dewey. We have a very interesting discussion on the end with relation to the process. I take part and am pleased to see that Dewey appreciates my point of view. In Suzzallo's class it becomes increasingly evident that he is no teacher of mathematical matters. Sandiford and I give most of the discussion to the satisfaction of the class so many say.
>
> Hear a good discussion by Dewey in the psychological ethics on the distinction between the voluntary act of the mature and the immature. Read on Colonial schools, hear Woodridge. I have never listened to a more incomprehensible man. In the evening attend meeting of Graduate Club. The ladies had arranged a Halloween Party which was quite a success. I preside. Walked home with Miss Pinckney.
>
> November 9 — Rise after sleepless night. Hear Dewey, magnificent. Fail thru misunderstanding to have a paper prepared to hand in to him. Hear Dewey on Psychological Ethics; he is evidently killing time today. Get a note from Miss Pinckney.[18]

Miss Pinckney was Margaret Manigault Pinckney, the daughter of Charles Cotesworth Pinckney of the distinguished Pinckney family of Charleston, South Carolina. Miss Pinckney and Kilpatrick had met inauspiciously in November of 1907, when he had mistakenly appeared at a meeting of the Southern Club, only to be turned away — the organization was for females only. The two southerners began to take long walks, discussing literature and, of course, the South. Tenenbaum implies that Kilpatrick may have been as taken with her distinguished genealogy and Southern background as he was with her personally.[19] This may indeed have been the case. Kilpatrick was a great admirer of southern culture, style, and manners. After attending a school meeting, he contrasted northern females with their southern counterparts:

> A pleasing occasion, tho' I find a very mediocre type of woman in general as compared with our Southern girls. Probably the academic preparation of the women I met was much ahead of an average group of Southern Women; but in mutual alertness and in charm of conversation, there was no comparison. I enjoyed the evening, but should have got more from any one of a number of Southern women I know.[20]

It may indeed have been a relationship more of cultural similarities than of personal magnetism on the part of either. There was also the issue of age. Miss Pinckney, born on December 4, 1861, was ten years older than Kilpatrick and looked it. The difference in their ages was not readily made known to friends or family, and it was Kilpatrick's son-in-law who ferreted out the information many years later. Kilpatrick was aware of attractive women and would, on occasion, take note of them in his diary, even when the woman was his future fiancée's niece. "Walk home with Miss Pinckney and her niece Miss Means, the latter a beautiful young woman." He never made such statements about Margaret Pinckney's appearance, either before or after they were married. And there was certainly no romance or excitement evident on his part. A week before his marriage he wrote, "I feel much older than I did a year ago. Father has died in the meanwhile; I have the responsibility of the family in a measure. I am about to be married the second time. All this brings home to me that I am nearing the apex of life's hill, soon to start down the other side. Now I begin to feel that I am in the home stretch." Although he referred to her as Margaret (or MPK in the diaries), at home he used the shortened version of her name, "Rita." On the day of the wedding he tells of witnesses signing the proper papers and

of coming home to "our own apartment to begin our new common life. I cannot here tell what all that this means to me."[21] And it would not be until her death that he did.

The six-month courtship (the proposal was made on a park bench on Riverside Drive near Teachers College) resulted in a wedding on November 26, 1908, at the Church of the Holy Apostles in New York City. At the end of the year Kilpatrick wrote, "I have married a woman who will help me to be and to do all that in me is."[22] But Rita's help would not be in his academic or educational work. She appears to have been of counsel to her husband in the social arena. Within six months of their wedding, he joined her to hear a young woman speak on the kindergarten. "More veritable rot I have never heard on any subject," he later wrote, and he compared the lecture to the "crazy literature" on such Biblical topics as the end times and Ezekiel's dreams. He continued his ranting on the way home, and "Afterwards, I am sorry to say that I express myself so extremely to Margaret . . . I unavoidably hurt her feelings. After which I forswear its discussion."[23] The following September, Kilpatrick's daughter, Margaret Louise, joined her father and stepmother in the North, and the newly established family moved into an apartment at 506-08 122nd Street.

Following the wedding, it was back to his classwork (mainly under Dewey and Thorndike) and attendant financial pressures. Kilpatrick was forced to borrow money from his sister, mother, and wife, and his father's estate, to keep financially afloat as he strove to complete his doctorate. Dean James Russell added to the pressure when he suggested that another scholarship would not be in Kilpatrick's best interest, adding that "he better get out and go to work." Although he held Russell in high regard, Kilpatrick did not care to have the dean or anyone else "pass judgment on him." He wanted to complete his work and "rejoin the fight," but the need to finish the degree concerned him also. Tenenbaum has suggested that Kilpatrick's regionalism and age may also have contributed to Russell's urging him to seek employment in the South. The concern over age might have been attributed to his premature graying. The trials of the past five years had turned his hair from brown to the silky white that would become one of his trademarks.[24]

The pressure Kilpatrick felt from Russell may have been for naught. The dean awarded Kilpatrick another fellowship, although still urging him to find a position. At the same time, Russell indicated that if Kilpatrick's southern prospects fell through, he would "take care" of him. "I am much relieved," Kilpatrick wrote. His "southern plan" did fall through, both at George Peabody and at the University of Georgia. He wrote regretfully, "I had planned so many

things to be done in Georgia from the vantage ground of the University." Yet he was able to write, despite his disappointment, "The future looks quite uncertain now, but I recognize too well the littleness of our knowledge of the future to feel that I ought to be down-cast." A month later, though, he was still anticipating a move to "Athens or Peabody." Then in late May he received an offer from Professor Monroe to take Percival Cole's place as lecturer for the coming academic year, 1909-1910, at a salary of $1,600. The news caused him to move from feeling "distressed and down in the mouth" to "relieved and brightened." To bolster their modest income (Rita was working as a social secretary at Teachers College) and to assist in eradicating his debt, Kilpatrick reluctantly accepted what turned out to be a full-time teaching position at part-time pay at Pratt Institute. For him the assignment was an embarrassment. "I shall be in a hell on earth . . . to be compelled to teach as a mere hack seems almost more than I can stand. Surely, surely one more year will end this humiliation." He received $5 per hour for teaching sometimes as many as five classes each semester.[25]

The academic year 1909-1910 was a difficult one for Kilpatrick. On both the personal and the professional level he felt that life had passed him by. "The South may invite me back, but not with shouts of acclamation," he wrote. He was concerned that his shift from mathematics to education might have come too late in his career and that any respect he had enjoyed at Mercer had evaporated. His former colleagues might think he held a solid position at Teachers College, but if they really knew his situation they would realize he "was emptied of what he was." On the personal level, he was disturbed by a belief that there would be no more children, although he had been married only a year. Added to this were thoughts that he might lose his daughter, who had health problems. She had been taken ill with scarlet fever, and he had almost set the apartment on fire burning sulfur in order to purify the air.[26] This was doubly troubling to him as a student of genealogy; he was greatly worried over the possibility that his "line" would end.

In the professional arena, Kilpatrick's study with Dewey at this time indeed changed his life. "The work under Dewey," he told Tenenbaum, "remade my philosophy of life and education."[27] The feeling seems to have been mutual. Professor MacVannel told Kilpatrick that Dewey had said that the Georgia student was the "best I ever had." Kilpatrick wrote, "I am more gratified than at any other estimate that could have been made."[28] Kilpatrick found that Dewey appreciated his comments in class and often found his ideas, especially those in a paper dealing with predeterminism, "proper . . .

novel . . . and valid." Unfortunately, Dewey's notorious absentmindedness had caused him to misplace Kilpatrick's paper, and the two men were unable to continue this particular conversation.[29] As others have suggested, Dewey's approach to teaching was one of intellectually working his way through a question or issue in front of the entire class. This would often lead to long pauses, blank gazes out the window, and then sudden encounters with a solution. According to Kilpatrick, Dewey would come to class "with a problem on his mind and sit before the class thinking out loud as he sought to bring creative thinking to bear on his problem." On occasion, Kilpatrick would assist his mentor. He once proctored an examination for Dewey, but he had such difficulty reading the philosopher's writing that he was unable to replicate the questions for the students.[30] While John Dewey and Kilpatrick remained in continual contact for the next half century (Dewey was twelve years older and both died at the age of ninety-three), they were never close personal friends. Kilpatrick often attributed this lack of personal interaction to his own difficulty in making "small talk."

Although later critics would suggest that Kilpatrick "misinterpreted" Dewey's thought, as will be seen, over a fifty-year period the great philosopher never repudiated his "best" student. In 1911, on the eve of the publication of Kilpatrick's book on the Montessori method, Dewey wrote to him, "Since you have asked me specifically about your understanding of my ideas, I do say that I would not desire a more sympathetically intelligent interpreter."[31] To be Dewey's interpreter had been one of Kilpatrick's goals since he had arrived at Teachers College. One diary entry records, "Hear Dewey, very good. I am wondering, however, whether I might not come to be an interpreter of Dewey," adding bluntly, "He needs one." A year later he wrote, "I feel in some measure that I am best qualified of those about here to interpret Dewey. His own lectures are frequently impenetrable to even intelligent students. If . . . I am called upon to teach the philosophy of education, I shall endeavor to make Dewey's point of view more accessible to people in general." But even Kilpatrick struggled at the task. He later admitted that it took him two years to fully understand and appreciate what Dewey was "driving at."[32]

Two concepts in Dewey's work were points of departure for Kilpatrick: interest and effort. To some, "interest" meant a sugarcoating of experience — a device to make things interesting for a student. And to some, "effort" meant coercion or threats used to make the student do the desired work. Dewey rejected both of these definitions, arguing that interest was the first state of an ongoing experience, in which correlative personal effort is the effecting state.

Thus, proper interest and proper effort could not be opposed. In addition, Kilpatrick agreed with Dewey's emphases on the concepts of process, continuity of nature, and the inductive method of science, all of which were later folded into a new philosophy called experimentalism.[33]

It did not take long for Kilpatrick to become a total convert. "Professor Dewey's fundamental point of view seems as unassailable as science," he wrote.[34] Kilpatrick next abandoned neo-Hegelian philosophy and accepted Dewey's experimental method. Absolutes, authority, a priori thinking, and dogma were all rejected. The universe was not fixed or static — it was an ever-changing world, or, as William James had stated it, a "universe with the lid off." In his diary, Kilpatrick took copious notes on an after-dinner talk by Dewey. These notes read, in part, "It is similarly urged that philosophy is forever changing, i.e., does not make a permanent deposit of truth on which it builds; this is true in a measure, but the explanation is that in an ever-changing society the old solutions will not fit."[35] Intelligence became the end and the means of living. Within the context of pragmatic philosophy, inductive reasoning and its practical outcomes became the process by which one sought the "good life." And, as Kilpatrick put it, "A thing is good or evil according to whether it makes life good or evil for all concerned."[36] "John Dewey taught me that we should use the methods of science as far as we can in all affairs of life and that we should build our philosophy on that," Kilpatrick later told Tenenbaum. He also thought that by "using intelligence, man should be constantly striving to make things better."[37] These were the first underlying principles that Kilpatrick generated from Dewey's work. He would redefine, refine, and extrapolate on these ideas as both his thinking and Dewey's evolved. Students, then, were to become:

> more capable of thinking and deciding wisely and not only capable of thinking but disposed to get at the best possible thinking and to act according to the best thinking that could be had. We want the whole person to be built up to do this. We further want him to be disposed to study those ways of behaving, those social customs, traditions, mores, those institutions of life which affect life, which help in making life good or the reverse.[38]

The purpose of education became, then, learning not only what to think but how to think. The free play of intelligence would be used to confront new

and novel experiences in light of previous ones. The implications of such a wide-open experiential approach to life were indeed radical, if taken to their logical conclusions. The fixed, staid world of traditional education was at odds with this new strategy. Some would claim that Kilpatrick took Dewey's thought beyond the reasonable limits of extrapolation and interpretation. But such charges would come many years afterward and will be examined in detail in later chapters.

For Kilpatrick, in the year 1910, a period of formal graduate education had now been coupled with more than a decade of experience in elementary, secondary, and higher education. What would be known as the "new education," and later as progressive education, was now emerging. It had been seen in the work of Colonel Parker in Chicago and also in the isolated, innovative laboratory schools that were being formed around the country, often in association with universities. Social critics, from Jacob Riis to Randolph Bourne, would join the voices of educators in calling for sweeping changes in the methods by which children were schooled in the classrooms of America. And Kilpatrick's thinking continued to grow as he became steeped directly in Deweyan thought and began to consider the most effective and appropriate means to put these new ideas into practice.

Another figure on the American scene at this time, also a southerner who had come north to seek his place in education and politics, was the president of Princeton University, Woodrow Wilson. At the same time that Kilpatrick was working with Dewey at Teachers College, Wilson came to the city and addressed an audience on the topic of education. The future governor of New Jersey and president of the United States declared that education must change. Suggesting that the old ways of schooling were detrimental to children, and even to university students, he stated, "We must remember that information is not education." Sounding positively progressive, he then quoted his father, who had said, "The mind is not a prolix gut to be stuffed." Wilson concluded that "one of the principal objects of education should be enlightenment, or the unloading from the minds of the pupils the misinformation that they have received."[39]   A new education was on the horizon, and the next stage in Kilpatrick's career, like Woodrow Wilson's, would place him on the national scene in the coming transformation of educational practices.

A PLATFORM FROM WHICH TO SPEAK

"He was now on his own, and this was what he liked best of all."
                                                    Samuel Tenenbaum [1]

Long after his retirement, Kilpatrick was asked why so many progressive educators, including himself, had been schooled more along the lines of a classical education than according to the principles that he and his colleagues were advocating. He didn't have an answer. His diary at the end of 1910 corroborated this inconsistency, though, as he was undertaking a second education along very traditional lines. He was in the midst of preparing for his doctoral examinations and had not been, it should be remembered, either a philosophy or a history major at the undergraduate or the graduate level. His readings were diverse, yet very traditional: included on his list were Plato, Boccaccio, Comenius, the history of education in Maryland and the Carolinas, books on John Knox and John Locke, biographies of Rousseau and Galileo, the letters of Martin Luther; and the diaries of Samuel Pepys and John Wesley. He was particularly taken with Wesley's diary, calling it fascinating and of genuine human interest and still quoting from it forty years later.[2] He also read, for the first time, *Émile* and *The Social Contract*, by Rousseau, and squeezed in a history of the Pinckney family, no doubt to become more knowledgeable about Rita's family.[3] At this time he was reading Dewey's *Moral Principles in Education* and *My Pedagogical Creed*. From among more recent writers, he credited J. Mark Baldwin, author of *The Individual and Society*, with being next to Dewey as a great American thinker.[4]

As 1910 opened, Kilpatrick took stock of his prospects, as was his custom each New Year's day:

> The beginning of another year seems more serious to me than formerly. I feel myself to be outside the genuine current of activity; so that I am impatient at the passing of time. Each year as it goes but records so much of this apparent waste. Especially do I feel this as my future seems so chaotic. I cannot stay here with satisfaction, nor can I now go. I hope

the future will soon open for me an opportunity for work in
the South, preferably in Georgia, where I can take hold with
all my soul and feel that every stroke counts.[5]

While Kilpatrick almost always gave Dean James Russell a great deal of
credit for the success of Teachers College, the ambivalence that Russell showed
toward Kilpatrick, added to his own indecision about remaining in New York,
often left him frustrated. After an evening lecture he recorded in his diary, "The
Dean speaks as dry as usual. I dislike him."[6] But this was one of the rare
occasions when he vented his critical feelings toward Russell. It was a trying
time for Kilpatrick. Able to translate simple Dutch prose, he began to devote a
great deal of time to reading colonial history. But Kilpatrick was able to take
advantage of the intellectual life at Columbia, attending the lectures of Charles
Beard and others. He also attended meetings of the "Black Cat," an intellectual
club in New York City, and the annual suffragist parades, in which his wife and
other college women marched. (In one suffrage parade, Dewey reportedly
carried a sign which someone had handed him that said, "Men Can Vote —
Why Can't I?") Kilpatrick enjoyed the demonstrations very much, although one
year he noted that some men jeered.[7]

The academic year 1910-1911 found Kilpatrick teaching history of
education at Teachers College for Professor Monroe for $1,200 and at Pratt
Institute again for $1,000. With his summer school stipend of $300, his
combined salary was $2,500 — the most money he had ever earned. But, as
he noted, the cost of living in New York City was substantial, even with his wife
working at Teachers College. In October, just after the plans for the year had
been set, what Kilpatrick called a "parting of the waves" occurred. The health
of Professor MacVannel, who taught philosophy of education, had broken,
even as Professor Monroe was urging Dean Russell to retain Kilpatrick on a
full-time basis. Kilpatrick turned to Suzzallo and Dewey, his confidants and
main sources of advice. (Suzzallo, as usual, functioned as the clearinghouse
for campus gossip.) Rita wanted him to take MacVannel's place in philosophy,
and he agreed that it was his first love and his main reason for being at Teachers
College. For some reason the dean's icy feelings toward Kilpatrick thawed, and
Monroe communicated to Kilpatrick that Russell was coming to the conclusion
that he might just want to keep him. By November of 1910 an offer came from
Monroe for Kilpatrick to teach full-time at Teachers College for $1,000 —
which was, of course, much less than the instructor's base pay. Kilpatrick
counteroffered $1,500 the next day and finally settled for $1,200.[8]

The holidays found Kilpatrick a bit depressed as he and Rita prepared Christmas for Margaret. He was saddened by the thought that she was an only child and would be raised alone. The fact that it was Christmas made him feel doubly guilty that he could not rise above his own melancholy and make others merry.[9] But New Year's Day found him in much better spirits, due in large part to his new standing with the Dean and the improvement in his daughter's health. Age ten and a student at Horace Mann School, Margaret was more and more becoming her own person, and the result was the opening stages of what would become an increasingly fractious relationship with her stepmother. "I am much troubled by the lack of harmonious relationship between my wife and daughter," Kilpatrick wrote. "Neither one seems to understand the other, nor to be willing to judge the other leniently." Kilpatrick, too, struggled with parenthood. In an undescribed incident, Rita had evidently questioned the veracity of one of Margaret's statements, and an argument ensued. But, wrote Kilpatrick in exasperation, "when a child says she forgot, what can a parent say?"[10]

Back in his academic world, Kilpatrick successfully defended his dissertation on January 11, 1911. Dean Russell, Henry Suzzallo, Paul Monroe, and five other professors were present. John Dewey, according to form, was late. Thirty minutes were spent on the dissertation, which, being historical, found Monroe the major inquisitor. It was then John Dewey's turn, as philosophy was Kilpatrick's minor. Dewey informed the group that Kilpatrick "had much more philosophy than was required" and began a traditional line of questioning on Spinoza. Kilpatrick described the rest:

> He [Dewey] went from Spinoza to Descartes and then to Liebnitz. The questions were not all such as I had before considered and some I did not answer off hand; but on the whole I seem to satisfy Dewey and even to interest the others. Occasionally they smiled audibly [sic]. The Dean asked Dewey if he were satisfied and he said yes.[11]

The dean disposed of the final vote before Kilpatrick could leave the room. There were then congratulations from the committee all around. The new Dr. Kilpatrick was invited to lunch, but he declined, saying that "Mrs. Kilpatrick was anxious to know." Two weeks later came his appointment as assistant professor at Teachers College. Although Kilpatrick still wished for a position in the South, the offer gave him time to consider his future further, and

the option to stay or leave would be his. On the same day as his appointment a publisher in Chicago invited him to write a history of educational theory, and accolades for his summer teaching soon followed from the campus conduit of information, Professor Suzzallo, who strongly encouraged Kilpatrick to stay at Teachers College.[12]

Maneuvering for academic positions for the school year 1912-1913 began in earnest almost as soon as classes started in 1911. The University of Tennessee offered Kilpatrick an attractive position, but at almost the same time Professor MacVannel suffered a second stroke. Suzzallo pressured the dean to give Kilpatrick a temporary appointment in philosophy of education, which he preferred to history. Kilpatrick, for his part, expressed an interest in removing himself from what he viewed as his odious obligations at Pratt. Declining to use the Knoxville offer for leverage with Teachers College, he wrote to Tennessee, indicating that he could not let his name be considered. The various stratagems and paradoxes of his career often wearied him. At one point that fall he wished he had entered law, had stayed away from Mercer, and had never accepted neo-Hegelian philosophy. But in the margin of that diary entry is written, "I now think differently on all three. August 2, 1954." His annual reflective birthday entry (on a milestone — his fortieth) expressed regret again over his lack of a son, his absence from the South, and the fact that getting older meant fewer and fewer chances to make his mark. On the positive side of the ledger, he pointed to his original thinking, his potential to achieve a "higher place," and his success in comparison with his ancestors in terms of education and worldly goods. On New Year's Day 1912 he turned melancholy again, mentioning that he was not satisfied with a subordinate place at Teachers College, not satisfied that he lived away from the South, and not satisfied that he did not have a real home of his own.[13] These comments were perhaps more symptomatic of his high ambition than of mild depression. Kilpatrick would display unhappiness later in his life, even anger at times, and in old age despondency over his failing health. But once he achieved a solid place of significance at Teachers College, further mentions of dissatisfaction with his life disappeared altogether.

By April 1912, Kilpatrick had orchestrated plans for a summer trip to Europe, at a cost of $350, in order to observe firsthand the work of Maria Montessori, the innovative Italian educator and physician. Dean Russell encouraged this fact-finding venture, on which Kilpatrick would be accompanied by colleagues Milo B. Hillegas and Annie Moore. In preparation for the journey, Hillegas and Kilpatrick took the subway to Fifth Avenue and

purchased, for $50, the Montessori "apparatus," a set of educational manipulative materials and toys that the children utilized in her schools in Italy. They also secured a secondhand language book on Italian.[14] One week later, on April 12, the *Titanic* sank in the North Atlantic, giving pause to many, including Kilpatrick. But the tragedy did not discourage the plans for the mission to Italy. Kilpatrick, as he read Montessori's book, speculated that there might be value to her unorthodox scheme after all. But he remained skeptical:

> I am reasonably sure that we cannot use it (the Montessori method) just so in America. I do not object to the notion of the liberty, in fact that seems very good. The sense of training seems to be carried too far and to include some indefensible areas.[15]

In the midst of preparations for his European journey, he was called to Dean Russell's office on May 1, where he was offered an administrative position as head of the Appointments Committee, which functioned as the placement bureau for Teachers College. The office had fallen into administrative disarray and was in need of a person holding professorial rank to direct the operation. During the discussion, Russell bluntly asked Kilpatrick if he wished to go to Peabody in Tennessee. Kilpatrick responded, just as frankly, yes, if Peabody did "the thing right and got in a position so to do," but he also added that he hadn't been approached for a position there. As for the offer to head the Appointments Committee, if the position included some teaching, he was drawn to the idea in that he would be able to give up teaching at Pratt Institute. He told Russell that he did not care for purely administrative work and inquired whether this meant that he would be forced to abandon his teaching and scholarship. The dean replied that he wished Kilpatrick to gain exposure for Teachers College through his writing and that they needed men such as he. The dean then added that he thought it only a matter of time before a full-time opening would emerge. Kilpatrick's salary was set at $2,500, with an extra stipend for summer school, and it was stipulated that the administrative work was to take no more than two days each week. Kilpatrick asked for a day to think the offer over. Russell gave him until two o'clock. They settled on four o'clock, and Kilpatrick quickly cloistered himself with Suzzallo and then his wife. Accepting the position that afternoon, he was pleased to quit Pratt, to have a well-respected position, and to have more contact with the faculty, students, and outsiders. He was also pleased to be thrown in more

with the dean — "not that I especially like him, but I wish the power that comes with intimacy." Concerned about the drain the position might have on his teaching and writing, he pledged himself to prevent that from occurring.[16]

The next day Kilpatrick told Pratt that he would not be joining them for another year, and officials there expressed their regret. He suggested Isaac Kandel for the open position.[17] However, within two weeks Kilpatrick was regretting his decision to take on the Appointments Committee. It would not be the last time he second-guessed himself. "For the second time recently," he wrote, "I fail to sleep well at night. In many ways I am sorry it was my lot to take up the work. The scholar's life is a very tranquil one; and just at present I regret even this temporary departure."[18]

Putting the newfound burden aside temporarily, Kilpatrick, with Milo Hillegas and Annie Moore, departed on May 18 for Europe aboard the steamship *Canada*. The trip would take nine days, and Kilpatrick weathered the journey with minimal discomfort. The voyage was uneventful, save for a party at which the costumes were too "coarse" for Kilpatrick's taste and at which he detected evidence of drinking, which also disturbed him. Ever the serious observer, he arose early one morning in order to see Gibraltar. The ship arrived in Naples on May 29, where, almost as soon as he disembarked, he was approached and propositioned by a prostitute. "One girl, apparently about 17, made a determined effort at me," he wrote. The Teachers College troika first visited the local historic sites and then took a side excursion to Pompeii. It was then off to Rome, where Kilpatrick saw the Colosseum by moonlight, and Saint Peter's by day, and caught a glimpse of the king and queen of Italy on the street.[19]

Sightseeing was now put aside as Kilpatrick and his colleagues commenced their firsthand observations of Maria Montessori's schools and of the innovative educator herself. In 1890, at age twenty, Montessori had left her studies in engineering to become the first woman to enter an Italian medical school. She had endured many of the indignities and discriminatory practices against women of that day, such as not being allowed to dissect when the men were present and being asked to enter the classroom only after all the men had been seated. Following her graduation in 1896, she had undertaken further study and research on mental illness and psychological disorders, areas in which she was especially influenced by the writings of the Frenchman Edouard Seguin. From 1904 to 1908 Montessori had lectured in the University of Rome's School of Pedagogy, bringing to her teaching an eclectic approach by drawing upon the disciplines of anthropology, psychology, and medicine.

In 1907 she had opened Casa dei Bambini, her first school, in one of Rome's poorest tenements, known for its vice, disease, and crime. Stressing cleanliness, order, developmental stages, freedom, the importance of motor skills, language instruction, and social adaptation, Montessori began accepting children aged three through seven. The children utilized her famous self-correcting didactic materials. Montessori had written about her approach in a book, *The Montessori Method*, in 1912. By 1913 there were 100 Montessori schools in the United States, with an organization — the Montessori Educational System — presided over by Mrs. Alexander Graham Bell. Montessori gave an American lecture tour in 1913, but the initial enthusiasm was, according to one sympathetic educational historian, "short lived."[20] Kilpatrick had read Montessori's work and had, as has been seen, strong preconceived notions about the program.

Before their visit to Casa dei Bambini, the Teachers College party visited other schools influenced by the Montessori method. Kilpatrick's first impression was that "the children seemed free; free almost to the point of doing nothing at times." He noted in his diary that he was especially struck by Signorina Anna Guastalla, "a bright young woman about 21 who has had two years with Dr. Montessori." But the tour guide, a baroness, accused Kilpatrick of merely being "smitten."[21]

Kilpatrick and his colleagues finally gained access to Madame Montessori's inner sanctum on Wednesday, June 4. Kilpatrick did not consider the interview a great success. The fault was due in part to the interpreters and in part to differing views held on each side. The first topics raised in the interview were the educational apparatus and who represented Montessori's financial interests in America. This latter question may have arisen because of the comments by Professor Walter Hallsey of the University of Omaha that the Montessori method was a "fad promoted and advertised by a shrewd commercial spirit."[22] There seem to have been vague pleas for funds to establish a Montessori-oriented training institute. The figure of $250,000 was mentioned. The interview then began in earnest. Kilpatrick felt that it was crucial to determine Montessori's beliefs about formal discipline. Her response astounded Kilpatrick: she had never heard of the concept. He also queried her on her views of memory, reasoning, and sensory discrimination. Then something went awry with the interpreter. Kilpatrick suspected that someone "had tried to queer our visit" and that there were "crooked dealings" going on somewhere. The interview concluded on an incomplete note. Montessori gave the group a card to allow them to visit one of her other schools on Saturday.[23]

The party learned much more about the Montessori method on the school visit than they had during the interview with the innovator herself. "On the whole I was favorably impressed with the value of the experiment as such. How much of it I should retain," Kilpatrick concluded, "is a matter more difficult to answer."[24]   On Monday, after visiting the Sistine Chapel, he observed another Montessori school:

> This was a better Montessori school to my notion than the Via Giusti school. In some respects I should not accept what was done, grammar being the most remarkable, tho I am bound to say that the children enjoyed it. The reading of the action slips was very good. The children were happy. I cannot say that all were equally engaged, the contrary I should think, but they were on the whole well occupied.[25]

On June 12, Kilpatrick visited Beni Stabile school, which he liked very much. "Here we find the best school yet," he wrote. "Liberty without license, children doing what they wish, but not allowed to become noisy. The children use the material for all manner of construction not intended by Madam M."[26] This met with his approval, no doubt, as he had little use for the controversial apparatus.

With their task in Rome complete, the Teachers College team left for Pisa, where they climbed the leaning tower, before going on to Florence, Venice, and Milan. The group then traveled through the Alps, staying in Lucerne before arriving on June 22 in Paris, where they came upon Abraham Flexner, reformer of twentieth-century medical education. Four days later they boarded the *Olympic*, sister ship to the *Titanic*. Arriving in New York City on July 3, Kilpatrick took the subway home and there read his mail, which contained an invitation to give two lectures on Froebel for $500. Sitting on a Riverside Drive park bench with Rita that evening, Kilpatrick read in the newspaper with "much interest" that Woodrow Wilson — a native of Virginia and the governor of New Jersey — had been nominated for president by the Democratic Party.[27]

Kilpatrick utilized his trip to Italy and his observations of the Montessori method to his advantage, lecturing both inside and outside Teachers College on his critique of all he had observed. His main contention was that, while there were admirable, even positive points in the method, the system had little new to offer American educational theory. "There was a good crowd and they gave excellent attention," he later wrote of the first of these lectures, held on August

7, 1912, in Horace Mann Auditorium. "I felt that I gripped the crowd and from the number of expressions that came to my ears, I judge that I made a good talk." A month before, Thorndike had come out against the formal sensory training of the Montessori method, and Kilpatrick found himself "gratified" that he and a colleague of Thorndike's stature and influence were in critical agreement. Kilpatrick also discovered that criticism of formal discipline raised a greater stir than any other comment he made on the Montessori system itself.[28]

One historian of education has suggested that Kilpatrick's foremost criticism of the Montessori method was that it lacked "sufficient initiatives for encouraging children's socialization and experimental attitudes and skills."[29] However, Kilpatrick's analysis of Montessori and her system went much deeper. His entire critique was published in 1914 in a small monograph entitled *The Montessori System Examined*. Both John Dewey and Naomi Norsworthy are credited in the preface with reading the manuscript and making suggestions.[30]

The monograph traced Montessori's educational thought and found it to be rooted in the Aristotelian idea of development as "unfoldment," in which the child is seen as containing at birth all that he or she will become. From almost the beginning, the book on Montessori became an essay as much on Kilpatrick's beliefs as on the thoughts of the Italian educator. Those who have placed Kilpatrick within the extreme wing of the Rousseauean "child freedom" movement would be surprised to note that as early as 1914 he questioned this philosophy of freedom, believing that it would inevitably lead to embracing the Enlightenment philosopher's opposition to man's entire institutional life. Kilpatrick wrote in the first chapter:

> It further fails to provide adequately for the most useful of modern conceptions, that of intelligent, self-directing adaptation to a novel environment. If education is to prepare for such a changing environment, its fundamental concept must take essential cognizance of that fact. This erroneous notion of education gives to the doctrine of child liberty a wrong and misleading foundation.[31]

Kilpatrick concluded this first chapter by stating that "we must reject Madam Montessori's interpretation of the doctrine of development as inadequate and misleading."[32]

Kilpatrick acknowledged that Montessori had advanced beyond Froebel

and the modern kindergarten, but he had reservations about both approaches. Montessori, he thought, had not provided situations in which children could engage in a more adequate social cooperation, and Froebel's environment included too many outside suggestions and adult considerations.[33] Kilpatrick then contributed his own thoughts on the issue:

> In a democracy, self-direction must be the goal of education. Under Professor Dewey's influence it has become commonplace that no thinking worthy of the name goes on apart from a felt problem, a thwarted impulse. The problems set by the teacher are too often not so felt by the children. The current of real life . . . can flow only when the child has freedom to choose, to express himself. And life does not flow in twenty-minute periods. Real thinking and real conduct demand freer rein.[34]

Kilpatrick had a deeper faith "in the ability of the natural working-out of the child's interest than many of us have dared to believe." He did admit that some "positive pain association," or punishment, might prove necessary for the prekindergarten child, but he maintained that, on the whole, the most effective method of managing recalcitrant behavior would be to encourage positive behavior when it could be found. The goal, as he saw it, was to put children under conditions that would enable them to learn gradually the fine art of living with their fellow students. The teacher must intervene, he added, to "draw distinctions and direct wisely the course," but the real "agency" for the child should be his or her own "comrades."[35]

The famous apparatus on which much of the Montessori system was based was a cause of real concern for Kilpatrick, who found it too limiting, remote, and formal to engage the student in social interactions and connections. He described the process as "relatively mechanical manipulation of very formal apparatus." Games in Montessori's scheme, he observed, were too restrictive, and there seemed to be little or no place for stories or imagination. His tone bordered on the patronizing when he wrote that no doubt Montessori would have incorporated better practices had she been aware of them. Essentially he found the curriculum of the Montessori system limiting in opportunity and nothing less than repressive. What was needed, he suggested, were situations arising from life itself, from which self-education could truly derive, whenever a student was able to make the connection between effort and success. The

apparatus, Kilpatrick concluded, was more of a "danger than a help."[36]

When activities within Montessori's system did approach life outside the classroom, Kilpatrick was both encouraging and positive in his assessment. In fact, his observations of Montessori's work in the tenement houses of Rome were distinctly late-twentieth-century in tone:

> Where mothers are so closely confined to duties either at home or on the outside that the children cannot receive proper attention, all-day care of the young children by the kindergarten would be highly desirable. If, then, the kindergartens for the very poor everywhere, and for practically all classes in the large cities, could have an all-day session with much time spent in the open air, the results would probably be highly beneficial.[37]

With regard to Montessori's emphasis on sensory training, Kilpatrick once again became an unsympathetic critic, maintaining that he could not see how one could improve the sense organs, and rejecting out of hand the notion that faculties of the mind could be enhanced by general training. He questioned the idea of general transfer and formal discipline ("the old analogy of mind and body"), or, as he had described it in an earlier article, the theory that, "if you learn to observe birds you have trained a general power of observation."[38] It was a theory, he stated, that had been discarded in both Germany and America.[39] Kilpatrick himself had rejected a portion of it, concluding that children can learn faster and better how to lace shoes by lacing their shoes.[40] He was not persuaded that any such transfer could take place in the learning process unless two activities had common elements. The theory, Kilpatrick concluded, uniting as it did sensory training and the highly suspect apparatus, was "worthless." Better experiences and learning could be had through "properly directed play with wisely chosen, but less expensive and more childlike, playthings."[41]

However, Kilpatrick found the idea of Montessori's curriculum, which reflected the needs of the community, extremely attractive. He firmly believed that the curriculum must grip the interest of the students, who, in turn, must attach themselves to actual and immediate social demands. In fact, what he had observed in this arena at the Montessori schools was but part of a "world-wide demand that the school shall function more definitely as a social institution, adapting itself to its own environment."[42] When the social reconstructionists of the 1930s emerged, and Kilpatrick joined their ranks (in fact, he would be one

of their leaders), he would be accused of dropping his interest in the child for social activism. However, as his views here — from some twenty years earlier show — he considered the child and society to be directly related and necessarily fused, not mutually exclusive.

When it came to an appraisal of Montessori's method of teaching reading and arithmetic, Kilpatrick found his task more difficult. He returned to his previously stated disdain for the lack of real-life applications in the schoolwork — mathematics, in this case — and then made comments that would later suggest, even support, charges of his being anti-intellectual and antiacademic. Holding to the theory that formal education should not begin before age six, he wrote, "Education . . . is more than the acquisition of knowledge from books. There . . . is reason to fear that the presence of books makes more difficult that other part of education." To Kilpatrick, "a school for the young without books was Froebel's chiefest glory."[43]

Kilpatrick did list similarities between Maria Montessori and John Dewey, including their development of experimental schools, their emphasis on freedom and independent activity, and their use of practical life activities. He stated that Dewey would never simplify education by using apparatus as Montessori did; that Dewey, while recognizing the need for school subjects, stressed the mastery of a complex social environment; and that "sense-qualities" as taught by Montessori, in isolation, were diametrically opposed to Dewey's idea that education is the differentiation and organization of meanings through real-life experiences, particularly since a child's experience may be vastly different from an adult's.[44]

As for the curriculum and its implications, Kilpatrick maintained that Montessori had not begun to grasp what Dewey was suggesting. Kilpatrick was willing to grant that Montessori's experiment in the tenement houses at Casa dei Bambini might prove "distinctly suggestive" and might turn out to be "her greatest contribution." But in a biting conclusion, Kilpatrick suggested that those who found Montessori a significant contributor to educational theory were ill-advised. "Stimulation she is," he wrote, "a contributor to our theory, hardly, if at all."[45] He was even more stinging in his private comments. To his mother he wrote, "The same psychology that leads people to expect panaceas in medicine, even in such humbugs as electric wells . . . leads them to look favorably upon any well-advertised scheme of a get-educated-quick process."[46]

Upon his return from Europe, Kilpatrick published his dissertation on the Dutch schools, thinking that people would neither read it nor enjoy it and certainly that few would know how much work he had put into it. That same

month, July 1912, the Kilpatricks moved into 88 Morningside Drive (later 106 Morningside Drive), apartment 85. It had a fine southern view, it was entirely new, and the rent was $65 per month.[47] This would be his home for the next fifty-three years. His return to the work of the Appointments Committee perturbed him a great deal; he viewed it as a waste of time that took him away from his other work.

Kilpatrick voted for Woodrow Wilson in November of 1912 and would remain devoted to the Democratic president for the next decade. Later that month, on his forty-first birthday, he wrote that while some might consider that to be middle age, he thought himself still a young man, and his work was going well. He was better satisfied than he had been for some years and seemed "to be gaining."[48] That fall he undertook speaking tours in the Midwest and Northeast, which included Chicago; Grand Rapids, Michigan; Hartford, Connecticut; Oneonta, New York; and Mankato, Minnesota. At Mankato he spoke to an audience of 3,000, his largest up to that point. "I seem to carry the crowd with me," he wrote in his diary.[49] He was indeed beginning to carry the crowds, and this tour was a portent of the future. The large audiences that thronged to hear him continued to grow, as would his fame. In four brief years — from doctoral student to sought after lecturer — he was truly gaining a national platform from which to speak.

6

THE RISE OF A PROGRESSIVE EDUCATOR:
THE WAR YEARS, 1914-1918

"I have . . . made a success in teaching Dewey's ideas.
Perhaps I am on a plateau, getting ready for a later rise. At
any rate I can yet hope so."

William Heard Kilpatrick, January 1, 1915.[1]

"Maybe we New Yorkers were just suckers for a Southern
accent."

David Ment, Archivist, Milbank Library
Teachers College

There were dramatic changes in art, science, and technology during the
first two decades of the twentieth century. As industrialization continued,
scientific breakthroughs brought into question not only how men and women
viewed the world, but the very nature of reality itself. Planck, Einstein, Freud,
Picasso, and Braque were introducing novel and unique approaches for
looking at and understanding the world. In a similar way, Teachers College of
New York City, "the school on the hill," embodied change and innovation in
the field of education. And, as with every institution, certain members of the
faculty were emblematic of the institution's new ideas. By the end of the Great
War, that individual at Teachers College would be the silver-haired native
Georgian who was a direct intellectual descendant of John Dewey, William
Heard Kilpatrick. The second decade of the new century would see his mete-
oric rise to national attention as an educational leader of the first rank.

Several reasons can be suggested for Kilpatrick's remarkable rise during
the years of the Great War. First, he was able to communicate and popularize
the ideas of John Dewey while at the same time providing insightful critiques
of educational thinkers past and present, such as Froebel and Montessori.
Second, Kilpatrick had the ability to inspire a classroom full of students and to
grip an audience in packed public halls with both his manner and his message.

Third, there can be little doubt that as a faculty member at Teachers College in New York City, he was all the more likely to be popular and famous. Almost any public school teacher, administrator, normal school professor, or graduate student would have leaped at the opportunity to sit before the charismatic Kilpatrick. And it was during this time that opportunities for him to spread his philosophy of education increased. In 1916 alone, Kilpatrick received invitations to speak from eighteen states.[2] Additional avenues of influence were opened for Kilpatrick by virtue of his work on the Appointments Committee — a placement bureau of sorts for teachers and administrators. Although he loathed the duties the committee involved, it did provide him with numerous contacts — and no doubt a list of unsolicited IOUs — as he placed hundreds of Teachers College students and graduates in key administrative and teaching positions across the country.

And yet with Kilpatrick there was substance as well as style. In the vanguard of the "new education," he had a message to deliver and an audience eager to receive it. The ideas of Edward L. Thorndike were providing the basis for a new psychology of education. Much of what was taught to teachers and administrators dealt with a reworking or critique of Herbart and Froebel. Under the leadership of Dean James Russell (and John Dewey, across the street at Columbia University), Kilpatrick, Thorndike, and others at Teachers College were challenging the conventional wisdom and stale practices of schooling in America. As Teachers College held its twenty-fifth anniversary in 1912, experimenters and educational leaders from across the country visited the campus. Two such innovators were Marietta Pierce Johnson of the Organic School in Fairhope, Alabama, and William Wirt from northern Indiana, who discussed his "Gary Plan." Although never a convert to the efficiency movement, Kilpatrick was impressed with Wirt's plan, especially its "financial economy and flexibility."[3]

A possible return to teaching in the South never left Kilpatrick's mind entirely, but the idea now occurred with less frequency. In a way, what he desired most was respect and influence in his former homeland. "I am definitely trying to win back my place in Georgia, which apparently has slipped from me," he wrote in 1914.[4] And yet his influence in the South became directly related to his successes in the North. In March of 1913, Professor Henry Suzzallo reported that Charles Hubbard Judd of the University of Chicago had decided *against* "wishing" Kilpatrick to join his faculty in history of education — apparently the reason was that Kilpatrick had too much of Professor Monroe's "point of view." Suzzallo carried the further news that

Kilpatrick was being considered to succeed Charles DeGarmo, at Cornell upon DeGarmo's retirement. "Piqued" over Judd's "not wishing him," Kilpatrick had no interest in going to either northern institution. The following year he was approached by the University of West Virginia for its presidency, and in 1916 Abraham Flexner repeatedly invited Kilpatrick to join his new experimental high school as a mathematics instructor.[5] He declined all these offers.

For all his commitment to Teachers College, though, Kilpatrick's work with the Appointments Committee continued to vex him. Always conscientious, he delved deeply into every case. One college president from a small denominational school requested a psychologist who was Calvinistic in his public as well as his private life. Kilpatrick told the story of another episode which illustrated how sexism often played a part in the selection of teachers. After he had informed a superintendent that Columbia did not have a candidate matching the position requested, the superintendent nevertheless requested an appointment the next day to meet the candidates in person. "Among the group was a young school teacher who was undoubtedly less qualified to fill the position than any of those present, but, if I do say it, she was good looking, attractive, a good personality and all of that," said Kilpatrick. After a brief conversation with her, the superintendent told Kilpatrick that if he would only give the word, he would give the young woman the position. "But I did not give the word," wrote Kilpatrick.[6] He found such requests preposterous, making his work that much more irritating.

A colleague finally complained to Dean Russell that Kilpatrick was too valuable a man to waste as a mere functionary in a placement office. Russell agreed, stating that "he had this other thing in mind for Kilpatrick." The dean, who had high prospects for Kilpatrick at Teachers College told him privately, "You may have to wait a little longer than you like, but ultimately you will get what you want." "His tone and manner were more cordial even than his words," wrote Kilpatrick of the meeting. Bolstered by the positive turn in the conversation, Kilpatrick inquired about an advancement from assistant to associate professor. Unusual, but not impossible, came the reply from the dean, who added that an executive position might help. Not missing a beat, the assistant professor asked for a change in title from secretary to chairman of the Appointments Committee. Russell agreed. In early 1914 Kilpatrick wrote, "I am certainly glad to be allowed to work here."[7]

Although the placement work remained a struggle, he did find time to join two discussion groups — one called the Tawse, the other Scholia. Usually centered on topics germane to education, the debate in these groups was often

lively. Kilpatrick wrote of a Teachers College colleague "fairly skinning a city principal alive," and remarked that he had never witnessed the equal of such a "performance." At another meeting Kilpatrick was attacked by a colleague for talking too much about the future. But, according to his diary, "I held my own and won the crowd." In May of 1913 Kilpatrick joined Phi Delta Kappa. A year later, a photograph of the education fraternity, *sans* females, was taken on the steps of a 120th Street entrance to Teachers College. Dean Russell, in the center of the front row, was flanked by Edward Thorndike and John Dewey. The group members were almost uniformly dressed in three-piece suits, starched collars, and high-ankled black-laced dress shoes. Kilpatrick was also in the front row. Near the back of the photograph was young Will Russell, son of the dean. Kilpatrick was one of William Russell's professors and even attended his dissertation defense, at which time he recorded in his diary that he considered Will "a very promising young man." Twenty years hence, as his father's successor, the younger Russell would become Kilpatrick's nemesis.[8]

Aside from academic activities, Kilpatrick and Rita attended a variety of college-related social events. Of course, the meetings of the Southern Club, no longer exclusively female, remained central to their calendar. During the summers, entertainment would be provided, with each state presenting a brief skit. One year, Georgia presented characters dressed up as Uncle Remus, a peach, Ty Cobb, and, much to Kilpatrick's surprise, "a small man dressed in a light gray suit — similar to mine — in rather long powdered hair" with the title "brainiest man in all the world."[9] But frequently the activities of this organization bothered the socially conservative side of Kilpatrick, the dancing being especially problematic for him. He found the crowd at one such gathering much too engrossed in the "bunny hug," calling it an "extreme of modern dance." On another occasion the dance in question was the "one step," which he described as "a sort of invitation, a rehearsal of the most fundamental of social acts."[10]

In November of 1913 Kilpatrick emerged from his self-imposed mold of teaching the ideas of others. Professor MacVannel's health had worsened, allowing Kilpatrick to move from teaching history of education to teaching the philosophy of education. This shift provided him with the avenue for which he longed. His work in the history of education had given him an excellent foundation, but students were not satisfied with MacVannel's, nor even, for that matter, with Dewey's approach to philosophy of education. "I must do better as a teacher," he confided in his diary. "My pupils must leave me better satisfied." At the same time, the Teachers College summer school classes were

growing — one summer, enrollments went up, in this prewar period, by 25 percent to over 4,500 students. "I find," he wrote, "that I am coming to be known far more widely each year."[11]

There was also interest in Kilpatrick's writing. He was asked by the historian Paul Monroe to rewrite some of Dewey's contributions to Monroe's *Cyclopedia of Education.* He agreed, and the clarity of Dewey's writing was, as usual, problematic. The official reason for the rewrite, according to Monroe, was to "adapt to the demands of the public." Although still uncomfortable with his own writing, Kilpatrick was also approached by the educational historian Ellwood P. Cubberly, who asked him to contribute to the Houghton Mifflin series on the philosophy of education. Kilpatrick declined. He also refused a request to write a book for an unknown individual whom he dismissed as a "clod-hopper." On another occasion, he noted in one of his classes that "two ignoramuses ask too many questions." And he also mentioned that one of his doctoral students was a "sloppy thinker." While flawlessly polite, Kilpatrick was not a man to suffer fools gladly.[12]

In a day and age when there was no popular radio and few gramophones or silent movies, and the theater, musical performances, and public lectures were the major forms of entertainment, it was not unusual that a man such as Kilpatrick could make a deep impression on those who heard him speak. As early as 1913, Kilpatrick would be brought back to the stage after a lecture by standing ovations, to take two or three extra bows. And the crowds were large. On October 31, 1913, in Boston, he addressed a hall holding 3,000. His fee at this time was $50 plus expenses. During 1913 his trips were restricted, for the most part, to the east coast — Boston, Philadelphia, Washington, D.C., Providence, Rhode Island, and also North Carolina and Virginia. At first he continued to speak on Montessori, but, becoming weary of the topic, he dropped his lecture on the Italian educator by the end of the year. The topics began to change to the so-called "newer thinking" in education. One lecture was entitled "Is There a New Education?" Another frequent topic was the reconstruction of education due to changed social conditions, "following essentially Dewey and Cubberly." He also ventured into psychology, with the title "What Would Happen to the Curriculum If We Really Gave Up the Dogma of Formal Discipline?" His lectures were breaking new ground, and he knew it. He went so far as to describe one of his talks as "radical."[13]

Kilpatrick's lectures struck a chord because there was a need for a "new education" from both the practitioner's and the theoretician's point of view. The endless reworking of Froebel and Herbart had failed to provide a new synthesis.

In fact, by 1914 no one even debated from a Froebelian perspective.[14] Kilpatrick's book *Froebel's Kindergarten Principles Critically Examined*, was published in 1916. It broke no ground analytically but was, rather, a restatement of his evolving thought with regard to Froebel. He disagreed with Froebel's main tenet of the child's "unfoldment," arguing instead that the child was a social organism. Kilpatrick believed that the theory of unfoldment lacked structure, which he deemed essential. A child who would live in an interdependent society needed to interact with peers, parents, institutions, and teachers.[15] Kilpatrick gave Froebel full credit for suggesting that education was more than intellectual tasks alone. In addition, he recognized Froebel's emphasis on games and his rejection of the doctrine of total depravity and applauded his emphasis on self-motivation and self-expression. But Kilpatrick concluded that the twin ideas of interest and activity, as demonstrated by Patty Hill of Horace Mann School, were closer to his own thinking than any of Froebel's theories.

Additional topics which entered Kilpatrick's lecture repertoire were the liberty of the child, the nature of the learner, and the need to move the curriculum away from a total reliance on the printed word. In an undated newspaper article (c. 1914) found in his scrapbooks, Kilpatrick discussed the conflict between the individual and society, saying, in part:

> What is to be learned cannot be foreign to individual nature. Books can include but a small portion of any true curriculum. Since the content of the curriculum consists essentially of solutions to problems, the child must first feel something of the problem and be placed where he can most adequately live the solution provided. This means that the school must take on more of the characteristics of life itself.[16]

Another concept with implications for the curriculum that intrigued Kilpatrick was variation. He observed that a high premium was placed on variation in the commercial world, while in other realms of endeavor severe penalties were attached to such ventures. It was "so frowned upon," he wrote, "that only the lawless and disorderly and ignorant vary. So much stress is put on conventionality that variation mainly comes from the bottom."[17] This observation transferred to his concern over the orthodoxy practiced in grammar and language, where no experimentation was permitted or allowed. The issue literally came home to him in connection with his daughter Margaret's being

upset at school when, in Kilpatrick's words, she was found to be "grammatically wrong, but logically correct." He was unable to tolerate "scholastic subtleties," as he termed them, when the children themselves were unable to make the distinctions.[18]

One minor paradox in Kilpatrick's career at this time was his apparent lack of recent firsthand knowledge of schooling, especially of young children, the stage to which he was devoting much of his writing. True, he had been an elementary and high school principal and had taught mathematics at both the secondary and the collegiate level. And, of course, there was also his daughter, who had just entered her teenage years, for him to observe. But he had not taught in the public schools for almost ten years, and when he had taught, it had been for only a single year at the high school level. He did make occasional visits to the Horace Mann School and also talked with Milo Hillegas, his colleague and partner on the Italian trip, who was an expert on elementary schools. "These talks help me because Hillegas works with the practical and brings that element to bear by asking questions which I then discuss theoretically," he wrote in his diary.[19] His observations at Horace Mann School included the first-grade and second-grade classrooms of Miss Burke and Miss Batchelor, who were both implementing his ideas.[20] And so, while it cannot be said that he spent much time in public school classrooms, he did keep abreast of life in the schools in more than a passing manner. And he was certainly a closer observer of school practices than other progressive theoreticians such as Boyd Bode or even John Dewey himself.

It was also during this period, before the United States entered into the Great War, that ideas related to the child-centered movement of progressive education began to emerge in Kilpatrick's lectures around the country. One talk given before the Michigan State Teachers' Association in 1914 had the lengthy title "Greater Spontaneity in the School Room and Limitations Upon Spontaneity." Kilpatrick concluded (in what had begun as a speech on democracy) with a call for less emphasis on obedience and for allowing children more freedom to follow their own spontaneous interests. Maintaining that the psychology of a child was different from that of an adult, he noted that various stages of growth should be taken into consideration and that children must be dealt with in a rational, nonpunitive manner. Children, he stressed, should enter into a full partnership with the country's philosophy — namely, democracy. In the same address he also advocated that women be included in the democratic process.[21]

Kilpatrick's travel increased rapidly during the war period. His stops

usually included normal schools, such as those in Kalamazoo, Michigan, and Muncie, Indiana, in addition to gatherings of public school teachers and administrators. These midsemester trips were enjoyable, and once, during a rail journey, he mentioned that he could have been quite "at home in Indiana or Iowa." The trips were also financially beneficial. In 1917 alone he earned $2,400 plus expenses for his lectures.[22] In addition to the theme of military training and preparedness in the schools (which will be discussed later), his lectures included "Interest and Education," "Education as Socialization," "The Project Method," "Principles Underlying Kindergarten and Primary Education," "Education as Activity," and "Democracy and Education."

Examples of his lecture tours are well-documented,[23] but a brief description of one eight-city, nine-day trip to Indiana, Ohio, and Michigan in early 1917 will provide the flavor. While this particular trip was made during the dead of winter, his reception was, without exception, warm and enthusiastic.[24] The audiences often greeted him in song. The lyrics would extol the virtues of the speaker, while the melody would be a tune familiar to most. A number of such songs survive in his scrapbooks:

To the tune of "Dixie":

If you want to know all of philosophy
That's found in Thorndike and Dewey,
   See "Killie" See "Killie"
   See "Killie" See "Killie"
Cooperation, communication,
This is the way to education,
   Democracy Democracy
   Democracy Democracy
Individual realization, Hooray! Hooray!
In "Killie's" brand I take my stand
To have a real democracy, Hooray! Hooray!
It's all to be found in "Killie" Hooray! Hooray!
It's all to be found in "Killie."

Another ditty was sung to the tune of "Tipperary":

Here's a long, long toast to our Kilpatrick
   Here's a pledge of good-will;

Here's a long, long toast to his keen vision
  From the college on the hill.
Goodbye old-time teaching,
  Welcome T.C. kind.
Here's a long toast now to our Kilpatrick
  He's ours! Never Mind!

Such trips allowed Kilpatrick to see some of the facilities of newer schools across the country. While in Indianapolis, he visited Arsenal Technical High School, of which he wrote, "A magnificent site for a magnificent plant." This stop in the Hoosier capital led to an incident from which Kilpatrick learned an important dictum: involvement in local school politics can be precarious. The superintendent, J. G. Collicott, was in the process of being dismissed by the school board. Several friends of Collicott's approached Kilpatrick, almost before he left his train at Union Station, requesting a letter to the school board in support of Collicott. Numerous drafts were produced until finally Kilpatrick, in exasperation, gave the group several sheets of Teachers College stationery. Although he felt uncomfortable at the time and "pushed" by the deputation to compose a letter, he finally did so, albeit reluctantly. The letter maintained that the school board was not practicing "fair play," and that the board would put itself in an adverse position across the country, "risk serious injury to the name of Indianapolis," even "cast a blight upon your city," hampering its efforts to find a new superintendent. Without doubt, the letter was heavily revised by Collicott's supporters after it left Kilpatrick's hands. Still, it speaks of Kilpatrick's influence throughout the country, which, while significant, was something he never spoke of publicly. Upon returning to New York, he discovered that Collicott had been given timely that notice that his work was unsatisfactory, had been asked to leave the year before, and, according to other reports, had been treated with full consideration. Upon learning this, Kilpatrick wrote letters both to the school board and to those who had gotten him involved in the fiasco, expressing his regret.[25] As he wrote in the margin of his scrapbook next to the original letter (which was published in the Indianapolis newspaper), the incident had been an "error of judgment."

One of Kilpatrick's journeys across the country almost proved fatal. On a night train to Pittsburgh on March 15, 1918, he was involved in a frightening and deadly wreck near Harrisburg, Pennsylvania. At 1 a.m., while Kilpatrick was dressed in nightclothes and asleep in a lower berth, the train derailed, rolled down an embankment and struck several large boulders below. Kilpatrick,

turned upside down, landed on the ceiling of the compartment with his mattress and bedclothes on top of him. As he later recalled, at first a series of thoughts flashed through his mind: that he would not see his wife and daughter again, that he hated "to go this way away from home," that he had failed to purchase life insurance for the trip, that he still had a "third to a fourth of his life left." As for his actual physical situation, although trapped, he felt quite comfortable. He even considered falling asleep until someone came for him. At that moment, though, he began to feel suffocated in the pitch-black compartment. Finally, freeing one of his arms and pulling aside the curtain to the berth, he was struck in the face by a cool breeze, and his fear of suffocation left him. Hearing groans and cries for help, Kilpatrick decided to call out his berth number — "Get lower nine out, get lower nine out." Almost immediately, his fellow passengers began shouting out their own berth numbers. Once this useless exercise ceased, Kilpatrick struck up a conversation with the passenger in berth upper nine, who was now below him and possibly injured. On discovering this, he began calling out, "Get upper nine first, he is hurt." The two men then exchanged promises to bring assistance back once one of them was freed.

At that moment, the voices of rescuers were heard, but simultaneously a new fear arose. Kilpatrick felt water seeping into his berth and thought that the car had possibly landed in a river. It had not, though, and the rescue crew began removing the passengers. Kilpatrick was eventually pulled from the wreck and later recorded in his diary, "It did indeed feel good to get back to the world of freedom and action." He was given a blanket for both warmth and modesty and laid on a mattress by the rail bed. One woman, brought out breathing, was laid near him, but soon died. Kilpatrick, no doubt in mild shock himself, yelled to the doctor not to give up on her. The passengers were all examined by a physician and then taken to Harrisburg and placed for the remainder of the night in an infirmary, where Kilpatrick tried, without success, to send a telegram to his wife. The next morning he was sent to a clothier, outfitted in a new suit and undergarments, and placed on a train back to New York. While some clothes were recovered, most of his belongings were lost. Upon arriving home, he told his family and colleagues of his brush with death. A few days later, bruising and pain commenced. But it could have been worse: the newspapers wrote that he had been killed. The *Philadelphia Evening Public-Ledger* reported that a loosened boulder had fallen onto the cars, causing the crash near Elizabethtown. Kilpatrick's railroad ticket from that fateful night is pasted in the scrapbooks.[26]

During the war, Kilpatrick considered leaving apartment living and

moving to one of the new suburbs of New York City. He and Rita looked at one home in Forest Hills Gardens, priced at $10,000. But train connections were inconvenient, and with his wife and daughter also involved at Teachers College, they demurred.[27] Although he never again considered leaving 106 Morningside Drive, the family did move to a seven-room apartment on the eighth floor in April of 1914. The new apartment had a fine view to the east, overlooking Morningside Park and, beyond that, Harlem. The rent, though, was a steep $1100 per year. The Kilpatricks also engaged the services of a cook and, later, a part-time maid.

As for his daughter, Margaret was becoming a young woman, and Kilpatrick took note of it: "Today M.L.K. ceases to be a child," he wrote just after her twelfth birthday. (Noting her strong-willed personality, he wrote on her thirteenth birthday that "If she were a boy, her stock would be rather more promising."[28]) What did not cease were the minor disagreements between daughter and stepmother. "My wife and daughter do not always get on well together," he wrote in his diary, and this made him "sick at heart." Margaret could also be recalcitrant at school. She became amused on one occasion when a teacher lost his temper. When the teacher took her to task for her behavior, she responded discourteously — bringing on an immediate parent conference. Always even-handed in such situations, Kilpatrick wrote, "I have a suspicion that he [the teacher] will regret the occurrence. I shall try to see that Margaret regrets it." Margaret's grades were mixed: she excelled in the subjects she enjoyed, such as art, history, and English, while barely passing in algebra and Latin. Kilpatrick blamed himself for the latter, saying that he had made his opposition to those disciplines too well-known and that therefore Margaret herself had rebelled. Helping Margaret one evening with factoring, he wrote, "A waste of time if there ever was. I chafe under it." Although he would emerge as a critic of standardized testing, he was enough of a scientific educator to utilize some of the first intelligence tests on Margaret. There is little doubt he had high hopes for her. "She draws well and writes well for her age. I am hoping she may do something significant along this line," he wrote.[29]

Kilpatrick's love for his daughter and concern for her well-being were deeply felt. After attending a play based on *David Copperfield*, in which Margaret appeared, Kilpatrick commented in his diary, "As I thought of little Emily and Steerforth's wrong treatment of her, my parental feelings were much stirred."[30] Margaret had a bout with typhoid fever in May of 1914, which caused him to cancel a trip to South America. The fall of 1916 brought a momentous decision, when he sent Margaret to school at Ashley Hall in

Charleston, South Carolina. It was a struggle for him because, in addition to his desire to keep her at home, he believed that Horace Mann was a stronger school. On the other hand, he was concerned about her social development and what he called "companionship." And, of course, there was the issue of Southern culture. "My wife's family is too prominent for my daughter not to profit somewhat therefrom," he wrote. At the end of one semester, Margaret's Christmas visit brought with it a mixed report. Kilpatrick was surprised to learn that certain young ladies from good families at Ashley Hall freely used profanity. But it was for the most part a structured environment. "The relatively severe discipline rubs her [Margaret] the wrong way, naturally," Kilpatrick noted.[31]

Margaret eventually returned to New York and finished school at Horace Mann. On her seventeenth birthday Kilpatrick ruminated on a perceived lack of closeness between the two of them, thinking that the loss of her mother at so young an age was partly the cause. While quite proud of her artistic and writing ability, he was slightly concerned about her lack of interest in books. But, he added, "I am not much troubled on this score except so far as comes the artificial standard of school record."[32] During Margaret's senior year he watched his daughter dance in a school play and thought she did rather well. The evening also brought back memories of Marie, and a touch of melancholy set in. "Margaret reminded me so of her that I was quite carried back to the days of the past."[33] In the fall of 1918 Margaret entered Teachers College as a resident student in Whittier Hall. Kilpatrick gave her a clothing allowance of almost $400 a year in addition to paying for her tuition, books, and board. She was also given $1.50 per week for incidentals. All of this was a bit unsettling for Kilpatrick, who felt uncomfortable, as a man, dealing with these matters. "Unfortunately," he wrote in his diary, "my wife and my daughter do not get on well, so that it seems better for them not to try to arrange matters."[34] The conflict between daughter and stepmother would eventually ameliorate, and the Southern influence of the Pinckney family would leave a lasting impression on Margaret. But at this time differences in temperament and opinions between the two lingered on.

Kilpatrick's wife continued working part-time at Teachers College as assistant social director for a salary of $700 a year, with additional income from a home she owned in Charleston. Kilpatrick earned $3,100 for the school year 1913-1914. His income would rise only a few hundred dollars the next few years. Kilpatrick's younger brother, Howard, who worked in a patent office, had moved to New York City and lived nearby. A bachelor, Howard was

slightly handicapped, walking with a closed-step shuffle. He was also as conservative as his older brother was liberal. Kilpatrick considered Howard "conceited and stubborn" and especially opinionated, amazingly enough, on the topic of education. "I have ceased to argue with him. I only lose my temper without in the least convincing him," wrote Kilpatrick soon after Howard moved to the city.[35]

The Kilpatricks did manage to take vacations after summer school and before the fall semester. There was usually a trip to the South during the late summer, with peaches and jellies brought to New York on the return journey. During the summer of 1914, while his daughter was at camp in New England — an activity Kilpatrick strongly endorsed — he and Rita visited the Catskill Mountains. The following summer they returned to New Hampshire and Maine. The summers also gave Kilpatrick time to work on his genealogy, by occasionally interviewing distant relatives. Genealogy would become his single hobby. ("Possibly those who contribute least to the family line are most interested in the history of the line," he modestly, but inaccurately, wrote at one time.) He eventually traced his family line back to Charlemagne. He again took up tennis for fitness and recreation, and attended an occasional play, such as George Bernard Shaw's *Pygmalion*, although he refused to attend musicals unless compelled to do so. A Victrola "talking machine" was purchased at this time, and Howard would bring records from his collection to the Morningside Drive apartment.[36]

In the summer of 1917 the Kilpatricks bought a Buick. The purchase was the result of an apparent disagreement that arose one Saturday morning. "Work at odds and ends as I do not feel like more serious work, having become exasperated by a remark of my wife at the breakfast table," Kilpatrick wrote in his diary. Although the issue in dispute was not mentioned in the diary entry, within a week an automobile was secured at a price of $950 and Kilpatrick was less than enthusiastic over the purchase. The attendant costs of the vehicle in this early era of automotive history included protective driving apparel, a license, oil, tires and inner tubes, the rental of a garage, and, of course, gasoline, at a cost of 26 cents a gallon. Still, Kilpatrick learned to drive, took a trip to New England in late August, and made weekend jaunts to the suburbs beginning in September. Two weeks later his first minor accident occurred. The whole process proved rather "fatiguing" for him. "I wondered why I had paid so much good money for so much trouble," he wrote in his diary. The car trouble continued. "I have bought a gold brick, a white elephant," he lamented as the Buick continued to give him problems and costs escalated. Not even

sleep provided a reprieve from his newfound worries: "In the night I wake, troubled by the car." The vehicle proved problematic even when idle. Once, after leaving it near Teachers College, he returned to find that President and Mrs. Wilson were visiting relatives in the neighborhood and the Buick had to be moved because it was in front of the home of Mrs. Wilson's "kinsmen." To add insult to injury, Kilpatrick then had "a vexatious time starting" the troublesome vehicle. By the end of the year he yearned for "any genuine excuse not to use the car."[37]

Excuses not to use the car arose but were never sufficient, it seemed, to rid him of this albatross. In July of 1919 the Buick was stolen, but it was then found. Two years later Kilpatrick had an accident (not his fault apparently), whereupon he pursued those who had struck him. When he caught the perpetrators, they pretended to be deaf. Less than a year later, he turned the car over to his wife, never to drive an automobile again. "I formally and legally give the car to my wife. This I do partly because I wish not to have the responsibility of deciding about a matter that has practically been in her exclusive hands for years, partly to avoid trouble, partly to avoid the danger of heavy damages. If she has to pay, being a woman she will have more influence with the jury and if the damage be very heavy (beyond her fortune) it would cost us less. She begins by going to the notary to swear to the license officiation." Thus ended a frustrating yet mildly amusing episode in Kilpatrick's life, which may have contributed to his lifelong aversion, if not to the potential of technology, at least to its practical applications.

Although the European war would not directly involve the United States until 1917, events across the ocean were certainly on the minds of many Americans. Never one to compartmentalize his activity in the field of education to the exclusion of national and world events in the political arena, Kilpatrick was an unusually close observer of events on the world scene. He read liberal journals of opinion, such as *The New Republic* and *The Nation*, as well as the daily city newspapers. (He read the *New York Post* before the war and then the *New York Times* after the war.) Throughout his life he commented on and analyzed world events, recording his insights in his diary. While it cannot be denied that he was decidedly left of center on the political spectrum, his assessments of issues of the day were enlightened, perceptive, and often, though not always, accurate in their predictions. His comments were never those of an uninformed observer.

During the winter of 1914–1915, Kilpatrick became involved in the work of the local Belgian Relief Committee. On campus, the war was on the minds

of many, including Dean James Russell, who often devoted entire faculty meetings to the topic of how the war would affect Teachers College as well as the nation. In one meeting he attributed the emergence of Germany's "war attitude" directly to German education.[38] Kilpatrick recorded his own thinking on the war in the pages of his diary:

> I am reading and thinking on the problems raised by the present war in the field of education, efficiency, democracy, academic freedom, the utilization of a system of education to support a social system. As I see it, the lesson of the war is that of appraising our fundamental conceptions as to the nature of social control.[39]

As for the German educational system, he too, was highly critical. "I object to her educational system in which the lower classes are trained to obedience and unquestioning loyalty. Even the university professors seem to have been made subservient to the government."[40]

As mentioned earlier, the topics of Kilpatrick's lectures on his tours during the war years included militarism and preparedness. Early in 1917, in Toledo, Ohio, he told a group of teachers that military training had no place within the school curriculum. "Unquestioning obedience is not to be desired," he said. "In a democracy we should know a reason for obedience. The idea of subordinating the many to the will of a few is an aristocratic idea and not in keeping with a democratic nation." As for the argument that preparedness would carry over into peacetime as a virtue, Kilpatrick once again raised an objection: "The man who is prompt to obey in the service may not always be on time at his church in later life or the soldier whose attire is immaculate may not keep his wardrobe in perfect order ten years later." And yet he understood the nation's compulsion toward a militaristic response and its motivation for preparedness: "This is the greatest spectacle the world has ever seen. We feel we must do something." But he also recognized the human dimension and the larger implications of settling disputes with violence:

> Today law should settle controversies. Murder is no longer respectable, war is not now close to human nature. Today the man in a balloon directs the one below who shoots at something over the hill — at those whom he has never seen.

> Conditions have changed; the world is about to demand a
> new method of settlement.[41]

The year before the United States entered the war, Kilpatrick was still solidly behind Wilson on "all points except on preparedness." By comparison, he called Theodore Roosevelt a "hotheaded knock-him-down and run-him-over type," who stood for the past, not the future. He concluded, "there is a final separation between those who wish to minimize and those who wish to maximize (if I may coin a word) the use of force. For myself I am a peace man."[42] He once spoke on militarism to an audience at Teachers College, stressing all these points in addition to what he termed the danger of imperialism and the hysteria for war.[43] When Theodore Roosevelt's book *Fear God and Do Your Own Part* appeared, Kilpatrick was livid:

> I am ashamed for America that such a slap dash and mushy
> book should appear from one counted to be among the
> foremost of our citizens. I think he is losing his mind. I may
> be somewhat prejudiced by his attack on Wilson, but I think
> my judgment is still correct.[44]

He voted for Woodrow Wilson in 1916, along with the Democratic Party candidates for the Senate, the House, and the governorship. But he voted predominantly for Republican judges, and he split his ticket on local candidates.[45] Kilpatrick was delighted when Wilson won the close election over Charles Evans Hughes, and he described in his diary why he was so devoted to the president:

> He stands as I see it for economic justice as opposed to special
> privilege, to progressive as opposed to "stand pat" policies,
> for peace and international democracy as against a military
> imperialism, for a reasoning as against a force diplomacy, for
> low tariff as against protectionism. Besides, he views the
> South as a vital part of the nation.[46]

Wilson's ideas and ideals closely mirrored Kilpatrick's own political notions. As 1917 opened, he wrote:

> I do not think that Wilson is a great man in the strictest sense,

but among our presidents he will rank high. On the whole I support his policies, regretting the apparent political necessity for preparedness. I am myself opposed to war, believe in a strong league of nations to enforce peace. I believe in free trade, in the total abolition of the spoils system. I oppose socialism, but believe that we need much wider extension of regulation and cooperative enterprise. I am anxious to see scientific thought enthroned in democratic fashion.[47]

When the United States entered the European conflict in April of 1917, Kilpatrick expressed his basic opposition to war and his concern over the capitalists' potential for involvement in "selfish exploitation." And yet he stood ready to support Wilson. Although against war, he was not a pacifist. To his way of thinking, Germany was the aggressor, and if by no other justification than tradition, the western powers had the right to prevent a victory which would "burden, if not stifle civilization." He was also continually optimistic: "War now to the defeat of Germany might mean a new face on world politics." But he added his wish that "the nation would not lose many of our young men." His position can be encapsulated in his own words: "I must say I think war is inherently anti-democratic, justifiable only to ward off something worse."[48]

The politics of war also came home to Columbia University when, in the fall of 1917, two professors were dismissed by President Nicholas Murray Butler. Kilpatrick, extremely disturbed and troubled over the incident, considered Butler's action misguided, autocratic, and "lacking in appreciation of freedom of thought and speech." But he decided to say nothing publicly until he was granted his full professorship, fearing that Butler and Dean Russell might oppose his promotion because of his support for Dewey. "Dewey . . . is *persona non grata* to them," wrote Kilpatrick, "in part I believe, for his radical views." He later went so far as to liken Columbia to the German universities. The episode caused him to conclude glumly that "America has a good deal to learn before it really believes in democracy or education."[49] When the historian Charles Beard resigned in protest, Kilpatrick was in full agreement with Beard's charges that the trustees were reactionary, medieval, and narrow in their outlook. He thought he himself might have to leave. "I hate to think of myself getting out again," he concluded, "yet it may come."[50]

In 1917 Kilpatrick gave a lecture in North Carolina entitled "What Changes Will the War Bring to America?" In his talk he suggested that the increase in scientific thought would lead to greater efficiency and the possible

exploitation of "nations and backward people." The success of the suffragists in England would be mirrored in the United States, he thought, with suffrage for "women, negroes, and foreigners." He had little doubt there would be a greater centralization of government, reflected in more state regulation and control. He supported continued high taxes and government spending. Although this sounded socialistic, for him it was not orthodox socialism. Kilpatrick foresaw a move toward equality for women as the greatest change that would be brought about by the war. Opportunities for women in business, he thought, would possibly result in the "identical functioning of the two sexes." Finally, family life would be problematic, divorce would increase, and other institutions would be questioned as women became more independent.[51]

During 1918, the last year of the war, Kilpatrick's mind turned to the issue of peace and the postwar world:

> To me democracy is at stake. If we do not now make the proper peace terms, the clock is turned back and civilization starts to commit suicide. Arming and preparedness must go on until another crash comes, either another world war or a revolution. Perhaps never before has a greater opportunity been offered to constructive thought. The President is our stronghold, and just now at any rate he is the greatest man in the world, the best thinker, most strategically placed.[52]

Kilpatrick's warning of another world conflagration if peace did not succeed rings prophetic. He truly thought the world was at a distinct historical juncture, analogous to, and as momentous as, the Renaissance, the Reformation, or the French Revolution. The United States — and Teachers College, specifically — was strategically placed to play a large role in the hoped-for transformation. But the results of the off-year election in November deeply disturbed him; he believed that the Republican victories in the Senate would make it difficult, if not impossible, for Wilson to achieve his postwar aims. Historians have explained the anti-Democratic sentiment as a result of Wilson's partisan political activity during the election. In Kilpatrick's view, however, it was the result of several factors: the war spirit, the feeling that Wilson would make a generous peace with the vanquished, and the inability of the American people to accept change.[53] For Kilpatrick, democracy, education, and events at home and abroad were always interdependent.

In the professional arena, Kilpatrick was promoted to associate professor

in 1915, with a salary of $3,300. His advancement was due mainly to his performance in the classroom, with his national lecture tours and his popularity among the students as contributing factors. With Henry Suzzallo leaving to become president of the University of Washington, Thorndike and McMurray both on leave, and Monroe "not popular as a lecturer," Kilpatrick wrote, "I am distinctly among the higher men on the general faculty."[54] The situation also left him acting head of the philosophy of education department. His hope for advancement to full professor in the near future was coupled with concern over whether he would ever be considered as more than a mere disciple or expounder of Dewey's philosophy. The following year, 1916, the title of his major course was changed from "Educational Theorists" to "Foundations of Method." He also found himself second only to McMurray in summer school enrollments, with one class of 240 students — a tribute to his growing reputation as a teacher. The same year, Dean James Russell merged the history of education and philosophy of education departments, thereby putting Kilpatrick back under Monroe, something the rising star did not especially care for. But the dean did need a person of Kilpatrick's rank and caliber to fill in for Monroe in the event of absence or disability. At the same time, Russell brought to the attention of his faculty the students' concerns over excessive travel by the faculty, assignments thought to be negative and destructive, and a general lack of harmony among faculty members.[55] Some perennial issues in higher education apparently never change.

In 1917 Dean Russell brought to Teachers College the conservative educator William Bagley — possibly, according to Kilpatrick, to offset the perceived "Dewey-McMurray-Kilpatrick attitude towards individualism." But Kilpatrick thought the Dean was mistaken regarding "individualism." In fact, he was not sure that Russell even knew what he meant by the term. Bagley's stance on educational issues emerged during the new man's first year at Teachers College. In his diary, Kilpatrick reported a conversation with a student and Russell's misconceptions regarding the schools of philosophy thought to exist within Teachers College:

> The Dean is partly responsible for this idea that Dewey and I are "individualistic" while he and others are guardians of the social point of view. It is however hard for me to see how anyone could stress the social point of view more than does Dewey or I. We do not stress the vested interest side either of property rights or of age rights. The Dean has said in my presence that Dewey has

no social philosophy. I told Miss Day I thought it not wise to have a debate with Bagley at the beginning of his career here lest we make him take a stand which he will afterwards feel compelled in self respect to maintain.[56]

Apparently Russell was seeking someone who could combine the thinking of John Dewey and Edward L. Thorndike. Many students, and Kilpatrick himself, thought that such a synthesis was already taking place, although when told this by a student, the dean apparently seemed surprised. All of this was upsetting to Kilpatrick, who thought that his chances for promotion were being held up by a dean who knew nothing of his work, let alone understood it. "I get so angry," he wrote after talking with a student and a colleague about the situation, "that I can hardly study for an hour."[57]

There was once again in 1917 the annual prospect of an offer from George Peabody College in Tennessee, but his work at Teachers College was going extremely well. "I hate to leave here," he wrote, "where the work is so congenial." At the same time the realization came that he would have to publish more if he was ever to establish a reputation beyond his own classroom. But at this juncture fewer passages of self-doubt or gloomy talk of his days running out are found in the diaries. His career was on the move. Only the need for reading glasses just before his forty-sixth birthday gave him pause.[58]

The vexing issue of Kilpatrick's full professorship remained unresolved as 1918 opened. Apparently feeling that there was little to lose, he had a frank talk with Russell soon after his train accident. Uncharacteristically blunt, he charged the dean with being inconsistent in desiring a faculty of "stand-patters," and with often being uninformed with regard to issues and thinking in the Teachers College community. Although risky, the exchange may have cleared the air. Within a week Kilpatrick was notified of his promotion to full professor, beginning July 1, with a salary of $4,500, representing a $700 raise. Ill feeling lingered, though. He continued to believe that his promotion had been stalled by Nicholas Murray Butler, by his own connection with Dewey, and by the vexing issue of publishing. The promotion, while marking the height of his ambition, left him feeling that he still had to make a contribution in terms of his own thought.[59]

But the work was, as he had indicated, "congenial," and it continued to bring him attention and even adulation from educators across the country. He himself realized that the war years had brought about a definite increase in his influence. On his forty-seventh birthday, in late 1918, he wrote:

I am getting further along now. Since last November I have
been promoted to a full professorship. My philosophy of
education course has made a distinct name for me. I feel
myself to be accumulating ideas. I can present pretty well
orally, but my writing is slow and painful. If I can overcome
this I shall make a much better name.[60]

The war years had witnessed a remarkable rise in the career of William
Heard Kilpatrick. In the eyes of students, colleagues, and the administration,
he had emerged among the top tier of professors at Teachers College. And he
received the same accolades across the country as he enjoyed on his home
campus. Kilpatrick's contributions in teaching, speaking, and analysis were all
considered significant and worthy of attention. The only area that concerned
him, and possibly others, was his relative lack of publications. However, in the
final year of the war, a brief but influential scholarly contribution by Kilpatrick
would fill that void and mark him as a major force in educational thought in his
own right. The article was eighteen pages in length and appeared in the
Teachers College Record under the title "The Project Method."

7

BRINGING DEMOCRACY TO THE CLASSROOM: THE PROJECT METHOD

"Education is life, not a preparation for life."[1]

"But it is democracy which we contemplate and with which we are here concerned. As the purposeful act is thus the typical unit of the worthy life in a democratic society, so also should it be made the typical unit of school procedure.[2]

"Knowledge we still wish, perhaps more than in the old days, but we demand that it be gained under such conditions and be organized in the mind in such a way as to make it more likely to serve us in time of need."[3]

William Heard Kilpatrick

Of the several suggestions put forth by Kilpatrick during the course of his swift and impressive rise to prominence in American education, none may have been as significant as the theoretical treatise he developed during the war years. One historian, Lawrence Cremin, considered "The Project Method," published by *Teachers College Record* in 1918, to be Kilpatrick's major contribution to the dialogue on progressive education.[4] Two more recent historians have been expansive in their assessment of its publication: "The article created the biggest wave of pedagogical excitement since the Herbartians' five formal steps. More than sixty thousand reprints poured forth into the education world in the next quarter century [and] brought Kilpatrick immediate and enduring fame."[5]

The seminal idea for the manuscript had emerged in 1892 (see Chapter 2), when a science teacher in Savannah, Georgia, related a unique classroom experience to Kilpatrick. Although the teacher had left the classroom, the students continued to work conscientiously at their various tasks. This scene of engaged students, actively involved without the threat of coercion or the need for constant direction from a teacher, left a vivid impression on the young Kilpatrick. This episode, coupled with his reading of Pestalozzi and other child-centered

educators, launched him on the road toward the "project method."[6]

The larger philosophical suppositions supporting Kilpatrick's thinking on what eventually emerged as the project method were rooted both inside and outside education. His biographer Tenenbaum asserted that:

> With Huxley, he [Kilpatrick] maintained that "the great end of life is not knowledge, but action"; with Goethe, he held that "in the beginning was the act"; with Montaigne, he concurred "that the object of education is to make not a scholar but a man."[7]

Tenenbaum also maintained that Kilpatrick strongly believed in an education which stressed the development of character and personality, not solely "the acquisition of bookish information."[8] Although Tenenbaum did not attribute this idea directly to Kilpatrick, such a statement lends credence to the charge of anti-intellectualism. This issue will be given fuller treatment later, but there is little doubt that Kilpatrick had reservations concerning education exclusively oriented toward the printed word. Years later he would call such an approach "Alexandrian," after the vast library upon which a word-oriented education in the ancient world was based. In Kilpatrick's view, education should encompass not only the intellectual but the aesthetic and the social. These ideas would be further developed in two of his later works, *Foundation of Method* and *Education for a Changing Civilization*. In brief, this assumption was predicated on the idea that children could not be adequately prepared for an unknowable future through a static curriculum. Knowing how to think, rather than what to think, would be an oversimplification. Kilpatrick was not calling for education to be devoid of content. Rather, the ideal was to involve the student actively in the process of education and to emphasize the experiences and knowledge the child might bring to the subject matter, rather than solely what the subject matter brought to the child. In a way, this harked back to Dewey's book *Interest and Effort*, with the purpose being not necessarily to make a subject interesting as an end in itself, but to deeply engage the interest of the child in the subject as the first step in an evolving process.

Years later, Kilpatrick would say that if called upon to state his "activities approach" to education in a phrase, it would be "acting on thinking."[9] Tenenbaum used the phrase "tested thought," which he defined as having a child participate in deed and action, or, to use Kilpatrick's own term, "purposeful activity." From such a scheme emerged the idea that the process of

education should be life itself rather than a preparation for life. As an example, Tenenbaum quoted Kilpatrick's suggestion that the best preparation for a six-year-old child was happy, adequate, successful living as a five-year-old, and so on for a ten-year-old, a fifteen-year-old, or a twenty-year-old. One must be careful with Kilpatrick as interpreted by Tenenbaum, though. The biographer wrote that "bookish, factual information should at all times be subservient to living" and also that "books as the beginning and the end of education are a sterile and meaningless kind of education that shrivels up life." [10] Such remarks by Tenenbaum misrepresent Kilpatrick. In actuality, Kilpatrick, addressing the issue of books in 1917, the year before "The Project Method" was published, put his concern in historical perspective:

> Our traditional school was organized to supplement the education of the practical life. It thus became predominantly bookish and mental. The body was even despised as material and antispiritual. Aristotle's God spent his time thinking on thought, not on matter; and this was deemed the ideal life of man. Christianity, pagans, aristocrats and the practical world of affairs agreed on restricting physical manipulation in the schools to a minimum. We are heirs to this tradition. [11]

The role of books and the place of subject matter within the schools would both be addressed by Kilpatrick at a future date. What he was advocating at this juncture in connection with purposeful activity resulted from a strong desire to see children interacting with peers, parents, and society at large. Learning truly took place, he believed, only when students internalized what they had heard or seen and then practiced it in their own lives. Learning was incapable of being passive; such a suggestion was a contradiction in terms. Memorization of a poem or lines from Scripture, for example, would not necessarily make people moral, unless they acted upon those thoughts in their own lives. "Ideals, attitudes, appreciations, correlative habits can be acquired only in life situations where they will find their natural habitat," Kilpatrick wrote. [12] The debate arose, of course, over how one defined "intellectual." While not opposed to reading, as will be seen later, Kilpatrick did view reliance on books as suppressing any opportunity for "emotions, feelings, hoping, ideas, attitudes." [13] Unfortunately, the often coercive, uncaring teaching practiced at the time under the guise of print-oriented intellectual education may have blinded Kilpatrick to the possible educational and emotional applications of the printed word.

"The first quality in life is that which leaves us eager," said Kilpatrick to his classes.[14] Kilpatrick sought an emphasis on action and, as he termed it, "leading on." He captured this concept in the phrase "activity leading to further activity." Any activity may, in time, become boring, tedious, lifeless, and lacking in creativity. What was needed, suggested Kilpatrick, was experience that would expand and develop a child's world, providing opportunity for both growth and progress. "The unifying idea I sought," he wrote in the opening pages of "The Project Method," "was to be found in the conception of wholehearted purposeful activity proceeding in a social environment, or more briefly, in the unit element of such activity, the hearty, purposeful act."[15]

The steps in the project method were straightforward enough: conceive, plan, execute, judge, and evaluate. And the key to the significance or worthiness of the project was purpose:

> In the case where no purpose is present, there the weak and foolish teacher has often in times past, cajoled and promised and sugar-coated, and this we all despise. Purpose then — its presence or its absence — exactly distinguishes the desirable . . . interest from the mushy type of anything-to-keep-the-dear-things-interested or amused. It is purpose then that we want, worthy purposes, urgently sought. Get these, and the interest will take care of itself.[16]

The sources of these ideas are clearly evident in John Dewey's influential work *Democracy and Education*, published in 1916. Dewey wrote:

> The essentials of method are therefore identical with the essentials of reflection. They are first that the pupil have a genuine situation of experience — that there be a continuous activity in which he is interested for its own sake; secondly, that a genuine problem develop within this situation as a stimulus to thought; third, that he possess the information and make the observations needed to deal with it; fourth, that suggested solutions occur to him which he shall be responsible for developing in an orderly way; fifth, that he have opportunity and occasion to test his ideas by application, to make their meaning clear and to discover for himself their validity.[17]

"The Project Method" linked purpose and democracy; in fact, Kilpatrick could not conceive how a person might exercise responsibility without being afforded freedom and opportunity. But for Kilpatrick and other progressive educators, the definition of democracy was not exclusively political. George Counts in *Dare the School Build a New Social Order?* later suggested that democracy, in part, meant "glory in every triumph of man in his timeless urge to express himself, providing adequate material and spiritual rewards for every kind of socially useful work . . . and genuine equality of opportunity."[18] His point was that for a political democracy to prosper a hospitable social environment must be present. In one talk in 1917, Kilpatrick said that faith in democracy was a belief in a fair chance for everyone, an unselfish regard for the public good, and social control by ethical persuasion. Thus, Kilpatrick labeled the two-tiered school system, divided between vocational and college-directed preparation, "Prussian" — a value-laden term, considering the time. For a democracy to truly function, neither the classroom nor the teacher could be managed along autocratic lines, nor — at the other end of the spectrum — with a laissez-faire style.[19] In accordance with his democratic ideal, Kilpatrick believed strongly, as did Dewey, in the importance of community and the involvement of the student in that community. The difference between the activities of the school and the activities of the community should be not dichotomous, but intertwined. Projects would necessarily lead the child to be more socially-minded and, therefore, more apt to become a participating and contributing member of a democratic society.

Alongside the social implications of the project method's underlying principles were psychological issues of motivation, competition, and coercion. Kilpatrick viewed intrinsic motivation as essential to the success of any learning experience. Accordingly, as we have seen, he was opposed to any form of extrinsic incentive, such as awards, honors, or grades. For him this was a moral issue. "To build in a child the habit of doing an otherwise good deed from an habitual wrong motive is to build an immoral character," he would later write.[20] In the same manner, competition was seen as extrinsic in nature and, once again, not conducive to growth or progress. Therefore, cooperation was prized, in that it derived from an intrinsic, self-initiated motivation. As for coercion, Kilpatrick would accede to its use only in emergencies. As a method for building lifelong practices, he saw in it little value. "How is it possible," he asked, "by punishing a child into practicing a thing ever to make that practice satisfying?"[21] For him, the project method seemed a much preferred answer to these psychological concerns.

As a Deweyan who viewed life as a social process, Kilpatrick was searching for a unit of behavior that offered the potential for growth in the ethical, moral, social, and intellectual aspects of life. The individual would then be prepared to interact within society — certainly, within a democratic society — and would be able to link personal and social progress as one and the same objective. In the spring of 1908, barely a year after arriving at Teachers College, he wrote in his diary of a "wild day dream of an experiment in education that banished formal discipline, utilized a social and scientific approach to education, providing a method in which particular motivation and technique [were] to be found in real situations."[22] Attached to this specific line of thinking was his overall interest in guided, yet open, freedom for children, encapsulated in the concept of an "abundant life."[23] This was embodied in a familiar verse from the Gospel of John, which he often quoted: "I came that you might have life and have it more abundantly."

Returning to Dewey's writings on interest and effort, Kilpatrick sought a single unit of work that elementary and secondary students could undertake, which would cross disciplinary lines. He expanded on this concept as he discussed the issue while strolling with his colleague Milo B. Hillegas and as he watched his daughter, Margaret, become engaged with a history lesson through her artwork. He was intrigued by how this "childish play" retained both her attention and her interest and by how the technique of art could be learned through concrete work.[24] After another walk with Hillegas, he wrote:

> Talk with Hillegas about history method. He accepts my opinion that connected historical sequence (of cause and effect) is the end state and not the initial method. Little children should get topics which interest them. The full organization should come later.[25]

In describing Margaret's successful project on Tudor and Stuart history to another professor, Kilpatrick quoted his daughter as saying at the end of the year, "I am cured of history."[26]

While his firsthand experiences did not always involve direct observation in public school settings, he was always a close observer of people. He spent one afternoon timing the work and rest periods of a construction crew near Central Park, and he devoted three pages in his diary to describing the actions of trained gorillas in a zoo. The behavior of the gorillas amazed him. His crucial observations, though, went beyond the primates. On another afternoon,

in 1914, Kilpatrick visited the Horace Mann playground and observed a Miss Rankin's class. "This is a scheme of free play which seems to me to contain the germ of a better educational practice. I am much interested by it," he wrote. Thirty years later, in the margin of this diary entry, he noted, "Project idea coming close." During this summer he made other references to the project method, writing in the margins of his diary, "project idea at work," or "project idea brooding here." Kilpatrick also mentioned the connection between his project concept and Dewey's thought. "It would be well to give the whole time to Dewey, and pay more attention to the scientific organization of his ideas," he wrote in describing a summer school class. "In this way the application would apparently come incidentally." After discussing with his class the application of Dewey's ideas, he was "much interested to see how slow the class is to believe that Dewey really means to revolutionize things." Although the project idea was definitely percolating during 1914, by the end of that year he was still unsure of his contribution and doubted that he would "originate any important point of view." The next year found him more optimistic. "I should like to hope that some small portion of it all may be a valuable addition to the world's thought." It was at this juncture that he also began to differentiate between Dewey's approach and his own project method.[27]

The concept of the project method continued to germinate until Kilpatrick reached a breakthrough. "I am much pleased at a thought I have got hold of or evolved, as to the worth of any activity being its tendency to connect up with or lead to other activity. The principle needs criticism, but it appears very fruitful." Near the end of 1915, he shared the concept with students.[28] And by 1916, after further observation of children at play at the Horace Mann School, Kilpatrick referred to the phenomenon he was seeking as "purposeful activity."[29] Such activity by students, he believed, would in turn lead to further activity — a crucial aim, in his view, for education. To one class he explained it thus: "I lay down that the three elements to be sought in the kindergarten, and really elsewhere, are wholesouledness, tendency to lead on, and variety. Activity meeting these three tests will almost certainly get what we wish."[30]

By 1917 Kilpatrick's colleague David Snedden, who had also written on projects, believed that the project method would prove helpful for lower elementary as well as university research and in disciplines as varied as English literature and manual training.[31] Kilpatrick eventually put his ideas down in a formal work for publication but, as usual, struggled with his writing. "I make some progress, but find it difficult to make a satisfactory outline. I can work out some details but not yet can I get the whole," he wrote.[32] Writing

was indeed a difficult task for him. The internal torment he felt as a result of putting his ideas down on paper can be seen in his attempt to make light of his sluggish pace with an analogy to the insect world: "I am like the centipede whose self-consciousness stood in the way of his walking."[33] By April of 1917 an 8,000-word first draft of the project method manuscript was complete, and Kilpatrick began to seek reactions and critiques. As he shared and discussed his ideas at conferences, criticisms did arise. Some could accept the idea of "child purposing" in the project method, but others raised concerns over the portion concerned with activity. Kilpatrick also attempted to implement the project method in his own thinking and teaching, believing that raising "difficulties," or controversial questions, would lead to activity. Conversely, answering all the questions raised in the classroom himself would, as he termed it, "put activity to sleep."[34]

Those who had attended Kilpatrickv talks compiled and published a collection of his ideas about the project method in *General Science Quarterly.* With this article several additional ideas emerged. For example, Kilpatrick was uncomfortable with foisting upon children what he termed, "adult formulations" or "predigested knowledge." Such learning, he contended, did not allow for personal experience or activity. While he did not enumerate an "ages and stages" formula for the process, Kilpatrick thought that children would progress and grow as they matured chronologically. While endorsing physical and manipulative activity, he did not rule out intellectual exertion. In fact, regarding the cognitive aspects of projects, he said, "Projects may vary with age and differentiate as the person gets older. Among these projects will be some that are predominantly intellectual. In all these activities considered above there has been a progressively higher intellectual activity." He added that he was striving for science, via the scientific method, and that "under proper guidance should come an increase of the more purely intellectual element."[35]

By May of 1918 Kilpatrick had completed the final draft of what would become "The Project Method," yet he remained apprehensive over the arguments put forth at several points.[36] On July 17 the article appeared in *Teachers College Record.* Apparently keeping an eye on a local bookstore, he noted, "a goodly number buying it."[37] Under its full title, "The Project Method: The Use of the Purposeful Act in the Educative Process," the article ran a mere eighteen pages.

Kilpatrick began by openly questioning whether "project" was the most suitable term, indicating that "purposeful act" might prove superior. He also readily confessed that he did not consider the work original. Others had used

the term "project," he admitted, though they had used it in what he described as a "mechanical" or "general way." Previous theorists had not made the crucial point of connecting a unit of conduct (which would be a sample of life) to the concept of "wholehearted purposeful activity." According to Kilpatrick, projects might be for either individuals or groups and might include producing a newspaper, a dress, a painting, or a speech, as well as listening to a story, solving a geometry problem, or organizing and playing a baseball game. He considered such projects most often social in nature and certainly psychological — with the psychological value depending on the degree of "wholeheart-edness." If the purposeful act was the typical unit of life in a democratic society, then there was no reason why it should not also be replicated in the schools. Any relationship between education and democracy, Kilpatrick suggested, was apparently absent in the schools. And yet he made this message very clear: "It is a democracy which we contemplate and with which we are here concerned."[38] Accordingly, the point often made by Kilpatrick and other progressive educators was that actually living through experiences that approximated life itself was the best preparation for life.

From this larger context of democracy and the schools, "The Project Method" undertook to outline, in universal yet precise terms, how the theory would function in practice. The project method was based on Thorndike's psychology, specifically Volume 2 of *Educational Psychology*. Kenneth Benne has suggested that this attempt to wed Edward L. Thorndike's connectionism or stimulus-response (S-R) bond psychology with Dewey's philosophy limited Kilpatrick somewhat.[39] Moving beyond primary responses to activities, Kilpatrick believed that both associate responses (thoughts suggested by primary responses) and concomitant responses (attitudes and generalizations also suggested by an activity) were essential by-products of the process. By "concomitant" Kilpatrick meant the inculcation of concepts such as self-reliance, initiative, cooperation, respect for law, confidence, and even joy. But, he was quick to add, the terminology "was not entirely happy."[40] The associate and concomitant learning developed through the project method, which included both knowledge and skills, would be more lasting because the student would be engaged in "wholehearted purpose."[41] This purpose had implications for the curriculum, in that Kilpatrick would later indicate his opposition to a "curriculum set in advance," admittedly one of his more controversial phrases. "The purpose must be the child's not the teacher's. Properly educative experiences cannot be so ordered in advance as to yield designated outcomes," he wrote, "let alone be ordered months in advance." "The essence of life,"

Kilpatrick maintained, "is spontaneity and its outgrowth." He went on to write, "I accordingly propose the following as the most general test to apply to evaluate our school activities. Do the activities of our children leave these and others whom they influence more disposed and better equipped to go on to other like fruitful activity? The two terms then 'growing' and 'leading on' are the touchstones that we must apply."[42]

Thus far, according to Kilpatrick, the associate and concomitant responses were as meaningful and consequential as the primary responses so often emphasized in the schools:

> Do we not too often reduce the subject matter of instruction
> to the level of this type alone? Does not our examination
> system — even our scientific tests at times — tend to carry us
> in the same direction? How many children at the close of a
> course decisively shut the book and say, "thank gracious, I am
> through with that!" How many people get an education yet
> hate books and hate to think?[43]

The final psychological point Kilpatrick developed in "The Project Method" was the need for truly educational experiences and activities extending into further activities. The value of any educational activity, he believed, rested on this element. He did not advocate, as many critics of the child-centered movement have suggested, that children be permitted unlimited freedom. In fact, Kilpatrick was precise in his caveat regarding this potential aberration. He did not believe that simply any purpose a child might pursue should be considered appropriate. Nor should the judgment of the child always be taken as valid. Following such a course would prove, he wrote, both "ineffective and unfruitful." "We contemplate," he stated unequivocally, "no scheme of subordination of teacher or school to childish whim."[44]

With this understood, Kilpatrick went on to suggest an essential role for the teacher. Rather than having the child be an independent agent in the learning process, he conferred upon the teacher the crucial roles of both guide and discriminator, especially with regard to selecting projects that might yield the best results. Specifically, he believed that:

> It is the special duty and opportunity of the teacher to guide
> the pupil through his present interests and achievement into

the wider interests and achievement demanded by the wider
social life of the older world.[45]

If anything, he saw the teacher as responsible for building bonds
between students. And yet, the successful teacher would gradually be
eliminated from the process as the child advanced, so that growth would
occur internally and independently. Moral considerations were also integral
to the project method, and, according to Kilpatrick, the building of moral
character was one of the "strongest points in its favor." Character would be
developed through shared social relationships with direct reference to the
welfare of the group.[46]

Near the end of "The Project Method," Kilpatrick classified four basic
types of projects: Type 1 was a creative idea or plan, e.g. building a boat,
writing a letter, presenting a play; Type 2 was an aesthetic experience, e.g.
listening to a symphony or appreciating a work of art; Type 3 was problem
solving, or, as he termed it, "straightening out some intellectual difficulty";
and Type 4 was obtaining some item or degree of skill or knowledge. He did
not elaborate at great length on the categories, other than encouraging schools
to devote additional time to Type 1. As for the aesthetic experiences of Type
2, he admitted that he had no definite process to suggest for undertaking such
endeavors. He believed that Type 3 lent itself to analysis of thought as
described in Dewey's book *How We Think.* For Type 4 projects, he was
persuaded that a process similar to Type 1 — including purposing, planning,
executing, and judging — should be followed, as this would be most appropriate for gaining skills and knowledge. He did fear an imbalance, or, as he
termed it, "danger of overemphasis" in this category. In addition, he was also
apprehensive that teachers might not adequately discriminate between drill as
a project and drill as a set task.[47]

Kilpatrick sounded several warnings in the conclusion to "The Project
Method." If such an approach were to be adopted, changes in textbooks,
curriculum, grading, and promotion would be needed. Even classroom
furniture and school architecture would need to evolve. He also predicted
opposition from taxpayers and from incompetent or unprepared teachers. He
reiterated that the project method should be viewed not as a license for the
"foolish humoring of childish whim," but rather as utilizing a native capacity
too frequently wasted. With these cautions understood, Kilpatrick was
optimistic about the results of subscribing to this method. It would develop a
more informed citizenry, able to think and act intelligently and to adapt to new

social conditions.[48] In the concluding lines of his article, Kilpatrick envisioned what the project method could mean to education:

> With the child naturally social and with the skillful teacher to stimulate and guide his purposing, we can especially expect that kind of learning we call character building. The necessary reconstruction consequent upon these consider-ations offers a most alluring "project" to the teacher who but dares to purpose.[49]

Kilpatrick was keenly aware that the ideas suggested in "The Project Method" were tentative, incomplete, and certainly untested — a beginning at best. He later suggested that systematic evidence be gathered on the process and that possibly, in the future, educators would learn how "to make scales or measuring rods that will tell us whether our children are growing in the way we wish."[50]

When the project method was put into practice, actual projects varied in scope and content and were undertaken both inside and outside the classroom. Projects within the classroom setting were often simulations of real-life activities taking place in the community. Those projects that took place outside the four walls of the school included investigations of health problems, construction ventures, or agriculturally related schemes. For example, Kilpatrick's grandson tells of painting a figurine of a Roman soldier, which led on to his study of Latin.[51] (A mixed blessing, one might surmise, from his grandfather's point of view.) Of all such experiences Kilpatrick later said, "I have not a doubt that the experience will make every child who participated a different citizen. That shouldn't happen once in a lifetime with children, but should happen every few weeks."[52]

Criticism of The Project Method commenced almost immediately upon its publication. In the popular press, Ella Frances Lynch, writing in the *Philadelphia Public Ledger*, was skeptical about the project method after hearing Kilpatrick address the Pennsylvania State Education Association. She found the ideas of this professor from "the Columbia Cafeteria" too "painless" and wondered if every purpose undertaken by a student would result in interest. "Does any normal human adult believe such flapdoodle?" she asked. Lynch mocked Kilpatrick's idea of permitting students half an hour a day to determine their abilities for choosing their purposeful activity. In her opinion, more "obedience" and "discipline" were necessary to improve the schools. An editorial in the same paper entitled "Mush, Slush, and

Schools," labeled Kilpatrick's ideas "namby pamby" and echoed Lynch's call for more "drill and discipline." [53]

Within the field of education itself, professional meetings became a forum for debating the project method. A motion picture was made in 1921 by the Detroit Public Schools to demonstrate that handwriting could be taught by the project method, thus refuting the charge that the method ignored the "fundamentals." On the other hand, Ernest Horn and others attacked the project method at the National Society for the Study of Education in 1921, while Kilpatrick, always able to hold his own and usually able to carry the audience, presented a defense. [54] The Elementary Section of the Annual Alumni Conference at Teachers College took place on March 18-19, 1921. A symposium was held entitled "Dangers and Difficulties of the Project and How to Overcome Them." Although the title was onerous and presupposed that there were troubles with Kilpatrick's notion of the project, he chaired the session, which was more a mix of positive reaction and guarded criticisms. William Bagley and Frederick Bosner of Teachers College raised the concerns while James Hosic, also of Teachers College, provided a spirited defense.

Bagley questioned whether all learning had to be purposeful and suggested that certain subjects, such as history and literature, did not lend themselves to the project approach. He ended, though, by calling the project method "an educational achievement of the very first magnitude." Bosner raised the issue about whether all expressed interests of the child were of equal worth; he argued that calling a topic a "project" did not necessarily make it one. He echoed Bagley's apprehension over the possibility that some subject matter might be lost if children would not choose to delve into it.

Hosic, as usual, defended the project method, mentioning a number of psychological, pedagogical, and social reasons for its use. In fact, he was almost carried away by his own rhetoric, stating emphatically that the project method "could not make things any worse than they are." R. W. Hatch, a teacher at Horace Mann, may have shed the most light on the project method by cautiously listing the positive and negative features of the approach. On the constructive side he mentioned enhanced preparation, organization, discussion, and independence on the part of the student. He indicated that more "lasting information" was learned without relying on textbooks. Students seemed to work harder and for some reason not explained, they had a greater interest in current literature than before. From the negative standpoint, less formal homework seemed to be assigned or undertaken, discussion often got off track, too much time was spent on one project, and an inequality of effort

emerged as some students tended to do less while others did more.

Kilpatrick concluded the symposium with several remarks aimed at dismissing some of the misconceptions regarding the project method. He told the audience that his approach did not advocate turning children loose to make their own decisions and he stressed that the project method did not give up control by adults or the teacher's contributions to the classroom. In a remark aimed, no doubt, at Bagley's and Bosner's concerns about a loss of literature, Kilpatrick replied, "I should wish the boy to read *Ivanhoe*, but I should not be satisfied if he read it under compulsion. I should wish him to put heart and soul into his reading." [55]

No doubt the most exhaustive implementation of Kilpatrick's theoretical treatise at the time was that of Ellsworth Collings, a professor of education at the University of Oklahoma. Kilpatrick would point to Collings as the best example of opertionalizing his ideas. Collings published his findings in 1923 in a work titled *An Experiment with a Project Curriculum*.[56] He noted in his foreword that because his experiment was limited to rural schools and was a single enterprise, the results would have to be considered tentative. While Collings's work was descriptive in nature, it did make claims of gains in the areas of students' achievement and of changes in their attitudes. Diverse projects were reported and documented through a series of photographs depicting classroom activity. The projects recounted ran the gamut from a traditional woodworking shop to drama, music, and reading. Kilpatrick had written the Introduction to Collings's book and gleefully reported the positive outcomes Collings had achieved: "Enrollment and attendance rose . . . tardiness and punishment dropped. A great increase in the number [going] on to high school." [57]

In 1995, Michael Knoll, in a superb piece of investigative historical inquiry, determined that Collings's dissertation, and a subsequent book based on the dissertation, were fabrications. Knoll has shown that Collings basically used a curriculum he had written for a class in health education in 1918 as the basis for his "research" on the project method. Knoll states that this original work by Collings failed to meet any of Kilpatrick's definitions of a project. While establishing that Kilpatrick was unaware of the deception, Knoll's study of the episode does destroy the case Collings subsequently made for the effectiveness of the project method in the school setting.[58] This does not detract from Kilpatrick's own creative derivation of the project method, but it does raise the issue of efficacy of the approach. And yet, its popularity with practitioners, as demonstrated by its sales and multiple printings, again proves Kilpatrick's talent for interpreting theoretical constructs and applying them to the classroom setting.

Boyd Bode, a progressive philosopher of education from The Ohio State University, was a constant critic of Kilpatrick's ideas, especially the project method. He saw an irreconcilable contradiction in the concept of "purposing." If the child was truly doing the purposing, then Bode was willing to admit that there was a unique element in Kilpatrick's concept. But if the teacher could also suggest an activity and the student could accept it "wholeheartedly," then, in Bode's view, the process was compromised. In the end, Bode could not consider the idea of purposeful activity truly "revolutionary in tone" but rather saw it as bordering on the "commonplace." [59]

More recent critics, such as Tanner and Tanner in their *History of the School Curriculum*, have noted several problematic areas in Kilpatrick's project method. One specific concern was, again, the issue of child-centeredness and Kilpatrick's definition of the term "project":

> For all intents and purposes, Kilpatrick was saying that the child must make his own curriculum. Kilpatrick's definition of project is so general that one would be hard pressed to find anything done in the classroom that did not qualify as a project as long as it was done "wholeheartedly." "Child purposing" appears to be nothing more or less than child interest under a different label. [60]

Tanner and Tanner also noted differences between Dewey and Kilpatrick arising out of "The Project Method." These were the lack of a social theory in the project method, the use of Thorndike's behavioristic psychology in the project method, and, finally, the concern for a balance between subject matter and the interests of the child. In this last category, Tanner and Tanner (quoting Cremin) saw Kilpatrick "shift the balance of Dewey's pedagogical paradigm to the child," a move that they claim Dewey had rejected in both *The Child and the Curriculum* and *Experience and Education*. Tanner and Tanner, reviewing the criticisms which emerged during the "dangers and difficulties" symposium held at Teachers College during 1921, mentioned a narrow concept of the curriculum, an emphasis on manipulative activities in lieu of higher intellectual inquiries, and a failure to develop the power of thinking. Therefore, according to Tanner and Tanner, the "biggest danger to Kilpatrick's project method was its associations with child-centeredness." The legacy of the project method, they concluded, was to be found mainly within industrial arts, science, and vocational subjects such as agriculture. [61]

Another historian, Herbert Kliebard, has also been critical of Kilpatrick's project method. In *The Struggle for the American Curriculum, 1893-1958*, Kliebard expressed mild astonishment at the reaction to "The Project Method." Kliebard did call its publication "the single most dramatic event in the evolution of the movement to reform the curriculum through projects," but then pondered "exactly why that particular article aroused such an explosion of interest." Kliebard implied that Kilpatrick's emergence as a leading voice in education may have been related more to style than to substance, depicting Kilpatrick, albeit the brightest star in Dean Russell's galaxy of faculty, as a man in his late forties having difficulty being promoted to full professor. (Kilpatrick had actually advanced from being a doctoral student to full professor in seven years.) Kliebard described Kilpatrick's style as "felicitous," suggesting that his way with words contributed greatly to his popularity. He further charged that Kilpatrick's ideas were rough extrapolations of concepts Dewey had been sounding for at least twenty years. As for the project idea itself, Kliebard viewed Kilpatrick as taking a successful, though restricted, area of the curriculum — vocational agriculture — and attempting to reconstruct the entire curriculum around it. And for the four types of projects discussed in the article, Kliebard declared that Kilpatrick "managed to obfuscate some of the issues," suggesting that while he discussed intellectual and knowledge-related projects, his sympathy obviously lay with physical activities.[62]

Another historian, Joel Spring, in his analysis of "The Project Method," placed much less emphasis on its pedagogical implications. For Spring, the purposeful act was directed toward a socially useful end, with the projects growing out of social situations. According to Spring, the key to Kilpatrick's article was that "the purposeful act was the basic unit of the worthy life and democracy."[63]

There were indeed problems with many of the concepts in Kilpatrick's "project" as presented in 1918. And there is little doubt that he had to define, refine, and explain the implications of his manuscript for the next thirty years. Kilpatrick did become a bit more specific over time, but not much. Yet Spring may have struck upon the essence of what Kilpatrick was striving for at the time "The Project Method" was written. While not by any means unschooled in learning theory, Kilpatrick clearly directed his emphasis toward what might be termed the "larger picture," especially toward a more democratic approach to education. The historical context of Kilpatrick's references to democracy should not be lost. As he was writing "The Project Method," he had just completed reading and making suggestions for Dewey's

Democracy and Education. For Kilpatrick, schools in the second decade of the twentieth century were not free places where students could pursue their interests and inquiries. Neither did he find tangential connections between classrooms and the problems and issues of life in the real world. What it meant for the schools to become examples of democracy; what the precise role of subject matter was; and what the implications were for the curriculum — these were all questions that demanded a response.

A perspective that had been lost in discussing "The Project Method," was the broader political and social milieu in which it was written — the era of Wilsonian democracy. This was a time of international conflict on a grand scale, and of progressive legislation on a variety of social issues. Woodrow Wilson was calling for a new world order in both politics and morality, and, as has been seen, Kilpatrick was an admirer of the president's rhetoric and idealism. This idealism pervaded public discussion, with liberal beliefs in the reasonableness of man, the inevitability of progress, and the power of public opinion. As Wilson was fashioning a new world order in the arena of international peace, so too, on a more modest scale, were Kilpatrick and his followers attempting to change the world of the classroom for students.

In an article on the genesis of projects and the project method, Michael Knoll has demonstrated that its origins were as early as the seventeenth and eighteenth centuries in Europe. Therefore, according to Knoll, "the project method should not be considered a child of the progressive education movement" in the United States. He has also shown that the twentieth century models of the project method have been in use in the nineteenth century, specifically in agriculture, and that the work of Kilpatrick and other progressive educators in the early twentieth century included basically broader definitions of earlier constructs, emphasizing the concept of purposeful activity. Knoll has written:

> At the beginning of the twentieth century, a movement arose among American progressive educators that attempted with great energy to replace the traditional narrow definition of the project with a new, broad one, and instead of the constructive activity to make 'purposeful' action the crucial feature of the project method. This new definition was not able to gain the ascendancy in the United States, but in other countries it was taken over as an innovation and a truly democratic achievement, with the

paradoxical result that in Europe today the broad "American" concept predominates, while in America the narrow "European" approach plays the leading part.[64]

"The Project Method" was extremely popular during the heyday of the progressive education movement, and did, to a large extent, make Kilpatrick a revered name in educational circles; but its legacy is mixed. And yet, more than sixty years after its publication, educators still considered it one of the ten documents that had most influenced the curriculum.[65] The problem with examining "The Project Method" in isolation, or as a strictly pedagogical tool, is that one loses sight of its larger impact. Whether it was unique or separate from other ideas about projects and activity may be less important than its influence on the curriculum for the rest of the century. It focused the debate squarely on the child and the role of subject matter. Where others, including Kilpatrick, took the debate is the next issue to be pursued in these pages. There can be little doubt that the suggestions contained in Kilpatrick's eighteen-page essay did "lead on," to borrow his phrase, to further educational ideas. As he would say to a newspaper reporter several years later, "The project method is not a device but an ideal to be developed in education."[66] Almost fifteen years after its publication, Kilpatrick had this to say about his much touted work:

> Many expected more of my "project method" ideas than has turned out. In this I think they are twice mistaken, first in expecting a panacea, a get-rich-quick scheme, second, in not seeing that it still underlies best modern practice and is worthy of further study.[67]

8

THE TWENTIES: TRAVELS, TEACHING, AND TRANSITIONS

One young woman said she did not know me by sight when
I came in so she asked her neighbor who it was. 'It is
Kilpatrick and now we'll have something good.'"
                                    Diary of William Heard Kilpatrick[1]

Whistles and bells were heard on the campus of Teachers College at eleven o'clock on the morning of November 11, 1918, as word came that Germany had signed the armistice: the Great War was finally over. Dean Russell canceled afternoon classes, calling a half holiday, and a number of students went downtown for the celebration. Others gathered on the steps of the college to sing patriotic songs and heard the dean call for magnanimity toward the defeated enemy. When Russell had finished, the popular Professor Kilpatrick was beckoned by the crowd to address them. He believed that the day was a turning point in world history. While the war had begun as a conflict between nations, he said, it had ended as "a war against war in order to enthrone a new type of universal justice." Speaking of Woodrow Wilson, Kilpatrick added that the "penetrating wisdom of our great leader" had allowed this transformation of purpose to occur. Kilpatrick believed that what the soldiers had won on the field of battle was now up to men and women alike to make permanent. "We have to bring a new democracy and this depends on us as teachers," he concluded. He later wrote in his diary, "I thought I caught the crowd."[2] On January 1, 1919, Kilpatrick drank to the victory with what he called his "first and last" glass of champagne.

Six months before the hostilities ended, Kilpatrick had rethought his earlier views on the war and had arrived at very different conclusions. Rather than wishing for a redistribution of national possessions, he now saw postwar developments as necessarily including a League of Nations to abolish war, a repudiation of selfish imperialism, and a renunciation of the "domestic exploitation of man by man." To this end, Kilpatrick felt compelled to cast his

vote for officials, especially state senators, who would stand with Wilson on these issues. In a deviation from his usually peace-oriented thoughts, he asserted that "we must whip Germany" so as to discredit it among the nations of the world.[3] But as 1918 came to a close he was unsure whether the peace could actually be won. He was especially upset with Theodore Roosevelt's wing of the Republican Party. "[They] have sold themselves, soul and body, to the cause of evil. The Republican newspapers are incredibly and viciously reactionary. They are denying every spark of ethical idealism and unselfishness." He considered this opposition to Wilson the "most disappointing factor in public life in my generation." "The future looks black," he concluded; "I almost despair." And yet he remained hopeful that Wilson might succeed with the League of Nations, thereby building a structure for future world peace. "The world is getting smaller, which means that wars must in time cease," he wrote.[4]

When Wilson fell ill in 1919, on his western tour designed to pressure the Senate to accept the League by garnering public support, Kilpatrick called the president the "one indispensable man right now." He also thought that within five years the "process of canonization" would begin for Wilson. "If the League succeeds," wrote Kilpatrick, "it will be a permanent monument to his memory." When the Republican reservationists came forward to oppose Wilson and the League in late 1919, Kilpatrick feared for the worst. "I am sick at heart, mortified and ashamed," he wrote. When the League was finally defeated in the Senate, he found himself "too sick at heart to analyze the situation." While willing to support some reservations to the treaty, he considered this lack of courage on the part of the Republicans "criminal."[5]

Although not a pacifist, Kilpatrick was repelled by war. As the troops came home in great numbers during the spring of 1919, Kilpatrick took the bus down to Fifth Avenue to greet them. One soldier, a former student just back from France, told the Kilpatricks one evening at dinner of battle atrocities, such as an American regiment that prided itself in taking no prisoners. These stories disturbed Kilpatrick and strengthened his resolve against war. Yet he extended his financial support of the war.[6] He and Rita had purchased a large number of Liberty Bonds — almost $8,000 worth by the end of the war — and while he was never in financial difficulty, the investments left him short of cash on occasion. The postwar period found him attending a League of Nations Discussion Group and even writing to Georgia Senator Hoke Smith, urging him to support the League.

Not only did Kilpatrick have concerns regarding the nation's plight in

foreign affairs, but he also began to detect the coming xenophobia that would characterize the decade of the twenties:

> Well meaning people are very apprehensive of "Bolshevistic" uprisings. The 100% Americanism crowd are taking advantage of the situation to inculcate what is in fact an "America über Alles" doctrine. There is now a rather violent recrudescence of the outworn notions of suppressing thought and speech. The general position now would have ten or twenty years ago seemed impossible.[7]

Beginning in the fall of 1919, Kilpatrick began to spend time at the newly opened Teachers College Country Club in Ossining, New York. It provided him with the opportunity to resume his golf game and sunbathe. In the evenings he read and played pool. His personal reading, outside books on education, in the years following the war included fiction by Jane Austen and Sinclair Lewis, plays by George Bernard Shaw, the works of Bertrand Russell (whom he always read, but with whom he rarely agreed), Walter Lippman's *Public Opinion*, and Henry Adams's *The Degradation of the Democratic Dogma*. He called this last book "heavy and stupid" and added that if it had been written by him, rather than Adams, it would have had no sale.[8] He also read Albert Beveridge's *Life of John Marshall*; Lytton Strachey's *Queen Victoria*; and southern studies, which always interested him, such as William E. Dodd's *The Cotton Kingdom* and Alexander Arnett's *Rise of Populism in Georgia*. Of course, he read everything penned by John Dewey and in 1925 Abraham Flexner's study, *Medical Education*. He also began to read novels and works of nonfiction with an international flavor, including *A Passage to India* by E. M. Forster and *With Lawrence in Arabia* by Lowell Thomas.

Plays, films, and light reading did interest Kilpatrick, but he reflected on the popular arts after viewing a Charlie Chaplin film:

> I see myself losing interest in any entertainment which remains mere entertainment. I seem to care less for novels, unless they open up vistas of thought or supply food for further thinking. So with the stage, particularly cinema. I will admit that I laughed almost immoderately at Chaplin trying, while seasick, to set up a steamer chair. I have myself encountered such a chair — tho I solved the puzzle.[9]

As for newspapers, he had become a "*Times* man" after the war, but he also took the *Evening Sun* in order to see, as he said, "the worst opposition to the policies I approve." He read the *New York Post* on Saturday evenings and subscribed to *The New Republic*, the *Manchester Guardian*, and the *Atlantic Monthly*. His professional reading included subscriptions to *School and Society* and the *American Journal of Sociology*.

As can be seen from his diverse reading, Kilpatrick's interests clearly went beyond schools and education. Kilpatrick's lectures also began to shift from themes surrounding the project method to broader topics such as citizenship, moral education, and education as growth; one talk was entitled "The Social Mind in the Making." Other lecture titles were "College Teaching," "How to Train People to Think," "Education for Character," "How Shall We Conceive Subject Matter?" and "Intrinsic versus Extrinsic Subject Matter."[10]

Kilpatrick became involved more and more in a variety of community and intellectual organizations. New York City provided him with unlimited opportunities to broaden his interests and extend his experiences beyond the strictly educational arena. One afternoon he attended a rather liberal discussion group at the Rand School on the topic of what constituted the good life. "Wine, women, and song," came one response. One young lady advocated "free love" rather than marriage. "On the whole," commented the ever open-minded Kilpatrick, "they were quite like any other group, only more earnest."[11] He also lectured to a labor group at the New School for Social Research and was troubled by the experience. "It was only a small group; and I must say it, a lousy looking lot. I have to keep a firm hold of my democracy not to revolt." Special schools for the laboring class bothered him. "Good public schools with decent laws and treatment would obviate the necessity of any special provision for the labor people," he later stated.[12]

Kilpatrick's reputation had indeed grown, and at this time in his life he probably traveled and lectured more than at any other period before his retirement. His thoughts on his teaching were ambivalent, although he felt that his classroom techniques were becoming more original. They still consisted, in his opinion, of translating and applying more systematically what he termed the "James-Dewey position." He realized, though, that it was through the printed word, not from the podium, that he could make his greatest contribution. "I think . . . I have accumulated a goodly stock of thoughts worthy of presenting to the education public, if only I could write more easily and more successfully."[13]

In February of 1920 Kilpatrick took his first sabbatical leave from

Teachers College. He decided to travel and lecture in England, accompanied by his wife. Sailing from New York, they arrived in Plymouth on February 15 and took lodgings in London at 56 Russell Square. He had no research agenda other than visiting schools and universities and lecturing whenever possible. His work at the British Museum was connected more with his avocation, genealogy, than with education. Kilpatrick did compare notes with English professors on numerous occasions, but he considered the British approach to education void of any scientific method and, therefore, inferior to the American system. He seems to have had a good time with these professors, even "jolly," as he put it once, although he drank only water when visiting pubs.[14]

Kilpatrick did find the English approach to the study of education different from that taken in the United States. "Our method work seems to be more general than theirs," he wrote, "i.e. based on the grouping of principles rather than the teaching of specific subject devices." He found a kindred spirit on occasion, as in the Burmondsey Central School, where the headmaster was a "democrat," according to Kilpatrick. But he still had reservations. The "custom here subdues the individual or at any rate the boy to the system." He reported hearing the word "sir" more times in one day than he would have heard it in a year in America. He was also troubled by the English concept of "instinctive obedience," or what he termed "habituation to subordination." Such authoritative approaches were anathema to Kilpatrick. The predominance of the classics in British education also concerned him — although it was actually the lack of experimentation in the curriculum, rather than the classics themselves, that he found troubling. One day in an economics class he was called upon to discuss labor, politics, and the economy. He held forth for an hour and then answered questions from the class, composed mostly of working-class men. There was a visit to a meeting of the Fabian Society, where Kilpatrick heard a lecture by George Bernard Shaw and was duly impressed by the great man.[15]

There were also visits to schools at Oxford, where he observed several of the colleges and met with a number of masters. In addition, he spoke to the "boys" and found them interested in what he said, even moved. "I believe that my philosophy appeals to youth and its stirring." Later in May, he lectured to a group of teachers at the University of Manchester on "The Demands of the Times Upon Our Schools" and, according to his account, "gripped my hearers and they responded appreciatively throughout." During another talk his cultivated Georgian accent prompted one man to question whether Kilpatrick

was really an American. The lack of a nasal tone caused this man to comment, "You have the best voice and speech of all the Americans I have met."[16]

There was a side trip to Paris in mid-April of 1920 and a tour of the scarred and devastated battlefields of the Great War. Kilpatrick and Rita visited Belleau Wood, Chateau-Thiérry, and Verdun, in addition to Reims, where they saw the great cathedral — roofless, but still standing. "An awful sight," recorded Kilpatrick. He visited several cemeteries, including Romagne, where 28,000 Americans were buried. At one stop he viewed a "cave-in" where an unknown number of soldiers had been entombed — with their rifles still projecting above the surface. "Nothing on the trip has touched me so much," he inscribed in his diary. Although many of the cemeteries were incomplete, already row upon row of white crosses stood in stark relief. Kilpatrick reflected "It is a great, tho sad sight, to see these graves. I hope they will continue to lie there forever to cement the nation; for war must be abolished."[17]

Kilpatrick and his wife returned to England for the month of May, where Kilpatrick purchased a pair of knee breeches for their trip to Scotland and the Highlands. Setting aside education for one evening in Scotland, he gave a talk on American politics, discussing the presidency and the role of the Senate, describing the historical differences between the two institutions.[18] The Kilpatricks visited Edinburgh and Dundee in addition to a number of the more famous Scottish lochs. While in the Highlands, he received word that James Cox, the governor of Ohio, and Warren G. Harding, that state's junior senator, had been nominated by the Democratic and Republican parties, respectively. Kilpatrick found both candidates mediocre but considered the Democratic platform the more honest of the two. He pined for Wilson and thought the vice presidential nominees, Franklin D. Roosevelt and Calvin Coolidge, might be superior candidates to those heading the tickets. And yet Kilpatrick's main passion that summer in Scotland was not politics but golf. At the Glasgow Golf Club, he observed the Kilpatrick Hills in the distance. Engaging a professional golfer, he took hour-long lessons and purchased a new pair of golf shoes, which "almost broke him before he broke them." His favorite Scottish course, as might be expected, was Saint Andrews.[19]

The Scottish leg of the trip was not all lochs and links: Kilpatrick gave five lectures at the Dundee Training College for teachers. Tickets went for sixpence a session, or two shillings for all five lectures.[20] Kilpatrick also observed several physical education classes. He was mildly shocked that the female gymnasts did not wear the traditional bloomers, but tights with skirts above the knee. "I wonder what Queen Victoria would have done if she had been here," he

pondered. He also delivered a series of lectures to the training schools of Scotland but was uncertain as to what they accomplished. He espoused the idea that American schools, and Teachers College in particular, were attempting to place teaching on a more scientific basis. In addition, he urged that a prototype institution for the professional preparation of school administrators, along the lines of Teachers College, be established at the University of Edinburgh. Upon leaving Scotland, he remarked that he and his wife enjoyed the Scots more than the English.[21]

In late August there was a hurried series of day trips to the cities of Canterbury, Bath, Bristol, and Birmingham, the last of which he likened to Cleveland or Detroit. On September 8, Kilpatrick and his wife departed for New York on the *Olympic*. En route, he argued "a little on Dewey with Dr. Hough, president of Northwestern University."[22] The day the ship docked in New York City, September 15, he printed in large letters in his diary, "GLAD TO BE HOME."

As noted earlier, the sabbatical trip had not been scholarly in nature. After two and a half decades of teaching and administration, a "tour," rather than a traditional sabbatical had been in order. But now Kilpatrick found himself unready to reenter the world of the classroom. As the semester began, he caught himself being "too dogmatic" and blamed the trip for having gotten him out of the "classroom attitude." Even his lecturing, always a strong point for him, had gone astray. After speaking to a group of English teachers on the project method, he felt ashamed that he had gone over his time limit. "I am resolved to take myself seriously in hand on this matter," he vowed. He pledged also to outline his talks and not to accept every invitation that came along.[23] But the requests for speaking engagements continued to increase.

To be visited by Kilpatrick and to hear him lecture was a memorable event. "So polished, so cultured, and so complete," raved the *New Rochelle* (New York) *Daily Star* after one speech.[24] And a journal in Boston wrote that "Professor Kilpatrick is always entertainingly impressive and impressively inspiring."[25] Paradoxically, as his oratory continued to be more powerful, he became more and more aware of its negative potential: "I am becoming too much given to trying to carry the populace and so use oratory rather than science or careful reasoning. There is a danger." In 1925 he gave his first radio talk on a topic now lost to us. It lasted twenty minutes, and he gauged it to within fifteen seconds of the allotted time. His wife, his secretary, and his graduate assistant listened to him on a neighbor's radio set.[26]

The 1920 presidential campaign proved boring for him, and he described

it as a low water mark of political thinking.[27]   When Harding was elected, Kilpatrick wrote that he had expected a Republican victory, but was "sorry this man was no better. I am ashamed for America of the low ebb to which our thinking and moral attitude are reduced. Surely politics has scraped the bottom now."[28] Kilpatrick had voted for Cox but was more concerned over the fate of the League of Nations and the treatment of Wilson. He also noted that women were voting for the first time and thought he already detected what he called "a higher tone." He also supported the other social experiment of the twenties — prohibition. But with the attitude of "a plague on both your houses," he found labor "blind" and capital "selfish." Society, in general, he believed, was in a "moral slump." In 1924 he voted for John W. Davis and the Democratic ticket on the national and state levels, while voting Republican for local officials. His wife voted the typical Southern ticket: straight Democratic. Coolidge's election was "a bad sign for real democracy," according to Kilpatrick a triumph for vested interests. Senator Lodge's death that same year, though, was "a good thing for the world," Kilpatrick thought: he believed that Lodge had done more harm than any other man in modern times. In late 1924 he attended a meeting of the Foreign Policy Association to hear James Shotwell and Norman Angell on the Protocol of Geneva to outlaw war. John Dewey, also present, was questioned, and Kilpatrick was surprised that Dewey was so strong a pacifist, seeing no place for force to combat force. "He answered poorly," thought Kilpatrick.[29]

Resuming his golf game during weekend outings at the Teachers College Country Club in Ossining, Kilpatrick thought his lessons at Saint Andrews had enhanced his game. He could drive much better and said that he enjoyed competition. Ever the educator, after one exceptional drive he told his partners, "I thought that one through." But he took his golf game very seriously. He was angered during one outing when his play was interrupted by another party's inquiry as to whether he had a ticket. He replied, with "some heat, but still exactness of tone," that he had a ticket and would show it to anyone who had a right to ask to see it. But if they didn't have such a right, then they "had better mind their own business." They did.[30]

Realizing that publication was the one sure route to fame, in addition to giving permanence to his ideas, he published nine articles during 1921 — his greatest output up to that point — and completed his syllabus for the course in philosophy of education. He also began work on what became his *Source Book in the Philosophy of Education* (it would sell almost 2,400 copies in the first six months of 1924) and on its successor, *Foundations of Method* (whose

preliminary title was "Talks on Teaching"). The former was a compilation of brief quotations and lengthy segments of narrative that he used in connection with his philosophy of education course. The latter would become a "dialogue" on a variety of issues in education. At the same time, he cut back on his lecture itinerary. He gave up a $600 fee offered for speaking in California, feeling that he should begin to reduce his hectic pace. At one point he also expressed his wish not to speak to small groups, or even crowds, that were not of strategic importance. But lecturing was an excellent source of income. He received as much as $1,000 for a series of lectures in the early 1920s.[31]

While he took on fewer speaking engagements at individual institutions, he did attend with regularity a number of professional conferences and conventions. During the war he had been asked by Clarence Kingsley to chair the mathematics committee for the Commission on Reorganization of Secondary Education of the National Education Association. After some soul-searching, he accepted the assignment. In light of his own unconventional views on the subject of mathematics, he wondered if the committee would ever reach consensus. His unorthodox opinions included the belief that geometry should be taught only in large high schools, and then only as an intellectual luxury. He did not think that either algebra or geometry should be required of students who were not going on to college, and that even students preparing for technical careers could survive quite nicely if the algebra curriculum was "cut horizontally by one third." Traditional college-bound students should also take a cultural or informational course in mathematics. He also contributed to the general philosophic statements of the committee's report, which became known as the "Cardinal Principles of Education." One point in particular in the Cardinal Principles — "worthy use of leisure" — was suggested by Kilpatrick and remained in the final draft.[32]

In February of 1925 Kilpatrick spoke to 3,000 people at a conference in Cincinnati, during which he was interrupted by applause several times and greeted most cordially at the beginning and end. "Clearly I have many friends in the audience," he wrote. In June of 1925, he took a summer trip west. He gave the commencement address at Northern Colorado Teachers College in Greeley, followed by a workshop in Estes Park. The gathering in Estes Park included several evangelicals, and some of Kilpatrick's ideas were met with polite skepticism. Some of his hearers did admit, though, that they had learned from him, especially how to facilitate a group and reach consensus. Kilpatrick also visited Pike's Peak, the Garden of the Gods, and the Royal Gorge before leaving Colorado. The next stop was Salt Lake City, the capital of Mormonism.

There he met the historian Frederick Jackson Turner, who was also visiting the city. Kilpatrick took great interest in the Mormon religion and even read the *Book of Mormon.* He found the Mormons' practice of plural marriages and their economic, political, and social hold on the state of Utah of great interest. Next he went on to Yellowstone, where he stayed at the Old Faithful Inn and saw the eruption of the famous geyser: "Wonderful, beautiful, surpassing all that we had expected." He also sighted what he oxymoronically termed a "very tame wild bear."[33]

There has been much speculation on Kilpatrick's motives during his career. Were his professional actions for personal aggrandizement, as some have suggested, or did he have an ideological ax to grind? In a quite clear statement of his aims in education given at this time, Kilpatrick wrote:

> I am now pretty well determined to keep on the attack on
> conventional schooling. I believe it is wrong. That I have most
> of the educators against me makes it a more serious matter.
> The administrators all wish definite aims because it increases
> ease of control. The measurers (both theoretical and practical)
> stress definite formal aims, because they can measure them.
> The teachers of children are nearly all with me. The teachers
> of subjects are apprehensive lest they may lose out.[34]

The emerging issue of testing and measurement was disturbing to Kilpatrick. As can be seen from the paragraph above, the "measurers," as he called those involved in assessment and evaluation, placed severe restrictions on both students and teachers. An increasing emphasis on standardized tests drove the curriculum. As for intelligence tests, he did not believe that they "measure native intelligence, but a compound of this and learning." Years later he would tell a colleague that because of the powerful and stifling grip that testing held over the schools, "Thorndike was the worst thing that ever happened to education." He also told a student that the way the New York Regents examinations dominated the curriculum forced students to cram for the tests for one month each school year before students and teachers could spend the remaining eight months on activities and curriculum that they viewed as worthwhile.[35]

The term "million dollar professor" — referring to the tuition his courses generated — would not be attached to Kilpatrick until after his retirement, but it was during the 1920s that he reached the pinnacle of his teaching, a summit from which he never fell. In 1914 he was ranked as one of the top three teachers

at Teachers College, and by 1919 he was considered its foremost teacher. By 1916 he realized that the large classes he was drawing for Teachers College were making a significant contribution to the coffers of the university. Still a competent mathematician, he figured that at $12 a course, during one summer session he was amassing for the institution ten times his salary of $550. He continued to have doubts, though, about his career and whether teaching, in and of itself, would be enough. The analysis almost approached self-doubt: "To many I am deemed a mere teacher — a good one to be sure, but still a mere hander-on of the thoughts of others."[36]

While Kilpatrick was a magnificent platform speaker, he did not fashion his teaching around oratory or lecturing. In fact, he devised an approach unique for the time. As early as 1911 he vowed not to "lecture much because I have determined not to give out simply." At times, he was positively reticent about giving any opinions, lest he be doing the thinking for the class. But of course he frequently let the class in on his thoughts. He devised a method in which a series of discussion questions were distributed to the class in advance. Students were divided into groups in order to study together in advance, and were then called upon, during class, by both question and group. The approach "gets more work from the class, I am satisfied. They all seem to think so and it practically abolishes the old nervous strain." In what was no doubt a reference to his own project method, he said that this technique generated both "interest and activity."[37] The discussion approach was not without controversy. Many students took Kilpatrick's classes because they wanted to hear his views and opinions, not those of their classmates, but after the term got under way these concerns diminished, and the students very much enjoyed the free exchange of ideas and opinions.[38]

Kilpatrick was an exacting taskmaster in the classroom. "I forced [students] to think by refusing to accept careless thinking and effected this by questioning and by pitting them against each other." Philosophically, he was in the child-centered camp, but in his own classes he could be a strict disciplinarian. He did not hesitate to warn habitual offenders about attendance and punctuality, cautioning them that their lapses would be dealt with.[39] Although opposed to coercion, he did at times use his presence and authority to bring not-so-subtle pressure to bear on students. An example is his handling of students who came to his classes unprepared:

> I hate very much to have a student answer "unprepared," and
> for the psychological effect I don't allow many to pass

unnoticed. I seldom say anything, but I frequently call attention by standing perfectly still so as to draw the notice of all to the delinquency. I must "break" this class in.[40]

Students often paid tribute to Kilpatrick's teaching, and the accolades took various forms, often a book or a small gift with an inscription. One such memento was inscribed with the words: "We the members of the Dr. Kilpatrick's classes of 1911 and 1912 wish to express to him our appreciation of the loftiness of his character and ideals, the charm of his personality, and the greatness of his work as scholar and teacher." Applause and even standing ovations were not uncommon, especially at the close of a term. Usually a student would rise, pay homage to Kilpatrick, and then lead the class in a round of applause. At times the compliments were personal. One young man sought Kilpatrick out after a class and said that as a teacher of long service himself, he found the lecture he had just heard "nearly ideal." A young woman told Kilpatrick that his class was the "most puzzling and most fascinating she ever had."[41] Another student wrote on an evaluation sheet, "I couldn't make suggestions about improving this course any more than I could make suggestions to Lindbergh about how to fly. I have enjoyed it immensely and am thankful for it." Even his philosophical rival, William Bagley, said in a public meeting, "Why, look at Kilpatrick and how his teachings have changed instruction all over America in the last fifteen years."[42]

The sizes of his classes were at times mind-boggling. Chairs were packed into classrooms, with students in the back often unable to hear during the summer owing to street noise coming through the open windows. In addition to the paying students, there were always visitors, especially when Kilpatrick lectured on Dewey.[43] Eventually, even large classrooms would not contain his courses, and he was forced to move them to the Horace Mann Auditorium. "I do all I can to hold the numbers down so that I won't have to change rooms. I dislike the H. M. Auditorium. One of the students tells me quite seriously that I am the biggest man of the summer school." But the large classes put pressure on him and on one occasion brought forth a rare display of the Kilpatrick temper. The inability of the secretaries to reproduce copies of his question sheets caused him to deliver an ultimatum to the staff, followed by a trip to the dean. After a good bit of consultation and overtime, his materials were prepared as he desired.[44]

The classes continued to increase, with his sections on philosophy of education growing from 250 students in 1921 to 400 by 1925. His other major course, "Foundations of Method," expanded from 335 in 1921 to 450 in 1925

though he also taught smaller sections of advanced courses in philosophy.[45] Eventually, as the numbers exceeded 600 per class, even Horace Mann Auditorium would no longer hold the immense throngs. He would often have to move his class to the Macmillan Theater on the Columbia campus. But even with Kilpatrick's great skill as a pedagogue, the vast numbers made teaching almost impossible; some students could not see the blackboard and some could be heard only by shouting their comments from the back of the hall or the balcony.

In the mid-1920s Kilpatrick added a teaching assistant to his course. R. Bruce Raup became an instructor, an assistant professor, and finally a full-time professor and close colleague of Kilpatrick's at Teachers College. And both Raup and Dewey taught Kilpatrick's classes during his absence. As to whether he graded all the papers in those large classes, the answer is probably no. However, one former student indicated that he did grade one of her papers and initialed it WHK.[46]

In his book *Education for a Changing Civilization* Kilpatrick addressed the centrality of teaching:

> The sooner we proclaim that teaching is not a factory-hand job but a profession, the better. Too much is at stake. Advancing civilization too much depends on education to allow the school to continue as a trade with mere rule of thumb procedures. Teaching must be a higher art based on freedom in both science and philosophy. Only to such can society trust its own perpetuation.[47]

Kilpatrick's teaching was important to him, regardless of his frequent thought that he was not an originator but an interpreter. A serious man in all he undertook, he often engaged in reflective self-evaluation in order to improve his teaching. "Take stock of myself as to my teaching work," he wrote. "First I raise a number of questions as to how well I am doing and wherein I might improve; second, I point out certain specific improvements to be made; then I make a list of certain specific problems about which I may well think." This introspection regarding teaching continued to the end of his career. But the estimation of his colleagues was another matter. Several evidently went to the dean to complain that Kilpatrick was requiring too much from his classes, especially too much reading. The criticism "dazed" him, and after a meeting with the dean he blamed himself and told his classes he had no intention of encroaching on other professors' time. He closed his apology by suggesting how his students might

read to "better advantage."[48]

But Kilpatrick's classes continued to grow, and his fame extended throughout Teachers College and the entire nation. Stories about "Kilpatrick of Teachers College" grew, reaching what some might consider legendary proportions. In the 1930s a newspaper in North Carolina repeated the story about one fellow who went to New York City to attend Teachers College. "Well," said a registrar when he arrived on the campus, "you will want to take a course from Kilpatrick." "And who is Kilpatrick?" asked the student. "Why, he is the man that looks like God and talks like God," the official replied solemnly.[49]

As his daughter entered college, the Kilpatricks' domestic life still remained bumpy at times. Kilpatrick's younger brother, Howard, had visited the Morningside Drive apartment once a month since moving to New York. Soon though, his visits occurred with less frequency — neither Kilpatrick nor his wife seemed to get on with him in a "congenial" manner. As for his daughter, Kilpatrick very much wanted to retain a close relationship with her, yet at times he felt it slipping away. Margaret Louise Kilpatrick did seem to be a free spirit. While a student at Teachers College, she threw a cat into a swimming pool, a prank which cost her father $25 — the fee for replacing the water. While not condoning his daughter's action, calling it childish, he did think that the officials had overreacted and called them "squeamish old maids." (Since Kilpatrick does not reveal the fate of the feline, it must be assumed that its nine lives had not been exceeded before it was immersed or that Margaret rescued the animal from a watery grave.) On another occasion, Margaret hosted a tea for her sorority in the Kilpatricks' apartment. When Kilpatrick had withdrawn, half of the young women began smoking. Although Margaret was not among them, Kilpatrick still did not approve. He was gratified that his daughter thought less of those who took part in this questionable activity.[50]

Kilpatrick admitted in his diary that he often responded with much "sympathy" toward Margaret because he wanted to maintain his relationship with her "at any cost." Margaret did admire and look up to her father and would do so for the rest of her life, while he felt that he had to be "mother, father, older sister, and brother" to her. She reciprocated and, according to Kilpatrick, shared with him "a good deal that many girls would not tell their fathers." This included discussions of religion and the nature of God. During one such discussion she told her father, who had not attended church for years, that she said her prayers every night. While he may not have agreed with her on all points, he was proud of his daughter and in a moment of parental self-congratulation he wrote, "I can see reflected in my daughter both my own psychology

and my training, it is a pleasure to see her developing into a responsible character."[51]

Margaret studied art at Teachers College and enrolled in the teacher training course. She student taught in art during the fall of 1921 in first-grade classes at Horace Mann School. Her IQ was assessed at 107 in 1920, but Kilpatrick disagreed, thinking the heavy emphasis on mathematics might have hurt her score. He judged her to be at least 120, and in 1930 he upped the number to "fully 130." Yet he had little faith in such tests, especially in the higher reaches of the IQ scales. Kilpatrick was deeply interested in Margaret's future, although in a traditional way. He had hoped she would teach for a while, then enter commercial art, and eventually get married. After dinner one evening, Margaret told her father that she found teaching "tiring." "She is, poor child, troubled about her future," wrote Kilpatrick. "Girls have nowadays even more uncertainty than boys."

Taken ill with appendicitis in the spring of 1922, Margaret underwent an emergency appendectomy. She convalesced in White Plains, Georgia with her grandmother and aunt and took her degree, a B.S. in education, *in absentia*. Her father, against his better judgment, allowed her to buy a pistol to protect herself in the rural South. Later that year she wrote to her father that she wished to undertake commercial artwork for the Howard Theater in Atlanta. Kilpatrick's old friend, Dr. Ashby Jones, warned him that public dancing took place at the Howard. Margaret soon received a letter from her father strongly suggesting that she not take the job, if dancing was indeed involved. Even this mild recommendation bothered him. "I believe I am right," he wrote, "but each generation I know wishes to curb the next."[52] For whatever reasons, Margaret chose not to take the position in Atlanta.

In late 1922 and early 1923 Margaret came close to becoming engaged to a man from White Plains, but these plans came to naught. Back in New York in the summer of 1923, Margaret met and invited to dinner one evening Theodore (Ted) Baumeister. Kilpatrick was favorably impressed. Baumeister was a rising young professor of engineering at Columbia. By November there was talk of an engagement, and Kilpatrick approved. On February 3, 1924, Baumeister formally asked for Margaret's hand in marriage, and her father "freely gave consent." He told Margaret that he approved of her choice, and then father and daughter had a long talk. They decided that no announcement would be made until Ted had received a permanent appointment at Columbia.[53]

The wedding was held on Friday, January 23, 1925, in the Kilpatricks' Morningside Drive apartment. The president of Union Theological Seminary,

Arthur C. McGiffert, presided. Margaret's dress, made of white velvet, had been sewn by her own hands. A wedding breakfast was served in the apartment, after which the bride and groom left for their own apartment. "I do not feel sad," Kilpatrick wrote. "I think it is best, and I feel as sure of him as I could ever expect to feel of any young man."

Two other important women in his life were, of course, his sister Helen and his mother. He once wrote of Helen: "Of all people I know there is none who surpasses her in my estimation as a dependable character and counselor. She is more capable in practical affairs of life, and lovable in all human relationships. She is the kind of woman I should most choose to be mother of my children, were I choosing freely."[54]

It was therefore jarring news when word came in 1920 that Helen had been diagnosed with breast cancer. The two brothers, Heard and Howard, immediately brought her to New York City for treatment. In the short term, the surgery and treatment were successful, and Heard and Howard covered all the bills.

Although his mother's health had been failing during 1924, it was still a shock and a blow when word came that she had died, on March 26, 1925. Kilpatrick left immediately for White Plains. Howard, Heard, Sarah, Helen, and their half brother, Jimmy, were all together for the first time since the family had attended the Chicago World's Fair in 1893. Writing in his diary about the funeral brought tears to Kilpatrick's eyes. "No children ever had, it seems to me, a better mother," he wrote. Mother and son had been extremely close, exchanging weekly letters. Kilpatrick gave her full credit for his moral, social, and personal education. Even as a child, he had been treated as a person by her, with full sympathy and encouragement at every stage. He remembered with pride her trip to New York City in 1915, when she saw him march in full regalia in the Columbia University graduation exercises, and how she had been full of pride when she saw his modest but adequate Morningside Drive apartment, marveling at how well her son had done despite his humble origins.[55] Although Helen stayed on at the home place, with his mother's passing another connection to the South had slipped away.

As he reached the apparent height of his career in the mid-1920s, it seemed as if the South held less and less sway over him. With his mother gone now, and his adored sister's health in a precarious condition, his ties to his roots were loosening. The first half of the decade had indeed been a time of travels, teaching, and transitions. As his teaching reached its zenith, so did his writing. Ahead were two round-the-world trips before the decade ended, and two major books outlining his educational thought.

EDUCATION FOR A CHANGING CIVILIZATION

Children have had to be massed together into a schoolroom just as cotton looms have had to be massed together into a factory. The difficulty is that, unlike cotton looms, massed children make a social group, and that the mind and personality can only be developed by the freely inter-stimulating play of minds in a group. Is it not very curious that we spend so much time on the practice and methods of teaching, and never criticize the very framework itself? Call this thing that goes on in the modern schoolroom schooling, if you like. Only don't call it education.

Randolph S. Bourne in The New Republic, 1914[1]

The school, like the factory, is a thoroughly regimented world. Immovable seats in orderly rows fix the sphere of activity of each child. For all, from the timid six-year-old entering for the first time to the most assured high school senior, the general routine is much the same. The lesson-textbook-recitation method is the chief characteristic of education. Then a bell rings, on the instant books bang, powder and mirrors come out, there is buzz of talk and laughter as all the urgent business of living resumes momentarily for the children.

Robert S. Lynd and Helen Merrell Lynd from
Middletown, 1929[2]

The two quotations above neatly bracket the period during which William Heard Kilpatrick endeavored to radically change the classroom as Bourne and the Lynds had found it between the Great War and the Great Depression. Kilpatrick's work on his project method had been germinating as early as 1914. By 1929, the end of the "roaring twenties," the shift to the child-centered

approach of progressive education was well under way. A crusade to do no less than remake the schoolrooms, the curriculum, and the teachers in American education was the objective of some members of this generation of progressive educators. Kilpatrick was, of course, familiar with the New York City schools which Randolph Bourne referred to in the inaugural issue of *The New Republic*. And the Columbia professor had also been to Muncie, Indiana, the Lynds' "Middletown," lecturing several times at the teachers college on the west side of town. Beyond his teaching and speaking, Kilpatrick next made his presence felt in American education during this phase of his career by writing three widely read books.

The three books Kilpatrick published in the 1920s were diverse, yet all were influential. The first was a compilation of brief quotations, with a few lengthy pieces of social, political, philosophical, and educational writing, which was used to accompany his philosophy of education courses. Published by Macmillan in 1923, and entitled *Source Book in the Philosophy of Education*, the volume contained 557 selections. His second and possibly best known book, published in 1925, was *Foundations of Method: Informal Talks on Teaching*. The final book, drawn from a series of lectures at Rutgers, was entitled *Education for a Changing Civilization*. These works were different in focus, content, even style, but together they formed a logical connection between "The Project Method" of 1918 and the ideas that would become known as social reconstructionism in the 1930s.

From his vast reading, Kilpatrick had always collected quotations, epigrams, and excerpts from articles, organizing them meticulously on index cards filed according to topic. As he developed and refined his philosophy of education courses and seminars during and after the Great War, he also developed a question-filled syllabus which ran to almost 100 pages. In 1921, Kilpatrick assembled an anthology of quotations drawn from history, philosophy, psychology, politics, literature, sociology, and, of course, education, to create *Source Book in the Philosophy of Education*. It included topics such as democracy, progress, curriculum, thinking, moral education, the nature of society, and the concept of experience. There were also sections on the wider areas of philosophy of education and on what constitutes the good life.

The quotations included Thucydides, Aristotle, Plato, Goethe, Shakespeare, Kant, Voltaire, Hobbes, Rousseau, and the Bible. Contributors of more recent vintage were Bertrand Russell, Edward L. Thorndike, William James, Mohandas Gandhi, Charles Beard, and Henry Adams. The person most

often quoted was, to no one's surprise, John Dewey. Kilpatrick quoted himself eight times.³ While the vast majority of the quotations supported progressive education, occasional references were diametrically opposed to Kilpatrick's beliefs. One, drawn from John Wesley, had been quoted by William James in his *Talks to Teachers*:

> Break your child's will in order that it may not perish. Break its will as soon as it can speak plainly — or even before it can speak at all. It should be forced to do as it is told, even if you have to whip it ten times running. Break its will, in order that its soul may live.⁴

But the plethora of quotations from Dewey, Pestalozzi, and Kilpatrick himself, in addition to selected citations from Plato to Jefferson, supported the progressive approach to education, making it clear where the author's sympathies lay.

A remarkable aspect of the *Source Book* is Kilpatrick's desire to provide his students and other readers with a rich and diverse body of knowledge and wisdom from which they were to undertake their own thinking. Although the selections were slanted in support of the progressive position, there were multiple points of view, representing a long and distinguished list of notable thinkers and demonstrating that Kilpatrick could draw upon an eclectic array. This collection stressed the theme of change — a theme that would drive his thinking on curriculum and education for the next decade and beyond. He was in solid agreement with John Dewey, who wrote that the only useful definition of reality was change.

Foundations of Method: Informal Talks on Teaching was conceived for use in one of Kilpatrick's two major courses, "Foundations of Method." As will be seen, despite his use of the word "method," Kilpatrick gave himself wide berth in defining it, so as to include a variety of topics and issues. This book made a significant impact on the thousands of students who read it during the course. Individuals have testified that, as a result of reading this book, either their views on education were changed or they decided to enter the teaching profession.⁵ For an education textbook, the organization is unique. It takes the form of a dialogue between two, sometimes three, students enrolled in a course very similar to Kilpatrick's own. While Kilpatrick is never mentioned by name, one of the teachers always seems to have a better understanding of the progressive point of view than the others. For dramatic effect, on occasion one

of the students feigns, with utmost sincerity, a point of view that provides a perfect foil for the teacher, who — serving as the Kilpatrick proxy, then makes a crucial point. At times a new student joins the group who needs to be apprised of what has been said, thus offering a subtle but effective opportunity to summarize or review the material. In his preface, Kilpatrick makes it readily apparent that his aim was to venture beyond the conventional definition of method — a "wider" view of method, he calls it. In fact, the first chapter is entitled "The Wider versus the Narrow Problem of Method." Kilpatrick also indicates in the preface that habits and attitudes had been overlooked in the larger picture of the intellectual and emotional development of the child.[6]

In the opening chapters of *Foundations of Method*, Kilpatrick has his speakers examine the larger problems of education: the need for a more scientific basis for learning; the necessity of students' enjoying as well as learning subject matter; the lack of concomitant learning on the part of the child; and, of course, the essential task of students: practicing what they learn. The "wider sense" of method also necessarily leads to moral, ethical, psycho-logical, and philosophical considerations. There is, in addition, a desire to establish more democratic schools; using the recent example of Prussian schools and their disastrous results, Kilpatrick writes, "A democratic society should have a democratic school system, and in this system a democratic method will play a most important part."[7] But the philosophical treatment of the "wider method" must wait while Kilpatrick takes the reader on a concise, but thorough journey through Thorndikian psychology.[8] In one chapter, there is also a discussion of Woodworth's physiological approach to psychology, complete with diagrams of neurons and synapses.[9]

Two chapters in *Foundations of Method* are devoted to the topic of coercion and learning (or, actually, lack of learning). Coercion was a practice that Kilpatrick railed against at almost every opportunity, often using examples from every century except the present. Predictably, his conclusion is that more undesirable traits and habits are learned than positive ones — the "evil attendants" outweigh any good. Coercion is acceptable in an emergency, but is almost always a sign of bad teaching. Kilpatrick does not dwell long on practices he finds untrustworthy. Interest can be built, he proclaims, only through activities which bring success and growth. The next step thus becomes intrinsic effort, a crucial element in Kilpatrick's scheme.[10]

One of the central tenets of Kilpatrick's thought had to do with the development of attitudes: "The wider problem (of method) is much concerned to build attitudes and appreciations. In so doing, it builds the

heart of the child; and out of the heart are the issues of learning." In fact, he states that "attitudes come pretty near to being the stuff of which character is built," and he goes even further in writing that "attitude building is then about the most important part of education." His view was that concomitant learning was paramount in the learning process and that concomitant "learnings" were attitudinal and were often ignored by the schools. A concomitant learning could be defined as an indirect or unanticipated outcome that occurred during a planned educational experience. The new and overriding influence of tests also became problematic in the struggle between what Kilpatrick called primary learning and what he considered superior — concomitant learning.[11] Teachers, realizing that their own success eventually depended on whether their students met externally set standards, would be compelled to adjust classroom activity toward what could be measured. But, counters Kilpatrick: "Sooner or later . . . they will find themselves rated according to these records." "Let them use tests," Kilpatrick concludes, "but with a clear sense of their limitations and dangers."[12]

A companion to the concept of concomitant learning in *Foundations of Method* is building within students what Kilpatrick terms "centers of interest." These could be, of course, either positive or negative, but such impressions would bear heavily on the child's perception of the teacher, the subject matter, the school, and the self.[13] For the time, this was a significant shift in thinking. While it was based on Dewey's thought, the concept went beyond Dewey. (Whether it was with the master's blessing will be examined later.) As Kilpatrick had tentatively posited in "The Project Method," the crux of this approach was the assumption that free citizens think for themselves. He reiterates this in *Foundations of Method* but adds:

> They must also be able and disposed to accept responsibility,
> and to put the common good ahead of everything else, and to
> subordinate to it all mere private or personal advantage. We
> want citizens who are open-minded, yet critical-minded, who
> are informed and intelligent, who accept the rule of law and
> responsibility for the common good.[14]

Kilpatrick based one chapter "Interest," on Dewey's *Interest and Effort in Education*, and once again he countered the critics who insisted that his method was riddled with undisciplined, unstructured approaches to education. One of

the speakers in *Foundations of Method* expresses this criticism, describing the theory of interest as "the best known device to spoil the child," "wishy-washy, namby-pamby," and, finally, "the worst educational doctrine known." Kilpatrick responds that the emphasis in the doctrine of interest is not to cajole or amuse students, but rather to guarantee attention and effort in order to best apply the laws of learning. Activities should be both challenging and difficult, though adjusted to the strength of the individual child. With that in mind, Kilpatrick defines curriculum building as, first, knowing what interests, both native and acquired, lie within a student; and second, knowing how these may be "stimulated, guided, and directed to bring about growing." He returns to the concept of freedom later in the book, when the question of how much should be allowed is raised: "Freedom, yes, but not unlimited freedom; freedom for practice, and as much freedom as does in fact bring growth from practice. Growth is always our criterion."[15]

The discussion of interest and growth concludes with an analysis of a lecture in which Dewey spoke of three stages of choices: the first a reaction to stimuli without thought; the second an action with general but not specific thought as to outcome; and the third, true "purposing" — action based on both experience and consequences.[16] The topic is raised so that Kilpatrick can further discuss his idea of growth as a continuous phenomenon, not ceasing at any specific age. A challenge to the doctrine of growth is raised by one of the speakers in *Foundations of Method*: "I teach grammar and history. How will all of this help me teach my very unwilling children? I ask for bread and you give me a stone." The rejoinder is swift: "Children too have asked for bread, but been given stones. But more important, children under the old regime have not learned." For Kilpatrick, the definition of growth was not in the least vague, ambiguous, or vacuous:

> Primarily . . . growing means more thoughts, more meanings, finer and finer distinctions, better ways of behaving, higher degrees of skill, broader interests, wider and better organizations — all things that go along with a growing interest span.[17]

The best known illustration in *Foundations of Method* is this exchange regarding the conundrum of "boy or corn":

> I should like to ask about planning. Don't you think that the teacher should often supply the plan? Take a boy planting corn,

for example; think of the waste of land and fertilizer and effort. Science has worked out better plans than a boy can make.

And in such case you would advocate furnishing the boy with the best plan the teacher could find or devise?

Yes wouldn't you?

I think it depends on what you seek. If you wish corn, give the boy the plan. But if you wish boy rather than corn, that is, if you wish to educate the boy to think and plan for himself, then let him make his own plan.[18]

As one critic later said, Kilpatrick always seemed to choose boy over corn.

Kilpatrick returns, in *Foundations of Method*, to *Dewey's Democracy and Education* and the concept of education as the "continuous reconstruction of experience."[19] Traditional, more formal lessons in school only postpone, rather than remake, life for the student. As to when an experience is truly educative, Kilpatrick provides an interlocking, extraneous definition: the experience must stay with the present interest span, reaching beyond the known, yet causing gain rather than discouragement or loss. Even when questioned about allowing the student to engage in vicarious experiences, Kilpatrick is reticent. While never explicitly denouncing secondary experiences, he extols firsthand encounters with life as superior in what he calls both "vividness and definiteness."[20]

Having offered this extensive introduction to psychology and philosophy, Kilpatrick takes up once again, his idea of the purposeful act, mainly reviewing "The Project Method." He then pursues Dewey's "complete act of thought," drawing from *How We Think* and describing a six-stage operation: (1) drive to action; (2) presence of a difficulty; (3) examination of the situation; (4) suggestions for a solution; (5) elaborating the implications of the hypothesis; and (6) trying out by actual test one or more of the implications. Kilpatrick states the caveat that these steps are meant to be logical, not necessarily chronological.[21]

Kilpatrick next enters the area of curriculum and paints a more detailed picture than before of the implications of his new education. The study of controversial issues, especially public policy affecting the daily lives of students, would be essential. His curriculum would be questioned-centered, rather than answered-centered. Admittedly, some components of the curriculum would change less than others. Change remained his thesis, though;

in fact, the title of this chapter is "Why Education Is Changing." When Kilpatrick is again confronted with the question of "boy or corn," this time expressed as "teaching children" versus "teaching subjects," his answer is similar; but it is not entirely dogmatic, nor is it without cautions. "We don't teach unless children learn," proclaims Kilpatrick's proxy, "So teaching children must mean that they learn something. But I quite agree with you that we are properly concerned first with our children that they shall grow, and only secondarily with subject-matter that it be learned."[22]

This essential conflict between the primacy of subject matter and the primacy of the child in the educational process would remain the point of contention between essentialists and progressives throughout the century. But while it profoundly challenged the conventional wisdom of the time, this controversy may have been a dialectic without a distinction. If any subject matter is to have meaning, purpose, or significance, it has to interact in some meaningful fashion with the mind. For Kilpatrick, just as it was true that the child must have something to learn, so it was also true that a book on a shelf, a work of art in a museum, or an unsolved mathematical problem was absent of meaning without interaction with a person. It was not a matter of the traditional three R's being irrelevant or extraneous. The reality for Kilpatrick was that the basics were merely insufficient as ends unto themselves. Change, innovation, reformation — even "transformation," as Lawrence Cremin would later call it — were all critical if the schools were indeed to make a significant difference in the lives of students.

As to why such changes needed to take place in education, it is Kilpatrick's thesis in *Foundations of Method* that the demands of the time were much different from those of even a century before, when frontier American society was much simpler, a pioneer era in which individuals were closer to the real problems of the day. The society of the twentieth century was more complicated, and the opportunities by which children could learn were further removed from real life. Kilpatrick remarks that modern children are less involved politically, having become mere "onlookers."[23] He goes on to describe a situation that many in the late twentieth century would find familiar: "The home and community no longer supply the same sort of education they once did." Therefore, it is left to the school to stand in the aperture and provide for the child what the family is not providing.[24]

The curriculum, then, would have to be unique, not only for each child but for each particular situation. Kilpatrick describes the teachers of the two types of schools, separated by a century, as "fixed civilization teachers" and "changing civilization teachers." Kilpatrick's preference was, of course, for the

latter, in that he wished schools to educate students to become self-reliant and adaptable citizens. This brought Kilpatrick full circle, as with the project method, to democracy. "Democracy," says one of the figures in *Foundations of Method*, "has been at work slowly remaking the school to a greater sensitiveness to child nature, and perhaps especially to make us see that we must get our children where they can and will think for themselves."[25]

Near the end of *Foundations of Method*, Kilpatrick describes subject matter as experience and what he terms "ways of behaving." By this he meant a curriculum that had an immediate and relevant aspect. The reason for such a recipe was based as much on the needs of the learner as on the needs of an unknown future society. That "which comes into the child's life because it is thus needed . . . will sooner and more frequently and more viably be called on to serve again in that child's life." Was this method, then, to become a dogmatic, lockstep approach to education like the approach he himself was battling against? "As I told you what I should wish," comes the response, "in this world we often are compelled to take less than we wish." Also at issue is "intrinsic subject matter" versus "extrinsic subject matter." The intrinsic, Kilpatrick claims, makes the student and teacher allies; the extrinsic leads only to a separation of the two. He also believes in what might be termed an integrated curriculum, one that allows the various disciplines to play a part in the whole. "No person ever finds arithmetic or geography or history by itself in life. It always comes embedded in a situation involving much more," says a participant in one of the dialogues.[26]

The concluding chapter of *Foundations of Method* deals with a variety of matters including textbooks and curriculum. As for textbooks, Kilpatrick urges their use in a new and — for that day — unconventional, manner:

> Would you use any textbooks in your school?
>
> Again a difficult question. Many textbooks of the present day aim only at presenting children with pre-digested thinking. Such I should not use, or at any rate I should not use them as was intended by their authors.
>
> But what kind would you use?
>
> Only time and fuller experimentation can tell. At present I can only prophesy, and you know what a bad business that is.

I can see several different kinds possible. One kind would be simply a reading book, one that would tell in a fascinating way the story of history or geography or travel or adventure, or of insect life — all the other wonderful things that have come down to us. Another would be a compendium of ready reference or possibly a systematic treatise to be consulted as need might arise. Still another would be a book that raised questions, stimulated inquiries and activities.[27]

As for curriculum and what constituted the basics, Kilpatrick wished for characteristics such as truth telling and honesty to be added to reading, writing, and spelling. "Do you think truth telling less essential to life than certain words in the spelling list?" he asks.[28] He admits that there would be a list of essential skills, but not essential subject matter. The only two such "basics" he names in *Foundations of Method* are reading and counting. The curriculum needs to be problem-centered, and he suggests that at least a half an hour of free time per day be provided for students to work on their own projects.[29] Kilpatrick's overall intent in this book is captured as one speaker inquires:

Would you mind telling your general aim of education?

My aim as I work with children is to have them live more richly and successfully right now in the belief that this will mean most to them and to others both now and hereafter.[30]

The third book that Kilpatrick produced in the 1920s was a compilation of three lectures given in 1926 at Rutgers University and published the same year by Macmillan: *Education for a Changing Civilization*.[31] This slender volume went into a dozen reprintings and was still in print in the 1990s. It unites his original thinking on the project method with his shift to what would become the social reconstructionist point of view of the 1930s and contains some of his most creative, innovative, and radical thinking on schools, curriculum, and society. Kilpatrick begins by examining the phenomenon of change and its causation. His immediate conclusion is that science and communication — both elements deriving from a new technology — have always had the greatest impact on change in western civilization. The superiority of mind over matter in Platonic thinking and the authority represented in Aristotelian thought were both challenged by Galileo and others during the Renaissance and subsequent

scientific and cultural revolutions. All of this was brought about through what Kilpatrick calls "tested thought," which led to the accumulation of reliable information. The shift had been away from an authoritarian approach to issues, and toward the scientific method.[32]

As Kilpatrick further probes the multiple causation for change in modern life, he arrives at three deep-lying tendencies: changes in attitudes, industrialization, and democracy. Attitudinal changes are seen as a result of scientific thought being brought to bear on societal institutions and "the increasing tendency to change . . . according to the results of criticism." The view which emerges is that "progress has caught the popular fancy," in tandem with the pragmatic belief that society has become increasingly disposed "to judge institutions by their consequences for life." The "hold of tradition," as Kilpatrick calls it — especially Christianity — has been too strong, but a new tendency to test thought is slowly permeating the general intellectual attitudes of the day, and human beings have found, in his words, "a new faith."[33]

As for changes in industrialization, Kilpatrick writes that he is hesitant to even touch upon a topic about which so much had been written. But he does offer a possibly original concept: interdependence. This is a term, and a concept much more in vogue today — at the century's end — than it was when the century began. Kilpatrick's vision of a globe shrinking because of increased communication, with an attendant spread and integration of ideas, is similar to the work of Marshall McLuhan, the Canadian media guru who saw the emergence of a "global village." Drawing an analogy with the nervous system, Kilpatrick suggests that speed in communication and travel is yet to subside, as innovation continues unabated. State lines mean less and less, and communication does not halt at national boundaries. "The application of thought to invention coupled with diversity of natural resources — these together make for an ever growing and ever diversified industry." Even in this seemingly strong social context, Kilpatrick continues to be attentive to the needs of the individual in a changing society. He concludes that the individual counts for less without the opportunity to manage his or her own business. As a result, "personal responsibility tends to decline" and "selfish individualism easily follows."[34]

For Kilpatrick, the third tendency deeply imbedded in modern society was democracy. Although democracy had previously been defined in different ways in other works, in *Education for a Changing Civilization* he writes that "democracy was essentially life, ethical life." Democracy was a growing, expanding, irrepressible force that ran deep in any society where it was allowed to flourish. "If we would learn democracy, we must then practice it. Possibly

one reason for the disappointments of democracy is that we have never really tried it," writes Kilpatrick.[35]

In addition to democracy, Kilpatrick sees other trends emerging. Authoritarianism was on the wane because of the Great War, a decline in family life, the vogue of higher criticism in religion, and psychoanalysis in psychology — and, of course, the suffrage movement, with attendant opportunity for women in education and the workplace. Individuals had to move from the older, external authority toward an internal authority grounded in scientific thought and inquiry. The fruits of the scientific revolution had been an ever-growing number of inventions, which then produced further change. The world had seen more inventions in the past hundred years than in the past millennium.[36] Kilpatrick concluded that:

> Increase in inventions means increase in social change. It appears that we must have a philosophy that not only takes positive recognition of the fact of change, but one that includes within it change as an essential element.[37]

According to Kilpatrick, Plato had proposed a state that would remain permanent, and Aristotle had advanced the theory that change must be severely restricted, which is what occurred under feudalism in the Middle Ages. Then, in the nineteenth century, Charles Darwin loosened the bounds for change. William James went so far as to suggest — in "startling words" for Kilpatrick — that "the lid is thus taken off the universe." No prior formulations held in any realm, and all the old certainties were questioned. There was thus a material advance in civilization that raised issues and problems outrunning the social and moral capabilities of the citizenry. All of this brings Kilpatrick to the conclusion that a new moral and intellectual response must be made in order to deal effectively and wisely with the ever-changing material and scientific world. He calls this phenomenon a "moving equilibrium" for our social affairs. Youth, especially, would no longer accept authoritarian answers to the issues of the day.[38]

The authority represented by the establishment is selected for special attention. "The upholders of the established group opinion have always seen in the school a chief means of perpetuating the established opinion," writes Kilpatrick. In even blunter terms, he adds, "Education has been the process by which those at present in charge of affairs determined what the rising generation should think and do." This was certainly radical talk by any measure, and more than one former student of Kilpatrick's has suggested that the sustained

criticism he endured throughout his life, as well as the criticism that persisted after his death, was caused by his vigorous challenge of the establishment. Kilpatrick also suggests, predating the social reconstructionists by almost a decade, that "schools be brought abreast of changes already effected in our social life. Our basic theory of education must be so reconstructed as to include as an essential determining element the recognition of . . . rapid and increasing change." Authority had to be challenged so that any attempt "to fasten our conclusions on our children vanishes." The rising generation had to be free to think for itself, even if this meant that current thought and conventional wisdom were revised or rejected altogether.[39]

As in *Foundations of Method*, the topic of the curriculum arises in *Education for a Changing Civilization*. The "out-of-date and merely conventional subject matter" taught in the schools, claims Kilpatrick, does not prepare students for present-day life, let alone the life they will encounter when they become adults. Education "pretends" that the future will be like the present. While not hurling out all subject matter — some "older stock subject matter" might survive to the next generation — Kilpatrick calls for more generalized methods and attitudes in attacking and meeting novel situations.[40] But he addresses specific subjects in *Education for a Changing Civilization*. Science has to be taught, but absent superstition, writes Kilpatrick, mentioning the Scopes trial. As for social science, it has to become more scientific in its methodology. There will also have to be a new history and a new geography in order to ward off the divisiveness of unbridled nationalism. The major impetus for heightened expectations in subject matter, according to Kilpatrick, is the result of colleges demanding strict entrance requirements from the secondary schools. Such domination has to be broken, he claims, or the high schools will continue to be nothing more than "cramming schools."[41]

According to Kilpatrick, outdated subject matter was supported by the new move toward assessment. In an article written prior to *Education for a Changing Civilization*, he takes direct aim at the testing process: "We find a tendency to reduce the content of what is studied and learned to such things as lend themselves readily to assignment and testing. Anything else tends to be ignored. If we cannot test it, how can we assign it? If we cannot assign it, how can we hold pupils responsible for it? If pupils cannot be held responsible for it, how can teachers?" Such an approach, thought Kilpatrick, often led to teaching a curriculum that was not alive — such as ancient history, ancient languages, mathematics, and physical sciences — because such a curriculum is much "safer" than modern history, modern languages, biology, economics, and politics.[42]

Kilpatrick's thought on subject matter was not constructed in a vacuum. In November 1925, at a remarkable meeting in a hotel room in Cleveland, Ohio, several educators discussed the preparation of the Twenty-Sixth Yearbook of the National Society for the Study of Education (NSSE). It was an impressive group. Present were Charles Hubbard Judd, Franklin Bobbitt, W. W. Charters, Ernest Horn, Harold Rugg, George Counts, and William Heard Kilpatrick. Teachers and subject matter were on the agenda. Teachers needed safeguards in the classroom, and this was one of the major reasons Kilpatrick did not believe in "fixing the curriculum in advance and furnishing it to the teachers." Only if teachers and pupils were free could similar freedom be built within society. Such arguments seemed to stun the group. "Rugg was a bit troubled. He and Counts looked quite serious. It is a line of thought I must develop," wrote Kilpatrick.[43] A year before, in Milwaukee, Kilpatrick, in the context of education as the reconstruction of experience, challenged the concept that subject matter should be selected on an intrinsic basis.[44] And still earlier, in 1922, he had provided the groundwork for his thinking on subject matter as a "way of behaving." Of course, he also opposed setting subject matter out in advance:

> The difference it would introduce is the difference between will and can. Now we ask, can this child read or multiply or locate Bolivia? On my plan we should ask: Does this child of himself read or use multiplication or use his knowledge of Bolivia in his own living? I am inclined to say that our children would in the end know as much, but probably not the same things.[45]

The passage most frequently quoted on the issue of subject matter in *Education for a Changing Civilization* is this:

> The American people, if we are not to disintegrate through inability to grow, must learn, as hitherto it has not learned, to tolerate the discussion of controversial issues. Increasingly it must learn how unethical and how socially hurtful it is to bind the minds of the defenseless young and shut their eyes to social evils. As we plan for a better world, to deal with the old is difficult, but for the young, prospective social problems furnish us the best intellectual subject-matter they can have.
>
> If some wonder how, in an already crowded curriculum, we

can find time for the extended study of social problems here demanded, one answer is clear. Rid the schools of dead stuff. With those who are in fair touch with educational thought the opinion grows that the present secondary curriculum remains not so much because it is defensible as because we do not have assured material in workable form to put in its place. For most pupils, Latin can and should follow Greek into the discard. Likewise with most of mathematics for most pupils. Much of present history study should give way to study of social problems (where more history will be gained than in the old way). Modern foreign languages can hardly be defended for most who now study them. With reference to English and the sciences, they need remaking from within rather than rejection.[46]

This may be the strongest and most specific assault Kilpatrick ever made on what could be considered traditional, discipline-centered subject matter. And yet his exclusions were not absolute. While not in favor of extensive mathematics, or Latin and Greek, he did speak of "some of the essentials" as being English, history, literature, and philosophy. Kilpatrick was often given credit for placing emphasis on the child rather than the subject matter — which he did — but, he was never fully ready to dispense with subject matter *per se*, as some critics have charged. In a brief newspaper article that used the same format as *Foundations of Method*, he has a questioner ask, "What should I teach, children or should I teach lessons?" Comes the reply, "There is only one answer: you teach both children and lessons."[47]

As noted above, Kilpatrick called for subject matter that was primarily defined as "ways of behaving." "The mind is not best used as a granary or as a place for cold storage," wrote Kilpatrick, "It is best used when it's put to work . . . meeting problems that call for our present efforts." He defined the new curriculum as comprising experience which uses "subject matter, but does not consist of subject matter."[48] He also believed that "to get subject-matter as it is needed was thus to bring growth," but to "give subject-matter before it is needed is exactly to lose by that much the opportunity for growing."[49]

Kilpatrick gave a more comprehensive exegesis on subject matter in an article titled "Subject Matter and the Educative Process." In it, he questioned the four presumptions: (1) that children ever use the current subject matter they learn, (2) that school is the only place where children learn, (3) that nothing

beyond skills and knowledge can be learned in the classroom, and (4) that once children learn something, it remains. He also stated, "What a change in a school it would be, what a shaking amongst the dry bones, if only we should with one accord demand that school learning be lively enough to break out of cold storage, and should agree to accept no other kind."[50] A prearranged or ordered curriculum, "set-in-advance" as Kilpatrick would often call it, would produce passive, docile youth. Activity was necessary. Teachers were to make themselves "progressively unnecessary," but teachers did have a crucial role. They would be ready to guide, assist, suggest sources of information, and, at times, provide direction. In fact, the teacher, not the curriculum, would be prepared in advance.

When in *Education for a Changing Civilization*, he raises the question, "What then of subjects?" his response is similar: "Learning follows use rather than subject arrangement. It must be so. We must know this and teach accordingly." He stated this succinctly elsewhere when he wrote, "My thesis today is that we must not start with subject matter foremost in mind; for subject matter is primarily means, not primarily end."[51] The final chapter of *Education for a Changing Civilization* is full of controversial statements on the topic of subject matter, and the following passage was a direct assault on the essentialist camp:

> It is a matter of regret that at this moment some thinkers otherwise most modern, while much concerned to bring the content of the curriculum up to date, still think in terms of fixing in advance the content for both teacher and pupil. We grant them that their expert thought has an invaluable part in the more scientific selection of useful problems and of correlative material, and we grant equally that the informed and discerning teacher must make appropriate use of materials so collected, but we cannot consent to settle the matter solely on grounds of content.[52]

As if to anticipate the criticism that would emerge in the decades ahead, Kilpatrick asks the penetrating question, "One wonders how these thinkers holding their respective university chairs would feel teaching curriculum material that some super-expert had handed out to them fully organized and documented."[53]

In Kilpatrick's new education, more than curriculum would change. If real life and real experiences were to take place in the schools, changes in buildings

and equipment, textbooks, and administration would also be required. There would be movable desks and, more important, "movable" children, who worked together in groups. There would be less repression and a greater sense of community. Finally, there would be an expansion of freedom. At this point, Kilpatrick becomes less prescriptive — in fact, deliberately ambiguous. "How much freedom shall we accord the child?" he asks. "As much as he can use wisely," is the immediate, if vague, response. Kilpatrick concludes that all education is experimental. Therefore, such an answer may not be as equivocal as it appears — though it has certainly been viewed as equivocal by critics.[54]

Kilpatrick not only called for a new educational paradigm; he also saw a need for new rhetoric and new language. "Such words as learn, teach, study, subject matter, curriculum, promotion, textbook, objectives, and norms, with their appropriate actual procedures, generally imply the static outlook and so prejudice in advance any discussion in which they occur," he writes.[55] The one word that remains for Kilpatrick at the end of this volume is "growth." Referring again to John Dewey's *Democracy and Education*, he calls growth the only goal that fits a growing world — both in its essence and in its end. In the closing pages, Kilpatrick, weaves the diverse threads of his thinking together to establish this central point. Such schools would require not only bricks and mortar, but a new teacher of high caliber and character, immersed in a new philosophy. Civilization depended on education, whatever the cost. Freed and given true support, education could be the "maker of a better civilization."[56]

The reviews of *Education for a Changing Civilization* were mixed, but it was taken seriously. Two religious journals were quite affirmative. *The Christian Leader* and the *Congregationalist* both praised Kilpatrick's work for its emphasis on reform supported by an attendant educational philosophy. The *Congregationalist* wrote, "No hasty characterization, however, can suggest the freshness, power, and originality of much of Professor Kilpatrick's analysis."[57] Two other periodicals assigned an economic interpretation. *School*, a journal published in New York City, indicated that Kilpatrick's philosophy could not be applied "on the hearts and minds of jaded, overworked teachers"[58] *Worker's Education* emphasized the importance of "actual experiencing" and "real enterprises" for students — both of which were topics discussed in the book. Its reviewer, Eduard C. Lindemann, also mentioned Kilpatrick's illustration of a paradoxical society in which modern science builds skyscrapers while the owners refuse to have a thirteenth floor in them.[59]

Two of the more critical reviews of *Education for a Changing Civilization*

were by Lewis Mumford and Kilpatrick's colleague at Teachers College, Isaac Kandel. Both men agreed that the book provoked reflection and could not be ignored. But its significance notwithstanding, these reviewers identified problems in Kilpatrick's thesis. Using metaphors from the theater, Mumford placed Kilpatrick in a band of social thinkers who were "overwhelmed," as he put it, by external characteristics of a changing civilization based on faith and historical choice as much as "the age which preceded it." "Characters and action," wrote Mumford, could not be downplayed in favor of technology and science. "The sceneshifters, mechanics, and property men have had the stage to themselves these last two centuries. Much as I agree with Professor Kilpatrick in a hundred details," concluded Mumford, "I feel that an educational plan that rests upon this illusion is unsound."[60]

Kandel approved of Kilpatrick's discussion of personality if for no other reason than that it had elicited significant interest on the part of laypeople and parents. But he had great difficulty with the concept of "tested thought" as a panacea for modern societal problems. Authoritarianism ran too deep. As for the validity of what Kilpatrick termed "internal authority," Kandel was skeptical. In his view, Kilpatrick seemed to have lost track of the work of psychologists on individual differences, and of the most recent statistics on crime. But the conservative Kandel found his real issue with the treatment of subject matter. For him, the problem resided not so much in the subjects themselves as in the teachers' unfamiliarity with the subjects they were teaching. Still Kandel concluded on a positive note: "If Professor Kilpatrick's general survey has any value, it lies in directing attention to the incompatibility between new theories of education and old systems of organization."[61] Kandel quoted Walter Lippmann's *The Phantom Public*: "If the schools attempt to teach children how to solve the problems of the day, they are bound always to be in arrears. The most they can conceivably attempt is the teaching of patterns of thought and feeling which will enable the citizen to approach a new problem in some useful fashion."

One informal review came from Edward L. Thorndike, another of Kilpatrick's colleagues at Teachers College. In a letter which Kilpatrick received in early 1927 while in China, Thorndike wrote of reading *Education for a Changing Civilization* and then spoke of the lectures from which they were derived: "I felt like putting in black and white my appreciation of your effective lectures at Rutgers. I wish I could have been there and seen you carry the audience along as you must have done."[62] It was one of the rare notes that Kilpatrick received from Thorndike, and it moved him deeply.

Education for a Changing Civilization contained some of Kilpatrick's most provocative ideas and rhetoric and brought to completion the dialogue begun a decade earlier in "The Project Method." Kilpatrick finally treated subject matter specifically and made the intellectual, philosophical, and educational connections that had eluded the earlier work. The second half of the 1920s would find Kilpatrick on two around-the-world trips, during which he would observe both changes and stagnation — the stagnation he feared — in the civilizations of the West and the East. In early 1926, before embarking on his travels, he delivered a lecture in Omaha, Nebraska, which expressed, in a simplified form, the essence of *Education for a Changing Civilization*. Described in the local newspaper as "silvery-haired, with keen blue eyes, looking every inch the educator," Kilpatrick told a group of high school teachers that education had problems larger than were generally supposed. Civilization was leading the race, with the schools next and those opposed to change following in third place. Uninformed critics were resisting any change, labeling progressive ideas as fads because advances were unknown in their own experience. Kilpatrick gave an example: while typewriters and adding machines used in the business world were not considered fads, analogous items in the schools were. He suggested that students were academically better prepared than previously. He noted that many voiced concern with regard to students' behavior, but he countered that the same charge had been made "five hundred years before Christ." He saw the new education bringing about a fresh disposition among students that would not pit them against teachers. In conclusion, he proudly noted that this new agenda for the nation's schools was the result of the continued study of education being led by the United States.[63]

The legacy of Kilpatrick's books written during this decade would be impossible to measure. A Harvard study conducted in 1927 found that *Foundations of Method* was the third most used textbook in education classes, behind texts by Inglis and Dewey, but ahead of Cubberly.[64] All of Kilpatrick's texts sold exceedingly well for the next thirty years. His call for education to embrace a new set of ideas and ideals was clear. A static and, in some cases, irrelevant curriculum had to be replaced with scientific thought, critical thinking, and open-mindedness. The new civilization Kilpatrick envisioned was built on cooperation and a commitment to social progress, even at the risk of questioning conventional educational wisdom and a number of established economic and social institutions. In 1928 H. L. Mencken wrote, "School days, I believe, are the unhappiest in the whole span of human

existence. They are full of dull, unintelligible tasks, new and unpleasant ordinances, brutal violations of common sense and common decency."[65] By involving teachers and schools in preparing future citizens for the reality of a changing civilization, Kilpatrick was attempting to eradicate what Mencken saw and too many children were experiencing.

10

A WIDER WORLD

This Mr. Fielding had been caught by India late. He was over
forty when he entered that oddest portal, the Victoria
Terminus at Bombay, and — having bribed a European ticket
inspector — took his luggage in the compartment of his first
tropical train.

A fictional educator arriving in India for the first time;
From E. M. Forster's *A Passage to India*, 1924.[1]

For Kilpatrick, there was a shift — midway through the decade of the
1920s — from the domestic scene, in both education and politics, to the
international arena. When he reviewed the past year in his diary on New Year's
Day 1926, he wrote pejoratively of the current occupant of the White House:
"Coolidge seems to satisfy the popular demand which is perhaps an adequate
commentary." He then moved on to describe the world scene, including the
League of Nations, Locarno, the Dawes Plan, and the World Court. His
increasing interest in the international sphere was evident, and there was good
reason for it: an upcoming round-the-world trip. As with the trip to England a
few years earlier, his wife Rita would accompany him. Their itinerary included
the Low Countries, Germany, Eastern Europe, Turkey, Greece, Egypt, India,
China, Japan, and Korea. The passages from New York to Rotterdam, Port Said
to Bombay, and Colombo to Hong Kong cost Kilpatrick and his wife $1,342.[2]
On August 28, 1926, they sailed for the Netherlands on the Holland-American
vessel *Valendian*.

On board ship, Kilpatrick read Gordon Hullfish's attack on the philosophy
of Edward L. Thorndike. Although he believed the article had been engineered
by Hullfish's mentor at The Ohio State University, Boyd H. Bode, it gave
Kilpatrick pause. He noted to himself that he would need to examine his own
positions more carefully. "Not that I consider any of my own positions
endangered," he added, "but my advocacy of them may need revising." Upon
arriving on the continent he was impressed with the beauty of the Dutch
countryside, the well-kept cows, and, of course, the marvelous tulips. But the
schools of the Netherlands were another matter. "The children are intelligent,

or they should be, belonging to the upper classes," he noted, thus attributing intelligence to socioeconomic causation, rather than to the schools. The teachers knew little of pedagogy, in Kilpatrick's opinion, and the principals were totally "innocent of education as I think of it."[3]

The Kilpatricks were impressed with Cologne, their next stop and the Rhine River. They stayed in a hotel across the street from the great cathedral in Cologne, and as they journeyed down the Rhine Kilpatrick noted, "I cannot soon forget the cities and the old castles." On September 17, they arrived in Prague. Within the week Kilpatrick had visited a *Realschule*, where he found 300 boys, down from 800 because of losses in the war and subsequent lower birthrates. What Kilpatrick saw there was everything he was fighting against: an unsympathetic master, frightened boys, dull textbooks, and rote lessons in anatomy. "I saw the best example I have ever seen I think of what McMurry and Dewey oppose," he wrote. "I see more clearly than ever just how far in our thinking we have proceeded on the road from structure to function, from repetition of cultural content to functional creative thinking." Kilpatrick also noted that on a wall of the classroom, a picture of the president of Czechoslovakia had replaced one of the emperor. The crucifixes remained; Czechoslovakian bureaucracy and the political situation made their removal unwise, he was told.[4]

From Czechoslovakia the Kilpatricks journeyed to Austria where in Vienna he lectured on October 9 at the Austro-American Institute of Education. The distinguished audience included the first president of the Austrian federal republic, Michael Hainisch, the president's wife, and a group of ministers. After the talk a German representative said he had heard several new lines of thinking, which deserved more thought. Kilpatrick's topic was "Education for a Changing Civilization," and it was given coverage in the Paris edition of the *New York Herald*, the major newspaper for Americans on the continent.[5]

The tour continued on October 13, as they pushed on toward Turkey via Hungary and Bulgaria. On October 17, they arrived in Constantinople. Kilpatrick was clearly taken by the city. Hagia Sophia and the mosques, museums, and minarets all mesmerized him. "The views of the Bosphorus of Asia, of the Golden Horn, of the city from various hills — all this is wonderful I believe beyond compare," he wrote. In Athens, they were greeted in the harbor by a spectacular view of the Acropolis. By October 24, 1926, they were in Egypt, where Erdman Harris, a professor of educational philosophy at the American University in Cairo, took the Kilpatricks out in his Dodge to see the pyramids and the Sphinx. Kilpatrick was not overly impressed. The rest of the week in Egypt was spent visiting schools and lecturing. He was surprised to

find that the Egyptian students thought of themselves as essentially democratic and subject to little interference from the religious authorities. Kilpatrick's observations led him to disagree. He was appalled at the rigidity of the universities and the heavy use of the Koran, which he felt monopolized the curriculum.[6] Unable to avoid accepting an invitation to attend services at the American mission church in Cairo, Kilpatrick found the experience worse than he had feared. Uncharacteristically passive aggressive, he endured the bilious evangelistic format by "analyzing the hymn numbers into their prime factors and the same with their sums and differences."

From Port Said the next leg of the journey took the Kilpatricks through the Suez Canal; this was followed by several days at sea en route to Bombay. On board ship Kilpatrick found the British passengers reserved and could not decide whether to attribute this to shyness or to the fact that he was mingling with and talking a great deal to the Indian passengers. One British officer, a Major Benson-Cooke, assigned to the Punjab, did discuss prohibition with Kilpatrick and was happy to hear that it was not the failure it was portrayed as in the English press. He also asked advice regarding the education of his two young daughters. Kilpatrick found several of the Indian passengers "strongly anti-British." Always well prepared, he completed Mason Olcott's book *Village Schools in India* just before arriving on the subcontinent.[7]

On November 12, the Victoria Terminus of Bombay — the portal that had for generations greeted those entering India — came into sight, and the Kilpatricks disembarked, pleasantly surprised to find the climate "not hot, but only warm." H. W. Bryant of the Y.M.C.A. collected them at the quay and delivered them to the Majestic Hotel, where their adequate room and bath cost them twenty-eight rupees.[8] They spent three days in Poona before returning to Bombay in preparation for their visit to Mahatma Gandhi in Ahmadabad. Gandhi sent a telegram to Bryant at the Y.M.C.A. in Bombay regarding the visit, stating succinctly: SHALL GLADLY SEE DOCTOR KILPATRICK WEDNESDAY AFTERNOON.[9]

The Kilpatricks arrived in Ahmadabad by rail on November 17, 1926, and hired a taxi for the forty-minute, four-mile drive to Gandhi's Sabarmati ashram outside the city. Gandhi had spent all of 1926 at his ashram in the political wilderness. Having been jailed from 1922 to 1924, he was consequently suffering from ill health. His days were spent meditating, reading, and spinning (swadeshi) at his wheel, working during the twelve hours of daylight. And yet he did not consider his self-imposed exile wasted time. "Sometimes even silence is a form of action," he wrote.[10] The year of Kilpatrick's visit fell

between the two major fasts that Gandhi undertook in 1924 and 1927. His recuperative retreat was also an attempt to discourage the constant stream of journalists and visitors.[11] Kilpatrick was indeed fortunate to get an interview. (Incidentally, Gandhi and Kilpatrick were almost exact contemporaries — just a year and a half apart in age.)

Kilpatrick recorded the visit in detail in his diary. He compared Gandhi's one-story house, with its large piazza, to the older country homes in his native South. There were several clerks working outside on the porch, one busily using a typewriter. Gandhi himself was inside, sitting on a low couch, at work at his spinning wheel, dressed only in a loincloth with a light shawl wrapped loosely around him. Kilpatrick described him as rather dark, with several teeth missing and a pigtail. Gandhi rose to greet the Kilpatricks, then returned to his couch while they sat on a nearby bench. An associate or aide sat nearby.[12]

Kilpatrick explained to Gandhi that the purpose of his visit was to discuss the type of civilization to be sought for India and the role of education in bringing this about. He first inquired as to what aspects of westernism the East should accept in its culture. Gandhi replied that at present the East should reject all of westernism, although he realized that such a rejection could not keep out all external influences. He granted that in the future, as India progressed further, the people could select what was to come in and what was to be rejected. When asked what he viewed as acceptable in western culture, Gandhi mentioned its industry — though not its industrialism — and its disposition to seek truth. He suggested that by comparison he found too much lethargy and laziness in the East. When queried by Kilpatrick about testing truth by its results, Gandhi demurred, saying that in terms of means and results only two characteristics could be considered invariably good: the doctrine of nonviolence and the existence of an unchangeable God behind the world. Since the soul finds expression not in building or changing, he "pleasantly" rejected Kilpatrick's attempt to find out what kind of civilization would work for India, as both typically western and lacking in "proper humility." Gandhi's purpose was not to change the world but to seek out what his duty might be in the world and to perform it.[13]

Kilpatrick next introduced the topic of education. Gandhi had been sufficiently critical of European schools in the 1890s to educate his own children at home. Although he later admitted that such an experience lacked many of the essential components of what would be considered a liberal arts education, he thought the regimen less artificial than it would have been had his children attended the westernized schools in either Africa or India.[14] There was

also the problem of the heavy British influence on the curriculum. One of Kilpatrick's Indian students, Stephen Khrishnayya, stated that the only historical period studied in Indian schools was the era of British colonialism.[15]

In discussing education, Gandhi spoke of the village schools and of a new experiment he and his colleagues were undertaking and seemed surprised that Kilpatrick was unaware of his ideas. When Kilpatrick asked if he was referring to the revival of household industries, Gandhi said yes. Gandhi saw this as the best way to improve the economic situation of the people. Also attractive was the element of contemplation involved as workers labored at home; this relaxed tension by letting the mind run its own course. He disagreed that "absentminded" contemplation might occur. When Kilpatrick attempted to bring Gandhi back to the more conscious attributes of education, Gandhi replied that some of his colleagues were pursuing this, but that he himself had little interest in it.[16]

Kilpatrick next asked Gandhi what kind of education he believed in. He would relate this portion of the interview to relatives and colleagues for years after the meeting. Gandhi pointed to a nearby loom and placed his hand upon it. "Do you mean this?" asked Kilpatrick. "Yes," replied Gandhi, "that's what I mean, the cottage industries; that is the education which India needs."[17] The loom, which would eventually appear on India's flag, had several meanings apart from education. It was an economic symbol, indicating a move away from dependence on imported goods that would keep Indians employed rather than idle; it was also political, pointing the way to freedom from the British Viceroy and all that he represented. One biographer of Gandhi has suggested that the wheel also had theological significance — but its educational meaning was never lost. Gandhi often encouraged English-educated Indian doctors and lawyers to abandon their professions and to both weave and wear the cloth made from hand-spun thread.[18]

Although they never discussed Kilpatrick's own philosophy *per se*, there may have been more agreement between the two men than either would have acknowledged. More and more, Gandhi emphasized character training over the accumulation of knowledge, and the importance of practical skills as opposed to book-bound study. Yet at times Gandhi's educational philosophy seemed inconsistent, even contradictory. While calling for a more spiritually oriented education and often castigating English-educated Indians, he would also praise his own people when they succeeded within the system of which he was so critical.[19]

The final topic of the interview was science and superstition. Kilpatrick indicated that the more thoughtful people in the West were trying to banish

superstitions. Gandhi agreed that India also had too much of superstitious practices. When asked what he was doing about this, he replied that his main effort was living a life free of superstition himself, for others to observe. At this point a "German woman follower," as Kilpatrick described her, joined the group. This woman — a "breezy type," according to Kilpatrick — soon had Gandhi laughing about Henry Ford and airplanes. She offered her opinion on western technology, saying that while she approved of using tractors, Gandhi did not. With this incongruous conclusion, there was a round of handshakes and the interview ended.[20]

Several years later, while visiting in Charleston during a time of crisis for both Gandhi and India, Rita Kilpatrick discussed the meeting with a newspaper reporter:

> He is one of the most interesting men I have ever seen. As you listen to him you forget all about his emaciation, his ugliness and his baldness and all you see are his beautiful eyes. He is perfectly sincere and though you may disagree with him, you are fascinated by what he says. I think he touches the imagination of Hindu, Moslem and, in fact, the whole world.

Mrs. Kilpatrick added that her husband had tried to point out Gandhi's inconsistency regarding western technology by noting that Gandhi himself used telegrams and the typewriter. Gandhi responded, rather coyly, that he would not introduce any more American innovations — though he might in the future, if it would help the East. (Upon being asked if he would consider taking a plane to America, he said yes. His female German disciple then asked, "Master, if you fly, will you take your little sparrow with you?") Mrs. Kilpatrick told the reporter she had formed the impression that Gandhi's primary goal was to help his people, and if it meant facing death he was perfectly willing to accept it.[21]

To Kilpatrick, Gandhi seemed more a saint, albeit a modern one, than a thinker. Gandhi, he felt, was unable to trust thought as a means to an end. He also felt that Gandhi's belief in a static universe boded little good for the people of India and would prove useless in shaking them loose from their superstitions. Kilpatrick's concluded that Gandhi reminded him of his former Mercer colleague J. R. Mosely — "one of the best men I know." As for India, Kilpatrick firmly believed that the paternalistic British education system had helped the country, but that Indians themselves had "no conception of what education should do and almost no place for new ideas" in their system.[22] He told

Tenenbaum years later that he believed Gandhi had wielded the most powerful influence of any man, and "I exclude no one." But he also believed that Gandhi's plans for India's revival were unworkable and intrinsically undesirable. India, ventured Kilpatrick in a lecture during his trip, would follow a different path. He retained this view almost twenty-five years later.[23]

In Benares Kilpatrick humorously noted that the merchants had closed their silk mills for the afternoon "to go and pray for better trade." The next day he described the scene on the Ganges River:

> The scene one can neither forget nor describe, brown bodies scrubbing themselves, some soaping, brushing their teeth, praying, more men than women, more old women than young, a holy man (more holy than fakir kind) sitting silent in prolonged and motionless prayer, a well dressed priest reading a sacred book, sacred bulls high on steps, doves flying; high, high flights of steps, the noisy chatter, some boys playing in the sand, wrestlers exercising with enormous Indian clubs, grown men pushing each other in the water, women bathing with their clothes on, some scrubbing clothes, maidens with shapely brass water jugs to carry home the sacred water.[24]

The Kilpatricks spent almost two weeks in Calcutta and a week in Madras before concluding the Indian portion of their world tour in Madura. Kilpatrick paused to reflect on his time in India as the year 1926 came to a close. Regarding the relative merits of eastern and western culture, he came to the (admittedly prejudiced) conclusion that he discovered little in the East that was superior to the West. He was especially troubled by the spirituality and mysticism in Indian culture. He found the Indian people on the whole to be good-natured, in spite of poverty, overpopulation, and inequality. But when superstition, religious intolerance, and caste were thrown into the mix, it made for a bleak situation. As Kilpatrick saw it, there were two solutions: first, an improvement in the economic lot of the people through the use of reason rather than superstition; and second, educational reform through real-life experiences and the project method, based on home, village, and agricultural life.[25]

On January 13, 1927, the Kilpatricks boarded ship at the Rameswaram Pier in Madura. Their next stopover, a lengthy one, was China. Under the auspices of the National Association for the Advancement of Education and the Y.M.C.A. in China, they spent five months. This time was to prove significant

not only for the Kilpatricks, but also for the Chinese people. The Nationalist Party, or Kuomintang, was being led by Sun Yat-sen's successor and brother in-law, Chiang Kai-shek. The goal of the Kuomintang was to unify the nation and to gain ascendancy over both the warlords and the emerging Communist Party. The military situation and the political situation were both extremely volatile during the spring of 1927.

The Kilpatricks arrived in Hong Kong on February 4 and were greeted by a representative of the Y.M.C.A. They refreshed themselves at the King Edward Hotel before leaving for Canton that evening. On February 7, Kilpatrick's host, Dr. Ping Ling, director of educational research for the National Association for the Advancement of Education in Peking, held a dinner jointly sponsored by the national government, the provincial government, the municipal government, the teachers' association, and two local universities. Shunning the knives and forks set out for them, Kilpatrick preferred "struggling" with the chopsticks to honor his hosts. He believed that the Chinese were striving to gain his favorable opinion. This they did.[26]

As Kilpatrick traveled in China, he found pictures of Sun Yat-sen everywhere, along with the threefold program of nationalism, democracy, and socialism espoused by all. He was stirred by this and felt that the United States had much to gain by recognizing the government of Sun Yat-sen's successors. But the political climate went beyond slogans and was often fraught with danger. On February 10, Kilpatrick and his host, Dr. Ling, found themselves in the middle of a mob scene. Kilpatrick at first thought it was an antiforeign tirade, but they seemed intent on making a point to the Chinese members of his party. A former student, a Canadian who spoke Chinese and recognized her professor, addressed the throng, eventually bringing calm to the situation. But the crowd, deeply troubled, swept Dr. Ling off his feet and began to carry him away. Finally, a contingent of soldiers rescued the group. Kilpatrick found the experience exhilarating as well as educational. "It was a great experience — at no time was I frightened," he wrote in his diary, "I thought I saw too how, in part, a mob differs from an individual."[27]

The next day Kilpatrick lectured at Sun Yat-sen University on "Educational Tendencies in Europe and America" and had tea that afternoon with President Chiang Kai-shek, although nothing is noted about the leader in the diary. That evening he lectured again, through an interpreter, this time on the now familiar topic "Education for a Changing Civilization." In addition to his educational duties, Dr. Ling also served at this time as a courier for Chiang Kai-shek. On a train one day, as Ling was accompanying Kilpatrick through the countryside,

he pointed out a man who he said was a spy following him. On another occasion, Ling greeted a surprised Kilpatrick dressed as a Japanese merchant. Kilpatrick even received a mysterious telephone call one night asking if he knew where Ling might be, but he told the caller nothing. Although he was once reported killed, Ling apparently survived his adventures.[28]

At the time of Kilpatrick's arrival the Kuomintang Party controlled the government and the army, while the Communist Party controlled propaganda. This arrangement lasted until Chiang turned on the communists. Kilpatrick went to the American consul in Hong Kong to inquire as to what the exact situation might be. The consul listened, confirmed what Kilpatrick had been hearing, but provided him with little new information. Turmoil was erupting with greater frequency. After visits to Canton and Amoy, the Kilpatricks went on to Shanghai, where they were delayed by a communist attack on foreigners in Nanking. Even the president of Nanking University was killed. Chiang then turned the army on the communists. The killing on both sides was to continue for years, halted only by a truce to fight the Japanese in World War II. In his diary entries of February and March 1927, Kilpatrick was critical of the Kuomintang, but twenty-five years later he noted in the margin that in hindsight, the trouble had been probably caused by the communists, not the Kuomintang. Whether this was his considered opinion, or simply Cold War sentiment is hard to tell. He did record that the violence in Nanking, while terrible, could have been worse and was more an attempt to embarrass Chiang and influence foreigners than to do actual harm.[29]

There was more than the political and military scene to observe. Socially, Kilpatrick was impressed by China's comparative freedom from class structure, in contrast to what he had observed in India. The Chinese had the opportunity to sit for the civil service exams regardless of their social or economic status. And the positive influence and role of the family also stood out as Kilpatrick scrutinized Chinese society. The downside of this family loyalty, though, was a seeming lack of empathy for anyone outside the family. He found men and women starving on the street, but rarely did anyone offer help.[30]

In Canton that February, Kilpatrick spoke on a new education for China, stressing character building. At the end of one such talk, he inquired what the Chinese would like him to advocate at the Institute for Pacific Relations, an international group of diplomats and scholars who were to gather in Honolulu in July to discuss the Far East. After insisting that China be given full autonomy from outside powers, his respondents listed a number of discriminatory practices that Americans of Chinese ancestry were enduring in the United

States. These included the inability of Chinese-American veterans to bring their Chinese brides into the United States, harassment by immigration officials when Chinese-Americans traveled into the interior of the country, and the refusal of the Los Angeles Y.M.C.A. to let a Chinese student swim in its pool. These incidents vexed Kilpatrick, and he promised to look into them.[31]

While believing in sovereignty for the Chinese, he still held onto a mild form of paternalistic colonialism. He noted that Shanghai might be jointly controlled for some time and that, in his opinion, Hong Kong might never be returned by the British.[32] By late March of 1927, the revolution had reached Shanghai, and Kilpatrick was to witness it first-hand. Coming out of the Shanghai Y.M.C.A. on March 21, he noticed the nationalist flag flying from the old post office building. He wrote of the scene:

> I could not but feel the excitement myself, a nation was being born. I was pleased of the event and excited to be present while events of such historic importance were being enacted. There was evident excitement everywhere, but I saw no disorder.[33]

But the scene was not entirely peaceful. Later the same day he saw cannons being conveyed through the streets and several thoroughfares barricaded with barbed wire and sandbags.[34]

On April 27, 1927, Kilpatrick dined at the Y.M.C.A. compound in Peking with John L. Childs. During the academic year 1922-1923, Childs, a missionary, had been a student in the joint masters program between Union Theological Seminary and Teachers College. Childs had taken two courses from Kilpatrick, who taught philosophy of education in the program, and had been invited to the Kilpatricks' apartment for one of their Sunday afternoon teas. During their meeting in Peking, Kilpatrick had persuaded Childs to take coursework at Union and combine it with further study for a doctorate at Teachers College. This Childs did. With his wife Grace, he left for America that summer after eleven years as a missionary in China.[35] Childs and Kilpatrick would develop a close relationship both during and after his doctoral studies.

When Kilpatrick left Peking to travel to Mukden, he was given a government armed guard who accompanied him until he left the country. From China, the Kilpatricks traveled to Korea, which was at that time under the control of the Japanese. The situation was obviously painful, with the Korean population resentful and indignant over their treatment. Kilpatrick noted that

the Japanese purposely degraded Korean holy places by placing Shinto shrines on hallowed ground and forcing the Koreans to worship the emperor of Japan. The Koreans were further alienated when the names of their cities were changed by the occupying forces. After the stop in Korea, Kilpatrick went on to Japan, where he lectured under the auspices of a Japanese newspaper, the *Osaka Asahi*. While in Japan, he asked students about their interests and found that they were fervent in their desire for peace, but he also noted that a militaristic element was equally strong.[36]

The voyage from Japan to Honolulu lasted from June 30 to July 8. Aboard ship, Kilpatrick lectured one evening; read *The Plastic Age*, which he found rather depressing; and attended a costume party. Although the voyage was quite smooth, the day before they disembarked he noted that, while "not actually sea sick, he was thoroughly sick of the sea."[37] Upon arriving, the Kilpatricks were met by Arthur A. Hauck, president of Oahu College — site of the conference — and George Axtelle, who would be a friend to Kilpatrick for the next forty years.[38] That evening, by prior arrangement, Kilpatrick spoke to 800 people at a parent-teacher meeting.

Kilpatrick's reason for being in Honolulu was to attend the Institute for Pacific Relations (IPR). The IPR had been founded in Honolulu in 1925 to improve American understanding of Asia by bringing together leaders for frank discussions of their differences. The organization, which was to meet on alternate years, would gain a reputation as a prestigious discussion group. This second international IPR conference, again held in Honolulu, was composed of six national councils, from the United States, Canada, Australia, New Zealand, China, and Japan. The United Kingdom, Korea, the Philippines, and the League of Nations also sent delegations. Distinguished delegates in Honolulu included W. W. Astor and Lionel Curtis from Great Britain, Herbert Croly and James T. Shotwell from the United States, and J. W. Beaton and Sir Arthur Carrie from Canada. James D. Dole, the agriculture magnate, represented a local delegation from the Hawaiian Islands. There were also women delegates representing the Philippines, the United States, and Great Britain. While the delegates saw the IPR primarily as "nonsectarian, noncontroversial, and nonpropagandist," with the goal of being a cross-cultural conference for the exchange of individual views in a private framework, the British and Chinese governments did use the forum to carry on semiformal negotiations.[39]

At this 1927 conference, Kilpatrick's major assignment was to serve as facilitator for the various discussion groups. He soon took on the additional role of negotiator, suggesting formats for the speakers and assisting in framing

questions for the opening sessions of the conference.   One of the British delegates, Malcolm MacDonald, son of the British prime minister Ramsay MacDonald, served as secretary to Kilpatrick's discussion group.   Both the Japanese delegate, Yusuka Tsurmumi, and a United States delegate, E. C. Carter, expressed their indebtedness to Kilpatrick for his expertise in ironing out numerous problems with the program of the conference.   Later, Malcolm MacDonald also praised Kilpatrick for his work with the discussion groups.   "I am clearly becoming a figure in the Institute," wrote Kilpatrick.[40]   Near the end of the conference, Kilpatrick was made chairman of a discussion group, "Roundtable on the Future of the Institute," and he believed that the conference was achieving much, especially in Sino-British relations.   Unfortunately, the conference yielded little progress for relations between the Chinese and Japanese, though this had been the goal of many of the delegates.[41]   Considering that this was Kilpatrick's first real experience with international relations, he performed admirably.   He was well-read and always a close observer of world events and this foundation, in addition to his own ability to facilitate group interactions and suggest workable solutions to problems, served him well in the international arena.

On July 30, the Kilpatricks sailed for the United States; they arrived in Los Angeles on August 5. They visited friends and former students in the Los Angeles area before working their way up the coast to Yosemite Valley and then Sacramento before departing eastward.[42]   On August 13, they arrived in Lincoln, Nebraska, where Kilpatrick checked into the Cornhusker Hotel and began teaching a two-week course to 200 students in the University of Nebraska summer school.   Rita continued her trip by train to New York.

On August 28, 1927 — one year to the day after he had left New York for his round-the-world trip — Kilpatrick returned to Morningside Drive.   After changing the contents of his bags in preparation for a week at the Teachers College Country Club at Ossining, he had lunch with his brother Howard, and his sister Helen, his daughter and son-in-law, and his grandson, Teddy (Theodore), born the previous year.   He had purchased a collapsible ball for the infant and found him "quite bright, good looking, and good natured."   He then caught the 5:46 p.m. train.   Upon arriving home, he greeted Rita and met a few old friends and several strangers before retiring to read his accumulated mail.[43]   The momentous journey was at an end.

Although Kilpatrick kept extremely active with his numerous professional duties, his international interests often returned to the forefront.   Students from abroad who were in residence at Teachers College often presented him with

gifts in recognition of his contributions to them. Officers of a Chinese organization spoke of Kilpatrick's lectures in China and his hour-long dialogue with a Buddhist monk on Eastern philosophy and religion. "He, more than any other, gave to our teachers a keener insight into the teaching and learning process," said Franklin Huang at the ceremony: "Our only regret was that he could not stay longer." In response, Kilpatrick called China the most interesting and significant place in the world and characterized the people as courteous and as lovers of learning and beauty.[44]

These strong feelings made Kilpatrick very much want to return to the next meeting of the Institute for Pacific Relations to be held in the fall of 1929 in Kyoto, Japan. Following both direct and indirect signals to the dean (including a strong hint from Rita to Russell at a tea), Kilpatrick received word in January that he would be allowed to attend the conference at full pay, with Teachers College underwriting a portion of the cost and the Carnegie Foundation covering the rest. He was deeply moved and extremely pleased. This time he would go to the IPR conference as an official delegate. The Kilpatricks left for the Far East on August 15, 1929 aboard the *Mauritania*, since they would be going via Europe. Crossing Europe by rail, they stopped in Germany for another education conference, in Mainz, before arriving in Poland on September 3. Although the Nazis were not yet in power in Germany, Kilpatrick discerned disturbing attitudes, which were harbingers of the decade to come. The Poles were wary of both the Soviet Union and Germany, believing that the Germans wanted to recapture the land taken from them at Versailles; there was a fear of democracy; and Kilpatrick detected a definite "acceptance of the anti-Jewish attitude."[45] These thoughts were recorded almost ten years to the day before Germany attacked Poland in 1939.

From Poland, the trip across the Soviet Union began. While not entirely primitive, the journey by rail was uncomfortable at times and tedious. To pass the time, Kilpatrick had secured a copy of D. H. Lawrence's novel *Lady Chatterley's Lover*, banned in both Britain and the United States. Ever analytical, Kilpatrick found the book unique in two ways: "the use of the old Saxon words for certain usually unwritten bodily parts and function" and "the unusual detailed frankness of 'the way of a man with a maid.'"[46] The Kilpatricks were met in Moscow by Miss Nucia Perlmutter, George Counts's secretary from Teachers College, who read and spoke Russian. Counts was in the country, but he was away from Moscow at the time. There were reports that both Dewey's and Kilpatrick's ideas were influential with officials and that progressive education was in vogue in the Soviet Union at this time. After the

revolution the Soviet schools had indeed begun from scratch, building into their methodology many of Dewey's ideas. Kilpatrick's books were also well-known in the Soviet Union, and a few had been translated and were in use in teacher-training institutes.[47]

Later in the week Professor Pinkevich, president of Moscow University, showed Kilpatrick a copy of *Education for a Changing Civilization*, for which he was writing an introduction. When Kilpatrick was asked if this met with his approval, he replied yes, since there were no copyright agreements between the two countries at the time. Just before leaving Moscow, Kilpatrick was approached by a young woman who had heard he was in the country. She had failed an examination in one of her education courses because she had not been able to identify Kilpatrick or describe his contribution to education. This amazed him.[48] Kilpatrick also went for an interview with the widow of Lenin. There he found Patty Hill of the Horace Mann School, who also had an interview with Madam Lenin. Miss Perlmutter acted as translator, although Kilpatrick believed that the dour and formal Madam Lenin, as she was called, could speak passable English. The interview was a flop. She was asked excellent questions about the role of education in the revolution and was complimented on the Soviet experiment, but she repeatedly answered with only a single word: "Obviously." Kilpatrick next turned to the topic of the Institute for Pacific Relations, wishing, as an official delegate, to persuade the Soviet Union to send more than observers. The only answer he could get from Madam Lenin was "The party will decide." Before he left, however, he did have his picture taken with the widow of the revolution's founder. Kilpatrick finished the day by attending *The Armored Train*, a play that dealt with the revolution in Siberia. He found it pure propaganda intended more to inspire a spirit of war than to depict economic conditions. Nuncia Perlmutter again served as translator. He noted in his diary that they were forced to leave their overcoats in the lobby; the management feared someone would carry a bomb into the theater.[49]

While in Moscow, Kilpatrick met with Comrade Shatsky, an administrator of twenty village schools, who was well-versed in American education. Shatsky was especially impressed with Collings's work on the project method and indicated that his own plan was to have his schools "100% on the project basis" within three years. Kilpatrick was skeptical as to how free the educators were to criticize the Soviet system. Shatsky told him such criticism was possible, to which Kilpatrick responded, "I hope you are right." The more he saw, the more skeptical Kilpatrick was becoming about the Soviet system. There was freedom in the area of teaching methodology, but no freedom as to which topics were to

be explored. He found the system saturated with a militaristic mentality and propaganda. One poster he saw in a classroom, depicting a Catholic priest engaged in scandalous behavior, was especially repulsive to him. "It was sad," he wrote in his diary. "This is propaganda of the worst type, a caricature of truth." Kilpatrick was himself put on the defensive when asked about the lack of freedom to teach evolution in the American schools and also about whether there was segregation of lower-class students. He heard that morals, specifically sexual relations, were rather loose, and he made persistent inquiries of the students about this. They repudiated such promiscuous behavior, yet he later heard that abortions were encouraged by the government, with the only restriction being that the procedure be done by a physician.[50]

When asked by Tenenbaum what he thought of the Russian schools, Kilpatrick responded that "the best was not as good as our best, but the worst I saw was much better than the worst I knew to exist here." As George Counts would later say, it was highly questionable how truly progressive the Soviet school system ever became. And all that Kilpatrick observed — the propaganda, the restrictions on topics to be discussed — painted a very bleak picture. "Now I understand how they do things," he told Tenenbaum twenty years later; "at that time I did not fully understand." Kilpatrick never did see Lunacharsky, who had been the architect of the new Soviet education. It was later revealed that he had probably been liquidated just before Kilpatrick's visit. Of the two educators Kilpatrick met, Shatsky committed suicide in 1931 and Pinkevich was never heard from again. While some, such as William Bagley, later made much of the Soviet's repudiation of progressive education, Kilpatrick strongly believed that it was Stalin's need to indoctrinate the population which finally came into diametric opposition to the beliefs and practices of the Dewey-Kilpatrick model.[51]

On September 15, 1929, the Kilpatricks left Moscow on the Trans-Siberian railway, cutting through the Ural Mountains and across the vast expanse of Siberia. The trip was monotonous, the food was bland, and the bathing facilities were primitive. The journey took eight days, punctuated only by twenty-minute walks at railroad stations along the way. To pass the time, Kilpatrick listened to a member of his party translate the Russian newspapers to the group and read several books on China and Japan in preparation for the IPR conference. On September 23, the party arrived in Vladivostak and were met at the rail station by members of the Society of Cultural Relations. After a brief visit to Korea, they returned to the mainland for a tour of Manchuria, which Kilpatrick found "fertile and prosperous." The week of October 5 to 12 was spent in Peking, with a day in Nanking and then almost a week in Shanghai, before

sailing on October 19 for Kobe, Japan, on the *President Lincoln.*[52]

Kilpatrick was surprised to learn while in China that the authorities, having little interest in or seeing no need for education as a subject of study, had abolished all normal schools except the National Normal University in Peking. All departments of education in the colleges were abolished, and teacher training was moved to the high schools. As a result, few, if any, students were entering the teaching profession. The dean of the National Normal University, a Columbia Ph.D., also told Kilpatrick that since Sun Yat-sen's death there had been a crackdown on freedom of expression. He himself had been forced to soften an article he had written, which was critical of the regime. Kilpatrick also heard that few students were being allowed to study in the United States, especially at Teachers College. While this troubled him, he wrote that such actions might be expected, since education was "a growing subject, hard to test."[53]

On October 27, 1929, the Kilpatricks left for Osaka. Kilpatrick's first assignment at the IPR Conference was to lead a roundtable discussion "The Machine Age and Traditional Culture." As an official member of the American delegation, Kilpatrick took a more active role in the proceedings this time than in 1927. Two days later the conference moved on to the topic of industrialization, and Kilpatrick met Yosuke Matsuoka, an intriguing Japanese diplomat who had been assigned to the Japanese ambassador to the United States in Washington, D.C. Matsuoka told Kilpatrick in confidence that he had been surprised at the actions of his government, especially in connection with the "Twenty-One Demands." (The "Twenty-One Demands" were economic and trade stipulations that Japan coerced upon China during World War I. Similar provisions were mandated for China by European nations in the previous century.) Matsuoka later became Japan's foreign minister in 1940, but he resigned in 1941, six months before Pearl Harbor. Kilpatrick was completely taken in by this diplomat, who was later considered a militarist, a conspirator with Hitler, and according to his obituary in the *New York Times*, one of "the world's greatest talkers." Matsuoka died in prison in 1946, under indictment as a war criminal.[54]

Sino-Japanese friction was a major problem at the conference. Japan had no wish to discuss its activity in Manchuria, but China viewed the IPR as an excellent forum for raising this increasingly bitter and contentious issue. Before the meeting began, Merle Davis, the IPR's secretary-general, resigned, believing that the organization's original intention of having individuals discuss economic and cultural issues had been superseded by political agendas and that

group opinions had achieved primacy in the discussions.[55]

But the topics were not primarily political. On October 30, the IPR discussed architecture, manners, art, marriage, and ethics. The historian Arnold Toynbee was in attendance and at this particular session assisted in framing the fundamental position on ethics. Later, Toynbee and Kilpatrick took several walks, discussing not only the conference, but also philosophy, education, and culture. Kilpatrick described as delightful one conversation on the differences between British and American attitudes. Kilpatrick viewed the British system as heavily influenced by remnants of the feudal class system, which, in turn, reflected upon the educational system — a system that he saw as Aristotelian, in the sense of being stagnant and divorcing thought from action. Conversely, in the United States he observed a vibrant, changing industrial society striving for democracy. Kilpatrick felt that the "buoyancy of outlook" he noted in America was based on a "chance economic prosperity." (Back in the United States the stock market had crashed a week before, but if he knew of this, he did not mention it.) He also saw American society as being grounded on solid thought and philosophy. Toynbee agreed with part of Kilpatrick's analysis but also demurred. He spoke of a spiritual depression resulting from the economic depression in Great Britain. The dialogue between the two men was enlightening, causing Kilpatrick to "see much more" than he did previously.[56] Toynbee was enjoying seeing Asia for the first time; years later, during a visit to New York, he would continue his discussion with Kilpatrick. Kilpatrick also met Owen Lattimore, who went on to become the editor of the IPR's journal *Pacific Relations* and would be a target, along with the IPR, of Senator Joseph McCarthy in the 1950s.

On November 6, the four roundtable groups were brought together to discuss Sino-Japanese differences. Kilpatrick was chosen to lead the discussion, both for his perceived impartiality and for his ability as a discussion leader. Although a tense atmosphere permeated the meeting, in an opening statement Kilpatrick made it clear that the session was not a debate, but rather an attempt to clarify positions and search for solutions. Except for a few extremists on both sides, the meeting was productive. Kilpatrick felt that the discussion had been a success and that he himself had done well. One Chinese delegate told him he felt as though he had "been at chapel." The British were also complimentary. The next day Toynbee and Kilpatrick were in charge of a discussion on the League of Nations, but despite thorough planning, several long-winded delegates spoiled the session.[57] The conference closed on November 9 with hopes all around that Japan and China could lessen their

differences in a positive way.

After the IPR conference, the Kilpatricks toured Japan, where Kilpatrick lectured several times, once to the Tokyo Women's Club. One evening at dinner, near the end of their stay, they were surprised to be entertained by teenage geisha girls. Some of the people in their traveling party disapproved, but Kilpatrick, not a prude, found the girls dull, though well-behaved. On November 26, the Kilpatricks boarded the liner *President Taft* at Yokohama for Hawaii. After a brief stay in the islands, where Kilpatrick lectured to teachers and normal school students at McKinley High School, the Kilpatricks sailed on to California. In San Francisco he attended a state conference held by public school leaders to advance a new education agenda — an agenda which, after his presentation, had a definite Kilpatrickan bent. Having just come from the IPR, Kilpatrick suggested a curriculum for California built around the issues of the Pacific Basin. High praises were sung of his work during the conference, held the week of Christmas, with one official saying that the service he rendered was the finest given by any single individual in memory.[58]

Kilpatrick was to summarize his visits to India, China, and Japan with an article in *Childhood Education* the following year: "Vacation Retrospect." Of India he mentioned the heavy hand of the British Commonwealth, with its uniform, centrally administered examination system, which he called the clearest and worst example of such assessment he had ever seen. On the positive side, he mentioned that the project method was being utilized in several missionary schools. As for China, he urged openness, patience, and a retreat from foreign paternalism. Japan was undergoing "pain," in his estimation, much of it due to feelings of inferiority and pride.[59] Kilpatrick's travels had once again broadened his intellectual horizons. He had met a number of major figures, had visited key nations, and had been exposed to a number of diverse cultures. These experiences would leave him both changed and enlightened as to the world scene in the era after the Great War.

COLUMBIA'S MILLION-DOLLAR PROFESSOR: FROM RIVERSIDE DRIVE TO MORNINGSIDE HEIGHTS

> In the country at large, I am increasingly well known. I do not feel that I am in the class with John Dewey or Thorndike as an originator. I mainly see good things, put them together, explain them better than others perhaps. My teaching gives me in the aggregate my greatest power.
>
> William Heard Kilpatrick, Diary, 1931[1]

> Dr. Kilpatrick is a man rather small in stature, with a mild ruddy countenance, a wealth of silvery white hair and clear, keen blue eyes that startle one with their penetrating force. He is a simple likable man with a whole-hearted friendly manner toward old friends and a quiet diffidence toward strangers. When he begins to talk one is first attracted by his quiet matter of factness and independence, then awed by the power of his intellect and charmed by the 'teacher.' He seems, indeed, a man who by the magnitude of his intellect would be an outstanding figure in whatever spot of the world he might be placed.
>
> Description of Kilpatrick by a southern reporter, 1929[2]

There is little doubt that during the decade before his retirement in 1937, Kilpatrick was at the pinnacle of his influence and productivity. With world travels behind him and the challenges of social reconstructionism ahead of him, he was involved in a number of activities at Teachers College. Kilpatrick's domain ran from Riverside Drive, along the Hudson River (where John D. Rockefeller, Jr., had just built Dr. Harry Emerson Fosdick an impressive new church) east down 120th Street past Union Theological Seminary to Teachers College, at the corner of Broadway and 120th. Two long city blocks farther east,

running north and south, was Morningside Drive, where the Kilpatricks had lived since 1914. Their apartment building, at one time known as Seth Low Hall, was numbered 106 Morningside Drive.

The door to the Kilpatricks' eighth-floor apartment (number 84, just a few steps from the elevator) opened onto a long hallway — a perfect example of what was commonly known at that time as a railroad flat. Kilpatrick had turned one of the four modest-sized bedrooms, the first room to the right along the hallway, into a study. A guest room came next, and then the Kilpatricks' bedroom — they slept in twin beds, and he wore a nightcap on cold nights — followed by the bath and another bedroom, which was daughter Margaret's until she married. Near the end of the hallway was a large "front room" composed of a sitting room and a dining room joined by a large opening, which gave the area a feeling of spaciousness. Adjacent to that room were the kitchen and a small pantry. The view from the sitting room windows was to the east, overlooking Morningside Park and Harlem. The East River was visible, as well as Hell's Gate and even Astoria Gas Works on Long Island, from which flames shot periodically. Kilpatrick kept a small pair of binoculars near the dining room window, with which planes taking off from LaGuardia Airport could be seen. One chair in Kilpatrick's study had broad wooden arms across which he placed a large flat board. He called this his "writing table," and here, rather than at his desk, he did his writing and some of his reading. There was another chair in the study for visitors. His grandson remembers that on visits he often found his grandfather in a contemplative pose, chin resting on fist, similar to Rodin's "The Thinker."[3]

Kilpatrick kept a very detailed record of his professional life in his diary, but only occasionally did he note what occurred in his personal life. At the conclusion of his diary for 1923, though, he took the time to describe a Sunday on Morningside Drive:

> *December 30, 1923 Sunday* — Rise as usual on Sunday at 8. Lower the window shade so that Margaret (Rita) may sleep till 9. Put on my heavy woolen dressing gown, sit by my study window, wrap up "steamer like" in my steamer rug, put my feet on the footstool and against the radiator and read. As usual I read the *New York Times*. The news section comes first, then the pictures, the editorial page, certain miscellaneous pages, then finally the Magazine Section and the Book Review. The articles are not always of the highest quality, but on the whole I rather like this Sunday paper.

Before I have finished Margaret comes with breakfast for two on a tray, and we eat in my study. I do not move from my chair, having previously cleared my little table to receive and hold the tray. We always have Sunday breakfast so. We begin with fruit, today with grapefruit. Then we have coffee, two cups and buttered bread. I drink no other coffee during the week.

Today before I copy the accounts into my big book, my daughter Margaret L. comes in as usual to dine with us. She comes so each Sunday and each dining holiday as Thanksgiving, Christmas, and New Year. In a few minutes Margaret P. (who reads till about 12 noon, then bathes) calls out to me that it is time to bathe.

I go to the bath room. Shave, and get into a tub of warm water. I take Packer's liquid tar soap and shampoo my head. This I do twice a week to keep down dandruff.

About one I come out, dress in street dress, except my bed room slippers which with no more company present, I retain. In a short while dinner is ready. Our cook is a student, Miss Alberto Alexander from Atlanta, who cooks dinners in return for her room rent. Our menu is turkey hash (brought over from Christmas dinner), and also a mutton chop each, egg plant, rice, salad of tomato and lettuce, plum pudding.

After dinner I lie out at full length on the lounge. Margaret P. sits in the large chair at my head, Margaret L. sits at my feet. We have music from our new Dao Art piano, electrically played. I try to recall a piece I heard played last evening, Chopin, Bach, Paderewski, but in vain, I can never quite recall it.

We sit there — or lie there, till about 3:30, when Margaret L. and I go to walk. We walk about an hour each Sunday afternoon, this time down Morningside to the rear entrance of the Cathedral, through the grounds to 110th and Amsterdam

and then to Riverside, down R. to about 100th Street, then back to 120th street and home.

Read a little on genealogy, which is a hobby of mine.

Have supper about 7:30, light. Then talk and listen to music.

Read the *Atlantic Monthly*. An article on the novelists' treatment of sex interests me. I wonder what the future has in store.

Write a little. 12/30/23.

This Sunday afternoon did not include a monthly event that Kilpatrick called his "at home." Kilpatrick's secretary would invite about thirty students to the apartment, taking special care to include international students. Possibly owing to Rita's southern decorum and etiquette, the structure of such an afternoon took on a very formal air. When the students arrived, their names would be announced, after which Rita would assemble half a dozen together and bring them to Kilpatrick, where they would be served tea and would chat for a few minutes. After a proper amount of time for pleasantries had elapsed, according to Rita's estimation, the groups would be rotated. Of twenty-two in attendance for one "at home," the countries represented included Nicaragua, New Zealand, Ecuador, China, Spain, Puerto Rico, Canada, and South Africa. Never one to forget his roots, Kilpatrick had also invited some young women from Georgia.[4]

Kilpatrick's family was growing: a second grandson was born on January 20, 1929, and named for him — Heard Kilpatrick Baumeister. In the mid-1930s his daughter and son-in-law built a new home in Riverdale, at 4711 Iselin Avenue. The cost was $25,000; Kilpatrick and Theodore Baumeister, Sr., contributed several thousand dollars each toward the purchase price. The relationship between Kilpatrick and his daughter continued to be close. Kilpatrick was an inveterate walker, and during these outings he had many meaningful talks with colleagues, friends, and family. After one such walk with Margaret, he wrote, "It is a pleasure to see how she has blossomed into a fine and sensible woman. She has learned how to profit from her experiences." They often spoke of the boys, Teddy and Heard. In another conversation with his daughter he noticed that she was developing a decidedly conservative bent

in her thought and attributed part of the shift to the influence of her father-in-law. Yet, never one to preach, he gently pointed out to her the proper place of change in the world and suggested that more open-mindedness should enter into her own thinking.[5]

At Teachers College, a change in leadership occurred in late 1926. Dean James G. Russell had rather unexpectedly retired and, after a rapid search, his son, William F. Russell, was appointed as the new dean. Kilpatrick, in Europe at the time, immediately wired congratulations to his former student. Eighteen months later, on April 11, 1928, the younger Russell was inaugurated as dean of Teachers College. President Butler of Columbia University and John Dewey gave the major addresses. "Will," as Kilpatrick had formerly called him, responded "well, tho not profoundly." Kilpatrick wore his orange-and-black Mercer LL.D. hood (he had been awarded an honorary doctorate in 1926) as the procession marched from the Dodge building to 120th Street, on to Broadway, and then into the Horace Mann Auditorium. Dewey's address was the highlight of the ceremony: "Professor Dewey makes the address and excellently. He was clear, concrete, interesting, and at times almost light in touch," wrote Kilpatrick.[6]

Kilpatrick's relations with the new dean began well. In September of 1927, during the Russell's first year, Kilpatrick found that his salary would be $10,000 for the coming academic year and $11,000 for the following year, one of the highest in the university. He credited the dean's assistant, Dr. Robert J. Leonard, for this.[7] Word spread across campus that there were two professors at Teachers College who made more than the dean and that Kilpatrick was one of them. But Kilpatrick himself was sure that Thorndike was one of the two, and that the other was more likely to be Bagley.[8] By the school year 1929-1930 Kilpatrick's salary had jumped to $13,000 per year, with an additional $2,000 for his summer school teaching. This clearly made him one of the highest-paid professors in the Columbia University community.[9] A decade later, Kilpatrick's compensation in relation to the revenue he generated for his institution would earn him the moniker "Columbia's million-dollar professor." Although his salary never approached that number, the tuition his classes garnered for Columbia's coffers did exceed that amount during his quarter century of service to Teachers College. And, at the modest fees charged during the first third of the century, that was a remarkable feat by any measure.

Another event of note at Teachers College in 1928 was the unveiling of a bust of John Dewey by Jacob Epstein. Among those contributing toward the commission of the bust were Oliver Wendell Holmes, Rabbi Stephen S. Wise,

Clarence Darrow, and Alice Vanderbilt. A small gathering of seventy-five attended the unveiling. Kilpatrick gave the presentation speech and was lavish in his praise, likening Dewey to Socrates, Plato, and Aristotle. "No school child in this country but feels the effect of his teaching," declared Kilpatrick. He went on to enumerate Dewey's contributions to education, including his concept of experience and intelligence, his ideas on biological psychology, and the significance he placed on the social factor in experience. Kilpatrick closed by lauding Dewey's personal attributes: modesty, kindliness, generosity, and friendliness.[10]

Dewey and Kilpatrick chatted briefly after the ceremony. Dewey did not know whether the bust actually resembled him, but at least, he said, it reflected the way he felt when he had sat for the sculptor. It was his hope that the bust would go down in history as a work of art rather than a likeness. Privately, Kilpatrick was astounded and repelled by the bust: "The mouth seemed too heavy and the head too high," he concluded. Ever the mathematician, he reached the conclusion that the best view was at a 105-degree angle from the right-hand front side of the bust. Dewey expressed his appreciation to Kilpatrick for his earlier remarks and added "playfully that he would have to thank me or kill me, meaning I had over praised him."[11]

During the latter half of the decade, Kilpatrick became intensely involved in the institutional life of the campus and was called upon more and more to represent Teachers College at civic functions. In October of 1927 he attended a luncheon at the offices of *The New Republic*, where the editor, Herbert Croly, placed Kilpatrick next to the honored guest, Bertrand Russell.[12] At times in this flurry of activity, Kilpatrick approached the breaking point, and he became concerned that life was just too full. "I am in danger of doing nothing through trying to do all. I feel so much the need of thinking and digesting, reading and thinking, lest I live and think on a lower plane than is necessary."[13] One November day in 1928 is emblematic of his hectic pace. The day began with Kilpatrick preparing for two talks, one to the female students at Horace Mann High School and the other at Harry Emerson Fosdick's church that weekend on "What's Right with Our Schools." He then met with the dean to consult on the marital difficulties of several staff members and the intolerant attitudes which had emerged over the situation. Kilpatrick then hurried away to a meeting with representatives of the Institute for Pacific Relations to plan the 1929 Kyoto conference. The session concluded at 11:30 p.m., and he did not reach his apartment until almost midnight.[14] Such days were not atypical. Yet Kilpatrick did find time to continue his wide reading, especially in psychology. He recorded in the index of his diary for 1928 that he had read Alfred Adler on

psychiatry and *The Self, Its Body and Freedom* by William Ernest Hocking, as well as unspecified works on behaviorism and gestalt psychology. He also read Dewey, Chesterton, Beard, Mencken, Lewis Mumford, and *Middletown*, the Lynds' sociological study of Muncie, Indiana.

During this time between international trips, Kilpatrick worked with, nurtured, and got to know a number of individuals who were newly associated with Teachers College. This unofficial mentoring often occurred during the many long walks that Kilpatrick took along Riverside Drive or south to the northern edge of Central Park. Goodwin Watson, who taught psychology at Teachers College and was considered by many a political radical, was one of the new personalities on campus. Kilpatrick found him both bright and creative.[15] Hilda Taba, a doctoral student and a future innovator in the area of curriculum, gave a memorable presentation at one of Kilpatrick's seminars. "It was quite good, showing a quality of thinking and breadth of command of thought not often found. We were all pleased," he wrote. Kilpatrick wrote the introduction to Taba's first book, *The Dynamics of Education*, in 1932. At one point he even seems to have saved Taba's career. She was evidently the victim of some vicious gossip, and Paul Monroe had called Kilpatrick and instructed him to "get rid of her." Kilpatrick calmed the waters, and Monroe eventually assisted her in finishing her dissertation. Kilpatrick, having read the dissertation, judged her to be "a very good thinker," but predicted her work would have few readers, as it was a bit ponderous and covered ground already staked out by Dewey and Whitehead.[16]

Kilpatrick later advised both Florence Stratemeyer and B. O. Smith on their dissertations. During 1930 he worked with John Childs — the former missionary — on his dissertation, and was pleased with the quality of Childs's work. Childs was also teaching philosophy of education for Kilpatrick, along with R. Bruce Raup. Raup eventually took over Kilpatrick's research course so that Kilpatrick could devote more time to an advanced course on current issues in education. Kilpatrick also turned one of his classes over to Raup because he thought his own reputation "overawed" the class. Kilpatrick, while he had an ego, usually kept it in check. "In some quarters I am even counted a great man, but I know better," he wrote, "and hope I always let it be seen that I know better." In 1928 Kilpatrick had been able to cap his enrollments at approximately 465 students per course, and he viewed this as a great improvement over 1926, when he had taught one class with 669 students and another with 630. Many students had to be turned away, though, and the circumstances often became emotional for both student and professor. "I hate very much to shut out

of the classes so many serious students — so anxious to get in," he wrote; "one girl could not restrain her feelings and gave way to tears."[17]

Kilpatrick extended his mentorship by attempting to secure John Childs a permanent position on the Teachers College staff. This proved a difficult task, however. The dean wished for diversity in philosophical thought among the faculty, as had his father before him, and was hesitant to employ full time another disciple of Dewey. Kilpatrick was always able to bring his powers of persuasion to full effect when an important issue was at stake and he now emphasized Childs's intellect, showing the dean a copy of the recently completed dissertation. As Childs's biographer puts it, Kilpatrick continued to press the reluctant Dean Russell on this issue and was finally able to secure an assistant professorship for Childs, which was made permanent on the publication of Child's dissertation in June of 1931.[18]

One of the new ventures Kilpatrick undertook at this time was the formation of what became known as the Kilpatrick Discussion Group. On May 8, 1928, eight men met in the Teachers College Faculty Club for the first time: William Bagley, Harrison Elliot, Jesse Newlon, George Counts, Percival Symonds, Goodwin Watson, Bruce Raup, and Kilpatrick. Another member, Harold Rugg, was ill that evening. According to Kilpatrick, the aim was to "discuss the more significant matters that interest us in the education field. We decide to limit the number to 12." Isaac Kandel was soon added to the list, and John Dewey also attended. Each man (the inclusion of women was apparently not considered) brought to the group a series of issues he was personally interested in, there being few, if any, limitations on the subjects to be discussed. The group ate dinner, and then one member was assigned to make an introductory statement on the topic. Kilpatrick's topic, "Is there now a need for some unifying outlook or point of view?" was selected as the first issue to be undertaken at the second meeting, and he was chosen as factotum.[19]

Kilpatrick had belonged to other discussion groups while in New York City and, as evidenced by his work with the Institute for Pacific Relations, was a deft and accomplished discussion leader. Discussion and intellectual stimulation were essential to Kilpatrick's professional life. In an interview with a journalist from Georgia he said:

> Education to my notion of thinking is a process of studying,
> thinking, and discussing what we are really interested in. And
> by discussion I mean clear frank discussion of whatever subjects

are of paramount interest to us at the immediate time. Whatever subject should be discussed, cleared up — that's education.[20]

Later questions addressed by the discussion group included whether the scientific procedure of psychology was adequate in addressing life as a whole and whether the curriculum should be prescribed so that students could acquire expertise.[21] This latter topic brought on an extensive attack by Bagley on progressive education. Although Kilpatrick would never agree with Bagley on this issue, he found such discussions informative and concluded that he was "delighted we are having them." Kilpatrick and Bagley were perpetual philosophical adversaries, with the former often amused at the inconsistencies in the latter's arguments: Kilpatrick had as much trouble with Bagley's logic as with his ideas. "I admire Bagley as a gentleman very much, tho I cannot say so much of his ideas," he wrote, "I wonder that so good a man can be guilty of so much poor reasoning." Two years later his opinions had not altered. "He nearly always seems superficial to me."[22]

John Dewey was present on the evening when Harold Rugg opened the discussion with his notion of creative learning versus assimilative learning. Both Dewey and Kilpatrick objected to the dualism it implied for teaching. On another occasion, Counts, possibly playing the devil's advocate, said that the accomplishments of progressive education were of doubtful validity and possibly indefensible. Kilpatrick arose quickly to say that he would defend his brand of progressive education "against all comers" as the only position upon which any current philosophy of education could be built.[23] Such controversy was endemic to the Discussion Group, and the members seemed to thrive on it. The breach between the progressives and the essentialists opened in 1932, when three Englishmen were invited to attend for a dialogue on American education. The trio advocated teaching the classics and other conventional subjects. Bagley, of course, quickly signed on to this approach, as did Kandel, but the lack of inquiry into current social problems caused Kilpatrick to repudiate this line of thought and wonder "how his (English) colleagues got this way" in their thinking. "We have thought all around them and beneath them," he concluded.[24]

Years later Harold Rugg, one of the group's charter members, recalled its beginnings:

> It served us on the social-educational frontier as Peirce's Metaphysical Club served the young intelligentsia of

Cambridge sixty years before and his similar one at Hopkins in the 1880s. We held our bimonthly dinner-discussion meetings, conversing informally, without programs planned in advance, on the roots of every phase of our culture. In hundreds of hours of friendly argument we dug to the social foundations of education.[25]

The Discussion Group did become influential on campus and was even invited to the dean's home for one meeting. In late 1931 Kilpatrick noted: "My discussion group is, I believe, the central fact in the thinking of the institution." A year later he added "my discussion group is, by odds, the chief life in the institution and is slowly influencing all else." Although there was no formal membership list, on occasion additional members were explicitly invited to join, including John Childs. During 1931 as many as seventeen members would be in attendance. That same year the group decided to ask Bruce Bliven of *The New Republic* and Harry Emerson Fosdick from the nearby Riverside Church to attend meetings. Walter Lippmann's name was also suggested, but tabled.[26] The Discussion Group was plainly Kilpatrick's creation, and he was its nurturer. When he was out of the country in 1929, the group failed to meet, although it happily resumed its activity when he returned. The group met regularly from 1927 to 1934 and then intermittently from 1934 to 1938. During World War II the members resumed their gatherings on a more regular basis. According to Rugg, they were a "cohesive" circle, standing together on the concept of the welfare state and agreeing in general on what constituted democratic principles. "This was practicing what we preached," wrote Rugg, "vigorous adult education."[27]

In addition to Kilpatrick, the other great educational philosopher of the day — also a disciple of Dewey's — was Boyd H. Bode of The Ohio State University. The rivalry between the two men never erupted into open intellectual warfare, but a palpable tension was always present, lasting until Bode's death in 1952. In February of 1929, Bode came from Columbus to Teachers College to lecture. Bode's lecture was a plea to make intelligence central within the curriculum. After hearing him lecture, Kilpatrick wrote: "I cannot but admit Bode's real ability and insight. I quite envy his facility of thought in his field." But the compliment was paired with a criticism: Kilpatrick found Bode's use of Thorndike's psychology careless and thought it unfortunate that Bode did not have closer contact with children in school. Kilpatrick concluded that Bode's criticisms of his own work were "founded but

slightly" on solid ground.[28] Later in the week, during a conversation between the two men, Bode amused Kilpatrick by asking him how he was able to work with such large groups of students "as if by magic." "He was very genial," wrote Kilpatrick. However, when Bode lectured to a standing-room-only audience in Horace Mann Auditorium during the summer of 1931, Kilpatrick found him more of an entertainer than a deep thinker.[29]

Kilpatrick also continued to separate himself from Thorndike's thinking. But while Kilpatrick was moving away from the S-R focus and the emphasis on measurement, he still employed Thorndike's ideas when they were consistent with his own. After reading Thorndike's book on adult learning, he noted that one idea — "the best time to learn anything is when you need it" — supported his own psychology. On New Year's Day 1930 he recorded: "I have launched a fight to break the present thralldom of American education to objective measurement. I deem this the greatest present handicap to growth of a better idea. It will be no easy task and I may not live to see victory, but I think things are moving already in that direction." After hearing Thorndike speak later that year, he concluded that Thorndike was still using the term learn "as of old." Another major figure in education with whom Kilpatrick rarely found common ground was Dean Charles H. Judd of the University of Chicago, who seemed to be diametrically opposed to Kilpatrick on almost every issue in education. Judd's antagonistic attitude and opinionated diatribes made Kilpatrick himself turn obstinate in his presence. "I am sorry that I cannot be dispassionate where he is concerned," he noted after one meeting.[30]

But Kilpatrick could raise hackles himself. In June of 1929 he returned to Macon, Georgia, to deliver the commencement address at his alma mater, Mercer University. His message dealt with modernity, societal unrest, and authoritarianism. "The most outstanding feature of modern life," he told the graduates, "is the breakdown of the inherited authoritarian outlook on life." Taking what was no doubt a calculated risk, he gave evolution, higher criticism, divorce, birth control, and contemporary literature as examples of areas of modern life in which what were previously held to be divine institutions were becoming human ones. Science, a changing intellectual outlook, and modern conditions were all providing what he called a "new authority." Quoting Dewey, Kilpatrick told the audience that "if ever there were a civilization divided against itself it is ours today." He concluded that a new viewpoint was needed to provide a synthesis. Only by integrating the best thought, especially in science, with the ever-novel experiences which the Mercer graduates would encounter, could the problems of the day be successfully faced and dealt with.[31]

The Associated Press carried Kilpatrick's remarks and his focus on unrest and independent thinking was lost in the uproar over his remarks on marriage. Unfortunately, after a twenty-year absence, he was still considered the "devil's disciple" by certain parts of Georgia society. Julia Collier Harris, associate editor of the *Columbus Enquirer-Sun*, came to his defense when P. G. Stovall of the *Savannah Press* attacked him on the editorial page. Stovall had wondered how such statements could emerge from a person who came from "such God-fearing people," and Mrs. Harris responded that she not only found nothing objectionable in Kilpatrick's advice to men — make up their minds in their own way — but thought it "pragmatic advice" and probably the only advice young people would heed. In his scrapbooks Kilpatrick noted that he was misquoted on the marriage issue by the Associated Press. There is also a handwritten note from Mrs. Harris, saying that Stovall probably "still keeps slaves, rides in a buggy, uses an oil lamp, and forbids his wife short skirts and the suffrage."[32] As the editorials by Harris and Stovall were reprinted across the state that summer, Kilpatrick was finally compelled to respond. In a humorous and good-natured letter to the *Greensboro Herald-Journal*, Kilpatrick raised the point that 3 percent of his speech had received 90 percent of the attention: "I feel like the old woman in the nursery rhyme who, waking to find her skirts cut short, did not recognize herself."[33] This would not be the last time he raised eyebrows in his native state.

In January of 1930, at a conference in Des Moines, Kilpatrick met Henry Wallace and had a long conversation with him. His diary does not record whether it was Wallace Sr. or Wallace Jr. — only that he was "quite a character." Later that year he heard Will Durant speak about India. "A more unfair and prejudiced presentation I have never heard," he wrote. Durant was so vehemently pro-Indian that it almost caused Kilpatrick, who followed him on the program, to respond with a pro-British rebuttal. In 1932 Norman Thomas, the Socialist candidate for president, visited Teachers College, speaking to an audience that filled Horace Mann Auditorium. Kilpatrick thought Thomas "did well, but not excellently." Another public figure with whom Kilpatrick shared the platform during this time was Frances Perkins. Perkins was secretary of Labor for New York state before taking the same position in Franklin Roosevelt's cabinet upon his election to the White House in 1932. Kilpatrick found her "intelligent and sincere," but he was surprised to hear her mention a husband and child. For some reason, he had not thought she was married.[34] He also appeared on the platform at the Mecca Temple in New York City with W. E. B. DuBois and Harry Emerson Fosdick, discussing the topic "How May

Another War Be Averted?"[35]

During the summer of 1929, Kilpatrick saw his first talking film. Although the movie was of poor technical quality, he was mesmerized at seeing and hearing Lloyd George and George Bernard Shaw. "Truly we live in wonderful era," he wrote enthusiastically.[36] On April 8, 1930, Kilpatrick himself was approached with an offer to make a "talkie-movie," approximately twenty minutes in length, in which he would discuss some of his ideas on education. He was immediately taken with the proposal, unabashedly recognizing its self-promotional aspect. "I am much interested in the possibilities of thus multiplying myself throughout the country," he wrote, with the aplomb of a modern promoter.[37] Ten days later he visited the studios of the Electric Research Products Company at 250 West 57th Street. After viewing several other educational films made by the company and being assured that the picture and sound were constantly improving, he further warmed to the idea. But if such a movie were to be made, he decided that he would want a composite picture, with actual scenes in schools and discussions between him and his students.[38]

For unknown reasons, the project was postponed until late in 1930, when Kilpatrick began working on the script. Apprehensive that he was writing too much dialogue for a twenty-minute film, he decided to work from an outline of notes, as he usually did when speaking, hoping it would appear more natural. His knowledge and his sophisticated approach to this still primitive art form are impressive. On January 6, 1931, he went to the old Edison laboratory in the Bronx to film the project, calling the experience the most difficult "talking" he had ever done. He was "made-up," he noted ironically, "to look like himself." Studio lights blazed like the sun on all sides. He attempted to relax and to throw off the image of respectability, but this made it even more difficult to concentrate on his outline. In the end he used his notes very little, because he had to "talk against time." Action was halted as the cameras repeatedly broke down — they were incapable of filming for more than ten minutes at a time. When the long shots were completed, the entire scene had to be repeated for the close-ups. Although the producers complimented Kilpatrick on his performance, he found it tiring and was "thoroughly glad when it was over and I could come home."[39]

The film, titled *Dynamic Learning*, captures the essentials of Kilpatrick's learning theory at the time, emphasizing the new education versus the old education, activity and the child, and finally Dewey's notion of interest and effort. The film also affords a rare opportunity to see Kilpatrick move, talk (in,

according to him, the voice of a "cultivated southerner"),[40] gesture, and deliver what may have been very close to one of his classroom lectures. A viewer might well think that Kilpatrick was on the platform of Horace Mann Auditorium rather than on a sound stage in the Bronx. Throughout almost the entire twenty-three minutes, he intersperses his remarks with questions, simulating a response to a real class or audience. The famous hair, finely groomed and parted in the middle, gently cascades over each side of his brow, and his gait is sprightly as he moves to and from the blackboard. While the sound is a bit primitive, the multiple cameras, the close-ups, and the excellent editing make the film technically well done, especially considering the year it was produced.

The first half of the film establishes Kilpatrick's stress on the need for active, age-appropriate, internally generated experiences for students; that which engages the student from the inside motivates best. An animated segment representing the "old education, displays a book — labeled "adult learning" — which is then subdivided into portions for children to digest and learn. Repudiating such an approach, Kilpatrick contrasts the old education with the new by using three brief episodes in which children are actively involved in the learning process. The first is a fictional depiction of a child asking questions of other children as to what it means to go on a picnic. Kilpatrick uses this scene to demonstrate how active learning involves children in their environment and captures their interest. The other two vignettes drawn from actual classroom settings, show elementary students cooperatively building a playhouse and older students demonstrating a science experiment. Kilpatrick concludes *Dynamic Learning* by contrasting the newer dynamic approaches to education with the old static approaches.

One recent observer, Regina Wilkes, has noted that Kilpatrick's emphasis on democracy in this film places socialization over politicalization. Kilpatrick's brand of learning reaps the moral benefits of democracy, which include cooperation, responsibility, and shared values. A resulting commitment to the education of the whole child emerges in the film, as body and mind blend in the learning process, leaving an indelible imprint on the learner. Wilkes also notes the importance attributed to critical thinking when Kilpatrick states that knowledge must be "freed from the docile acceptance of authority." It is clear that Kilpatrick believes that all subject matter and experiences must be questioned, tested, and tried. This is the essence of what he means by "meaningful learning." Wilkes does question Kilpatrick's apparent assumption that only those situations and experiences which are drawn from the present can

be meaningful. The implied presumption is that theoretical, esoteric, or vicariously experienced subject matter has minimal use in the learning process. In the end though, Wilkes cannot see how Kilpatrick, the advocate of progress and innovation, can justify excluding such experiences.[41] But this, of course, would not be the first time Kilpatrick has been charged with over-emphasizing the practical approach to learning at the expense of the theoretical.

A month after completing the film, Kilpatrick viewed unedited portions of it. While he found his speech distinct and sensible, he also noted that it was "slow and quite solemn," at times almost unnatural.[42] The *Christian Science Monitor* described the film and its impact in an article titled "Talkies for the Classroom." The writer of the piece stated that a superintendent could educate a recalcitrant school board to more progressive thinking in twenty-two minutes rather than twenty-two months. The article glowingly praised Kilpatrick ("We were not inclined to argue over a single point made by the reasonable and persuasive Dr. Kilpatrick") and reported that, at a conference of the National Education Association, the film ran continuously for attendees until 3 a.m.[43]

The enrollment in Kilpatrick's summer school classes dropped slightly in 1930, and the waiting list for his fall courses was shorter than usual. This bothered Kilpatrick. Since the end of the war, every doctoral student had been required to take his philosophy course. But now, although his popularity remained high, the curriculum for many of the students, especially those in the school administration program, no longer required his course. Pondering this "troubling" situation, he concluded that he probably had as many students as ever — he just didn't have them all. But then, neither did his intellectual foil, William Bagley. Bagley's course "Techniques in Teaching," the essentialist counterpart to Kilpatrick's "Foundation of Method," had decreased from 320 to 170 students within a two-year period.[44]

It was true that Kilpatrick probably did not have access to the same percentage as before of students coming through Teachers College. Matriculation exams, formerly required in either philosophy or sociology of education, had meant that Kilpatrick's courses were in great demand. The numbers at Teachers College were on an upward trend, although the Depression had dampened growth somewhat. But not only did course requirements change; so too did the faculty. Kilpatrick admitted that rising stars within Teachers College often siphoned students from his courses. Discussing the situation in his diary, he mentioned several "new people" who attracted students into their courses. Four names in particular were mentioned— George Counts, Goodwin Watson, Harold Rugg, and Isaac Kandel.[45] However, Kilpatrick's comments

never convey a sense of competition. How could there be competition? Three of the four rising stars at Teachers College were original members of the Kilpatrick Discussion Group and were his close kinsmen intellectually.[46] And he himself could, of course, still attract a solid audience. In a summer lecture series in 1931, he outdrew Reinhold Niebuhr ten to one (on July 9 Kilpatrick's audience numbered 2,500, while Niebuhr filled only 225 seats). During the summer session of 1934, Kilpatrick filled Horace Mann Auditorium when he held a standard, unscheduled question-and-answer session.[47]

Next occurred one of the celebrated and highly volatile affairs in which Kilpatrick was wont to become involved. It centered on his frank, some might say ill-advisedly blunt, comments regarding certain civic and patriotic organizations. This series of events began at a dinner meeting of the Flushing Peace Society on March 9, 1931, where Kilpatrick stated that in order to eliminate war, the traditions of war, inextricably woven into the fabric of American society, had to be attacked. For Kilpatrick, these traditions included patriotic legends, saluting the flag and the uniform, Decoration Day, and the Monroe Doctrine. Among the organizations espousing such traditions, he named the Daughters of the American Revolution, the Reserve Officers' Training Corps, the American Legion, the Boy Scouts, the Army, and the Navy. Rather than blindly following these outmoded practices and organizations, he called for new methods and better communication in settling disputes. Cooperation, international order, reason, and morality, he avowed, should be the hallmarks in dealing with conflicts — not physical prowess. Kilpatrick firmly believed that another war might wipe out western civilization and maintained in his address that war should be attacked through adult education.[48]

Scarcely had the speech in Flushing been delivered when Kilpatrick waded into another controversial issue — censorship. The New York City schools had, according to the directive of an assistant superintendent, excluded any textbook found by the public to be objectionable. At a meeting sponsored by the American Civil Liberties Union on March 30, 1931, Kilpatrick heaped scorn on the decision, asking: "Could you devise any means of making education more innocuous or futile?" "Real education," according to Kilpatrick, could take place only when controversial issues were openly discussed by students. Although Kilpatrick was one of five speakers on the program, his comments were the ones that drew press coverage.[49] That summer Kilpatrick challenged the use of "mere devices such as games, prizes, or badges" as a substitute for encouraging children to ask questions and face realistic problems. The failure to have children ask "why," Kilpatrick said, "was the unpardonable sin in

modern education."[50]

What prompted Kilpatrick to engage in such highly public and controversial issues is a difficult question to answer. He mentions nothing in his diaries of his blistering attacks on civic organizations, the military, or the schools. And he wasn't finished. In the Columbia gymnasium, in front of a packed audience of summer school students and teachers, Kilpatrick called the United States government "one of the worst among civilized nations" in terms of facing the political and economic problems of the day. In this talk, titled "Responsibility in Planned Government," he charged that the schools had vaccinated students against thinking about such problems and called the situation "traitorous." Moving ever deeper into controversy, Kilpatrick suggested that the United States should follow the Soviet Union's Five Year Plan in order to address the problems of the Depression: production, health, poverty, and farm shortages. A planned and cooperative venture was needed, according to Kilpatrick, and the teachers should organize in order to study the major aspects of world affairs.[51] This blast predated Counts' speech "Dare the Schools Build a New Social Order?" by eight months.

But it took an almost verbatim repetition of his Flushing speech to trigger the strongest response. On December 2, 1931, by invitation Kilpatrick gave a talk in Milbank Chapel at Teachers College under the rather general title "War and Peace." In his remarks he named again the American Legion and the Daughters of the American Revolution as organizations committed to keeping the war tradition alive. He also added to his list the Ku Klux Klan. He then confirmed upon the members of these organizations the alliterative appellation "professional patriots." The incendiary quality of the talk was further inflamed by the use of phrases such as "saluting the flag is morally vicious" and by intimating that the United States could learn much from the Chinese, who abhorred war.[52] Kilpatrick's remarks were carried only in several smaller New York papers, and mentioned only briefly in the *New York Times*; but two days later they were picked up by both the Associated Press and the International News Service. A firestorm was under way.

"The professor should go back to the kindergarten and study history," retorted the vice president of the Reserve Officers' Association, going on to describe Kilpatrick's comments as those of an "extreme pacifist." Mrs. Lowell Fletcher Hobart, President General of the Daughters of the American Revolution, told the press, "How mistaken he is. We are just as opposite from the way he describes us as we could be." George Counts and Paul Limbert, a professor of religious education at Teachers College, both came to their

colleague's defense. Limbert called Kilpatrick's comments "sound psychology and good religion." The *New York Evening Post* reported that Kilpatrick was mildly amused over the uproar his talk generated but was standing by his remarks. "I still insist that these organizations keep up a war spirit in this country," he said. He went on to suggest that people should ignore the D.A.R. and noted that he had been on the R.O.T.C.'s blacklist for years and would not be concerned if other groups followed its example.[53]

An editorial in the *Boston Journal of Education* quickly came to Kilpatrick's defense:

> There is no question but that the Manchuria situation has created a determined world demand for the toning down of everybody and everything that promotes nationalism and internationalism without magnifying the peace note. Any one who anywhere loosens a phrase that can possibly stir animosity in anything should be silenced at once, regardless of the way it is done. Thank the Lord for William H. Kilpatrick.[54]

Letters began to be published in the newspapers and also arriving at Kilpatrick's office. His scrapbooks include a letter from a housing developer in Erie, Pennsylvania, who indicated that he would stand by the American Legion and the D.A.R. against "the vociferous minority, of which you apparently are a member" and concluded by saying that these two "real" American institutions would endure "long after you and your kind have been forgotten."[55] The March issue of the *National Republic* wrote that the public and the government had been "harangued by this army of pinks for long enough"; that it would be difficult to know whether Kilpatrick was a "red, a pink, or a dupe"; and that the president of Columbia University, Nicholas Murray Butler, should let the American public know where he stood on these matters."[56] As it happened, a letter to Butler from the D.A.R. allowed him to do just that.

On December 13, 1932, President Butler received a letter from Mrs. Evaline Watson Northrup, a member of the Committee on National Defense of the D.A.R. She called Kilpatrick's comments "un-American and dangerous" and wrote that such sentiments "must give great joy and satisfaction to the ever-active communistic citizens in this country." Butler came to the Teachers College professor's defense and informed Mrs. Northrup that her dispatch was the only one which had reached his desk. Butler concluded his letter with these words:

I invite your attention to the fact that a University is the carefully protected home of freedom of thought and freedom of speech, that its object is to seek and to proclaim this truth as a scholar may find it, subject only to the obvious limitations set by good manners and by good morals. Professor Kilpatrick is an American gentleman and scholar of high standing and deservedly wide influence. His associates in the University take pride in his service and in his reputation.

Very truly yours,
Nicholas Murray Butler[57]

Butler sent Kilpatrick a copy of the letter and also released it to the press.

Kilpatrick felt deeply about these issues and saw them as relevant to what it meant to live and teach in a democratic society. So strong was his "dislike for the flag cult" that he was personally disturbed when required to stand for the national anthem. He also felt that Decoration (or Memorial) Day had been absorbed by "pinhead patriots" such as the D.A.R. and the American Legion, whose "chauvinistic reactionary patriotism is highly antithetical to all I stand for."[58] While in Washington, D.C., in early 1933, he attended a dinner of the Civitans, a civic organization with a strongly patriotic sensibility. A creed was recited by the members which vowed total allegiance to the government. Deciding to pursue the issue with the chairman, Kilpatrick inquired as to what was meant by the pledge. "It means what it says with no 'ifs, ands, or buts,'" came the reply. "Including the 18th Amendment?" asked Kilpatrick, referring to prohibition; he knew that many Civitans privately broke the Volstead Act. The chairman's face fell, but he replied yes, as long as it was in the Constitution. Not willing to leave the issue there, Kilpatrick solicited one more response from the man: "And this holds for all Civitans?" The weak and troubled answer was "It ought to." Kilpatrick concluded that such episodes only illustrated the hypocrisy and "crudities" that Sinclair Lewis had exposed in *Babbitt*.[59]

On the Fourth of July 1933, at the Teachers College Country Club in Ossining, several faculty members dressed in colonial attire and spoke against the D.A.R. The following year the issue of loyalty oaths for teachers emerged in the New York state assembly, and Kilpatrick immediately wrote the Senate Committee on Education in protest. That same week a colleague warned him that Dean William Russell was apprehensive, even distressed, over this issue and the previous controversies with the D.A.R. and other civic and military

organizations. Although disappointed with Russell's stance, Kilpatrick vowed to "keep on at it."[60]

The activities of Kilpatrick and his colleagues at Teachers College had not escaped the attention of the Hearst press. And Kilpatrick's hostile opinion toward newspapers such as the Hearst chain cannot be overemphasized. "When I read the *Chicago Tribune* I find myself growing resentful, with tendencies toward violence," the ever rational and peaceful Kilpatrick wrote: "It [and] Hearst's papers [are] . . . intentionally lying newspapers." Tenenbaum reports that the attacks on Kilpatrick "did not bother him excessively" and refers to an article in the *Teachers College Record* in which Kilpatrick alluded to the fact that Socrates had been accused by the Athenians of corrupting youth. But in fact, the attacks disturbed Kilpatrick more than Tenenbaum suggests. One article in the *New York Times* during this period "exasperated" him: a Catholic priest, Father Duffee, was quoted as chastising local foundations for giving money to "Columbia Red Professors" for the purpose of producing more "Red Professors and propagating Communism." "I think much of the 'red baiting' is stirred by Catholic educators," Kilpatrick wrote in his diary.[61]

Kilpatrick's polemical attitude toward the so-called "professional patriots" became most intense when William Randolph Hearst himself became actively involved in an attack on progressive education in general and Teachers College in particular. Kilpatrick had publicly censured Hearst's tactics and called for a congressional investigation of the publisher's "insidious and un-American attack upon our educational institutions."[62] "Insidious" was an apt term. Reporters from the Hearst press wrote letters to John Washburne of Syracuse University and to George Counts under the guise of asking for the "liberal side" of political issues, and for guidance as to which communist organizations they should join. Counts soon ferreted out the scheme and got the reporter to admit his real reason for requesting an interview. A Hearst reporter also called on Kilpatrick, trying to get information on radical organizations under the pretense of being a naive, questioning student. Kilpatrick, knowing what was afoot, had a stenographer present and confronted the reporter. Kilpatrick asked the man if he was not ashamed of what he was doing, and of the motive behind Hearst's actions. The reporter pleaded expediency, saying that either he did Hearst's bidding, or he would find himself working in a slaughterhouse. But at least, Kilpatrick wryly observed, a man could do that work with a "clear conscience."[63]

In refusing to be silenced by the voices of orthodoxy, Kilpatrick demonstrated a great deal of fortitude. Norman Cousins would later say that

Kilpatrick was attacked with such vehemence because he was a threat to the political and economic power structure that Hearst, and other men like Hearst, represented. On December 23, 1934, Counts and Kilpatrick went public and asked that the McCormack-Dickstein Congressional Committee on Un-American Activities investigate these episodes. Kilpatrick described Hearst's efforts as "the destruction of the school as a preparation for intelligent democratic citizenship. Students could not be encouraged to think, but only made to conform to predetermined positions authoritatively promulgated." John Dewey, Harry Emerson Fosdick, and Charles Beard joined Kilpatrick and Counts in signing the telegram to the congressional committee.[64]

The issue of "professional patriots" would decline, but it would emerge again before the end of the decade. In 1936 and 1937 the issue shifted to oaths for teachers and mandatory saluting of the flag by students in the classroom. Kilpatrick rejoiced when a number of state legislators who had favored teachers' oaths were defeated for reelection. Attention was also drawn to Kilpatrick when his picture appeared in the summer of 1936 in *Fortune* magazine over the caption "opposed flag saluting." As C. A. Bowers has indicated, the problem Dewey, Kilpatrick, and others had with such symbolic gestures was that "by accommodating their activities to the wishes of conservative social elements, the schools had also assumed responsibilities in areas that possessed dubious educational value."[65] Kilpatrick was eventually vindicated in his crusade against what he considered the coercive and inappropriate use of the nation's symbols by public school children. Ironically, it was on Flag Day, June 17, 1943, that the Supreme Court struck down a West Virginia law which required public school students to salute the flag. In his majority opinion Justice Robert Jackson wrote that the purpose of the Bill of Rights was to withdraw certain subjects "from the vicissitudes of political controversy, to place them beyond the reach of majorities and officials." Kilpatrick concurred and was "glad to see the flag saluting case reversed."[66]

While capable of being critical, Kilpatrick could also be creative. One project in which he was deeply involved and which spanned portions of both the 1920s and 1930s was the creation of Bennington College. In 1923 Frank P. Graves, the New York state commissioner of education, sent Edith Arthur McCullough, a wealthy New Englander, to discuss with Kilpatrick ideas about how a college for women might be developed. Mrs. McCullough's husband, Hall Park McCullough, had inherited a large sum of money and hoped to support a venture in higher education. Kilpatrick indicated that "if they would make it not simply new, but a new kind, then I would be interested." "How new in kind?"

asked Mrs. McCullough. "That is a longer story," Kilpatrick replied. Mrs. McCullough did not delay in finding out. The next evening Kilpatrick was invited to meet with other potential trustees for dinner at the McCulloughs' home. The guests were impressed with what they heard, and Kilpatrick became the principal educational advisor to the Bennington College trustees for the next decade.[67]

In a meeting at the New York Colony Club on April 28, 1924, Kilpatrick outlined his ideas, which were very much along the lines of his philosophy of progressive education. The college would emphasize living and experiences, with the goal of developing self-directing, independent young women. All academic subjects had to be defended in terms of their ability to assist the women in building on their present plans and purposes. Courses would be based on the needs of the student, not the subject matter. There were questions at the end of Kilpatrick's address, especially about the curriculum. One member of the audience contended that the curriculum would have to be the same for women as for men if women were to "reach an equal position." Kilpatrick quickly retorted that the current curriculum had been started for the clergy and was patently unsuitable for either sex.[68]

Kilpatrick visited Bennington in the summer of 1924 and was impressed with both the site and the McCulloughs who reciprocated his admiration. Kilpatrick became a pillar of educational advice to whom many turned. Although Mrs. McCullough remained chair of the trustees at this time, she asked Kilpatrick to preside at the meetings, and in 1925 he was elected to a six-year term on the Bennington College board. He also continued to keep the trustees in the dark, so to speak, regarding the curriculum. "His rhetoric was virtually unmarred by specifics," wrote a historian of the college, Thomas Brockway. The only exception was his specific ban on mathematics and foreign languages. The prohibition on mathematics would linger for a while, with only the physics professor teaching the subject when a need for it arose in other classes. Kilpatrick believed that no matter how progressive an institution was in the beginning, in time it became "stupidly conservative." It was his hope that Bennington College would escape this fate through continual and enlightened criticism.[69]

In 1926, upon returning from his trip around the world, Kilpatrick became actively involved in the selection of the new college's president. Robert D. Leigh was suggested for the post. Leigh, a summa cum laude graduate of Bowdoin in political science and who was a professor at Williams College, had been a student in one of Kilpatrick's classes before the war. It was there that he had met his future wife, Mildred Boardman, who was taking a degree in

education. After the war they had returned to Columbia, where Mildred completed a masters degree at Teachers College.[70] Kilpatrick had originally argued for a female president — he had thought that his colleague at Teachers College, Lois Meek, would be a good choice — but to no avail. The characteristics and experience desired by the trustees, considering the stranglehold males held on administrative positions at this time, made the appointment of a woman impossible. Also, Mrs. McCullough confronted Kilpatrick in a meeting, getting him to admit (somewhat sheepishly, she later said) that he himself might have reservations about taking an appointment under a woman. Later, Dr. Leigh had a positive private interview with the McCulloughs and Kilpatrick in New York City, and his appointment was assured. Regarding Leigh's appointment, Kilpatrick wrote in his diary in late December of 1927, "I am not jubilant, but still not opposing." One of his own disciples (such as Lois Meek) would have given him more influence, he thought, but he was relieved that at least he did not "carry the responsibility" for Leigh's appointment. The trustees found Leigh acceptable, and he was appointed in January of 1928 as president of Bennington College, at a salary of $10,000.

The next step in the process of establishing Bennington College was fundraising and publicity. According to the official historian of Bennington College, Kilpatrick and Nathalie Henderson Swan were the major contributors to the first two college brochures. Kilpatrick's hand was not hidden: "The first half of the text might well have been based on Kilpatrick's lecture notes," wrote Brockway. He added that Mrs. Swan and Kilpatrick "rushed into print [the brochure] to provide the new president with sound guidelines."[71] As for fundraising, by the summer of 1928 Kilpatrick thought that the "outlook seems not bright for any early success with the necessary funds." With the crash of the stock market in 1929, the situation looked even bleaker, and at a trustee's meeting in June of 1930, it seemed quite likely that the entire project might fold. A number of "soft" votes on the board had emerged over whether starting a college in the midst of an ever worsening economic situation might be inadvisable. With two businessmen apparently firmly opposed to continuing the project, Kilpatrick, who was presiding at the meeting, took a straw poll of support, calling first on those he knew were firmly in favor of the new institution. With several positive votes cast before the resisters had been called upon for their opinions, the project was saved. Kilpatrick's skill in reaching a consensus and working with groups had again proved more than adequate to the task. Hall Park McCullough said later that had it not been for Kilpatrick's quick thinking, the vote would have gone the other way. There had also been a

vote on the issue of a women's college versus a coeducational institution, with the women's college prevailing by a vote of 19 to 5.

The trustees' meeting of June 1930 thus ended on a high note with Kilpatrick pleased with the emerging physical plant, the growing list of prospective students, and the increasingly stable financial outlook. And yet for all these positive institutional indicators, Kilpatrick felt his personal influence waning. "I have grown to count less and less in the enterprise," he wrote; "Partly I surmise because I am counted radical by some, but this I think, is not the whole thing."[72] He was "partly right" in his assumption: college trustee James S. Dennis, basing his opinion on observations at board meetings, told a friend that he considered Kilpatrick "the most dangerous radical he ever met."[73]

When Bennington College opened its doors, the tuition and board expenses for an academic year totaled $1,600. In order to admit capable women who did not have sufficient financial means, the trustees labored diligently to provide scholarships. Admission was based on a high school education and the potential to profit from the Bennington experience. There were no classroom recitations, no examinations, no sororities, and few extracurricular activities. Music, art, drama, and dance were all part of the regular school program. One of the first women to attend Bennington wrote of the experience fifty years later: "We were clear enough only about several negatives; no courses, no requirements, no lectures, no grades, no exams, no pre-determined curriculum." This former student also added that the women of the period were "liberated" and welcomed a new kind of college. "Our mothers had fought for and won the battle for women's suffrage. Their mothers had fought for higher education for women." The only required component of the curriculum was community involvement in either the public or private sector, which included the arts, journalism, and social agencies.[74]

In lieu of traditional grades to evaluate class work, Bennington students were assigned advisers who kept folders containing narrative remarks about their work and progress. A committee would later review the folders to ascertain whether each student was profiting from the Bennington experience. Heavy emphasis was placed on students' participation, and the relatively novel idea of soliciting students' feedback on the quality of instruction and activities in the classroom was also practiced. A student committee canvassed the opinions of the student body regarding the quality of instruction and then discussed the results with the professors. "Many eyebrows were raised," Kilpatrick later told Tenenbaum, "when outsiders heard that the girls were making their own rules." But while some raised their eyebrows, others were

persuaded that Bennington College was succeeding. The husband of one trustee, who had been skeptical at first, was later converted to the Bennington process and stated that he wished for "a college that will do for the boys what Bennington is doing for the girls."[75] Eventually, under Dr. Leigh's leadership the curriculum became a blend of traditional subject matter with individualized studies, emphasis on the development of personality, and a pointed aversion to grades, prizes, and tests. Kilpatrick did not get his way on all issues, however. It is reported that he wished to create a department of education at Bennington College, but Leigh refused. It apparently was not a crucial issue with Kilpatrick, though, as he never mentioned the suggestion in his diaries. "I myself approve what they are doing, both act and attitude," he wrote.[76]

Kilpatrick served on the board of trustees for thirteen years and was chair from 1931 to 1938. In September of 1933 the students at Bennington asked permission to name a dormitory hall after him. He did not think it wise to name buildings after living persons, but since it was being done for others he wired to the students: "Am pleased to accept the honor." He marched with the first group of seniors in June of 1936 and at the time of his retirement from the board was awarded an honorary doctorate — one of only seven the school gave between 1938 and 1981.[77] After Kilpatrick stepped down from the board, Dr. Leigh wrote that he had given the college "its educational form and direction." Brockway, concurred, adding that, setting aside Leigh's role, "no one need quarrel with that judgment."[78] Kilpatrick later said that not all of the faculty were committed to the philosophy of the school and some could have been better selected, but in the end Bennington College "represented more nearly at the time what I believed a school should be than any other college."[79] In 1935 he wrote: "My educational position is winning out I think, certainly in elementary education, with some significant beginnings in the college field (Bennington, Sarah Lawrence, Bard College, etc.) and some hopeful signs in the secondary field. But the fight is just warming up."[80]

Such were the activities that occupied Kilpatrick in several areas of his life — teaching, speaking, and personally — in the mid-1930s, when his influence was at a high point. A group of visiting Brazilian educators declared in 1935 that the "trinity of American educators are Dewey, Thorndike, and Kilpatrick.[81] But at this same time, he was also deeply immersed in addressing the social and economic issues which had arisen with the onset of the Great Depression. A notable dichotomy had emerged between the child-centered proponents of the progressive education movement on one side and — on the other side — likeminded men and women who saw a national crisis which called for a response

from all Americans, especially educators. The latter group became known as the "social reconstructionists," and Kilpatrick, as a major voice in the progressive movement, found himself deeply immersed in their crusade.

THE GREAT DEPRESSION AND
THE SOCIAL RECONSTRUCTIONISTS

I see one-third of a nation ill-housed, ill-clad, ill-nourished.
>Franklin D. Roosevelt, Second Inaugural Address

The very foundations on which we have been trying to build our economic civilization stand challenged . . . Never before, in this country at least, have so many so openly questioned . . . the actual basis and organization of our economic system.
>William Heard Kilpatrick from *Education and the Social Crisis*, 1932.[1]

Unlike the popular image of the educator as a supine and socially weak if not indifferent figure, these educators — led by George Counts, John L. Childs, William Heard Kilpatrick, and Harold Rugg — were social radicals who had a deep commitment to social planning and public ownership of the means of production.
>C. A. Bowers in *The Progressive Educator and the Depression: The Radical Years*[2]

In the middle of Herbert Hoover's single term, Nicholas Murray Butler, president of Columbia University, concurred with the occupant of the White House that there was no need of heroic measures to deliver the nation from the ever-deepening Depression. "Courage will end the slump," said Butler to the students on his campus. He evidently had not been on any walks similar to those taken by William Heard Kilpatrick, his popular professor at Teachers College. There were two "Hoovervilles" close by the campus: one below Riverside Drive, and another near the obelisk in Central Park. Others were not as optimistic as Butler. When asked if there had been anything like the

Depression before, the economist John Maynard Keynes replied, "Yes. It was called the Dark Ages, and it lasted four hundred years." In 1930 there were an estimated 4 million Americans unemployed. A year later the figure had risen to 8 million.

The Depression was no respecter of persons. It struck the uneducated, the uneducated, and the educators. In 1932 a college degree was required to get a job as an elevator operator in New York City department stores. When a Russian trading agency advertised 6,000 skilled jobs in the Soviet Union, 100,000 Americans applied, including teachers and librarians. The nation's schools were hit especially hard. By 1932 a third of a million students were out of school because of a lack of funds. Teachers in Kansas were being paid $35 per month, on an eight-month contract. In Iowa teachers received $40 a month. Akron, Ohio, owed its teachers $300,000 in back pay. Chicago owed its teachers more than $20 million and dismissed 1,000 of them outright. And in Atlanta, where the schools went completely bankrupt in the 1930s, Rich's Department Store paid teachers in scrip. Regardless of location, the schools hit bottom during the school year 1933-1934.[3]

The personal toll the Depression took on students was even more devastating. In October of 1932 the New York City Health Department reported that over 20 percent of the pupils in the public schools were suffering from malnutrition. One teacher suggested to a student that she go home and eat something. "I can't," the child replied; "this is my sister's day to eat." In 1932 a deputation of teachers visited Kilpatrick in his apartment to solicit assistance for their unemployed colleagues.[4] It is little wonder that the band of men and women at Teachers College, who saw education as inseparable from the social and political milieu, became activists in response to the economic disaster that was taking place in the nation.

In 1941, in his book, *Intellectual America*, Oscar Cargill warned his readers not to let October 29, 1929, mark too sharp a break in the nation's intellectual history. His advice could be heeded only up to a certain point. Almost every sector of the economy had been damaged by the Depression. Farm prices had spiraled downward, manufacturing came to a virtual standstill, and banking in every state was either wholly or partly suspended. The first four years of the Great Depression saw farmers losing their land and veterans marching on the nation's capital. Funding for schools began a steady decline, from which it never fully recovered. Most severe of all may have been the blow dealt to the nation's confidence. The country's loss of faith in institutions — political, social, and, of course, economic — cannot be dismissed. Sidney

Hook wrote: "Of course, the general feeling was that the economic system was completely finished, but there was no unanimity or even general agreement on what was to replace it."[5] The old system did not seem to work, and there seemed scant hope that any new model would prove a successful substitute. The White House referred to a whole "lost generation of young people." A little over a year after the stock market crash, Kilpatrick, along with a large group of educators attending the Conference on Child Health and Protection in Washington, was invited to the White House. He noted, after shaking hands with President Hoover, "It was pathetic and otherwise disturbing to see how tired and worn he looked as of a man determined to do his duty at any cost."[6] Kilpatrick's observation captured the beleaguered president's response to the economic crisis.

With even the business world questioning capitalism, it is not surprising that many intellectuals veered sharply leftward. John Dos Passos, Sherwood Anderson, Malcolm Cowley, Upton Sinclair, and Edmond Wilson openly espoused communism. Governors in Mississippi and Minnesota were also sympathetic to communism. The journalist William Allen White called the Soviet Union the "most interesting place on the planet," and Will Rogers was quoted as saying that "those rascals in Russia have got mighty good ideas." Both George Counts and Kilpatrick had journeyed to the Soviet Union in 1929 to observe the new experiment for themselves; John Dewey had been there two years before them. In early 1934 the College League Against War and Fascism, a communist-led organization, called a strike at Teachers College. One third of the staff and two-thirds of the students struck. Several of those who did not walk out of classes, Kilpatrick amongst them, met to study the situation. Personally, Kilpatrick had little sympathy for the communists. "I find myself more and more out of patience with communist tactics," he wrote. Nevertheless, not a week later he wrote "I wish we could end the capitalist system."[7] Kilpatrick agreed with Counts that the current economic system was deeply flawed, possibly anachronistic, and greatly in need of more social planning and control. But moderation and amelioration would best describe Kilpatrick's philosophical approach to addressing economic and social issues. Kilpatrick desired classrooms where cooperation reigned, while Counts exhorted teachers to capture power and to utilize it to a specific end.

As with any movement, what would become known as "social reconstructionism" evolved through several stages and lasted, in some fashion, from the late 1920s until the 1980s and beyond. Several philosophical presuppositions underlay its attempt to broaden the definition of education to include promoting

a clearly reasoned program of social reform. The social reconstructionists felt that civilization faced possible self-annihilation, like that envisioned by H. G. Wells. Educators felt compelled to fill the breach by creating a new social order based on genuine democratic principles. The social reconstructionists believed that educators must identify the prevailing social problems in society and then attempt to ameliorate them, beginning with the schools. The schools, as a social institution, could not escape the social, political, or cultural forces pressing upon them, and neither could the students. Teachers had no choice but to take an active, vigorous, and leading role in building a new social order.[8] As C. A. Bowers has put it, the social reconstructionists believed that "only by combining political ideology with education . . . would it be possible for the movement to become truly progressive and to be in harmony with both the needs of the student and the needs of society."[9]

But this aspiration for harmony had within it the seeds of disunity for the progressive education movement. Merging politics with education and the student with society would prove an arduous task. This new movement of social reconstructionism appeared to be diametrically opposed to the reigning ideas and ideals of child-centered progressivism.[10] Since that time, educators have continued to debate about the struggle between political indoctrination and experimentalism, and about whether the teacher should focus on improving society or improving the child. To make the matter more confusing, both wings of progressive education, in order to reinforce their respective positions, returned to Dewey for their inspiration, appealing to his idea that schools must deliberately improve society by strengthening democratic values within classrooms.

The roots of social reconstructionism have been traced to George S. Counts and a speech he gave in February of 1932 to the Progressive Education Association (PEA) in Baltimore. Counts had joined the faculty of Teachers College in 1927. He had taken his doctorate from the University of Chicago in sociology of education, but was equally at home with history and economics. One of his biographers has suggested that Counts was simultaneously calling for teachers to become "statesmen" while critically evaluating their culture in terms of the new technology and the ever changing socioeconomic scene. It was clear that Counts was more interested in the economic, historical, and sociological dimensions of educational problems than in the pedagogical implications of his position. He was also at this point further to the left politically than most of his colleagues, including his friend and collaborator, the historian Charles Beard. There was no room for neutrality in Counts's proposals for America's teachers.

Educators must recognize the transition from an agrarian to a technological society, and he said as much, in 1930, in his book, *The American Road to Culture*. And since Counts's writings were published in *The New Republic*, his ideas were carried beyond the immediate audience of teachers.[11]

The speech Counts gave to the PEA in February of 1932 was titled "Dare Progressive Education Be Progressive?" In it, Counts acknowledged that progressive education had been instrumental in bringing about positive changes within the schools, but held that educators were now compelled to confront the economic and social issues peculiar to the industrial age. His speech contained such politically loaded words (for the time) as "planning," "welfare," "class," and "indoctrination." According to Counts, teachers could not be neutral — they had to choose either capitalism or socialism. A new social order was needed, and teachers were to be in the vanguard of its creation. The speech so astounded the audience that when it ended they sat in silence. The assembly then changed the agenda for the remainder of the conference, meeting in small groups to discuss the implications of Counts's clarion call. As one group of historians put it, the message of social reconstructionism was "intoxicating." Lawrence Cremin called the response to the speech "electric."[12]

And the enthusiasm continued. Three weeks after the speech, Kilpatrick, along with Counts, Jesse Newlon, and several others from Teachers College, met in a rather seedy restaurant with officials of the PEA to discuss Counts's challenge further. After what Kilpatrick called "radical talk," a "sensible discussion" followed, which he led.[13] In April, leaders of the PEA and several special participants, including Kilpatrick, Counts, and Bode, met at Vassar College to continue the dialogue. Teachers were ready to listen because there appeared to be no escape from the grinding economic conditions they were enduring. But the talk of class conflict and the generally Marxist tone of Counts's rhetoric did give some educators pause.[14] Agnes De Lima, a frequent contributor to *The New Republic*, though sympathetic to progressive education, was skeptical. She found it doubtful that teachers could really lead the citizenry out of the "morass": "A class long trained to social docility and economically protected by life tenure of office . . . is unlikely to challenge unduly the status quo," she countered.[15] This opinion apparently was not shared by the faculty at Teachers College. As a group, they neither looked nor acted like radicals or revolutionaries. Yet they saw, as did many Americans, a civilization in crisis. They wanted a more equitable and just society based not so much on *The New Masses*, as one group of historians put it, as on *The New Republic* — in other words, one in alignment more with George Counts and Charles Beard than with Karl Marx.[16]

The leadership for much of what occurred in social reconstructionism in the 1930s fell to the Teachers College group, which included Kilpatrick and Counts, John L. Childs, Harold Rugg, Jesse Newlon, and R. Bruce Raup. The Kilpatrick Discussion Group had begun to consider the "social outlook," as they put it, in the fall of 1930. If the tone of their rhetoric often took on a religious aura, this was no doubt due to the background shared by several of these men. Whether religious or secular, the tone was idealistic: this group was out to change the status quo. Terms such as "propaganda," "planning," and "clashes" all pointed to change writ large. But even among this small band of brothers, the extent to which each carried his ideology often differed. C. A. Bowers has written that if you placed the social reconstructionists on a spectrum ranging from those who came close to embracing the Communist Party agenda to those in sympathy with John Dewey's allegiance to the democratic process (and Norman Thomas's brand of socialism), George Counts would be closest to the former position, Boyd H. Bode nearest the latter, and Kilpatrick would be squarely in the middle.[17]

Regardless of the wing of the movement to which they were allied, the social reconstructionists were all agreed that education was the key to progress, and they were ready to do battle with economic injustices and with those in political power. These "frontier thinkers" saw technology and rational social planning as a panacea which would raise the Depression-era economy from its apparently inescapable slump. The central tenet and guiding principle for these individuals remained democracy. Industries, communities, and schools should all be established and run along democratic lines. As Counts had stressed, teachers should play a pivotal role in the reconstruction, even devising the blueprint for the future society.[18]

The social reconstructionists were not always united in thought. Kilpatrick, for example, disagreed with Counts on the issue of indoctrination. Kilpatrick's devotion to the idea of free inquiry and his belief that the individual, in most circumstances, would make responsible decisions, led him to abhor any regimented, preset parcel of ideas. Just as he rejected the idea of a curriculum set in advance, so too he rebuffed a prescription for culture or democracy. Such presuppositions would enslave children both intellectually and morally. "Simply to indoctrinate them with what has been taught is to indoctrinate them against thinking," he wrote in 1935.[19] The ever revolving nature of society meant that students needed to grapple with real problems and controversial situations. In the end, to Kilpatrick, indoctrination meant that students would be dependent on the thinking of the teacher, unable to come to their own conclusions rationally.[20] John

Dewey agreed with Kilpatrick about indoctrination, writing that "there is an important difference between education with respect to a new social order and indoctrination into settled convictions about that order." Others, such as Henry Holmes of Harvard, George Coe of Teachers College, and Horace Kallen of the New School for Social Research, were also openly critical of indoctrination, and advocated, as did Kilpatrick, the need for open and free discussions in the classrooms. According to Daniel Tanner, both John Dewey and Sidney Hook were troubled over the issue of indoctrination "on both social and historical grounds." In a letter written near the end of his life, Hook indicated that even "Counts himself at heart was really opposed."[21]

Kilpatrick's own formal response to the nation's economic situation came in September of 1932, when he published *Education and the Social Crisis*. One of Dewey's biographers has suggested that Kilpatrick, "ever alert to shifting trends," moved quickly into the social reconstructionist camp, apparently abandoning his long-held belief in child-centeredness for the political and educational expediency of joining "educational reform to radical politics." But Kilpatrick did not come late to the social aspect of the progressive education gospel. In fact, it may be a disservice to Dewey's disciples to label them with single theoretical categories. This is especially true of Kilpatrick. In 1936 he recounted the evolution of his thinking:

> My social theory was greatly developed from say 1928 onward, and largely under the influence of my Discussion Group, but the germs of it — and much of the development — were there in 1918-20. My notions of democracy are much the same from 1917.[22]

And in an article that predated Counts's landmark speech, Kilpatrick rank-ordered his educational agenda, declaring that the social program was the primary element, followed by seeking the good life and building integrated personalities. He also noted that these three components were not separate entities to be pursued independently. And yet:

> I believe my insistence on a social program for education is the emphasis now most needed. The water is stirring even at this moment. People are thinking possibly as never before. The times demand it. I have chosen this occasion as a fitting

one in which to announce what is now for me the chief
demand on American education.[23]

Kilpatrick's brief book, *Education and the Social Crisis,* was drawn from
his Kappa Delta Pi lecture series given in Washington D.C., in February 1932,
the same month that Counts made his "Dare the Schools" speech in Baltimore.
Kilpatrick had called one speech "A Social Program for American Education"
and had given it to his discussion group a week later. He emerged from the
experience with ambivalent feelings. "There were those who thought I was too
"red," others not so. Some wished a more positive program. I am not brilliant
and I have not done anything profound. Possibly it will help the cause."[24]

Building on his work from the previous decade, Kilpatrick opens *Education
and the Social Crisis* with a historical portrait of an ever changing civilization
that diminishes the individual through mass production, an impersonal industrial
system, and an economic machine controlled by a few in order to selfishly
"extort as much as possible from the rest." The concept of "rugged individualism" had become incongruous with the passing of an economic order built
on modest-sized farms and small industries. Freedom has been lost, declares
Kilpatrick, with autonomy left only to those who control the capital or the means
of production — owners, managers, and bankers. He then suggests that only in
a demand-oriented economy, in which workers can generate enough income to
become significant purchasers, can future depressions be avoided.[25]

But how does such a new economic system develop? The twin solutions
Kilpatrick suggests are planning and technology. (Both proposals echo those of
Counts, although Kilpatrick arrived at them independently.) Kilpatrick saw the
possibility of a future wage earner working twenty hours a week, thirty or forty
weeks a year, and making $20,000 a year — the present-day equivalent would
be $200,000. Economic success would depend on a cooperative effort among
all Americans, rather than on the competitive profit-motive system that pitted
worker against worker. Kilpatrick strongly criticizes capitalism, particularly as
embodied in the stock market. He implies that certain similarities exist between
speculation and racketeering. "Success must prevail over honesty. When the
stock market goes up," he asks, "where does the new wealth come from?"[26]

As George Counts trumpeted the need for teachers to build a new social
order, so too did Kilpatrick include educators within his scheme for a modern
approach to social change. A major cause for these static economic conditions
is an educational system that inculcates the status quo. Society's attention is
diverted from the major social issues of the time "to prohibition or the Atlantic

flights of an aviatrix." Addressing, as Counts had, the need for educators to take the lead, Kilpatrick wrote that "school thinking becomes thus too often utterly inane, and teachers too often the most timid of professional workers." Just as medicine had moved beyond its origins in barbering, so too must education discover its own new day. Teachers must become "the responsible guardians of society's conscious and intentional education." At this point in *Education and the Social Crisis*, Kilpatrick returns to the curriculum, noting that, at a time when it was imperative to think in terms of social responsibility, teachers had not yet thought beyond subject matter or the mere daily routine of schools.[27] He states his deep concern with the vacuous nature of the curriculum as plainly as he had stated it a decade earlier:

> The curriculum, too, is largely bookish, often conventional and snobbishly "cultural." From the point of view of controversial issues and institutional criticism, the content is on the whole surprisingly "safe," and innocuous . . . [with] typically no critical consideration of life's problems as the young face them. The final results . . . are tested by examinations which in effect encourage cramming.[28]

Democracy is not forgotten in *Education and the Social Crisis*, even in the area of parental rights. Society's duty to build open-mindedness within the student, it might be argued, is itself democratic indoctrination. Kilpatrick writes:

> Parents, for example, do not have the right — though probably most still claim it — to fix the future thinking of their children. Teachers have at times obligations to help children to free themselves from the limitations which ignorant parents have with the best of intentions attempted to fasten irrevocably upon them.[29]

But a note of caution accompanies this strong assertion: Any teacher attempting to "ride rough-shod over community sensitivities" would come to "grief." Once again, Kilpatrick advocates moderation and gradualism by means of "prudence. . .courtesy. . .and consideration."[30]

As discussed earlier, indoctrination became one of the most controversial issues within the social reconstructionist camp. Bowers states that Kilpatrick was as much a believer in indoctrination as Counts, differing only in degree. In

fact, he and Counts did share similar personal views on the economy, social change, and the role of schools in the process of change. Nevertheless, Kilpatrick refused to dictate that process within the system or to impose his personal beliefs on others. At the same time, Kilpatrick realized that endless planning, speculation, and group processes would come to naught if some sort of conclusion was not reached. Lack of convictions in the cause of impartiality was unacceptable. In the end, he placed his faith in applied intelligence rather than a dogmatic set of beliefs. "A zeal based on another foundation," he wrote, "would be a dangerous kind of zeal to have around."[31]

Kilpatrick concludes *Education and the Social Crisis* by calling for a deeper understanding of the individual within the social context. He does not abandon his commitment to the individual, nor does he repudiate his philosophy by conceding many disputed points to the social reconstructionists. A group transmission of culture is what he is striving for, not an uncritical acceptance of any philosophy. The moral obligation of the teaching profession and a commitment to adult education, especially discussion groups, are put forth as keys to future success. And that success is to be measured by an increase in social responsibility and social intelligence.[32] In Kilpatrick's view, the two competing wings of progressivism could live and prosper together.

Conservative reaction to *Education and the Social Crisis* was strong. While admitting that criticism of the current political and economic situation was warranted, the Catholic journal *Commonweal* issued a quick response to Kilpatrick's call for a new moral structure. "It would be a great help to know the author's definition of moral," wrote the reviewer. If it were the same as Dewey's, which reduced morality to sociality, then "it was a flagrant case of begging the question." But an acquaintance of Kilpatrick's from the Institute of Pacific Relations, Bruno Lasker, found the author himself the embodiment of what was being advocated in *Education and the Social Crisis*: "The educator . . . is not to be measured by the degree in which he aims to indoctrinate others . . . but rather by the degree in which he succeeds in stimulating others to think effectively through their problems." This "dialectic skill" that Lasker saw in Kilpatrick was the key by which democratically controlled planning could succeed. Robert Morss Lovett in *The New Republic* viewed Kilpatrick's book as an example of the author's concern about competitiveness, lack of social responsibility, and the need for the schools to change society. Kilpatrick himself was mildly disappointed in the book's reception. For him it represented a "new social-economic position" that he had been developing for the past two years. "Some have spoken well of it, but on the whole I had expected a more definite reception."[33]

What *Education and the Social Crisis* had established was Kilpatrick's attempt to formulate a synthesis between the two camps of progressivism. It also demonstrated that he was reaching conclusions similar to Counts's in an independent and creative fashion. But as one scholar has written, the contents of *Education and the Social Crisis* were not as important as the fact that "Kilpatrick had lent his tremendous prestige, which in progressive education was second only to Dewey himself, to the social reconstructionist faction which was emerging to challenge the child-centered educators for leadership of the progressive education movement."[34]

Yet it would be Kilpatrick's contribution to, and editorship of, his next work that would draw the most attention. Published in 1933, *The Educational Frontier* was a collaboratively written yearbook that had been commissioned by the National Society of College Teachers of Education. In addition to Kilpatrick, the writers included John Dewey, Boyd H. Bode, John R. Childs, R. Bruce Raup, H. Gordon Hullfish, and V. T. Thayer. In February of 1932, Kilpatrick had met with Raup, Bode, Hullfish, and two other professors "in a discussion of a possible yearbook in philosophy of education. In the end we seem to agree on the desirability of a book in which philosophy of education attempts to deal — in a philosophic fashion — with the social situation as far as concerns education." In April the general outline and writing assignments were agreed upon, and another meeting was scheduled for early July. The group was bolstered in its task by a lecture at this time given by one of the future New Deal "brain trusters", Rexford "Guy" Tugwell, and sponsored by Teachers College. "We are indeed in a new era," wrote Kilpatrick, "when an American audience will applaud Tugwell's statements of how we need a new economic orientation." Kilpatrick also noted a new sense of awareness within his classes. That summer he noted, "There is a very marked change of outlook in two years. I failed in 1930 to get much response to social problems. But then I myself have grown in my thinking." Feeling in high spirits, in the spring of 1932, the Kilpatrick Discussion Group began working on a manifesto that would address social, economic, and educational problems.[35]

When *The Educational Frontier* group reconvened in July at the Teachers College Country Club in Ossining, New York, it took all of Kilpatrick's skill as mediator, discussion leader, and editor to bring these independent thinkers together. It was never an issue of disparate points of view or lack of consensus on the direction of the project. Apparently, however, the stereotypical traits of absentminded professors came to full fruition during the project. At first, the 74-year-old Dewey seemed in top form, but Boyd Bode had "slipped back,"

according to Kilpatrick, forgetting all that had been accomplished in the previous meeting three months earlier. Once Bode got on track, then Dewey's focus lapsed, as did Hullfish's. Kilpatrick at one point felt as though he had two conferences on his hands, and after adjournment one day he went to bed discouraged. A round of golf the next day, with John Dewey observing, seems to have cleared the minds of the group, and the following day progress was made. Although a mild philosophical rift developed between the Ohio State group and the Teachers College delegation — the former wanting to focus on changing the school, the latter on changing society — by the end of the stay Kilpatrick was again hopeful. "I feel that we still have a chance to write a good book," he wrote, "but it will take a good deal more conference to do it." The book reached closure in mid-November of 1932, with Dewey leading the others in expressing to Kilpatrick their appreciation for his leadership of the group.[36]

As Lawrence Cremin has written, since all of the men were of Dewey's persuasion and four were from Kilpatrick's discussion group, "It is no surprise that the volume which emerged is for all intents and purposes a restatement of Dewey's philosophy appropriate to Depression America." Cremin goes on to describe the book as "the characteristic progressivist statement of its decade" and the "most hardheaded and realistic" of all the "post-war versions of progressive education." But Cremin also notes a dichotomy between the Kilpatrick of *The Educational Frontier*, in which the social outlook was advanced, and the Kilpatrick of *Foundations of Method*, in which his proposals for classroom practice had been suggested. In addition to these "differing Kilpatricks," Cremin notes that despite the repeated calls for practicality, *The Educational Frontier* "stops short at the very point of what to do."[37] Kilpatrick recognized this weakness at the time, if not in his own contribution, in that of Boyd Bode. The group seemed concerned that Bode's first chapter dealt solely with "looking intellectually at life instead of grappling with life." As for the chapters by Dewey and Childs, however, there was a consensus among the collaborators that their offering was strong, thanks in large measure to John Childs.[38]

Although Kilpatrick served as editor and wrote two chapters, Dewey and Childs's two chapters formed the philosophical foundation of the volume. Lawrence Dennis, in his biography of Childs, indicates that Dewey and Childs mirrored the philosophy of the rest of the group. He quotes from *The Educational Frontier* their conception of education as "a process of social interaction carried on in behalf of consequences which are themselves social —that is, it involves interactions between persons and includes shared values."

Dennis notes that the reviews of the book were very positive, particularly the one by Sidney Hook, who called it "by far the most progressive and significant statement of the new educational philosophy which is emerging from the depression."[39]

But John Almack of Stanford University was not persuaded. Stating that it was "not Dewey at his best," Almack concluded, "That they have not succeeded is due to several reasons, most notably that they have no new place to go and no means of conveyance." He likened the authors to "beaters in a wood where there is no game." The Catholic journal *Commonweal* found it a "monotonous chant" by utopians "wandering about in the clouds of an abstract and bloodless ideology." *Commonweal* could not reconcile the new role outlined for teachers in *The Educational Frontier* as "social apostles" with its own perception of what educators should be — followers, not leaders.[40]

Kilpatrick's contribution to the volume — often overlooked because of John Dewey's participation in the project — consisted of two chapters, one on adult education and the other on the professional preparation of educators. Chapter Four, "The New Adult Education," was built around three major areas: the concept of educating the whole child; Kilpatrick's definition of adult education; and, finally, groups and organizations outside the school which could contribute to adult education. On the whole, the chapter on adult education was not one of the better entries in the book: Kilpatrick made it clear that he did not relish the topic or have any particular expertise in it, and he wondered if he really had anything worth saying. During the writing, he noted that "all the interesting chapters have gone to others."[41]

Kilpatrick felt much more comfortable with his other chapter, "Professional Education from the Social Point of View," which examined the education of educators. It is creative and remarkably modern in its outlook on the preparation of teachers and administrators. If there is a thesis, it is that a social outlook, as well as the traditional components of subject matter and pedagogy, must be inherent in the professional preparation of teachers. He quickly dispatched the often used term "training" in connection with educating teachers, noting that animals, not people, are trained. He argued strongly for a longer and more rigorous period of preparation for teachers and pointed out that the major reason that the public had not yet demanded a quality of preparation analogous to that of medicine and law was the "lack of any very clearly observed connection between the extent of teacher preparation and the educative results in the children."[42] He also recommended a move from a two-year to a four-year course and, within fifty years, to an even longer period of

study. Kilpatrick firmly believed that future teachers needed to develop an understanding and personal knowledge of "how the less-favored among us live and feel. First-hand contacts carry great potency." He then wisely added, "We easily disregard the needs of those we do not know."[43] He also held that, on the personal level, teachers needed to be psychologically balanced:

> The maladjusted teacher means, in tendency, at least, maladjusted children. Only as the teacher has brought order and clarity and integration into his own or her own grasp of life can we expect the children to profit by the teacher's leadership.[44]

He also felt compelled to respond once again to the controversy over the role of subject matter. In doing so, he gave what may be his most direct statement on the issue:

> Neither an instructor in a professional school for teachers nor a teacher of young people can expect really to succeed without a knowledge of what he is teaching far in advance of what most teachers can now show. No amount of educational theory or skill can take the place of full and exact knowledge. But, on the other hand, it is equally true that no mere subject-matter acquisition as such can hope to succeed in the long run apart from the general educational preparation (i.e. professional education preparation) discussed above.[45]

Kilpatrick also stressed the need for teachers to become more involved in the community if crime, poverty, and lack of health care are having a detrimental effect on children's achievement in school. Within the school, he pointed out the need for shared decision making and "a new place for teachers in the management of education." He also criticized superintendents for too easily following the lead of business in its style of management, including a "firing and hiring" model, overcautiousness on controversial issues, and preservation of a hierarchical style of leadership — which he viewed as the worst aspects of business. He charged that this whole prototype of school administration was patently antidemocratic. The chapter closes with a comprehensive and often quoted statement: "From top to bottom the social outlook must permeate and dominate the school system."[46] This chapter is one of the more

frank, plainly written, direct statements on a topic on which there had been a minimum of creative thinking, and it clearly demonstrates Kilpatrick's ability to weld social philosophy to the world of practice. A sense of modernity pervades this chapter, referring as it does to the empowerment of teachers, decentralized decision making, the impact of poverty and social class on educational achievement, and the need to professionalize teachers' preparation and examine anew the role of the school superintendency.

As the final touches were being put on *The Educational Frontier* in November 1932, the nation went to the polls. Kilpatrick voted for Norman Thomas: "Not that I am a Socialist," he wrote in his diary, "but I wished to help move in that direction."[47] John Dewey had similar inclinations in 1928, but as a matter of practical politics he had voted for Al Smith — he thought the Democrats would face the issue of economic reconstruction more forthrightly than the Republicans. While he supported Roosevelt during the Depression years, Dewey did not believe that the New Deal had gone far enough; it was always in danger of repeal because of its business interests. In 1932, Kilpatrick knew that the conventional wisdom indicated a victory for Roosevelt; he only wished that the New York governor "were a stronger man and that the vote for him was on more positive grounds." Pleased though he was with the inaugural address, Kilpatrick echoed Dewey's disappointment that Roosevelt did not go as far as he would have wished. Nevertheless, Kilpatrick admitted that Roosevelt held a great deal of promise. As Roosevelt's famous first hundred days neared an end, Kilpatrick noted that the country was entering upon a "new deal" and that the administration was consciously planning the economy. "If I am right," wrote Kilpatrick in his diary, "this is a very significant thing in history."[48]

During the summer of 1933 Kilpatrick gave a radio talk on WEVD, "Education to Help the New Deal," in support of Roosevelt's new program. He called the president's program "the beginning of a half-century of social experimentation" shifting away from what he termed a selfish, laissez-faire regime to an inclusive social plan devised by all for the good of all. He envisioned support for the New Deal generated by thousands of study groups, including both young and old, across the country, wherever social problems were honestly discussed and attacked with "social intelligence." By the following year, his talks almost always included a plea to his audiences that the New Deal be "extended and developed."[49] Kilpatrick's enthusiasm for the New Deal was due to the program's advocacy and application of the concepts of moderation, experimentation, and amelioration. Technology would bring economic interdependence, democracy would deliver equality of opportunity, and education

would produce — in the long term — lasting socioeconomic changes in society.

In marked contrast to the more strident utterances of the time, Kilpatrick's was a voice of reason, and his emphasis on moderation was demonstrated during one Sunday talk with students. Rather than calling for the "smashing of the capitalist machine," or declaring that the choice was either "communism or starvation," he told students that the corroded parts of the broken capitalist machine could be replaced through thinking, by an intelligent citizenry. An article in the *Student's Weekly*, "Dr. Kilpatrick Speaks," remarked favorably on both "the old fashioned cut of his hair and the slow soothing tone of his voice, richly flavored by the South." Although Kilpatrick abhorred the pain, disorder, and harm he saw occurring with the old system, he continued to advocate a democratic and extended response to the crisis. He agreed with Franklin Roosevelt's observation made in 1932, that "the country needs bold, persistent experimentation."[50]

Soon after the election of 1932, the Kilpatrick Discussion Group began working on a "manifesto," as they termed it, to send to President-Elect Roosevelt. Counts, Childs, Paul Hanna, and William C. Bagley worked on a rather lengthy first draft. It was then turned over to Kilpatrick, Childs, and Counts for editing. All except Isaac Kandel agreed to the document in principle. It began by describing the plight of American children, stating that one-fourth of those in New York City schools were suffering from malnutrition. Idleness and fear were turning adolescents to lives of crime and despair. With 12 million adults out of work, many more children were directly affected. The manifesto stated that educators could not stand by while such conditions continued unabated, with schools and health agencies undergoing "reckless budget cutting" that caused "irreparable damage." Democracy demanded that institutions work impartially for the benefit of all. The answer, said the authors of the document, was to move away from the self-regulating status of modern corporate life toward more cooperative measures that would be able to deal with modern industrial conditions. They called for a planned economy of "consciously devised arrangements," which would supplant "selfish opportunism." This goal was then detailed in seven specific points, including coordination of production and consumption, apportioning national income between investment and purchasing, equitable distribution of occupational opportunities, and the effective provision of essential services such as health and education. After calling for the objectives to be met through democratic means, the document requested the formation by the president, with the cooperation of Congress, of a National Coordinating Council to devise and implement them.[51]

The "manifesto" was delivered to President-Elect Roosevelt by Rexford Tugwell. But it arrived in the midst of the banking crisis and it did not result in the desired audience with the president, nor even a formal response from him. Apparently, Roosevelt had little interest in educational issues; Kilpatrick would suggest years later, that this was due to the president's private schooling. Some historians agree, at least in part, holding that Roosevelt did not view the federal government as an appropriate conduit for public school support and that there was a lack of harmony between national educators, especially the NEA, and the president. For example, Roosevelt is said to have seen public school teachers as "fussy," and educators are said to have seen him as "a private school snob." Kilpatrick, for one, is named as an educator who thought this way. Ralph Tyler has suggested that the public schools and college educators had indeed been "overlooked" by the New Dealers, although both had a great deal to contribute.[52]

One potential contributor was the commissioner of education, a former student of Kilpatrick's, John Studebaker. Studebaker, who was appointed to his post in 1934, proposed a more reformist agenda for the education program of the Civilian Conservation Corps; but this simply demonstrates how marginalized progressive educators were during the New Deal — they were fighting to influence a peripheral segment of a conservation program. And yet one historian, Arthur Schlesinger, Jr., has suggested that John Dewey was one of four intellectuals who helped shape the philosophy of the New Deal. During the 1936 campaign, the progressives attempted again to gain attention, in order to influence and promote educational policy at the national level. Kilpatrick and Jesse Newlon, on behalf of the *Social Frontier*, sent a telegram to President Roosevelt, Governor Alf Landon of Kansas, Norman Thomas, and Earl Browder asking three questions. The first dealt with the role of schools in a democratic society; the other two concerned the need for greater and more equitable funding of schools. After speeches by Kilpatrick and Harold Rugg, the answers from the presidential candidates were read to an audience of 1,200 in Horace Mann Auditorium on August 10, 1936.[53]

A year after the publication of *The Educational Frontier*, what could be called its companion in journal form, *The Social Frontier*, was launched. Proposed by two Teachers College graduate students, it was eventually underwritten and edited by several members of the Kilpatrick Discussion Group. Kilpatrick himself became chairman of its board of directors, in addition to christening it, and George S. Counts was selected as its first editor. John Dewey and Sidney Hook were also on the board of directors. The first issue was published in October of 1934. An announcement for the first issue of

The Social Frontier, subtitled *A Journal of Educational Criticism and Reconstruction*, promised that it would be the arena where major battles of education would be intelligently fought while serving the emerging consciousness of American teachers.[54] *The Social Frontier* provided an educational forum, according to Lawrence Cremin, that "achieved a level of polemical journalism that frequently rivaled *The Nation* and *The New Republic*." The diverse contributors included Dewey, Kilpatrick, Charles Beard, Robert Hutchins, Merle Curti, Lewis Mumford, the Roman Catholic F. J. Sheed, Harry D. Gideonse — an economist from the University of Chicago — and advocates of both fascism and communism. There was even an article by Leon Trotsky.

Although the vitality of *The Social Frontier* was apparent, Cremin saw its quality as inconsistent and judged that, in the end it had little impact on New Deal educational policies and even less on classrooms or teachers. "The brilliant polemicists of *The Social Frontier*," he wrote, "were simply finessed by less imaginative men with more specific pedagogical nostrums to purvey. In the end, the journal left one more image of progressive education in the public mind, the caricature of the radical pedagogue using the school to subvert the American way of life." Herbert Kliebard has called *The Social Frontier* "a lively forum for debate on social reconstructionism generally and on the schools' role in creating a new social order in particular." For Kliebard, the "persistent theme running through the articles and editorials was the evils of laissez-faire capitalism and rampant individualism." C. A. Bowers described the articles and editorials in the new journal as "redolent with crusading zeal" and alerting its readers to "the weaknesses of both the capitalistic system and the programs of the New Deal." By the mid-1930s, Bowers noted, the journal had abandoned Dewey in favor of Marx as its "new spiritual guide." The social reconstructionists eventually moved outside the mainstream of radical liberalism, in Bowers's opinion, becoming too radical for labor, but unable to persuade the communists that the schools could be used for revolutionary purposes. The issue of extremism was a serious one. Bode and Kilpatrick, for example, were considered "safe" convention speakers by the Pennsylvania State Education Association, while the editors of *The Social Frontier* asked these two to explain their conservatism.[55]

Kilpatrick's major contribution to the thinking of *The Social Frontier* was his recurring criticism of capitalism as detrimental to the citizenry, because of its unbridled stress on individual self-interest. In its pursuit of profits, inattention to the economic security of the population led to a debasement of the individual and to a potential for political corruption. Technology, argued

Kilpatrick, made a more just and adequate distribution of goods and services possible, without resorting to selfishness and greed. Kilpatrick believed that social values, as well as social institutions, needed to be addressed and advanced. Personally, Kilpatrick believed that private ownership of the means of production should be abolished. He did not think that there should be a differentiation between workers, believing that this was "the only way to abolish the struggle of man against man and usher in a regime of all for all." Kilpatrick's belief about self-interest and cooperation were deeply held and fervent, but only on rare occasions would he express them publicly. However, he felt that children could be educated only if institutional impediments were set aside; and at a meeting of the discussion group Scholia, he did propound that belief with, as he later said, "considerable earnestness." In fact, a colleague called Kilpatrick's fervent declaration the "most thrilling occasion" he had ever witnessed. Although restrained, refined, and courteous to a fault, Kilpatrick could bring his intellect and persuasive powers to bear to great effect. It should be noted, though, that not everyone agreed with him. Professor Reisner arose and told the group that he "never expected to see the leader of thought in education renounce thought and commit himself to emotion instead."[56] If nothing else, the episode demonstrates Kilpatrick's commitment to advancing the social outlook within the educational arena.

As a group, the "frontiersmen" were also willing to put their ideas into practice. When reductions in secretarial salaries at Teachers College were suggested in early 1933, several professors suggested that their own salaries, at least those at the higher end of the spectrum, be reduced rather than permit the staff to suffer. "We cannot propose plans for social justice," wrote Kilpatrick in his diary after the meeting, "unless we are willing to begin at home." When the issue came up later in a faculty meeting, Dean Russell declined to accept the professors' proposal, on the grounds of cost. For the first time, a breach arose between the dean and his most influential professor. Kilpatrick believed that Russell had "assumed the role of benevolent despot," viewing him as the antagonist in the debate. By the close of the meeting the dean seemed apprehensive about his decision, but Edward L. Thorndike, as usual, supported him. The issue emerged again, with Kilpatrick directly challenging the dean on the issue of pay and staff morale. He repeated the call for a shared approach to the budget predicament, with higher-paid faculty members taking the larger cuts. Counts supported him, but once again Thorndike opposed the idea, saying that job security had little to do with morale and that the situation would provide an opportunity to remove inferior employees. This seemed to seal the

issue. An overall 15 percent reduction in all salaries took place in 1933. In 1934 Kilpatrick challenged the dean again, asking him to use a $60,000 surplus to "assist those who stand in need." Russell did not act upon the recommendation, but did reduce the previous year's salary cut from 15 to 10 percent.[57]

Harold Rugg continued to raise the issue of compensation throughout the summer of 1933, and more criticism of the dean emerged. In August Kilpatrick pushed Russell to accept the National Reconstruction Act (NRA) regulations for the nonprofessional employees, but once again the dean responded that the costs would be prohibitive. In a remarkable covert meeting at the home of Harold Rugg, Kilpatrick met with Newlon, Counts, Childs, Watson, Ernest Johnson, Clyde Miller, and Lois Meek to discuss the future of Teachers College. Their major concern was not Russell, but the larger issues of the economy and the actions the trustees might take if the New Deal failed. They discussed founding a college of their own and considered establishing a group similar to the Committees of Correspondence during the American Revolution or the Jacobin Clubs in France. Their purpose was to democratize Teachers College and gain support among like-minded colleagues. Another suggestion was to found a campus chapter of the American Association of University Professors and secure an agreement, similar to Columbia's, regarding the dismissal of professors. Most of those present agreed with what was said that evening, with the exception of the more radical Childs who thought that little of tangible effect had been accomplished.[58]

There was a similar evolution of thought among the editors of *The Social Frontier*, who had departed from their initial dictum of 1934 that collectivism should supplant individualism in economic activity, saying in 1936 that class warfare was the solution. This resulted in an exodus from the group, and Kilpatrick was among those who left. He had made his own position clear in 1935 in an address to the NEA's Department of Superintendence. In that speech, he reiterated his belief in technology, interdependence, and the need to bring about socioeconomic changes through the study of social changes and the application of intelligence to specific situations. What was new was his explicit rejection of the inevitability of class warfare. "Such a position seems for this country false and wrong in almost every detail," he declared. A great deal of the responsibility for "applying intelligence" resided with the universities, he believed. "When this happens, schools will be the dangerous outposts of a humane civilization," he said, "but, they will also begin to be supremely interesting places."[59]

In addition to Bode and Kilpatrick, Dewey and Harold Rugg soon rejected

Marxist ideology.   Personally, Kilpatrick had little hope for reforming capitalism in 1935; reform would require a democratic renewal, and he acknowledged that such a process would take decades.   He took the argument a step further in his diary, writing that if a majority could not bring this change about, then "what our fathers called the right of revolution may be the only wise step." But he never made such statements in public.   Indeed, in June of 1936, he warned *The Social Frontier* against propagandizing on behalf of socialism. As chairman of its board of directors, Kilpatrick editorialized in "High Marxism Defined and Rejected," that while other contributors were free to advocate the Marxist doctrine as a viable option, given the current economic morass, such a stand by the editors would not be tolerated.[60]

With *The Social Frontier* under way, a larger group of like-minded progressive educators began to explore the possibility of forming a national organization to study the broader issues of school and society.   On February 6, 1935, Counts, Rugg, and Newlon invited a number of people to attend the annual meeting of the NEA's Department of Superintendence at which Kilpatrick was to be a major speaker.   Sixty-seven men responded to the letter and met in the Hotel Traymore in Baltimore.   Although the new organization was as yet unnamed, its first minutes were taken.   Daniel Tanner, in his history of the John Dewey Society, as it would eventually be called, states that the letter from Counts, Rugg, and Newlon — who were all members of the Kilpatrick Discussion Group — had been initiated by Henry Harap and Paul Hanna in meetings held the previous year.   Harap, a graduate of Teachers College, was a professor at Case Western Reserve University; Hanna, an assistant professor at Teachers College, was working as a research associate with Jesse Newlon at the Lincoln School.   While *The Social Frontier* was clearly an outgrowth of the Kilpatrick Discussion Group, Harry Harap later pointed out that the John Dewey Society was national in scope, based on a wider constituency.   Harap also contended that it was a letter he wrote to Paul Hanna on January 3, 1934, which persuaded Jesse Newlon to call this gathering of educational liberals.[61]

Tanner went to great lengths, in discussing the origins of the Dewey Society, to document the fact that Harold Rugg, Lawrence Cremin, and Adolphe E. Meyer are all in error when they argued that the new organization grew out of Kilpatrick's Discussion Group.   But in his diary for October 3, 1934, Kilpatrick records attending a meeting of a group, ironically called the Fundamentalists, at the home of Ralph Spear.   He notes at the end of this entry that "out of this group actually grew the John Dewey Society" and also mentions the dates: February 5, 20, and 24, 1935.[62]   Little else is said, though,

to show that this meeting played a major role in the formation of the society.

Harap's recollection of the organizational meeting at the Hotel Pennsylvania in Atlantic City on February 24, 1935, is limited, as is Tanner's description. Kilpatrick's diary fills in some of the blanks. Newlon, Hanna, and Kilpatrick had undertaken much of the planning for the breakfast session, and it was composed, according to Kilpatrick, of "the left wing in education — Rugg, Newlon, etc." Counts, George Stoddard of Iowa, Hollis L. Caswell of George Peabody, and others were present. A proposal to include some "middle of the road" people as fellows was rejected, and later Dewey, Beard, and others were named as the first fellows. At a luncheon, Kilpatrick was named chairman of the board of directors. This was done in spite of a fear on the part of John Childs and others that the Teachers College contingent would be perceived as controlling the new society. The group then moved to the Rose Room, which seated 500, and found it filled to standing room only. Hanna announced "Building America" — his pictorial reference magazine series — and then Rugg took the platform and announced the new organization to study the school and society. Kilpatrick noted in his diary that he was hoping against hope to call it the Dewey Society. He also recorded that Charles Beard, one of several speakers that afternoon, made a blistering attack on William Randolph Hearst, calling for a congressional committee to investigate the press lord.[63]

Overall, Kilpatrick seems to have played a much larger role in the society, including actually naming it, than Harap and subsequent chroniclers have discerned. A majority of the board of directors, of what Kilpatrick was now calling in his diary the John Dewey Society, met on March 27 and discussed the organization's name. Kilpatrick and Newlon favored the Dewey Society, Rugg was opposed, but not militantly so, and Counts and Robert Spear acquiesced. They also discussed a yearbook related to the nation's high schools. The next meeting of the group was held in May 1935, at Teachers College, where the chairmanship of the first yearbook, to be titled *The Teacher and Society*, was assigned to Kilpatrick, along with the responsibility for the next program, to be held the following year in Saint Louis in conjunction with the Department of Superintendence. A gathering of the executive board in late October of 1935, again at Teachers College, finally agreed to present to the membership the name "The John Dewey Society," with the subtitle "For the Study of Education in Its Social Relations."[64]

But closure was not reached on a formal name until the following year. In January 1936, Kilpatrick, Rugg, and a few other Teachers College faculty members involved in the organization met to determine the name to be

presented to the membership in Saint Louis that spring. "The John Dewey Society for the Study of Education and Culture" was ratified by the group, although Kilpatrick was unwilling to approve the latter half of the designation. He was also asked to approach Dewey to get approval to use his name — through all the discussions over the last eighteen months, no one had sought Dewey's approval. Two days later, Kilpatrick called on Dewey in his office, and he described the meeting in his diary:

> He [Dewey] agrees without demur, "graciously" as they say of royalty, to allow the society to be named for him. He thinks the subtitle "for the Study of Education and Culture" ambiguous because the American people take usually the other meaning of culture. He also says it is a mistake to name the society after him, but I thought he counted it a pardonable mistake. He declined to go to St. Louis. His health has not been good.[66]

What was the effect of the social reconstructionists on schools in the 1930s? The nation's teachers were significant in number — there were over a million of them in classrooms across the country. But the response of teachers to the call of the "frontiersmen" (and the occasional "frontierswoman") was mixed at best. Teachers who took summer classes at Teachers College were often hesitant to return to Iowa or Minnesota and tell their administrators that they had studied under Counts or Kilpatrick, since both men were considered radicals and there was little protection at the time from arbitrary actions by school boards. With a surplus of teachers, it was difficult for these men and women to speak out. The only teachers with enough courage to do so seemed to be urban, and usually unemployed. Cremin has also noted that calling on teachers — "not the most courageous element of the population" — to take on the Herculean task of reforming the schools and society, without any specific guidance as to curriculum, methods, or organization, left many educators at a loss. Another critic has also noted that the overwhelming number of classroom teachers were women, at a time of insensitivity to gender issues. In addition, many teachers, concurring with Kilpatrick, did not really believe in indoctrination.[67]

One historian, though, Merle Curti, does not agree that Kilpatrick and his like-minded colleagues suggested to teachers only a vague, nonspecific approach for dealing with the Depression. Curti, who later went on to a distinguished career at the University of Wisconsin, worked beside Kilpatrick in the mid-1930s as a teaching assistant at Teachers College. He later wrote:

Kilpatrick, exploring democratic ideals and ethics, unhesi-
tatingly showed how they are emasculated by traditions and
by vested interests, and insisted that creative, integrated
personalities can be achieved only through genuine sharing of
social activities. If his call for humane and intelligent control
over a rapidly changing world was too general to endow many
with militant and socially effective zeal in basic economic and
cultural conflicts, his teaching definitely challenged the social
structure as well as existing education aims and procedures.[68]

Curti went on to say that democracy could not be fully realized without an
explicit statement about the actual social and economic setting within which the
schools functioned. Rather than accept the rigid dichotomy that critics have
claimed tore progressive education apart — "individual versus social outlook"
— Curti believed that both components had to be present for the movement to
be successful and have intellectual integrity. He added that while the
Depression did accentuate the social tendency within the ranks of the progressives, this was a line of thought which went back to Dewey and Parker, and
which "others, notably Kilpatrick, were responsive to even before 1929."
Curti's statements seriously challenge C. A. Bowers's contention that in the mid-
1920s "Kilpatrick was still vacillating between the child-centered approach . . .
and Dewey's idea that the school should be used as an instrument for social
action," as well as Robert Westbrook's charge, in *John Dewey and American
Democracy*, that Kilpatrick was an opportunist.[69]

Whether the social reconstructionists failed to apply their thought to the
schools is also debatable. Harold Rugg produced his famous — later, some
would say infamous — textbook series, which embodied the reconstructionist
approach to the teaching of social studies during the 1930s and 1940s. One of
Kilpatrick's friends, Paul Hanna, who went on to Stanford University, headed
a group that published a pictorial magazine, *Building America*, for use in social
studies classrooms. The series was devoted to various social problems such as
housing, nutrition, and industry. Although it was considered to be on the fringe
of the social reconstructionist movement, *Building America*, according to one
critic, "yielded the most concrete results by involving a great many students in
an analysis of the social crisis."[70]

George Counts, as a productive writer and teacher, also had an impact on
educators for years — well into the 1970s. Many educators heard him say,

during the Depression: "Teachers must inform the new generation that a new society is here, that the system of private capitalism for private gain is dead."[71] He and John Childs were active in New York state politics through the Liberal Party and the labor movement, specifically the American Federation of Teachers. Much to Dean William Russell's chagrin, they were deeply involved in the Teachers College cafeteria strike in the mid-1930s. In 1952 Counts ran for the United States Senate and received almost half a million votes. Two other prominent members of the Kilpatrick group, Jesse Newlon and Goodwin Watson, were highly visible in translating their beliefs into action. Newlon, as superintendent of the Denver schools in the 1920s, had pushed for greater decision making on the part of teachers; Watson integrated the social reconstructionist gospel into his field, educational psychology.

Possibly the best case study on the influence of social reconstructionism on the nation's public schools took place in California during the Depression era. The debilitating economic situation had affected California by the time Counts addressed the PEA in 1932. Helen Heffernan, a stalwart Deweyan and chief of the Bureau of Elementary Education in the state department of education, was advancing progressive education to "every city and hamlet." *California Schools*, the official organ of the department of education, encouraged all teachers and administrators to read and discuss Counts's *A Call to the Teachers of the Nation*. A superintendent in Orange County in 1933 had questioned the profit motive, calling for the "ethics of success to be founded on justice and morality." Even the relatively conservative superintendent of public instruction, Vierling Kersey, saw social reconstructionism as a way of moving toward economic recovery, increased attention to social welfare, and the control of excessive private profit. The state's affiliation with social reconstructionism was brief. In 1935, the communist scares had begun. By 1947, it was prohibited to buy Paul Hanna's *Building America* series with state funds. But as Irving J. Hendrick notes in his examination of progressivism in California in the 1930s, the concept of social reconstructionism was viewed as a way to apply "moderate and appropriate solutions to pressing economic problems" within the educational context.[72]

The ideals of social reconstructionism did persist, especially through the large enrollments in the summer school programs of Teachers College and like-minded institutions. Many superintendents and other school administrators were exposed to the philosophies of Kilpatrick, Counts, Childs, Rugg, and other leading progressive educators. Such tutelage was also taking place at The Ohio State University under Bode and Hullfish, and at other less known

institutions. And *The Social Frontier* and other substantive activities by the social reconstructionists continued beyond the 1930s. Kilpatrick continued to contribute his monthly "Page" to *The Social Frontier*, even after 1937. As for the social reconstructionists' influence, certain historians have written that the devastation of teachers' local districts focused more attention on their own plight than on the numerous speeches and articles by the "frontier thinkers." It is true that these frontier thinkers were a small group — there were only 3,751 subscriptions to *The Social Frontier* in 1936. But as Tyack, Lowe, and Hansot have written:

> They appealed to conscience, to hope, to professional pride.
> They were certain at a time when many others were confused
> and vacillating. They gave educators a reason to feel
> important, a utopian cause. They also gave life to a
> compelling vision of social justice.[73]

What the social reconstructionists achieved or failed to accomplish will continue to be debated. Their legacy may lie less in their economic suggestions and prognostications than in their attempt to reframe the educational debate within the edifice of Deweyan thought. On this deeper level, the social reconstructionists provided, as James Giarelli has pointed out, a philosophy of education which allowed a serious discourse on education to take place:

> Social reconstructionism, with *The Social Frontier* and its
> failures as well as successes as a starting point, provides a set
> of problems and possibilities around which an educational
> philosophy of the public could be worked out.[74]

Kilpatrick himself reviewed his thinking on the social implications of reconstructionism in 1935 in his article "The Social Philosophy of Progressive Education." The dichotomy between personal interdependence and economic competition placed the individual between two competing and potentially irreconcilable forces. The question became how social responsibility could be learned when, to change education significantly, there had to be a change in culture. He concluded that societal ills were organic, not functional, and were ameliorated only by systemic change:

I see now that the present evil social system educates more powerfully in behalf of itself than anything the schools can do to change it. We cannot educate our children properly except as we have another system. So that as an educator, I must now join hands with other citizens to change the system.[75]

Kilpatrick can be placed at the midpoint of the social reconstructionist spectrum. While never embracing the more extreme elements of the movement — such as indoctrination, the class struggle, and Marxism — he did, during the 1920s, anticipate portions of social reconstructionist thought. There was, admittedly, a mild radicalism in his thinking, but it was tempered by a reflective, Deweyan philosophical process. For Kilpatrick, the consequences of any action — economic, political, or educational — had to fall within the parameters of intelligent, democratic procedures. For this reason, during the darkest days of the Depression he was able to reiterate his deeply held conviction that "the new condition of economic interdependence seems to demand drastic changes in our economic system, not in violation of human freedom but to preserve and to extend it."[76]

A PROGRESSIVE AT THE PINNACLE:
THE RETIREMENT CRISIS

Progressive educators, so-called, were at work in the schools. Subjects taught for generations were being demeaned and abandoned.

Progressive education had certainly developed Tarquin's sense of being an individual, but some of the results were so startling that Mrs. Bridge was reduced to a bewildered silence.

Evan S. Connell, from *Mr. Bridge* and *Mrs. Bridge*[1]

I now know that my days are numbered, eight years at the most of university work, possibly less — compulsory retirement at 65 is a possibility.

William Heard Kilpatrick from Diary, January 1, 1934

In 1937, an article titled "Is Progressive Education on the Wane?" was published. It raised the question whether a connection might exist between Kilpatrick's retirement and a decline in the movement so closely associated with him. While respectful of Kilpatrick, the article was skeptical as to the soundness of the progressive movement and included a stock vignette of the progressive schools:

A lady visited a progressive school. In the first classroom several boys were hitting each other with sticks and some were reeling around in a strange fashion. "Oh," cried the visitor, "these boys are hurting each other, and some of them are behaving as though they were drunk." The teacher calmly replied, "Of course, they are drunk and soon they will be sick. You see, they are studying the Whiskey Rebellion." After a moment's pause, the teacher continued, "Would you care to visit the class studying *The Murders of the Rue Morgue*?"[2]

Kilpatrick's connection with progressive education was a salient feature of his career. And yet he was never formally linked to the established professional organization under which progressive education was advanced in the world of practice: the Progressive Education Association (PEA), established in 1919. As Patricia Albjerg Graham has suggested in her history of the PEA, educators after the Great War had no intention of allowing the seminal ideas that had emerged during the previous quarter century to wither on the vine. "Scientific education, child study, and learning by doing were well on the way in before the American Expeditionary Force sailed for Europe," writes Graham — although after the war, the influence of progressive education had shifted away from the public schools, becoming more concentrated in private schools and classrooms found mainly in the more affluent suburbs of America.[3] The PEA was committed to the individual child and to an activity curriculum, and John Dewey lent his name to the group as its honorary president. And there was, of course, a distinct bond between Kilpatrick and progressive education. He was clearly, as Graham says, "The most prominent exponent of progressive education of the period between the wars.

Graham tells of a fictitious New Year's party of progressive educators — a spoof — at which only two or three members of the Teachers College faculty are present, the others being unwilling to get involved in "popularizing" progressive education. Graham notes that by PEA's first decade many of the Teachers College group held important positions in the organization. (Years later, when the glory days of PEA had faded, its founder Stanwood Cobb complained to Lawrence Cremin that the Teachers College crowd "took it away from us.") And Kilpatrick, by his own admission, was a populiazer *par excellence*. But it was the PEA's own journal, *Progressive Education* — rather than Teachers College or Kilpatrick — that became the most effective vehicle of popularization, exalting child-centeredness, classroom freedom, and creativity.[4]

Providing an exact definition of progressive education was often difficult; and since by its very nature progressive education was a modern, dynamic, growing process, definitions could and would change. Kilpatrick addressed the issue in 1930, in an article titled "What Do We Mean by Progressive Education?" For him, progressive education attempted to base itself on a careful study of educational processes rather than relying on tradition for answers. A distinction was drawn between "careful study" and "scientific study," though. The latter, according to Kilpatrick, excluded the personality of the child in order to examine "separate pieces" such as knowledge, skills, and habits. "To begin by cutting up life . . . is to fail to care for the whole child," he

wrote. A second element of progressive education was the emphasis on activity. Behaving and learning could not be separated. Such experimental learning allows for the adjustment of conduct toward the positive. In comparison, traditional education stressed facts, skills, grades, marks, and credits to the exclusion of character and personality development. Progressive education, then,

> seeks to care for the whole child. Not that it does not care for
> reading and writing and literature and all the like things. It
> will get these and even more than does the old school, but it
> seeks first the whole child.[5]

Progressive education was both ignored and spotlighted by intellectuals and the popular press between the wars, and later, during the critical reassessment of the 1950s. Graham notes that Arthur Link, an influential historian and Woodrow Wilson scholar, completely overlooked progressive education in his article in the *American Historical Review* in 1959: "What Happened to the Progressive Movement of the 1920s?" On the other hand, James M. Wallace, in his book *Liberal Journalism and American Education, 1914-1941*, has described the great interest two journals of opinion — *The Nation* and *The New Republic* — took in progressive education. Social commentators such as Malcolm Cowley and Frederick Lewis Allen lauded the child-centered, psychologically appropriate elements of educational progressivism. In addition, such proponents as Margaret Naumburg, Lucy Sprague Mitchell, and Harold Rugg were all active participants in the intellectual life of New York City in the period between the wars.[6] And of course, both Dewey and Kilpatrick were frequent contributors to journals such as *The New Republic* and often gave radio talks on social and educational issues of the day.

The goal of the Progressive Education Association in the 1930s was to move the nation beyond mere recognition of progressivism to a point of public endorsement and wide support of the movement. To disseminate the progressive message, a series of regional meetings were held, beginning in the East in the early 1930s and moving, by the midpoint of the decade, across the entire nation. Kilpatrick was an indefatigable leader at these gatherings. At one such meeting in 1933, he shared the platform with Eleanor Roosevelt, Norman Thomas, Louis Howe, and Sidney Hook. And two issues that the PEA stressed in the 1930s were also to become matters of concern for Kilpatrick in the coming decade and beyond — academic freedom and the role of the federal

government in education. One sign of the increasing public acceptance of progressivism was that on October 31, 1938, *Time* magazine had PEA's executive secretary Frederick L. Redefer (a partisan of Kilpatrick) on its cover and carried a major story on progressive education. The article in *Time* said that progressive education had moved from "a tiny, and in many eyes, crackpot movement quarantined in a handful of private schools" to a status where "no U.S. school has completely escaped its influence." Two model public school districts where progressive education was being practiced were Glencoe, Illinois, and Denver, Colorado. In Denver, according to the article, a "core curriculum" was in place: all studies were built around core topics such as modern living or specific social problems. *Time* also noted that the Progressive Education Association, under Redefer's guidance, had received large financial contributions from the Carnegie and Rockefeller foundations. The article quoted Boyd H. Bode to the effect that progressive education needed to move away from its child-centered emphasis and encompass democracy as a way of life — defining democracy as the "continuous extension of common interests." The article closed by citing a number of studies comparing progressive education students with those in traditional schools. According to data collected by J. Wayne Wrightstone of The Ohio State University, progressive students were clearly superior in both academics and the less tangible areas of development such as leadership, honesty, and cooperation.[7]

But Kilpatrick was not totally convinced of the PEA's success, or of progressive education's impact. In 1933, he noted a decline of interest in progressive education and speculated that the decrease in attention was due to the fact that progressive education had been generally accepted in school practice and had failed to "bring on a millennium" in teaching — something Kilpatrick himself had never promised. There were also the "measurers," or advocates of testing, who were championing an agenda quite different from that of the progressives. On this issue, at least, Kilpatrick and the PEA were in agreement. One problem was that the terms "fads" and "frills" were often coupled with progressive education during this era. But Kilpatrick came to its defense. In the *New York Times* he asked critics if they saw health, physical education, and after-school athletics as "frills," the teaching of morals and manners, of which many homes were bereft, as "fads."[8] Despite the critics, Kilpatrick still believed strongly in his message, which, while not new, was, in his opinion, still sound.

On one occasion, Kilpatrick unwittingly became involved in what the *New York Times* referred to as an "unscheduled debate" on the topic of progressive

education. Professor Douglas Bush of Harvard attacked progressive education during a conference, telling of a young woman who was asked if she could teach English history and who replied that she could because she had "had it twice, once in clay and once in sand." Unbeknownst to Bush, Kilpatrick was in the audience, and he was invited to the platform to respond. He denounced Bush's anecdote as a "caricature" of what he and other progressive educators stood for. Undeterred by the response, Bush indicated that he did not intend any reflection on Kilpatrick's achievements and offered another vignette: a child at a progressive school who told her mother that "she had to rest during recess because she played so hard at school."[9] Mortimer Adler, disciple of Robert Hutchins, also joined the assault on progressive education at a conference of school administrators in 1939. Calling progressive education "an unsavory mess," Adler went on to charge that:

> Progressive education is a racket. And the biggest racketeers are the professors of education at Teachers College, Columbia University. Progressive education is throwing the curriculum out of the school and putting extra-curricular activities in its stead. It is supplanting curriculum of the schools with claptrap.[10]

One of the strongest broadsides against progressive education came from the "Essentialist Committee for the Advancement of Education" in 1938, during a meeting of the American Association of School Administrators in Atlantic City. Led by William Bagley and other like-minded thinkers, the committee charged that test results proved that progressive education had failed American elementary students who did not measure up scholastically to their European counterparts. There were deficiencies not only in arithmetic and grammar, but also in the social arena: "Ours is the only nation in which the expansion of universal school education has not been paralleled by a significant decrease in the ratio of serious crime." Louis Shores of George Peabody College stated that "the progressives have tuned the American education system to the ability of the lowest class of morons." Conferees even pointed to John Dewey's recently published *Experience and Education* as an indictment of the movement. Dewey quickly responded that his book was not a criticism of progressive education but merely noted some of the problems it had to meet. He went on to argue that the faults of which the essentialists were complaining "have been accentuated because of the failure of the type of education which

this new essentialist group seems to represent." Kilpatrick was less restrained; in fact, he was uncharacteristically contemptuous: "This is the same sort of reactionary movement that always springs up when a doctrine is sweeping the country. The astonishing thing is . . . that it is so small and on the whole comes from such inconspicuous people."[11]

The 1930s did find progressive education at a crossroads. The division between the social reconstructionists and the advocates of child-centered education left a breach which scholars — Cremin and Graham included — saw as sowing the seeds of the movement's destruction. There were also attendant issues that eroded the highly identifiable philosophy of progressive education which had dominated educational thought for much of the period between the wars. There was, for example, a brief but public debate between John Dewey and Robert Hutchins of the University of Chicago in 1936, which Kilpatrick himself joined a year later. In addition, there was the perennial problem in educational reform of how best to advance and replicate the central tenets of the movement in the classrooms of America. If Cremin is correct as to the multiple reasons for the decline of the PEA and progressive education in the 1950s, these same root causes were at work in the 1930s.

Just as the philosophy of social reconstruction was being redefined during the mid-1930s, so too were the often nebulous underpinnings of progressive education. In February of 1935, at the annual meeting of the Progressive Education Association, Kilpatrick shared the platform with the historian Charles Beard. Kilpatrick outlined the major presuppositions of progressive education as he saw them. They included respect for personality and the social origin of character, a moral obligation to consider the consequences of one's acts, a consideration of the new demands on education in a time of rapid change, a need for the individual to rise above culture through creative intelligence, and finally, the necessity that schools be immersed in life. Such definitions were crucial.

During a regional conference of the PEA held at Colorado State College of Education in the summer of 1935, Kilpatrick gave one of his most complete statements on progressive education in an address titled "Why Progressive Education?" He began by declaring what progressive education was opposed to — tradition as opposed to thinking, reliance on measurement, and the theory of "cold storage" whereby organized subject matter is separated from life. In reliably pragmatic fashion, Kilpatrick asserted that final authority rested on tested and criticized experience in an ever novel world. Democracy becomes indistinguishable from education, in that self-directed individuality becomes

the chief aim of the developing personality. The teacher's role in this process is to assist the learner to act on thinking, while being knowledgeable about the whole child. In a Churchillian turn of phrase, Kilpatrick did not claim that progressive education was the superior approach, only that its competitors were inferior. Voicing a notion he would continue to develop for the next two decades, Kilpatrick maintained that "we learn along any line only as we practice along that line." He was leaving behind the S - R (stimulus-response) bond and theory of conditioning that had been part of his earlier thinking, comparing the shift to scientists' abandonment of Newtonian physics for modern physics. He concluded his address by saying that progressive education provided the best basis for a democratic reconstruction of the social order.[12]

The breach within the progressive education movement between advocates of the child-centered approach and those stressing the need to reconstruct society was ever-widening. Attempting to narrow that divide, in 1935 Kilpatrick wrote an article for *Progressive Education,* "The Social Philosophy of Progressive Education," in which he asked: "Can we educate our children properly in school so long as the surrounding order hinders, either by withholding opportunities or by educating against us?" He firmly believed that the progressive philosophy would hold if its essential components could be further developed. To change education significantly, then, the culture had to be changed. The answer, wrote Kilpatrick, lay within a process of intelligent study and criticism of the culture on the part of the young child. Society was at war with itself, with interdependence and morality combating the self-centered interests of business and capitalism. The two sides were irreconcilable. The solution rested in the development of social science and its attendant "cumulative intelligence for dealing with human affairs," just as development in the natural sciences had led to prodigious strides during the last decade. On the most elementary level, "the true unit of educative experience was . . . some cooperative community enterprise where young and old work together for a common good." Kilpatrick admitted that he had previously thought that the ills of society were functional, not organic. He now believed that they were indeed organic, curable only by changing the system. But that change had to be democratic. What was needed was "not less democracy, but more and better democracy."[13]

On July 2, 1936, Kilpatrick published *Remaking the Curriculum*, his most comprehensive examination of progressive education since *Education for a Changing Civilization.* A short work, *Remaking the Curriculum* was drawn from a series of previously published articles. The book was well received, both

critically and by the public, although Kilpatrick admitted that the collection was "simply written."[14] He opens with the expected and consistent call for pragmatism and a rejection of "atomistic and dualistic" scientific education. By this he meant a renunciation of the S-R psychology for an as yet unnamed approach that was more creative in nature, involving the "conscious pursuit of personally felt purposes with ever more self-direction as the goal." Kilpatrick was careful, though, to include the need for directing attention toward the social and economic situation, declaring that a properly planned economic system would bring comfort and security for all. An "educational program not of propaganda and indoctrination, but to build social intelligence among the people" became his formula for developing democracy in both word and practice. In discussing the post-Thorndike approach to psychology, Kilpatrick wrote that feelings and emotions are central to learning, because they either increase or decrease the effort put forth by the learner. Addressing learning once again as a process for the "whole organism," he reiterated the Deweyan concept of education as a reconstruction and reorganization of experience. Education thus facilitates and advances the entire process by assisting and guiding the choices made by the learner. From this emerges the essential advocacy of child-centeredness, still alive in Kilpatrick's philosophy:

> The new curriculum must then put first things first. The child must for us come before subject matter as such. This is the everlasting and final condemnation of the old curriculum. It put subject matter first and it bent — or if need be, broke — the child to fit that. The only way to put the child first is to put first the child's present living. Subject matter — if any reader be concerned for it — will be called this way better into play than is usual now, and more of it, but probably not the precise subject matter of the customary school and most certainly not in the usual order.[15]

Such a strong emphasis on the child at the expense of subject matter makes explicit the fact that Kilpatrick views the drill and repetition of the school as antithetical to the creativity he desires to be loosed in each child. For him, an educative experience is present "whenever a person faces a challenging situation and undertakes responsibly to deal with it." The elementary school has begun; he predicts that the secondary school must follow. The competition endemic in large corporations and the factory system, he maintains, makes

personal and societal advancement difficult, if not impossible. Paying homage to the home for its role in the inculcation of cultivated living, Kilpatrick submits that the emergence of selfhood — and the recognition of the self as separate from others — advances both social and moral thinking, thus enhancing social life. This "citadel of selfhood," as he calls it, is socially built and conditioned. Any distinction between the individual and society is, according to Kilpatrick, a chimera. To hold, with Hobbes, Locke, and Rousseau, that humans are endowed with natural rights does not address the central issue that pitting the individual against society raises an "impossible artificiality." Paraphrasing Aristotle, he says that cooperation began to make life possible, and so it exists to make life good.[16]

Returning to curriculum, in *Remaking the Curriculum*, he defines it broadly as a process for living. As for motivation, Kilpatrick places great faith in the child if teachers will only begin at the point of a child's interest and implement a process of planning, choosing, doing, and evaluating. Responding directly to the criticism that progressive education is all "motion and commotion," Kilpatrick acknowledges the need for guidance by parents and teachers, but in the end "it is the process itself, especially as socially conditioned, that educates." In one chapter, "Safeguarding Curriculum Results," Kilpatrick defends the "life process" curriculum from the charge of being haphazard and lacking in thoroughness and organization; he argues that the teacher can and will either veto or redirect a proposal, but that real progress is made through the student's ability to generalize and think abstractly. This higher-order thinking could be developed only by "much thinking . . . orderly thinking . . . and many connections."[17]

Kilpatrick's ideas were used by one of his students, and later his collaborator, William Van Til. As a young teacher in Columbus, Ohio, in the 1930s, Van Til invited his high school class to select an area of investigation that fell within the purview of language arts and social studies. "We can study whatever we want, Mr. Van Til, right?" "Right," came the reply. "We'd like to learn about crooks," they said. Unwilling to abandon his progressive philosophy, Van Til took a leap of faith and engaged his students in the topic. Attempting to follow the interests of the students, the youthful teacher and his class piled into several automobiles and began their "life process curriculum" at the local police station. After receiving a demographic profile of urban "crooks" from the desk sergeant, they moved on to their own research, locating a dusty dissertation on criminals in The Ohio State University library. From that point, they undertook individual research, interviewing specialists in the field, making hypotheses on

the causes and cures of crime. An English teacher assisted them in writing reports based on their findings. A science teacher helped some of them as they took cameras into the inner city to document conditions found on the Depression-era streets of Ohio's capital city. The class began to make connections between health and housing, social class and race, and other interrelated urban problems. The school librarian, who had not witnessed such intense activity before, was drawn further into the enterprise. She loaned the class display cases in the hallway, where the students exhibited their research in the form of essays, photography, graphs, and maps. What makes this anecdote even more astonishing is that the class was considered by the principal to be a "problem group." It was such ventures, by young teachers like Van Til, that Kilpatrick advocated in *Remaking the Curriculum*. The freedom to allow children and young people to judge, to decide, to establish independence was central to his philosophy. "Putting all of these ever more precisely to work in the actual situations of life, deliberating ever more carefully over what is to be done, reasoning ever more precisely in connection with doing. It is in these varied but interrelated processes that one learns better how to think."[18]

The final chapter in *Remaking the Curriculum* addresses the issue of which direction the secondary school should follow in substance and structure. While Kilpatrick admits that some specialization could and should take place in high school, he also argues for an "extended acquaintance" between teacher and pupil, permitting a degree of personal counseling and guidance that is often lost in the transition from elementary school to the upper grades. Suggesting a 6-3-3 organizational pattern for the twelve years of schooling, he focuses on the need to make the sixth, seventh, and eighth grades transitional in nature, using a variation of the "sliding scale" in the curriculum, with greater specialization as the child proceeds. He continues to stress the education of the "whole child" and the need for the activity curriculum at every level, holding tenaciously to his argument that life itself is not compartmentalized by subject matter and that individuals certainly do not solve problems by remaining within the confines of a subject or discipline. Adults, and children, need to attack issues through an interdisciplinary approach to life's daily demands. Such a plan for secondary schools, he concludes, permits "adjustment to meet each particular case," and thus allows the more intellectually inclined and the more specifically interested to pursue their work under conditions more favorable to them.[19]

Unfortunately, the year 1936 would be notable in Kilpatrick's career for more than the publication of *Remaking the Curriculum*. While the hypothesized relationship between his retirement and the decline of progressive

education can be debated, there is little doubt that the departure of the "million-dollar professor" from active teaching at Teachers College led to what can be described only as a crisis. As early as 1934, Kilpatrick had indicated that he would be compelled to retire at age sixty-five, and the probability of mandatory retirement was raised in a blunt exchange with Dean William Russell in February of 1935. At that time, Kilpatrick told Russell that he did not wish to retire at age sixty-five — only two years away. But the dean replied that he would decide that issue and would be, according to Kilpatrick, "hard-boiled" about it. Russell suggested the possibility of a year-by-year contract, adding that July 1937 was still far in the future. The forced retirement, in 1934, of a female faculty member had been significant enough for Kilpatrick to note in his diary, but at the time of his talk with the dean, he did not seem to be unduly concerned for himself.[20] As July 1937 edged nearer, though, he became adamantly opposed to leaving the classroom.

As relations between the dean and Kilpatrick became more strained, a series of events took place on the Teachers College campus that engulfed Kilpatrick and several of his colleagues. "The revolutionary spirit is gripping many of the young people," wrote Kilpatrick in early 1936. The student council at Teachers College had begun a weekly paper, which often advocated revolutionary tactics in response to the Depression. In this climate, the Teachers College cafeteria cut the wages of several workers, but not of the supervisors. The situation became tense when the Cafeteria Workers' Union began picketing in the summer of 1935, and soon thereafter four of the workers were dismissed for being "uncooperative." Ferment among the students increased. Kilpatrick suggested that an investigation be undertaken, which he thought would prove the innocence of the cafeteria management, and the dean asked him to head a committee to suggest whether further investigation was required. The decision was that a further examination of the issues was necessary, and John Childs was asked to chair the investigating committee. Childs's committee concluded that there had been injustices on the part of the authorities.[21]

In January of 1936, when Dean Russell appeared before the faculty to respond to the findings of Childs's committee, Kilpatrick found the dean making the situation worse and was puzzled over whether he was not in full control of himself or whether there was actually a "method to his madness." Lawrence Dennis, in his biography of Childs, suggests that although Russell opposed unionization and was troubled by Childs's political activity in the 1940s, the two held each other in high regard professionally throughout their years together at Teachers College.[22] Yet for some reason, Russell considered

Kilpatrick, rather than Childs, the ringleader of the more radical element of the faculty. Kilpatrick did view himself as one of the "revolutionary party," but leaned more toward the middle of the group and was certainly not as extreme in his views as Childs — or as George Counts or Goodwin Watson.

At times, Russell seemed obsessed with the actions of unions, especially those within his purview. In March of 1936 he called the faculty together again to express his distress over another strike — this time by elevator workers — and his concern that the students, staff, and faculty had encouraged the strikers. While supporting freedom of speech, at least freedom of academic speech, he indicated that any incitement to strike was to be considered interference with his administration and that he wished to have on file the resignation of anyone who disagreed with him. Kilpatrick was shocked that Russell would call the faculty together "while angry" and also ask for resignations *en masse*, and further appalled that at the close of the meeting Russell received "widespread and vigorous applause." The dean then decided to hold yet another meeting, but Kilpatrick used all his influence with senior faculty members and Russell himself to cancel the meeting, concerned that matters might become worse. He succeeded.[23]

In 1935, John Childs had joined the Columbia University Chapter of Local Five of the American Federations of Teachers (AFT). Although John Dewey had resigned from the organization at about this time, several of Childs's fellow faculty at Teachers College, including Counts and Watson, were also AFT members. One highly visible name that was not found on Chapter Five's roll was Kilpatrick's. With the cafeteria crisis at its height in March of 1936, Russell called Kilpatrick to his office. The dean was much agitated over Childs's report and alarmed that a union might replace the current faculty governance system. Russell wondered aloud whether it might mean either he as dean, or the faculty activist Goodwin Watson, might have to go. Kilpatrick patiently explained his own views on unions, but Russell returned to Watson and Childs, asking whether there might be communists on the faculty. Kilpatrick responded that he did not know of any, but added that it was the right of any faculty members to hold such views if they so chose. Russell agreed with the latter statement, but reiterated that he thought Watson might be a communist and was apparently irritated that Watson did not stick to psychology rather than slipping into philosophy. Kilpatrick replied that Watson ought to teach psychology as he saw best and urged the dean not to take any hasty actions until he, Kilpatrick, could speak with Childs and Watson. Russell then said that this was what he wished and was the reason he had called Kilpatrick.[24]

This amazing meeting clearly indicates that Russell viewed Kilpatrick as the leader of the radicals, or at least as someone who had influence with them, and that the dean thought he knew exactly where Kilpatrick stood on the issue of unions. Kilpatrick did meet with Newlon and Counts and urged caution on the part of all, because of the dean's emotional state — especially his concern for what Childs and Watson might do. Kilpatrick arranged to take Childs on one of his celebrated walks and found his younger colleague the very picture of restraint and good judgment. He told Childs that he personally did not wish to join the AFT chapter, but did not have the slightest problem with others' doing so. He reiterated the need for caution with the dean and added that he was concerned about the "balance" of some union members. A similar walk took place with Goodwin Watson the following week. Watson too denied having knowingly done anything to upset the dean and disavowed that he was a communist. But Kilpatrick found himself troubled by the conversation, not so much by Watson's behavior during it as by the young man's psychological analysis of the dean, the essence of which was that Russell was paranoid and that his actions were unpredictable. A follow-up meeting with the dean proved fruitless. Privately, Kilpatrick wished that he could extricate himself from the whole situation.

Then, in the midst of the cafeteria crisis, Russell felt compelled to dismiss the staff of the *Teachers College News*, the student newspaper subsidized by the institution, because it had published a letter accusing him of taking "sadistic pleasure" in his actions against the strikers. "I must confess to myself," wrote the confounded Kilpatrick, "that I am greatly amazed and made fearful as to what may happen." Kilpatrick was able to take a respite from the situation, although involuntarily. He spent the month of June and a portion of July 1936 in a lengthy convalescence after a hernia operation.[25]

It is appropriate at this juncture to pause and briefly examine Kilpatrick's role in the liberal-radical issue of the Teachers College faculty and specifically to explore his beliefs on unionism. A point of stability, having been at Teachers College for a quarter of a century, he was respected as a facilitator and articulate spokesman for progressive education. But Counts, Rugg, Watson, and the others in the Teachers College circle were highly independent thinkers and men of action. While they may have looked to Kilpatrick for leadership and counsel, they did not receive their marching orders, so to speak, from anyone. If Kilpatrick's meticulous diaries during this period prove anything, it is that there was no collusion, grand design, or conspiracy being directed by him. As for unionism, Kilpatrick believed that labor had been the school's most consistent

friend, and he had no reservations about teachers aligning themselves with such groups. His reluctance in supporting unionism for teachers arose from his concern that teachers, as professionals, should remain independent, so as to maintain their autonomy within the classroom on social and political issues. His other apprehension about unions was their propensity, in his view, to foster class struggle as the means for social change. He rejected class conflict, as has been seen, and this often put him at odds with his colleagues, especially John Childs.[26]

While the summer of 1936 did provide a hiatus on both sides of the union controversy, the conflict emerged again in the fall at the first faculty meeting. The dean ridiculed faculty reports (mentioning Kilpatrick's by name), suggested abolishing the faculty committee system, and spoke disparagingly of the teachers' union.[27] On the surface, though, Kilpatrick and Dean Russell continued to work together, and on the personal level, they were always cordial. Kilpatrick even represented Russell on numerous occasions at campus functions, including, at times, the introduction of Columbia's president, Nicholas Murray Butler. But the overall situation was clearly deteriorating.

In an article in *The Nation*, James Weschler traced what he saw as the decline of Teachers College, laying much of the blame at the door of Dean Russell. His article, "Twilight at Teachers College," was written at the end of 1938. Weschler suggested that summer school enrollments had been dropping from an all-time high of 14,000 students in 1930 owing to competition locally from New York University and across the country from other teacher education institutions. As financial problems increased, positive publicity was essential. It was no longer the Strayers and the Thorndikes, though, who were receiving attention, but the progressives — Counts, Rugg, and Watson. Since the "drawing power" lay with the progressives, their anti-Hearst campaign of 1935 was deeply troubling to Russell.

According to Weschler, the cafeteria workers' episode widened the breach between Kilpatrick and Russell, with the latter viewing the former as the acknowledged head of the progressive bloc. The fact that Childs was one of Kilpatrick's protégés and the author of the critical report on the episode did not help his mentor's situation with the dean. It was all this, along with the faculty's support for other labor actions and its criticism of his removal of financial support from the student newspaper, that led Russell to "invite" the resignations of those who disagreed with his views on unions. Although he indicated that he would not accept the resignations, he did wish — as noted above — to have them "on file." Weschler went on to report that at a party in the dean's home

for a group of like-minded students and administrators, Russell bragged that he was going to "purge" the faculty, naming five professors specifically: Kilpatrick, Counts, Watson, Childs, and one woman, Roma Gans. The story quickly spread across campus. Russell first replied that the remark had been made in jest, then switched his story to say that the statement had been made by an anonymous trustee. Finally, at a faculty meeting, he denied the whole thing. Weschler implied in his article that the forced retirement of Kilpatrick, which was to occur in 1937, proved the threat was real.[28]

The response from the faculty to Weschler's article was immediate: a letter to the editor appeared in *The Nation* one week later. Eleven faculty members, including Counts, Rugg, Childs, Newlon, Watson, and Raup, wrote that, while "true in some respects" (they did not state exactly which portions were true), the article was "full of insinuation and misrepresentation . . . taken as a whole . . . profoundly false and misleading." This rather nebulous letter concluded with an odd non-sequitur: that Teachers College remained one of the most liberal institutions of higher learning in America. Childs wrote a separate letter indicating that his recent withdrawal from the Columbia Teachers Union had nothing to do with Dean Russell. The editors of *The Nation* responded in the same issue, supporting Weschler's article and finding it amazing that Counts, who in their opinion was himself a victim of oppression by Teachers College, would sign the letter. They thought Childs's letter even more baffling in that Weschler had never made the charge regarding union membership which Childs rebutted.[29]

The most telling fact as to the veracity of this entire interchange may be that Kilpatrick was not a signatory to the letter, nor did he rebut the article, which in other cases he was quick to do. But then again, neither did Russell, who was actually the major focus of the article. Another telling fact is that in October of 1938, (before Weschler's article appeared), Childs had told Kilpatrick that Counts had indeed been "restrained" by Russell from discussing issues publicly. The episode of Weschler's controversial publication so vexed the Teachers College group that it even disrupted a Kilpatrick Discussion Group meeting, when John Childs and Goodwin Watson exchanged heated remarks over the article.[30]

An earlier article is also illuminating. This was in *Fortune* magazine in July 1936, and it did not present Dean Russell in flattering terms. "William Fletcher Russell, the forty-six year old dean of Teachers College — tall, heavy-set, lip-smacking, and bald far back — speaks of himself as an old-fashioned liberal and is spoken of in radical circles as a Fascist." The article repeated

Russell's demand that faculty members showing sympathy with the elevator workers' strike "quietly and quickly resign." *Fortune* also said that "conservative students have the inside track to his office."[31]

Russell finally showed his hand on November 18, 1936, when he told Jesse Newlon that Kilpatrick would probably be retired before the next academic year. Newlon quickly relayed this information to Kilpatrick who wrote in his diary the next day, "Do not sleep well. I am worried over what seems the injustice of retiring while I am as strong and capable as I am, for a reason which has no justification." On his birthday, two days later, he received a letter of congratulations from President Butler, but took it as portentous. "I think of the Chinese custom of giving a rose and a glass of wine as the notification of dismissal," he wrote.[32]

Further word came to Kilpatrick via Roma Gans. Gans, one of the newer members of the Teachers College faculty, was a popular activist known to encourage her students to visit flophouses, accompany applicants to welfare offices, and observe people wrapped in newspapers in Central Park. In its article of July 1936, *Fortune* gave a description of her that seemed to focus as much on her appearance as her ideas: "Tall and trim, black-haired and black-eyed, answering to forty and looking thirty."[33] Gans indicated to Kilpatrick that the dean was definitely "hostile" toward him and that Milo B. Hillegas, also of retirement age, was pushing the Elementary Education Department to request a continuance on his behalf. Gans repeated stories similar to those which would be reported by Weschler two years later in *The Nation* that Russell had been talking to students and trustees in his home, saying that while he could not prove it, he was convinced that Kilpatrick had contrived Childs's whole investigation to make trouble for him. She alluded to other pieces of information which suggested that the dean's state of mind was not stable, but no specifics were recorded by Kilpatrick. Gans then suggested a campaign on Kilpatrick's behalf to make him Alumni Professor on his retirement. While not approving the campaign, Kilpatrick did permit Gans to discuss the situation with Newlon and other colleagues. Evidently taking the stories seriously, he began scrutinizing his financial portfolio in case the dean succeeded in retiring him. One other hint of what was to come emerged in December, when Russell openly told Bruce Raup that he would receive his sabbatical during the academic year 1939-1940, after the "shock of Kilpatrick's retirement" had passed.[34]

As 1936 drew to a close, Kilpatrick, with the counsel of colleagues, decided to test the dean's resolve. He submitted his name in the new budget, using the rationale that he had informed Russell the year before that he did not

wish to retire and that he had received no formal notice in the fall. This he thought, would make it "more difficult" for Russell to "settle the question adversely."[35] On Christmas Eve he reflected on recent events, mustering all the reasons it would be in the best interest of Teachers College to retain him. He was considered the best teacher in the college and, along with Strayer and Thorndike, he was the most widely known. He was second only to Dewey and possibly Bode in philosophy of education — his ideas on the "activity movement," drawn from Dewey's philosophy, having been adopted across the nation. "It will be absolutely impossible to fill my place for some years to come," he stated, "but the dean will retire me, if he does, for no valid reason." Kilpatrick then speculated on why Russell was intent on forcing his departure. "The Dean has been from childhood not quite adjusted 'emotionally' — as the slang goes," he wrote bitterly. He went on to record that the dean had been "emotionally disturbed" over the strikes, the picketing, and Childs's investigation, especially the investigation imagining disloyalty on the part of Childs and Watson. Kilpatrick then connected his own chairmanship of the foundations at Teachers College and his leadership in the John Dewey Society and *The Social Frontier* with the dean's perception that this radical wing of the faculty was challenging his administration. Kilpatrick surmised that Russell hoped to "break up the Social Frontier group."[36]

The first three months of 1937 would bring the denouement. It began on January 4, 1937, when Kilpatrick confronted Dean Russell about his retirement issue during a discussion of the budget. During the meeting, Russell had asked what would become of a certain staff member when Kilpatrick retired. "But I do not mean to accept the idea of retiring," Kilpatrick said; "I wish to discuss that." Russell tersely replied, "But not now." After the others had been dismissed, Russell said that he would take the issue up with the board of trustees, but that the rule called for retirement at age sixty-five. Kilpatrick clearly desired a yearly appointment, or even part-time teaching. Russell again referred to the "rule," which Kilpatrick privately did not think existed, at least not as the dean was interpreting it. Russell then said he would think the matter over and indicated that an appointment prevented further discussion of the issue that day.

Kilpatrick left the meeting not unhappy, since the session had been for the most part pleasant, with no break between the two men. But while Russell had said he would think about it, Kilpatrick had little hope for a positive resolution to the impasse. Within the week information filtered back to Kilpatrick that the dean had made up his mind. At the same time, Russell kept up the pretense that

all was well between them, sitting next to Kilpatrick at a dinner at the Faculty Club, where he again denied the rumor that he intended to fire five staff members. Russell then went on to read a statement of strong support for academic freedom. This cynicism and dishonesty, in Kilpatrick's opinion, was almost too much. He felt "humiliated to see a group of sycophants look on with coerced interest while an egotist talked about himself and basked in their smiles of interest and approval."[37]

In early February, Kilpatrick had a frank talk with the dean, presenting his case for being kept on, reporting what he knew about the actions being taken in his behalf, telling Russell he had no knowledge of a regulation compelling retirement, and noting that it was his understanding that year by year extensions were possible if both parties approved. Russell responded that the rule had been in place all along and that at the trustees meeting in the fall there had been a decision to enforce the rule for everyone, including Thorndike. The option to continue teaching on a yearly basis was not mentioned. Kilpatrick informed Russell that he was not behind the attempts by faculty members and students to retain him and did not know who was engineering those actions. Russell, apparently well connected to the information chain in higher education, said it was William Gellerman of Northwestern University. A few days later, Kilpatrick mentioned the possibility of his teaching at other institutions and, much to his chagrin, Russell encouraged him. He again began to question Russell's motives, suspecting that the dean was taking a hard line to impress the Columbia trustees and improve his chances for an administrative position at Columbia.[38]

In mid-February of 1937, the scene of the retirement crisis shifted to New Orleans and the convention of the National Education Association, where, as if for melodramatic effect, all the major players were present. While no official announcement had yet been made, Dean Russell made it known that he was going to enforce the mandatory retirement age of sixty-five, which would affect Kilpatrick and Milo B. Hillegas. Immediately, Frederick L. Redefer, executive secretary of the Progressive Education Association, led a vocal contingent of people who wished to see Kilpatrick retained. Redefer intimated that the real reasons for Kilpatrick's retirement were not related to age, but, when pressed, he refused to specify them. Intermediaries for his Teachers College colleagues came to Kilpatrick's hotel room, warned him not to make any statements to the press, and said that Newlon and others were trying to set up a meeting for him with Russell. They also advised against any joint statement from Kilpatrick and the dean.[39]

But prominent articles in several newspapers made the issue central during the entire week of the conference. One paper noted that Kilpatrick had been identified with a group of left-wing educators at Teachers College, including George Counts, John Childs, and Goodwin Watson. The article stated that the group had been under fire from the Hearst papers and that Dean Russell had been urged by colleagues to expel the radical professors. The previous day, Kilpatrick had spoken to journalists (who literally followed his every step at the conference) and was quoted as suggesting that since other professors had been permitted to teach beyond age sixty-five, he would like to be granted the same privilege. As was his custom, though, he conveyed this opinion in a reserved, noncombative manner. The dean did meet with Kilpatrick on the 20th of February, with a reporter present, but was unsure what to say. Kilpatrick told him to tell the truth. Still unwilling to concede what was nearly a *fait accompli*, Kilpatrick said nothing regarding the retirement issue, much to Russell's chagrin. The situation distressed Kilpatrick inordinately, and he was unable even to record the events of these days until three months later.[40]

On February 21st Russell stated explicitly that retirement was automatic and that no exceptions would be made, explaining that exemptions made during the Depression were due to "special circumstances" which no longer "governed the situation." The John Dewey Society also met that day at a Spanish-American restaurant (where they dined for 35 cents a plate). Kilpatrick was asked to edit *The Social Frontier*, and he told the gathering he would give the invitation consideration. After the meeting, Paul Hanna, who was now at Stanford University, informed him that Gellerman's efforts had produced over 10,000 signatures to a petition urging the Teachers College trustees to retain him. This news "overwhelmed" Kilpatrick. Hanna also extended an invitation to him to teach during the summer of 1938 at Stanford in Palo Alto. "It all touches me very deeply," he wrote.[41]

On the fifth day of the convention, in what had become daily volleys, a threat was made that 30,000 petitions would be dispatched to New Orleans in support of Kilpatrick. In addition, Russell was asked whether the popular professor was being retired because he was a radical; the dean issued an immediate statement insisting that no violation of academic freedom was involved. To complicate the issue, thirty educators, including Kilpatrick, in good social reconstructionist fashion, sent a letter to President Roosevelt supporting his plan to "pack" the Supreme Court — a plan that hinged on the question of age. Charles Evans Hughes, Jr. — son of the aged chief justice and a member of the Board of Trustees at Teachers College — had approved of

Kilpatrick's retirement, although this had happened before the events in New Orleans.[42]

The next day John Dewey himself waded into the controversy, saying, "I am not in sympathy with the rule of the Teachers College unless there is provision for exception. It is strange that those who say that justices should not be retired at age seventy hold that teachers should be retired at sixty-five."[43] His argument, not surprisingly, was immediately turned against Kilpatrick's supporters by the conservatives, who countered that it was "inconsistent to approve of retiring at seventy Supreme Court justices while insisting at the same time that Dr. Kilpatrick's services are far too useful to be cut short by a similar retirement rule."[44]

On the final day of the New Orleans conference, at a Teachers College alumni dinner, Dean Russell was formally presented with the 10,000 signatures collected by William Gellerman, asking that Kilpatrick be retained. The names included John W. Studebaker, United States commissioner of education, who called his former professor "one of the greatest teachers in the world." Diplomatically, Dean Russell called the petition a tribute to Kilpatrick and then, for reasons unknown, proceeded to attack the social reconstructionists by saying that he deplored "efforts to make teachers class conscious" and that he did not think teachers should organize or think of their own welfare.[45] According to Kilpatrick's diary, the beleaguered dean went into detail regarding the retirement issue, quoting the 1929 rule and insisting that all professors had accepted appointment with this understanding. Kilpatrick said that both statements were false and indicated that he had a copy of the 1929 memorandum, which offered as another option a yearly extension beyond retirement. (January 4, 1937, was the first time Kilpatrick had written in his diary that he had heard of the rule, stating privately that it was being invoked at this time for the "explicit purpose of retiring me.") Russell went on, in an attempt to soften the blow, by announcing that Kilpatrick would give the Macy lectures during 1938 and that the college would commission a portrait of him.

All this was still not apparently enough to salve Russell's conscience. The dean caught Kilpatrick after the meeting to deny the rumor that he had made a wager with a colleague (now long dead) that he would retire Kilpatrick. The colleague had had heart trouble, said Russell, and was no doubt under the influence of some sort of drug when he made the charge. Russell also disavowed any intention of retiring Kilpatrick for the purpose of improving his own chances at Columbia. This final, odd, and unsolicited denial was a rather bizarre conclusion to an eventful five days.

The *New York Times* observed that the alumni dinner had taken on a "religious fervor." But Kilpatrick again refused to enter the fray directly, saying judiciously that he did not regard academic freedom as the major issue and adding that he had "always talked freely and pleasantly" with the dean and that "the college has never brought pressure on me. To the best of my belief, the dean has been pretty straight on the matter of academic freedom. I have never been interfered with and I have always said what I wanted to say."[46]

It was then on to Saint Louis for another conference, where Kilpatrick spoke and was greeted in a manner that went beyond even the receptions he normally received in public. "It is clear that my forced retirement gives people . . . different feelings toward me." He was also honored at a banquet arranged on the spur of the moment, at which Boyd Bode paid tribute to him. Looking both forward and into the recent past in Saint Louis, he wrote:

> It is clear that I am ending the main period of my career and am entering upon its conclusion. What has happened has given me a clearer and more assured place than I would otherwise have had. Without exactly knowing the inside causes, the feeling is that I have been treated unjustly and that it endears me as nothing has heretofore done.[47]

In 1951, in his biography of Kilpatrick, Samuel Tenenbaum wrote that the true story behind the retirement issue could not, at that time, be fully disclosed. Now, with the diaries available, the reason behind Tenenbaum's statement has emerged. The retirement issue was to vex Kilpatrick as no other during his life. And, as will be seen, he frankly expressed his frustration and displeasure in the pages of the diary. While he had referred to innuendoes that his retirement was imminent, it was not until a month after the NEA convention that he displayed his anger fully. "It appears that the dean has been talking recklessly again," wrote Kilpatrick on April 7, 1937, "blaming the petitions in my behalf on the communists — than which nothing could be farther from the truth."[48]

A week later, formal word was received from the dean that July 1, 1938, would be the date of Kilpatrick's retirement. After July 1937, he would be on leave for one year at half pay. At the same time Kilpatrick was informed that he had been selected to give the promised series of lectures during the academic year 1937-1938 with an honorarium of $2,000. (His salary in the 1930s was in the range of $11,000 per year.) Still piqued over the controversy in New Orleans, Kilpatrick wrote of the lectures, "It would have been kinder to have

got this in my hands before the public announcement." The dean then visited Kilpatrick on April 14 to discuss the retirement dinner, which was to be held in three weeks. The haste of all this suggests that Russell was leaving nothing to chance. When word came that the board had voted for his retirement, Kilpatrick had considered making a plea for a part-time teaching assignment, but colleagues told him that this would look like begging, and he dropped the idea. When the dean visited him, Kilpatrick felt that "he is clearly determined to make it appear that he is friendly to me." The two men decided that, rather than conduct the usual laudatory biographical retirement dinner, there would be a discussion of the way in which competing viewpoints vie for ascendancy in higher education.[49]

The retirement dinner for Kilpatrick and Milo B. Hillegas was held at the Teachers College Faculty Club on Wednesday, May 5, 1937. Kilpatrick noted in his diary, "Nothing unpleasant happens except the background reason that the dean has, I am convinced, willed my retirement from irrational grounds and lied publicly to make it appear a long-standing rule requires it." At the dinner, Professor Edward Reisner presided, with dean emeritus James Russell having been assigned the topic of how consensus is built within higher education. But the senior Russell instead reminisced about the early days of Teachers College, and Hillegas, who spoke next, also failed to address the question of the hour. This left Kilpatrick to close the discussion with a prepared paper, for which he showed little enthusiasm. Reisner concluded the evening by speaking at length about Hillegas, though few were in doubt as to who had made the more significant contribution to Teachers College. To add insult to injury, Kilpatrick and Hillegas were given gold-banded walking sticks, a conventional gift, but a thoughtless reminder of the unwelcome retirement. At the close of the evening presentations and remarks, Hillegas said a few words, but Kilpatrick only bowed. "The occasion lacked open speaking and candor," wrote Kilpatrick, "It could not be otherwise." When Kilpatrick met with his last class of the regular academic year a week after the dinner on May 12, he wrote that he was "embittered": "It is administrative stupidity and wrongheadedness that is retiring me, to the hurt of the college."[50]

With the bitter taste of the previous week's ceremony still in his mouth, Kilpatrick could, however, look forward to a more fitting tribute, planned by the students. On May 14, 1937, 175 students were in attendance for a markedly different event at the same Faculty Club. One of them, Kenneth Benne, served as toastmaster, and there was a distinctly international flavor to the evening. Chinese, Greek, Indian, Iraqi, Iranian, Canadian, and African students all made

special presentations. Bruce Raup and John Childs, colleagues who had both been teaching assistants under Kilpatrick, spoke. They were followed by John Dewey, who spent twenty-five minutes analyzing Kilpatrick's *Education for a Changing Civilization.* "He quite surprised me by the praise," wrote Kilpatrick. In contrast to the preceding week's fiasco, the emphasis this evening was not that Kilpatrick's work had reached closure, but that it was just commencing. The Chinese students presented him with a statue of Wisdom, and the other students gave him a silver bowl and candlesticks. Kilpatrick spoke for thirty minutes, reminiscing about his parents, his brother Macon, his early educational experiences and readings, and his work at Mercer before he had come to Teachers College. He spoke of how he had channeled his efforts in philosophy of education to remake the schools in order to help society meet its problems. "The sadness of retirement was largely forgot," he later wrote, "It was a truly memorable event in my life."[51]

The contrast between the two dinners held that May at Teachers College could not have been more stark. One witness, in attendance at both affairs, was a young historian from the University of Wisconsin, R. Freeman Butts, who had come to Teachers College on a half-time assistantship. He would go on to serve there for forty years, and while he was not especially close to Kilpatrick (he found Kilpatrick a bit forbidding at times), Butts did become part of the Discussion Group and lived for several years in the same building as the Kilpatricks on Morningside Drive. As with most of Kilpatrick's relationships, the interaction between the two men was quite formal. He "always addressed me as Dr. Butts. I always addressed him as Dr. Kilpatrick. Only once in my life did I ever hear anyone speak of Kilpatrick as other than Dr. Kilpatrick. One time Harold Rugg called him Heard and I don't think I ever heard that from anybody else."[52]

The faculty dinner of May 5 had been a somber affair, according to Butts, and left such acrid feelings that no other collegewide dinner to honor a retiring faculty member was held for more than thirty years. There was no doubt that the ideology of the "social frontiersmen" had been an element in the retirement crisis, but Butts also thought, as did many others, that the 1929 rule was ironclad and that no exceptions could be made. Kilpatrick himself made a number of direct and indirect charges regarding Russell's psychological state, but these cannot be proved at this distance. Freeman Butts suggests simply that the personalities of the two men were diametrically opposed. Kilpatrick was "austere, determined, self-confident" and held "quite rigid views of others," while Russell was "bombastic, hard driving, outspoken, aggressive, a real personal administrator

type." Butts remembers that even years later, when he was a department chair, the telephone would ring and Russell would bellow, "Butts, this is the dean!" When the gentlemanly reserve of Kilpatrick met the bluntness of Russell there was inevitably "fire," according to Butts. Almost forty years later, Butts noted in an address at a Teachers College alumni day that Kilpatrick must have sworn to "outlive the perpetrators of that idea — and almost did."[53]

The student dinner held on May 15, recollected Butts, was much more a celebration and a look toward the future. Kilpatrick signed most of the programs and, as his diary indicates, was deeply moved by the evening. It should be noted that although the child-centered approach and social outlook approach were at the time battling for ascendancy in progressive education, the quotation from Kilpatrick chosen for the program was, "From top to bottom the social outlook must permeate and dominate the school system. In the light of this must everything else proceed."[54]

One legacy of the retirement crisis was an action undertaken in the early 1940s by Counts, Childs, Gans, and others to challenge the perceived dictatorial methods of running the college by the dean. This involved the formation of the Committee on Policy, Program, and Budget which moved toward collaborative deliberations, and joint decision-making by the faculty and administration. Butts suggests that the impetus was the dean's allegedly heavy-handed style of which the retirement episode was emblematic. As Butts later wrote, it was "regrettable that this particular rite of passage — or lack of it — should so often result in alienation and bitterness." Actually, the entire retirement episode seems to have tempered Russell. Dennis, in his biography of Childs, provides evidence that Russell and Childs resolved their differences over the years and even became friends. In his observations of Russell, Freeman Butts suggests the same healing process. Despite calling him "arbitrary, brusque, and remote" and noting that he could be "authoritarian and infelicitous" in his manner toward underlings, he believed that Russell had an abiding interest in the foundations of education and a strongly "proprietary and paternalistic" feeling toward Teachers College, due to his father's long service.[55]

Kilpatrick would continue, privately, to protest the retirement decision for years. His fury reached a crescendo on May 26, when he wrote in his diary that Russell was the "biggest liar I know personally." At the commencement exercises on June 6th he heard President Nicholas Murray Butler of Columbia University declare that chronological age, mental vigor, and creativity have no certain correlation. Kilpatrick found this ironic and wondered if the president was being cynical, especially since Butler himself was seventy-five. Kilpatrick

seemed mentally unable to escape the issue of age and retirement. After that commencement, he observed a colleague and noted that the fellow, though five years younger than he, moved much less sprightly.[56]

During the retirement crisis, a few prestigious offers had arrived for temporary or part-time positions. (Economic difficulties, apparently made it impossible for any institutions to offer a full-time position — such appointments were at a premium.) Northwestern University, New York University, and Stanford all offered semester or summer school work, as did the Progressive Education Association. In June Kilpatrick completed plans to teach that summer and fall at Northwestern University in Evanston, Illinois, and the following summer at Stanford.

Kilpatrick and Rita arrived in Chicago that June of 1937, and he immediately entered a controversy when he gave an interview to a reporter from the *Chicago Daily News* in which he was highly critical of the philosophy of education advanced by Robert Hutchins, president of the University of Chicago. Kilpatrick said that Hutchins was trying to revive the philosophy of education that had been dead 400 years. Charging that Hutchins's theories were based on the scholasticism of Thomas Aquinas, he denounced them as altogether unscientific, even antiscientific. Kilpatrick's most severe criticism was that Hutchins' methods were deductive rather than inductive.

Warmly welcomed to the Evanston campus, Kilpatrick taught two moderate-sized sections of his usual courses. As ever, his reputation had preceded him. During his first week on campus, while he was reading a newspaper, a man called him by name, then apologized, saying, "I thought you were Dr. Kilpatrick." When Kilpatrick responded, "I am," the man said, "When I saw your white hair I thought it was you, but when you looked up I thought the face too young."[57]

Kilpatrick returned from Evanston that July to teach in his final summer session at Columbia. The Columbia Summer School, in its thirty-eighth year in 1937, was a phenomenon unto itself. As noted earlier, *Fortune* magazine had profiled it — and the entire campus — the year before in an illustrated article, which noted that automobiles from all forty-eight states could usually be found parked between 116th and 120th Streets. Seven of every eleven students who attended Columbia in the summer were teachers, generating 75 percent of the revenue of the entire operation. As one caption — accompanying a picture of a demonstration classroom–noted, "A.B.s for some, ABCs for others." Of the 12,000 students who crowded the campus, the article said:

Their resources are anything from $1,000,000 to needing help to pay for broken glasses. Their standing is anything from the *Social Register* in Philadelphia to a fear of being lynched in Vicksburg. Their politics are anything from royalism to Marx. Their religious beliefs are anything from Hard-Shell Baptist to noisy atheism. And their purpose is anything from learning about running a large city school system to wanting a lover.[58]

The three-day registration process, with its long alphabetized lines in the gymnasium and its precious orange enrollment cards, was exhausting and highly competitive. Students paid $12.50 per point, with each point equaling one classroom period a week. The maximum was eight points. (A student could complete an M.A. in four summer sessions or in two summer sessions and one winter semester.) Upon paying their fees, students often moved to the "Grove," a shady park across the street from Teachers College which has long since disappeared. Here, students would read notices nailed to the trees and exchange information — usually more social than academic in nature. *Fortune* magazine reported that discussion groups from Kilpatrick's classes could be found in the Grove as early as seven-thirty in the morning, going over study questions.[59]

Columbia's administrators formulated a profile of a typical summer attendee: a single, female, high school history teacher from Kentucky, thirty-eight years of age, who made approximately $1,200 per year. She could find a room for the entire session for as little as $30 or take a two-room suite at Barnard College for $108. The reputation of the school's faculty, efficiency, the variety of course offerings, and the opportunity to speak one's mind without fear of losing one's position were all reasons why the classes of Kilpatrick and his colleagues were filled. Living expenses would run at least $200 per session, but as *Fortune* remarked, much of the New York City environment — such as its museums and the class field trips to the labor unions, flophouses, and birth control clinics — was free. And, of course, on Sunday morning there was the nearby Riverside Church, where Dr. Harry Emerson Fosdick would return from his vacations in Maine especially to preach to the large crowds that filled the pews.[60]

Photographs of a number of professors were featured in the *Fortune* piece, including historian Allan Nevins, Mark Van Doren of the English department, and the philosopher Irwin Edman. Teachers College was represented by George Strayer and Nickolaus Engelhardt, from school administration; by George Counts; and, of course, by Kilpatrick, of whom *Fortune* said:

> The G.O.M. [grand old man] of the radical group is William
> Heard Kilpatrick, professor of education — a gentle-looking,
> blue-eyed, white-haired man in his sixties who has taught at
> T.C., with a tremendous following, for twenty-six years.
> Thousands of students have heard him say: "From the broad
> point of view all life thoughtfully lived is education."[61]

Kilpatrick taught two final classes that summer of 1937. One, with 622
enrollees, had to be moved from Horace Mann Auditorium to the Macmillan
Theater on the Columbia campus. "How can anybody teach 500 students?" one
student asked another, for probably the thousandth time. "Come and see; he
does it," was the reply. The other class remained in Horace Mann Auditorium
where, when Kilpatrick arrived, for a session, it was not uncommon for him to
be hailed with a round of applause. On one occasion, a messenger witnessed
this display of enthusiasm and remarked on leaving, "Lord, they applaud him
like he was Sally Rand."[62] Near the end of summer term, Kilpatrick reflected,
albeit somewhat immodestly, on those last two Teachers College classes:

> I believe I was never so much personally appreciated as now.
> People seem personally drawn to me as never before, I think.
> Not that they feel intimate, perhaps the reverse, but still they
> feel I might almost say tender. Much of it is admiration. I
> have become a great man and they feel it. They get me to
> autograph copies of my books. They applaud what I say.[63]

On August 9, Kilpatrick gave his final campus wide lecture in the
Columbia gymnasium, the only space on campus that could hold the audience
of 4,000. The day before, in a newspaper interview, he had stated that
"progressive education had been adopted by many teachers and administrators
as a fad and that many things they did were stupid." Thursday, August 19, 1937,
was Kilpatrick's last day as a classroom teacher at Teachers College, and he felt
the need to revisit privately the reasons that had brought him to this juncture of
his life. He concluded once again, with regard to Russell, that in the final
analysis, "the facts which argue his emotional unbalance are many and strong.
I think he is the biggest liar by all odds I have ever personally dealt with."
Publicly, in class, he spoke for almost an hour — something he rarely did —
but that day the students in his class wished to hear from him directly. Near the

end of the class time a student came forward with a matched set of golf clubs in a leather golf bag, which he presented to Kilpatrick on behalf of the class. The student said that the class did not know about his prowess as a golfer, but as a teacher and discussion leader he was a "champ." The class had been successful beyond Kilpatrick's expectations, and he noted that he could not remember ever before signing as many copies of his books for his students.[64]

In that final class of 622 students was Betty Hovey, a teacher from Shaker Heights, Ohio, who was a card-carrying member of the Progressive Education Association. She had spent four summers at Teachers College working on her M.A., and she had heard Dewey speak on several occasions in New York City and Ohio. In her opinion, she had never encountered two more intelligent, well-read, intellectually disciplined men than Dewey and Kilpatrick. Betty Hovey, like other students, was clearly overwhelmed by Kilpatrick's presence. Even in a class of more than 600 students, each one had to be ready to respond to questions. After a quarter of a century the Kilpatrick trademarks were still in evidence: the pink face, the full head of white hair, the stately bearing, the meticulous dress — even in the heat of summer — and the resonant speaking voice with the accent of a cultured Southerner. In that last session a student rose and said, "We believe in what you are telling us, Dr. Kilpatrick, but how can we go back to our little towns and schools and put your ideas into practice?" Kilpatrick walked to the front of the platform and said, "I'll tell you how to implement what I have been telling you. You do what the greatest of all teachers said to do, 'I came that you might have life and that you might have it abundantly.' And those are my final words to you."[65]

In September, one month after the final class, word came from White Plains, Georgia, that Kilpatrick's sister Helen was dying — her recurring cancer had reached the brain and was inoperable. The imminence of his beloved sister's death impelled him to remember their closeness. And in his diary, he divulged that at one time in her youth Helen had been forbidden by their father to marry. Apparently, the elder Kilpatrick had not approved of the young man who had asked for Helen's hand, and he also wished to keep his daughter at home as housekeeper and companion for her mother. Kilpatrick remembered how Helen had taken care of little Margaret after Marie's death, and how Helen had kept the home place alive in memory and reality after their mother's death. He also pondered the history of breast cancer in his family and began to calculate how long his relatives had lived, realizing — as he thought — that his own days were also growing short. The end of Helen's suffering came six months later, on February 21, 1938. The family arrived in White Plains two

days later, but Kilpatrick could not bring himself to look at his sister in her coffin, not wishing to remember her in that way. Devastated, he wrote "This day ends for me much of my life. Helen has been since Macon's death the closest of my born family to me and I to her. I feel the end approaching. Life is already shrinking."[66]

Late September of 1937 found Kilpatrick and his wife Rita back in Evanston, Illinois, preparing for the coming semester at Northwestern. They lived in room number 611 of a residence hotel known as the Homestead. (He quietly gloated when friends in New York sent him the enrollment figures for his old classes, which were greatly reduced from the numbers he had enjoyed.) He was well received at Northwestern, with many students visiting his classes, wishing to shake his hand, or asking him to sign books of his. His Foundations of Education course had an enrollment of 420 students, and he consulted weekly with the faculty at large on a variety of issues confronting the institution. During one such faculty meeting the question of democracy in relation to an issue on the Northwestern campus emerged, and Kilpatrick gave his frank opinion, which he later regretted. "Possibly I seemed too radical," he wrote in his diary. At Northwestern, the Kilpatricks became better acquainted with Dr. and Mrs. George Axtelle. Of Axtelle, Kilpatrick remarked, "I find him very intelligent, unusually well read . . . the best thought man in the seminar."[67]

In addition to teaching at Northwestern, Kilpatrick accepted several speaking engagements in the Midwest, including the "charge to the president" address for the inauguration of F. Marion Smith at Evansville College in southern Indiana. Smith was a graduate of Columbia and a Methodist minister. The inaugural festivities were held in early October in conjunction with a brief educational conference. As usual, Kilpatrick served as the conference discussion leader. At a banquet the evening before the inauguration, one of the trustees told a racial joke about a black Baptist minister from Georgia, using the phrase "we'uns," which Kilpatrick noted privately was most certainly an inaccurate imitation of the dialect.

The next day there were other activities on campus before the party drove to the downtown area of Evansville, on the Ohio River, and marched in procession into the civic auditorium. Kilpatrick's address touched on the relationship between the practical and the theoretical and on the need for social solutions to problems in higher education. His conclusion centered on the good life, incorporating his now familiar quotation from the Gospel of Saint John about living life abundantly. He also alluded to certain unnamed patriotic pressure groups, not learning until later that Dr. Smith's predecessor, a

philosophy professor, had been virtually run out of town by the American Legion. Later that month, Kilpatrick spoke at the University of Kentucky in Lexington and visited several thoroughbred stables in the surrounding counties. Throughout his life, Kilpatrick was to meet innumerable prominent and distinguished men and women. On this trip through the Kentucky countryside he added to that list a horse — the celebrated thoroughbred Man O' War.[68]

Kilpatrick and Rita returned to New York in February of 1938 and resumed their usual busy lives, absent his regular teaching. Kilpatrick was involved in both *The Social Frontier* and the new John Dewey Society yearbook, a project he was laboring on with Harold Rugg and others. In addition, he and John Dewey were collaborating on a new edition of William James's *Talks with Teachers*, preparing an introduction and notes to accompany the text, highlighting the differences between James's thought and their own. During this work, Dewey told Kilpatrick that he owed his psychology largely to James. That spring, Kilpatrick was officially informed by Teachers College that he would no longer be provided an emeritus office. This meant that he would be compelled to work from his apartment, and the action deeply hurt him. He still clung to the dream that he would have some role at Teachers College, but this hope was again dashed. "It may very well be that I shall find it better to move on elsewhere, say Northwestern or North Carolina or Florida," he wrote.[69] While not the last such insensitive gesture, it made for one less connection with his beloved Teachers College.

In the spring of 1938 he made a solo trip to California, speaking at several places along the way, including the Mormon Tabernacle on April 25. Two days later he arrived in Oakland, California, and was greeted by Lois Meek and her husband of one month, Dr. Herbert Stoltz. They drove Kilpatrick to the Stanford campus, where Paul Hanna showed his former colleague his new home, designed by Frank Lloyd Wright. Having recently read the architect's autobiography, Kilpatrick wrote, "I do not accept the aesthetic theory underlying it, tho I am glad to see it." He explored possible accommodations for the coming summer, when he would be teaching at Stanford, and the day concluded with a private talk with Lois Meek regarding her divorce, her remarriage, and a recently written harangue from Dean Russell, virtually asking for her resignation. Kilpatrick personally thought that she had remarried too soon, but he also considered Russell obsessive about sex and divorce. And the situation was made worse by the fact that "busybodies on his staff" had filled the dean with false information.[70]

Kilpatrick returned to Stanford in late June with his wife, daughter, and

younger grandson, nine-year-old Heard. Margaret Baumeister had accompanied the Kilpatricks because of her stepmother's continued ill health: the cross-country train journey was a strain on the older woman's heart. They stayed in a house across the street from Paul Hanna's at 736 Coronado and found the residence a virtual paradise: "We find peaches blooming. The grass is green. Birds abound. There are rabbits hopping about."[71] At Stanford, Kilpatrick had sixty-five and thirty-eight students in his philosophy and foundations courses, respectively. After his enormous classes at Teachers College, he called teaching such numbers "playing at dolls," but he did cherish the fact that he could know the students as individuals. There were also frequent visitors and a number of auditors, which raised the attendance in each class session.

The time in Palo Alto turned out to be an idyllic summer for husband and wife, daughter and grandson. But by the time they returned to New York in the fall of 1938, all eyes were on Europe and the gathering storm. Ever a careful observer and commentator on world events, Kilpatrick was filled with apprehension over Hitler's actions in Czechoslovakia. "It begins to appear," he wrote in mid-September, "that the democracies will have to fight to preserve any decent sort of world." A few days later he lamented the appeasement of Hitler, and to a certain extent he blamed America for the failure of the League of Nations to stand up to Japan, Italy, and Germany. But the potential for destruction made him ponder whether compromise might be preferable to war. "It is a terrible state of affairs," he concluded. After the Munich agreement, he wondered whether the price of peace might have been too high. Still, while aware of a lack of decency and an unscrupulous use of might, he continued to hope that the agreement might prevail, in spite of its injustice.[72]

Meanwhile, he found himself considerably occupied closer to home, consulting with Adelphi University on Long Island, reading the dissertations of the few remaining students who were finishing their degrees under him, and sitting for his portrait, which would hang outside the main room on the third floor of the Teachers College library. A small ceremony was held on November 16, with Dean Russell in charge of the event and John Dewey and Bruce Raup speaking briefly. Kilpatrick's grandson and namesake Heard was supposed to pull the cord to reveal the portrait, but someone mistakenly grabbed his older brother Teddy, who did the honors. With regard to events in Europe, he attended a rally by the Friends of Republican Spain at Madison Square Garden.[73]

Much of the fall was spent in preparation for his four V. Everit Macy Lectures, which were to be delivered in mid-November. Before the lectures were

given he had signed a book contract with Macmillan for them, though he was not optimistic as to its success: "The subject is too abstruse and the contribution too slight," he wrote.[74] On the evening of the final lecture, members of the Discussion Group invited Kilpatrick to the Grace Dodge Room. When he arrived, he saw that the old group was well represented: among the fifteen in attendance were Bagley, Benne, Butts, Childs, Counts, Raup, Rugg, Newlon, and Watson. They asked their former colleague what he wished to discuss, and he responded that they should consider the lectures he had just given and raise questions regarding them. "We had a vigorous discussion for about two hours," he wrote.[75]

Although the retirement crisis was a year and a half past, and although it was six months since he had been asked to remove his books from his office, this evening's discussion with the resurrected circle of progressive educators represented the formal termination of Kilpatrick's connection with Teachers College. Still convinced that he had been retired early and unjustly, Rita lay critically ill in their apartment on Morningside Drive. And he himself, after delivering four major lectures within a week, was physically exhausted. Attending the first lecture, his daughter, Margaret, detected both the strain and the grandeur within him. In her diaries she wrote:

> Father gave the first of the Macy lectures. It was about self and other. It was difficult to follow, because the thought conceptions were not easy to conceive. They are not for the layman. Father looked old and worn, and the light reflected disagreeably from his glasses. Yet his voice and quietness were compelling. Decidedly, he is a master.[76]

14

MARION

Far from "managing," she deferred to her famous husband. She had early lost her faith and substituted it for what Henry James called "genius worship." She had married Hardy, forty years older than herself, "that I might have the right to express my devotion and to endeavor to add to his comfort and happiness."

Robert Gittings and Jo Mawtow
The Second Mrs. Hardy[1]

On September 29, 1920, William Heard Kilpatrick met Marion Ysabelle Ostrander for the first time. His colleague, Milo B. Hillegas, had recommended her as a full-time assistant to help with Kilpatrick's over-enrolled classes and workload. It is not known how Hillegas, who had connections in Vermont, had become aware of her. "Miss Ostrander," as she would be called in Kilpatrick's diaries for the next twenty years, was from the village of Schuylerville, in upstate New York, where her father had been a county surrogate judge. Marion was a graduate of Simmons College in Massachusetts and had served with the Y.W.C.A. during the Great War. She and her sister Gretchen Murray had come to New York City after the war to take a teacher preparation course at Teachers College. Kilpatrick offered her $1,500 for the year's position. This was the year when women received the vote, and Miss Ostrander was apparently an independent woman; she told Professor Kilpatrick that she would "take time to think over" the offer. She was twenty-nine years old.[2]

Miss Ostrander accepted the position the next day, and jointly she and Kilpatrick attacked the ever-growing problem of seating in his classes. "I find that she works well," he concluded at the end of their first day together. Two years later, when Teachers College was unable to increase her salary by $100, Kilpatrick offered to pay the sum from his own pocket. Miss Ostrander objected, telling Kilpatrick that if she was worth the raise to him then she was worth the raise to the college. Mildly surprised by the response, Kilpatrick was unable to explain the inequalities of the college's pay structure. Thanks to his expanding classes, though, six months later Kilpatrick was able to secure Dean

James Russell's permission to make Miss Ostrander his full-time assistant. She was to grade papers and to have her own clerical help. The following year, 1923, he found her contribution to the compilation and preparation of his *Source Book in the Philosophy of Education* so crucial that he gave her one-third of the royalties, which in the book's first printing amounted to over $700.

Although she was only in her early thirties, James Russell raised the issue of keeping Miss Ostrander on past her fortieth birthday. In what today would be considered an overt case of both agism and sexism, the dean said that it was his policy "not to keep these people beyond forty years of age." Kilpatrick valiantly defended her on the basis of her competence, and Russell agreed to keep her for at least another five years. Hoping to secure her place at Teachers College, Kilpatrick pushed to have her name included in the catalog, and a few years later he championed her claim to the rank of instructor. Kilpatrick's personal involvement with Miss Ostrander's security intensified after the death of her father in 1924, when he began to watch over her financial affairs, even keeping her important papers in his own safe-deposit box. Marion's sister Gretchen married in 1922; had two children, David and Mary; divorced, and later taught at the Lincoln School.[3]

In 1928, Miss Ostrander was finally upgraded to the staff classification of "associate," which was equal or slightly superior to the faculty status of "instructor" and which allowed her some academic perquisites, including taking part in the dean's inauguration that year. During the academic year of 1926-1927, when Kilpatrick was on his second trip around the world, Miss Ostrander accepted a position as secretary to the dean of the medical department at the American University in Beirut, Lebanon, and during most of the academic year 1930-1931 she lived in Japan under a similar exchange arrangement. During this latter absence, Kilpatrick seemed to be at a loss without her, indicating that he depended on her a great deal in his professional life, especially for her revision of his classroom and examination questions. The vocational status of Miss Ostrander continued to concern Kilpatrick, and yet his compulsion to take personal responsibility for it diminished. In May of 1930 he had a long talk about "her problems," especially the lack of a position for the coming academic year, noting "I am very sorry for her."[4] Having undertaken course work during her years at Teachers College, Miss Ostrander began working in earnest on her Ed.D. degree in the mid-1930s and took her doctoral matriculation exam in September of 1935. She completed the doctorate in 1938, writing a dissertation entitled "Value-Aims to Be Taken into Account in an Introductory Course in Philosophy of Education: An Effort at

Schematization." It was hoped that the degree would give her an opportunity to teach at the collegiate level sometime in the future.

Certainly Marion Ostrander's intelligence and capability have never been questioned, nor is her reputation as a scholar impugned by noting that the influence of Kilpatrick's thought permeates the dissertation. Early on, she states that the experimentalist philosophy is the basis of her formulation, and the process advocated is clearly pragmatic. The dissertation itself is a schematic outline of essential components of an introductory course in the philosophy of education, providing a sampling of current thought on educational topics before focusing on the philosophy its author was in greatest agreement with. Education is defined as "the actual upbuilding of individuals and the immediate enrichment and improvement of the process of living." There are occasional jabs at traditional subject matter, but these are not overdone. An argument against indoctrination is taken directly from the master. But if the Ostrander dissertation is not highly original in its thinking, Kilpatrick's influence is probably the result of osmosis, rather than premeditated scholarly borrowing. By this time, Marion Ostrander had sat through innumerable classes for almost twenty years, and that such phrases as "the good life," "abundant living," "criticized experience," and "personality building" should appear is not remarkable. Though the 100-page dissertation does not have footnotes, it does have an extensive bibliography, including the major names then current in education: Bobbitt, Charters, Counts, Childs, Bode, Dewey, Bagley, Kandel, Thorndike, and, of course, Kilpatrick.[5] Stripped of its narrative form and outlined, the dissertation provides what might be a verbatim record of the master's rare classroom records, now preserved only in long-forgotten notebooks, if not lost altogether.

No suggestion of impropriety has ever been made about Kilpatrick's personal life, and Tenenbaum's biography makes it clear that his only sexual relations were marital. Kilpatrick did dine alone with Miss Ostrander at her apartment during the summer of 1933, when Rita was at the Teachers College Country Club in Ossining; but since he recorded the dinner in his diary, he apparently was not trying to conceal the evening. In their professional relations, Miss Ostrander was capable of making suggestions, warning him if he was pushing his ideas to excess, and even making criticisms which Kilpatrick would heed. On one occasion, several students wished to inaugurate a philosophy club in his name. He rather summarily rebuffed the idea, and Miss Ostrander informed him that his attitude in the matter had been "cold." But she clearly worshiped him, and also, as one witness has suggested, "protected" him,

knowing of his painful shyness.[6]

Miss Ostrander's future after his departure became a major concern for Kilpatrick, and it was over her that Dean William Russell and he had words during the retirement crisis. Though she did stay on at Teachers College after his retirement, her position was always precarious. Despite the fact that she had her doctorate at this time, Jesse Newlon — quite accurately — thought that she would be better off taking a position at another institution where she would not be thought of as Kilpatrick's secretary and assistant. Miss Ostrander herself thought that Raup and Childs were attempting to move her out of the department for their own reasons. Kilpatrick, troubled by the prospects, also did not think it wise for her to stay at Teachers College, believing that her decision to move from the clerical to the instructional staff made her vulnerable. Apparently, John Childs continued to make his opposition known. "I am amazed and indignant, but am not sure I can do anything," wrote a distraught Kilpatrick. "The idea of turning Miss Ostrander loose to shift for herself after all these years of faithful service is very repugnant to me."

In February of 1938, Dean Russell informed Miss Ostrander that 1937-1938 would be her last year at Teachers College. Once again Childs was blamed for leading the move against her, with Raup, Newlon, and finally the dean agreeing. As for the dean's decision, Kilpatrick took it personally, viewing it as an attempt to "get rid of all trace of me." While yet unwilling to compare her abilities to those of the men in the department, he did believe that she was "too good in comparison with other women about the College to turn her out in this way." He observed her teaching the next month and declared after the visit, "I see enough to see that she has learned how to teach, and teach well." He continued throughout the rest of 1938 to help her secure teaching positions, even asking his old philosophical nemesis William Bagley for assistance.[7]

During November of 1938, Margaret Pinckney Kilpatrick's health began to deteriorate rapidly. She reduced her physical activity to a minimum, so as not to bring on her debilitating heart palpitations. Kilpatrick ministered to her every need, from assisting her to and from the bedroom, bathroom, and living rooms, to filling her hot-water bottles, rubbing her back, and making sure she had reading material for her frequently sleepless nights. On November 15, Rita was stricken with a paralytic stroke affecting the right side of her body. Two days before this stroke she had told her husband that she would be glad if it were all to end and regretted that there was no way the end might be brought on — that is, as Kilpatrick wrote, "no available way." At this time, Kilpatrick was in the midst of his Macy lectures and brought in round-the-clock nurses. On

November 20 he realized that she faced either death or permanent disability, and it made him, he wrote, feel much older than his own sixty-seven years. With Helen gone, his wife moving in and out of consciousness, and his daughter Margaret caught up in the busy affairs of her own life, no one remembered that this was his birthday.[8]

Dr. Mary Nelson, who had been the family doctor for a short time, attended to Rita in the apartment, but on November 23 she stopped eating. Thanksgiving Day, November 24, was passed with Rita's niece, the nurse, and the cook joining Kilpatrick for the traditional turkey dinner. That afternoon he had held up a hand mirror so that Rita, unable to move, might see the snow outside. In the early evening the nurse called for the doctor, who arrived soon after, and Rita rallied momentarily. But around 7:25 the end was near, and Kilpatrick was summoned back into the room. He called "tell me good-bye," but it was too late. This 24th of November was their thirtieth wedding anniversary.[9]

Kilpatrick first called his daughter, and soon after that his brother Howard. He then telephoned the relatives in Charleston, indicating that Rita's wishes were to be buried there, near her father at Magnolia Cemetery. The undertaker took the body away for embalming and preparation for shipping. Margaret selected a casket the next morning, and Marion Ostrander came to the apartment to assist Kilpatrick in handling the day-to-day details of his personal business. A short viewing was held at Saint Luke's Chapel at noon, but there was no service. At 2:15 p.m. Margaret, her husband Ted, and the two grandsons accompanied Kilpatrick to Pennsylvania Station, where the casket was placed on the train for the journey to Charleston. Margaret accompanied her father to South Carolina and was of inestimable help: "My wife and my daughter never quite got on together, from the very first for various causes, but my daughter has done her part whenever there was need," he wrote.[10]

The funeral was on the 26th of November. Kilpatrick spent some time alone with the casket at the undertaker's. Rita's wedding ring was left on her hand. As they had no child for her to leave it to as an heirloom, he wished her to have it, even in the grave. A short service was given by a Mr. Stuart, minister of Saint Michael's in Charleston; there were no other eulogies. Margaret Pinckney Kilpatrick was then buried near her father and sister in Magnolia Cemetery of Charleston.

Although the Kilpatricks' match may not have been entirely a matter of love at first, they had certainly been comfortable together. He likened her death to the loss of his sister Helen earlier in the year. "We had lived thirty years

together. We had traveled together and worked together and lived together," he wrote. His final thought on that was: "She has been even more indignant than I at the ill treatment I have received from Dean Russell." Rita's will distributed the heirlooms she owned to her relatives and left what financial holdings she had in a trust to her husband, sisters, and unmarried nieces. Upon Kilpatrick's death the income was to revert to the nieces, and upon their deaths, to the South Carolina Historical Society.[11]

The relationship between the couple is difficult to assess with so little documentation in the diaries and no witnesses who knew them well during their marriage. Kilpatrick was clearly taken with Margaret Pinckney's southernness and family history when they met during the first decade of the century, although, it has been suggested that he may also have felt socially inferior to her. With the possible exception of the minor disagreement over their automobile during the Great War, there had been no detectable difficulty or problems in the marriage. He did confess in his diary on Christmas Day in 1919 that he "felt cheated of much of life. Here I am with only one child and nothing much to call home." And the one child and her stepmother, as has been seen, did not get along well. He had moved Margaret into a dormitory in 1920 with the specific intent of lowering the level of conflict between the two women by keeping their interaction to a minimum. As Margaret matured, left home, and married, the relationship ameliorated to a point where the earlier altercations were all but forgotten. And yet, beneath the surface certain doubts about the relationship and a certain discomfort with it remained, at least for Margaret. Just before the elder woman died, Margaret had questioned the need for her to stay in the apartment during a ten-day trip of her father's. She demurred at this request (made by a family friend) and then wondered, "Is it just that I am not so fond of Mother? Am I being a 'bad daughter'?" But at the Magnolia Cemetery, emotion gave way to any long-standing conflict, when she wept during the service.[12]

Kilpatrick's life as a widower became the immediate topic of conversation in the apartment from which he was now absent. Margaret returned to find that the state had closed her father's account and that state tax waivers would be needed to reopen them. She called Marion Ostrander, who had power of attorney. While Kilpatrick's maid, Sally, and Margaret's maid, Lessie, cleaned the apartment, Margaret received a call on December 2 from Rita's niece, Esther Barnwell Means, who wished to discuss Dr. Kilpatrick's future. Margaret said that she planned for him to live with her family; Esther responded that he would surely marry again, that he was very attractive, and that women

"had always been crazy about him and one would get him." (A Northwestern coed once said of him, "He is a saint. I should like nothing better than to run my fingers through his hair.") Margaret did not care for this idea: "Mama was a distinct disappointment to me, and I can't fancy another stepmother I could care for." As to who the next stepmother might be, the intrusive Esther Barnwell Means had a distinct idea — Marion Ostrander. She suggested that Margaret quickly get whatever possessions she wished from the apartment, because if her father did remarry, his daughter would never be able to get the items from another woman. And, Esther added, "I just can't bear the idea of Miss Ostrander "getting the silver spoons." After this conversation, Margaret took stock of the situation and concluded that her father would probably marry after a year and would possibly want a son. She would have a year with her father, though, and would make the most of that time — a year of companionship and then good-bye.[13] It would not be good-bye, of course, but her calendar regarding the rest of the scenario was only six months off.

When Kilpatrick returned from his brief stay in the South after Rita's funeral, he retained his maid and attempted to carry on life as best he could. While mentally he was grieving, his physical health continued to be quite good. He walked, played an occasional round of golf, and maintained his normal weight (142 pounds). Financially, he estimated his personal wealth to be $119,000. He considered editing another book on curriculum, no doubt stung by the ever-increasing charges among the public that progressive education was an overly permissive philosophy giving children the license to frolic and romp unimpeded in the classroom. He also mentioned Miss Ostrander as a potential contributor.[14]

Kilpatrick's encounters with the celebrated and prominent figures of his time continued. At the sixtieth anniversary celebration of the Ethical Culture School, Kilpatrick was invited to sit at the head table with Eleanor Roosevelt. He was to meet Mrs. Roosevelt on a number of occasions in the future, once appearing with her in a photograph in the *New York Times*. That year — 1939 — he attended what he considered a very fruitful discussion meeting, which included Margaret Mead, at the City Club. At a dinner at the Urban League he sat next to the author Pearl Buck, and at a Philosophy of Education Club luncheon he challenged Bertrand Russell, who had propounded the idea of giving universities final approval of all textbooks. A few years later he heard Russell speak and concluded that he was "brilliant, but not thoughtful. I don't like him." Kilpatrick's meetings with the great and near-great even included royalty. During the summer of 1939 he saw George VI and the queen when

they were on the Columbia campus as part of a state visit to North America. As an emeritus faculty member, he was given an excellent seat and noted that the queen was much more alert than the king (as was usual, since she was much more attuned to public opinion than her husband) and that there was genuine enthusiasm on the part of the crowd. Kilpatrick did not think such an outpouring would have occurred a generation earlier, or even a year earlier; it had required the perception of a common and immediate military threat from Germany and Italy.[15]

In February of 1939 Kilpatrick attended a conference at the University of Florida, where he stayed with his former student Dean J. W. Norman. The previous year Kilpatrick had begun to do occasional *pro bono* consulting work for Adelphi University on Long Island, and Adelphi had even dedicated its 1938 yearbook to him. April found him in Washington, D.C., where he visited Mount Vernon for the first time and felt "impressed and subdued" as he approached Washington's tomb. He went on to Statesboro, Georgia, that month to visit the teachers college there. He had also been approached by a Miss Stone, a "visionary," who had talked him and John Dewey into exploring the establishment of a school. Nothing emerged from the discussions. Meanwhile, he maintained his connection with the Institute for Pacific Relations whenever it met in New York. All of this activity troubled him and kept him awake at night. "I am an easy mark. The more I think about [it] the wider awake I become and more appalled. I need a guardian." A month later the same notion emerged again, when he almost missed an appointment. "I need a guardian or nurse or somebody to check up on my thinking."[16]

June 1939 found him back at Evanston for a summer teaching stint. He renewed his friendship with George Axtelle and was a frequent visitor at Axtelle's apartment. Axtelle enjoyed classical music and had what Kilpatrick described as the most expensive combination Victrola and radio on the market. Unfortunately, though, he played it late into the evening, and this often disrupted serious conversation. Kilpatrick clearly liked Axtelle and thought him highly intelligent, though at times obtuse. Kilpatrick's summer at Northwestern was a mixture of teaching, discussion, brief side trips, and golf. He went with a group one evening to see the film *The Nazi Spy*. Although he hated the Nazis, his ever-analytical mind and sense of fairness made him view the use of propaganda as inequitable. Ready to leave at the film's conclusion, his party decided to stay for the second feature, an unnamed melodrama which Kilpatrick described as "silly, improbable, and unconvincing to the nth degree." When he returned to New York at the end of the summer, Margaret took him to

the World's Fair. Greatly impressed, he spent most of the time visiting the international buildings; those of the Soviet Union and Britain stood out in his judgment. In the British pavilion, he saw one of the original Magna Cartas.[17]

The summer ended, of course, with war in Europe, which Kilpatrick called "simply Hitler's choice." Kilpatrick was concluding a conference, which was all but abandoned at the news of the invasion of Poland. "How it will turn out I do not see," he wrote. "I hate war, but think it will have to be stopped by force by the combined forces of orderly nations." Forever a Wilsonian, he declared from the platform that but for Senators Lodge and Borah, the United States might have entered the League of Nations and the world would be much different. He received a generous round of applause for this comment.[18] Barely a month into the war, Kilpatrick put his thoughts into writing:

> My own feeling is that we should try to keep out, but meanwhile use all legal means to help the allies (so as, however, not to hurt China). In the end we may have to go in; for civilization in a sense is at stake. I do not like Chamberlain or his Tory supporters, but they can be voted down. Hitler and Stalin and Mussolini represent a return to barbarism (from which Japan never emerged). The world cannot run on their formula, and we are selfish to refuse to see and help subdue the upholders of that formula.[19]

Again, Kilpatrick's careful, insightful analysis of world events was very close to the most accurate assessments of the fascist threat. Although somewhat ahead of public opinion, he could see that intervention by the United States, as yet more than two years away, was a distinct possibility. "At last they [the British Tories] have seen what many of us had earlier seen. I hate war," he reiterated, "but am no pacifist."[20]

The Kilpatrick Discussion Group reorganized in October of 1939 at the prodding of Harold Rugg and with Kilpatrick's blessing. It permitted him an intellectual outlet that had been missing since his retirement and also gave him the opportunity to interact with former colleagues from Teachers College. In addition to Rugg, others present that first evening — at Union Theological Seminary — included Childs, Newlon, Raup, Watson, Harold Cottrell, and Ernest Johnson. Merle Curti, Kenneth Benne, and Freeman Butts were invited to attend at a later date. The topic for this first reunion meeting was "the fundamental problem of modern civilization." A week later, the topic was

whether the United States should stay out of the war. In November Kilpatrick was asked to be the main speaker at John Dewey's eightieth birthday celebration. He spoke for twenty minutes on "John Dewey in American Life."[21] The guest of honor was in absentia.

Another meeting of the Discussion Group, in late November, again raised the issue of America's entrance into the war. Merle Curti began the discussion and was followed by Kilpatrick, who stated his position at length. It was very Wilsonian, with Rooseveltian overtones, its salient concerns being establishing justice in the international community; America's moral obligation to enter the war if the forces of Germany, Italy, or Russia threatened to prevail; and a warning against a repetition of the mistakes of the Versailles Treaty. One evening a guest, Peter Drucker, spoke to the group about the economic breakdown of Europe. Kilpatrick found the presentation interesting, but he thought Drucker had been given too much to the "paradoxes and quibblings which we see in the European scholar." He also thought that Drucker "showed too, too much of the Jesuit in him." At times, points of contention arose in the Discussion Group, once almost breaking up the gathering. Kilpatrick, frustrated when Rugg, "as usual" shifted the conversation away from the topic under consideration, while Childs was fearful that the need for economic reconstruction would be missed, called that entire episode an "utter waste of time." But the circle continued, its members at one point uniting to defend their colleague Goodwin Watson, who had been accused by a congressman from Texas, Martin Dies, of being a communist.[22]

Accusations of communism continued to plague several left-wing educational progressives: John Dewey had been a target, on and off, for four decades. Beginning in the 1920s, Kilpatrick himself had become the subject of a file at the Federal Bureau of Investigation, though that did not dissuade J. Edgar Hoover's agents from calling on Kilpatrick to gain information. In early 1942, an F.B.I. agent inquired about Frederick Redefer's wife and Redefer himself. Kilpatrick did not know Mrs. Redefer, but he told the agent that her husband was loyal to the government and democracy. At the time, such visits did not seem to be out of the ordinary, and Kilpatrick apparently saw nothing sinister about them, and nothing amiss in answering the questions. A year later the agents returned to ask again about Redefer, and once again Kilpatrick vouched for his friend.[23]

Concern about his personal life arose again, and on his sixty-eighth birthday he wrote, "My home life is at times lonely, true I am busy and too contented as to outlook to brood, but I begin to feel that it is not good for man

to be alone." His thoughts may have already been directed at someone who might alleviate the loneliness he was feeling. Since the previous summer, Kilpatrick had been writing to "Miss Ostrander," who had been in Florida teaching summer school. When she returned in the fall, she began to take dictation for him, and he often visited her apartment at 160 Claremont Avenue in the evenings. Miss Ostrander — actually Dr. Ostrander — also had a part-time position with the Progressive Education Association in the city. In 1940, a twelve-day, forty-one-speech trip was undertaken by Kilpatrick to the Northwest, on behalf of the Progressive Education Association. He seemed indefatigable. The next month he was on the NBC Blue Network, where he answered questions from an announcer designated as "Mr. Average Citizen." It was during this excursion that the issue of Harold Rugg's textbooks arose. Kilpatrick responded by saying that, while "progressive education" as such, had nothing to do with the books, he knew Rugg intimately and "Rugg is no communist."[24]

Upon returning, Kilpatrick continued his visits to Apartment 3K, 160 Claremont Avenue. On February 9, he noted, "Don't dictate much, there are too many things to talk over," and on a Sunday evening, February 18, he finally made his intentions known to Miss Ostrander: "Talk at some length with Miss Ostrander, more definitely than hitherto. Now I must tell Margaret what I plan and in time others concerned." The evening seems to have unsettled him so much that he forgot to bring his usual dictation with him. Informing Margaret was a problem, and he decided to communicate the news to her in writing while he was in Chicago, 1,000 miles away. On February 22 he wrote, "Write letters, one to Margaret telling her of my engagement with Miss Ostrander. I hope she will not take it too hard." The letter arrived two days later. "How do I feel? Stunned," Margaret noted in her diary, "And yet it is not a surprise. I seem to have expected it. Do I regret it? Am I upset? Jealous?" Yet she did wish him happiness: "She can, and will, I believe, give him a happy home. I believe I can like her a lot."[25]

But two days later Margaret's mood reversed: "I have a feeling of distaste for the whole thing — Father included. So many silly old men marry their secretaries. I would have expected something superior of him," she wrote. It was not that she disliked Marion Ostrander; she simply desired something "more dignified." Having her father live with his brother Howard would have been acceptable, but she was deeply concerned that this marriage would ruin his reputation: "A year has passed, mercifully, but just barely, and I think Mother's old friends will resent it, even if I don't." It was a very painful situation

for Margaret, who believed that her unusually close relationship with her father would end with his marriage. She also wondered whether there would be children. Margaret added that Rita (the "duchess" as she had called her, though not to her face) had "talked bitterly against Miss Ostrander to everyone," but "no one outside can know how hateful our duchess was at times." Ted Baumeister found the news humorous, and this probably made her feel that others would think the same. But when Kilpatrick returned from the trip, Margaret greeted him graciously, indicating that she understood his need for someone in his life. "She talks very sensibly about my proposed marriage with Miss Ostrander," he wrote in his diary, "recognizing that I need something and was very thoughtful regarding Miss Ostrander in every way."[26]

The wedding was set for early May, and in the meantime Kilpatrick worked assiduously to secure a position for Dr. Ostrander. Eventually, she took a part-time position at Adelphi, to complement her half-time work with the Progressive Education Association. Her suitor's almost nightly visits to 160 Claremont Avenue continued; these evenings were a mixture of business and socializing. While the relationship was almost certainly chaste, it did have a physical aspect. One evening, six weeks before the wedding, Marion was suffering from a cold, which, according to Kilpatrick, was "an interference with happiness." He noted that he returned home earlier than usual and "gargled my throat." Marion was also assisting Kilpatrick as he turned his Macy Lectures into a book for publication. "She is *very* helpfully criticizing," he wrote. "I had not before known how much improvement she can give by her suggestions." Marion's niece would later say that the process of authorship was very much collaborative in the latter stages of Kilpatrick's manuscripts.[27]

A diamond engagement ring was purchased at Tiffany's and placed on the bride-to-be's finger on April 15. The bridegroom-to-be informed his brother Howard of his plans the next day. Still unsure about the reaction he would receive from others, he waited until almost a week before the wedding to write and inform Rita's nieces Esther and Caroline Means, hoping, as he put it, that "they will not be troubled." He then made plans for a wedding trip to Quebec and informed his maid, Sally, of the upcoming event. That evening he entertained Marion in his apartment for the first time. Four days before the wedding he told John Childs of his intentions and found that his younger colleague was surprised and a bit dazed. Childs later told Marion that he was "dumbfounded not as an earthquake, but a cosmic quake."[28]

Margaret had apparently recovered from any quaking she may have experienced and offered Marion the Baumeisters' home for the wedding. After

showing Marion the house, Margaret noted that "she seemed very nice, wholesome, sincere, and good." Margaret and Marion's sister, Gretchen, both dove into preparations for the wedding. Marion sent flowers to Margaret for a pre-wedding party, and Margaret was struck by her future stepmother's thoughtfulness. Margaret, for her part, assisted her father in moving the Pinckney furniture from the Morningside Drive apartment. Several pink upholstered chairs were sent to the Charleston Museum. As the burly moving men were carrying them to the truck, Kilpatrick told them that the chairs had once belonged to the first ambassador to Great Britain and had been sent to Ambassador Pinckney by George Washington.[29]

Wednesday, May 8, 1940, dawned clear and cool. Flowers in the garden were just beginning to bloom, and the florist had decorated the house to elegant effect with roses, gladiolus, snapdragons, and delphinium. The wedding cake was decorated with lilies of the valley and white roses. The ladies were dressed in long chiffon of delicate colors, the men in evening clothes. Kilpatrick wore full dress and, according to his daughter, appeared "with his white hair shining like satin, the boutonniere matching it." Marion wore a long, graceful, but simple gown and white slippers, but neither gloves nor veil." Photographs of Marion show her to be of slightly below average height, a buxom woman, but not heavy. She kept her hair relatively short. Her appearance has been described as simple or plain. Kilpatrick's colleague Dr. Ernest Johnson, who clearly approved of the marriage, had agreed to officiate, using a shortened version of the Episcopal Prayer Book, and Ted Baumeister's mother played the wedding march. Candles and flowers made the temperature and fragrance of the room heavy. Twenty-four people were in attendance, including the bride and bridegroom. A dinner followed the ceremony, and then the wedding cake was cut. Mrs. Baumeister, Sr., played "Good Night, Ladies" as Kilpatrick and Marion went upstairs to change into their traveling clothes. After Marion threw her bouquet, the couple departed at 8:40 p.m., under a hail of rice, for Pennsylvania Station to catch a northbound train at 9:35. In the excitement of it all, Kilpatrick almost forgot his suitcase.[30]

The newlyweds had engaged a drawing room on the train for the journey to Canada. Arriving in Montreal the next morning, they changed for the trip to Quebec City, but not before securing a copy of the *New York Times* carrying the notice of the marriage of "Dr. Ostrander and W. H. Kilpatrick." They arrived that afternoon in the old city and checked into the historic Château Frontenac, room 1307, overlooking the Saint Lawrence River to the east. After resting briefly, they walked over the hills of the city, visiting the provincial parliament building,

the citadel, and the old city walls. The following day a provincial education official, a former student of Kilpatrick's, showed them the city — though he was taken aback at first when "Miss Ostrander was introduced as Mrs. Kilpatrick."

Their honeymoon could not shield the couple from the news of the day: the German army had invaded Holland and Belgium. That evening they went to see a new film by Alfred Hitchcock, *Rebecca*, starring Joan Fontaine and Laurence Olivier, based on Daphne du Maurier's best-seller. The rest of the week was spent visiting schools, shopping, and closely following the war news — they bought every newspaper they could find. They spent much of their time walking about the walled city: "We go much of the time hand in hand," he wrote. Then, they went on to Montreal for two more days of sightseeing, staying at the Windsor Hotel (for $8 a night). They arrived back in New York City on the 18th, ending "as perfect a wedding journey . . . as could be imagined."[31]

Several items of business filled the Kilpatricks' days after their return. He immediately set up bank accounts for Marion so that, in case he should die suddenly, she would not be without funds until the estate was settled. Marion, on the advice of Dr. Mary Nelson, saw a gynecologist in Bronxville and was told that conception was possible but not probable. The Kilpatricks did attempt to conceive a child. In the summer of 1940 Marion flew from Florida to Chicago to spend a weekend at Northwestern, where Kilpatrick was teaching. As Kilpatrick put it in his diary, "If we are to have any child, we cannot afford to waste any opportunity. To wait even a week longer would certainly lose this opportunity as we are told."

The newlyweds were fêted in late May by members of the Kilpatrick Discussion Group at the home of Dr. and Mrs. Harold Rugg. Next on the agenda was redecorating the Morningside Drive apartment, which, according to Margaret, was much in need of refurbishment. The changes would be made while the couple were away for the summer, with major improvements in the living rooms and kitchen. Marion left on June 7 for six weeks of teaching at the summer school of the University of Florida. Before going to Evanston for his own stint of summer school teaching, Kilpatrick made a trip to the state college in Fort Hayes, Kansas, and a brief trip to Carbondale, in downstate Illinois, to speak at the local college. In Carbondale he was told, much to his amusement, that Ohio State's Laboratory School was operating on his principles, but not saying so.[32]

Kilpatrick arrived at Northwestern on June 23, where he was greeted by a

class of over 100 students, plus a sizable number of auditors. Marion joined him in late July after completing her teaching in Gainesville, Florida. It was an extremely hot summer, and during one class session a woman told Kilpatrick that they would all be much happier if he took his coat off. He did.[33] He and Marion ate fruit lunches, took walks along the cool shore of Lake Michigan, and spent evenings with Dean Ernest Melby and the Axtelles, discussing the war. He also worked for the first time with Willard Goslin, the impressive superintendent from Webster Groves, Missouri. It would be more than a decade before Kilpatrick and Goslin would meet again — in California, for an episode neither man would forget.

In Chicago, Kilpatrick met with a national education group to produce a philosophy of education yearbook. The gathering included Mortimer Adler, and the meeting did not go well: "Adler is personally pleasant, but impossibly Thomist. We find it impossible to agree on any questions to discuss and finally leave each man free to discuss what he conceives to be his conception of the problem of education in his own way." Later that fall, Adler pulled out of the project altogether, claiming he could not follow the procedure agreed to by the rest of the group.[34] This was one of the rare defeats Kilpatrick met as facilitator, discussion leader, and consensus builder.

The Kilpatricks left Chicago on August 16, 1940, arriving at their newly furnished apartment the next day. New rugs, draperies, and furniture greeted them, in addition to a renovated kitchen. In September they made the first of what would become almost yearly summer trips to Marion's hometown, Schuylerville. The cool weather of upstate New York was a pleasant relief for the annual month they would spend in August or early September. There would be long walks, and side trips to Vermont, Lake Champlain, Saratoga Springs, and Fort Ticondaroga. Most of all, the time provided an opportunity to read and write, away from the heat of New York City. The only drawback was the Sunday evening family cookouts, which Kilpatrick grew to dislike, stridently, as the years passed. When necessary, he made quick trips back to Morningside Drive to take care of his numerous professional and organizational responsibilities. Other than his New England vacations during the years of World War I, his trips abroad, and his visits to the Teachers College Country Club in Ossining, Kilpatrick took little time off for relaxation. Consequently, these brief respites were all the more welcome, and he once told his sister-in-law, Gretchen, that in 1943 he found the time in Schuylerville the most restful he had experienced in twenty years. Gretchen's children addressed Kilpatrick as Uncle Heard, but they referred to him as H.P. — "Herr Professor" — good-

naturedly behind his back.[35]

Kilpatrick kept quite active with his numerous voluntary responsibilities. He agreed to serve as the editor of the *Frontiers of Democracy* (formerly *The Social Frontier*) as long as others would do the legwork and the major tasks associated with publishing the journal. He was also chairman of the Service Bureau of Intercultural Education; acting chairman, and later full chairman, of the New York City Urban League; and chairman of the Board of American Youth for World Youth. Kilpatrick disliked the fact that Marion was working at two positions, one as a part-time faculty member (albeit head of the education department) at Adelphi College in Garden City, Long Island, where she spent three to four days per week; and the other at the national headquarters of the Progressive Education Association, where she was in charge of the Service Center. But after six months of marriage he wrote, "We are living together very happily." The couple spent evenings on Morningside Drive either going over a current manuscript, reading, or in conversation. Kilpatrick also gave abbreviated tutorials to Marion on Herbart, Froebel, and other thinkers as she prepared for her classes. On occasion, he also read Uncle Remus stories aloud. His younger brother Howard was a frequent visitor, and Marion quickly learned during one of Howard's first visits that one did not debate with the patent lawyer, a fact Kilpatrick apparently already knew: "I learned many years ago never to argue with Howard on any point. It never pays," he wrote, after Marion's baptism by fire. Howard's endless complaints did aggrieve Kilpatrick, but he patiently endured the outbursts on the topic of the patent office. "I also get tired of his reactionary social and political attitudes," he wrote. Apparently, Howard was also "rabidly anti-Negro" and on one occasion almost disrupted a gathering of several of Marion's friends by making inappropriate comments.[36]

Kilpatrick did find time to read an occasional work of fiction, and his thoughts on one novel reveal a rare instance of naiveté on his part about the nation's underclass. While reading *The Grapes of Wrath*, he recorded that he had never personally known of a situation such as that described by Steinbeck, unless it was that of the tenant "poor white folks" of his youth in the South. He found the treatment of the characters convincing psychologically, but less convincing sociologically. Still the book deeply moved him. "It is a good many months since I have got lost in a work of fiction," he wrote. He began Tolstoy's *Anna Karenina*, but did not finish it: "Do not wish to get interested in such love affairs." He also abandoned a Henry James novel after encountering a three-page paragraph. On another occasion he stopped reading a work of fiction when the hero "behaved badly," admitting that doing this "reflects on me, but

it is true."[37]

The Kilpatricks continued to follow events in Europe on the radio and in the newspapers. That September, of 1940, they watched with the rest of the world as Britain held off the German Luftwaffe over the skies of southern England and the English Channel. "Britain is fighting our battle," he wrote. "There is some growing spirit that we should help more positively." The war news, he felt, made Roosevelt's election that much more probable, and on November 5 Roosevelt was indeed reelected to an unprecedented third term. Kilpatrick had foreseen Roosevelt's third term as early as August of 1939. and "rejoiced" for the sake of foreign affairs, but not for the domestic agenda. He still did not think the New Deal had gone far enough with regards to economic control. Everyday aspects of the war on the home front began to affect the Kilpatricks. Blackouts, in particular, became a nuisance. At one meeting, a total blackout occurred, but the lecturer continued speaking for an hour. Later, in mid-1944, Kilpatrick took umbrage at a call for a blackout and considered "formal disobedience," but later acquiesced, though he considered the drill "the outrageous act of the military mind."[38]

Life in the Morningside Drive apartment had changed appreciably for Kilpatrick as he neared the first anniversary of his marriage. New furnishings and appliances, fresh paint, and the transformation of the décor were only the beginning: Marion's divorced sister, Gretchen, and her two children, Mary and David Murray, paid frequent visits, which altered the atmosphere markedly. Mary, who would graduate from high school during the war and go on to Smith College, visited the apartment for tutoring in French from Marion and in mathematics from Kilpatrick. Some of the more difficult problems (and answers) he assisted her with still survive in the diaries. An element of sexism in his thinking emerged when he noted, "To make girls study such [trigonometry] is nothing short of a sinful waste. The returns are nearly nil." Whether he meant returns in terms of the female students or the subject itself is unclear. Marion was also able to get Kilpatrick to sing folk songs he had learned as a youth to her and the immediate family. It was the first time in his adult life, he admitted, that he had sung a solo where others could hear him. Marion was also fond of games and introduced them into the once-sedate apartment, much to the disgruntlement of Howard and occasionally, Kilpatrick himself. On holidays, when family were present, they played the rather boisterous game "Turn the Plate." Kilpatrick often won the calmer game of "Categories."[39]

Marion also managed to get Kilpatrick to change his famous pompadour slightly. Rather than his customary part in the middle, which, when his hair was

long, had allowed it to fall down on each side of his face, he now had it cut in "the new way of simply brushing it all back — Marion likes it so." The celebrated hair was an almost constant focus of attention. One man pointed to his head and muttered something one day on the elevator, and Kilpatrick thought he had brushed into some wet paint. Kilpatrick inquired and the man said louder, "Your hair is so pretty." "I had just washed it," admitted Kilpatrick, "and it was rather fluffy."[40]

Kilpatrick even allowed himself to be persuaded to attend movie theaters more frequently than before, at times almost every other week. He and Marion went to see *Gone With the Wind*, and he described its accuracies and inaccuracies in great detail from his firsthand knowledge of the South during Reconstruction. He would have wished for a more historical story line, but overall he thought the presentation "excellent." They also went to see Charlie Chaplin's *The Great Dictator*, Steinbeck's *The Forgotten Village*, the classic *How Green Was My Valley*, and a comedy, *Life with Father*. He took pleasure in the numerous motion pictures he saw, especially *Mrs. Miniver* with Greer Garson and Walter Pidgeon — he discarded his usual reserve to proclaim it a "stirring experience, very well done." The Macmillan Theater, on Columbia's campus, featured newsreels and "patriotic pictures," so that Kilpatrick managed to see not only R.A.F. raids, the fighting in Greece, and films from the Soviet Union, but also a Donald Duck cartoon which found little favor in his eyes: "The Donald Duck makes me wonder how the American people can possibly enjoy such."[41]

These first few years of marriage certainly changed the staid professor's daily habits and customs. Moreover, the feeling between him and Marion ran deep — surpassed only by what he had felt in his marriage to Marie. On Marion's fifty-first birthday, in December of 1942, he paid her a glowing tribute in his diary: "Few women are more capable or more attractive — none more devoted to what she accepts as her cause and duty." The home he had felt somewhat cheated of during the holidays a few years before was now filled with family and friends. Margaret, Ted, and the two boys were joined by Marion's sister and her two children, along with Kilpatrick's brother Howard and two nephews, William Kilpatrick and Frank Jenkins, who were now living in wartime New York. The apartment was filled to overflowing with presents, food, and the conversation of adults and teenagers.[42]

Some of Kilpatrick's time was spent with diverse — even eclectic — appointments. On a single day all the following occurred: he counseled two former students, one facing the draft, the other a missionary to India. The latter

sought advice on how best to secure friendly relations between the United States and India. Next, a woman who had been recently dismissed from the W.P.A. came to ask if she could sue the government; after indicating that he thought not, Kilpatrick made arrangements for her to see a professor at the Columbia Law School. Following a meeting with another woman regarding an upcoming conference featuring Norman Thomas, two Chinese students begged for an audience, though the hour was approaching five o'clock. Kilpatrick treated each of these individuals with the greatest courtesy, even if at times their requests seemed trifling or bordered on the bizarre.[43]

Financially, the Kilpatricks were faring well, much better than he had expected before his retirement. His yearly income in the 1930s had averaged approximately $20,000. In 1940, his income was a bit over $14,000, while Marion earned almost $3,000 — though Marion's income dropped in mid-1941 when she lost her position in the Progressive Education Association owing to the organization's financial difficulties. Kilpatrick celebrated his seventieth birthday on November 20, 1941. He found his health to be excellent, although he was not quite as "supple or sprightly" as in his youth. He had begun to take vitamins A, B, and C, and his weight had dropped ten pounds, to 130. His hearing was beginning to deteriorate, as well as his memory, he suspected, especially for names. Yet, on one occasion a Northwestern student greeted Kilpatrick on a visit to Canada and said in passing that the professor probably did not remember him. "You sat in the next to the back row on my left." The student was "quite overcome."[44]

In May of 1941 Yuichi Saito, son of an old friend from the Tokyo Y.M.C.A. and the Institute for Pacific Relations days, made a visit to Kilpatrick's apartment. The young Japanese man asked him numerous detailed questions about America's thinking in terms of the war and the world scene. Margaret Baumeister was present, and a distilled version of the conversation fills several pages of her diary. Kilpatrick understood that there was a good possibility that much of what he was telling Saito would be conveyed to Mansakuto, another acquaintance of his in the IPR during the 1920s and 1930s. He was frank in expressing what he viewed as America's commitment to destroy Hitlerism, and he implied strongly at more than one point during in the discussion that he placed Japan within the Axis camp.

On December 7, 1941, Saito and a friend returned for another visit. Kilpatrick turned on the radio in the afternoon, but there proved to be too much static for good listening. Later, Marion's sister, Gretchen, called with word that Japan had attacked Pearl Harbor. With their two Japanese guests still in the

apartment, the Kilpatricks said nothing until the two men had left. That evening, writing in his diary, Kilpatrick once again demonstrated his discernment on current issues. He knew that this reckless act had united the American people in one stroke and noted that even the isolationist Senator Burton Wheeler had been quoted immediately as saying, "We must go in and beat hell out of them." He also looked toward the future and the complete defeat of the Japanese military that would free the occupied territories of Manchuria and Korea. After the defeat he thought Japan should be remade so that it had practically no military, be put back on its feet economically, and be reestablished with a democratic political system and equal access to raw materials. Kilpatrick's speculation, just hours after the surprise attack on Honolulu, proved remarkable for its accuracy and political acumen.[45]

When the war had reached its midpoint for the United States, in 1943, others joined Kilpatrick in thinking about the economic and social reconstruction that would follow the conflict. In that year, Robert Merrill Bartlett interviewed fifteen prominent Americans on their thoughts regarding the war and the future. This group of distinguished men and women — Bartlett called them "defenders of thought and pioneers of truth" — included Wendell Wilkie, Pearl Buck, Cordell Hull, Mordecai Johnson, Henry Wallace, and John Foster Dulles. The lone educator in the assembly was William Heard Kilpatrick. Bartlett's book, *They Work for Tomorrow*, characterized his interviewees as believers in democracy, forward-looking individuals who were working to advance civilization and who were in the "thick of the fight," doing something constructive "to create a better world order."[46]

Bartlett began his sketch of "the dean of American educators" by describing the silver-haired Kilpatrick as he sat in a Morris chair in a room full of books. Democracy launched the discussion, but for Kilpatrick it was tribute not to an inert form of government, but rather to a developing social and economic arrangement. Asked about his faith in the common man, Kilpatrick quickly responded, "I have more faith in the common man than in the wise, the good, and the rich, who are much quicker to sell out. When the common people are aroused, they don't sell out; that is why England is holding out today." Kilpatrick of course touched on what he termed the "profound revolution in philosophy" effected by science and on the need to face new facts and theories rather than turning away and retreating to fascism or communism. He suggested that the American people needed to maintain faith in their ideals and pointed out that fear had caused many to turn to astrology, numerology, outworn religious positions, and even lotteries as a substitute for taxes. "To

retreat from reason is to surrender our one guide to progress. What we must do is face these problems of our time and try to solve them. It will take time, and we must be patient. The democratic way is the only route to permanent progress."

In envisioning the postwar era, Kilpatrick indicated that as the chief power, with money and ability to make significant changes, the United States must be ready to "act quicker than we did in the last war." It seemed to him that Americans had lost faith at a crucial point, in failing to join the League of Nations. The subsequent aggression of Japan, Italy, and Germany could have been avoided, in his opinion, with a strong world organization, and he made it clear that the experience must not be repeated. "If we don't achieve this, we shall have to live in an armed camp," he said. "This is clear as any lesson from history. We can't have peace unless we have an effective organization to enforce it. Our failure was a moral failure. We must not fail again." He foresaw disease, hunger, isolationism, and economic selfishness after the war. Another legacy of the war that would have to be dealt with, according to Kilpatrick, was nationalism. "The conception of absolute sovereignty is quite as unworkable as is the theory of absolute personal sovereignty," he stated to Bartlett. "Absolute nationalism, or unrestrained sovereignty is nothing more than anarchy or state chaos."[47]

In the concluding portion of the interview, Bartlett raised the issue of whether human nature could be changed. Kilpatrick rejected out of hand the concept that it could, indicating this idea was Aristotelian in origin and had been destroyed by Darwin. Learning, he maintained, was the chief feature of the human organism:

> We learn the correlative of each new situation, and what we thus learn we build into character. We are what we learn. We are continually building ourselves out of new situations. It is thus a mistaken idea to think of human nature as a fixed thing. Our nature at any given time is what we have learned to be under the coercion of our past circumstances.[48]

There is little doubt that Kilpatrick saw the human experience as one which was improving and being enhanced at an ever greater pace. Americans, he was convinced, were now ready to enlarge their moral ideals through economic justice and collective security. Nevertheless, he was not naive about the magnitude of the current conflict: he called the war "this awful holocaust now before us."

As with most who spent any amount of time with Kilpatrick, Bartlett was clearly impressed. "The dictators would scorn his [Kilpatrick's] mission of the mind as a puerile project in a day when might is measured by tanks and bombers. But I wondered whether the judgment of this distinguished philosopher of education were not destined to triumph over the vaunted power of the militarists, realizing that the most powerful thing in the world was still an idea." Kilpatrick's inclusion in this book placed him in very distinguished company, and once again he held his own intellectually, as much in the political and economic arena, as in his own specialty, education. When he received a copy of *They Work for Tomorrow*, he said that, while he did not know how Bartlett had "hit" on him, he felt honored to be included.[49]

The war would strike close to home for both Kilpatrick and Marion. Teddy Baumeister, his grandson, would eventually serve in the military, although he enrolled at Yale first. Marion's nephew David Murray was inducted into the Army in early February of 1943. This troubled Marion greatly and proved to be an especially difficult situation in that her sister, Gretchen, as a single mother, believed she needed a male figure for David turn to. Kilpatrick filled this role as best he could and met with the young man just before he left for basic training in electrical engineering. He told David that the college class which emerged from the Civil War was of a higher caliber than any previous classes. David was certainly troubled by the prospect of war, and Kilpatrick did his best to emphasize the positive nature of the experience in terms of character building, adding that it would be an episode in life that many of his friends would probably miss. He concluded the session by advising David to write to his mother, save his money, and buy war bonds. "He shook hands," wrote Kilpatrick, "as if he appreciated [the advice] and would try." As Kilpatrick stated on several occasions, although he was against war, he was not a pacifist; but he did, on one occasion, reluctantly sign a petition for a conscientious objector to work at an interracial boy's camp in lieu of active service.[50]

In the midst of war and death, there was also a birth in the family. After a difficult pregnancy, on May 15, 1943, Margaret gave birth to her third child, a girl, Mary Berrien Baumeister. Kilpatrick suggested the middle name of Berrien from among four choices, apparently from the family ancestry, which also included Beran, Guyton, and Stryker. Margaret was delighted at having given birth to a girl, in spite of the fourteen years' difference in age between the baby and her younger son, Heard. Looking through the window of the hospital nursery during the once-a-day viewing allowed to parents and grandparents, Kilpatrick noted that little Mary was "quite attractive, very much alive, and

appeared intelligent." He was also amused that the nurse observed a resemblance to Marion.[51]

Professionally, 1943 found Kilpatrick working on editing the seventh John Dewey Society Yearbook, *Teaching the Spiritual Values of Civilization in the Public Schools*, and turning his talks, now becoming more frequent than his teaching stints, to topics such as "Moral Obligation and World Peace." Speculation began during the summer of 1943 regarding the future of the journal *Frontiers of Democracy*. Although Harold Rugg wished to continue the publication, its financial backers in the Progressive Education Association disapproved, and, apparently, there was neither the will nor the means to continue. In November the decision was made to discontinue the journal.[52] In 1943 Kilpatrick began meeting with Norman Cousins, a young journalist who had been a student of his at Teachers College in the 1930s. "This is my first meeting with Norman Cousins; I liked him." Another young man whom he met at this time was William Van Til, also a former student. Previously a teacher at The Ohio State University Laboratory School, Van Til had undertaken an assignment with the Bureau of Intercultural Education in New York City.

At this time, too, the Kilpatrick Award was created. This prize, envisioned by Bruce Raup and other colleagues, was an honor given to both young and more senior scholars in education. Kenneth Benne was its first recipient in 1944. Kilpatrick's long-standing opposition to prizes or awards had apparently been laid aside. Neither was it mentioned a year later when the American Education Fellowship, formerly the Progressive Education Association, gave Kilpatrick himself an award for his lifetime of thinking and achievement in education.[53]

Though he thought his teaching was finally coming to an end, Kilpatrick did spend a month at two institutions in North Carolina during the summer of 1943 and two weeks at the University of Florida in Gainesville, through an invitation from Dean J. W. Norman. The unwritten dress standards at Florida perturbed him, in that at unpredictable times coats were worn, carried, or dispensed with altogether. He wished that one day "we may dress as we reasonably please as we may now think as we reasonably please." But apparently the progressive gospel of independent thinking still had ground to cover. He was told by a professor in Florida that a traditional local teacher had fainted and lay prone on the floor for some time before the principal found her. When he inquired of the class as to why they had taken no action, they responded that the teacher had not told them what to do. On Kilpatrick's last

day in Gainesville, a group of students and faculty sang "Dixie," "The Battle Hymn of the Republic," and "God Be With You Till We Meet Again," three songs which probably meant little to him, given his dislike of the Confederate cause, groundless patriotism, and religion. Kilpatrick was then given a billfold made of Florida alligator skin, and he received expressions of appreciation from many students, including a nun in the class. Dean Norman, who had audited the class, called it the "Number one of all I have ever taken."[54]

During the war years and beyond, Kilpatrick attended many of the same social and political gatherings as Eleanor Roosevelt. She maintained an apartment in Washington Square and was very much a part of the life of New York City. At a meeting of the Harlem Sydenham Hospital Fund in September of 1944, he met her again, and, according to Kilpatrick, "as soon as she saw me, [she] came across the room to greet me." Having seen or met every president since Grover Cleveland, Kilpatrick was also to be present for one of the most notable days in the life of Franklin D. Roosevelt. During Roosevelt's election race against Thomas Dewey in 1944, the president's health became a major issue, with New York newspapers often mentioning that six presidents had died in office. *Time* magazine wrote, "Franklin Roosevelt at sixty-two is an old man." And it was later learned that the White House physician put out reports which were at times misleading. In order to confront the issue, Roosevelt decided to squelch the rumors of ill health, as William Manchester has written, "by submitting himself to a physical ordeal" at the first opportunity.[55] That opportunity was a four-hour, fifty-mile motorcade through New York City on October 21, 1944. The day's ordeal included stops at Ebbets Field, Harlem, Queens, and the Bronx, all during a torrential downpour of cold fall rain. Twice Roosevelt was taken from his open-top car, stripped of his soaked clothes, given a massage and a shot of whiskey, and then dressed in a dry suit. The estimate was that 3 million people saw him that day.

The president's final event of the day was a speech that evening at the Waldorf Astoria, to the Association of Foreign Affairs. Through his connections with the newly formed Liberal Party, and his numerous other relationships with civic and cultural organizations, Kilpatrick and Marion obtained seats for this event at Table 1, next to the speaker's platform. Kilpatrick successfully intervened with an official to get his daughter Margaret and John Dewey better seats before the speech began. Kilpatrick noted that the room was full of measures for the president's security, with even the waiters wearing special tags. The photographers and newsreels were in evidence, with klieg lights illuminating the ballroom to spectacular effect when the program began. The presi-

dent was in fine form, touching upon his Good Neighbor Policy, the inter-war years, the League of Nations, Germany's reemergence, and the status of the Soviet Union, in addition to making a strong defense of his actions in the face of the isolationists. After a quick strike at the McCormick-Patterson-Gannett-Hearst press — an attack that must have warmed Kilpatrick's heart — Roosevelt moved into a fervent argument for a future United Nations. All of these themes found great favor in Kilpatrick's eyes. The cheers were deafening, and the delivery of the president's speech was "euphoric, accompanied by elaborate gestures and facial expressions." FDR left the podium to "cheers and stomping of feet ringing in the ballroom." A presidential aide wrote in his diary, "misgivings about the President's health under the terrific load he is carrying are dissipated."[56] Kilpatrick concurred, and in his own diary wrote:

> The question of his health had entered the campaign. A whispering campaign had it that he was too feeble to carry the load. He had spent the forenoon driving in the rain all over New York City to show his vigor, and he certainly appeared well and strong to us. He spoke very pleasantly, in evident good humor, and carried the group with him. We greatly enjoyed the occasion.[57]

Kilpatrick's thinking was validated two and a half weeks later when Roosevelt triumphed over the forty-two-year-old Thomas Dewey by a four-to-one ratio in the Electoral College. Kilpatrick had thought of Dewey as inexperienced and "a man with no real personal convictions." He and Marion were especially delighted in the defeat of Senator Gerald Nye and several others who had been thorns in Roosevelt's side.[58]

Although his retirement was now seven years in the past, the fiftieth anniversary of Teachers College during the third week of November in 1944 brought memories and still unhealed emotions to the surface. (Earlier in the year, he had not been recognized by the library staff in the Columbia University Periodical Room: "I left in a kind of sorrowful anger, that these underlings do not know me.") When the formal ceremonies were held on November 15, the environment seemed entirely unsuitable. Nicholas Murray Butler, who had been attacking progressive education, gave a brief history of the college and was followed by James Conant, who spoke on the split between the liberal arts and teacher education in the academy. To add insult to injury, Cleveland Dodge, chairman of the board of trustees, referred to several distinguished faculty

members during his speech but failed to mention Kilpatrick. "He left me out. I wonder why?" Kilpatrick pondered. He recorded that Paul Monroe and Edward L. Thorndike, both within two years of him in age, "looked bloated and not long for this world." When the dean emeritus, James Russell, was brought into the room in his "rolling chair," Kilpatrick was deeply stirred by memories of the past. The old dean was a mixture of wrongheadedness and honesty, thought Kilpatrick, but always "honorable, as his son is not."[59] A picture was taken for *Life* magazine, and William F. Russell gave Kilpatrick a place of honor on the front row with Thorndike — one to the dean's left and the other to his right.

Kilpatrick was to have his first encounter with television in December of 1944, when he was invited to the studios of WCBW, the NBC affiliate in New York City, to take part in a mock courtroom debate on the topic "New Major Party Alignments in the United States Are Desirable." The format was that of a courtroom trial, with Norman Thomas and a number of local politicians and journalists appearing as witnesses. Kilpatrick took the affirmative on the issue, gave his testimony, and was recalled later in the program to be cross-examined. "It went fairly well and was mildly interesting. This was my first contact with television on the operating end."[60]

As 1944 drew to a close, the war would be brought home tragically to the Kilpatricks. Before the Thanksgiving Day meal, Kilpatrick requested that the family stand for a full minute of silence to remember the two young men who were in harm's way. Teddy Baumeister, in the medical corps, was on the western front, as was Marion's nephew, David Murray, serving in the artillery corps. Their exact locations were, of course, unknown. The next month the Germans, in an act of desperation, struck out at the Allies, driving them over fifty miles back toward the west. In his diary, Kilpatrick mentioned the "German surprise" on December 16, better known as the Battle of the Bulge. Young David was killed the next day by Nazi soldiers in an unwarranted act of cruelty. During the second week of January word came that David was "missing in action," which the family took to mean that he had been captured. There was then no word at all for two months, as the Allied troops fought to regain the lost ground. Then on March 17, Gretchen Murray's birthday, word came to her from the War Department that her son, David, had been killed in Belgium on December 17. Without telling her sister or Kilpatrick of the news until the following Monday, she went through a birthday celebration at Morningside Drive, with only Marion detecting the slightest hint of tears. Later, Kilpatrick marveled at her courage and self-control. Marion was, of course, deeply troubled by the news and stayed Monday night at her sister's

apartment. Kilpatrick was also profoundly affected by the incident. "My heart aches for them both," he wrote sympathetically. Gretchen later learned that David had been among 150 American prisoners in Belgium who were wantonly shot by the Nazis; their bodies had been left for months before the Americans regained the ground. This news came at the same time as the death camps were liberated, causing Kilpatrick to state that "Germany will stand disgraced before the world for centuries to come."[61]

The next casualty of the war, which jarred Kilpatrick with equal intensity, was the death of Franklin Roosevelt. Kilpatrick was heading for the subway in the early evening of April 12 when he glimpsed a placard in a store that read "F.D.R. Died This Afternoon." The sign was confirmed by fellow passengers, who spoke with one another regarding the implications of the president's passing. Kilpatrick said to one man, "It's the worst news we could hear," to which there was no reply. When the man got off the subway a woman said to Kilpatrick, "He didn't agree with you, but I do." That night Kilpatrick pondered the transfer of power and whether the new president, Harry Truman, was capable of the task: "He has seldom been counted great; but now he has the hardest task in the world."[62]

As the dark paint from the wartime blackouts was being removed from the windows at Morningside Drive, a fresh light of hope began to appear in the form of the new United Nations. Kilpatrick hoped that the meeting in San Francisco to frame the new organization would forgo the errors of Versailles a generation earlier. He was looking for "a beginning that can grow as the spirit of man more and more accepts the moral obligation to maintain world law and order."[63] But before peace could be given full consideration by the world, the war in the Pacific had to be brought to a successful conclusion. The Kilpatricks had left in late July for their annual stay in Schuylerville and were there on August 6 when a B-29, the *Enola Gay*, dropped an atomic bomb on the city of Hiroshima, killing 200,000 people, according to estimates by the Japanese. Kilpatrick, reading the *New York Times* on the following day, immediately grasped the significance of splitting the atom. He contrasted a description of a thousandfold bomb with his own view of a world greatly changed:

> The effecting of this process is very, very significant — I judge the most significant event in my lifetime. When we think of magnifying war a thousand fold, the idea is very sobering. The world has become a thousand fold smaller and thousand fold more dangerous. The problem will be man himself.[64]

With the surrender of the Japanese after a second atomic bomb was dropped on Nagasaki, the world could truly consider the peace. "Now we must do all we can to start the world off again right," wrote Kilpatrick on the cessation of hostilities, "with no chance to war again and if possible with no wish again to war. It will take all the wisdom we can muster, but it can be done." He believed that civilization had been saved "from the awful degradation of murderous subjugation" as the unspeakable details of the concentration camps and the fate of the Jews became known to the world. "It is literally incredible," he wrote at the end of 1945, "that any 'civilized' nation could sink to such moral depths." While he never publicly criticized Truman's decision to drop the bombs on Japan, he did question privately whether "we can morally defend these two uses of such bombs considering the destruction to the unwarned civilian population."[65]

Kenneth Benne — the recipient of the first Kilpatrick Award, and one of his best students — had returned from the war where he had served in the Navy on the carrier *Independence* in the Battle of Luzon and at the formal surrender in Tokyo Bay. Invited to the Morningside Drive apartment for dinner, Benne discussed his wartime experiences and agreed with Kilpatrick that in ten years his twenty-four months in the service would mean little to him. According to Benne, Marion demurred: "But Heard, the great philosopher of experimentalism does not see development in all experiences?" To which Kilpatrick quickly replied, "Experiences can develop and develop, but they can also wither and wither." In his diary, Kilpatrick's analysis of the evening was that his wife doubted his judgment. Benne remembers Kilpatrick saying on another occasion, "Marion has a good mind, but it is a made-up mind."[66] Hal Lewis, of the University of Florida, who knew Marion quite well, took this to mean that she had and would voice her own strong opinions.[67]

Postwar events seemed to mark, in more ways than one, the passing of an age. Dean Emeritus James Russell died in late 1945. Kilpatrick paid tribute to Russell for having built the most renowned and most advanced institution for the study of education in the world, outranking all European universities. There was but one caveat: "He could have made it a much greater institution if he had not had an antagonism to John Dewey." Kilpatrick felt that the old dean had done everything he could to destroy Dewey's influence "except turn me off." In addition to Russell, Kilpatrick's old foil William Bagley died. Always blunt, Kilpatrick judged his nemesis to be a "hurtful reactionary," incapable of understanding the concepts of Dewey's interest and effort, but he said that Bagley's death ended an era, in that no one alive would "henceforth stand forth

in opposition" to Kilpatrick as Bagley did.[68]

During the summer of 1946, Kilpatrick taught again, this time for two weeks at the University of Minnesota. Nevertheless, at times he must have felt, if not that he himself was included in the changing of the old guard, at least that the battle of ideas had not yet been won. Marion had been made a full professor at Adelphi during the summer of 1946 at a salary of $3,300, but in the fall she felt compelled to resign because Adelphi had accepted a large gift to institute the Waldorf Schools Plan, a program opposed to her educational beliefs and those of her husband.[69] Kilpatrick's seventy-fifth birthday took place that same year, and while he thought his "vigorous work" was at an end, he did not see any less strain in his weekly activities. The war years had coincided with the first years of his marriage to Marion, and, as he said on one anniversary, "it is a happy one." He may have thought that this milestone — seventy-five years — was finally bringing to a close his "vigorous work," but just as he kept ratcheting up his estimate of the years he had left, so too did his activity after retirement continue: personal and professional controversies awaited him in the coming decade and beyond. As he turned to his birthday cake that evening, with family around him, he noted that there were actually seventy-five candles on the cake. "With one great breath I blew them all out," he wrote.[70]

LIVING AND LEARNING:
THE MATURE THOUGHT OF A
PROGRESSIVE EDUCATOR

We learn what we live, only what we live, and everything we live. We learn each thing we live as we accept it to act on and we learn it in the degree that we count it important and also in the degree that it fits in with what we already know.[1]

Sufficiently considered, the study of democracy brings us into society itself, into a study of associated living and how this should be managed that men may together live best.[2]

William Heard Kilpatrick

Although Kilpatrick struggled as a writer early in his career, at about the same time that he reached the apex of his reputation as a teacher, he developed a greater confidence in the proficiency and adeptness of his composition. Yet even late in his life, a nagging element of self-doubt about his writing style remained. In 1949, after Marion had given a manuscript a rather rigorous review, he wrote:

Marion has made many suggestions. I find myself much discouraged. It looks as if I cannot write. If I did not already have a dozen books to my credit, some of which have sold well, I would feel pretty hopeless about our finishing this book with any sort of satisfaction. I can now understand better those people who have attempted more than they could do and built various maladjustments from their frustrations.[3]

His issues changed, but — like other prolific writers — Kilpatrick often restated, reiterated, and reworked his major themes. Up to the mid-1920s Kilpatrick's topics focused on the learner, establishing his leadership in the child-centered movement. During the period of social reconstructionism his

attention turned to the social agenda. And then as the Depression drew to a close, there emerged a melding of the two, with a definite emphasis on the social side of the progressive agenda. But Kilpatrick cannot be pigeonholed. New thoughts and points of reference emerged from his writings in the 1930s and 1940s, not only in articles in the major educational journals, but also in radio broadcasts and addresses to professional meetings.

James Wallace has written that journals such as *The Nation* and *The New Republic* were blessed with active and articulate readers who responded to the writings of George Counts, John Dewey, and William Heard Kilpatrick.[4] In a lead article in *The New Republic*, in 1924, Kilpatrick addressed the contemporary status and problems of the elementary school, an institution that he considered critical for the continued success of the United States. While his central theme was the breach between society and the school brought about by the breakneck speed of industrialization and urbanization, other notions appeared. Kilpatrick called for experiences outside the classroom that would move beyond the printed page. Newer methods and curriculum would thereby thwart current practices, which drive children in "herds to acquire in formal fashion a formal pabulum." There would be significant financial considerations — superior teachers, smaller classes, and better equipment would all prove costly. However, in light of the ever increasing social problems among the "underprivileged," a refusal to invest the appropriate funds would be suicidal.[5]

The connectedness of learning within the social setting was crucial for Kilpatrick. In an article written in 1929 he stressed the need for group learning opportunities, approving the use of tests only to provide direction for the study at hand. Schools, he felt, should be encouraging and rewarding places of growth for teachers as well as students. Kilpatrick was never reluctant to criticize what he deemed "hindrances" to the educational process. These included textbooks "as at present made," university entrance requirements, and assorted schemes for classification and promotion. Kilpatrick consistently emphasized the growth of the child in outlook and insight. The writer Agnes de Lima agreed with Kilpatrick and quoted him in one of her essays in *The New Republic*: "It has been the more disheartening because that part, being chiefly formal and mechanical, was easy to be seized upon by the mechanically minded and by them treated as if it were in effect the whole."[6]

In the 1930s Kilpatrick also grappled with the relationship between scientific research and the role of philosophy. He was willing to concede certain psychological principles, but was troubled by the idea of teachers using quantitative methods at the expense of pragmatic thinking. Consequently, he

tended to denigrate testing and formal measurement, while still paying homage to Thorndike for his work on learning. Though applauding the scientific method as applied to education in general, he could never bring himself to fully appreciate the advances of quantitative research, or to concede the limitations of the qualitative approach.[7] In his diary at this time he wrote:

> I suffer somewhat from the present "scientific" reaction against philosophy. Many have been led to believe that "science" will take adequate care of all our educational problems. This I am fighting on all fronts and thanks to the general thought movement — with some success I think.

As the 1930s opened, Kilpatrick began to incorporate into his public lectures topics that he had not hitherto addressed. The possibility of war after little more than a decade of unstable peace concerned him. Demagogic appeals, the use of propaganda, and the danger of unthinking mass responses to public issues deeply troubled him. The new media of mass communication — motion pictures and radio — provided soil for dangerous ideologies to take root and flourish. He bluntly stated in one article, "First Things in Education," that no one should be deceived by either "Mussolini or Lenin" — fascism or communism. In the same article he chastised school administrators for following the practices of the business world by advocating docility in teachers, economic efficiencies, and the vested interests of the privileged few. This is one of Kilpatrick's more strident pieces. In it he strikes out at the use of the term "training" to describe normal schools. "Hateful term," he writes, "we train dogs, but educate intelligent people."[8]

Another issue which absorbed much of Kilpatrick's energy for a number of years was academic freedom. In a speech to the National Education Association (NEA) in 1935, he outlined a three-part program to secure this crucial value in higher education. First, he believed, the NEA should work for adequate tenure laws throughout the country; second, a careful study of academic freedom in the nation's classrooms should be undertaken; and third, a number of educational organizations should collectively investigate any infringements within these two areas of concern. Kilpatrick firmly believed that a democratic society demanded a free exchange of ideas and that change could only occur when autonomy and independence existed in the classroom.[9]

In 1937 Kilpatrick collaborated with John Dewey, Hilda Taba, Jesse Newlon, and five other progressive educators on *The Teacher and Society: The*

First Yearbook of the John Dewey Society. This was the inaugural work sponsored by the newly formed society, and as the title indicates, that often forgotten entity in the educational process — the teacher — was selected for special attention. Kilpatrick authored the first three chapters, providing generic treatments of democracy and education and the connection between social problems and the teaching profession. Alonzo Myers's review of this book in *The Social Frontier* was, predictably, positive. Myers succinctly summarized its emphasis on the need for better education and more freedom for teachers, and on the teacher's central role in social change, a change which, Myers concluded, was literally a "frontier task."[10]

In 1939, Kilpatrick's picture, along with those of sixteen other prominent American thinkers, including Thomas Mann, Archibald MacLeish, Lewis Mumford, and Charles Beard, appeared on the cover of *The New Republic*'s twenty-fifth anniversary edition, to which each had contributed. Kilpatrick's contribution, under the title "The Promise of Education," addressed the differences between democratic and totalitarian education. The primary distinctions had to do with three elements: the individual, innovation, and indoctrination. In Kilpatrick's estimation, society needed much more of the first two and very little of the third. Twentieth-century society was still following eighteenth- and nineteenth-century dogmas, and he quoted, in admonishment, Voltaire's dictum that "men will continue to commit atrocities as long as they believe in absurdities." Interdependence was contrasted with dependence, and absolutist thinking with the free play of intelligence. On the topic of education, he returned to his familiar themes of personality development, socially useful work, acting on thinking, and the need to build social intelligence. The article was illustrated with positive educational examples, such as rural and urban progressive schools that solved community-based problems as part of their curriculum. Kilpatrick concluded the piece with a prediction and an endorsement of the new education: "If our democracy is headed for neither social chaos nor native fascism, we still need a program, and this remains the best if not the only one."[11]

During this period, Kilpatrick also began to offer advice, in a limited way, on child-rearing practices. In an article titled "My Child as a Person," Kilpatrick explored the meaning of the phrase "becoming a person" and included in his concept of personhood a consideration of the child's thought processes. While at times verbose and indirect in his counsel, Kilpatrick made it clear that he viewed parent's efforts to suppress children, especially in curbing the number of experiences or the kinds of questions permitted, as counter-

productive. What, then, is the role of parents? It is to provide ancillary support and measured guidance. "You can directly hurt, but only indirectly can you help," Kilpatrick wrote. Growth was given as the chief aim in the educative process, but terms such as "responsibility" and "stability" also made their way into the discussion. Kilpatrick closed the article by noting that traditional schools "largely disregard and even oppose what is here advocated."[12]

Some of Kilpatrick's "advisory" talks included vignettes of occurrences he had witnessed and then woven into his presentations. In a radio talk, he reproved a mother he had heard on a train; she had told her child that if he didn't stop crying, the conductor would stop the train and put him off. "I wondered," said Kilpatrick, "whether that child would probably grow up to be truthful and I thought not." Sometimes he overgeneralized, as when he said, "Show me a spoiled child and somewhere I will show you a father or a mother or an aunt or uncle or grandparent responsible for spoiling the child." He went on, in this instance, to admonish adults to "deny the child what it should not have the first time it demands it." In an article on the misuses of punishment, Kilpatrick made an example of a wise aunt who had dealt creatively with a nephew who had a propensity for throwing temper tantrums. He suggested that self-control, honesty, industry, and truthfulness be reinforced through habit-building devices. Punishment or success, he felt, had to be internalized for any true growth to take place. Kilpatrick also pointed out that, owing to the strength of association in learning, children might end up disliking the punisher more than the act they were being punished for.[13]

To Kilpatrick, the most repugnant tool being utilized by parents or practitioners of the old education was testing. The tests themselves assessed only the "more mechanical school learnings which are the easiest to test." As for the finer and more significant experiences of schooling, such as appreciation of music and literature and such moral qualities as thoughtfulness, responsibility, and persistence, these tests were of little value. Kilpatrick admitted that tests might have a valid diagnostic purpose, but only when used wisely. The New York state Regents examinations, he felt, were harmful because they "fixed attention back at examinations instead of working intelligently at present problems." Report cards should be used only in exceptional cases to inform the parent of a specific problem, he added. Once, when he was asked about the Regents tests, he indicated that each teacher should, of course, make up his or her own mind on educational issues. But in his opinion, only one month should be spent preparing for the examinations; the other eight months of the school year should be devoted to what the students and teacher thought worth

studying.[14] Kilpatrick's antipathy toward testing was virtually unbounded. When the principal of the Horace Mann School, Dr. Rollo G. Reynolds, called those who made use of intelligence tests "test-crazy psychologists," Kilpatrick concurred. Once again calling for an education that was more inclusive, rather than solely intellectual, he stated:

> The labeling of students as dull and bright has done a great deal of harm by making one group feel inferior and the other conceited. The belief in the magic of intelligence tests rests upon a false analogy between natural science and psychology. The whole may be the sum of its parts, but a personality is more than a composition of legs and arms. This the intelligence testers have failed to realize.[15]

In the late 1930s Kilpatrick slightly recast his theory of learning; his new keynote was the phrase, "We learn what we live, then live what we have learned." This dictum was built on the idea that learning could take place only when the individual accepted and acted on what he or she experienced. Each new experience permeated and remade previous experiences — a concept derived from Dewey's "reconstruction of experience." For Kilpatrick, though, new experiences were not merely an addition to an individual's life but became unique events, events unto themselves. He also strongly believed that the human organism acted as a unified whole, that its physical, psychological, and aesthetic facets often performed in concert. Accordingly, he subscribed to Kant's rule that each person must be treated as an end, not a means. It became imperative, then, to allow children to act with as much autonomy as parents and teachers could "morally" permit. Democratic ethics were also part and parcel of this learning process, with each student permitted to strive for the highest attainment in life and growth.[16]

The active component of learning was essential to any theory Kilpatrick espoused. He quoted Dewey, who said that thinking was an adventure into the unknown. At times, Kilpatrick provided serviceable suggestions for teachers, even those at the college level. At a conference in North Carolina on teaching, soon after his retirement, Kilpatrick spoke of the need for students to be connected concretely to the subject under study. Their work, he felt, should be neither too difficult nor overly simple, but should afford all of them the opportunity to make significant contributions to others. Courses should be developed internally, directed by the focus and interest of the class. Using the

now familiar adage that teachers teach students, not subject matter, Kilpatrick categorically condemned using laboratory manuals and teaching history chronologically. Specific practices came in for harsh rebuke: "Grades are unfair measurements of a student's ability. One cannot measure another's friendship by 'A' or '94,' neither can he determine another's knowledge with any accuracy." He also rejected required college entrance examinations, calling for their abolition: "I do not believe in examinations for they distract attention from education."[17]

He also offered counsel to teachers. For approximately five years after his retirement, Kilpatrick traveled extensively for the Progressive Education Association, giving talks, leading workshops, and espousing the progressive gospel. His scrapbooks contain a plethora of newspaper clippings from his numerous stops across the country. He visited the urban centers — of Saint Louis, Philadelphia, and Chicago — as well as outposts in Nebraska, Wyoming, and the rural South. Photographs from newspapers, usually taken with local school leaders, dignitaries, and children, are found in great number in Kilpatrick's scrapbooks. Reporters were almost always granted interviews. Though frequently overwhelmed by the argot of educators, these journalists provided their readers with direct quotations from Columbia's former resident philosopher of education:

> A school is a place of living, and our aim should be to make sure that living is as fine, as efficient and as moral as we can. We must work, therefore, on the child's inner attitudes by supplying favorable and stimulating influence, and by positive guidance. But this does not mean the teacher should stand idly by, smiling, hoping and praying that it will turn out all right. The teacher must work more and harder than ever before — but indirectly.[18]

On a trip to Oregon in 1940, Kilpatrick lashed out against prohibiting married women from teaching (adding that married women have wider experiences with children than many men) and said that sex education programs should be instituted whenever children begin to raise questions on the topic. On the same trip he proposed doing away with textbooks and workbooks, abolishing report cards (they teach the pupil to cheat), and making much less use of paper-and-pencil activities. And what he termed "newer reference books" should replace traditional textbooks.[19] Kilpatrick always

entertained questions from the audience. When asked how he knew his psychology of learning was the best, he responded that he didn't, but it was better than any of the alternatives currently available. Only by persistent testing could the process be affirmed. Not everyone was impressed by Kilpatrick. A letter to the editor written by a critic soon after Kilpatrick had left one town, charged that "gullible" teachers were being taken advantage of financially by being asked to pay a fee to the Progressive Education Association and then placed in study groups to be "indoctrinated with the progressive gospel."[20]

Even the topic of "baby talk" merited an opinion from Kilpatrick. During his stint teaching at Stanford in the summer of 1938, he discouraged parents' use of "baby talk" in communicating with their children. "Exact language helps exact thinking," he told a meeting of the Conference of the Early Childhood Education Association. The next day the *San Francisco Chronicle* supported Kilpatrick in an editorial, "Whose Itty Bitty is Oo?" It concluded, "Dr. Kilpatrick has struck a blow for the rights of the helpless young that deserves to be heard round the world." There is little doubt that Kilpatrick was a champion of children. "Children show an astonishing ability to be mistreated without being ruined," he stated at one conference in the late 1930s, "but it is dangerous to go on mistreating them." The mental hygiene of the young — the personality — was paramount: "It is vastly more important than spelling, or grammar or subject matter standards." In a letter to the journal *Progressive Education* Kilpatrick endorsed the pamphlet "Teaching Reading" because its thesis was that reading skills develop best in a well-planned scheme of day-by-day living and that the scheme worked well for students at all levels of ability.[21]

During this same period Kilpatrick's thought moved beyond elementary schools, where his ideas had had their greatest impact, to the high school. In 1936 he suggested eliminating departments and instead assigning secondary students to a single teacher. Obliterating subject divisions would give students a greater opportunity to examine what he called "life process subjects." Although he did not consider specialization to be an important need for either children or adults, he did acknowledge that in some circumstances such distinct subjects and departmentalization might be permitted. As unemployment continued throughout the 1930s, striking the older adolescent population especially hard, Kilpatrick called for an extension of the secondary school system. "This is our greatest blot," he said: "I am afraid we are going to ruin several million children before we learn what to do with them and what to do for them."[22]

In an editorial written in 1940 for *The High School Journal*, Kilpatrick

decried the fact that over 3,500 boys had run away from home in 1939 in New York City, with 90 percent of them giving school as their reason for fleeing. He proposed that men and women choose to enter the teaching profession more for their love of children than for their affinity with a particular subject matter. Kilpatrick was not surprised that, emerging as they did from college settings where professors "have little or no knowledge of education or sympathy with it," teachers became enamored with their subject matter to the detriment of the child. In another article on this topic, Kilpatrick stipulated that changes in the secondary school be made only with thorough study and experimentation. He believed that the alarming dropout rate was due to strict organization of subject matter that failed to engage students in the practical problems of life.[23]

Kilpatrick did, on occasion, blame the schools themselves for some of the ills befalling students. At a meeting of New York City principals, Kilpatrick charged that teachers did not treat pupils as personalities, helping them to interact with each other and grow into socially cooperative persons. Even the teachers' tones of voice conveyed the impression that they did not want students to reason together with them — rather, the teacher wanted to "lay the law down." Their pupils would become autocrats themselves, he warned, "learning rebellion and to hate school and books." Adding that such practices were taking place in at least two-thirds of the city's schools, Kilpatrick called on educators to build quickly a "social antidote against the autocratic forces which make fascism."[24] These frank comments came back to haunt Kilpatrick almost immediately after he made them. He had been unaware that there were reporters in the audience and his remarks became headline news. (This was one danger of attempting to be supportive of schools while serving as an "in-house critic.") His comments sounded harsher than he wished, though there were a number of principals who communicated their appreciation to him for raising the issue. Actually, five years later — in 1941 — he would give a very favorable review of the city schools. In an editorial in *Frontiers of Democracy*, "Better Teaching of Democracy," he boasted that the activity program, adopted by seventy local schools, had been recommended for extension throughout the entire system. The *New York Times* reported that pupils in the activity schools excelled in cooperation, self-confidence, creative ability, self-discipline, and scientific outlook. Such a report encouraged Kilpatrick to exhort all teachers to practice democracy in their schools and classrooms.[25]

Although the rudiments of Kilpatrick's philosophy of higher education had been established at Bennington College, on occasion he would make further suggestions. In 1937 he predicted that eventually all students would, after high

school, attend two-year junior colleges and would most likely go on to additional collegiate education. At the time, a few high schools and junior colleges had linked themselves physically, providing a continuous four-year educational experience. Kilpatrick also recommended that colleges be kept smaller, so that the faculty and administration could know each student.[26] During World War II, Kilpatrick elaborated on his ideas about higher education. In "The Proper Work of the Liberal Arts College" he stressed the need for more seminars and fewer lectures, an adviser for each student, an advisory committee for every 250 students, and greater freedom of choice by students in formulating the curriculum. He encouraged unique courses throughout the curriculum — no two alike. Seminars should devote themselves to the personal problems of students, a more social and scientific outlook, and the development of a philosophy of life. The college major, while being "semi-vocational or pre-professional," should above all simply reflect a predominant interest of the student.[27]

In 1948, Kilpatrick provided greater detail about his thoughts on instruction in higher education, in his article "Securing Better College Teaching." He began his critique of college teaching and general education requirements by noting that much of the "inert information" taught is "soon forgotten." An emphasis on research and publication in the professors' graduate education, with little or no attention to teaching, was the cause for much poor instruction and insufficient learning. Quoting a college president, Kilpatrick noted that, with the G.I. Bill, more mature students with an unusually wide variety of experiences were entering the halls of higher education. What had been considered an adequate education for the traditional undergraduate student no longer sufficed. The development of character and personality, of course, headed the list of what he considered an appropriate general education, but he also added health, intelligence, moral responsibility, and a personal philosophy of life. As for how general education was to be taught, he suggested that it be done experientially so as to involve active citizenship and a positive reconstruction of personal life. He concluded by proposing the establishment of a new graduate-level school to prepare college instructors, much as teachers' colleges prepared elementary and secondary teachers for the nation's public schools.[28]

In 1939 Kilpatrick and John Dewey jointly agreed to prepare a new edition of William James's *Talks to Teachers* (originally published in 1899). Other than Kilpatrick's contributions to *Democracy and Education* and their work on *The Educational Frontier*, this would be the only time the master and his disciple collaborated on a publication. They wrote a new introduction, in which they

said that because this short work held so much truth, expressed in such clear and vigorous language, "we who knew it when it first came out are not willing that it should stand unused on library shelves." While dissenting with James on a number of points, Dewey and Kilpatrick both considered the original book a seminal contribution to the education of teachers. Dewey and Kilpatrick found a new psychology in the pages of *Talks to Teachers*, despite James's earlier disavowal of such an intention. They acknowledged James's emphasis on active learning, the unity of the physical and mental elements of the individual, and a sound approach to "behaviorism." There was also agreement with James's objection to "making things interesting," which was criticized as soft pedagogy. And yet there were also a number of elements in *Talks to Teachers* with which Dewey and Kilpatrick disagreed. For example, they were unwilling to concede that school would necessarily be dull and repulsive, with an attendant need for external incentives such as marks and prizes.[29]

In the social and political arena, Kilpatrick developed a unique definition of democracy for progressive educators in the classroom. In an address to the Progressive Education Association in 1937 — "What Can Education Contribute to Democratic Living?" — Kilpatrick warned of the dangers of class struggle and the possibility of a Hitlerian youth movement in the United States. "American education must renounce its own autocracy," warned Kilpatrick, "if it expects to teach democracy to others." This statement was no doubt aimed at the dogmatism, in both belief and behavior, that he observed in administrators and many classroom teachers. He believed that the "downtrodden schoolma'm" should be given a new, higher status in a more democratic school setting. Teachers should share in the making of policies, and when they arrived at the top of their profession, they should be compensated equally with principals. As for superintendents, most whom were directly elected at the time, Kilpatrick called for indirect election by teachers and school boards jointly, to give teachers a greater say in their governance.[30]

In 1940, a collection of Kilpatrick's writings appeared under the title *Group Education for a Democracy*. In his introduction, Kilpatrick wrote that it was intended for those involved in working with "teen-age young people." The book's purpose was to bring parents, teachers, and youth workers closer together. Democracy was its theme: it looked toward equality of opportunity and the development of individuals capable of managing their personal and social lives. One of the articles reprinted here was "Watchman, What of the Night?" from *The Social Frontier*, 1939; it warned against using undemocratic means to bring about democratic ends. In this article, Kilpatrick criticized the impediment to

social progress for the masses brought about because the affluent class controlled the press, radio, motion pictures, and churches. He expresses his conviction that only by bringing more citizens into the dialogue could crucial changes be achieved. *Group Education for a Democracy* also included Kilpatrick's thoughts on two issues that received little attention prior to World War II — the environment and the status of women. He wrote of businesses that had laid forests bare, causing soil erosion and unjustly depriving future generations of essential natural resources. "They refused," he wrote passionately, "to include the unborn in their decisions."[31] As for women's rights, he again excoriated the practice of prohibiting female teachers to marry; this denied to half the teachers "an important part of healthy normal life." He declared:

> If the proposal were made to treat men so, the outraged cry of indignation would shake the very heavens. It would be an unwarrantable interference with the just rights of citizens. And so it would be, and so it is — to male or female — an immoral encroachment on life itself.[32]

Group Education for a Democracy received the reviews that were usual for Kilpatrick's works. Those within educational circles found much to laud: those outside were more critical. R. L. West, president of State Teachers College in Trenton, New Jersey, though, gave it a rather rigorous critique. While agreeing that the old education would not pass muster in modern society, West doubted that idealism was the path out of civilization's troubles. He also differed with Kilpatrick on the topic of interests, stating that "vital interests often develop from initial coercions." West did, nevertheless, agree that much hard thinking was needed to change the schools, which were inadequately funded and handicapped by competing voices in the public sector. Lawrence Hall, in *Progressive Education*, found the compilation helpful and the fact that the themes of articles were repetitive a strength, noting that Kilpatrick put "his whole philosophy in each thing he writes."[33]

Democratic citizenship was a recurrent theme of Kilpatrick's during the war years. Creative study was, in his opinion, essential to a democratic society in order to make people more intelligent regarding the issues confronting them. In his article "School Preparation for Democratic Citizenship," Kilpatrick pointed out that twentieth-century developments such as technological advances, labor unions, and large corporations had left laissez-faire economic doctrines bankrupt. "Interdependence gives a content to teach; the fact of rapid

change, coupled with democracy, tells us how to teach this content." Civics, he thought, had been taught on a structural rather than a functional basis, and institutions had been studied as static entities, rather than for their strengths and weaknesses. Controversial issues and current unsolved problems, he asserted, should become the curriculum, since students are motivated to learn when the subject matter is pertinent and meaningful and there is an appeal along socially approved lines. He did hold the rather puritanical view that on some topics the sexes might need to be separated, and he felt that meaningful activities might prove more difficult to implement in urban areas than in rural settings.[34]

During a visit to Georgia, Kilpatrick was interviewed by the *Atlanta Constitution* and called on to defend progressive education as he was espousing it. The reporter remarked that the phrase "good old days" set Kilpatrick's mind in motion. He reminded his interviewer that in Horace Mann's day fifty schools in Massachusetts had closed because teachers were run off by students. And in Boston in 1844 it was recorded that it took sixty-five beatings a day to maintain any kind of order. In contrast, Kilpatrick pointed to Omaha, Nebraska, as an example of a place where students' participation had reduced discipline cases to nine per day, out of a population of 4,000 students. "It isn't perfect," said Kilpatrick: "We cannot expect perfection in this world, but the new way is more lifelike."[35]

Another outstanding model for education outside the formal school structure which Kilpatrick found exemplary was camping. In what must be considered the most affirmative article written by Kilpatrick during this period, he heartily endorsed it. (Without its militaristic bent, he also thought that scouting could prove a positive experience.) Taking up his now familiar theme of "learning what we live," Kilpatrick stated "Hour for hour, a camp is often more educative than school because in it the children can better live what they are to learn." Not only were there activities such as swimming, boating, cooking, and becoming more familiar with nature through firsthand experiences, but campers and counselors were on the same side rather than being opposed to each other, as was often the case between student and teacher in the formal school setting. In fact, Kilpatrick believed that, because strong control was often extended in the home, the family setting itself made it difficult for children to emerge emotionally and morally in their own right. Camping, by contrast, provided an optimal opportunity for youngsters to interact with their peers with minimal "adult domination." Boyd Bode had, similarly, described the scout leader as an excellent metaphor for how teaching should ideally operate, since the scoutmaster is one "who leads his group into

a country familiar to himself but filled with adventure and wonderful opportunities for the moral and intellectual development of his followers."[36]

Contrasting the school and the camp, Kilpatrick wrote, "The good camp builds up decisions from within the group. Insofar as the conventional school is emotionally and morally miseducative, the well-run camp can be truly educative." He also noted how learning would lead to further activity: "Life is forever different because of having lived these enrichments. Books have richer content and life has different meanings. If the camp is wise, there is much opportunity for discussion and shared decisions. It is this sort of living democracy that best teaches democracy." With his own philosophical opposition to "subject matter set out in advance to be learned," he was pleased to find in the camp setting "no fixed-in-advance learnings to be achieved. The camp is free to be a place of real living and therefore a real educational institution as most schools are not." He concludes this synthesis of his educational theory with ideal practice in the world by celebrating the fact that youthful campers are able to "live in their hearts the kind of traits worthy to be fixed in habit and character."[37]

Another channel for the dissemination of Kilpatrick's ideas was his column in *The Social Frontier* and its successor, *Frontiers of Democracy*. "Professor Kilpatrick's Page" gave him a platform from which to address social, cultural, and political topics. Many of his columns touched on education, of course. One, for example, discussed the attempt by the President's Advisory Committee on Education to promote financial support to private and parochial schools. Kilpatrick's major concerns in his response were the democratic principle of free communication and a nondoctrinaire approach to issues. "The free play of intelligence is the very breath of democracy," he wrote. He also aimed a strong blast at President Roosevelt for his lack of "enthusiasm for the public schools." Personalizing his attack by alluding to FDR's private school background, Kilpatrick stated, "CCC camps, yes; American youth, yes; but public schools, no. The superior attitude, we may believe, still survives. Groton and Harvard mold too effectively." In another article in *The Social Frontier* — this one based on an address he had given at Teachers College — Kilpatrick discussed the significance of two of the six "underlying principles" the editors had suggested for the next four years. "All the wealth of all the people must support a program of education for all the people," he declared, and "actual equality of educational opportunity — equal as far as thought and money — can reasonably make it so."[38]

The economy in general concerned Kilpatrick and often served as food for thought in his page in *The Social Frontier*. In "Questions About the Stock

Market" he asked whether the so-called "psychological fluctuations" of the market were anything more than mere speculation, otherwise known as gambling. Kilpatrick found it unacceptable that such actions should be sanctioned and observed by children: "How far speculation is inherently tied up in business processes may well be a matter of discussion." In a companion article six months later, Kilpatrick attacked, in what might be his most frank and explosive language, the notion that the American people had to provide "confidence" to the business system, or it would not work properly, thereby causing the nation to suffer. Why should "this goddess of Confidence rule over us?" he asks. "As we study further the ways of this Confidence, we find her always in the company with that evil acclaimed bitch goddess Success, the two consorting together with speculators and money-changers and with everyone that seeketh not the good of man, but instead profits."

Walter Lippmann's economic ideas did not receive such harsh treatment from Kilpatrick, but they were nevertheless rigorously scrutinized in a review of the columnist's book *The Good Society*. Lippmann's mistake, according to Kilpatrick, was equating collectivism with absolutism and failing to honor the pragmatist's central tenet that no course of action could be declared ineffective until tried. Kilpatrick found the book's saving grace in Lippmann's criticism of "old guard" Republicanism and the evils of the old system. In the end though, Kilpatrick could not be persuaded that "excessive competition" might lead to anything other than further insecurity in the nation.[39]

This was a heady time for the journal *The Social Frontier*. William Gellerman, the provocative professor at Northwestern University who had championed Kilpatrick's retention at Teacher's College, published an emblematic essay in the November 1937 issue entitled "Tradition Be Damned." There seemed to be no end to news and controversy in education. The same issue reported that the schools of Spain were just beginning to reopen after the Civil War of 1936. On the domestic front, the state superintendent of public instruction in Indiana had recommended that teachers place emphasis on teaching patriotism, temperance, the Bible, and the Constitution. The Boston public schools had banned Shakespeare's *Merchant of Venice* in response to complaints that the character Shylock was offensive to Jews. And the archbishop of Cincinnati had called the city school system "counterfeit" and the state's collection of taxes for educational purposes "unjust." At the same time, the Detroit Teachers Association had spent over $750,000 in the past six years to meet the personal needs of the city's school children.[40]

In the spring of 1939 Kilpatrick confronted the growing menace of

Hitlerism and Nazism, and the results, both domestic and international, of fascism. He noted in *The Social Frontier* that anti-Semitism was a blight not only in Germany, but also in the United States. Using a letter sent to one of his Jewish friends as an example, Kilpatrick documented how narrow definitions of Americanism lead to racial hatred and stereotyping. He viewed an unthinking confusion of group and individual behavior as the core of the problem. In a simple yet highly effective indictment of such prejudice, Kilpatrick wrote:

> Any instance of bad conduct by a member of the majority group is ascribed to the individual, he is to blame. But any instance of bad conduct on the part of a member of a minority group is, for all who dislike that group, charged rather to the group than to the individual.[41]

Only a conscious and concerted effort by the schools to broaden the outlook and sympathies of the young could counteract the venom spewed forth by this type of thinking. The article also called for collective approaches to law and order and for greater democracy and planning through the dual ideals of liberty and security.[42]

As 1939 drew to a close, Kilpatrick, writing in *Frontiers of Democracy*, stated that the consensus of his colleagues was that the United States should keep out of the war. But the failure of the League of Nations, the growing interdependence of the world, and the grave threats to law and order on a global scale had given him pause. "It may be that we can render the world a greater service, by not passing by on the other side." Kilpatrick's ambivalence is obvious. He believed that his country could stay out of the conflict, but should nevertheless play a part in reconstructing peace and order afterward. Kilpatrick's message was not isolationist in tone, but was within the mainstream thought of the time: even Roosevelt was suggesting that America could remain out of the armed struggle in Europe.[43]

Attendant issues arose in connection with the war, and one of the first was alleged "un-American activities." Congressman Martin Dies of Texas had been appointed chair of the House of Representatives' Committee on Un-American Activities (which preceded Joseph McCarthy's infamous Senate committee by more than a decade). Kilpatrick immediately questioned its purpose and methods. "It was un-American *activities*, not un-American *opinions*" the committee was charged to investigate, he pointed out in his column. The committee's actions, according to Kilpatrick, violated democratic principles, sowed dissension among groups, and questioned the allegiance of many loyal

Americans. Public "smearing" of individuals with the "taint of Communism" and denying them the opportunity to deny or explain the charges against them were unwarranted. "We cannot expect undemocratic means to produce democratic results," concluded Kilpatrick, adding that most "un-American practices have their root in economic distress and inequalities."[44]

In the end, Kilpatrick's estimation of the Dies Committee proved correct. Charging that the New Deal was communistic, Congressman Dies failed to notice the activities of a number of right-wing groups who were attempting to intimidate Congress, including Father Coughlin's Crusaders, the Citizens' Protective League, and the German-American Bund. The same month that his editorial against the Dies Committee appeared, Kilpatrick joined seventy-five other educators, authors, and artists — members of the Committee for Cultural Freedom — to protest the committee's inability to distinguish between "subversive activity and honest, open criticism." The signatories of the petition included Frederick Lewis Allen, John Dewey, Elmer Davis, Arthur M. Schlesinger Sr., and Norman Thomas. The following year, Kilpatrick wrote a similar editorial about a committee in the New York State Assembly — the Rapp-Coudert Committee — that was investigating subversive activities and connections with the Communist Party.[45]

Kilpatrick employed *Frontiers of Democracy* to promote a liberal agenda in economics, politics, and education. In an editorial that asked, "What Is Holding Us Back?" Kilpatrick, using a wartime metaphor, wrote that a convoy was only as fast as the rate of its slowest boat. The past decade of thinking on social, economic, and political issues should not, he felt, be curbed by reactionaries who hated Roosevelt. He accused T. S. Eliot in literature, Robert Hutchins and Mortimer Adler in education, and the *Saturday Evening Post* in journalism of shutting their eyes to reason and harking back to "various mystical authorities." Although sympathetic to Roosevelt during the Depression, Kilpatrick had voted for Norman Thomas in 1932 — wishing a more liberal program on the domestic front. But by 1940 Kilpatrick gave his full backing to Roosevelt's bid for a third term. In writing an editorial for *Frontiers of Democracy* titled "The Election: What Is at Issue?" Kilpatrick threw the journal's support to the incumbent, explaining that, while Wendell Willkie was committed to the democratic process and had a "certain attractiveness" as a candidate, Roosevelt was a "symbol of the most determined effort America has yet made to reconstruct our business system in the interest of the common good and democratic fair play." Speaking for the editors, Kilpatrick said that Roosevelt's reelection would give energy and hope to the

youth of America. In a piece appearing in the same issue under his own signature, Kilpatrick echoed his justification of an earlier war; he wrote that the conflict now raging was "not simply a struggle between nations to see which shall win. It is a struggle over civilization itself."[46]

"The heart of the educative process is the self-other process at work building personality, or selfhood, within the social milieu," Kilpatrick wrote in 1941, in his book, *Selfhood and Civilization: A Study of the Self-Other Process*. This major work grew out of the V. Everit Macy Lectures — "Self, Freedom, and Individuality" — which he had delivered at Teachers College in 1938, a year after his forced retirement. He spent the next three years refashioning and expanding these original lectures into a 250-page volume. "It comes pretty close to disclosing my philosophy without being exactly an exposition of it," he wrote in his diary, upon the book's completion.[47] In his introduction Kilpatrick paid homage to J. Mark Baldwin and George Herbert Mead — with, of course, acknowledgment of John Dewey's writings on ethics. But in his preparation for the lectures and the book, Kilpatrick had also read works by a variety of anthropologists and sociologists and a number of psychologists, including J. B. Watson, William James, and Jean Piaget. Kilpatrick had previously referred to the self (*ego*) and other (*socius*) in his *Remaking the Curriculum*, and it had been a topic of discussion in his classes. In a rare moment of intellectual uncertainty, he had experienced deep reservations about his mastery of this subject matter. When he was developing the lectures, he had noted in his diary, "I begin to fear that I have bit off more than I can chew." In the midst of delivering the lectures he admitted, "the subject is too abstruse and the contribution too slight."[48] A year after the publication of *Selfhood and Civilization*, Kilpatrick considered the book a "failure" in terms of sales.

Critics have charged that Kilpatrick moved from an emphasis on the individual during his early career, into the mainstream of the social reconstructionist movement in the 1930s, and then back to his original child-centered views as the Depression faded. But this analysis may be too simple. Kilpatrick's thesis in *Selfhood and Civilization* is that "human personality, in any desirable sense, is inherently a social product." Human beings, as he saw it, developed through a process of social maturation in stages and degrees, and this could occur only within a social milieu and a particular cultural context. It is this amalgamation of primary and vicarious experiences from which the concept of self-other emerges. This concept does not necessarily or absolutely support the child's self-concept. Kilpatrick, although he was alleged to be a Rousseauean, offered little sympathy here for the idea of the child as inherently

good: "Some children build a pathological self-centeredness. Few things are more annoying, or more hurtful to healthy growth, than this maladjustment in its worst forms."[49] The ideal outcome of the self-other concept occurs, he avows, when children view themselves as others, allowing for the critical use of experience in their own lives.

A secondary theme developed in *Selfhood and Civilization* is the way in which language and culture enable individuals to realize their full potential. The title of the book differed from the original lectures because Kilpatrick now viewed selfhood, language, and culture as the three factors that interacted to create what we know as civilization. For Kilpatrick, the central phases of the self-other process — agency, accountability, self-consciousness, and self-direction — were also central to progressive education, as exemplified by the activity program and the project method. Activity, language development, communication, and cooperation were all revealed to be directly associated with the self-other process.[50] A convergence of activity and thinking was Kilpatrick's goal, and no doubt his ideal. The same was true of the joining of selfhood and civilization. Whether such a state may be permanently reached is, of course, problematic — hence the pragmatists' concept of an "open-ended future." But Kilpatrick clearly saw culture, through reason and intelligence, moving in a positive direction.

In his discussion of moral development, the self and the other had partitions between their internal and external dimensions. Thus, a moral conflict, as defined by Kilpatrick, occurred when the "internal self" struggled against the demands of the "internal other." The much criticized educational approach to moral development known as "values clarification" may have had its genesis in this work. Kilpatrick suggested and partially endorsed choices freely made, consciously acted upon, and willingly acknowledged. His only reservation was that moral acts must be based on a concept of the "good life." The good life, a theme he would develop over the coming decade, was based on ethical character, service to humanity, nobility of outlook, and sensitive discrimination. Kilpatrick provided personal models, including Plato, Spinoza, Kant, Locke, Lincoln, Florence Nightingale, and Jane Addams, but admitted that few people attained such high levels of moral development.[51]

Kilpatrick moved from his discussion of the individual in *Selfhood and Civilization* to a discussion of culture. Defining "intelligence" as cumulatively acquired cultural wisdom and "culture" as communicable intelligence, Kilpatrick gave his strong approval to national and international forms of law and order. He endorsed a neo-Rousseauean view of perfectibility as "still within

limits a valid possibility." Whereas William James had said that old-fogeyism begins at twenty-five, Kilpatrick took it a step further and noted that of all conservatives, children are the most consistent. He refused to believe in any inherent racial differences between Caucasians (whites), African-Americans (Negroes, in his nomenclature), Jews, and Germans, pointing to culture, not innate biologically transmitted differences, as the basis for behavioral variations. Although *Selfhood and Civilization* was written prior to America's entry into the Second World War, Kilpatrick was aware to some extent of the Nazi's treatment of the Jews, calling it "outrageous beyond words."[52]

Kilpatrick next traced the emergence of cultures through language and thought. According to his model, after the Greeks had developed new methods of inquiry, civilization waited 2,000 years before its next significant advance, when Galileo brought forth the experimental method of modern science. Darwin and Einstein had then extended that process during the nineteenth and twentieth centuries. From these roots, Kilpatrick's pragmatic definition of selfhood grew. It included: (1) moral consideration of and respect for others on the basis of equal and just treatment, a concept from which modern democracy is derived; (2) ability to engage in self-conscious criticism of self and culture; and (3) acceptance of tested experience as the final authority of thought and action. "Only a self built on these principles," wrote Kilpatrick, "can constitute the type of individuality that we of the modern world are willing to accept." The rapidity with which modern scientific and cultural advances had been made in the past three centuries could be directly attributed, according to Kilpatrick, to the working of these suppositions. The progress made by the natural and biological sciences should next be applied to the social sciences. And to what purpose? To the development of personality — the "sanctity of the human personality," grounded in ethics, the Hebraic-Christian outlook, and democracy.[53]

In order to develop the self-other process as a means to a more complete understanding of selfhood, Kilpatrick used Piaget's *Moral Judgment of Children* to demonstrate the importance of experiences and interactions in the lives of students. He noted his surprise at the immaturity of the young subjects in Piaget's study, implying that a sheltered cultural background had impeded their development. All experience, for Kilpatrick, ultimately led not to absolutes, but to intelligent objectivity — an ability to confront novel situations successfully. All thought must submit to testing as the final authority, "or I renounce human effort, or I am insane." All ideas are to be tried in this way, even democracy, even the scientific method.[54]

Kilpatrick devoted considerable space to the implications of the self-other process for learning. During his first ten years at Teachers College he had been an unabashed Thorndikean, and he had based the psychology of his *Foundations of Method* on the S-R bond theory. Later, totally disenchanted with Thorndike's emphasis on measurement, he became equally disillusioned with his colleague's learning theory. In the 1920s, Kilpatrick had begun to explore the concepts of habit and conscious action, noting that the "atomistic S-R bond people had overlooked much in this field." Yet *Selfhood and Civilization* assailed, not Thorndikean psychology, but rather behaviorism, for attempting to reduce higher human traits to baser ones. While admitting that even S-R bonds could make a contribution, Kilpatrick remained repulsed by the reduction of psychology to physiology. Educationally, in Kilpatrick's opinion, behaviorism shifted attention away from the child to an overemphasis on subject matter, drills, and tests. With J. B. Watson in mind, Kilpatrick wrote that "psychological reduction has much to answer for." Branding Watson's behaviorism as "mechanistic and subhuman," Kilpatrick subscribed to what he called the "Darwin-James-Dewey" line of psychological development, which closely paralleled gestalt psychology, but without its "lumbering terminology."[55]

There is no doubt that with *Selfhood and Civilization*, Kilpatrick completely broke away from Thorndikean S-R bonding in favor of the gestalt approach to learning and thinking. (Goodwin Watson had suggested the connection between Dewey's philosophy of education and gestalt psychology a decade before.) Kilpatrick described his own approach as a more humane psychology based on components which included the moral, the aesthetic, and respect for the personality of each individual. Dewey's suggestion that "thinking is often and essentially dramatic rehearsal" had influenced Kilpatrick's depiction of an ongoing dialogue between internal self and internal other. Kilpatrick also presented a psychological hierarchy, albeit incomplete and rudimentary, beginning with intelligent purposing, critical thinking, and artistic creation, and culminating with moral conduct.[56]

Returning to morality, Kilpatrick stated his conviction that individuals are originally amoral and gain moral qualities — either good or bad — through the inevitable working out of the self-other process. There is, of course, no assurance that an individual will always choose the morally good deed — nor did Kilpatrick define what might constitute such an action. He did state that the "intelligent self-conscious organism" would, in the long term, work toward democracy, though even democracy can be destroyed in a world with no absolutes. And he firmly believed that only democracy could facilitate justice

and peace. Ethical principles emerged but were always based on the process of conscious criticism and consistency. Almost a decade after the controversy over "indoctrination for democracy," he was still incapable of endorsing the use of undemocratic means to teach democracy: "Specifically democracy can hardly if at all be taught in an undemocratic way. It must be taught in the spirit of democracy or the results are dangerous."[57]

The issues addressed up to this point in *Selfhood and Civilization* served as a prologue for Kilpatrick's discussion of the education milieu, in which he argued that it was the self-other process that assisted and supported children as they observed and examined their environment and made decisions in their daily life. The internal development of self was, in a sense, an independent process enhanced by an increase in self-worth, with teachers and parents providing security for the learner. "The better the child can feel both the self and other inherently checked by the conditions, the more inherent and binding does he feel the standards to be." For Kilpatrick, personality adjustment and character building were always at the core of the educational process, and here he ascribed a strong element of "fixedness" to character development, quoting Dewey's concept of habit: "In actuality each habit operates all the time of waking life."[58] Kilpatrick's model of the development of character on an experiential basis was the Hegelian approach, in which the self is remade after each experience — a balance between the abiding self and the proposed self. The educational key to such development, as Kilpatrick saw it, was for young people to have "abundant opportunities" to make decisions — always under wise guidance — in order to build a strong character, consisting of rational thinking and the habit of acting on rational thinking. Guidance could assist, but it could not and should not compel, and the rational could never outweigh the emotional.[59]

The concept of freedom in *Selfhood and Civilization* was also closely tied to character development, but the propositions put forth called more for amelioration than for radical transformation. Kilpatrick attacked prejudice and championed greater freedom of thought, but he did not censure institutions, as one might have expected. In fact, he suggested that they are necessary for building any good life. Surprisingly, in light of Kilpatrick's personal antipathy toward belief in the supernatural and toward formal religion, he praised Protestantism for encouraging individual freedom and for remaking institutions to meet the challenges of the new world. However, Kilpatrick's views on another institution, the press, were shaded by his antipathy toward the empire of William Randolph Hearst and its attacks on the "reds at Columbia

University." Leaving Hearst unnamed, he described the potential social harm that might be inflicted by unchecked freedom of the press, whose excesses were often rewarded by the economic system. However, he conceded that abridging the freedom of the press in any way would do greater harm in the end.[60]

Kilpatrick concluded *Selfhood and Civilization* with a review of the global political situation. The good life in a civilization, he maintained, was built upon a complex culture, safeguarded by law and order, and a belief on the part of the citizenry that progress was feasible. His strong emphasis on law and order certainly differed from the skepticism with which it had been traditionally viewed by liberals. However, this book, written just prior to Pearl Harbor, when the outcome of the European war was still uncertain, reflected the peril of the times. If Hitler won the war, Kilpatrick postulated, America would find no security other than living in an armed camp. Always convinced that the refusal of the United States to enter the League of Nations had been a moral lapse, he reminded his readers that the votes of ten men in 1920 might have made the world a much different place, and he gloomily hinted that civilization might wander in a wilderness of wars for the proverbial forty years. But a note of optimism prevailed as Kilpatrick pointed out that a structure for lasting peace must be built both internally and externally — in selfhood and in civilization — in the manner espoused in this volume.[61]

In a relatively recent review, "A Critical Analysis of *Selfhood and Civilization*," (1993) Regina Wilkes raised a number of salient points addressing the logical consistency of Kilpatrick's work. One was Kilpatrick's insistence that his approach was inductive in nature, when this is not, strictly speaking, his methodology. Wilkes observed that *Selfhood and Civilization* was "an explication of observable facts in a manner logically consistent with his own faith in rational, orderly processes and the self-other theory of personality development." Wilkes thus found what she saw as hasty conclusions and a failure to consider alternative inferences from the data he presented: "The conceptual or philosophical system has been preformulated, selected beforehand, not developed in a purely inductive fashion." In the political realm, Wilkes also noted a tendency toward ideological imperialism when Kilpatrick spoke of "natural tendencies toward democracy" and advocated industrialism by defining the good life almost exclusively in terms of western values. A variation of colonialism was also suggested by phrases such as "unmapped areas still benighted by superstition" and "qualitatively inferior civilizations" as opposed to "the better culture" and "more advanced societies . . . inhabited by right-minded people." All this, as Wilkes saw it, led to an apparent equivalence

between complexity and superiority.[62]   On this point, one is reminded that Kilpatrick had been disturbed by Gandhi's lack of pragmatism in wishing to return India to cottage industries.

At the time it was published, the critics uniformly saw *Selfhood and Civilization* as too generic, lacking depth and expertise in the numerous disciplines discussed. But this presumed weakness may actually have been the work's strength.[63]   Kilpatrick was at his best synthesizing and interpreting diverse disciplines in his role as philosopher. He could seize upon topics in psychology, anthropology, history, and sociology and use them to suggest new lines of thought on the global situation. (Norman Cousins, a former student, thought that Kilpatrick was a master at creating such connections.[64])   The seminal idea of the book may have been the self-other process, but the final work was a pragmatist's response to a world gone awry. Addressing both the individual and the culture, this volume might be considered an educator's first draft for reconstructing the postwar world. *Selfhood and Civilization*, therefore, is best viewed as a transitional work, pointing in a definite direction, noting landmarks along the way, but never fully describing the journey's final destination.

As the war neared its end, Kilpatrick's writings began to examine the need for a just and lasting peace. He had been disillusioned by the failure of the United States to align itself with Wilsonian idealism and the League of Nations a generation before, and he was now deeply committed to the cause of avoiding such errors a second time. In May of 1944, in *Educational Forum,* Kilpatrick wrote an article on "Education and Enduring Peace," arguing that peaceful reconstruction could proceed only when the new leaders of the defeated countries convened with professional educators to reach a consensus on what the schools would do. Kilpatrick also realized that economic prosperity and self-respect would need to be reestablished. On this latter point, he drew on his own experiences as a boy during Reconstruction in the South, noting that lack of self-respect "crystallized contrary attitudes," particularly attitudes about race. Mindful of the approach of postwar Reconstruction, Kilpatrick looked to history and to the monitory example of the Weimar Republic, which had been a breeding ground for rearmament and revenge. He also mentioned the internment of the Japanese Americans on the West Coast, calling it both a blemish and a break of a "Gentleman's Agreement."[65] This article once again demonstrated Kilpatrick's facility in integrating history, current events, and the educational world, making possible a coherent and constructive analysis of major world phenomena.

Kilpatrick's views on race will be examined in greater detail later (see Chapter 17), but it is important to note here that, during the war, he became involved in the Bureau for Intercultural Education, which focused on combating cultural intolerance and prejudice, and fostering better relations among Americans of all races, religions, and ethnic backgrounds. An announcement written by Kilpatrick stated the organization's intention: to address tension within society caused by "socially advantaged groups" that attempted to "retain their traditional domination over the folkways and wishes of the minority people." These conflicts were seen in the "practice of personal prejudice, social discrimination, in-group bigotry, out-group suspicion, and intergroup strained feeling which at times eventuates in violence." The goals of the bureau were to "immunize the younger generation from the divisive attitudes that burden adults" and to "integrate pupils of all cultural backgrounds into an intelligent, purposeful American society."

Kilpatrick served as chair of the bureau's board of directors and worked closely with the staff in producing books and workshops. One young staff member and teacher with whom Kilpatrick worked especially closely was William Van Til, who conducted a number of workshops on intercultural relations for teachers throughout New York City. Another former student of Kilpatrick's, Hilda Taba, was leading similar workshops at Harvard. Strategies of the bureau included using population figures to integrate mathematics with the study of intercultural relations and also examining achievements of different racial and cultural groups in order to build respect for diversity. According to the *New York Times*, the organization's budget for 1944 was $100,000.[66]

In the postwar era, Kilpatrick intensified his work with the Bureau for Intercultural Education. He visited schools where intercultural issues were being discussed and new teaching strategies were being employed. There were also visits to the intercultural education workshops sponsored by the bureau and led at the Lincoln School by William Van Til, who was now an employee of the organization. In the mid-1940s the John Dewey Society asked Kilpatrick to edit a yearbook on intercultural education. As director of publications for the bureau, Van Til became what he called the "legman" for the project, and he observed Kilpatrick's skill in matching the best intellects with gifted writers to create an excellent product for the John Dewey Society. Kilpatrick liked Van Til, calling him a good man, and believed that the book would be a solid contribution to the literature on the subject.[67] Van Til had taken a course from Kilpatrick in the 1930s and, on his first visit to the Morningside Drive apartment in 1945 had mentioned this fact by way of conversation. Kilpatrick

immediately left the room, returned, and "like a cat that had just finished off a bowl of cream," said to Van Til, "And you got a B+." As he worked week after week with Kilpatrick, Van Til described his mentor:

> I soon discovered that Kilpatrick tolerated rather than welcomed small talk. The man was innately courteous, dignified, formal, reserved, intent. His mind worked like a Swiss watch, precise, accurate, orderly. He raised the important questions, suggested good procedures as to problems, gave careful instructions.

When Van Til delivered the completed manuscript of the yearbook, ready for publication (by Harper Brothers), to the Morningside Heights apartment, the title page read "*Intercultural Attitudes in the Making*, Edited by William Heard Kilpatrick." After thumbing through the pages, Van Til rose and was on his way to the door when Kilpatrick stopped him. Years later Van Til recollected the conversation:

> "Mr. Van Til." (I was always Mr. Van Til to him.)
> Yes, Dr. Kilpatrick." (I would no more have called the Dalai Lama by his first name than call Dr. Kilpatrick Heard.)
> He said, "I want you to make a change on the title page. It is to read, 'Edited by William Heard Kilpatrick and William Van Til.'"
> I was thunderstruck. The 35-year-old legman had become the co-editor of *Intercultural Attitudes in the Making* with the eminent philosopher of education born six years after the end of the Civil War.
> "Thank you," I gasped.
> "If I make any other changes, I'll call you," he said. And the door closed.

Van Til also had a preview of the pressure that would emerge in the 1950s, during the McCarthy period. A group of supporters of the pro-Nazi, anti-Semitic Father Charles Coughlin met with Kilpatrick and the staff of the bureau over some educational materials the group found unacceptable. According to Van Til, Kilpatrick was subjected to a tirade filled with economic threats and thinly disguised abuse. After hearing the critics out, Kilpatrick reaffirmed the right of young people to use the educational materials, and their own intelligence

to make their own decisions. He courteously dismissed the censors by stating, "You have given me an insight into the sensibilities of some persons that I have not had before." The bureau continued to publish the materials.[68]

These numerous contributions to the educational literature of the day reveal that Kilpatrick was at the height of his scholarship, thought, and production from 1925 to 1950. The last five years of this period were largely devoted to what he hoped would be his magnum opus: *Philosophy of Education*, published in 1951. *Philosophy of Education* had only modest sales, although it did go into a limited second printing. And it received very few, if any reviews in the popular journals of opinion. Only those professional journals directly connected with progressive education undertook reviews, but these were uniformly and benignly complimentary.[69]

Philosophy of Education can best be described not as a revision but rather a reiteration and a reestablishment of the author's past positions and opinions. As with many aggregate works, the parts are greater than the whole, because of Kilpatrick's ponderous and sometimes tedious prose. However, *Philosophy of Education* is workmanlike in its construction, complete in its coverage of educational topics, and filled, of course, with quotations — mainly from Dewey.

This work begins by addressing the larger philosophical issues found in science, culture, and society. Kilpatrick then turns to the application of philosophy, discussing the educational process in areas such as learning, curriculum, and teaching. In the early chapters he confirms his conviction that education is a social process and underscores his belief that institutions must be malleable to meet the ever novel demands of society. Although he emphasizes the social process, he again disapproves of any school program whereby teachers plan and execute, by indoctrination, a new social order. He also repeats his rejection of psychological behaviorism, as he did in *Selfhood and Civilization*. There is little doubt, when one sets this book down, that democracy reigns supreme in Kilpatrick's heart and mind.[70]

What is most useful about *Philosophy of Education* is the compilation of Kilpatrick's thinking and the definitions provided for the terms he frequently used: personality, character, and education. For Kilpatrick, the development of character and personality was always paramount in a child's education, and character and personality were often interrelated in meaning and function. Although he interprets it broadly, Kilpatrick defines "character" as an inclusive term for what takes place in all aspects of the organism's behavior in relation to itself and its environment — the sum of one's tendencies toward regularized and

predictable behavior, including personality. "Personality," then, is seen as the self-conscious, self-directing self — how one thinks and feels about oneself, how one interacts with others, and what one values.[71] His definition for "education" is both personal and interpersonal:

> Education must aim at developing in the individual the best possible insight into life's problems as they successfully present themselves before him; at helping him to make ever finer distinctions in what he does, to take more and more considerations ever better into account, and finally to bring the best social-moral attitudes to bear on each decision as made and enacted. For the only proper aim of education is fullness of living through fully developed character.[72]

While this is an already highly comprehensive definition, Kilpatrick goes on to place education in an even broader context, viewing it as the development of both practical knowledge and attitudes, the ability to add richness to one's life, the capacity to develop positive control over one's thoughts, and finally, the fostering of an attitude of justice for others. All this demonstrates that Kilpatrick stood very much with John Ruskin, whom he quotes as saying, "Education does not mean teaching people what they do not know. It means teaching them to behave as they do not otherwise behave."

In addition, Kilpatrick provides a number of aphorisms that would become conventional wisdom for much of the world of education. These would include the teacher's need to "start where the learner is" academically and base as much education as possible on the student's experiences; and the obligation to attend to the concept of the "whole child." In terms of democracy, he stressed that even "the humblest may know of bearings missed by the more intelligent," a call for all voices to be heard in any democratic discussion.[73]

While much of *Philosophy of Education* could be perceived as armchair philosophizing with heavy doses of platitudes and warmed-over generalities, Kilpatrick did see a measurable difference between "the old education and the new education." And while he was consistently critical of testing, assessment, and measurement in relation to students and schools, he was willing in this work to draw on the most sophisticated longitudinal study of the time. The research he cited to support his lifelong commitment to progressive education was a comparative study of high school and college students during 1932–1940 that became known as the Eight Year Study; its formal title was *Adventure in*

American Education, and it filled five volumes. Wilford Aiken brought the entire work together in his book, *The Story of the Eight Year Study: With Conclusions and Recommendations* (1942). Kilpatrick was so taken up with this work that, as he noted in his diary, he was fined 55 cents for returning it late to the Columbia Library.[74]

The Eight Year Study encompassed thirty American high schools, which could be categorized along a spectrum from what Kilpatrick would pejoratively term "Alexandrian" or traditional, to progressive or experimental schools representing the "new education." Students from the experimental schools, without having the standard college preparation courses or credits, were given waivers to enter a college or university as if they had met the usual prerequisites. Each of these students was then matched with a counterpart from a traditional school — a student with a similar academic and socioeconomic profile. For example, the daughter of a dentist who attended a traditional high school, had a grade-point average of 97, and lived in a midsize midwestern suburb would be paired with a young woman of similar characteristics and background who attended a progressive school. These pairs were then followed through four years of high school and four years of higher education — the "eight years" of the study.

The results of this sophisticated research design (1,475 matched pairs took part in the study, at a cost of $700,000 in Depression-era dollars) generated data that the progressives, including Kilpatrick, saw as establishing their case against the "old education." The study found that the students who graduated from the six high schools most unlike the traditional schools had consistently higher academic averages and won more academic honors, were clearly superior in intangible intellectual traits — curiosity and drive — demonstrated willingness and ability to think logically and objectively, and had an active and vital interest in the world about them. They more frequently held democratic values and assumed shared responsibility. In addition, they were more cooperative, more tolerant, more self-directing, and less selfish in orientation.[75] In a talk at The Ohio State University in 1949, Kilpatrick listed these results and added that the only area in which the traditional group exceeded the experimental group was that greater numbers of traditional students joined the Y.M.C.A.

Kilpatrick's decision to close his magnum opus with a review of the Eight Year Study is striking. The results of this exhaustive longitudinal study, as he would continue to argue until the end of his life, confirmed the practice and substance of the new education. But his claim of victory has not gone unchallenged. Critics have suggested that the numerical differences separating the two

groups, although they did favor the experimental group, were not statistically significant, except for those schools categorized as highly experimental. Thus in effect the two groups had reached a "tie." Also, it has been noted that the experimental group had not followed, collectively or individually, any particular curricular pattern — other than what could be considered experimental as such. For some analysts, this made the results difficult to interpret. And for one critic, the findings spoke more about the control higher education had over the nation's high schools, in terms of entrance requirements, than it said about the value of educational progressivism.[76]

Still, some historians have agreed with Kilpatrick's assessment of the significance of the Eight Year Study for American education. A fairly recent review (1994) of the history of American curricula called the Eight Year Study "the most important and comprehensive curriculum experiment ever carried on in the United States." This review went on to conclude that the more experimental the school, the greater the success of students in college, and, conversely, that "college success did not depend on a prescribed sequence of subjects in high school." This second conclusion was an endorsement of Kilpatrick's long-held belief that "subject matter set in advance" was an unproductive means of reaching meaningful educational ends. More important, the Eight Year Study endorsed the idea — basic to Kilpatrick's thought — that it was possible for schools to develop educational programs that would engage students, meet educational needs, and at the same time provide the preparation needed to succeed in college."[77] In reconsidering the entire Eight Year Study fifty years after its completion, Craig Kridel saw the project as neither a myth, a monument, nor a forgotten remnant of American educational experience. He concluded that the project provided a way for schools to improve their programs through a collective process of thinking, experience, and experimentation without the artificial restrictions of administrative hierarchies or external authorities.[78] Such an aim succinctly describes Kilpatrick's message as expressed in his collective writings when he was at the height of his creative and intellectual powers.

THE BATTLE FOR THE SCHOOLS: PROGRESSIVISM, POLITICS, AND PASADENA

The battle for free schools, like the battle on other fronts, is moving from the cold to the hot stage.

Theodore Brameld, *The Nation*, October 27, 1951[1]

We are in an exceedingly difficult position. Each of us feels that our freedom is in jeopardy. We are threatened from without. I think we are threatened even more from within. I know of no better way to wreck everything that we think is good in America than to begin to destroy ourselves, one by one, institution by institution, community by community throughout the land.

Willard Goslin, 1950[2]

If we are ridden by fear, we lose faith in our fellow man — and that is the unforgivable sin.

John Dewey, at his ninetieth birthday celebration

A pantheon of progressive educators gathered on the stage of the Horace Mann Auditorium at Teachers College on November 10, 1947. The event was the presentation of the William Heard Kilpatrick Award for significant contribution to the philosophy of education. Present on the platform were the eighty-eight-year-old John Dewey; the award's namesake, William Heard Kilpatrick; and the recipient of the award, Boyd H. Bode. George S. Counts, who presided, told those present that few would have ever expected to hear "these three giants of educational thought" speaking from the same platform. R. Bruce Raup gave a brief statement, as did H. Gordon Hullfish, Bode's protégé at The Ohio State University.

Boyd Bode's personal thoughts on this occasion are unknown. But Bode, the "in-house critic" of progressive education, had proved himself ever ready to hurl cogent volleys of criticism into the camp of the child-centered wing of the

movement. (Later, while Bode was living in retirement in Florida, someone suggested that he and Kilpatrick have a "debate." Possibly he did not view Kilpatrick as his equal, but he refused on the grounds that he would take part in such a forum only if John Dewey were also present. The interchange was never to take place.[3]) To receive an award named after Kilpatrick himself, therefore, may have been more difficult for Bode than he let on during the ceremony. But he was gracious as always, speaking for forty minutes on democracy and education. This was followed with a few brief remarks by Dewey and then a fifteen-minute appraisal by Kilpatrick of Bode's contribution to educational thought. Dewey alluded to Bode's application of philosophy to life and his emphasis on freedom rooted in morals and intelligence. Kilpatrick was profuse in his praise of Bode, saying that Ohio State's School of Education was second to none as a result of Bode's influence, and crediting Bode and Hullfish with revealing Thorndike's failure to accord conscious choice and behavior a place in his psychology. The crowd that day lined the walls of the auditorium and spilled out the rear doors into the hallways. *Time* magazine reported on the occasion in an article entitled "Rebel," which described Dewey and Kilpatrick's eulogies and characterized Bode as a forgetful, agnostic, inflammatory gadfly, beloved by students. The article quoted Dewey as saying, "Whatever of mine goes through Bode, comes out different."[4]

Lawrence Cremin's history of progressive education gave the movement only ten more years of life after this event. In fact, such a gathering of the giants in educational progressivism did not occur again, and none of these men's disciples had the intellectual authority or personal popularity of the cadre that occupied center stage in Horace Mann Auditorium that day. Bode and Dewey were dead within five years. On the other hand, Counts and Hullfish continued their notable careers actively for many years more, with Counts making a foray into politics in the early 1950s. And Kilpatrick, aged seventy-six in 1947, seemed indefatigable; by the end of the decade he would begin to take part in a national controversy over politics, communism, and education. Joseph McCarthy did not officially begin his hunt for communists in government and the media until his 1950 speech in Wheeling, West Virginia. But for Kilpatrick, the acrimonious mixture of politics and education began earlier, on what appeared to be a benign, conventional trip to Pasadena, California, in 1949.

The postwar events in Kilpatrick's personal and professional life provided no indication that the Pasadena episode would become a *cause célèbre* for the mild-mannered educational philosopher, now more than a dozen years into his retirement. His marriage to Marion Ostrander had been a distinct success. On

their ninth anniversary in 1949 he wrote, "I am sure that few marriages have been more successful. We have both been happy in it, with remarkably few situations of stress or strain." Marion had resigned from Adelphi College in 1947 over a philosophical issue in the education program, and the following year she began teaching part-time at Hunter College, an assignment she continued until 1957. She was elected to the National Board of the Y.W.C.A. in 1948 and reelected in 1955 for a six-year term. Within the Kilpatricks' immediate family, his son-in-law, Ted Baumeister, had recently stepped down as head of Mechanical Engineering at Columbia. His grandsons, Ted III and Heard, were at Yale University and Columbia College respectively. The Baumeisters' daughter, Mary, a preschooler, was, according to Kilpatrick, "the chief charm of the household." In 1950, the Baumeisters purchased a hundred-year-old home on the most spectacular bluff of the Edisto River in South Carolina. Their five-acre piece of land held fifty-five live oaks with hanging Spanish moss. Kilpatrick visited the Rectory, later renamed the Parsonage, at Willtown Bluff in late 1952 and pronounced that "the live oak trees with their flowing Spanish moss are among the most impressive I have ever seen."[5]

As the years passed, Kilpatrick continued to revise his estimated life span each year, moving beyond the ages reached by both his immediate and his distant relatives. But his health did concern him. In 1947, the loss of a lifelong friend, the Reverend Ashby Jones, coupled with a persistent cold, made him feel mortal. And while he believed that his creative powers were as great as ever, his short-term memory slowly continued to decrease. Marion held a birthday party for him, celebrating his seventy-sixth year, with a dozen friends in attendance, including John Dewey, who entertained those present with nonstop conversation. Hormone and vitamin treatments seemed to arrest Kilpatrick's perceived physical and mental deterioration, and his weight rose from 140 pounds to 148. "These seem to give me a new lease on life," he wrote in his diary. A neighbor even commented that Kilpatrick, on foot, had beaten her back to their building while she rode in a car. On another occasion, a former student told Marion that her husband "looked ten years younger than he did ten years ago."[6]

In his professional life, Kilpatrick continued as president of the Urban League of Greater New York and chairman of the Bureau for Intercultural Education and American Youth for World Youth. In 1949 he became chairman of the John Dewey Society; in 1952 he accepted a position on the board of the New Lincoln School; and in the mid-1950s he became chairman of the League for Industrial Democracy (which caused him some internal conflict, due to his stand against teachers joining unions). He spent six weeks teaching at the

University of Minnesota during the summer of 1946, in what was to be his last lengthy stint in the classroom. His connections with Teachers College continued to be infrequent, although he did attempt to get Columbia's new president, Dwight Eisenhower, involved in John Dewey's ninetieth birthday celebration, and he attended Eisenhower's inauguration on October 12, 1948. Kilpatrick was impressed with both the content and the style of Eisenhower's address. A year later, according to Kilpatrick, at the presentation of an honorary doctorate to Jawaharlal Nehru, the prime minister of India, Eisenhower recognized Kilpatrick's name when it was mentioned, possibly from their consultations in connection with Dewey's birthday celebration.[7]

Kilpatrick was also called as a witness in a case at the state supreme court involving an attempt to save the experimental Lincoln School: Dean Russell and the Teachers College trustees wanted to close it. Testifying on behalf of the parents and students who desired to keep their school, Kilpatrick persuaded the judge to allow him to move beyond the attorney's questions to give a strong and coherent defense of experimental schools and the need for New York City to be a national leader in this area. The opposing counsel was so flabbergasted by the speech that the only question he asked of Kilpatrick before he left the stand was his age. Once again, though, Dean Russell prevailed and the school was closed.

Kilpatrick now took fewer trips, though he did go to southern California in early 1948 to lead a workshop on intercultural education. On this trip Kilpatrick saw Howard Hughes's "Spruce Goose" in Long Beach Harbor; and he also saw his first television set. He was impressed by the former but "cared little" for the latter. His encounters with celebrities and well-known politicians continued. Upon meeting Helen Keller, he recorded, paradoxically, that he "spoke" to her. He and Marion also heard Edward R. Murrow and David Sarnoff speak on several occasions. At one New York fund-raiser for two Jewish organizations he shared the dais with Raymond Massey, Jackie Robinson, and Gloria Swanson. In the political arena Kilpatrick was in the audience to hear President Truman, Chief Justice Earl Warren, and even the cartoonist Herbert Block.[8]

The domestic and international scenes were both fraught with danger in Kilpatrick's ever perceptive assessment of events. At home, strikes and inflation hit at the core of everyday life for Americans. The birth of Israel and the ensuing Arab-Israeli conflicts became a hotly debated issue in the Morningside Drive apartment. Kilpatrick was sympathetic with the Jews and their need for a homeland, while Marion saw merit in the Arabs' counterargument. One evening a visitor filibustered on the highly emotional topic for over an hour. In early 1949, after several such incidents, Kilpatrick noted that there were "echoes of the

conflict in our own home, so keenly did our Jewish and our Arab friends differ." The Soviet Union's behavior in eastern Europe and the fall of Czechoslovakia to communism deeply disturbed Kilpatrick. As for China, he had little sympathy for either Mao Tse-tung or Chiang Kai-shek, and when the communists later took control he called the situation "very discouraging." Kilpatrick's political views reflected postwar ideas about the Cold War, and his own continuing bias against communism.[9]

On the educational front, Kilpatrick was informed that his philosophy was being disseminated in several countries throughout the postwar world. A professor of comparative education involved in Japanese educational reconstruction related that his program was greatly influenced by Teachers College and specifically requested works by Kilpatrick in addition to those of Charles Beard and John Dewey. In California in 1948, Kilpatrick was told that his former student, Nishimoto, had drafted a document that closely mirrored the philosopher's educational thinking. Once Kilpatrick indicted postwar German secondary education, telling a group of visitors to Teachers College that "no one could learn a generalization from another person" — individuals had to make their own generalizations out of their own experience. In 1951, the *Report of the Royal Commission on Education in Ontario*, sent to Kilpatrick by Chief Director J. G. Althouse, noted the acceptance of Kilpatrick's ideas in the elementary school. The report stated that "the principles of the project or enterprise method should be utilized as far as possible in the elementary school."

Kilpatrick also received a communication that India was still stressing the project method, a quarter century after his visit there. And a former graduate told him that, whereas two decades earlier the new education had been ridiculed in England, twenty years later, four out of five books on education in Great Britain were written by Americans. Ernest Papanek's article in the *Jewish Forum* claimed that Kilpatrick's influence was recognized in France, Belgium, India, China, and the Canadian province of Saskatchewan. To acknowledge the high international esteem in which he was held, the organizers of the first International Humanist and Ethical Culture Conference, to be held in the Netherlands in July of 1952, invited Kilpatrick to serve as one of four vice-chairmen. He regretfully declined, citing the strain it would place on his health and finances, and his decision deeply troubled Marion, who viewed the invitation as a high honor.[10]

In the late 1940s Kilpatrick tilted with two intellectual titans of the time, Jacques Barzun of Columbia University and the British historian Arnold Toynbee. One night in 1947 Barzun was the guest of the Discussion Group on Higher

Education, a gathering Kilpatrick and Marion attended for several years after the war. Barzun held forth about his belief in intellectual values but negated the possibility of moral, social, or political values on the grounds that such proofs were impossible, given people's differing views. Two or three members of the group attempted to point out the fallacies in Barzun's thinking, but they were brushed aside. Kilpatrick was unable to "stand it any longer." Suspicious of Barzun's French education, he waded into the fray, raising the issues of character-building and habit. Barzun had no theory of learning, according to Kilpatrick, and was an "Alexandrian" in his thinking on education. Barzun admitted that, beyond teaching his students logic, he had no other concern for their moral or personal development. "I pushed him hard at that point, perhaps too hard for good manners, but I had the satisfaction that he left his patronizing condescension."[11]

Kilpatrick's exchange with Toynbee was less confrontational. Having known the historian since 1929, and being familiar with his works, Kilpatrick was of the opinion that Toynbee had missed something "which Dewey could have given him." Kilpatrick was impressed by Toynbee's brilliance and astonished to learn that he thought first in Greek and then translated his thoughts into English. But the historian's compulsion to weave theology throughout his works troubled Kilpatrick. "I think if he had thought through the self-other selfhood argument, he would conclude differently, or at least describe his conclusion differently," wrote Kilpatrick. "He comes pretty close to convincing me that he is hopeless. In fact, he seems to be playing with the idea of joining the Catholics."[12]

Toynbee and his wife lunched with the Kilpatricks in their Morningside Drive apartment in April of 1948. On the personal level, the meal was pleasant. Marion was as taken with the historian as her husband had been twenty years earlier. But after lunch Kilpatrick felt compelled to raise a point of contention. It dealt with Toynbee's notion that God was the principal authority in ethics — an idea that implicitly denied the possibility of inherent ethics and relegated the process of morality to authoritarianism. He went on to instruct Toynbee that the Greeks had not gotten their ethics from religion, nor had they endorsed the concept that the individual existed for society. "To preach such doctrine was to educate for the docility demanded by totalitarianism," Kilpatrick informed his guest. Surprisingly, Mrs. Toynbee agreed with her host, and, according to Kilpatrick, Toynbee himself was quite shaken by the exchange. Hearing Toynbee lecture at Columbia the next day, Margaret told her father that afterward Mrs. Toynbee had described the previous afternoon's discussion between the two men "a real set-to." Kilpatrick

himself had thoroughly enjoyed the interchange and looked forward to Toynbee's next visit to New York. Toynbee did visit New York again, but he never called at Morningside Drive.

Another visitor was Mainbel Gandhi, son of the Mahatma. He was part of a contingent of Indians who visited the Kilpatricks in 1949. Gandhi was the editor of *Indian Opinion*, a South African newspaper his father had founded, and was in New York City to cover events at the United Nations. The Kilpatricks immediately took to him. "Gandhi was to my mind the best mind and character of them all. We were quite pleased with him," he wrote.[13]

Kilpatrick continued to be active in the New York Liberal Party, and as the presidential election of 1948 approached, he followed the conventional wisdom of the time: though few held the Republican candidate Thomas Dewey in high regard, Harry Truman was weak, and the country was ready for change. Although Kilpatrick had voted Socialist at least once in his life, his leftward-leaning political proclivities did not take him into the camp of the ultraliberal candidate Henry Wallace, a former vice-president and secretary of agriculture. Ultimately, Kilpatrick — and Marion — voted for Truman. He also voted for Jacob Javits, the Republican congressman who was endorsed by the Liberal Party. While Kilpatrick believed the president would lose, he did not believe Dewey's margin of victory would be as large as the polls indicated. He was as shocked as the rest of the nation when Truman upset Dewey, fulfilling the incumbent's prediction that the "pollsters' faces would be red on the day after the election." While he thought Truman "no great man," Kilpatrick believed Truman's advisors were superior to Dewey's and rejoiced in the fact that the voice of the people had been heard.[14]

It was after the election that Kilpatrick next became involved in one of the most celebrated episodes in the history of postwar American education. Although he was not the sole cause of Willard Goslin's departure from the super-intendency of the Pasadena schools, Kilpatrick's very presence added to the furor and brought him face to face with the decidedly ugly nature of an emerging polit-ical force in American life: McCarthyism, named of course, for Wisconsin's junior senator, Joseph McCarthy. Heightened tension on the international scene had led to ever increasing domestic turmoil over the issues of communism, loyalty, and foreign espionage. Soviet expansion in eastern Europe, the Chinese communists' victory over Chiang Kai-shek's regime, and later the invasion of South Korea were all ominous events. As 1950 began, even Kilpatrick viewed the situation as the most difficult he had known in peacetime: "The commu-nists," he wrote, "are succeeding in a degree I had not thought possible." The

invasion of South Korea by the North Koreans in June of 1950 only reinforced his thinking on this topic. For him, the congressional elections of 1950 made the duplicitous nature of McCarthyism even more apparent. Kilpatrick was not deceived by McCarthy's maneuvers: "The hysteria that has been created against alleged communism in the administration . . . is 100% bunk," he wrote.[15]

The change in the public perception of education coinciding with the onset of McCarthyism was indeed dramatic. A study published as the century reached its midpoint had presented a highly favorable view of public education and significant support for progressive educational ideas. An article in the *University of Illinois Bulletin* "What Popular Magazines Say About Education: 1946-1948," revealed that public opinion supported "a functional curriculum with real-life problems" and "active learning characteristics of method"; it also found that the American public was favorably disposed toward financially supporting education. But this popular patronage of public education was soon to evaporate along both curricular and financial lines. The progressive educator Harold Benjamin, dean of education at the University of Maryland, viewed the political threat to the public schools as real. In 1950, addressing the annual conference of the National Education Association, he said, "The enemy is trying our lines with a number of local probing raids, attempting to find out where we are weak or strong, testing his methods of attack, recruiting and training his forces, building up his stockpiles." Benjamin and others had little doubt that the situation developing in Pasadena would be the test case.[16]

Two newspapers in southern California began questioning the efficacy of the public schools in early 1950. The *Los Angeles Herald-Express* published a series called "What's Wrong with the Schools?" These articles charged that the schools were being taken over by progressive educators, who were replacing the "three R's" with the "three C's" — "calcimine, clay, and confusion." The *Los Angeles Times* followed suit with an editorial opposing federal aid to education: "If the Schools Would Only Educate." After this a series of six articles appeared which coincided with the school board elections in Pasadena. (An election, incidentally, that drew no more than 4 percent of an apathetic electorate to the polls.) Describing a variety of real and perceived ills in the schools, the articles took up issues that clearly went beyond school funding. One observer noted that "a discerning reader might have concluded that the *Times*, in the guise of stalking John Dewey, was inciting voters to rebel against an increased tax levy." The campaign in Pasadena had prompted the Los Angeles superintendent of schools to soft-pedal a program of expansion in that city. And the success of the forces opposing progressive education in the Pasadena elections caused a similar

attack to be launched in San Diego, where the schools, according to the critics, had been "redefined and reanalyzed" in 1948 by William Heard Kilpatrick.

The emphasis of Kilpatrick's San Diego trip was to discuss intercultural and minority-group issues as they related to the schools, and Kilpatrick and William Van Til's book *Intercultural Attitudes in the Making*, was used during the seminars. There was extensive coverage of this visit to San Diego in the papers, complete with photographs. When reporters raised questions regarding communist influence in the schools, Kilpatrick downplayed the issue. "I don't think there is much of it," he responded. "Some communists have tried to get into key positions, but were discovered."[17]

The Pasadena controversy had begun innocently enough for Kilpatrick, in early 1949, when Willard Goslin, the city's charismatic superintendent of schools, and his wife were invited to dinner at the Morningside Drive apartment. Ironically, while discussing communist hysteria in America, Goslin invited Kilparick to lead a summer conference for his staff, and Kilpatrick gladly accepted. Kilpatrick, who had known Goslin for several years, had long been a champion of Goslin's, even pushing for his appointment to the superintendency of the New York schools in 1947. When Goslin's appointment in New York failed to materialize, the blow to Kilpatrick was both personal and professional. "I am sick at heart," he wrote; "I had been fearing this, but the actuality is very, very discouraging." A dynamic speaker, Goslin could inspire an audience of civic leaders or a roomful of teachers to action, frequently with only a few well chosen words on democracy and education. Kilpatrick, writing of Goslin's rhetorical skills, told of the superintendent's moving a Rotary meeting to "applause as I have seldom heard before." And Goslin reciprocated Kilpatrick's admiration.[18]

Beginning their trip westward to California in early July of 1949, Kilpatrick and Marion first stopped at The Ohio State University, where he was to be the major speaker for the Bode Conference, an annual meeting planned by the graduate students in education. Kilpatrick spent two days at the conference, using as his theme "The Essential Difference Between the New and Old Education." Beginning his thesis with an examination of what he termed "Alexandrian" education, an approach based solely on the printed word, he moved through the history of education, skillfully making his case for progressive education. Kilpatrick could still inform and entertain audiences, regaling them with stories from his wide reading. He told of Martha Washington scolding her husband for letting his "dirty democrats" into Mount Vernon after she spotted a handprint on the wall. He quoted Blackwell's Law to illustrate the lack of women's rights: "The

man and woman shall be one and the man is that one." And he also condemned racial discrimination, though in a circumspect manner.[19]

After a layover of a few hours in Chicago, the Kilpatricks boarded the "Super Chief" for California on July 9. The ride was so smooth that Kilpatrick was unable to tell whether the train was running, even when it was traveling at full speed. The Kilpatricks arrived at Union Station in Los Angeles on July 11 and were greeted by "flower princesses" bearing roses. A photograph of the occasion showed Kilpatrick, wearing a bowtie and a light-colored summer suit, with an uncomfortable-looking Marion holding the bouquet; the caption read, "Savant to Confer Here."[20] Taken to the Huntington Hotel and assigned to a lovely bungalow, they were overcome by both the extravagant attention and the potential cost. The conference for the Pasadena schools' administrative staff began the next day. A near verbatim account of the conference, accompanied by recordings, was published under a familiar Kilpatrick title, "We Learn What We Live." In the foreword, Goslin called Kilpatrick "one of the great teachers of modern times," a "citizen of vision, integrity, and courage." According to the booklet, the thirty conferees included teachers, principals, counselors, and central office administrative personnel. Topics encompassed the aims and objectives of education, human relations, the nature of the learning process, the curriculum, and principles of guidance.

Since subversion, loyalty, and allegiance to democracy would all become issues later on in the Pasadena controversy, a number of statements Kilpatrick made during this conference are germane. He held that democracy and discussion were correlates, and the antithesis of absolutism. The democratic outlook, he maintained, also included responsibility, respect for the rights of others, freedom, and equality of opportunity. Kilpatrick also forthrightly addressed concerns regarding minorities, remarking that prejudices involving race, religion, and socioeconomic differences often emerged early in a child's life. In support of this last point on equality, he quoted the Declaration of Independence, the Constitution, the Bill of Rights, and Jesus.[21] Any fair reading of these proceedings reveals a moderately liberal viewpoint on race relations and Kilpatrick's standard beliefs on educational issues. It would certainly be difficult to discover in them the genesis of the confrontation between Goslin and the community of Pasadena.

During the conference, Kilpatrick was clearly at the height of his rhetorical and persuasive powers. An author who later chronicled the events wrote that the thirty educators, who spent five days with him, came away "according to well substantiated reports intellectually refreshed and inspired." After one of the

sessions Goslin scribbled a brief note and slipped it to Kilpatrick: "You have never been more effective than this morning. I wished that every teacher in America might have been in this room. I am greatly indebted to you for coming." Midway through the conference, the man who was managing the recording equipment — not a teacher — told Kilpatrick that he had learned more in two days than he had in years. Kilpatrick even gave an extra lecture at U.C.L.A. Frances Davenport later wrote to him suggesting that Hollywood might have been his calling: "It was thrilling to hear you at U.C.L.A. and never have I seen such an audience reaction. I sometimes think you should have been an actor. You can hold an audience in the palm of your hand." On July 20, Kilpatrick wrote, "They all seemed to feel that the Conference has been a success. I certainly enjoyed it and I think they did. Not in a long time have I had a group work with such discernment."[22]

The actual conflict between Willard Goslin and the Pasadena Board of Education did not begin in earnest until a full year after Kilpatrick's visit. But the reverberations of educational McCarthyism buffeted Kilpatrick much sooner. Upon returning from a speaking engagement in April of 1950, he found that the superintendent of the Buffalo schools had been spreading reports that Kilpatrick was a communist, or at best a fellow traveler. (The language used was that of the political communist-hunters; it quickly spread to the educational arena.) A congressman had informed the superintendent that a congressional committee on un-American activities had named Kilpatrick as a prewar member of two groups recently labeled communist fronts. If this was, in fact, the case, reflected Kilpatrick, "these represent two instances in which in spite of all my effort to the contrary, I was duped by the communists." Checking his diaries, he discovered that indeed he had allowed his name to be associated with the two organizations in question.[23] Kilpatrick, like other Americans, soon began to recognize that McCarthyism entailed guilt by association, intimidation, misrepresentation, and basing current judgments on past allegiances. Attention was usually directed at left-of-center politicians, journalists, union leaders, and Hollywood filmmakers, but with ever-increasing frequency, academicians, too, came under scrutiny.

In retrospect, it seems to have been inevitable that Willard Goslin, one of the most highly visible superintendents in the country, would become a target for those taking aim at public schools and the increasingly controversial ideas surrounding progressive education and its advocates. One of the most successful school administrators in the country, Goslin had led the Webster Groves system in Missouri and the Minneapolis public schools prior to going to Pasadena. While in

Minnesota, Goslin, with the assistance of Hubert Humphrey — who was then the mayor of Minneapolis — had settled a difficult labor dispute involving the school system's nonteaching support staff. But the long and acrimonious strike weakened Goslin's political clout. Having made his reputation nationally by being elected president of the prestigious American Association of School Administrators, Goslin decided to search for a new post. In 1948, he was aggressively recruited for and appointed to the highly attractive superintendency in Pasadena, California.

Efficient and charismatic, Goslin was also perceived as remote, especially by the more influential circles in the community. Arthur Zilversmit, in his book *Changing Schools: Progressive Education Theory and Practice, 1930-1960*, has noted that "Goslin was no radical." Progressive education was to become an inflammatory issue, but Zilversmit considered Goslin only a "mild supporter" of that philosophy. Another historian, however — Michael James — dissents. According to James, "Goslin was a firm proponent of the core curriculum and a non-hierarchical, child-centered school setting. And Goslin's progressivism went beyond pedagogy to include establishing an egalitarian culture, also an essential outcome of progressive education." Goslin did indeed become linked to the most radical progressive educators and thus became vulnerable to the charges of instituting "fads and frills" in the classroom, increasing the school budget, and neglecting the traditional academic subjects — the standard criticisms of progressive education. ("Frills" in this case included hiring a psychiatric caseworker, placing greater emphasis on guidance and mental health, and stressing a need for improved human relations and interracial understanding.) According to Zilversmit, critics associated these issues with Dewey's philosophy, which they viewed as relativistic and therefore inimical to traditional values. Under these circumstances, attacks on the schools easily took on the atmosphere of a "religious crusade."[24]

By May of 1950, Goslin and the Pasadena schools were once again placed in the spotlight by the *Los Angeles Times*. The reporter John Copeland ran a six-part series on the growing controversy in Pasadena. This time half the articles focused on Kilpatrick's influence on Goslin and the schools. Copeland, giving Kilpatrick the alliterative description "most famous present day patriarch of pragmatic philosophy," credited him with the current status of the San Diego school system. (Whether Kilpatrick's influence was positive or negative, Copeland did not state, but he drew great attention to Kilpatrick's fee of $700 for a week's services at Goslin's summer workshop.) Also highlighted was the fact that the Pasadena workshops had been recorded, the tapes were being heard by educators not in attendance, and that Kilpatrick had defined the good life as a

noncompetitive, group-oriented activity. While Copeland fully acknowledged Kilpatrick and Goslin's commitment to democracy and deemed it a worthy goal of education, he subtly questioned the means by which it was to be achieved.[25]

In September of 1950 word came to Kilpatrick that Goslin had lost the confidence of the public and the teachers in Pasadena and had only a "fifty-fifty" chance of surviving. Kilpatrick first thought that Goslin's tax increase and the opposition of the American Legion and older teachers to progressive education were the crux of the superintendent's problems. Additional criticism had come down on Goslin because he had brought Mary Beauchamp, his administrative aide in Minneapolis, to assist him in Pasadena. But by March of 1950 Beauchamp's candid remarks based on her staunch and deep-rooted beliefs in progressivism, became a liability for him. He called her into his office and asked for her resignation, indicating that the superintendent knew he was in political trouble much earlier than would subsequently be suggested. The story that she was leaving to undertake further graduate work was not accurate, and Goslin's treatment of Mary Beauchamp somewhat tarnishes his otherwise heroic behavior during this critical time.[26]

Goslin's predicament became national news in late November of 1950. *Time* magazine interpreted the conflict between superintendent and school board as a series of thwarted efforts on Goslin's part to introduce his progressive pedagogical ideas into the school system. According to the article, preschool workshops for teachers were viewed as too expensive; summer camps for students smacked of collectivism ("camps for communists" according to one critic); and Goslin's professional involvements, which entailed extensive travel, mere "gallivanting." *Time* also reported that Goslin's insistence that pupils attend schools in their own districts had "infuriated" parents, especially those who wanted to send their children "to whatever schools suited them (i.e., those without Negroes or underprivileged children)." Progressive education, too, came in for its share of criticism; the *Pasadena Independent* suggested that "there is far too much paint-daubing [and] far too little discipline."[27]

While Goslin had his supporters, his detractors were organized and certainly more vocal. The School Development Council (SDC), led by a local osteopath, Ernest Brower, charged that the Pasadena schools were riddled with communism. One pamphlet distributed in the campaign asked, "How Red Is the Little Red School House?" Allegedly, classroom competition was being downplayed, while sex education was finding its way into the science and health curriculum. (Brower utilized a pamphlet "Progressive Education Increases Delinquency," by Allen Zoll of American Patriots, Inc., who held a doctorate

from a diploma mill.[28]) Unfortunately for Goslin, all this coincided with the arrival in town of the California State Senate Education Committee, to investigate communism in the schools. Goslin was permitted to testify and did so eloquently in defense of the democratic process:

> I have never seen a community in America where the school system was better than its people wanted it to be. What the people want not only should govern, it does in fact govern. Here in Pasadena we are going through one of those typically American procedures to find out what we believe in and what we want.[29]

Since Goslin's predicament was, by most accounts, the result of multiple causes, the question becomes how much of it can be ascribed to progressive education in general and to William Heard Kilpatrick in particular. At the time of the 1949 workshop, Kilpatrick's visit had "raised a few eyebrows," but there had been no public outcry or criticism. In fact, the investigation of the episode by the National Education Association, *The Pasadena Story* (published in June of 1951 with the clearly pro-Goslin subtitle "An Analysis of Some Forces and Factors That Injured a Superior School System"), concluded that Kilpatrick's role had been solely to lead a four-day workshop and had been brief, benign, and innocuous. In his book *This Happened in Pasadena,* the journalist David Hulburd chronicled the entire episode in great detail, (his account was published immediately following the denouement of the case). For Hulburd, Kilpatrick's role was significant — both because of his visit in the summer of 1949 and because of his reputation. The journalist described Kilpatrick as "a man who among modern educational philosophers and students is known and respected throughout the world" and also as a "liberal, a progressive in education, and at all times a controversial figure." According to Hulburd, the citizens of Pasadena viewed Kilpatrick as a disciple of "old John Dewey . . . anathema to many people," as well as a man whose name was on several lists of organizations suspected of communist attachments. For these conservative Californians, any scholarly and educational achievements by these progressive educators were overshadowed by their radical political or economic theories.[30]

As Kilpatrick continued to be a point of contention for the anti-Goslin forces, the school board (with the superintendent's guidance) found itself obliged to make some statement about his involvement. While Kilpatrick was indeed influential in educational circles, they explained, he had not dictated his beliefs to Goslin, to the teachers of Pasadena, or to the members of the board of

education. The board also asked that the School Development Council, which had attributed "unwholesome influences" to Kilpatrick, to explain exactly what they meant. In another statement, the board of education declared that the teachers would continue to use Kilpatrick's recorded lectures and published materials from the 1949 workshop. But in response to an explicit question posed by the SDC, "Does the administration agree with the socialistic philosophy of Professor William Heard Kilpatrick?" the board equivocated. "The Board of Education and the administration do not agree with any socialistic philosophy," it responded, leaving the question about Kilpatrick's beliefs unanswered. The SDC had also alleged that Goslin's assistant, Mary Beauchamp, by this point no longer an employee of the school district, had left behind an organization to perpetuate and accelerate Kilpatrick's philosophy. The board categorically denied this charge. The SDC had also mentioned, as significant to the debate, Kilpatrick's association with the Bureau for Intercultural Education. Much of the SDC's literature was again provided by Allen Zoll, an anti-Semite and former Coughlinite, who continued to print such pamphlets as "Progressive Education Is Subverting America" and "Progressive Education Breeds Delinquency."[31]

Other accounts of the Goslin affair were to emerge later. Mary L. Allen's book *Education or Indoctrination*, written four years after Hulburd's, claimed that the progressive educators under Goslin's leadership had mounted a full-scale attack against public education. Allen also raised the issue of race, claiming that "minority groups, racial and otherwise, were propagandized with the idea that the majority discriminated against them, exploited them, and held them in subjection." She further alleged that under Goslin's leadership, intercultural dances were held and that children who failed to dance with those of other cultures were made to feel "uncomfortable." Allen is clearly misinformed on the race issue. The National Association for the Advancement of Colored People (N.A.A.C.P.) and the Council on Racial Equality (C.O.R.E.) did work in the 1950s to desegregate Friday night dances at the Pasadena Auditorium, but there was no connection between this effort and Goslin or school policies. Charles M. Wollenberg, in his book *All Deliberate Speed: Segregation and Exclusion in the California Schools, 1855-1975*, has claimed that racial and ethnic prejudice continued to be ingrained in the citizenry of Pasadena well into the 1970s. And the professional baseball player Jackie Robinson, a native of Pasadena, would call his hometown racist.[32]

Educational historians have since put the episode into a larger context. Lawrence Cremin viewed the Goslin case as emblematic of the post-World War II milieu, in which a myriad of problems arose for public schools, including

increased enrollments, rampant inflation, teachers leaving the profession, an escalating demand for a competent and educated workforce, and, finally, the perception of communist influence at home and communist expansion abroad. The result, according to Cremin, was "the most vigorous, searching, and fundamental attack on progressive education since the beginning of the movement." This assault was initially led by Bernard Iddings Bell, in his book *Crisis in Education,* and Mortimer Smith, in his book *And Madly Teach*; both books were published in 1949. Bell, an educator, and Smith, a layman, represented "the intellectual thrust of a polyglot political movement" that made serious inroads into education in the late 1940s.[33]

In discussing the McCarthy period, the historian Joel Spring has pointed to a widening gap between traditional free-market capitalism, with its emphasis on rugged individualism, and the more group-oriented, cooperative basis for social and economic interaction which had been stressed in the schools since the onset of the Great Depression. Spring's analysis was more educational than political, suggesting that progressivism became a focus of attention owing to an increasing emphasis by the public on teaching the "basics" — rather than the "extras" — which were consistently associated with progressive education. Spring also found significance in Kilpatrick's visit as it related to Goslin's fall. In addition, he placed the Pasadena episode in a larger context, linking it to similar cases in Denver, Colorado, and Scarsdale, New York, and noting the chill felt by administrators across the country. Spring's careful documentation of the censorship which arose in curriculum and textbook selection cannot be dismissed.[34]

Diane Ravitch, however, downplayed the impact of McCarthyism on the educational scene and its connection to Goslin and Pasadena in her book *The Troubled Crusade: American Education, 1945-1980.* As Ravitch saw it, a "substantial" segment of the community disliked progressive education, which it believed was equivalent to a communist conspiracy within the schools. When the community's "objections were ignored" by the professional educators in charge of the schools, according to Ravitch, the situation became more serious. The lesson of the episode was not that reactionary forces had irrationally smeared a reform-minded administrator or that outside agitators were on the verge of taking over the school district. Rather, concluded Ravitch, "what happened in Pasadena revealed an extraordinary lack of understanding" between educators and the community, which "became entangled in the language of McCarthyism." Ravitch's seemingly evenhanded assessment of the Pasadena affair as a "lack of understanding" ignores the fact that individuals like Goslin,

Mary Beauchamp, Robert Gilchrist, and other educators outside this particular case were unjustly smeared, and their careers were significantly harmed. In fact, even Ravitch's handling of McCarthy is gentle to an extreme.   Never condemning McCarthy's unfounded accusations (although she does call his rhetoric "inflammatory"), Ravitch treats the era as a temporary circumstance that had no lasting influence and did no discernible damage to individuals or institutions.[35]

A more recent assessment of the episode, by Michael James, places the cause of Goslin's dismissal squarely in the superintendent's continuous drive to desegregate the city schools. James admits that typical reactionary criticisms of progressive educational practices were present, but the attempt to eliminate the neutral zones by redrawing school boundaries remained central in the controversy. (He views Kilpatrick's visit as minor to begin with, but taking on greater significance as events proceeded.) James also notes that the affair left its mark on the Pasadena community. The issue of desegregation continued after Goslin's departure as the N.A.A.C.P. picked up on it, taking depositions that pointed to a three-decade practice of allowing whites to avoid sending their children to schools with African-Americans and Mexicans. In an interview with Charles Johnson, counsel for the N.A.A.C.P., James reports that if the Pasadena school board had not backed away from its student transfer policy, the city would have found itself one of the companion cases in the landmark suit *Brown v. Board of Education*.[36]

Goslin was finally forced to resign on November 21, 1950. The *Los Angeles Times* ran the headline "Progressive Education Tossed Out — Pasadena Schools to Abandon Policy After Years of Trial." *Life* magazine gave the resignation full coverage, with pictures. Goslin was shown on the playground of a Pasadena elementary school, a mother was captured weeping upon hearing the news of his dismissal, and photographs of the school board members were accompanied by captions noting how each had voted. The brief narrative mentioned integration, taxes, the curriculum, and politics as reasons behind the superintendent's departure. *Life* suggested that the community had tried too late to hold on to its superintendent and quoted Goslin as saying, "People are worried and they are hunting for scapegoats." The $23,250 settlement Goslin received was mentioned, along with the fact that he was leaving, with no bitterness, to go quail hunting in his home state, Missouri.[37]

When the episode was finally concluded, Kilpatrick, personally wounded and in sympathy with Goslin, wrote with uncharacteristic vehemence:

It is a disgrace to Pasadena and a hurt to American education. I am involved, having been accused of Communism. If there is an open minded, liberally disposed person in these United States more opposed to Communism I don't know it. Our people suffer from hysteria.[38]

Kilpatrick's outrage was shared by others. The president of Harvard, James B. Conant, reviewing Hulburd's book on the front page of the *New York Times Book Review*, said that the campaign against Goslin was "an orgy of misrepresentation" propelled by an "irrational mob," revealing the "reactionary temper of our times." According to Conant's biographer, this forceful outburst was unusual for him, but because of the "paranoia gripping Washington and the nation," he had felt compelled to denounce the smear tactics of those attacking progressive education. Conant was especially incensed by the linking of John Dewey, William Heard Kilpatrick, and the philosophy of pragmatism with communism and Karl Marx, concluding that "against government by intimidation all believers in democracy must be ready to stand, whatever their personal views about education."[39]

Other voices censuring the Pasadena activists were heard. In an article for *The Christian Century*, Carey McWilliams declared that an alliance of "apoplectic frenzies, superpatriots, and religious zealots" had permitted "their fear of Mao Tse-tung to become displaced and directed against such symbols as Willard Goslin, John Dewey, and William Heard Kilpatrick." In McWilliams's opinion, though, the "shamelessly demagogic attacks" had less to do with Goslin or progressive education than with a concerted effort to control the public schools. Even the conservative Isaac Kandel, writing in *School and Society*, was incensed by Goslin's resignation. Indicating that this was an issue around which progressives and essentialists alike should unite, Kandel went so far as to suggest that anyone who filled a position vacated under such circumstances should be denied membership in professional organizations. In late 1951, *The Nation* published an eight-part series, "The Battle for Free Schools." The first article, written by Morris Mitchell, focused on the ramifications of the Goslin episode, attributing the problem to four related groups: "real-estate conservatives, superpatriots, dogma peddlers, and race haters." The predicted consequences were fear among teachers, ruined careers, and threats to free speech. Mitchell also defended the philosophical basis of pragmatism; he said that the "dogma peddlers oppose pragmatism because pragmatism opposes dogmatism. They fight such protagonists of the Yankee way of thinking as John Dewey and

William Heard Kilpatrick."[40]

The Goslin episode took on national significance as a symbol of the emerging reaction to perceived threats to both internal security and the country's educational system. Admittedly, communism and progressive education were not the only issues in Pasadena. The proposed tax increases, attempts at racial integration, and even the superintendent's style of leadership were undeniably all major points of contention. Yet Kilpatrick's reputation and his advocacy of progressive education made his very appearance at Goslin's side an unanticipated lightning rod. While Kilpatrick had been criticized since the days of "The Project Method," the child-centered movement, and the social reconstructionists, the nature of this latest attack was different: it was political rather than pedagogical. Kilpatrick's indirect involvement in the Goslin episode would be his first rather remote experience of what would become a virulent anti-public school sentiment, one which would continue to appear at regular intervals in various forms throughout the rest of the century.

As author Zilversmit has pointed out, the Goslin case was indeed a prime example of McCarthyism at work in the educational arena. Other examples emerged in the early 1950s. Harold Rugg was enjoined from speaking at The Ohio State University when the board of trustees passed a "Speaker Screening Rule," which the dean of education, Donald Cotrell, called a "McCarthyite fuss." Kilpatrick, in the *New York Times*, saw it as an issue of academic freedom and condemned the trustees for their "totalitarian methods." Charges that the educational progressives had socialistic and communistic associations came with ever greater frequency. It is now known that the Federal Bureau of Investigation monitored John Dewey's activities and associations from the 1920s until his death.[41]

Kilpatrick also became the subject of an F.B.I. file and two intergovernmental requests for information about him were made in 1956 and 1960. The declassified portion of the file states that "no actual investigation of William H. Kilpatrick has been conducted," but the records kept by the New York office of the F.B.I. are quite extensive. The information kept on Kilpatrick enumerated his organizational connections, which included the International Relief Association, the Urban League of New York, the Bureau for Intercultural Education, the Liberal Party of New York State, the Committee on Academic Freedom of the American Civil Liberties Union, and the John Dewey Society. A number of these organizations were listed by the F.B.I. and Congress as communist, pro-communist, or communist front groups. Kilpatrick's voluntary service as head of the board of education's advisory committee during the search for a superin-

tendent of schools for New York City was described in the F.B.I. file as "an attempt to have the Board of Education appoint a pro-Communist superintendent of schools." Kilpatrick's candidate was, as noted earlier, Willard Goslin.

In 1960, a request from an unnamed petitioner in the United States government listed Kilpatrick's connection with the American Institute for Pacific Relations and the Institute for Pacific Relations from 1927 to 1936, noting that he had chaired the IPR's Education Committee from 1927 to 1930. (The entire program from the July 1927 IPR Conference was placed in the file, no doubt because of McCarthy's interest in the organization and one of its more prominent members, Owen Lattimore.) The F.B.I. report noted that Kilpatrick and others utilized the trip to Japan in 1927 to visit Moscow and that Soviet officials considered the IPR "an instrument of communist policy, propaganda, and military intelligence." The file also scrutinized the "Social Frontier" group, naming Dewey, Beard, Rugg, Counts, Newlon, and Kilpatrick as members and emphasizing their belief that the age of economic individualism was closing and an age of collectivism was beginning. The Pasadena episode, of course, found its way into the files, as did Kilpatrick's appearance in the summer workshop and the inquiry by the Senate Investigating Committee on Education. The file also refers the reader to the House Committee on Un-American Activities for further information. Unable to let the racial element pass without comment, the F.B.I. documented that Kilpatrick was one of six white members on the board of directors of Sydenham Hospital in Harlem.[42]

In January 1951, two months after his resignation, Goslin had dinner with the Kilpatricks, spending the evening going over the entire ordeal with his highly sympathetic hosts. Although familiar with most of the details, Kilpatrick was deeply troubled by what he heard: "It is disheartening to see the antagonism to decent public schools and to learn how it was able to manipulate an unguarded population to the destruction of Goslin's administration and program." Goslin considered his career as a superintendent at an end and was considering a post at George Peabody College in Nashville, which he later accepted. "We could not but admire his poise, his well-balanced analysis of the situation, and his forward outlook," wrote Kilpatrick, "but we could not fail to see that the experience has hurt him." Goslin, along with his wife and daughter, made a round-the-world trip and spent the summer working in German schools before joining the faculty at Peabody to teach courses in administration. Kilpatrick continued to support Goslin, introducing him at professional meetings and excoriating the Pasadena community whenever the opportunity arose.[43]

In April, Marion purchased Hulburd's book, *This Happened in Pasadena*,

for Kilpatrick, who was astonished to read about the strong public opposition to himself. Kilpatrick listed in his diary, in abbreviated form, each of the negative references and charges described in the book, rebutting each. As for the charge of communism, he considered himself far from any Marxist thinking, writing that he had opposed it "in every way and on every occasion." He tersely responded to the pejorative connection with Dewey by writing, "as to being indebted to John Dewey for my essential philosophy, yes; as for letting John Dewey do my thinking for me, no." He considered himself no more a political radical than Franklin Roosevelt, and the charge of undermining patriotism in Pasadena "100% false in every respect." He categorically denied ever advocating socialism and defended the Bureau for Intercultural Relations, maintaining that it was guilty only of applying democracy and practicing the golden rule. He took most offense not for himself, but for Goslin: "If ever a man was unjustly accused and unjustly treated, it was Willard Goslin. As I see it, Pasadena is for a long time degraded by what went on there."[44]

The Pasadena case refused to go away. Word came to Kilpatrick in May of 1951 that the California Legislative Committee on Un-American Activities had issued a report accusing both him and the Bureau for Intercultural Education of communist affiliations, according to information gained from the United States House of Representatives' Un-American Activities Committee. (Much was made of certain quotes in the first John Dewey Society yearbook, *The Teacher and Society*, some in chapters which Kilpatrick had not written.) As usual, he prepared a detailed response to the charges, and he sent it to his supporters in California. His response was strident, especially in defense of his association with John Dewey — he called the connection an honor — and his advocacy of progressive education, of which he was equally proud. A former student, living in California, sent him clippings of the report, writing, "It destroys me completely when they speak of you, the greatest teacher in America, as subversive. If you are a subversive, so is God." Surprisingly, another individual who came to his defense was Eugene Nixon, in the *Los Angeles Times*. Calling himself a "hidebound conservative Republican," he criticized the Pasadena School Development Council and other groups for making a "terrible monster" out of Kilpatrick. If the public would read Kilpatrick's works, wrote Nixon, they would conclude that "everything he says sounds reasonable." With remarkable clarity in the confines of a two-column article, Nixon synthesized Kilpatrick's better-known ideas by relating them to his call for meeting the needs of a changing society. If children were failing to learn the "three R's," wrote Nixon, it was partly because teachers and the public had misunderstood Kilpatrick's

ideas, and partly because of severely overcrowded classrooms, which might have as many as 50 children.[45]

Interestingly, Kilpatrick never let his personal turmoil surface during this period. His grandson Heard Baumeister was a college student at the time and has noted that the Goslin issue never emerged in conversations during his frequent visits to the Morningside Drive apartment, nor was he, for years, even aware of the firestorm that surrounded his grandfather. While maintaining a stoic face in public, though, Kilpatrick was stung by the accusations of communist connections. He termed the attacks "highly artificial . . . thoroughly manufactured almost entirely out of whole cloth." He was ideologically opposed to communism, and he saw no place for the followers of Marx as leaders of the classrooms of America. For him, a card-carrying communist was not free to think and, therefore, not fit to teach.

One book that emerged at this time especially irked him: Howard David Langford's *Education and Social Conflict.* This proved to be a source for much of the California legislature's information on Kilpatrick in the aftermath of the Pasadena case. Langford attempted to establish that, under Kilpatrick's guidance, a widespread effort had been undertaken to introduce communism into the public schools. Kilpatrick was hurt most by the way McCarthyite tactics threatened to work against him personally and professionally. "For one who does not know the facts," he wrote in his diary, "it may sound a plausible indictment." He was affected so deeply by the attacks that he even considered writing a book to refute the charges, lest people actually believe that he "had dabbled with Communism." Viewing himself as having been "smeared" by the California senate committee, Kilpatrick wrote that "those who know me know that at no time have I in any degree dallied with Communism or the Communist Party. On the contrary, I have been a consistent opponent."[46]

While he never penned a full-length book in defense of his political views, Kilpatrick did not remain silent. In a speech to the New York Humanist Association in late 1952, "The Current Retreat from Reason," he spoke frankly of the communist hysteria and its troubling repercussions, warning of the danger of authoritarianism. The following summer in his commencement address at Mercer, "Watchmen, What of the Night?" he became more explicit in his criticism:

> With McCarthy still going strong, and so many agreeing with
> him, the hysteria threatens to grow worse. So far as I can see,
> we have never before had in this country an hysteria equal to

this, and we must expect appreciable damage to result. Unwise political moves are possible, and this at every level. Upright and innocent individuals will be unjustly smeared. Teachers will think twice before they face angry crowds. Controversial discussion in the classrooms will suffer, academic freedom will be threatened.[47]

Others within the progressive education movement raised their voices to counter the onslaught. The John Dewey Society and the National Education Association's Commission for the Defense of Democracy responded in their publications. Two books which courageously rebutted educational McCarthyism were *Forces Affecting American Education*, edited by William Van Til, and *Educational Freedom in an Age of Anxiety*, edited by Gordon Hullfish.[48] Others defending American education at this time included Ernest O. Melby, V. T. Thayer, and Harold Benjamin. But the personal and professional toll suffered by academics and the nation's schools from these assaults may never be known.

As the century reached its midpoint, a number of Kilpatrick's friends and associates slipped from the scene, either by retirement or through death. Edward L. Thorndike died in August of 1949, and Kilpatrick gave his usual frank opinion of the man and his work:

> Thorndike was a near genius. He also put educational psychology on the map as did no one else. Unfortunately, he did not give his followers his best impulses in education. They formalized his Stimulus - Response bond theory so as to run it in the ground. A practical mistake was in the failure to discuss with his colleagues. Had he developed this practice he might have been saved some specific errors. But he was a great creator and his influence will never die.[49]

In 1953, Boyd Bode died in Florida, after a long bout with cancer. But the old rivalry was still very much alive for Kilpatrick. Alongside the obituary, pasted into his personal scrapbook, Kilpatrick noted that, while Bode was an effective teacher and thinker, a follower of Dewey, and a defender of democracy and free thought, he had lacked a practical side — and had never "fully appreciated the best available insight into the educative process." The following year, J. R. Moseley died at age eighty-four. Moseley, as an itinerant nondenominational religious workshop leader and writer, had taught with Kilpatrick for three years

at Mercer and had visited Kilpatrick frequently over the years, often writing about his former colleague in a column for a Macon newspaper. "If there has ever been a saint among my acquaintances," wrote Kilpatrick of Moseley, "he was that one." So often was he losing friends and colleagues now that he prepared a "model" condolence letter for his stenographer to personalize and send out, rather than writing a fresh one each time he received word of a passing.[50]

As others were retiring or dying, Kilpatrick took stock of his own position and toyed with the idea of writing his autobiography. But work on his books on philosophy of education and learning delayed this project. It was further postponed in October of 1948 when Ordway Tead of Harper Brothers approached him with the suggestion that he cooperate on a biography with his former student, Samuel Tenenbaum, now a full-time writer. Tenenbaum — who had been a teacher — was an admirer of Kilpatrick's and sympathetic to progressive education. Kilpatrick was open to the idea, although he was skeptical about whether Tenenbaum could do justice to the first half of his life. But he agreed to read some of Tenenbaum's works, including *Why Men Hate*, and made an appointment to meet with the young author. The following week, Tenenbaum visited the Kilpatricks' apartment where the two men discussed potential problems with the project while the diaries, scrapbooks, and letters were displayed. During this first visit, Kilpatrick found Tenenbaum sincere and genuinely interested in the educative process. In early November of 1948 he informed Tenenbaum that he would be glad to have him undertake his biography, with the understanding that two years after its publication Kilpatrick would be free to publish his own autobiography.[51]

The process of writing the biography was to be an arduous task for author and subject alike. The two men recorded their interviews on a wire recorder, and a secretary transcribed them. The recording itself took place in one of the apartment bedrooms, and there was much playing, rewinding, and replaying to ensure accuracy. When Tenenbaum was not interviewing Kilpatrick, he would be in the front rooms talking with Marion. Kilpatrick would then be shut in his study, trying to work with the recorder and two people talking at the same time. "With all this, it seems a full day," he noted once. The amount of written material Kilpatrick had collected astounded Tenenbaum. Just working with the letters, he was "aghast at the amount of material to be read." Kilpatrick again had his inexplicable influence over others. When Tenenbaum and his wife were invited to dinner during the writing of the book, Mrs. Tenenbaum told Marion that her husband's association with Kilpatrick had made him more thoughtful, less assertive, and kinder. She added that the

effect of one visit lasted as much as a week.[52]

Tenenbaum continued writing the biography, completing a final manuscript by the fall of 1950. Kilpatrick had declined to read it during development, in order to distance himself from the final product, and from responsibility for the contents. But Tenenbaum continued to plead with Kilpatrick to read the manuscript, indicating that his devotion to Kilpatrick's thinking was sincere. Kilpatrick assented and, on his first reading, was pleased with Tenenbaum's use of the sources and the description of his educational philosophy. He was concerned, though, by his biographer's exploitation of his "differences and opposition" with other educators. "Some of them I shall have to soften," he wrote. Marion agreed, and negotiations began to persuade Tenenbaum to make certain modifications. In a meeting of the three of them, Marion conveyed an agreement on the part of the Kilpatricks that the extensive use of quotations made it appear as if Kilpatrick was praising himself. Tenenbaum reacted rather excitedly to this, and it took the well known Kilpatrick diplomacy to pour oil on the troubled waters. Taking Tenenbaum aside, Kilpatrick urged him to eliminate any direct reference to the major figures in the Mercer "heresy trial," and to the retirement crisis of 1937. His major concern was the use of the names of Charles Lee Smith (president of Mercer in 1906) and William F. Russell of Teachers College. Marion and Tenenbaum later "argued vigorously," according to Kilpatrick, over a passage that discussed William James's *Talks to Teachers*.[53]

By the end of November 1950, all issues were resolved save one. Kilpatrick, who described the next meeting as a "painful conference," believed that the use of his diaries to belittle Dean William Russell, who was now the president of Teachers College, would be criticized in some quarters. Tenenbaum countered that leaving Russell out would decrease interest in the book and, more important, would increase the chances that Russell's behavior would be repeated by others. Kilpatrick agreed with this logic, but still could not approve the manuscript as it stood. The next day Ordway Tead, Tenenbaum's editor at Harper Brothers, praised the biography, but agreed with Kilpatrick on excluding Russell. For Tead it was a matter of taste: it was not fitting for a man of Kilpatrick's reputation to become entangled with a man of "inferior status" like William Russell. Tenenbaum finally conceded the point, and the manuscript was completed on Kilpatrick's terms. Kilpatrick later wrote that Tenenbaum had "done a good job in many respects, but many emphases are very different from what I would publish." When the biography appeared in September of 1951, the Kilpatricks agreed that they "liked the way" Tenenbaum had drafted the work and, with the exception of a few minor matters, on the whole found it "very acceptably written."[54]

Tenenbaum's *William Heard Kilpatrick: Trailblazer in Education*[55] certainly cannot be considered a critical study of Kilpatrick's thought and work. The reviews, with few exceptions, were basically positive, but they appeared for the most part in journals sympathetic to progressive education. One strength of the book is its consistent references to and examples of Kilpatrick's commitment to democracy and to the activity curriculum. Tenenbaum's extensive interviews with his subject may be the most important aspect of the work. If the quotations can be trusted, Kilpatrick is presented in his own words circa 1950. Unfortunately, however, Tenenbaum, ever ready to take Kilpatrick's opposition to the now infamous "Alexandrian theory" of print-oriented education to an extreme, often obscured the distinction between his own opinions and those of Kilpatrick. The biography also lacked analyses of Kilpatrick's major works and his philosophical relationship to Dewey. And Tenenbaum was unable, owing to Kilpatrick's reticence, to describe in detail either his resignation from Mercer in 1906 or the retirement crisis at Teacher's College in 1937. Finally, the book was written in 1950 and therefore preceded the Goslin affair and the attacks on progressive education by the back-to-basics movement. But as the only full-length work on Kilpatrick, it remained the standard reference for almost fifty years.

To coincide with the publication of the biography and the approach of Kilpatrick's eightieth birthday, Helen Parkhurst arranged for the production of five recordings in which Kilpatrick served as both discussion leader and participant. Parkhurst was the founder of the Dalton School in New York City, which was patterned after Carlton Washburne's Winnetka Plan, and she had been a longtime supporter of progressive education. The records included "The World Situation," with Ralph Bunche and Hu Shih; "Personal Characteristics Necessary to Civilization," with Theodore Brameld, Harold Taylor, Walter Anderson, Harry Overstreet, and Bruce Raup; "The Educative Process," with Roma Gans, Truda Weil, and Ernest Melby; "Civilization and the Good Life," with George Axtelle, John Childs, and Eduard Lindeman; and a unique exchange between Kilpatrick and a group of young teenagers. Parkhurst planned a sixth recording with John Dewey and John Childs, but because of Dewey's ill health, the project never materialized. Lawrence Cremin, who was then an assistant professor at Teachers College, reviewed the recordings for the *Teachers College Record* and noted Kilpatrick's keen knowledge of political and social movements. "The way in which Dr. Kilpatrick's personality stands forth in each of these discussions, will be gratifying to admirers of Kilpatrick the man," he wrote. At their best, the Parkhurst records captured the flavor of what the Kilpatrick Discussion Group might have been like. For the most part, though,

the discussions wavered between Kilpatrick's attempt to lead a discussion by drawing broad generalizations on social trends and the participants' efforts to connect Kilpatrick's educational thinking to the topic at hand.[56]

The actual observance of Kilpatrick's eightieth birthday was held on November 17, 1951, in two parts. A morning session, sponsored by the American Education Fellowship, began at the Hotel Commodore with Theodore Brameld presiding. After giving a ten-minute speech, Kilpatrick was followed by Willard Goslin, Eduard Lindeman, and Harold Taylor. The crowd was so large that it overflowed into adjoining rooms, where loudspeakers were used. After lunch, Kilpatrick autographed copies of Tenenbaum's book and Parkhurst's records. The evening celebration, sponsored by a number of organizations, also drew a large audience and filled the room to capacity. A letter from Eleanor Roosevelt was read, after which George Axtelle shared a selection of other greetings. Then followed speeches from honored guests, including Willard Goslin, William F. Russell, Kenneth Benne, David Dubinsky, Hollis Caswell, and Lester Granger. The honoree also received greetings from the National Education Association, the American Federation of Teachers, and the New York public school system.

After the guests blew out the birthday candles at each table, Kilpatrick spoke on the need for American education to stress moral and spiritual values and gave what the *New York Times* called a spirited defense of his progressive theories. Describing him as one of the most "controversial figures in American education," the *Times* reported that the "white-maned professor emeritus assailed teaching methods based on repetitive memorization of textbook information." Stressing his idea that we learn only what we accept into our lives, Kilpatrick added that by this he did not suggest any "depreciation of books or of book learning," and that his concerns were aimed directly at the secondary schools and colleges.[57] He spoke for twenty-five minutes, and, although the hour was late, few left early. Originally, 600 seats had been expected to be sold, but the final figure passed 1,000. "All in all the evening was a distinct success," wrote Kilpatrick in his diary. "It is seldom in one's life so momentous an occasion comes to stir one's feelings."[58] For the man from tiny White Plains, Georgia, to be feted by the elite of New York society was indeed memorable.

In the Sunday edition of the *New York Times*, Benjamin Fine, a former student of Kilpatrick's and now the paper's education columnist, presented a profile of the octogenarian based on a recent interview. Describing Kilpatrick as "vigorous, alert and youthful-looking," he also noted that "his bushy snow white hair, long his distinguishing feature, is as heavy and well-groomed as it was

when the standing room only signs were placed outside the rooms in which he taught." Fine wrote of Kilpatrick's influence at home and abroad and noted that Kilpatrick saw a threat to democracy internationally and a need for ever higher educational standards at home. Suggesting that teachers be given more money and be held in higher esteem by society, Kilpatrick outlined the characteristics he viewed as necessary for a good teacher. These included a moral commitment to democracy, a well-adjusted personality, intelligence and knowledge, leadership, and a positive regard for children. Educators, he felt, must improve the quality of living to build within students the attributes of kindness, generosity, and social-mindedness. He concluded that children must learn democracy by practicing democracy and that it must be grounded in respect for the individual regardless of social or economic status. From this, the nation's best-known newspaper, to the lesser-known daily presses, tributes flowed in. Even in the small Pennsylvania town where John Dewey had begun his teaching career (on a note that was none too successful), the *Oil City Blizzard* carried an editorial lauding Kilpatrick: "America's Greatest Teacher."[59]

In 1956, modest, but deeply appreciative celebrations marked Kilpatrick's eighty-fifth birthday. The League for Industrial Democracy sponsored the largest of the festivities, which was held, appropriately, in Horace Mann Auditorium. A volume of letters from friends and former students had been compiled, including a message from President Eisenhower. Kilpatrick spoke six times during the month of his eighty-fifth birthday, including once at the presentation to John Childs of the resurrected Kilpatrick Award. He concluded this busy month by sponsoring a fund-raiser for the New Lincoln School and a scholarship in his name. Eleanor Roosevelt and Ralph Bunche cosponsored the event, and Louis Gimble hosted the party at his residence. Ten thousand dollars were raised, and Kilpatrick had his picture taken with the Gimbles' daughter.[60]

These two milepost birthday celebrations for Kilpatrick had been preceded by John Dewey's ninetieth birthday fete in 1949. Dewey had been so overwhelmed on his seventieth birthday that he failed to appear at a similar celebration held a decade later. For his ninetieth, though, he did arrive at the Commodore Hotel (somewhat tardy, in his usual fashion), to the rousing applause of a crowd of 1,500 and the strains of "Happy Birthday." *Time* magazine, reporting on the event, claimed that almost every public school in America had been "Deweyized": "In five decades the emphasis has shifted from the subject to the pupil, from rote-learning to problem-solving, from drilling to creative thinking." *Newsweek*, also reporting on the celebration, quoted a wag who remarked that Dewey must be half as old as God. Dewey himself declared,

"Development and growth are two of my main ideas. I hope I'm sticking by them." *Life* magazine linked the roots of progressive education to Dewey and also alluded to the fact that Dewey had been labeled a "red" twenty years before.[61]

Kilpatrick had worked diligently on the preparations for this evening honoring Dewey, especially in securing a tribute from the president of Columbia, Dwight Eisenhower. Because of his connection with Dewey, Kilpatrick was seated on the dais. Harold Taylor, president of Sarah Lawrence College, led the festivities, and a number of guests gave one- to two-minute tributes to Dewey. Several others, including Kilpatrick and Supreme Court Justice Felix Frankfurter, were given ten minutes. John Childs called Kilpatrick's homage the best of the evening. Kilpatrick compared the old philosophies, grounded in eternal verities, cosmic purposes, and deductive logic, with the new tools of modern science and inductive, experimental logic. Pragmatism, experience, and interests were also woven into Kilpatrick's own notions concerning personality and character development. He concluded his tribute by stressing the centrality of the formation of social life: "The obligation of society to make its education all that it should be becomes the paramount social duty."[62]

President Truman sent greetings to Dewey, as did the prime minister of Great Britain, Clement Attlee, who said, "The impact of your writings and teachings has reached thinking men and women throughout the English-speaking world, showing them the true nature of democracy and thereby strengthening their faith in the democratic way of life."[63] Dewey's late arrival — well after the program had begun — puzzled Kilpatrick, as did the philosopher's behavior during a surprise visit from Nehru to pay tribute: While the prime minister of India was talking, Dewey stood on the dais waving to friends in the audience. But Kilpatrick considered the evening a great success and was astonished at the strong international following that Dewey had developed over the years.

Two nights later, on October 22, 1949, another meeting to honor Dewey was held at Teachers College, where Eisenhower, Henry Steele Commanger, and Horace Kallen all gave major addresses to an overflowing crowd in Horace Mann Auditorium. Kilpatrick provided a brief opening talk and made the introductions. Although later, when he became president of the United States, Eisenhower would say that Dewey had had a negative impact on American education, on this evening the two men chatted amiably. On the way out of the hall, John Childs overheard someone say, "Well, you can count on old Kilpatrick to say more in ten words than most will say in ten minutes." Kilpatrick called on the Deweys the following week to deliver a photograph of Dewey and

Eisenhower. Dewey was in good health and apparently gratified by the celebrations held in his honor.[64]

Dewey died three years later on June 1, 1952, at the age of ninety-three. His death so troubled Kilpatrick that he was obliged to take a sedative to get to sleep, and even that did not bring him rest — he dreamed he was managing Dewey's funeral. As for the actual funeral, Kilpatrick was at first scheduled to be a speaker, but Mrs. Dewey later requested that Max Otto, professor emeritus at the University of Wisconsin, be the sole speaker. The service was held at Community Church on 35th Street and Park Avenue. This location perturbed Kilpatrick, who thought a church an odd choice for the site and would have preferred either Hunter College or Carnegie Hall. Kilpatrick was seated near the front and was greeted by Jane and Evelyn Dewey and later the widow and the Deweys' adopted children, John and Adrienne. The following month, Kilpatrick recorded a radio tribute to Dewey at the Museum of Modern Art.[65]

In addition to his own birthday celebrations, other honors came Kilpatrick's way. The Jewish community acknowledged his contributions more than once in the early 1950s. In 1953 he received a doctorate of Hebrew letters from the College of Jewish Studies; in the same year he and the Nobel laureate Solman Waksman, developer of streptomycin, received the prestigious Louis Brandeis Award presented by *The Jewish Forum*. The citation spoke of Kilpatrick's international influence as a teacher, his impact on America's schools, and his constant advocacy for the development of character, personality, and behavior. The solid gold medal was placed around his neck, and he gave a fifteen-minute speech, "Attacks on Modern Education." In December of 1953, *The Jewish Forum* published an entire issue honoring Kilpatrick and his life's work. Also in 1953, Kilpatrick received the Abraham Lincoln Award from Lincoln High School, and a portrait of him was unveiled at Mercer University.[66]

The cool, distant relationship between Kilpatrick and the formal power structure at Teachers College, embodied in William F. Russell, began to thaw a dozen years after the retirement crisis. The rapprochement began in 1950, when Kilpatrick made a significant decision about his personal finances. He and Marion approached Teachers College with an offer to donate $100,000 to the institution, with the understanding that they would receive the income from the investment of the contribution as long as they lived. It was a generous offer on Kilpatrick's part, in that the total worth of his estate at this time was approximately $150,000. (Marion's holdings were near $40,000.) But with the addition of his Teachers College annuity, the Kilpatricks were able to make this contribution and still live comfortably, even in the inflationary postwar economy. Randolph Burgess, a

prominent banker and one of the most influential members of the Teachers College Board of Trustees, was greatly surprised that a professor had been able to accumulate so much money. Kilpatrick wanted the gift to be used to carry on his work in the philosophy of education, either through funding an actual lecture series or through research and publication. He also stipulated that a faculty committee in the philosophy of education department should have control over the funds.[67]

Relations between Kilpatrick and Teachers College seemed even brighter as William Russell, who had been made president of Teachers College, neared the end of his tenure, and Hollis Caswell, as dean and then as Russell's successor, took control. When Kilpatrick attended the 200th anniversary of the founding of Columbia, Caswell intimated that he would be seeking his advice on a number of issues. Soon after, Caswell invited Kilpatrick to his office, indicating that he was concerned over the future of the institution. The two men discussed appointments to faculty committees and the naming of four endowed professorships — one of them in Kilpatrick's honor. After being relegated to virtual obscurity by Russell, Kilpatrick found such words from Caswell music to his ears. He reciprocated by offering Caswell the use of a portion of his earlier donation to support the proposed chair in his name. At the end of the conversation, Caswell mentioned a number of friends of Teachers College who had signified their appreciation for Kilpatrick as a teacher and thinker. Caswell later sought Kilpatrick's advice on a potential $5 million gift to Teachers College from the Ford Foundation to explore the uses of radio and television in teaching. Caswell and Kilpatrick, possibly uncomfortable with the new technology, both viewed the offer as an attempt to put teacher education "back fifty years," and it was declined.[68]

The summer of 1954 saw the publication of *A History of Teachers College, Columbia University* by Lawrence Cremin, David Shannon, and Mary Evelyn Townsend. Kilpatrick had mixed thoughts on the chronicle: on the one hand, he viewed the work as having been written by "newcomers and outsiders, anxious to please . . . not sensitive to the inner feelings of the participants"; but on the other hand, he considered that the "net result is on the whole good." He thought that he himself came off "rather well." The authors portrayed Kilpatrick as the popular Teachers College professor who had taught innumerable students, including those from sixty foreign countries, while bringing the legendary "million dollars" into Columbia's coffers. His distinguishing philosophy, according to this account, included the need for the schools to have a social orientation, for children to be engaged in purposeful activity, and for the curriculum to look more to the current needs of students than to future demands. The authors called Kilpatrick the "chief elaborator and popularizer" of Dewey's

philosophy.   His commitment to democracy and to acting with intelligent forethought was also mentioned. The book reviewed the debate between Bagley (standing for essentialism) and Kilpatrick (standing for progressivism) and mentioned the Discussion Group, though without giving Kilpatrick credit as its leader. The retirement issue went unmentioned, and the social reconstructionist movement during the Depression received only passing notice as a "stimulating and fascinating adventure" and an "unforgettable educational experience" for the students.[69]   Cremin would later have more to say about Kilpatrick in *The Transformation of the School*, published in 1962.

The Kilpatricks continued to take great interest in national politics, especially in the presidential election of 1952 between Adlai Stevenson (the governor of Illinois) and Columbia University's Dwight Eisenhower. Kilpatrick supported both Stevenson and his running mate, Senator John Sparkman. While he understood that Sparkman's presence as a southerner on the ticket would lessen the Democratic Party's commitment to civil rights, Kilpatrick erroneously assumed that blacks would vote Republican, an outcome that he felt sure would encourage a strong two-party system in the South and thereby advance minority rights. Although the Kilpatricks did not own a television, Marion was addicted to the convention and election coverage, watching the political events on a neighbor's set — once until three in the morning. While Kilpatrick voted for Stevenson — there was even a Stevenson sticker on their apartment door — he realized that a change in political parties would not be altogether bad for the country. He also voted for George Counts, who ran, unsuccessfully, for the United States Senate in New York on the Liberal Party ticket. Kilpatrick thought that his former colleague was a fine extemporaneous speaker, but when giving a prepared speech he was enough to "kill any ordinary political assembly." After voting on November 4, the Kilpatricks listened to the election returns.   In Kilpatrick's opinion, the reasons for Eisenhower's victory were communist hysteria, the need for a change, unfair charges of corruption in the Truman administration, and, finally, Eisenhower's pledge to end the war in Korea.[70]

In the early 1950s, Kilpatrick began to participate in the exchange of "Robin-Trot" letters among his college classmates, an activity undertaken by the Mercer class of 1905. He kept up-to-date on recent happenings in the region near White Plains through the *Greensboro Herald-Journal*; his brother Howard was a subscriber and would drop it off after reading it. In 1953, Kilpatrick and Marion experienced an innovation in motion pictures, "Cinerama" — a large semicircular screen with amplified sound, which placed the viewer vicariously within the action of the film. While a Cinerama river ride gave Kilpatrick

"seasickness," he enjoyed the travelogue aspects of the film. The Kilpatricks also attended the Broadway production of *Inherit the Wind*, which, despite "exaggerations," as he put it, he found engaging. He was unusually profuse in his admiration for Lawrence Olivier's film *Richard III*. "This was a great movie," he declared, in part, no doubt, because he had seen this Shakespeare play as a sophomore at Mercer sixty years before. But the Kilpatricks' entertainment — such as it was — consisted more of attending United Nations events and meetings and luncheons of the American Jewish Congress, the American Civil Liberties Union, the American Association of University Professors, and the Urban League. Speakers at these events included Roger Baldwin, Sol Hurok, Marian Anderson, and Nelson Rockefeller. It was at one of these meetings that Kilpatrick first met Robert Hutchins, with whom he had parried in newspaper articles twenty years before.[71]

The weeklong summer workshops at schools and colleges, such as the one at Pasadena that had sparked so much controversy, occurred with less frequency. While not himself a viewer, he did make an occasional appearance as a panelist on television — frequently on local affiliates or New York City network flagships. His topic had shifted to the moral and spiritual (as distinct from religious) aspects of teaching, and he still received significant coverage in the press, usually of a positive nature. Retrieving ideas that he had espoused more than fifty years earlier, he suggested eliminating examinations and warned against the dubious consequences of coercion. "You know," he told a reporter from Louisville, "a great many people who are made to go to church learn not to go to church." Reiterating the Constitution's prohibition of teaching religion in the schools, Kilpatrick maintained that children nevertheless should and could be taught moral and spiritual values, advocating integrity and decision-making. "Nobody learns somebody else's formulation unless he's had considerable experience along that line," he declared. Although he was well received during these appearances, such events had lost their satisfaction for him. "I do not feel any great success or any great personal pleasure in connection with the week," he wrote in his diary.[72] There were brief two- or three-day visits, during which he would be the keynote speaker for the PTA or for a university conference. But while he was still in excellent health for a man in his eighties, his active days of travel, with extended stays at an institution, were drawing to a close.

While advocating nonsectarian moral and spiritual education, Kilpatrick did become deeply involved, along with Eleanor Roosevelt, in opposing legislation to provide federal aid to private and parochial schools. Kilpatrick argued that "the glory of our country" was the manner in which the public schools had

brought various immigrant groups together. (He was careful, though, not to push the idea of conformity too far, quoting Chief Justice Hughes, who said, "When we lose the right to be different, we lose the right to be free.") He conceded a religious group's legal right to establish separate schools in order to indoctrinate its children, though the morality of such instruction was questionable. However, that such a school should be funded by the federal government was unacceptable. Although many nonsectarian private schools had been on the forefront of the progressive movement, Kilpatrick stated that federal financial assistance could increase the number of private schools, which were concerned not with democratic goals, but rather with class snobbishness.

The issue was magnified when, during the summer of 1949, Eleanor Roosevelt and Cardinal Spellman entered the fray on opposite sides and the debate came to center on questions of religion. Mrs. Roosevelt stated in a meeting of the Committee on Federal Aid to Public Education that she opposed legislation proposed by John F. Kennedy, then a congressman from Massachusetts, that would allow federal monies to be spent on parochial schools' transportation. Kilpatrick also spoke to the group, voicing his objections to actions which would damage the wall of separation between the state and religion. A photograph appeared in the *New York Times*, showing Kilpatrick sharing the rostrum with Mrs. Roosevelt and a number of congressmen. Kilpatrick and Mrs. Roosevelt found themselves together on numerous other occasions, as they were both part of the liberal political circle in New York City that often banded together on such issues. In 1954 he attended her seventieth birthday celebration, where Edward R. Murrow was master of ceremonies and Ralph Bunche was one of the major speakers. Kilpatrick was especially honored in 1955, when he was privileged to introduce Mrs. Roosevelt, Margaret Mead, and Norman Cousins at the "Education for the Atomic Age" conference in New York City, supplying glowing remarks about each.[73]

With regards to the national political scene, Kilpatrick believed that although during his first term President Eisenhower was a "good and well meaning man," he "lacked the insight and drive necessary to make a successful leader." The Kilpatricks were in Schuylerville during the political conventions of 1956 and once again watched portions of them on television. Although still an enthusiastic supporter of Stevenson, Kilpatrick found the lengthy traditions associated with the political conventions to be tedious. After viewing the Republican convention, he told Marion that he did not wish to watch these party gatherings again. The Kilpatricks continued to faithfully support the Democratic ticket: once again they placed a Stevenson sign on their apartment door and they

worked with the Liberal Party of New York at several functions on the Columbia campus that fall. When Stevenson lost his second bid to become president, Kilpatrick noted tersely in his diary that he "regretted" it, but "rejoiced to hear that Wayne Morse (a liberal westerner) had been elected to the Senate over Eisenhower's special efforts to the contrary."

As the decade reached its midpoint, the seemingly ever-youthful Kilpatrick began to suffer the inevitable setbacks of a man in his eighties. He became a bit more absent-minded and had two nasty falls, which seemed to point to a lessening of his equilibrium. His hands also began to "behave unreliably," and by his eighty-third birthday, he had to admit that he was indeed beginning to feel older. Kilpatrick was forgetting many things, especially names; but creatively, he believed he could still function quite adequately. His eyes began to fail him by his eighty-fourth birthday, and he found himself sleeping more — taking both morning and afternoon naps — and wishing for less interaction with other people. Kilpatrick's famous walks had all but ceased. He made one more attempt, in 1956, to take an extended constitutional, but it proved too taxing for him.[75]

But all this did not seem to affect Kilpatrick's schedule and he began to travel by air rather than rail, though at first he was concerned about possible damage to his ears. During his travels, usually undertaken in connection with family visits, he was invariably recognized by former students and by people who had heard him speak at conferences and conventions. And his family continued to grow.[76] His grandson, Ted Baumeister III was married in 1955, and Kilpatrick became a great-grandfather the following year. His other grandson — his namesake Heard Kilpatrick Baumeister — was married in 1957. More great-grandchildren soon began to follow. And so a decade which had begun with continued professional involvement, even on the national stage, was now winding slowly down as health problems and family interests superseded a life of nonstop activity that had begun a half-century before when he first arrived in New York City.

RACE, RELIGION, AND THE SOUTH

Listening at an early age to the stories of the grandparents and also to reminiscences of the more ancient blacks, the boy had puzzled over the vanished condition of slavery. For the life of him he could see only superficial differences in the former and present systems.

Ferrol Sams, from *Run with the Horseman*[1]

The South, one might say, is a tree with many age rings, with its limbs and trunk bent and twisted by all the winds of the years, with its tap root in the Old South.

W. J. Cash, *The Mind of the South*[2]

There must no longer be exploitation of so-called "backward" peoples or ill-treatment of minority groups. We must create a system to help all people toward legal equality with all others in self-government.

Segregation is the polar opposite of democracy and any defensible ethics.

William Heard Kilpatrick, 1943[3]

Two issues ran through the life of William Heard Kilpatrick that are not easily placed within the confines of a chronological account. They were the questions of race and religion, and how his native region — the South — influenced the development of his thinking on both of them. His concern with these issues originated in his childhood and youth. If the word "struggle" does not exactly describe the manner in which he grappled with race and religion, he certainly devoted a significant amount of thought and action to each during his adult life. The development of Kilpatrick's thought on race will be considered first, followed by an examination of his ideas on religion.

It could be said that while Kilpatrick held racist views the first half of his life, he renounced those ideas and moved further and further toward being an

integrationist as the years passed. As will be seen, while never taking part in or condoning overt acts of persecution, he believed in a restrained and gradual implementation of the social component of racial relations. While he would eventually entertain African-Americans in his home, push for total and unqualified equality of minorities in all aspects of life, and support the rapid and changing practices in race relations as a result of court decisions, Kilpatrick maintained a moderate and cautious approach toward each of these steps. Terms such as "gradualist," "patient," "prudent," and "ameliorist" have been used to describe Kilpatrick's approach toward racial justice. While he never personally employed a justification for racial inequality grounded in Southern traditions, to expect Kilpatrick — born in the Georgia of Reconstruction — to be on the forefront of the civil rights movement would be unrealistic. Yet his personal growth toward what could be considered a liberal view on racial matters was profound.

Kilpatrick was the son of a fifth-generation (possibly eighth-generation) slaveowner. A photograph of a former slave and Kilpatrick's grandsons, taken during the Depression, can be found in a family album. In 1940, on accepting the chairmanship of the Bureau for Intercultural Education, he stated: "You know, my family was probably the largest owner of slaves in the state in Georgia. I have a responsibility in this cause."[4] While never defending the practice of enslavement, he remained, for a great portion of his life, closely attached to his native region. A quarter century after his birth, he placed in his diary the words to "Rah! Rah! Rah! Georgia!" which included the lines:

> Tho' this world I've traveled over, and have sailed its many seas,
> My home is sunny Georgia, the dearest spot to me.
> Her sons and daughters fair — a joyous, happy band,
> At Freedom's shrine still worship, and love their Georgia land.[5]

Without bringing postintegration historical interpretations to bear on this song, one still must realize that the state described in its lyrics was certainly not one that all citizens of Georgia would identify with. The idea of the "lost cause" was conspicuous, even unavoidable, during the post-Reconstruction era. One historian has pointed out that the period from 1885 to 1912 — when Kilpatrick was an adolescent and a young adult — saw the founding of the United Confederate Veterans and the Daughters of the Confederacy, and the erection of numerous monuments to the South's fallen.[6] In fact, Kilpatrick never accepted the idea that Reconstruction had a positive legacy. Even after the

decision in *Brown v. Board of Education* in 1954, Kilpatrick continued to argue that Reconstruction "did not solve the problem" of racial relations in the South, but rather created a caste system in the region in response to the North's heavy-handedness. On being asked by his sister-in-law in 1955 how slaves were treated, he gave the frequent southern response that most upper-class owners dealt with them "considerately."[7] The lines from "Rah! Rah! Rah! Georgia!" become even more ironic when one considers that they were copied by him just one year after the Atlanta race riots of 1906. Apparently, Kilpatrick could separate his own notion of the state from the more egregious collective actions of its citizens.

And yet not even the deep South could remain immune to the changes emerging in the early twentieth century. While teaching at Mercer in 1904, northern professors visiting the campus would engage their guests in conversation on the race issue. Kilpatrick noted in his diary the lynchings of blacks. One lynching that he read about took place in Statesboro in 1905 and included a burning, the body being doused with the contents of a five-gallon oil can. Apparently, only the ministers and lawyers in the town objected to the act. In his biography, Tenenbaum reported that Kilpatrick joined with other citizens in Columbus, Georgia, during his year as principal there (1906-1907), to study local conditions in order to prevent the spread of further violence. Tenenbaum claimed that Kilpatrick moved north as an "unreconstructed southerner" and that even after he had lived in New York City for many years, his "emotional living and thinking" was bound up with the South. Tenenbaum concluded that the South was where Kilpatrick ultimately wished to work and serve.[8] This was not exactly accurate. While he always preferred the social niceties of southern friendliness, hospitality, and regional traditions, Kilpatrick's connections with the South diminished as the years passed, especially after the death of his mother and his sister Helen. And it can be stated with certainty that he had no desire to leave Teachers College. Even when, early in his career, he was approached with offers to return to the South, he never pursued them. In fact, at the Teachers College Alumni Conference in March of 1921, he outlined in great detail his affinity for the institution which had become his home and his base of operations in the battle for the "new education."[9]

When Kilpatrick moved to New York in 1907 he began to hear views that were rarely, if ever voiced in his native South. One lecturer speculated on a time when racial differences, even skin color, would disappear as a distinction. While open to progressive thinking on race at this time, Kilpatrick found it difficult to accept the views of people with New England abolitionist roots.

Upon reading a biography of John Hay, he became irate that the former Secretary of State had nothing good to say about the South and its leaders — even a single Democrat. "The more I see of the abolitionist mind," he wrote, "the less admirable it appears." He was often reinforced in his thinking. A colleague, after seeing the play *Birth of a Nation* (soon to become a D. W. Griffith film) stated that if it was anywhere near the truth, it was no wonder that the South did all it could to regain white control during Reconstruction. Even Elwood Cubberley's *History of Public Education in the United States* irritated him as being rabidly pro-New England while understating the role of the South.[10] And yet, reading biographies of Southern leaders, such as Jefferson Davis, written by northern historians, gave him pause. Kilpatrick realized there was an element of truth in what they wrote, and a greater sensitivity to racial injustice eventually emerged in his life. Upon reading that in 1853 white women in Virginia had been imprisoned for teaching free blacks to read, he wrote, "I am mortified and ashamed."[11]   In 1912, after reading Olmstead's *Seaboard Slave States*, he became even more troubled:

> I must confess it has influenced me powerfully. Slavery appears more certainly an economically unwise system and a morally wrong institution. I confess it comes to be a hateful scheme whereby a few exploited others. Not only did the slaveholder exploit the slave, but the slaveholding regime suppressed the poor white, and in all to the detriment of the community. I feel less proud of the South.[12]

But there remained room for further growth in Kilpatrick's thinking on the so-called "Negro problem." In 1909, he privately advocated continued white political control — a difficult proposition, given the 13th, 14th, and 15th Amendments — and a continuation of the "separate but equal" status of blacks in the schools, churches, theaters, and streetcars. The euphemism he used was a "dual economic and social system." An even more racist comment was recorded by Kilpatrick in 1913, when he noted with approval that the death rate for blacks in Kansas City ran higher than the birthrate. He indicated that if such figures could only be replicated in rural areas, the "problem" might solve itself. "As it is," he wrote, "the Negro is a fearful handicap to the South."[13]

While reading John Bright in 1914, he became outraged over the fact that the South was attacked on the slavery issue. Heartened that the Union was strong and slavery gone, he still could not at times abide the fact that the South

had lost. He made the familiar rejoinder that the slaves in the South were better taken care of than the poor in England at the same time, and that while certain practices — such as separating families, sexual license, and cruel punishments — made him "shudder," these occurrences were not common. We have paid for our "sinning," he asserted, and he resented the holier-than-thou attitude of those whom he felt had profited from the Confederacy's misfortunes. This diatribe, like others, he later revised. A line added to his diary in 1947 states simply, "I find that I cannot subscribe to the foregoing in any full degree." At this same time, Kilpatrick, upset that his maid, an African-American, had left during their move to a new apartment, called the behavior irresponsible and "characteristic of the race." He also later retracted and regretted this outburst.[14]

The diversity of race and culture Kilpatrick encountered in New York City, especially in the student body of Teachers College, eventually began to transform his thinking. Concern for the treatment of other minority groups also emerged, but with mixed results. Kilpatrick was always troubled about the plight of women in society, but more from an economic or social point of view than from a concept of outright equality. He was often frustrated by the fact that women were unable to rise within the academic world. In a remark exemplifying his ambivalence on the gender issue, he attributed such sexual discrimination to "general prejudice against women in authority and partly the fault of old maidishness." Later on, he noted that agism was added to the discriminatory treatment of women when he observed that society would not give a woman over the age of fifty a decent position, no matter how talented or educated she might be.

Kilpatrick also included rare anti-Semitic statements in his diary, which — as with his inappropriate comments on the race issue he would repudiate years later when rereading and indexing his early entries. One example is an entry he made in 1909 regarding the inability of some of his Jewish students at the Pratt Institute to compete with non-Jewish students, especially in "ethical qualities." Forty years later, he placed in the margin of this page: "History, not heredity to blame." During the First World War he was troubled over the problem of assimilation of immigrants, especially Jews, and he even debated the issue with Dewey. (Ethnic bias also reared its head when, upon meeting his future son-in-law, Theodore Baumeister, Kilpatrick expressed mild concern over the German surname.) A part of Kilpatrick's problem with what he once termed the "Jewish mind" was philosophical. He could not countenance any closed system of thinking — in the case of Judaism, one based on the Talmud — that caused thought to turn in on itself.[15]

When outsiders criticized the South, Kilpatrick could become quite

defensive. The Southern Club of Columbia University Summer Session, the organization that he and Rita had helped to found in 1910, had a speaker one evening who made a number of disparaging remarks regarding the standard of living in Eatonton, Georgia. Kilpatrick rose and challenged the speaker with such uncharacteristic vehemence that the chair for the evening decided to adjourn the meeting. Actually, the Southern Club itself frequently displayed not-so-subtle racism in the themes and skits the members presented at their annual meetings. Kilpatrick noted them in his diary, but he did not condemn them. On one occasion, South Carolina was ruled out of a competition because it had allowed a black to play the part of a "Negro." (By the 1930s the Southern Club, which had reached a membership of 3,000 in 1921 and had become a mainstay for Columbia students from below the Mason-Dixon Line, would begin to lose both numbers and interest.)

At this point in his life, Kilpatrick remained unabashedly pro-southern. As was indicated earlier, his marriage to Rita was in part based on his predisposition for all things southern, a predilection evidenced by his decision to send his daughter, Margaret, to school at Ashley Hall in Charleston. (His granddaughter, Mary, would also enroll at Ashley Hall, in the 1950s.) Kilpatrick wanted Margaret to meet the "best-bred" girls and concluded that his wife's family, the Pinckneys, were too prominent for his daughter not to profit from being in the South. According to him, northern women were too loud, usually morally loose, and far less refined — even cruder — than their southern counterparts. He would note Memorial Day in Georgia in his diary, believing that while much had been gained for the nation through the conflict, much was also lost by the South. On one occasion, in the 1920s, he stated that he held the day sacred, not because of the merits of the Confederacy, but as recalling a movement that had protested the interference of outsiders. In 1930 Kilpatrick used a familiar argument of southern liberals which placed the blame for racism on the northern military occupation during Reconstruction. This use of force rather than reason had resulted, he said, in an "orthodoxy founded on ignorance." And, always defensive in connection with his own and the South's favorite son, Woodrow Wilson, he even associated the Confederacy's defeat and the domination of the North in arts and letters to "Senator Lodge and his vile crew," blaming them for their actions against the president and the Versailles Treaty.[16]

One illustration of Kilpatrick's attachment to the South can be seen in the extraordinary bond he felt with Woodrow Wilson. Beyond common political viewpoints, Kilpatrick's lifetime affinity to Wilson can be explained only in the "southernness" and personal traits the two men shared. Both were born in the

South and had fathers who were ministers. Both did graduate work at Johns Hopkins University before moving on to successful teaching careers at prestigious northern universities. Charismatic idealism and strong oratorical skills in the classroom then boosted their careers. And finally, these two men, who both lost first wives to tuberculosis, ended their years of forced retirement — one due to health, the other to campus politics — in the company of much younger wives who proved to be staunch protectors and aggressive defenders of their husbands' legacies.

One scholar, Walter Feinberg, has suggested that progressive education lacked any clear appraisal of Negro education until almost 1940. Even John Dewey, active in the formation of the National Association for the Advancement of Colored People, had a "limited vision" of Negro education in America. Feinberg noted that in *Schools of Tomorrow*, by Dewey and his daughter Evelyn, Dewey accepted Booker T. Washington's philosophy: that Negroes should accept the vocational or trades path offered within the schools, rather than aspire to the professional tracks. As John and Evelyn Dewey examined Public School 26 in Indianapolis, Indiana, they failed to ask what role education could play in promoting equal opportunity or social justice for minorities.[17]

Kilpatrick, though, did make progress on this issue well before World War II. Kilpatrick agreed with a report published by the United States Bureau of Education in 1917, which found that damage was occurring from the South's ill-treatment of Negroes. He also agreed at this time that there was no scientific evidence of transmission of acquired characteristics ("It is education broadly considered that makes the differences.") and mentioned a need for "amalgamation" of the races. Privately, he advocated a more active role for the federal government in the education of Negroes and in the relocation of Negroes outside the South. As a southerner, he "abominated" such a procedure, but as a man of science and ethics he had to approve of it.[18] The rational man was slowly overtaking the emotional man, but it was a struggle. By the end of the 1920s, one could say that Kilpatrick was within the mainstream of southern liberalism, as exemplified by W. J. Cash, author of the classic study of the region, *The Mind of the South*. Southern liberals gave no credence to the view that Negroes were inherently inferior, nor did they provide justifications for slavery. Yet on other topics, such as Reconstruction, the mystical southern way of life, and the superiority of his native culture to the culture of the North, Kilpatrick was not as enlightened. He could look at the South and see inequity, injustice, and also a path toward a better way; but it may be said that when he

looked, he occasionally flinched.

Kilpatrick took the moderate, but significant, step of expressing his opinions on the race issue during a southern speaking tour in the midst of the First World War. In May of 1917 he publicly called upon the South to be more tolerant, to read more, and to allow greater diversity of opinion. His talk was "Education as Socialization," and he gave it to the Georgia Educational Association, a local history club, and several other groups during a trip to the South.[19] Issues of race would occasionally confront him in New York. During the 1920s, in response to the queries of a black woman who was attempting to stop lynchings in the South, Kilpatrick suggested that such a movement be led by a white southern woman and gave her the name of his minister friend, Ashby Jones, who might provide further advice. Jones, usually even-tempered, took Kilpatrick to task for even referring the woman to him.[20] The topic of lynching emerged again during his trip to India in the mid-1920s. Kilpatrick was asked point-blank about the practice and how it could be defended. Kilpatrick could not justify the atrocities, of course, and he was surely stung by the evident contradiction between democratic theory and practice that his hosts had brought to his attention.[21]

Thus Kilpatrick began to examine more closely his own presuppositions about race. In 1924, during an evening seminar led by Goodwin Watson on the topic of prejudice, a questionnaire was distributed, and Kilpatrick was "chagrined" to see more personal bias on his part than he cared to admit. And yet the following month, when Marion — who was then his secretary — "mistakenly" invited a "colored girl" to one of the Sunday afternoon teas at the apartment, he noted that, while he and Rita would not mind, they would "hate for it to be talked about back home." Whether the liberal Marion had actually done this by "mistake" is open to conjecture. Later blacks were welcomed to the Kilpatrick apartment, but it would not be until 1942 that an African-American shared the Kilpatricks' dinner table. Kilpatrick made a record of that event; he noted, as well, the first time he gave up his seat to a black female on the subway, two years later. Despite his eloquent writings on the self-other process, he himself would on occasion view blacks as a group rather than as individuals. When he and Marion attended a performance by Paul Robeson in *Othello*, his comment was that "Negroes . . . must have felt pride that one of their group could win such applause."[22]

And yet, despite the prejudices Kilpatrick brought with him, personal breakthroughs on race did occur. In 1925, some African-American students moved into his building, and while as a southerner he found it "awkward," as

"a thinker and a moralist" it marked the breakdown of the "indefensible color line." At other times, though, he continued to be torn over the issue. For example, at one point rumors circulated that blacks were being excluded from a student dinner to be held at Teachers College. When a Canadian student asked, in class, if the rumor was true, Kilpatrick refused to allow the matter to be discussed. On another occasion in Hampton, Virginia, Kilpatrick was asked whether Gandhi's method of passive resistance might be applied in the South in connection with the "black-white situation." He did not record his own opinion, but he noted that the consensus of the group, mainly blacks, was not in favor of such action.[23] But his two trips around the world in the 1920s increased Kilpatrick's receptivity to the reality of cultural diversity.

As the 1920s progressed, Kilpatrick began to take an active role in advancing the status of blacks. He went with a Negro minister to the Lincoln School to meet with Jesse Newlon in an attempt to get the clergyman's daughter enrolled in classes. The minister had heard the false report that Newlon, as an administrator in Denver, had advocated segregation. In the 1930s, during an address given at a conference in Talladega, Alabama, on "The Function of the Negro Liberal Arts College," Kilpatrick shared the stage with W. E .B. DuBois, and argued that the best way to improve the culture was through the family. Kilpatrick held Du Bois in high regard. When told in 1931 that DuBois had said that any man who had not known the South in the last five years was a fool to talk about it, Kilpatrick found the statement significant. At the same time, his audiences at white schools and colleges were often segregated — either by holding separate meetings or by blacks being required to sit in the balcony.[24]

Fred Hobson has written that "rare indeed was the southern liberal who had decided against racial segregation by the 1930s, rarer still the southerner who would announce such a decision." In a way, Kilpatrick was becoming as much a northern liberal as a southern one. And there would remain, despite all his actions, involvements, and stands against racial inequality, a dichotomy between what he affirmed on the conceptual level and what he believed personally regarding blacks. Kilpatrick was caught in what Ronald Goodenow has called a "double bind." He no doubt wished to protect the southern mores, folkways, and culture he considered important, including the literature of the South, its emphasis on decorous interpersonal relations, and its social customs. Yet he realized that economic and social progress had to be made or the South would be doomed to third-class status for years to come.[25]

Kilpatrick did begin to articulate these ideas, at least in a restrained manner, during his Weil lectures at the University of North Carolina in 1928. (These

lectures were later expanded and published as a book, *Our Educational Task as Illustrated in the Changing South.*) For the first time on a large scale, Kilpatrick spoke in the South to the South. The local press gave the addresses significant attention, with headlines such as "Warns South to Shun Bigotry" and "South Shaken."[26] The *New York Times* noted the series, which had been carried over the Associated Press wires. Kilpatrick knew that the South had to end its isolation in order to prosper economically. He pointed out that "defensive mechanisms" too often took the place of constructive thinking, "inferiority complexes" emerged, and a "stagnant orthodoxy" had become prevalent in the South. Kilpatrick directly mentioned the adverse effect of the Ku Klux Klan, not only on Negroes, but on whites. He went on to speak directly of "discrimination against the Negro" and the unwillingness of Southerners to allow "the Negro to live on just and equal terms." As Goodenow has pointed out, he did employ "rhetorical scare tactics" in the lectures, stating that "the South must do justice to the Negro. Wrong begets wrong. A day of reckoning will come. 'Radicalism' is too easily bred not to be feared. The only way out lies along the road of fair play." Kilpatrick also blamed mindless religious fundamentalism and a general lowering of social mores as additional causes of the South's persistently low morale and low economic status.[27]

If such rhetoric was indeed meant to frighten his fellow southerners, it was a strategy Kilpatrick rarely used. His emphasis was, rather, the need to reconstruct attitudes through communication, tolerance, and better understanding between individuals. In fact, he rarely touched upon the products of discrimination — political oppression, poverty, and lack of economic opportunity — choosing instead to focus on the process by which blacks could emerge from the condition they currently endured.

In 1933 Kilpatrick heard for the first time his future adversary, Governor Eugene Talmadge of Georgia. The governor's demagoguery, and his poor grammar, irritated Kilpatrick, who felt "ashamed for my state." A decade later, during an educational conference in Georgia, Kilpatrick struck at Talmadge for the first time. Some in the audience laughed when Kilpatrick indicated, in humorous terms, what a disgrace Talmadge was to the state. He also criticized a state judge, J. B. Jackson who was a graduate of Mercer and a former student of Kilpatrick's. Jackson, had made the statement that "any unintelligent white man, if only he was white, was better than any nigger no matter how well educated."[28]

By 1935 Kilpatrick's thinking had advanced to the point where he believed that racial equality must be attempted by democratic measures. (Whether he

meant full social equality at this juncture is uncertain.) Speaking to the Negro Education Club at Columbia, he stressed his view that a gradual, ameliorative approach to racial divisions was needed, but he speculated that it would take as long as fifty years to achieve the goal. He totally rejected maintaining the status quo by undemocratic methods or overturning the current system by violent means. In the South, he continued to give strong speeches expressing these views — on one occasion in 1936 before the largest group of teachers ever assembled in Richmond. There were also lectures at segregated colleges in the South, such as Southern University in Louisiana.[29]

New thinking and new approaches to the issue of race were to emerge during the Depression years, and they became topics of conversation at discussion groups and seminars at Teachers College. An example would be the views of two of Kilpatrick's former students, Buell Gallagher and John Childs, who differed on the methods to be employed to reach equality. Childs thought it best that Negroes run their own schools, while Gallagher, who was president of Talladega College, a black institution, was not persuaded. (There was a school of thought that assistance to Negroes should take place through support and training to "intermediaries" — teachers, administrators, and givers of child care — rather than working directly with minorities.) While Kilpatrick did not share Childs's passion on the issue, he did tend to agree with him.[30]

As regards Gallagher, Kilpatrick took a step in 1938 which he believed would be viewed by his friends and family in the South as a betrayal. His former student's doctoral dissertation was being published by Columbia University Press under the title *American Caste and the Negro College*. Gallagher had asked Kilpatrick, who had been his major professor, to write the foreword to the book. "I hate to do it," he wrote in his diary, but did believe strongly enough in both the book and Gallagher to grant the request. The foreword sets out very clearly Kilpatrick's thoughts on race in the period before World War II, and yet at some points his conclusions are puzzling.

Kilpatrick began by acknowledging the importance of integrating Negroes into the mainstream of American society and by frankly admitting that the process was being impeded. The cause of such delays in assimilation, he felt, was a lack of understanding between the races. In an aside, he added that many believed that interference by "outsiders" had hindered progress, and he presented a halfhearted explanation, as a southerner, of how such a postulate could emerge. But he immediately returned to the issue of understanding, placing much of the onus on the "dominant group" — whites. Whites were also held accountable for denying blacks access to education and for erecting a

"master-slave paradigm," causing both races to create false personalities in order to deal with the condition they found themselves in. One critic has suggested that Kilpatrick was accusing blacks of compliance in such a situation, in effect blaming the victim, but this was not the case. Kilpatrick explicitly stated that the "master class wished it." Kilpatrick went on to reject once more the claim of innate racial differences and with notable sensitivity, he briefly discussed the insurmountable obstacles Negroes faced in attempting to build a culture after being torn from their African homelands. He struck one final blow at his native South, asserting that many in that region "still uphold to a greater or less degree the historic relationship" between the races.[31]

While significant, Kilpatrick's words cannot be extolled as consistent with the most progressive thinking on race at the time. Paradoxically, he claimed that Negroes, through schools, literature, and the media, had the means to secure a better understanding of the situation they found themselves in. (Exactly what blacks were to do about the situation was not addressed.) And yet whites, he maintained, have no similar recourse, leaving them in "danger of not understanding . . . the modern phase of the problem." But he did not see the need for taking immediate steps to alleviate the injustices, beyond promoting increased understanding through the educative process. Kilpatrick did make a notable personal admission — that Gallagher's work had given him a "clearer view of the problem," particularly what it meant to live "a life of perpetual denial of full life and opportunity." He concluded the foreword by stating that both the South and the nation needed to address the problem of race more resolutely, providing justice to all regardless of color or lack of opportunity, and characterizing the situation as a wrong which could result only in "multiplied evil."[32]

Four years prior to the publication of *American Caste and the Negro College*, Kilpatrick had given the inaugural address at Talladega College, a black institution, when Gallagher, a white, had become its president. In the speech he emphasized that it was individual characteristics, not group differences, which resulted in perceived racial disparities in behavior and intelligence. This line of thinking, taken to its logical conclusion, could imply that a cultural lag or miseducative process might be occurring in the black family, requiring formal education to remediate it.[33] But educational progress was slow. A significant number of minority and international students were enrolled in Kilpatrick's classes during his tenure at Teachers College, yet from 1876 through 1936 (the year Kilpatrick retired) Columbia awarded only twelve doctorates to blacks. Even in institutions where segregation did not hold sway,

the inclusion of blacks was meager at best. The total number of degrees awarded to blacks in the United States from 1876 to 1936 was 148. The University of Chicago ranked first, with Columbia, Harvard, and Cornell tied for second place.[34]

With the approach of World War II, Kilpatrick's interest and involvement in the rights of black Americans continued to grow. He would often repeat a talk in the South when local custom refused to let blacks meet in the same hall with whites, even in a separate section. After one talk to 150 black teachers in South Carolina, he was given an envelope with $10 in it. He quietly returned it, asking that it be spent in behalf of the group. In 1939 he gave an address in the chapel at Howard University in Washington, D.C., and noted that several of his former students were on the faculty. The same year he spoke at Carnegie Hall at the Inter-Racial Unity Meeting held under the auspices of the American Society for Race Tolerance.[35]

During the war years, Kilpatrick espoused his gradualist philosophy on race in the pages of the *Frontiers of Democracy* when he wrote, "Remaking the fundamental institutions takes time to . . . contrive the needed new institutional machinery . . . because time is always needed before a people can change any deep-set ideas."[36] Race was the topic of two of his other editorials in *Frontiers of Democracy*: "The Problem of Minorities" and "An Immoral Cultural Lag: Our War Treatment of Negroes." In the former, he spoke of the issue of race in generalities, indicating that the world was becoming too interdependent and the future of children was too crucial to let prejudices rule the day. In the latter, he likened the status of blacks to the caste system of India, stating that no evidence could support the charge of inborn inferiority in ability, morals, or talent. Kilpatrick said that discrimination was clearly present in the war factories, despite President Roosevelt's claim that none existed. The matter was made worse, according to Kilpatrick, in that educated minorities had become conscious of their unjust treatment. Racial discrimination was a moral problem, and he concluded that whites could not treat others unjustly without hurting themselves in the process. An array of social problems could be ameliorated, he believed, if economic inequity in America were rectified.[37] Even before the attack on Pearl Harbor, Kilpatrick took note of the ill-treatment of Japanese Americans, calling for both these citizens and Negroes to be permitted to share in the fruits of the nation's move toward "cultural democracy." One student of Kilpatrick's racial views and practices classified his overall position on race and ethnicity as "advanced, if not radical, for his times."[38]

In early 1940 Kilpatrick began his long association with the New York

Urban League. The Urban League had been founded in 1910, and the New York Urban League organized eight years later. James H. Hubert, a fellow Georgian — who was black — had gotten Kilpatrick involved, as well as a few other prominent whites. At the first meeting, Kilpatrick gave a fifteen-minute talk stressing his usual theme in racial matters — the importance of culture. But at one point in his presentation, he also mentioned the need for "patience" and was immediately aware that he had "struck a wrong note," even with this moderate audience. No doubt because of his southern upbringing, he often felt uncomfortable discussing racial matters in the presence of blacks. On this occasion, the "wrong note" may also have been due to an earlier verbal miscue, the exact nature of which was never made clear. After the meeting, he noted that "I find more sensitivity among the Negroes than I had been aware; I must be more careful." But the organization appreciated his presence and his interest, and in 1941 Kilpatrick became acting chairman (and later chairman) of the board of the New York Urban League, a position in which he oversaw organizational and financial matters.[39]

The Urban League was committed to assisting blacks who had migrated North, its function being one of reorientation rather than rehabilitation, and it was concerned more with cultural orientation than with economic or political issues. Goodenow has noted that these were aims with which Kilpatrick was entirely comfortable. He was able to take the "moribund and conflict-laden organization" and form it into an effective and visible group. (Also, through his affiliation with the Urban League, he became in 1944 a member of the board of Sydenham Hospital in Harlem.) He also played a key role in uniting the New York branch of the Urban League with the Brooklyn branch, forming the Urban League of Greater New York. In 1944 he went so far as to loan the Urban League $500 to keep the organization afloat financially. The association would last almost twenty years, and Kilpatrick would receive complimentary tickets to Urban League functions long after his active participation had ended.[40] At this same time, at a meeting of the American Civil Liberties Union, Kilpatrick met the writer Roger Baldwin. A decade later, writing a letter recognizing Baldwin's contributions to the A.C.L.U., he recorded that although they had "not always seen eye to eye," he did admire the controversial Baldwin for his work, especially after the organization broke with the communists.[41]

Kilpatrick also continued to take bolder steps in the South. In 1941, during an educational conference in Georgia, he asked Negroes to come down from the balcony and sit on the right-hand side of the room. He went a step further, placing four blacks on discussion panels. This was done, he later reported, in

total ignorance of some ugly words on both sides regarding the seating arrangements of the previous night. During the war, Kilpatrick addressed a different type of segregation. Meeting with sixty school principals to discuss the question of Jewish, Catholic, and Protestant teachers sitting separately at lunch, he suggested assailing such segregation, and that the principals should be "morally responsible for leading the attack." The assistant superintendent, who had called the meeting, adjourned it quickly after this proposal, and Kilpatrick noted that few spoke to him on the way out.[42]

The racial atmosphere was far from calm in New York City at this time. In the summer of 1941, what was referred to as the "Harlem crime wave situation" developed. In December, just four days after the bombing of Pearl Harbor, a meeting was held in Horace Mann Auditorium to address the issue, with Kilpatrick presiding. Speakers included George Counts, J. H. Hubert of the Urban League, and Dr. Adam Clayton Powell, Jr. (Powell was a member of the City Council and pastor of the Abyssinian Baptist Church and had been a student of Kilpatrick's in the early 1930s; he had taken an M.A. from Teachers College in 1932, finding the experience highly useful in his religious and political work.) Roma Gans called for a boycott of the press for misrepresenting the situation and Powell spoke vigorously, according to Kilpatrick, about the ill-treatment of blacks in Harlem. At the close of the meeting, Counts was called on to draft a telegram to President Roosevelt regarding it.[43]

Kilpatrick worked with other black leaders in the Urban League, such as Warren Brown and Edward Lewis. With racial tensions at what some believed to be a fifty-year high, the Urban League was seen as a moderate organization, as compared with the National Association for the Advancement of Colored People (N.A.A.C.P.). While never publicly or privately critical of the N.A.A.C.P., Kilpatrick evidently felt more comfortable with the Urban League. As a result of his chairmanship of the Urban League, Kilpatrick was called upon to represent the organization at numerous events such as war bond rallies. Also present at such events were Pearl Buck, Thomas Dewey, Olivia DeHaviland, and the black dancer Bill Robinson. Kilpatrick's exceptional human relations skills and his ability to lead discussions brought a complement on his sensitivity from Judge Herbert Delany, one of Fiorello La Guardia's black advisors. Delany called Kilpatrick a "perfect man." A vignette supports this tribute by a leader of the black community. One day a black courier from the Urban League, bringing checks for Kilpatrick to countersign as chairman of the board, mentioned that one of his college instructors had been a student at Teachers College and had admired Kilpatrick's work. Kilpatrick took time to show the man several of the

translations of his textbooks, after which the man said, "Dr. Kilpatrick, to know you is to love you. You are so kind. That's what they all say." To his diary, Kilpatrick confided, "I must confess I was much touched."[44]

The war years also brought the defeat of Eugene Talmadge as governor of Georgia. In 1942, during one of his trips to the South, Kilpatrick had given a strong speech, "Building National Unity on the Basis of Democracy," in which he had called for the majority to grant equal rights to minorities, the most urgent case being that of the Negroes. In one of his most forceful statements, leveled directly at Talmadge, he declared:

> But as a southerner, the descendant of a long line of
> slaveholders . . . and as a Georgian, I have to say that I think
> the Negro suffers most, and in most places, most unjustly. I
> am pleased however, to believe on the other hand that there is
> a positive movement among the better southern whites — I do
> not include the present governor of Georgia among these —
> to try to improve the situation of injustice. But much, very
> much, remains to be done.[45]

Before his defeat, Talmadge had severely damaged the state's University System by packing the board of regents with his own appointees in an attempt to force out two allegedly pro-integrationist administrators. One was Walter Cocking, dean of the College of Education at the University of Georgia; the other was Marvin Pittman, president of Georgia Teachers College in Statesboro, a former student of Kilpatrick's. Kilpatrick supported Pittman from afar as much as possible, earning the enmity of Talmadge in the process. Talmadge's attempt to remove these two respected educators, along with his subsequent packing of the board of regents with his own people, cost the state's higher education system its regional accreditation. Kilpatrick was to become strident, almost uncontrollably so, in his criticism of Talmadge over this issue. He used his bluntest language on the editorial page of *Frontiers of Democracy*: he called Talmadge a "politically scheming dictator" and a "demagogue," "subject to the limelight complex," "emotionally maladjusted," and, finally, in need of the services of a psychiatrist. Several major Georgia newspapers and a number of distinguished public figures were also highly critical of Talmadge's arbitrary action and Kilpatrick wrote that he had never seen such ridicule directed toward a public figure. According to him, Talmadge had pandered to the "lowest strata of white men," playing on race prejudice in Georgia in order

to win reelection. If these men were better educated and more economically secure, Kilpatrick concluded, Talmadge's message would have no effect.[46]

Kilpatrick rejoiced when Ellis Arnall defeated Talmadge in the Democratic primary. "It is very, very good," he wrote: "Good for the college system in Georgia, good for recognized education throughout the South, good for the Negro." Two months later, on a tour of the state with his friend Guy Wells, president of Georgia State College for Women in Milledgeville, Kilpatrick met with Ralph McGill of the *Atlanta Constitution*, who had, according to some, directed the fight against Talmadge's reelection. Wells, Kilpatrick, and McGill had lunch together and discussed the revival of the board of regents under the new governor. Kilpatrick told newspaper reporters that it would be "a long time before a politician would touch the school system again" and that he looked for great strides in education under Arnall. On January 22, 1943, Governor Arnall signed House Bill 1, which established a new board of regents and removed the governor as a member. Eight days later, the Southern Association of Colleges and Secondary Schools notified Arnall that accreditation had been restored to the University System of Georgia.[47]

Even after Talmadge's defeat, Kilpatrick was wary of him. Talmadge still had power, and that might pose a threat to the people and institutions that hosted Kilpatrick on his trips to Georgia. Kilpatrick was especially concerned for Guy Wells, who had been rumored in 1944 to be a possible candidate for chancellor of the University System. Talmadge's propaganda organ, ironically entitled *Statesmen* — which Kilpatrick labeled "a vile sheet" — accused Guy Wells of bringing Kilpatrick to Georgia at state expense. The charge was false. Kilpatrick was surprised to learn that comments he had made on his trip to Georgia in November 1942 "had got so keenly under Talmadge's skin." An editorial in the *Statesmen* declared that those who assisted in funding Kilpatrick's expenses (mainly public schools, which paid him a modest honorarium) were "crackpots," paying to have "false doctrines taught them." "It is not a question of racial prejudice in the South that moves us against co-education of blacks and whites," stated the editorial: "It is racial pride, pride of the white race to keep it pure!!!"[48] Kilpatrick concluded that Wells should not take the risk of extending any more invitations, at least not until Talmadge was out of the picture. Kilpatrick was "greatly saddened" when Talmadge regained the governorship in 1946. But then he suddenly died before taking office.[49]

During World War II, Kilpatrick finally set aside his seemingly blind devotion to the South's position in the Civil War. He had based this attachment on the ideal of states' rights, ignoring the overriding cause of the conflict —

slavery. In 1944, on the anniversary of Lee's surrender at Appomattox, he stated, "I used to fasten my attention on the local self-government aspect of the dispute. Now I believe that was an evasion of the real issue." As a result Kilpatrick now spoke more frequently, especially to parents' organizations, on the topic of how to improve race relations in the schools. He theorized that racial prejudice had its genesis in the tendency of individuals to fear groups perceived as threatening their way of life. He used as a text Shakespeare's line, "What we often fear in time we hate."[50]

In one of his most personal articles, Kilpatrick outlined his moderate yet progressive vision of intercultural education in America. Written in 1940, "Intercultural Education: A Program for American Democracy," stressed that inherent in the very notion of democracy was the human right to be different. He attacked unscientific beliefs in innate racial qualities held by many Americans with regard to Mexicans, Jews, Japanese, and Negroes. He specifically mentioned the Nazis' attacks against the Jews as being "cruel in their moral bearing." He emphasized the need in intercultural education for communication, mutual respect, and understanding. While noting the need for free elections and for effective use of legislation and the courts, he had reservations: "mere legal enforcement of legally defined rights" might prove insufficient. He closed this lengthy article with two personal vignettes —something he rarely did in his professional publications. First, he described how, having been raised in the South, he had taken the view that Negroes were "naturally inferior in mind and morals" and how he had overcome this belief. The second account dealt with a Jew he had known before World War I who had inexplicably distanced himself from Kilpatrick. He had inadvertently offended the man through a lack of sensitivity on some issue, though Kilpatrick did not know what it was. For Kilpatrick, attitudes were of extreme importance. The circle of distrust must be broken, he concluded, or "it will break us."[51]

On more than one occasion Kilpatrick was present at awards ceremonies for Jackie Robinson, who broke the color line in professional baseball when he joined the Brooklyn Dodgers in 1947. But Kilpatrick, who had little interest in sports, never seemed to appreciate the importance of this milestone step and privately questioned the practice of giving such recognition to a baseball player. In 1951, he received a gold watch marking his ten years of service as president of the Urban League of Greater New York; the inscription read, "Devoted President of the New York Urban League, 1940-1950." At about this time, however, African-Americans were coming to believe that white leadership had a moderating effect on their organizations and moved more toward black

control. There was also the continued competition, intentional or unintentional, between the National Urban League and the N.A.A.C.P. After *Brown v. Board of Education*, in which the N.A.A.C.P. Legal Defense Fund had played the preeminent role, the rivalry would become more intense.[52]

The Bureau for Intercultural Education was a New York-based organization that focused on combating intolerance and prejudice by fostering better relations among racial, religious, and ethnic groups through improved communication and education. This strategy fit well with Kilpatrick's philosophical approach to such issues. He began his association with the bureau in 1940 and went on to serve as the chair of its board of directors. The bureau was funded by the American Jewish Committee and the Anti-Defamation League of B'nai B'rith, and also received gifts from a number of wealthy individuals in New York City. Stewart Cole, a Protestant clergyman, undertook the fund-raising for the organization; Ernest Melby served as vice-chairman and Frank Trager as executive secretary. As leader of the Bureau for Intercultural Education, Kilpatrick has been given high marks for his well-known ability to overcome "interpersonal rivals" within organizations and to "negotiate the fine line between pluralism and assimilation through the espousal of cultural democracy."[53]

In a public announcement that Kilpatrick wrote for the bureau in 1944, he said that its mission was to address the tension caused when "socially advantaged groups" attempted to "retain their traditional domination over the folkways and wishes of the minority people." Such conflicts, the announcement read, were manifested in the "practice of personal prejudice, social discrimination, in-group bigotry, out-group suspicion, and intergroup strained feeling which at times eventuates in violence." The goals of the bureau, according to this declaration, were to "immunize the younger generation from the divisive attitudes that burden adults" and to "integrate pupils of all cultural backgrounds into an intelligent, purposeful American society."[54] In his role as chairman of the bureau, Kilpatrick worked closely with the staff during the war and the postwar years, producing books and workshops for teachers and student teachers. Strategies developed in the workshops included utilizing population figures to integrate mathematics with the study of intercultural relations and examining the achievements of different racial and cultural groups to build respect for diversity. According to the *New York Times*, the Bureau's budget for 1944 was $100,000.[55]

A move toward intercultural education had begun in the late 1920s at Teachers College, and the first workshop had been held on the campus in 1943.

By 1950 the number of workshops and institutes had increased to more than sixty.[56] One young staff member at the Bureau for Intercultural Education with whom Kilpatrick worked especially closely was William Van Til. Van Til, a former teacher at The Ohio State University Laboratory School, had joined the staff during the war, delivering a number of workshops for the Bureau throughout New York City, including some at Teachers College and the Lincoln School. Another former student, Hilda Taba, led a series of similar workshops from Harvard University.

In the mid-1940s the John Dewey Society asked Kilpatrick to edit a yearbook on intercultural education. One of his most extensive statements on minority issues is found in the preface and first chapter of this yearbook, *Intercultural Attitudes in the Making*. Calling intergroup tensions and the accompanying prejudice and discrimination "a most serious evil in our modern world," Kilpatrick, not surprisingly, pointed to education as the antidote. Stating that discrimination was "fundamentally opposed to democracy, to ethics, and to any adequately sensitive religion," he reminded his readers that the Constitution called for equal protection under the laws. Intercultural education, which he defined as moving beyond just race, must be based on acceptance of and respect for others. Since all bias and prejudice were the result of learned behavior, he maintained, education was the key. But it would not be feasible to teach interrelational skills solely through textbooks. Children in the majority group had to actually practice democratic living and develop empathy by placing themselves in the position of the minority group. (The model provided by the home and family was also mentioned as a factor.)

Kilpatrick concluded by noting the heavy responsibility this sort of education placed on the teacher, who would have to identify "maladjustments" — as he termed intercultural problems — and then either address the milder forms of bigotry and prejudice or be able to refer more difficult cases for further "expert consideration and treatment."[57] Other contributors to *Intercultural Attitudes in the Making* discussed the role of parents, teachers, youth organizations, and the curriculum, making suggestions for addressing the problem of inappropriate intercultural attitudes. Rather than making proposals of his own, Kilpatrick mainly addressed results of such inappropriate attitudes — such as emotional instability, humiliation, and insecurity, which often led to "abiding grudges." Kilpatrick made a similar entreaty in a pamphlet for the Anti-Defamation League, noting the social and psychological dangers of continued prejudice and discrimination.[58]

Although he frequently offered penetrating insights into the racial problem,

Kilpatrick could at the same time, be naive regarding life for blacks in the South. An example would be stereotypical depictions in popular literature. When Margaret Mitchell's *Gone With the Wind* appeared in 1936, Kilpatrick read the best-seller immediately, and was surprised that he enjoyed it. Dr. Keys, the family physician, was also reading the novel and asked Kilpatrick whether it was a true account of the war and Reconstruction. Historiographically uninformed, Kilpatrick responded, "Yes, I think it is." He also read the controversial novel *Strange Fruit*, written by a fellow Georgian, Lillian Smith, about a love affair between a white man and a black woman in the South. Kilpatrick admitted that the book was skillfully written but found it unconvincing. He bluntly claimed that such a relationship "had never happened in that part of the world," although if it had, it might have taken place in such a manner. In his opinion, the book would also prove unconvincing to other southern white men; he commented that the "lynching seems truer than the lovemaking." In 1949, after reading Smith's *Killers of the Dream*, Kilpatrick said that it was not her support of equal rights for Negroes that concerned him, but rather the Freudian treatment of sex. Yet he went on record apologetically, "She seems to me not to recognize how deep this [caste system] is in our historic culture and how easy it was for our people to think that the Negro was an inferior people."[59]

At the same time, Kilpatrick suggested that the root causes of prejudice against blacks included an institutionalized attitude of exploitation and a psychological bias on the part of whites toward minorities. He also believed that removing blacks from the mainstream of culture was the kind of method used by totalitarian regimes to keep minorities in a subservient position. Still, there were occasions his thinking reverted to paternalism. For example, during the early days of the Cold War, Kilpatrick attended a meeting at which a Negro minister spoke on how racial discrimination in the United States provided the Soviet Union with excellent material for propaganda. While conceding that the presentation was eloquent, Kilpatrick questioned whether speaking so bluntly to "an audience predominantly Negro" was wise.[60] Interestingly, though, Kilpatrick himself had made an almost identical point of view just one year earlier, when discussing race in his *Philosophy of Education*:

> The world asks in amazement how we can speak so loudly in behalf of democracy and yet fall so short of decent democracy in our treatment of Negroes and other minorities in our population. During the last war, Japan took advantage of each outrage against Negroes here to show the Indonesians

and other Asiatics what to expect from us. The U.S.S.R., which long long ago abolished racial discrimination within its borders, points the finger of scorn at us that we pretend to uphold the doctrine of equality, yet so flagrantly refuse it to non-whites.[61]

Well before *Brown v. Board of Education*, Kilpatrick was presented with more than one opportunity to strike a blow at segregation, and to do so in his native South. His determination not to act may have been one of his most notable errors of personal judgment regarding race relations. The crucial issue was what role the courts should play in extending minority rights. It was a question that had been argued among members of the black community for twenty years. As Goodenow has pointed out, Kilpatrick "failed to acknowledge that there is a point at which people may reasonably demand rapid changes in many of the conditions which oppress them."[62] In fact, Kilpatrick had argued against this in the 1935 Yearbook of the *Journal of Negro Education*, in a chapter that carried the title "Resort to Courts by Negroes to Improve Their Schools a Conditional Alternative." Kilpatrick rejected using the courts to seek relief from inequitable situations, except when such efforts were directed by white "friends" of the Negro. Since making a change in the status of minorities was the decision of the "dominant" — that is, white race — Kilpatrick reasoned that it should also be up to the whites to initiate the change. His reasoning seemed to be grounded in the belief that the South was not ready for court-mandated change in the deeply ingrained practice of racial segregation in the schools, and that such change could not occur peacefully. In the end, for Kilpatrick, the potential for violence outweighed the continued injustices being endured by blacks.[63]

Not surprisingly, Kilpatrick was quickly taken to task — within the pages of the same Yearbook — by two blacks, Alain Locke of Howard University and Charles Thompson, editor of the *Journal of Negro Education*. Locke argued that those who counseled against court action (Kilpatrick was not named) did not understand the hopelessness of the current situation. Although Locke was a supporter of progressive education, he contended that it was fallacious to rely solely on educating the public as a foundation on which to build; rather, as the courts would provide both redress for Negroes and education for the public. Thompson's criticisms were stronger. He characterized Kilpatrick's position as naive, failing to distinguish between challenging cultural patterns — which concerned Kilpatrick — and confronting the abhorrent "separate but equal"

doctrine.[64]

Outside the pages of academic journals, of course, there were the real-life struggles of a segregated society. Four carefully selected cases which were to challenge the separate-but-equal doctrine slowly, but methodically, evolved into the test case in the Supreme Court in 1954: *Brown v. Board of Education of Topeka, Kansas*. Led by the N.A.A.C.P. Defense League and its chief counsel, Thurgood Marshall, a case involving Clarendon County, South Carolina, had reached a federal district court by 1950. Kilpatrick was invited by Marshall's second-in-command, Bob Clark, to travel to Charleston, South Carolina, to testify as an expert witness. He refused to go. Kilpatrick replied that he did not think at this stage "such a step would be wise." In his opinion, it would alienate the whites in much of the South and thus would "thwart progress in better thinking." Kilpatrick was also concerned that in school districts where blacks outnumbered whites, a "white flight" to private schools would occur, which indeed happened. He also believed, for unstated reasons, that black teachers would be harmed. Kilpatrick, despite his many activities in intercultural organizations, did not believe that segregation should be fought through the courts, or at least not at this time. Yet he offered no viable alternative. When preparing for a speech two years earlier on this issue, he had noted that it would not be a good talk because it did not offer any detailed solution and concluded, "I do not know too well [what to suggest], anyhow."[65]

One observer who was not reticent about offering his opinion was Richard Kluger, author of *Simple Justice*, a history of the 1954 landmark school desegregation case. Kluger considered Kilpatrick "the most impressive and effective professional educator that the N.A.A.C.P. could have put on the stand in Charleston." Kluger noted Kilpatrick's many positive attributes and character traits, such as his professional bearing, his noble looks, and the "dulcet tones of his native Georgia speech." He believed that as a witness, Kilpatrick would not have been perceived as a "wise-guy carpetbagger down for the day to lecture the rednecks." But Kluger also described "the great Kilpatrick" as a "genial follower" of John Dewey and was highly critical of Kilpatrick's refusal to testify in the integration case. Despite being considered the "perfect witness for the N.A.A.C.P.," Kilpatrick cordially, but repeatedly questioned the wisdom of pressing the Supreme Court to abolish segregation. In a letter to Clark, he "rejoiced" in the recent successes of the N.A.A.C.P. in dealing with desegregation in graduate and professional schools, but he was doubtful about abolishing segregated elementary and secondary schools, fearing that the "results in the South would put back the long-run cause." He pleaded for more

time for the South to "digest the change at the highest levels." Without Kilpatrick, the N.A.A.C.P. would have to look for other, less visible and less influential witnesses from the field of education.[66]

Walter Feinberg, in his book *Reason and Rhetoric: The Intellectual Foundations of 20th Century Liberal Education Policy*, was not quite so harsh in his judgment of Kilpatrick, mentioning that he spoke out with "some strength for the equality of the black man" and was active in organizations such as the Bureau for Intercultural Education. Feinberg also pointed out that during World War II, Kilpatrick had emphasized the country's need to live up to its principles of democracy and had argued that suppressing Negroes hurt blacks and whites alike. But Feinberg also noted Kilpatrick's gradualist approach toward full integration, contrasting him with W. E. B. DuBois, who had, of course, rejected the idea that blacks could persuade whites to accept the fact that segregation should end. In addition, Feinberg noted the irony that, while Kilpatrick and Dewey were considered radicals by many in the progressive education movement, neither of them were able to generate a strategy for including blacks on an equitable basis in the schools.[67]

Yet some who knew Kilpatrick well and worked with him during the postwar years had nothing but high praise for his contribution to racial and cultural understanding. Helen Trager, Frank Trager, and William Van Til have all written of his extensive contributions of time and effort to the cause of better interracial understanding. Even the controversial civil rights activist Bayard Rustin was present at Kilpatrick's memorial service.[68] Tenenbaum, whose biography was written before *Brown v. Board of Education*, thought that Kilpatrick had made great strides on the issue of race from his early life, when he had held a narrow and highly prejudicial point of view, to his later "better attitudes." And Goodenow reported that Buell Gallagher, who knew Kilpatrick's mind on the race issue as well as anyone, considered him an early convert to the integrationist position.[69] In sum, then, Kilpatrick based his hopes for better intercultural relations on education but failed to use his substantial influence to end segregated schools; thus he missed an opportunity to facilitate the democratic experience that he so strongly advocated for America's classrooms.

While Kilpatrick could not bring himself to render this important service to the campaign for desegregation, when the decision was finally reached, he fully supported it. Acknowledging the significance of the case in his diary ("one of the most important in our history"), he perceptively identified the two key elements of the ruling — the unanimous vote by the nine justices and the fact that the specifics on implementation were delayed. It was a decision he had

expected. The previous month he had spoken before the Children Apart Conference, jointly sponsored by the Urban League, the N.A.A.C.P., and a number of other civil rights and educational organizations. In his talk he speculated on the forthcoming decision:

> I do not myself see how the Court can fail to rule against segregation. Under the existing conditions there can be no such thing as "equal but separate" school arrangements. The physical arrangements might be equal, but they cannot be equal as long as separate *implies* superiority on the one hand and inferiority on the other. This denies the spirit of democracy as it does the spirit of our best religions.

At the conclusion of his talk, Dr. Kenneth Clark, the psychologist who had been one of the chief witnesses in the *Brown* case, told Kilpatrick that what he had said "was exactly right."[70]

The Supreme Court decision proved to be only the beginning of the struggle to desegregate the schools, and portions of the South resisted strongly. This response deeply disturbed Kilpatrick, and he called the white opposition "reprehensible." He himself firmly believed that desegregation would be fully won only when the black population as a whole became more fully integrated throughout the entire country. Kilpatrick assisted the Urban League in formulating a strategy to implement the Court's decision, although he continued to prefer to fight the issue on northern, rather than southern, ground. After the decision, the Urban League felt itself under pressure to support the actions of the N.A.A.C.P., by endorsing the Powell Amendment in the House of Representatives, which withheld funds from communities contesting desegregation.[71]

In 1956 Kilpatrick wrote a very clear statement regarding integration, utilizing an array of arguments to undermine any support for segregation. Genetics, psychology, politics, economics, and even international condemnation were all presented, as were the legal grounds — in particular, the unanimous decision of 1954. In what may have been his strongest statement on the subject, he wrote:

> This doctrine of "equal rights" with respect for personality means equality of opportunity for all so far as social institutions can provide such opportunity.[72]

While he had been reticent prior to the *Brown* decision, this sanction of the use of "social institutions," including legal avenues, finally placed Kilpatrick within the mainstream of liberal thought on race. That same year, 1956, he attended the N.A.A.C.P.'s second anniversary celebration of the Supreme Court decision held at the Waldorf Astoria. The evening's program presented almost all the distinguished figures in the civil rights movement, including Thurgood Marshall, Ralph Bunche, Roy Wilkens, and Rosa Parks — who received a standing ovation. The final talk of the evening was given by the still relatively unknown pastor of the Dexter Avenue Baptist Church in Montgomery, Alabama, the Rev. Martin Luther King, Jr. Kilpatrick was impressed with the young minister's speech.[73]

Thus Kilpatrick's endeavors in this area did involve some activism. He can be credited with bringing racial issues to the forefront in the pages of *Frontiers of Democracy*. He supported efforts to integrate businesses and hospitals, playing a crucial role in the integration of Harlem's Sydenham Hospital, the first interracial voluntary hospital in the country. And he helped keep Morris High School in the Bronx racially mixed by supporting an unpopular redistricting plan. Goodenow has likened him to another gradualist, Booker T. Washington — though this is no great compliment, considering the recent criticism of Washington. But Goodenow also saw Kilpatrick's contributions as "comfortable," "long on democratic rhetoric," and offering "benign forms of pluralism."[74]

The country, too, was advancing in its thinking on the issue of race, but a dichotomous path was being taken in the South. There, the *Brown* decision was met with deep resentment and frequent obstruction. Public schools were closed in Virginia, where whites set up "private" classrooms in church basements and other makeshift locations. Some black students were thus forced to leave their homes and live with relatives in neighboring counties. Several states — including Kilpatrick's home state, Georgia — resurrected the Confederacy's battle banner and incorporated it into their flags as a symbol of defiance. At the same time, though, two southerners — Lyndon Johnson, majority leader of the Senate, and his fellow Texan, Sam Rayburn, Speaker of the House — were able to pass, in the summer of 1957, a civil rights act to secure voting rights for blacks.

Kilpatrick was ashamed, once again, of the South's stand on race and its insistence on passing state legislation to thwart blacks' voting rights. The federal legislation, in his opinion, would result in "Negroes actually voting," and thus a two-party system would develop in the South. This was based on his

continued erroneous belief that blacks would vote Republican. When Eisenhower sent federal troops into Little Rock, Arkansas, Kilpatrick fully supported the move. Although he noted the "bitterness it would provoke," he could see no other step to be taken after the arbitrary actions of Governor Orval Faubus. Kilpatrick found it more and more difficult to justify such intransigence. Speaking of voting rights and school integration in 1959, Kilpatrick remarked, "The South is holding out against the rest of the civilized world except South Africa. It seems strange to me that so many in the South still hold to the slavery doctrine that the Negro must be kept on a lower grade level."[75]

Kilpatrick's developing thoughts on desegregation emerged in his review of *Schools in Transition*, which examined twenty-four border states and their handling of desegregation. On the evidence contained in this book, he concluded that school boards were the key to the success of any desegregation plan, and that lack of "reasoned appeal" and "full communication" between blacks and whites was the major cause of failure. This, of course, reflected his own endorsement of a gradual, rational policy of better interracial understanding and education. He did, though, depart from his own long-held view that "outsiders" could only impair the process. Calling whites who used such an argument ignorant, and admitting that Negroes did desire change, he believed the move from segregation to integration could occur smoothly, with little or no friction.[76]

Kilpatrick's earlier concern about a backlash against his friends in the South proved justified when, in 1956, Guy Wells was stripped of his status as president emeritus of Georgia State College for Women by the University Board of Regents. Following quickly on the heels of this decision, the Georgia State Board of Education asked that his pension be discontinued. At the time Wells was executive secretary of the Georgia Council on Interracial Cooperation and was, therefore, labeled an "integrationist." The news was carried in the *New York Times*, and Kilpatrick was — uncharacteristically — livid when he read of it. Writing to Wells, he said, "Not in a long time have I heard of such outrageous treatment as that given you. We would have to go back to the Inquisition to get a parallel case to this effort to stop public discussion." He went on to write that as a Georgian he "hung his head in shame" and pondered the "shallow roots of democracy" in his home state.

As a result of this episode, and because of an article he had written on desegregation for *Progressive Education,* Kilpatrick canceled a trip to the South in 1956, lest he "embarrass my friends and perhaps bring upon myself most unpleasant reactions."[77] His trips to the South had already decreased in the

1950s, although he took one nostalgic trip to Blakely, Georgia, in 1953, after an absence of almost fifty years. (He made this trip without Marion.) Kilpatrick was warmly received and fondly remembered, even after five decades, and as he traveled by bus into the deep South, he was recognized on more than one occasion by other passengers. Local and regional newspapers, as well as the *Atlanta Constitution*, gave the trip full coverage.[78]

A deep-rooted sense of religion, as well as race, was part of Kilpatrick's southern experience. As a young man Kilpatrick had followed the teachings of his father's church — the Baptists — even joining the congregation during his adolescent years. But then his reading of Charles Darwin, the influence of his older half brother Macon, and his introduction to higher biblical criticism had caused him to suspend belief in the supernatural, at least privately. Out of respect for his father and because of his own close connection with Mercer University, as both professor and administrator, Kilpatrick had kept his religious opinions to himself, at least as far as was possible ethically. When his disagreement with certain church dogma finally emerged, the "heresy trial" of 1907 resulted. After that episode he felt less inclined, in his outward behavior, to meet the expectations of his Baptist upbringing. His attendance at church ceased, and he no longer masked his true convictions on religious questions. The only qualification would be his continued adherence to a self-imposed rule not to do or say anything that would reflect adversely upon his father. He did believe that the situation at Mercer and his departure from the Baptist faith had caused some tension between him and his father.

However, Kilpatrick was to some extent ambivalent about religion. Even at Mercer, he had been considered "religious" by his students. In the Mercer University alumni correspondence, known as the "Robin-Trot" letters, one student said of Kilpatrick, "He was the most active man on that faculty religiously speaking and had the most influence over the student body in a constructive way." In fact, this ambivalence about religion troubled Kilpatrick greatly. In a retrospective diary entry, he admitted being at odds with certain aspects of his father's religion, especially piety, evangelical theology, and church attendance. "All my life it has been easy for me to live a divided existence," he admitted, "which I now feel as most unfortunate."[79]

After leaving Georgia, Kilpatrick continued to have an interest in religion, although not from a traditional vantage point. (While still at Mercer, he was attempting to frame an outlook on religion based on neo-Hegelianism.) His lifelong friendship with Ashby Jones, the liberal Baptist clergyman from Georgia, had a significant impact on him. The two held long conversations and

apparently agreed on a number of issues. Upon arriving in New York City, Kilpatrick briefly attended an Episcopal church, admiring a number of its features, including the education of its clergy, the beauty of its architecture, and the aesthetics of its worship. On the other hand, he had difficulty with its "sacramental superstitions" and its snobbery. At this point he even considered breaking his already tenuous ties with his family's Baptist background. Paradoxically, in his New Year's resolution for 1908 he stated that he was determined to live so as to hide nothing from "God or man." Kilpatrick finally ceased attending services of any kind, with two exceptions: when he visited White Plains, or when he was asked to speak in a church during one of his lecture tours. In 1909 he wrote to his friend J. R. Moseley, telling him that under Dewey's influence, he had put out of his mind any thought of God as a supernatural being.

And yet Kilpatrick was troubled over how to come to terms with the phenomenon called "religion," pondering its worth as an area of study. The week after his letter to Moseley, he answered his own question, in a sense, deciding that one must move beyond the "bible" (his term for the Scriptures) and place religion in the area of empiricism. But his daughter's religious education was another matter, and he bluntly stated his thoughts on that and his own beliefs in his diary for 1911:

> I have definitely given up all religion in the revealed or theological sense. I see no God of any sort anywhere. The bible however is a part of literature and it is therefore well to know it. Moreover, other people will teach theology to my child, and those of the crudest type are the quickest to impart it. So I have determined to fight the devil with fire — let her learn a mild form of biblical theology with the hope that it will the more readily go away.[80]

For himself, in 1914, Kilpatrick flatly stated that he could not hope for any "life beyond the grave." He was not alone in this; many Americans in the 1920s were turning from religion. Frederick Lewis Allen would write that the impact of scientific doctrines and methods of thought on churches was enormous: "The prestige of science was colossal."[81] By the end of the First World War, Kilpatrick would privately enter into his diary his staunch faith in science and an admission of atheism. After attending a funeral, he wrote:

> I must admit that the religious ceremonies and words lose me
> and exasperate me. I think they do positive harm. I feel myself
> a distinct and almost militant atheist. I believe the whole
> religious worship machinery and dogma to be a hindrance to
> the much needed scientific effort to direct progress.

Yet while religion, at least in its traditional form, held little sway over him, questions of morality deeply interested him. For example, in one of his classes he was nearly "floored" by a question as to why he would deny the moral influence of a good story, but admit the evil influence of a bad one. He gave a talk in chapel in 1920 in which he advocated a religion of ethics, by which he meant democracy, and advised the audience to cease trying to base religion on "God, the bible, or immortality." The following year in the Columbia University chapel he called religion "bad science, doubtful philosophy, and improbable history."[82]

During Kilpatrick's visits to the South, religion would occasionally cause him to feel both uncomfortable and embarrassed. As with race, he seemed to be greatly concerned about what others might think of his views and practices. During one summer visit he attended a service with his sister Helen in a nearby town and found himself seated in front of a minister who had known him for many years. During the service this man, referring to the presence of a Columbia University professor, asked that "Christian kisses" be blown toward others in the congregation. Kilpatrick went this far, but then the minister asked all Baptists to stand. Kilpatrick remained seated. The minister next asked for all Christians to stand, and Kilpatrick again refused. He later told a friend that he had almost stood, to keep others from misunderstanding, and that ethically he could almost have done so if he had chosen to "play with words" and definitions. It was a troubling episode for him.

In 1922, when he was asked by President McGiffert of Union Theological Seminary to teach a course in education there, Kilpatrick jumped at the chance. He wished to help his friend Harrison Elliot, a professor at Union, but he was also eager to have it known in Georgia that he had been asked to lecture at a theological seminary. During one class, he was buttonholed by a missionary who attempted to draw Kilpatrick out on whether or not he was a Christian. "I told him," wrote Kilpatrick, that "he who asks about my belief in order to find out what to believe may be told what I think, but anyone who has any other idea in view will not find out if I can by any honest 'side stepping' keep him from knowing." A number of students seemed to find wisdom in what Kilpatrick had

to say; one student told him, "You give us more religion than we get at church."

Kilpatrick continued to take care so he would not be drawn into any discussion that might label him an atheist, although by this time he clearly was one. It might be argued that he lacked the courage of his convictions, or that he saw no need to make a controversial stand in an area which he did not see as worth the risk. Kilpatrick did feel compelled, though, to demonstrate that one need not be religious, in a formal way, to be interested in morals and ethics. Religion often became an academic subject for him. On one occasion he debated his Syrian seatmate on a train as to whether the garden of Eden was in the man's home country and whether Adam and Abraham spoke Hebrew.[83]

In the 1920s Kilpatrick continued teaching a single course at Union Theological Seminary, which was located just across the street from Teachers College and was adjacent to the site of Riverside Church, which was soon to be built. Riverside Church was underwritten by John D. Rockefeller, Jr., for its minister, Dr. Harry Emerson Fosdick. Kilpatrick knew Fosdick and would occasionally take part with him in discussion groups and formal programs on Union's campus. Although theologically liberal, Fosdick's views did not match Kilpatrick's. The one point of agreement between the two men concerned fundamentalism, which was sweeping the country: Fosdick was as vehemently opposed to it as Kilpatrick was. Kilpatrick blamed William Jennings Bryan and his crusade against evolution for much of the religious controversy of the time. For his own part, he considered the dispute over evolution a "hornet's nest" and was confident that scientific reasoning was on such firm ground that continued attacks would only cause great harm to organized religion.

Religion became the focus of controversy in the 1920s not only because of the Scopes trial, but also because of Sinclair Lewis's novel *Elmer Gantry*. When Kilpatrick read *Elmer Gantry*, he was uncertain whether Lewis was exposing "humbugary and sex immorality" among the fundamentalists or was actually directing an attack against the American people and their gullibility in the area of religion.[84] Kilpatrick did touch upon religion in his own two major works of the 1920s, *Foundations of Method* and *Education for a Changing Civilization*, in the context of teaching morals and the deterioration of an authoritarian point of view. These ideas came in part from Dewey, who maintained that religion had to allow freedom to permit the organization of one's deepest insight. Once, at a meeting Kilpatrick attended, Dewey was asked how he would define religious education. His enigmatic and nebulous response was, "Any education fit to be."[85]

Just before the onset of the Depression, Kilpatrick published a number of articles setting forth his thinking on religion. In a talk in the chapel at Teachers

College — later published under the title "How Shall We Think About Religion?" — he concluded that humanity was probably incurably religious in the aggregate, but not on an individual basis. He defined religion as "a certain way of giving one's self to what one counts most significant." Religious thought had to evolve, or it would die. To support this, he noted that every religious hero worthy of a place in history had undertaken some deed that was either new or difficult. But for Kilpatrick, reconstructing a religious experience meant remaking a philosophy of life.[86] In other writings he continued to separate the teaching of morals from traditional religious thought or dogma of any kind. In part, his argument was based on his deep opposition to any type of indoctrination. For Kilpatrick, not only was indoctrination a poor and ineffective teaching method; it was no guarantee of the validity of any espoused doctrine. It would even prove harmful to the child, who would be rendered incapable of rational thought in later life. He went so far in one article as to say that the psychology of the Bible was extraordinarily true, but much of its history and science was false. And he bluntly advised parents to tell children that "while people used to believe such things," they no longer did.[87]

Religion seemed to engage Kilpatrick at the deepest levels, even the subconscious. He occasionally wrote of his dreams in his diary, and he recounted one that was about religion. It had to do with his observing someone with a gun setting off to kill God. God and Satan, in Kilpatrick's dream, took the form of two rats. "Satan" was able to escape, but the person with the gun shot "God." Kilpatrick denied any Freudian implications that this was a wish to destroy God; he simply looked on this dream as an example of framing a concept in one's thinking.

While he never intentionally set out to undermine anyone's religious faith, Kilpatrick was capable of raising doubts in the minds of his students. One woman, a Mormon, told him years later that he had "destroyed" her religion." Kilpatrick offered quite a different interpretation: he had merely induced her to think, and "her religious dogma could not stand the test."[88]

Kilpatrick placed those interested in religion in three categories: (1) those who wished to escape the troubles of life through prayer, ritual, and forgetfulness; (2) those who wished to work for a better world, attempting to gain the deepest insight they could through religion; and (3) those who desired to gain power over others. Kilpatrick was skeptical about the first group, respectful of the second, and contemptuous of the third — and he placed the Catholic church squarely in the third category. Kilpatrick's opinion of Catholicism bordered at times on blind intolerance. While Kilpatrick was at Northwestern University in

1939, he, George Axtelle, and two other colleagues met at DePaul University with Father Cunningham of the Notre Dame School of Education and several of his Catholic associates for a discussion. After an evening of conversation, Kilpatrick came away with a high regard for the men, but little respect for their philosophy, which he termed neo-Thomism. "It is simply bad thinking that couldn't make a stand outside the authoritarianism of the sheltered cloisters of the R.C. schools. It is a pitiable affair, looking backward only. Whatever thinking these people do, they have to do it in spite of their philosophy." Roman Catholics increasingly exasperated Kilpatrick. At one lecture he gave at the New School for Social Research, a Catholic questioned him closely on his concept of morality as being built upon foreseeable consequences and concluded that Kilpatrick was advocating "that anyone can do whatever he can get away with." This and several other queries "irritated much more than for many a long day," he wrote in his diary.[89]

Kilpatrick's feelings regarding Catholicism went beyond personal annoyance. He viewed the Catholic church as a menace to education, with its advocacy of federal aid to parochial schools and its criticisms of progressive education. In 1950 he confided to his diary his concern about "the ambitious aim of the Roman Catholic Church to capture America." He believed that Catholics controlled Rhode Island, Massachusetts, and a number of large cities. "Catholicism represents reaction in thought and religion and the hierarchy is very ambitious and not too scrupulous," he wrote. He even likened the Catholic church domestically to the Soviet Union internationally. On another occasion he said that Catholicism was "the most active enemy to intelligent civilization we have."[90]

In public, Kilpatrick's assertions regarding Catholicism were much more circumspect. During the same month that he made these comments in his diary, he addressed the Christian Fellowship Club with Dr. Oswald Hoffman of the Lutheran church, Missouri Synod. He mainly discussed issues such as released time in schools for religious instruction, the role of inductive ethics, and the historical background of relations between church and state. His reception was polite, with no hostile questions from the audience, but, then again, he left out any direct attacks on the Catholic hierarchy. On another occasion, though, he was less restrained. To an audience of early childhood educators, he quoted from a textbook from Mussolini's Italy which stated, "As the Catholic Church must have a blind belief in the Catholic faith and obey the Catholic Church blindly, so the perfect Fascist must have a blind belief and obey blindly." Kilpatrick had not always had such deep anti-Catholic sentiments. He had

voted for Al Smith in 1928 precisely because the New York Democrat was Catholic; Kilpatrick wished to further the process of assimilation. At about the same time, he also endorsed the use of a European history textbook by Carlton Hayes, a Catholic, so that students could encounter the history of the Reformation from both sides.[91]

Kilpatrick's declarations on religion at semipublic affairs, such as dinner parties, fell somewhere between what he would state in his diary and what he espoused from the platform. A Presbyterian minister at a dinner party once asked his opinion on teaching morals from a religious point of view, and Kilpatrick replied so sharply that Marion quietly expressed her disapproval to him. He quickly explained to the clergyman his experiential approach to the teaching of values, and the situation calmed down. At the same gathering, he advised Willard Goslin, then a superintendent in Minneapolis, not to permit the Gideons to distribute New Testaments to elementary students. Although he was uncomfortable about testifying on the racial issue in the South, Kilpatrick did appear as an educational expert witness before the New Jersey state supreme court in a case concerning the distribution of Gideon Bibles in the schools. The suit had been brought by Catholics and Jews, and Kilpatrick indicated that he thought the practice was motivated by "Protestant selfishness" (because the Gideons had chosen the King James version) and that distributing the Scriptures would alienate people who did not believe in the New Testament. In a unanimous decision, the court agreed with Kilpatrick. Oddly enough, given his stalwart defense of the separation of church and state, he did work on composing an alternative to a school prayer proposed by the New York Regents. The revised prayer for both high school and elementary students was a pledge to uphold the golden rule, to accept personal responsibility, and to maintain the standards of the school.[92]

Kilpatrick could become quite angry over attacks of any kind on his theory of moral development. When Dr. Robert McCracken, Fosdick's successor at Riverside Church, criticized people who made decisions on grounds of expediency, national interest, or their own values, rather than appealing to a supreme being or a set of absolutes, Kilpatrick was incensed. Kilpatrick mused on "how an intelligent and honest man can so unfairly state the position he opposes is hard to see."

His own position was close to that of his former colleague, George Coe, who defined religion as that to which one gives supreme authority and value; and he praised the theologian Paul Tillich, upon hearing Tillich speak one evening, for echoing that definition.[93] The closest Kilpatrick himself came to

defining religion was in his *Philosophy of Education* in 1951. Excluding any consideration of the supernatural, he wrote it was "the spirit with which one holds one's supreme value and the outworking of this attitude appropriately in life."[94] That same year, in a response to a series of questions on his religious views, he concluded a talk by stating:

> I hope for a time when religion can be studied objectively and freely on its merits and not on tradition. When that time comes, I should be ready to answer yes to each of your four questions. In that day we can helpfully guide students and older pupils to build a defensible religion, to the improvement of our troubled world and of the people in it.[95]

Sometimes Kilpatrick's views on religion bordered on contempt. One Easter Sunday he noted the day by stating that, to Marion and him, "it means nothing. We are both glad that we have no ritualistic or other impulse to observe the day." On other occasions, for no apparent reason, he would reiterate his view that there was no rational evidence to support the existence of God.[96] Yet at times, when personalities became involved, he could be highly sympathetic. He wrote the foreword to the deeply personal book *Manifest Victory* by his longtime friend J. R. Moseley, who had been his colleague at Mercer. Moseley, an evangelical, who traveled the country giving workshops on practical Christianity, earned Kilpatrick's praise, not for his beliefs, but for living his faith. Kilpatrick called Moseley a saint. Still, he took care to avoid any appearance of endorsing Moseley's beliefs, stating simply that, while he himself might use different "language," one could not fail to recognize true insight when it was presented.[97] At the same time, though, he seemed to have no opposition to the attachment of his daughter and her family to the Episcopal church, and he never attempted to undermine her faith in any way.

In 1954, after reading an article in the *New York Times* on the mixed status of religion around the world, Kilpatrick noted in his diary that his own views were beginning to take hold, especially in America. While orthodoxy and fundamentalism still held sway in many places across the country, emphases on higher criticism and the social gospel were predominant, even in seminaries. The more "liberal view" was certainly gaining, he concluded.[98]

The development of Kilpatrick's attitudes on race and religion owed much to his experiences as a southerner. Paradoxically, he was able to advance his opinions on race beyond his native prejudices, while at the same time falling

into an ever narrowing intolerance of Roman Catholicism. He was able to argue eloquently that the worth of a group should never be judged by the acts of a single individual, yet he frequently described the entire Catholic church in highly derogatory terms because of the actions of its leadership. Even when he interacted with Catholics on an individual basis, he came away condemning their philosophy, logic, and intellectual standards. How much his personal distaste for the supernatural accounted for this aberration, in a man who was usually so tolerant, is difficult to gauge. As with all bigotry, his was learned, but his distaste seems to have expanded in his later life.

As for race, by the 1950s Kilpatrick was able to progress from his reservations about the social and intellectual equality of African-Americans — reservations typical of a young man in the turn-of-the-century South — to a solidly liberal stance. He continued for many years, though, to rationalize about not pressing the South on the issue of race. While Kilpatrick was able to make advances conceptually, his deep-seated affection for the South kept him from more vigorous activism on behalf of comprehensive equality. When the opportunity arose, he could not strike a forceful and essential blow against segregation. Ultimately, Kilpatrick's record on interracial relations, including his numerous speeches and writings, may be seen as testimony to the degree to which cultural biases could be overcome and horizons expanded through education and intellectual effort. At the same time, his failure to act at a crucial point in the history of the civil rights movement would be a chastening reminder as to the persistence of cultural limitations.

18

THE DISCIPLE AND THE MASTER

There is no god but Dewey, and Kilpatrick is his prophet.

Chant heard on the Columbia Campus[1]

During his last years, Kilpatrick spent a significant amount of time responding to attacks on progressive education. But these years also brought an ever-increasing number of physical ailments. Kilpatrick was plagued with chronic prostate trouble, which led to surgery in 1957, as well as minor lapses in memory, inner ear problems, cataracts, and bouts of fatigue. With embarrassing frequency there were falls resulting in minor injuries. And the death of his younger brother, Howard, of an apparent heart attack in 1957, made his own mortality all the more real to him. Kilpatrick also seemed more disposed to episodes of crankiness associated with old age, as exemplified by his sudden disapproval of men wearing beards. Increasingly, he found himself involved in inconsequential disputes with local governmental and retail services, even writing notes requesting that cracks in the sidewalk be repaired and becoming testy over returning clothes that did not fit. By 1958 he had abandoned work on the manuscript he had labored on for over a decade, *We Learn What We Live*. He began working occasionally on an autobiography, but it never moved beyond his youth and his days at Mercer.[2] He did dictate a dozen letters every other week, but the interactions between him and the public at large decreased as the 1950s drew to a close. In sum, he was slowing down, making mistakes, and realizing that his active days would soon cease.

The Kilpatricks continued their month-long summer stays at Schuylerville. This village in upstate New York was the only place where Kilpatrick, approaching his ninetieth year, felt safe enough to take brief walks. The marriage between Kilpatrick and Marion, as it approached the twenty-year mark, continued to be a close one. At Christmas in 1959 he gave a note to her, accompanied by a potted plant, which read, "To my darling wife, whom I love the more fully because she very kindly forgives my serious shortcomings."[3]

In January of 1957 Kilpatrick was feted by Goddard College for his contribution to that institution. The next year he was honored by the American Humanist Association as Humanist Pioneer of 1958 and by the Little Red

Schoolhouse for his lifetime of work in American education.[4] And in that same year the John Dewey Society also paid tribute to him, making him its permanent honorary president. Kilpatrick donated another $25,000 to Teachers College in 1959, and President Caswell continued to seek his advice on appointments. On occasion, Kilpatrick marched in the summer graduation exercises at Teachers College, enjoying the interaction with the faculty and students. One graduate student remembers Kilpatrick engaging a group in conversation at a graduation until Marion located him and suggested that he might be boring the *ad hoc* gathering with his stories. "But they seem to be interested in what I'm saying," Kilpatrick protested.[5]

Attacks on progressive education were to fill the 1950s. They had begun with Arthur Bestor's *Educational Wastelands*, to be examined later, and continued with Rudolf Flesch's *Why Johnny Can't Read*. Astonished to learn that Flesch had attended Teachers College, Kilpatrick called the registrar and discovered that his degree had been in adult education (1943) and that Flesch also had a law degree from Vienna. He then contacted his former colleague, Roma Gans, who concluded that the book was dishonestly written, seeking "notoriety at the cost of integrity."[6] A personal attack upon Kilpatrick came in Albert Lynd's *Quackery in the Public Schools*, in which one chapter was entitled "The World of Professor Kilpatrick." Lynd began with Dewey, and unlike other critics of the time, who handled Dewey gently, Lynd argued that his thought rested on questionable assumptions such as "There are no eternal truths," "There are no fixed moral laws," and "Democracy is a moral value." From there Lynd went on to link the social reconstructionists with communism, stating that progressive educators, using the shield of pragmatism, had duped the public through the use of an esoteric vocabulary. Lynd concluded that, despite Dewey's unquestioned intellectual stature and integrity, "his educational doctrines have opened in our schools a door wide enough to admit a legion of pedagogical boondogglers."[7]

In the chapter "The World of Professor Kilpatrick," Lynd noted that Kilpatrick had been Dewey's most influential interpreter and called Kilpatrick "the greatest box office attraction in Educationdom." Drawing on Tenenbaum's biography, Lynd mocked Kilpatrick's temperate personal habits, writing that "one might easily believe that a Providence of Progressive Education sent the professor to redress the very different career of Jean Jacques Rousseau." Kilpatrick's philosophy was characterized as both dogmatized Deweyanism and Deweyanism "heavily adjectivized."[8] As other critics would, Lynd attacked Kilpatrick's emphasis on democracy and growth.

As for curriculum and teachers, Lynd wrote:

> It is in the name of such a philosophy that an army of
> Kilpatrickians is throwing out of our schools the disciplines of
> formal grammar, mathematics, and the like. It would be
> pedantic and pointless to expect our classroom teachers and
> our local administrators to be logicians; no one expects
> philosophical erudition in them. The mischief, however, is in
> the assurance given them, through our schools of education,
> that they have a "philosophy" as justification for putting the
> ax to traditional curriculum. What they have, in fact, is a
> collection of emotive words.[9]

Lynd was also disturbed by Kilpatrick's manner of explicating Dewey's
ideas. According to Lynd, Kilpatrick merely "translated them into a riot of
hosannas about joy, richness, zest, and so forth. It is understandable that when
this stuff gets down from Teachers College and other institutions to the humbler
workers in our schools, it becomes even more farcical." He concluded that
"while education is responsible for the multiplication of courses filled with
trivia, Kilpatrick and his admirers have heaped the trivia with verbal meringue,"
dismissing Kilpatrick as a mere echoer of the academic leftism popular in the
1920s and 1930s.[10] Lynd attacked teacher education and its avoidance of
teaching the basic subject knowledge areas in the schools, pejoratively referring
to teachers as "educationists" and their jargon as "educationese."

While some critics thought Lynd's attacks excessive, many agreed with the
underlying assumptions. These criticisms would emerge time and again over
the next forty years whenever the pendulum swung toward progressive
pedagogy or public schools came under scrutiny.[11] After reading the book,
Kilpatrick noted in his diary, "His [Lynd's] attack on me misses the mark
widely. So far as I can tell, he has not read at all in my books, but attacks me
solely on Tenenbaum and his prejudices." He also concluded, after noting the
numerous negative comments regarding teachers, teacher educators, and
principals, that the book would have been better titled "Quackery *about* the
Public Schools."[12]

In the spring of 1958, *Life* magazine ran a censorious series on progressive
education. Although Kilpatrick was not named in it, he was nonetheless
disturbed by the attack, which did include Dewey. Variations on the theme of
"Why Johnny Can't Read" were featured, including "What Johnny Doesn't

Know" which was hardly novel — students' inability to list and locate assorted geographical and historical places was a popular criticism, especially in newspapers. The blame for perceived declines in adolescents' knowledge was laid at the doorstep of progressive education, in particular its shift from stand-alone courses in geography and history to the allegedly amorphous collection of disciplines known as social studies.

In general, Kilpatrick took a longer view of the issue: "John ain't the man he used to be," he would say, and then quickly add, "No, and he never was." Kilpatrick never became excessively defensive, choosing to respond in a rational, moderated voice. Twenty years before the assaults began in earnest, he had written that many people expected too much from the project method, even looking to it as a panacea for all educational ills. This specific application of progressive education, he maintained, was never a "get rich quick scheme," but rather the underpinning for modern practice — one approach among several.[13]

The Catholic church also continued to be a critic of public education. It even attacked Kilpatrick on his eighty-fifth birthday: in the Jesuit weekly *America*, he was denounced for the "scars his antiintellectualist philosophy had left on American education." The American Legion entered the controversy with an especially vicious attack "Your Child Is the Target" in the June 1952 issue of the *American Legion Magazine*. This article attacked Kilpatrick, Harold Rugg, indoctrination, and teachers' organizations. "Never before," he wrote in his diary, "so far as I know, has truth been so disregarded as now in these United States." The harassment even extended into his personal life. As he was sending a manuscript to a publisher, a postal worker, seeing his name on the package, asked if he was the same man who advocated progressive education. When Kilpatrick said yes, the man said he knew of his attacks on parochial schools and insisted on first class postage, rather than allowing the book rate. Compliments were so scarce at this time that at dinner one evening with William Van Til, Kilpatrick pulled a small newspaper clipping from his pocket sent to him from a friend in California; deeply moved, he told Van Til that it was the only positive thing that had been written about him in that section of the country.

Other notable critics during the 1950s and early 1960s included Admiral Hyman Rickover and Max Rafferty, California state school superintendent. Rickover, in *Education and Freedom* (1959), took pride in blaming progressive education for what he viewed as the nation's bureaucratic mentality, its lack of scientific knowledge, and its inability to produce leaders. Soon afterward Max Rafferty, in a broadside against progressive education, likened Dewey, Rugg,

and Kilpatrick to the fascist dictators of the 1930s and 1940s, who had "denounced learning for the sake of learning" thereby "discouraging nonconformity just as had Stalin."[14]

After a number of these accusations had accumulated, Kilpatrick responded one evening in an after-dinner speech at a major conference. In a reserved but rational reply, he outlined five distinguishable groups, which, he said, were behind the attack on modern public education: (1) college and university teachers who could not accept education as a proper area of study; (2) parents still tied to their own type of schooling; (3) the wealthy, who sent their children to private schools and were affronted by being taxed for the education of other people's children; (4) people obsessed with anticommunist hysteria and therefore opposed to anything new; and (5) agitators who took advantage of the fears of the other groups to advance their own agendas. On a broader scale, in 1955 he wrote, "I might add that the [attack on public education] troubles me personally. So far I have heard nothing that, properly considered, really calls in question the education I have been standing for forty years, though there is danger many will be mis-led."[15]

As another decade began, the Kilpatricks followed the presidential campaign of 1960 with great interest. Kilpatrick had read John Kennedy's book *Profiles in Courage* and had approved of it. He also kept track of political events through his southern cousin, Carroll Kilpatrick, who was a journalist for *Newsweek* and later the *Washington Post* and had accompanied Richard Nixon to the Soviet Union in 1959; he was now covering Lyndon Johnson during the 1960 presidential campaign. Carroll Kilpatrick would be the *Post*'s White House correspondent from Kennedy's presidency through Gerald Ford's. He and his older relative had an exceptionally close relationship; Carroll was at times treated like the son Kilpatrick never had. Although considered an outstanding reporter and man of integrity, he would bear the brunt of the Nixon administration's anger at the *Washington Post* during the Watergate scandal, when he was relegated to the back row at press conferences. Carroll died in 1984.

In July of 1960 Kilpatrick accurately speculated that John Kennedy would be the "most effective vote getter and perhaps the most promising candidate." He had, after all, been sizing up Democratic presidential candidates since Grover Cleveland's second term. As the Kilpatricks did not own a television, Marion orchestrated an invitation from a neighbor to watch the Kennedy-Nixon debates in October, and Kilpatrick went along. But his lifelong interest in politics was beginning to wane, and he admitted to his diary that he was eager for the debates to end, so he could return to filing his personal papers. The

Kilpatricks voted for Kennedy in November despite their frequently expressed suspicions and distrust of Catholicism. They listened to the inaugural address on the radio and were impressed by the young president's challenge to the American people. In his last yearly diary entry, as to world events, Kilpatrick observed that although the United States was the strongest free nation in the world, with that distinction came "great responsibility for which we are hardly prepared."

Lawrence Cremin's history of progressive education, *The Transformation of the Schools*, appeared in 1961. Kilpatrick had allowed Cremin limited use of his diaries, in addition to lending him Tenenbaum's recordings, made almost a decade before. The Kilpatricks had also entertained Cremin and his wife Ruth, the daughter of Bruce Raup, on more than one occasion. Kilpatrick had reacted positively to an early copy of the book, in spite of several tacit criticisms of himself: One example was Cremin's implication that Boyd Bode had been a more reliable disciple of Dewey than Kilpatrick was. But, as he had been with Tenenbaum's biography, John Childs was critical of Cremin's work, disapproving of certain unspecified "excesses." Kilpatrick, nonplused, encouraged him to put these criticisms in writing for Cremin's benefit.[16]

Marion's health remained excellent as she entered her mid-sixties, but she narrowly escaped death in January of 1959 after being struck by a taxi while crossing Amsterdam Avenue at 120th Street on her way to Hunter College. Her pelvis, two ribs, and an arm were broken. She recovered rapidly from the mishap, and Kilpatrick got along fairly well on his own during her convalescence at Saint Luke's Hospital. For her part, Marion began to become increasingly protective of Kilpatrick's health, making sure that visitors and friends kept their stays brief and that his evenings never got too late.

Even the entries in Kilpatrick's diary, which he had kept faithfully since 1903, now began to diminish. In early 1960 his clear handwriting deteriorated, literally overnight. He had at first thought it was the result of his sleeping on his right hand, but the entries continued to degenerate into an almost unintelligible scrawl for the last two years he kept the diary — 1960 and 1961. The exact physiological cause of the problem remained a mystery, although the symptoms would seem to indicate a mild stroke. As a result, he decided to make 1961 the final year of chronicling his life.[17]

As Kilpatrick's ninetieth birthday approached, in November of 1961, both *Newsweek* and the *New York Times* took note. For its article "Learn by Living," *Newsweek* interviewed Kilpatrick in his Morningside Drive apartment. The article described him as "aristocratic in appearance, zealous in outlook," and

"Dewey's foremost apostle, interpreter, and propagandist" in the area of education. Mentioning his mellifluous Georgia drawl, the interviewer quoted at length Kilpatrick's rigorous defense of Dewey's philosophy. While admitting that progressive education in the early 1960s did not have the momentum it once did, Kilpatrick said that "every school now accepts and teaches an intelligent form of progressive education." Stating that American schools needed more, not less, progressivism, Kilpatrick concluded, "During my lifetime, I have tried to build up a proper outlook on educational procedures. That counts for something, I hope."[18]

The *New York Times* covered Kilpatrick's appearance before about 100 students at City College the week before his ninetieth birthday, noting his increasing problems with vision. In this talk Kilpatrick admitted that the Soviet Union's successful space program had been a factor in the retreat of American schools from Dewey's philosophy. But he made no defense of the philosophy itself, preferring to cite his achievements on a personal level one last time: "I tried to get each student to think for himself. I tried to develop self-direction, independent thinking, a democratic process, and I believe I succeeded reasonably well." His last recorded public words were these:

> Well, I think I'll stop now. I can look back over a long period of years. I have seen a real change take place in American education. There is not a teaching institution in this country preparing teachers on the elementary level that does not employ some of my methods.[19]

A small gathering recognized him on his ninetieth birthday, and newspaper articles again appeared with photographs of the still vigorous-looking Kilpatrick and stories about the "million-dollar professor." A William Heard Kilpatrick Day was held at Jersey City State College on April 17, 1962; this was his last public appearance. A symposium on his thought was held in Horace Mann Auditorium on his ninety-third birthday, but he was too ill to attend.[20]

The last three years of Kilpatrick's life become difficult to document. Unfortunately, they were filled with illnesses, strokes, and hospitalizations. Margaret recorded one last conversation between father and daughter sometime after his first stroke. He was deeply concerned about the youth of the 1960s turning against their parents, criticizing them, blaming them when things went wrong — even hating them. "Did you ever feel that way toward me?," the old man asked. When Margaret said no, he responded, relieved, that he had not

thought such was the case, but he wanted to know.[21]

William Van Til, teaching at New York University, had kept in fairly close contact with Kilpatrick. But one day when he visited the Morningside Drive apartment a sad-eyed Marion said that her husband no longer wished to see visitors. "He's a proud man, you know," she told Van Til, "and he doesn't want people to remember him as he is now." As Van Til walked back to the subway, he saw Kilpatrick wrapped in a blanket in a wheelchair, being pushed by a young man. He stood and watched for a while, then turned and walked away. He never saw Kilpatrick again.

Kilpatrick's final stay in Saint Luke's Hospital lasted over a year; he was in a coma, connected to various feeding tubes and life support systems.[22] Margaret was unsure if it was Marion or the doctors who kept the inevitable at bay. But Marion's protectiveness increased as she kept vigil at her husband's bedside, never failing to make two lengthy visits each day to his room. One person close to the family indicated that this routine broke Marion's health, and when the end finally came, she was a shell of the woman she once had been. According to Margaret's diaries, the only time she could slip in to see her comatose father was when Marion had an appointment elsewhere or happened to be momentarily absent from the hospital room.

The end finally came on the afternoon of February 14, 1965. William Heard Kilpatrick was ninety-three years old. Lyndon Johnson was president, and both *Time* magazine and the *New York Times* were reporting the impending escalation of the United States' involvement in Vietnam.[23] Born during the days of Reconstruction following the Civil War, Kilpatrick died as America was entering another armed conflict. His life had spanned more than half the life of the nation, and half of its presidencies — he had lived during the administrations of eighteen presidents.

Margaret and Marion's relationship had deteriorated over the last ten years of Kilpatrick's life, and at the time of his death communication between the two women was nonexistent. Margaret's feelings regarding the situation were mixed. She was appreciative of Marion's ministrations to her father during his long illness, but vexed over the excessively protective attitude of the woman who continued, even in the final stages of the old man's life, to be the keeper of the flame. And so it was that when the end came, Margaret was informed by the attending physician, Dr. Mary Nelson. Margaret, like her father, had kept a diary, in which she recorded relief at her father's passing, writing that Marion had finally lost him, and that he was now "accessible to us all — Grandmother, Aunt Helen, my own dear Mother, the little boys — his sons, and even Mama

(Rita), that other outsider." She willingly admitted that Marion had been faithful, good, and devoted, except for her possessiveness. Margaret believed that, as the only child, she had a special responsibility to pass what she called "the preciousness of the heritage" along to her family and, therefore, to behave accordingly.

Marion attended the funeral with a small group of her family from New York and her brother, Paul, who lived in Georgia. The two families — the Ostranders and the Kilpatricks — met at the old homestead in White Plains. The doorbell to the old house rang incessantly as guests and local relatives came to call. All three grandchildren were present, along with two great-grandchildren. The service, apparently planned by either Marion or Kilpatrick's nephew Frank Jenkins, was held in the White Plains Baptist Church where James Kilpatrick had been the minister for so many years. Flowers filled the front of the chancel, with the urn containing Kilpatrick's ashes, placed on a blanket draped over a pantograph stand. There were some prayers, a hymn — "Abide with Me" — and a "motley collection" in the choir, joined by an inept pianist who frequently took the singers off-key.

Next came the sole eulogy, delivered by Francis Robert Otto, a junior professor of philosophy and religion from Mercer University, who had been invited by Frank Jenkins to perform this service. Otto recalled that when Jenkins had invited him and mentioned White Plains, he had first thought of New York state. Otto was accompanied by Mercer's current president, Rufus Harris, who gave a brief statement. Harris attended the funeral, according to Otto, because of both his sense of duty and his great respect for Kilpatrick. A memorial service for Kilpatrick was also held on the Mercer campus.[24] The presence of the contingent from Mercer University, the heirs and representatives of the institution that, six decades before, had persecuted the now-celebrated man, was indeed ironic. But it seems that both parties had long since made their peace with each other, as witnessed by the numerous occasions on which Kilpatrick had returned to Mercer to give talks and graduation addresses.

Margaret doubted whether any eulogist could adequately address the religious and intellectual diversity represented by the audience in White Plains that day. According to Margaret there was "the aggressively atheist, humanist" Marion, along with the Roman Catholic Ostranders, the high church Episcopalian Baumeisters, the local Baptist Kilpatricks, and, of course, Kilpatrick himself — "the iconoclast, the heretic, the agnostic." But Margaret thought Professor Otto rose to the occasion. "He has come home," he began simply, "to be with his fathers," and he repeated that refrain throughout the

eulogy. Several years later, Margaret remembered that her father had always thought of himself as a southerner and a Georgian. There had been talk of retiring in Georgia, but Rita's connection to Charleston may have made such a move difficult. "The [New York] apartment was large and comfortable," Margaret said, "but it was not 'home.' 'Home' was White Plains, Georgia."[25] The eulogist's words, therefore, struck an emotional chord within Margaret, who, deeply moved by the experience, felt as though a miracle had taken place during the eulogy. At the graveside there were the customary "dust to dust" references from Scripture, followed by the comforting biblical maxim, "In my Father's house are many mansions; if it were not so, I would have told you. I go to prepare a place for you." The interment followed. The urn was a square bronze box, which looked to Margaret like a large tea caddy with handles. She had never seen one before and was unable to make the connection between it and her father.[26]

Marion was later to erect what proved to be a controversial grave marker. Rather long and made of limestone, it was inscribed in large letters "KILPATRICK," under which was written "Delightful Task . . . to Teach the Young Idea How to Shoot," a line from James Thomson's *The Seasons*. The family seemed to be unanimous in the opinion that this nebulous phrase was not appropriate. Questions may have also been raised about whether Marion should or would be buried alongside Kilpatrick. In fact, the decision had been made during one of the couple's summer visits to Schuylerville. As they strolled through the village cemetery examining gravestones, they had made plans to be buried together in White Plains.[27] A decade after Marion's death, members of the Kilpatrick family in White Plains brought the offending monument down and had it replaced with twin black marble slabs over the gravesite.

Even more controversial was Marion's decision to overturn her late husband's will. Throughout his life Kilpatrick had taken great care in connection with his will, having it rewritten on numerous occasions. He no doubt thought that Marion would be able to live in relative comfort after his death on the income from the two Teachers College gifts made in the 1950s, in addition to her own modest estate.[28] But after his death Marion invoked the New York state law for widows, which effectively disinherited Margaret and the other major heir, Kilpatrick's grandson Heard Kilpatrick Baumeister. A certain number of personal items did make their way to daughter and grandson, in addition to a number of Kilpatrick's books, his genealogy collection, his diaries, his scrapbooks, and his personal papers. The diaries and scrapbooks given to Teachers College had a twenty-year seal placed on them, no doubt because of

Kilpatrick's frankly stated reaction to the "heresy" episode at Mercer and the retirement crisis in 1937.

Marion continued to live in the Morningside Drive apartment, along with her sister Gretchen, who would precede her in death. According to relatives, as Marion's physical health deteriorated, so too did her mental capacities. Her last years are clouded, as she lived alone, with occasional stays in a nursing home in Ossining, New York, no doubt clinging to and defending the legacy of her late husband. She died on January 29, 1975, at the age of 83, was cremated, and was buried a week later in White Plains alongside her husband, whom she had served as loyal assistant for over twenty years and as wife and partner for almost a quarter of a century. Margaret attended the funeral service in White Plains, which was — ironically, considering Marion's beliefs — given by a local minister who went by the name of "Preacher Williams."[29]

Tributes to Kilpatrick after his death were remarkably few. This may have been due in part to a traditional lack of esteem and respect for teachers and philosophers. The major newspaper in his home state, the *Atlanta Constitution*, however, took note of his passing with a prominent story with the heading "William Heard Kilpatrick Dies at 93; Dean of U.S. Education."[30]   The newspaper also paid glowing tribute to Kilpatrick in an editorial the next day, "State, Nation Honor Dr. W. H. Kilpatrick":

> No man in this century has had a greater impact on the nation's educational programs than Dr. William Heard Kilpatrick. It is he who gave meaning to the principles of John Dewey, famous exponent of the theory of progressive education. Because of him, many of those principles have become standard in modern education techniques. Their value, still a matter of controversy, is yet to be fully evaluated but no one questions the fact that variations of the philosophy exist in most schools today. His fellow Georgians pay him tribute and acknowledge his great contribution to the times in which he lived.[31]

Apparently forgetting the long-standing feuds over Kilpatrick's liberalism and his disagreements with Eugene Talmadge in the 1940s, the Georgia General Assembly, in session at the time of his death, passed a resolution lamenting the educator's passing and stating in part:

During his long and distinguished career as an educator, he was recognized as one of the leading exponents of progressive education, having been principally responsible for the practical translation of the philosophical principles of progressive education espoused by John Dewey.[32]

William Van Til arranged for a memorial meeting in New York City on March 4, 1965, placed an announcement in the *New York Times*, and fretted over the possibility that the room he had reserved would be too small. He need not have worried. Although Kilpatrick had taught over 35,000 students during his long career, only fifty-six signed the guest register that evening. They included his longtime friends and colleagues Bruce Raup, V. T. Thayer, Ernest Johnson, George Axtelle, Frederick Redefer, and Frank and Helen Trager. Also present was a young philosopher of education who would one day teach at Teachers College, Maxine Greene. One notable registrant stands out — Bayard Rustin. The controversial black civil rights leader evidently felt compelled to pay tribute to this son of slaveholders for his tireless efforts to achieve equality and dignity among the races. Later, at Teachers College, there would be an endowed William Heard Kilpatrick Professorship in Philosophy and Education; and in 1977, his daughter Margaret and his grandson Heard would make brief remarks at the dedication of the Kilpatrick Education Center at Georgia College in Milledgeville. Thus ended the formal recognitions of his life and work.

Any examination of Kilpatrick's life and work would be incomplete without an understanding of his relationship to John Dewey. As Lawrence Dennis has written, "As long as Dewey remains important to modern education, then so too do his disciples." One of Dewey's early biographers, George Dykhuizen, said to Kilpatrick: "Your name is so clearly associated with that of John Dewey in the world of education that one hardly thinks of one without the other." John Childs — student, colleague, and chronicler of the pragmatist philosophy — viewed Kilpatrick as the spokesman for progressive educators and as the one who had given pragmatic principles "their most mature expression in the formulations of John Dewey."[33] The association between Dewey and Kilpatrick spanned over fifty years, encompassing both the professional and the personal areas of their lives. Yet, once the connection between the two philosophers had been made, the public perception of progressivism quickly became entangled with a combination of Rousseau's philosophy, classroom permissiveness, and anti-intellectualism.

As documented earlier, Dewey considered Kilpatrick one of his most outstanding students and the two men occasionally worked together on editorial tasks. Dewey had read and approved of Kilpatrick's *The Montessori System Examined* in 1912, and the favor was returned in 1916 when Kilpatrick critiqued the first ten chapters of Dewey's *Democracy and Education.* Dewey then asked for a list of other topics in order to complete the book, and Kilpatrick raised a number of philosophic problems from his philosophy of education course and turned them over to Dewey. Though he first rejected the list, Dewey later redefined a number of the problems, and they appeared in the completed book. While reading the manuscript in galley form and making additional criticisms, Kilpatrick admitted his envy of Dewey's "genius in making for himself of a point of view." Dewey gave Kilpatrick sole acknowledgment for his assistance in the introduction to *Democracy and Education,* one of the essential texts in twentieth-century educational thought. Dewey would occasionally call upon his former student for advice. On one occasion the topic was educational values, for which Kilpatrick provided his mentor an outline. Later, when Dewey was retired and was teaching a course in philosophy of education as a visiting professor, he again requested aid from Kilpatrick, who gladly provided it. But on occasion, Dewey would baffle even Kilpatrick in the process of providing an explanation of a concept. "Sometimes I understood the explanation and sometimes I didn't," Kilpatrick told Tenenbaum.[34]

Much of the information regarding the relationship between Dewey and Kilpatrick is contained in an article Kilpatrick wrote in 1959, on the 100th anniversary of Dewey's birth. Kilpatrick noted that, soon after his arrival in New York City, Dewey had told him that he had never read Rousseau or Froebel, giving William James and Francis W. Parker most of the credit for his concepts of education. In a conversation with Kilpatrick in 1912, Dewey acknowledged Franklin Ford, Herbert Spencer, and George Herbert Mead as other influences on his thinking.[35] Kilpatrick wrote that Dewey's belief in equality had emerged as a result of "the creative frontier background which he shared with his Vermont family." Kilpatrick judged Dewey to be next to Plato and Aristotle in the history of philosophy (above Kant and Hegel), and without peer in the history of philosophy of education. When asked in 1959 about this comparison, Kilpatrick responded that he ranked Dewey so high because of the completeness of his philosophical thinking. Undoubtedly, Kilpatrick's high praise for his former professor sometimes verged on the extravagant. Merle Curti once quoted Kilpatrick as saying, "Like Socrates, [Dewey] too has brought philosophy down from the clouds to dwell among men." Yet, as he

remarked in a more moderate vein, "How [Dewey] would hate us if we did not try to improve upon him."[36]

As early as 1911 Kilpatrick had come to the conclusion that Dewey needed an interpreter — "His own lectures are frequently impenetrable even to intelligent students" — believing that by teaching philosophy of education, he could make Dewey's point of view more accessible. Kilpatrick did not personally find Dewey intellectually confusing; in fact, he compared Dewey to Shakespeare and William James in his clarity of presentation and argument. He considered Dewey deliberate and thoughtful when lecturing and not without humor and wit on occasion. But in Kilpatrick's opinion, he was "poor in marshaling his principles so as to make them form a communicable whole." Dewey gave Kilpatrick his blessing to provide an interpretation. In 1915, the younger man asked Dewey's permission to give a synoptic view of his educational thought. "He gave cordial permission," reported Kilpatrick, "saying he knew no one who could probably do it better, in fact, no one who could do it so well." After this endorsement, Kilpatrick's major concern was that he found so little within Dewey's position to reject.[37] Even a decade after his retirement, Kilpatrick still considered himself the ascendant interpreter of Dewey:

> My principal interest now in my educational theory is to get it before the world and to see it put into American education. While Dewey has given the underlying philosophy, he has not worked it out into school procedures. I think I can do this better than he.[38]

At the same time, Kilpatrick was evidently sensitive to any suggestion that his own work was merely imitative. While acknowledging Dewey's influence, he noted, "My indebtedness to Dewey is profound and far-reaching; but I do not think that any one will justly accuse me of not adding my part." And on one occasion he bristled at being compared to Dewey, particularly in his style of teaching. One notable distinction that Kilpatrick drew between himself and Dewey was based on a famous epigram in education: "learning by doing." This was frequently attributed to Dewey and was consistent with the activity curriculum, but Kilpatrick rejected it. "Personally, I don't like the phrase 'learning by doing' because so many people misconceived 'doing' as being merely the physical aspect of it. And so I put it under 'living.' We learn by living. That carries you deeper." Fundamentally, however, his devotion to Dewey's principles was total.[39]

By the early 1920s Kilpatrick was making great strides in spreading Dewey's ideas, or "telling his own tale," as he put it, although he was admittedly alienating the school administrators ("who wished for something to make control easier"), the measurers ("who were looking for formal aims to assess"), and the subject matter specialists ("lest they lose out in the philosophical battle"). However, Kilpatrick added triumphantly, "the teachers of children are nearly all with me." The heavy emphasis of the time on the scientific approach to teaching often drove educators into what the historian Merle Curti called the "socially conservative camp," as they became more interested in measurement, administration, and instrumentation applied to the school setting. Curti pointed out that, in contrast, both Dewey and Kilpatrick provided the schools a "humanitarianism and realistic concept of democracy" for the educational process.[40]

Just before the outbreak of World War II, as his contribution to a collection of essays on Dewey, Kilpatrick summarized the influence of Dewey's educational philosophy. Dewey had brought about a new attention to the schools and to students. He also credited Dewey with bringing about more interaction between teacher and student, in addition to a community-focused, student-centered orientation. Finally, democracy, scientific thinking, and human values were now central in the educational milieu. "There is not to be found in this country a single child," wrote Kilpatrick, "whose life has not been made somewhat happier because John Dewey has lived."[41]

One important distinction Kilpatrick drew between his work and that of Dewey was his own development and discussion of learning. During World War II Kilpatrick explained his own ideas on learning to Dewey in the latter's apartment. Dewey "caught on at once, seemed to accept it, caught on readily to certain implications," wrote Kilpatrick in his diary. Kilpatrick firmly believed that his own thought on education had begun prior to his going to Teachers College in 1907 and taking classes under Dewey. In 1951 he wrote, "John Dewey did shift me from neo-Hegelianism to experimentalism, but in a way to let me keep much of what had previously been developing." The application of educational thought to the classroom was, for Kilpatrick, his major contribution as distinguished from Dewey's.[42]

Yet there was a strong connection between the two philosophers' ideas. One of the most incisive explications of Dewey's educational thought was undertaken by John Childs in his article of 1958, "An Evaluation of Dewey's Theory of Education." Childs was a student of both Dewey and Kilpatrick — the article is filled with "Kilpatrickan" phrases and concepts — and he found a number of remarkable similarities between their ideas. For example, Childs

saw Dewey as proposing education that was something more than merely "acquiring a certain amount of information." In addition, he saw Dewey as endorsing "experiences which originate as a felt need," learning through the use of "purposeful efforts," and learning as the connection between what we do and what happens as a consequence." According to Childs, Dewey was also a promoter of an activity curriculum that would provide the conditions essential for reflective thinking. Childs concluded his review of Dewey's educational philosophy by stating in almost Kilpatrickan terms that:

> Respect for the individuality of the child, respect for his capacity for independent thought, and respect for his ability to share in our system of democratic self-government, should not be opposed to the mastery of whatever methods, techniques, knowledge and attitudes are required to enable our country to meet the responsibilities of this critical time.[43]

Kilpatrick's own interpretation of Dewey accentuated, in particular, the child's experiential learning process, as opposed to rote memorization; the child's self-direction, self-motivation, and self-control as espoused in *Interest and Effort*; the importance of moral development and character in education; and the essential role of the community in the development of citizenship and public welfare. In "John Dewey and His Educational Theory," written on the occasion of Dewey's death in 1952, Kilpatrick stressed the paramount importance of the developmental nature of the child. Furthermore, quoting William James, as well as Dewey's *My Pedagogic Creed* and *The Child and the Curriculum*, he pointed out the necessity of taking into account the child's crucial interaction with life's social dimension. In this article he also stated, though without documentation, that Dewey believed that the "child should precede any choice of subject matter, that nothing should be presented to the child for learning except as it answered the felt demands of the child's own self." Kilpatrick's second in-depth analysis after Dewey's death was in 1953, in an article for the *Educational Forum* titled "Dewey's Philosophy of Education." Here he relied heavily on *Democracy and Education*, footnoting more than was his usual practice. Restating Dewey's commitment to the educational concept of growth, Kilpatrick emphasized the necessity of purposeful activity and experience. He also reiterated Dewey's opposition to drill and repetition, while cautioning against any attempt to indulge the child.[44]

Despite Kilpatrick's intimate professional acquaintance with Dewey, the

two men were never close personal friends. Neither was an extrovert, although Dewey could be much more affable than Kilpatrick, if the mood struck him. The protégé would however, call upon the older man on occasion at his Fifth Avenue apartment. Kilpatrick had always been painfully aware of his inadequacy at making small talk and often disparaged his "incapacity either to make or receive pleasure in triangular company." This was especially true with Dewey. "I have to confess," Kilpatrick wrote after a dinner party, "that he and I do not stimulate each other to talk. There is no one to whom I am more indebted or for whom I have greater admiration, but we never get on very well talking generally." Sometimes though, the problem was the subject at hand. He once attempted to engage Dewey in a conversation regarding Pestalozzi but soon discovered that Dewey "didn't know the facts."[45]

While admiring Dewey, Kilpatrick could also step back and see the human side of the man. He often good-naturedly noted Dewey's invariable absent-mindedness and chronic tardiness. On one occasion, before his marriage to Roberta Grant, Dewey was unable to join the Kilpatricks for dinner and had Mrs. Grant drive the party to the restaurant. The evening ended with Mrs. Grant running out of gas and kissing Kilpatrick on both cheeks when she bid him and Marion goodnight. The relationship between Mrs. Grant and Dewey frequently baffled Kilpatrick, who was unable to discern much about it other than to note that "though not related she acts as a member of the family." On a visit to Dewey's apartment in 1945, he noted that Dewey's "kinsman" (he also mistakenly referred to her once as "Dewey's adopted daughter") was present, and on another occasion, when asked what the relationship between Grant and Dewey was, Kilpatrick responded with a laconic southern, "I don't rightly know." When they did marry, the event completely surprised Kilpatrick. While he hoped the union would mean greater happiness for Dewey, he also added enigmatically that there might be a "price to pay." Newspaper reporters even telephoned Kilpatrick for his reaction, but he gave them none.[46]

One of the more amazing conversations between the two men consisted of a confession by Dewey. After he had taken his baccalaureate degree from the University of Vermont and gone to Pennsylvania to teach high school, he had received a score of 20 percent on a state teacher's examination.[47] The preeminent philosopher of American education had failed a teaching proficiency test. Kilpatrick continued to visit Dewey's apartment on occasion, though at times not without effort on the part of both men. Once Kilpatrick was unable to rouse Dewey (whose hearing was impaired), and the elevator man opened the apartment for him. He found Dewey busy at his typewriter, and the

two men chatted for an hour. There was also the rare tea party for the Deweys, hosted by the Kilpatricks. In May of 1947, for example, the guests at Morningside Drive included the Counts, the Childs, the Herbert Schneiders, the Raups, Sidney Hook, and Kenneth Benne. Kilpatrick could still be critical of his mentor, bluntly stating in his diary, "As too often happens, Professor Dewey was not too interesting," and "I doubt that most got much from it."[48]

Although Kilpatrick's diary never recorded a visit by John Dewey to any of his protégé's classes, legend has it that the philosopher once slipped unnoticed into the back of Horace Mann Auditorium. According to this apocryphal account, after listening for a while, he sadly turned away, disclaiming any ownership of what Kilpatrick was teaching. Conventional wisdom has held that Dewey's disciples and interpreters distorted and misapplied his ideas for a generation of educators, amplifying the flaws in their interpretations as they passed them on in their own teaching. Kilpatrick never seemed to be aware of the charge that he himself was one of the primary malefactors.

Kilpatrick carefully read *Experience and Education*, Dewey's work of 1938, in which many suggested Dewey separated himself from the progressive educators who had strayed from his original message. In it, Dewey warned that not all experiences were educational and that "unless the problems of intellectual organization be worked on the ground of experience then a reaction to progressivism would set in."[49] If Dewey's criticisms were aimed at Kilpatrick — and there is no evidence to suggest they were — he failed to take note of them. Commenting on the work, Kilpatrick wrote, "It is of course excellently done. I learn little, but like his treatment all except what seems to me ambiguous wording about the organization of subject matter."[50] Twenty years later, he continued to believe that *Experience and Education* was the "least satisfactory work by John Dewey," especially since Dewey had adopted the experimentalist philosophy. Kilpatrick added that in his opinion, Dewey's daughters had urged him to give the lectures to "clear himself of the charges . . . against certain excesses committed in the name of progressive education." And on Dewey's death, Kilpatrick wrote that his mentor clearly believed the study of the child came before subject matter."[51]

To many there was a discrepancy between what Dewey thought regarding progressive education and what Kilpatrick thought he meant. But in 1948 the two men stood shoulder to shoulder in defense of modern education when Francis Crowly, dean of Fordham University's School of Education, charged that New York City schools had "slipped" and that the system was not receiving an adequate return on its educational dollar. The assault prompted the Bronx

Chamber of Commerce to demand that the mayor conduct an investigation of the school system. Dewey said it was "silly to regard the lack of discipline in the schools as a result of progressive education." He assigned the blame for juvenile delinquency to "conditions in the home, on the street, and to the lack of suitable playgrounds and to our slum areas." Kilpatrick also responded, saying that when "a maladjusted child is forced into the traditional school patterns he resorts to truancy and then becomes delinquent." He went on to defend the "activity program," which had been adopted five years earlier by the city schools, as not only ensuring mastery of the three R's, but also advancing character and personality development and decreasing the need for rewards and punishments. Such charges against Dewey continued to appear with regularity, including one by President Dwight Eisenhower, who regarded Dewey as the source of deterioration in the American educational system. Kilpatrick frequently came to his mentor's defense, even responding to an article in a newspaper in Atlanta that blamed John Dewey for the misbehavior of some local college students.[52]

That Dewey ever disavowed Kilpatrick, even indirectly, would be difficult to prove. In 1953, a reviewer of Kilpatrick's article in *Educational Forum*, "Dewey's Philosophy of Education," noted, "It was often said by students who did not understand Dewey's point of view that the philosopher would say to them, 'Go to Dr. Kilpatrick. He can explain it more clearly than I can.'" In Dewey's last written exposition on the new education in 1952 — the year of his death — his words are positive, overly so at times, in defense of the progressivists' record. According to Dewey, progressive education liberated students and schools from "repressive modes of life," enlightened the intellectual and social aspects of the community, brought about greater awareness of the needs of human beings, and humanized and democratized relations between students and teachers. He concluded that making such changes is a long and arduous task, as apparent in the lack of progress in secondary schools, but that much success could be seen in the kindergarten and elementary schools.[53]

The major refutation of the charge that Kilpatrick strayed considerably from Dewey is provided by Dewey himself, in his introduction to Tenenbaum's biography of Kilpatrick, a book it is doubtful Dewey ever read. The introduction comprised an assessment of Kilpatrick's work, independent of Tenenbaum's interpretation, which read, in part:

> In the best sense of the words, progressive education, and the
> work of Dr. Kilpatrick are virtually synonymous. I say in the

best sense because the phrase "progressive education" has been and is frequently used to signify almost any kind of school theory and practice that departs from previously established scholastic methods. Many of these procedures, when they are examined, are found to be innovation, but there seems to be no sound basis for regarding them as progressive. Dr. Kilpatrick has never fallen victim to the one-sidedness of identifying progressive education with child-centered education. This does not mean that he has not given attention to the capacities, interests and achievements and failures of those who are still students, but he has always balanced regard for the psychological conditions and processes of those who are learning with consideration of the social and cultural conditions in which as human beings the pupils are living. The aims and processes of learning, which have been so fully and concretely stated by Dr. Kilpatrick, form a notable and virtually unique contribution to the development of a school society that is an organic component of a living, growing democracy.[54]

In 1951, Kilpatrick made one last visit to Dewey, just a few months before the philosopher's death. When he arrived at 1158 Fifth Avenue, he noted with disgust — apparently for the first time — that the fourteenth floor apartment was actually on the mislabeled thirteenth floor and knew that this superstitious act would have irked Dewey. Dewey had recently been released from yet another hospitalization, and Kilpatrick waited patiently until he awoke. Although Dewey was confused at times, the two men talked for fifteen minutes, at long last seemingly at ease with each other. Dewey even made an attempt at humor, saying he was suffering from "hospitalitis." When he left, Kilpatrick noted they "shook hands warmly."[55]

In October of 1959, Kilpatrick gave a recorded interview in his apartment to mark the century celebration of Dewey's birth, responding to many familiar questions regarding progressive education and Dewey. The session was arranged by William Van Til, who brought together several colleagues and reporters. Almost immediately the issue was raised of Dewey's heirs and their alleged and documented deviations from the master's path. "Had some 'out-Deweyed' Dewey?" came the first question. Horace Kallen, who was present, quickly retorted that it was a case of being "de-Deweyed" rather than "out-Deweyed,"

which brought a chuckle from the usually reserved Kilpatrick. But Kilpatrick agreed that there was truth in this, indicating that many had made a "fad" out of Dewey's ideas, though he considered Freud rather than Dewey the culprit. By this Kilpatrick meant that after World War I educators were urged to recognize the unconscious as the source of motivation and behavior. The aim of education thus became interests, instincts, and tendencies, knowledge of which would remove the major obstacles to cognitive development.[56]

Once again, as with the publication of *Experience and Education*, if Kilpatrick was the intended target of the critics who made this charge, it was entirely lost on him. For Kilpatrick, Dewey's message went beyond pedagogy, or at least beyond strict classroom nostrums, to a democratic way of life, including social, intellectual, and personal elements. In 1939 he wrote, "When Dewey speaks, we know the voice. It is, in a sense, our own best selves speaking, instructed by him how to think, what to wish, what to do." For Dewey, democracy consisted of mutual respect, of citizens actually thinking about their dealings with others.[57] For Kilpatrick, the voice of Dewey was what American democracy and American education could be, and it had been his mission to spread that message across the world.

LEGACIES: PROGRESSIVE PATHS
TO THE FUTURE

> It has become fashionable to criticize American education for
> being unduly influenced during the last fifty years by
> Dewey's ideas. But it would be accurate to say that insofar as
> our schools have failed to develop the tough-minded habits of
> intelligence, they have failed to be influenced by what is most
> basic in Dewey's concept of the function of education in a
> democratic society.
>
> Richard Bernstein[1]

As Bernstein suggests, the flow of Dewey's ideas into twentieth-century
schooling — for good or ill — is a controversy that has yet to abate. And
Kilpatrick's legacy, in turn, cannot be viewed apart from the progressive
education movement so intimately connected with him. Inevitably, fundamental questions about his life and work have remained: Which held primacy
in Kilpatrick's philosophy — child centeredness or the social outlook? What
did Kilpatrick believe the role of subject matter should be in the classroom?
Was Kilpatrick's progressivism anti-intellectual, antiacademic, or neither?
These issues continue to be debated within the context of school reform as
teachers and educational leaders grapple with how best to improve society
through education.

In the mid-1950s, Howard Whitman went on a journey of inquiry into
progressive education, tracking down Kilpatrick, Counts, and Rugg. The latter
two seemed mildly reserved about their pasts, both calling themselves "New
Dealers" and disavowing much of their Depression-era rhetoric. Counts even
told Whitman that his "Dare the Schools" talk had been "polemical." Kilpatrick,
on the other hand, told Whitman that he remained more enamored of the child-
centered phase of progressive education than the social-centered phase and that
he stood with Dewey on "no indoctrination, no orthodoxy, no absolutes." When
asked where his ideas were being implemented, Kilpatrick mentioned the
UCLA University Elementary School, but Whitman found only a mild form of

progressivism still in practice there. And in the face of ever-mounting criticism that the collectivist ideas of progressivism were not carrying the day, Kilpatrick suggested that pragmatism called for further experimentation and change. "The whole idea is to try [a principle] out in practice to see how it works," he said, "and then decide — depending on whether it works — whether to hold on to this belief or not." Whitman's article stridently emphasized some of the failures of progressive education, but he came away from his meetings with Kilpatrick impressed, won over by the man and his message:

> When I left Kilpatrick's apartment, the quiet, tasteful abode of a scholar, I knew that regardless of posterity's final verdict on Progressive Education, no one could gainsay this man's contribution to education. Kilpatrick did much to force America to sweep the cobwebs and the hickory sticks and the dry-as-dust rote learning out of some schools as he found them one and two generations ago.[2]

Criticism, even ridicule, of progressive education has a rich history. As has been seen, it began first "in-house," at Teachers College, with the arrival of William Bagley in the 1920s. The tone of the dispute was then kept on a formal and "gentlemanly basis," reflecting both the era and the personalities. Thomas Hopkins, a professor at Teachers College and a philosophical soul mate of Kilpatrick, does, however, tell the story of walking into a room on the campus and finding Bagley holding forth on the sins of progressive education to a group of colleagues. In the 1930s another dissenting voice emerged at Teachers College, that of Isaac Kandel, who in one article pointed out inconsistencies in Kilpatrick's open system of exploration, which denied the need for subject matter fixed in advance. Kandel directly attributed the nation's social disorder during the Great Depression to what he perceived as progressive education's unstructured approach to both social conditions and learning. In 1942 Kandel again ridiculed progressive education, this time chiding the New York City schools' for their recent commitment to the activity curriculum. He focused particularly on a suggestion that orange crates be used in connection with certain projects in the classroom and "orange crates" soon became a typical point of derision among critics of progressive education.[3]

Derogatory and skeptical observations moved from the halls of academe and philosophic treatises to the pages of the *New Yorker* magazine, current novels, and even stage plays. As Lawrence Cremin pointed out in 1959 in a

speech titled "What is Progressive Education?," after World War II the movement became an "anathema, immortalized only in jokes," or merely a "delightful caricature." One sympathetic observer of progressive education saw a grain of truth in the comedy that imperiled the movement in general: "The unskilled teacher attempting to follow Dewey and Kilpatrick," wrote Fred Hechinger, "is likely to turn education into a farce."[4] Patricia Graham saw a failure both within the progressive education movement itself and by the organizations that supported it, due to an unwillingness to recognize "the extreme and irresponsible nature of their position" on curricular reform. The phrases "child-centered" and "democratic education" lost their power when definitions became more and more difficult to formulate. Nevertheless, Graham concluded that progressive education would have flourished in any environment where it was enthusiastically and intelligently presented and that, indeed, the movement had "affected children in nearly all socioeconomic classes at some time between 1876 and 1955," a broad acknowledgment from a frank, rigorous critic.[5]

The most extensive assault on progressive education, though, came in the early 1950s with the publication of several books, all blaming the movement for real and perceived failures of schools. In addition to the books by Flesch and Lynd mentioned earlier (see Chapter 18), one of the harshest and longest-lived attacks on progressive education came from the historian Arthur Bestor. In his book *Educational Wastelands*, Bestor discussed the "limited contributions" of pedagogy to the improvement of public education, arguing that pedagogues overstepped the bounds of their mission when they concerned themselves with what subject matter should be learned in the classroom. (This linking of pedagogy and curriculum occurred when pedagogues ventured into a discussion of the aims of education. E. D. Hirsch concurred with Bestor's conclusion in his book *Cultural Literacy*, where he contrasted the work of the Committee of Ten with that of the Cardinal Principles group.) Bestor evidently had felt a deep sense of betrayal when, as a student at Lincoln High School in New York in the 1920s, he saw "educationists" assume control, inventing social studies, which he called "social stew." Charging that the pedagogic mind has "grave limitations," Bestor went on to state that "American teacher training colleges" are "the most blatantly vocational and anti-intellectual of our institutions." He asserted that one cannot really be trained to be a teacher and that "nothing original, creative, or significant" had ever been accomplished by these "narrowly conceived vocational programs."[6] After reading *Educational Wastelands*, Kilpatrick was of the opinion that Bestor's argument was erroneous

because it had defined education narrowly to include only subject matter, and had not considered other aspects of a student's life or experience.

Bestor's charges were instrumental in exposing teacher education, and thereby the work of Kilpatrick, to accusations of anti-intellectualism. At three separate points in his book, Bestor contended that education was not a legitimate field of study, that those making educational policy had no faith in the value of intellectual endeavor, and that teacher education programs were devoid of intellectual content — he suggested they taught people how "to blow their noses and button their pants." He summarily defined the process as "a pedagogical program that is superficial and blatantly anti-intellectual and that solemnly and tediously re-instructs him [the student] in vocational skills he already possesses."[7]

The influence of Bestor's work made itself felt during the decade of educational reform in the 1980s. Its staying power can been seen in the writings of Timothy Noah and Mickey Kaus, two journalists who have written for both *The New Republic* and *Newsweek*. They have denounced the practice of certifying teachers to teach in the public schools; referred to educators as "snake-oil salesmen"; poked fun at pedagogy classes, calling them "sterile"; and labeled the doctorate in education (Ed.D.) a technician's degree, not a scholar's degree.[8] Lynne Cheney, chair of the National Endowment for the Humanities at this time, arrived at conclusions similar to those in *Educational Wastelands*: that there was a need to reduce the influence of schools of education; that teachers should major in a discipline, not in education; and that professors of the arts and sciences know more about public schools and educating future teachers than do teacher educators.[9]

The other monumental work associating teacher education with anti-intellectualism was Richard Hofstadter's *Anti-Intellectualism in American Life*, which contained three chapters on education, one of which was devoted entirely to John Dewey. The book's title, the amount of space it devoted to education, and a number of the conclusions it reached all contributed to the continuing perception that progressive education was an anti-intellectual movement. Hofstadter, too, questioned the idea of growth as an educational aim in itself as well as the dictum that education is not only a preparation for life, but life itself. His sharpest criticism was for those holding administrative posts in schools and for teacher educators, who were, he said, "far from enthusiastic about the new demand for academic excellence." He likened attempts at educational reform to the difficulties encountered by a new political regime saddled with a civil service of determined opponents.[10] Nevertheless, Hofstadter provided an even-

handed critique of progressive education, noting that "Dewey has been praised, paraphrased, repeated, discussed, apotheosized, even on occasion read." And in a lengthy passage, containing words and phrases often used by Kilpatrick, Hofstadter paid tribute to the movement:

> Although its reputation suffered unwarranted damage from extremists on its periphery, progressivism had at its core something sound and important. The main strength of progressivism came from its freshness in method. It tried to mobilize the interests of the child, to make good use of his need for activity, to concern the minds of teachers and educators with a more adequate sense of his nature, to set up pedagogical rules that would put the burden on the teacher not to be arbitrarily authoritative, and to develop the child's capacity for expression as well as his ability to learn. It had the great merit of being experimental in a field in which too many people thought that all the truths had been established.[11]

Actually then, Hofstadter's monumental work on anti-intellectualism is, if anything, mildly positive on the whole topic of progressivism. This may be due, in part, to the influence of Lawrence Cremin. Before leaving Hofstadter, three brief points should be made. First, as he attempted to define anti-intellectualism, Hofstadter referred to the work of Merle Curti, who had taught with Kilpatrick at Teachers College. Curti had publicly praised Kilpatrick's teaching abilities, paying tribute to him in his survey of educational thought.[12] Second, while making an occasional criticism of Teachers College, Hofstadter never mentioned Kilpatrick by name. And third, as James Wallace has noted, Hofstadter analyzed only eight of Dewey's works from 1897 to 1938, ignoring his journalistic writings, which forcefully repudiated anti-intellectual mutilations of his ideas.[13]

Hofstadter's comments brought the criticism of progressive schools back from the extreme points it had reached in the 1950s. There followed a brief renaissance of progressivism in the mid-1960s and early 1970s. In 1962 William Van Til wrote a widely anthologized article for the *Saturday Review*, "Is Progressive Education Obsolete?" It was Van Til's contention that education could not escape the essential questions raised by Kilpatrick and his colleagues: What are the aims of education? Upon what foundations should the school program be built? Given such aims and foundations, what should the schools

teach? According to Van Til, Kilpatrick's work, taken along with George Counts's advocacy of the connection between school and society and Boyd Bode's emphasis on democratic values and the development of intelligence, formed a progressive triad. Kilpatrick's contribution emphasized the interests and needs of the individual learner, the necessity for classroom planning and activity, and the importance of intrinsic motivation.[14] The revival of progressive practices that began shortly after Kilpatrick's death was led by a group of urban educators whom Van Til described as "compassionate critics." They included John Holt, Herbert Kohl, and Jonathan Kozol. These men and others resurrected and extrapolated from earlier progressive ideas and practices, such as the open classroom and team teaching, and their innovations took hold in selected schools and certain curricular programs in the 1960s and 1970s.

But this brief interest in progressive practices was not to last. In 1983, a national report on education, titled *A Nation at Risk*, launched a return to the back-to-basics philosophy, which reemphasized outcomes and efficiency, standardized testing, and a uniform curriculum. In fact, the literature that accompanied this wave of educational reform in the 1980s was brutally critical of the progressive movement — progressivism in general and William Heard Kilpatrick in particular. In 1983, in a book that was not untypical of the genre — *Necessary Lessons: Decline and Renewal in American Schools* — Gilbert Sewall ridiculed Kilpatrick and spoke patronizingly of progressive education:

> Kilpatrick propounded a simplified version of progressive education that even students at provincial normal schools could grasp. The outlook was Manichaean: In one dark universe, ten-year-olds sat at attention in straight-backed chairs, memorizing facts from drab primers, speaking only when spoken to. Solemn schoolmasters drilled students without mercy, impelling effort, if need be, with hickory sticks and dunce caps. In the universe of light, schools served the "felt needs" of students, possibly through Kilpatrick's own "project method."

Sewall continued: "In Kilpatrick's wonderful world, the modern learning process was free of tension. It was painless. It was liberating. How appealing! How magical! And how specious! For pure cornfed 'Progressive' insensibility — looking straight at the intellect and seeing in it something repressive and irrelevant."[15]

Another work of the 1980s on educational reform, *The Shopping Mall High School: Winners and Losers in the Educational Marketplace*, by Arthur G. Powell, Eleanor Farrar, and David K. Cohen, also singled Kilpatrick out for special attention:

> This prolific professor taught at Columbia University, but he was militantly anti-academic: "The mind is best used when it is put to work on conducting enterprises and meeting problems." Teaching must be centered on "activities," or an "activities curriculum," in which students took responsibility for solving problems that interest them. Students would learn whatever academic content they really needed, because they would stumble on things they needed to know in order to solve the problems.[16]

These authors went on to establish their thesis by quoting selectively, but accurately, from Kilpatrick's *Education for a Changing Civilization*: "Rid the schools of dead stuff. For most pupils, Latin should follow Greek into the discard. Likewise with most of mathematics for most pupils. Much of present history study should give way to the study of social problems. Modern foreign languages can hardly be defended."[17]

The role of subject matter in Kilpatrick's thought is also at the core of E. D. Hirsch's (1996) critique in *The Schools We Need and Why We Don't Have Them*. Citing Kilpatrick more than forty times, Hirsch concedes both his popularity and his influence, but calls his legacy flawed. Hirsch describes Kilpatrick as the "charismatic codifier" of current educational ideas and maintains that his name should be better known, yet views most of Kilpatrick's contributions as negative. For Hirsch, these include his overemphasis on innate talent, his call for a dynamic and uniquely American approach to education, and his crusade against a common core of content. It is Hirsch's opinion that this last point was undertaken by Kilpatrick in order to protect teachers' autonomy. Hirsch comprehensively suggests a dozen dubious outcomes of late-twentieth-century educational practice that he finds rooted in Kilpatrick's *Foundations of Method* of 1925. He considers Kilpatrick much more dangerous than John Dewey and laments the fact that the hearts and minds of a generation of education professors were won over by the progressive Kilpatrick rather than the essentialist William Bagley. The result, according to Hirsch, has been "suspicion and contempt" on the part of the American public toward schools,

and six decades of "antiknowledge extremism" in the nation's classrooms.[18]

Historians and philosophers of education have also grappled with Kilpatrick's legacy, often with a mixture of penetrating insight and conventional wisdom. Charles Frankel, a professor of philosophy at Columbia University, gave a major address at Kilpatrick's ninety-third birthday celebration: "Appearance and Reality in Kilpatrick's Philosophy." Having given Hyman Rickover favorable reviews, Frankel may have seemed an odd choice to honor the dying man. But as he said in his opening remarks, the appraisal would be a dispassionate one, an effort to discover what in Kilpatrick's philosophy could be used and what should be rejected. Frankel questioned Kilpatrick's emphasis on cooperation and self-reliance and his propensity to favor freedom to the detriment of authority. Teaching how to think rather than what to think is problematic, and therefore Frankel views Kilpatrick's idea of educating children for a changing world as an incomplete statement — psychologically, logically, and morally. But amidst this seemingly withering assault, Frankel states that "it is impossible to face up to this man and be trivial. We may think, after considering his doctrines, that we have rejected them, [but] second thought suggests that we retain a good deal." As for the charge of anti-intellectualism, Frankel responds: "But did anyone in the history of American education have greater faith that the school could be made the center for active, energizing youthful purpose, or for serious, independent intellectual work?" Frankel even endorses Kilpatrick's notion of the "whole child," arguing that teaching is impossible unless attention is paid to the home, the neighborhood, the economy, and the child's physical and emotional condition.[19]

In *The Transformation of the School* (1961), Lawrence Cremin presented a number of contrasts and outright differences between the ideas espoused by Dewey and Kilpatrick on progressive education. Dewey is portrayed as pursuing a new subject matter during his days at the Chicago Laboratory School, while Kilpatrick is depicted as making "unrelenting attacks on subject matter 'fixed-in-advance.'" According to Cremin, Kilpatrick was primarily, and even dogmatically at times, "child-centered" in his outlook, while Dewey rejected this solitary approach in both *The Child and the Curriculum* and *Experience and Education*. With regard to disseminating the progressivist message, Cremin ultimately held that Kilpatrick's version of Dewey — conveyed from the stage of Horace Mann Auditorium for mass consumption to 35,000 students — was "quite different from the original." Cremin's final concern in examining Kilpatrick's contributions was what he called the "problem of the two Kilpatricks." He saw a paradox: students looked to the

Kilpatrick of *The Social Frontier* to guide their social outlook, but then turning to the Kilpatrick of *Foundations of Method* to inform their classroom practice. This was a philosophical dichotomy that Cremin observed throughout progressive education, especially in the 1930s.[20]

While some saw *The Transformation of the School* as the death knell for progressivism, Cremin nevertheless remained intrigued with the Deweyan aspects of progressivism, so much so that he was at work on a biography of Dewey at the time of his death. In one of his last interviews, Cremin stated, "I believe we are going to have a revival of interest in Dewey. His works are a point of departure from which to think about education." In the same interview he called attention to the renewed interest in child-saving agencies, day-care facilities, and the recreation movement, all of which had boomed during the progressive period and all of which Kilpatrick had endorsed.[21] *The Transformation of the School* and Tenenbaum's biography have become the primary sources and the conventional wisdom on Kilpatrick. Although he actually preferred Boyd Bode's version of Dewey to that of Kilpatrick's, Cremin contributed significantly to current thought regarding Kilpatrick's legacy.

Diane Ravitch, a student of Cremin's who taught at Teachers College as a visiting lecturer, was also a frequent critic of progressivism, especially in her history of post-World War II education, *The Troubled Crusade* (1983). Ravitch did praise progressivism for easing the transition to mass secondary education and for offering a rationale for including vocational and nonacademic studies, thus enabling high schools to retain a larger proportion of young people. Also, she never confronted Dewey directly — in fact, she called him "humane, pragmatic, and open-minded." But she did go on to state that "progressive educators rejected . . . the belief that the primary purpose of the school was to improve intellectual functioning." Ravitch was much more comfortable with progressive education before World War I than the form that developed afterward, which she called a "bastard version" of Dewey's vision.[22] Using Tenenbaum as her source (as others had done before), Ravitch denounced the progressives' apparent promotion of "dancing, dramatics, and doll playing" over "Greek, Latin, and mathematics." She concluded with a stinging assessment of Kilpatrick, stating:

> Not only did Kilpatrick combine in his work the romanticism
> of the child-centered school, the full-blown scientism of the
> authoritative pedagogue, and the anti-intellectualism of the
> social utilitarians, but he contributed to progressivism many

of the phrases that became part of the arcane language of the education profession.[23]

Clarence J. Karier, in *The Individual, Society, and Education: A History of American Education* (1986), recognized the close intellectual kinship between Kilpatrick and Dewey, but he also observed in Kilpatrick's thought an affinity with the ideas of both Pestalozzi and Francis Parker. Karier pointed out that Kilpatrick popularized familiar education epigrams such as "Students need to know how to think and not what to think" and "Teachers teach children, not subjects." Unfortunately, Karier noted, many educators turned these clichés into a philosophy that became, if not anti-intellectual, at least antiacademic. He suggested that many of the failures of progressive education were unfairly attributed to Kilpatrick, but still Kilpatrick's "war on fixed subject matter was to discredit the functional role of the disciplines" among the nation's youth. Karier justified this criticism by appealing to Kilpatrick's own tenet that the thinking of the next generation must not be limited, even if such freedom eventuates a total revision of current ideas and practices. Karier's strongest criticism of Kilpatrick concerned the concept of the "good life," which he found excessively idealistic. "While thousands flocked to hear Kilpatrick at Teachers College . . . books were burning in front of the University of Berlin," he wrote.[24]

One of the most severe critical appraisals of Kilpatrick has come from Dewey biographer Robert B. Westbrook, in *John Dewey and American Democracy* (1991). Westbrook relied heavily on primary sources, especially Kilpatrick's "The Project Method" and *Foundations of Method*, rather than Tenenbaum and Cremin. Kilpatrick is placed within what he calls the school of "romantic progressivism." He also refers to "negative freedom" in which children are left to their own "spontaneous impulses." And the familiar caricature of absolute freedom for students emerges once again as Westbrook refers to the famous *New Yorker* cartoon in which a gloomy child asks her progressive teacher, "Do we have to do what we want today?" By contrast, Dewey's *Experience and Education* is said to refute the extremes of progressivism and to direct students toward the intelligent use of spontaneity, creativity, and self-control.[25]

Westbrook does devote a significant amount of space to Kilpatrick, unlike other figures in this intellectual biography. He begins by stating unconditionally (but also without documentation), "Though Dewey rarely named names in his criticisms of progressive education reform, one of his principal targets was William H. Kilpatrick." After briefly examining Kilpatrick's "The Project

Method" and quickly reviewing the debate over student versus subject matter, Westbrook concludes that this exchange "tipped Kilpatrick's thinking toward the sort of romanticism which troubled Dewey and made Kilpatrick's program, to a significant degree, little more than an updated version of the child-centered pedagogy Dewey had been criticizing since the 1890s." Westbrook agrees that Kilpatrick followed Dewey's thinking in terms of interests, the project method, and the need to reorganize subject matter to meet the needs of the new pedagogy. But he sees Kilpatrick as having abandoned the child's mastery of organized subject matter — and this is what distresses Westbrook most. Quoting Herbert Kliebard, Westbrook writes that reorganizing the teaching of science became a substitute for science and that what critics attacked as aimless, contentless "Deweyism" was in fact aimless, contentless "Kilpatrickism."

Westbrook returns to Kilpatrick again in his discussion of the social reconstructionists, stating that, while Dewey "clearly felt most at home with this group," he differed with Counts on the question of indoctrination. Dewey's work with the *Social Frontier* and *The Educational Frontier* is discussed, but not in depth. In listing the social reconstructionists, Westbrook includes Childs, Counts, Raup, Rugg, and Watson. Kilpatrick is also included, but after his name, Westbrook writes, parenthetically and pejoratively, "ever alert to shifting trends," implying a lack of conviction, on Kilpatrick's part, in the goals and beliefs of the group. Westbrook views Dewey's impact on education as marginal, owing to its lack of a following in the world of educational practice, once again implying that Kilpatrick's connection to the world of practice was negligible and making the parting remark, "some (like Kilpatrick) continued to think of themselves as Deweyans."[26]

Alan Ryan, in *John Dewey and the High Tide of American Liberalism* (1995), has also pointed to Kilpatrick as a disciple who strayed from Dewey's fold. Although cautious, even circumspect, in his criticism, Ryan sees a "degeneration" of Dewey's ideas in his "supposed disciple William Heard Kilpatrick." But he adds, albeit in a footnote, that by this he does not mean that Kilpatrick was not by intention or fact a disciple of Dewey. Ryan does, though, blame Dewey for a goodly portion of the criticism that came his way over education, because of his obsessive "harping" on the child and growth of the child as the be-all and end-all. Ryan's overall portrayal of Kilpatrick is drawn heavily from Cremin's history of Teachers College (1954), in which Kilpatrick is portrayed as flamboyant and "readier to take ideas to extremes than his hero." But Ryan moves beyond conventional critiques of progressive education. He characterizes Dewey's educational philosophy as an "obsessive concern with

using elementary education to re-create social ties" that might be lost if the child were not able to experience the world as a meaningful, rather than mechanical, entity. Ryan's Dewey sees education as political, holding "that it was not a matter of what went on in the classroom" so much as how citizens approached what went on in the classroom. In the end, Ryan compliments Kilpatrick for the pedagogy he taught in the classroom but ignores Kilpatrick's social outlook.[27]

Kilpatrick's social outlook was not lost on Arthur Zilversmit, who drew generalizations about progressive education from his case-study approach to midcentury classrooms in Chicago in *Changing Schools: Progressive Education Theory and Practice, 1930-1960* (1993). Kilpatrick is considered a popularizer — not a true philosopher or an abstract thinker — who distorted Dewey by way of classroom applications and anti-intellectual theory. Zilversmit uses a combination of Dewey's *Democracy and Education*, Westbrook's *John Dewey and American Democracy*, and Tenenbaum's biography to contrast Dewey's allegiance to subject matter and Kilpatrick's support of the child as the school's primary focus. Zilversmit links Kilpatrick to Dewey during the 1930s, when Kilpatrick revived Dewey's social reform agenda as leader of the "frontier" theorists who fought to have the schools reshape society by making "America more equal and more democratic."[28]

Such criticism of Kilpatrick, when contrasted with his vast popularity and his apparent influence, calls for a response with both a broad brush and a bill of particulars. The strongest statement in defense of Kilpatrick would be that elementary schools were much more positive places for children at the end of Kilpatrick's career — which was also the end of the progressive era — than they had been before. Between the two world wars, the needs of children were taken into greater consideration than at any time earlier. There was also an emphasis on activity, experiences, and solving future problems. A new respect for personality and character, key elements in Kilpatrick's philosophy, emerged during this time, as schools became more sensitive to children's emotional, social, and physical development as well as their intellectual achievement. Despite the critics, according to Cremin, progressive education at the end of World War II "enjoyed a substantial measure of acceptance in many quarters, particularly among intellectuals and other influential segments of the middle class."[29] Even subject matter became more integrated as disciplines merged and thus better met the needs of the child through the social studies, language arts, and a closer relationship between the natural and physical sciences.

As has been demonstrated by the selective discussion above, reconstructing

the era of progressive education in the light of late-twentieth-century essentialism has become a cottage industry. One eyewitness to the progressivism earlier in the century is Agnes de Lima, who, in an interview in 1965, rebutted the major charge against Kilpatrick and the progressives — that of anti-intellectualism. She reported that in most child-centered classrooms the children were surrounded by good books and undertook excellent academic work. De Lima conceded that a few schools became too Freudian, while others approximated the caricature of students running amok. But, she concluded, even in these settings more learning took place than in the traditional schools of the time.[30]

Kilpatrick's supposed antipathy to formal study of the disciplines and subject matter, a perception which formed the basis for accusations of anti-intellectualism, has remained the most serious of criticisms aimed at him. Therefore, it may be helpful to return to Hofstadter's original charge of anti-intellectualism. To assess Kilpatrick's position Hofstadter defined the term as follows:

> The common strain that binds together the attitudes and ideas which I call anti-intellectual is a resentment and suspicion of the life of the mind and those who are considered to represent it: and a disposition constantly to minimize the value of that life. This admittedly general formulation is as close as I find it useful to venture toward definition.[31]

An examination of an individual's intellectual practices would provide strong evidence of belief or disbelief in the life of the mind. Kilpatrick's life was one of books, writing, attending conferences, and attending and leading discussion groups. His interests were multidisciplinary, spanning the sciences, arts, and humanities. John Childs, his colleague and former student, concluded that "Kilpatrick was in full accord with Dewey's insistence that the deepest discipline is *intellectual* in nature; it involves taking responsibility for having ideas, for developing ideas, and for testing ideas by the consequences they produce in human experience."[32] Kilpatrick's commitment to the intellect, though, had to serve a purpose by meeting the needs of the individual.

On this point, Kilpatrick's stance on textbooks and subject matter has continued to be the overriding point of concern and contention in examining his legacy. Once again, certain aspects of this discussion must be clarified. Kilpatrick himself held books in high regard and read voluminously, usually nonfiction, but also novels, newspapers, and journals. His pedagogic quarrel was with school programs that were book-centered to the exclusion of other

sources of experience. As John Childs has written on this subject, "It is one thing to regard books as an indispensable means for the enrichment of the meaning of life; it is another and very different thing to assume that the study of books can become a substitute for learning through living."[33] The external authority that books could assume in the schooling process, the tendency to make learning a mechanical and rote affair because of a central focus on books, and a disregard for the vital examination of the community all made Kilpatrick wary of overdependence on the written word. Concern about subject matter "set in advance" thus became a crucial point in Kilpatrick's criticism of the curriculum, which frequently set the agenda for all that occurred in the school. Because the child must be able to respond to actual situations in life, Kilpatrick considered the reconstruction of experience in authentic acts — thought included — to be essential to an individual's education.

That Kilpatrick himself repudiated subject matter, especially in *Education for a Changing Civilization*, must be understood within a larger context. Kilpatrick did not believe that subject matter "set in advance," as he termed it, was as helpful as material which allowed students the opportunity to become involved themselves in the problem-solving process. This explains, in part, his comments on closed systems within mathematics. Even though he questioned the efficacy of certain disciplines, it should also be noted that there is no evidence that he categorically denied the importance of subject matter. Although rather lengthy, the following passage, from 1928, clarifies his thinking on the issue:

> We teach knowledge and skills for their service in life. The conditions of true learning, that is for the appropriation in life for life, seem to demand that subject matter be taught, typically if not exclusively, when and as it is needed in order to carry on some enterprise which the learner (preferably in a group with others) has then under way. Such enterprises, which always include the thought aspect, will with the very young perhaps usually show an emphasis upon motor activity. With increasing age the successive enterprises (activities, problems, projects, experiences of whatever kind) will increase in social outlook and in thought content. Any teacher who has worked primarily with problems rather than with the fixed content of ordinary textbooks will testify that the quantity of knowledge thus brought into play is far and away

greater than any textbook writer would dare place in his book. The plan of teaching subject matter as it is needed seems, if reasonably directed, to promise not less, but more and better learning of both skill and knowledge.[34]

Not surprisingly, this was a highly utilitarian approach as to what should be learned in the schools. The debate turned as much on *how* one learns as *what* one learns. But with regard to subject matter, Kilpatrick focused directly on the practical needs of the students for "their service in life." The move from the physically oriented activities of the young child to the more intellectual experiences of adolescents occurred naturally along a continuum. And the concept of freedom was not lost in the process. Kilpatrick was unwilling to justify the imposition of arbitrarily selected subject matter on the learner. As he reminded his colleagues from the traditional disciplines of the arts and sciences, they would take strong exception if their own academic research and pursuits were externally directed by others or their own subject matter were preordained and "set in advance" by others.

The consequences of Kilpatrick's intellectual suasion can be seen in the way his contributions swayed the debate. Winston Churchill once said that great men control the weather. Likewise, Sol Cohen has gauged the influence of the movement which Kilpatrick led by suggesting that the debate was determined by those who controlled its language.[35] While he may not have always been the dominant voice, Kilpatrick did to a large extent establish the parameters around which the discussion of modern schooling practices took place. He was also able to extend his ideas beyond the high tide of progressivism by suggesting topics and issues of a social nature that would receive attention in the decades to come. He believed the low status of women was in need of rectification, found the current penal system indefensible, saw labor problems as demanding better theory and practice, and thought instability in the family structure presented serious problems for future consideration.[36]

But it remained the educational arena in which his prognostications proved most accurate and influential. During the Pasadena conference in 1949, Kilpatrick conjectured about a number of educational trends that did come to fruition. College students, he believed, should take part in community volunteer work as part of their commitment to citizenship. He supported extracurricular activities but hesitated to endorse athletics, calling for the "abolishment of the present cult of interscholastic athletics." He suggested released time for kindergarten teachers to hold parent-teacher conferences. He called for

confining the uses of standardized tests within individual classrooms, abolishing scholarship societies, reducing classes to twenty-five pupils, allowing children to remain with one teacher for up to three years, and encouraging the use of anecdotal observation records (what today would be called portfolios) for valuation purposes. And he stated his firm opposition to the segregation of students then referred to as mentally retarded; he considered it "stupid" to label these children in such a way. Kilpatrick also affirmed his belief that the first six years of the child's life were the most crucial and during the last decade of his life he advocated the concept of year-round schools.[37]

On a broader scale, innovations of progressive education, first proposed over fifty years ago during the time of Kilpatrick's ascendancy, have returned under fresh titles or in modified form. These include cooperative learning, which is reminiscent of the progressive idea of students working in group settings; and the call for professional development schools — a major recommendation of recent teacher educators — which is a variation of the laboratory or demonstration schools promoted earlier in the twentieth century. A further parallel is the movement toward what is termed "site-based management" of schools, with greater authority and responsibility being assumed by those at the grassroots level, similar to efforts to bring about more participatory and democratic schools during the progressive era. And one can easily imagine Kilpatrick endorsing the recent attention to learning styles espoused by Howard Gardner and others, with its interest on how best to discern and engage an individual's mode of learning.[38]   John Pulliam has documented additional progressive influences on contemporary educational practices in his *History of American Education*, noting the current emphasis on individualized instruction, the inquiry approach, differentiated staffing, and a host of child-centered teaching strategies, which exist in many modern elementary and middle schools. In fact, it has even been suggested that the inspiration for the middle school model grew out of the progressive education movement.[39]

What ideas, then, were at the core of this man's life and philosophy? First, life and behavior are transactional — there must be activity, and it must significantly engage the environment one lives in. Neither the unheard piece of music nor the unseen work of art has an inherent value solely unto itself. Accordingly, it is the reader, as much as the writer, who gives ultimate meaning to a text. Second, an experimental and scientific view of life must be present, continually testing and connecting solutions to problems. The more experiences are employed and absorbed, the more possibilities there are for learning. Kilpatrick

reiterated this belief in his dictum "We learn what we live," but he added to it in his *Philosophy of Education* when he concluded, "We learn our responses, only our responses, and all our responses; we learn each as we accept it to live by, and we learn it in the degree we accept it."[40] Third, democratic ideals must be at the core of both individual and group value systems. And morality was essential to Kilpatrick's conception of democracy. Only when the individual is accepted for the full potential he or she represents as a person — a moral stance — can democracy function and flourish. Once again, in *Philosophy of Education*, he stated, "When we so treat another that he too can set up ends and live and develop himself . . . then we are treating him as an end in himself." Democracy itself had to be taught in a democratic fashion. Uncritical, irrational, indoctrinated citizens made the democratic model unworkable. "I have faith in democracy and I have faith in the free play of intelligence," Kilpatrick once said, "Those are the two things I want to base my procedure on."[41] As Norman Cousins saw it, Kilpatrick's strength derived from his ability to make connections throughout his philosophy. "I think he recognized," said Cousins:

> the need for connections and the need for correlation. One of the unfortunate trends in education has been toward specialization of knowledge. But that tends to produce compartments. Kilpatrick didn't believe in compartments and to that extent he provided the antidote to over specialization which enabled people to think across these compartments.[42]

And yet, for all these significant contributions, there remain both paradoxes and enigmas regarding the man and his work. Ronald Goodenow, who wrote about Kilpatrick's views and activities with regard to racial issues, said of him: "Democratic in outlook and aristocratic in bearing, he was in many respects a quintessential liberal, a man so prolific and complex that he defies easy description and comparison with his peers."[43] When examining a legacy, one finds that individuals most often belong to one of two groups: those who have successfully dealt with issues which are no longer important today, and those who have grappled, relatively successfully, with themes that are still relevant. Kilpatrick seems to belong to the latter group, particularly when one takes into consideration James Wallace's succinct statement of the problems faced by our society as it nears the end of the millennium. Wallace points out that our age faces new versions of old problems, such as creating a more democratic polity and a more humane economy, and providing an educational

system that serves justice and excellence rather than privilege and mediocrity.[44]

That Kilpatrick was concerned with just such perennial issues is illustrated by his statement, near the end of his life, that he wished for an economic and educational system where the son of a General Motors president and the son of a cobbler would have equal opportunities to develop, grow, and achieve.[45] Such a declaration raises again Lawrence Cremin's conundrum of the "two Kilpatricks" — pedagogue or social interventionist? The only reasonable response to this seemingly irreconcilable breach is that Kilpatrick was at home in both camps, and residence in either camp did not preclude intellectual habitation in the other. Staunchly child-centered from his early days as a teacher and principal in the South, he remained comfortable with this approach until the end of his life. What emerged, though, in the 1920s, was the informed addition and considered integration of the social outlook into his educational philosophy. While this latter viewpoint would become the dominant feature in his thinking from the Depression on, he never abandoned his commitment to the former position, nor did he see sufficient reason, intellectually or philosophically, to shift away from this point of view.

For what changes was Kilpatrick responsible, and what makes him significant in the history of American education? The time period during which he emerged on the national scene cannot be overlooked in answering these questions. The progressive era must be seen as a time during which individuals perceived unlimited possibilities — a time when creativity was set free in politics, health, communication, psychology, and the arts, as well as education. Prior to the Great War the application of scientific and democratic principles held the promise of solving, in time, any given problem. It was a time when the authoritarian practices of the nineteenth century were beginning to be questioned. As John Maynard Keynes once said, "The real difficulty in changing the course of any enterprise lies not in developing new ideas, but in escaping from old ones." The human condition was being examined in the light of new thinking on education, which took into account both the way students learned and what they studied in the curriculum. Kilpatrick was able to balance the roles of critic and defender in the new movement. Although very much a part of the institutional and bureaucratic mainstream of formal education, owing to his position at Teachers College, through his writing and speaking he placed himself outside the establishment in order to make his disagreements with the current system heard. When progressivism became the conventional wisdom in many schools across the country and the attacks began, he then found it necessary to switch from the role of critic and mount a formal defense of its practices.

We are reminded by the historians David Tyack and Larry Cuban, in *Tinkering Toward Utopia: A Century of Public School Reform*, that the pragmatic concept of change was to constantly reassess goals in the light of experience. This Kilpatrick was able to do, while at the same time making the reform of schools a forum for debating the future of a democratic society. Tyack and Cuban suggest that school reform and shifts in classroom practice are a process of amelioration, with reform gradual and perennial rather than immediate and dramatic.[46] What Kilpatrick contributed to this process was essentially mainline pragmatism matched with unyielding idealism. His type of reform proved to be substantive while appearing subversive, gradually changing the system while always remaining reflective at its roots.

What Kilpatrick provided in terms of educational theory was not on the same scale as what he offered to the world of classroom practice. This was due, in part, to his struggles as a writer and his strength as a stirring and charismatic orator. Yet there were distinct contributions. He took credit for the concept of concomitant learning. And the project method did provide an alternative approach to classroom activity, although it tortuously attempted to wed Dewey's philosophy to Thorndike's psychology. Some, such as Kenneth Benne, considered Kilpatrick's suggestion of the "complete thoughtful act" to be as original as Dewey's "complete act of thought." And ultimately, Kilpatrick was responsible for rendering Dewey's educational thought accessible and understandable to several generations of teachers and their students, who would have been the poorer had the message never been given voice. If Kilpatrick at times pushed his interpretation of the Deweyan gospel beyond what has since seemed accurate or even appropriate, the suggestions he put forward rarely crossed over into documented heresy or whole-cloth improvisation. And if he challenged conventional ideas on the role of subject matter, he did so in the belief that more would be learned by the progressive approach to schooling than by the process being espoused by the essentialists.

As for the world of educational practice, in examining Kilpatrick's life one cannot escape his power as a classroom teacher and communicator. And since teachers have rarely been afforded the prestige or acknowledgment they deserve, this is no mean accomplishment. Edward Thorndike would send graduate students to the Horace Mann Auditorium to observe Kilpatrick teach, so highly did he think of his colleague's example in the classroom.[47] The originality with which he managed classes of several hundred students was in itself a testament to his pedagogic skill. Through preclass questions and group work, consensus building in teams, and finally full class overviews of the issues

at hand, the process became a model for schools and organizations across the country. But what may have been most impressive regarding Kilpatrick's teaching was the close personal identification each student felt with him, while sitting in a hall with 500 others. That great talent transferred itself to group settings, organizational gatherings, and professional meetings. The wide acceptance of his ideas, in conjunction with his personal reticence and the absence of a public ego, can suggest only that his message was so passionately received because it was so passionately felt. The faith Kilpatrick put into the democratic process — and in the need for students to discern and appropriate the truth for themselves — was put into practice in his classes as he demonstrated his lifelong belief in the centrality of the individual and the worth of each person's ideas.

Kilpatrick's success was, admittedly, enhanced by the fact that his forum was in New York City — the major center of intellectual life in the United States and the home of world-renowned newspapers, journals, and publishing enterprises. What occurred in New York was augmented beyond normal expectations. In addition, his personal charisma and style cannot be discounted as factors in his professional achievements and accomplishments. The presence he carried onto a platform — with his immaculate dress and grooming, his abundant silver hair, his mellifluous southern accent — combined with his message of progressive change, made Kilpatrick and his ideas attractive to a nation seeking new approaches and workable solutions to the educational issues of the day.

But his style did not overshadow the substance of his message. Kilpatrick stands the test of time when one examines the best practices in the elementary and middle schools of today, where the focus is on the individual student, the need for activity, the integration of subject matter with real-life experiences, and the importance of engaging the inherent interests of the child in the daily lessons of the classroom. Even in adult education, another field on which Kilpatrick wrote and to which he applied his theories, the need for experiential learning remains a key element. Only the modern high school, as in Kilpatrick's time, remains most resistant to substantive change and creative experimentation. In the end, Cremin may have been correct when he stated, "I think we will find that some of the best of what the progressives tried to teach has yet to be applied in American schools." But the world of practice had to be coupled to a supportive social outlook. Kilpatrick understood that schools without a social purpose or a social vision are incomplete systems. As Dewey had suggested in the titles of his books, such as *The Child and the Curriculum*

and *The School and Society*, the emphasis was to be on the conjunctive. In Kilpatrick's mind, the cultivation of intelligence for character formation had to serve the democratic elements of a unified educational process. "The philosophy of education will not recover its importance or excitement," wrote Charles Frankel, "until it recovers something like Kilpatrick's large-minded view of its function."[48]

Kilpatrick's students often heard him say that the process of learning never ceases. The pragmatic philosophy of tested thought, activity, and reconstructing life's experiences was inescapable. It is not surprising, then, that he concluded *Foundations of Method* with the following dialogue. The student inquires of the master teacher, "Are you not sorry that we've reached the end?" Comes the response: "Reached the end? We haven't reached the end. There's plenty more. We have merely paused. It is the term that has ended."[49]

NOTES

Chapter 1

1. Helen M. Kilpatrick, "What One Must Absorb to Be Intelligent," *Macon Telegraph*, June 16, 1929. (Helen Kilpatrick was not related to William Heard Kilpatrick.) Article located in William Heard Kilpatrick Scrapbooks (unpaginated), collected by year in Milbank Memorial Library, Teachers College, Columbia University, New York, NY. (Hereafter cited as Scrapbooks.)
2. Edward L. Ayres, *The Promise of the New South: Life after Reconstruction*. New York: Oxford University Press, 1992, pp. 422-23.
3. Autobiography of William Heard Kilpatrick, tentatively titled *Two Halves of One Life*, unpaginated. Stetson Library Archives, Mercer University, Macon, GA. (Hereafter cited as Kilpatrick, Autobiography.)
4. Thaddeus Brockett Rice and Carolyn White Williams, *History of Greene County Georgia*. 1786-1886, Macon, GA: J. W. Burke, Company, 1961, pp. 4, 5, 50-1.
5. Kilpatrick, Autobiography, Federal troops actually stayed in Greene County until 1872, one year after William Heard Kilpatrick's birth. Rice and Williams, p. 427.
6. Kilpatrick, Autobiography.
7. Ayres, pp. 154-59.
8. Kilpatrick, Autobiography.
9. Kilpatrick, Autobiography.
10. Rice and Williams, p. 414. J. G. Randall and David Donald, *The Civil War and Reconstruction*, 2nd ed. Lexington, MA: D. C. Heath and Company, 1969, pp. 99, 114-15, 424-33, and 516.
11. Letter from Washington L. Kilpatrick to James Hines Kilpatrick, December 31, 1864. Papers of Heard Kilpatrick Baumeister (HKB).
12. Kilpatrick, Autobiography.
13. Kilpatrick, Autobiography.
14. Kilpatrick, Autobiography.
15. Letter to author from Heard Kilpatrick Baumeister, July 28, 1992.
16. Kilpatrick, Autobiography.
17. Kilpatrick, Autobiography. Letter to author from HKB, July 28, 1992.
18. Diary of William Heard Kilpatrick, Milbank Memorial Library, Teachers College, New York, NY. Dated January 5, 1936, but unpaginated. (Hereafter cited as Diary or Diaries.)
19. Kilpatrick, Autobiography.
20. Kilpatrick, Autobiography.
21. Kilpatrick, Autobiography.
22. Samuel Tenenbaum, *William Heard Kilpatrick: Trail Blazer in Education*. New York: Harper and Brothers Publishers, 1951, p. 4 (Hereafter cited as Tenenbaum.)
23. Kilpatrick, Autobiography.
24. Tenenbaum, p. 8.

25. William Heard Kilpatrick, "People Who Made Me," *Educational Leadership*, March 1944, 1(6): 323.
26. Tenenbaum, p. 4.
27. Untitled article in Scrapbooks, 1929.
28. HKB Papers.
29. William Heard Kilpatrick, unpublished biographical sketch of Macon M. Kilpatrick from HKB Papers. (Hereafter cited as MMK.)
30. Kilpatrick, Autobiography.
31. Kilpatrick, Autobiography.
32. HKB Papers.
33. Kilpatrick, Autobiography.
34. Tenenbaum, p. 4.
35. Kilpatrick, Autobiography.
36. Diary, September 18, 1928.
37. Kilpatrick, Autobiography.
38. Taped Recording of "Proceedings of Boyd H. Bode Conference," The Ohio State University Archives, July 1949.
39. Tenenbaum, p. 5.
40. Diary, April 30, 1943.
41. Diary, April 30, 1938.
42. Tenenbaum, p. 7.
43. Kilpatrick, Autobiography. After the death of his mother, Kilpatrick wrote in a burst of frankness, "My mother was much more sensitive to such than my father, but she was both too hard worked and too much over-awed by my father and his awful religion."
44. Kilpatrick, Autobiography.
45. Kilpatrick, Autobiography.
46. Tenenbaum, p. 10.
47. Kilpatrick, Autobiography.
48. Kilpatrick, "People Who Made Me," p. 323.
49. Kilpatrick, Autobiography.
50. Tenenbaum, p. 9.
51. Kilpatrick, Autobiography.
52. Kilpatrick, "People Who Made Me," p. 324.
53. Kilpatrick, Autobiography.
54. Helen M. Kilpatrick, "What Must One Absorb to Be Intelligent,"
55. Letter to author from Heard Kilpatrick Baumeister, July 28, 1992.
56. Kilpatrick, Autobiography.
57. Kilpatrick, Autobiography.
58. Kilpatrick, Autobiography.
59. Kilpatrick, Autobiography.
60. Kilpatrick, Autobiography.

61. Tenenbaum, pp. 11-12.
62. Kilpatrick, Autobiography.
63. Arthur Powell, *I Can Go Home Again*. Chapel Hill: University of North Carolina Press, 1943, pp. 105, 108.
64. Powell, pp. 110-113, 115.
65. Kilpatrick, Autobiography.
66. Tenenbaum, pp. 13-14.
67. Tenenbaum, p. 14.
68. MMK.
69. MMK.
70. MMK.
71. Diary, September 18, 1928.
72. Kilpatrick, Autobiography.
73. Ayres, p. 423.
74. Diary, September 18, 1928.
75. Tenenbaum, p. 15.
76. Tenenbaum, pp. 16-17.
77. Kilpatrick, Autobiography.
78. Kilpatrick, Autobiography

Chapter 2

1. Donald Chipman, "Young Kilpatrick and the Progressive Idea," *History of Education Quarterly*, Winter 1977, p. 408.
2. Letter from William Heard Kilpatrick to Marie Guyton Kilpatrick, July 20, 1902, from Knoxville, TN. Papers of HKB.
3. Kilpatrick Autobiography.
4. Kilpatrick Autobiography.
5. Kilpatrick Autobiography.
6. William Heard Kilpatrick, "People Who Made Me," *Educational Leadership*, March 1944, 1 (6): 326.
7. Kilpatrick Autobiography.
8. Chipman, p. 410.
9. Kilpatrick, Autobiography. Also Kilpatrick, "People Who Made Me," p. 327.
10. Chipman, p. 410.
11. Kilpatrick Autobiography.
12. Kilpatrick Autobiography.
13. Tenenbaum, pp. 21-22.
14. Tenenbaum, p. 25.
15. Arthur G. Powell, *I Can Go Home Again*. Chapel Hill: University of North Carolina Press, 1943, pp. 154-156.
16. Kilpatrick Autobiography.

17. Chipman, p. 414.
18. Kilpatrick Autobiography.
19. Kilpatrick Autobiography.
20. Tenenbaum, p. 28.
21. Kilpatrick Autobiography.
22. Tenenbaum, p. 28.
23. Tenenbaum, pp. 30-31; and   Kilpatrick,   Autobiography.
24. Tenenbaum, p. 31.
25. Tenenbaum, pp. 29-30.
26. Diary, November 14, 1943.
27. Hoyt Ware, "Noted Educator Spans Years Recalling His Teaching Here," *Savannah Press*, January 11, 1941.
28. Tenenbaum, p. 31.
29. Tenenbaum, p. 33.
30. Kilpatrick Autobiography.
31. Tenenbum, p. 35.
32. Tenenbaum, pp. 41-42.
33. Tenenbaum, p. 36.
34. Kilpatrick Autobiography.
35. Tenenbaum, p. 38.
36. Kilpatrick Autobiography.
37. Letter from William Heard Kilpatrick (WHK) to Marie Guyton Kilpatrick (MGK), June 22, 1902, Knoxville, TN. Letters located in the Papers of HKB.
38. Letter from WHK to MGK, July 6, 1902, Knoxville, TN.
39. Kilpatrick Autobiography.
40. Tenenbaum, pp. 42-43.
41. Tenenbaum, pp. 34-36.
42. Kilpatrick, "People Who Made Me," p. 328.
43. Tenenbaum, p. 37. This self-doubt in his mathematical ability is not borne out in actual fact. He continued throughout his life to use his mathematical background in a variety of applications, from assisting students and relatives with their calculus and other mathematical assignments to the processing of income tax forms for himself and relatives.
44. Kilpatrick Autobiography. Also Kilpatrick, "People Who Made Me," p. 328.
45. Tenenbaum, p. 37.
46. Tenenbaum, p. 37.
47. Kilpatrick Autobiography.
48. Kilpatrick, "People Who Made Me," p. 328.
49. John Dewey, *The Child and the Curriculum*, 1902 from Jo Ann Boydston, *The Middle Works of John Dewey*. Carbondale: University of Southern Illinois Press, 2:276.
50. Tenenbaum, p. 43.
51. Kilpatrick Autobiography.

52. Letters from WHK to MGK, July 17 and July 27, 1902, Knoxville, TN.

53. Letter from WHK to MGK, July 12, 1902, Knoxville, TN.

54. Letter from WHK to MGK, July 20, 1902, Knoxville, TN.

55. Letter from WHK to MGK, July 20, 1902, Knoxville, TN.

56. Letter from WHK to MGK, June 28, 1903, Macon, GA.

57. Letter from WHK to MGK, July 1, 1903, Macon, GA. Twenty years later, while reading a scene in *Rebecca of Sunnybrook Farm*, Kilpatrick was taken back to the tragedy of his son's death. "The little grave was touching to me. My son would have been half through college now. He died the victim of ignorance. Esthetic cleanliness was supposed to be also antiseptic cleanliness. Life would have had a very different outlook to me." Diary, August 27, 1923.

58. Letter from WHK to MGK, June 16, 1903, Macon, GA.

59. Letter from WHK to MGK, August 5, 1903, Macon, GA.

60. Tenenbaum, p. 39.

61. Letter from WHK to MGK, July 5, 1903, Macon, GA.

62. Tenenbaum, p. 39.

63. Letter from WHK to MGK, June 28, 1903, Macon, GA.

64. Tenenbaum, p. 48.

65. Diary, July 14, 1904.

66. Letter from WHK to MGK, February 6, 1904, Macon, GA.

Chapter 3

1. Diary, January 1, 1904, Preface.

2. William Heard Kilpatrick, *Selfhood and Civilization: A Study of the Self-Other Process*. New York: Macmillan Company, 1941, p. 189.

3. Kilpatrick, Autobiography.

4. Diary, January 10, 1904.

5. Tenenbaum, p. 50.

6. Tenenbaum, p. 51.

7. Diary, January 31, 1904.

8. Diaries, February 7, 1904; March 16, 1906.

9. Diaries, February 21 and May 4, 1905.

10. Diaries, June 7 and July 22-23, 1905.

11. Diaries, July 28 and September 15, 1905.

12. Diaries, October 5 and 25, 1905.

13. Diaries, November 20 and 22, 1905.

14. Diaries, November 27 and December 5, 1905; February 9, 1906.

15. Diaries, February 19-20, 1906.

16. Diaries, February 23, 24, and 28, 1906.

17. Diary, March 16, 1906. Tenenbaum, pp. 50-52. See also Kenneth K. Krakow, "William Heard Kilpatrick and Heresy at Mercer," 1970; unpublished paper at

Stetson Library Archives, Mercer University, Macon, GA.

18. Diaries, March 21, 27, and 30, 1906.

19. Diary, March 22, 1906. Tenenbaum, pp. 52-53.

20. Tenenbaum, p. 53.

21. Tenenbaum p. 53.

22. Diary, June 1, 1906. Tenenbaum, pp. 53-54.

23. Diary, June 5, 1906. Tenenbaum, pp. 53-54.

24. Diaries, June 6-7, 1906.

25. Tenenbaum, p. 54. Diary, December 15, 1917.

26. Editorial in *Christian Index* (June 1906) by Rev. T. P. Bell.

27. Diary, November 27, 1913.

28. Diaries, July 22 and September 3, 1921.

29. Tenenbaum p. 55.

30. Diary, September 30, 1932.

31. Spright Dowell, *A History of Mercer University*. Macon, GA: Mercer University Press, 1958, p. 225.

32. Diaries, August 13 and September 12, 1906.

33. Tenenbaum, p. 58. Margaret Kilpatrick Baumeister, interview by John Lounsbury, July 1978, Georgia Museum and Archives of Education, Milledgeville, GA.

34. Diaries, November 20, October 11, and January 6 and 23, 1906.

35. Tenenbaum, p. 59.

36. Diary, October 5, 1906.

37. Tenenbum, p. 59.

38. Diary, December 22, 1906.

39. Diaries, January 27-28, 1906; February 24, 1907.

40. Diary, May 25, 1907.

41. Diary, May 29, 1907.

42. Diary, May 30, 1907.

Chapter 4

1. Diary, May 19, 1909.

2. Tenenbaum, p. 60.

3. Diary, July 9, 1907.

4. Tenenbaum, p. 60. Diary, September 2, 1907.

5. Diaries, September 26 and 29 and October 19, 1907.

6. John Dewey, "Education As a University Study," *Columbia University Quarterly*, June 1907.

7. Tenenbaum, pp. 64-66.

8. Diary, October 11, 1907.

9. Diaries, October 30, 1907; January 3, 1908; December 14, 1907.

10. Diary, September 26, 1907.

11. Diary, October 4, 1909.
12. Diary, October 10, 1907.
13. Diaries, October 10, 1907; January 27, 1908.
14. Diary, November 20, 1907.
15. Diary, December 31, 1907.
16. Diary, March 28, 1908.
17. Tenenbaum, pp. 70-71.
18. Diary, November 2 and 9, 1908.
19. Tenenbaum, pp. 84-85.
20. Diary, March 8, 1908.
21. Diaries, March 1 and November 20 and 26, 1908.
22. Diary, December 31, 1908.
23. Diary, April 29, 1909.
24. Diaries, August 20 and March 17, 1909. Tenenbaum, pp. 71-72.
25. Diaries, March 19 and 27, April 29, May 25, and September 20, 1909.
26. Diary, November 20, 1909.
27. Tenenbaum, p. 75.
28. Diary, May 19, 1909.
29. Diary, November 15, 1909.
30. William Heard Kilpatrick, "Personal Reminiscences of Dewey and My Judgment on His Present Influence," *School and Society*, October 10, 1959, pp. 374-75. Diary, February 2, 1910.
31. Quoted in a letter from Kilpatrick to his mother July 16, 1913.
32. Diaries, November 27, 1910; October 8, 1911. Tenenbaum, p. 78.
33. Kilpatrick, "Personal Reminiscences of Dewey and My Judgment on His Present Influence." pp. 374-75.
34. Diary, May 14, 1909.
35. Diary, April 27, 1908.
36. Tenenbaum, p. 79.
37. Tenenbaum, pp. 78-79.
38. Tenenbaum, p. 80.
39. "Dr. Wilson Sees No Real Education," *New York Times*, December 2, 1909.

Chapter 5

1. Tenenbaum, p. 85.
2. Diary, January 25, 1912.
3. Diary, Index of 1910.
4. Diary, April 5, 1911.
5. Diary, January 1, 1910.
6. Diary, March 18, 1910.
7. Diaries, April 19, 1910; March 12 and May 6, 1911; May 4, 1912.

8. Diaries, September 28, October 21-22, and November 10, 1910.

9. Diary, December 24 and 25, 1910.

10. Diaries, January 1, May 18, and March 25, 1911.

11. Diary, January 11, 1911.

12. Diaries, January 11 and 25 and August 15, 1911.

13. Diaries, September 27, October 31, and November 20, 1911; January 1, 1912.

14. Diary, April 5, 1912.

15. Diary, April 7, 1912.

16. Diary, May 1, 1912.

17. Diary, May 2, 1912.

18. Diary, May 12, 1912.

19. Diaries, May 18-29 and June 1, 1912.

20. This biographical sketch of Montessori has been drawn from Gerald Gutek, *Cultural Foundations of Education*, chapter titled "Maria Montessori: Pioneer in Early Childhood Education." New York: Macmillan Publishing Company, 1991, pp. 304-324.

21. Diary, June 4, 1912.

22. Gutek, p. 315. Kilpatrick did write a letter to his mother intimating that Montessori's having patented the apparatus made him wonder about her commitment to pedagogical ends as opposed to financial ones (Letter, April 7, 1912, Kilpatrick to his mother).

23. Diary, June 4, 1912.

24. Diary, June 8, 1912.

25. Diary, June 10, 1912.

26. Diary, June 12, 1912.

27. Diary, June 26-July 3, 1912.

28. Diaries, August 7, July 16, and October 5, 1912.

29. Gutek, p. 315.

30. William Heard Kilpatrick, *The Montessori System Examined*. Boston: Houghton Mifflin Company, Riverside Press, 1914. (Hereafter cited as *Montessori System*.)

31. *Montessori System*, pp. 9-10.

32. *Montessori System*, pp. 10-11.

33. *Montessori System*, pp. 19-20.

34. *Montessori System*, pp. 18-19.

35. *Montessori System*, pp. 22, 24-25.

36. *Montessori System*, pp. 27-30, 33-35.

37. *Montessori System*, p. 38.

38. William Heard Kilpatrick, "Montessori and Froebel," *Kindergarten Review*, April 1913.

39. *Montessori System*, pp. 44-48.

40. Tenenbaum, p. 96.

41. *Montessori System*, p. 52.

42. *Montessori System*, pp. 39-41.
43. *Montessori System*, pp. 59-60.
44. *Montessori System*, pp. 61-65.
45. *Montessori System*, pp. 66-67.
46. Letter from Kilpatrick to his mother, October 20, 1912.
47. Diaries, July 12 and 20, 1912.
48. Diary, November 20, 1912.
49. Diary, November 7, 1912.

Chapter 6

1. Diary, January 1, 1915.
2. Diary, November 20, 1916.
3. Diary, April 23, 1915.
4. Diary, September 1914.
5. Diaries, March 5, 1913; October 16, 1914; November 21, 1916.
6. Diary, January 21, 1916. Episode found in "Scores Reaching Only Newspaper Whose Opinions Agree with Own," unidentified, undated newspaper article in Kilpatrick Scrapbooks.
7. Diaries, March 7, and July 16, 1913; March 10, 1914.
8. Diaries, April 8, 1913; May 10, 1914; April 24, 1914.
9. Diary, August 8, 1916. In the *Columbia Spectator* (Georgia Issue), August 17, 1916, the students wrote of both Cobb and Kilpatrick, calling the latter "the child who has lived on Mount Parnassus and imbibed the lessons taught by Homer, Socrates, Aristotle and the other poets and philosophers of all time."
10. Diaries, February 7 and April 12, 1913.
11. Diaries, November 19 and July 7, 1913.
12. Diaries, November 30, 1914; August 15, 1914; and December 9, 1915.
13. Diaries, April 13, 1913; May 1 and February 9, 1914.
14. Diary, November 12, 1914.
15. William Heard Kilpatrick, *Froebel's Kindergarten Principles Critically Examined*. New York: Macmillan Company, 1916. For a somewhat more sympathetic view of Froebel, see Gerald Gutek's analysis in *Cultural Foundations of Education: A Biographical Introduction*. New York: Macmillan Publishing Co., 1991, pp. 220-241.
16. Many of the following accounts of Kilpatrick's lectures from local newspapers may be unreliable, especially if you believe Kilpatrick. Often he would write in the margin statements such as "a mistaken account of this talk," or "I said no such thing."
17. Diary, January 1915.
18. Diaries, February 16-17, 1915.
19. Diary, January 1, 1915. Hillegas left Teachers College in 1916 to become commissioner of education in Vermont. He later returned to the Teachers College faculty,

retiring in 1937, the same year as Kilpatrick.

20. Diary, November 16, 1917.

21. Kilpatrick Scrapbooks, Outline of talk by Kilpatrick titled, "Greater Spontaneity in the School Room and Limitations Upon Spontaneity."

22. Diaries, December 24 and 28, 1917.

23. Kilpatrick traveled throughout the country on lecture trips during his entire career and also during his retirement. In fact, although his heaviest commitments to lecturing fell during the period from World War I through World War II, he did make a number of trips and give a number of talks until the late 1950s, never really stopping until his health totally prevented him from traveling. The *Boston Journal of Education*, March 16, 1922, p. 285 wrote, "Professor Kilpatrick is always entertainingly impressive and impressively inspiring." In addition to conference speeches, he also made an occasional consulting trip to assist professors in the classroom. A few days spent at Pennsylvania State College School of Agriculture brought forth the comment by a student, "Went first out of curiosity; then could not stay away." *School Life* (U.S. Bureau of Education), March 1, 1921, p. 7.

24. Diary, January 25 through February 3, 1917.

25. Diary, January 29, 1917. Article concerning the case and the letter to a Mr. Keller, chairman of the City School Commissioners, is found in the February 1, 1917, issue of the *Indianapolis Star*. Diary, February 11, 1917.

26. Diaries, March 14-17, 1918. "Two Women Killed in Pennsylvania Railroad Wreck," *Philadelphia Evening Public-Ledger*, March 15, 1918.

27. Diary, February 15, 1913.

28. Diaries, February 8, 1913; and January 13, 1914.

29. Diaries, December 16, 1913; November 19, 1914; January 1 and January 20, 1916; April 12, 1915; November 20, 1914.

30. Diary, November 14, 1914.

31. Diaries, September 19 and December 16, 1916.

32. Diary, January 10, 1918.

33. Diary, March 22, 1918.

34. Diary, September 22, 1918.

35. Diary, November 25, 1915. Kilpatrick's half brother Jim Kilpatrick from Texas, reappears in the diaries during this period after an absence of several years. On May 3, 1916, Kilpatrick received word that Jim had shot two soldiers while on duty in Texas in connection with problems associated with the Mexican Revolution, killing one of them. He was sentenced to ten years in jail, although he appealed. Jim was later accused of running machine guns over the border. Another version of the incident has Jimmy merely attempting to protect his land from Mexican bandits owing to the inadequacy of the Texas Rangers. Jimmy won his appeal in district court. Letter to author from H. K. Baumeister, July 18, 1992.

36. Diaries, November 20 and January 30, 1915; November 11, 1914; November 30, 1916.

37. Diaries, August 11, 19, and 23, and September 1 and 15, 1917; November 3, 1918; July 9, 1921.

38. Diary, September 24, 1914.

39. Diary, October 23, 1915.

40. Diary, January 1, 1916.

41. Quotations from his remarks in Toledo are drawn from *Toledo* (Ohio) *News*, January 27, 1917, the *Toledo Blade*, January 27, 1917, and the *Toledo Teacher*, February 1917.

42. Diary, January 1, 1916.

43. Diary, August 9, 1916.

44. Diary, August 25, 1916.

45. Diary, November 7, 1916.

46. Diary, November 9, 1916.

47. Diary, January 1, 1917.

48. Diaries, April 6 and December 30, 1917.

49. Diary, October 4, 1917.

50. Diary, October 8, 1917.

51. This lecture is recorded in the *Greensboro* (North Carolina) *Daily News*, July 2, 1917.

52. Diary, January 1, 1918.

53. Diary, November 7, 1918.

54. Diary, September 22, 1915.

55. Diaries, November 20, 1915; March 1 and April 19, 1916.

56 Diary, November 28, 1917. A colleague of Kilpatrick's, Thomas Briggs, thought that Bagley might bring about "an unpleasant division" at the institution. Kilpatrick responded: "I tell Briggs frankly that I don't like Bagley or his position or the Dean's intention in bringing him (i.e. to counterbalance the Dewey tendency in the College)." But he also indicated that he would not confront Bagley and wished to know Bagley better. Diary, April 24, 1918.

57. Diary, May 1, 1917.

58. Diaries, March 19, August 5 and September 19, 1917.

59. Diaries, March 22 and 25, 1918.

60. Diary, November 20, 1918.

Chapter 7

1. Diary, January 18, 1916. A similar quotation is found on the cover of *The Bulletin of the Milwaukee Teachers' Association*, February 1922: "We of America have for years increasingly desired that education be considered as life itself and not as a mere preparation for later living."

2. William Heard Kilpatrick, "The Project Method: The Use of the Purposeful Act in the Educative Process," *Teachers College Record*, September 1918. 19:323. (Hereafter cited as "The Project Method.")

3. William Heard Kilpatrick, "Educational Values Underlying the Project," *Michigan State Teachers Association Quarterly Review,* June 1920.
4. Lawrence Cremin, *The Transformation of the School: Progressivism in American Education, 1876-1957.* New York: Alfred A. Knopf, 1961, pp. 215-24.
5. Daniel Tanner and Laurel Tanner, *History of the School Curriculum,* New York: Macmillan Publishing, 1990, p. 157.
6. Kilpatrick, Autobiography.
7. Tenenbaum, p. 135.
8. Tenenbaum, p. 135.
9. Tape recording, "Proceedings of Boyd H. Bode Conference," The Ohio State University Archives, July 1949.
10. Tenenbaum, pp. 135-36
11. Tenenbaum, p. 136.
12. William Heard Kilpatrick, "The American Elementary School," *Teachers College Record,* March 1929.
13. Tenenbaum, pp. 141-42.
14. Diary, August 28, 1923.
15. "The Project Method," pp. 320-21.
16. William Heard Kilpatrick, "Teaching by the Project Method," *Detroit Journal of Education,* October 30, 1919, and Tenenbaum, pp. 144-45.
17. John Dewey, *Democracy and Education.* New York: Free Press, Division of Macmillan, 1966, p. 163.
18. George S. Counts, *Dare the Schools Build a New Social Order?* Carbondale: Southern Illinois University Press, 1932 and 1978, pp. 36-38. Counts had originally published this work in two installments in *The New Republic.*
19. "Democracy Has Not Been Practiced Yet," *Greensboro* (North Carolina) *Daily News,* July 1, 1917.
20. William Heard Kilpatrick, "The Scaffolding of Character Building," *Women's Press of New York,* 43:584-86, August 1924.
21. William Heard Kilpatrick, "How Character Comes," *World Tomorrow,* 5:259-62, September 1922. The context of this paragraph is drawn from Tenenbaum, pp. 138-39.
22. Diary, May 17, 1908.   One individual has disputed the genesis and originality of Kilpatrick's work on the project method.   George Douglas Hofe, in an article in *Teachers College Record* entitled "The Project Method and Its Origins (1966)," asserted that Tenenbaum's biography overstates the claim that Kilpatrick was an innovator.   To be fair, Tenenbaum does discuss the project method as being not only a methodology but a philosophy of education.   Hofe's own article of 1916, "The Development of a Project," is not in the least similar to Kilpatrick's, nor does it follow Kilpatrick's vein of thought.   One of Hofe's more absurd accusations in the 1966 article is that Kilpatrick had taken the idea from a colleague at Teachers College, John Francis Woodhull, and from Hofe himself, when he borrowed several magazines which contained their articles.   Hofe's charge that Kilpatrick first

developed his own version of the project method in 1917 and 1918 is not consistent with the diaries, which document that his thought on the topic was in place by 1915 and was being formed as early as 1908, or even the 1890s with the episode in the Savannah school. It should also be noted that Hofe waited almost fifty years, until one year after Kilpatrick's death, to make his charge. See George Douglas Hofe, "The Project Method and Its Origins," *Teachers College Record*, February 1966, pp. 371-73 and "The Development of a Project," *Teachers College Record*, May 1916, pp. 240-46. As for Kilpatrick, he gave credit for the project method to Adam: "Just before I was to address a kindergarten association on the project method not long ago the chairman asked me whether she could credit me with being its inventor. I told her that Adam had doubtless been the first to use it and I could scarcely take the honor from him." Unattributed newspaper article in Scrapbooks.

23. Diary, January 13, 1916.
24. Diaries, June 30 and July 7, 1914.
25. Diary, December 12, 1914.
26. Diary, June 28, 1919.
27. Diaries, April 12, 1915; July 13, 1914; July 7, June 30, 1914, August 13, August 5, and November 20, 1914; April 6 and August 12, 1915.
28. Diaries, November 2 and 18, 1915.
29. Kilpatrick, Autobiography. See also Gerald L. Gutek, *Philosophical and Ideological Perspectives on Education*. Englewood Cliffs, NJ: Prentice Hall, Inc., 1988, pp. 290-94.
30. Diary, July 27, 1916.
31. Diary, January 15, 1917.
32. Diary, April 5, 1917.
33. Diary, April 13, 1918.
34. Diaries, April 9, December 2, and December 8, 1917.
35. Compilation of lectures given by William Heard Kilpatrick, but not written by him. *General Science Quarterly*, January 1917, 1:67-72. (As noted, this compilation is not by Kilpatrick but by those who attended the lectures.)
36. Diary, May 8, 1918.
37. Diary, July 17, 1918.
38. "The Project Method," p. 323.
39. Interview by author with Kenneth Benne, October 1990. Benne also suggested that Kilpatrick would probably have felt more comfortable with a Gestalt approach to psychology. Tenenbaum states that Kilpatrick later left the "atomistic" and "mechanical" elements of Thorndike's psychology for a more inclusive approach to the development of the whole person. See Tenenbaum, pp. 152-54.
40. "The Project Method," p. 10. An additional concept that Kilpatrick addressed in this article was the "interest span," or what might be termed today "attention span." He also noted that the length of time spent on a project was crucial; this is similar to the current concept of "time on task.." p. 15.

41. "The Project Method," p. 327.

42 William Heard Kilpatrick, *Twenty-Sixth Yearbook of the National Society for the Study of Education*, 1926. See also Kilpatrick, address to the Michigan State Teachers' Association, October 29, 1914 Kilpatrick, "Educational Values Underlying the Project," *Michigan State Teachers Association Quarterly Review*, June 1920 and Tenenbaum, p. 155.

43. "The Project Method," p. 328. Kilpatrick told Tenenbaum that he was aware of some colleges in which a traditional ceremony was the burning of calculus books. He objected: "That's exactly the thing I didn't want and that is exactly what the old type of teaching naturally led to." See Tenenbaum, pp. 154-55.

44. "The Project Method," p. 329.

45. "The Project Method," pp. 329.

46. "The Project Method," pp. 330-31.

47. "The Project Method," p. 332.

48. "The Project Method," p. 334.

49. "The Project Method," pp. 334-35.

50. Tenenbaum, pp. 151, 159-62.

51. Interview by author with Theodore Baumeister, III, July 1988.

52. Tenenbaum, p. 151.

53. Ella Frances Lynch, "Taking the Line of Least Resistance Doesn't Spell Success in Teaching," *Philadelphia Public Ledger*, January 2, 1920, and editorial, "Mush, Slush, and Schools," *Philadelphia Public Ledger*, January 2, 1920. Both found in Scrapbooks.

54. Diaries, February 24 and 26, 1921.

55. "Dangers and Difficulties of the Project Method and How to Overcome Them — A Symposium," *Teachers College Record*, September 1921, 23(4): 283-321.

56. Ellsworth Collings, *An Experiment with a Project Curriculum*. New York: Macmillan Company, 1923.

57. Collings, pp. xxiii-xxiv.

58. Michael Knoll, "Faking a Dissertation: Ellsworth Collings, William H. Kilpatrick, and the 'Project Curriculum,'" *Journal of Curriculum Studies*, 1996, 28(2):193-222.

59. Boyd H. Bode, *Modern Educational Theories*. New York: Macmillan, 1927, p. 191.

60. Tanner and Tanner, p. 160.

61. Tanner and Tanner, pp. 160-62.

62. Herbert Kliebard, *The Struggle for the American Curriculum, 1893-1958*. Boston: Routledge and Kegan Paul, 1986, pp. 159, 161-65.

63. Joel Spring, *The American School, 1642-1985*. New York: Longman, 1986, p. 176.

64. Michael Knoll, "The Project Method — Its Origin and International Dissemination," in *Progressive Education Across the Continents*, edited by V. Lenhart and H. Rohrs. New York: Peter Lang Press, 1995, pp. 307-18.

65. Harold G. Shane, "Significant Writings That Have Influenced the Curriculum: 1906-1981," *Phi Delta Kappa*, January 1981, pp. 311-14. Shane's survey found

Kilpatrick's "The Project Method" tied for eighth place. John Dewey's *Democracy and Education* and Ralph Tyler's *Basic Principles of Curriculum and Instruction* tied for first place. In a companion article, Franklin Parker, "Ideas That Shaped American Schools," *Phi Delta Kappa*, January 1981, pp. 314-19, Parker notes Kilpatrick's influence in relation to Dewey and calls the "The Project Method" a "much publicized Progressive Education teaching device," p. 316.

66. "Project Method as Old as Adam," *New York Evening Post*, December 31, 1921.
67. Diary, November 20, 1932.

Chapter 8

1. Diary, April 11, 1912.
2. Diary, November 11, 1918.
3. Diary, July 4, 1918.
4. Diaries, December 31, 1918; January 1, 1919.
5. Diaries, October 9 and November 13 and 20, 1919; January 1, 1920.
6. Diary, March 9, 1919.
7. Diary, January 1, 1920.
8. Diary, February 8, 1920.
9. Diary, March 11, 1920.
10. Diary, September 24, 1919; Indexes 1920 to 1923.
11. Diary, March 18, 1922. As for his own views on marriage, in speaking with two Chinese men on the topic, he found that they had become interested in Bertrand Russell's theory of free love. "I defend monogamous marriage," Kilpatrick wrote, "with liberal divorce." Diary, December 27, 1921.
12. Diary, October 21, 1922.
13. Diaries, November 20, 1919; January 1, 1920.
14. Diaries, March 4 and 13, 1920.
15. Diaries, March 12, 17, and 25-26 and May 3, 1920.
16. Diaries, April 26 and May 11 and 20, 1920.
17. Diaries, April 22-23, 1920.
18. Diary, June 10, 1920.
19. Diaries, June 18 and 27, July 7 and 26, 1920.
20. The five lectures given at Dundee Training College under the general heading "The Foundations of Method" were "The Necessary Psychology," "The Purposeful Act," "Coercion and Learning," "The Logical and the Psychological," "The Use of the Purposeful Act." Handbill advertising the lectures, Kilpatrick Scrapbooks.
21. Diaries, June 30, and July 24 and 30, 1920.
22. Diaries, September 9-13, 1920.
23. Diaries, October 8 and 30, 1920.
24. *New Rochelle* (New York) *Daily Star*, June 9, 1923.
25. *Boston Journal of Education*, March 16, 1922, p. 285.

26. Diaries, November 15, 1920; January 7, 1925.

27. Diaries, November 26, 1921; October 13, 1920.

28. Diaries, October 30 and November 2, 1920.

29. Diaries, January 1, 1921; November 7, 1924; January 1, 1925; November 15, 1924.

30. Diaries, October 16, 1920; and September 12, 1923; also, Interview by author with Kenneth Benne, October 31, 1990.

31. Diaries, September 9, 1922; August 4, 1923; February 3, 1922.

32. Diaries, January 8-9 and February 20, 1916; August 13, 1920.

33. Diaries, February 24, June 5-25 and June 28 and 30, 1925.

34. Diary, October 24, 1922.

35. Diary, August 31, 1923. Interview by author with R. Freeman Butts, June 1990 and interview by author with Kenneth Benne, October 31, 1990.

36. Diaries, January 1, 1919; July 31, 1916; November 20, 1917.

37. Diaries, October 21, 1911; July 29 and August 18, 1918. Although the concept of hierarchical levels of questions and questioning was several decades in the future, he devised what he termed "problem questions" and then used "corollary" or follow-up questions to delve deeper into the topic. See Diary, June 20, 1928.

38. Transcripts of Tenenbaum-Kilpatrick interviews on Columbia University tape recording, Stetson Library Archives, Mercer University, Macon, GA, p.152.

39. Diaries, August 4, 1916; December 18, 1913.

40. Diary, July 11, 1914.

41. Diaries, May 16 and April 12, 1916; July 7, 1916.

42. Diaries, June 11 and July 11, 1928.

43. There have been apocryphal stories of Dewey himself slipping into Kilpatrick's lectures, only to shake his head sadly and mutter that what he heard was not consistent with his own principles. But there is no proof that the philosopher ever surreptitiously attended one of Kilpatrick's lectures, nor that he directly criticized what Kilpatrick was teaching.

44. Diaries, July 8, 1919; September 18, 1920.

45. "Education 241-242 — Philosophy of Education. Lectures, readings, and discussions. 2 points each Session. Professor KILPATRICK. Section I: M. and W. at 4.10. Section II: M. and F. at 9. Open only to graduate students. In the Winter Session education will be studied as a social agency in relation especially to other factors at work in a democratic society. During the Spring Session the effort will be made to construct a satisfactory working theory of democratic education, considering principally such topics as the nature of education, the principles of the curriculum, and the bases of method." From "Teachers College Announcement," 1922-1923.

46. Diary, October 9, 1925. Interview by author with Betty Hovey, July 1987. In his diary, Kilpatrick mentioned that he usually only read the A's, D's, and F's. Diary, August 14, 1928.

47. William Heard Kilpatrick, *Education for a Changing Civilization*. New York: Macmillan and Company, 1926, p. 128.

48. Diaries, November 19, 1915; November 12 and December 19, 1919.
49. T. Bost, "Kilpatrick Arrives," *Greensboro* (North Carolina) *Daily News*, March 18, 1938.
50. Diaries, February 16, 1919; December 18, 1921.
51. Diaries, March 21, 1919; November 21, 1920; January 30, March 10 and November 6, 1921.
52. Diaries, June 15, 1920; November 20, 1921; June 9 and November 14, 1922.
53. Diaries, July 15 and November 14 and December 23, 1923; February 3, 1924.
54. Diary, November 23, 1922.
55. Diary, March 28, 1925.

Chapter 9

1. Randolph S. Bourne, "In a Schoolroom," *The New Republic*, November 7, 1914, 1(1): 23-24.
2. Robert S. Lynd and Helen Merrell Lynd, *Middletown: A Study in American Culture*. (New York: Harcourt, Brace and Company, 1929, p. 188.
3. William Heard Kilpatrick, *Source Book in the Philosophy of Education*, New York: Macmillan Company, 1923. Index of sources, pp. 341-49. (Hereafter cited as *Source Book.*)
4. *Source Book*, p. 334.
5. Interviews with author: Everett Jarboe, October 20, 1990, and Kenneth Benne, October 1990.
6. William Heard Kilpatrick, *Foundations of Method: Informal Talks on Teaching*. New York: The Macmillan Company, 1925, pp. vii-viii. (Hereafter cited as *Foundations of Method.*)
7. *Foundations of Method*, pp. 5-6, 9, 13, 17.
8. As with "The Project Method," Kilpatrick continued to wed Thorndikian psychology to Deweyan philosophy. Midway through *Foundations of Method* he states, "In general we seem to have made progress in connecting psychology with education and ethics by joining more closely the doctrine of interest and the psychology of learning with the conceptions of self and will. If we have succeeded in doing this, surely the gains have been worth the trouble." p. 181.
9. *Foundations of Method*, pp. 43-53.
10. *Foundations of Method*, pp. 92, 94, 98.
11. *Foundations of Method*, pp. 100-103, 135. An excellent example of Kilpatrick's thinking on this topic can be found in "What Shall We Seek from a History Project?" *Ethical Culture School: School and Home*, March 1922, pp. 1-3, where he speaks of the several concomitant "learnings" that can take place in a history lesson, including the attitudinal, critical thinking, and moral areas. See also "The Effect of the War upon the Teaching of History and Civics," *Detroit Journal of Education*, February 1922, 2:48-50.

12. *Foundations of Method*, pp. 107-108.

13. *Foundations of Method*, p. 121.

14. *Foundations of Method*, pp. 126-27.

15. *Foundations of Method*, pp. 136, 140, 146, 148, 211.

16. *Foundations of Method*, pp. 183-84.

17. *Foundations of Method*, p. 189. In an undated article in the Kilpatrick Scrapbooks, "The Project Method," Kilpatrick used the example of a boy learning twelve batting averages and learning twelve dates in history: Which one was learned more readily?

18. *Foundations of Method*, p. 212.

19. John Dewey, *Democracy and Education*. New York: Free Press paperback ed., 1966, p. 80. (Originally published in 1916.) On the previous page (p. 79) Dewey summarizes and reminds the reader that experiences "do not consist of externally presented material, but of interaction of native activities with the environment which progressively modifies both activities and the environment."

20. *Foundations of Method*, pp. 196, 222-23. When Kilpatrick stressed experiences he evaluated them according to three criteria: gripping, novel, and varied.

21. *Foundations of Method*, pp. 236-37, 239.

22. *Foundations of Method*, pp. 252-53.

23. *Foundations of Method*, pp. 256-59.

24. *Foundations of Method*, pp. 260-61. Kilpatrick returns to this theme in *Education for a Changing Civilization*. There he speaks of prehistoric tribal activities of hunting and fishing, in which the young first observed and then took part actively in the learning process.

25. *Foundations of Method*, pp. 263, 266-67, 270.

26. *Foundations of Method*, pp. 276-78, 290, 358.

27. *Foundations of Method*, p. 360.

28. *Foundations of Method*, p. 365.

29. *Foundations of Method*, pp. 366, 368-69. In addition to Dewey and Thorndike, the bibliography of *Foundations of Method* includes W. W. Charters's *Curriculum Construction*. New York: The Macmillan Company, 1923; E. P. Cubberley's *Changing Conceptions of Education*, Boston: Houghton Mifflin, 1909; William James's *Principles of Psychology*, New York: Henry Holt, 1909; and J. L. Meriam's *Child Life and the Curriculum*, Yonkers on the Hudson: World Book Company, 1920.

30. *Foundations of Method*, p. 367.

31. William Heard Kilpatrick, *Education for a Changing Civilization*. New York: Macmillan and Company, 1926. (Hereafter cited as *Changing Civilization*.) Frequently reprinted, this volume may have had its genesis in an address first given on October 31, 1919, to the Michigan State Teachers Association, "The Demands of the Times Upon the Schools of America." *Michigan State Teachers Association Quarterly Review*, January 1920, pp. 5-8.

32. For Kilpatrick this included motion pictures, radio, and print communication. See *Changing Civilization*, pp. 10-12, 15.

33. *Changing Civilization*, pp. 16, 18-21.

34. *Changing Civilization*, pp. 21-26.

35. *Changing Civilization*, pp. 28, 75.

36. *Changing Civilization*, pp. 30-37, 39-40.

37. *Changing Civilization*, pp. 40-41.

38. *Changing Civilization*, pp. 42-44, 47-50.

39. *Changing Civilization*, pp. 57-60. Interviews by author with Hal Lewis, December 1991, and Norman Cousins, June 1990.

40. *Changing Civilization*, pp. 61-62.

41. *Changing Civilization*, pp. 65-67, 74. For more on the Scopes trial, see "Professor Kilpatrick Condemns Tennessee Law" in *Phi Delta Kappan,* Summer School Publication, 1925. For discussion of college entrance requirements see William Heard Kilpatrick, "College Domination Over Secondary Schools Attacked," *Christian Science Monitor*, December 17, 1924, p. 5. The article went on to say that Kilpatrick thought the best teaching took place in the grammar schools, the next best in the high schools, third best in universities, and the poorest in colleges. He also suggested that a year of teaching first grade would improve the skills of university professors.

42. William Heard Kilpatrick, *The Journal of Educational Method - Part II*, March, 1923, 2:235-36.

43. Diary, November 22, 1925.

44. Diary, February 28, 1924.

45. Diary, April 16, 1922.

46. *Changing Civilization*, pp. 110-12.

47. William Heard Kilpatrick, "The Essentials of the Activity Movement," *Progressive Education*, October 1924. See also Tenenbaum, p. 163. Diary, September 21, 1918. William Heard Kilpatrick, "What Should Teachers Teach?" *Maryland Oriole*, Towson, Maryland, February 1922.

48. *Changing Civilization*, pp. 122, 125.

49. *Changing Civilization*, p. 123.

50. William Heard Kilpatrick, "Subject Matter and the Educative Process," *The Journal of Educational Method*, November 1922, 2:94-102.

51. *Changing Civilization*, pp. 118, 123, 125-26. He had stated this previously in "How Shall We Select the Subject Matter of the Elementary School Curriculum?" *Journal of Educational Method*, 4(11):3-10. This article may be the best overview of his ideas on subject matter, which include the issues of method, testing, and growth. Diary, August 24, 1923.

52. *Changing Civilization*, p. 127.

53. *Changing Civilization*, p. 127.

54. *Changing Civilization*, pp. 85, 90-91, 129-30. For the critics, see Chapter 19.

55. *Changing Civilization*, pp. 134-35. See also Postman and Weingartner's *Teaching as a Subversive Activity*, written in the late 1960s, which provides a similar list of

terms and phrases that the authors suggest be prohibited from educational discourse: "teach, syllabus, covering ground, I.Q., makeup test, disadvantaged, gifted, accelerated, enhancement, course, grade, score, human nature, dumb, college material, and administrative necessity." Neil Postman and Charles Weingartner, *Teaching as a Subversive Activity.* New York: Delacorte Press, 1969, p. 140.

56. *Changing Civilization*, pp. 130; 134-36.
57. Reviews in *The Christian Leader*, July 23, 1927, 30: 955; and *Congregationalist*, June 30, 1927.
58. *School*, April 7, 1927, p. 544.
59. *Worker's Education*, July 1927, pp. 62-63.
60. *Progressive Education*, August 1927, 4:139-41.
61. *Saturday Review of Literature*, October 15, 1927.
62. Diary, February 5, 1927.
63. "Children Never Better" in *Omaha Evening World-Herald*, January 25, 1926. While Kilpatrick did defend the "deportment of students," he also noted forms of escapism that had pervaded the lives of students in the post–World War I era: "On the one hand there are now vastly more stimulations to excitement than formerly, with varied educative effect, some good, some bad." See *Changing Civilization*, p. 64.
64. Diary, October 27, 1927.
65. L. Mencken, "Travail," *Baltimore Evening Sun*, October 8, 1928.

Chapter 10

1. E. M. Forster, *A Passage to India.* New York: Harcourt, Brace and World, Inc., 1924, p. 61.
2. Diaries, January 1, May 10, and August 16, 1926.
3. Diaries, September 1, 7, and 13, 1926.
4. Diaries, September 14-15, and 20, 1926.
5. Diaries, October 8-9, 1926; "Vienna Institute Hears American Discuss Education," *New York Herald* (Paris Edition), October 14, 1926.
6. Diaries, October 16-17, 24, and 29, 1926; and Tenenbaum, p. 253. See also the transcripts of the Columbia University Tapes of Kilpatrick-Tenenbaum conversations in Stetson Library Archives, Mercer University, Macon, GA, p. 137.
7. Diaries, October 30 and November 8-11, 1926.
8. Diary, November 12, 1926.
9. Telegram is in Kilpatrick Papers, Stetson Library Archives, Mercer University.
10. Gandhi later called the Sabarmati ashram his best and only creation, despite its failures and problems. Judith M. Brown, *Gandhi: Prisoner of Hope.* New Haven: Yale University Press 1989, pp. 190, 199.
11. Brown, p. 190.
12. Diary, November 17, 1926.
13. Diary, November 17, 1926. On another occasion when he was asked what he

thought of Western civilization, Gandhi responded that it would be a good idea. George Will, "After the Dust Settles," *Newsweek*, February 25, 1991, p. 70.

14. Brown, pp. 37, 41. Gandhi's eldest son, Harilal, did break away and attended the local high school in Ahmadabad in 1911. The decision by the son seemed as much personal as educational.

15. Tenenbaum, p. 254.

16. Diary, November 17, 1926. Gandhi once said, "I have always felt that the true textbook for the pupil is the teacher." Myra Pollack Sadker and David Miller Sadker, *Teachers, Schools, and Society*, New York: McGraw-Hill, 1991, p.5.

17. Tenenbaum, p. 257; and interview by author with Mary Murray Steele, June 1990.

18. Brown, p. 90.

19. Brown, pp. 90, 107. Gandhi encouraged agricultural education, health education, and schooling to promote the individual's self-worth; see pp. 106 and 111.

20. Diary, November 17, 1926.

21. "Charleston Woman Who Met Gandhi Terms Him a Saint," *Charleston* (South Carolina) *News and Courier*, May 8, 1933.

22. Diary, November 17, 1926. William Heard Kilpatrick, notes for lecture "My Impressions of India," given in Canton, China, January 27, 1927. Kilpatrick Papers, Stetson Library Archives, Mercer University.

23. Tenenbaum, p. 257. Diary, January 27, 1950. Kilpatrick was very critical of Gandhi's book *Basic Education*. He reiterated this opinion four months later in his diary after attending a conference at Teachers College on "Modern Indian Education."

24. Diary, December 9-10, 1926.

25. Diary, December 30, 1926.

26. Diary, February 7, 1927.

27. Diary, February 10, 1927.

28. Diary, February 11, 1927. Transcripts of Columbia University Tapes, pp. 149-151.

29. Diary, March 31, 1927.

30. Transcripts of Columbia University Tapes, pp. 144-48.

31. Diary, February 13, 1927.

32. Diary, March 26, 1927.

33. Diary, March 21, 1927.

34. Diary, March 21, 1927.

35. Diary, April 27, 1927. Lawrence J. Dennis, *From Prayer to Pragmatism: A Biography of John L. Childs*. Carbondale: Southern Illinois University Press, 1992, pp. 44-46, 53-54.

36. Transcripts of Columbia University Tape, pp. 152, 154-56.

37. Diary, July 7, 1927. Details of voyage June 30 to July 8, 1927.

38. Diary, July 8, 1927.

39. John N. Thomas, *The Institute for Pacific Relations: Asian Scholars and American Politics*. Seattle: University of Washington Press, 1974, pp. 3-4.

40. Diaries, July 14, 16, and 19, 1927. In his diary on January 1, 1928, Kilpatrick wrote that his work as go-between for China and Japan had been especially helpful. As for his work as discussion leader, he wrote that E. C. Carter and others gave him credit for fathering the program structure. Diary, February 25, 1928.

41. Diary, July 28-29, 1927.

42. Diaries, August 5-11, 1927.

43. Diary, August 28, 1927.

44. William Heard Kilpatrick, *Teachers College Record*, "Philosophy of Education," March, 1929, 30:620-21.

45. Diaries, January 15, August 15-20, and September 3, 1929.

46. Diary, September 5, 1929.

47. Tenenbaum, pp. 263-65.

48. Diary, September 10 and 14, 1929.

49. Diaries, September 7, 1929; Tenenbaum, p. 269.

50. Diaries, September 8 and 10-11, 1929; Tenenbaum, pp. 266-67.

51. Tenenbaum, pp. 267-68.

52. Diary, September 28, 1929, provides the itinerary in China.

53. Diaries, October 9 and 15, 1929.

54. Diary, October 27-29, 1929. Obituary of Yosuke Matsuoka, *New York Times*, June 28, 1946, p. 27.

55. Thomas, *Institute for Pacific Relations*, p. 6.

56. Diaries, November 2-4, 1929.

57. Diary, November 6, 1929.

58. Diaries, November 14, and December 12 and 26, 1929.

59. William Heard Kilpatrick, "Vacation Retrospect," *Childhood Education*, May 1928, 4(9): 403-404. See also Kilpatrick, "Promising Educational Experiments in the Far East," *Progressive Education*, July-August-September, 1930, 5:246-50 for analyses of six schools — two each in India, Ceylon, and China.

Chapter 11

1. Diary, November 20, 1931.

2. "What Must One Absorb to Be Intelligent?" by Helen M. Kilpatrick (no relation), *Macon Telegraph*, June 16, 1929. Kilpatrick Scrapbooks.

3. The description of the Kilpatrick apartment is from the remembrances of his grandson, Heard Kilpatrick Baumeister. Letter to author, November 28, 1989.

4. Diary, November 5, 1922.

5. Diaries, January 1 and August 28, 1934; September 9, 1935.

6. Diary, April 11, 1928.

7. Diary, September 15, 1927.

8. Diary, May 17, 1928.

9. Diary, February 11, 1929.

10. William Heard Kilpatrick, "Remarks at the Unveiling of Dr. Dewey's Bust," *School and Society*, December 22, 1928, pp. 778-80. See also *New York Times*, "Columbia Unveils John Dewey Bust," November 10, 1928; and *New York Evening Post*, "Dewey Bust Unveiled," November 10, 1928.

11. Diary, May 16, 1928.

12. Diary, October 14, 1927.

13. Diary, September 13, 1928.

14. Diary, November 1, 1928.

15. Diary, April 5, 1928; see also Diary, February 4, 1929.

16. Diaries, February 14, 1929; January 30, 1930; June 23, 1933; April 18, 1930.

17. Diaries, March 26, 1929; October 10, 1933; January 1, 1931; November 20 and 30, 1927; July 10, 1928. He decided in the fall to cease his practice of seating men and women in alternate rows. "Now I find that the women don't like it. I am not so sure of the men." See Diary, October 1, 1928.

18. Diary, January 31, 1931 and Lawrence J. Dennis, *From Prayer to Pragmatism: A Biography of John L. Childs*. Carbondale: Southern Illinois University Press, 1992, pp. 57-58.

19. Diary, May 8, 1928.

20. Helen M. Kilpatrick, "What Must One Absorb to Be Intelligent?"

21. Diary, July 19, 1928.

22. Diaries, August 5, 1928; January 21, February 16, and May 6, 1929; and November 3, 1931.

23. Diaries, October 4, 1928; January 14, 1929.

24. Diary, August 1, 1932.

25. Harold Rugg, *Foundations for American Education*. New York: World Book Company, 1947, p. 578.

26. Diaries, November 20, 1931; February 4, 1932; January 6, 1931.

27. Rugg, p. 579.

28. Diaries, February 5 and 7, 1929; January 1, October 28, 1930; August 18, 1954.

29. Diaries, February 7, 1929; July 28, 1931.

30. Diary, February 22, 1930.

31. "Mercer Gives 83 Degrees Today," *Macon Evening News*, June 4, 1929; "Kilpatrick Analyzes 'Unrest' in Address to Mercer Grads," *Greensboro* (Georgia) *Herald-Journal*, June 7, 1929.

32. "Dr. Kilpatrick and the Changing Status of Marriage," *Columbus* (Georgia) *Enquirer-Sun*, June 9, 1929.

33. William Heard Kilpatrick, "A Much Puzzled Professor," Kilpatrick letter to the editor, *Greensboro* (Georgia) *Herald-Journal*, July 12, 1929.

34. Diaries, January 7, and November 1, 1930; July 26 and November 22, 1932.

35. Kilpatrick Scrapbooks, poster-advertisement, undated, c. 1927.

36. Diary, July 25, 1993.

37. Diary, April 8, 1930.

38. Diaries, April 18 and May 15, 1930.
39. Diaries, January 1 and 6, 1931.
40. Diary, November 28, 1935.
41. Untitled review of film by Regina Wilkes, September 15, 1993. (Unpublished.)
42. Diary, February 5, 1931.
43. "Talkies in the Classroom," *Christian Science Monitor*, June 13, 1931.
44. Diaries, October 27, 1930; July 13, 1933.
45. Diary, November 20, 1931.
46. After taking one of his famous strolls with Counts, he commented: "I like him and like his mind, but I recognize that he lacks the close reasoning which indicates the philosophic training." Diary, January 14, 1932.
47. Diaries, August 31, 1931; August 14, 1934.
48. "War Will Cease If Traditions Die, Speaker Declares," *Flushing* (New York) *North Shore Daily Journal*, March 10, 1931. See also *Brooklyn Standard Union*, March 10, 1931, for comments on the Boy Scouts. It should be noted that Kilpatrick was usually supportive of scouting and camping because of its emphases on activity and real life experiences.
49. "Educator Hits N.Y. Schools," *Washington Times*, March 31, 1931; "City's School System Futile, Says Educator," *New York American*, March 29, 1931.
50. "Says Schools Fail to Stress Reality," *New York Times*, July 9, 1931; "Childrens' Prizes Classed As Bribes," *Brooklyn Times*, July 9, 1931.
51. "Educator Urges Economic Reform," *New York Evening Post*, July 10, 1931.
52. "Attacks D.A.R., Legion for Glorifying War," *Brooklyn Eagle*, December 3, 1931; "Patriotic Groups War Makers, Says Teacher," *New York Journal*, December 3, 1931. See also Diary, December 2, 1931. One year earlier he had supported a student campaign against military training at the College of the City of New York, calling such drills "inferior to other forms of physical exercise" and as "education in democratic citizenship . . . worse than worthless." He found such a program paradoxical in a country that had committed itself to the Kellogg Pact. "Deny Military Drill Has Value in Schools," *New York Times*, December 12, 1930.
53. "'Warlike,' Says Kilpatrick," *New York Evening Post*, December 3, 1931. See also "D.A.R. Not War-Like, Mrs. Hobart Declares," *Boston Evening Transcript*, December 4, 1931. "Two Educators Back Kilpatrick Thrust at Legion, D.A.R.," *New York Evening Post*, December 4, 1931.
54. "Fostering the War Spirit," Editorial in *Boston Journal of Education*, January 4, 1932.
55. Letter from Forrest F. Friedly, December 6, 1931. Kilpatrick Scrapbooks.
56. Article from *National Republic* (Washington, D.C.) March 1932. Kilpatrick Scrapbooks.
57. Letters between Nicholas Murray Butler and Evaline Watson Northrup, December 13 and 16, 1932. Kilpatrick Scrapbooks.
58. Diaries, May 30 and August 2, 1935.

59. Diary, February 14, 1933.
60. Diaries, July 4, 1933; March 11 and 14, 1934.
61. Diary, June 26, 1937. Tenenbaum, pp. 284-85. See also William Heard Kilpatrick, "Limitations upon the Academic Freedom of Public School Teachers," *Teachers College Record*, November, 1935, 37:94-99. Diary, July 12, 1936.
62. *New York Herald Tribune*, December 24, 1934.
63. Tenenbaum, pp. 285-87. Original in *Journal of the NEA*, February, 1935, 24:51-52, February 1935.
64. Interview by author with Norman Cousins, June 1990. "Twenty Educators Ask Curb on 'Red Scare,'" *New York Times*, December 24, 1934.
65. A. Bowers, *The Progressive Educator and the Depression: The Radical Years*. New York: Random House, 1969, pp. 99-100. See also Diary, January 1, 1937.
66. Diary, June 17, 1943
67. Tenenbaum, p. 210, Diaries, December 21-22, 1923.
68. Tenenbaum, p. 210; Thomas P. Brockway, *Bennington College: In the Beginning*. Bennington, VT: Bennington College Press, 1981, pp. 8-9.
69. Diary, August 23, 1924; Brockway, pp. 11-12, 15, 18-19, 202.
70. Tenenbaum, pp. 210-211; Brockway, p. 28.
71. Brockway, pp. 31-34.
72. Diaries, June 5, 1928; June 10, 1930; March 18, 1930. Tenenbaum, p. 211; and Brockway, p.45.
73. Brockway, p. 46.
74. Tenenbaum, pp. 211-213; Brockway, p. ix.
75. Both quoted in Tenenbaum, pp. 212-13.
76. Brockway, pp. 52-54, 60, Diary, June 2, 1934.
77. Diary, September 7, 1933, Brockway, pp. 98-100.
78. Brockway, p. 61.
79. Tenenbaum, p. 214. Kilpatrick also told Tenenbaum that he thought Sarah Lawrence College, under the direction of its first president, Marion Edward Coates (who had heard Kilpatrick's address at the Colony Club) attempted to put Kilpatrick's ideas into practice.
80. Diary, January 1, 1935.
81. Diary, January 16, 1935.

Chapter 12

1. William Heard Kilpatrick, *Education and the Social Crisis*. New York: Liveright, Inc., 1932, p. 3. (Hereafter cited as *Social Crisis*.)
2. Bowers, *The Progressive Educator and the Depression: The Radical Years*. New York: Random House, 1969, p. ix.
3. James M. Wallace, *Liberal Journalism and American Education 1914-1941*. New Brunswick, NJ: Rutgers University Press, 1991, p. 109.

4. The material that opens this chapter is drawn from the prologue and first three chapters of William Manchester, *The Glory and the Dream: A Narrative History of America, 1932-1972*. Boston: Little, Brown, and Co., 1973, pp. 1-149. Diary, March 25, 1932.

5. Daniel Tanner, *Crusade for Democracy: Progressive Education at the Crossroads*. Albany, N.Y.: State University of New York Press, 1991, p. 25.

6. Diary, November 20-22, 1930. The cereal magnate W. K. Kellogg was also in attendance at this conference and was so moved by the proceedings that when he returned to Battle Creek he launched a foundation into which he poured the bulk of his fortune.

7. Manchester, pp. 66-67. Diaries, April 13 and 18, 1934.

8. Lloyd Duck, *Teaching with Charisma*. Boston: Allyn and Bacon, Inc., 1981, pp. 112-16.

9. Bowers, p. x.

10. Bowers, p. 24. Bowers has suggested that the child-centered approach had all but disappeared by 1935. It can be argued, though, that the strategy is still with us today.

11. Gerald Gutek, *George A. Counts and American Civilization*. Macon, GA: Mercer University Press, 1984, p. 17. Lawrence J. Dennis, *George S. Counts and Charles A. Beard: Collaborators for Change*. State University of New York Press, Albany, NY, 1989. George S. Counts, *The American Road to Culture*. New York: John Day Co., 1930, p. 8. See also James Wallace, "'Red Teachers Can't Save Us': Radical Educators and Liberal Journalists in the 1930s" in Michael E. James, ed., *Social Reconstruction Through Education: The Philosophy, History, and Curricula of a Radical Ideal*. Norwood, NJ: Ablex Publishing Corporation, 1995, pp. 43-56.

12. David Tyack, Robert Lowe, and Elisabeth Hansot, *Public Schools in Hard Times: The Great Depression and Recent Years*. Cambridge, MA: Harvard University Press, 1984, p. 19. Lawrence Cremin, *The Transformation of the Schools*. New York: Knopf, 1961, p. 260. For a remembrance of the speech see Frederick Redefer, "Resolutions, Reactions, and Reminiscences," *Progressive Education*, 1948-1949, 26:188.

13. Diary, March 18, 1932.

14. Tyack et al., p. 24.

15. Agnes de Lima, "Education for What?" *The New Republic*, August 3, 1932, 71(922):317-18.

16. Tyack e. al., p. 25.

17. Diary, October 14, 1930. Bowers, p. 40.

18. Tenenbaum, pp. 288-89.

19. William Heard Kilpatrick, "Freedom in Schools," *New York Times*, July 14, 1935.

20. Much of the argument in this paragraph derives from Tenenbaum, pp. 292-93.

21. John Dewey, *Education and the Social Order*. (New York, 1934), p. 10. Bowers, *The Progressive Educator*, pp. 38-39. Tanner, *Crusade for Democracy*, p. 25.

22. Diary, November 20, 1936.

23. William Heard Kilpatrick, "First Things First," *School and Society*, December 26, 1931, 34(887):855.

24. Diary, February 23 and 29, 1932.

25. Kilpatrick, *Social Crisis*, pp. 6-12, 81-82.

26. Kilpatrick, *Social Crisis*, pp. 16, 21-24, 26-27.

27. Kilpatrick, *Social Crisis*, pp. 28-29, 46, 48-49.

28. Kilpatrick, *Social Crisis*, p. 56.

29. Kilpatrick, *Social Crisis*, p. 64.

30. Kilpatrick, *Social Crisis*, p. 65.

31. Bowers, pp. 21-22 and Kilpatrick, *The Social Crisis*, pp. 70-72.

32. Kilpatrick, *The Social Crisis*, pp. 83-85.

33. Gregory Feige, "The Scholastic Dilemma," *Commonweal*, January 25, 1933, pp. 360-62. Bruno Lasker, "Educational Planning," *The Survey*, March 1933, p. 128. Robert Morss Lovett, *The New Republic*, November 23, 1932, 73:51-52. Diary, January 1, 1933.

34. Robert B. Westbrook, *John Dewey and American Democracy*. Ithaca, NY: Cornell University Press, 1991, p. 506. Bowers, pp. 20-21.

35. Diaries, February 23, April 15-16, 23, May 9, and July 11, 1932.

36. Diaries, July 2-4 and November 13, 1932.

37. Cremin, pp. 229-31.

38. Diaries, November 11-12, 1932.

39. Lawrence Dennis, *From Prayer to Pragmatism: A Biography of John L. Childs*. Carbondale: University of Southern Illinois Press, 1992, See pages 64-72 for an excellent description of the genesis of *The Educational Frontier*. William Heard Kilpatrick, ed., *The Educational Frontier*, New York: The Century Company, 1933, p. 290. (Hereafter cited as *The Educational Frontier*.) Review of *The Educational Frontier* by Sidney Hook, *The New Republic*, May 24, 1933, pp. 49-50.

40. Reviews of *The Educational Frontier* by John C. Almack, *Elementary School Journal*, December 1933, pp. 307-10 and Arpad Steiner, *Commonweal*, November 3, 1933, pp. 23-4.

41. Kilpatrick, *The Educational Frontier*, pp. 140-44, 157-58. In *Education and the Social Crisis*, Kilpatrick stated that women were more open-minded than men because "business tends to close the minds of men," while organizations like the League of Women Voters and the American Association of University Women were more inclined to present opportunities for discussion and debate (pp. 53-4). Diary, August 25, 1932.

42. Kilpatrick, *The Educational Frontier*, pp. 263-65.

43. Kilpatrick, *The Educational Frontier*, pp. 267-69.

44. Kilpatrick, *The Educational Frontier*, p. 261.

45 Kilpatrick, *The Educational Frontier*, p. 274.

46. Kilpatrick, *The Educational Frontier*, pp. 280-82. He also called it a crime that women teachers were forbidden to marry by many school districts. "American men

would never have tolerated it for themselves." pp. 281, 284-86.

47. Diary, November 8, 1932.

48. George Dykhuizen, *The Life and Mind of John Dewey*. Carbondale: Southern Illinois University Press, 1973, pp. 228; 253-54. Diaries, November 8, 1932; March 4 and May 22, 1933; November 7, 1936.

49. William Heard Kilpatrick, "Education to Help the New Deal," Radio Talk on August 22, 1933, over WEVD. Transcript in *High School Quarterly*, October, 1933. See also Diary, August 22, 1933.

50. "Dr. Kilpatrick Speaks." *The Student's Weekly*, April 7, 1935. Kilpatrick Scrapbooks.

51. Diary, January 4, 1933. "An Address to President-Elect Roosevelt by a Group of Educators," *School and Society*, February 25, 1933; 37:259-62. Kilpatrick did the major writing of this document which is also in the Kilpatrick Scrapbooks.

52. Diary, January 1, 1934. Tyack et al., p. 134. Tanner, p. 34.

53. Wallace, p. 152. Arthur M. Schlesinger Jr. and Morton White, eds., "Sources of the New Deal," in *Paths of American Thought*. Boston: Houghton Mifflin, 1963, pp. 377-81. The other three Schlesinger named were Herbert Croly, Charles Beard, and Thorstein Veblen. See *Social Frontier*, October 1936, 8:8.

54. Diary, May 23, 1935. Announcement, Kilpatrick Scrapbooks.

55. Cremin, pp. 231-33. Herbert Kliebard, *The Struggle for the American Curriculum, 1893-1958*. Boston: Routledge and Kegan Paul, 1986, p. 196. Bowers, pp. 97, 105, 141, 144, 148-51.

56. Bowers, pp. 98-101. Diaries, January 9, 1933; January 1, 1936.

57. Diaries, February 9 and 17, November 1 and 23, 1934.

58. Diaries, July 17, and August 5 and 15, 1933.

59. Kilpatrick's speech was later reprinted: "Public Education as a Force for Social Improvement" *School and Society*, Vol. 41, No. 106, Saturday, April 20, 1935, 41(106):521-27.

60. Bowers, p. 152. Diary, January 1, 1935. William Heard Kilpatrick, "High Marxism Defined and Rejected," *The Social Frontier*, June 1936, 2(9):274.

61. Tanner, pp. 5-8. Henry Harap, "The Beginnings of the John Dewey Society," *Educational Theory*, Spring, 1970, 20:157-63.

62. Tanner, pp. 18-20. In a letter to Tanner in February 1986, Sidney Hook stated that he was "intellectually and educationally quite close to George Counts, Jack Childs, William Kilpatrick, and Jesse Newlon" and that he was closer to *The Social Frontier* than the John Dewey Society. p. 38. This is a remarkable statement in that Hook paid little attention to these men in his autobiography. See Sidney Hook, *Out of Step: An Unquiet Life in the Twentieth Century*. New York: Harper and Row, 1987. Diary, October 3, 1934.

63. Diary, February 24, 1935.

64. Diary, March 27, 1935. Tanner, pp. 18-20, 23.

65. Diary, January 13, 1936.

66. Diary, January 15, 1936.

67. Interview by author with Mrs. Leland Moon, April 1990. Cremin, pp. 230-31. Bowers, p. 165.
68. Merle Curti, *The Social Ideas of American Educators*. Paterson, NJ: Pageant, 1959, pp. 561-62.
69. Curti, pp. 562; 574. Bowers, p. 81. Westbrook, p. 506.
70. Bowers, pp. 124-25.
71. "Columbia Summer Session," *Fortune*, July 1936, p. 98.
72. Irving J. Hendrick, "California's Response to the 'New Education' in the 1930s," *California Historical Quarterly*, Spring 1976, pp. 25-40.
73. Tyack et al., 26-27, 61.
74. James M. Giarelli, "Public Philosophies and Education," *Educational Foundations*, Winter 1990, 4(1):16.
75. William Heard Kilpatrick, "The Social Philosophy of Progressive Education," *Progressive Education*, 1935, p. 292.
76. Kilpatrick, "The Social Philosophy of Progressive Education," p. 293.

Chapter 13

1. Evan S. Connell, *Mr. Bridge*. New York: Alford A. Knopf, Inc., 1969, p. 355; and *Mrs. Bridge*. New York: Viking Press, 1959, p. 44.
2. William Withers, "Is Progressive Education on the Wane?", *School and Society*, September 25, 1937, 46:401-403. For accurate contemporary descriptions of progressive education at this time, see Agnes DeLima, *Our Enemy, the Child*. New York: *New Republic*, 1926, Harold Rugg and Ann Shumaker, *The Child-Centered School*. Yonkers-on-Hudson, NY: World Book Company, 1928, Lawrence A. Cremin, *The Transformation of the School*. New York: Knopf, 1961.
3. Patricia Albjerg Graham, *Progressive Education: From Arcady to Academe, A History of the Progressive Education Association 1919-1955*. New York: Teachers College Press, 1967, pp. 1, 8.
4. Graham, pp. 16, 33.
5. William Heard Kilpatrick, "What Do We Mean by Progressive Education?" *Progressive Education*, December, 1930, 7:383-86.
6. Graham, pp. 58-59.
7. "Progressives' Progress," *Time*, October 31, 1938, pp. 31-35.
8. Diary, July 10, 1933. William Heard Kilpatrick, "Plea for School 'Fads,'" *New York Times*, February 5, 1933.
9. *New York Times* article, September 11, 1941, in Kilpatrick Scrapbooks.
10. "We Have With Us - The Progressives" *Education*, October 1939, 60(2):67. (Editorial.)
11. Eunice Barnard, "Study Row Stirred by Essentialist," *New York Times*, March 1, 1938. See also "Essentialist Group Urges Pupils Be Coddled Less and Taught More," *Newsweek*, March 14, 1938.

12. Federal Council of Churches Information Service, May 25, 1935, 14:4. William Heard Kilpatrick, "Why Progressive Education?" (Address delivered at the regional conference of the Progressive Education Association, Colorado State College for Education, June 28, 1935.) Greeley: Colorado State College for Education, 1935, pp. 1-16.

13. William Heard Kilpatrick, "The Social Philosophy of Progressive Education," *Progressive Education*, Ma, 1935, 12(5):289-93.

14. Diary, January 1, 1937.

15. William Heard Kilpatrick, *Remaking the Curriculum*, New York: Newson and Company, 1936, pp. 14-18, 20, 24, 28, 31-32. (Hereafter cited as *Remaking the Curriculum*.)

16. *Remaking the Curriculum*, pp. 33-43.

17. *Remaking the Curriculum*, pp. 46-56, 58-65.

18. William Van Til, *My Way of Looking at It*. Terre Haute, IN: Lake Lure Press, 1983. pp. 82-84. *Remaking the Curriculum*, pp. 84, 87.

19. *Remaking the Curriculum*, pp. 99-107.

20. Diaries, January 1 and April 26, 1934; February 15, 1935.

21. Diary, January 1, 1936.

22. Diary, January 10, 1936. For a description of the cafeteria worker's issue see Lawrence Dennis, *From Prayer to Pragmatism: A Biography of John L. Childs*. Carbondale, IL: Southern Illinois University Press, 1992, pp. 85-92.

23. Diary, March 16, 1936.

24. Diaries, March 30 and April 2, 1936.

25. Diaries, April 2, 3, 4, 9, and 13, 1936.

26. Diary, January 14, 1936.

27. Diary, September 23, 1936.

28. James Weschler, "Twilight at Teachers College," *The Nation*, December 17, 1938, pp. 661-63.

29. Letters to the editor, *The Nation*, December 24, 1938. p. 703.

30. Diaries, October 5, 1938; December 18, 1939.

31. "Columbia Summer Session," *Fortune*, July 1936, pp. 98, 100. See also "Trouble at TC," *Time*, November 28, 1938, pp. 36-37.

32. Diaries, November 18 and 20, 1936.

33. "Columbia Summer Session," *Fortune*, p. 100.

34. Diaries, November 21 and December 15, 1936.

35. Diary, December 18, 1936.

36. Diary, December 24, 1936.

37. Diaries, January 1, 4, 6, and 8, 1937.

38. Diaries, February 8 and 15, 1937.

39. Diary, February 20, 1937.

40. *New York World Telegram*, February 18 and 19, 1937. *New York Herald Tribune*, February 20, 1937. Diary, February 20, 1937.

41. *New York Times*, February 21,1937. Diary, February 21, 1937.

42. *New Orleans Item-Tribune*, February 22, 1937 and *New York Herald Tribune*, February 22, 1937.

43. *New York Times*, February 22, 1937.

44. *New York Herald Tribune*, February 23, 1937.

45. *New York Herald Tribune*, February 24, 1937.

46. Diary, February 24, 1937 and *New York Times*, February 24, 1937.

47. Diary, February 26, 1937.

48. Diary, April 7, 1937.

49. Diaries, April 8 and 14, 1937.

50. Diaries, May, 5 and 12, 1937.

51. Diary, May 14, 1937.

52. Interview by author with R. Freeman Butts, June 27, 1990.

53. Butts interview. See also R. Freeman Butts, "Reflections on Forty Years in the Foundations Department at Teachers College," in *In the First Person Singular: The Foundations of Education*, San Francisco: Caddo Gap Press, 1993, pp. 17-18.

54. Butts Interview.

55. Butts, "Reflections on Forty Years" pp. 17-20.

56. Diaries, May 26 and June 6, 1937.

57. *Chicago Daily News*, June 3, 1937. Diaries, February 12 and June 24, 25, and 29, 1937.

58. "Columbia Summer Session," *Fortune*, p. 69.

59. "Columbia Summer Session," *Fortune*, pp. 73, 74, 95.

60. "Columbia Summer Session," *Fortune*, pp. 95-96.

61. "Columbia Summer Session," *Fortune*, p. 97. While Kilpatrick's attacks on the D.A.R., the R.O.T.C., the American Legion, and loyalty oaths for teachers are mentioned, it is George Counts who is described as the true radical of the group. Counts is quoted as saying, "Teachers must inform the new generation that a new society is here, that the system of private capitalism for private gain is dead." But *Fortune* also noted that Counts was not a communist and that the communists agreed.

62. Diaries, July 16 and 17, 1937.

63. Diary, August 9, 1937.

64. "Schools Closing Pupils Minds, Says Kilpatrick." *New York Herald Tribune*, August 8, 1937. Diary, August 19, 1937.

65. Interview by author with Betty Hovey, July 1987.

66. Diaries, September 8, 1937; and February 23, 1938.

67. Diaries, September 29 and November 14, 1937; January 8, 1938.

68. Diaries, October 9, 10, and 30, 1937. William Heard Kilpatrick, "Charge to the President," October 10, 1937 in Archives, University of Evansville, IN.

69. Diaries, May 17 and 27, 1938.

70. Diary, April 27, 1938.

71. Diary, June 22, 1938.

72. Diaries, September 14, 19, and 30, 1938.

73. Diaries, October 5 and November 16, 1938.

74. Diary, November 3, 1938.

75. Diary, November 21, 1938.

76. Diary of Margaret Kilpatrick Baumeister, November 14, 1938. Diary, January 1, 1939.

Chapter 14

1. Robert Gittings and Jo Mawtow, *The Second Mrs. Hardy*. Seattle: University of Washington Press, 1979, p. 3.

2. Diary, September 29, 1920. Interview by author with Marion Ostrander's niece, Mary Murray Steele, June 28, 1990. Marion Y. Ostrander was born December 6, 1891.

3. Diaries, September 30, 1920; July 27, and September 28, 1922; November 8, 1922; April 29, and June 1, 1923; July 24, and December 17, 1924; and March 14, 1928.

4. Diaries, August 25, 1926; April 9, 1928; February 10, 1931; May 10, 1939.

5. Marion Y. Ostrander, *Value-Aims to Be Taken into Account in an Introductory Course in Philosophy of Education: An Effort at Schematization*, dissertation for Ed.D., Advanced School of Education, Teachers College, Columbia University, 1938, 100 pp.

6. Diaries, June 12, 1933; August 9, 1932. Interview by author with Kenneth Benne, October 1990.

7. Diaries, September 17 and 20, 1937; February 1, March 5, and December 20, 1938.

8. Diaries, November 19-20, 1938; January 1, 1939.

9. Diaries, November 23-24, 1938.

10. Diaries, November 24-25, 1938.

11. Diary, November 26, 1938.

12. Interview, Benne. Diaries March 7, 1908; December 25, 1919; December 6, 1920. Diary of Margaret Kilpatrick Baumeister (MKB), November 23 and 27, 1938; collection of Mary Baumeister.

13. Diary, August 8, 1939. Diary of MKB, December 2, 1938.

14. Diary, January 6, 1939.

15. Diaries, January 8 and 21, April 14, and June 10, 1939; March 13, 1942; December 3, 1943.

16. Diary, February 15-18, June 14, and July 18, 1939.

17. Diaries, June 18, July 1 and 15, and August 22, 1939.

18. Diary, September 1, 1939.

19. Diary, September 30, 1939.

20. Diary, January 1, 1940.

21. Diaries, October 9 and 16 and November 10, 1939.

22. Diaries, November 23, 1939; March 10, October 13, and November 19, 1941.

23. Diaries, January 27, 1942; December 7, 1943.

24. Diaries, November 20, 1939; February 6 and March 30, 1940.

25. Diaries, February 9, 18, and 22, 1940. Diary of MKB, February 24, 1940.

26. Diary, MKB, February 26, 1940. Diary, February 27, 1940.

27. Diaries, March 5 and 24, 1940. Interview with Mary Murray Steele, June 28, 1990.

28. Diaries, May 1 and 4, 1940.

29. Diary, MKB, April 6, 16, 24, and 25, 1940.

30. Diary, MKB, May 8, 1940. Diary, May 8, 1940.

31. Diaries, May 9-17, 1940.

32. Diaries, May 24 and 28-29, June 7 and July 8, 1940.

33. Diaries, June 12-14 and June 20-22 and July 24, 1940.

34. Diaries, August 13 and October 25, 1940.

35. Diary, July 19, 1943 and interview with Mary Murray Steele, June 1990.

36. Diaries, January 12, 1939; September 15 and November 20, 1940; October 31, 1943; July 29, 1944.

37. Diaries, December 22, 1940; July 12, 1943; August 28, 1945.

38. Diaries, August 9, 1939; September 22 and November 5, 1940; May 11, 1943; September 5, 1944.

39. Diaries, April 17, May 1, June 2, and 10-20, and November 20, 1941; May 6, 1943.

40. Diaries, June 4, 1942; March 20, 1946.

41. Diaries, February 1, 1941, January 7 and 20 and August 7, 1942; April 3, 1943.

42. Diaries, December 23 and 25, 1942.

43. Diary, March 25, 1942.

44. Diaries, March 12 and April 18, 1941.

45. Diaries, May 20 and December 7, 1941.

46. Robert Merrill Bartlett, *They Work for Tomorrow*. New York: International Committee of Young Men's Christian Associations, 1943, pp. v, vi.

47. Bartlett, pp. 116-22.

48. Bartlett, p. 123.

49. Bartlett, pp. 124-25 and Diary, December 8, 1943.

50. Diaries, February 2, 1943; March 5, 1944.

51. Diary, May 16, 1943.

52. Diaries, May 24 and November 11, 1943.

53. Diaries, September 14 and November 4, 1943; February 2 and March 4 and 25, 1944.

54. Diaries, June 23, 25, 26, 30, 1944.

55. Diary, September 6, 1944. William Manchester, *The Glory and the Dream: A Narrative History of America, 1932-1972*. Boston: Little, Brown, and Company, 1973, pp. 392-93.

56. Diary, October 21, 1944. The description of this day's events are drawn from Jim Bishop, *FDR's Last Year: April 1944 April 1945*. New York: William Morrow and Company, Inc., 1974, pp. 168-75.

57. Diary, October 21, 1944.

58. Diary, November 8, 1944.

59. Diaries, March 30 and November 15, 1944.
60. Diary, December 8, 1944.
61. Diaries, March 17 and 19 and April 22, 1945.
62. Diary, April 12, 1945.
63. Diary, April 20 (addendum), 1945.
64. Diary, August 7, 1945.
65. Diaries, August 14, 1945; January 1, 1946.
66. Interview, Benne, October 1990. Diary, December 5, 1945.
67. Interview by author with Hal Lewis, December 1991.
68. Diaries, November 8, 1945; July 5, 1946.
69. Diary, July 29, 1946.
70. Diaries, November 7 and 20, 1946.

CHAPTER 15

1. William Heard Kilpatrick, "The Role of Camping in Education Today," *The Camping Magazine*, February 1942, 14(2):15.
2. William Heard Kilpatrick, "Democracy and Respect for Personality," in *Group Education for Democracy*, New York: Association Press, 1940, p. 18.
3. Diary, September 14, 1949.
4. James M. Wallace, *Liberal Education and American Journalism: 1914-1941*. New Brunswick, NJ: Rutgers University Press, 1991, p. 168.
5. William Heard Kilpatrick, "The Elementary School: Its Status and Problems," *The New Republic*, November 12, 1924, 40:1-3.
6. William Heard Kilpatrick, "The Philosophy of the Classroom," *The New Era* (London) April 1929, 10:85-90. Agnes de Lima, "From Infancy On," *The New Republic*, July 1, 1925, 43: 157-59.
7. William Heard Kilpatrick, "The Relation of Philosophy to Scientific Research," *Journal of Educational Research,* September 1931, 24(2):97-114.
8. William Heard Kilpatrick, "First Thing in Education," *School and Society*, December 26, 1931, 34(887): 847-54.
9. William Heard Kilpatrick, "Freedom in the Schools," *New York Times*, July 14, 1935, Sec. 5, p. 9. "Limitations upon Academic Freedom for Public School Teachers," *Teachers College Record*, November, 1935, 37:94-99.
10. Alonzo F. Myers, Review of *The Teacher and Society: The First Yearbook of the John Society,* in *The Social Frontier*, October 1937, 4(28):28-29.
11. William Heard Kilpatrick, "The Promise of Education," *The New Republic*, November 8, 1939. 101:57-59, 62.
12. William Heard Kilpatrick, "My Child as a Person," *Teachers College Record*, March 1932, 33:488, 491, 493.
13. William Heard Kilpatrick, "New Aims in Education," *Hawaii Educational Review*, February 1930, 18:141-42, 157-58. "How to Build Character," radio talk manuscript

in Kilpatrick Scrapbooks. "Some Parents to Blame for Spoiled Children," *The Citizen*, c. 1924, Kilpatrick Scrapbooks. "New Ideas on Discipline Supplant Old Methods of Punishment," *Children: The Magazine for Parents*, Kilpatrick Scrapbooks, circa 1929.

14. William Heard Kilpatrick, "New Trends in Education," *Parents' Magazine*, October 1932, 8:13, 42-43. Interview by author with Kenneth Benne, October 1990.

15. "Mentality Test Ended as Guide at Horace Mann," *New York Times*, November 24, 1930.

16. William Heard Kilpatrick, "Education as Living for Better Living," *Journal of Educative Method*, January, 1938, 17:149-56. For Kilpatrick's thinking on this topic, see also "Living and Learning: A Fresh View of the Education Process," *Journal of Arkansas Education*, December 1939, pp. 3-4, 24. "The Philosophy of the New Education," *School and Society*, November 29, 1941, 54(29):481-84.

17. William Heard Kilpatrick, "College and University Teaching," *Proceedings of the Seventeenth Annual (Greensboro) North Carolina College Conference*, November 3-4, 1937, pp. 13-18. "Kilpatrick Says Grades Are Unfair Measurements," *Kansas State Collegian*, October 31, 1939.

18. "Keep Anniversary of Community School," *Saint Louis Post Dispatch*, October 26, 1939.

19. "Teachers Hear Answers to Education Problems from Dr. Kilpatrick," *Eugene (Oregon) Daily News*, February 1, 1940. "Teachers Told to Live Broad Life by Expert", *Eugene (Oregon) Register-Guard*, January 31, 1940.

20. "Teach Children How to Think," *Spokane Spokesman Review*, February 5, 1940.

21. "Baby Talk Held Detrimental to Child Thought," *San Francisco Chronicle*, July 6, 1938. "Whose Itty Bitty Is Oo?" Editorial, *San Francisco Chronicle*, July 8, 1938. "Teachers Discuss 30 Questions," *School Management*, June 1939, 8:10. William Heard Kilpatrick, letter to editor, *Progressive Education*, February 1942, 19(2):136.

22. "High School Revision is Suggested by Kilpatrick," *Teachers College News*, April 4, 1936. "Leader of Teachers' Conference," *Saint Louis Post Dispatch*, October 27, 1939.

23. William Heard Kilpatrick, "The Crux of the Secondary-School Problem," *The High School Journal*, December 1940, 23(8):345-47. "A Suggested New Secondary Curriculum," *National Education Association Journal*, April 1936, 25:111-12.

24. "Most City Schools Held Anti-Social," *New York World Telegram*, May 4, 1936.

25. Diary, May 2, 1936. William Heard Kilpatrick, "Better Teaching of Democracy," *Frontiers of Democracy*, December 15, 1941, 8(65):70-71.

26. "Conference Lends Support to Aims of College Here," *Evansville (Indiana) Courier*, October 10, 1937.

27. William Heard Kilpatrick, "The Proper Work of the Liberal Arts College," *Bulletin of the Association of American Colleges*," March 1943, 29:37-44.

28. William Heard Kilpatrick, "Securing Better College Teaching," *The Educational Record*, January 1948, pp. 5-10. In *Philosophy of Education*, New York: Macmillan

Company, 1951, pp. 327-28. (Hereafter cited as *Philosophy of Education*.) Kilpatrick broadened his list to include the humanities, psychology, citizenship, and personal philosophy.

29. William James, *Talks to Teachers on Psychology*, with an Introduction by John Dewey and William Heard Kilpatrick, New York: Henry Holt and Company, 1939, pp. iii-viii.

30. William Heard Kilpatrick, "What Can Education Contribute to Democratic Living?" *The Missouri School Journal*, March 1937, pp. 7-14. "Educators Urged to Aid Democracy," *New York Times*, March 1, 1938. "School Discipline Much Improved," *Chattanooga Evening Times*, January 18, 1941.

31. William Heard Kilpatrick, *Group Education for a Democracy*, New York: Association Press, 1940, pp. v-vii., 1-2, 4-17, 21.

32. Kilpatrick, *Group Education for a Democracy*, pp. 33-34.

33. Review by R. L. West of *Group Education for Democracy* in *Saturday Review of Literature*, August 3, 1940, 22:19. Review by Lawrence Hall of *Group Education for a Democracy* in *Progressive Education*, October 1940, 17:433-34.

34. William Heard Kilpatrick, "School Preparation for Democratic Citizenship," *The American Citizen*, June 1940, 6(10):3-9.

35. Bernice Brown McCullar, "Georgia Folkways," *Atlanta Constitution*, June 25, 1944.

36. Lawrence Cremin, *Transformation of the School: Progressivism in American Education, 1876-1957*. New York: Alfred A. Knopf, 1961, p. 224.

37. William Heard Kilpatrick, "The Role of Camping in Education Today," *The Camping Magazine*, February 1942, 14(2):14-16.

38. William Heard Kilpatrick, "Proposed Support for Non-Public Schools: A Serious Threat," *The Social Frontier*, April 1938, 4(34):210-11. "A Four Year Educational Program: The Underlying Principles," *The Social Frontier*, October 1936, 4(15):3, 11.

39. William Heard Kilpatrick, "Questions About the Stock Market," *The Social Frontier*, December 1937, 4(30):74-75. "Awaiting Business Confidence: A Modern Version of an Ancient Superstition," *The Social Frontier*, March 1938, 4(33):177. William Heard Kilpatrick, "Searching for the Good Society," *The Social Frontier*, January 1938, 4(31):106-107.

40. "On the Education Front," *The Social Frontier*, November 1937, 4(29):63.

41. William Heard Kilpatrick, "Anti-Semitism: Over There and Here at Home," *The Social Frontier*, January 1939, 5(1):103-104.

42. William Heard Kilpatrick, "Wanted by America: A Policy on War and Peace and Foreign Relationships," *The Social Frontier*, May 1938, 4(35):242-43, "Democracy and Social Planning — How to Unite Liberty and Security," *The Social Frontier*, July 1938, 4(37):311-12.

43. William Heard Kilpatrick, "The War: Our Country and the World," *Frontiers of Democracy*, December 15, 1939, pp. 69-70.

44. William Heard Kilpatrick, "The Dies Committee and True Americanism," *Frontiers of Democracy*, January 15, 1940, pp. 102-104.

45. "Replace Dies, Committee for Cultural Freedom Urges," *New Leader*, January 6, 1940. William Heard Kilpatrick, "The Coudert Investigation," *Frontiers of Democracy*, January 15, 1941, pp. 88-89.

46. William Heard Kilpatrick, "What is Holding Us Back?" *Frontiers of Democracy*, May 15, 1940, pp. 231-33. Editorial, "The Election: What Is at Issue?" *Frontiers of Democracy*, October 15, 1940, p. 8. "The Threat to Civilization," *Frontiers of Democracy*, October 15, 1940, p. 7.

47. William Heard Kilpatrick, *Selfhood and Civilization: A Study of the Self-Other Process*. New York: The Macmillan Company, 1941, p. 138. (Hereafter cited as *Selfhood and Civilization*.) Diary, November 27, 1940.

48. William Heard Kilpatrick, *Remaking the Curriculum*, New York: Newson and Company, 1936, p. 117. Diaries, November 3-4, 1938.

49. *Selfhood and Civilization*, pp. 2-3, 8-9.

50. *Selfhood and Civilization*, p. 23.

51. *Selfhood and Civilization*, pp. 26-32, 151-52, 200-203.

52. *Selfhood and Civilization*, pp. 40-41, 62.

53. *Selfhood and Civilization*, pp. 46-50, 60.

54. *Selfhood and Civilization*, pp. 72-74, 80-83.

55. *Selfhood and Civilization*, pp. 85-94, 98, 100, 107.

56. *Selfhood and Civilization*, pp. 101, 112, 114.

57. *Selfhood and Civilization*, pp. 122, 127-37, 155.

58. *Selfhood and Civilization*, pp. 138-40, 148 and John Dewey, *Human Nature and Conduct*. New York: Henry Holt, 1922, p. 37.

59. Kilpatrick, *Selfhood and Civilization*, pp. 153, 156-57, 161, 195.

60. Kilpatrick, *Selfhood and Civilization*, pp. 184-85, 188.

61. Kilpatrick, *Selfhood and Civilization*, p. 227.

62. Regina Wilkes, "A Critical Analysis of *Selfhood and Civilization*," unpublished essay, 1993, pp. 11, 13-15.

63. Marten Ten Hoor gave *Selfhood and Civilization* a negative review in *The American Journal of Psychology*, April 1942, 55:296-97, as did Stuart Henderson Britt in *American Sociological Review*, June 1942, 7:457-58. John Brubacher of Yale University wrote a sympathetic review in *Curriculum Journal*, January 1942, 13:42-43. This critique is drawn from the author's "A Reconsideration of *Selfhood and Civilization: A Study of the Self-Other Process*" *Educational Studies*, Summer 1994, 25(2):115-20.

64. Interview by author with Norman Cousins, June 1990.

65. William Heard Kilpatrick, "Education and Enduring Peace," *The Educational Forum*, May 1944, 8(14):375-81.

66. William Heard Kilpatrick, "Announcement: The Bureau Expands Its Services," *Intercultural Education News*, June 1944, 5(4). "Tolerance Study Will Be Expanded," *New York Times*, March 23, 1944.

67. Diaries, July 5, October 18, and November 1, 1945.

68. William Van Til, "William Heard Kilpatrick: A Memoir," *Teaching Education*, Winter 1988, 2(2):38-39.

69. An example is Ernest O. Melby's review of *Philosophy of Education* "To Know How to Know," *Saturday Review*, October 1951, 18-19.

70. William Heard Kilpatrick, *Philosophy of Education*, New York: Macmillan Company, 1951, pp. 43, 57, 124, and 283.   (Hereafter cited as *Philosophy of Education*.)

71. *Philosophy of Education*, pp. 357-58.

72. *Philosophy of Education*, p. 120.

73. *Philosophy of Education*, pp. 121, 301, 304, and 313.

74. Diary, November 20, 1944.

75. *Philosophy of Education*, pp. 231, 432.

76. Herbert M. Kliebard, *The Struggle for the American Curriculum, 1893-1958*. New York: Routledge and Kegan Paul, 1986, pp. 213-22.

77. Daniel Tanner and Laurel Tanner, *History of the School Curriculum*. New York: Macmillan Publishing Company, 1990, pp. 227-35.

78. Craig, Kridel, "Reconsideration of the Eight Year Study," *Educational Studies*, Summer 1994, 25(2):101-14.

Chapter 16

1. Theodore Brameld, Introduction to "The Battle for Free Schools," *The Nation*, October 27, 1951, 173(17):344.

2. David Hulburd, *This Happened in Pasadena*. New York: The Macmillan Company, 1951, pp. 152-53.

3. Interview by author with Hal Lewis, December 1991.

4. "Conference on Philosophy of Education," *Teachers College Record*, January 1948, 49(4):263-76.   Includes John Dewey, "Boyd H. Bode: An Appreciation"; William Heard Kilpatrick, "Bode's Philosophic Position"; and Boyd H. Bode, "Education for Freedom." "Rebel," *Time*, November 24, 1947, p. 73.

5. Diaries, January 1 and May 8, 1949.   See also Diary, September 25, 1950. Kilpatrick's grandson, Heard Kilpatrick Baumeister, now owns and lives at the Parsonage.

6. Diaries, November 20, 1947; May 22 and June 12, 1948; January 1 and July 7, 1949.

7. Diaries, October 12, 1948; October 17, 1949; January 1, 1950.

8. Diaries, January 8-30 and May 18, 1948; February 6-7 and December 6 and 13, 1947; June 16, 1949.

9. Diaries, April 27, September 10 and December 27, 1947; March 18, 1948; January 1, 1949.

10. Diaries, January 18 and October 24, 1947; June 15, 1949; June 7, 1951; June 7, and July 23, 1952; and November 23, 1954.   Ernest Papanek, "William Heard

Kilpatrick: Teacher of World Teachers," *The Jewish Forum*, December 1952, pp. 207-208.

11. Diary, April 7, 1947.

12. Diaries, May 26, 1947; August 23 and 25, 1948.

13. Diaries, April 21-22, 1948; May 26, 1949.

14. Diaries, June 25 and November 2-3, 1948.

15. Diaries, January 1 and November 8, 1950.

16. Evelyn Luecking and William Van Til, "What Popular Magazines Say About Education: 1946-1948," *University of Illinois Bulletin*, September 1949, p. 51. Carey McWilliams, "The Enemy in Pasadena," *Christian Century*, January 3, 1951, 68:10.

17. McWilliams, pp. 11-13. "Dr. Kilpatrick Plans Conferences," *San Diego Union*, January 12, 1948. "Educator Here for Seminars," *Tribune-Sun* (San Diego), January 13, 1948, p. 10. "Minority Group Problem Probed by N.Y. Visitor," *San Diego Union*, January 13, 1948. "Growing Trend of Inter-Cultural Education Told," *Riverside* (California.) *Enterprise*, January 20, 1948.

18. Diaries, July 12, 1946; January 10, 1947; February 12, 1949.

19. Tape recording of William Heard Kilpatrick at Bode Conference, July 7-9, 1949. The Ohio State University Archives, Columbus. Diary, June 8, 1949.

20. Diary, July 9, 1949. Undated newspaper clipping in Kilpatrick file of Archives, Stetson Library, Mercer University, Macon, GA.

21. *We Live What We Learn*, Proceedings of the William Heard Kilpatrick Workshop, Pasadena, CA, July 1949. (Published by Pasadena City Schools. Pasadena United School District Archives.)

22. David Hulburd, *This Happened in Pasadena*. New York: Macmillan Company, 1951, p. 53. Diaries, July 13-17 and 19-20, 1949.

23. Diary, April 14, 1950.

24. Letter from Michael James to author, April 27, 1994. Arthur Zilversmit, *Changing Schools: Progressive Education Theory and Practice, 1930-1960*. Chicago: University of Chicago Press, pp. 103-105.

25. John Q. Copeland, *Los Angeles Times*, "Pasadena Becomes Schools' Test Tube," May 25, 1950; "School Zones Stir Debate in Pasadena," May 26, 1950; "Pasadena Studies Camp Experiment," May 27, 1950; "Short Visit by Noted Educator Had Profound Effect on Teaching System in City Schools," May 28, 1950; "School Goal Told by Progressives," May 29, 1950; and "Teacher Drilling Key to Progressive Plan," May 30, 1950.

26. Diary, September 19, 1950. See also Mary L. Allen, *Education or Indoctrination*. Caldwell, ID: Caxton Printers, Ltd., 1955, pp. 88-89, 151, for heavy criticism of Mary Beauchamp. Another Goslin "lieutenant," Robert Gilchrist, also brought to Pasadena from Minneapolis, was "blacklisted" for other administrative slots in California, and the Goslin's shadow even followed him to his next position in the midwest. Interview by author with Robert Gilchrist, March 26, 1994. Information

on Beauchamp's firing comes from Michael James letter to author, April 27, 1994.

27. "Quandary in Pasadena," *Time*, November 27, 1950, pp. 85-87. *Newsweek* also reported the conflict, mentioning the racial rezoning, the tax increase initiative, and educational progressivism. "Pasadena Free-for-All," *Newsweek*, November 27, 1950, p. 75.

28. Mitchell Morris, "Fever Spots in American Education," *The Nation*, October 27, 1951, 173(17):345.

29. "Quandary in Pasadena," p. 87.

30. McWilliams, pp. 10-11. *The Pasadena Story: An Analysis of Some Forces and Factors That Injured a Superior School System*. Washington D.C.: National Education Association, June 1951, p. 13. Hulburd, p. 53. Hulburd noted that many of these radical theories of the 1930s were views that the educators no longer held. But Kilpatrick, for one, never rejected the economic ideas he espoused during the Depression, which he did not consider radical.

31. Hulburd, pp. 105-106; 112-13; and 144. Carey McWilliams, p. 12.

32. Allen, pp. 54, 147, 149. Charles M. Wollenberg, *All Deliberate Speed: Segregation and Exclusion in the California Schools*, 1855-1975. Berkeley: University of California Press, 1976, pp. 168-71, 183. In 1952 the Pasadena schools published a 1000 page survey of the district. It included financial, curricular, and demographic information, referred once to Goslin's "brief stay," and played down the recent conflict as the community's merely "taking stock." Clyde M. Hill and Lloyd N. Morrisett, *Report of the Survey of the Pasadena Schools: A Cooperative Study*. Pasadena: City Board of Education, 1951, pp. xxix-xxxiii; 1-5.

33. Lawrence Cremin, *The Transformation of the School: Progressivism in American Education, 1876-1957*. New York: Alfred A. Knopf, 1962, pp. 338-43.

34. Joel Spring, *The Sorting Machine: National Educational Policy Since 1945*. White Plains, NY: Longman, Inc., rev. ed., 1989, pp. 2-10. For a contemporary view of the Scarsdale episode, see Robert Shaplen, "Scarsdale's Battle of the Books," *Commentary*, December 1950, 10(6):530-40.

35. Diane Ravitch, *The Troubled Crusade: American Education, 1945-1980*. New York: Basic Books, Inc., 1983, pp. 45, 82, 92, 103, 107-13.

36. Letter from Michael James to author, April 27, 1994.

37. McWilliams, p. 14. "Man Out of a Job," *Life*, December 11, 1950, 29:95-6.

38. Diary, November 22, 1950.

39. James B. Conant, "The Superintendent Was the Target," *New York Times Book Review*, April 29, 1951, pp. 1, 27. See also James G. Hershberg, *James B. Conant: Harvard to Hiroshima and the Making of the Nuclear Age*. New York: Alfred A. Knopf, 1993, pp. 584-85.

40. McWilliams, pp. 13-15. Isaac Kandel, "The Challenge of Pasadena," *School and Society*, December 30, 1950, 72(1880):444-45. Morris Mitchell, "Fever Spots in American Education," *The Nation*, October 27, 1951, 173(17):344-47.

41. Daniel Tanner, *Crusade for Democracy: Progressive Education at the Crossroads*.

Albany, NY: State University of New York Press, 1991, pp. 28-29, 41. Benjamin Fine, "Kilpatrick at 80 Bars Retirement," *New York Times,* November 17, 1951, p. 19. John A. Beineke, "The Investigation of John Dewey by the F.B.I.," *Educational Theory,* Winter 1987, 37(1):43-52.

42. United States Department of Justice, "Federal Bureau of Investigation File on William Heard Kilpatrick," released October 7, 1987, and December 23, 1993. (51 pp.)

43. Diaries, January 14, 1951, February 9, 1952. Another indication of Goslin's anguish is the fact there is an intentional absence within his papers of any material relating to the Pasadena years. Letter from Michael James to author, April 24, 1994.

44. Diary, April 30, 1951.

45. Diaries, May 11, 15, and 17 and July 1, 1951. Eugene Nixon, "Educator Defended," *Los Angeles Times,* June 27, 1951.

46. Letter from H. K. Baumeister to author, April 24, 1994. Diaries, January 1, 1952; July 14, 1953; September 13 and 17, 1953; and January 1, 1954. See Howard David Langford, *Education and the Social Conflict.* New York: Macmillan Company, 1936.

47. William Heard Kilpatrick, "The Current Retreat from Reason," speech to the New York Humanist Association, October 17, 1952. "Watchman, What of the Night?" commencement address at Mercer University, June 8, 1953. Archives, Stetson Library, Mercer University, Macon, GA.

48. William Van Til, ed., *Forces Affecting American Education.* Washington, D.C.: Association for Supervision and Curriculum, 1953. H. Gordon Hullfish, ed., *Educational Freedom in an Age of Anxiety.* New York: Harper and Brothers, 1953.

49. Diary, August 9, 1949.

50. WHK Personal Papers, comments on Boyd H. Bode dated March 29, 1953, in Archives Stetson Library, Mercer University, Macon, GA. Diaries, March 14 and September 28, 1954.

51. Diaries, October 7, 8, and 11 and November 10, 1948.

52. Diaries, December 17 and 30 and June 8, 1949.

53. Diaries, September 18 and November 3, 6, and 13, 1950. See also Diary, August 25, 1951.

54. Diaries, November 27-28, 1950; May 18, and September 3 and 5, 1951.

55. Samuel Tenenbaum, *William Heard Kilpatrick: Trailblazer in Education.* New York: Harper and Brothers Publishers, 1951.

56. Susan F. Semel, *The Dalton School: The Transformation of a Progressive School.* New York: Peter Lang Publishing Inc., 1992, p. 12. Lawrence Cremin, "The William H. Kilpatrick Birthday Records," *Teachers College Record,* February, 1952, pp. 280-81. William Heard Kilpatrick's eightieth birthday recordings produced by Helen Parkhurst. "Civilization and Life," "The Educative Process," and "The World Situation." Transcripts in Archives, Stetson Library, Mercer University, Macon, GA.

57. These addresses, with an introductory essay by John Childs and Kilpatrick's own talk, "The Pursuit of Moral and Spiritual Values," were printed the following year in *Teachers College Record*, February 1952, 53(5):241-69. "Kilpatrick Scores Learning by Rote: At Birthday Dinner, Educator Defends Theories — 1,000 Pay Tribute to Him," *New York Times*, November 18, 1951.

58. Diary, November 17, 1951.

59. Benjamin Fine, "Education in Review: Dr. Kilpatrick at 80 Champions the Teaching Profession and Defines the Good Teacher," *New York Times* (Week in Review section), November 18, 1951. "America's Greatest Teacher," *Oil City* (Pennsylvania.) *Blizzard*, November 26, 1951.

60. Diary, November 9, 1956. For L.I.D. celebration see Diary, November 17, 1956, and see Diary for New Lincoln School fundraiser, November 20, 1956.

61. "Perpetual Arriver," *Time*, October 31, 1949, pp. 35-36. "John Dewey at 90," *Newsweek*, October 24, 1949, p. 80. "*Life* Congratulates John Dewey," *Life*, October 31, 1949, 27:43.

62. William Heard Kilpatrick, "John Dewey and Education," speech given October 20, 1949, New York. Archives, Stetson Library, Mercer Library, Macon, GA. See Diary, October 20, 1949, for Childs's comment.

63. Kalman Siegel, "World Cheers Dewey at Lively 90; 1,500 Hear Educator Extolled," *New York Times*, October 21, 1949.

64. Diaries, October 20 and 22 and November 1, 1949.

65. Diaries, June 1-4 and July 20, 1952.

66. Diaries, October 29, 1953; January 1, 1954.

67. Diaries, January 1, February 9, and June 9, 1950.

68. Diaries, June 1 and October 22, 1954; May 6, 1956.

69. Diary, July 26, 1952. Lawrence A. Cremin, David A. Shannon, and Mary Evelyn Townsend, *A History of Teachers College Columbia University*. New York: Columbia University, 1954, pp. 47, 48, 139, 144-47, 151, 152, 160, 250, 251.

70. Diaries, July 26, October 29, and November 4-5, 1952; and January 1, 1955.

71. Diaries, August 10, 1952; January 20, 1953; July 13, 1955; January 31, and April 7, 1956.

72. Diaries, June 21-23, 1951; July 10, 1953.

73. William Heard Kilpatrick, "Proposal of S. 2499 a Serious Threat," *The Nation's Schools*, April 1947, 39:4. Richard H. Parke, "Barden Denounces Spellman Here as 'Cruel' Critic of Mrs. Roosevelt," *New York Times*, March 7, 1950, pp. 1, 16. Diaries, October 11, 1954; February 3, 1955.

74. Diaries, March 28, May 29, 1954; January 27, August 17 and 21, September 11, and November 7, 1956.

75. Diaries, November 20, 1954; February 28 and November 20, 1955.

76. Diaries, December 11-12, June 6, 1954; September 22-23, 1955.

Chapter 17

1. Ferrol Sams, *Run with the Horseman*. New York: Penguin Books, 1984, p. 4.

2. J. Cash, *The Mind of the South*. New York: Alfred A. Knopf, 1941, p. x.

3. Kilpatrick, quoted in Robert Merrill Bartlett, *They Work for Tomorrow*. New York: International Committee of Young Men's Christian Associations, 1943, p. 120. Diary, December 21, 1943.

4. Ronald K. Goodenow, "The Southern Progressive Educator on Race and Pluralism: The Case of William Heard Kilpatrick," *History of Education Quarterly*, Summer 1981, 21:149. Goodenow's source is Stewart Cole, an official in the organization. Cole must have misinterpreted Kilpatrick's comment: his family was not among the largest slaveowners in the state, and Kilpatrick was never one to exaggerate. Kilpatrick's grandson H. K. Baumeister has suggested that his grandfather may have been including enslaved individuals owned by his extended family through both his fraternal and his maternal lines. Letter to author, February 17, 1995.

5. Diary, July 4, 1907.

6. Edward L. Ayres, *The Promise of the New South: Life After Reconstruction*. New York: Oxford University Press, 1992, pp. 334-35.

7. William Heard Kilpatrick, "Modern Educational Theory and the Inherent Inequality of Segregation," *Progressive Education*, March 1956, 33:41. Diary, February 20, 1955.

8. Tenenbaum, p. 60.

9. William Heard Kilpatrick, "Teachers College as a Contribution to Education," address delivered at Teachers College Alumni Conference, March 1921. Kilpatrick Scrapbooks. Milbank Library, Teachers College.

10. Diaries, March 15 and December 7, 1915; July 19, 1919.

11. Diaries, February 25, 1904; July 14, 1905; April 25, 1910; February 18, 1912; April 20, 1910.

12. Diary, February 27, 1912.

13. Diaries, July 15, 1909; September 20, 1913.

14. Diaries, March 22 and April 3, 1914.

15. Diaries, December 3, 1909; February 2, 1916; February 22, 1921; July 15, 1923; May 8, 1931; January 25, 1942.

16. William Heard Kilpatrick, *Our Educational Task as Illustrated in the Changing South*. Chapel Hill: University of North Carolina Press, pp. 52-53. See also Diaries, November 6, 1909; September 19, 1916; April 9, 1922; August 15, 1925; April 26, 1927.

17. Walter Feinberg, *Reason and Rhetoric: The Intellectual Foundations of 20th Century Liberal Educational Policy*. New York: John Wiley and Sons, Inc., 1975, p. 111. See also John Dewey and Evelyn Dewey, *Schools for Tomorrow*. New York: E.P. Dutton and Co., 1915, pp. 207-08.

18. Diaries, September 9 and 17, 1917.

19. William Heard Kilpatrick, "Education as Socialization," *High School Quarterly*,

July 1917, 5:267-70. See also "Spread Reading and Bring South into Proud Leadership," *Macon Telegraph*, May 5, 1917, p. 7.

20. Diaries, August 7 and 18, 1922.

21. Transcripts of Tenenbaum-Kilpatrick interviews, Columbia University tape recordings, p. 136, Archives, Stetson Library, Mercer University, Macon, GA.

22. Diaries, February 9 and March 14, 1924; August 1, 1942; May 4, and April 10, 1944.

23. Diaries, November 8, 1925; July 30, 1926; January 24, 1931.

24. Diaries, March 15, 1928; May 15, 1931; March 24, 1934; January 28, 1935.

25. Lillian Smith, *Strange Fruit* with Foreword by Fred Hobson. Athens: University of Georgia Press, 1985, p. vii. and Goodenow, p. 150.

26. See "Unrest Blow at Religion, Says Kilpatrick," *Charlotte Observer*, May 5, 1928; "Warns South to Shun Bigotry," May 6, 1928.

27. Kilpatrick, *Our Educational Task*, pp. 8-9, 34-36, 43-45, 96-97.

28. Diaries, April 2, 1933; July 29, 1941.

29. Diaries, May 19, 1935; November 6, 1936; February 10, 1945.

30. Diary, December 7, 1933.

31. Buell G. Gallagher, *American Caste and the Negro College*. New York: Columbia University Press, 1938; Foreword by William Heard Kilpatrick, pp. vi-ix. For a criticism of Kilpatrick's views in this volume, see Goodenow, p. 156.

32. Gallagher, pp. x-xii.

33. "Inaugural Conference at Talladega College," *Quarterly Review of Higher Education Among Negroes*, April 1934, 2:143-44.

34. See Harry W. Greene, "Sixty Years of Doctorates Conferred upon Negroes," *Journal of Negro Education*, January 1937, 6(1):30-37.

35. Diary, February 12, 1939. Program, Inter-Racial Unity Meeting, April 14, 1939. Kilpatrick Scrapbooks.

36. William Heard Kilpatrick, "Social Planning: Today's 1776 and 1787 — An Editorial" *Frontiers of Democracy*, March 15, 1940, 6(18):165-66.

37. William Heard Kilpatrick, "The Problem of Minorities," *Frontiers of Democracy*, April 1940, 6(19):135-36. "An Immoral Cultural Lag: Our War Treatment of Negroes," *Frontiers of Democracy*, February 15, 1942, 8(67):134-35.

38. William Heard Kilpatrick, "Cultural Democracy in War and Peace," *Intercultural Education News*, January 1941, 4:1. Goodenow, p. 148.

39. Diaries, January 11, March 21, and August 1, 1940; February 3, 1941. He also had the unpleasant duty of assisting in the unseating of J. H. Hubert, who had, according to Kilpatrick, not kept the organization committed to its original goals.

40. Goodenow, p. 162. Diary, September 28, 1944.

41. For comments about Roger Baldwin, see Diary, December 1, 1949. Kilpatrick had worked with Baldwin and the A.C.L.U. as early as 1943. Diary, April 29, 1943.

42. Diaries, January 10, 1941; May 22, 1944.

43. Charles V. Hamilton, *Adam Clayton Powell, Jr.: The Political Biography of an*

American Dilemma. New York: Atheneum, 1991, pp. 55, 83-84. Diary, December 11, 1941.

44. Diaries, June 3, 1942; October 19, 1943; November 1, 1944.

45. William Heard Kilpatrick, "Building National Unity on the Basis of Democracy," *Peabody Reporter*, April 1942, 15:125-26, 134-35.

46. William Heard Kilpatrick, "What Shall We Say of Governor Talmadge?" *Frontiers of Democracy*, October 15, 1941, 8(63):17-19. Diary, February 28, 1954.

47. Diaries, September 11 and November 18, 1942. Harold Paulk Henderson, *The Politics of Change in Georgia: A Political Biography of Ellis Arnall*. Athens: University Press of Georgia, 1991, pp. 36-54. See also James F. Cook Jr. *Politics and Education in the Talmadge Era: The Controversy Over the University System of Georgia, 1941-1942*. Ph.D. dissertation, University of Georgia, 1972.

48. Editorial, *Statesmen*, April 6, 1944.

49. Diaries, August 3, 1946; April 21, 1944; September 9, 1948. When Eugene Talmadge's son, Herman, entered the United States Senate in 1956, Kilpatrick thought him wrong on every controversial issue and glumly noted that "in these days one from Georgia can feel but small pride in his native state." See Diary, May 21, 1956.

50. Diaries, November 6, 1943; April 9, 1944; May 21, 1944.

51. William Heard Kilpatrick, "Intercultural Education: A Program for American Democracy," *Jewish Social Service Quarterly*, September 1940, 17(1):58-64. Kilpatrick also made a strong statement regarding the Nazis' public treatment of Jews in *Selfhood and Civilization*, p. 62.

52. Diary, November 3, 1951. See Jesse Thomas Moore, Jr., *A Search for Equality: The National Urban League, 1910-1961*. University Park: Pennsylvania State University Press, 1981, pp. 162-67. While Kilpatrick would certainly fall into the category of moderate white leadership discussed by Moore, neither he nor other nonminority members of the Urban League are mentioned in this or other histories. Diary, February 12, 1947.

53. Goodenow, p.157.

54. William Heard Kilpatrick, "Announcement: The Bureau Expands Its Services," *Intercultural Education News*, June 1944. 5(4).

55. "Tolerance Study Will Be Expanded," *New York Times*, March 23, 1944.

56. Helen G. Trager and Frank N. Trager, "W. H. Kilpatrick and Intercultural Education," *Progressive Education*, March 1957, 34:52-53, 58.

57. William Heard Kilpatrick and William Van Til, eds., *Intercultural Attitudes in the Making*. New York: Ninth Yearbook of the John Dewey Society, 1947, pp. vi-ix and 1-16.

58. Kilpatrick and Van Til, p. 15. An early entry in the literature on youth gangs is included in the volume. *Modern Education and Better Human Relations*, (Freedom Pamphlet). New York: Anti-Defamation League, 1949, pp. 1-43.

59. Diaries, July 18-19 and September 10, 1936; March 5, 1944; October 17, 1949.

60. Kilpatrick, "Modern Education and Better Human Relations," pp. 7-8. Diary, March 25, 1952.

61. William Heard Kilpatrick, *Philosophy of Education*. New York: Macmillan Company, 1951, p. 205.

62. Goodenow, p. 153.

63. William Heard Kilpatrick, "Resort to Courts by Negroes to Improve Their Schools a Conditional Alternative," *The Journal of Negro Education*, July 1935, 4:414-17. (Kilpatrick again notes his ancestors' slaveholding, reporting that former slaves continued to call his father "master" after emancipation. p. 414.)

64. Alain Locke, "The Dilemma of Segregation," *Journal of Negro Education*, July 1935,4: 407-18. Charles H. Thompson, "Court Action Only Reasonable Alternative to Remedy Immediate Abuses of the Negro Separate School," *The Journal of Negro Education*, July 1935, 4:419-20.

65. Diaries, August 19, 1948; October 17, 1950; December 22, 1955.

66. Richard Kluger, *Simple Justice*. New York: Alfred A. Knopf, 1976, pp. 335-37.

67. Feinberg, pp. 116-21.

68. Trager and Trager, pp. 52-53, 58. William Van Til, " William Heard Kilpatrick: A Remembrance, *Teaching Education*, Winter 1988, 2(2):32-35.

69. Goodenow, p. 156. Goodenow, while positive toward Kilpatrick's activity, remained skeptical regarding Gallagher's statement, reserving judgment on the philosopher's overall status on the race issue pending data on the influence he brought to bear on the audiences he addressed.

70. Diaries, April 24 and May 18, 1954; December 22, 1955.

71. Goodenow, p.163. See also Diary, April 25, 1956, for a discussion of a strategy session. Also Diaries, February 23 and July 6, 1956.

72. William Heard Kilpatrick, "Modern Educational Theory and Inherent Inequality of Segregation," *Progressive Education*, March 1956, 33:41-42.

73. Diary, May 17, 1956.

74. Goodenow, pp. 162-64.

75. Diaries, July 12, August 31, and September 25, 1957. At times, Kilpatrick would vocally support the continued progress of integration. He even sent a letter to the head of TWA congratulating the airline on being the first to hire Negro stewardesses. Diaries, May 22, 1958; January 1, 1959.

76. William Heard Kilpatrick, "How to End School Segregation," a review of Robin M. Williams Jr. and Margaret W. Ryan, eds. *Schools in Transition* in *The New Leader*, March 7, 1955, p. 27.

77. "Georgia Would Bar Pension of Bias Foe," *New York Times*, March 15, 1956, p. 56. Letter from Kilpatrick to Dr. Guy H. Wells, March 20, 1956. Archives Stetson Library, Mercer University, Macon, GA.

78. Diaries, June 2-5, 1953. Articles by Ameila Barksdale, "Famed Educator Revisits Former Blakely Students," *Albany* (Georgia.) *Herald*, June 14, 1953. "Famed Dr.

Kilpatrick Visits Blakely Family" *Atlanta Constitution*, June 12, 1953. Also *Early County News*, June 11, 1953.

79. Diaries, November 8, 1907; September 18, 1928; September 29, 1959.

80. Diaries, December 23, 1951; October 10, 1907; January 1, 1908; August 25 and September 5, 1909; February 26, 1911.

81. Frederick Lewis Allen, *Only Yesterday: An Informal History of the Nineteen-Twenties*. New York: Blue Ribbon Books, Inc., 1931, p. 197.

82. Diaries, May 15 and November 20, 1914; March 31, 1919; ; January 9, 1920, July 19, 1921.

83. Diaries, June 4 and September 16, 1922; January 19 and October 29, 1923; April 7, 1924; March 30, 1934.

84. Diaries, January 1, 1924; June 26, 1927.

85. Diary, February 18, 1926.

86. William Heard Kilpatrick, "How Shall We Think About Religion?" *Child Study*, November 1930, 8:67-69, 84.

87. William Heard Kilpatrick, "The Philosophy of American Education," *Teachers College Record*, October 1928, 30(1):13-22. "Thinking in Childhood and Youth," *Religious Education*, February 1928, 23:132-40.

88. Diaries, August 19, 1935; October 4, 1950.

89. Diaries, July 21, 1939; March 25, 1951; November 5, 1941.

90. Diaries, September 1, 1942; January 1, 1950; April 30, 1949. Upon reading William Buckley's *God and Man at Yale*, Kilpatrick wrote, "Only a Catholic and a snob could write such a book." See Diary, June 6, 1953.

91. Diaries, January 25, 1950; March 22, 1952; June 2, 1956.

92. Diaries, July 18, 1946; April 30, 1952; March 16 and December 8, 1953.

93. Diaries, February 2 and 26, 1953.

94. Kilpatrick, *Philosophy of Education*, p. 157.

95. Diary, December 23, 1951.

96. Diaries, April 1, 1945; January 25, 1958.

97. J.R. Moseley, *Manifest Victory*. New York: Harper and Brothers Publishers, 1941. Foreword by William Heard Kilpatrick, pp. xiii-xv.

98. Diary, April 12, 1954.

Chapter 18

1. Reported in Howard Whitman, "Progressive Education: Which Way Forward?" *Collier's*, May 14, 1954, p. 32. The Chant is possibly apocryphal.

2. Diaries, March 18, 1957; October 28, 1958.

3. Diary, December 26, 1959.

4. Diaries, January 28 and February 28, 1957; March 1, 1958.

5. Diaries, July 8,1959; June 6, 1961. Interview by author with Robert Oana, April 1994.

6. Diary, May 25, 1955.
7. Albert Lynd, *Quackery in the Public Schools*. New York: Grosset and Dunlap, 1953, from chapter 8, "The Influence of John Dewey," pp. 183-211.
8. Lynd, pp. 212, 213, and 216.
9. Lynd, p. 231.
10. Lynd, pp. 236, 241, 245, and. 250.
11. See book reviews in the *New York Times*, September 13, 1953, p. 31; *San Francisco Chronicle*, September 27, 1953, p. 12; *Saturday Review*, September 12, 1953, 36:26; and *Christian Century*, November 4, 1953, 70:1262.
12. Diaries, October 17 and 20, 1953.
13. Diaries, May 4, 1958; June 17, 1951; November 20, 1932.
14. Neil G. McCluskey, "Dr. Kilpatrick's Eighty-fifth Birthday," *America*, December 1, 1956, p. 253. Diaries, June 17,1952; December 4, 1950. William Van Til, "William Heard Kilpatrick: A Memoir," *Teaching Education*, Winter 1988, 2(2):32-35. Theodore Rockwell, *The Rickover Effect: How One Man Made a Difference*. Annapolis: Naval Institute Press, 1992, pp. 278-79. Max Rafferty, *What They Are Doing to Your Children*. New York: New American Library, 1963, p.18.
15. Diaries, July 9, 1953; January 1, 1955.
16. Diaries, May 27, 1961; April 5, 1957; September 19, 1961.
17. Diaries, January 12-16, 1959; January 4, 1960.
18. "Learn by Living," *Newsweek*, November 20, 1961, p. 62.
19. Nan Robertson, "Nearing 90, Kilpatrick Salutes Progressive Education Gains," New York Times, November 15, 1961.
20. Program, "William Heard Kilpatrick Day — 90th Birthday Celebration," Collection of H. K. Baumeister.
21. Margaret Kilpatrick Baumeister, "William Heard Kilpatrick as a Georgian," Address at dedication of Kilpatrick Education Center at Georgia College, Milledgeville. Collection of H. K. Baumeister. Kilpatrick's concern about youth seems to be real. Edwin Blue told the author that he sat next to Kilpatrick on an airplane in the early 1960s and Kilpatrick told Blue that he predicted an uprising of the young in the 1960s against their parents and the conformity of the times. Interview with Edwin Blue by author, April 1992.
22. Interview by author with Mary Murray Steele, June 1990.
23. "Attacks in Retaliation," Time, February 12, 1965, 85(7):13.
24. Interview by author with Francis Robert Otto by author, May 30, 1995.
25. Margaret Kilpatrick Baumeister, "William Heard Kilpatrick as a Georgian."
26. Descriptions of the funeral come from the Diary of Margaret Kilpatrick Baumeister and remembrances of Heard Kilpatrick Baumeister in a letter to the author, July 18, 1990.
27. Diary, July 26, 1957. As early as 1945, Kilpatrick considered being buried in White Plains. After hearing Roland Hayes sing several Negro spirituals at Columbia, he noted that he was "carried back to my childhood as not in a very long time. It made me feel that I wished to be buried at White Plains." Diary, April 15, 1945.

28. Last Will and Testament of William Heard Kilpatrick." Collection of H. K. Baumeister.

29. Interview with Mary Murray Steele and Diary of Margaret Kilpatrick Baumeister, February 6, 1975.

30. "Dr. Kilpatrick Dies at 93; Dean of U.S. Education," *Atlanta Constitution*, February 16, 1965, p. 9.

31. "State, Nation Honor Dr. W. H. Kilpatrick," *Atlanta Constitution*, February 16, 1965, p. 4.

32. State of Georgia, General Assembly, resolution, February 19, 1965, Archives, Stetson Library, Mercer University, Macon, GA.

33. Diary, October 28, 1959. John L. Childs, *American Pragmatism and Education: An Interpretation and Criticism*. New York: Henry Holt and Company, 1956, p. 179.

34. William Heard Kilpatrick, "Personal Reminiscences of Dewey and My Judgment of His Present Influence," *School and Society*, October 10, 1959, pp. 374-75. Diaries, October 16, 1915; October 5, 1914; April 4, 1947. Samuel Tenenbaum, "An Informal Essay on William Heard Kilpatrick," *Educational Theory*, January 1966,16(1):44.

35. Diary, February 6, 1912. In this same conversation, Dewey told Kilpatrick that he had come to the conclusion that "philosophy is education and not anything else. The problem of interaction of mind and matter, e.g., is not a scientific, but an educational affair." Kilpatrick admitted, "I confess I don't know what this means."

36. William Heard Kilpatrick, "Personal Reminiscences," p. 375. Merle Curti, *The Social Ideas of American Educators*, Paterson, NJ, Pageant Books, Inc., 1959, p. 499. Diary, March 18, 1935. Boyd Bode agreed with Kilpatrick's evaluation of Dewey's place in the history of philosophy.

37. Diaries, October 28, 1915; October 16, 1913; April 17, 1930.

38. Diary, November 20, 1949.

39. Diaries, November 16, 1917; January 1, 1916; July 3, 1914. William Heard Kilpatrick, *We Learn What We Live*. Conference Proceedings, Pasadena City Schools, July 13-20, 1949, p. 38. Diary April 10, 1910.

40. Diary, October 24, 1922. Merle Curti, "The Social Ideas of American Educators," *Progressive Education*, January-February 1934, 11:26-31.

41. William Heard Kilpatrick, "Dewey's Influence on Education," in Paul Arthur Schlipp, ed., *The Philosophy of John Dewey*, Evanston, IL: Northwestern University Press, 1939, pp. 472-73.

42. Diaries, November 20, 1941; September 30, 1940; March 15, 1951.

43. John L. Childs, "An Evaluation of Dewey's Theory of Education," *University of Michigan School of Education Bulletin*, May 1958, 29(8):113-21.

44. Interview with William Heard Kilpatrick by Dale DeWitt, "John Dewey: Humanist and Educator," *The Humanist*, July-August 1952, pp. 161-65. "John Dewey and His Educational Theory," *Educational Theory*, October, 1952, 3(4):217-21. See also "John Dewey and His Contributions to American Education," *Journal of*

Educational Sociology, March 1947, 20(7):395-400. "Dewey's Philosophy of Education," *The Educational Forum*, January 1953, 17(2):143-54.

45. Diaries, May 30, 1911, November 7 and December 15, 1945. Dewey was able to get Kilpatrick to drink a glass of sherry on one visit, against both his "custom and conviction" regarding alcohol, but Kilpatrick later noted that he probably could defend neither.

46. Diaries, December 24, 1945, November 19, 1944; November 7, 1945. Interview with Kenneth Benne, October 1989. Diaries, December 11, 1946.

47. Diary, December 9, 1949.

48. Diaries, May 9 and 16 and November 13, 1947.

49. John Dewey, *Experience and Education*. New York: Macmillan, 1938, pp. 13, 107.

50. Diary, April 11, 1938.

51. Diary, January 30, 1958. William Heard Kilpatrick, "John Dewey and his Educational Theory," *Progressive Education*, October 1952, p. 7.

52. Murray Illson, "School Program Sharply Debated," *New York Times*, May 6, 1948. William Heard Kilpatrick, letter to editor, "John Dewey Was Not Responsible for Misbehavior of College Men," *Atlanta Journal*, June 11, 1952. Kilpatrick Scrapbooks.

53. Kilpatrick Scrapbooks, attached to article by Kilpatrick "Dewey's Philosophy of Education," 1953. John Dewey, "An Introduction," in Elsie Clapp, *The Use of Resources in Education*. New York: Harper and Brothers Publishers, 1952, pp. vii-xi.

54. Tenenbaum, pp. vii, viii, x.

55. Diary, September 26, 1951.

56. Diary October 14, 1959. Tape recording of meeting on October 14, 1959, from the collection of William Van Til.

57. William Heard Kilpatrick, *The New Leader*, November 25, 1939. William Heard Kilpatrick, *John Dewey*, undated article in the Kilpatrick Scrapbooks.

Chapter 19

1. Richard Bernstein, *John Dewey*. New York: Washington Square Press, 1966, pp. 144-45.

2. Howard Whitman, "Progressive Education — Which Way Is Forward?" *Collier's*, February 14, 1954, pp. 32-36.

3. Interview with Thomas Hopkins by O.L. Davis, University of Texas Collection. I. L. Kandel, "Education and Social Disorder," *Teachers College Record*, February 1933, 34(5):359-367; "The Educative Value of Orange Crates," *School and Society*, January 3, 1942, 55(1410):17-18.

4. Lawrence A. Cremin, "What Was Progressive Education?" *Vital Speeches of the Day*, September 15, 1959, 25:721-25. Fred Hechinger, "Progressive Education Versus Spectatoritis," *Reporter*, August 5, 1952, pp. 35-37.

5. Patricia Albjerg Graham, *Progressive Education: From Arcady to Academe: A History of the Progressive Education Association*, 1919-1955. New York: Teachers College Press, 1967, pp. 151, 156, 162.
6. Hirsch, *Cultural Literacy: What Every American Needs to Know*. Boston: Houghton Mifflin, 1987, pp. 116-123. Arthur Bestor, *Educational Wastelands: The Retreat from Learning in Our Public Schools*, 2nd ed. Urbana and Chicago: University of Illinois Press, pp. 47, 64-65. Diary December 9, 1959.
7. Bestor, pp. 37, 64-65, 90-91, 114, 131, 138.
8. Timothy Noah, "Yes, Our Schools Can Be Saved," *Newsweek*, May 2, 1988, 111(18):60. "Washington Diarist: Blobs," *The New Republic*, July 11, 1988, 199:43. Mickey Kaus, "Bush's New Ideas," *Newsweek*, August 22, 1988, 112(8):27.
9. Lynne V. Cheney, *American Memory: A Report on the Humanities in the Nation's Public Schools*, Washington, D.C.: U.S. Government Printing Office, 1988, p. 24.
10. Richard Hofstadter, *Anti-Intellectualism in American Life*, New York: Alfred A. Knopf, 1966, pp. 358, 361.
11. Hofstadter, p. 360.
12. Merle Curti, *The Social Ideas of American Educators*. Paterson, N.J.: Pageant Books, 1959. Hofstadter, p. 6; Diary, July 20, 1937.
13. Lawrence Cremin, *The Transformation of the School: Progressivism in American Education, 1876-1957*, pp. 348-53. James Wallace, *Liberal Journalism and American Education*, 1914-1941. New Brunswick, NJ: Rutgers University Press, pp. 88-89.
14. William Van Til, "Is Progressive Education Obsolete?" *Saturday Review*, February 1962, pp. 56-57, 82-84. "The Compassionate Critics," in *My Way of Looking at It*. Terre Haute: Indiana State University Press, pp. 27-30.
15. Gilbert Sewall, *Necessary Lessons: Decline and Renewal in American Schools*. New York: Free Press, Macmillan, 1983, pp. 22-23.
16. Arthur G. Powell, Eleanor Farrar, and David K. Cohen, *The Shopping Mall High School: Winners and Losers in the Educational Marketplace*. Boston: Houghton Mifflin, 1985, pp. 264-65. See also Robert L. Hampel, *The Last Little Citadel: American High Schools Since 1940*. Boston: Houghton Mifflin, 1986, p. 18, which, in guarded language, is also mildly critical of the progressives.
17. William Heard Kilpatrick, *Education for a Changing Civilization*. New York: Macmillan, 1926, pp. 111-12.
18. D. Hirsch, Jr., *The Schools We Need and Why We Don't Have Them*. New York: Doubleday, 1996, pp. 52, 90, 94, 98, 108, 122-23, 126.
19. Charles Frankel, "Appearance and Reality in Kilpatrick's Philosophy," *Teachers College Record*, January 1965, 66(4):352-64.
20. Cremin, *The Transformation of the School*, pp. 219-21, 231.
21. Lawrence Cremin, "History: A Lamp to Light the Present," *Education Week*, March 16, 1988, pp. 5, 20. Interview with Lynn Olsen.

22. Diane Ravitch, *The Troubled Crusade: American Education, 1945-1980*. New York: Basic Books, 1983, pp. 44-46, 79. Ravitch also quotes William C. Bagley to the effect that there are no proven laws of learning.

23. Ravitch, p. 51.

24. Clarence J. Karier, *The Individual, Society, and Education: A History of American Education*. Urbana: University of Illinois Press, 1986, pp. 247-51.

25. Robert Westbrook, *John Dewey and American Democracy*. Ithaca, NY: Cornell University Press, 1991, pp. 503-04.

26. Westbrook, pp. 505-08.

27. Alan Ryan, *John Dewey and the High Tide of American Liberalism*. New York: W.W. Norton and Company, 1995, pp. 145, 146, 162, 277, 378.

28. Arthur Zilversmit, *Changing Schools: Progressive Education Theory and Practice, 1930-1960*. Chicago: University of Chicago Press, 1993, pp. 14-16 and 195-96.

29. Cremin, "What Was Progressive Education?" p. 723.

30. Wallace, p. 198.

31. Hofstadter, p. 7.

32. John L. Childs, *American Pragmatism and Education*. New York: Henry Holt and Company, 1956, p. 197.

33. Childs, p. 188.

34. William Heard Kilpatrick, editor, *The Twenty-Sixth Yearbook of the National Society for the Study of Education, Part II, The Foundations of Curriculum-Making*. Bloomington, IN.: Public School Publishing Company, 1928, p. 133.

35. Sol Cohen, "The Influence of Progressive Education on School Reform in the USA," in Hermann Rohrs and Volker Lenhart, eds. *Progressive Education Across the Continents*. New York: Peter Lang, 1995, pp. 321-32.

36. William Heard Kilpatrick, "Getting Grown: What It Means; How to Do It?" *Thames Magazine*, July 1947, pp. 12, 13, 16, 18.

37. William Heard Kilpatrick, *We Learn What We Live*. Pasadena, CA: Conference Proceedings, Pasadena City Schools, July 13-20, 1949, pp. 40-42, 57-59, 60, 62, 64.

38. Much of this material is drawn from John A. Beineke, "Is Progressive Education Obsolete: A Reconsideration," *Teaching Education*, Spring-Summer, 1993, 5(2):175-81.

39. John Pulliam, *History of American Education*, 4th ed. Columbus, OH: Merrill, 1987, pp. 178-80, and interview by author with John Lounsbury, June 1993.

40. William Heard Kilpatrick, *Philosophy of Education*. New York: Macmillan Company, 1951, p. 244.

41. Kilpatrick, *Philosophy of Education*, pp. 114, 135. Kilpatrick-Tenenbaum Columbia University tapes, transcripts in Archives Stetson Library, Mercer University, Macon, Georgia, p. 102.

42. Interview by author with Norman Cousins, June 15, 1990.

43. Ronald K. Goodenow, "The Southern Progressive Educator on Race and Pluralism: The Case of William Heard Kilpatrick," *History of Education Quarterly*, 21(2):147.

44. Wallace, p. 173.
45. Tenenbaum, p. 291. This included even more free enterprise than he had advocated in the 1930s.
46. David Tyack and Larry Cuban, *Tinkering Toward Utopia: A Century of Public School Reform*. Cambridge, MA: Harvard University Press, 1995, pp. 84, 109, 136.
47. Geraldine Joncich, *The Sane Positivist: A Biography of Edward L. Thorndike*. Middletown, CT: Wesleyan University Press, 1968, p. 219.
48. Cremin, "What Was Progressive Education?", p. 725. Charles Frankel, 66(4):364.
49. William Heard Kilpatrick, *Foundations of Method: Informal Talks on Teaching*. New York: Macmillan, 1925, p. 371.

INDEX

TABLE OF CONTENTS

support. Both a student and professional acquaintance of Kilpatrick's, Dr. Van Til represents for me, both intellectually and through the world of practice, what is best about progressive education.

Two individuals undertook significant labors for me in word processing the manuscript at various stages in the development of the manuscript. Jill Fulkes and Jill Grant contributed their skills to this work and took a deep interest in the numerous revisions. Their patience, hard work, and suggestions made the process much less painful than it would normally have been. And Brad Latty provided much-appreciated technological support in the production of the photographs and the formatting of the text in this book.

Five mentors who were not directly involved in this manuscript but who have had a major impact on me in the fields of history, education, and scholarship are Jay C. Thompson, Jr., Robert M. Mitchell, Rod A. Camp, Lawrence Dennis, and J. Stephen Hazlett. Jay Thompson sensitized me to the issues, challenges, and opportunities within the field of educational studies, while Bob Mitchell served as a role model and mentor in the field of history. Rod Camp emerged as an exemplar of dedicated scholarship as I watched him research and write in his own area of Mexican politics. Lawrence Dennis became a colleague *in absentia*, keeping alive my interest in progressive education through personal interaction and professional collaborations. And Steve Hazlett proved to me that one could be an administrator and maintain one's interest and integrity as a scholar.

At the W.K. Kellogg Foundation, the support and encouragement of Rick Foster and Roger Sublett is noted with appreciation. In addition, Dee Grubb — on more than one occasion — provided me with quick and accurate counsel on thorny issues of grammar and syntax. And last, but far from least, my profound indebtedness to Sharon Cutler, also of the Kellogg Foundation, who took of her personal time and energy to solve baffling computer-related problems that arose during the final stages of the manuscript's preparation.

Because this work was ten years in the making, it became in one sense a member of the family. As a result, my real family learned more about Dr. Kilpatrick than probably they wished to know, always gamely listening to my many stories about both the process and the subject of the book. Above all others and most importantly, I recognize and pay special tribute to my wife Debbie — for her belief in me and in this book. She spent countless hours discussing, proof reading, and in general, supporting all my efforts. Her love is what sustains me. A final acknowledgment to my three children — Eric, Colin, and Kaitlin — whose lives as students in the public schools have no doubt been different because of the life of Professor Kilpatrick of Teachers College.

John Beineke
January 1998

script could never have been successfully developed without the essential contributions of Kilpatrick's grandson and namesake, Heard Kilpatrick Baumeister. As conservative as his grandfather was liberal, this retired engineer cooperated with me through my many questions, culminating in a correspondence lasting several years. He graciously received me in his home, took my phone calls, and gave me access to his personal files and those he had inherited from his grandfather via his mother. I am deeply thankful for his interest and assistance. I also am indebted to several members of the Marion Kilpatrick Ostrander family for the time they afforded me in interviews and questions answered. The numerous individuals whom I interviewed, literally from coast to coast, added context and background to the mosaic of Kilpatrick's life. I especially think of my conversations with two men now gone, Norman Cousins and Kenneth Benne, who were students of Kilpatrick.

A number of libraries provided service and support for the research. David Ment, archivist at the Milbank Memorial Library of Teachers College at Columbia University, showed me much hospitality and responded to my many requests with graciousness and promptness. M. E. Overby, retired archivist and librarian at the Stetson Library of Mercer University in Macon, Georgia, lent valuable aid on a number of occasions as I worked with its Kilpatrick Collection. Special materials were secured for me by Craig Kridel of the Museum of Education at the University of South Carolina and O. L. Davis, Jr. of the University of Texas at Austin. Mary Hargaden, Museum Manager at the Museum and Archives of Georgia Education in Milledgeville, also offered special assistance in securing photographs and recordings connected with Kilpatrick. Jane Reese of Vanderbilt University facilitated obtaining the cover photograph from the *Peabody Reflector*. In addition, my research was aided by the good offices of the libraries at the University of Evansville and Kennesaw State University through interlibrary loan assistance and technological support. And quite early in my research, while at the University of Evansville, a small but crucial grant was awarded to me by Dianne Garnett and the institution's Development Office.

I had the good fortune of having the weighty task of reading the manuscript and making editorial suggestions undertaken by three marvelous and remarkable individuals. Regina Wilkes of Atlanta, Georgia, a writer and philosopher, provided stylistic and grammatical suggestions and in two places provided her own perspective on the subject of this book. James Wallace, a writer on progressive education and historian from Portland, Oregon, read the many drafts and contributed both content and stylistic options for me to consider. He also spent an enormous amount of time on E-mail, in correspondence, and on the telephone, assisting me in innumerable ways. Susan Gamer provided final editing suggestions which were most welcome and helpful. The final product is infinitely stronger because of the contributions of these three individuals, but any factual errors, misinterpretations, or stylistic lapses remain solely my responsibility.

I also acknowledge the many ideas provided to me by the veteran progressive educator, William Van Til. From my first interview with him early in the project, he became a source of information as well as a voice of constant encouragement and

ACKNOWLEDGMENTS

The research and writing of this book, a decade-long process, began in a church basement in Iowa. I had written an article on the FBI investigations of John Dewey. Betty Hovey, who had begun her teaching career in the 1930s, had read the piece and stopped me somewhere near the end of the line at a community supper. She told me that she had heard John Dewey speak in Shaker Heights, Ohio, and had been a student of William Heard Kilpatrick's while at Teachers College. In fact, Mrs. Hovey was one of the 622 students in the last class Kilpatrick taught during the summer of 1937. According to this retired teacher, the critics had gotten Dewey and Kilpatrick all wrong. Progressive education had been portrayed as a haphazard approach to education, in which students did as they pleased and studied whatever took their fancy. Allegedly, under progressive philosophy, playing with orange crates and making things out of clay and sand held supremacy over serious schoolwork. "This has been one of the great inaccuracies in educational history," said Mrs. Hovey, "John Dewey and Professor Kilpatrick were two of the most intelligent, disciplined men I have ever met. And they could hold their own intellectually with anyone at that time."

I had heard of Kilpatrick of Teachers College, of course — "Columbia's million-dollar Professor," Dewey's major disciple, "the project method," and of the legendary classes in which more than 500 students were held enthralled by the charismatic Southerner in the cavernous Horace Mann Auditorium. Having always enjoyed biographical studies, and looking for a new research undertaking, I thought, "Why not take a stab at Kilpatrick?" Only one full-length treatment of his life existed — written fifteen years before his death — and I thought this controversial educator deserved a reexamination and reassessment after almost fifty years.

Two strokes of good fortune got my project off to an exceptional start. First, Kilpatrick's sealed diaries had just become available through Milbank Memorial Library at Teachers College. Second, through a bit of detective work, I located the two grandsons of Kilpatrick (and later his granddaughter), one of whom was the family genealogist. Work on the diaries began, primary and secondary sources were read, and the list of those I needed to interview took shape. The fascinating women and men I met in the process of writing this book were the major unexpected pleasure of this project.

I must first thank Susan F. Semel and Alan R. Sadovnik, editors of the Peter Lang series of which this volume is a part. Their confidence in this work, their informed suggestions about the manuscript, and the overall support they have provided were of inestimable help in bringing this work to fruition. The excellent work of Jacqueline Pavlovic at Peter Lang is noted for her outstanding management of the numerous details involved in the production of this book.

This treatment of Kilpatrick's life cannot be considered an authorized biography, in terms of a blessing bestowed or permission granted from the family. But the manu-

Library of Congress Cataloging-in-Publication Data

Beineke, John A.
And there were giants in the land: the life
of William Heard Kilpatrick / John A. Beineke.
p. cm. — (History of schools and schooling; 5)
Includes bibliographical references (p.).
1. Kilpatrick, William Heard, 1871–1965. 2. Educators—United States—Biography.
3. Progressive education—United States—History. I. Title.
II. Series: History of schools and schooling: v. 5.
LB875.K54B44   370'.92—dc21   97-8539
ISBN 0-8204-3773-5
ISSN 1089-0678

Die Deutsche Bibliothek-CIP-Einheitsaufnahme

Beineke, John A.:
And there were giants in the land: the life of William Heard Kilpatrick /
John A. Beineke. –New York; Washington, D.C./Baltimore;
Boston; Bern; Frankfurt am Main; Berlin; Vienna; Paris: Lang.
(History of schools and schooling; 5)
ISBN 0-8204-3773-5

Cover design by Nona Reuter.
Cover photograph of Kilpatrick in 1943 at George Peabody College, Nashville,
Tennessee, 1943. Photograph courtesy of Peabody Reflector, Vanderbilt University.

The paper in this book meets the guidelines for permanence and durability
of the Committee on Production Guidelines for Book Longevity
of the Council of Library Resources.

© 1998 Peter Lang Publishing, Inc., New York

Printed in the United States of America.

John A. Beineke

And there were giants in the land

THE LIFE OF
WILLIAM HEARD KILPATRICK

PETER LANG
New York • Washington, D.C./Baltimore • Boston
Bern • Frankfurt am Main • Berlin • Vienna • Paris

History of Schools and Schooling

Alan R. Sadovnik and Susan F. Semel
General Editors

Vol. 5

PETER LANG
New York • Washington, D.C./Baltimore • Boston
Bern • Frankfurt am Main • Berlin • Vienna • Paris

*And there were
giants in the land*

To my wife, Debbie;
and my three children,
Eric, Colin, and Kaitlin

Why didn't you eat last night? (Example A)

PAST

NIGHT

YOU

EAT

NOT

WHY

Why didn't you eat last night? (Example B)

PAST	NIGHT	WHY

YOU	EAT	NOT

Which do you want, coffee or tea? (Example A)

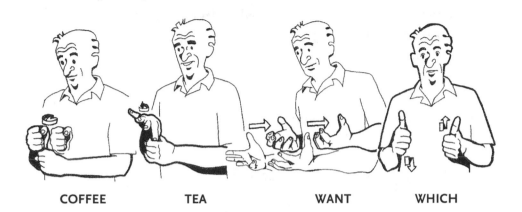

| COFFEE | TEA | WANT | WHICH |

Which do you want, coffee or tea? (Example B)

| WANT | WHICH | COFFEE | TEA |

Naturally the signer makes a questioning facial expression when using these *wh-* sign questions.

Do not use a *wh-* sign in statements that do not ask questions. In English, for example, we may make such statements as, "When I say 'frog,' jump!" or "Where there is smoke there is fire." In these statements the *wh-* word does not ask a question; therefore, *wh-* signs are not used. A different way of making the statement is used.

3. Rhetorical Questions (RHQ). This type of question does not require an answer. For example, "What's in a name?" and "You know why he won't go? I'll tell you why." In English, an RHQ is usually used to set off or emphasize a point, but in ASL it is used much more frequently.

I didn't go because it rained.

I

GO TO

NOT

WHY

RAIN

I flew./I went by airplane.

I   GO TO

HOW   AIRPLANE

4. Negative Questions. These are questions such as "Don't you understand?" or "Why didn't you tell me?" Ask them the same way you would a yes/no or a *wh-* sign question, but put in some form of negation. Usually you just shake your head as you ask the question, but you may add a sign of negation as well.

Why didn't you tell me?

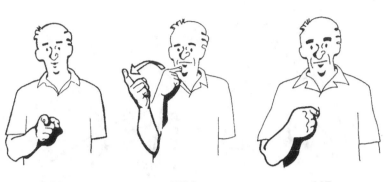

YOU   TELL   ME

NOT   WHY

Statements That Do Not Ask Questions

1. Simple Statements. These are called "simple" because they are signed exactly the way they are spoken in English. Some examples are "I know you," "You tell me," "He loves you," "She likes movies." They have what is called the subject-verb-object arrangement.

I know you.

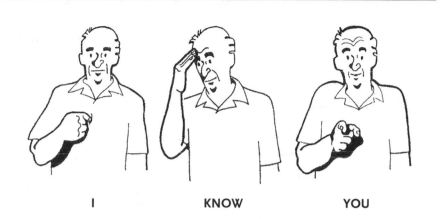

I	KNOW	YOU

You tell me.

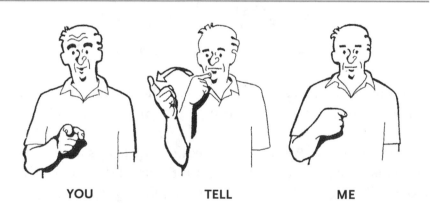

YOU	TELL	ME

She likes movies.

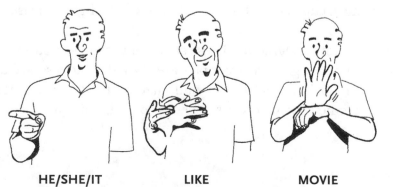

HE/SHE/IT	LIKE	MOVIE

2. Complex Statements. These are called "complex" because they involve two objects and are *not* signed exactly the way they are spoken in English. In the statement "You give me the book," the subject is "you," the first object is "me," and the second object is "book."

You give me the book.

BOOK   GIVE ME

More explanation about how to make these complex statements is given in the next section, "Stringing the Signs Together."

3. Commands or Requests. The command tells someone to do something. Some examples are "Shut the door!" "Get out of here!" "Keep off the grass!" Generally speaking the signs are made vigorously and are accompanied by a frown (lowered eyebrows).

The request differs from the command only in that it is followed by the sign PLEASE and there is no frown. Some examples are "Bring me a cup of coffee, please," "Turn off the lights, please."

4. Exclamatory Statements. These statements express a strong reaction to something. Some examples are "What!" (surprise), "Ouch!" (pain), "Yahoo!" (elation), "Far out!" (admiration). As in English, these statements usually consist of only one sign in ASL.

Stringing the Signs Together

The fascinating part of any language is learning how to put the words together correctly to make a statement. The way words are strung together is the syntax of a language. Except for simple statements, commands, requests, and exclamatory statements, ASL differs considerably from English in syntax.

First, we need to deal with the concept of topicalization, which means that a statement begins with a topic. The topic may be a person, a thing, an action, or an event. In the example used earlier, "You give me the book," the topic is *the book*. If we topicalize this statement in English, it comes out "The book, you give it to me." Although there is nothing wrong with saying it this way, it sounds awkward to our ears because we are not used to topicalizing in English. The statement "Do you see the woman in the red hat?" if topicalized, comes out "The woman in the red hat, do you see her?" The topic here is *the woman*, a person. "I enjoy going for long walks" comes out "Going for long walks, I enjoy them." Here the topic is *going for long walks*, an activity. "It was a long and difficult test" comes out "The test, it was long and difficult." The topic is *the test*, an event.

The topic of a statement is always followed by the comment. In the above examples, the comments are *you give it to me*, *in the red hat*, *I enjoy them*, and *it was long and difficult*.

Topic-Comment Statements

To topicalize a statement in ASL, you must first identify the topic and the comment. Because this is something you are not used to doing, it may appear difficult, but with practice it becomes easier. Topic-comment statements fall into one of several categories, which makes them easier to identify. Let's look at these categories.

1. Descriptive Statements. In these statements the topic is described and the description is the comment. An example is "I bought a new, red car." The topic is *car*, the comment is *new, red, I bought*. In ASL, the color of an object usually takes precedence over other qualities, so the comment would be *red, new, I bought*. The signed statement comes out CAR RED NEW BUY ME. (We will talk more later about the pronoun *me* coming after the verb *buy*.)

I bought a new red car.

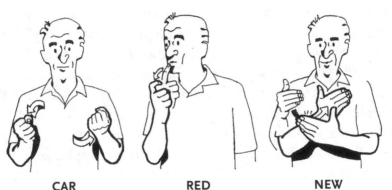

CAR   RED   NEW

BUY   ME

In the statement "I really enjoyed living in that big old house," the topic is *house* and the comment is *big, old, I really enjoyed living there*. In ASL, the size of an object generally comes first, and the emotional reaction comes last (more about this later, too). The statement is signed HOUSE BIG OLD LIVE THERE ENJOY ME TRUE.

I really enjoyed living in that big old house.

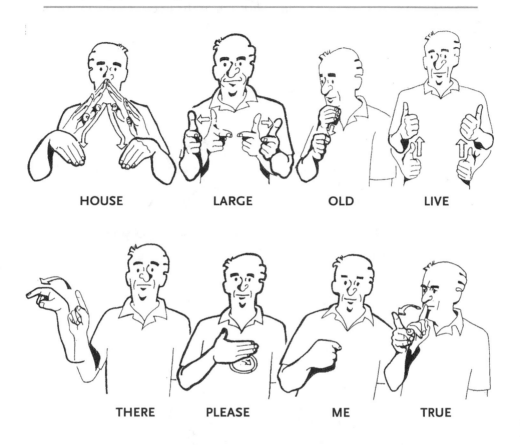

| HOUSE | LARGE | OLD | LIVE |

| THERE | PLEASE | ME | TRUE |

2. Cause and Effect or Stimulus-Response Statements. In real life, you cannot have an effect without first having a cause, or a response without first having a stimulus. I cannot, for example, scream before a safe falls out of the sky and lands a few feet from me. Neither could I yell "Ouch!" before stubbing my toe on a chair leg. The safe (the cause) must fall first, and the stubbing of my toe (the stimulus) must happen first. The cause/stimulus in these kinds of statements is the topic, the effect/response is the comment.

In the statement "I'm scared of thunder and lightning," the cause/stimulus is *thunder and lightning,* and the effect/response is *scared of.*

I'm scared of thunder and lightning.

LIGHTNING   SHAKE

SCARE   I

In the statement "I felt better after I took the medicine," the cause/stimulus is *took the medicine,* and the effect/response is *felt better.*

I felt better after I took the medicine.

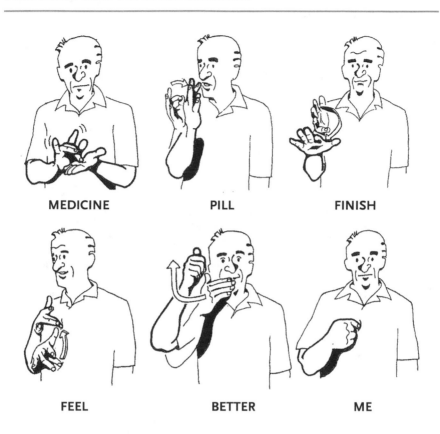

MEDICINE   PILL   FINISH

FEEL   BETTER   ME

3. Statements That Require Real-Time Sequencing. "Real-time sequencing" means that the events in a statement must be arranged in the chronological order in which they occurred in real life, another way of saying that the cause/stimulus must come before the effect/response.

In the statement "I was happy that no one was hurt when the plane landed safely," the events are not in chronological order. Rearranged to conform to real-time sequencing, the statement reads, "When the plane landed safely and no one was hurt, I was happy." Picture the scene in your mind as if you were watching it happen.

First you see the plane land, then you see everyone get out and that no one is hurt, and then you feel happy.

I was happy that no one was hurt when the plane landed safely.

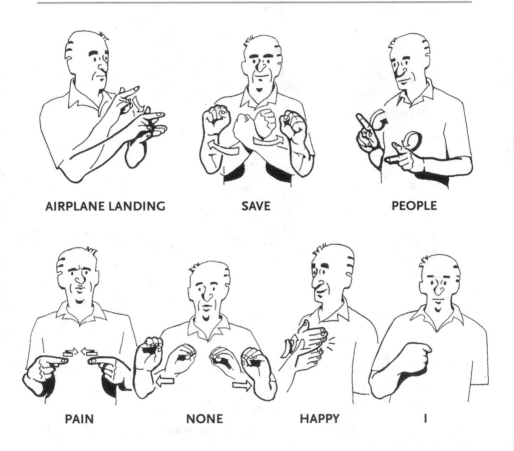

AIRPLANE LANDING   SAVE   PEOPLE

PAIN   NONE   HAPPY   I

4. Statements That Move from General to Specific. These statements require that you visualize the whole scene, just as you did with the airplane, but this time you move from the large to the small. An example is "There's an old man in the white house on that farm."

First see the whole picture of a farm with a white house on it; then move in closer to see an old man in the house.

There's an old man in the white house on that farm.

FARM   THERE   HOUSE

WHITE   IN   MAN   OLD

Another example is "I was exhausted by the time I arrived at the hotel in New York." Start with the largest thing, "New York"; then work down to the next largest thing, "hotel." The next largest thing after "hotel" is "I." See yourself arriving at the hotel and then feeling exhausted.

I was exhausted by the time I arrived at the hotel in New York.

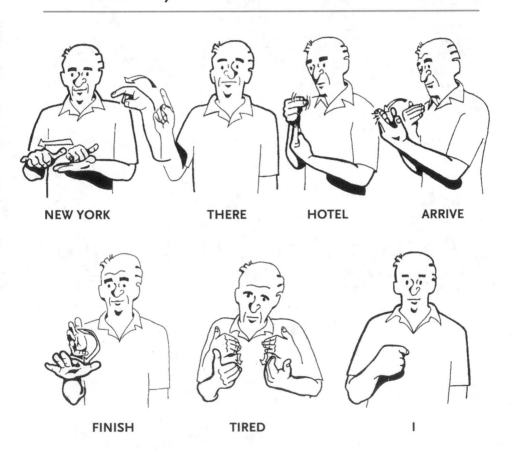

NEW YORK   THERE   HOTEL   ARRIVE

FINISH   TIRED   I

Your success in putting the signs in the correct order, as you probably can tell by now, lies in your ability to imagine, to visualize a scene. ASL is, after all, a visual language, so you must develop this skill.

Pronouns

Pronoun signs tend to come before verbs, at the end of statements, and often in both positions. As a rule, they tend to appear at the end of a statement more often than at the beginning, but this rule is honored as much in the breaking as in the keeping of it. As a result, you will not be wrong if you put it in either or both places.

All the pronouns may be expressed by just three hand shapes. The first group is made up of the pointing pronouns. Simply point to get: *I, me, you, he, she, him, her, it.*

The second group is the possessive pronouns:

MY

HIS/HER/ITS

YOUR

OUR

The third group is the self pronouns:

MYSELF

HIMSELF/HERSELF/ITSELF

YOURSELF

OURSELVES

Third person plural pronouns move in a very small arc:

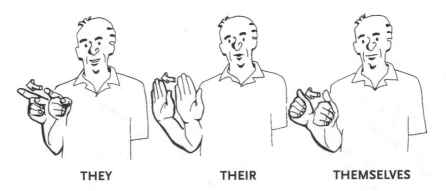

THEY   **THEIR**   **THEMSELVES**

First and second person singular pointing pronouns tend to come at the end of a statement:

I want to go to the movie.

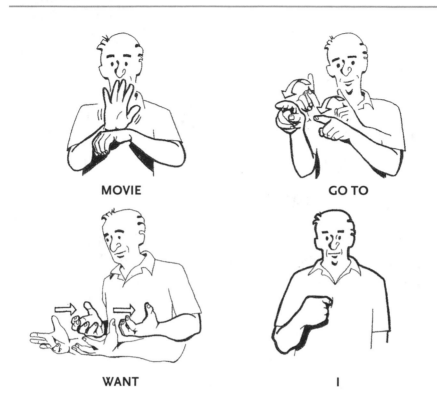

MOVIE

GO TO

WANT

I

Sometimes the first and second person singular point pronoun is dropped entirely, especially in questions:

Do you like to watch TV?

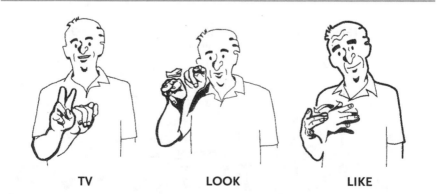

TV

LOOK

LIKE

I told him/her.

TELL   FINISH

The statement above is a simple declarative statement of fact, so you may assume the subject is "I." If the intent were "You told him," then the sentence would be:

You told him/her.

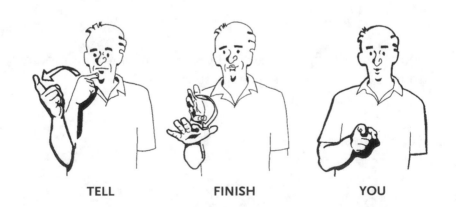

TELL   FINISH   YOU

The second person singular pointing pronoun is usually dropped in questions, as here:

Did you tell him/her?

TELL	**FINISH**

If the intent here were "Did I tell him?" then it would be signed:

Did I tell him/her?

TELL	**FINISH**	**I**

Command forms rarely use pronouns:

Tell him/her!

TELL

Negation

The most common way to negate a statement in ASL is to shake the head while you are making a sign. For example, to say "I do not understand," shake your head as you sign "I understand." The shaking of the head negates the statement so that it means "I do not understand." This practice applies to nearly all signs, including negative signs themselves. If the signer adds NOT in the above statement, and simultaneously shakes the head, the negation is emphasized. We know that English grammar does not permit double negatives, but in Spanish one may say "Yo no sé nada," which literally means "I not know nothing." Spanish here may be compared to ASL, where one may sign UNDERSTAND NOTHING while shaking the head, thus creating a double negative.

In general, a negative sign follows the thing it negates. It may also come before, and it may come both before and after. For emphasis, however, it always follows the thing it negates. The latter is especially true in negative commands.

She tells me nothing.

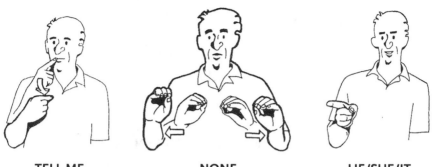

| TELL ME | NONE | HE/SHE/IT |

I didn't tell him.

| TELL | NOT | I |

You can't go.

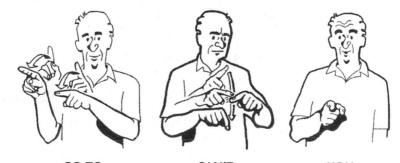

| GO TO | CAN'T | YOU |

Many signs have negation built into them:

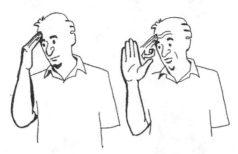

KNOW   **DON'T KNOW**

LIKE   **DON'T LIKE**

WANT   **DON'T WANT**

The signer should always shake the head while simultaneously making the negative form of the sign.

More Final Signs

In addition to the final position of the pronoun, there are other signs that tend to appear in the final position. For example,

I want to go to the movies tomorrow.

TOMORROW MOVIE GO TO

WANT I

The WANT sign comes after the verb because it belongs to a class of signs that expresses obligation, necessity, feelings, moods, states of mind, and intentions. Some other signs in this class are HOPE, CAN, MUST, and WILL. They do not always follow the verb, sometimes they precede it, and often they appear both before and after the verb.

I hope it clears up this afternoon.

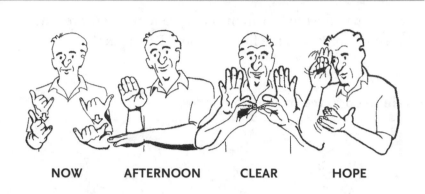

NOW   AFTERNOON   CLEAR   HOPE

Can you read lips?

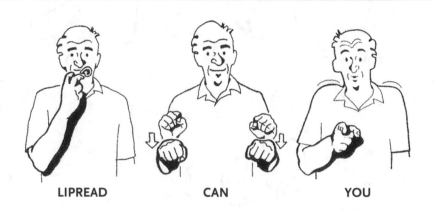

LIPREAD   CAN   YOU

The WILL sign is often confusing because it expresses both future tense and intention.

I will never tell.

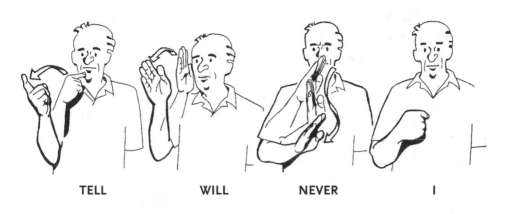

| TELL | WILL | NEVER | I |

A final word about signs in the final position is that if you want to emphasize something, put it at or near the end of the statement. The last thing seen is the thing best remembered.

Plurals

Often signs are repeated or moved in a way that shows plurality.

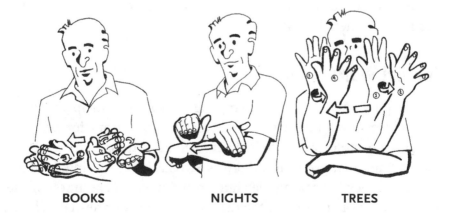

| BOOKS | NIGHTS | TREES |

When a sign does not lend itself to this kind of repetition or pluralizing movement, then signers use such signs as MANY, FEW, and SOME, or they use specific numbers such as NINE or FIFTY.

Names and Titles

When deaf people are talking to each other they rarely use each other's names. For example, "How are you, Bob?" becomes simply, "How you?" If, however, the signer asks the watcher about another person, then the signer uses that person's name. ("How is Bob?")

A person's name must be fingerspelled, but most deaf people also have name-signs. A name-sign is one that stands for that person, not for the name. Two people with the same name will have different name-signs. When you first meet a deaf person, you fingerspell your name. You tell him or her your name-sign only if he or she asks. Usually name-signs are not asked for until the relationship develops beyond that of a casual acquaintance.

Titles such as "Mrs.," "Dr.," and "Rev." are fingerspelled and used only when the person is being introduced. You never use them when you are talking directly to the person. "How are you, Dr. Smith?" becomes simply "How you?"

Articles

A discussion of articles (*a, an, the*) in American Sign Language is beyond the scope of this book. Please refer to a book on ASL linguistics for more detailed information.

A Final Word

The acquisition of a spoken language involves principally learning grammar, pronunciation, and vocabulary. Except for pronunciation, the same applies to learning ASL. Forming signs clearly is the equivalent of pronunciation in ASL. Clarity in signing depends upon accuracy in making the sign, smoothness in execution of the sign, flow from one sign to the next without jerky or hesitant movements, the use of facial expressions, the use of head and body movements, and the proper use of space. The only way to develop these is through using the language with deaf people. They will correct you when you err, and by watching them carefully you will correct and fine-tune yourself.

Greetings, Salutations, and Everyday Expressions

Hello.

HELLO

Good morning.

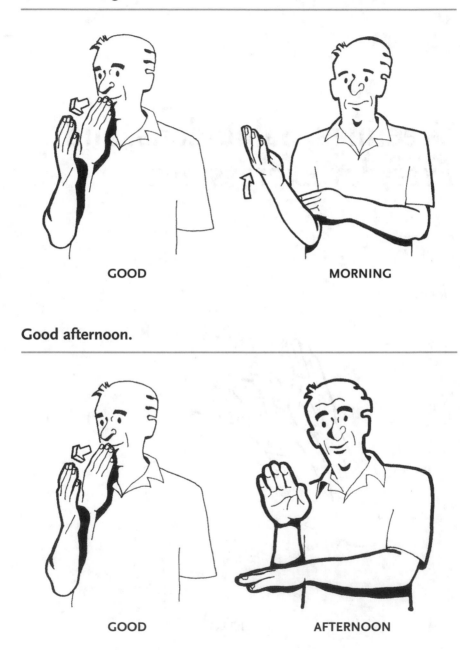

GOOD   MORNING

Good afternoon.

GOOD   AFTERNOON

Good night.

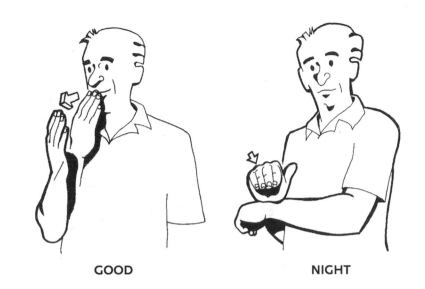

GOOD   NIGHT

How are you?

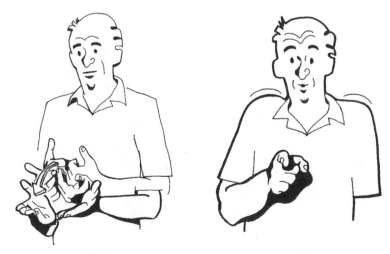

HOW   YOU

How have you been?

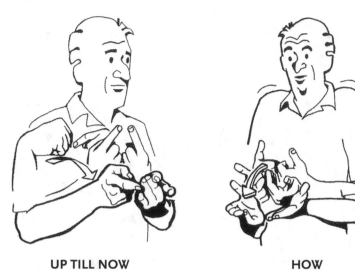

UP TILL NOW   HOW

I'm glad to see you.

HAPPY   SEE

See you later.

SEE   LATER

Good-bye.

GOOD-BYE

I feel fine.

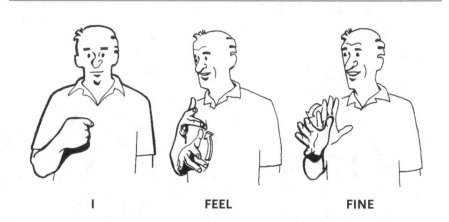

| I | FEEL | FINE |

Additional vocabulary

| SICK | TIRED | LOUSY |

ALL RIGHT   WONDERFUL

I haven't seen you for a long time. (Example A)

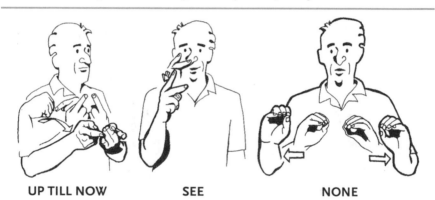

| SEE | NONE | LONG | TIME |

I haven't seen you for a long time. (Example B)

| UP TILL NOW | SEE | NONE |

Thank you.

GOOD

Please.

PLEASE

No, thank you.

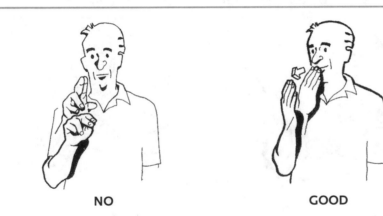

NO   **GOOD**

Pardon me.

EXCUSE

Where is the restroom?

TOILET

WHERE

Close the door.

CLOSE DOOR

Open the door.

OPEN DOOR

Close the window.

CLOSE WINDOW

Open the window.

OPEN WINDOW

Do you like to watch TV?

TV   LOOK   LIKE

Do you want to go to the movies?

MOVIE   GO TO   WANT

What's your phone number?

PHONE NUMBER WHAT SHRUG

Do you have a TTY?

Note: The TTY or TDD is a device that permits one to type messages back and forth over the telephone.

T-T-Y HAVE

Do you have a car?

CAR   HAVE

May I go with you?

I   WITH

Have a seat, please.

SIT

PLEASE

What time is it?

TIME

I have to go home.

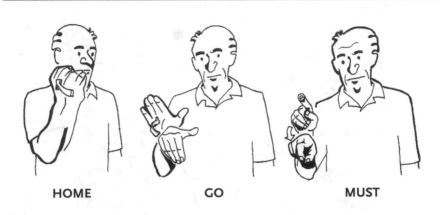

HOME   GO   MUST

Where are you going?

GOING   WHERE

I'm sorry.

SORRY

Have a nice Thanksgiving.

HAVE   **NICE**   **THANKSGIVING (1)**   **THANKSGIVING (2)**

Merry Christmas.

Note: For Christmas Eve, the word *Eve* is fingerspelled.

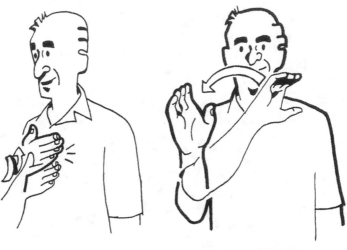

HAPPY   CHRISTMAS

Happy Hanukkah.

HAPPY   HANUKKAH

Happy New Year.

Note: For New Year's Eve, the word *Eve* is fingerspelled.

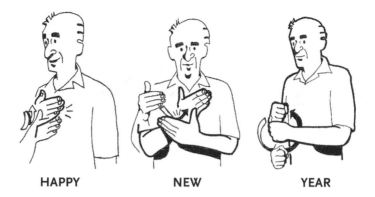

| HAPPY | NEW | YEAR |

Happy birthday.

| HAPPY | BIRTH | DAY |

4

Signing and Deafness

I'm learning sign language.

The sign LANGUAGE is usually not signed in this expression, so that it reads literally: "I am learning to sign."

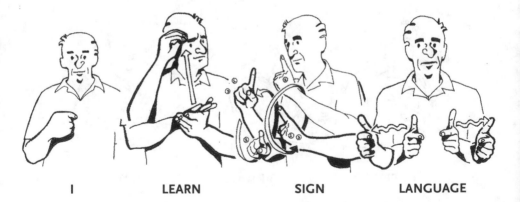

I   LEARN   SIGN   LANGUAGE

Sign slowly, please.

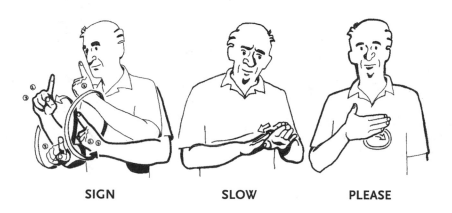

SIGN   SLOW   PLEASE

Please repeat.

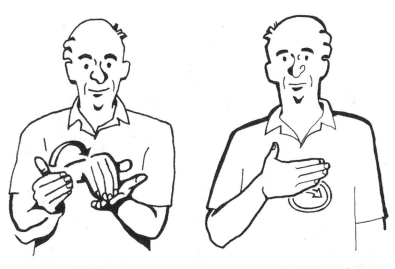

AGAIN   PLEASE

I can't fingerspell well.

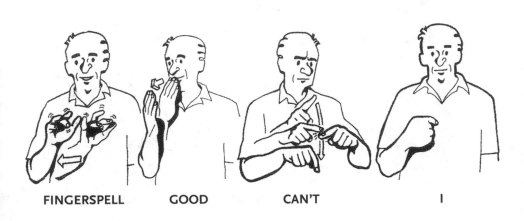

FINGERSPELL   GOOD   CAN'T   I

I can fingerspell, but I can't read it well.

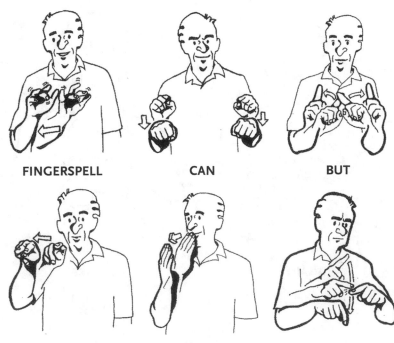

FINGERSPELL   CAN   BUT

READ   GOOD   CAN'T

You sign fast.

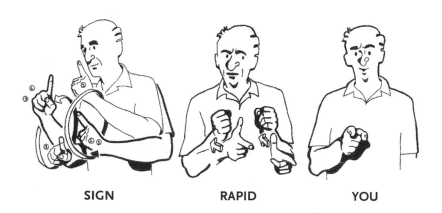

SIGN   RAPID   YOU

I don't understand.

UNDERSTAND

Would you write it, please?

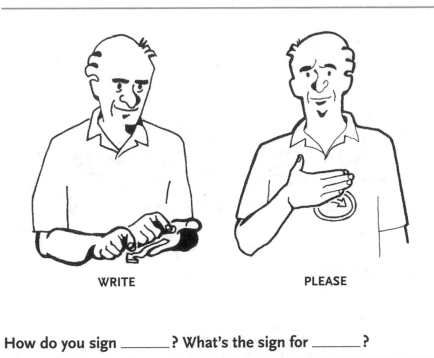

WRITE   PLEASE

How do you sign _____? What's the sign for _____?

Ask these questions by pointing to whatever it is you want to know the sign for or by fingerspelling the word.

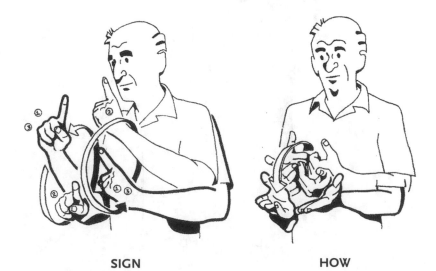

SIGN   HOW

There's no sign for that; you have to fingerspell it.

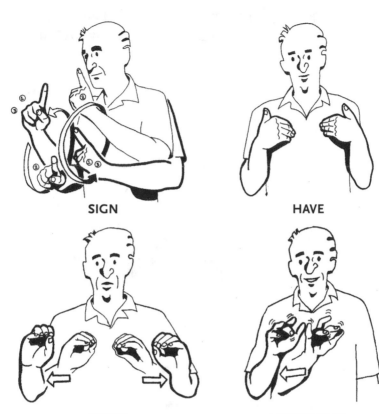

SIGN   HAVE

NONE   FINGERSPELL

MUST

What does _____ mean?

To ask this question, first make the sign of whatever it is that you want to know the meaning of, then sign MEAN WHAT SHRUG.

MEAN

WHAT SHRUG

Are you deaf?

Either way of signing "deaf" is acceptable, but deaf people use the first one shown below more often than the second one.

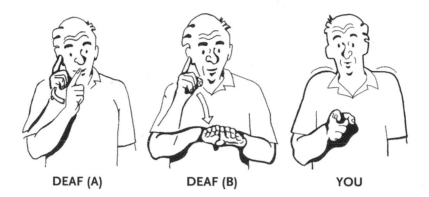

DEAF (A)   DEAF (B)   YOU

I'm not deaf, I'm hearing.

Hearing people are referred to as "speaking" people.

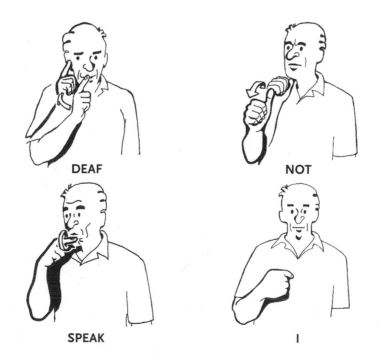

DEAF   NOT

SPEAK   I

I'm hard of hearing.

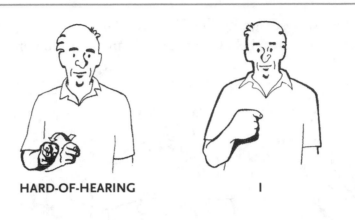

HARD-OF-HEARING   **I**

Do you use a hearing aid?

The first two signs for "hearing aid" shown here represent the kind of aid that is attached by a cord to a unit worn on the body. The third kind is the type worn behind the ear.

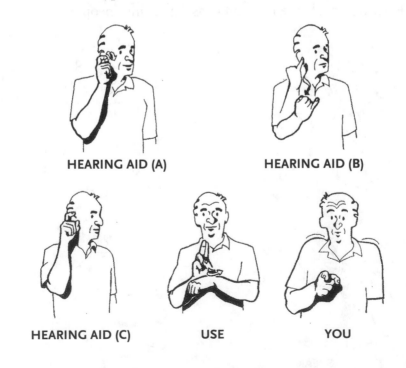

HEARING AID (A)   **HEARING AID (B)**

HEARING AID (C)   **USE**   **YOU**

Can you read lips?

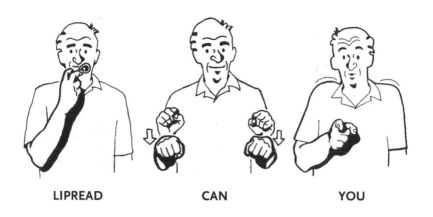

LIPREAD   CAN   YOU

I speak a little.

SPEAK   LITTLE BIT

How did you lose your hearing?

HEAR　　　　　　　LOSE　　　　　　　HOW

How old were you when you became deaf?

BECOME　　　　　　DEAF

OLD

HOW MANY

I was born deaf.

BIRTH   DEAF

Are your parents deaf?

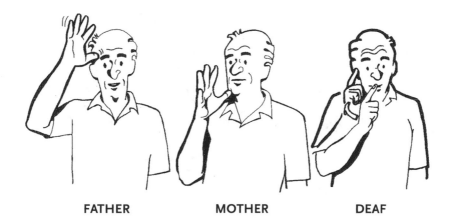

FATHER   MOTHER   DEAF

I want to visit the club for deaf people.

Fingerspell CLUB at the beginning of this sentence. It is not necessary to sign "for deaf people," because the word *club* implies that.

C-L-U-B   VISIT   WANT   I

I enjoy TV with captions.

TV   SENTENCE   PLEASE   I

I saw a captioned film last night.

Note: See Chapter 18 for more phrases on open and closed captioning.

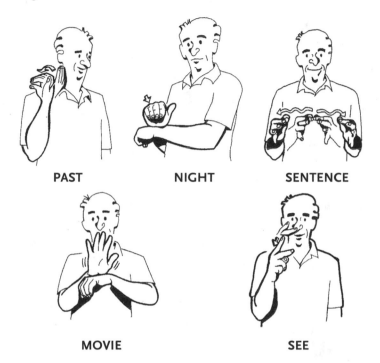

PAST   NIGHT   SENTENCE

MOVIE   SEE

Did you go to a residential school for deaf children?

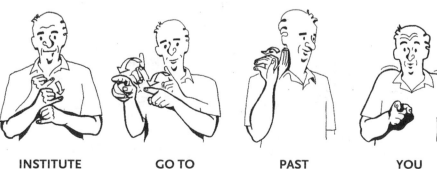

INSTITUTE   GO TO   PAST   YOU

I went to a school for hearing children.

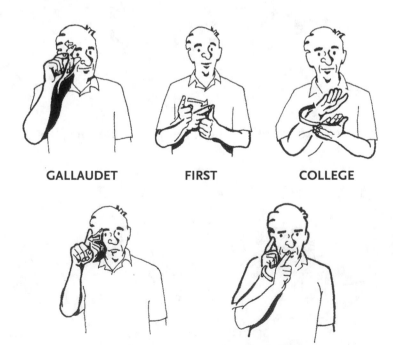

SPEAK   SCHOOL   I

Gallaudet was the first college for deaf people.

Note: Gallaudet is now a university and is the world's only liberal arts university for the deaf.

GALLAUDET   FIRST   COLLEGE

FOR   DEAF

Many deaf students enter hearing colleges.

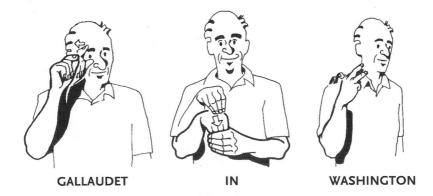

| MANY | DEAF | LEARN | AGENT |

| ENTER | SPEAK | COLLEGE |

Gallaudet University is in Washington, D.C.

Sometimes the letters "D-C" are fingerspelled after the sign for "Washington."

| GALLAUDET | IN | WASHINGTON |

Getting Acquainted

What is your name?

NAME   WHAT SHRUG

My name is _____.

Fingerspell your name.

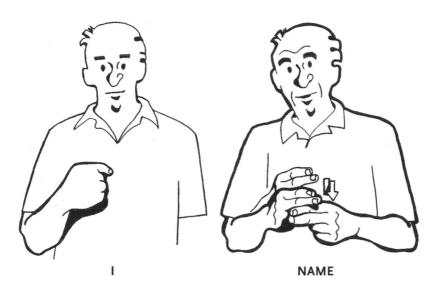

I   NAME

I'm happy to meet you.

HAPPY   MEET

Where do you live?

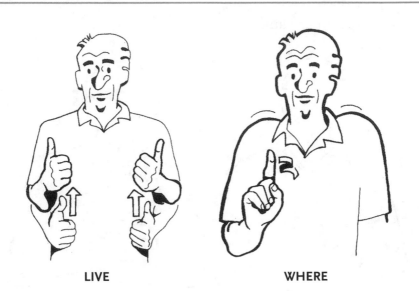

LIVE   WHERE

Where are you from?

FROM   WHERE

Where were you born?

BIRTH WHERE

May I introduce my wife?

After making the sign for the person you are introducing, you then fingerspell that person's name.

INTRODUCE WIFE

Additional vocabulary

HUSBAND   SON

DAUGHTER   FRIEND

Where do you work?

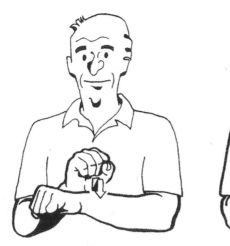

WORK   WHERE

What kind of work do you do?

WORK   MAJOR   WHAT SHRUG

I'm a doctor.

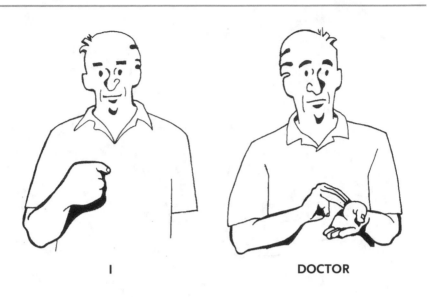

I   DOCTOR

Additional vocabulary

The AGENT sign is often added to a verb or noun sign to indicate that one does or is what the verb or noun sign says. Here the AGENT sign could be added to TEACH, LAW, ACT, and ART, but would not be added to DOCTOR, POLICE, HOMEMAKER, or FIREFIGHTER. The use of the AGENT sign is optional.

LAW   TEACH

ACT

ART

AGENT

FIREFIGHTER

POLICE

Homemaker

Note: To sign "househusband," use the signs for HOUSE and HUSBAND (see page 112). The phrase below cannot be used for a househusband.

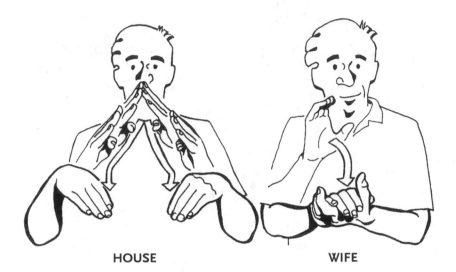

HOUSE   WIFE

Do you go to school?

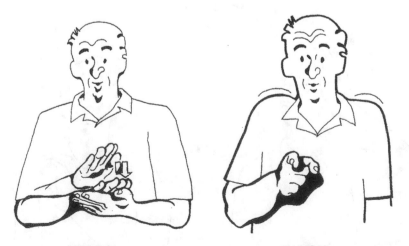

SCHOOL   YOU

Are you married?

MARRY   YOU

I'm single.

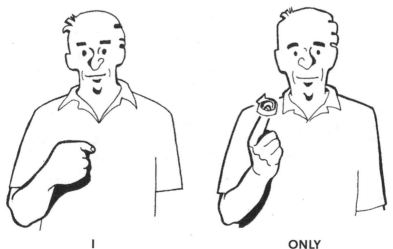

I   ONLY

I'm divorced.

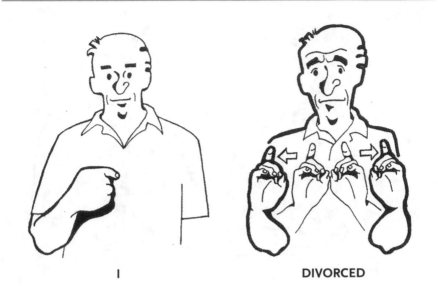

I   DIVORCED

My husband/wife is dead.

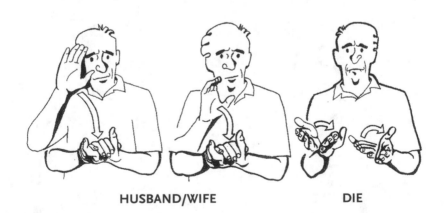

HUSBAND/WIFE   DIE

Do you have any children?

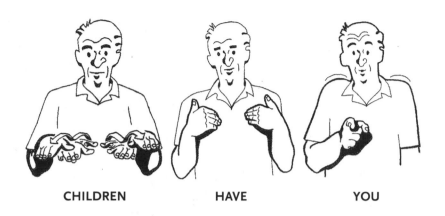

CHILDREN   HAVE   YOU

How many children do you have?

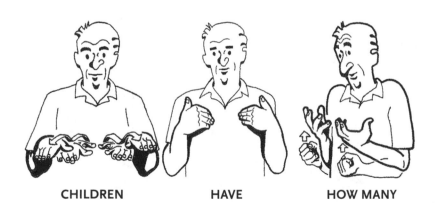

CHILDREN   HAVE   HOW MANY

How old are you?

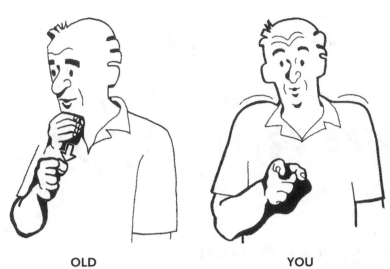

OLD   YOU

Do you mind if I smoke?

SMOKE CIGARETTE   COMPLAIN

It's all right. It's OK.

ALL RIGHT

Smoking is not allowed.

SMOKE CIGARETTE **PROHIBIT**

Health

How do you feel?

HOW

FEEL

Do you feel all right?

FEEL   ALL RIGHT

I don't feel well.

FEEL   GOOD   NOT

Where does it hurt?

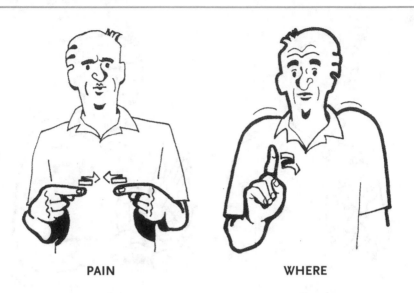

PAIN   WHERE

My stomach is upset.

When done alone, as it is done here, this sign may also mean that something is disgusting. Context determines which meaning is intended.

DISGUST

I have a cold.

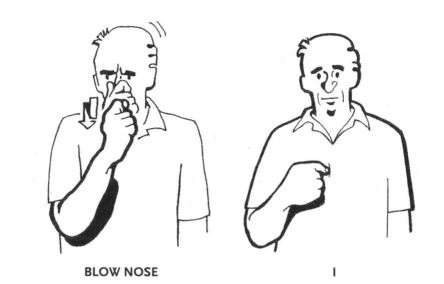

BLOW NOSE   I

My nose is runny.

RUNNY NOSE   I

My head aches.

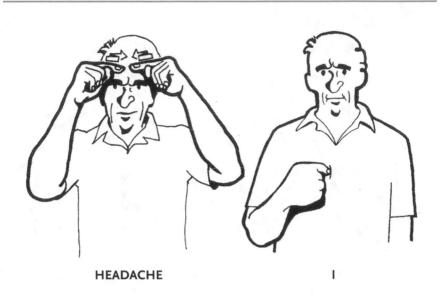

HEADACHE   I

I have a toothache.

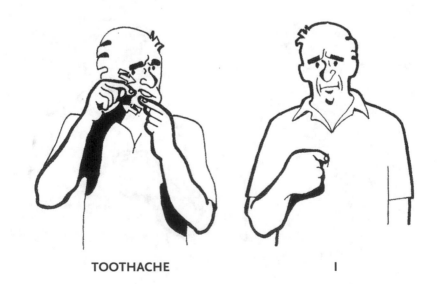

TOOTHACHE   I

I have a stomachache.

The sign PAIN may be placed anywhere on the body to denote that you are hurt or have a pain in that part of the body.

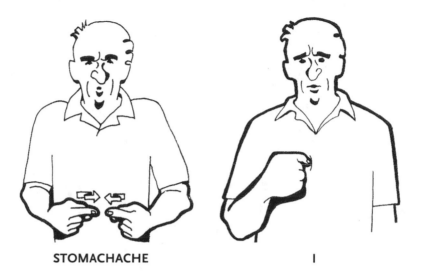

STOMACHACHE   I

I need a dentist/doctor.

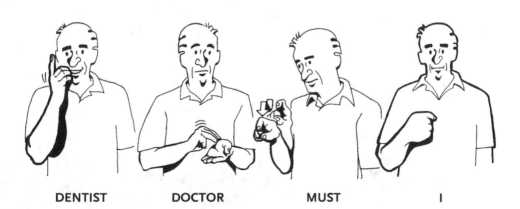

DENTIST   DOCTOR   MUST   I

Do you have any aspirin?

Fingerspell ASPIRIN.

A-S-P-I-R-I-N

HAVE

I've run out of medicine.

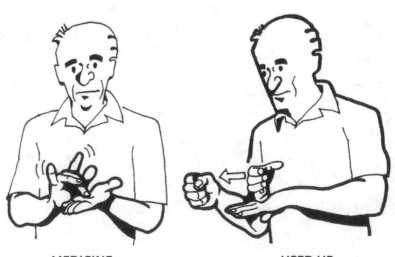

MEDICINE   **USED UP**

I have to buy some medicine.

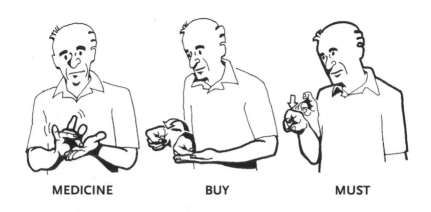

MEDICINE   BUY   MUST

I have to take pills.

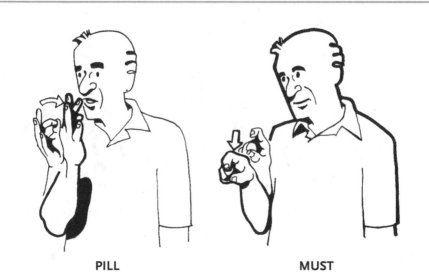

PILL   MUST

You need to have an x-ray.

Fingerspell X-RAY.

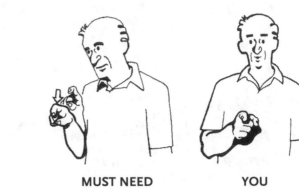

X-R-A-Y

MUST NEED	YOU

It's time to take your temperature.

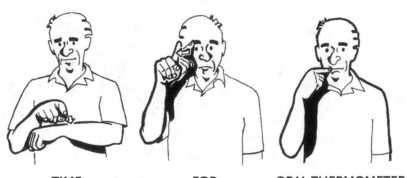

TIME	FOR	ORAL THERMOMETER

You have to have a shot.

The MUST sign may mean "need" or "should" and is done differently depending upon the meaning desired. If something is mandatory, then make one movement down. If something is optional but desirable, then make two gentle downward movements.

| HYPODERMIC | MUST NEED | YOU |

I feel better now.

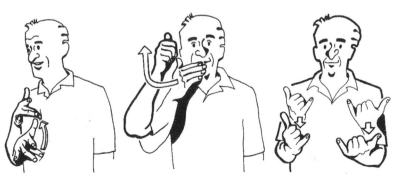

| FEEL | BETTER | NOW |

I was in bed for two weeks.

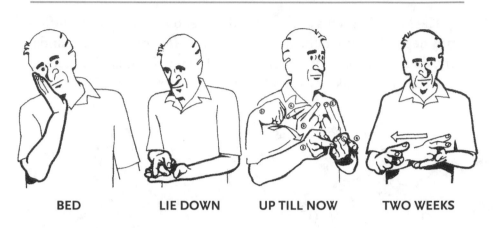

BED   LIE DOWN   UP TILL NOW   TWO WEEKS

Were any bones broken?

There is no standard sign for "bone," so the statement here is more generally read as, "Is anything in your body broken?" If you wish to sign "bone" specifically, then you must fingerspell it or find out what the local sign for it is.

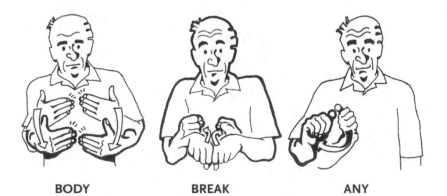

BODY   BREAK   ANY

You lost a lot of blood.

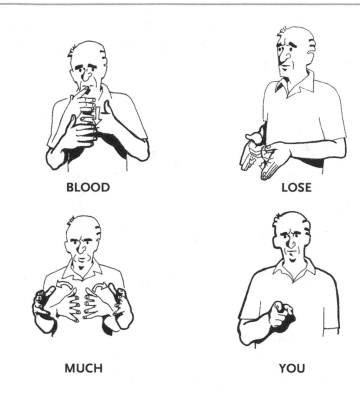

BLOOD

LOSE

MUCH

YOU

They have to draw some blood.

DRAW BLOOD

MUST

Have you ever had a tooth pulled?

The signs PAST and FINISH both refer to the past. Either one may be used alone here, but it is very common to see them both appear in a statement.

PULL TOOTH   **PAST**   **FINISH**

I had a physical last week.

The use of the FINISH sign here denotes the idea that I "already" had a physical last week.

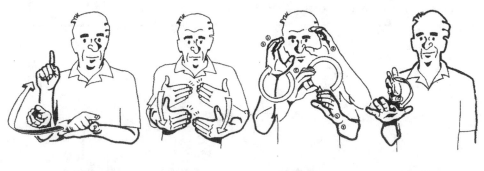

A WEEK AGO   **BODY**   **SEARCH**   **FINISH**

My husband had an operation.

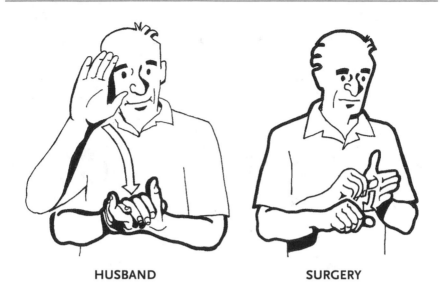

HUSBAND   SURGERY

My wife is in the hospital.

The HOSPITAL sign is made by drawing a cross on the sleeve.

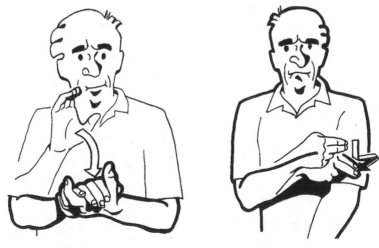

WIFE   HOSPITAL

My father passed away last month.

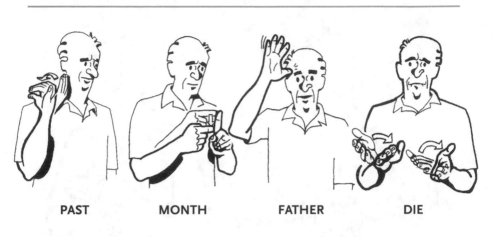

PAST MONTH FATHER DIE

Call the ambulance.

The sign for "ambulance" indicates the spinning red light on top of the vehicle and may refer to any emergency vehicle or just the flashing red light itself. Also, instead of the sign BECKON, you may sign PHONE.

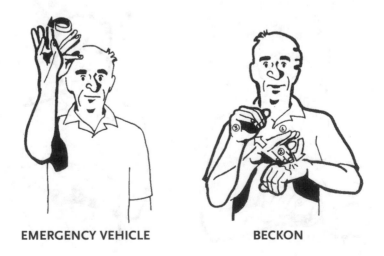

EMERGENCY VEHICLE BECKON

Do you have hospitalization insurance?

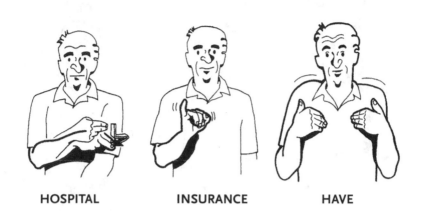

HOSPITAL INSURANCE HAVE

I have an appointment at 2:30.

APPOINTMENT TIME 2:30

Where's my toothbrush?

TOOTHBRUSH   MY   WHERE

I want to brush my teeth.

TOOTHBRUSH   WANT

I already took a bath/shower.

BATH   SHOWER   FINISH

Wash your hands.

This sign, shown in three steps, is a mime of actually washing the hands, as the sign at the top of page 140 is a mime of actually washing the face.

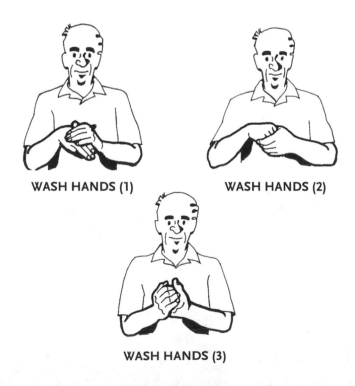

WASH HANDS (1)   WASH HANDS (2)

WASH HANDS (3)

Wash your face.

WASH FACE

I haven't shaved yet.

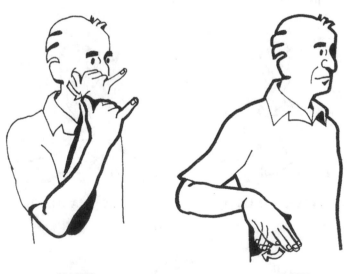

SHAVE   LATE

May I borrow your hair dryer?

HAIR DRYER

LEND

Brush your hair.

BRUSH HAIR

I lost my comb.

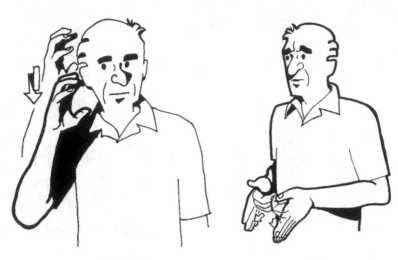

COMB   LOSE

Weather

It's beautiful today.

| NOW | DAY | PRETTY |

The sun is hot.

SUN   HOT

I enjoy sitting in the sun.

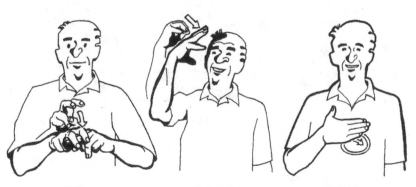

SIT   SUNRAY   PLEASE

It was cold this morning.

NOW   MORNING   COLD

It will freeze tonight.

NOW   NIGHT   ICE

Maybe it will snow tomorrow.

TOMORROW   SNOW   MAYBE

There was thunder and lightning last night.

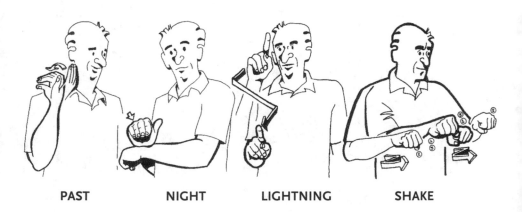

PAST   NIGHT   LIGHTNING   SHAKE

It rained yesterday.

YESTERDAY   RAIN

Do you have a raincoat?

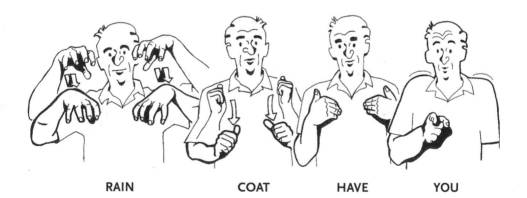

RAIN   COAT   HAVE   YOU

I lost my umbrella.

UMBRELLA

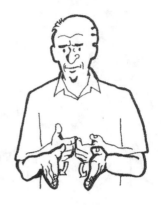

LOSE

Where are your galoshes/rubbers?

YOUR

GALOSHES (1)

GALOSHES (2)

RUBBER

WHERE

It's windy today.

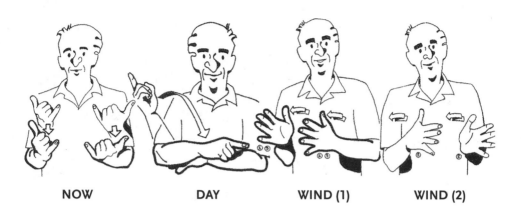

NOW   DAY   WIND (1)   WIND (2)

Yesterday evening at sunset, the clouds were beautiful.

YESTERDAY   LATE AFTERNOON   SUNSET

CLOUDS   PRETTY

I hope it clears up this afternoon.

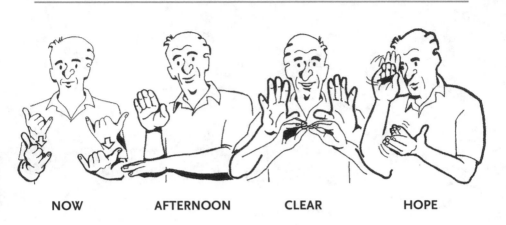

NOW   AFTERNOON   CLEAR   HOPE

I like spring/summer/autumn/winter best.

I   LIKE   GROW   SUMMER

AUTUMN   COLD   BEST

You have to have chains to drive in the mountains in winter.

DURING   COLD   CAR

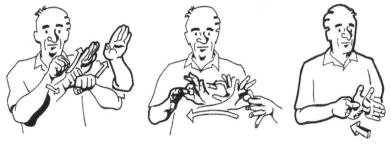

MOUNTAIN   CHAIN   REQUIRE

I'm afraid of tornados.

TORNADO   SCARE   ME

What's the temperature?

TEMPERATURE　　　　　　WHAT SHRUG

Has the snow melted?

SNOW　　　　　MELT　　　　　FINISH

There was a flood last year.

LAST YEAR   WATER   FLOOD

The temperature is below zero.

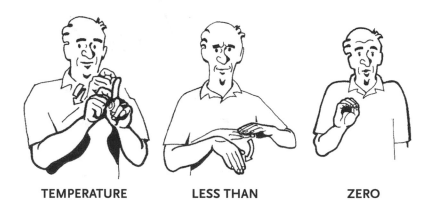

TEMPERATURE   LESS THAN   ZERO

Have you ever been in an earthquake?

EARTH

SHAKE

FINISH

YOU

8

Family

Your father is nice looking.

| YOUR | FATHER | FACE | NICE |

You look like your mother.

YOU   FACE   AS

YOUR

MOTHER

My brother is younger than I.

MY BROTHER YOUNGER

THAN I

My sister speaks several languages fluently.

The repetition of a sign, as SKILL is repeated here, is a common practice.

MY

SISTER

SKILL

TALK

FEW

LANGUAGE

SKILL

His son wants to be an astronaut.

HIS/HER/ITS   SON   AIM

ROCKET   AGENT

Her daughter works here.

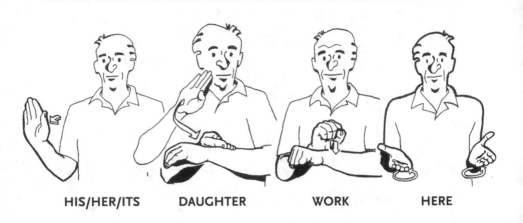

HIS/HER/ITS   DAUGHTER   WORK   HERE

My uncle is a farmer.

MY   UNCLE   FARM   AGENT

My aunt lives in town.

MY

AUNT

LIVE

THERE

CITY

Your nephew gave me a book.

YOUR   NEPHEW   GIVE ME   BOOK

His niece will help you.

HIS/HER/ITS   NIECE   SHE HELP YOU   WILL

Her grandfather gave her grandmother a book.

Normally the sign GRANDMOTHER would have been made with the right hand, but since the action of the GIVE sign moves from the signer's right to the signer's left, making the GRAND-MOTHER sign with the left hand makes it visually clearer who is on which side. (For further explanation, see the "Placement of Signs" section in Chapter 2.)

 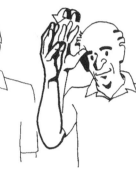 

HIS/HER   **GRANDFATHER**   **BOOK**

HE GIVES HER   **GRANDMOTHER**

My cousin is a pilot.

Note: American Sign Language distinguishes between male and female cousins: the signs are gender-specific. Here, the sign is for a male cousin. For a female cousin, use the same sign handshape but in a different location: the jaw area.

MY

COUSIN (MALE)

AIRPLANE

PILOT

Who is that man?

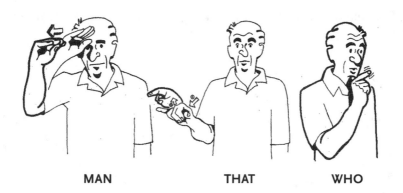

MAN   THAT   WHO

Did you see the woman?

WOMAN   SEE   FINISH

The baby is cute.

BABY   SWEET

The girl told the boy that she loves him.

The use of both hands in making the sign helps reinforce visually who is doing what to whom.

 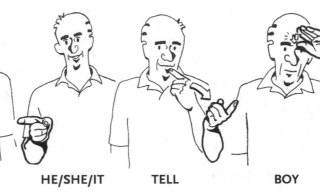

GIRL   HE/SHE/IT   TELL   BOY

HE/SHE/IT   LOVE   HIM/HER/IT

Father told the little boy to play outside.

The TELL sign moves downward to denote that the person being told is a child. The same thing occurs in the following sentence with the HER sign.

| FATHER | TELL | BOY |

| SHORT (height) | PLAY | OUT |

The little girl's doll is broken.

GIRL　　　　　SHORT (height)　　　　HIS/HER/ITS

DOLL

BREAK

How many children are coming?

CHILDREN   COME HERE   HOW MANY

Our family is large/small.

OUR   FAMILY   LARGE   SMALL

We had a family reunion last summer.

The idea "we had" is understood and therefore not signed.

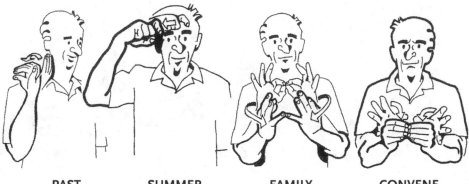

| PAST | SUMMER | FAMILY | CONVENE |

We met at Grandfather's farm.

| WE | CONVENE | GRANDFATHER |

FARM   THERE

Additional vocabulary

ADOPT (+ daughter/son/brother/sister)

FOSTER (+ children/daughter/son/brother/sister)*

STEP (+ father/mother/brother/sister)

*The same sign is used for FOSTER and FALSE; the context of the sentence will determine which concept is being conveyed.

HALF (+ brother/sister)

IN-LAW
(+ mother/father/daughter/son)

GAY

LESBIAN

PARTNER (A)

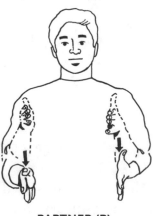

PARTNER (B)

School

Do you go to school? Are you in school?

SCHOOL

YOU

I go to college.

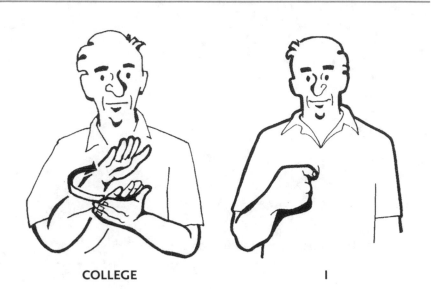

COLLEGE   I

I'm majoring in English.

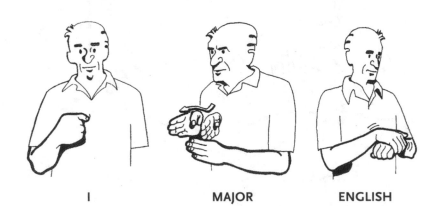

I   MAJOR   ENGLISH

Additional vocabulary for majors or courses of study

HISTORY

SCIENCE (Chemistry)

MATH

BUSY (Business)

ART

MUSIC

PSYCHOLOGY

ACT (Theater)

EDUCATION

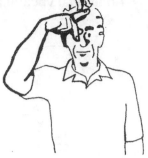

ADVISE (Counseling)   **HEALTH**   **PHILOSOPHY**

Special education

SPECIAL   **EDUCATION**

Physical therapy

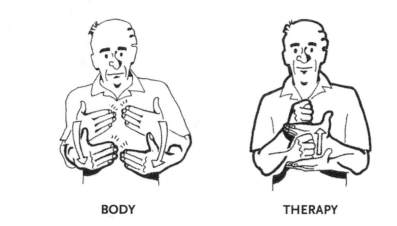

BODY   THERAPY

Computer science

The sign for "computer" varies a good deal around the country, so check it out with your local deaf people. See also Chapter 18, "Technology."

COMPUTER

Other academic fields are fingerspelled, either in full or in abbreviated form. "Physical Education" is "P-E," "Library Science" is "L-S," "Sociology" is "S-O-C," and so on.

What course are you taking this semester?

NOW   SEMESTER   LESSON

LESSON (rear view)   TAKE UP   WHAT SHRUG

I'm a student.

LEARN   AGENT   I

Additional vocabulary

PREP

FRESHMAN

SOPHOMORE

JUNIOR

SENIOR

GRADUATE

I graduated last year.

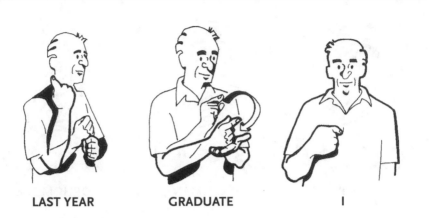

LAST YEAR   GRADUATE   I

I'm in graduate school now.

NOW   GRADUATE   SCHOOL   I

I like to study.

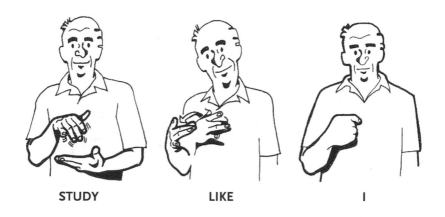

STUDY   LIKE   I

Where's the administration building?

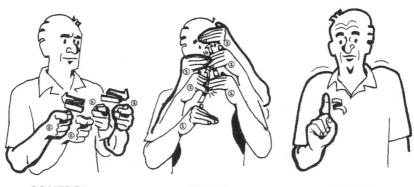

CONTROL   BUILD   WHERE

You've got to go to the library and do some research.

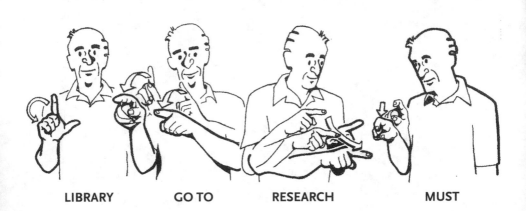

LIBRARY   GO TO   RESEARCH   MUST

I got an A on my paper.

PAPER   A

I studied all night.

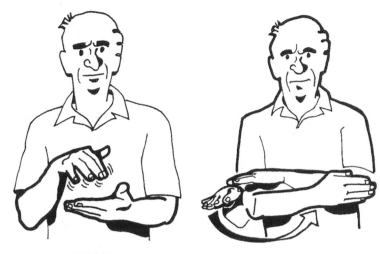

STUDY   ALL NIGHT

Where's my calculator?

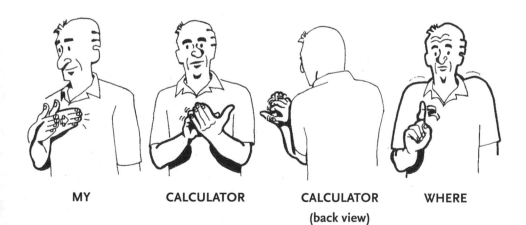

MY   CALCULATOR   CALCULATOR   WHERE
                                (back view)

My roommate and I live in a dorm.

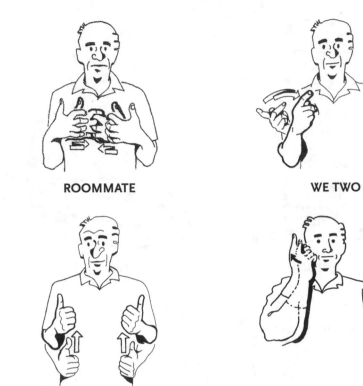

ROOMMATE

WE TWO

LIVE

DORM

I have a question.

QUERY

Did you ask him?

QUERY   FINISH   YOU

The teacher asked me a lot of questions.

The repetition of the QUERY sign using both hands indicates that many questions were asked.

TEACH   QUERY ME

No talking during the test.

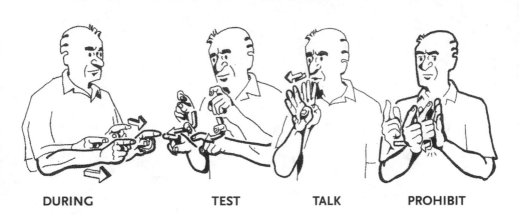

DURING   TEST   TALK   PROHIBIT

We have a test tomorrow.

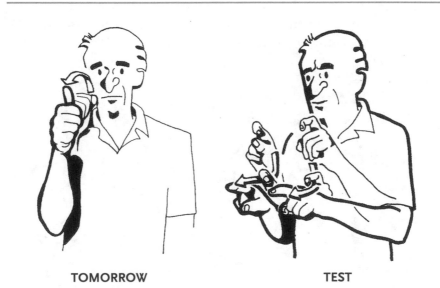

TOMORROW   TEST

Close your books.

CLOSE BOOK

Open your books.

OPEN BOOK

Begin writing.

WRITE   START

Stop writing.

WRITE   STOP

I lost my pencil.

The sign WRITE also stands for "pen," "pencil," and any other writing instrument.

WRITE   LOSE

Please don't erase the board.

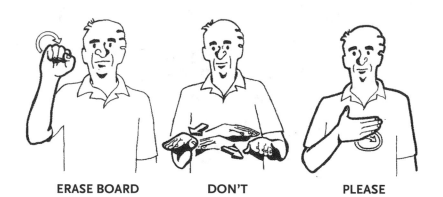

ERASE BOARD   DON'T   PLEASE

Did you pass or fail/flunk?

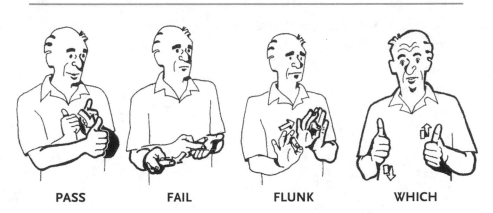

| PASS | FAIL | FLUNK | WHICH |

Any questions?

| QUERY ME | ANY |

You haven't turned in your paper to me yet.

In order to sign GIVE, reverse the movement of the GIVE ME sign.

PAPER   **GIVE ME**   **LATE**

She and I discussed it.

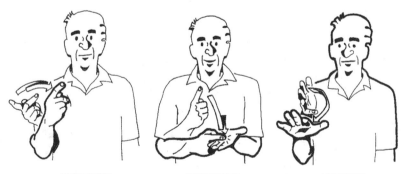

WE TWO   **DISCUSS**   **FINISH**

Let's take a break.

BREAK

When you've been absent, you must bring an excuse.

Conditional statements such as "When you've eaten, you may go" or "If you're good, I'll tell you" are usually changed to questions. In the sentence shown below, the ABSENT sign is made with a questioning expression.

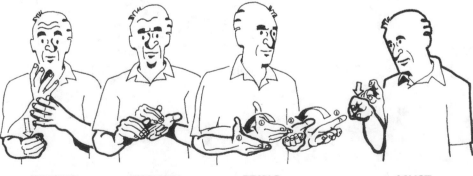

ABSENT   EXCUSE   BRING   MUST

Food and Drink

Have you eaten? Did you eat? Are you finished eating?

EAT   FINISH

I haven't eaten yet.

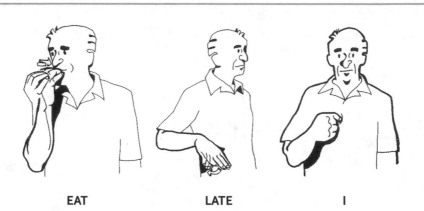

EAT   LATE   I

He eats too much.

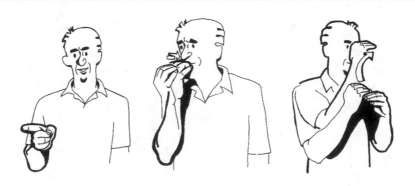

HE/SHE/IT   EAT   TOO MUCH

Are you hungry?

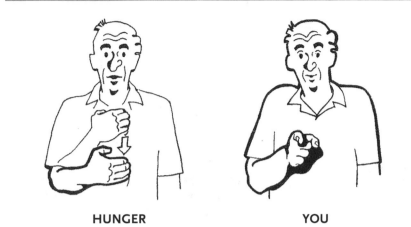

HUNGER   YOU

Let's you and I go to a restaurant.

YOU AND I   GO TO   RESTAURANT

What are you going to order?

ORDER   WHAT SHRUG

Do you want a cocktail?

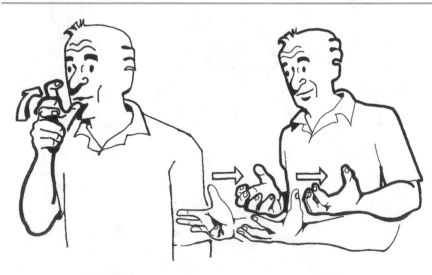

COCKTAIL   WANT

Do you want red or white wine?

RED

WHITE

WINE

WANT

WHICH

I'll have a scotch and water.

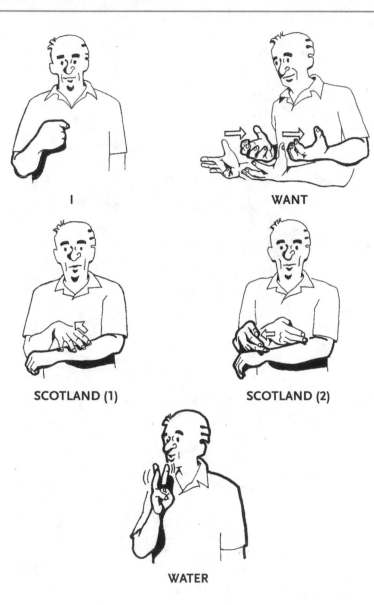

I

WANT

SCOTLAND (1)

SCOTLAND (2)

WATER

They have a lot of different beers.

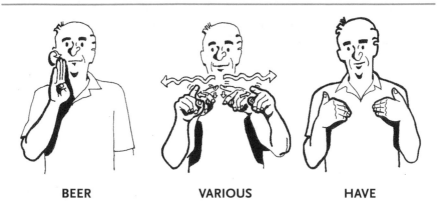

BEER   VARIOUS   HAVE

He never drinks whiskey.

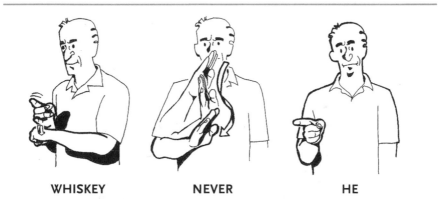

WHISKEY   NEVER   HE

Do you want a soft drink?

SOFT DRINK (1)   SOFT DRINK (2)   WANT

I want a tall Coke/Pepsi.

Coke and Pepsi are the only soft drinks with signs; all others are fingerspelled.

TALL (glass)

GLASS

COKE

PEPSI

WANT

I like sandwiches and hamburgers.

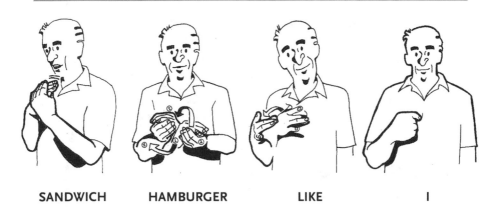

| SANDWICH | HAMBURGER | LIKE | I |

Where's the waiter/waitress?

| SERVE | AGENT | WHERE |

The service is lousy.

SERVE   LOUSY

I've been waiting 20 minutes.

WAIT   20   MINUTE

I want a large/medium/small milk.

TALL (glass)   **MEDIUM (glass)**   **SMALL (glass)**

GLASS   **MILK**   **WANT**

I'll have iced/hot tea.

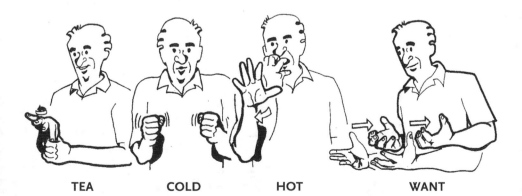

TEA   **COLD**   **HOT**   **WANT**

I'll have coffee after I eat.

EAT   FINISH   COFFEE   WANT

Do you want milk/cream and sugar?

MILK   CREAM   SWEET   WANT

I take it black, please.

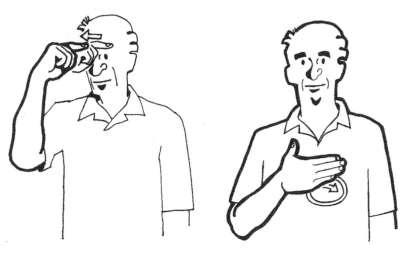

BLACK PLEASE

Sugar only, please.

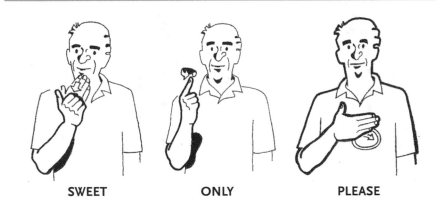

SWEET ONLY PLEASE

Both, please.

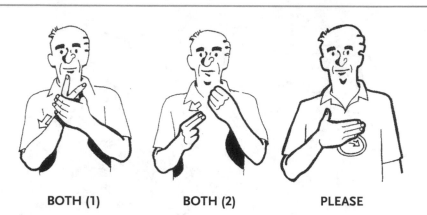

BOTH (1)   BOTH (2)   PLEASE

The food is delicious.

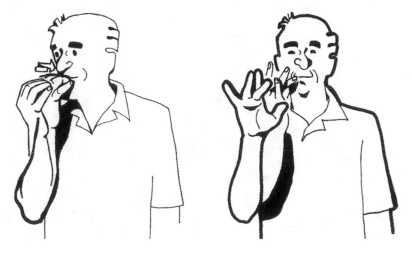

EAT   DELICIOUS

The meat is too rare.

MEAT

COOK (1)

COOK (2)

ENOUGH

NOT

He/she does not eat meat. He/she's a vegetarian.

HE/SHE/IT

EAT

MEAT

NOT

The vegetables are overdone.

V-E-G

COOK (1)

COOK (2)

TOO MUCH

Fingerspell "V-E-G" at the beginning of the sentence. Most vegetables, fruits, and meats are fingerspelled. Some of those that have signs follow.

Additional vocabulary

APPLE

BACON

BANANA

CABBAGE/LETTUCE   **CARROT**   **CHICKEN (A-1)**

CHICKEN (A-2)*   **CHICKEN (B)**   **COCONUT**

CORN   **FISH**   **LEMON**

*This is the sign for "BIRD," but it is often used for "chicken."

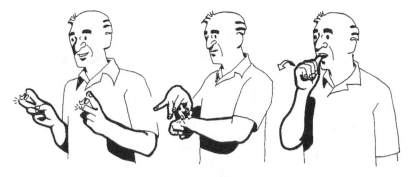

LOBSTER   **MELON**   **NUT**

ONION   **ORANGE**   **PICKLE**

POTATO   **SAUSAGE**   **TOMATO**

CAKE (1)   **CAKE (2)**   **CATSUP**

DESSERT   **FORK**   **GREASE**

ICE CREAM   **KNIFE**   **PEPPER**

PIE (1)

PIE (2)

SALAD

SALT

SPOON/SOUP

TOAST

BREAD

BUTTER

Breakfast

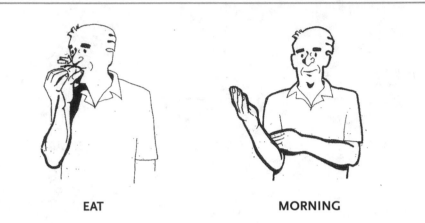

EAT   MORNING

Lunch

EAT   NOON

Supper/dinner

EAT   NIGHT

The following signs are for describing how you want your eggs.

Scrambled

To indicate whether you want your scrambled eggs moist or dry, sign WET or DRY after EGG MIX.

EGG   MIX   DRY   WET

Soft-/hard-boiled eggs

EGG

BOIL

SOFT

HARD

Eggs sunny-side up

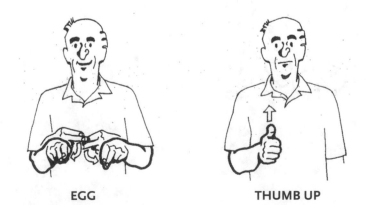

EGG   THUMB UP

Eggs over easy

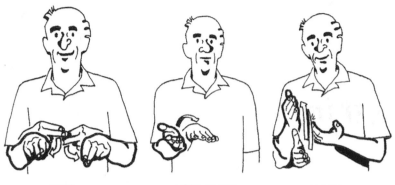

EGG   FLIP OVER   EASY

Clothing

I have to go shopping.

The BUY sign is repeated to convey the idea "shopping."

| GO TO | BUY | MUST |

What are you wearing tonight?

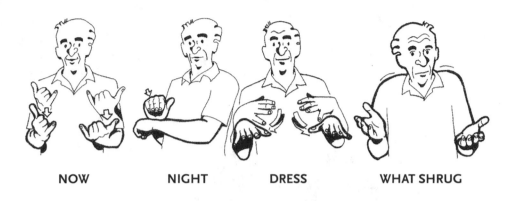

NOW   NIGHT   DRESS   WHAT SHRUG

That dress is an odd color.

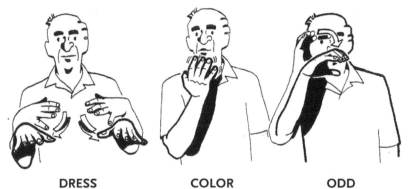

DRESS   COLOR   ODD

Do you have any dirty clothes?

DRESS   DIRTY   HAVE

I need to do some laundry.

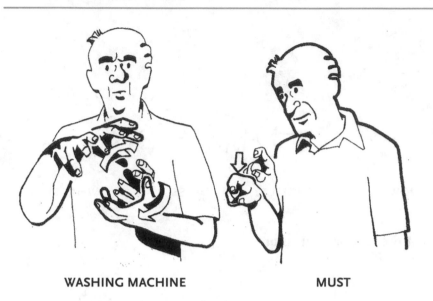

WASHING MACHINE   MUST

Is there a laundromat nearby?

The NEAR sign is done so that the hands do not actually touch each other.

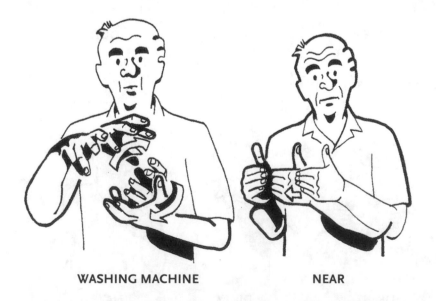

WASHING MACHINE   NEAR

He always dresses nicely.

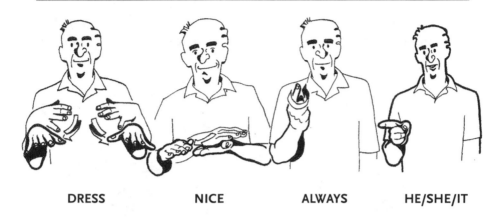

DRESS   NICE   ALWAYS   HE/SHE/IT

The shirt and tie don't match.

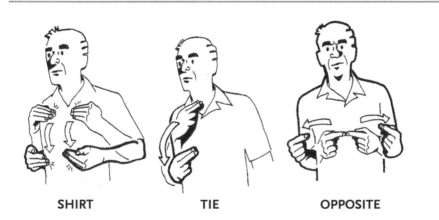

SHIRT   TIE   OPPOSITE

Blue agrees with you.

Ordinarily the AGREE sign just moves downward, but when it is used in the expression above, it must move toward the watcher.

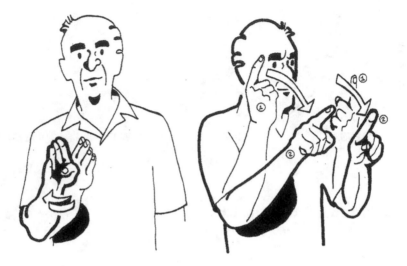

BLUE   AGREE

My trousers are torn.

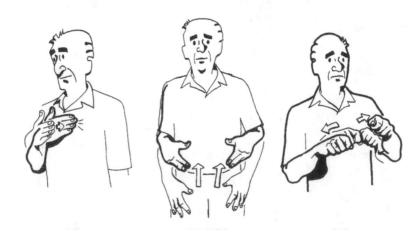

MY   PANTS   RIP

Can you sew a button for me?

Fingerspell BUTTON at the beginning of the sentence before the sign SEW.

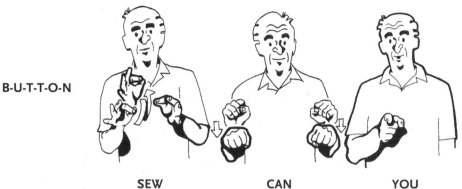

B-U-T-T-O-N

SEW   CAN   YOU

I can't tie a bow tie.

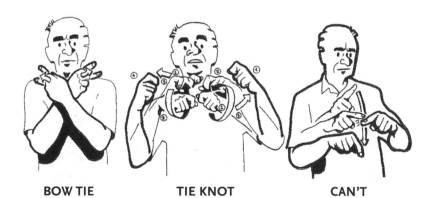

BOW TIE   TIE KNOT   CAN'T

Most women wear slacks nowadays.

NOW

DAY

MOST

WOMAN

USE

SLACKS

Shirt and shoes are required.

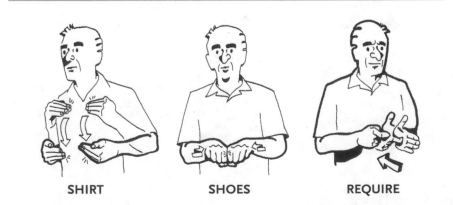

SHIRT

SHOES

REQUIRE

I wear shorts every day in the summer.

DURING

SUMMER   **SHORTS**

EVERY DAY

I

She needs to wash out her skirt.

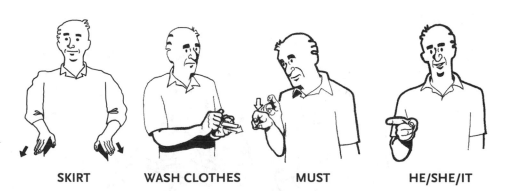

SKIRT   **WASH CLOTHES**   **MUST**   **HE/SHE/IT**

Your socks don't match.

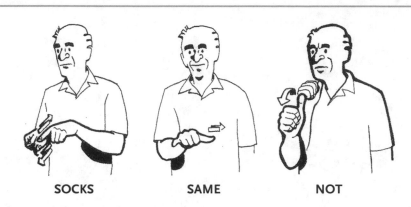

SOCKS   SAME   NOT

Who took my hat?

MY   HAT   GRAB   WHO

I can't fasten my belt.

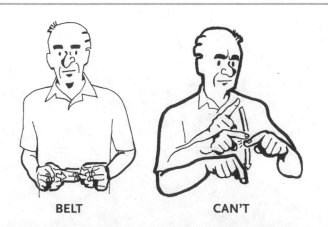

BELT   CAN'T

When I took my coat to the cleaners, it shrunk.

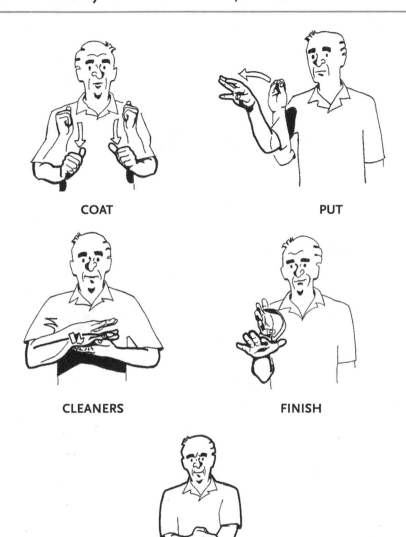

COAT

PUT

CLEANERS

FINISH

SHORTER SLEEVE

Sports and Recreation

Do you like to play baseball?

PLAY   BASEBALL   LIKE

Additional vocabulary

BASKETBALL

BILLIARDS

CARDS

CHECKERS

DOMINOES

ELECTRONIC GAMES

FOOTBALL

GOLF

HANDBALL

SOCCER

TABLE TENNIS

TENNIS

VOLLEYBALL

I run every day.

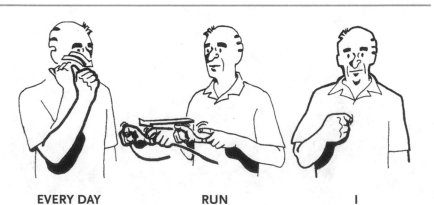

EVERY DAY   **RUN**   **I**

I enjoy going to the mountains to fish.

MOUNTAIN GO TO FISHING PLEASE

Can you ski?

SKI   CAN

I went camping last summer.

PAST   SUMMER   TENT   I

I can roller-skate, but I've never tried ice-skating.

ROLLER-SKATE   CAN   BUT   ICE-SKATE

TRY   NEVER   I

We went canoeing every day.

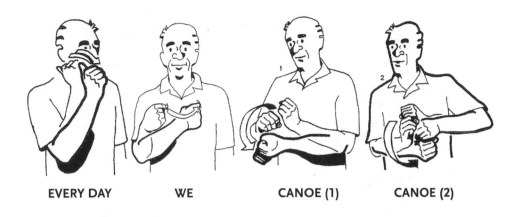

EVERY DAY   WE   CANOE (1)   CANOE (2)

He has a sailboat.

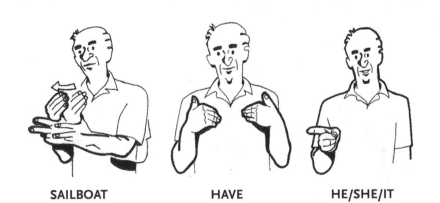

SAILBOAT   HAVE   HE/SHE/IT

She's an expert surfer.

SURFBOARD   SKILL   HE/SHE/IT

I don't like to swim in the ocean.

It takes four signs to express "OCEAN"—WATER, WAVE (1), WAVE (2), and WAVE (3).

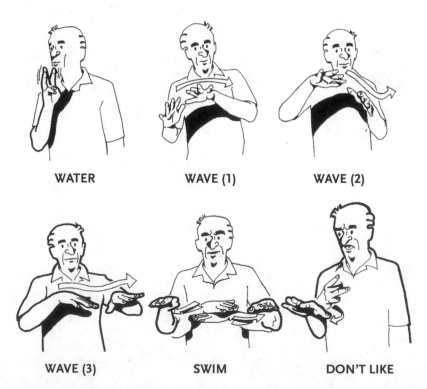

WATER   WAVE (1)   WAVE (2)

WAVE (3)   SWIM   DON'T LIKE

Many people hunt in the fall.

DURING

AUTUMN

MANY

PEOPLE

HUNTING

He's crazy about betting on the horses.

HORSE   COMPLETE   BET

CRAZY   HE/SHE/IT

She loves to ride horses.

RIDE HORSE   LOVE   HE/SHE/IT

He hopes to compete in the Olympics.

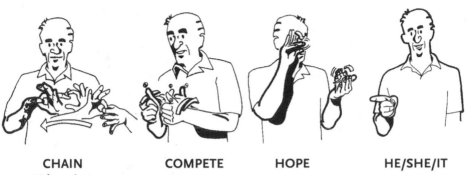

| CHAIN (Olympics) | COMPETE | HOPE | HE/SHE/IT |

I hate calisthenics/exercising.

| EXERCISE | HATE (1) | HATE (2) | I |

What do you do in your spare time?

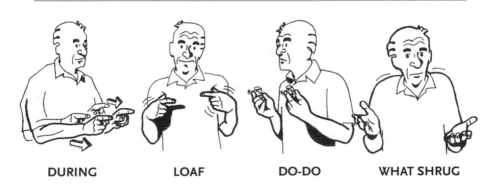

| DURING | LOAF | DO-DO | WHAT SHRUG |

Do you like to dance?

DANCE   LIKE

Do you want to learn to dance?

DANCE   LEARN   WANT

Let's stop and rest now.

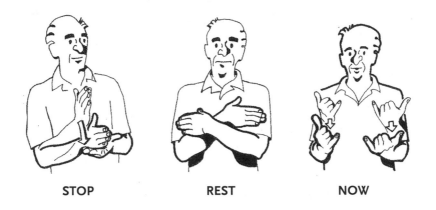

STOP   REST   NOW

I go bowling every week.

WEEKLY   BOWL   I

Travel

IN RECENT YEARS, there has been a movement among U.S. deaf people to replace ASL signs for other nationalities with the signs used by the deaf people of those nationalities. The reasons for this were, first, to show respect for the sign language of those nationalities by using their sign. The second reason was that the ASL sign sometimes was a derogatory sign in the sign language of another country. The ASL sign for Sweden, for example, means "drunk" or "crazy" in Swedish sign language, so naturally Swedes objected to our using the sign to refer to them and their country. Japanese and Chinese deaf people did not like the ASL signs for their countries because they highlighted the facial features of Asians.

In this chapter, the signs marked with an asterisk (*) indicate the sign used by the deaf people of the nation to which the sign refers and are commonly known everywhere. Only those signs that are known by the international community to be truly representative of the signs used by the deaf people within the country are asterisked. (Please keep in mind that not all country signs will be listed here—instead, a select number will be demonstrated due to space limitations. I apologize in advance should any reader take offense.)

Areas of the World

Someday I'm going to Africa.

ONLY

DAY

I

GO TO

AFRICA

Additional vocabulary

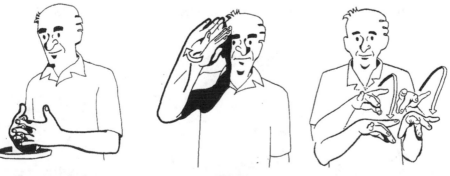

AMERICA　　　AUSTRALIA　　　AUSTRALIA*

CANADA

CHINA

CHINA*

DENMARK

DENMARK*

EGYPT

ENGLAND

EUROPE

FINLAND

FINLAND*

FRANCE

GERMANY

GERMANY＊

GREECE

HOLLAND

HOLLAND＊

INDIA

IRAN＊

IRELAND

ISRAEL

ITALY

ITALY*

JAPAN

JAPAN*

KOREA

MEXICO

MEXICO*

NORWAY

NORWAY*

POLAND

RUSSIA

SCOTLAND*

SCOTLAND (1)

SCOTLAND (2)

SPAIN

SWEDEN

SWEDEN*

SWITZERLAND

Have you ever been to Japan?

TOUCH   **FINISH**   **JAPAN**   **YOU**

States and Cities of the United States

Almost all states are fingerspelled using the standard written abbreviations such as Penn. or PA, ND, and Wyo. States such as Ohio that have short names are spelled out. The few states that have signs that are used throughout the country are shown below:

ALASKA

ARIZONA

CALIFORNIA

COLORADO

HAWAII

NEW YORK*

OREGON

TEXAS

WASHINGTON*

*Note that NEW YORK and WASHINGTON can signify the state as well as the city.

I'm flying to New York tonight.

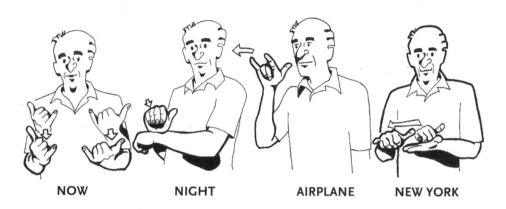

| NOW | NIGHT | AIRPLANE | NEW YORK |

Almost every city has a sign, or a fingerspelled abbreviation. Often, however, the sign is either not common outside the state or it is the same sign for another city in another state. For example, Berkeley and Boston share the same sign. Therefore, one must inquire of local deaf people how the cities in their state are signed. A few cities do have signs that are used all over the country. New York is one such city, and others are shown on page 248:

ATLANTA

CHICAGO

MILWAUKEE

NEW ORLEANS

PHILADELPHIA

PITTSBURGH

SAN FRANCISCO

WASHINGTON, D.C.

San Francisco is abbreviated to "SF," and so are many other cities. Take care with Los Angeles, since its abbreviation can also mean Louisiana.

Traveling

Are your bags packed?

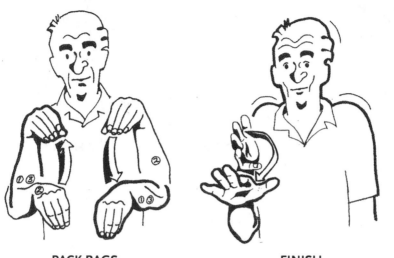

PACK BAGS   FINISH

I'll take you to the airport.

I   BRING   AIRPLANE

Which airline are you taking?

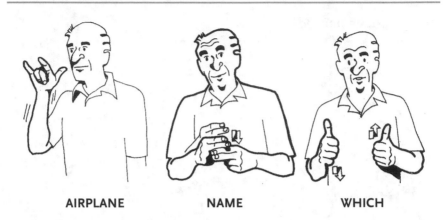

AIRPLANE   NAME   WHICH

What time does the plane take off?

AIRPLANE TAKEOFF   TIME

Do you have your ticket?

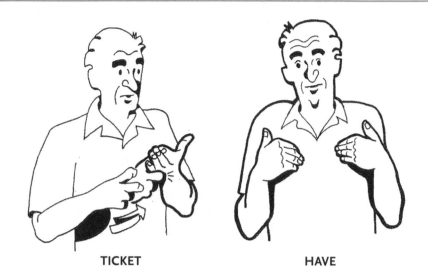

TICKET   HAVE

May I see your ticket, please?

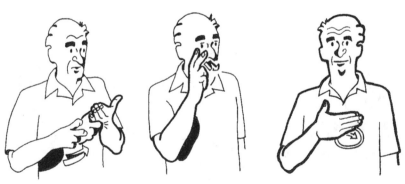

TICKET   LET'S SEE   PLEASE

The airport is closed due to fog.

There is no sign for "fog," so fingerspell it at the end of the sentence, after the sign BECAUSE.

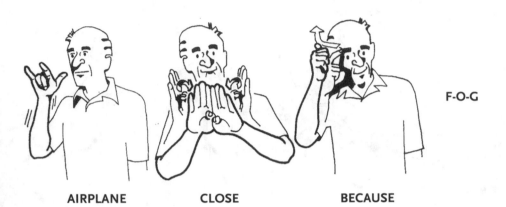

AIRPLANE   **CLOSE**   **BECAUSE**   **F-O-G**

The flight has been delayed an hour.

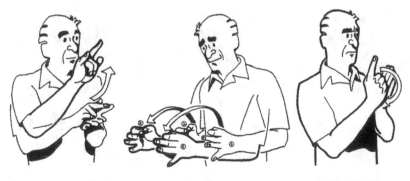

AIRPLANE TAKEOFF   **POSTPONE**   **ONE HOUR**

The flight has been canceled.

AIRPLANE   CANCEL

I have to change planes in Chicago.

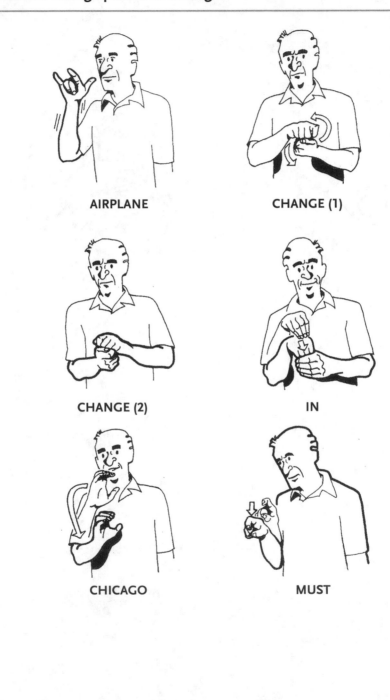

AIRPLANE

CHANGE (1)

CHANGE (2)

IN

CHICAGO

MUST

There's a two-hour layover.

WAIT   TWO HOURS

The seats are not reserved.

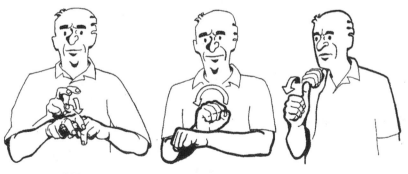

SIT   APPOINTMENT   NOT

The plane is ready for boarding now.

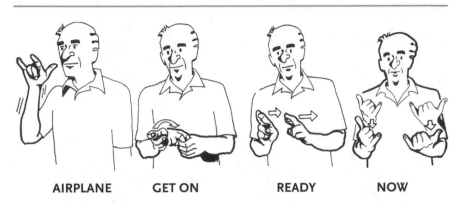

AIRPLANE   GET ON   READY   NOW

Have you checked your luggage?

LUGGAGE   TICKET   FINISH

Please fasten your seat belt.

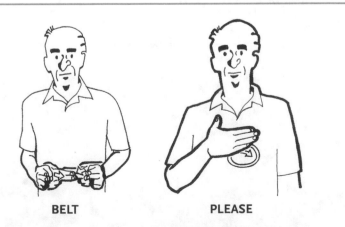

BELT   PLEASE

Would you like a magazine or newspaper?

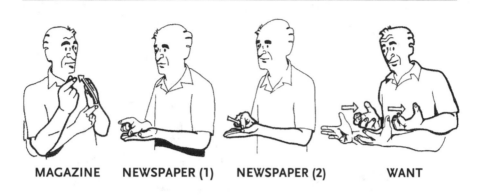

MAGAZINE   NEWSPAPER (1)   NEWSPAPER (2)   WANT

We will land in 10 minutes.

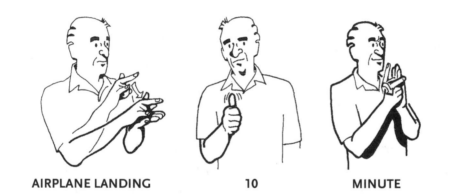

AIRPLANE LANDING   10   MINUTE

Is somebody meeting you?

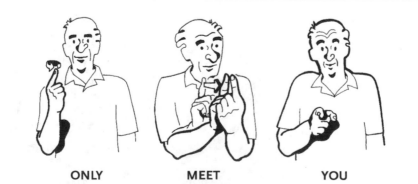

ONLY   MEET   YOU

I enjoy riding the train.

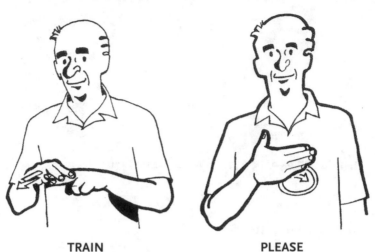

TRAIN   PLEASE

What time does the bus arrive?

A good many languages will share some vocabulary when they come into contact with each other; ASL is one of them. Certain words have been borrowed from the English language and incorporated into the ASL lexicon through a process called *lexicalized fingerspelling*. When this process occurs, many of these fingerspelled words undergo a special transformation and end up looking like a single sign rather than a bunch of letters. In the phrase below, BUS is one example of a lexicalized fingerspelled sign.

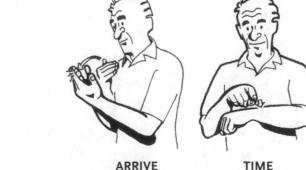

B-U-S

ARRIVE   TIME

What time does the train leave?

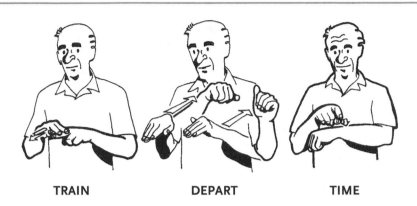

TRAIN   DEPART   TIME

Have you bought your ticket?

TICKET   BUY   FINISH

I'm going to the hotel to take a bath.

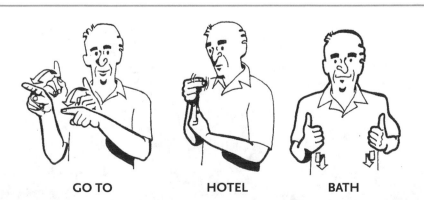

GO TO   HOTEL   BATH

How long are you staying?

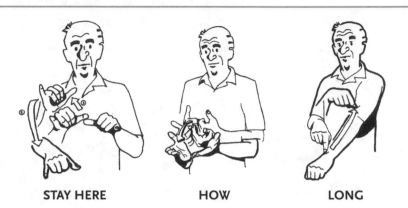

STAY HERE   HOW   LONG

The elevator is stuck.

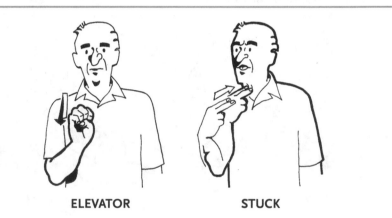

ELEVATOR   STUCK

Do you have a car?

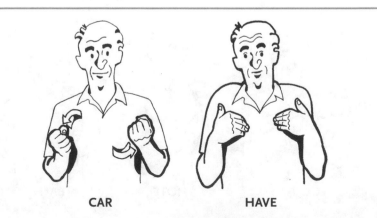

CAR   HAVE

Can you drive?

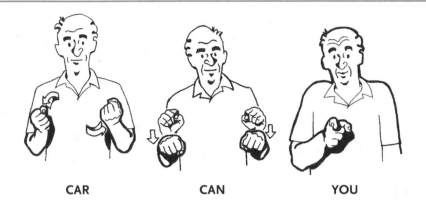

CAR   CAN   YOU

I don't have a license.

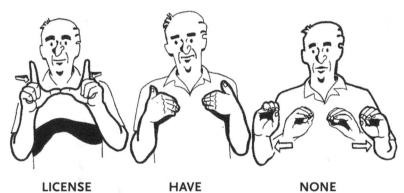

LICENSE   HAVE   NONE

Do you know how to use a manual shift?

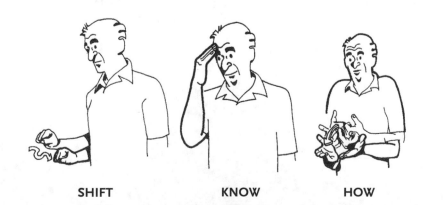

SHIFT   KNOW   HOW

It's illegal to park here overnight.

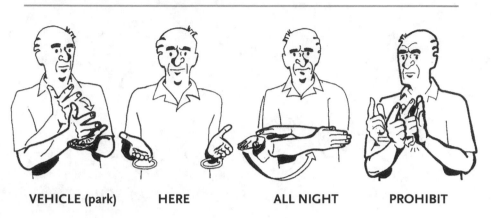

VEHICLE (park)   HERE   ALL NIGHT   PROHIBIT

Slow down and make a right turn.

"RIGHT" means "as opposed to left," but "RIGHT TURN" is one sign.

SLOW   RIGHT   RIGHT TURN

Make a left turn and stop.

"LEFT" means "as opposed to right," but "LEFT TURN" is one sign.

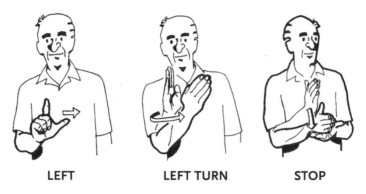

LEFT   LEFT TURN   STOP

Would you call me a cab, please?

The sign CAB is an example of a lexicalized fingerspelling. Fingerspell "cab" at the beginning of the sentence, before the sign PHONE.

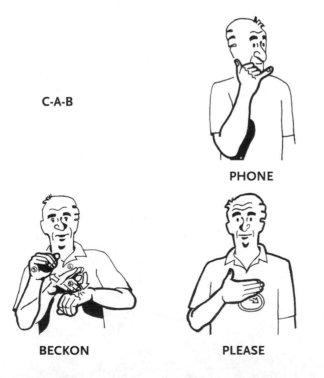

C-A-B

PHONE

BECKON   PLEASE

Come visit me sometime.

ONLY

TIME

COME

VISIT

Animals and Colors

Animals

ASL does not have a sign for every animal. Presented here are nearly all the animal signs that do exist. All other animal names are either fingerspelled or have signs that are known only in a particular area.

ANIMAL

ALLIGATOR (1)

ALLIGATOR (2)

BEAR (1)

BEAR (2)

BEE (1)

BEE (2)

BIRD (1)

BIRD (2)

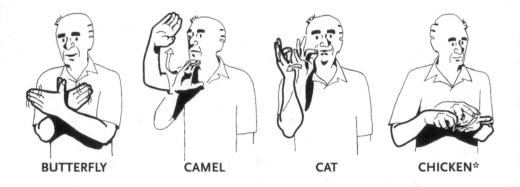

BUTTERFLY   **CAMEL**   **CAT**   **CHICKEN***

*While this sign means "chicken," the sign "BIRD" is also often used to mean "chicken."

COW **DEER** **DOG**

EAGLE **ELEPHANT (A)** **ELEPHANT (B)**

FROG **GIRAFFE** **GOAT**

HAWK

HORSE

INSECT

LION

MONKEY

MOUSE

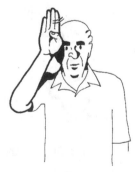

MULE

RABBIT (A)

RABBIT (B)

RAT   **SHEEP**   **SNAKE**

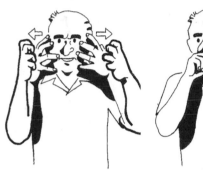

TIGER   **TURKEY (A-1)**   **TURKEY (A-2)**

TURKEY (B)   **WORM**

Colors

ASL does not have a sign for every color, so "beige" and "fuchsia" have to be fingerspelled. Colors such as "blue-green," however, may be signed by combining the two signs BLUE and GREEN.

BLACK

BLUE

BROWN

GRAY (1)

GRAY (2)

GREEN

ORANGE

PINK

PURPLE

RED

WHITE

YELLOW

Varying shades of colors can be signed by using the signs DARK and CLEAR. In this sense, CLEAR means "light."

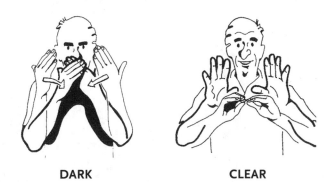

DARK

CLEAR

Civics

I'm a Democrat/Republican/Independent.

DEMOCRAT   REPUBLICAN   INDEPENDENT   I

I voted; did you?

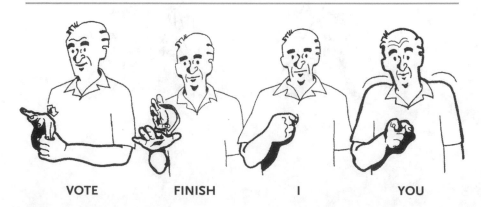

VOTE   FINISH   I   YOU

Who's the new president?

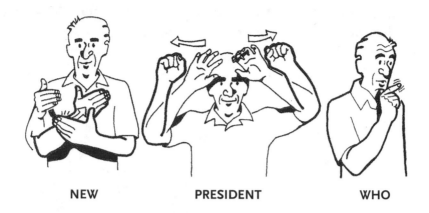

NEW   PRESIDENT   WHO

Who won the election?

VOTE   WIN   WHO

The legislature/congress is responsible for passing laws.

This is an example of the rhetorical question, where the signer asks, then answers, the question. It is used a great deal in ASL. There is a slight pause at the end of the question—after the sign WHO in this example—and then the answer is signed.

LAW

PASS

RESPONSIBLE

WHO

LEGISLATURE

CONGRESS

She is a congresswoman.

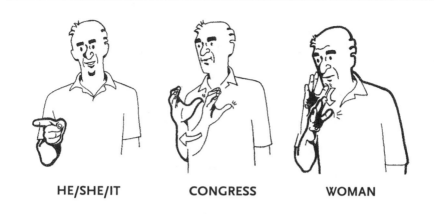

| HE/SHE/IT | CONGRESS | WOMAN |

He is a senator/governor/judge/lawyer.

The AGENT sign shown below is usually done following the SENATE, GOVERNMENT, JUDGE, and LAW signs to indicate senator, governor, judge, and lawyer, respectively.

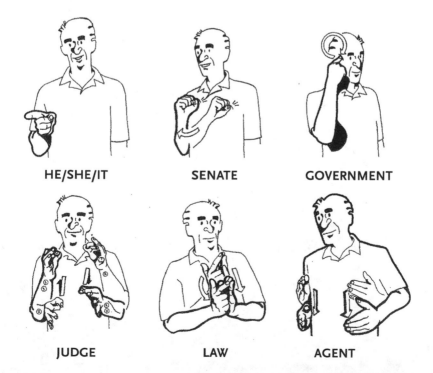

| HE/SHE/IT | SENATE | GOVERNMENT |

| JUDGE | LAW | AGENT |

We must pay taxes to support the government.

COST

PAY

MUST

WE

FOR

SUPPORT

GOVERNMENT

Our country is large.

Either sign for "country" is acceptable.

| OUR | COUNTRY (A) | COUNTRY (B) | LARGE |

I had to pay a parking fine.

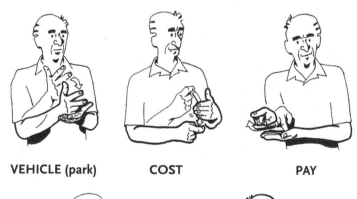

| VEHICLE (park) | COST | PAY |

| MUST | I |

Which city is the capital?

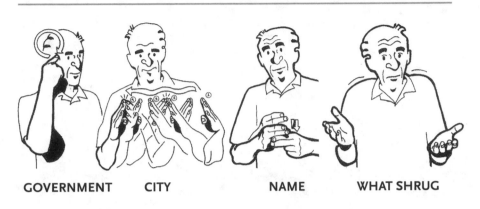

GOVERNMENT   CITY   NAME   WHAT SHRUG

If you break the law, you might go to jail.

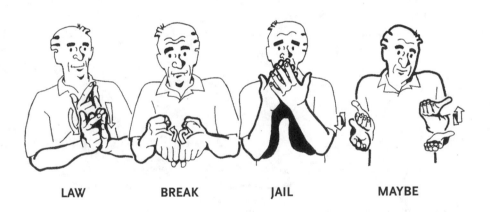

LAW   BREAK   JAIL   MAYBE

The idea of "if" is often expressed in ASL by stating the sentence as a question. This requires a questioning expression. In the above sentence the expression would be done on the BREAK sign, and then there is a slight pause before you sign the consequence. In the following sentence, the questioning expression happens with the DISOBEY sign, which is followed by a pause before the rest of the statement is signed.

If you disobey the law, you will be punished.

LAW   DISOBEY   PUNISH   WILL

You must obey the law.

LAW   OBEY   MUST   YOU

The police arrested him for speeding.

POLICE   ARREST (1)   ARREST (2)

BECAUSE   CAR

RAPID   TOO MUCH

She plans to sue them.

HE/SHE/IT   PLAN   AGAINST

They are on strike against the company.

There is no sign for "company," so fingerspell "C-O" at the end of the sentence after the sign AGAINST.

THEY   PROTEST   AGAINST   C-O

Last year the students protested.

LAST YEAR   LEARN   AGENT   PROTEST

I was on the picket line all morning.

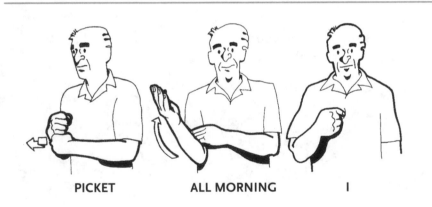

PICKET   ALL MORNING   I

I move we pass it.

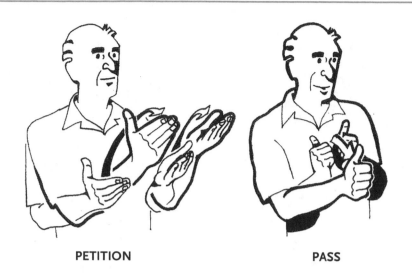

PETITION   PASS

I second the motion.

This sign is also used idiomatically to show that you agree with someone.

SECOND A MOTION

Did you receive a notification to appear in court?

NOTIFY

GO TO

JUDGE

GET

FINISH

Do you belong to the PTA?

There is no sign for "PTA," so fingerspell it at the beginning of the sentence before the sign JOIN.

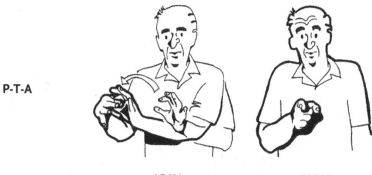

P-T-A

JOIN   **YOU**

He's on Social Security.

Fingerspell "S-S" to indicate "Social Security" at the beginning of the sentence before the sign PENSION.

S-S

PENSION   **HE/SHE/IT**

She gets the Supplementary Salary Income.

Fingerspell "S-S-I" to indicate "Supplementary Salary Income" at the beginning of the sentence before the sign PENSION.

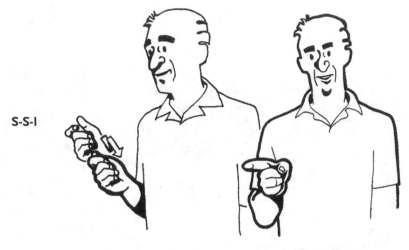

S-S-I

PENSION　　　**HE/SHE/IT**

If you go to court, you should have a good lawyer.

Do not forget the questioning facial expression, since this is an "if" statement. It should occur with the sign GO TO.

JUDGE　　　　GO TO　　　　GOOD

LAW　　　　AGENT

MUST　　　　YOU

Religion

SIGNS FOR VARIOUS denominations differ considerably around the United States, so it is suggested that you make local inquiries about how specific denominations are signed in your area. Those that follow are fairly standard.

Are you a Christian?

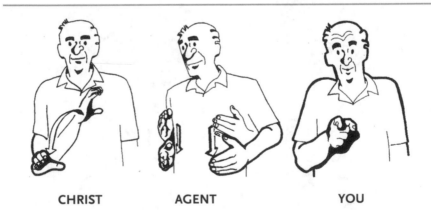

CHRIST   AGENT   YOU

Judaism is an old religion.

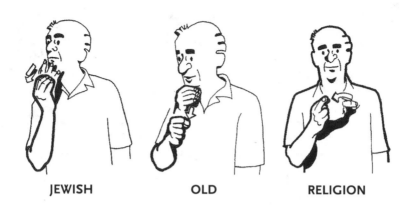

| JEWISH | OLD | RELIGION |

Note: Although the signs CHERISH and STINGY are very similar, the facial expression is quite different in each case, naturally. The sign JEWISH looks as if you are stroking a beard. It would, obviously, be offensive if you signed STINGY and meant to sign JEWISH, so be careful.

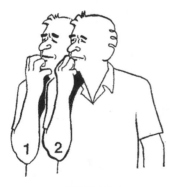 

| CHERISH | STINGY |

Are you a Roman Catholic or a Protestant?

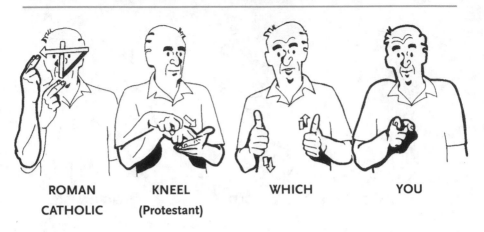

ROMAN
CATHOLIC

KNEEL
(Protestant)

WHICH

YOU

He's an atheist.

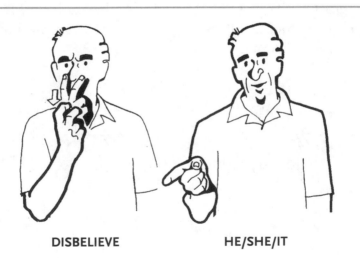

DISBELIEVE

HE/SHE/IT

Additional vocabulary for religious denominations

BAPTIZE (Baptist)

BUDDHISM/BUDDHIST

EPISCOPAL

ISLAM/MUSLIM

LUTHERAN

MORMON

Have you been baptized?

BAPTIZE   **FINISH**   **YOU**

If a particular denomination baptizes by sprinkling rather than by immersion, then one of the following signs is used:

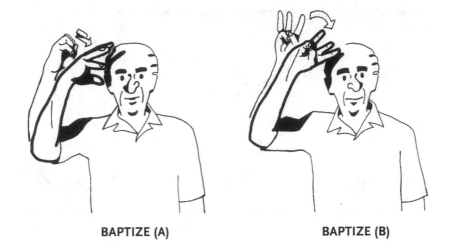

BAPTIZE (A)   BAPTIZE (B)

I go to church every Sunday.

CHURCH   GO TO   EVERY SUNDAY   I

Jewish people go to temple on the Sabbath.

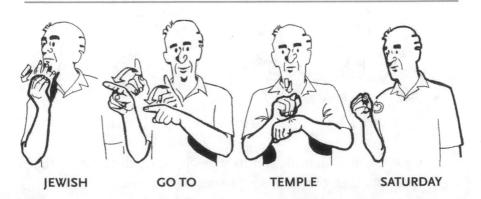

JEWISH   GO TO   TEMPLE   SATURDAY

Which church to you belong to?

CHURCH   JOIN   WHICH

He used to be a preacher/minister/pastor.

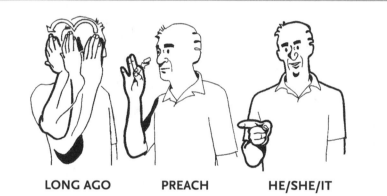

LONG AGO   PREACH   HE/SHE/IT

She's a missionary.

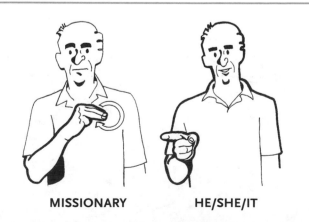

MISSIONARY   HE/SHE/IT

Do you want me to interpret the sermon?

ME

INTERPRET (1)

INTERPRET (2)

PREACH

WANT

YOU

Choir

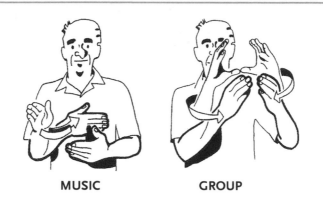

MUSIC   GROUP

Additional vocabulary

ANGEL   BELIEVE   BLESS

COMMUNION   CONFESSION   CRUCIFY (1)   CRUCIFY (2)

CRUCIFY (3)   **DEVIL**   **FAITH**

FUNERAL   **GOD**   **GRAVE**

HEAVEN (1)   **HEAVEN (2)**   **HELL**

JESUS (1)

JESUS (2)

LORD

MASS

CRACKER (Passover)

PITY

PRAY

PRIEST

PROPHECY

RABBI **SABBATH/ SUNSET** **SAVE** **SIN**

SOUL (A) **SOUL (B-1)** **SOUL (B-2)** **WORSHIP**

Resurrection

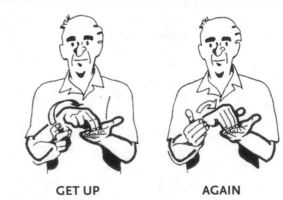

GET UP **AGAIN**

Numbers, Time, Dates, and Money

Numbers

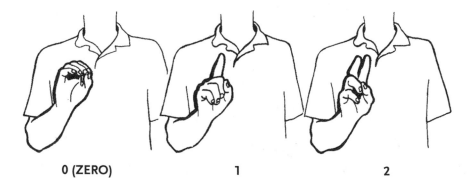

| 0 (ZERO) | 1 | 2 |

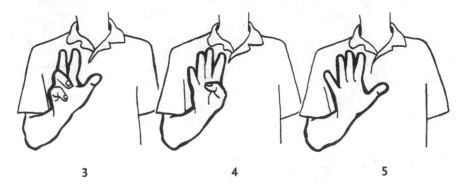

3   4   5

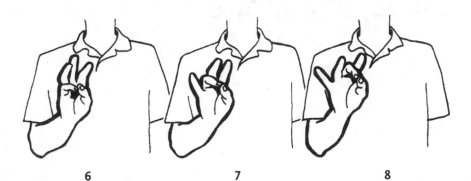

6   7   8

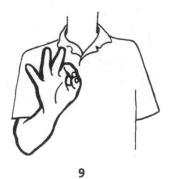

9

The signs for the number 6 and the letter *W* are exactly the same, and the sign for the number 9 is the same as that for the letter *F*. Context tells you whether the number or the letter is intended.

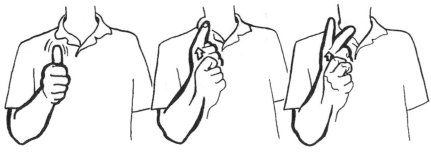

10

11

12

13

14

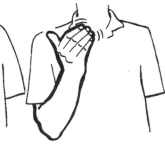

15

16

17

18

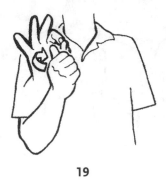

19

The numbers 16 through 19 are actually a very fast blend of 10 and 6, 10 and 7, 10 and 8, 10 and 9.

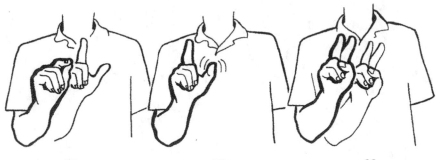

20   21   22

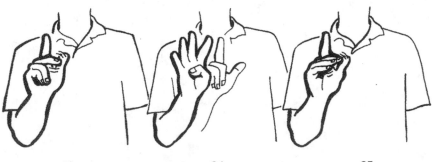

23   24   25

26

27

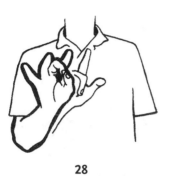

28

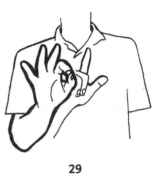

29

That the "2" in the twenties is made with the thumb and index finger rather than the index and second fingers—as it appears in the number 22—is probably due to the fact that ASL has its roots in the old French sign language. In Europe, even hearing people count *one* with the thumb, and *two* with the thumb and index finger.

The remaining numbers from 30 through 99 are done with the numbers 0 through 9. Examples follow:

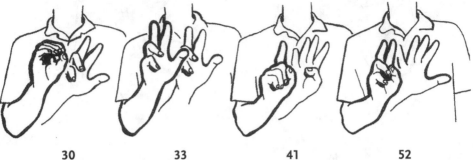

| 30 | 33 | 41 | 52 |

| 64 | 75 | 86 |

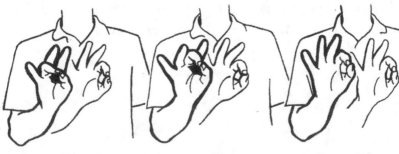

| 97 | 98 | 99 |

The number 100 is made by signing the number 1 and the letter *C*:

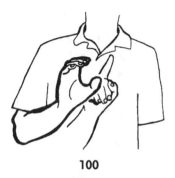

100

The numbers between 100 and 999 are made in one of two ways. One may make the number "7-7-7" or one may sign "7-C-7-7":

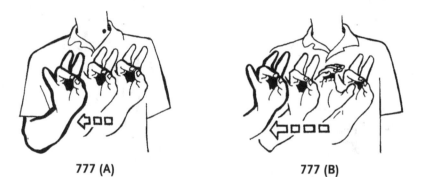

777 (A)   **777 (B)**

The numbers 1,000 and 1,000,000 are signed like so:

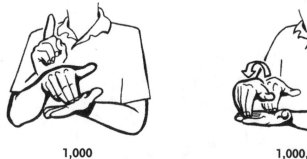

1,000   **1,000,000**

The numbers "billion" and "trillion" are fingerspelled—there is not a specific sign for them.

Fractions are made the same way they are written, one number above another:

½ (A)

The one-half sign as shown above is usually made more quickly as shown below:

½ (B)

¾

Percentages are made as follows:

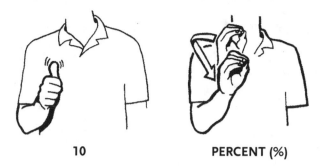

10   PERCENT (%)

Numbers with decimals can also be expressed:

1-.7-5

The sign for the decimal may also mean the punctuation mark "period."

What's your number?

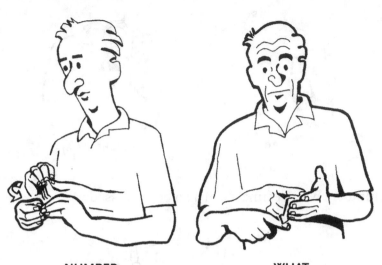

NUMBER   WHAT

My phone number is _____.

Fingerspell your phone number after the sign NUMBER.

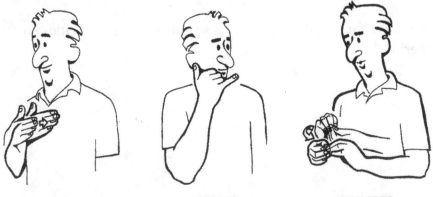

MY   PHONE   NUMBER

Time

Telling time in ASL is usually done exactly in the same way as it is done in English.

It is 4:45.

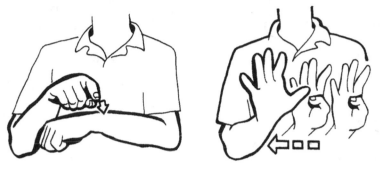

TIME   4-4-5

It is 6:15.

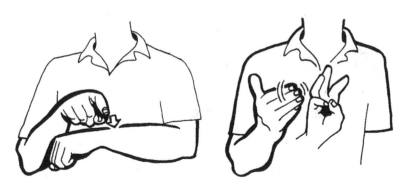

TIME   6-15

It is ten till nine.

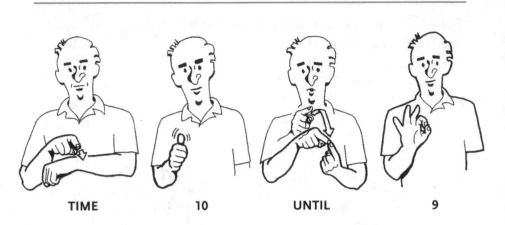

| TIME | 10 | UNTIL | 9 |

Dates

He is 87 years old.

| HE/SHE/IT | OLD | 87 |

I was born in 1911.

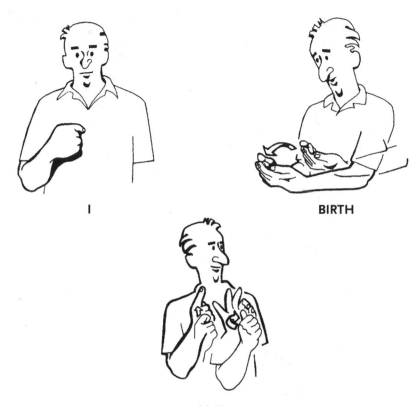

I

BIRTH

19-11

Most of the months are abbreviated in fingerspelling. Only the short ones—March, April, May, June, and July—are spelled out completely.

My birthday is April 3, 1948.

MY

BIRTH

DAY

A-P-R-I-L

3

19-48

Additional vocabulary

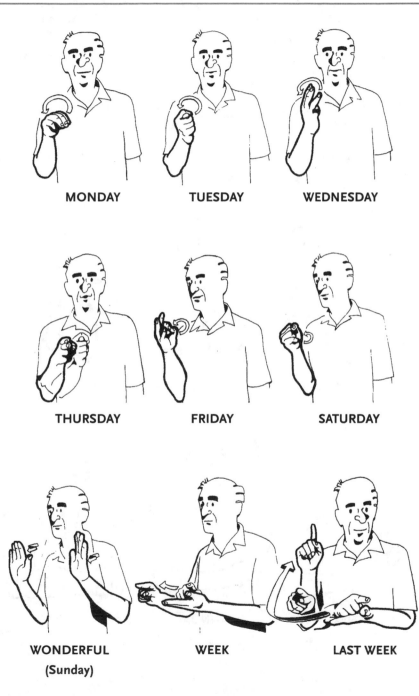

MONDAY　　　TUESDAY　　　WEDNESDAY

THURSDAY　　　FRIDAY　　　SATURDAY

WONDERFUL　　　WEEK　　　LAST WEEK
(Sunday)

NEXT WEEK   **WEEKLY**   **MONTH**

MONTHLY   **YEAR**   **LAST YEAR**

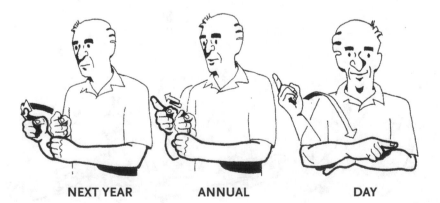

NEXT YEAR   **ANNUAL**   **DAY**

ALL DAY

NIGHT

ALL NIGHT

MORNING

NOON

AFTERNOON

EVERY DAY

GROW (Spring)

SUMMER

AUTUMN

COLD (Winter)

I'll see you next Monday.

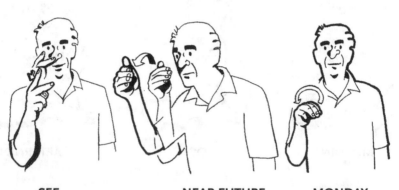

| SEE | NEAR FUTURE | MONDAY |

I visited my aunt two months ago.

| TWO MONTHS | PAST | AUNT | VISIT |

I bought a new house two years ago.

| TWO YEARS AGO | BUY | NEW | HOUSE |

I graduate in two years.

| TWO YEARS FROM NOW | GRADUATE | I |

I pay every three months.

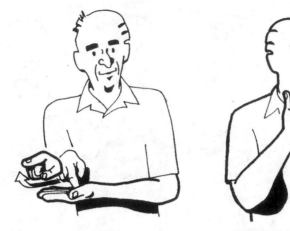

PAY   EVERY THREE MONTHS

He goes to the movies every Tuesday.

By moving the sign for a day of the week downward, as done with TUESDAY here, you convey the idea of every week on that day.

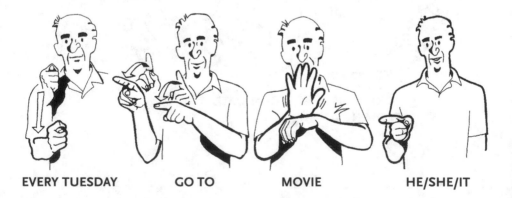

EVERY TUESDAY   GO TO   MOVIE   HE/SHE/IT

I see her every Saturday.

EVERY SATURDAY   **SEE**

The Fourth of July is a holiday.

Fingerspell JULY at the beginning of the sentence before the sign 4TH.

J-U-L-Y

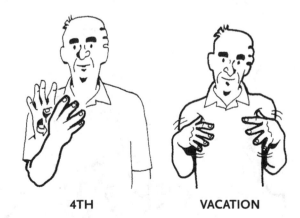

4TH   **VACATION**

Money

These signs also serve as ordinal numbers—i.e., first, second, third, etc.

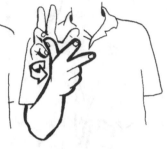

$1.00 $2.00 $3.00

$4.00 $5.00 $6.00

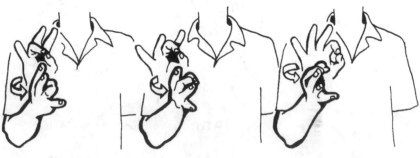

$7.00 $8.00 $9.00

The sign DOLLAR is used when the amount is over nine dollars or when speaking specifically of a bill, as in "a dollar bill." As here:

10

DOLLAR

1¢

2¢

3¢

4¢

5¢

6¢

7¢

8¢

9¢

10¢

These signs are used only when speaking of these amounts by themselves, not when they are preceded by a dollar amount. For example, $3.09 would be signed as follows:

$3.-0-9

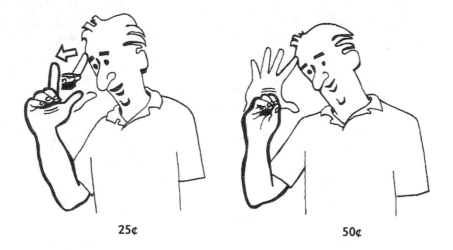

25¢   50¢

The same applies to the following two signs as to the cent signs above. Use them only when speaking of these amounts alone, and not with a dollar amount.

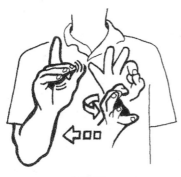

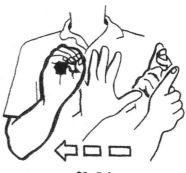

$9.-25 $1.-5-0

How much does the book cost?

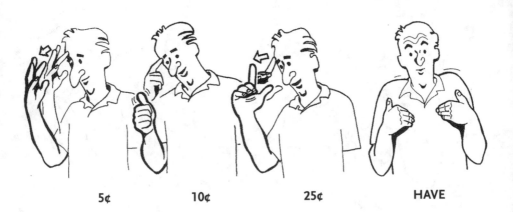

BOOK   COST   HOW MANY

Have you a nickel/dime/quarter?

5¢   10¢   25¢   HAVE

Can you change a five?

| $5.00 | SHARE (make change) | CAN |

How much did you pay?

| PAY | HOW MANY |

It's under five dollars.

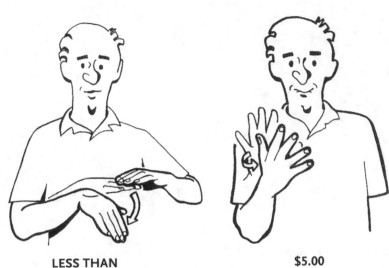

LESS THAN $5.00

It's over five dollars.

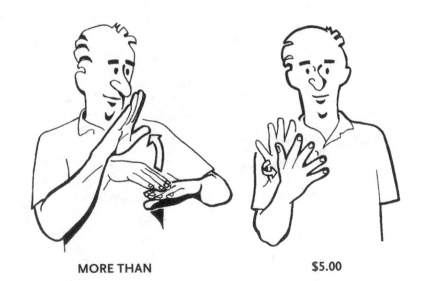

MORE THAN $5.00

I paid less than you.

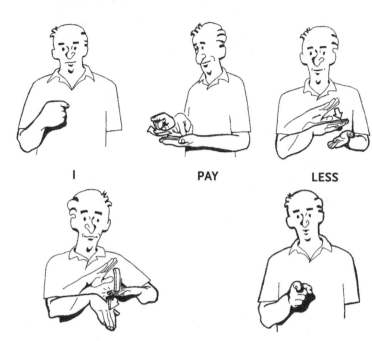

I PAY LESS

THAN YOU

I have no money.

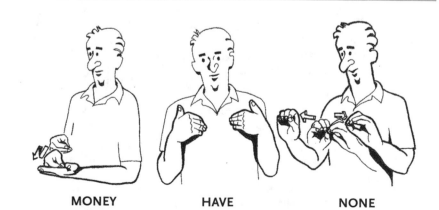

MONEY HAVE NONE

I'm broke.

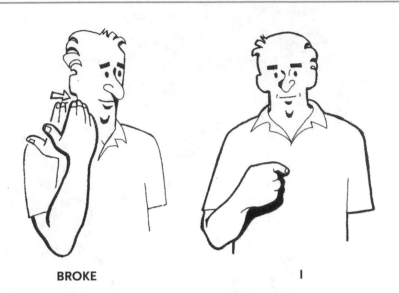

BROKE   I

How much does it cost to get in?

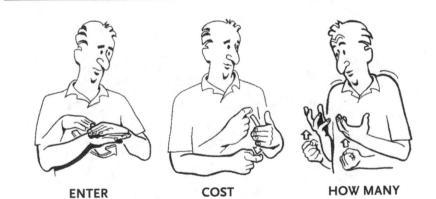

ENTER   COST   HOW MANY

How much does he owe?

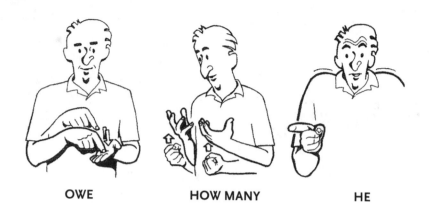

OWE   HOW MANY   HE

Technology

PLEASE NOTE THAT this chapter illustrates several variations of the word *computer*, as commonly used by deaf people.

I have e-mail.

___

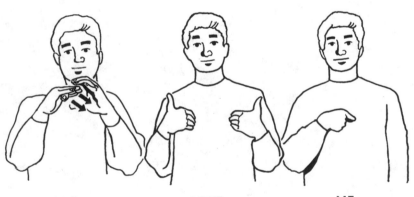

E-MAIL   HAVE   ME

Would you mind giving me your e-mail address?

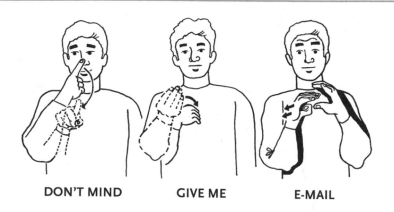

DON'T MIND   **GIVE ME**   **E-MAIL**

Which Internet service provider do you use? AOL or MSN?

Fingerspell "A-O-L" and "M-S-N."

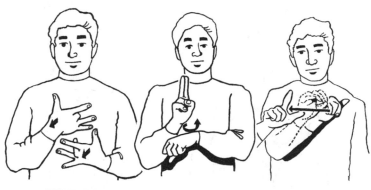

TEND TO   **USE**   **A-O-L**

M-S-N   **WHICH**

Do you have cable TV?

Fingerspell TV and CABLE.

T-V   C-A-B-L-E   HAVE   YOU

Where's the remote?

REMOTE CONTROL   WHERE

I do not have cable service.

Fingerspell CABLE.

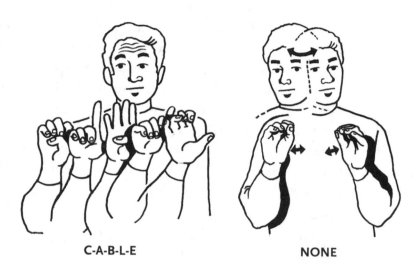

C-A-B-L-E   NONE

He/she has a high-definition TV.

Fingerspell "H-D T-V."

H-D T-V   HAVE   HE/SHE/IT

Please fax me your résumé.

Fingerspell FAX. *Fax* is another example of a word borrowed from English through the lexicalized fingerspelling process that has taken on the appearance of a single sign. With frequent usage, signers have added movement, dropped letters, or altered palm orientation to certain lexicalized fingerspelled signs, which is the case with the word *fax*. The letters "F" and "X" move toward the signer's chest, the letter "A" has been dropped, and the palm orientation of the letter "X" has been shifted toward the signer's chest. Lexicalized fingerspelled words do not follow the rules of regularly fingerspelled words (e.g., P-T-A, D-V-D, S-S-I). Refer to the Appendix for more information on the manual alphabet.

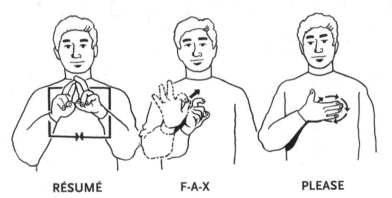

RÉSUMÉ   F-A-X   PLEASE

I bought a laptop.

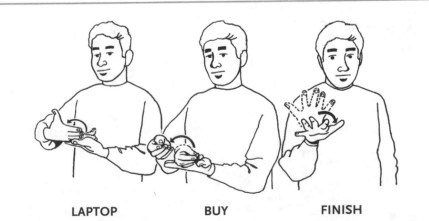

LAPTOP   BUY   FINISH

What make is your computer?

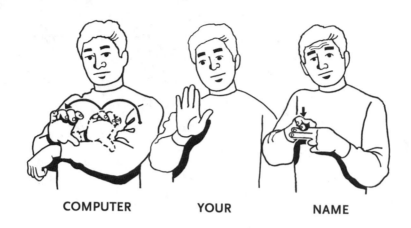

COMPUTER   YOUR   NAME

How much memory does your computer have?

YOUR   COMPUTER   MEMORIZE   HOW MUCH

I don't have high-speed Internet access.

FAST INTERNET NONE ME

Copy and paste your document.

COMPUTER TEXT COPY PASTE

Download this program.

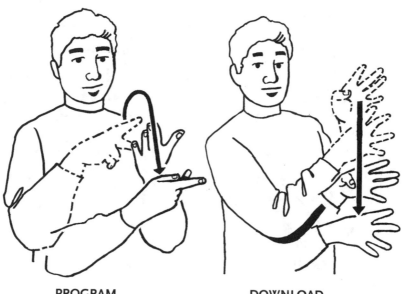

PROGRAM   DOWNLOAD

Have you printed your document?

PAPER   PRINT   FINISH

My printer is broken.

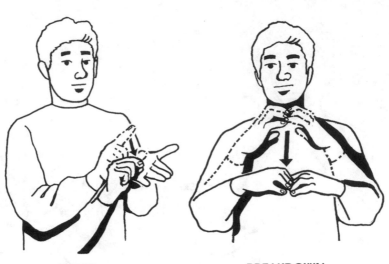

PRINT   BREAKDOWN

Please save your file.

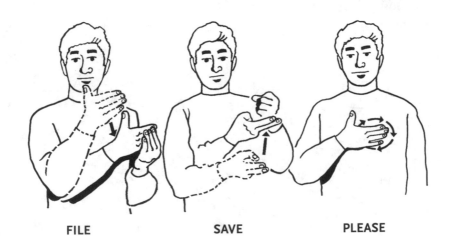

FILE   SAVE   PLEASE

I accidentally deleted my file.

Note: You can use either the MISTAKE or CARELESS sign with this phrase.

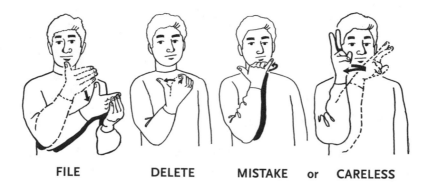

FILE   **DELETE**   **MISTAKE**   or   **CARELESS**

Did you scan your photograph?

Note: You can use either version of SCAN for this phrase.

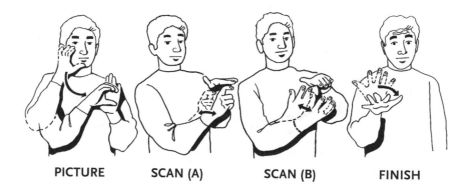

PICTURE   **SCAN (A)**   **SCAN (B)**   **FINISH**

Send your picture as an attachment.

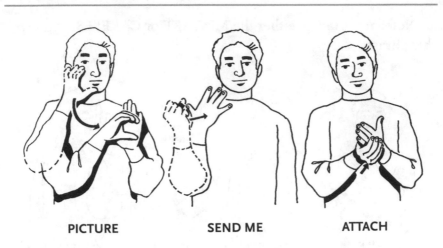

PICTURE   SEND ME   ATTACH

My computer crashed!

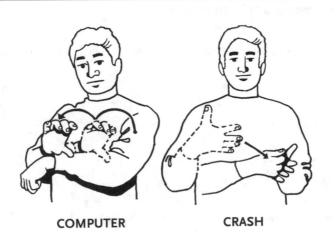

COMPUTER   CRASH

A virus destroyed my hard drive.

Fingerspell "H-D" and VIRUS.

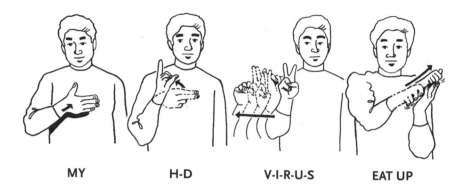

| MY | H-D | V-I-R-U-S | EAT UP |

Which software do you prefer?

Software is another example of the lexicalized fingerspelling process becoming like a sign. The word has been shortened or abbreviated to the letters "S" and "W." The sign movement starts with the palm orientation of the letter "S" reversed inward toward the signer's chest. The "S" palm orientation swings outward away from the signer and the next letter, "W," is fingerspelled.

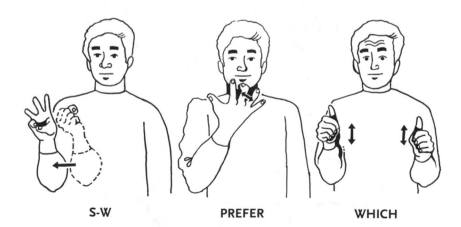

| S-W | PREFER | WHICH |

Please burn a CD.

Fingerspell "C-D."

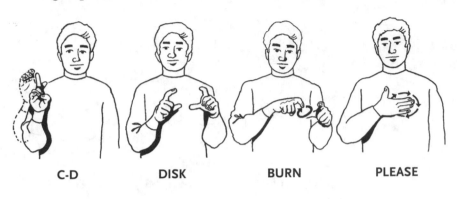

C-D   DISK   BURN   PLEASE

I will buy a DVD/VHS player.

Fingerspell "D-V-D" and "V-H-S."

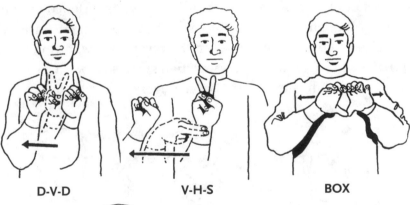

D-V-D   V-H-S   BOX

BUY   WILL

A satellite dish is expensive!

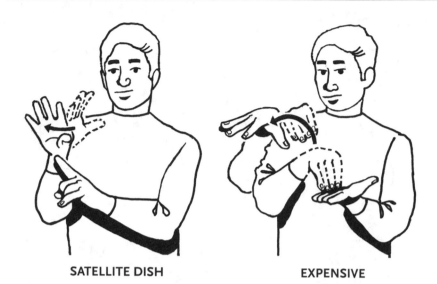

SATELLITE DISH

EXPENSIVE

My camcorder works fine.

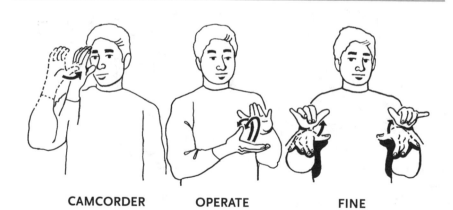

CAMCORDER   OPERATE   FINE

My parents gave me a 35-mm digital camera for my birthday.

"M-M" and DIGITAL are fingerspelled.

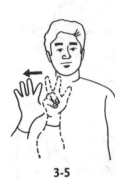

3-5

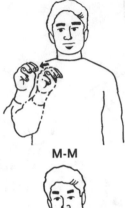

M-M

D-I-G-I-T-A-L

CAMERA

MY

PARENTS

GIVE-ME

BIRTHDAY

My aunt got a GPS for her boat.

Fingerspell "G-P-S." This is an example of a rhetorical question where the signer asks, and then answers, the question. It is used a great deal in ASL. There is a slight pause at the end of the question—after the sign FOR-FOR in this example—and then the answer is signed.

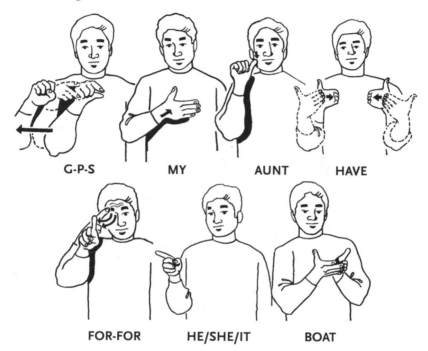

G-P-S   MY   AUNT   HAVE

FOR-FOR   HE/SHE/IT   BOAT

iPods are very popular!

Fingerspell IPOD.

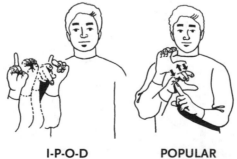

I-P-O-D   POPULAR

That coffeehouse doesn't have wi-fi access.

Fingerspell WI-FI.

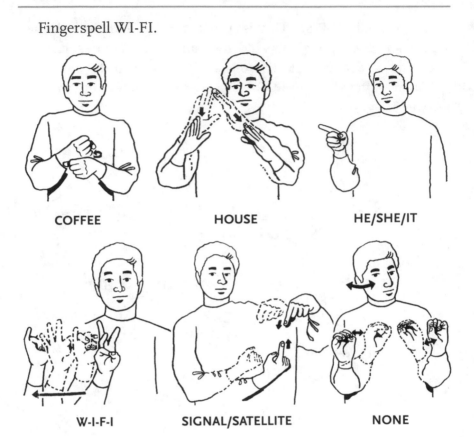

COFFEE   HOUSE   HE/SHE/IT

W-I-F-I   SIGNAL/SATELLITE   NONE

What's the link to that blog?

Fingerspell BLOG.

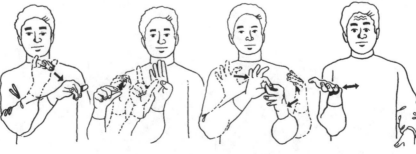

THAT   B-L-O-G   CONNECT   WHAT

This theater downtown has open captioning.

HE/SHE/IT

MOVIE

DOWNTOWN

HAVE

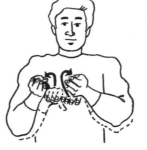

OPEN

CAPTION

My TV has closed captioning.

Fingerspell TV.

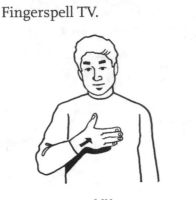

MY

T-V

(CLOSE) CAPTION

HE/SHE/ IT

Which pager did you choose?

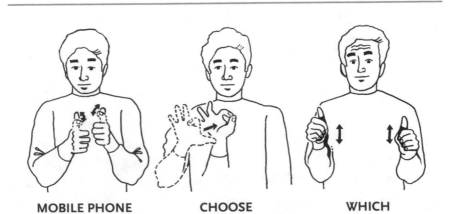

MOBILE PHONE

CHOOSE

WHICH

I need to recharge my pager.

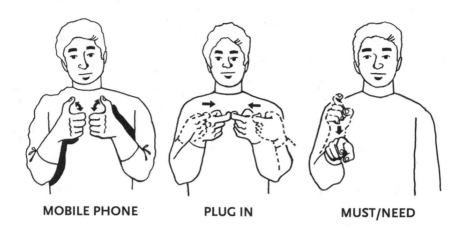

MOBILE PHONE   PLUG IN   MUST/NEED

Mine's a BlackBerry pager.

Fingerspell "B-B."

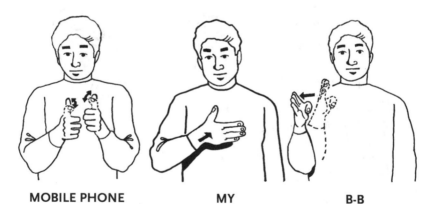

MOBILE PHONE   MY   B-B

I will buy a Sidekick III pager.

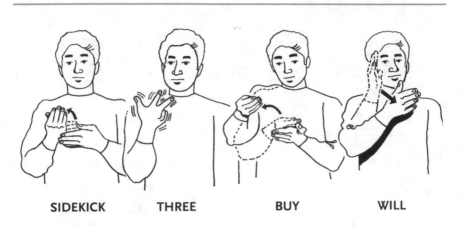

SIDEKICK   THREE   BUY   WILL

I love video relay service!

Fingerspell "V-R-S."

V-R-S   ME   LOVE

A few people use the voice carryover feature on the video relay service.

Fingerspell "V-R-S."

FEW	**PEOPLE**	**USE**

VOICE	**TALK**	**V-R-S**

When you get home, check your video relay mail.

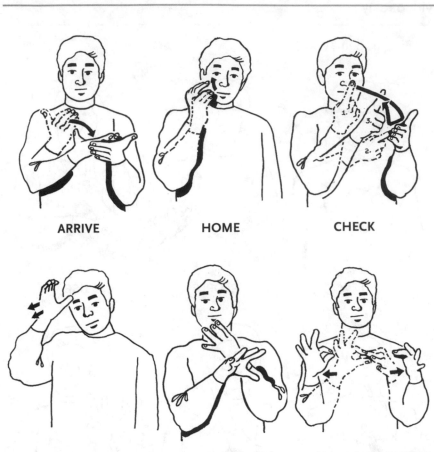

ARRIVE   HOME   CHECK

COMPUTER   VIDEO RELAY   MESSAGE/COMMENT

The wireless Internet relay on my pager is terrific!

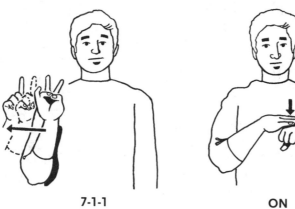

7-1-1

ON

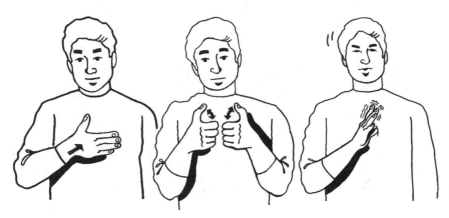

MY

PAGER

FINE

Sometimes I use the IP relay on my computer.

Fingerspell "I-P" and RELAY.

I-P   R-E-L-A-Y   ON

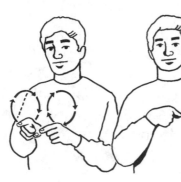

COMPUTER   ME   USE   SOMETIMES

Deaf people text message their hearing friends.

Fingerspell TEXT.

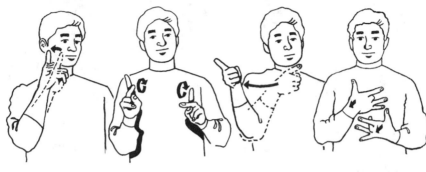

| DEAF | PEOPLE | THEY | TEND TO |

| HEARING | FRIEND | T-E-X-T | SEND |

Some deaf people have gotten cochlear implants.

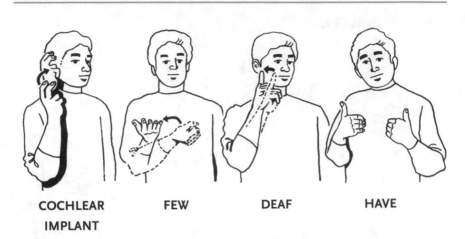

COCHLEAR IMPLANT | FEW | DEAF | HAVE

How do you feel about cochlear implants?

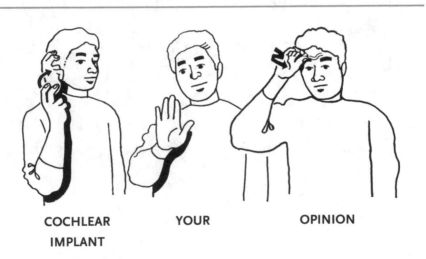

COCHLEAR IMPLANT | YOUR | OPINION

My deaf-blind friend has a closed-circuit television magnifier.

Fingerspell "C-C-T-V."

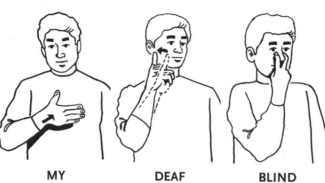

MY	DEAF	BLIND

FRIEND	HAVE	C-C-T-V

Did you see that vlog?

Fingerspell VLOG.

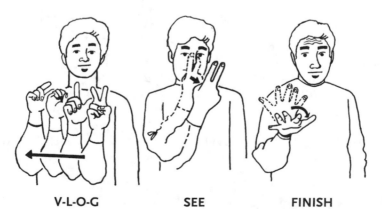

V-L-O-G	SEE	FINISH

Most deaf people use light-signaling devices for their doorbells, alarm clocks, videophones, and TTYs, and to alert them to a baby's cry.

Fingerspell "T-T-Y."

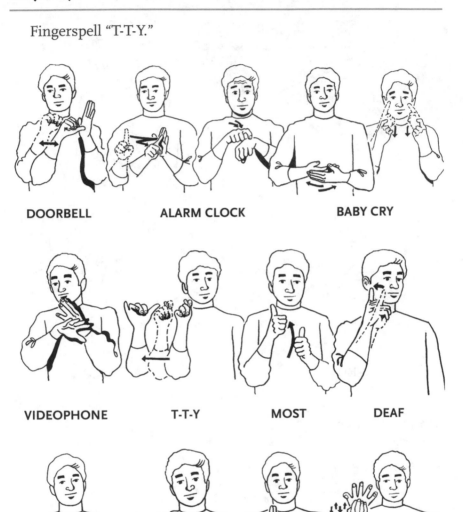

DOORBELL   ALARM CLOCK   BABY CRY

VIDEOPHONE   T-T-Y   MOST   DEAF

PEOPLE   ALL OVER   USE   LIGHT FLASH

Nowadays, deaf people are using video relay services rather than TTYs.

Fingerspell "T-T-Y."

DEAF

ALL OVER

T-T-Y

LESS

NOW

VIDEO RELAY

APPENDIX

The Manual Alphabet

THE MANUAL ALPHABET allows us to fingerspell English words. When there is not a sign for an idea, then fingerspelling is used. This occurs most often with proper names. Mastery of fingerspelling is relatively easy if you form good habits from the very beginning.

First, relax your fingers. This may require bending and stretching the fingers so that they fall easily into the proper hand shapes. Next, relax your arm and shoulder. Tension is the greatest obstacle to clear formation of the letters, so strive to remain relaxed as you work at it. Let the arm hang down with the elbow to your side and the hand slightly in front of your body as the pictures show. Do not let your elbow start moving away from your side and rising upwards.

Rhythm is the most important quality to develop in fingerspelling. A rhythmical spelling is much easier to read than an unrythmical one, even when the letters are not perfectly formed. Rhythm is also critical for indicating when one word has ended and the next word has begun. This is done by holding on to the last letter of a word for about one-fourth of a beat of the rhythm you are using, then going on to the first letter of the next word. As you practice rhythmical fingerspelling, be sure you do not let the rhythm cause you to bounce your hand. Hold it steadily in one place.

Speed is not a goal to pursue. Work on rhythm, and then speed will come naturally in time. The tendency is to attempt to fingerspell too fast. Then the rhythm becomes broken when you cannot remember how to make a letter. A slow, rhythmic pattern is far more desirable than a fast but erratic rhythm.

Do not say the letters, either aloud or to yourself, as you make them. This is a very bad habit to get into and exceedingly hard to break once established. As you fingerspell a word, say the whole word. For instance, as you spell "C-A-T" do not say the letters, but say the word *cat*. You may say it aloud or without voice. It will seem awkward at first, but you will quickly become used to it.

The reason for speaking the word rather than saying the letters has to do with lipreading. Deaf people are taught to lipread words, not letters. When you fingerspell they see both your hand and your lips, and the two complement and reinforce each other. (This is also the reason you do not let your fingerspelling hand wander out to your side, too far away from your face.) It is not necessary to speak the word aloud; you may mouth it without using your voice.

When fingerspelling long words, pronounce the word syllable by syllable as you fingerspell it. For example, say, "fin" as you fin-gerspell "F-I-N," then say "ger" as you fingerspell "G-E-R," and then say "spell" as you fingerspell "S-P-E-L-L." (Double letters are moved slightly to the side or bumped back and forth slightly.) Caution: Do not pause after each syllable, but keep the rhythm flowing.

Practice spelling words, not just running through the alphabet. Begin with three-letter words, then work your way up to longer ones. A first-grade reading book provides excellent practice mate-rial because most of the words are short and are repeated often. Practice fingerspelling as you read a newspaper, listen to the radio or television, and see street signs and billboards. You may get some odd looks from some people, but never mind, you are on the road to mastering an intricate skill.

You will find that fingerspelling is much easier to do than to read. This happens because, initially, you tend to look for each individual letter as it is fingerspelled to you so that when you reach the end of the word you cannot make sense of the letters. You must learn to see whole words, not individual letters, just as you are doing as you read this printed material. You will have to find someone to learn and practice fingerspelling with you, since you cannot practice reading your own fingerspelling. As the two of you practice, do not speak or mouth the words since you would then hear or lipread them instead of reading the fingerspelling.

Here, in summary, are the tips to follow:

1. Relax.
2. Keep your elbow in and your hand in front of you.
3. Maintain a constant rhythm, but do not bounce your hand.
4. Pause for one-fourth of a beat at the end of each word.
5. Do not try to fingerspell rapidly.
6. Mouth or speak the word, not the letters.
7. Practice with someone so you can gain experience reading fingerspelling. (In this kind of practice, do not mouth or speak the word aloud.)
8. Look for the whole word, not individual letters.

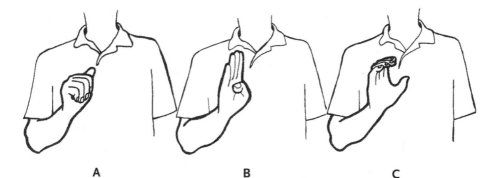

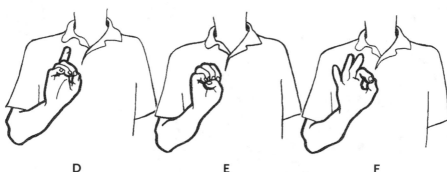

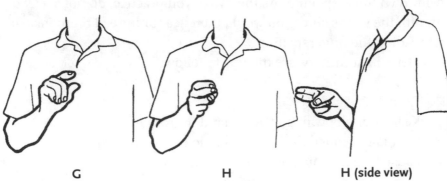

G

H

H (side view)

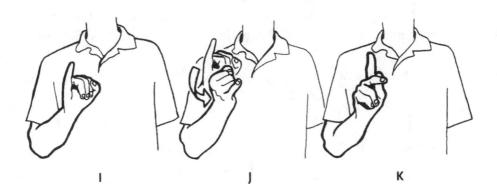

I

J

K

L

M

N

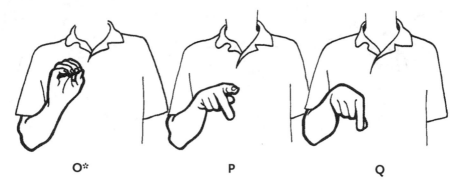

O*   P   Q

*Note: The sign for the letter *O* is the same as that for the number "0" (zero).

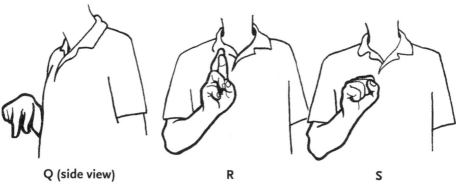

Q (side view)   R   S

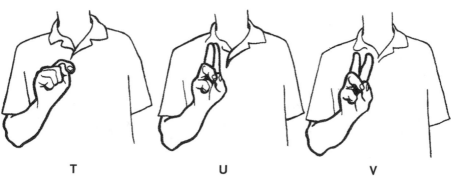

T   U   V

W   X   Y

Z

Dictionary/Index

THE DICTIONARY/INDEX consists of a combination of three things:

1. All the signs in this book listed by sign labels. All sign labels are in capital letters. When the meaning of the sign is not evident from the sign label, additional definitions and explanations are given.

2. English words that are glossed by signs in this book. The word is printed in lowercase letters, and the correct sign is in all capitals within parentheses following the word. Example: food (EAT). It is suggested that you refer to the sign label in the Dictionary/Index to see if an additional definition or explanation is given before looking up the picture of the sign.

3. Topics that are discussed in various sections of this book. They are printed as titles. Examples: "Past, Present, Future," "Labeling of the Drawings."

Abbreviations used:

SM: Single movement. The movement of the sign is made only once.
DM: Double movement. The movement of the sign is repeated once.